PENGUIN C1

TILISM-E-HOSHRUBA

Shahnaz Aijazuddin has spent several years researching the *Tilism-e-Hoshruba* and is deeply interested in Urdu and Persian. She has been a columnist with a leading Pakistani newspaper and has written for several other publications in India and Pakistan. A collection of her articles, *Lost from View*, was published in 1994. Shahnaz Aijazuddin is married and has three children. She lives in Lahore, Pakistan.

TILISM-E-HOSHRUBA

THE ENCHANTMENT
OF THE SENSES

ABRIDGED AND TRANSLATED
BY
SHAHNAZ AIJAZUDDIN

PENGUIN BOOKS

PENGUIN BOOKS
Published by the Penguin Group
Penguin Books India Pvt. Ltd, 11 Community Centre, Panchsheel Park,
New Delhi 110 017, India
Penguin Group (USA) Inc., 375 Hudson Street, New York, New York 10014, USA
Penguin Group (Canada), 90 Eglinton Avenue East, Suite 700, Toronto, Ontario,
M4P 2Y3, Canada (a division of Pearson Penguin Canada Inc.)
Penguin Books Ltd, 80 Strand, London WC2R 0RL, England
Penguin Ireland, 25 St. Stephen's Green, Dublin 2, Ireland (a division of Penguin Books Ltd)
Penguin Group (Australia), 250 Camberwell Road, Camberwell, Victoria 3124,
Australia (a division of Pearson Australia Group Pty Ltd)
Penguin Group (NZ), 67 Apollo Drive, Rosedale, North Shore 0632,
New Zealand (a division of Pearson New Zealand Ltd)
Penguin Group (South Africa) (Pty) Ltd, 24 Sturdee Avenue, Rosebank, Johannesburg 2196,
South Africa

Penguin Books Ltd, Registered Offices: 80 Strand, London WC2R 0RL, England

First published in Penguin Books India 2009

Copyright © Shahnaz Aijazuddin 2009

All rights reserved

10 9 8 7 6 5 4 3 2 1

ISBN 9780143102724

Typeset in Sabon by Eleven Arts, New Delhi
Printed at Chaman Offset Printers, Delhi

For my parents
Nayyar Agha and Col. Agha Asghar Ali Shah
my 'keystones' to the *Tilism*

CONTENTS

III

IV

V

VI

VII

ACKNOWLEDGEMENTS

When I began this translation of the *Tilism-e-Hoshruba*, I had no idea of the number of worlds through which I would have to traverse. My journey has taken me backwards and forward in Time, oscillated me in Space, and admitted me to magic kingdoms that have no boundaries. It has been an exhilarating experience—one that I hope will be shared by my readers. As I read and reread the original text, I became aware of the layers of meaning and allusions secreted into the narrative. This increased my respect for the ingenuity of Muhammad Husain Jah and Ahmed Husain Qamar—the writers of the printed version of the *Tilism-e-Hoshruba*.

In a sense they were more fortunate than I was because to them, the length of the story was not a constraint and nor was effusion of language a disadvantage. Compressing the voluminous and seemingly endless text of the *Tilism-e-Hoshruba* into one book was as much of a challenge to me as it must have been later to my editors at Penguin India. For much sound advice and clarity of thought I am deeply indebted to Anupama Ramakrishnan, my editor at Penguin. For the initial encouragement to tackle this ambitious assignment, I owe thanks in particular to Meru Gokhale and Ravi Singh. In addition, R. Sivapriya provided invaluable help for which I am grateful. Collaborating with them has proven the adage that ideas know no frontiers and that technology knows no boundaries. Yesterday's magicians are today's computer wizards. Their sorcery has made the instantaneous transmission of drafts and proofs between New Delhi and Lahore a modern miracle.

I am grateful to the scholar and *dastangoh* Mahmood Farooqui for his unstinting support and inspiration; to the writer Intizar Hussain who has encouraged me through the years that this project came to fruition; to the *dastan* scholar Musharraf Ali Farooqi for his generosity of spirit; and to the Urdu scholar Dr Moazzam Siddiqi who provided valuable insights during an afternoon with me in Washington DC. And to countless other friends, in particular Pinni Mehta, who have encouraged me on every step of this journey, my sincerest and heartfelt thanks.

My husband Aijaz has been my rock and guide in the journey through the Tilism. For his love and support I am deeply grateful. My sister

Lalarukh has always provided clear advice about my work and I cannot thank her enough for her loving faith in me.

One of the reasons I embarked on this project was to share the text with my children. For me they were the profile of the reader I was writing for. I am obliged to my daughter Mubarika for patiently sitting through impromptu readings to test the readability of the text. I thank my other daughter Momina and her husband Khalid Saeed for their loving support in a project that started before their marriage! I hope that my young grandchildren Raeya and Ramiz will some day be drawn to read this text just as I was on that distant day when my mother bought the *Tilism-e-Hoshruba* for my father.

I share my love for fantasy literature with my son Komail and thank him for nudging me in this direction and for his continuous faith in me. Finally, I thank my parents for the happiest of childhoods and for my understanding of Urdu and Persian. This book and its dedication are my belated tribute to them. My only regret is that they are no longer alive to read it.

Lahore   Shahnaz Aijazuddin
August 2009

INTRODUCTION

The dastan of *Tilism-e-Hoshruba* is to Urdu literature what Homer's epic poems were to Greek literature and what *A Thousand and One Nights* were to the Arabian bardic tradition. For years, it was believed that the *Tilism-e-Hoshruba* was translated from an original Persian version composed by Faizi to entertain the Mughal emperor Akbar. This was due to the established tradition of giving the credit for a dastan to an irreproachable source to establish its credibility as a historical document. It is now almost certain that the bulk of the *Tilism* dastans were composed not in the sixteenth century but later, in that unique period of aesthetic refinement and cultural decadence which distinguished Lucknow as the capital of the former kingdom of Awadh. The storyline of the Hoshruba chronicle was probably delineated by one Mir Ahmed Ali, a dastangoh or narrator from Lucknow who later moved to Rampur. The story was further embellished by his disciples like Amba Prasad Rasa and numerous other dastangohs, including Rasa's son, Ghulam Raza.

In the late nineteenth century, the Naval Kishore Press in Lucknow commissioned dastangohs to compile the primarily oral tradition of dastans into written form. The first to be published were the seven volumes of the *Tilism-e-Hoshruba*, already very popular in its oral form. For this purpose, the canny Munshi Naval Kishore employed Muhammad Husain Jah, a leading dastan narrator and *marsia* reciter in Lucknow. Jah was familiar with the Hoshruba chronicles and composed the first four volumes of this classic for publication. Ahmed Husain Qamar, another dastan professional, wrote the final three volumes. Qamar had a longer association with his distinguished patron Naval Kishore and continued to compose other Tilism dastans.

Although the *Tilism-e-Hoshruba* is a narrative complete in itself, it is deemed to be a sequel to the original epic of the legendary Persian hero, Emir Hamza. The Hamza dastan is said to have originated in eleventh-century Persia and was greatly influenced by the national epic *Shahnama*—the Story of Kings. The story of Hamza is derived from the life of a real-life hero—Hamza bin Abu Muttalib, the paternal uncle of the Holy Prophet Mohammad. The original Hamza was known to be the strongest man in his tribe, a warrior, a hunter and an outdoor man. The fictional

Hamza travels to Persia where he fights the enemies of the emperor Nausherwan and is later trapped in Qaf, the land of *jinni* and fairies for fourteen years. The last part of Hamza's story involves his return to Arabia. Here, the fictional Hamza becomes the real Hamza bin Abu Muttalib who defends his nephew, the Holy Prophet, against the kafirs of Mecca and is subsequently martyred at the Battle of Uhud.

The Hamza stories travelled through the Middle East and Central Asia and gained immense popularity. Inevitably, the itinerant dastan narrators added local touches or nuances to the recited text to broaden its appeal. This was particularly apparent during the spread of the Hamza legend in India. The emperor Akbar gave the Hamza story an imperial stamp of acceptance by commissioning a series of 1600 illustrations, painted in the Perso-Mughal miniature style, but on cloth. The size of each illustration and the use of cloth rather than paper was done to allow each illustration to be unfolded simultaneously before the audience while the narrative was being recited.

Gradually, over the centuries, dastan narration became an intrinsic part of court ritual in India. It became increasingly popular in an age when the self-indulgent philosophy to live only for the moment had permeated from the monarch through the aristocracy to all levels of society. Story-tellers were as essential a feature of the entertainment at a royal court or of a nobleman as were retinues of musicians, singers and courtesans. They enjoyed a mass appeal that encouraged the narrators to tailor their stories to suit their audience. The original Hamza stories were translated from Persian into Urdu and spawned another genre of epic fantasies known as the Tilism dastans. Emir Hamza remained the pivotal character, but now was supported by his dynasty of sons, grandsons and great grandsons, all of them like their illustrious forbear—brave, chivalrous and stunningly handsome.

The word '*tilism*' or magic was applied now to describe magic-bound lands created by an ancient pantheon of gods such as Samri and Jamshed, and in some cases, by sages. The enchantments the dastangohs contrived in their narratives were complex creations unlike the simpler magic in the original Hamza story. Tilism dastans usually involved a quest for the Lauh-e-Tilism—the magic keystone closely guarded by the ruler of the Tilism. Only the person destined to vanquish the Tilism, known as the Tilism Kusha, was able to find it. To gain it, the keystone demanded some sort of sacrifice—usually of blood—before it yielded its secrets to the Tilism Kusha and guided him.

Although at first glance the *Tilism-e-Hoshruba* story seems to be the metaphor for the advent of Islam in India, Hoshruba is in a time and place of its own. Its villains are sorcerers or sahirs and it was therefore popular with every religious sect. Its backdrop is more Central Asian and Middle Eastern than Indian. Its Muslim heroes are not averse to drinking wine even if it was served by one of their own faith. There is another view that the *Tilism* dastans had a hidden, esoteric dimension and that a tilism was a metaphor for the real world. The vanquishers are the people of this world and their hearts are the keystones that guide them in their journey. The theory applies equally to the invisible worlds in the dastans. Most dastan scholars though are sceptical about this view and maintain that the composers had no other agenda than to entertain their secular audience.

In volume two of *Tilism-e-Hoshruba*, Hamza's great grandson Iraj goes through an elaborate procedure to vanquish the Tilism of Mirrors. He is guided by the keystone to act according to the hours of the day that correspond to the signs of the zodiac. Similarly, recurring expressions like 'the rust of disbelief dissolved from the mirror of the heart' have a resonance in Sufi thought. There is perhaps a need to research these aspects of the stories for their deeper meanings.

Whether or not they were influenced by Sufi thought, the composers of the tales of *Tilism-e-Hoshruba* were endowed with intelligent, imaginative and febrile minds. They competed with each other to make their dastans lengthier and increasingly elaborate, which explains the sheer bulk of the final text when printed. Although they were not soldiers, their understanding of military strategy and the use of weaponry was immense. They were not statesmen but were aware of statecraft and the art of diplomacy sufficiently enough to capture and hold their select and discerning audience. They were as familiar with the names of women's costumes and jewellery as they were with the names of foods sold in Lucknow fairs.

As in most classics the characters created in *Tilism-e-Hoshruba* outlived their creators and were complex, almost split personalities. Hamza's childhood companion and trickster Amar ayyar has been given a key role in the epic. While Hamza waits in the sidelines at Mount Agate, having occasional skirmishes with the false god Laqa's forces, it is Amar who accompanies Hamza's grandson Asad into the Tilism to vanquish it. While Asad Sherdil languishes in Afrasiyab's prison, Amar is left to make most of the alliances with powerful sorcerers. He is much ridiculed for his greed, his low birth and ugly form, and yet endears himself with his sharp wit and audacious disguises. Amar resorts to the most underhand, ruthless and rapacious behaviour but remains the most popular and memorable character with dastan aficionados.

The real hero of *Tilism-e-Hoshruba* is Afrasiyab Jadoo, the King of Magic, who faces a rebellion within his favourite sardars when Amar forms the Islamic army. Here is a Jupiter-like character who has to merely wave his fingers to release lightning bolts, but on several occasions shields his turncoat sardars from certain death believing optimistically that they might switch back to his side. Capable of incinerating the rebel camp within moments, he nevertheless goes through the formality of deputing his officers to fight them. The writers of Hoshruba maintain his dignity and majesty throughout the narrative; even his constant humiliations by the tricksters take place mainly when his replica is on the throne. The reader empathizes with him when he talks longingly of a past when he was at school with those who are now his enemies or when he laughs despite his rage at the comical name Amar uses in one of his trickeries. Hoshruba seems a dreary place after his death, bereft of all magical illusions.

The Islamic army within Hoshruba is quite different from Emir Hamza's camp in Mount Agate. Hamza's female relatives have walk-on parts unlike Amar's army in Hoshruba, which is led by a woman, Mahrukh Magic-eye. Several other powerful princesses from Afrasiyab's court have defected to the Islamic side and fight for Asad and Amar against their former overlord. There is a certain amount of ambiguity about the relationship of Asad Sherdil with the women who fall in love with him. Asad lives openly with his beloved Mahjabeen and later, with the other princesses who are also besotted with him. The implication throughout is that they remain chaste until he vanquishes Hoshruba and marries them. Afrasiyab too is surrounded by powerful women—his wife, the loyal Hairat, his maternal and paternal grandmothers, and several other sorceresses whom he has awarded kingdoms. Even his most powerful minister is a middle-aged woman called Sannat Magic-maker, who is his rock when he is heartbroken over the death of his favourite mistress Zulmat.

❦

When I started reading *Tilism-e-Hoshruba* as a child I was unaware of its historical stature in Urdu literature, of the oral tradition of the *Tilism* stories, and that the epic was a reflection of the highly sophisticated and ephemeral culture of Lucknow with its extremes of refinement and cruelty. I was not sensitive to its political nuances or its Muslim prejudices. For me, it was simply a portal into the magical world of Emir Hamza and the nefarious Amar ayyar. It was a world of enchantments and magical snares, of demons and fairies, of trickery and valour, and of the primeval struggle of good against evil.

For the three months that it took me to read the entire epic, the real world that I lived in became an unwelcome intrusion, a bleak, drab place where the robot in me ate, slept and attended school; but the real me lived and breathed within the pages of the *Tilism*. I worried about the lives of the princesses who had to forswear magic and go into purdah after they married Hamza's grandsons in the last chapter and I wept when Afrasiyab died.

My parents, torn between pride in my obsession and alarm at my exposure to erotic verses with which the book is replete, understandably prevented me from reading it. But by that time, I was hooked, so to speak, and like every addict sneaked fixes of the book late at night, reading it by torchlight. For years, the dog-eared copy of *Tilism* was blamed for my increasing myopia. Its archaic style, the beauty and richness of the language, and the sheer magic of the story have captivated me over the years.

The copy I used was Rais Ahmed Jafri's magnificently compiled and edited version of this classic published in 1960. Years later, when I sought out the original seven (eight in some versions) volumes of *Tilism*, I discovered that Jafri had not tampered much with the original beyond deleting some repetitive text and verse. He had organized it into paragraphs, introduced rudimentary punctuation and compressed the seven volumes of *Tilism* in one large tome while keeping the bulk of the classic intact.

For this translation, while being influenced by the model of Jafri's literary compression, I have translated or interpreted what I considered the essence of the story and some of my favourite passages. My narrative is essentially about the conquest of Hoshruba and I have kept those events that moved the story forward. Like the earliest Qurans, published dastans have running text without punctuation. The punctuation here is mine as are the subheadings that I have used to contain the material into episodes. A fascinating element in these dastans is the significance of sobriquets to indicate the personality or powers of the individual mentioned. Magical personalities in particular are given names that underscore the kind of magic they practise. I have provided equivalent terms in English in many cases to give the reader an instantly recognizable image.

Naturally, as in any translation, something had to be sacrificed in the process, not least the poetry and the wonderful rhythmic cadence of the language of Hoshruba, composed by Jah and Qamar. This has been revived in the recent dastan narrations, in which the text familiar to me has been brought to life in brilliant performances by two modern Indian dastangohs—Mahmood Farooqui and his partner, Danish Husain. The future of this genre of dastans will owe as much to the discerning scholar Mahmood Farooqui for single-handedly reviving interest in this art form as it already does to Munshi Naval Kishore, who through his publications over a century ago disseminated the dastan to a wider public.

Tilism-e-Lahore   Shahnaz Aijazuddin

THE STORY OF TILISM-E-HOSHRUBA
OR THE FALSE GOD LAQA

I

In the name of Allah,
the Compassionate, the Merciful

PREAMBLE

Let it be stated that the *dastan* of Emir Hamza has seven *daftar*s in all. Therefore, this narrative should be read as part of that whole to understand the roles of Emir Hamza, Amar bin Ummayyah, Zamurrad Shah and Bakhtiarak within context. To summarize, Emir Hamza is the son of Syed Khwaja Abdul Muttalib, the sardar of the Khana Kaaba in Mecca. Amar bin Ummayyah is his ayyar or trickster. Emir Hamza has appointed his grandson Saad bin Qubad as the Badshah-e-lashkar or the king of his army. All of Hamza's sons and numerous grandsons pay homage to Saad as their king. There are, however, several other kings with equally large armies who will also be mentioned during the course of this narrative. One of them, a Persian king of considerable stature, claims divinity and expects to be revered as Khudawand. He is Zamurrad Shah Bakhtri, also known as Laqa.

Emir Hamza fights Laqa so that he can be prevented from spreading such a false claim. Emir has defeated Laqa several times, but he always manages to flee to countries where the rulers and their people are prepared to acknowledge him as a Living God and fight on his behalf. Laqa is supported by Faramurz bin Nausherwan, son of the great Persian king Nausherwan, who has earlier fought many battles with Emir Hamza and is now allied with Laqa against Hamza.

Divinity also requires the counterforce of a Satan or Shaitan. Therefore, Faramurz's vizier, Bakhtiarak bin Bakhtak, has been appointed the Shaitan in Laqa's durbar. Earlier, Laqa had sought protection from Emir Hamza in the Tilism of a Thousand Faces. When Emir Hamza conquered that Tilism, Laqa fled to Kohistan.

Thus, the narrative begins . . .

1 Tilism-e-Hoshruba and the Story of Laqa

The cupbearers of the wine of storytelling and the imbibers of the wine of thought from the goblet of paper tell us the story in this manner . . .

When Zamurrad Shah Bakhtri, better known as the false god Laqa, escaped from the Tilism of a Thousand Faces, his resourceful vizier, Shaitan Bakhtiarak suggested that they both take refuge with the ruler of Mount Agate in the Garden of Sulaiman. The wily Shaitan advised the great oaf Laqa that the mighty ruler of Mount Agate, Sulaiman Ambreen, maintained a huge army with many famous warriors and wrestlers in it. This kingdom also shared a border with Tilism-e-Hoshruba. The ruler of Tilism-e-Hoshruba, Afrasiyab Jadoo, was the King of Magic and Sahirs—the mighty sound of his sword made the rebels of the earth tremble and quiver; and the followers of the great magicians Samri and Jamshed were in awe of his magical skills. Bakhtiarak advised his master that Afrasiyab would be an invaluable ally in his fight against Emir Hamza.

Therefore, Zamurrad Shah departed with his followers for Mount Agate and reached it after a journey of several days through the steep mountains of Kohistan. Its ruler Sulaiman Ambreen came out of the walled city of Agate to receive Laqa and welcomed him after giving him gold trays heaped with precious stones. The city was illuminated in Laqa's honour. Laqa was visibly delighted with all the pomp and ceremony. After he sat on a jewelled throne in the royal palace, all the viziers and high-ranking nobles kneeled before him in homage. *Saqi*s began singing melodiously as they served wine to the guests assembled in the durbar.

Ravi, the legendary narrator, tells us that when Laqa fled from the Tilism of a Thousand Faces, his adversary, the mighty Emir Hamza Sahibqiran, sent his fleet-footed spies to keep track of Laqa's movements. After the conquest of this Tilism, Emir Hamza, the Shah of the Islamic army, Saad bin Qubad, and his sardars relaxed in the pavilion of Solomon. The flaps of the pavilion had been drawn up and provided a view of verdant plains.

The badshah of the *lashkar*, Saad bin Qubad, was sitting in all splendour on the throne of Solomon when Hamza's spies returned from their mission; exhausted from the long journey, their lips were cracked and parched. They first performed a *mujra*-greeting for the Shah and kissed the ground before him; then they raised their hands and praised him before giving him a detailed account of Laqa's latest hideout.

The Shah looked at his commander-in-chief, Emir Hamza, inquiringly. The Emir, in turn, directed Amar bin Ummayyah to prepare the Islamic lashkar to move. All the soldiers were excited by the prospect of another campaign; army bazaars packed their wares and pack-mules were loaded with tents and other equipment and necessities of war. The army travelled the whole day and camped in the evening on a pleasant meadow. The pavilion of Solomon, with its pillars soaring to the skies, was erected there. Bazaars reopened and the platoons set up their tents in neat rows.

One of Hamza's sons, Prince Badi-uz-Zaman, tempted by the temperate climate and the surrounding verdant plains, sought permission to hunt from the Emir, who assented graciously to his request. Early next morning, the noble Badi-uz-Zaman set off with his men for the hunt. There was a morning breeze while the evening lamps still glimmered in the camp; blossoms smiled as bulbul birds trilled noisily, peacocks danced in the jungle, and birds sang in praise of the one true Lord. Suddenly, a deer as winsome and beautiful as a beloved mistress leapt into sight. The deer captivated Badi as it frolicked and he ordered his companions to capture the animal alive. 'I am warning you,' he cried, 'it is not to be harmed at any cost!'

The prince's men tried to ambush the deer, but it eluded them. Leaving his group behind, Badi rode hard after it. When he realized that he could not capture the deer alive, the prince reached reluctantly for his bow and arrow and released an arrow that soon found its mark. When the deer died, a fearsome voice that shook the Bull of the Earth cried out, 'O Son of Hamza! You have done grave harm by killing Ghazzal Jadoo! This is the land of Hoshruba—it is impossible to escape from here!' The lush green plains were darkened by a mighty dust storm and the prince fell unconscious. When he opened his eyes, he found himself bound in iron shackles.

The Great Name

Ummayyah bin Amar, Badi's childhood friend and *ayyar* or trickster, had been following him during the hunt. Ummayyah waited for the dust storm to settle and saw the prince lying lifeless on the ground, his moon-like face covered with blood. He tore his robes in grief and hugged the limp body, weeping bitterly. After a while, he lifted the prince and placed him on his horse gently. He returned to the camp with the prince's companions who had smeared their faces with dust in sheer grief. Emir Hamza and his army wept on seeing the body of Badi-uz-Zaman and his mother collapsed at the sight of his bloodied face. In cold fury, Emir Hamza ordered the ayyar Amar bin Ummayyah, to saddle his horse Ashqar so that he could find his son's murderer and return with his head.

Amar bin Ummayyah implored the Emir to stay calm and said, 'O Ruler of the World! I have heard that no man murdered the prince. The desert suddenly went very dark and then this corpse was found.' Emir exclaimed, 'By Allah! There is a mystery here. Call the sons of the astrologer Khwaja Buzurjmeher, the vizier of Nausherwan!'

When the astrologers arrived, Emir received them respectfully and sought their advice on unravelling the mystery of Badi's murder. Khwaja Buzurg Umeed, Khwaja Siahvash and Khwaja Darya Dil, sons of the legendary Buzurjmeher, cast astrological charts and after studying them declared, 'O Sheheryar! The prince is still alive, but he is in captivity. This corpse is a dummy. Sprinkle some water of the Great Name, the Ism-e-Azam, over it and you will witness the miracle of Allah!'

Emir recited the Ism-e-Azam and blew on some water. He sprinkled it over the corpse, which was revealed to be nothing more than moulded lentil flour. Emir Hamza fell on his knees and thanked Allah for His mercy. He rewarded the astrologers with costly robes of honour and the dummy corpse was thrown away. Everyone in the camp rejoiced as the prince was still alive.

Later on, Emir Hamza summoned Amar, and after bestowing gifts of gold and precious jewels on him, asked him to find his son, Prince Badi-uz-Zaman. Amar returned to his tent where he armed himself with his tools of *ayyari* and the divine gifts of the prophets. Ravi tells us that when Emir Hamza decided to conquer Hindustan, Amar had spent a night at the tombs of the prophets to pray for victory. During that night, he was blessed with visions of several prophets who spoke to him and revealed that treasures (each of which had enchanted properties) were hidden in their tombs.

The first prophet told him, 'Zambil is a pouch with several worlds within it. Whatever you require, you can draw out from it, and place in it whatever you like.' The second said, 'Jaal-e-Ilyasi, the Net of Ilyas, has the property of converting any weight, be it millions of *maund*s, into only a seer and a half when you cast the net over it.' The third spoke of the blessed Tent of Nabi Danyal and said, 'It will protect you from all magic. It can expand as wide as you like and reduce likewise.' The fourth mentioned the Asifi Kamand or snare-rope of Asif and said to Amar, 'It will extend and reduce to any length you require.' The fifth prophet described a *devjama* that reflected the seven colours of the rainbow.

Amar awoke from his trance and found these items lying beside him. Since then, he always carried them on special missions.

Princess Tasveer and Sharara Jadoo

After equipping himself, the honourable Amar, moon of trickery and star of swordplay, set forth on his search for Prince Badi-uz-Zaman. When he reached the place where his son had discovered the substitute body, he saw a group of maidens emerging out of a grove of trees. Amar hastily dived behind a bush. He saw that the maidens milled around a beautiful princess adorned with rich silks and precious jewels.

These maidens walked past the bush where Amar was hiding and he silently ambushed one of them who had fallen behind in order to relieve herself. He stuffed a ball in her mouth to prevent her from screaming and rubbed an unguent on her face to render her unconscious. After dragging her behind the bush, he took out a hand-mirror from Zambil and used special paints of ayyari to transform his face into looking like her. Finally, he stripped her of her outer garments and wore them himself to complete his disguise. After a final reassuring look at the mirror, he ran to catch up with the group of maidens. One of them looked at him in surprise and exclaimed, 'Shagoofa, you took a long time! Where have you been?' Amar mumbled, 'I did not take that long!'

The princess and her group walked towards a walled garden. The doors of the garden were open like the eager eyes of a waiting suitor and as they entered it, Amar marvelled at the beauty of the garden, which was like paradise on earth. Its pathways sparkled with crushed jewels and its trees and plants gleamed with flecks of silver thread. Henna bushes and grapevines were adorned like new brides, and a soft cool breeze wafted across the garden. In the middle of all this splendour was a marble platform covered with rich carpets and a velvet, gold-embroidered *masnad*. A middle-aged woman was reclining on the masnad with bowls of betelnut, flowers and perfumes laid out before her.

The woman was the powerful sorceress Sharara Jadoo, who had lured the prince using the beautiful deer as bait; the young princess was Tasveer, the daughter of Hairat Jadoo, wife of Shahanshah Afrasiyab of Tilism-e-Hoshruba. Tasveer was also Sharara's niece.

Sharara greeted the princess with affection and sat her down on the masnad next to her. Beautiful young dancers began performing for the princess and wine was served. Sharara asked her niece, 'My daughter, what brings you to this wilderness?' Tasveer responded eagerly, 'I have heard that you have captured a son of Hamza. I am keen to see Muslims as I am told that they have conquered several lands and have reduced powerful Tilisms to ashes.'

Sharara laughed and ordered an attendant witch to fetch her prisoner. Badi-uz-Zaman was dragged forward with his magical shackles weighing him down. Tasveer beheld a young man of radiant beauty, bound with heavy iron chains that were virtually eating into his body. She felt a sudden rush of love for the prince and fainted because of the intensity of her emotion. The women gasped when they saw this and Sharara anxiously tried to revive her niece. The prince too looked up and on seeing the lovely Tasveer, felt that he could lose his life a thousand times for her love; his heart yearned for her but he controlled his feelings and remained silent.

Sharara revived the princess with rose and musk waters. Seeing her so distressed, she immediately ordered her handmaidens to remove the prince. She told them, 'My poor daughter has never seen anyone in such a dire plight and has fainted as a result; she has the delicate disposition of an unmarried girl; her body-blood is very light!'

Tasveer woke up and her eyes again began searching for that rare flower in the garden. When she could not find him, she sighed deeply, but remained silent. Sharara asked her, 'My daughter, how do you feel now?' 'Dear aunt,' Tasveer replied, 'what can I say? My heart seems to be sinking and there is a feeling of dread at the thought that people go through such suffering!'

Sharara murmured sympathetically, 'O my daughter, you are a royal princess. You should have a stouter heart. So many sinners are captured every day. Some are hanged and others, forgiven. This is a prisoner of Afrasiyab. He is the enemy of all magicians and sahirs, and cannot escape. Otherwise, I would have released him for your sake and even rewarded him with money. Return to your garden and blossom again. Think no more of him.'

That full moon Tasveer then rose and bowed to Sharara so gracefully that her body formed the shape of a crescent. Sharara made the traditional gesture of taking the princess's troubles upon herself and bid her farewell. The handmaidens who had been strolling in the garden gathered when they heard that Tasveer was leaving. Amar, still disguised as her maid, thought to himself, 'I should kill this wretch Sharara and rescue my prince.' He pleaded with Sharara with folded hands, 'Huzoor, allow me to remain with you. It will be my singular honour to entertain you tonight and earn your appreciation.' Sharara graciously invited the false Shagoofa to stay for as many days as she wished to and requested Tasveer to leave Shagoofa with her.

Princess Tasveer left the garden and after a while encountered the real Shagoofa, naked and wailing about the loss of her clothes. Though Tasveer was puzzled, she told her companions to provide clothes for

Shagoofa and then said, 'Look at this slut! She pretended to stay back with Sharara but who knows where she went to be stripped!' Poor Shagoofa tried to relate what had happened to her but the princess refused to believe her and returned to her garden with a heavy heart, her thoughts still absorbed by Prince Badi.

Now hear about the slayer of sahirs and apostates, the incomparable Khwaja Amar. Disguised as the handmaiden Shagoofa, he mingled with Sharara's maids, teasing and flirting with them, pinching one on the cheek, caressing another, and all the time quietly slipping silver betelnut holders and gold vases into Zambil.

After dinner, Sharara had the marble platform in the garden adorned with carpets and silk cushions. Her attendants illuminated the garden with crystal chandeliers and suspended lamps that shed the light of heaven on every tree. Praise be to God for that place— the spouting waters of the marble fountains and canals gleamed with gold and silver glitter. Then Sharara sent for Shagoofa, who came wearing a costly *peshwaz* and dancing bells sewn to her anklets. Shagoofa ordered the musicians and singers to provide the accompaniment to Shagoofa's dance.

Amar tucked a flask of wine under his arm and took out his flute. Then he held a goblet in his hand and started dancing. The false Shagoofa's dancing was so skilled that she looked like a flame leaping in the twilight. The reader should know that Amar had been fed three grapes by the angel Gabriel. One endowed him with a melodious voice; the second enabled him to assume any face or form he wanted and the third gave him the ability to speak any language fluently. There were loud cheers of appreciation from Sharara and her companions. Enthralled with the ghazal that Shagoofa sang for her, Sharara cried, 'You have entertained me royally tonight, O Shagoofa! From tonight, you will be one of my special companions. Come here and serve some more wine to me!'

The false Shagoofa offered five gold coins as homage to Sharara, who, in turn, awarded her with a costly robe. Shagoofa donned the robe, arranged the green and red cut-glass wine flasks in a bouquet, and while doing so, slipped a strong narcotic into the wine. After impressing everyone present with her skills as a cupbearer, she filled a wine cup and served it to Sharara even as she continued dancing. Just as Sharara leaned forward to take the cup, Shagoofa tossed it and caught it on her head without spilling a drop of wine.

'Huzoor, nobles and royals are served this way!' Shagoofa announced, and bowed low to offer the cup to Sharara. As Sharara extended her hand to take the cup, the wine suddenly burst into flames. Sharara realized that Shagoofa must be an ayyar in disguise and muttered a spell. The paints of ayyari on Amar quickly evaporated to reveal his real face. Sharara cried out, 'You wily wretch, you would have killed me! Now see how horribly I execute you!'

'Listen witch,' Amar retorted, 'where will you escape from me? Wherever we go, we fulfil our purpose. Now watch how I send you straight to hell.'

The Empire of Hoshruba

Ravi tells us that when Sharara captured Prince Badi, she had alerted her magical spirits to protect her against ayyars who came to rescue the prince. That was how the wine had turned into flames, thus exposing Amar. On realizing that Amar was unrepentant, Sharara had him tied to a tree. Then she sent a detailed note of the evening's events to Afrasiyab through her trusted companion, Shola Rukhsar.

The empire of Afrasiyab Jadoo, ruler of Tilism-e-Hoshruba, included sixty thousand countries populated by powerful *sahir*s and *sahira*s. The rulers of these countries were his subjects and vassals. Tilism-e-Hoshruba consisted of three distinct areas—Zulmat or the Veil of Darkness, the hidden Tilism of Batin, and the visible Tilism of Zahir. Afrasiyab's elders, including his grandmothers Mahiyan Emerald-robe and Afat Four-eyes lived in Zulmat, the Veil of Darkness. Nobles and aristocrats of the court such as Malika Hairat lived in the invisible Tilism of Batin, while the public and officers of the state lived in the visible Tilism of Zahir.

Between the visible and hidden Tilisms flowed the River of Flowing Blood, spanned by the Bridge of Parizadan. Two lions made of smoke guarded the bridge, which had a three-tiered tower of smoke on the Batin side. *Parizad*s played trumpets and flutes on the first tier of this tower. On the second tier, more *pari*s or fairies stood with armfuls of pearls, which they tossed into the river, where silver fish leaped out to catch the pearls. On the third tier, naked African warriors fenced with each other. Blood spilled out of their wounds into the water, thus giving the river its name. Shahanshah Afrasiyab had access to all three Tilisms and there were monuments and gardens in each one that he had conjured with his magic.

Sharara's messenger flew to the River of Flowing Blood, stood on its banks and cried out, 'O King of Sahirs! I have been sent by Sharara Jadoo and request an audience with you!' It is said that Afrasiyab was so powerful that if anyone called out to him from any corner of his vast empire, he could hear the call. He also possessed the magic Book of Samri, which could reveal any secret to him. Besides, an army of clay and iron puppets carried out his commands. The puppets could snatch anybody Afrasiyab needed from anywhere with a swipe of their hands.

On hearing Shola Rukhsar's call, Afrasiyab sent his magic *panja* to bring her to his court in the Garden of Apples. The panja brought her to him in a flash and disappeared. Shola found herself in the *baradari* of a garden that was furnished with chairs studded with priceless rubies and crystals. Seated on these chairs were the nobles of Tilism such as Bahar Jadoo, Zafaran Jadoo, Surkh Mu Deadly-locks and Makhmoor Red-eye.

The empress, Hairat Jadoo, sat beside Afrasiyab in the place of honour on a throne encrusted with precious stones. To her right stood her special attendants, the five ayyar-princesses—Sarsar Sword-fighter, Saba Raftar Swift-footed, Shameema Tunnel-woman, Sanobar Whip-lasher and Tez Nigah Dagger-woman. The Malika's two *vizierzadis*—Yakut and Zamurrad—stood behind her and were fanning her. Afrasiyab's four viziers—Baghban Qudrat, Sannat Magic-maker, Abriq Mountain-breaker, and Sarmaya Ice-breaker—were fanning the King of Sahirs silently. There was a respectful hush in the durbar.

Shola performed a *mujra*-greeting and presented Sharara's note to Afrasiyab, who read it and wrote a terse message: 'Kill Amar.' He sent Shola back to the other side of the River of Flowing Blood, from where she flew back to Sharara.

Meanwhile, the nightingale of the garden of trickery, Khwaja Amar, lay tied to a tree while Sharara slept in her baradari. Amar was thinking of ways of escape when he noticed a maiden walking by. He beckoned to her with the words, 'O Daughter of Laqa, please hear my plea!' Weeping bitterly, he continued, 'You know, I will be killed in the morning and the executioner will take all my possessions. I will give them all to you if you fulfil my last wish.'

The maiden, Saman Azar, tempted by the mention of wealth, trotted up to him eagerly and asked, 'What is your will then and how much wealth do you have?' Amar said, 'Untie my arms so I can hand it over to you.' Saman eagerly untied his left arm and Amar immediately pulled out his pouch of ayyari. Then he asked her to help him unpack it. As she unpacked the contents of the bag, he explained the use of each item to her: 'These are the tools of my trade. This is how I can transform myself into a woman, a beggar or even a king. These sweets, for example, are drugged and these are doctored fruits.' He took out a bag of gold coins and some gems that he gave to Saman, who greedily rummaged for more. She found a carved cornelian box that Amar hastily snatched from her.

'What is in that box?' Saman asked Amar. Amar replied, 'My life is in it! Whatever I have earned is in it!' Saman pleaded, 'O Amar, you will surely die tomorrow! Give this to me as well.' Finally, Amar relented and asked her to open the box and show its contents to him for the last time. When Saman tried to open the box and could not, Amar urged her to press it to her bosom and use both hands to open it. When she did so, the box snapped open and released powerful narcotic vapours that made her sneeze and faint.

Amar quickly freed himself from the ropes, painted his face to resemble hers, and then painted her so that she looked like him. He exchanged his clothes with her and applied toxic oil to her tongue that made it swollen and prevented her from speaking. After tying Saman to the tree, he found her bed and quietly laid down on it.

Sharara woke up with the light of the morning sun. Her companions and maidservants prepared the baradari for her. Meanwhile, Shola Rukhsar had returned with Afrasiyab's reply. Sharara declared that Amar was to be executed immediately. Saman (now disguised by Amar to look like him) was therefore dragged before Sharara. Although she wept and did her best to gesture, she could not speak because of her swollen tongue and no one could understand her. She was beheaded with one stroke of a sword, but because she was a sahira, her magical spirits created an uproar when she died. 'Alas!' they cried, 'You have actually murdered Saman Azar Jadoo!' Darkness descended on the garden and taking advantage of the confusion, Amar hid in a secluded corner.

The ill-fated Sharara was horrified when she realized that the tree of Saman Azar's life had withered and that Amar had escaped. She went to her room and took out a gold bracelet from a magic box. The bracelet was enchanted and could expose any impostor who wore it. Sharara made all her companions and handmaidens try the bracelet on, but no one was caught. Eventually, she proclaimed, 'Amar is obviously not amongst you! Return the box to its place. I will awaken my magic tonight so that we can find him.'

Amar watched all this from his hiding place. He spotted a gardener's hut in a far corner. Darting behind trees, he reached the hut and saw an old woman lying on a string cot. Amar asked her, 'Who are you?' 'My name is Champa,' the old woman replied. Amar easily overcame her with a narcotic bubble that he burst in her face. Depositing her in Zambil, he disguised himself this time as Champa. Leaning heavily on a walking stick, he hobbled to Sharara to pay homage.

'How are you Champa?' Sharara asked the old woman kindly. The false Champa replied, 'I can forfeit my life for you, my mistress. I have heard that there is a thief in the garden and you have tested everyone here. I have come to be tested as well.' On hearing this, Sharara laughed and exclaimed, 'Champa, you don't need to be tested! My magic will bring Amar himself to me tonight.'

Champa however insisted on being treated like the other inmates of the garden. Finally, Sharara asked her to bring the magic box from her room. Champa shuffled off and on finding the box, quietly filled it with a sleep-inducing dust and walked slowly back to Sharara. Impatient with her painstakingly slow progress, Sharara asked her handmaidens to help the infirm old woman and finally took the box from her.

As soon as Sharara opened the box, the dust in it made her and all those near her sneeze and fall unconscious. The false Champa swiftly decapitated Sharara and it was as if the sky had fallen—there was thunder, lightning and a downpour of stones. Amar quickly made himself invisible in Galeem and then called out loudly to everyone else in the garden, 'Run away quickly, lest the rest of you are killed!'

Sharara's guards and her other servants panicked and ran out of the garden. Becoming visible again, Amar slaughtered Sharara's unconscious companions. There was yet more thunder and darkness. Finally, the sky cleared and Amar saw that the ground was strewn with the corpses of dead sahiras. All the trees and buildings in the garden conjured up magically suddenly disappeared, leaving only the original houses and trees. In the distance, Prince Badi, who was now free, stood watching Amar's antics with interest.

Badi-uz-Zaman and Amar met and embraced with joy. Suddenly, there was a sharp gust of wind in the garden. It whipped up sand from the ground into a whirlwind that picked up Sharara's corpse, which started spinning as well. The whirlwind blew out of the garden carrying Sharara's corpse.

Badi and Tasveer meet at last

Amar said to Prince Badi, 'My son! You should leave quickly. It appears that the corpse will be taken to the ruler of Tilism, which means there will be trouble any moment!' The prince replied thoughtfully, 'If I had a mount, I could leave faster.' Amar said somewhat furtively that a horse could be made available, but that it would cost him dearly. Badi-uz-Zaman pledged to pay him one lakh rupees, at which Amar pulled out a pen and paper and said, 'Then write that down! You are a young man and if you do not keep your word, at least I will have something to sue you with!'

The prince laughed heartily and wrote out a pledge, promising to pay Amar once he had rejoined his army. Amar carefully folded the letter and put it in his pocket. He went out of the garden and took out a saddled and harnessed steed from Zambil. He presented this to the prince, claiming that he had just acquired it from a merchant.

As they rode out of the garden, the prince said to Amar, 'Respected elder, I cannot return to the army because I am in love with Princess Tasveer. What will she think of me if I desert her now?' Amar looked hard at Badi and cried, 'You idiot, what nonsense is this? Get going, or by Allah, I will flay you alive!' Badi-uz-Zaman pleaded with Amar to find a way of uniting him with his beloved. He even offered his valuable jewelled armband to Amar. Eyeing the precious amulet, Amar pretended to become angrier. 'Just what kind of a pimp do you think I am?' he screamed. 'However, I suppose, as she is a princess, I could try for her sake. Hand over that armband!' The prince untied his armband and gave it to Amar, who then led him in the direction of Tasveer's garden.

Now hear of the plight of Princess Tasveer. She had been pining for the prince and was constantly restless and tearful. Seeing her condition, one of her handmaidens said, 'Princess, may I die for you! I know that you may be angry with me, but the fact is that you have been in this state of melancholy ever since you saw that prisoner.' Another one said, 'That rogue was so beautiful! Even I have been in a state ever since I saw him. My heart is entangled in his winsome locks; I cannot sleep at night and can think only of seeing his face again.'

Listening to their expressions of solicitude, the princess confessed her love for the prisoner. She asked her handmaidens to transform themselves into pigeons and doves and fly to Sharara's garden. 'Bring me news of him as soon as you can!' she pleaded with them. They returned the next morning and brought her news of Sharara's death. Tasveer laughed like a bed of blossoming flowers and told them, 'The prince must now be returning to his lashkar. Pray, find him and lead him to me!'

The handmaidens went in search of the prince. Meanwhile, the prince and Amar were walking towards the garden and came across five fairy-like young damsels. Their hair parting was reddened with vermilion and they seemed to have emerged from a river of jewels. They greeted the prince respectfully and said, 'Our Princess Tasveer sends you salaams and greetings. She invites you to rest in her garden for a while before you return to your people.'

Amar interrupted scornfully, 'We do not consort with witches. We will not allow you to help us even with our ablutions!' The maidens looked in his direction and saw a thin, reedy-looking man sneering at them. Giggling amongst each other, they began teasing him and continued to do so until they reached their garden, which had been bedecked to welcome Prince Badi. The soft-eyed Princess Tasveer stood waiting at the entrance to receive him. Supported by her maidens, she came up to the prince and held his hand. 'Prince,' she whispered, 'by coming to my garden you have graced this humble abode. You honour me!' The prince looked deep into her eyes and sighed, 'My princess, I am besotted!' Thus whispering to each other, they sat side by side on a velvet masnad in a pavilion by the lake in the garden. Crystal goblets of wine were laid out on silver trays for them.

Amar sat in front of them and looked closely at Tasveer. Suddenly, he exclaimed, 'O Badi-uz-Zaman! Just look at this woman, how ugly she is! She is cross-eyed and her hair is moth-eaten!' The beautiful Princess Tasveer felt acutely embarrassed on hearing this unflattering description of her, but the prince whispered to her, 'My dear princess, this man is very greedy. If you give him something, he will surely sing your praises as loudly as he has criticized you!'

Tasveer quickly offered Amar a chest of jewels. Seizing it, Amar declared, 'O Badi-uz-Zaman, you have done well! She is truly a princess of the realm! How lucky you are that you, a son of a lowly keeper of the Kaaba, can consort with her!' Everyone laughed to hear Amar change his tune so quickly.

The princess filled a goblet of wine and offered it to the prince. 'This is an offering of love, pray accept it!' she said. The prince replied, 'Nightingale of this garden! You are a sorceress and I am a Muslim. Only if you promise to forswear magic can I drink with you and even be your slave forever!' The princess responded gently, 'Sheheryar, I have not yet learnt to use magic as I am young, but I do wish to adopt your faith.' Thus, the princess converted to Islam and the festivities began. Wine flowed freely and dancers entertained the gathering with a mujra performance.

Just then, the waters of the nearby lake began to boil. There was a loud noise and a huge black ogre rose out of the water. Calling out to the prince, he cried, 'Come forth you intruder, you are my victim!' The prince drew his sword out and slew the ogre in half with one swift cut. Both parts of the ogre's body fell into the lake. Moments later, he re-emerged, intact and whole again. Vizierzadi Nairang whispered to the princess, 'Huzoor, this ogre will emerge out of the lake seven times in all and can be slain each time. But the eighth time, he will not die!'

The princess exclaimed, 'Nairang, if you know how he can be killed, tell me now!' Nairang replied, 'I just know that this ogre was kept here by Sharara Jadoo for your protection. She had also kept a bow with three special arrows that can kill him in a hut in the garden. If all three arrows miss him, he will not die. Sharara had made the hut invisible with her spells, but as she is dead, I am sure we will be able to see it.' The princess and

Nairang then searched the garden and found a hut near the baradari, which no one had seen before. The princess quickly rushed in, found the bow and arrows, and ran back to the lake where she handed them to the prince.

By this time, Badi had already slain the ogre five times. The princess urged him to use the enchanted arrows. Badi waited for the ogre to appear again for the sixth time, and as he emerged, Badi charged towards him and shot an arrow straight at his chest. Where the arrow pierced the ogre, a flame sprang out and within moments, reduced his body to ashes. There were fearsome noises and a disembodied voice called out, 'You have killed Muhafiz Jadoo!'

The prince first kneeled down in gratitude to Allah Almighty and then embraced the princess. Amar, emerged from Galeem, his protective cape of invisibility, and pleaded with the prince to leave before there was more trouble. The prince turned to Tasveer to say farewell, but before he could speak, she said, 'I must go away with you. When Afrasiyab learns of this, he will surely kill me!' So Badi-uz-Zaman sent for his horse and lifted the princess on it. He then addressed her handmaidens, 'You are servants and will not be blamed. You are free to go or you can join us in Mount Agate!' The prince, the princess and Amar left the garden together for the Islamic camp, leaving her handmaidens in tears.

Meanwhile, Afrasiyab was waiting in the Garden of Apples to hear of Amar's death when the whirlwind blew Sharara's body into the garden. Her ghostly spirits cried out, 'O King of Magic, Sharara has been killed!' Trembling with fury, Afrasiyab opened the oracle Book of Samri, which informed him that Amar and Badi-uz-Zaman had slain both Sharara and Muhafiz Jadoo.

Afrasiyab summoned Azhdar Jadoo, a sahir with flames pouring out of his nostrils, mouth and eyeballs. Clay idols adorned his arms from the elbows to the shoulders. Afrasiyab ordered, 'Go in haste, Badi and Tasveer are on their way to the Islamic camp with Amar. Arrest the two of them, but do not arrest Amar. He must be left free to warn Hamza and to make him fearful of attacking us!'

While this was happening, Badi and Tasveer had already travelled several miles from Tasveer's garden. Suddenly, from behind a bush, a large dragon reared up, emitting flames from its mouth. Amar ran away, leaving the prince to defend himself and the princess against the dragon. The dragon incinerated the arrows shot by the prince. All of a sudden, it breathed in, and swallowed both Badi and Tasveer.

Realizing that he was now alone, Amar emerged from his hiding place and tried to kill the dragon by firing huge stones from his catapult. They missed the dragon that called out, 'O Amar! Go and describe this mishap to Hamza. This is the sacred land of Tilism-e-Hoshruba. Be warned that no one should enter it. It will now be difficult for anyone to rescue Badi-uz-Zaman!' The dragon then disappeared. Amar wailed in grief at losing his prince and returned to the Muslim camp.

Emir Hamza was seated in the durbar when Amar walked in. He paid the appropriate homage to his master and sat on the Hoopoe Chair. Hamza Sahibqiran, the badshah of the lashkar asked Amar, 'Khwaja, how are you faring?' Amar then related all that had transpired. Emir heard the news calmly and said, 'Praise be to Allah, my son is alive! We must find a way to conquer Tilism, but at this moment, we are facing Sulaiman Ambreen Kohi. We must plan a strategy for this battle and will worry about who to send to Tilism later.' Then the Emir became absorbed in his battle plans.

c⁓ꝋ

2 Afrasiyab Sends Ajlal Jadoo to Help Laqa

The narrators and storytellers who wielded the magic of eloquence relate the story thus:

When the victorious army of Emir Hamza followed Zamurrad Shah, the heretic, to Mount Agate, Sulaiman Kohi saw the strength and might of the Islamic army and thought that he would not be able to confront such a formidable force by himself.

He dispatched messages to neighbouring rulers appealing for help: 'It is because our Khudawand is so merciful that his created mortals are harassing him. His divinity does not kill them because he tells us, "I created these people in my sleep. My pen of destiny ordained that these mortals would be rebellious and arrogant. What has been written once cannot be erased." This is the reason why Khudawand cannot destroy these people. Therefore, it is incumbent upon you to at once ally with him.'

One of these messages was sent to Afrasiyab Jadoo, the ruler of Tilism-e-Hoshruba. On the border of Hoshruba and Mount Agate was a great mountain and a massive *naqara* drum had been placed on it. To communicate with Afrasiyab, Sulaiman placed his letter on the mountain and struck the enchanted drum with a wooden mallet. The magic sound reached Afrasiyab and he dispatched one of his magic hands to bring the message.

After reading Sulaiman's letter, Afrasiyab wrote back to him, 'It will be my privilege to help my Khudawand. It seems that he does not destroy these rebels deliberately, just so that I can have the honour of destroying them. Be assured, Hamza is doomed. I am sending the powerful Ajlal Jadoo with forty thousand sahir soldiers who will crush Hamza's army in a day.' A panja threw the message on the mountain and it was retrieved by Sulaiman's attendant. Sulaiman was delighted with the response and started to chart his own battle strategy.

The next morning, Zamurrad Shah and Sulaiman Kohi were holding court when the sky clouded over and there was unseasonable snowfall. Sulaiman realized that these were the auguries or signs of the impending arrival of a sahir and stepped out of the fortress to receive him. Ajlal and his fire-breathing sahir soldiers arrived, mounted on dragons, peacocks and swans, all conjured from lentil flour. They held wands and batons in their hands, and had tied their pouches of magical tools around their waists. Sulaiman welcomed them all and led them to Laqa. They all prostrated in front of Khudawand and submitted offerings of gold and silver to him. Sulaiman lodged Ajlal in a sumptuous palace within the city and that evening, Laqa joined them in the Garden of Pleasure.

The agents of Islam soon conveyed the news of Ajlal's arrival to Emir Hamza. Amar immediately exclaimed, 'Ya Emir! I have still not seen Fort Agate. Please give me leave to see it and to enjoy Ajlal's feast.' The Emir looked doubtful and said, 'Amar, they are sahirs in there, and you could be recognised.' Amar shrugged and replied philosophically, 'What has to happen, will happen. At least I may be able to earn a few coins while I am in the Fort.' The Emir relented and said with a smile, 'Bismillah! No one can stop you from trading!'

Amar reached Fort Agate and managed to enter it disguised as a sahir. He wore a loincloth, a pouch of magic around his neck, clay idols on his forearms and wooden clogs. Inside the gates, the city buzzed with activity. Its prosperous citizens traded with each other and the air positively hummed with hawkers' calls. It was a model city with clean wide roads and handsome buildings.

A moonlight tryst

Amar entered the royal palace and mingled with Ajlal's sahirs. Sulaiman was entertaining Ajlal with a performance by his dancing girls in the garden. Amar managed to station himself right behind Ajlal. He noticed that Ajlal's eyes were drawn to the gauze curtains of a house on the far side, through which a beautiful woman was watching him. This was Princess Nasreen Ambreen, daughter of Sulaiman, who had also come to watch the dancing.

Amar went to a secluded corner of the garden and transformed himself into a uniformed palace attendant there. He perfected the disguise with a long white beard, a starched turban, a gold baton in one hand and a silver and gold staff in the other. Transformed thus, he walked to the house where Princess Nasreen sat. Grasping the curtain, he held it down firmly. Nasreen tried to lift the curtain but when she detected some resistance, she let go. Amar whispered loudly through it, 'What is there to prevent me from informing the king that the women behind this curtain were making eyes at Ajlal Jadoo?' The princess hastily drew back out of sight, but did not say a word.

On the other side, Ajlal was surprised to see an elderly attendant guarding the curtain, but he could hardly complain to his host about the security around the palace of his women. A short while later, he noticed the elderly attendant signalling to him. He felt sure that there must be a message from the beautiful maiden behind the curtain. Making an excuse to his host about having to retire for ten minutes, he hurried to meet the old attendant.

'Why have you called me?' Ajlal asked him. Amar replied, 'O Ajlal! I have brought up the princess from infancy and she keeps no secrets from me. She loves you and wants me to tell you that if you at all return her love, you should demand an isolated house from her father. Be there only with those attendants who you trust completely. She will sleep on the rooftop of her palace tonight. Command your friends to transport her bed by magic to your house, so she can spend the night with you. But she must return before daylight.' Amar concluded by asking, 'Now tell me Ajlal, what message should I to convey to my princess?'

Overjoyed at receiving this message of confessed love, Ajlal bestowed a string of pearls on the old attendant and whispered to him, 'Tell the princess I too long for her. I will do as she says.' He then returned to his seat beside Sulaiman.

Meanwhile, cloaked in Galeem, Amar entered the room where the princess was sitting among a throng of women. He arranged the cloak such that only his arms and legs were visible. Then he walked in on the women with his arms outstretched. The women fainted with fright on seeing this horrible apparition. Amar locked all the doors and painted his face to look like the princess. After exchanging his clothes with her, he deposited her in Zambil and woke up the women. They awoke, trembling with fear and insisted on taking the princess to the safety of her chambers. Amar saw that these were richly furnished and asked them to prepare a bed on the roof. She murmured, 'We will enjoy the moonlight and sleep there.'

Ajlal asked Sulaiman for a private house by reasoning that he needed to practise his magic alone. Sulaiman obliged him at once and ordered that a house be furnished for Ajlal's use. Chalak bin Amar, who had followed his father into the city disguised as a labourer, joined a group of labourers hired to carry furniture into Ajlal's house. Ajlal had also ordered that carpets, a bejewelled bed, masnad seating, wine and sweetmeats be arranged on the roof. Chalak bin Amar cleverly managed to hide under the bed when the other labourers were leaving.

That night, Ajlal confided in his trusted aides Intizam and Munsarim about his love for the princess and asked them to bring her to him. Both bowed deeply and said, 'We hear and obey.' The two sahirs flew to the roof of Princess Nasreen's palace and saw that she was fast asleep—a vision of loveliness in the moonlight. They cast a spell to conjure a cool breeze, which made the maidens around her go into deep slumber. Both sahirs descended on the roof and lifted her bed. Amar as the princess was actually awake, but kept his eyes shut, sensing that these were Ajlal's men.

Within moments, the two sahirs flew with the bed to Ajlal's rooftop. Ajlal asked his aides to stay downstairs to make sure that there was no disturbance. He then turned to the sleeping princess. He nervously removed the veil from her face and was so dazzled by her beauty that he began to massage her feet. The false princess opened her eyes and drowsily called for her maidservants. Ajlal laid his head at her feet and said, 'The maids are not here, but I am your humble slave.'

The false princess pretended to be startled and frowned at Ajlal. Then she turned her face away and tied her loose tresses into a knot. Ajlal pleaded with her to be kind and told her that he was her humble servant. The Princess retorted sharply that he could be a humble servant to his mother and sister and how did he even dare to speak to her this way. After making him plead for a while, the princess walked over to the masnad with Ajlal and tantalized him with her smiles. When she saw that Ajlal was quite overcome with passion, the false princess said, 'You are a silly fool Ajlal. Your claims of love are hollow. How can you invite me here and not offer me wine or refreshments? Is this how you treat a guest? It is true that all men are alike and only after one thing?'

Ajlal was embarrassed and thought that she was right—wine would remove her inhibitions and she would yield to him. He quickly filled a crystal goblet with choice wine and offered it to her. The princess frowned as she sipped it and immediately threw its contents over him in a temper. 'This wine is no good!' she shouted. 'Alas! You call yourself a king but drink cheap liquor!'

Then she took out a small flask of wine from inside her robe and added a few drops of colour from a phial, which turned the wine rosy pink. She poured it into a crystal goblet and held it out to him. Delighted with her attentions, Ajlal drank the wine in one gulp and exclaimed, 'You certainly drink a strong wine my princess, I feel dizzy with just one goblet!' The false princess advised him to walk to dispel the dizziness and when he took a few steps, he fell down heavily and collapsed.

Amar drew his sword to decapitate Ajlal when his son Chalak darted out from his hiding place under the bed and stopped him. Startled, Amar attacked him instead. Chalak ducked neatly and cried out, 'I am your son, Chalak!' Amar was furious, 'Why are you here, you no good scoundrel? How dare you prevent me from killing an enemy of Emir?' Chalak explained patiently, 'Because, respected father, whenever a sahir is killed, his magical spirits will raise a hue and cry and you will be arrested immediately by the two sahirs downstairs.'

'You are right,' Amar acknowledged, 'so what am I to do?' Chalak suggested that he could become the princess and Amar could assume Ajlal's face after depositing him in Zambil. Amar could then order Ajlal's two attendants to take the princess back to her roof. Thus, they could both escape from the palace. Amar did as his son suggested and after the disguises were complete, he called out to Intizam and Munsarim to take the princess back.

The battle with Hamza

The next morning, Amar, disguised as Ajlal, asked Laqa and Sulaiman to announce the battle against Hamza. The mighty doors of Fort Agate opened and the elephants emerged first, followed by sixty thousand armed soldiers on horses. Behind them walked seventy thousand foot soldiers equipped with bows and arrows, and swords and shields. An army of sahirs emerged next, mounted on magical lions and dragons. They wore earrings and thick metal bands on their throats, and called out 'Ya Samri! Ya Jamshed!' even as they conjured dazzling spectacles of magic. Last of all, forty elephants were tethered together to make a platform for the thrones of Laqa, his son Yakut Shah and Faramurz, the son of King Nausherwan. The two young men flanked Laqa and Shaitan Bakhtiarak stood behind them, fanning Laqa. Several sardars accompanied them on the platform.

The false Ajlal made his aides Intizam and Munsarim conjure a dragon mount for him and told them that he was saving his powers for the battlefield. So a fire-breathing dragon was conjured and when Amar mounted it, both his companions held its reins and led it through a magical rain of stones and fire flames.

Emir Hamza saw the might of this army from his camp and prayed to the Almighty for success in battle. He then asked for the Naqara of Alexander to be struck to announce the battle. When the keeper struck it, it seemed as if the very Bull of the Earth trembled. Even mountains quivered as its sound travelled in full strength for sixty-four miles. The braves in the army of Islam prepared to meet the angel of death as they sharpened their swords. The daredevils amongst the men looked to the battlefield and laughed with their faces flushed while the cowards turned pale. The sahirs were also fully prepared—pig's blood had been smeared on the sacred ground during the night, red chillies were burnt and incense lit in anticipation of the battle.

Emir Hamza armed himself with the divine gifts that the prophets had bestowed on him. These were the chain armour of David, the spear of Saam bin Noah, the *tegha*s or swords Sumsaam and Qumqaam from the Garden of Abraham, Solomon's spear, the *neemcha* or dagger of Sohrab and the shield from Koh Qaf. Then Hamza sent for his great horse Ashqar and traced the name of Hazrat Ali with his forefinger on the horse's mane before mounting him. There were shouts of 'Bismillah' all around and after reciting the powerful verses of the *Naad-e-Ali*, the Emir went, followed by five hundred of his faithful sardars, to the pavilion of the Shah of the Islamic army, Saad bin Qubad.

From the Shah's pavilion emerged a posse of twelve hundred handsome youths wearing costly uniforms and heavy gold bracelets, and holding jars of *oudh* and *umber* incense. Foot soldiers followed in red uniforms and were holding gold and silver tapers. Maidens emerged next with jars of crystal and hundreds of eunuchs milled around them. Everyone cried 'Bismillah' when the Shah's throne held by *kahari*s dressed in costly silks and gleaming jewellery emerged from the pavilion.

Hamza Sahibqiran bowed low and the Shah in turn touched his breast to indicate 'Your place is in my heart'. All the other sardars also greeted the Shah and he ordered them to lead the way to the battlefield. Camp sweepers had swept the field clean of all bumps, thorns and nails, and *saqa*s or water carriers had sprinkled water on it to settle the dust. Both forces fell into battle formations with the foot soldiers standing in front of the artillery. Poets and singers exhorted the soldiers of Islam to fight bravely and sang verses like,

'O brave men, this is your moment and all that will endure are the tales of your valour. Conduct yourself with honour for if you falter, you will not find honour anywhere!'

Amar, disguised as Ajlal Jadoo, had his magic dragon flown to the battlefield and shouted, 'Ya Hamza! Come and prostrate at once in front of Khudawand Laqa or I will cut your head off!' As the Emir went forward to face him, Ajlal rebuked him for harassing the Living God and drew a coconut out from his bag of magic and muttered a spell. In fact, this was not a spell but the language of Jinni that Amar and Hamza had learnt during their extended visit to fairyland. Therefore, what Amar said to the Emir was this: 'I am not Ajlal but your faithful servant Amar. You should arrest me but please be gentle lest a miserable creature like me should be harmed by a person of your strength and lose a limb in the process!'

Emir Hamza looked closely at Amar who pulled his eyelid down and showed him his hidden mole. The Emir smiled at Amar's disguise and Amar immediately threw the coconut at him. Emir shattered the coconut with one blow and then chanted the Great Name. Amar's dragon collapsed under him into a heap of lentil flour. The false Ajlal, now on foot, attacked the Emir with his baton and wand but the Emir ducked, grasped Amar firmly by the waist and shouted, 'O sahir army, I have arrested your officer!'

There were cries of 'Get him! After him!' and the sahir army rushed on to the battlefield. Emir handed Amar over to his faithful archer Muqbil and while reciting the Great Name, turned to attack the enemy. Faramurz and Sulaiman also ordered their forces to attack and the Shah of Islam led his forces into battle. The warriors formed a black cloud with swords flashing like lightning within it. In the heat of the battle, Intizam and Munsarim ordered their sahir troops to back off. They shouted, 'Our officer has been captured. We should wait to see which way he will go before fighting.'

The armies of Sulaiman and Faramurz, however, fought until they were overcome by Hamza's forces. When Shaitan Bakhtiarak realized that their forces were about to surrender, he wisely had the drums of peace struck. The warriors of Islam sheathed their swords in triumph and the enemy forces returned to Mount Agate, broken and defeated. They had lost three lakh men, while the Emir had lost eight hundred. Emir Hamza had his dead soldiers' corpses removed from the battleground and the living had their wounds stitched and bandaged.

The next morning in the durbar, Emir Hamza asked the false Ajlal, 'Now what do you say in praise of the immortal lord of the worlds?'

Amar replied, 'Till I am alive, I am your man!' Emir presented him with a costly *khalat* robe and Amar went to Ajlal's army and told them that he, Ajlal, had joined Hamza and that they were free to join the pure faith or return to Afrasiyab. Except for a few, most of them swore allegiance to Emir, who graced them with the robes of his army.

It was then that Amar took the real Ajlal out from Zambil and tied to him to a post of the pavilion of Hisham. He woke him up after putting a needle through his tongue so that he could not cast spells.

To inform the reader, Emir Hamza had three legendary pavilions— Danyal, Hisham and Solomon. The pavilion of Hisham had originally belonged to the wrestler Hisham of Nausherwan's court. It also had a naqara drum, which made a sound that could be heard for miles. Emir Hamza had acquired the pavilion and the drum after killing Hisham in battle. The fairy queen Asmaan Pari had bestowed the pavilion of Solomon on Emir. Its peculiar feature was that it was completely secure—any sahir who entered it would be burnt, no one could dig a tunnel under it or slash or tear its flaps and no one could jump over it. Because of its fatal effect on sahirs, the Emir always met them in the safer pavilion of Hisham.

The conversion of Ajlal Jadoo

Ajlal was startled to see his double facing him in Hamza's court. As he stared at him, Amar said, 'Ajlal Jadoo, open your eyes wide and reflect on your condition. I am Amar bin Ummayyah, the king of ayyars. Do you see the hand of Allah in how I tricked you? That was not Sulaiman's daughter but I who deceived you. I have your beloved in my possession and your army has joined Emir. Join us too and you will be rewarded with love and Emir will bestow four kingdoms on you for losing your own to Afrasiyab.'

Ajlal nodded his assent, having arrived at the conclusion that Laqa must be false for Amar to have been able to humiliate him. Amar untied him and withdrew the needle from his tongue. Ajlal ran towards the Emir and knelt at his feet. Emir Hamza bestowed a khalat robe and the title of sardar on Ajlal and asked him to choose his chair. Ajlal looked at both the left and right rows and was drawn to the leader of the left row. The leader welcomed him with affection and after choosing his chair, Ajlal forswore magic and became a Muslim. There were cheers of celebration and toasts were raised to his health.

Suddenly, a beautiful woman walked into the pavilion and greeted the Emir. Ajlal recognized her as his beloved, Princess Nasreen, and was embarrassed that she was so shameless as to walk into durbar alone. This woman was actually Chalak bin Amar disguised as Princess Nasreen.

The false princess had sent for a palanquin under the pretext that she wanted to visit her father and when it reached Fort Agate, Chalak darted out of it and ran like a hare right into Emir's camp. Astonished, the princess' attendants made a vain effort to chase him, but Chalak was too quick for them.

The attendants returned to Sulaiman and gave him the news of his daughter's elopement. Sulaiman swore to follow and kill her for the shame she had brought upon him but Shaitan Bakhtiarak held him back and said, 'Where do you think you are going? You are not the only victim in this tragedy of fate. Our esteemed Khudawand Laqa who sits here has two daughters, Jahan Afroze and Gaiti Afroze, who have also eloped with Hamza's sons.'

'Haramzadeh Shaitan! Why must you mention my daughters?' shouted Laqa. 'A thousand pardons my lord; your humble servant wished only to provide a worldly example,' Shaitan apologized as members of durbar sniggered into their beards. Just then, Sulaiman's spies in Hamza's camp informed him that the runaway was not his daughter but the ayyar, Chalak bin Amar.

Sulaiman sank back in relief but Shaitan Bakhtiarak laughed aloud and cried, 'Very good Sulaiman! Ajlal came from Tilism-e-Hoshruba but the great Amar did not even let him fight and he was captured by Hamza. As for you, you are not even aware of what goes on in your household! How will you fight Hamza?' Sulaiman mumbled sheepishly, 'Malik-ji, I will send another message to Afrasiyab and ask for more help. This time we will remain on guard against ayyars.'

Afrasiyab addressed his courtiers in anger after reading Sulaiman's second message. 'Have you all heard what happened? Ajlal Jadoo, the traitor, has converted to Islam. I would like one of you to go immediately to help Khudawand Laqa. Destroy Hamza's army and bring Ajlal back to me, tied in chains.' Haseena Jadoo, a beautiful sahira, volunteered to go. Afrasiyab rewarded her and cautioned her against the ayyars. Haseena Jadoo left for Mount Agate with twenty thousand sahiras.

Back at Mount Agate, Emir asked Amar to release Princess Nasreen from Zambil to ask her if she would like to be converted to Islam. Amar replied with a malicious glint in his eyes, 'I will bring her out only if I get something in return. Whatever goes into Zambil stays there even if it is a pinch of salt!'

Emir Hamza laughed at Amar's greed and promised to reward him with a bag of gold coins. Amar first had the coins issued from the treasury and then returned to his tent. He took out the princess from Zambil and presented her with the costly silk garments that Emir had sent for her. Nasreen wore the clothes but was still confused as to what had happened to her. The Emir explained the situation to her and said, 'Your lover is with me. You can live here and marry him or I can send you back to your father.' Moved by the Emir's nobility and sense of justice, the princess indicated her wish to stay and convert to Islam. Emir Hamza himself conducted her marriage to Ajlal and bestowed great riches and countries on both of them. Hamza then sent for the sons of the Persian astrologer Buzurjmeher. He requested them to tell the court who was destined to conquer Tilism-e-Hoshruba and which brave warrior would kill Afrasiyab. After consulting their charts, the astrologers said, 'Sahibqiran, only God knows the future for sure. We can only indicate through our calculations that to conquer this Tilism, your grandson, Prince Asad bin Karb Ghazi should be sent with five ayyars—Mehtar Qiran, Barq Firangi, Zargham Sherdil and Jansoz bin Qiran. We cannot name the fifth ayyar, but his name begins with the letter A.

Amar realized they meant him and at once quipped, 'Ya Emir! An astrologer should also be sent, ayyars alone will not be enough!' The astrologers took offence at this and protested that the reason they did not want to name Amar was because of his caustic tongue; only the Emir could deal with him. Emir Hamza turned to Amar and said, 'Khwaja your name comes up in the charts and you will have to go!'

'Never!' retorted Amar, 'I refuse to go!' Emir Hamza ignored Amar and calmly sent the astrologers off with gifts. He then asked Asad to prepare for the journey. After this, he sent for ten lakh dinars from the treasury and gave five lakhs to the ayyars whose names had been drawn and asked Amar if he wanted to accept the rest. When Amar saw such a large sum being dispensed freely, he cried out, 'Ya Emir! I am not a greedy man and have no desire for money. I do not wish to go to Tilism but your son is in prison there, so I have to go. I beg you, do not spoil my disciples by awarding them such large sums of money.'

Amar then turned to the four ayyars and shouted, 'Listen, you no good scoundrels! You will waste this money, so give it to me for safekeeping. You are supposed to earn money when you are in Tilism, not take it from here! I have greater need for my share, therefore I will keep it.' The ayyars knew that once Amar had seen the money, they would not hear the end of it. So they handed it over to him and returned to their tents to prepare for the journey. Emir Hamza discreetly sent each of them a large sum of money later.

3 ASAD SETS FORTH TO CONQUER TILISM-E-HOSHRUBA

Travellers to wondrous places and victors of the magic of eloquence walk into the realm of imagination to say this:

The brave Prince Asad Lion-heart was allocated a powerful force of over forty thousand soldiers to conquer Tilism. Before his departure, he had the armoury opened to equip his men with the turquoise-studded armour of the defeated army of Tilism-e-Jamshedi. Elephants and camels carried silver and gold drums, while tents and furniture were loaded on to mule carts.

The naqara drum of travel resounded early next morning. After offering his prayers, the prince went into the women's palace to bid farewell to his mother, Zubaida Sherdil, daughter of Hamza. He kissed her feet reverently and knelt before his grandfather Emir Hamza to take his leave. Then he mounted his horse and led the army through the camp to the sound of drums, bugles and naqaras with great pomp and ceremony.

As Emir Hamza watched Asad's army leave, his attention was diverted by the sound of bugles announcing the arrival of the king of ayyars, Amar bin Ummayyah, and his four disciples. All the ayyars were armed with their unique weapons—the *kamand* or snare-rope that they wrapped around their arms, the *gophan* or large catapult for which they carried strings of stones wound around their necks, and the distinctive pouches of ayyari tools that they had tied to their waists. Each ayyar came and knelt at Emir's feet and wept at the prospect of parting from so gracious a master.

After taking their leave of the Emir, the ayyars travelled together for a while before Amar suggested, 'Brothers, it is wiser for us to travel separately. That way, if one of us is in trouble, the others can rescue him.' Accordingly, the ayyars parted company and went in different directions. Amar decided to follow the route Prince Asad had taken.

First, hear of what happened to the noble Asad. He had already crossed the border of Hoshruba at Mount Agate and had reached the mountain of the magic drum. He saw that the mountain was so tall that it seemed as if it was beyond the reach of the rope of thought and the bird of imagination. An ancient man, who appeared to be almost a hundred years old, was sitting next to the drum. On seeing Asad, he cried out, 'Wait, wait, young man! What are you doing? You are deliberately entering the very mouth of the dragon. The land beyond this mountain is magic-bound. It is a fearful place! Whoever steps in there never returns. He only finds the path to the land of eternity. Take pity on your own youth and turn back or you will lose your life!'

The prince, riding on undeterred, answered back, 'Old man, the brave have no fear of death! Once they go forward, they never turn back. I am the destroyer of Tilisms, the grandson of Hamza, Prince Asad Lion-heart. Do you think you can stop me now? I go into Tilism with no fear for my life!'

As soon as the prince entered the mountain range with his lashkar, the magic drum sounded on its own. The birds in the forest, who were Afrasiyab's spies, flew at once to inform him that Prince Asad and his army had entered Tilism-e-Hoshruba with the intention of conquering it. Afrasiyab immediately sent word to the guardians of the borders of Tilism-e-Hoshruba that a prince called Asad, grandson of Hamza, had infiltrated Tilism. He ordered them to arrest him on sight.

The prince passed through a lush plain that was green as far as the eye could see. He went through a forest that was fragrant with the scent of blossoms; where thorns seemed to be a garland for the flowers; where the bushes were so glossy that they could humble the tresses of the beloved; and where the flowing rivers reminded lovers of the way their beloved walked towards them.

Asad continued riding through lush meadows and forests until he reached a garden with an imposing gateway of white marble latticework. There, his men suggested that they all rest for an hour. The gateway was open like the arms of a beloved and there was no guard or keeper. The only custodian here was spring itself. The garden was a pleasing sight to the weary soldiers with its water channels, fountains and shady trees laden with blossoms and ripe fruits. In the middle of the garden stood a marble pavilion on a huge square slab of marble, a hundred feet in diameter. In spite of this splendour, the garden was quite deserted.

The army camped around the pavilion. As Asad strolled on to the marble platform, sounds of laughter emanated from the tulip flowerbeds around the pavilion and suddenly, the tulips opened and expelled thousands of pythons that were spewing flames. Within a split second, the snakes swallowed not only all of Asad's men, but also his horses and elephants, and then reverted to being tulips, swaying innocently in the breeze. The prince was startled by the sudden disappearance of his army and had stepped off the platform to investigate when he heard a loud sound. Asad turned and saw that his horse had sprouted wings and was flying out of the garden.

Asad was completely alone now. He consoled himself that since this was a magic-ridden place, such incidents were bound to occur. 'Move on,' he told himself, 'and do not be deterred by such illusions!' Asad left the magic garden and after travelling for three days and three nights on foot, reached a city enclosed within crystal walls adorned with murals of landscapes and portraits of kings. The gates of the city were swaying in the wind like rogue elephants. Inside, sahirs were everywhere, their foreheads smeared with sandalwood paste—some were tossing iron balls; other sahirs had the heads of animals and bodies of men; still others had transformed into giant birds and beasts. The sahirs chanted their spells as they sat around blazing sacred fires.

The prince entered the city unchecked. He saw that it was orderly and had numerous shops glittering with gold jewellery and rolls of gleaming brocade and *gulbadan* cloth. There were confectionery shops with sweetmeats laid out neatly on gold and silver trays, food shops with kebabs and *nan*s, and flower shops fragrant with rose and jasmine garlands. Courtesans dressed in costly saris and jewellery dallied with their clients. The city certainly looked prosperous.

Exhausted and hungry after his arduous journey, Asad walked up to a sweet shop and asked for a tray of *barfi*. He offered some gold coins as payment, but the shopkeeper threw the coins back at him and said, 'We cannot trade in these!' The prince asked him about the local currency and the shopkeeper showed him a paper bearing Afrasiyab's portrait and the name of the city, Napursan.

Asad tried to buy food from some more shops, but every one of them refused to accept his gold coins. Finally, in sheer hunger and frustration, he seized a tray of barfi from a shop and tossed a few gold coins at the shopkeepers. When the shopkeepers protested, he banged their heads together. Then he found a stool and sat in the middle of the road, defiantly consuming the barfi. He soundly thrashed anyone who was foolhardy enough to approach him. The aggrieved shopkeepers withdrew and decided to report him to their ruler.

Ravi, the legendary narrator, tells us that Afrasiyab had established this city for his wife Malika Hairat. In the middle of the city was the huge, three-tiered Dome of Light. Twelve hundred sahir soldiers stood on the first tier. The second tier housed several thousand magic drums and bugles, which, if sounded together, could strike all the residents of Tilism-e-Hoshruba senseless. From the third and highest level, Hairat could view all of Tilism. The city of Napursan was located in the visible tilism of Zahir and was well provisioned so that whenever the Malika came to the Dome of Light, she did not want for anything.

When Asad had entered the city, Hairat had been sitting in the dome, glancing occasionally at the view and then at the dancing held in her honour. Seventeen hundred ladies in waiting adorned with jewellery stood in the durbar with folded hands. When the wailing shopkeepers approached the dome, Hairat sent her vizierzadi, Zamurrad Jadoo, to bring them to her. After hearing their complaint, she ordered an attendant named Gulshan Jadoo to arrest Asad.

Gulshan Jadoo accompanied the shopkeepers to the spot where Asad was sitting and saw instead of the common thief she expected, a young man whose radiant beauty seemed to illuminate the bazaar. He sat in the middle of the road with a sword in one hand and a tray of sweetmeats in front of him. Gulshan, who had never seen such noble beauty in a man adored him at first sight. She called out archly to him, 'Sir, who are you? And how dare you commit such injustice to the citizens of our Malika by seizing their goods without paying for them?'

Asad looked up and saw a young sahira dressed in a sari with a red vermilion *tilak* on her forehead and a pouch of magic tools tied to her waist. He thought quickly, 'Asad, if she casts a spell on you, you will look like a fool. It would be better to deceive the venal wretch first and then get her!' Smiling at her, he replied, 'Come to me first. I promise I will go with you to your Malika!' As Gulshan Jadoo drew nearer, he winked at her and encouraged her to come closer. Gulshan held out her hand and grasped his hand, but Asad lifted her off the ground, stuffed her mouth with a cloth before she could cast a spell, and then tied her to a pillar in a shop. Then he whipped her a few times for good measure.

The shopkeepers shouted at Asad from a distance but did not dare approach him. Eventually, they returned to Hairat. She was amused when she heard of Gulshan's fate and decided to send her powerful counsellor Zamurrad Jadoo to deal with the thief. The vizierzadi flew to the bazaar and instantly cast a spell on Asad that rendered his limbs lifeless. She then released the terrified Gulshan and flew back to the dome, holding Prince Asad by his waist.

When they reached the dome, Asad looked up at the throne and saw a beautiful woman in bejewelled garments. Hundreds of women stood in attendance around her. The Malika looked at Asad and marvelling at his noble beauty, asked him, 'O prisoner of grief, you are the blossom of which garden?'

The prince replied without fear, 'I am the grandson of Hamza Sahibqiran and am here to conquer Tilism!' Hearing Hamza's name, Hairat smote her forehead with fear and ordered her women to take him away and leave him in the Plain of Tilism. She told them, 'If he is indeed Tilism Kusha, he will manage to escape. If he is not, he will perish there.'

The sahiras, thus commanded, cast a spell on the prince that made him fall into a deep slumber, after which they transported him to the enchanted Plain of Tilism. When the prince awoke, he found himself in a lush meadow. He strolled about in it until he came upon a garden where some men were tending to the flowerbeds. 'Who are you?' Asad asked them, 'and what are you doing here?'

'Ours is a long story,' one of them said. Another explained, 'In short, we are all princes of various countries who were on hunting expeditions when we were trapped in this enchanted plain from where there is no escape. We now survive by growing flowers for a princess who likes to wear fresh flowers every day. We string the flowers into jewellery for her. In return, her women provide us with food. Now that you too are trapped here, you might as well live and work with us. This is the only way you can survive here.'

'God forbid,' Asad retorted, 'that I should become a gardener. You are welcome to this life.' 'You are young and fresh still,' said another of the men, 'but in a few days, when you will begin to starve and the fat starts melting from your body, you will do as we do!'

Asad did not respond to this and sat separately from them under some trees. After a while, he began to feel hungry and noticed some luscious fruit hanging from the trees. He reached out to pluck them but the branches instantly rose out of his reach. Then he turned to the fruit that had fallen to the ground, but at his touch, they vanished. He tried to climb the trees, but could not get a foothold on them. Likewise, streams ran dry when he tried to drink water from them. In the evening, the maidservants of the princess arrived with trays laden with hot, steaming food and handed these to the gardeners in exchange for the garlands and bracelets of fresh flowers. Poor Asad kept watching the men eat from a distance, but they consumed the food without offering a single morsel to him and he had to sleep hungry that night.

The next day went by in a similar manner, but this time, when the maidservants arrived with the trays of food, Asad blocked their way and rudely asked them to leave the food and go away. The women called out to the other captives for help. When the men ran towards him, Asad wounded a couple of them, slapped the maidservants and kicked the *kahari*s who had brought the trays. Then, he sat down and calmly ate his fill while everyone watched him in horror. The maidservants were in tears and ran off to inform Princess Mahjabeen.

Mahjabeen meets Tilism Kusha

Mahjabeen Diamond-robe was Afrasiyab's niece and Afrasiyab had declared her as his daughter and heir. There had been celebrations throughout the realm during the annual spring festival, Nauroze, when it had been announced that Mahjabeen would take her place on the throne in due course.

The princess had taken a fancy to the verdant Plain of Tilism and so her uncle Afrasiyab had built a small palace for her there. She lived with Afrasiyab's sister Sunddal Jadoo, who was also her guardian. Sunddal was away at Afrasiyab's court when the maidservants arrived looking distraught. Mahjabeen asked them what had happened and they cried, 'Huzoor, there is a new prisoner who does not pick flowers or make garlands. He beat up the other prisoners and snatched the food trays from us!'

Mahjabeen decided to send more trays of food to the prisoners, this time through Mahaldar, the keeper of the palace. The Mahaldar held her gold and silver wand of office, marched straight up to Asad and said, 'Are you crazy to invite death by attacking state servants? And look how shamelessly you have seized the food—as if it was prepared only for you!'

Enraged by her taunts, Asad slapped the Mahaldar, threw her veil aside, pulled off the gold bracelets on her wrists, and snatched her wand of office from her. The kaharis saw the Mahaldar being treated this way and ran for their lives while the gardeners hid behind some bushes. Asad chased the kaharis for good measure and reached as far as the palace of their mistress, Princess Mahjabeen. On hearing the commotion, the princess came out of her room and beheld a young man of overpowering beauty and nobility, drunk on wine, chasing her screaming servants. She called out to him, 'Now, now, young man, what do you think you are doing?'

The prince stopped in his tracks at the sound of her voice. He looked up and saw a fairy-like young maiden whose dark tresses could shame the darkness of Zulmat; the glitter in the parting of her hair could have been a path to the Milky Way. Asad saw this vision of light and immediately lost his heart to her. Mahjabeen smiled as she approached him and softly said, 'Listen! It is not good to rob people. Tell me what you need, and I will provide it. Why do you feel the need to steal?'

Asad was enchanted by these words that dropped like pearls from her mouth and murmured, 'I have been hungry for many days and I needed to eat.' The princess smiled again and said coquettishly, 'That is quite obvious, but what can I do about your hunger? If you are not happy, then find another place for yourself if you can!' The prince grasped her hand and blurted, 'Princess, in truth my eyes thirst for you and I hunger for your love!' Mahjabeen, though she kept holding his hand, replied, 'How shameless you are! Be gone from here!' Asad persisted, 'O Princess, where can I go when the stone of your palace is my pillow? A man is helpless when he is in love!'

While they gazed at each other, rapt with desire, the princess's attendants advised her to move inside the palace lest her aunt Hairat's spies reported on her. The princess looked at Asad demurely and said, 'If you are that hungry, come into my home and I will provide you with everything that you crave for.'

The prince laughed and followed her into the palace. Mahjabeen Diamond-robe went in first but as soon as Asad followed her, an invisible hand pushed him out. Asad tried to enter the palace several times, but failed each time. The princess laughed at seeing him getting angry, and said, 'Did you think you could enter someone's house that easily?' She then directed her vizierzadi, Dilaram Jadoo, to remove the protective spell that Sunddal had cast to keep intruders out of her palace.

Dilaram broke the spell and Mahjabeen led Asad to the roof garden. She sat next to him on a velvet masnad and her handmaidens laid out fragrant and delicious food for them. The princess offered Asad food and wine, but hungry as he was, Asad said, 'Princess, it is enough for me to feast on your beauty. If you want me to eat with you, you must first enter the Garden of Islam. Abjure the use of magic!'

The princess looked troubled and replied, 'I cannot practise magic as I am still too young, but I cannot give up the religion of Samri and Laqa. They are such powerful and great deities.' Asad told her gently, 'Princess, if Laqa had been that powerful, he would not allow himself to be chased by my grandfather Emir Hamza from one country to another.'

Asad continued to speak to her and by the power and sincerity of his words, he convinced Mahjabeen to abjure idolatry and embrace Islam. After her formal conversion, they both began eating and talked lovingly to each other.

Suddenly, the skies grew cloudy and dark with dust, and lightning flashed through the churning clouds. Prince Asad was startled to see an old hag mounted on a fire-breathing dragon descend on the roof. The hag's hair and face were streaked with mud and she wore only a blue loincloth, a black veil and a garland of skulls around her neck. She looked first at the prince and then called out to Mahjabeen, 'You shameless one, you have disgraced our family! Who is this man with you?'

Mahjabeen trembled with fear as she told Sunddal, 'Aunt, this is a poor hungry prisoner who had come in to eat some food. He was just leaving!' Sunddal Jadoo peered closely at Asad and said, 'I am going down to my room. Send him to me there and I will see if I can forgive you. Otherwise, you can expect to be punished for your folly!'

After the old hag left them, the princess turned to Asad and said caustically, 'Well, congratulations! Aunt has taken a fancy to you! How will I matter to you when you can have a beloved who is only seven hundred years old! Go downstairs and enjoy her!'

Ignoring this jibe, Asad followed Sunddal to her room and saw that Sunddal had transformed herself from a hideous old hag into a ravishingly beautiful woman. She sat on a masnad with flasks of different wines laid out before her and a bed with jewelled posts stood gleaming in a corner. Asad walked in and sat down beside her on the masnad.

The sahira acted coy at first and then poured a goblet of wine for him. Asad accepted it readily. 'Drink from it first,' he said, 'so I may savour its taste from your lips.' Sunddal pretended to resist when Asad took her in his arms and carried her to the bejewelled bed. Laying her down, he put one hand on her throat and held her feet with the other. Delighted with his ardour, Sunddal lay motionless. Still clutching her throat, Asad pressed down on her with such strength that he strangled her.

There was an almighty furore the moment she stopped breathing and Asad leapt to one side to escape the onslaught. The skies went dark and there was a hail of stones and flames as a voice called out, 'O, he has killed me with deceit, my name was Sunddal Jadoo. Alas for seven hundred years I plucked no flower from the garden of youth and now the breeze of death has withered the blossom of my life!'

Mahjabeen had been watching Asad and Sunddal Jadoo through a peephole and had been feeling increasingly jealous. 'How besotted this wretched man is with that old woman!' she thought. Then realizing that Sunddal was dead, the princess whispered to Dilaram, 'This is dreadful! He has killed my aunt!' Instead of sympathizing with her, Dilaram looked delighted and said, 'Huzoor, think of it. For his love of you, he risked his own life! You should express your gratitude to him!'

The princess and Dilaram entered the darkened chamber and when light returned, they noticed Sunddal lying naked on the floor with Asad looking at them triumphantly. The princess sniffed, 'You have killed my aunt!'

'Yes, my princess!' Asad replied happily. 'Did you see how I sent her straight to hell?' The princess, taken aback by his casual manner, asked him sardonically, 'I suppose you think it is praiseworthy that you should first kill my aunt and then ask me to admire you for it.' Asad put his arms around the princess and tried to placate her by kissing her, but she turned her face away and said, 'Do you intend to strangle me as well?' Asad hugged her even tighter and said, 'If I strangle you, my love, then how will I survive?'

Even as they spoke, Sunddal Jadoo's skull cracked open and a bird of many hues emerged from it and flew off shrieking, 'Alas! Alas!' Dilaram said, 'Princess, this was not a bird but actually the shadow of sorcery from Sunddal's impure body. It will fly straight to Afrasiyab and inform him of Sunddal's death. You should leave Tilism at once or you will be caught like Badi and Tasveer.'

'I have come to conquer Tilism!' Asad declared. 'I will not return without first killing Afrasiyab!' Mahjabeen appealed to Dilaram to help them. Dilaram said that although she was not powerful enough to face any of Afrasiyab's subordinates, she could attempt to provide a safe refuge for the prince and Mahjabeen. Losing no time, Dilaram stepped out of the palace, rolled on the ground and magically transformed herself into a mountain. Asad and Mahjabeen climbed on to the mountain and hid in a ravine. As the mountain heaved into motion, all of the princess's attendants and maidservants started weeping. Dilaram, however, ignored them and moved slowly into the plain with the fugitive lovers in her protection.

Meanwhile, the magic bird that had emerged from the dead sahira Sunddal's skull flew to Afrasiyab's durbar in the Garden of Apples and delivered its doleful message that Prince Asad had killed Sunddal. Moments later, the bird expelled a flame from its beak and incinerated itself. Afrasiyab was very grieved on hearing of Sunddal's murder and ordered the court to go into mourning. His wife Hairat rushed over from Napursan to offer condolences and wept loudly to express her grief.

Later, Afrasiyab, with his ministers and advisers, travelled to Mahjabeen's palace. Mahjabeen's attendants threw themselves at his mercy and pleaded that they were innocent. 'Where is Mahjabeen?' Afrasiyab asked them coldly. They informed him that Dilaram had left with Asad and Mahjabeen. 'They will never be able to leave Tilism!' Afrasiyab declared. 'I will arrange for my sister's funeral and then punish that shameless hussy!'

Sunddal's last rites were conducted with due solemnity in the tradition of the religion of Samri and Jamshed. Saddened by his sister's death, Afrasiyab returned to his favourite garden and after some thought, sent messages to all the kingdoms in his realm, alerting them that Mahjabeen had run away with the grandson of Hamza. He urged them to arrest the two fugitives at sight.

Mahrukh Magic-eye rebels against Afrasiyab

At the same time, Afrasiyab sent a letter to Malika Mahrukh Magic-eye, Mahjabeen's maternal grandmother. Mahrukh was a powerful sorceress, skilled in the science of astrology and experienced in statecraft. Afrasiyab was her blood relative and moreover, her son Shakeel Jadoo was in love with the Shahanshah's daughter, Khubsoorat Jadoo. Wary of Afrasiyab's antagonism towards her son, Mahrukh had confined herself to Fort Rangeen Hissar in Zahir, the visible Tilism. Mahrukh Magic-eye was a powerful overlord and was privy to the secrets of Tilism.

Somewhat in awe of her strength and intelligence, Afrasiyab maintained cordial relations with her but feared her secretly. Therefore, in his letter to her, he wrote, 'Your granddaughter has eloped with Asad. Despite the fact that I had designated her as the future Malika, she has dishonoured me and lost all shame. You must arrest her with Asad and I will spare her for your sake.' He added, 'If you do not obey this order, your entire kingdom and all your property will be confiscated, and you will have to face a traitor's death.'

On receiving this letter, Mahrukh immediately cast the horoscopes of both Afrasiyab and Asad. She reached the conclusion that Asad would indeed overcome Afrasiyab. She found that anyone allied with Asad would prosper and that his enemies would be destroyed. Mahrukh reflected carefully on these findings and thought to herself, 'Mahjabeen is my granddaughter. It would be proper for me to side with her. Afrasiyab, on the other hand, is a proven traitor. He snatched the throne of Hoshruba from Shah Lacheen, the actual ruler. Besides, he nurses a grudge against my son Shakeel and torments his beloved Khubsoorat for loving him. Shakeel might just die of a broken heart for her. Perhaps it is best that I save my son and granddaughter and join Asad, Tilism Kusha.'

Accordingly, Mahrukh wrote to Afrasiyab, 'It is not possible for a lowly woman like me to deliver Mahjabeen to certain death. You are the ruler and have the right to honour me or to punish me. I do not have anything to do with you, nor would I want to punish Mahjabeen. I send you my most respectful greetings, etc., Mahrukh Magic-eye.'

As soon as the messenger from Afrasiyab departed with her reply, Mahrukh sent for her son Shakeel who lived in the desert. She told him through her emissary that there was trouble brewing with Afrasiyab. On hearing this, Shakeel was delighted and thought, 'Now I will either die at Afrasiyab's hands or gain my beloved Khubsoorat!' Accompanied by a combined force of twenty-four thousand soldiers from her own army and twelve thousand sahirs from Shakeel's forces, Mahrukh set out to look for Mahjabeen and Asad.

Afrasiyab received Mahrukh's letter and was naturally furious on reading its contents. He ordered his subordinates to arrest all the rebels at sight and declared, 'I will not demean myself by fighting with this woman. A few of you should be able to dispose of her army.'

Meanwhile, Dilaram, who had transformed into a mountain, travelled a considerable distance but still could not find a way out of Tilism. Asad and Mahjabeen, still hidden in the ravine, gazed upon the many wonders of Tilism—the mountain ranges of porcelain and lapis lazuli, the desert of thorns, the meadows of flowers and River Zakhar. Eventually, when Dilaram changed back into her original form, they found themselves in a pleasant green meadow with streams, trees and flowering bushes. Mahjabeen pleaded, 'O Dilaram, this is such a soothing place. Let us rest here for a while. I am hungry and thirsty.'

Dilaram was saddened on hearing the princess's plaintive words. She thought to herself, 'How alike a king and a beggar are in the court of love. Here is the same princess behind whose carriage seventy thousand princesses walked in attendance and now she is struggling in the wilderness, without a throne or a crown, hounded by Afrasiyab's men.'

Asad suggested that the women could rest while he went hunting in search of food. When he did not return for a while, Dilaram was worried and decided to follow him in case he was in trouble. Princess Mahjabeen was now left alone.

It was then that one of Afrasiyab's officers, Zulmat Jadoo, found her. Smitten by her beauty, he thought, 'This maiden is beautiful and laden with jewellery. If I take her home, I can enjoy her and her wealth. No one will suspect me as she has run away with Asad.' The princess shuddered at the sight of Zulmat but he addressed her gently and concocted a story about Prince Asad having converted him to the true faith. He told Mahjabeen that Asad was waiting for her in his garden. The princess arose and followed him unsuspectingly to the garden. After seating her on a jewelled couch, Zulmat said to her, 'Mahjabeen, forget Asad. You can see that I am besotted with you. You will be safe with me. Once Asad is killed, the Shah's fury will abate and you can return home.'

By now, the princess was terrified of him. She warned Zulmat not to touch her and even threatened to kill herself if he did. Zulmat pleaded with her to relent, but she refused. He then began threatening her. Mahjabeen raised her hands in prayer and at that very moment, another sahir, Dakhan Jadoo, who had been looking for Mahjabeen entered the garden. On seeing Zulmat threatening the princess, he challenged him to a duel. Zulmat responded by casting a spell that caused the garden to be engulfed in inky darkness. In response, Dakhan sprinkled some magic water that made the darkness fill with light instantly. Dakhan then sprinkled the same water on Zulmat. Each drop seared him like a live ember and he succumbed to his burns.

Dakhan waited for the storms and darkness that usually followed a sahir's death to dispel and then approached the princess. Like Zulmat, he fell in love with her and offered to plead for her life with the Shahanshah if she accepted him. She rejected him bluntly. Dakhan thought, 'If she is in love with Tilism Kusha, she will never come with me willingly.' He cast a love spell on her that made her become completely besotted with him. Thus bewitched, the princess followed him out of the garden.

When Asad Lion-heart returned from his hunt, he saw the princess running after a sahir and suspected that she was under some sort of spell. He aimed an arrow and shot it straight through Dakhan's heart. Released from Dakhan's spell, Mahjabeen ran to Asad and wept uncontrollably in the safety of his arms. Asad comforted her and sat down with her in a comfortable spot where a hill shielded them from view. There, he grilled succulent kebabs cut from the deer that he had hunted and brought fresh water for them to drink from a nearby mountain stream. They had barely finished their meal when there was a flash of lightning in the sky followed by the sound of thunder. A black-faced sahir sent by Afrasiyab suddenly materialized and shouted, 'I am Shola Jadoo! How will you escape now, traitors?'

Asad immediately reached for his sword but Shola muttered a spell that caused Asad to sink into the earth up to his waist. Just then, Dilaram arrived on the scene. She aimed a magic coconut at Shola, but he shattered the coconut. He then conjured a chain of flames that bound Asad, Mahjabeen and Dilaram. Shola flew up into the air with his three prisoners dangling on the flaming chain. It then occurred to Shola that it was best to kill his captives before any ally of theirs could rescue them.

Accordingly, he descended to the ground and drew out his sword to kill Asad. Mahjabeen cried out, 'Kill me first, you cruel beast. I will not be able to see my beloved's lifeless form covered in blood and dust!' Shola obligingly turned to kill her when Asad shouted, 'Listen, you godless heathen! How can a man live after his woman is dead? Kill me first!' When Shola turned to Asad again, Dilaram pleaded, 'O treacherous one, can a lowly handmaiden watch her masters die? Kill me first!' Shola hesitated, uncertain as to whom he could strike first.

At that instant, Asad raised his hands and pleaded with the Almighty to deliver them from this cruel sahir. Miraculously, a *dev* emissary of Asad's grandmother, who was flying to Mount Agate with a message from her, saw them. Asad's grandmother was the fairy queen Aasman Pari, who sometimes exchanged letters with her husband Emir Hamza. On hearing cries for help from the ground, the dev looked down and saw Asad being threatened by a sahir. Without a moment's hesitation, he swooped down, caught Shola by the neck, folded him into a small morsel and swallowed him.

The usual outbreak of thunder and lightning and darkness following a sahir's death occurred. Having never eaten a sahir before, the dev was bewildered by the tumult in his stomach and ran about in great discomfort, wailing, 'What kind of an ill-fated morsel was this? My insides are twisting in pain!' Eventually, the noise and the darkness dispelled and the dev, who was feeling somewhat lighter, went up to Asad. He greeted Asad and introduced himself as his grandmother's loyal servant, on his way to deliver a message to Emir Hamza.

'Well,' said Asad, 'then you can greet Emir and all the sardars from me and convey what has befallen me since I entered Tilism.' After describing to him all that had happened, Asad gently admonished the dev, 'You should not have killed the sahir. If that had been our intention, we could have had all the sahirs swallowed by ogres. That is the way of cowards. It is enough for us to counteract their magic with the trickery of ayyars. Leave now, my friend, but you must promise not to do this again!'

The dev sheepishly promised to obey Asad's injunction and then flew away. Asad led Mahjabeen and Dilaram to a sheltered gully within a mountain where they remained hidden from sight for the time being.

✺

4 KHWAJA AMAR ENTERS TILISM-E-HOSHRUBA

The incomparable ayyar, Amar, and his four honourable disciples had followed different paths into Tilism and entered it disguised as sahirs. Each of them marvelled at the wondrous sights of verdant fields and mountains of every hue and size. They came across sahirs everywhere, practising their magic and conjuring hailstorms and fire-rains.

Amar walked into a meadow where, for miles in sight, the grass was made of silver. He thought to himself, 'If only I could mow all of this grass! Alas, that would be difficult, but let me get as much of it as I can!' He set to work using a sharpened scythe, but soon heard a distant cry of 'Wait, you wily thief! I was searching for you! Where will you hide now?' Amar sighed deeply and looked up. He saw a sahir whose body was made of pure silver and whose hair was silver threads. Black cobras were wound around his head and his pouch of magical tools was hanging at his waist. Amar tried to flee but the sahir gestured lightly and Amar's feet remained rooted to the earth. The sahir then drew out his sword and said sharply, 'You must be Amar! I had created this enchanted forest to trap you and now I have been rewarded!'

Amar pretended to look helpless and pleaded, 'I am but a poor grass cutter, afflicted with sorrow!' The sahir remained unmoved and was about to kill him, when another sahir hailed him. The silver sahir saw that the second sahir was impressive and wore metal loops in his ears and huge snakes coiled around his neck. He was holding a massive *bughda* in one hand and when he came closer, he glared at Amar and said, 'Please get my goods out of this thief before you kill him. Not only has he robbed my home, he has also stolen the pair of this priceless pearl!' The sahir held out a pearl the size of a hen's egg, which glowed in his palm, as if alight.

The silver sahir was entranced by the pearl and exclaimed, 'Brother, from where did you acquire this precious jewel?' The stranger hesitated and then replied casually, 'I live on Pearl Mountain which produces these miracles of nature from the earth of the great god Samri. I obtained this pearl with great difficulty and this wretched thief has robbed its pair!'

The silver sahir examined the pearl and praised its sheen. The second sahir advised him to breathe on to the pearl so that its true lustre could be revealed. As the silver sahir brought the pearl closer to his mouth, it split open and released a deadly vapour. The silver sahir immediately fell unconscious. The stranger drew up and called out, 'I am the wielder of swords and slayer of dragons! I am Mehtar Qiran, the Lion-hearted!'

In a flash, he had smashed the sahir's skull with his mighty bughda and there was a huge din as the silver forest disappeared within moments of his death. Amar was now free and embraced Qiran, warmly complimenting him on his clever ayyari. Qiran bowed his head modestly and said, 'Huzoor, this is all due to your teachings. What is your plan, where do we go?' Amar suggested that they continue to travel separately and the two ayyars parted.

Meanwhile, Afrasiyab's spies, the enchanted birds, flew away to inform him of the silver sahir's fate. When Afrasiyab heard the news, he knocked in the air and an iron puppet appeared before him. Afrasiyab sent the puppet to Mehtab, his officer in the desert of Dakhshan with a message. He warned him of the silver sahir's death and urged him to be vigilant against Amar and his four ayyars. After sending the puppet to Mehtab, Afrasiyab had the silver sahir's corpse cremated when it was brought from the forest.

Mehtab Jadoo and the magic sparrows

As soon as Mehtab Jadoo received Afrasiyab's message, he conjured a house in the middle of the desert and had it richly furnished with silk carpets and jewel-inlaid furniture. He appointed some of his sahir soldiers to guard the house, and then cut out a paper moon and cast a spell on it so that it looked real. The magic moon floated up and stayed suspended over the entrance of the house. Then Mehtab poured himself a cup of wine and began thinking of ways to identify the ayyars.

He cut seven sparrows out of paper and breathed spells on them that made them come to life. They flew off and perched on a ledge overlooking the doorway. Satisfied with his security precautions, Mehtab relaxed and drank his wine.

When Amar reached this area, he saw the house with the full moon shining on the doorway with sahirs all around. Some of them were cooking food in huge copper vessels and some others were playing drums and singing hymns in praise of Samri. Amar quickly disguised himself as a sahir and thought, 'Let me purify this desert of these impure bastards!' Soon, he mingled with the guards and entertained them with a lilting melody. Mehtab heard his voice from inside the house and asked the guards to bring the singer to him. As soon as Amar entered the room, one of the sparrows cried out, 'Amar is here!' and fell off its perch before going up in flames. Amar heard his name and quickly vanished under his cloak. Mehtab was stunned and told his guards, 'That was no singer, but Amar! Now remain alert!'

Amar waited in the desert for a while and then blew Zafeel, the secret whistle of ayyari. Of the four ayyars, Barq Firangi heard his signal and reached him quickly, 'O my Teacher, is all well with you?' Amar whispered, 'My son, I would like you to disguise yourself as me and be arrested by Mehtab's men. They will be satisfied and I will rescue you soon.' Barq complied with Amar's wishes and deliberately walked past Mehtab's soldiers who arrested him immediately and led him to their master.

As soon as Barq entered the doorway, another sparrow cried out, 'Barq is here!' Mehtab exclaimed, 'So you are Barq?' Barq replied, 'No! I am Amar!' 'Impossible!' said Mehtab, 'My sparrow would not lie!' 'If I was Barq,' said Barq convincingly, 'would I get into trouble by pretending to be Amar? Do I not know that all the sahirs in Tilism are hunting for me?'

Mehtab remained doubtful, but suggested, 'Could it be that your name is also Barq?' Barq pretended to relent and said, 'My real name is

Barq, but I am famous as Amar.' Mehtab shouted with delight, 'Did I not tell you that my magic would not lie!'

He compared Barq's face to Amar's portrait that Afrasiyab had circulated amongst all his subordinates and found that it matched perfectly. Satisfied, he tied up Barq and left him in a corner.

Amar watched Barq's capture from a distance and then disguised himself as a beautiful young maiden. The maiden was so lovely that she glowed like the full moon; her lips were like rubies and her teeth, like pearls; her cheeks shone like the mirror of Alexander and her arms gleamed like lamps. Amar then wore a bride's jewel-embroidered red costume, but tore the chemise and spread heavy black tresses on his face to suggest that the maiden was in distress. He placed himself behind a bush close to Mehtab's house and wailed loudly, 'O faithless lover, why have you punished me this way!'

Mehtab heard the maiden's plaintive call and emerged from his house to check. Peering through the bushes, he saw a young bride overcome with grief. Seeing him, the girl backed off in fear. Dazzled by her beauty, Mehtab asked her, 'Tell me, what troubles you and I may be able to help.'

The maiden sighed deeply and wept even more but when Mehtab pleaded again, she said, 'What can I tell you? I am the daughter of a powerful sahir and was to marry my uncle's son whom I loved. On the eve of my marriage, a Habshi low-caste, who had also claimed my hand, slaughtered my beloved. I ran into the desert to escape from him and I will surely die of grief here!'

Mehtab wept on hearing her sad story and said, 'O beloved! How long will you grieve for the dead? I am Afrasiyab's companion and quite rich and powerful. I will be your slave for life and will look after you well if you accept me.' The maiden recoiled in horror and while touching her ears, cried, 'I am afraid of sahirs and magic. They live to be a thousand years of age and you can never tell what sex they are!'

Mehtab regretted revealing his identity and pleaded, 'My beloved, I would never practise magic in front of you. I assure you that I am young yet . . . only three hundred and twenty-five years old!' The false maiden still played coy and relented only after Mehtab had sworn in the name of the great idol of Jamshed to give up magic.

Mehtab led her into his house and as soon as she stepped inside, the third magic sparrow called out 'Amar comes!' Mehtab was startled and thought, 'The bird must be wrong, I have just caught Amar.' The false maiden cried, 'This is why I did not want to come with you. I will leave before your magic takes my life!' Mehtab, who was bursting with love and desire for her, placated her and recited a spell that reduced all the sparrows to ashes.

Barq Firangi, who was tied up in a corner, recognized Amar but remained quiet. Mehtab seated his beloved on a masnad and sent for food and wine, and urged her to gain some nourishment after her ordeal. That flower-petal gently said, 'I have not tasted wine for several days, pray give me a glass.' Mehtab filled a goblet for her and they began to speak lovingly to each other.

Meanwhile, Afrasiyab consulted the oracle Book of Samri and discovered to his alarm that Amar was about to kill Mehtab. Afrasiyab quickly sent a puppet to warn Mehtab about Amar and Barq. Amar had already slipped a drug in Mehtab's wine and the sahir was about to drink it when the floor in front of them trembled and the puppet emerged from it. Amar quickly threw himself on Mehtab with a scream of fright and at the same time, blew some sleeping dust on his face that made him unconscious.

The puppet shrieked Afrasiyab's message to Mehtab, but Mehtab was dead to the world. When the puppet leaned closer to examine him, Amar swept him into the blessed Net of Ilyas and tied him up before releasing Barq. He beheaded Mehtab with one stroke of his sword and there was an almighty uproar and sudden darkness. Mehtab's soldiers rushed inside but Amar and Barq disposed them off easily.

Eventually, the darkness gave way to light. Amar untied the puppet and told it, 'Go now and tell that joker Afrasiyab that I will get his hide soon!' Shaking with fear, the puppet fled and left Amar and Barq to plunder all of Mehtab's furniture and carpets.

The puppet reached the court and conveyed the news of the carnage in Mehtab's house and Amar's message to Afrasiyab. The Shahanshah was livid and rose from his seat, ready to capture Amar himself, but his courtiers pleaded with folded hands, 'O King of Sahirs, it is beneath your station to capture a lowly deceiver. You have many servants who can fight with his master Hamza, so what is the relevance of his ayyar? Please appoint someone to arrest him but enable him to recognize Amar and the ayyars in whatever disguise they assume.'

Afrasiyab felt that they were right and turned towards a bed of flowers in the Garden of Apples. His eyes flashed with so much anger that the flowers caught fire. Without hesitation, Afrasiyab jumped into the flames. He emerged moments later with a polished and jewelled tablet of jade engraved with a portrait of a young woman. He then sketched a sign in the air and a dark and monstrous sahir emerged from the earth to greet the Shah. Afrasiyab said to him, 'Azar Jadoo, go forth and arrest Amar from Mehtab's desert. Consult the magic tablet whenever you meet someone on the way. If he is an ayyar in disguise, the portrait will reveal his true face to you. If he is not an ayyar, the magic tablet will remain unchanged.'

Azar and the ayyars

Azar Jadoo left with the tablet for Mehtab's desert and started looking for Amar. Amar was roaming the desert disguised as a sahir and was very anxious. He thought furiously, 'How many sahirs can I kill? There are millions in Tilism. Where is Asad, is he dead or alive? How will we find the *Lauh-e-Tilism*?' Ravi, the narrator tells us that the Lauh-e-Tilism—the magic tablet or keystone—was closely guarded by the ruler of Tilism because it could guide the Tilism Kusha to destroy the ruler and his Tilism. The keystone requires some sort of sacrifice, usually of blood before it reveals its secrets to the Tilism Kusha and guides him.

At that moment, Amar saw Azar Jadoo looking for someone in the forest and thought, 'Oh well, let me kill this *haramzada* first, one less sahir in the world!' Amar called out to him and Azar Jadoo looked up to see a sahir with flames coming out of his mouth and nose.

After exchanging greetings, Amar told Azar that he was Mehtab's relative and that he was looking for Mehtab's murderer. As they spoke, Azar remembered the Shahanshah's instruction to consult the magic tablet if he came across a stranger. When he looked at it, the portrait in the tablet changed into the image of a man with a little round head, beady eyes, a reedy neck, ears like dried apricots, cheeks like *kulcha* bread, and limbs like ropes. The man was six yards long from the waist down and three yards from the waist up.

Startled by this image, Azar quickly muttered a spell that caused Amar to lose all power over his limbs. Azar also conjured an iron chain to tie him up. Amar howled in protest, 'O Brother, why do you torture an innocent man like me?' Azar replied, 'You are a deceitful rascal, I was warned about you!' Amar lost his temper and said, 'It seems you want to be sent to hell very soon. Do you know a million ayyars have invaded this Tilism? One or the other will kill you any moment!' Azar calmly dragged him along and said, 'I will kill them all!'

From a distance, Zargham Sherdil saw Amar being dragged by a sahir. He disguised himself as a cowhand with a loincloth, a turban and a waistcoat, and then stole a cow from a nearby pasture. As Azar came closer, he saw Zargham milking the cow and asked him for a tumbler of water. Zargham bowed low and said, 'My lord, you have travelled in the sun, let me offer you some fresh milk from my cow!' Zargham quickly milked the cow and gave Azar a tumbler of fresh milk into which he had mixed some powder of unconsciousness.

Just as Azar was about to drink the milk, he remembered the tablet and saw the portrait in the magic tablet turning into an image of the real Zargham. Azar disabled him with a quick spell and tied him to the same chain as Amar, who spoke up again, 'Did I not warn you that there are scores of us? Anytime now, you will be killed! It is better to join us.' Azar felt apprehensive when he heard these words and vowed to himself that he would check the tablet whenever he met someone new.

From the top of a nearby hill, Barq saw his friends in custody and disguised himself as a beautiful young wine seller. He mixed sleeping potion into a flask of wine and half revealing his face through a gauze veil, walked saucily past Azar. Azar saw the young wine seller swaying, as if walking for the eyes of a lover, and called out, 'O Bibi, let me taste your wine!' The young damsel peeped at him through her veil and retorted with a smile, 'My wine is not for sale!' Encouraged by her smile, Azar asked her where she was going. 'Wherever I like!' replied the young wine seller, 'and who are you to ask?'

Suddenly Azar seized her wrist, which brought forth a cry of outrage from her: 'Let go of me you brute! My reputation will be in shreds!' Azar smiled and holding on to her wrist, said, 'Come and sit with me under the shade of that tree and we will chat for a while!' The fair damsel giggled and said, 'I cannot consort with passing strangers!' Azar assured her that he was an officer of the king and not just any passing stranger, but the young damsel cried, 'You may be anyone, but I am not so shameless as to strike up friendships with strange men!'

Azar knew that she was willing though and picked her up and placed her under a tree. He also tied Amar and Zargham to the tree. Barq flirted shamelessly with the sahir before pouring him a glass of the deadly wine. Just as Azar was about to sip it, he remembered the tablet and of course, Barq's identity was revealed. Azar breathed a spell on his face and Barq's paints of trickery peeled off.

Azar tied Barq to the same chain as Amar and Zargham, muttering all the while, 'These ayyars are incredible—they deceive me at every step!' Amar laughed and said, 'Listen, haramzadeh! How will you escape? Any moment now you will be murdered!' Azar was suitably terrified but determined to continue travelling with his prisoners. He rested for a while in a garden where the gardener offered him a bouquet of flowers with fruit cleverly arranged in the centre. Azar tossed a few coins at him and reached out for the fruit but remembered to check the magic tablet first and discovered that the gardener was the fourth ayyar, Jansoz. Azar was really frightened now and thought of sending a message to the Shah for help.

From a safe distance, the blessed of the king of brave-hearts, Mehtar Qiran, saw Azar with the four ayyars in chains and realized that he would have to be trapped in a different way. He thought deeply for a while and then walked into the forest and quickly cut some branches from the trees to assemble a rudimentary shack covered with leaves and vines. He piled some logs and lit a fire, on to which he sprinkled a quantity of sleeping potion. He then stuffed his own nostrils with wads of cotton soaked in an antidote. Qiran then squatted behind the fire and patiently waited for Azar.

A little later, Azar emerged with his band of prisoners and saw a fakir swaying in ecstasy behind a fire. Azar greeted him with folded hands. The fakir looked at him with bloodshot eyes and said, 'I am also an ayyar waiting to kill you!' Azar lunged towards him but overcome by the drugged fumes, fell into a dead faint. Qiran stood up and smashed his skull with one blow of his bughda. There was sudden darkness and a hail of stones and fire from the sky. A colourful bird flew out of Azar's skull crying, 'Alas, alas!' It flew straight to Afrasiyab.

The ayyars were now free. Qiran greeted Amar respectfully, who in turn complimented Qiran on another brilliant trick. The ayyars parted company again and hid separately in the forest. At night, all the ayyars took out their dry rations of nan and drank water from streams, and then finally slept fitfully after a hard day. The miserly Amar was reluctant to take out food from his Zambil, and lamented, 'This is the problem with Hamza's employment! You have to use your own resources. It is too late to find food anywhere so I will sleep without eating!' Later that night, Amar was awakened by hunger pangs and finally took out some pieces of stale bread from his Zambil to assuage his need, while cursing the expense to himself at the same time.

Meanwhile, the bird from Azar's skull had reached Afrasiyab. It cried, 'O Shahanshah of Tilism, Azar was killed!' Afrasiyab bit his lips in fury but ordered one of his sahirs to bury Azar's body and retrieve the magic portrait tablet. He cautioned him, 'It is late so do not linger in the forest, just bury him quickly and bring the tablet to me.' Afrasiyab tried to distract himself from his problems with wine and dancing when the sahir went off to retrieve the tablet from Azar's body. By the time he returned to give the tablet to Afrasiyab, the night was almost over and the sahir of the East emerged in all radiance.

Amar and Mahrukh

The ayyars woke up at dawn and bowed their heads in submission to God. Later, they braced themselves and set forth on their separate paths. In another part of Tilism-e-Hoshruba, Afrasiyab woke up as well and held court in the Garden of Apples. After the state officials presented themselves in court, dancing commenced and wine was served. When Afrasiyab was refreshed, he told his men, 'Amar and four ayyars have entered Tilism. They have killed sahirs and have almost reached the River of Flowing Blood. Mahrukh is looking for Asad and Mahjabeen in the Plains of Nargis. Proceed to where Asad hides in the mountains as both Mahrukh and the ayyars are headed that way. Capture them all together.' He gave his men some magic dust from the graves of Samri and Jamshed and told them, 'Sprinkle this on any sahir, no matter how powerful, and he will fall unconscious.' A group of sahirs flew off with the magical dust in search of the rebels.

Now hear about the ayyars. They were very alert when they crossed mountains and deserts, suspicious even of their own shadows. Amar, who was looking forward to foraging a meal from somewhere, reached a mountain that was mighty and adorned with many blossoms like a bride of the first night. Its base was like the conscience of the righteous one—pure and clean. Refreshed by this sight, he walked on and saw that a sahira stood guard in a shady spot on the mountain where Asad was sitting with a beautiful maiden. It was as if the sun and moon sat together, so radiant did they look!

Amar called out, 'Boy! Have you come to conquer Tilism or court young prostitutes?' Asad recognized Amar's voice and rose to greet him, 'Welcome, my grandfather!' Amar considered Karb Ghazi, Asad's father, as his own son, and thus, Asad called Amar his grandfather. They embraced and Amar prayed for his long life. Then he walked to where Mahjabeen was sitting. Looking scornfully at her, he said, 'Who is this ugly woman you have with you Asad? God save me from her evil eye!'

The princess was outraged and embarrassed, but Asad whispered to her, 'My dear, he is very greedy—offer him a gift and he will sing your praises!' Mahjabeen at once took off her diamond bracelets and presented them to Amar who readily pocketed them and said, 'Princess, this lowly grandson of Hamza is not worthy of you. You are a royal princess and deserve a great king!' As Asad, Mahjabeen and Dilaram laughed at his words Amar smiled back at them and said, 'May Allah keep you laughing!' After this fortunate reunion, Asad assured

Mahjabeen, 'Dear princess, now that grandfather is here, he will slay the sahirs and I will deal with the warriors.' The princess felt happy and confident with Asad's assurance.

Meanwhile, Mahrukh Magic-eye, who set out with her son Shakeel to find Mahjabeen, had flown ahead of her army and came across their hiding place. Dilaram saw her first and warned the princess that her grandmother had arrived. Mahjabeen said in fear, 'Alas, she only comes to arrest us!' Asad unsheathed his sword and Amar vanished in his cloak but Mahrukh addressed the prince gently, 'O Esteemed Prince, why do you regard me as your enemy? I am your friend and Mahjabeen's grandmother. Where is my child?' Mahjabeen ran to her grandmother and knelt at her feet. Mahrukh embraced her and said, 'My child, let us see what happens to you and me. Afrasiyab is powerful. I have rebelled against him but cannot face his might . . . he can destroy us in no time!'

Asad said, 'How can that low-born scoundrel destroy us when we are in Allah's protection? You can rest easy, I am here to fight for us and you should trust the Almighty!' Mahrukh responded, 'You are right prince, but one has to face reality.' Asad said, 'The beard-shaver of kafirs and slayer of sahirs, Khwaja Amar is here now. He will kill Afrasiyab like an impure dog!' Mahrukh replied, 'I have seen many people but none could withstand Afrasiyab's power. However, I am here to stay and face him, whatever happens to me!'

Dilaram spread a rug for them to sit on but Amar kept himself hidden, in case Mahrukh showed any signs of treachery. After she was seated, Mahrukh addressed the prince again, 'Prince, I have drawn a natal chart and seen that you will overcome the Shah of Tilism. I was merely describing his power and might to you to test your bravery. Allah be praised, you are brave-hearted with the courage of a lion!'

As they were talking, one of Afrasiyab's officers, Rahdar Jadoo, was passing by the mountain and on seeing this group, called out, 'Wait you rebels! How can you live in a river and avoid the crocodile? You will not escape the Shah!'

Mahrukh quickly shot an iron ball at him. It burst into a thousand flames that leapt towards him like swords. The sahir sprinkled a pinch of the magic dust to dispel the flames. He then sprinkled the same dust on Mahrukh and Dilaram, causing them both to fall unconscious. Asad attacked him with his sword but Rahdar overcame him with a spell and tied all of them together.

Amar now emerged from Galeem and fitted a crystal ball in his gophan. The ball weighed five seers and was sculpted into an octagon. He then called out to Rahdar and aimed the ball straight at his head.

The impact of the ball shattered Rahdar's head into tiny pieces. There were fearsome sounds and dust storms following his death. The din woke up Mahrukh, who cleared the darkness and storms with a spell. She saw Rahdar's dead body and a strange-looking man standing nearby. Not knowing Amar, she was about to attack him, but realizing her intentions, he quickly burst a narcotic bubble in her face that caused her to faint yet again. Amar disappeared and Asad who was now free, revived her and explained, 'Grandfather saved us all from Rahdar, but when you wanted to attack him, he disappeared.'

'Then please call him back!' said Mahrukh. Asad advised her to do so herself. Mahrukh called out loudly, 'O king of ayyars! I am anxious to meet you. Show me your blessed face and do not hide from me!' Amar said, while still invisible, 'It will cost you dearly to see me!' Asad and the women laughed at this while Mahrukh took off her heavy gold bracelets and held them out. Amar appeared and accepted the offering graciously. However, on seeing Amar, Mahrukh thought with contempt, 'How will this ordinary man face anyone?'

Amar read her thoughts and said, 'You think a thin, reedy-looking man like me will not be able to fight?' Mahrukh was greatly impressed by this and said admiringly, 'You are a mind reader!' 'I have that talent,' Amar replied dryly.

As they were speaking, another one of Afrasiyab's sahirs, Folad Jadoo, reached the mountain and challenged the traitors. Amar looked at Mahrukh and said, 'Since you are a powerful sahira, deal with him!' Mahrukh said, 'I was unconscious when you tackled Rahdar Jadoo. Show me how you can kill this one!'

'Like a dirty dog!' declared Amar confidently and called out to Folad to stop talking nonsense and face him in battle. Folad drew a coconut out of his pouch of magic and muttered a spell. Amar also drew out a citron and started muttering on it to give the impression that he was a sahir. As Folad was aiming the coconut at him, Amar called out, 'You are a fool! You have come to fight me but another sahir follows you to kill you!' Folad turned around and on finding no one there, turned back in anger to Amar. By this time, however, Amar had reached him and burst a narcotic bubble in his nose. As he fell unconscious, Amar cut his head off with his sword.

Mahrukh dispelled the storms and darkness that followed the sahir's death and saw that Amar was standing to one side, counting worry beads as he muttered, 'Save me, O Allah!' Mahrukh walked up to him and said, 'O king of ayyars, all praise to Allah! How soon you sent this sahir straight to hell! I am your humble servant, come and sit with me.'

The rebel camp

Mahrukh, Amar and the others were talking to each other when they heard trumpets and drums, and the sounds of an approaching army. They saw twenty-four thousand sahirs mounted on fire-breathing dragons coming towards them. Many of them were conjuring flames and stones that fell from the skies. Shakeel was leading this army, seated on a king swan that shone like fire and was followed by thousands of elephants, mules and camels carrying tents and furniture. Amar turned to Asad and remarked, 'It almost seems like a sardar from Hamza's army.' Mahrukh said, 'My prince, this is your slave and my son, Shakeel Jadoo. Lay your blessed hand on him and comfort him.'

Shakeel got off his mount and greeted Amar and Asad who embraced him warmly and gave him their blessings. Mahrukh directed the army to camp on the fields around them. Gardeners cleared the fields of bushes and shrubs, and soldiers prepared bunkers and dug trenches. The royal tent was erected first next to the mountain spring. The women's tent was pitched besides it. Kitchen tents started preparing vast quantities of food and brisk trading began in the bazaars that had opened in the camp.

Mahrukh entered the royal tent with the others and invited Asad to preside as the badshah of the army. Asad declined her invitation and said, 'That title is only for the Badshah of the Islamic army. Princess Mahjabeen will reign as his regent and will send him gifts of money and goods every year.' Thus, Mahjabeen was crowned and it was she who sat on the throne of state. Asad and the other sardars presented her with gifts of gold coins and precious stones. There were jubilant cries of *mubarak* and wine flowed freely.

Dilaram was appointed the most important companion of the regent and Asad became the commander-in-chief of the army. Amar was awarded the title of special adviser with powers to guide the regent and to replace her in an emergency. Courts were established and magistrates and judges appointed. Mahrukh Magic-eye became the Grand Vizier and established a treasury. Heralds went to nearby villages to recruit soldiers. Amongst the ayyars, Zargham Sherdil, Mehtar Qiran and Jansoz bin Qiran heard the heralds and came to the camp to pay homage to the newly-crowned regent and grand vizier.

Soon enough, Afrasiyab's spies who had been disguised as birds reported all these events to him. Immediately, he sent for Hairat from her city. When she arrived on her flying couch with her companions, he said in anger, 'Malika, have you seen how this traitor to the salt Mahrukh has allied with Tilism Kusha to fight against me?' Hairat tried to placate him and said, 'Huzoor, I will write to Mahrukh and counsel her. She will never dare to face you in battle!' On hearing this Afrasiyab said, 'As you wish, she is related to you and I hesitate to punish her.'

Hairat wrote in a terse note to Mahrukh, 'You are informed that you should present yourself in haste as my lowly maid so that I can have your crime forgiven by the Shahanshah.' A messenger bird deposited the note in Mahrukh's lap. She read the note and trembled with fear. Seeing Mahrukh so distressed, Amar read the note and tore it deliberately. Then he composed the reply: 'Malika Hairat, I am the slayer of sahirs and kafirs. It was my dagger that slayed Damama Jadoo, the granddaughter of your idol Samri. It was I who killed Mishmish, the teacher of all sahirs, in his abode under the river. You must release Princess Tasveer and Prince Badi-uz-Zaman and present yourself in haste at the court of Princess Mahjabeen who is the real ruler of this Tilism. If you resist, your nose will be cut off, your face will be blackened, and you will be mounted on a donkey or my name is not Amar!'

Amar then gave the note to the bird and said, 'Tell that wretch Hairat that she should watch out as I will be shaving her head very soon. She can do what she likes. Allah will protect us!' The bird flew back to Hairat, handed her the note, and repeated Amar's verbal message. Hairat looked at the Shah and said, 'You are right. These people will have to be punished. Just look at how that lowly ayyar has humiliated us in this note!' Afrasiyab read the note and in sheer rage, bit his lips until they bled.

సౌ

5 AFRASIYAB SENDS IN AN ARMY AGAINST AMAR AND MAHRUKH

Hairat wanted to lead the army against the rebels herself but Afrasiyab dissuaded her by saying that there were plenty of officers in Tilism other than the Shahanshah's wife who could fight the rebels. Then he read a spell and knocked in the air. Within moments, the skies darkened and lightning flashed across the sky. This was followed by sheets of flames and stone-rains from the skies. Eventually, three sahirs descended from the clouds. They bowed before Afrasiyab in a mujra-greeting, kissed the base of his throne and asked, 'Why does the great Shahanshah summon us?'

Afrasiyab briefed them about his feud with Mahrukh and Mahjabeen and about their alliance with the Tilism Kusha. He also told the sahirs about the five ayyars from Hamza's army. He added, 'You three take an army of sixty thousand sahirs and bring these rebels to me with their hands tied!' The three sahirs, Jamosh Jadoo, Shahbaz Jadoo and Kohan Jadoo promptly reached their respective forts and left for the battle with sixty thousand sahir soldiers riding dragons and other magical animals. They crossed the River of Flowing Blood and marched towards Mahrukh's camp. When she heard the sound of thunder and lightning, Mahrukh turned to Amar and said, 'Khwaja, the sahir army is here!' All five ayyars headed for the desert, while Mahrukh and the other sahirs chanted counterspells to prevent injuries from the rain of flames and stones that preceded Afrasiyab's army.

Thus, the perfidious sahir army arrived in great pomp and splendour, and camped right opposite Mahrukh's army, leaving an area in between for the battlefield. Tents and pavilions were erected, and bazaars were set up. That evening, Jamosh ordered his commanders to give the signal for battle the next morning. Accordingly, his men struck magical drums and trumpets so forcefully that the ears of the sky were deafened. Spy birds flew to Mahjabeen's durbar and after praising and greeting Mahjabeen, the badshah of the lashkar, they announced, 'The enemy has struck battle drums and is prepared to attack!' Mahjabeen turned to Asad for advice, who in turn ordered Mahrukh, 'Let us repose our faith in the Almighty and also respond in kind!' Attendants rushed to strike the great magical kettledrum of war while Mahrukh and Shakeel sounded magic trumpets whose sounds shook the earth and reverberated in distant domes.

Across enemy lines, Jamosh smeared the floor of his tent with pig blood, moulded balls and puppets of lentil flour, and carved arrows out of animal horns. He breathed magical spells on the puppets and arrows to make them as hard as steel. Then he burnt incense and offered sacrificial meats to all the spirits in his command.

Mahrukh kept up a midnight vigil on her side of the battlefield. She poured wine in libation to the gods and moulded a wax doll with beautiful features and delicate straw jewellery. She placed the doll in the sacred fire and whispered softly, 'O Woman of Magic, leave now and come when you are needed!' The wax doll melted into the flames and Mahrukh finally went to bed.

Early next morning, Asad rose to say his prayers and went to the pavilion of the regent in battle dress. Several drums and trumpets sounded as kaharis emerged from the pavilion carrying Mahjabeen Diamond-robe on her throne. All the sardars bowed in mujra-greeting to her. The regent's throne was placed in the heart of the lashkar and the faithful Dilaram stayed close to Mahjabeen, riding a magic peacock. The regent's attendants and guards called out, 'Stay away!' They formed a protective ring around her throne and held the flags of the lashkar aloft.

Sahirs on both sides cleared the battleground. Some cast spells that made wild bushes and scrub burn down, while others had the fields cleared and sprinkled with magic rain to settle the dust. Heralds of both armies emerged and called out, 'Where are Samri and Jamshed? They have vanished behind the veil of time after dazzling the world with their magic. O noble sahirs, today is the day when you can make your name and fight to your heart's content!'

Shahbaz appeared first and challenged Mahrukh to confront him. As she flew towards him on her throne, he shot a magic arrow at her that she gracefully deflected back at him. He then hurled an iron ball that smashed her throne. Mahrukh quickly flew higher and transformed into a shimmering sword that fell on Shahbaz from a great height, slaying him along with his dragon. Stones and flames rained from the skies as he died and his soldiers rushed to attack Mahrukh. Shakeel signalled to his sahirs to conjure heavy raindrops that fell on the enemy sahirs and made them fall unconscious.

Seeing the commotion caused by Shahbaz's death, Jamosh cut out a paper sun that rose in the sky and shone so brightly that it turned Mahrukh's soldiers into stone. Jamosh and Kohan then jumped into the battlefield and killed thousands of sahirs with their spells. Asad, who had been holding back all this while, asked Mahjabeen for permission to fight. She smiled her assent but asked Dilaram softly on the side to protect him against magic. The prince had not yet reached the battlefield when Dilaram caused his horse to sprout wings and fly upwards. Asad tried to ride the horse back down to the ground, but it remained frozen in mid-air and Asad could only watch the battle being fought beneath him.

Meanwhile, Mahrukh dived into the earth to emerge behind Jamosh and shot an arrow at him. As he died, the magic sun that he had conjured crumpled into paper and the soldiers who had turned into stone became alive again. The third sahir, Kohan Jadoo, now stepped forward. He made a cut on his thigh and sprinkled his blood on some pebbles. For a moment, there was darkness and as light returned, huge boulders began raining down on Mahrukh's army. There was panic and Shakeel's soldiers fled from the battlefield. At this time, Mahrukh read a spell and said, 'O Woman of Magic, come forth!'

There was a flash of unearthly light accompanied by the sound of bells ringing. A beautiful maiden wearing rich garments and jewellery arrived on a flying throne. Her reddened lips glowed, her eyes sparkled with kohl, and her face put the full moon to shame. As Kohan continued fighting, she called out to him, 'O Kohan, I have come here for you and you ignore me? Shall I leave?' Kohan looked up and at the sight of her fairy-like beauty, he became weak with love.

'I am your slave and love you with all my heart,' he cried. The *parizad* came closer, fanned him with her jewelled fan, and said archly, 'It will be difficult to get me!' Enchanted by the magic breeze of the fan, Kohan lost all reason and recited verses of love as he followed her. 'I am Malika Mahrukh's handmaiden and you fight her? What kind of a lover are you? Stop your army and retract your spell!' whispered the parizad furiously.

Burning with desire, Kohan ordered his army to stop fighting and chanted a spell to turn the raining boulders back into pebbles lying on the ground. Kohan's army were as enchanted by the *pari* and she said to Kohan, 'If you claim to be in love with me, prove it by cutting your own throat!' Just as Kohan drew his sword to obey her, she laughed and held his hand, 'If you die, where will I find true love and who will appreciate my beauty? I am yours on the condition that you bring the head of Hairat as a gift for Malika Mahrukh!'

Kohan turned to army and called, 'O faithful lovers, go now and drag that low-born Hairat by her hair back to me!' Hearing him, his soldiers tore their tunics in frenzy and ran towards the Garden of Apples to do his bidding, all the while shouting, 'Get her! Get her!' They crossed the River of Flowing Blood and when Afrasiyab's guards stopped them at the gate of the garden, the soldiers began fighting fiercely.

Afrasiyab heard the din from inside the garden and came outside. On seeing Kohan's men fighting his guards, he consulted the oracle Book of Samri and learnt that Mahrukh had moulded a doll out of the dust of Jamshed. He realized that these men would never revert to normality again. Afrasiyab reluctantly smashed an iron ball through Kohan that killed him instantly. He then twirled his fingers so that several thousand bolts of lightning fell from the sky on the enchanted soldiers, who all burnt to death. As they died, the magic parizad in the battlefield caught fire suddenly and was burnt to ashes.

'It seems,' declared Mahrukh, 'that Afrasiyab has killed Kohan and his men.' There were joyous celebrations and Mahrukh's camp struck the drums of victory. The pavilions, furniture and goods of the defeated army were also appropriated. The Islamic camp moved several miles away from the scene of destruction and everyone enjoyed wine and nautch performances.

Bibran, the Lion-mounted

Afrasiyab said to Hairat in despair, 'It is a sad hour when one has to dispose of subordinates and allies oneself. Three great sahirs and a force of sixty thousand soldiers have been destroyed!' As Afrasiyab was speaking, there was a shower of water and flames at the same time and the sound of trumpets and gongs filled the air. Moments later, a hideous looking young sahir appeared on a lion with amulets of Samri and Jamshed tied around his neck. His army of twelve thousand sahirs waited outside the garden. He walked up to Afrasiyab and Hairat and greeted them respectfully. This was Hairat's nephew Bibran, the Lion-mounted. She rose to embrace him and asked him, 'What brings you here my son?' Bibran replied, 'I have heard that some of my uncle's subordinates are fighting him and have come to offer my services to you. Give me your permission to punish them!' Hairat said, 'My son, there are enough people to deal with them. Why should you go? They are being helped by ayyars from Hamza's army who deceive sahirs and kill them, or they would have been destroyed by now.' However, Bibran insisted and Afrasiyab relented. He sent him to fight with several thousand sahirs from his own army.

Bibran crossed the River of Flowing Blood and camped there. Mahrukh Magic-eye heard the fanfare and sent her spy birds to investigate. They returned and informed her, 'The lashkar of our stubborn enemy has camped near the river. It wants to be divested of the River of Life, otherwise all is well.'

Mahrukh declared, 'Then our lashkar should also move forward!' Accordingly, the army moved with its equipment. Sahirs surrounded Mahjabeen's throne and led her forward in great splendour. On the other side, Bibran did not declare the battle immediately. He posted a guard of twelve hundred sahirs around the camp and another guard of a hundred sahirs around his tent to prevent ayyars from entering his camp. All the soldiers were on high alert for the ayyars and the day went by in Bibran's camp in making these arrangements.

Meanwhile, Barq disguised himself as a holy man carrying a pitcher of wine. He slipped past the outer ring of guards and strolled past Bibran's tent. All the guards on duty outside the tent greeted him respectfully, but he remained silent and suddenly ran past them. The guards murmured amongst themselves that he had to be a gifted man of god and ran after him. The holy man halted unexpectedly, threw a handful of dust in the air, started muttering to himself, and then ran off again. The guards followed him, completely riveted by his antics. Thus, Barq lured them out of the camp. As the men watched him, he suddenly dropped the pitcher on the ground, ran away and hid himself behind a bush.

The guards said to each other, 'This man is truly holy and does not fraternize with other men. When we chased him, he fled but left this wine for us. Let us see what it contains.' They examined the pitcher and found it full of wine. One of them said, 'If we drink from his pitcher, all our troubles might vanish.' Another suggested that the wine would surely increase their lifespan. Eventually, all the guards drank deeply from the pitcher and fell unconscious because the wine was drugged. Barq now emerged from his hiding place and killed several of them. As the sahirs died, there were cries of outrage from their spirits followed by snowstorms and lightning in the sky. Bibran who had been drinking wine inside his tent rushed outside in panic and saw Barq killing his soldiers. He trapped Barq with a quick spell and brought him inside the tent.

'Who are you?' Bibran asked Barq, who calmly replied, 'I am the angel of death of sahirs and will presently kill you!' Bibran was suitably terrified and thought, 'My aunt Hairat was right. These ayyars are straight out of hell.' He tied Barq to a pillar and told him, 'You can threaten me all you want, but I will kill you tomorrow morning, and if some ayyar comes to rescue you, he will be killed as well!' Barq merely replied, 'Whoever comes will surely get you Bibran!'

Mehtar Qiran had been watching Barq's entrapment from a distance and did not want to risk being caught in case there was a magic circle around Bibran's camp. The next morning, Qiran thought of a rescue plan and went deep into the forest to look for a lion. He came across one sitting near a pool. Since Qiran was the favoured one of the lion of Allah— Hazrat Ali—he went fearlessly before the lion and challenged him. The lion arose with a growl, but Qiran caught his front paws and hit the lion so hard that he fell down in a stupor. Qiran then opened his pouch of ayyari to find a saddle like the one Bibran used on his lion. After saddling the cowed lion, he rode him to the enemy camp disguised as Bibran.

Bibran's soldiers greeted him respectfully and Qiran ordered them, 'Go to my tent and remove my spell off the prisoner. Bring him to me so I can kill him in front of his army.' When Barq was led to him in chains, the false Bibran instructed the soldiers to remain on guard and led Barq to the edge of the camp. He then revealed his identity, adding lightly, 'Run along now, and be careful the next time you attempt ayyari!' Barq said gratefully, 'Khalifa, only you would be so blessed by Allah that you overcame a live lion! I thank you a hundred times over!' Deeper inside the forest, Qiran released the lion and said, 'Off with you! You have served your purpose!'

Bibran had been away for an early morning ride and returned to his tent to find Barq missing. 'Where is he?' Bibran asked his men in fury. 'But huzoor,' they stuttered, 'you took him away just a while ago!' After much denial and debate, Bibran realized that he had been outwitted, but was stunned by the audacity of the tricksters and thought, 'Where on earth did they find a live lion! Surely, I will find it difficult to survive their attacks!' Bibran however kept his thoughts to himself and ordered the soldiers to let no one into the camp, even if the real Afrasiyab and Hairat came to visit him.

Meanwhile Hairat requested Afrasiyab to check on her nephew. Afrasiyab consulted the Book of Samri and informed her about Qiran and Barq's tricks. Hairat was aghast and cried, 'These ayyars will surely take his life. I cannot believe that they actually harnessed a live lion!' Hairat turned to her vizierzadi Zamurrad Jadoo and asked her to convey a message to Bibran. Now Zamurrad was very beautiful and had a face like the full moon, fragrant black tresses like the long night of parted lovers and a body that looked as if it was sculpted from light.

Zamurrad Jadoo flew with the power of magic to the camp. Bibran's soldiers surrounded her as she was about to enter his tent and only let her in after they got his consent. When she finally entered his tent, Bibran threw his ring on the floor and said, 'Lift this ring. If you are the real Zamurrad it will not harm you, if you are false, it will burn your hand!' Zamurrad replied, 'First I have been insulted by your men, now you play these childish tricks!'

The fair sahira chanted an incantation and picked up the ring easily. She joined Bibran on his masnad but declined his offer of wine angrily. 'Go away,' she said, 'I will not speak to such a simpleton as you. If you are so afraid of ayyars, why do you come here to fight them?' Bibran was smitten by her beauty and encouraged by the familiarity of her tone, stroked her cheek and said, 'Do not be angry my princess! I may be a simpleton, but have some wine at least.' Zamurrad looked at him, then bowed her head shyly and whispered, 'Do not speak to me this way or I will tell your aunt.' Bibran restrained his ardour and after reading his aunt's letter, politely told Zamurrad to convey the message to Hairat that he would visit her that evening.

After Zamurrad left, Bibran kept yearning for her. Barq, who had been trying to enter the camp, saw her fly off from the edge of the camp. Barq thought of a trick and wore emerald-coloured clothes and emerald jewellery, and painted his face to look like Zamurrad. Then, holding a flask of drugged wine, he found a pleasant green meadow where he waited for unsuspecting sahirs. Towards sunset, Bibran left his camp to visit his aunt. As he flew over the meadow, he heard someone calling out to him and saw Zamurrad Jadoo sitting on the ground. A surprised Bibran descended and asked her, 'O Princess Zamurrad, is all well? Why have you not gone to my aunt yet?' The false Zamurrad sighed deeply and said, 'Why do you ask the stricken by love of where they are? I have no measure of time and space!'

As soon as he heard this, Bibran thought that though Zamurrad had been willing in the camp, she had exercised restraint and waited for him, as she knew that he would be travelling this way alone. Delighted with this change in her, he held her hand and tried to kiss her on her sweet tender lips. She turned away and said, 'Stay away from me, faithless lover!' Bibran tried to embrace her again and murmured, 'I am yours forever, my love!' This time, the false Zamurrad responded by placing her cheek on his. Overcome with desire, Bibran wanted more but she held him back and suggested that they have some wine first.

Meanwhile, Hairat was worried about her nephew and asked Afrasiyab to consult the Book of Samri. Afrasiyab hit his head in frustration when he read the book and cried, 'Malika, Barq Ayyar disguised as Zamurrad is about to kill him in a meadow!' Hairat turned to Zamurrad and cried, 'Go quickly with this magic dust of Jamshed and warn Bibran!'

Zamurrad flew off and in no time reached the meadow where Bibran was just about to sip the drugged wine. Zamurrad called out, 'Bibran, you are courting your own death! It is an ayyar who sits next to you!' Barq quickly whispered to the besotted Bibran, 'It is not fated that we should unite. Even now an ayyar disguised to look like me comes to deceive you!' Bibran was in such rapture that he was convinced that Barq was right. He whispered, 'Hide yourself my love and I will take care of this wily ayyar!'

Barq darted behind a bush and Bibran stood up to face Zamurrad. As she came closer and asked where the trickster was, Bibran held her hand and slapped her hard even as he muttered a spell. Zamurrad was a powerful sahira and quickly turned her cheek to stone, or else Bibran would have struck her head off. Furious with Bibran, she sprinkled a pinch of the magic dust on him and he fell down unconscious. Turning around, she saw Barq cowering behind a bush and said the magic word '*gir*' that made Barq stuck to the ground. Zamurrad then cut two paper hands and chanted a spell that made them real. She ordered them to carry Barq and Bibran to the Dome of Light. The hands moved swiftly and deposited Bibran and the ayyar before the Shah and Hairat.

Zamurrad arrived soon after the magic hands and complained bitterly to Hairat, 'Bibi, your nephew cannot recognize friend from foe. He was so overcome with lust for this ayyar that he slapped me with a magical hand. Believe me, had it been another sahira, she would have died! Here is your nephew and here is the ayyar whom he was embracing. I cannot work for you now. I am not used to being slapped!'

Hairat placated the affronted Zamurrad and then revived Bibran. He woke up and on seeing Hairat, greeted her with some surprise. Hairat looked stern and said, 'You embrace an ayyar and slap my vizierzadi?

Can you not distinguish between friend and foe?' Bibran was embarrassed and apologized profusely to Zamurrad. Hairat looked at the captive Barq and said, 'What a perfect face this rascal has made. Why Zamurrad, he looks the image of you! It is no wonder that Bibran was mistaken!'

Hairat chanted an incantation that made the paint on Barq's face peel off and said, 'Go to your camp! Tell Mahrukh not to tempt fate and to present herself with Mahjabeen in my court; I will have the Shahanshah pardon her crime.' Barq retorted, 'You can make up fantasies as you sit here. Are you not aware that each day of your life is a boon and eventually carrions will eat you? Mahrukh is not your father's servant that she will come running to you!'

Enraged by his reply, Hairat ordered a sahir to cut off his head. Barq prayed desperately for help from the Almighty. The arrowhead of his prayer reached its target—Bibran stepped in and said, 'Aunt, this ayyar has caused my disgrace. Give me leave to have him slaughtered in front of his camp.' Hairat was reluctant to let Bibran return to the camp but he threatened to kill himself if she did not let him go back. Finally, Hairat gave him permission to leave. Bibran cut out a paper lion and breathed life into it. He mounted the lion and left for his camp with Barq tied up behind him.

As Barq had been missing for a while, Qiran became worried and had been looking for him through the day. Then came that moment when the beautifier of time adorned the ruler of the night with the ornaments of stars. Qiran eventually reached the place where Zamurrad had captured Barq. He stopped there for a while and suddenly saw Bibran dragging Barq in the distance. Qiran filled an envelope with drugged dust and put Hairat's seal on the envelope.

He stopped Bibran just before he reached his camp. 'Who are you?' asked Bibran of the false sahir, who replied, 'The messenger of Hairat.' 'I was with her just now,' Bibran said with some surprise, 'and I did not see you there! And why should she send me a message when I just left her?'

Qiran who did not know of any of this frowned and said, 'How should I know? She has given me this letter. O Bibran, do you think that servants constantly sit on Hairat's bosom that you claim not to have seen me with her? I was in my place and was summoned to convey this message to you.'

A chastened Bibran asked the sahir to accompany him to the camp as he could not read the letter in darkness. The false sahir taunted him, 'Very well, read it and send your reply through someone else. However, you claim to be a sahir, you could conjure some light and read the letter now, or perhaps I should do it for you?' Bibran felt that his honour as a sahir had been challenged. He instantly picked up a twig from the ground and transformed it into a flaming taper.

He then gave it to Qiran to hold so he could read the letter. Qiran quietly sprinkled the powder of unconsciousness on the flame too and as Bibran breathed in the fumes, he slumped over unconscious. Qiran smashed his head with his powerful bughda immediately. There were terrible sounds and a burst of stones and fire from the skies. Barq was now free and ran into the forest with Qiran.

Barq rushed back his camp and told Mahrukh Magic-eye, 'Alert the army! Bibran has been killed.' Mahrukh gave the order and her son Shakeel blew the battle trumpet. His army mobilized quickly and sahir soldiers mounted their magical peacocks and dragons. Mahrukh, Asad and Shakeel, along with forty thousand sardars and men attacked Bibran's camp. Bibran's army was taken by surprise as iron balls and arrows followed by bolts of lightning fell upon them.

Amar, who was in the forest at the time, heard the din and rushed over to discover that Bibran's army was being slaughtered. Amar took advantage of the situation to plunder the enemy tents of furnishings and objects of value. Eventually, Bibran's defeated soldiers ran towards the Dome of Light. Afrasiyab and Hairat were informed that Bibran's army had fled from the battlefield. On hearing this, an alarmed Hairat cried, 'Is all well with my son?'

Bibran's soldiers wailed, 'Your nephew was killed by the ayyars and is with Samri now!' Hairat smote her head and wept in grief. She cried, 'Alas, my poor son was killed by these cruel ayyars!' Afrasiyab muttered an incantation and knocked in the air. A whirlwind carried Bibran's body from the forest to the Dome of Light. Nobles of the durbar donned black robes and prepared for the funeral. The next morning, Bibran's funeral was conducted with great solemnity. After it was over, Hairat said, 'Shahanshah, give me leave to kill all the traitors!' Afrasiyab placated her and said, 'This time, I will send a man who will surely dispose the ayyars for he is not affected by drugs, potions or any of their tricks.'

Folad Shikan Iron-breaker

Afrasiyab roared, 'O Folad Shikan, come here at once!' Within moments, a sahir appeared on a fire-breathing bull. He was powerfully built and hideously ugly to look at. He bowed before Afrasiyab, who said, 'Take your army of twelve thousand and help me get rid of the ayyars who have created havoc in our domain. Bibran has been murdered. Until now, I have been soft on them as I wanted the traitors to come to their senses, but now they are asking for their doom. Here are twelve iron warriors who can neither be killed nor made unconscious. Use them when you fight the ayyars.'

Afrasiyab knocked in the air and twelve iron puppets armed with swords dug their way out of the earth and stood before him. Afrasiyab ordered them to accompany Folad. 'My lord,' said Folad bowing respectfully, 'what need have I of the warriors? I can face the enemy alone. I am never unconscious, I can only enjoy wine if it is mixed with huge quantities of the strongest potions and no ayyars or soldier can face my strength.' Afrasiyab looked at him doubtfully and said, 'Take them anyway as a precaution.' Folad smiled and left for the battlefield with his army, tents and animals. The twelve warriors too went with him.

As Folad and his army drew closer to Mahrukh's camp, the sound of their trumpets reached the ears of the champions of righteousness. Mahrukh sent her bird spies to investigate and they returned to report, 'May the life of the ruler be extended, the wretched enemy is on the march again. A sahir named Folad Shikan Jadoo comes with his army.'

Mahrukh turned to Amar in despair and said, 'Khwaja, may Allah protect us! This haramzada cannot be killed or even wounded. He is immune to drugs and potions; no weapon can wound him!' Amar replied calmly, 'Malika, we only need the Lord's help! Who is this joker Folad and what standing does he have when we are fighting his master Afrasiyab? Look at the way their living god Laqa flees in terror from Emir Hamza. Just have trust in Allah and do not lose faith even if things seem to be going against you. I will kill this shameless wretch very soon!'

After reassuring Mahrukh, Amar left his camp. The other four ayyars were already thinking of ways to tackle their latest adversary. Amar, Zargham and Jansoz, disguised as sahirs, set off for Folad's camp. Amar, disguised as a sahir, went to his guards and asked them to inform Folad that Maut Jadoo would like to meet him. When he was allowed into the pavilion, Amar saw that Folad Shikan Jadoo was sitting on a throne of fire with a crown of flames on his head and a chain of flames around his waist. Hundreds of fearsome-looking sahirs sat around him and iron puppets that breathed out fire guarded him.

When Amar greeted him, Folad looked up and was impressed by the appearance of the newcomer who seemed to be a powerful sahir as he had live snakes wrapped around his head and a gold chain around his waist. 'Who are you sir and what brings you here?' he asked Amar politely after offering him a chair. 'I am from the fort of Rangeen Hissar,' replied Amar, 'and Mahrukh has deprived me of my house and property. I am looking forward to her destruction by you huzoor!' Folad was pleased with his guest and bestowed the title of special companion on him and also presented him with robes of honour.

Elsewhere, Jansoz and Zargham were also trying to reach Folad. They had waylaid two of his servants and said conspiratorially to them,

'Brothers, we have a rare perfume but do not have access to your master. Try and sell it for us if you can.' Intrigued and flattered, the servants asked to see the perfume and became unconscious after they sniffed it. The two ayyars took away their clothes and hid the unconscious servants in a ditch. Then, after disguising themselves as the two servants, they went into the pavilion.

At the time when Amar as Maut Jadoo was offering Folad drugged wine, Jansoz and Zargham were already standing behind Folad. Folad drank the wine and remained unaffected but realized that the wine was drugged and that Maut Jadoo was probably an ayyar. He quietly whispered a spell that made Amar stuck to his chair and said, 'You can give me as many drugs as you can, I will not be affected!'

Jansoz and Zargham then decided to attack Folad openly but when they struck him, their swords broke on impact with his magically thickened skin. Folad had them all arrested immediately. The three ayyars were imprisoned in a tent next to Folad's tent and their tent was encircled by a ring of flames.

Mahrukh Magic-eye was agitated when she received the news of the ayyars' arrests and said to Mahjabeen, 'Have you heard that the ayyars have been captured? None of us can confront Folad Shikan. If you agree, I think that we should retreat. Since I know the secrets of this realm, I can take you all to Sahibqiran. Only he will be able to fight Afrasiyab!' Asad smiled and said, 'Malika, Amar has been captured and released a thousand times. Do not worry about him and let the drums of battle roll. To run like cowards is not part of our tradition. Even if we take refuge with Emir Hamza, he will throw us out of his camp. Perhaps he might be softer on you because you are a woman but I will certainly not return now!'

Mahrukh said, 'In that case, my prince, I am with you. Let us strike the drums of war in the name of Allah!' Battle drums were struck and everyone prepared for certain death. The next day, after his early morning prayers, Asad arrived in Mahjabeen Diamond-robe's durbar in battle dress. Shakeel and Mahrukh sent the army to the battlefield and went to the royal pavilion. Mahjabeen emerged in all splendour and greeted everyone. Dilaram escorted her to the battlefield.

Meanwhile, Folad had been awakening his magical powers all night. In the morning, he mounted his bull and went to the battleground with his army and the twelve invincible iron warriors. The first man to confront him after seeking Mahjabeen Diamond-robe's permission was Shakeel Jadoo. Before Folad could attack him, Shakeel cast a spell on him. Folad was enveloped in darkness and several unseen claws attacked him with swords and spears. Folad, in turn, threw a fistful of magic dust to the skies, which dispelled the darkness and the claws. Then he hurled an iron ball toward Shakeel that burst into smoke and made Shakeel unconscious. Folad's iron warriors ran and tied him up. A few other sardars of Islam attacked Folad but fell unconscious in the smoke and were captured.

Eventually, Mahrukh Magic-eye herself jumped into the fray and cast a spell that created a mighty storm that dispersed the magic smoke. Mahrukh then smashed a citron on the ground that burst and caused a huge dragon to rear up from the earth. It breathed out flames and as it breathed in, Folad was sucked into its mouth. He screamed, 'Save me magic warriors ! This venal Mahrukh has cast too powerful a spell!' The iron warriors fell on the dragon and tore him apart.

Then they turned to attack Mahrukh. She tried to fight them but they were immune to magic and soon overcame her. Seeing her plight, Mahjabeen ordered all her forces to save Mahrukh. The army attacked from all four sides crying, 'Get him! Get him now!' Lightning flashed on the battlefield and there were dreadful sounds. Folad assessed the situation and flung four coconuts in each corner of the battlefield. Flames shot out of the earth and Mahjabeen's army was trapped within walls of fire. The smoke from these flames covered them like a canopy and the army was now completely trapped.

Folad had all the sardars tied up with magical chains of fire and prepared to travel back to his master with his prisoners. He cast a spell that made the wall of fire around Mahjabeen and Asad's army move with them. All the prisoners within wailed at their plight and jubilant in his victory, Folad led his army to the Dome of Light.

Barq and Qiran watched all this from a distance. Barq wept to see their army in this state and said, 'Khalifa, I will go and either cut this haramzada Folad to pieces or give my life in the process!' Qiran said quietly, 'There is no point, my brother, for this sahir is immune to drugs or swords. Let us follow him and pray to Allah for deliverance.'

The land of Nafarman

In the Dome of Light, Afrasiyab consulted the Book of Samri and tilted his crown with pride when he saw Folad's triumph. He declared, 'Have you seen the fruit of rebellion? They are in a pitiable state now!' Afrasiyab sent some sahirs with precious robes of state and a message for Folad: 'Well done my commander! I will reward you handsomely! As for the rebels, there is no need to bring them across the River of Flowing Blood. Bring them to the Garden of Pleasure by way of Nafarman in Tilism-e-Zahir. We will reach there as well and punish them horribly!'

After dispatching this message, Afrasiyab entered his favourite garden in triumph and the area surrounding it was organized for the arrival of the rebels. Hundreds of executioners and hangmen were summoned. They came wearing the sliced off noses and ears of their victims as garlands around their necks. They sharpened and cleaned their swords with dust-cloths smelling of blood and praised Afrasiyab's might and glory. They clamoured, 'Whose lives are forfeit? Which sinners do we kill?' Afrasiyab ordered them to be ready to execute the rebel prisoners and went back to the garden to celebrate. Harps of victory played without musicians, trees were adorned with gold and silver glitter, water-channels flowed in the garden and fountains spouted sparkling water.

Folad entered the land of Nafarman with his prisoners and reached the fort of Nafarman, which had walls of pure gold. Thousands of sahirs milled around in magical disguises. For miles around the city, fields blazed with millions of red tulips and violet *nafarman* flowers. The ruler of this realm was Malika Nafarman, a powerful and high-born sahira, also renowned for her beauty. After learning of Folad's arrival, Nafarman went with gifts and jewels to welcome him. As she emerged from her fort on her magical white swan, she heard cries of agony from the prisoners trapped inside the blazing walls of fire that spread for miles.

Malika Nafarman met Folad and said, 'Huzoor, my fort is nearby. Rest a while so that you are refreshed.' Folad replied after some thought, 'I am anxious to take my prisoners straight to the Shahanshah but I cannot decline so gracious an offer.' Folad then left the prisoners and followed Malika Nafarman into the city. He observed that the city was prosperous and that its citizens seemed happy. He entered a garden that had been specially adorned for him and noticed the neatly laid-out blooming flowerbeds and singing birds. Folad sat in a *baradari* in the middle of the garden where royal masnad seating had been arranged for him. His iron warriors and nobles stood around him respectfully. Nafarman signalled for the dancing to begin and then became involved with making arrangements for a feast.

Qiran and Barq

Now hear about what happened to Qiran and Barq. They had followed Folad to Nafarman hoping to rescue their lashkar. After settling on a course of action, Qiran disguised himself as a chef and Barq became a common labourer. They bought huge quantities of vegetables from Folad's camp bazaars and Barq carried these in a straw basket balanced on his head. As they approached the city gates, Nafarman's guards refused to let them in. 'But we are cooks from Folad's camp,' the ayyars protested, 'and we bring these vegetables under Malika's orders!'

The guards asked them to wait while they took permission from the palace. Qiran pretended to be furious and threw the basket of vegetables at their feet. 'Very well,' he shouted, 'if there is a delay in the feast you answer for it. I am leaving; perhaps you can send the vegetables in yourself!' He turned around to leave but the guards called him back for fear of losing their jobs. Qiran and Barq entered the city and saw that it was prosperous and buzzing with activity. They sold the basket of vegetables to a vegetable shop, and in a secluded corner, disguised themselves as palace attendants.

Eventually, they managed to reach the garden where Folad was being entertained and consulted each other on what was to be their next move. 'We will have to kill him tonight,' whispered Barq, 'or it might me too late to save our army tomorrow. Khalifa, I am at my wit's end with this sahir! Even if we manage to get near him, he can neither be killed nor made unconscious.' Qiran pondered for a moment and said, 'Observe the sahir sitting next to Folad very carefully; then assume his form and capture Malika Nafarman. You will then have to disguise yourself as her. I have thought of a plan.'

After disguising himself as Mareekh Jadoo, companion of Folad, Barq walked into the palace with Qiran and asked for Malika Nafarman. She came out of the royal kitchens and on recognizing Folad's companion, greeted him cordially. Barq asked her to accompany him to a private corner so he could deliver Folad's message to her. The unsuspecting Nafarman went with him and was easily made unconscious. Barq tied her to a tree and pierced her tongue with a needle to prevent her from casting any spells.

Barq then used his paints to become the image of Nafarman. As the false Nafarman entered the palace, her companions and attendants greeted her with folded hands. A man wearing shabby clothes and holding a few firecrackers in his hands came forward to greet the Malika. Barq recognized Qiran immediately in the guise of an *atishbaz* and enquired casually, 'So how many fireworks do you have and how many can you make now?' Qiran looked thoughtful and replied slowly, 'Huzoor, I can prepare some right now.'

'How much will it cost me?' the Malika inquired. Qiran replied, 'It will be about one lakh rupees.' The false Malika looked shocked and said, 'That is too much!' 'Very well huzoor,' retorted the atishbaz, 'provide me with twenty-five kegs of dynamite; I will only charge you my labour cost.' The false Nafarman pretended to look closely at him for a while, then sent for the captain of the armoury and ordered him to provide the atishbaz with the explosives.

In no time, mule carts arrived, loaded with dynamite. The atishbaz asked for the explosives to be kept behind the garden in a tent where he could make the fireworks on his own. After he was left alone with the explosives, Qiran set to work and dug tunnels under the baradari where Folad was relaxing with his henchmen. Qiran was a strong young man of African origin and also a favoured one of the great Imam Ali. He managed to dig a network of tunnels under the baradari within an hour. He then placed the twenty-five kegs of dynamite in the tunnels and tore rags from his turban to use as makeshift torches.

Meanwhile, Barq as Malika Nafarman was waiting anxiously for a signal from his friend. Qiran soon appeared before the false Nafarman and requested her to inspect his work. When they reached the tent, Qiran whispered, 'Barq, I have placed the explosives in these tunnels. I will light the dynamite now and you go and revive Nafarman. She should also witness Folad's fate and shed tears for him, for her tongue is pierced with a needle and she will not be able to do anything!'

Barq revived Nafarman who woke up to find that she was tied to a tree and completely powerless. Just then, there was an almighty explosion as Qiran set off the dynamite. It sounded as if the sky had fallen down. Folad and his warriors and nobles were blown up and the whole garden was destroyed in an instant. The people of Nafarman panicked and ran out of their homes as the impact shattered windows and doors, and made pregnant women abort their foetuses. As Folad and his companions died, their escaping spirits added to the confusion and flames and stones rained from the sky. Qiran took advantage of the situation and torched several houses in the city, which caused fires all over and people ran out of the city crying, 'Ya Samri! Ya Jamshed!'

As soon as Folad died, the wall of fire around the Islamic army vanished. Amar and the two ayyars who were in captivity in Folad's camp were freed from their chains. Hearing the explosions in the city, Amar cried out, 'Malika Mahrukh, Folad has been killed! It seems that Barq and Qiran have sent him straight to hell! Let us rally our forces and destroy Folad's army.' Mahrukh and Shakeel's army attacked Folad's forces and conjured storms that made deadly arrows rain from the skies. Folad's army of twelve thousand sahirs was completely destroyed and not one sahir survived. The victors eventually fought their way into the fort of Nafarman. This is how that night ended.

The next morning, the victors saw that the army and people of the city of Nafarman were all gathered outside the fort and could hardly confront them. Nafarman's army surrendered in the first battle itself and the civilians begged for mercy. Mahrukh Magic-eye declared a general amnesty and entered the city triumphant. Barq shouted with joy as he saw her and ran to inform Qiran of the success of their plan. Both ayyars went to the durbar with Nafarman tied up in *pushtara*. Mahrukh was overjoyed to see both of them and embraced them with affection.

'How did you manage this?' she asked them. Qiran related the whole story and Mahjabeen Diamond-robe presented both ayyars with heavy robes of state, which they, in turn, presented to Amar in homage. He accepted their tribute and took out a homespun cotton scarf that he draped with great ceremony on Qiran's shoulders as a reward.

Qiran remarked with a smile, 'No apprentice could have received a greater honour from his teacher!' Seeing this, Barq pleaded with Amar that surely he too deserved praise because he had helped Qiran in his plan to kill Folad. 'You do not deserve it yet,' said Amar with a solemn face. 'Besides,' he continued, 'Qiran is my spiritual heir and you are not his equal in merit.'

Nafarman allies with Mahrukh

Nafarman had been tied to a pillar in the durbar. Amar revived Nafarman as she had fallen unconscious again because of the traumatic events of the previous night. Her last memory was of watching her city burning. She woke up to see Mahjabeen sitting on her throne with Asad beside her, surrounded by their nobles. Nafarman closed her eyes again in case she was having a nightmare. Amar called out to her, 'Nafarman, this is not a dream but reality. Your guests have been blown to bits; your kingdom is with Mahjabeen Diamond-robe. Join us and your life will be spared!'

Nafarman was a powerful and intelligent sahira. She knew that Tilism would eventually be destroyed and realized that Asad was Tilism Kusha. She nodded her head in acceptance of their terms and Amar untied her from the pillar. She knelt in submission before Mahjabeen Diamond-robe and was honoured with robes of state and promised several kingdoms besides her own after Tilism-e-Hoshruba was conquered. Nafarman's twenty-five thousand troops too joined their ruler and were rewarded richly.

Later, Amar suggested that it was safest for them to move from Fort Nafarman as Afrasiyab's forces could surround them easily there. Nafarman declared that she would also move with them, as she was convinced that Afrasiyab would not leave her alive now. As the lashkar prepared to move, the ayyars, sardars and Nafarman sat on magic birds and flying thrones to travel to their old campsite behind the fortress of Rangeen Hissar, where they had battled with Folad. Soon after the camp had settled in and the sardars were relaxing in the royal pavilion, a huge cloud suddenly blocked the sunlight and hundreds of stars started shooting out from it. Nafarman turned to Mahrukh and said, 'It seems that my friend Surkh Mu Deadly-locks is coming to visit us.' Mahrukh sent her son Shakeel and other nobles to receive Surkh Mu.

Surkh Mu had come to persuade Nafarman to return to the King of Sahirs. Both embraced each other warmly for they were childhood friends. Surkh Mu recognized Amar who was seated next to Mahrukh as by now his portrait had been circulated throughout Tilism. She addressed Nafarman with her eyes on him, 'O Nafarman you have doomed yourself by leaving the Shah. Alas, your life is now forfeit.'

Nafarman tried to convince her friend that Tilism-e-Hoshruba would be conquered soon and that it would be wiser for her to join forces with Amar, but Surkh Mu laughed and said, 'Are you out of your mind my sister? How can you compare the earth to the sky? What is Amar compared to Afrasiyab? Listen, Afrasiyab has an army so vast that just one of his forts has hundreds of wells that appear to be full of mosquitoes, which are in reality minute sahirs. At his command, if the sahirs of only one of these wells emerge, Tilism will be filled with sahir warriors. Who can confront Afrasiyab? Even if you think Amar can overwhelm the sahirs, where will he find the magic keystone of Tilism? Why, Afrasiyab himself does not know where it is! How will Amar find it?'

Amar remained silent but Nafarman replied, 'When the Almighty is with us he will find a way for us to obtain the magic keystone and Tilism will be conquered! Are you not aware that the enemy maybe powerful but our Protector is even more powerful?' Surkh Mu looked at her friend sadly and said, 'My dear friend, it seems that we must part as I will never join a base ayyar like Amar!' As Surkh Mu was Nafarman's friend and guest, none of the sardars challenged her opinion and continued to treat her with respect.

Meanwhile, Afrasiyab was waiting for Folad and his prisoners when some of the terrorized citizens of Nafarman arrived at his court to seek refuge. Afrasiyab slapped his thigh in sheer frustration and Hairat wept when the citizens related the horrors of the previous night. Afrasiyab tried to console his wife, but she cried, 'Shahanshah, it is best to fight our own battles. Give me leave now to round up all the rebels!' Afrasiyab replied gravely, 'My love, you have been told of how those infamous ayyars blew up Folad with dynamite. How can I risk your life by sending you? From today onwards, even I will reside physically in Zulmat and will not appear in Zahir.' Hairat looked worried and asked, 'How will I consult you on administrative issues?' Afrasiyab replied, 'You can visit me behind the veil of Zulmat. When I come here, I will be behind an invisible shield of glass. It will look like I am here in person but it will actually be my double.'

Thus, Afrasiyab's peacock throne rose from the court. As if in accompaniment, parizads emerged with musical instruments to dance in front of the throne and a crimson cloud that had floated in to form a canopy on the throne began to rain pearls. Afrasiyab's throne flew swiftly towards the Veil of Darkness, and trees, birds and people chanted, 'Ya Afrasiyab! Ya Afrasiyab!'

The arrival of spring

After Afrasiyab's departure, Hairat returned to the Garden of Apples with the nobles of the state and sat on the throne in great splendour. As soon as her sardars and nobles seated themselves, a nautch performance began and pretty cupbearers served wine in goblets. Suddenly, a cool breeze swept over the garden and the apple trees blossomed out of season. Magic birds flew in to inform Hairat that her sister Malika Bahar Jadoo had come to visit her. Hairat smiled and said, 'So that is why there is a feeling of spring in the air!'

Hairat ordered a few of her nobles to welcome Bahar. When Bahar entered the durbar, everyone stood up to greet her and Hairat embraced her warmly. Bahar was Hairat's younger sister and was of such incomparable loveliness that it seemed as if the Divine Gardener had nurtured the garden of her beauty with His grace. Afrasiyab secretly loved her and because she wanted to avoid his constant attentions, Bahar would rarely come to his court. Her permanent abode was a mountain in Tilism called Aram Koh. Many powerful sahirs were in love with her, but for fear of the Shahanshah, no one proposed to her. Hairat, in turn, was jealous of her younger sister but kept up a façade of friendship.

Bahar sat down and Hairat signalled to a cupbearer to serve wine. After she was refreshed, Bahar asked, '*Baji*, what is this fight in Tilism all about?' Hairat replied derisively, 'That trollop Mahrukh has invited her own death! She has rebelled against the Shah with a few of his subjects. I will have to give her a beating with my shoe before I kill her for such disloyalty!'

Bahar was close to Mahrukh and frowned when she heard these words. She said, 'My dear sister, how can you refer in such an insulting manner to Mahrukh who is not only a powerful sorceress, but also related to us by blood? She is equal to us in rank and power and can only be defeated by the Shah himself or perhaps by the sahirs of the seven Cells of Doom or the inmates of the Nile and the River of Seven Hues! I believe she even had the powerful Folad Shikan swallowed by her dragon and he had to be rescued by the magic iron warriors of the Shah. She certainly does not deserve such harsh words from you!'

Hairat was outraged to hear her sister defend Mahrukh and shouted, 'You silly girl, do you intend to frighten our commanders by describing Mahrukh's might? You defend the rebels as though you are secretly with them! This woman is our enemy! How else do you expect me to refer to her? Do you think I should kneel before her instead of punishing her?' Bahar too lost her temper and said, 'How dare you speak this way to me! A curse on you and your kingdom and your rebellion! Do not challenge me or I swear, I will teach you a lesson. You do not frighten me even if you are the Shah's wife!'

Afrasiyab returned from the Veil of Darkness on his flying throne when the sisters were fighting. He arrived smiling and was casually tossing a fragrant lemon in one hand. The whole court rose to greet him but he had eyes only for his lovely sister-in-law whose beautiful face was flushed with rage and whose eyes brimmed with tears. Afrasiyab was distraught on seeing her upset and cried, 'What ails you my beauty?' Bahar replied angrily, 'Shahanshah, I have been called a traitor in your durbar and to clear my name, I intend to fight Mahrukh and the rebel army and destroy them completely. But after that, I do not intend to live in Tilism and you will see no more of me!'

Afrasiyab turned to a guilty Hairat and told her sternly, 'If you call Bahar a traitor, who do you think will be loyal to us?' Hairat muttered, 'Well, if you don't spring to her defence, who else will?' Afrasiyab had no answer to this question and Bahar firmly told him, 'Shahanshah, you will have to send someone to fight the enemy, so send me.' Afrasiyab was taken aback with her offer. He thought that if he stopped her now, Hairat would accuse him of being soft on her. Therefore, he told Bahar, 'Go then, but do not fight them yourself, send one of your officers. I will also send somebody to be with you.'

Bahar gave him a withering look and said, 'I have never sought anyone else's help before. I will cut my own throat if you send someone, or even if you think of helping me yourself.' Afrasiyab smiled indulgently at her and said, 'Malika, you are quite capable of doing just that!' Sulking and frowning, Bahar took her leave and returned to Aram Koh to gather her forces. The next morning, her golden tent and furniture were loaded on golden dragons and she left on a flying throne with an army of sixty thousand sahirs. Parizads materialized in the air and sprayed coloured water from miniature gold water pumps as they sang Holi songs to mark the advent of spring. Thus, Bahar's magnificent procession travelled towards the battlefield.

The wrath of spring

As they drew closer to Mahrukh's camp, Bahar instructed her commanders to camp a few miles behind Mahrukh's lashkar. 'I will go on my own and tackle the enemy. The danger of going with my army is that ayyars often mingle with the soldiers and cannot be identified. I will arrest them all in no time!' Then she left with a few select companions. The Islamic camp was aware of her impending arrival and the five ayyars had left their camp to keep an eye on her army from a safe distance.

Meanwhile, Mahrukh's durbar was convened with pomp and splendour. The sardars were enjoying its pleasures when Amar whispered to Mahrukh, 'Farewell for now. Bahar will be coming and I should not remain here. Do not lose heart and do not worry.' After Amar left, the other ayyars also left for the forest. Mahrukh was thinking of ways to neutralize Bahar's magic when a cool breeze swept through the camp and there were shouts of 'Bahar, Bahar! The Queen of Spring is here!'

Surkh Mu was still in the Islamic camp and looked at Nafarman ruefully. She commented, 'It seems my friend that I will be in trouble as well because of you!' Mahrukh and all the nobles of the court, including Nafarman and Surkh Mu, came out eagerly from the pavilion to see Bahar floating above the camp on her magic peacock. As the whole army emerged from their tents and gazed at her, entranced by her beauty, Bahar quietly whispered a spell that made dark monsoon clouds rise up behind her. Mahrukh and the other sahirs tried to read counterspells, but a yellow dust rose from the earth and for a moment, everyone had to shut their eyes.

When their eyes opened, they found that for miles in sight, there was a beautiful garden with a low crystal wall enclosing it. During the time that their eyes were shut, Bahar had quickly sketched the picture of a garden with a magic pen and ink and conjured it. The garden enchanted whoever entered it and since it was drawn on paper, no one could dig tunnels underneath it. The sardars saw Bahar flying on her peacock into the garden and followed her.

Inside the garden stood a crystal platform, glowing with an unearthly light, shaded by a canopy of pearls sewed on to soft white leather. Bahar herself sat on a chair inlaid with precious jewels. She wore rich garments and jewellery, and held a diamond-studded wand. Costly perfumes and fresh bouquets were arranged before her and attendants were waiting on her with goblets of wine.

Mahrukh and Shakeel, Asad and Mahjabeen, and Nafarman, Surkh Mu and Dilaram were all mesmerized by the splendour of the spring garden and Bahar's beauty. They cried out in unison, 'O vision of beauty and grace, O Malika Bahar, accept us as your devoted slaves! We would die for just a favoured glance from you!'

Bahar seemed unmoved by their pleas and threw a bouquet of flowers straight at them. Its petals scattered to form bracelets and snapped around their wrists like handcuffs. Everyone started pleading, 'We repent! We repent! That wicked thief Amar misled us. Huzoor, have mercy on us and take us to Shahanshah Afrasiyab whom we have greatly wronged!' Bahar said, 'Very well! Follow me and I will take you to the Shahanshah.' She mounted her white peacock and flew out of the garden, followed by the nobles and soldiers of Mahrukh's camp who were in an enchanted frenzy and were reciting love poems and calling out her name. After they left, the magic garden vanished.

Khwaja Amar and Bahar Jadoo

The ayyars witnessed their army's enchantment from a distance and consulted each other. Barq declared that he would try to trick Bahar. 'There is no point,' said Amar, 'because she is a very powerful sahira and you will never overcome her. You can try if you promise not to kill her for I would like to have her on our side if I can manage it.' The ayyars could make no such promise and decided to leave the matter to Amar.

Amar kept his right hand on Zambil and prayed for a miracle. Within moments, he had transformed into a beautiful youth, about fourteen years of age. He waited for Bahar in a forest that was like the abode of Rizwan— an earthly paradise. As Bahar was flying over the forest, she heard a musical voice that touched her heart. She flew into the forest and saw a handsome, well-dressed youth standing beneath a tree with his eyes closed, singing so melodiously that the animals and the birds of the forest were all entranced by his voice. She approached the rosy-cheeked boy and called out, 'Who are you my child and what are you doing in this dangerous forest? Have your parents got hearts of stone?'

The young boy opened his eyes and trembled with fear when he saw Bahar. Greeting her with folded hands, he stammered, 'I am sorry, huzoor, I did not know this is your place, I will leave immediately!' Bahar leaped off her peacock to reassure him but he was even more frightened and kept edging backwards, apologizing for intruding in her area. Bahar stopped and called out softly, 'My son, come to me. I will not harm you!' Amar pouted and said, 'Promise you will not hurt me! Promise in the name of Samri!' Bahar promised and the boy took a few tentative steps towards her but ran back to hide behind a tree again.

Bahar drew out one of her bouquets and offered it to him. Amar thought, 'If she bewitches me, I am finished!' He smiled and ran eagerly up to Bahar to take it from her but she held him and kissed him on both cheeks first. 'You are my son from today. Where do you live?' The boy pointed through the trees and said, 'Far away, beyond this forest!' Bahar smiled and replied, 'Go on you liar! As if your house is so close that I can see it from here!'

Meanwhile, Bahar's handmaidens had followed her into the forest. Amar ran out of Bahar's arms when he saw them and cried, 'I must go now!' Bahar told her companions, 'The child is frightened of you. Go ahead and join the lashkar. I will be along soon.' A little later, Bahar coaxed the boy to mount her peacock and travelled to her camp with him. She then sent for her commanders and said, 'Mahrukh and the others are under a spell and will remain so as long as the flower bracelets are clamped around their wrists. Even so, be watchful and guard them well against the ayyars. I am tired and wish to rest alone in my pavilion. I am not to be disturbed.'

Bahar then led the young boy into her pavilion. It was evening by now and Bahar's attendants lit oil lamps before leaving. As the day ended, the dancer of the sky wore star-studded garments to perform a mujra nautch before the victor of the night. Bahar laid out sweetmeats, fruits and a sumptuous assortment of dishes before Amar. He declined to eat the food although he had no objection to consuming the fruit.

After dinner, Bahar laid back on the masnad and said, 'Young master, sing for me now.' Amar took out his flute to play for her. So sweetly did he play that the very air became still and the birds and beasts of the forest collected around the pavilion to hear the melody. Bahar Jadoo swayed with rapture and was lost in the music when Amar stopped abruptly and said, 'My head aches!' Bahar thought, 'If he has a glass of wine, he will play even more keenly.' She filled a goblet with wine and offered it to him, 'Have this sherbet!'

'You think I do not know wine when I see it?' the boy exclaimed. 'In my house, they drink it all the time!' He proceeded to arrange the wine decanters into a bouquet so that the green and red decanters set each other off. Bahar marvelled at his skills and thought that the boy was from a noble family. As he arranged the decanters, Amar managed to add a powerful drug to the wine. He poured Bahar a goblet and said, 'You must drink before me.' The unsuspecting Bahar swallowed the wine, asking for even more and urged the youth to have it too. Amar pretended to sip some wine but quietly poured it aside. He served her more wine and played his flute again.

Bahar Jadoo, drunk on the wine and music, sang along with Amar and finally succumbed to the drug. Amar found that after a while, she was snoring loudly, oblivious to the world; her pyjamas had climbed up her thighs, her veil was tossed aside and her bosom was exposed. He quickly pierced her tongue with a needle and tied her to a pillar. Then he lit an incense of consciousness and waved it under her nose. She awoke and was alarmed to see him. Amar called out, 'I am the king of ayyars and the slayer of sahirs, Amar bin Ummayyah. O Bahar, see how I have overcome you with Allah's help. You should yield lest you lose your life!'

Bahar signalled to Amar to release her and implied that she was willing to convert to Islam. Amar released her without hesitation but Bahar was thinking otherwise: 'Let me deceive this ayyar as he deceived me. Who is he to make an exalted princess like me convert?' Her feelings were evident as she glared at him in anger. Amar said, 'Bahar, I trusted and released you, but do not imagine you are safe even now. I can crush you like an ordinary insect. Do what you can and call for help if you like!' Amar then calmly walked out of the pavilion. Bahar called to her guards to arrest him, but Amar opened the blessed Tent of Danyal and held it over himself. He asked the tent to expand so that it became a vast pavilion with posts of rubies, and curtains and flaps embroidered with gold thread and precious stones.

Bahar's guards surrounded him and she cast a spell that made magic gardens appear around him, but it was of no use. The tent was immune to magic spells and Amar was safe within it. Amar only used his precious gifts when he had no other recourse. He had made a solemn oath to

Emir Hamza never to kill anyone while he was invisible or when he was within the tent as Emir believed that it did not behove a warrior to kill anyone who could not fight back.

Bahar saw that Amar was impervious to her magic. She ordered her officers to stand back and walked into the circle of the tent herself. As soon as she stepped inside, she was suspended upside down and could not move her lips to cast any spell. Her officers rushed in to help her, but suffered the same fate. Amar took out four parizads and a bed with jewelled posts from Zambil. He stretched out on the bed and the parizads began to massage his arms and legs. Amar looked at Bahar and said quietly, 'Princess I could have killed you earlier, but my master has forbidden me from killing anyone that way. You people use magic, so we retaliate with trickery and deceit.'

Bahar still looked furious, so Amar continued speaking: 'Fair princess, how can a beautiful, intelligent woman like you worship Zamurrad Shah Bakhtri? How can you equate him with the Almighty who is the ruler of the universe; who is alone in His power and who has no equal; who is just and kind and who is Creator of all things? Do not ruin your life by equating Laqa, who runs from Hamza from country to country with the one and only Allah! Emerge from the desert of thorns and enter the garden of righteousness.'

In short, Amar described the attributes of the One True God in such a manner that the rust on the mirror of Bahar's heart dissolved. She gestured to be released and wept at Amar's feet for some time. He embraced her and said, 'Princess, you are like my own sister and you will have a high rank once Tilism is conquered.' Bahar left the tent pavilion and addressed her commanders, 'I have joined Amar. If you are with me, you will have to pay homage to Amar. If that is not acceptable, you are free to leave me.'

Bahar's army vowed never to leave her side. Bahar then uttered a spell and knocked in the air to make Mahrukh's army come back to their senses. The enchanted bracelets of flowers withered and dropped off their wrists. Bahar approached Mahrukh Magic-eye and paid homage to Mahjabeen with *nazar*. Prince Asad and Mahrukh embraced her and said, 'You are a source of comfort and strength for us!'

They brought her back to their camp and the combined armies of Nafarman and Bahar now made them a formidable force. Everyone celebrated Bahar's arrival and the ayyars from the desert came in to meet their new ally. After witnessing the miracle of Bahar's surrender and conversion, Surkh Mu reconsidered her opinion of Amar and supported by Nafarman, approached Mahrukh Magic-eye. 'Huzoor,' she said, 'I am returning to my country now, but will return with my army to join you. Consider me now as one of your ardent supporters, even if I have to lose my life for you!' Mahrukh was moved by the sincerity of her words and embraced her warmly.

Afrasiyab sends a sahir army to confront Bahar

A day after Bahar left, Afrasiyab became increasingly restless as he genuinely loved and missed her. He travelled to Porcelain Mountain that was covered with thousands of shady, flowering trees. This pretty sight distracted Afrasiyab, but the blossoms reminded him of that rare flower, Bahar. He wrote a note to her that read, 'Return from this difficult campaign and provide your lover with the sweet sherbet of your vision. Someone else will be sent to face the rebels. You are worthy of resting on your lover's bosom, not to fight wars.' Afrasiyab then read an incantation so that a slave-boy emerged from the earth. He ordered the slave-boy to take the note to Bahar.

Bahar was in the durbar pavilion with Mahrukh and the other sardars when Afrasiyab's slave-boy approached her and handed her the note. Bahar read the note and wrote back, 'If you claim to love me, then release Tasveer and Prince Badi-uz-Zaman and present yourself to Prince Asad Sherdil with all the gifts of Tilism. I have allied myself with the forces of Islam and will die for them!'

The slave-boy flew to Porcelain Mountain with this missive. Afrasiyab read it and a sigh that seared his senses escaped from his heart. In his grief, he chanted a spell that produced dark rain clouds from which three sahirs appeared. They greeted the Shahanshah and saw that he looked unhappy and depressed.

Afrasiyab said quietly, 'O Shadeed Jadoo, Qeher Jadoo and Azab Jadoo, you must take a large army and persuade Princess Bahar Jadoo to return to my fold. She has joined the enemy as she is angry with me. Remember that she is very powerful and will not yield easily. I will send the shroud of Jamshed to you, so wait for it before you engage in battle.'

After dispatching the three sahirs, Afrasiyab returned to the Garden of Apples frowning in anger and did not respond to anyone's greetings. As he sat down on his throne looking obviously unhappy, Hairat asked him lovingly, 'O Shahanshah, how is your royal self?'

Afrasiyab snapped back, 'Hairat, Bahar has allied herself with Amar!' Hairat said angrily, 'Shahanshah, that girl is very spoilt and arrogant and thinks she is better than all of us. You should not lose any sleep over her as you have thousands of loyal subordinates who will arrest and present her to you within moments!'

Afrasiyab replied, 'This is just talk. I have spent so much time and money tutoring people like Mahrukh and Nafarman and Bahar. I have nurtured them like children. How can I now have them killed? I would much rather make them see the error of their ways. I am leaving now for the grave of Jamshed to obtain his shroud. You should proceed to the Dome of Light.'

The three sahirs, Shadeed, Qeher and Azab had reached the camp of the rebel army and sent Bahar several messages advising her to apologize to the Shahanshah. As Bahar ignored all of them, they consulted each other and decided, 'If we wait for Shahanshah to send Jamshed's shroud, we will be known throughout Tilism as cowards. What do we have to fear from Bahar? Let us strike battle drums and capture her before the shroud arrives!' Thus, they had the battle drums struck and Mahrukh's army also prepared to fight them. Asad performed the early morning Fajar prayers while the sahirs in the Islamic camp prayed to Allah in their hearts. Dilaram escorted Mahjabeen's throne to the edge of the battlefield and all the commanders gathered there to pay homage to her.

Suddenly, the field in front of them was lit by several bolts of lightning. There was thunder and heavy monsoon clouds rolled in. The armies of the three sahirs swept in like the waves of a stormy sea. Qeher, mounted on a fire-breathing dragon, rode forward and rained flames and stones. 'O disloyal subjects,' he shouted, 'face me if you can!' After gaining Mahjabeen's permission, Nafarman flew on her swan to the frontline of the battle. After a few exchanges of spells, Qeher aimed a magic coconut at her that went through her thigh like an iron ball and wounded her.

Surkh Mu Deadly-locks, who had just returned from her kingdom, sought permission to fight. Qeher aimed a coconut at her as well, but she deflected it, then loosened her long red tresses, and took out a tiny ruby box. This contained thousands of tiny stars and she tossed them up in the air. They flew to the skies, grew in size and fell like arrows that went through Qeher and thousands of his soldiers, killing them instantly. The battlefield boomed with the voices of magical spirits lamenting the dead.

Azab Jadoo now entered the battlefield and Shakeel confronted him, mounted on his fiery dragon. Azab attacked him several times with his spear but Shakeel dodged him and drew out his enchanted sword. The sword fell on Azab like a bolt of lightning and burnt him to ashes.

Trembling with fury, the third sahir Shadeed came forward and tossed a magic snake on to the field. The snake slithered towards Shakeel and bit him despite his counterspells. When Shakeel slumped on the battlefield, Mahrukh tended to him and Surkh Mu emerged to fight again. She cut out a paper peacock that came to life with her spell. The peacock swooped down, caught the snake in his beak and flew off with it. Surkh Mu received a warm round of applause from her army, which incited Shadeed to even greater fury. He shot a magic arrow that pierced through forty magic shields conjured by Surkh Mu and injured her in the shoulder. As she withdrew, Shadeed called out, 'Bahar, I have come to arrest you! How long will you hide from me?'

The vision of loveliness, Bahar, was watching the battle from her peacock throne while several thousands of her companions surrounded her with bouquets in their hands. Responding to Shadeed's challenge, she tossed a bouquet into the air. Suddenly, black clouds rose from the mountains and the skies darkened. Then Bahar applied a *tilak* of *afshan* on her forehead so that the field glowed in the moonlight. Shadeed started to murmur counterspells but Bahar tossed a second bouquet and called out, 'Come to me O spring!'

There were gusts of cool breeze and Shadeed and his army clapped with joy. As Bahar tossed the third bouquet, hundreds of beautiful parizads materialized with musical instruments and the sahir army became besotted with them. Bahar tossed yet another bouquet and the air became fragrant with the perfume of a thousand spring flowers that blossomed in a garden spreading for miles. Bahar descended from her throne and walked into the garden with the parizads. Shadeed and his army followed them in their enchanted state. When Shadeed set his eyes on Bahar in the gardens, he implored her to treat him kindly. She ignored him and signalled to her parizads. They approached the sahir soldiers with golden bowls and sharp knives and proclaimed, 'O lovers of the beautiful moon-like Bahar, make her an offering of your blood!'

Shadeed's soldiers rushed to be the first to offer blood and the parizads cut their wrists one by one and began collecting their blood in the bowls. As the soldiers fainted with the loss of blood, Bahar summoned Shadeed himself. He approached her trembling with anticipation. She tapped him gently with a wand of flowers and said, 'If you love me, you will kill Hairat!' Then she tied a bracelet of enchanted flowers around his wrist and the parizads did the same with the rest of the army.

Shadeed and his followers chanted Bahar's name and left for the Dome of Light, determined to kill Hairat. After they were out of sight, Bahar wiped the glitter off her forehead and tapped the air so that the moonlit garden and parizads vanished and the sun began to shine again. Drums of victory sounded in Mahrukh's camp and her soldiers seized the abandoned enemy tents. Mahrukh returned to the royal pavilion with her sardars and showered Bahar with jewels. She was presented with the most costly robes of honour and the lashkar was again at ease.

While there were celebrations in Mahrukh's camp, Shadeed and his followers had crossed the River of Flowing Blood and were creating havoc in the city of Napursan. In their enchanted frenzy, they attacked and killed several innocent citizens. Shadeed kept abusing Hairat loudly. 'Bring that slut Hairat out!' he screamed. Hairat, however, was safe in the powerful Dome of Light and although Shadeed tried to force his way in, unseen forces threw him out.

The shroud of Jamshed

Meanwhile, Afrasiyab had travelled to the Veil of Darkness and into the desolate wilderness of Hasti where he crossed the River of Fire. He reached the site of the great god Jamshed's grave where thousands of gruesome sahirs guarded a palace suspended in mid-air. In its gardens, the seven handmaidens of Jamshed sat on swings that swayed on their own. Afrasiyab flew upwards as hundreds of bells heralded his arrival. He saw that the palace was encrusted with precious jewels and the handmaidens of Jamshed came forward to greet him. Afrasiyab stood on one leg and said a prayer to Jamshed. He cut a piece of flesh off his foot and placed it on the dome of the palace as an offering, after which he was allowed to enter the palace. The handmaidens asked him, 'O King of Magic, what brings you here?'

Afrasiyab replied, 'Give me the shroud of Jamshed as I am surrounded by enemies. Amar has entered Tilism and has incited mutiny. Thousands of Jamshed's followers are being killed!' The handmaidens said, 'You are the Shahanshah and cannot be denied. Take the shroud from this box.' One of them tossed him the key and said, 'What about Sarsar Sword-fighter and her band of ayyar girls? Why have you not sent them out to foil the trickery of the ayyars?' Afrasiyab looked at her thoughtfully and said, 'You are right. It is the first thing I will do as soon as I get back!'

Afrasiyab then knelt to open the box, but had to hastily fall back as a flame leapt out from it and singed him. When he cut open his vein to offer sacrificial blood, the flame subsided and a silk sheet embroidered with jewels rose from the box, heavy with the fragrant dust of Jamshed's grave. This shroud was a powerful weapon of magic warfare as whoever held it could withstand any spell, no matter how powerful. If it was waved over any enemy force, it released a strong breeze that could render the enemy unconscious.

Afrasiyab folded the silk shroud carefully and flew with it to the Garden of Apples. Once he got there, he whispered an incantation and a sahir whose body glowed like embers appeared and bowed before the king. Afrasiyab greeted him and ordered, 'Rohtas Jadoo, take this shroud of Jamshed and go and arrest Mahrukh and Bahar. You are of noble birth and therefore eligible to be assigned this task.' Rohtas replied, 'Shahanshah is generous, otherwise I am an ordinary mortal of Samri and your humble servant.' He kissed the shroud and kept it carefully tucked within his clothes. He then asked Afrasiyab, 'Am I to go alone or take an army with me?'

'I have already sent Shadeed, Azab and Qeher with a large army,' Afrasiyab replied, 'but perhaps you should take twelve thousand men with you and leave immediately. I will be watching your progress from the Dome of Light.'

After dispatching Rohtas, Afrasiyab came to the Dome of Light and found Shadeed's hysterical army killing the citizens of Napursan, while the enchanted Shadeed was trying to climb the walls of the Dome of Light. Afrasiyab understood at once that they were under Bahar's spell. Furious with her, he thought of reversing the spell so that she would be in the same condition as Shadeed and his soldiers, but then thought, 'She might die if I turn the spell around. Even if she lives, she will be very angry with me. I will not get my heart's desire. It would not be right to make her angry or hurt her.' His expression hardened with resolve and he threw a magic orange at Shadeed that burst through his chest and killed him instantly. As spirits bewailed Shadeed's death, Afrasiyab waved his hands and bolts of lightning sprang from his fingers and burnt all of Shadeed's army.

After this, Afrasiyab went into the dome to meet Hairat who greeted him respectfully. Afrasiyab said dryly, 'This was your dear sister's handiwork. Shadeed lost his reason and I had to destroy such a large army!' Hairat folded her hands and said, 'O Shahanshah, give me leave to punish that rebellious girl!' Afrasiyab replied, 'Mahrukh has rebelled against me so I will deal with her. Bahar is your sister and her fate lies in your hands. I have sent Rohtas with the shroud of Jamshed to arrest them all. If he is unsuccessful, perhaps then you should lead the army!'

The princesses of trickery

After this exchange, Afrasiyab sat on his throne in a room with a view of the Tilisms of Zahir and Batin as well as the River of Flowing Blood. His ministers and viziers stood in attendance and a nautch performance began as Hairat offered him some wine. Afrasiyab then ordered one of his sahirs to summon the five ayyar girls. That sahir travelled to the kingdom of Nigaristan that been gifted to Sarsar Sword-fighter by the King of Sahirs; Saba Raftar Swift-footed was her vizierzadi, and Shameema Tunnel-digger, Sanobar Whip-lasher and Tez Nigah Dagger-woman were her special companions.

All the five ayyar girls were beautiful and young, and had grown up together. They were accomplished tricksters and loathed the practice of magic. On being summoned, they armed themselves with their weapons and pouches of ayyari and presented themselves in durbar. Afrasiyab looked at them favourably and addressed Sarsar, 'Amar ayyar has entered our realm with his companions and has killed hundreds of sahirs. You must match them in ayyari and arrest them immediately. You will have the freedom to move in the three tilisms, Zahir, Batin and Zulmat.'

The five ayyar girls left for the battlefront after the Shah awarded them with robes of travel. They passed through the forest close to Mahrukh's camp that was frequented by Amar and his friends. At the time, Amar had left the camp and was strolling in the forest with three ayyars when they heard the familiar sound of Zafeel, the whistle of ayyari. Moving stealthily to investigate, they came upon five spirited females armed with weapons of trickery. They were all dressed in costly garments and jewellery. Sarsar Sword-fighter, the most beautiful and accomplished of them all, led them proudly.

Amar decided that they had to declare themselves and whistled. Soon, Qiran also joined his friends. Alerted, the five women drew their swords out and each shouted out the name of the ayyar they would attack. Thus, Sarsar confronted Amar, as Saba Raftar attacked Qiran, Shameema fought Barq, while Sanobar and Tez Nigah tackled Jansoz and Zargham. All five ayyars were smitten by the arrows of love when they saw these fierce and beautiful creatures and recited verses of love even as they fought them.

Swords and daggers flashed in the air. The ayyar girls first used their snare-ropes, but each of the ayyars jumped high to escape and attacked with swords as they descended. The women jumped neatly out of the way. As they fought, the forest resounded with the sound of their mighty swords and the strong smell of narcotic vapours filled the air. The fight continued for two hours but eventually, the ayyar girls leaped and bounded out of sight shouting, 'You dwellers of misery, wait and see how we destroy you!'

The ayyars allowed them to get away. Later, Amar declared, 'I want to inform all four of you that Sarsar is my beloved. If any of you harm her, you will have me to deal with.' The four disciples looked at each other and after some hesitation, Qiran confessed his love for Saba Raftar, Barq for Shameema, Zargham pleaded for Tez Nigah and Jansoz for Sanobar. Each ayyar swore solemnly that he would not hurt the other's beloved.

On the other side of the forest, the five women were also exchanging notes on their first encounter with the ayyars. 'You seem out of sorts to me Saba,' said Sarsar, 'you look pale and your lips are dry.' Saba Raftar looked sheepish and retorted, 'Well, I was not going to bring this up princess, but do please observe your own image in a mirror. It is obvious that there are signs of love on your face!' Sarsar retorted sharply, 'God forbid! Only you have this tendency that wherever you see a young man, you fall for him. Even if I do fall in love, my lover would be the king of ayyars, Hamza Sahibqiran's vizier and companion. How can you compare yourself with me?'

Saba Raftar laughed and said, 'I will tell you if you do not get angry my princess. My beloved is Qiran, the king of Zanzibar, Amar's declared successor and the favoured one of the incomparable Imam Ali bin Abu Talib. But what about these three girls, why are they in such a state?'

Shameema piped up, 'My lover Barq Firangi is the king of one of the countries of the Firang and Amar's chief disciple. Need I say more?' Sanobar frowned at Shameema and said, 'Shameema there is no need to boast! My beloved Jansoz is better than all your lovers; but he can languish forever as far as I am concerned!' All eyes were now on Tez Nigah who blushed furiously and said, 'I have nothing to do with Zargham, but since you compare notes, like Qiran, he is favoured by the saints. Moreover, he is the special ayyar of Tilism Kusha who claims he will rule this land. So, in a way, he will rule over the other ayyars!'

'Oh really!' cried Sarsar, 'So what you are saying is that, in fact, you will rule over all of us. Well, well! Congratulations!' The other girls took their cue from her and teased Tez Nigah until she begged for mercy. The point of these exchanges was that each could now identify the other's lover. They made a promise that they would not harm each other's beloved ayyar.

Rohtas fights with the shroud of Jamshed

Rohtas had the war drums struck that evening to announce that a battle would take place the next morning with the rebels. His camp was up throughout the night in preparation for the battle. The next morning, Rohtas was the first to reach the battlefield and conjured stone rains and other magic tricks to impress Mahrukh's army. After blustering for some time, he called out insolently, 'Can any of you traitors face me and my magic?' Mahrukh's army valiantly moved forward to fight, but he cast a spell that caused thousands of birds to fly in from the forest. At a signal from the sahir, they perched on the soldiers who transformed into saplings with branches and leaves sprouting from them. Mahrukh, Shakeel and the other commanders immediately conjured magic shields to protect themselves.

Bahar, who was sitting regally on a peacock throne, realized that Rohtas was using her own tactics and came forward to meet him. She held his gaze and slowly uncoiled her tresses. She took out a filigreed gold case that contained a tiny ivory figurine. Still watching Rohtas who seemed mesmerized by her, she cut her forefinger and dropped her blood on the figurine as she pronounced, 'O Woman of Samri, did I shelter you in my hair for so long only to have my army turned into trees?' The ivory figurine laughed when Bahar spoke and vanished from the case. The next moment, everyone saw a net stretching for miles with the magic birds trapped in it. Bahar's ivory figurine now emerged as a woman holding a knife with which she slaughtered the birds. She sprinkled their blood on Mahrukh's soldiers so that those who had transformed into trees became men again.

Rohtas realized that he would need to tackle Bahar before she bewitched him. He flew to the skies quickly and dusted the shroud of Jamshed from a height on Mahrukh's army. As its dust scattered on the army, everyone fell unconscious, including the commanders—Mahrukh, Bahar, Nafarman, Dilaram, Asad, Mahjabeen, and many others. Rohtas had them all captured and chained. He then decided to travel to the Shahanshah with his prisoners the next day.

That night, Rohtas cautioned his guards against the tricksters and settled in his tent to dally with a courtesan. He cast a protective spell that made any ayyar who entered the tent fall unconscious. Zargham, Barq and Jansoz who went into the tent disguised as sahirs succumbed to the spell, and Rohtas had them chained. Amar disguised himself as the ayyar girl Saba Raftar Fleet-foot, and forged a letter, ostensibly from Afrasiyab, that he cleverly filled with sleeping dust. He sealed the letter and asked the guards on watch to announce his arrival to Rohtas. When the guards hesitated to go in, the false Saba Raftar realized that Rohtas had set a trap for the ayyars and called out loudly, 'Rohtas come and receive your Shahanshah's message!'

Rohtas rushed outside and took the letter from her. Then he removed his spell and took Saba Raftar inside the tent. As he opened the letter, a faint perfume filled the air and he immediately succumbed to the fumes of the drug. Amar decapitated Rohtas at once and his spirits raised a huge din while flames and stones fell from the skies. Amar stripped the courtesan of her jewels and released his companions. Unseen by Amar, Barq quietly took the shroud of Jamshed from Rohtas's magic pouch and while it was still dark, slipped out of the tent.

With Rohtas's death, the Islamic army was released from his magic chains and attacked his forces forcefully. Mahrukh and Bahar flew upwards and threw bunches of magic needles and iron pellets on Rohtas's soldiers that fell on them like bolts of lightning and a rain of flames. Bahar tossed her enchanted bouquets and infatuated thousands of soldiers into doing her bidding. Nafarman and Surkh Mu rained arrows and shooting stars and eventually, Rohtas's army was completely destroyed.

The victors celebrated after they had set up camp once again. However, Amar was busy hunting for the enchanted shroud of Jamshed and when he could not find it, whistled to summon the three ayyars who were in Rohtas's tent with him. Jansoz and Zargham responded to his call but there was no sign of Barq and Amar realized that he had fled with the precious shroud. Meanwhile, Barq was on his way to the hidden tilism of Batin for he knew that Amar would force him to give up the shroud if he stayed in Zahir. 'It is just not fair,' Barq thought, 'Ustad Amar has so many gifts like Zambil and the cape of invisibility and I have nothing. I must hold on to this shroud.'

Barq and the shroud of Jamshed

After Rohtas's death, the five ayyar girls were on the lookout for the ayyars of Islam. Sarsar Sword-fighter saw Amar looking for someone in the forest and after disguising herself as Barq, deliberately walked past him. Amar who had been looking for Barq accosted her immediately and shouted, 'Barq did you take the shroud?' Sarsar fell at his feet and pleaded, 'Sir, please gift it to me!' Amar took out his whip to teach his disciple a lesson but Sarsar tripped him and burst a narcotic bubble on his face as he fell. She spread a sheet of ayyari, placed the unconscious Amar on it and tied his hands and feet with a snare-rope. She tied the sheet around him and then hoisted the pushtara on her back to present him to her master in the Dome of Light.

On his way to Batin, the real Barq spotted Saba Raftar from a distance and after disguising himself as Sarsar, overcame her with a narcotic bubble. He painted her face as a spitting image of Amar and after tying her up in pushtara, went towards the River of Flowing Blood. The magic shroud he was carrying enabled him to cross the river without any hindrance and he reached the Dome of Light in the city of Napursan. Afrasiyab was holding court when Barq disguised as Saba Raftar deposited her bundle at his feet and declared, 'I have captured Amar!'

Afrasiyab smiled in triumph and ordered his sahirs to tie Amar to a pillar in the court. A little later, Sarsar arrived with the real Amar. This led to a furore in the durbar about the two Amars. Barq as the false Saba Raftar whispered to Afrasiyab, 'As I have already brought Amar, this must be an ayyar disguised as Sarsar. I will hide so you can catch the real culprit.' As soon as Sarsar deposited her bundle in front of Afrasiyab, he gestured to a sahir officer to arrest her. The false Saba Raftar emerged from behind the throne and wept on seeing Amar unconscious. 'Huzoor, this rascal has brought Princess Sarsar disguised as Amar and is impersonating her.'

At her insistence, Afrasiyab released Amar and tied Sarsar to another pillar. Sarsar protested vehemently, but no one believed her. Barq came up to her and whispered in her ear, 'O beloved of Amar, you have captivated my teacher and now parade naked before everyone; I should cut your nose off for this!' Sarsar protested loudly but was whipped a couple of times by Afrasiyab's sahirs on Barq's orders.

Eventually, Sarsar begged the Shahanshah to consult the oracle Book of Samri and he agreed. Just as Afrasiyab opened the book to consult it, the false Saba whispered that she wanted to say something of great importance to him. As he leaned towards her, Barq snatched his crown, struck a great blow on his head and shouted, 'I am Barq!' and quickly leapt out of reach. Afrasiyab cried, 'Catch him now!'

There was chaos in the durbar as sahirs chased the fleet-footed Barq. Amar, who had been eying the riches of Afrasiyab's durbar since his release, cast his Net of Ilyas and scooped up several precious vases and jewel-inlaid furniture. Afrasiyab stood up in alarm and read a spell that conjured several magical puppets to catch Amar. The slippery ayyar vanished under his cloak and Barq managed to escape from the dome because the shroud still protected him. Sahirs who tried to capture him felt as if their bodies were on fire and retreated immediately. Meanwhile, Afrasiyab had the real Saba and Sarsar released and placated them.

The two ayyars Barq and Amar then began to plunder the city of Napursan. Amar's powerful net emptied whole shops of gold and precious items and there was pandemonium in the city. Hearing the howls of protest from her citizens, Hairat cast spells to conjure a thousand magical dragons to look for the ayyars. Amar protected himself under the blessed Tent of Danyal while Barq remained safe because of the shroud. The dragons failed to locate them but swallowed hundreds of citizens instead, causing even more panic in the city. The dragons returned to Hairat and she declared triumphantly, 'Shahanshah, the dragons must have finished the two culprits!

Just then, a sahir entered Afrasiyab's durbar with a large bundle. 'What have you got?' asked the king. The sahir replied that he had caught Amar. When everyone leaned forward to inspect the bundle, the false sahir snatched the second crown from Afrasiyab's head and shouted, 'It's Barq again!' He then landed another hard blow on the Shah's head. Sannat Magic-maker, Afrasiyab's female vizier cast a spell so that everyone in court, save the Shahanshah and his wife, fell unconscious. Barq remained impervious to her spells and she reluctantly dispelled her magic. Afrasiyab wore seven different crowns and each time, Barq snatched it from his head in different disguises.

Vizier Sarmaya Ice-breaker, made huge icebergs fall on the city and it became so cold that several people were frozen instantly and many died. Everyone begged Sarmaya to cease his magic. Yet another vizier, Baghban Qudrat, plucked a string of pearls from his neck and tossed it in the air. Several beds of red roses immediately came into sight and from them flew out thousands of multicoloured birds that began looking for the tricksters. They could not find them but sat instead on the heads of hundreds of citizens who tore their garments in enchanted frenzy. Baghban quickly removed his spell when he realized what had happened.

Suddenly, Barq appeared in court as himself. As soon as Afrasiyab saw him, he vanished from his throne. The next moment, everyone saw a full-length mirror that seemed to reflect Afrasiyab's image. Barq threw a stone at the mirror, but it bounced back. The Shahanshah's fourth vizier, Abriq Mountain-breaker, flung a few pebbles at Barq, which transformed into huge boulders mid-air. Barq remained safe but the boulders fell instead on the innocent citizens of Napursan and buried thousands of them. This catastrophe in the city made Abriq neutralize his spell.

Amar made his way to Afrasiyab and opened his blessed Tent of Danyal again. Afrasiyab and his nobles saw Amar under a small, dome-like pavilion, relaxing on a jewel-inlaid cot as parizads massaged his feet.

Turning to his guards, Afrasiyab said, 'Amar seems to be a powerful magician! Which one of you will capture him now?' One of the sahirs came forward and chanting magic incantations, walked into the pavilion, only to be suspended upside down. Amar laughed and took out live coals from his Zambil and then swiftly cut off a piece of flesh from the sahir's thigh. The sahir howled in pain, but Amar shouted, 'Haramzadeh, I am going to roast your flesh and eat it as I am partial to sahir flesh!'

The sahir's brother went running up to the pavilion and pleaded with Amar to release his brother in exchange for a thousand gold coins. 'A figure of five thousand would be more acceptable,' was Amar's reply. The sahir at once sent for the coins and presented them to the merciless trickster. Amar released the brother, but quietly cut off the tip of his tongue. The sahir was enraged to see his brother's condition and conjured flames and boulders to fall over Amar's tent, but it was to no avail. Amar now caught the four posts of the dome pavilion, held it aloft like a canopy over his head and walked away, accompanied by Barq. Afrasiyab watched them leave, but remained helpless.

Afrasiyab's mirror image

Just after Amar and Barq left, the skies darkened with storm clouds and the city resounded with the thundering sounds of a thousand drums and trumpets announcing the real Afrasiyab's arrival. The whole durbar knelt down to greet him. Afrasiyab looked at his double in the mirror and said, 'Leave now, my image. You have suffered much and have been insulted by the ayyars.' The image in the mirror vanished and Afrasiyab consulted the oracle Book of Samri that pronounced, 'Barq was protected by the shroud of Jamshed and was impervious to magic. What need was there to bring out such a powerful treasure of Tilism from the Veil of Darkness? Your double suffered the consequences of your mistake and had you been here in person, it would have been much worse for you!'

Ravi, the legendary narrator tells us that during the confusion about Sarsar and Saba Raftar's identities in court, Afrasiyab had absently glanced at his left palm and realized that he would have to leave the court unless he wanted to be disgraced in the next few hours. Therefore, he quietly summoned his mirror image and vanished. In the confusion of the time, no one had noticed this event. Afrasiyab had the power to divine his future from both his palms. The right palm revealed events pertaining to his safety and welfare, while the left palm warned him against mischief and bad luck. There were only seven people in all of

Tilism who had doubles and were immune to death unless the doubles died first. Afrasiyab and Hairat were two of these select seven and we will witness during the course of this book how many attempts against their lives will end in failure.

We will now return to the main narrative. Afrasiyab observed the destruction of the city of Napursan and unleashed his anger on Sarsar and Saba Raftar. 'You disloyal wretches, is this how you protect us? You are responsible for the havoc in the city!' Sarsar pleaded in her defence, 'Huzoor, I did bring Amar to you and that is no small feat; he is after all the king of ayyars, but you released him yourself. Now your wish is my command.' A chastened Afrasiyab replied, 'Barq will be able to cross the River of Flowing Blood but Amar will not as he has no gift of Tilism with him. You will be able to capture him easily, but make sure you take him across the river for I want to hang him before his army!'

After they left, Afrasiyab looked ruefully at his courtiers and said, 'Whoever is sent to capture Bahar is killed himself! Is there no one equal to the task?' In response, a powerful noble, Namrood Jadoo, rose from his chair and volunteered to go. Afrasiyab advised him to take an army but Namrood said haughtily, 'Bahar is not worth so much trouble. Besides, a large army makes the detection of ayyars impossible. I will enter their camp alone and capture Bahar!' He then took his leave and flew to Mahrukh's camp.

Meanwhile, Barq had crossed the River of Flowing Blood without any mishap and came across the ayyar girls Shameema Tunnel-digger, Sanobar Whip-lasher and Tez Nigah Dagger-woman. The girls attacked him with swords but Barq was an excellent swordsman and tackled all three at the same time. Jansoz saw him fighting them and jumped in to help. Eventually, they warded off the women and continued on their journey. Barq was nervous about the shroud and slipped away from his friend but the women followed them and attacked Jansoz once again. They overcame him easily and tied up him in a pushtara. Sanobar undertook the task of taking him to the Shahanshah. She was on her way to Tilism-e-Batin when Zargham Sherdil ambushed her with a kamand. As she tripped and fell, Zargham released Jansoz from the pushtara.

Sarsar, who had been looking for Amar, came upon her friend in trouble and attacked the two ayyars ferociously. They fought back but teased her at the same time: 'Our teacher's beloved, the day he takes you home will be a black day for you. He does not treat his wives well and works them hard. They have to press his feet all night!' Sarsar was enraged by their taunts and screamed, 'Your teacher will be buried in a deep grave by me! Who is his beloved? How dare you take my name with his?'

After fighting them briefly, Sarsar decided not to waste her time on them and slipped away with her friend. Later, she spotted Amar on the shores of the River of Flowing Blood. He seemed to be trying to find a way across the treacherous waters. Aware of his greedy nature, Sarsar trapped him by dropping a silk scarf in his path. Amar came upon it and found that it contained fifty gold coins, betelnuts and a few cardamoms. Amar thought that it belonged to a court noble and took the coins, but the scarf was drenched in drugged perfume and he fell unconscious. Sarsar, who was hiding behind a bush, saw Amar fall unconscious and shouted in triumph. As she was carrying him back across the river bound and gagged, Barq saw her and thought of a plan to rescue his teacher.

So, he disguised himself as Sarsar's friend, Tez Nigah Dagger-woman. He wore moss green clothes and painted rosy lips and black locks on himself. Then he smeared his neck and chest with false blood and lay down on the path like a corpse. Sarsar stumbled across the body soon enough and on recognizing her childhood friend, flung Amar to one side and beat her breast in grief. She cried, 'Alas, the wretched ayyars have murdered my sister so cruelly! O my Sister, why have you abandoned me?'

In her grief, she knelt to embrace the lifeless form of her friend, and fainted from the fumes of the narcotic that Barq had added to the false blood. Barq emerged from behind a bush, untied and placed the unconscious Amar on a sheet and laid Sarsar next to him. Then he revived both of them with the incense of consciousness and addressed Sarsar, 'My teacher's beloved, greetings to you! Are you so desperate that you lie with my teacher on this public path? Could you not at least find a private garden or a tent? Such behaviour is beneath you!'

Amar woke up and found Sarsar lying beside him. He tried to take her in his arms but she kicked him hard so that he rolled off the sheet and cried, 'My beloved's kicks are as welcome as her kisses!' Sarsar slinked off in sheer embarrassment, but Amar persuaded Barq to return with him to the camp and promised not to take the shroud of Jamshed from him. Barq returned to the royal pavilion with him and offered the seven crowns of Afrasiyab as tribute to Asad and Mahjabeen. All sardars applauded his bravery and Asad rewarded Amar with the crowns. Mahjabeen awarded Barq with a gift of one lakh gold coins while Bahar bestowed another fifty thousand upon him.

At that moment, Amar said, 'My son, I ask you for the shroud of Jamshed as Emir Hamza has ordered us never to use such magical gifts until we have severe need of them. You misused this gift by trying to confront Afrasiyab with it. If it were so easy, nothing would prevent me from donning Galeem and beheading all our enemies. You should overcome the enemy with your cunning and bravery and give me the shroud.' Barq saw the wisdom of these words and declared, 'What need have I of this shroud? Inshallah, I will kill thousands of sahirs without it!' Saying this, he handed the shroud of Jamshed to Amar.

Moments later, a fearful shout, 'I am Namrood Jadoo!' was heard and a claw flashed into sight and swooped down on Bahar Jadoo. All the sardars in the pavilion shot magic coconuts and oranges at Namrood, but he was a powerful sahir and flew off with Bahar in his clasp. The ayyars too rushed out of the pavilion to follow him. Namrood landed on a mountaintop and saw that the ayyars were trying to climb the mountain. He conjured a puppet to keep watch as he waited for the ayyars to reach him.

Soon enough, Amar went to him him disguised as a sahir carrying a gem-inlaid bowl of pomegranate seeds. The puppet called out, 'Beware Namrood! Amar is here!' Namrood smiled arrogantly and said, 'Let him come!' Amar greeted him and said, 'Your puppet is a liar. I have been sent by Afrasiyab with the gift of this fruit from his garden.' Namrood burst out laughing and exclaimed, 'Amar you are an audacious rascal but you cannot deceive me. Let me see your fruit.'

He reached out for the bowl and as he examined the seeds, they began to release narcotic vapours. Moments later, Namrood fell unconscious. Amar decapitated him instantly and the mountain was engulfed in darkness. A little later, cries of 'You have killed me, my name was Namrood Jadoo,' were heard. The slain sahir's skull cracked open and released a multicoloured bird that flew to Afrasiyab. Bahar was now free and Amar took her back to the camp where they were greeted with cheers of triumph. Namrood's spirits informed Afrasiyab of his treacherous death and Afrasiyab clutched his head in despair. Hairat finally persuaded Afrasiyab to allow her to confront their enemies.

Now hear about Laqa. The last time that Sulaiman Ambreen had appealed for help, Afrasiyab had ordered Haseena Jadoo to go to Mount Agate. As it happened, after Haseena returned to her palace, she fell ill and therefore could not go to Laqa. Sulaiman now sent another letter and had it placed by the magic drum. Afrasiyab sent a magic claw to retrieve the letter and it reached him just as Hairat was preparing to fight the rebels. Afrasiyab ordered one of his sardars Sarmast Jadoo to go and help the Living God. Accordingly, Sarmast left for Mount Agate with his sahir army of twelve thousand men in great splendour.

6 HAIRAT LEADS AN ARMY AGAINST MAHRUKH'S ARMY

When Hairat set off to fight the forces of Islam, she organized a large army that included several powerful sahir commanders. Afrasiyab insisted that his viziers, the brothers Sarmaya and Abriq, accompany her. Her own vizierzadis, Zamurrad and Yaqut, stood behind her with fans made of *huma* feathers as she sat on her flying throne. Her throne flew upwards and vanished into a cloud that transformed into a gem-inlaid bungalow with ruby chairs.

Once she was seated on her magnificent diamond throne, Hairat's body seemed to glow like a flame and the air was filled with the sounds of a thousand drums and trumpets. Occasionally, Hairat would wave her hand and in response, her commander Toolan bin Shahab would toss a magic citron in the air. The citron would spin upwards and burst open to release the sound of a thousand cannons that boomed at the same time and a thousand stars would shoot down from the skies. Thus, Hairat advanced like a river in full flood towards Rangeen Hissar.

Mahrukh and Mahjabeen were in their durbar with other nobles when the sounds of the bells and drums of Hairat's army shook the earth. The sardars emerged from the durbar and the sight of that vast army made them feel anxious and insecure. A ripple of fear passed through Mahrukh's army when they realized that Hairat's camp would spread over several miles. In Hairat's camp, markets had already begun trading their wares and they buzzed with activity. Hairat walked into the durbar pavilion erected for her and held court there. The ayyar girls too came from the forest to pay her homage and guard her against the ayyars of Islam.

Sarmast and Nagin in Mount Agate

We will leave these two armies for a while and return to Mount Agate, toward which Sarmast was travelling to help Laqa in his fight against Hamza. He camped in a pleasant meadow enroute and decided to go hunting. One of Hamza's sons, Darab, was also in the forest on a hunting expedition at the time. As it happened, he shot the same deer that Sarmast was pursuing just moments before Sarmast appeared on the scene. Furious with the prince, Sarmast shouted, 'Who are you to have killed my prey!'

The prince smiled and replied gently, 'Brave warrior, I had no idea this was your prey or I would have left it alone. Please take this deer with my compliments as he is yours by right!' Sarmast was even more outraged by this and said, 'Do you think I crave for meat that you dare to offer your spoils to me? I am Sarmast Jadoo! I will kill you instead of the deer now!' Darab sighed in resignation, 'You sahirs are so proud of your magic tricks. Fight me with your sword if you can!'

Sarmast swore arrogantly to not use magic on him and then attacked Darab with all his might. Darab foiled his move and wounded him on his forehead, and Sarmast fell off his horse unconscious. Darab did not want to kill a defenceless man and was about to leave when there was a sharp gust of wind and an ugly old crone flew in. This was Nagin Jadoo, Sarmast's wet nurse, who had reared him as a child. Seeing him lying helpless on the ground with his face covered in blood, she angrily cast a spell that conjured a tower of flames around Darab.

As Nagin cradled Sarmast's head in her lap, his followers reached the spot, as did the companions of Prince Darab. There was a brief skirmish but the sahirs prevailed and the prince's companions raced back to Hamza to inform him of his son's capture. Nagin healed Sarmast's wound with a magic salve and urged him to travel to Mount Agate as soon as possible. Meanwhile, Prince Darab's ayyar, Fateh Kishwar who was disguised as a woodcutter, managed to slip into Sarmast's army as it moved towards Mount Agate.

Laqa was holding court when there was a sudden dust storm and an avalanche of stones and flames from the sky. Trembling with fear, Laqa hid under his throne. Sarmast Jadoo appeared moments later and looked perplexed when he saw Laqa's empty throne. Shaitan Bakhtiarak rose to greet him and offered him a chair; he then added that the Living God would appear shortly. Bakhtiarak had a sheet drawn across Laqa's throne and while bringing him out of his hiding place, whispered to him, 'My Lord, if you keep hiding for fear of the sahirs, people will lose faith in you!'

Laqa tried to look dignified when Sarmast prostrated before him. He gave orders that Sarmast was to be treated as a special guest and that his evening meal was to be prepared in the royal kitchen. Accompanied by a steward, the ayyar Fateh, now disguised as a labourer, carried the food from the kitchens to Sarmast's camp. He stumbled deliberately on the way and dropped a few vessels. The steward abused him roundly as they retrieved the dishes. Fateh apologized profusely and quietly drugged the food in the process. Later, the food was served to the commanders of Sarmast's army who collapsed as soon they ate, after which Fateh decapitated all of them.

When Sarmast was informed of this unfortunate turn of events, he immediately turned to Bakhtiarak in fury and cried, 'I am not going to rest after my journey. Have the battle drums struck this evening so that I can destroy the enemy now!' Hamza's army too was prepared to fight. The battleground was levelled, water carriers sprinkled water to settle the dust on the ground and both armies settled into their battle formations.

Sarmast first asked Laqa's permission to fight and then flew on his dragon to the battle lines, calling out arrogantly, 'O disbelievers, which one of you dares to confront me?'

One of Hamza's sardars accepted the challenge and went forward after seeking permission from the Shah. Sarmast cast a spell that produced a mysterious warrior who rode in from the desert admist great whirls of dust. Hamza's sardar attacked him with his lance and sword, but the warrior overwhelmed him with his supernatural strength. That day, the unknown warrior captured a hundred more of Hamza's sardars and Sarmast ended the first round of battle elated and triumphant.

In the evening, Bakhtiarak warned Sarmast, 'Hamza knows the powerful incantation of the Great Name and is immune to your magic warrior!' Sarmast pondered over this advice and called out to his foster mother Nagin Jadoo, who materialized immediately. Sarmast told her, 'We have to find a way to capture Hamza as he is immune to magic.' Nagin replied, 'In that case, I will make sure that he does not remember the Great Name.' Bakhtiarak urged Nagin to stay in her son's camp to guard him against the ayyars, but she refused. Instead, she gave Bakhtiarak an amulet and said, 'Place this amulet on fire if you need me. I will respond immediately!'

Meanwhile, Chalak bin Amar slipped into Sarmast's camp in order to get some information on the identity of the magic warrior. Eventually, he entered Bakhtiarak's tent disguised as an attendant. Bakhtiarak recognized him at once and welcomed him. Ever since the heinous incident when Amar had cooked a *hareesa* with Bakhtiarak's father, Bakhtak's flesh, and then fed this dish to Bakhtiarak, he feared the ayyars and treated them with respect.

He offered Chalak a place of honour and asked, 'What brings you here, O Son of my Teacher? Are my days over?' Chalak smiled, 'On the contrary Malik-ji, I bring you a gift of dates this evening!' Bakhtiarak paled visibly and pleaded, 'Ask me what you will. Why do you have to make me unconscious?'

On hearing this, Chalak drew out his dagger menacingly, which made Bakhtiarak quickly eat the dates and fall unconscious. Chalak then tied him into a pushtara and went towards the open desert. He revived Bakhtiarak there and asked him, 'Tell me truthfully, where does the unknown warrior come from?'

The wily Bakhtiarak tried to strike a bargain, 'If I tell you, will you spare my life?' Chalak frowned and said, 'Tell me quickly and do not negotiate. It can go either way for you!' Bakhtiarak lost his nerve and said, 'I cannot tell you anything about the magic warrior but Nagin has gone to make Hamza forget the Great Name. She has also given me this amulet to send for her in an emergency.' Chalak looked unconvinced by the amulet that Bakhtiarak held in his hand and said, 'Very well, summon her now!'

Bakhtiarak lit a fire and placed the amulet on it. There was a sudden hush and the next moment, Nagin appeared in front of him. Bakhtiarak tried to signal a warning to her, but just then, Chalak who had hidden himself emerged and aimed a large stone from his catapult at her. The stone smashed her head and she went straight to hell. There was a fierce sandstorm and Bakhtiarak closed his eyes in fear as her magical spirits raged and howled.

Chalak tied Bakhtiarak to a tree and after assuming Nagin's form, went to Sarmast's pavilion. Sarmast was happy to see his foster mother again and eagerly asked her, 'Did you get Hamza?' The false Nagin held his hand and spoke solemnly, 'The next three days will be hard on you my son and there is a threat to your life. I have brought you this life-giving apple from the orchard of the god Samri. Eat it and your lifespan will increase tenfold!' Sarmast ate the apple readily and became unconscious. Chalak swiftly beheaded him and Sarmast's spirits rained stones and flames, causing great chaos in the camp. Darab bin Hamza and his companions, who had been released from the tower of flames when Nagin died, signalled to their army that this was the time to attack Sarmast's troops. Sarmast's army was unprepared and agitated by the deaths of their commanders, and fled in defeat.

Afrasiyab was in the Dome of Light when he received the news of the rout of Sarmast's army, along with another message for help from Laqa. Visibly angry, he sent a message to Hairat instructing her to have the tricksters captured by Sarsar and her companions before she went to war. He sent another message to Haseena Jadoo that said, 'Malika, you had volunteered to help Khudawand but I heard that you had taken ill. If you have recovered, leave at once for Mount Agate, otherwise I will arrange to send someone else!' Haseena wrote back, 'I have recovered due to the grace of Jamshed and am on my way now.'

Amar's tricks and arrest

Hairat sent for Sarsar and told her that the Shahanshah wanted her to capture Amar. The ayyars had already left their camp when Hairat arrived with her army. Amar was in a village close to the Dome of Light and was thinking of ways to enter Hairat's camp when he heard the sounds of laughter and celebration. Going closer, he saw a wedding party with a number of sahirs seated under a marquee, being entertained with wine and a nautch performance. The bridegroom sat on masnad in a gold embroidered robe. Amar thought to himself, 'This is fortuitous. I am penniless and need to make money. Let me rob this gathering.'

Accordingly, he dressed up as a professional musician with a large turban and a beard down to his chest, and entered the marquee holding a flute and drums. He walked into the gathering singing so melodiously that everyone was captivated by him. The bridegroom's father, Taseer Jadoo, offered him a handsome reward for singing at his son's wedding and Amar settled down to enthral his audience.

Sarsar Sword-fighter had been looking for Amar when she heard him singing at the marquee. She went closer and recognized Amar in the guise of a singer at once. She listened to his voice for a while and swaying with enjoyment, thought, 'What marvellous talent my lover has!' However, Sarsar soon recalled her duty and quietly warned Taseer Jadoo that the wedding singer was the in fact an infamous trickster. Amar realized what she was up to and sprinted out of the marquee after snatching Taseer's emerald studded cap from his head!

Sarsar ran after him and soon engaged him in a sword fight. Barq saw them fighting and addressed Sarsar in his customary mocking manner: 'Greetings to you my teacher's beloved!' Sarsar fought on, gasping, 'Barq, your teacher claims to be the king of ayyars and yet he needs your help? If his claim is true, leave me to fight him alone!' Barq bowed gallantly and cried, 'Dare I intrude when two lovers are together? I realize this is just your excuse to have him to yourself!'

He left them fighting but Khumar Jadoo, who was looking for Amar on Afrasiyab's orders, swooped down like lightning and seized both Amar and Sarsar, and took off with them in her grasp. Amar had fainted with the rush of air and when he awoke, found himself in Afrasiyab's durbar. Amar greeted Afrasiyab respectfully. 'Amar!' said the Shahanshah, 'Did you think there would be a day like this?'

'Of course I did,' retorted Amar, 'This is the day I will plunder this durbar!' Afrasiyab was speechless with rage and had Amar locked up in an iron cage. Then he wrote to Hairat to come and witness Amar's execution. Hairat received the note and laughed with unrestrained joy. She sent for her camp commanders and ordered them to strike drums and trumpets to celebrate Amar's arrest. As the camp celebrated, Hairat wore red garments with ruby jewellery and flew to the Dome of Light on her magic peacock.

The news of Amar's arrest reached Mahrukh's camp as well. Many sardars wanted to attempt a rescue right away, even if that meant losing their lives, but Mahrukh insisted that it would be difficult to infiltrate the Dome of Light. Asad too advised them to wait. 'Who can execute Khwaja Amar? He is the favoured one of seven prophets and the slayer of sahirs!' he said confidently.

Hairat soon reached the Dome of Light where the courtiers received her respectfully. She sat besides Afrasiyab and offered him a betelnut leaf with great ceremony. Then she put her arms around his neck and said lovingly, 'Do not delay the execution my lord, and show this devil the day of doom!' Afrasiyab, however, wanted Amar to die the next morning in front of the whole city and breathed a spell on the door of the cage so that only he could open it. Heralds announced Amar's imminent punishment and the citizens of Napursan collected in the plain below the Dome of Light to witness his death. Hairat and Afrasiyab celebrated well into the night, confident that Amar could not escape from the cage.

Late that night, Amar took out a cardboard figure from Zambil and painted it to look like himself; then he became invisible in Galeem and hid in a corner. The celebrations for Amar's execution continued throughout the night. Huge crowds thronged the plain and every sahir swore, 'He has caused us damage, each one of us will strike him tomorrow!'

The next morning, Afrasiyab opened the cage himself and ordered his guards to bring the prisoner out. They dragged the dummy out of the cage while Amar slipped out unseen and cast his net on the valuable furniture and vases in the palace. Within moments, all precious items in the durbar had vanished. Amar whispered in a maiden's ear, 'I am leaving now!'

She was startled and screamed as Amar shouted loudly, 'You joker Afrasiyab! I am leaving!' Everyone heard him this time and saw that what they were slapping and kicking as Amar was actually a paper dummy, now torn to shreds.

Afrasiyab turned on Khumar Jadoo in his rage and embarrassment and said, 'You wretch, did you bring a paper dummy just to boast about capturing Amar?' Khumar Jadoo blanched in fear but spoke steadily, 'Huzoor, when I brought Amar to you last evening, you spoke with him yourself. If you doubt my word please consult the oracle Book of Samri and the truth will be known!' Afrasiyab consulted the book and read that Khumar was speaking the truth and that Amar had escaped under his Galeem when the cage was opened. Afrasiyab instructed his vizier Baghban Qudrat to look for Amar and bring him back quickly. Baghban chanted an incantation that gave rise to a pillar of smoke from the earth and at his command, the smoke dispersed to look for Amar.

Meanwhile, Amar was busy plundering the city of Napursan again. The long-suffering citizens of Napursan had locked their doors and windows against the invisible thief and town squares were deserted. Amar had taken off the Galeem to move around easily when the pillar of smoke descended on him and twirled him like a windblown leaf, right up to the vizier. Baghban took his hand and led him to the King of Sahirs. Afrasiyab asked Amar, 'How should I kill you?' Amar replied, 'I do not see anyone under this sky who can harm me!'

'You are in my power now and I can punish you as I wish!' said Afrasiyab. Amar smiled and said, 'Am I under your power or are you under mine?' Though Afrasiyab was angry at this remark, he asked pleasantly, 'Tell me, how are you so convinced that you cannot be killed?' To this question, Amar replied, 'O Shahanshah tell me first, what status do you give to Laqa?' Afrasiyab replied guardedly, 'He is our Khudawand of course!'

'So then,' said Amar, 'does Khudawand have power over life and death?' All the sahirs present murmured their approval as Afrasiyab replied, 'Of course Khudawand has power over everyone! He can kill and punish some while blessing others!'

'Correct!' exclaimed Amar. 'Therefore, I kill sahirs only because I have been sent to Tilism expressly for this reason by Khudawand Laqa! I am his angel of death and he has sent me here to punish the sinful and the disobedient!' All the sahirs present looked at Amar in wonder and cried out in unison, 'Amar is right, not a leaf moves without Khudawand's will! We are sinners and deserve this punishment!'

Afrasiyab approached Amar, respectfully kissed his hands and said humbly, 'O Angel of Death, greetings to you! Please tell us whose death is fated by Khudawand?' Amar sat on a jewel-inlaid chair and said solemnly, 'Shahanshah, I cannot divulge such divine secrets. But I can demonstrate other talents that Khudawand has bestowed on me. I can change faces and sing melodiously!' Afrasiyab nodded gravely at this and said, 'He is right! Who else can be privy to divine secrets? Very well, demonstrate your powers!'

As they spoke, Amar vanished from his chair and everyone cried, 'Without doubt, he is the angel of death!' Amar then emerged from his cloak behind a pillar and transformed himself into a beautiful woman with costly garments and heavy jewellery. He then walked up to Afrasiyab and bowed low in greeting.

'O flower of beauty, who are you? What brings you here?' asked Afrasiyab, overwhelmed by her beauty. That fairy-like creature replied softly, 'O Shahanshah I have loved you for some time and would willingly die for you!' On hearing this, Afrasiyab held her hand and sat her down next to him, all the while gazing at her. Hairat, meanwhile, looked visibly upset and resentful. The unknown beauty smiled and said, 'Malika Hairat, I am not a woman but the lion of ayyari, Amar bin Ummayyah!'

Afrasiyab looked stunned and thought to himself that Amar was indeed the favoured one of Khudawand. He applauded Amar and presented him with a robe of honour. Then he asked him to sing for them. Amar danced for the court and sang so melodiously that everyone began swaying in enjoyment. Even as the people were entranced by Amar's singing, he took charge of the *maikhana* and served wine to his audience after having drugged it cleverly. Afrasiyab drank several goblets and called out drunkenly, 'Amar, all the gods are here to hear you sing. Samri and Jamshed sing your praises!'

Amar replied, 'Shahanshah, drag them in by their legs and have them seated!' At this, Afrasiyab drunkenly pulled Hairat off her throne and both of them danced until they fell unconscious. Gradually, the rest of the court too fell down in a drugged stupor.

Amar beheaded a few sahirs quickly and as their spirits wailed their deaths, he cast his net and stole all the precious gold and silver objects in the palace. He drew closer to the throne and unsheathed his sword to kill Afrasiyab and Hairat, when the earth split open suddenly. Parizads emerged with pitchers of musk and rosewater. They gently placed Afrasiyab's head in their laps and sprinkled his face with the perfumed waters to awaken him. Amar quickly hid amongst the corpses and covered his throat and chest with false blood and gore to appear dead.

Afrasiyab awoke to find the court in chaos, with several people unconscious or dead. He pointed towards the sky and conjured a magic cloud that floated in and revived everyone with a light shower. Afrasiyab had the furniture and missing items replaced and consulted the oracle Book of Samri that told him, 'Amar is hidden among the dead bodies. Have him arrested but the next few hours are ill-fated for you so leave now for Batin.'

Afrasiyab whispered to his minions not to lift the dead bodies as Amar was hiding among them. Just then, Sarsar Sword-fighter reached the durbar and Afrasiyab ordered her to identify Amar among the bodies. As the court watched her, the Shah quietly sent for his double and vanished. Sarsar identified Amar among the corpses and was about to alert the sahirs when Amar leapt up, rubbed his palm on her face and made her unconscious. The next moment, Amar lifted her and sprinted out of the durbar. Afrasiyab's sahirs pursued him, but he ran out of sight into the forests close to the city of Napursan and threw Sarsar into a cave. However, as he emerged from it, Shameema Tunnel-woman and Saba Raftar Fleet-foot challenged him. While he fought them off, Sarsar woke up inside the cave. She was still groggy when she got out of the cave and drifted back to the city in a daze.

Amar managed to escape from the two ayyar girls and had reached the durbar again, this time posing as Hamnasheen Jadoo, a court singer. Pleased with his talent, Afrasiyab presented him with a costly robe. The false Hamnasheen bowed and said, 'Huzoor, I can light a candle and in its glow you will be able to see the legendary Raja Indra and his parizads dancing for him.' Afrasiyab agreed eagerly and so Amar asked for five seers of wax and oil for making the magic candle. Once these ingredients were provided, he sat behind a curtain and moulded a large candle and added a huge amount of the powder of unconsciousness to it. He emerged with the candle and dramatically placed it in the centre of the durbar. After lighting the candle, he urged the Shah to wait for a couple of minutes to witness the miracle. Then he drew back and muttered a few words in the language of Jinni as if he was casting a spell.

Hairat, Afrasiyab and the whole durbar watched the candle flame closely. Very soon, the drugged fumes from the candle assailed their senses and they cried out, 'There, we can see Raja Indra and his dancing fairies!' Some of the sahirs got up to dance and soon, everyone was unconscious. Amar again emptied the durbar of its costly furnishings and then decapitated a few sahirs that led to fierce whirlwinds and gales. He tried to kill Afrasiyab a second time, but when his guardian parizads emerged from the earth, he quickly became invisible in Galeem and left the Dome of Light.

The parizads revived Afrasiyab once again and the sight of his ruined durbar outraged him. He snuffed out Amar's lethal candle, revived his nobles and furnished the durbar again. He looked around at his courtiers who were still stunned and mockingly said, 'Without doubt, Amar is the special creation of Khudawand Laqa. I am beginning to believe he will be the death of us all!'

The magic water of Samri

While Hairat was preparing to fight the rebels once again, Afrasiyab sent for Hoshiar Jadoo. He handed him two glass jars filled with magic water and said, 'Go to Hairat's camp and capture the rebels. You will be able to do so easily if you sprinkle this water on the enemy. Dilute this water with a larger quantity of water and sprinkle it around Hairat's camp so that it is protected. Any ayyar trying to infiltrate the camp will become unconscious and you will be able to capture them as well.'

Hoshiar went back home to make preparations and later returned to Afrasiyab who bestowed a robe of honour on him and told him that he had been sanctioned a sahir army of twelve thousand soldiers. Hoshiar took his leave of the Shahanshah and left for Hairat's camp. His mother, Mughlia Jadoo, also flew along secretly to protect her son. Later, Hairat received Hoshiar who explained the Shahanshah's strategy to her. Hoshiar's army camped close to Hairat's lashkar and that evening, Hairat struck the battle drums in Hoshiar's name.

The next morning, Hoshiar waited for his army to arrange themselves into battle formations before seeking Hairat's permission to go into battle. He first conjured magical illusions to impress the rebels and then challenged them to fight. Surkh Mu sought permission from Mahrukh and came forward on her dragon mount. Hoshiar shot an arrow towards her but she conjured a magical hand holding a knife that sliced the arrow in half. Surkh Mu then loosened her deadly tresses and made thousands of stars appear in the sky and fall like fiery arrows on Hoshiar's army. Thousands of sahirs died in this onslaught.

Hoshiar was enraged and took out the glass jar containing the magic water of Samri from his pouch. For the reader's information, Afrasiyab had given Hoshiar two glass jars of the magical water, one for causing unconsciousness and the other for reviving the same people. Hoshiar sent for a pitcher of water and added a few drops of water from the jar. Then he soaked a large wad of cotton wool in the pitcher and read an incantation that caused the cotton wool to soar up to the sky in the form of a cloud. The magic cloud floated above Mahrukh's lashkar and burst into heavy rain.

Surkh Mu, who was standing in the battlefield, was the first to fall unconscious. Sardars like Mahrukh conjured magic shields above their heads, but the deadly raindrops seeped through the shields and soon, many in the Islamic army fell unconscious. There was chaos in the lashkar as the soldiers fled from the battlefield. Asad Ghazi, who rode forth to rally his fleeing troops, also fell unconscious. Hoshiar had the unconscious sardars tied up and returned to his camp as Hairat revelled in his triumph by showering fistfuls of jewels on him.

Hairat informed Afrasiyab about the capture of the rebel sardars before sending for the prisoners. Hoshiar recited an incantation that bound the prisoners in magical shackles and pierced their tongues with needles. Then he sprinkled water from the second jar on them. The sardars awoke to find themselves shackled in Hairat's durbar and bowed their heads silently. Hairat looked at Mahrukh and sneered, 'Why, Mahrukh, did you think a day like this would come?' Mahrukh pointed to the sky as if to say, 'Our God will protect us.' Thus, Mahrukh and her sardars responded to Hairat's taunts with gestures for they could not talk with their tongues pierced.

Hairat was infuriated by their calm indifference to her threats. She told Hoshiar to erect a scaffolding with gallows to hang the prisoners the next morning. 'Let the angel of death be active at dawn, spare no one!' she said. Hoshiar brought the prisoners to his own vast pavilion and tied each of them to a pillar. He ordered his guards that only one of them was to stay there and that they were to tell the water carriers that each one should visit him with his *mashkeeza*. He added, 'You will supervise them when they sprinkle the magic water around the camp.'

The water carriers approached Hoshiar's pavilion and went to him one by one. Hoshiar first gave them the water of consciousness to rub on their bodies and then added the water of unconsciousness to their mashkeezas. He then ordered the water carriers to sprinkle the magic water around the camp to form a magic circle.

Now hear about the ayyars. They had witnessed the rout of their lashkar and the capture of the sardars from a distance. Qiran disguised himself as an attendant and went towards the enemy camp. He saw the water carriers sprinkle the magic water on the edge of the camp and sensing danger, took a longer route to enter the camp. He came across one of the water carriers and called out, 'So, have you formed the magic circle yet?' The man replied, 'This will not be over in a day. It is a huge camp. It might days to complete the circle!'

Qiran inwardly applauded himself for his instinct as it was now confirmed to him that the magic circle was a trap for the ayyars. He went into the camp and stood outside Hoshiar's pavilion. After two hours, the attendant on duty inside emerged and called out for someone to relieve him. Qiran stepped forward and said, 'Brother, I was waiting here for you.' The attendant walked off and Qiran went inside and stood behind Hoshiar to fan him.

Meanwhile, the ayyars Jansoz and Zargham had walked into the camp, but heedless of the danger, immediately fell unconscious. They were carried to Hoshiar who breathed a spell on them that stripped them of their disguise. Hoshiar whooped in triumph and tied them along with the other prisoners.

Amar too approached the camp but cleverly avoided the magic circle. He went to the other side and saw that one of the water carriers was having his meal beneath a makeshift canopy. Amar quickly disguised himself as a water carrier and wore a handwoven loincloth, a loosely tied turban and a mashkeeza that he hung at an angle around his waist. He approached the water carrier and after greeting him, asked, 'Why do you eat at this odd hour my brother?' The water carrier replied, 'I have no time to eat, what with filling my mashkeeza and forming the circle.' Amar murmured sympathetically, 'These rich people are very odd. Now why does so much water need to be sprinkled?'

The water carrier found a willing audience in Amar and told him all about Hoshiar and the magic water of Samri. Amar then changed the subject and after chatting for a while, offered his new friend a sweetmeat. The water carrier slumped down unconscious as soon as he ate it. Amar hid him out of sight and went to Hoshiar's pavilion. He walked in boldly and said, 'Huzoor, I have run out of water.' Hoshiar handed him the jar of the water of unconsciousness and said, 'Add a few drops of this water to your mashkeeza.'

Amar asked Hoshiar, 'Huzoor, can I first have the water that will protect me?' Hoshiar looked at him suspiciously and asked, 'Did you not take it before?' Amar replied quickly, 'I have replaced my brother who is not well.'

Convinced, Hoshiar handed him both the jars. When Amar turned around, Hoshiar shouted, 'You fool, mix the water first!' Amar turned back and snarled, 'You are the fool and your father is a greater fool! Watch what I do to you!' Amar reached into the jar of unconsciousness and sprinkled its water on Hoshiar. As the sahir fell down, Amar immediately decapitated him with his dagger. When Hoshiar's magical spirits began wailing, Amar freed Jansoz and Zargham who set about releasing the other prisoners. Amar, meanwhile, was already busy plundering the precious items of the pavilion.

Hoshiar's mother Mughlia and the other commanders rushed to Hoshiar's pavilion when they heard spirits wailing his death. Mughlia chanted a spell so that Amar, who was rushing around plundering the pavilion, sank into the earth up to his waist. Mughlia went ahead to capture him when a voice called out, 'Listen to me!' That was Qiran, who was disguised as an attendant. As Mughlia turned around, Qiran smashed her skull with an almighty blow of his bughda.

Mahrukh, Bahar, Nafarman, Surkh Mu and the other sardars who had been set free left the pavilion and fell upon Hairat's army in sheer fury. Hairat had been celebrating their capture and was quite relaxed and happy, and her army too was at ease and completely unprepared for the attack. Thousands of men died as bolts of lightning and huge slabs of ice fell from the skies. Hairat's commanders hastily conjured magic tapers to dispel the darkness but Mahrukh cast a spell that snuffed them out. There was a bloodbath of such magnitude that it seemed this piece of earth would never be green again.

After it was over, Hairat travelled to the Garden of Apples to inform her husband of Hoshiar's death and the destruction of the army. Afrasiyab consulted the oracle Book of Samri that said, 'It was your own doing that killed Hoshiar and Mughlia for Amar got hold of the magical water of Samri.' Afrasiyab became thunderously angry and told Hairat, 'Return to your camp. This time I will send a curse on those disloyal rebels so that all of them will be killed!'

The seven bolts of lightning

Hairat returned to her camp to fight Amar and Mahrukh but Afrasiyab was chafing at his recent humiliation by Amar and summoned the seven Barqs or the seven bolts of lightning of Tilism. The legendary narrator Ravi tells us that these women fell like lightning on enemy forces and could annihilate thousands in one strike. A reddish cloud with flashing golden lights descended in front of Afrasiyab. Seven sahiras who had golden bodies and who were laden with jewels stepped out of the cloud. The sahiras prostrated before the Shah and he ordered, 'One of you should proceed to Hairat's camp and assist her in destroying the rebels. The rest of you return to your palaces and wait for my summons.' Barq Khatif volunteered to go and the Shah presented her with a robe of state before she left.

After her departure, Sarsar Sword-fighter and Saba Raftar Fleet-foot approached the Shah, but he turned his face away from them. The two girls cried, 'Huzoor, how have we failed you?' Afrasiyab looked angrily at them and said, 'Ever since Amar and his companions have invaded Tilism, they have killed such powerful sahirs. Despite being paid so handsomely, you have not managed to capture even an ordinary sardar from the enemy camp nor have you killed anyone. You have failed me miserably!'

Sarsar bowed her head in shame and said, 'Huzoor, I am going now to bring you Asad who claims to be Tilism Kusha and Mahjabeen who is the regent of the camp. Without them, Amar will lose his fighting spirit. Forgive me for being so lax and rest assured that I will deliver them to you!' Afrasiyab was pleased with this answer. He presented Sarsar with a costly robe of honour and asked her to leave at once to perform this task. Meanwhile, Amar had returned to his camp amidst great jubilation and related his adventures in Afrasiyab's durbar, causing much amusement among Mahrukh's sardars.

Haseena Jadoo in Mount Agate

Now let us return to Princess Haseena who was on her way to help Laqa. She travelled in stages with an army of sahirs. Laqa was in his durbar when clouds emerged on the horizon and there were signs of magic in the air. Bakhtiarak and Sulaiman knew at once that someone had come from Hoshruba and went outside to welcome Haseena. When the army of sahirs led by Haseena descended, her beauty struck everyone for she had enhanced her looks with magic.

Haseena prostrated in front of Laqa, who cried, 'Rise from the ground for I have blessed you with divine grace.' Haseena sat on a jewelled chair close to Laqa and asked him, 'Who are these rebellious mortals who dare to challenge you?' Laqa pronounced solemnly, 'It is a long story, my Shaitan knows it well!' Haseena turned to Bakhtiarak who said, 'Malika, have you no idea of Hamza's might from Asad and Amar's antics in your Tilism? Even Afrasiyab has not managed to stop them there!'

Hearing this, Haseena declared arrogantly that she could destroy Hamza's army with ease. 'Oh yes,' laughed Bakhtiarak, 'you have only just arrived. Enjoy your time on this earth for eventually you will be destroyed!' Haseena looked scornful at this remark and said, 'Malik-ji you would see a weapon even in a vessel of urine!' Bakhtiarak continued, 'I say this with good reason. Listen, there is one Amar in Tilism and a hundred thousand of his kind here! There is one Asad in Tilism and his fathers and grandfathers are here. Our god Laqa has created such rebellious creatures that no one can vanquish them!'

Haseena declared, 'I need only the blessings of Khudawand. Wait and see what I do with them!' She rested for a few days and then one evening, asked for the battle drums to be struck in her name. At dawn the next morning, Emir Hamza said his prayers and presented himself to the Shah of the lashkar along with the other sardars. As the Shah's retinue emerged from the pavilion, everyone bowed low in mujra-greeting and carried his throne into the heart of the lashkar. Bibran, a warrior from Haseena's army sought Laqa's permission to fight and entered the battleground. He exhibited his skills in wielding a spear and then challenged Hamza's army, 'Is there anyone who can fight with me?'

From Hamza's side, the noble Behram emerged to confront him. The two warriors fought with spears but Behram struck such a mighty blow that Bibran's spear went flying out of his hand. At that moment, Haseena recited an incantation and Behram felt the strength ebbing out of his body. As he slumped forward on his mount, Bibran held him by his iron belt and threw him on the ground. He climbed on to

Behram's chest and tied his limbs, after which Laqa's men carried Behram off the battlefield.

Bibran challenged Hamza's lashkar once again. The next sardar who confronted him suffered the same fate as Behram. One after the other, Hamza's sardars were defeated and captured. Seventeen of them were vanquished before Hamza's son, Prince Hashim, came forward to ask the Shah for permission to fight. Hamza placed a blessed amulet around his neck to protect him against magic, read the prayer of Abraham and embraced his son before sending him to confront Haseena.

Hashim thundered out on to the battlefield where Bibran attacked him with his spear. Hashim was well versed in the martial arts and soon had Bibran on his knees. Seeing this, Hashim too drew his sword and alerted Bibran. Haseena tried to use her magic on Hashim but he was immune to it because of his protective amulet. His sword sliced through Bibran and killed him. There were roars of victory from the Islamic army and Hashim challenged the enemy to send another warrior.

Everyone saw Haseena coming out on to the battlefield. In truth, however, it was not her but a magic puppet that she had conjured. The puppet attacked Hashim with a sword but he struck back hard and sliced through its body. Instantly, the two parts of the puppet's body flew to the skies. Moments later, there was a tinkle of anklet bells. Hashim looked up to see Princess Haseena, of the long tresses and fairy-like form, floating down towards him. Hashim, the brave warrior, gazed at her enchanting beauty and instantly lost his heart to her.

Haseena, of the moon-like face, held his hand and said, 'O Noble Prince! Why do you fight me? Hand me your weapons!' Entranced, the prince silently handed his sword and spear to her. Haseena said, 'That amulet is meant to protect your beloved. Put it around my neck.' Hashim silently put the holy amulet around the sahira's neck. Haseena turned around and walked back to her camp while Hashim followed her, reciting verses of love. In no time, Laqa's men shackled and imprisoned him with the other sardars. Soon, Laqa struck the drums of peace. Emir Hamza returned to his tent to bathe and then walked to the durbar. The durbar was in complete silence as everyone was depressed by the day's events. Emir calmly greeted the Shah and sat in his chair.

Another of Emir Hamza's sons, the young and brave Alamshah was the first to confront Haseena the next morning. Haseena watched him coming towards her and whispered an incantation so that her beauty dazzled him completely, making it impossible for him to attack her. As Haseena beckoned to him to follow her, the prince followed meekly with no thought for his father or army. The wily Bakhtiarak did not want

Emir Hamza to come forth himself and quickly had the drums of truce struck. Both armies turned back and Emir Hamza returned to his tent with a heavy heart.

The noble Alamshah followed Haseena to Laqa's pavilion and was completely mesmerized by her. Sulaiman and Bakhtiarak welcomed him, but had eyes only for the beautiful sahira and continued to recite love verses. Bakhtiarak said loudly, 'For what reason does huzoor visit us?' Alamshah, who kept gazing at the sahira, said, 'Malik-ji, I will be your unpaid slave if you can convince the princess to respond to me.'

Bakhtiarak held a whispered conference with the sahira and said, 'Noble prince, although the princess would not agree at first, I have pleaded on your behalf and she says that she will be yours if you prostrate before Khudawand and offer your father's head and the pavilion of Solomon to her.'

Alamshah immediately prostrated before Laqa who was delighted and bestowed a heavy robe of honour on the prince. He called out, 'I have ordained that this mortal should marry the beautiful Haseena Jadoo!' Alamshah cried, 'Strike the drums of war in my name and I will bring Hamza's head for the princess!'

Bakhtiarak then urged Haseena to keep the prince in her tent and quietly said, 'If he goes to fight his father, Hamza will soon neutralize your spell with the Great Name.' Haseena whispered back that she was working on a plan to take away Hamza's powers but that she would need a few days to perfect it. Bakhtiarak advised her to keep Alamshah captivated by her charms but not to succumb to his ardour completely.

Bakhtiarak then spoke to Sulaiman, the ruler of Mount Agate, who ordered that a garden of pleasure be vacated for the lovers. The garden had royal floor seating and rich drapes. Fragrant musk wine and delicacies were laid out, and beautiful handmaidens and cupbearers waited to serve the guests. Haseena walked in, hand in hand with Alamshah. After several goblets of wine had dulled their inhibitions, she and Alamshah embraced and kissed. Alamshah wanted to become intimate with her, but the sahira held him off with a frown. When she saw him becoming restless and angry, she wooed him back by embracing him again. In his enchanted state, Alamshah obeyed his beloved blindly and accompanied her to Laqa's durbar whenever she went there.

Meanwhile, Bakhtiarak instructed Tarrar Fleet-footed, an ayyar from his camp, to kidnap Hamza from his tent. Tarrar entered the lashkar of Islam disguised as an attendant and stood quietly in one corner of the tent of Solomon. As the durbar dispersed for the day, he hid under a couch. The Shah and all the sardars left the tent but Hamza stayed on. His faithful archer Muqbil stayed at the entrance to keep watch.

Tarrar stayed under the couch and waited for Hamza to go to sleep while his servants pressed his limbs. He threw a few drugged pellets into the tapers burning in the tent so that they released narcotic vapours. Hamza's servants soon fell into a drugged sleep. Tarrar then called out to the faithful Muqbil in Hamza's voice. As Muqbil entered the tent, Tarrar sprayed him with narcotic water and rendered him unconscious. He then tied the sleeping Hamza in a pushtara and staying close to the tents, dodged and darted out of the sight of the guards. Whenever he saw a posse of guards marching by, he would lie on the ground, as still as a desert lizard.

Tarrar was sweating by the time he emerged from the camp, both with fear and the heavy burden he was carrying. It occurred to him that he should hide Hamza in a place from where the Islamic ayyars would not be able to rescue him. He found a cave miles away where he placed Emir Hamza. He blocked the cave's entrance with huge boulders and then went and assured his master, 'I have put Hamza in a place where he will die without food or water within a few days!' Bakhtiarak was delighted and said, 'You were wise not to bring Hamza here, for his faithful ayyars would surely have rescued him.'

The next morning, there was an uproar in the Islamic camp when the soldiers found Emir was missing. The Shah immediately sent the ayyars Abul Fateh and Samak to investigate. Meanwhile, Bakhtiarak went to Haseena's garden and advised her to declare war, as the Islamic forces were vulnerable in Hamza's absence. Haseena turned to Alamshah and said, 'If you want me, you will have to fight against your people and bring your father's head to me!' Alamshah declared, 'Strike the drums of war. I will cut Hamza into small pieces!'

The war drums on Laqa's side were struck in Alamshah's name this time. The Shah was informed and the Naqara of Alexander was struck in turn. Laqa emerged, flanked by Haseena and Alamshah, as soldiers on both sides stood in battle formation. Haseena had made herself look particularly lovely that day with magic. After the battleground had been evened out and cleared, Alamshah respectfully sought Laqa's permission to fight. He went out into the battlefield and called out to his people, 'Come and fight me, whoever can match my strength!' Soldiers in the Islamic army wept to see their commander thus bewitched and cried, 'How can we fight our beloved prince?'

At this juncture, the pillar of the lashkar of Islam and the heart and life of Hamza Sahibqiran, the commander from Hindustan, Landhoor bin Sadaan sought permission from the Shah to approach the prince. As his elephant drew closer to the prince, Alamshah looked at him haughtily and said, 'Hindi, I am glad you have come to confront me!' The loyal Landhoor replied gravely, 'O Noble Prince! How could I dare confront you? You are my master's son and I am your devoted slave. But it is a sad day, huzoor, when you fight your father's army because of a wicked shameless strumpet who is also a black witch!'

The prince was enraged by his words, besotted as he was with Haseena. He shouted back, 'O Hindi, you have insulted one who is dear to me and who is your mistress. Watch what I do to you!' Alamshah attacked Landhoor who responded reluctantly and knocked the sword out of the prince's hand. Both men jumped from their mounts and began to wrestle. Alamshah was strong but Landhoor was a veteran of many battles and more than a match for him. It seemed as if two powerful elephants were fighting head to head in the battlefield. Haseena saw this and whispered a spell that made the strength ebb out of Landhoor's limbs and Alamshah overpowered him easily.

After handing him to the guards, Alamshah signalled to Laqa's army that fell upon the Islamic army. The sardars of the Islamic army were forced to fight Alamshah. The Shah himself mounted his horse and rode forth into battle. The two armies met like raging rivers and the din of clashing swords and armour filled the air. The sardars tried to avoid hurting Alamshah but he wounded several of them. He killed several Muslim soldiers himself and even wounded the Shah. Eventually, the Islamic lashkar began to retreat. The ayyars jumped into the fray and rescued the honour of Sahibqiran and his army. They managed to escape with the Shah and hid him in the mountains. The sardars soon followed their ruler. Alamshah triumphantly took over the pavilion of Solomon and declared, 'How long will they hide? I will kill all of them tomorrow!' Laqa personally escorted the prince back to Fort Agate, showering fistfuls of jewels on him.

There were celebrations in Laqa's durbar that evening and wine flowed freely. Alamshah was eager to wed Haseena now that he had captured the prized pavilion of Solomon. 'I will bring you my father's head in the same way!' he promised her. Haseena too was as eager to marry the prince and told Bakhtiarak that she could not wait any longer. Bakhtiarak told her, 'Princess, you will ruin everything with this haste, but no matter. Prepare for the wedding now.' Haseena told her servants to adorn the garden. Fresh water flowed in the channels, trees and bushes were trimmed and the baradari was lavishly decorated for the wedding feast. Alamshah, dressed as a bridegroom with costly robes and a jewelled turban, sat on the throne.

In the distant hills, the Shah lay unconscious because of the bleeding from his wounds while his injured sardars surrounded him. Occasionally, the Shah would become conscious and beg to be tied to his horse, 'Let me fight back. I would rather lose my life than bear this disgrace!' His sardars wept when they heard him. At one point, he cried out, 'We have been afflicted thus due to the absence of our dear Amar bin Ummayyah. No other ayyar can match his wiles!'

Stung by this remark, Chalak bin Amar vowed to kill Haseena even if he lost his life doing this. He reached Fort Agate in disguise and was intrigued by the signs of a wedding celebration. On learning that this was in fact the wedding of Alamshah and Haseena, he found his way into Haseena's garden and told the guards that he was Afrasiyab's messenger.

Haseena emerged from her bridal chamber to meet the Shahanshah's messenger. Chalak handed her a letter with Afrasiyab's seal that read, 'You have done well, my brave Haseena, by destroying Hamza's army. I have sent you this gift of fruit from the Garden of Samri through my messenger Makkar Jadoo. It will increase your life span but make sure you are alone when Makkar gives it to you and eat it right then!'

Haseena was delighted that the King of Magic had singled her out for this honour and led Chalak to a private chamber. Chalak took out some fresh fruit with an unearthly lustre. He arranged the fruit on a platter, recited a prayer over it and then offered it to Haseena. She kissed the platter and said, 'Shahanshah is kind to his handmaidens. O Makkar, I will eat the fruit now. Please inform Shahanshah that I was alone at this time.' She took a bite eagerly from one apple and collapsed at once in a dead faint. Chalak lost no time in beheading her. As her spirits raged and howled in protest, he wrenched off the blessed amulet of Emir Hamza from her neck. There was general panic in the garden as her attendants ran around confused.

Meanwhile, in Laqa's court, Alamshah was waiting, bedecked as a bridegroom. As soon as Haseena died, her spell waned and the prince immediately came to his senses. Looking around him, he saw the idol worshippers of Laqa's court and was puzzled. 'Where am I?' he asked Laqa's courtiers. 'It is your wedding day,' he was informed. When Alamshah realized that he had been worshipping Laqa and had destroyed his own army, he was enraged and cried, 'Alas, that I should worship this kafir and kill my own people!'

In his fury, Alamshah drew his sword on the people around him. Landhoor and other sardars of the Islamic army had already been released from Haseena's magical shackles following her death. They fought their way to the durbar and joined Alamshah. Chalak ran back to his people and informed them of the latest turn of events. The lashkar mobilized quickly and then attacked Laqa's men.

Emir Hamza, who had been lying unconscious in the cave for a few days, woke up and escaped from the cave after pushing the boulders aside. He wandered around before he came across a grass-cutter who led him back to his lashkar that was engaged in fighting Laqa's army. Emir also joined the attack and recited the Great Name, thus making his men immune to the magic of Haseena's sahir army. Heads rolled like begging bowls during the battle. Finally, Laqa managed to escape into the formidable fortress of Mount Agate and the remnants of the sahir army too fled towards the wilderness.

Emir plundered the sahir camp and found the precious pavilion of Solomon there. It was erected where it had stood earlier and the bazaars of the Islamic camp were restored to their former splendour. The Shah and sardars were brought back from the mountains and their wounds were tended to. Chalak bin Amar presented Emir with the blessed amulet and in turn, Emir rewarded him with a khalat robe.

On the defeated side, the wily Bakhtiarak once again sought Afrasiyab's help and made Sulaiman write a letter that said, 'O Afrasiyab, send someone else for Haseena fell in love with a son of Hamza, thus displeasing Khudawand. He has destroyed her and waits to see who you send next. Regard this letter as urgent and act immediately!' Sulaiman's soldiers placed this letter on the mountain with the magic drum and Afrasiyab received it through his messenger puppet.

◦~◦

7 THE CAPTURE OF ASAD LION-HEART AND MAHJABEEN DIAMOND-ROBE

The chroniclers of this narrative recite our tale of grief and woe in this manner. Sarsar Sword-fighter and Saba Raftar Fleet-foot, who had promised to deliver Asad and Mahjabeen to the King of Sahirs, crossed the River of Flowing Blood and went towards Mahrukh's camp. Sarsar disguised herself as a royal attendant. She wore a uniform, tied a turban around her head with an aigrette attached to it, and held a golden staff. Saba Raftar became a farmer and wore a homespun loincloth hanging down to her knees, a waistcoat and a loosely-tied turban.

Both the ayyar girls wandered around the camp until the great traveller of the sky settled in the west and a bazaar of stars and planets adorned the heavens. At that time, Mahjabeen left from her durbar and the sardars returned to their pavilions. Asad and Mahjabeen went to the palace of pleasure and settled down on a masnad. The ayyar girls hovered around the entrance to the palace and watched Turkish and African handmaidens going in and out.

Saba Raftar waylaid a Habshi slave-girl as she left the pavilion and presented her with a beautifully arranged basket of choice fruits and several gold coins. Saba Raftar pleaded with her, 'I am a modest farmer but the magistrate has increased the taxes in my village. My case is in Malika Mahrukh's court. Could you put in a good word for me with her when she is alone?' The maidservant was delighted and promised that she would help. She took Saba Raftar to her own tent where she tasted the fruit. Within minutes, she was unconscious. Saba Raftar quickly disguised herself as the maidservant and returned to the palace.

Sarsar approached another handmaiden and shouted, 'Why did you abuse all the staff holders yesterday?' The handmaiden snapped, 'Are you out of your mind, you lout? Do not speak to me this way or I will complain to the princess about you!' Then Sarsar deliberately slapped her hard (her palm was smeared with the powder of unconsciousness). When the woman promptly fainted, Sarsar dragged her to a dark corner, assumed her form, and entered the palace disguised as the handmaiden.

She saw that Asad and Mahjabeen were sitting together on a rich masnad with wine goblets laid out before them. Behind them lay a jewel-inlaid couch and beautiful singers were entertaining them with melodious songs. Sarsar mingled with the handmaidens and went around replenishing the wine and the kebabs, while quietly adding sleeping powder to them. Saba Raftar, disguised as the Habshi slave-girl also added sleeping powder to the food she served. After Asad and Mahjabeen had eaten, the ayyar girls made sure that the servants consumed the leftovers. The two lovers, overcome by the drug, staggered to the couch and fell heavily upon it. After some time, everyone lay in a drug-induced sleep.

Late at night, the two girls tied both Asad and Mahjabeen in sheets and left the palace with them. They stealthily eluded all the camp guards and reached the edge of the camp with their precious bundles. Once out of the camp, they bolted out of sight of the camp guards, crossed the River of Flowing Blood and happily made their way to the Garden of Apples where they spent the remainder of the night. When the night had passed and the bright face of morning was revealed, the kettledrums of Tilism were struck. Afrasiyab sat on his throne and all his nobles arrived in court. At that time, the ayyar girls placed the unconscious Mahjabeen and Asad before the Shahanshah. Afrasiyab was overjoyed and ordered that the two prisoners be rendered helpless with a spell before they regained consciousness.

Asad Lion-heart opened his eyes and saw the King of Magic in his durbar, surrounded by hundreds of courtiers. He looked around calmly and called out, 'My salaam to anyone here who believes in the One True God and his Prophet Mohammad!' The sahirs in the durbar stuffed their fingers into their ears to muffle his voice and cried, 'This sinner praises the Unseen God!' Afrasiyab was incensed and asked his guards to behead Asad right away. He then tried to persuade Mahjabeen Diamond-robe to ask for forgiveness but she wept and said, 'I am the nightingale that will sing only to this flower. If you kill me a thousand times I will remain faithful to Asad!' Afrasiyab became even angrier and asked his guards to execute both lovers at once.

The lovers looked at each other with tears in their eyes. Mahjabeen desperately prayed to the Almighty to save them from this peril and the arrow of her prayer soon reached its target. A few ministers and nobles advised the King of Magic against executing the Tilism Kusha just yet. 'The makers of this Tilism have advised against it huzoor,' they said. 'At least consult the oracle Book of Samri first!'

Afrasiyab sent for the book that told him sternly to refrain from killing Asad. The book went on to pronounce, 'All that will happen is that Amar will wear his cloak of invisibility and kill all of you. Imprison Asad and try and arrest Amar and the four ayyars before you execute anyone.'

Afrasiyab cried out to his ministers, 'You are right! The oracle advises us against killing Asad. Take both lovers to the dungeons of the Dome of Light. The doors of Napursan that face Tilism Zahir will be made invisible and no one will be able to rescue them!' Thus, the two leading lights of the gathering of the righteous were imprisoned in a narrow dark dungeon under the Dome of Light.

There was an uproar in Mahrukh's camp when Asad and Mahjabeen were found missing. Amar rushed to Mahjabeen's pavilion and after looking around for clues, Amar declared that he was sure that Sarsar Sword-fighter and Saba Raftar Fleet-foot had kidnapped both her and Asad because he recognized their footprints in the palace!

Mahrukh threw herself on the ground in grief and wailed, 'This is surely the end! Afrasiyab will never let them live now!' Bahar tore her shirt and her tears were as heavy as a cloudburst. 'O fickle skies,' she cried, 'why have you done this to me? I am all alone in this world, where will I go now?'

Amar consoled each of his commanders and dried their tears. He then addressed Mahrukh firmly, 'You have seen Asad's birth chart and you said that he will destroy Tilism and kill Afrasiyab. It does not behove you to be so despondent. You will be the regent instead of Mahjabeen from today and manage the camp. God willing, Asad will be freed soon!' On hearing this, Mahrukh controlled herself and reluctantly sat on the regent's throne, and all the nobles paid solemn homage to her.

Lightning strikes

Meanwhile, Barq Khatif reached Hairat's camp, flashing like a bolt of lightning within dark clouds. Hairat welcomed her and her army of one lakh sahir soldiers graciously, but Barq Khatif did not assume her human form for fear of the ayyars. So, only a bolt of lightning continued to flash on the throne. She sent a message to Mahrukh through a magic puppet that said, 'Surrender to me. I will have you forgiven by the King of Magic, who will restore your kingdom and property to you.' Mahrukh wrote back, 'O Barq Khatif, be warned that Amar is a slayer of sahirs! Ally yourself with him or you will be justly punished.'

When the puppet conveyed Mahrukh's message to Barq Khatif, she shot up like a flame from her throne and went towards the enemy camp. Her lashkar saw her leaving and hastily blew on war trumpets to announce battle. Mahrukh also speedily prepared to fight her but Barq Khatif fell on Mahrukh's army in the form of lightning and destroyed hundreds in one deadly flash. The sahirs on Mahrukh's side had to conjure shields to protect themselves from her onslaughts. All that could be seen were monsoon clouds and bolts of lightning that fell on Mahrukh's soldiers. By evening, several thousand sahirs from Mahrukh's army had left for their final journey. As she left the battlefield, Barq Khatif called out, 'Mahrukh! This was a small example of my wrath. I am leaving now, but tomorrow, I promise, you will all perish in the dust without coffins and graves!'

The young diver

Mahrukh returned to her camp with a heavy heart. Meanwhile, Amar had reached Barq Khatif's camp that sprawled along the banks of a river. Amar assumed the guise of a muscular young man and dressed only in a loincloth, began to dive into the river. Some of Barq Khatif's attendants began amusing themselves by tossing coins into the river for the young diver to retrieve for them. Amar engaged one of them in conversation and learned that he was about to prepare a hookah for his mistress. Amar took him to an isolated place and offered him a whiff of his own tobacco. He told the attendant, 'It is very rare; if you like it, I will tell you where to buy it from.' The attendant sniffed the perfumed tobacco and became unconscious. Amar immediately wore the attendant's clothes and painted his own face to look like the attendent. He went into Barq Khatif's pavilion and saw that the throne was occupied by a golden bolt of lightning. Amar called out to Barq Khatif that her hookah was ready and the flashing light condensed into the form of a woman whose body gleamed like the sun. As Amar offered her the smoking hookah, she looked at him closely. Amar was prepared for this and took out the container of magic water that he had stolen from Hoshiar Jadoo earlier. He threw a handful of the water on Barq Khatif who collapsed on her throne. However, as she fell, her throne moved on its own and whisked her out of the pavilion towards the sky.

Amar was very startled by this, but ran back to his camp and told Mahrukh to attack the enemy camp right then as it was without a commander. Mahrukh blew the magic trumpets of war and her army mobilized quickly to attack Barq Khatif's camp. Thousands of enemy sahirs were killed in the first onslaught. Hairat's army also joined the battle but Barq Khatif's army could not withstand this surprise attack and fled. Hairat's army was also defeated and Hairat finally had to ask for a truce. As both armies retreated, Amar was showered with praise and Mahrukh's camp celebrated victory.

Barq Mehshar and her son Ra'ad

Barq Khatif's magic throne flew her to the Garden of Apples. Afrasiyab revived her and consulted the oracle Book of Samri that read, 'She was defeated by your own weapon. Amar threw the magic water from Samri's well on her. He would have killed her but she is powerful and her magical spirits saved her and brought her to you.' The magic water had sapped Barq Khatif's powers and she asked Afrasiyab for leave to recover in her own palace. He gave her permission to leave but summoned her sister, Barq Mehshar. She arrived with her illustrious son Ra'ad Jadoo in a great burst of thunder and lightning, and Afrasiyab ordered her to help Malika Hairat in the fight against the rebels. Barq Mehshar returned to her place, mobilized her army of one lakh sahirs and left with Ra'ad for Hairat's camp.

A few hours before reaching the camp, Barq Mehshar decided to rest in one of the many beautiful gardens that Afrasiyab had created in his land. This garden was close to the estate of Rain Jadoo, a beautiful temptress whom Ra'ad Jadoo loved with all his heart. The young suitor bribed one of her maidservants into contriving a meeting for him with his beloved on her roof garden. Rain met him on the roof, but some of her other suitors saw them together and were consumed by jealousy at the sight of the lovers. The suitors waited for Ra'ad to leave Rain's palace and ambushed him on his way back to his camp, with the intention of getting rid of him in the forest.

Meanwhile, Amar had left his camp and strolled into the forest wondering who Afrasiyab would send as a replacement for Barq Khatif. That was when he saw three sahirs going into the forest with a young noble. Amar thought, 'I should help this young man as he looks like a powerful sahir.' Accordingly, he disguised himself as a demon by attaching several false heads on either side of his own head. The heads had mouths with snake-like tongues darting in and out of them. Amar also rubbed his body with an unguent so that it seemed as if his body emanated flames. To complete his disguise, he wore a devjama and blew loudly on his magic horn to produce a sound that could make Jinnis dance.

The sahirs who had kidnapped Ra'ad were stunned by the horn's sound and terrified by the sight of a ten-headed monster in a dazzling cloak that seemed to change colours. In sheer fright, they fell at Amar's feet who called out, 'I am Izrael, the Angel of Death!'

The sahirs stuttered, 'Why are you here?' Amar looked at them sternly and replied, 'You are about to kill this sinner and I have come to receive his soul! But your lives are over as well so prepare to leave this earth!' The sahirs fell at Amar's feet and cried, 'O Angel of Death! Help us so that we can live longer!' Amar advised them to be charitable in order to please the god Laqa. They quickly handed him all the money and jewels that they had with them. In turn, Amar gave them an apple and said, 'Eat this and your life spans will increase.' The sahirs eagerly cut the apple into slices and ate it. Within moments, they began feeling uncomfortable.

'O Angel of Death,' they cried, 'We feel so ill!' Amar replied, 'Your lives are getting longer, your arteries must be stretching.' Later, when they slumped unconscious, he ruthlessly beheaded all three sahirs and the forest resounded with the wailing of their spirits. Ra'ad was released after they died, but looked at Amar suspiciously. 'I have saved your life! Why do you look at me this way?' said Amar. The youthful sahir flushed and asked him, 'Are you really the Angel of Death?'

Amar nodded and Ra'ad respectfully said, 'O Angel of Death, these sahirs caught me by surprise; otherwise, I am the son of the powerful Barq Mehshar. In battle, we work as a team. I plunge into the earth and emerge within the ranks of the enemy soldiers and scream like thunder, which makes their heads split open . . . although powerful sahirs usually just fall unconscious. My mother then falls from the heavens as a bolt of lightning and slices the fallen soldiers in two. Afrasiyab has asked us to confront Mahrukh and I think that we should be able to destroy the rebels.'

Amar thought to himself, 'How fortunate that I met this rascal! Let me finish him before he can cause any trouble.' Just then, a dark cloud appeared on the horizon with lightning streaking through it. This was Barq Mehshar in search of her son. As the cloud hovered above them, Amar foresaw trouble and disappeared into Galeem. Ra'ad was now convinced that Amar really was the Angel of Death.

Barq Mehshar spotted her son and descended from the cloud in her real form. She embraced her son and looked at the bodies of the slain sahirs. She asked, 'Who has killed these people?' Ra'ad related his kidnapping and rescue by the Angel of Death and added, 'He was standing right here but saw you and disappeared suddenly.' Barq Mehshar said, 'Then he is unfortunate for I would have enriched him beyond his expectations for saving your life.' Ra'ad called out, 'O Angel of Death, grace us with your vision if you are still here!'

Amar appeared suddenly and Barq Mehshar humbly bowed to him and said, 'You are our saviour. Because of you, Samri has bestowed the khalat of life on my son again. Please come to my humble abode so that I can serve you in whatever manner I can.' Amar replied casually, 'There is no harm in that!'

Barq Mehshar uttered a spell and a jewel-studded throne flew in. Amar and Ra'ad sat on the throne while she rode alongside them in her magical form of lightning. She brought them into the garden where she had camped and Amar saw that the garden was blooming with flowers and fruit trees.

Barq Mehshar seated Amar on the masnad seating and laid out trays of gold coins and gems for him. She said, 'These are not worthy of you but please accept them and tell me truthfully, who are you really?' Amar replied, 'I have told you already, I am the Angel of Death so why do you ask me again?' Barq Mehshar sighed and sent for her casket that contained the oracle Papers of Jamshed. She was stunned to read the text that read, 'This is Amar the famous ayyar and ally of Mahrukh Magic-eye. He assumed this form to save your son's life. Get rid of with him with gifts or he will cause trouble.'

Barq Mehshar looked at Amar angrily and said, 'You are Amar and you are a liar and a cheat, but you have saved my son's life so I offer you these trays of jewels. Take them and be gone from here!' Amar retorted, 'I will go! Do you think I have come to live here?'

Meanwhile Afrasiyab consulted the oracle Book of Samri, and was furious when he saw that Barq Mehshar had brought Amar to her camp and was actually offering costly gifts to him. He was at the time sitting with the beautiful Makhmoor Red-eye, sister of Khumar Jadoo. A reminder here: both these sisters, like Bahar, were powerful sahiras and beloved of the king, but had not yielded to him for fear of his wife Hairat. Afrasiyab ordered Makhmoor Red-eye to immediately arrest Amar and punish Barq Mehshar if she resisted. Makhmoor flew to Barq Mehshar's garden and looked unmoved as the sahira greeted her with great deference.

Makhmoor spoke firmly, 'Barq Mehshar, you consort with our greatest enemy and the Shah is furious with you! I have come to arrest Amar and it will be wiser for you not to interfere!' Barq Mehshar replied softly, 'My sister, Amar has saved my son's life. It will be dishonourable for me to get him into trouble now!' Makhmoor said derisively, 'You are a foolish woman! Keep your honour and faith aside now and look to Afrasiyab who can destroy you in a flash! Anyway I am not bound by your scruples and will capture Amar myself!'

As the two women argued, Amar quietly took out the jar of the powerful magic water he had taken from Hoshiar and sprinkled a little on Makhmoor who immediately fainted. Amar drew his sword out to kill the fair sahira, but suddenly, a magic panja appeared and whisked Makhmoor out of sight. Barq Mehshar looked at him aghast and said, 'Amar, you better leave immediately and I will also hide myself somewhere in Tilism. Afrasiyab is now my enemy and will not refrain from killing me! It was unwise of you to attack Makhmoor!'

Amar replied calmly, 'Malika, if my enemy is strong, my God is stronger still. Come with me to my camp. You will suffer what we suffer. The final decision is yours, but this is my sincere advice!' Barq Mehshar pondered over his words and finally said, 'Of course you are quite right! Well, I am with you now. It is better to fight and lose than to hide like a coward!'

Saying this, she rose and ordered her army to follow her. She conjured a throne for Ra'ad and Amar, and left for Mahrukh's camp in a cloud emitting thunder and lightning. Meanwhile, the panja that had saved Makhmoor brought her to the King of Sahirs, who had her revived. Makhmoor looked confused and said, 'I was fighting with Barq Mehshar when I fell unconscious.' Afrasiyab consulted the oracle Book of Samri and learnt that Amar had used the magic water on Makhmoor and that Barq Mehshar had now allied with him. Afrasiyab immediately sent for the third sister, Barq Lameh, and ordered her to proceed to the rebel camp to arrest Barq Mehshar.

Barq Lameh reached Hairat's camp with a huge army. The next morning, the two armies faced each other on the battlefield. Barq Lameh came to the battlefield in the form of lightning and killed hundreds of soldiers in one strike. Soon, thousands had died as a result of her deadly attacks and Mahrukh's army began to retreat. A desperate Mahrukh took off her crown and kneeled in prayer to Bibi Fatima, the daughter of the Prophet, to help them in the name of Allah.

Her prayer was answered and a huge cloud appeared on the horizon with the signature flag of Barq Mehshar outlined in lightning. Several thousand sahirs appeared on magic dragons and Barq Mehshar arrived with Khwaja Amar and her son Ra'ad. Barq Mehshar lost no time in attacking Barq Lameh who had struck fear in the hearts of Mahrukh's soldiers. Now it appeared as if there were two sets of lightning in the clouds striking at each other. At one point, when the two sisters fell on the ground, Ra'ad Jadoo emerged from the earth where Barq Lameh was rolling and let out an ear-shattering roar. Barq Lameh fell down unconscious. Barq Mehshar flew upwards and was about to swoop down and cut her adversary in half when a panja swiftly removed Barq Lameh out of sight.

Barq Mehshar fell instead on the enemy forces and cut them to pieces. Her son Ra'ad kept emerging from the earth within the ranks of enemy soldiers and his thunderous roars caused hundreds to become unconscious or suffer injury. His mother completed the job by falling from the skies and killing the unconscious sahirs. Other commanders also joined in the battle. Bahar bewitched hundreds of soldiers with her spring gardens while Surkh Mu loosened her deadly tresses and thousands of stars that pierced the hearts of enemy soldiers fell from the skies. Nafarman's magic caused panic in enemy ranks and Shakeel ruthlessly killed so many enemy sahirs that their bodies piled up around him.

Hairat saw this carnage and had the drums of peace struck. Mahrukh Magic-eye entered her durbar in triumph as Barq Mehshar and Ra'ad came forward with nazar offerings for her. Mahrukh embraced them warmly and presented them with robes of honour. She gave Ra'ad a *naulakha* string of gems that she had been wearing herself. That night, the camp celebrated their arrival with wine and dancing.

The arrest of Afat Jadoo

Meanwhile, the panja that had retrieved Barq Lameh from the battlefield deposited her in front of Afrasiyab. The king had her revived and struck his head in frustration as she related the story of her defeat. He sent the wounded sahira back to her land and decided to summon the fourth lightning sister. At this point, Afat Jadoo, a powerful sahir in Afrasiyab's durbar, suddenly laughed. Afrasiyab said furiously, 'You impertinent man, how dare you mock your Shahanshah instead of being sorrowful!'

Afat replied courteously, 'O Badshah, I laughed at Amar and Mahrukh's daring. So many powerful servants of Samri and Jamshed have been humiliated and have fled from battle. The truth is that it will be impossible to win against Amar!' Enraged, Afrasiyab told Afat, 'You disloyal rascal, never enter my durbar again! You praise the enemy in order to dishearten my companions!'

Afat was a sahir of noble lineage and felt insulted by the Shahanshah. He responded quietly, 'Afrasiyab, it is because of your pride and arrogance that Samri has afflicted you with these troubles. Despite these humiliations, you have still not learnt a lesson! I told you that you will never be able to defeat Amar and I am beginning to believe that his faith might be the true one!' Afrasiyab hissed, 'It seems you are secretly his ally and that is why you praise and admire him. Well, I will make you eat your words. Let us see how Amar can save you now!'

Afrasiyab ordered his sahir-guards to arrest Afat. Afat tried to resist but was powerless against so many sahirs and they easily captured him. Afrasiyab shouted, 'Take him across the River of Flowing Blood! This unfortunate man will be kept alive tonight. Tomorrow morning, light a pyre on the plain of Zahir below the Dome of Light and burn him alive in front of Mahrukh's camp. I will watch him die from the Dome of Light and enjoy the weeping of his sympathizers. Let us see which of his new friends can rescue him there!'

Afat was taken across the river by several hundred guards while the news of his arrest caused a ripple of fear in the visible tilism. Afat's fair young wife, Hilal Sehr Afgan, was stunned to hear the news and left her house in a frenzy to meet her husband for the last time. Several hundred of his friends and attendants went with her. For fear of the Shahanshah's wrath, no one approached him for clemency. Hairat was informed of the impending execution and she left for the execution ground with her commanders. The kettledrums of Tilism were struck and heralds declared that anyone defying the Shahanshah would suffer the same fate as Afat.

The news of Afat's arrest also reached the rebel camp. Amar and Mahrukh heard that Afat was going to be burnt alive for sympathizing with them and immediately decided to rescue him. Mahrukh suggested a sudden attack to free Afat but Amar advised against any hasty action and said, 'I will think of a plan.' He went to the forest and summoned his companions with Zafeel, the whistle of ayyari. After they had joined him, he explained the situation to them. Then the ayyars got busy thinking of a plan to rescue Afat.

By this time, Afrasiyab's men had brought Afat across the river and had confined him to a tent in Hairat's camp. The sahir commander Tadbeer and his men had been assigned the duty of collecting wood for the pyre on which Afat was to be burnt. Barq ayyar, disguised as a soldier holding an axe in one hand, went to Tadbeer and said, 'As I was cutting down a tree, it released a flame which transformed into a fire-fairy. Come and see this wonder!' Tadbeer was intrigued and followed the ayyar who led him to an isolated grove and burst a narcotic bubble in his face that made him unconscious. Barq hid him behind a tree and quickly disguised himself as Tadbeer. He returned to supervise the pyre as Tadbeer Jadoo, making sure that the logs were arranged in a square, with a hollow centre.

Qiran kept an eye on Barq from a distance and when he was sure that Barq had been accepted as Tadbeer, he started digging a tunnel that brought him right underneath the hollow in the stack of logs. Zargham and Jansoz, disguised as sahirs, sprayed the pyre with oils and powders of unconsciousness.

The fair Sati

As the other ayyars were busy in these tasks, Amar walked along the shore of the River of Flowing Blood and came across a garden. He entered the garden and saw that it was as beautiful as the Garden of Paradise. This garden belonged to Afat's wife, the beautiful Hilal Sehr Afgan, who was spending the night there and intended to meet her husband the next morning to die with him. Amar saw that several women in mourning, clad in black, were wailing and weeping around her. In their midst, that honourable full moon of beauty, Hilal, seemed overwhelmed with grief. Tears rolled down her cheeks as her companions wailed in anticipation of Afat's death the next morning.

Amar disguised himself as a wizened, bent old woman and leaning heavily on a walking stick, approached the fair Hilal. He wept bitterly, embraced her and cried, 'I am your husband's nursemaid, my daughter, and have just heard the terrible news!' As Hilal sobbed even more, Amar whispered to her, 'I have thought of a plan to rescue him but we need to be alone.'

Hilal followed the false nursemaid to a corner of the garden hidden from her companions. Amar rendered her unconscious and dropped her in Zambil. Within minutes, he had transformed himself into the grieving Hilal and joined her companions.

Amar as the false Hilal cried out, 'Sati! Sati! I will burn with my husband on the pyre!' Her companions and maidservants implored her not to take this course and said, 'O beautiful mistress! You are too young to die; for the love of Samri and Jamshed give up this idea!' The false Hilal replied dramatically, 'It would be better for me to burn along with my beloved instead of burning in the fire of separation for the rest of my life!' Then, the false Hilal ordered her handmaidens, 'Bring my bridal finery, for tonight I will adorn myself for my spiritual awakening and for a last meeting with my beloved.'

The handmaidens brought all her jewels and rich red bridal clothes in trays and wept as they dressed her. Hilal remained composed as her flowing black tresses were adorned with pearls and diamonds. After she was ready, the false Hilal sat on a throne and her maidservants worshipped her as the divine Sati. She was surrounded by heaps of flowers and sweetmeats. As porters lifted her throne, the false Hilal laughed and tossed a coconut as she left the garden. Very soon, throngs of worshippers surrounded her throne, playing drums and dancing alongside her throne. Occasionally, the Sati would bestow a flower, a sweetmeat or a pinch of holy ash on the crowds. Early next morning, her procession reached the plain where her husband Afat was captive. Afat had been up throughout the night praying to Almighty Allah, 'O Unseen God, I am of your faith like Mahrukh. Deliver me from this calamity!'

While he prayed, there was a murmur of excitement in the crowds as the false Hilal came forth on her throne crying, 'Sati! Sati!' Afrasiyab who had come to watch Afat die from the Dome of Light heard the crowds shouting and was informed that Afat's wife had come to die with him. He sent for her and was moved by the sight of her magnificent beauty. He pleaded softly with her, 'Fair lady, I will be devoted to you and will honour you with land and money. Give up this idea of dying on your husband's pyre!' The beautiful Sati answered, 'Shahanshah, only when the fires of separation are cooled will I be happy. Riches and money are like ashes to me now!' Saying this, the false Hilal jumped off her throne and joined her husband on the pyre.

Hairat and other notable sardars stood around the unlit pyre. Jansoz and Zargham, disguised as supervisors of the pyre, had been busy and had added noxious potions to all the containers of oil and clarified butter. They poured these on to the pyre as Barq lit a taper and thrust it amongst the logs. As the logs burst into flames, Hilal, who was actually Amar, moved quickly and pushed Afat into Zambil. He then jumped down into the tunnel that Qiran had dug under the pyre. Qiran was in the tunnel and led his teacher to where it opened, well beyond where the crowds had gathered.

As the pyre burnt, fumes from the drugged oils and clarified butter rose to permeate the air for miles around. Hairat and her companions and soldiers who stood around the pyre became unconscious, as did the throngs of people who had come to witness the execution of Afat. At that time, Amar, Qiran, and the three ayyars fell on the army with their swords drawn. They had stuffed wads of cotton wool soaked in an antidote in their nostrils and the ayyars shouted out their names to declare their identities as they fought.

Mahrukh, Bahar and Nafarman heard their cries in the rebel camp and plunged into the earth or flew up to join the ayyars in slaying the soldiers as well. The spirits of the dead sahirs wailed and howled and Afrasiyab on his throne in the Dome of Light heard their cries. He went out to investigate, but when he leaned against the balustrade of the Dome of Light, he was overcome by the drugged fumes and went hurtling down the length of the Dome. His guardian puppets emerged from the earth just in time to halt his fall.

The drugged fumes had permeated the dome and many people inside had also become unconscious. Mahrukh and her commanders had killed scores of enemy soldiers by the time that the guardian puppets revived Afrasiyab, who now saw thousands of his men lying in a river of blood. Stricken with shame, he revived Hairat and fled towards the Veil of Darkness. Hairat quickly woke up her unconscious army by conjuring rain, but by that time Mahrukh had already struck the drums of peace and retreated to her camp.

Mahrukh Magic-eye, followed by the ayyars, entered the durbar amidst great jubilation. At that time, Amar took Afat and Hilal out from Zambil where they had reunited with joy. They were surprised to find themselves in a strange durbar and looked around confused. Amar addressed them, 'O Afat, I saved you in the guise of Sati with the help of Allah!' As Amar went on to relate the events that led to his rescue, Afat silently kneeled at his feet with tears of gratitude in his eyes. Amar smiled and embraced him with warmth. Mahrukh bestowed costly robes of state on Afat and Hilal and the camp rejoiced on account of their arrival.

Hairat had the bodies of her dead soldiers retrieved from the plain and returned to her camp with a heavy heart. She longed to punish Mahrukh for this latest defeat but decided to consult her husband first. Soon enough, Afrasiyab returned from the Veil of Darkness smarting with anger. From his durbar in the Garden of Apples, he ordered his vizier Baghban Qudrat to set off immediately to capture Amar and punish anyone who interfered with this task. Baghban plunged into the earth and made his way underground to avoid facing any ayyars.

The capture of Amar

Amar was chatting with his friends in the durbar when it occurred to him that after being humiliated publicly, the King of Magic was bound to send someone to capture him and that it would be prudent for him to hide. Accordingly, he took out a Kashmiri wrestler from Zambil. (To remind the reader, Amar's Zambil held a huge number of captive sahirs and non-sahirs. The Zambil, as has been explained earlier, was an enchanted pouch within which was a whole world with its own sun and moon, rivers and lakes, and cities and towns. The Jinni of Zambil looked after the prisoners and fed and clothed them.) Amar drugged the wrestler and painted his own face over the wrestler's. He placed him on a couch in the enclosed courtyard behind the durbar so that it seemed as if Amar lay asleep on it. Then the real Amar slipped into his Galeem and became invisible.

A little later, Vizier Baghban reached Mahrukh's camp and startled everyone by emerging from the earth within the durbar pavilion. Before anyone could attack him, Baghban cast a spell to create a cool breeze that lulled everyone into an enchanted sleep. He looked at all the sleeping commanders but could not find Amar in the durbar. He then began looking for Amar and found him asleep on a couch in the courtyard. Seizing the false Amar by his waist, he flew upwards and reversed his spell with a wave of his hand. Everyone woke up to see Baghban flying off with Amar. Baghban called out, 'Rebels and traitors! I was here just to capture Amar or else I would have cut your heads off. Look, I have taken him now. Rescue him if you can!'

As Amar's friends prepared to attack the vizier, Amar, invisible in his cloak, whispered to Mahrukh, 'I am safe. Do not let anyone follow him!' Mahrukh ordered her sardars to fall back, and declared, 'Let Baghban go! Khwaja Amar will be protected by Allah!'

Baghban flew with his prisoner to the Shahanshah's durbar and threw Amar in front of his master. Afrasiyab sent for the executioner and the false Amar was woken up with cold water. The Kashmiri wrestler opened his eyes to find himself in the durbar of an obviously powerful king. Overawed, the wrestler greeted the King of Sahirs respectfully. Afrasiyab smiled scornfully and said, 'Amar! I am going to punish you dreadfully now!' To this the wrestler said, 'O Badshah, I am no ayyar but huzoor's faithful servant and a worshipper of Laqa!' Afrasiyab laughed derisively and said, 'You rascal, I will not be deceived by you any longer!' Turning to the executioner, Afrasiyab ordered him to behead Amar right away.

The wrestler pleaded tearfully, 'Give me justice huzoor. I am from Kashmir; the worshippers of the Unseen God tried to convert me but I did not relent. Since then, for years I have been a prisoner in Amar's Zambil. I have no idea how I was rescued and brought to you!' Hearing this, Afrasiyab felt doubtful and consulted the oracle Book of Samri. The oracle informed him that the wrestler was indeed speaking the truth and that Amar had tricked Baghban by disguising this man as himself. Afrasiyab had the wrestler's face washed and when his real face emerged, Afrasiyab released him and bestowed a robe of honour and a position in the durbar on him. Then he frowned at Baghban who apologized sheepishly, 'Huzoor, I am unfamiliar with such trickeries, forgive me.' Afrasiyab let him go but sent for Sarsar Sword-fighter and ordered her to find the real Amar. He told her, 'If you do not find him, by my faith, I will kill you myself. Look at how the ayyars of the enemy camp are fighting so valiantly!'

In fear of the Shahanshah's wrath, Sarsar left the durbar. She came upon her companions in the forest and urged them to remain alert in case she needed assistance. Sarsar then made her way to Mahrukh's pavilion disguised as a maidservant and managed to render Mahrukh unconscious. Sarsar bound Mahrukh's hands and feet and placed her in a large trunk. Then she disguised herself as Mahrukh and waited for Amar. Sure enough, Amar called on her for a private audience before retiring to his tent. The false malika lured him into sharing a betel leaf with her and offered a scented handkerchief to him to wipe his face. As soon as Amar succumbed to the drugged perfume, she deftly tied him in a pushtara and walked out of the pavilion. Though Mahrukh's guards were surprised to see Mahrukh scampering out of the lashkar holding a large bundle, no one dared question the badshah and Sarsar breezed past the guards with the captive Amar.

Barq, who was keeping guard outside the camp recognized her from a distance and chased her, but Sarsar reached the Bridge of Smoke quickly and called out loudly for help. The smoke parted to make way for her and as Sarsar walked through the smoke, Amar regained consciousness but kept his eyes closed as he realized that Sarsar was carrying him through a fearful dark passage. A little later, when the ayyar girl reached the Desert of Fire, it also provided her with safe passage. Beyond the Desert of Fire was total darkness and Sarsar stopped here. A sahir whose body glowed like a torch emerged out of the gloom.

He put his arm around Sarsar's waist and spun her body like a top before tossing her into the air.

Amar, who had been peering out of the pushtara, closed his eyes in sheer fright. When he opened his eyes, he saw a puppet of fire flying with its arm around Sarsar's waist. Moments later, the puppet dived with her into a river of fire. After they crossed the river, the puppet handed over Sarsar with her bundle to a sahir who flew with his arm around her waist to the top of a mountain from where he pushed her off. The next time Amar opened his eyes, they had already reached the Shahanshah's Garden of Apples. Amar saw that the garden was alight with spring blossoms and that melodious magic birds were eloquently singing Afrasiyab's praises.

The Garden of Apples had been so designed that it was forever spring within its enchanted walls. A person just had to think of anything he desired for it to appear before him. It had lamps made of pearls that glowed at night and the garden vibrated with the sounds of bells and drums. Its floors were covered with velvet carpets that had magic symbols woven into them and its curtains opened and closed by themselves when people walked through.

Khumar, the bald sahira

Afrasiyab was seated on his throne in a baradari and was surrounded by hundreds of sahirs who stood in attendance with folded hands. Sarsar appeared and performed a mujra-greeting for Afrasiyab before depositing Amar's pushtara in front of him. 'As you had bidden me huzoor, I have brought this sinner to you!' she said. Afrasiyab was delighted with Sarsar and presented her with a priceless robe of honour. It was then that Sulaiman Ambreen Kohi's message arrived with the news of Haseena's death.

Afrasiyab sent a *nama* back to Laqa that read, 'Khudawand, your humble slave has captured your greatest enemy Amar. Please send Shaitan Bakhtiarak to execute Amar with his own hands. I will send an army back with him that will destroy Hamza's lashkar.' Afrasiyab entrusted this message to his beloved Khumar Jadoo and asked her to bring Shaitan back with her.

Khumar flew to Mount Agate and went directly to Laqa's durbar. As it happened, Chalak bin Amar had been spying on Laqa's durbar disguised as a guard. Khumar met him outside the durbar and said, 'Go and inform the durbar that Khumar Jadoo has come from Tilism-e-Hoshruba with a message from Afrasiyab.' Chalak went inside and returned after a while, and whispered to her that Laqa had asked him to convey a private message to her before she entered the durbar.

He led her to an isolated corner and produced a shiny red apple. He told Khumar, 'Khudawand has sent this gift for you. Eat it and you will be filled with his grace and light.' Khumar was happy to be singled out by Laqa and ate the apple quickly. Moments later, she slumped downwards, her feet in the air. Immediately, Chalak shaved off the hair on her head so that she became as bald as a newborn baby. He then exchanged the message that Afrasiyab had sent with one written by him.

Khumar regained consciousness a little later and thought that the blessed apple had caused her to fall asleep. She made her way into the durbar feeling light-headed but was unaware of her hair having been shorn. She prostrated before Laqa, whose courtiers laughed aloud at seeing a beautiful noble sahira completely bald. Laqa said, 'Rise with my blessing, my daughter.'

Khumar then produced Afrasiyab's nama and it was passed to the court scribe to read out aloud. As Chalak had replaced the message with one of his own, the nama was now full of insults and abuses. The scribe tactfully said that he could not understand the language of magic and the nama was then handed to Bakhtiarak who laughed aloud as he read the contents. He said, 'Listen my lord to what Afrasiyab has written to you: "O shameless haramzadeh! You silly ass with the face and intelligence of a pig! You ugly, black-faced apostate, Zamurrad Shah Bakhtri! A thousand curses on you for you have misled so many people of Allah! Go immediately, beg forgiveness of the brave Emir Hamza, and convert to Islam. If you do not, I, the King of Magic, will punish you so grievously that no one will remember what you looked like! This letter ends with a thousand curses on you!"'

Laqa was outraged and roared like thunder, 'Has that haramzada Afrasiyab taken leave of his senses? I will doom him to eternal damnation and hell!' Khumar Jadoo trembled with fear and stammered, 'Khudawand, this is not what the Shahanshah wrote. He had sent me to invite Shaitan Bakhtiarak to come and execute Amar! Someone must have tampered with this message. You are divine and must know what has happened.'

Bakhtiarak laughed even louder and said, 'I agree that this message has been changed. I am also sure that the real Amar has not been arrested. He must have accompanied you and changed the message on the way. By the way princess, is it customary for sahiras in Tilism to shave their heads?' Khumar smiled and said, 'O Shaitan of Khudawand, I know it is your function to tease people, but I am a devotee of his divinity, at least spare me! Tilism-e-Hoshruba is famous for its beautiful women whose lovely tresses have captured thousands of men in their coils. Shave their heads indeed!' Then Bakhtiarak said, 'Then did you take a vow that you would come to Khudawand with your head shorn? Touch your head if you do not believe me!'

Khumar touched her head and was startled at the feel of her smooth scalp. She wept bitterly and cried, 'Malik-ji you are right to say that Amar had travelled with me! In fact, I felt an invisible weight on my shoulders as I flew here. I am positive it was that rogue. He must surely have been the man who offered me fruit, as I was unconscious after tasting it. He had shaved my head once in Tilism as well!'

Bakhtiarak cried out, 'The blessings of Allah on the True Prophet and his family and a thousand curses on Laqa! Khumar, do you now see what a blessed man Amar ﷺ?' Bakhtiarak then called out loudly, 'O Teacher of Trickeries, reveal your presence to us sinners now!' Chalak bin Amar who was present in the durbar thought, 'If I can convince them that I am Amar, Khumar will inform Afrasiyab that Amar is in Mount Agate. Afrasiyab will become doubtful and will release the real Amar. I will earn praise for rescuing Amar from such a distance.' So, he left the durbar and painted his face to look like Amar.

While Bakhtiarak was still babbling about Amar, Chalak leapt into the durbar. He first lowered his eyelid to reveal Amar's telltale mole to Bakhtiarak and then addressed the bald sahira, 'Listen Khumar, be grateful that your life was spared, otherwise I would have surely killed you today!' Khumar ran towards him furiously crying, 'You shameless rascal, you dared to shave my head? You have disgraced me in the entire Tilism and the durbar of Khudawand!' Just as she was about to attack him, Chalak aimed an egg of unconsciousness at her face and when she collapsed, he bounded out of the durbar. Laqa's servants and courtiers remained calm as they were quite used to the antics of the ayyars. No one bothered to chase him.

Bakhtiarak had the sahira revived and told her to return to Afrasiyab with a reply from Laqa that read: 'Afrasiyab, you are one of my chosen favourites but you are a foolish man. You have been deceived and the real Amar accompanied your messenger to my durbar. You will lose your life if you are not more careful and it is unsafe for my Shaitan to grace your durbar. Now send someone to help me or my wrath will fall upon you and your land!'

This message, stamped with the seal of Laqa, was given to Khumar along with the note that Chalak had written. She pleaded with Laqa to grant her the bounty of a full head of hair and Laqa promised her that by Nauroze, the first day of the spring equinox, she would have a head full of hair. He said to her, 'At that time, I will bestow the beauty of a *houri* on you, my daughter, so that you will never grow old!' Thus, Laqa managed to placate Khumar and sent her back to Tilism.

Afrasiyab was keenly awaiting Khumar's return and was shocked to see her bald head. He read the message from Laqa and the nama written by Chalak, and trembling with rage said, 'O shame and dishonour! Alas, that Khudawand should have been so abused because of me!' He was now convinced that Sarsar had passed off some poor innocent as Amar just to prove her efficiency.

Amar was untied and brought before the Shahanshah who asked him, 'Who are you?' Amar had heard Khumar's story and realized that some friend of his in Mount Agate had deceived them. Accordingly, he had a story ready for the ever-gullible Afrasiyab: 'O Mighty King. I am a prostitute from Tilism-e-Zahir. Sarsar had promised to pay me five thousand gold coins for this deception. She brought me here disguised as Amar and said that she would set me free at night!'

Afrasiyab awarded the woman five thousand gold coins for her honesty and set her free. Amar left the durbar with the money and quickly became invisible in Galeem in case they suspected him again. Sarsar was duly summoned and Afrasiyab had her tied to a pillar in the durbar and ordered his minions to beat her soundly. As Sarsar howled in protest, Afrasiyab shouted, 'You trollop! You have disgraced me in front of Khudawand! How dare you bribe a prostitute into becoming Amar! I should cut your nose off for this!'

'Impossible huzoor,' Sarsar screamed as the beating continued, 'that was the real Amar! I brought him to you after making sure it was him!' Khumar stepped forward crying, 'Look at my shaven head you hussy! Would I be in this state just to prove you wrong?' Sarsar ignored her and addressed Afrasiyab again, 'Huzoor, consult the oracle Book of Samri. If I am a liar, you can behead me. If someone had her head shaved I should not be blamed for it!'

Khumar became even more incensed when she heard this and shouted, 'You lowborn slut! How dare you cast aspersions on me! First you deceive us and now you are defiant!' Sarsar shouted back at her, 'Whoever calls me a slut must be one herself! I am only answerable to the Shahanshah!'

Afrasiyab reprimanded both women for misbehaving in front of him and sent for the oracle Book of Samri. Naturally, it exposed Chalak's trickery. Sarsar was now untied from the pillar and gifted with a robe of honour. 'Amar will not be able to cross the River of Flowing Blood,' Afrasiyab told her, 'arrest him immediately!' Sarsar Sword-fighter left the durbar with her honour restored while Afrasiyab dismissed his courtiers to rest after an exhausting day.

Amar and Vizier Baghban Qudrat

Now hear about Amar: He was wandering along the bank of the River of Flowing Blood disguised as a vicious-looking Aghori fakir with a skull hanging on his chest and a bottle of wine in his hand. He was hoping to trick a sahir into taking him across the river. Sarsar recognized him at first glance and fell upon him with her sword. Amar was forced to retaliate and as they fenced, they saw a sahir walking towards them. For a moment, Sarsar was distracted and Amar quickly burst a narcotic bubble in her face. As she fainted, he caught her and threw her in Zambil. He thought of running away, but the sahir was puzzled by Sarsar's sudden disappearance and quickly cast a spell on Amar, making him immobile. Coming a little bit closer, he asked Amar, 'What have you done with the woman you were fighting with?'

Amar replied airily, 'She was my wife and as I was hungry, I swallowed her!' The sahir looked confused and then said to himself, 'I have never been to the Shahanshah's durbar before. This will be a good excuse to approach the Shah. He will surely be intrigued by the story of a man who has swallowed his wife alive!'

The sahir clasped Amar by the waist and flew with him to Afrasiyab's durbar. As he was flying to the durbar, Vizier Baghban Qudrat, who was drinking wine with his wife Gulcheen in their garden, looked up and saw him. The vizier chanted a spell that forced the sahir to land in the garden with his prisoner. On recognizing the vizier, the sahir greeted him respectfully and told him that he was taking the Aghori fakir to the Shahanshah as he had swallowed his wife. The vizier looked surprised and then stared at Amar intently. Baghban was a powerful sahir and his penetrating magical gaze stripped the ayyar of the paints of trickery and he felt as if his body was burning.

Baghban smiled at the sahir and said, 'This is not an Aghori but the infamous Amar!' Then the vizier asked Amar, 'So, who have you swallowed?' Amar grinned and said, 'It was my wife, O Noble Vizier! I never show her to anyone and she stays in my Zambil. I had taken her out by the river, but she was fighting with me when this sahir appeared and so I quickly put her back in Zambil. Naturally, I cannot swallow her!' At this, Baghban's wife Gulcheen cried, 'Amar do show us your wife!'

Amar replied, 'I will not expose her to the gaze of strangers. Ask everyone to leave and give me some money to show her to you.' At

Gulcheen's signal, everyone left the garden. Baghban and his wife presented Amar with a sack of gold and after securing the treasure in Zambil, Amar went to a secluded corner and took Sarsar out of Zambil. Sarsar was still unconscious and Amar disguised her as an extremely beautiful woman before dragging her in front of Baghban and Gulcheen. They were both impressed with the beauty of the unconscious woman and asked Amar to wake her up.

'She might run away!' Amar exclaimed. The vizier and his wife promised to restrain her if she did. 'She might even claim to be Sarsar Sword-fighter!' Amar warned them. 'And then you will turn against me!' Both assured him they would not believe his wife. Finally, Amar tied Sarsar to a tree and revived her. She woke up to see the vizier and his wife and cried out, 'O Vizier of State, why have you tied me up? Do not be deceived by this ayyar! I am Sarsar and was trying to capture Amar for my master!'

Amar slapped her and said, 'You dare to threaten me by speaking about your lover Shahanshah. I will cut your nose off today!' Hearing this, Sarsar started to abuse him too. Very amused with what she thought was a marital argument, Gulcheen commented, 'Amar your wife has a foul tongue!' Amar slapped Sarsar a few more times for being abusive and the vizier and his wife laughed again. Sarsar cried out, 'It is not right to jest with me. I will tell Shahanshah that your vizier has joined the enemy!'

Sarsar then gave an account of events in the durbar to which only she and Baghban were privy. Feeling doubtful after hearing this, Baghban plucked a fruit off the nearest tree and muttered a spell on it. It split open and a multicoloured bird flew out of it crying, 'The woman who is tied up is Sarsar!' Baghban immediately released Sarsar and apologized profusely to her.

While the vizier's attention was on Sarsar, Amar slipped into Galeem and became invisible. Sarsar and Baghban tried to find him, but Sarsar eventually took leave of the vizier to look for Amar elsewhere. After she had gone, Gulcheen confided in her husband, 'What a pity! I had heard so much about Amar's talents! I would have liked to have seen some of his skills.' Hidden behind Galeem, Amar called out that he was still in the garden but invisible for fear of being captured. Gulcheen promised not to betray him and also offered him money. Amar then emerged from the cloak and Gulcheen requested him to sing. Amar took out his flute and wore anklet bells. His music and dancing held his audience spellbound and even the birds fell silent in order to hear him. The flowers were still and no breeze rustled the leaves, but they moved of their own accord to applaud his talent.

Afrasiyab returned to his durbar and consulted the oracle Book of Samri. He was furious to learn that Amar was entertaining Baghban and Gulcheen. 'To think that my own vizier should be fraternizing with the enemy!' he thundered, and ordered a magic slave-boy to bring Baghban and Amar to him. Even as Amar was dancing and singing, he saw the puppet flying into the garden. Sensing trouble, he quickly became invisible. The puppet could not find Amar but swooped down on Baghban and took him to the Shahanshah.

Afrasiyab was waiting for his vizier and subjected him to several lashes of his whip. 'Why, you disloyal wretch,' he shouted, 'how dare you shelter my enemy!' Baghban begged for mercy and explained how he had waylaid a sahir who had captured Amar. He pleaded with Afrasiyab to release him so that he could find the wretched deceiver. Afrasiyab realized that the vizier was sincerely contrite and let him go. Baghban hastened back to his garden to capture Amar.

After the slave-boy had left with Baghban, Amar had become visible again and managed to render Gulcheen unconscious. He rolled her up in a carpet and left her in a corner before assuming her form. When Baghban returned to the garden, he greeted the false Gulcheen who informed him that Amar had disappeared yet again. Baghban sat with his wife and related how he had been humiliated in the durbar. 'Because of Amar,' he said, 'I was chastised publicly. I have to arrest him before he crosses the river.'

After Baghban left the garden, Amar thought of a plan to escape from Batin, the invisible Tilism. He sent for Baghban's daughters, Nihal and Samar. When they came to meet their false mother, Amar hugged them warmly and said, 'My daughters, your father has gone to look for Amar but I am worried as Amar is a seasoned ayyar and may harm him. Let us also help him in his quest.'

The girls agreed and the false Gulcheen asked them to summon a flying throne. Nihal smashed a citron on the ground and moments later, a throne flew into the garden. Amar and Nihal ascended the throne and left Samar to keep watch on the garden. 'Now my daughter,' said Amar to Nihal, 'let me see how much magic you know. Can you fly this throne to the river or do you just play around all day?' Nihal chanted a spell that made the throne fly to the River of Flowing Blood. The false Gulcheen muttered under her breath and declared, 'My magic informs me that Amar has crossed the river and is wandering in the forest beyond the shore. Let us quickly fly there and arrest him.' Nihal read another incantation and the throne flew over the river.

Baghban, who had been looking for Amar, untied a tiny figurine wrapped around his arm and chanted a prayer. As the figurine came to life, Baghban asked it, 'O Image of Samri, tell me where Amar is!' The figurine replied, 'He is disguised as your wife and has just crossed the river with your daughter. He is about to kill her!'

Amar had crossed the river with Nihal and was thinking of his next move when Baghban arrived on the scene shouting, 'Wait you wily rogue! I have arrived!' Nihal was astounded to hear her father's voice and looked around to see who he was addressing. Amar slapped Nihal, became invisible and jumped off the throne while calling out, 'I am the king of ayyari! Baghban, you are a lucky man or I would have sent you straight to hell today!'

Baghban looked ruefully at his daughter and told her, 'You enabled Amar to cross the river, my girl.' Nihal was still reeling from Amar's slap and Baghban took her home, where he looked for the real Gulcheen and found her rolled up in a carpet. After she regained consciousness and when the household had recovered from Amar's onslaught, Baghban told his family, 'Amar must have reached his tent now. I will capture him there and present him to the king.'

Gulcheen pleaded tearfully with her husband not to meddle with the tricksters. 'Have you not seen how helpless the Shah is against them? You will just get yourself killed!' Baghban was reluctant to openly agree with her, but saw the wisdom of her words. He returned to the durbar and related to Afrasiyab how Amar had escaped this time. Afrasiyab remained silent and did not chastise his vizier any more for fear of losing him to the rebels as well.

Sharara, the Warrior Witch

As Amar was making his way back to his camp, Qiran and the rest of his ayyar companions met him on the way. Mahrukh Magic-eye came out into the forest to meet them, delighted with Amar's return. A sahir from Hairat's army came upon them in the forest and on recognizing them, called out, 'You can be joyous today but tomorrow you will surely die!' Mahrukh called back, 'Who can kill us except Allah?' The sahir retorted, 'That may be so, but I was in Hairat's durbar when Afrasiyab sent her a message that Princess Sharara, the Warrior Witch will be sent tomorrow to tackle you.'

The sahir went on his way but Mahrukh paled visibly on hearing Sharara's name. Amar comforted her, 'Don't you worry Malika! I am back and Allah is great. I will go now to deal with Sharara before she reaches Hairat's camp!' The other ayyars also went in different directions to look for Sharara.

Barq Firangi reached the plains besides the River of Flowing Blood assuming that Sharara would have to pass that way. As he waited, he saw three beautiful women on a swing. The women called out to him in melodious voices and said, 'Come to us, O Barq, we are waiting for you!' Barq sensed that this was a trap and bolted in the opposite direction. When he stopped running, he saw the three women and the swing again. He turned in another direction and ran away. But wherever he stopped, he saw the same women calling out, 'Come here you silly man! How long will you escape from us!' Finally, Barq surrendered to them and said, 'Look I am an ayyar. You will regret capturing me!' The women laughed at him and after tying him to a chain, made their way to Afrasiyab.

Meanwhile, Amar had been looking for Sharara. He came upon a lush glade with trees on all sides and decided to set a trap for Sharara there as he felt that she would surely want to rest in such an attractive spot. He took out bottles of perfumed water that contained a powerful narcotic from Zambil and liberally sprayed all the trees and grass with it. He then took out garlands with flowers infused with the same perfume and hung them on the trees. Finally, he waited behind some trees in the guise of a frail old woman leaning on a stick.

Some time later, Amar saw some women dragging Barq on a chain. Amar, disguised as the old crone, hobbled over to them, wailing loudly. The women stopped to inquire out of sympathy and Amar said, 'My ladies, please retrieve my silver *paandaan* from this wily thief before I die for want of tobacco. This shameless man has robbed me thrice already! I am the royal custodian of this forest.'

Barq looked closely at the old woman and recognized Amar in an old woman's guise. He played along and begged the women to release him in exchange for the stolen goods. Furious with his impudence, the women hit him repeatedly until he cried, 'Don't be angry, I will give the container back to you. It is hidden in a cave close to where this woman lives.' The witches asked the old woman to lead them to her house and Amar led them through the glade that he had prepared for Sharara. As they walked through it, the drugged perfume affected them and they fell down unconscious. Amar and Barq promptly cut their heads off and the forest resounded with the howling of their spirits. There was a furious shower of stones and flames but Amar and Barq calmly stripped the dead witches of their expensive clothes and jewels and ran out of the forest.

The caretakers of the forest brought the corpses of the dead witches to the King of Sahirs. Afrasiyab was outraged when he saw the bodies and roared, 'O Sharara, Warrior Witch! Come to me at once!' Moments later, the skies reddened with flames and a pit of flames opened up before Afrasiyab. From this pit, a beautiful, fierce-looking woman emerged wearing ruby coloured robes and ruby jewellery that adorned her from head to toe. As she greeted the Shahanshah, he thundered, 'Proceed at once with your army to Hairat's camp. You are to destroy the enemy. Do not spare a single person!'

Sharara withdrew into the pit of flames and returned to her castle. She left for Hairat's camp with her army of one lakh sahir soldiers amidst blazing flames. After reaching there, she was entertained with wine and dancing. Later, Sharara wrote a message to Mahrukh that read, 'I am Sharara and as you know well, both magic and trickery are wasted on me. You cannot confront me, therefore, surrender to me. Otherwise I shall punish you hideously!'

Mahrukh received the note and wrote back, 'I am an ordinary servant of Amar and do not acknowledge that haramzada Afrasiyab or his immoral wife Hairat! Sharara do what you will; my God is greater than you!' Sharara became furious on reading this message but decided to wait until the night was over to deal with the forces of Islam.

The next morning, Mahrukh led her army into the battlefield. Sharara sprouted wings of flames and flew to the sky. From very high, she hurled a coconut at Mahrukh's forces. Suddenly, thousands of black snakes expelling flames appeared on the battleground. The flames spread throughout the battlefield and bound the soldiers like chains. Mahrukh and her commanders cast counterspells that made magical rain and cooled the flames.

Sharara signalled her army to attack at this time. Mahrukh, Bahar, Nafarman and the others fought bravely and caused a lot of damage to Sharara's army. Sharara then threw another coconut from the skies and produced a sheet of flames that extended over Mahrukh's army. Mahrukh and the senior commanders could not extinguish the flames this time and fled to save their lives, followed by their army.

Glowing with triumph, Sharara returned to her camp. That evening, a feast was held in her honour. The ayyars witnessed their army's defeat from a safe distance and prepared to tackle Sharara. Qiran was the first to approach her pavilion. As soon as he tried to step inside, a voice called out, 'Beware Sharara! Qiran is coming!' Qiran ran away and the other ayyars did not dare approach her pavilion for fear of arrest. They returned to where Mahrukh's army had taken refuge and told Mahrukh that they were helpless against Sharara. As this news spread, a ripple of despair passed through the ranks of the soldiers. Amar also reached at that time and wept to see the condition of his army.

Sharara was watching the dancing held in her honour when she got a message from Afrasiyab that read, 'We have consulted the oracle Book of Samri and learnt that the traitors to our salt are hiding in Mount Lajward. Attack now and capture them all.' Sharara mobilized her army and surrounded the defeated army with her sahirs. Amar then advised Mahrukh and the others to pretend to capitulate to Sharara.

Accordingly, Mahrukh and her commanders humbly approached Sharara holding trays heaped with jewels. Sharara saw them coming with their hands tied with scarves and smiled in triumph. Mahrukh ran forward, fell at Sharara's feet and begged for clemency. Sharara spoke to her enemies graciously, delighted that she had managed to resolve this matter amicably for the Shahanshah. She led them to her pavilion and seated the rebel commanders there.

Amar joined his commanders a little later and Sharara welcomed him as well. After offering wine to him, Sharara read an incantation so that a veil of flames hid her from sight. 'Will you not sit with us, O Malika?' Amar asked her. Sharara called out from behind the flames: 'Amar, for fear of you I keep myself hidden!' Amar responded, 'If you doubt my integrity, then why should I be here? I will leave at once!' Sharara replied, 'Do not be offended! I will emerge now!' A single flame leapt out from the wall of fire on to the throne and slowly petered out to reveal Sharara. Amar came forward and said, 'Malika, may I serve you wine?' Sharara laughed heartily, 'What? Will you make me unconscious?' Amar cried, 'Heaven forbid! I will never mention wine again!'

Meanwhile, Afrasiyab consulted the oracle Book of Samri in his durbar and discovered that Amar had every intention of tricking and killing Sharara. Afrasiyab sent a magic slave-boy with a message to warn Sharara. She read the warning and muttered a spell so that Amar and his commanders were trapped within a well of flames. They cried out, 'Malika, why do you punish us?' Sharara replied, 'You would have deceived me but my king has warned me of your intentions!' The rebel sardars were now truly convinced that this was the end for them.

Mehtar Qiran was waiting with the lashkar and heard of what happened to the sardars. He took a sahir soldier from his lashkar aside and asked him to conjure a peacock. The sahir sculpted a peacock from wax and brought it to life. Qiran harnessed the peacock with a saddle of gold cloth and strings of pearls and diamonds. Then he assumed Afrasiyab's form and mounted the peacock. His sahir attendant flew the peacock towards Sharara's pavilion, conjuring flames and stones all the while so that it looked as if a powerful sahir was on his way.

Sharara was about to leave with her prisoners when she saw the signs of the impending arrival of a high-ranking sahir. Soon, she saw Afrasiyab mounted on a magic peacock, wearing rich attire and his crown. Sharara emerged from behind her protective veil of flames and went forward to greet him with trays of jewels as homage. Afrasiyab jumped off his swan and called out, 'Praise be to you princess! How soon you have resolved this war!'

The false Afrasiyab came close to the sahira and whispered, 'Sharara, I went to the Dome of Samri and was blessed with a wondrous spell that enables me to foretell the future for twelve years. If you close your eyes and recite the name of Samri thrice, I will tell you how it can be done.' Sharara glowed with pride at being favoured thus and led the false Afrasiyab to a secluded area in the mountains, hidden from her army. There, she sat on the ground, closed her eyes and called out 'Ya Samri' three times. Qiran, who was waiting for such an opportunity, drew out his *bughda* and smashed her head. Sharara went straight to hell and her spirits howled with rage.

The circle of flames around Mahrukh and her friends disappeared suddenly and they heard loud voices calling out, 'Alas you have killed Sharara, the Warrior Princess!' Amar cried out in joy, 'Malika Mahrukh, that *harami* is dead! Attack her army right now!' Mahrukh and her commanders flew to the skies from where they wreaked havoc on Sharara's army. Surkh Mu loosened her tresses and thousands of stars fell from the skies and shot like arrows towards the soldiers. Bahar tossed her magic bouquets and her lethal gardens enchanted thousands of enemy soldiers.

Some of Sharara's soldiers managed to escape and ran to Afrasiyab's durbar. Hairat, who was on her way to meet Sharara, was informed that she had been killed and returned despondently to her camp. After annihilating Sharara's army, Mahrukh Magic-eye also returned to their old campsite and finally, her army rested after their recent ordeal.

The grandson of Samri

Afrasiyab called Hairat from her camp for a private consultation and told her, 'I have been thinking of informing the grandson of Samri who lives in our realm about this trouble with our enemies. He can destroy them within minutes from his own palace before they become too powerful!' Hairat was thoughtful for a while and then said, 'Khudawand Dawood is not an ordinary mortal that you can send him a message. You will have to call on him yourself. Perhaps it would be more prudent to call his half-brother Mussavir Jadoo. He is also as invincible and powerful as Dawood. The only difference is that Dawood's mother was

rt from their destination. Her army spread out in the plain and the
ls around it, and huge cauldrons of food were cooked for the soldiers.

To recollect recent events, Sarsar Sword-fighter had abducted Ra'ad
d was on her way to deliver him to Mussavir. She came upon Soorat
igar's camp on the way and thought with some relief, 'Now I won't
ave to travel that far. I can deliver Ra'ad to Tareek's mother directly!'
he went to the durbar pavilion where Soorat Nigar had summoned her.
here, Soorat Nigar was sitting on a throne surrounded by hundreds of
ahirs. Sarsar greeted the Malika deferentially, laid the pushtara with
a'ad tied in it at her feet and said, 'I have captured the sinner Ra'ad
nd offer him to you.'

Soorat Nigar was delighted with Sarsar and awarded her with a heavy
khalat robe and seated her in a place of honour. After a while, when Sarsar
had left, Soorat Nigar said, 'Summon Princess Almas to our durbar so that
she can execute her brother's murderer herself.' Almas Fairy-face had been
strolling in the hills with several of her companions when she was summoned
and came to the durbar adorned in rich robes and jewels. Soorat Nigar
glowed with pride at seeing her beautiful daughter and made a gesture
to ward off any evil eye. By this time, Ra'ad too had gained consciousness
and Soorat Nigar greeted him with a volley of abuses.

Almas looked at Ra'ad and saw a young man, about twenty-two years
of age, whose handsome, noble face shone like the moon. Almas Fairy-
face lost her heart a thousand times at this sight and felt as if she could
die for her beloved. At the same time, she was aware of the hopelessness
of her situation and began weeping softly. Soorat Nigar, unaware of
Almas's thoughts, tried to comfort her by saying, 'My daughter, your
tears will not bring your brother back to life, you will just ruin your
health with your grief.' Others in the durbar fussed over Almas as well.
When their attention was focussed on her, Ra'ad looked up and saw a
beautiful young damsel watching him with tears in her eyes. The young
sahir sensed her longing and fell in love with her as deeply, but remained
helpless and silent.

Just then, Soorat Nigar received a message from her husband that urged
her to take the young prisoner to Hairat's camp. The message said, 'We
can behead him in full view of his friends and punish anyone who tries to
rescue him.' Accordingly, she ordered her officers to keep Ra'ad in chains
within a circle of magic flames that night. After the guards took him away,
Almas felt restless and asked her mother if she could retire for the night as
she was exhausted. After her mother gave her permission to leave, she
returned to her pavilion with her special attendant, the eunuch Mian Ishrat,
who was in charge of her litter, riding alongside.

married to Samri's son and Mussavir's mother was a slave.' Afrasiyab
agreed with this plan and wrote a letter to Mussavir informing him of all
that had passed since Mahrukh's rebellion.

Mussavir the magic artist was in his durbar in the capital city of
Azhrang when he received Afrasiyab's message. He expressed great
sympathy with Afrasiyab and announced in his durbar, 'I must take an
army and help him out!' His son Tareek Face-sketcher offered to go
instead. 'It will give me a chance to exercise my magic Father,' said the
young prince, 'and besides, it is not appropriate for you to confront a
handful of rebels!' Mussavir was reluctant but finally relented on Tareek's
insistence. He sent a message to Afrasiyab that his son would represent
him. He then advised Tareek to confront and decimate the rebels before
meeting Afrasiyab. Mussavir spent the rest of the day tutoring Tareek in
battle strategies and gave him several tips on magic warfare.

Hairat received Tareek Face-sketcher in her camp with a guard of
honour and escorted him to her pavilion where a feast was laid out for
him. Spy birds informed Mahrukh of his arrival but Mahrukh was
unmoved and said, 'If it had been Mussavir the magic artist, I would
have been worried. But this boy can be confronted easily with Allah's
help!' Saying this, she prepared her forces for battle the next morning.

Tareek spent that night in his tent drawing portraits of his enemy
commanders. Finally, the spinning disc of time slashed the veil of night
and dressed the sun in robes of heavenly light. The hearts of the brave
ones filled with courage and fervour as the hour of battle approached.
Tareek rode on his magic dragon on to the battlefield and after displaying
some feats of magic, called out arrogantly, 'O traitors and rebels, see
how I will destroy you in minutes!'

Mahrukh came forward and said, 'Listen, you foolish boy, do not
be so proud for very soon, you will leave this world!' Tareek took out
a puppet likeness of Mahrukh and cried, 'In the name of Samri, arrest
Mahrukh!' The puppet came to life and started for Mahrukh who called
out, 'Alas, this puppet has Tareek's body but not his head. No matter,
I can provide that!' No sooner had she uttered these words than the
puppet assumed Tareek's features and turned back to attack him instead.
Tareek hurriedly muttered a spell to make his puppet lifeless. Mahrukh
cast other spells on him, which he neutralized just in time. As he was
fighting with her, Tareek tried to quickly sketch a likeness of Mahrukh
with an enchanted pencil. Seeing the inexperienced Tareek thus
absorbed, Ra'ad Jadoo stamped hard on the ground and tore into the
earth while his mother Barq Mehshar flew to the sky. Ra'ad emerged
close to Tareek who was busy warding off Mahrukh's attacks and did

not notice him. Ra'ad's piercing scream deafened Tareek and he fell down from his dragon mount. Just as his soldiers were rushing forward to help him, Barq Mehshar fell upon him in the form of a bolt of lightning and cleaved his body in half.

There was an almighty din as Tareek's spirits howled, 'You have killed me, Tareek Face-sketcher, great grandson of Samri!' Mahrukh and her army now fell on Tareek's soldiers who were devastated at the sight of their commander's slain body and fought back ferociously. A fierce battle ensued and it seemed as if there was a downpour of metal weapons on the battlefield. Finally, Tareek's lashkar fled from the battlefield with his body. Hairat saw that the course of the battle had changed in Mahrukh's favour and had the drums of peace struck. Mahrukh returned to her camp in triumph and showered Barq Mehshar and her son with jewels.

The defeated soldiers of Tareek's army took his maimed body to Afrasiyab who was deeply distressed. 'Alas!' he cried, 'Tareek was his father's only son! I feel responsible for his death!' Tareek was cremated with due honours, after which Afrasiyab sent a letter to Mussavir that read, 'O Grandson of Samri, your son fought valiantly and went into Samri's service. In other words, he is dead.' Then, Afrasiyab ordered Sarsar to capture Ra'ad Jadoo so that Mussavir could punish his son's killer.

Sarsar captures Ra'ad Jadoo

Sarsar set off immediately for the enemy camp disguised as a maidservant and managed to station herself behind Ra'ad Jadoo. Amar, who was in the durbar at the time, recognized her at once. He rose from his seat casually, but Sarsar realized that he had recognized her and moved swiftly out of reach. Amar called out, 'O slave-girl, why do you run?' Sarsar retorted sharply, 'O Ghulam, even your father cannot dream of owning a slave!' She then ran out of sight and though Amar chased her, she got away. Mahrukh was shocked at the maidservant's impudence and cried out, 'Who was that impertinent hussy who insulted Khwaja sahib?' Amar replied, 'It was Sarsar Sword-fighter and she is after Ra'ad. We must remain vigilant.' Mahrukh and her commanders retired to their tents, but did not rest for fear of Sarsar capturing Ra'ad.

Realizing that her presence in the camp had been detected, Sarsar disguised herself as Barq Mehshar and went to Ra'ad's tent late that night. After telling the guards on duty that she had come to protect her son from Sarsar, the false Barq Mehshar entered the tent. As Ra'ad was sleeping at the time, it was easy for Sarsar to render him unconscious. She did not

have the time to tie him up in pushtara and just hoisted hi her shoulder. Ra'ad's guards saw her running out of the tent and raised an alarm. Hearing their cries, Amar chased her who was entering the camp just then saw her dashing a about to smash her head with his bughda when Amar saw out, 'Harm her and you will have to answer to me!' Qiran s tracks and in the confusion, Sarsar dropped Ra'ad and ran urgency to escape from him.

Amar and Qiran untied Ra'ad and woke him up. They back to the camp and urged him to remain alert. Once everyon again, Sarsar re-entered the camp disguised as a saucy young She walked past Ra'ad's tent and smiled archly at the guards. their watch, the guards called out to her and asked her to s some wine. Sarsar poured out goblets of her drugged wine an the guards were unconscious. Ra'ad was asleep inside his tent a made sure that he was unconscious before she tied him up in a one was there to stop Sarsar this time and she went straig Shahanshah, who ordered her to deliver the captured sahir to Jadoo in the city of Azhrang.

Ra'ad and Almas Fairy-face

Now hear about what happened in Azhrang: After Afrasiyab's mes puppet conveyed the news of Tareek's death to his father, Mussavi bitterly and the whole court went into mourning. Tareek's mother S Nigar fainted when she heard of her son's death. After she awok tore her garments apart and cried, 'My son, you are hidden fron sight! Alas, where has death taken you? Who gave you the evil Soorat Nigar's grief touched the hearts of her companions and relat and their tears fell like the spring rain.

Later, Tareek's parents decided to avenge their son's death destroying the rebels and prepared their army for battle. Their daugh Almas Fairy-face also insisted on accompanying them. Her mother Soor Nigar tried to dissuade her daughter and told her, 'My child, you ai young and not well-versed in the arts of magic and warfare.' Howeve Almas was adamant and Soorat Nigar finally agreed to take her daughte along. Soorat Nigar and Almas Fairy-face left in a magnificent procession while Mussavir stayed behind for a day to hand over the state's administration to a regent in his absence.

Soorat Nigar and her army travelled towards Hairat's lashkar and by evening decided that they would camp in a place that was a day's march

We will now return to Mahrukh's camp where Ra'ad's capture had caused a great uproar. Barq Mehshar was sick with worry over her son's disappearance and Amar promised her that they would find Ra'ad. Amar left the camp to look for Ra'ad and met Barq on the way. Barq decided to assist Amar in his search for Ra'ad and soon enough, came upon Soorat Nigar's camp. Barq, disguised as a sahir, began wandering through the camp, and saw Ra'ad being led out of the durbar in chains. Immediately, he began thinking of ways to rescue him.

A little later, Barq saw Princess Almas and her attendants. When he realized that she was Mussavir's daughter, he followed her to her pavilion. He observed that Mian Ishrat, who had escorted the princess back to her tent, was now enjoying a smoke in a secluded place. Barq managed to engage the eunuch in gossip about Hairat's camp and soon overcome him with drugged vapours. Barq dragged him behind some bushes and then quickly disguised himself as the eunuch.

Princess Almas Fairy-face was still thinking of Ra'ad and dismissed her attendants as she wanted to be on her own. Barq approached her tent stealthily and overheard her sighing, 'O Ra'ad, I could die for one more glimpse of you!' Barq realized that Almas was in love with Ra'ad and went forward to speak to her. On seeing the royal attendant, the princess tried to compose herself, but Barq whispered in her ear, 'Princess, I am aware of your secret; do not hide it from me. I am your devoted slave. If you so desire, I will try and pluck stars from the sky for you.' Thus reassured, the princess confessed that she was in love with Ra'ad. At this point, Barq decided to take her into confidence and told her, 'Princess, I am not your eunuch but an ayyar and have come to rescue Ra'ad. Tell his guards that you want to interrogate your brother's killer. Once they open the ring of flames around him for you, I will manage an escape.'

The princess laughed like a blossoming flower when she heard this and lost no time in sending for her palanquin. Barq, still disguised as Mian Ishrat, accompanied her. Folad, the captain of the guards, received them both and on the princess's request, dispelled the ring of flames around the prisoner. While the princess was with the prisoner, Barq offered Folad and the guards drugged wine and when they fell unconscious, he promptly beheaded all of them. This was followed by total darkness and the camp resounded with the wailing of their spirits. The princess was terrified and Ra'ad's magical shackles melted with Folad's death. Barq wanted to leave the camp with Ra'ad immediately, but Almas insisted that her tent would be safe for Ra'ad to rest after his ordeal.

The news of the prisoner's escape soon reached Soorat Nigar who flew around the camp looking for him. She thought of warning her daughter against the escaped prisoner and walked into her tent, only to see Almas Fairy-face and Ra'ad in each other's arms. In sheer rage, she cast a spell that made the earth under them tremble and fly upwards. Ra'ad and Almas found themselves flying in the air and Ra'ad tried to chant a spell to release them both, but realized that he was tongue-tied. Then, Soorat Nigar cast another spell that made the piece of earth on which the lovers stood divide in mid-air. The two pieces of earth took Ra'ad in one direction and the princess in another and the lovers wept on seeing that they were being drawn apart. Soon, they were out of each other's sight.

Barq, who was watching all this anxiously, did not know which one of them to follow. Eventually, he went straight to Barq Mehshar and related to her all that had happened. Barq Mehshar rushed like lightning to the enemy camp and fell upon the piece of earth carrying the princess first. She caught the princess and flew upwards, holding her by the waist. Soorat Nigar saw what was happening and cast a spell that made several puppets fly towards Barq Mehshar. Soon, the puppets had brought her down to the ground.

Soorat Nigar now wrote something on a piece of paper and gave it to a messenger puppet that promptly vanished. Moments later, the earth cleaved open and a sahir emerged from it. Soorat Nigar addressed him solemnly, 'O Zalim Black-face, I have summoned you to entrust my daughter and these two prisoners to your custody. Taking them back to my camp will bring us disgrace. Everyone will come to know that the daughter of Mussavir is in love with a traitor. Moreover, it is easier for ayyars to rescue them if they are in the camp.' Zalim immediately conjured a tower around the three prisoners.

Soorat Nigar confronts the rebels

Soorat Nigar flew back to her camp and ordered that they were to move. The next day, they reached Hairat's camp and after the usual courtesies, Soorat Nigar confided in Hairat, 'We are both naked in the same bath my sister! Your daughter Khubsoorat is in love with Mahrukh's son and my daughter Almas is infatuated with that traitor Ra'ad Jadoo! Strike the battle drums in my name as I am determined to destroy the rebels and avenge my son's death!'. The drums of battle were struck on both sides and the night was alive with the sound of armour being prepared for battle the next morning.

Mahrukh and Bahar were the first to enter the battlefield the next morning. They conjured rainfall to settle the dust on the field and their soldiers fell into battle formations. Soorat Nigar and Hairat emerged with great ceremony, surrounded by their commanders. Soorat Nigar went forward on her magic dragon and challenged the rebels. Bahar Jadoo decided to face her first.

Soorat Nigar initiated the battle by smashing a coconut. Thousands of shadows emerged from it and rushed menacingly towards Bahar. In turn, Bahar smiled and a long string of pearls materialized before her. Bahar climbed up on the string, and conjured flames that fell on the spectres and burnt them to ashes. Soorat Nigar then sketched a portrait of Bahar and flung it on the string of pearls. The portrait came to life and expelled flames from its mouth that burnt the string of pearls. Bahar fell down, but recovered quickly and plucked a few strands of hair off her head, which she flung at the portrait. The strands of hair coiled around the picture like ropes and dragged it to Bahar, who shredded it with magic scissors.

Bahar then threw a bouquet that expelled a shower of gold and silver flowers at Soorat Nigar and her companions. In no time, they were all enchanted and swayed as they chanted lyrics in praise of Bahar's beauty. Just then, the earth opened and puppets emerged from it and gathered the enchanted flowers. They called out to Soorat Nigar, 'Malika, you are the wife of the grandson of Samri and you have been enchanted by a mere slip of a girl. Remember your status!'

Soorat Nigar was jolted back to awareness on hearing these words and fell upon Bahar with her sword. Hairat ordered her troops to attack at the same time and Mahrukh's army also joined in the fray. As the armies clashed with each other, there were fierce storms and bursts of flames and rain. The battleground looked as if it was blooming with flowers of blood. In the midst of battle, Soorat Nigar turned to Hairat in fury and declared, 'That chit of a girl Bahar has embarrassed me today. Tonight I will draw magic portraits of all enemy commanders and will kill them tomorrow!' 'As you wish,' replied Hairat. As they were talking, the earth before them split open as a slave-boy emerged from it and gave Hairat a message from her husband. Afrasiyab had summoned Hairat to meet him at the Dome of Light and Hairat left the battlefield to adorn herself for him. Before leaving, she ordered Sarsar to protect Soorat Nigar against tricksters.

That night, Amar and his comrades tried to kidnap and trick Soorat Nigar several times and even succeeded a couple of times. However, Sarsar was more than a match for them and saved Soorat Nigar from being executed. When Hairat returned the next morning, Soorat Nigar looked visibly pale and distressed and said, 'If it were not for Sarsar, my sister, you would have found me dead for sure.' As Hairat and Soorat Nigar talked to each other, Afrasiyab also arrived at the camp. After learning of Soorat Nigar's troubles with the ayyars, he said, 'Why do you bother to fight them? Rest easy and I will deal with the rebels now!' He sketched a magical sign in the air and within minutes, there was a shower of golden raindrops from the sky that came together to form a sahir. 'Baraan Jadoo, I appoint you as officer to confront the rebels. Arrest them for me!' said Afrasiyab to the young sahir, who kneeled low in obeisance. Then Baraan disappeared from sight in a shower of golden raindrops. A little later, Afrasiyab too returned to the Garden of Apples.

A magical shower or Baraan Jadoo

The youthful and confident Baraan Jadoo lost no time in assembling his army to confront Mahrukh's forces. Before settling into his quarters, he decided to call on the enemy and set off for Mahrukh's durbar. He walked into the durbar before his entry could be announced and calmly sat down on an empty chair. Then he addressed the rebel commanders in a contemptuous tone, 'Be warned you traitors, I have come to punish you for your treachery.' The durbar was too stunned by his audacity to respond, but Amar quickly flicked his whip and trapped Baraan in its coils. Baraan, in turn, transformed into a vaporous cloud and vanished amidst thunder and lightning. Amar turned to Mahrukh and asked, 'How does his magic work?'

'Khwaja, Baraan conjures a magical rainfall and the raindrops transform his enemies into trees,' explained Mahrukh. 'He was always a subordinate of Ra'ad and Barq Mehshar. Alas, had they been with us, we could have vanquished him with ease.' Amar decided that the two captured sardars needed to be released urgently and went to the edge of his camp. He summoned his ayyar colleagues using Zafeel, the whistle of ayyari. After directing them to find Barq Mehshar and Ra'ad, Amar and all the ayyars went off in different directions.

Baraan entered the battlefield early next morning. Too arrogant to lead the fight, he gestured to some of his officers to commence battle. Sardars like Surkh Mu Deadly-locks disposed of them with ease. Seeing this, Baraan angrily strode into the battleground and immediately muttered a spell that caused a large black cloud to drift in over the area where Mahrukh's forces were standing. As they looked up uneasily at the cloud, it released deadly raindrops and many of Mahrukh's soldiers slowly turned into trees with branches and leaves sprouting from them.

married to Samri's son and Mussavir's mother was a slave.' Afrasiyab agreed with this plan and wrote a letter to Mussavir informing him of all that had passed since Mahrukh's rebellion.

Mussavir the magic artist was in his durbar in the capital city of Azhrang when he received Afrasiyab's message. He expressed great sympathy with Afrasiyab and announced in his durbar, 'I must take an army and help him out!' His son Tareek Face-sketcher offered to go instead. 'It will give me a chance to exercise my magic Father,' said the young prince, 'and besides, it is not appropriate for you to confront a handful of rebels!' Mussavir was reluctant but finally relented on Tareek's insistence. He sent a message to Afrasiyab that his son would represent him. He then advised Tareek to confront and decimate the rebels before meeting Afrasiyab. Mussavir spent the rest of the day tutoring Tareek in battle strategies and gave him several tips on magic warfare.

Hairat received Tareek Face-sketcher in her camp with a guard of honour and escorted him to her pavilion where a feast was laid out for him. Spy birds informed Mahrukh of his arrival but Mahrukh was unmoved and said, 'If it had been Mussavir the magic artist, I would have been worried. But this boy can be confronted easily with Allah's help!' Saying this, she prepared her forces for battle the next morning.

Tareek spent that night in his tent drawing portraits of his enemy commanders. Finally, the spinning disc of time slashed the veil of night and dressed the sun in robes of heavenly light. The hearts of the brave ones filled with courage and fervour as the hour of battle approached. Tareek rode on his magic dragon on to the battlefield and after displaying some feats of magic, called out arrogantly, 'O traitors and rebels, see how I will destroy you in minutes!'

Mahrukh came forward and said, 'Listen, you foolish boy, do not be so proud for very soon, you will leave this world!' Tareek took out a puppet likeness of Mahrukh and cried, 'In the name of Samri, arrest Mahrukh!' The puppet came to life and started for Mahrukh who called out, 'Alas, this puppet has Tareek's body but not his head. No matter, I can provide that!' No sooner had she uttered these words than the puppet assumed Tareek's features and turned back to attack him instead. Tareek hurriedly muttered a spell to make his puppet lifeless. Mahrukh cast other spells on him, which he neutralized just in time. As he was fighting with her, Tareek tried to quickly sketch a likeness of Mahrukh with an enchanted pencil. Seeing the inexperienced Tareek thus absorbed, Ra'ad Jadoo stamped hard on the ground and tore into the earth while his mother Barq Mehshar flew to the sky. Ra'ad emerged close to Tareek who was busy warding off Mahrukh's attacks and did not notice him. Ra'ad's piercing scream deafened Tareek and he fell down from his dragon mount. Just as his soldiers were rushing forward to help him, Barq Mehshar fell upon him in the form of a bolt of lightning and cleaved his body in half.

There was an almighty din as Tareek's spirits howled, 'You have killed me, Tareek Face-sketcher, great grandson of Samri!' Mahrukh and her army now fell on Tareek's soldiers who were devastated at the sight of their commander's slain body and fought back ferociously. A fierce battle ensued and it seemed as if there was a downpour of metal weapons on the battlefield. Finally, Tareek's lashkar fled from the battlefield with his body. Hairat saw that the course of the battle had changed in Mahrukh's favour and had the drums of peace struck. Mahrukh returned to her camp in triumph and showered Barq Mehshar and her son with jewels.

The defeated soldiers of Tareek's army took his maimed body to Afrasiyab who was deeply distressed. 'Alas!' he cried, 'Tareek was his father's only son! I feel responsible for his death!' Tareek was cremated with due honours, after which Afrasiyab sent a letter to Mussavir that read, 'O Grandson of Samri, your son fought valiantly and went into Samri's service. In other words, he is dead.' Then, Afrasiyab ordered Sarsar to capture Ra'ad Jadoo so that Mussavir could punish his son's killer.

Sarsar captures Ra'ad Jadoo

Sarsar set off immediately for the enemy camp disguised as a maidservant and managed to station herself behind Ra'ad Jadoo. Amar, who was in the durbar at the time, recognized her at once. He rose from his seat casually, but Sarsar realized that he had recognized her and moved swiftly out of reach. Amar called out, 'O slave-girl, why do you run?' Sarsar retorted sharply, 'O Ghulam, even your father cannot dream of owning a slave!' She then ran out of sight and though Amar chased her, she got away. Mahrukh was shocked at the maidservant's impudence and cried out, 'Who was that impertinent hussy who insulted Khwaja sahib?' Amar replied, 'It was Sarsar Sword-fighter and she is after Ra'ad. We must remain vigilant.' Mahrukh and her commanders retired to their tents, but did not rest for fear of Sarsar capturing Ra'ad.

Realizing that her presence in the camp had been detected, Sarsar disguised herself as Barq Mehshar and went to Ra'ad's tent late that night. After telling the guards on duty that she had come to protect her son from Sarsar, the false Barq Mehshar entered the tent. As Ra'ad was sleeping at the time, it was easy for Sarsar to render him unconscious. She did not have the time to tie him up in pushtara and just hoisted his limp body on her shoulder. Ra'ad's guards saw her running out of the tent in this manner and raised an alarm. Hearing their cries, Amar chased her as well. Qiran, who was entering the camp just then saw her dashing away and was about to smash her head with his bughda when Amar saw him and cried out, 'Harm her and you will have to answer to me!' Qiran stopped in his tracks and in the confusion, Sarsar dropped Ra'ad and ran away in her urgency to escape from him.

Amar and Qiran untied Ra'ad and woke him up. They brought him back to the camp and urged him to remain alert. Once everyone was asleep again, Sarsar re-entered the camp disguised as a saucy young wine seller. She walked past Ra'ad's tent and smiled archly at the guards. Bored with their watch, the guards called out to her and asked her to serve them some wine. Sarsar poured out goblets of her drugged wine and soon, all the guards were unconscious. Ra'ad was asleep inside his tent and Sarsar made sure that he was unconscious before she tied him up in a sheet. No one was there to stop Sarsar this time and she went straight to the Shahanshah, who ordered her to deliver the captured sahir to Mussavir Jadoo in the city of Azhrang.

Ra'ad and Almas Fairy-face

Now hear about what happened in Azhrang: After Afrasiyab's messenger puppet conveyed the news of Tareek's death to his father, Mussavir wept bitterly and the whole court went into mourning. Tareek's mother Soorat Nigar fainted when she heard of her son's death. After she awoke, she tore her garments apart and cried, 'My son, you are hidden from my sight! Alas, where has death taken you? Who gave you the evil eye?' Soorat Nigar's grief touched the hearts of her companions and relatives and their tears fell like the spring rain.

Later, Tareek's parents decided to avenge their son's death by destroying the rebels and prepared their army for battle. Their daughter Almas Fairy-face also insisted on accompanying them. Her mother Soorat Nigar tried to dissuade her daughter and told her, 'My child, you are young and not well-versed in the arts of magic and warfare.' However, Almas was adamant and Soorat Nigar finally agreed to take her daughter along. Soorat Nigar and Almas Fairy-face left in a magnificent procession, while Mussavir stayed behind for a day to hand over the state's administration to a regent in his absence.

Soorat Nigar and her army travelled towards Hairat's lashkar and by evening decided that they would camp in a place that was a day's march short from their destination. Her army spread out in the plain and the hills around it, and huge cauldrons of food were cooked for the soldiers.

To recollect recent events, Sarsar Sword-fighter had abducted Ra'ad and was on her way to deliver him to Mussavir. She came upon Soorat Nigar's camp on the way and thought with some relief, 'Now I won't have to travel that far. I can deliver Ra'ad to Tareek's mother directly!' She went to the durbar pavilion where Soorat Nigar had summoned her. There, Soorat Nigar was sitting on a throne surrounded by hundreds of sahirs. Sarsar greeted the Malika deferentially, laid the pushtara with Ra'ad tied in it at her feet and said, 'I have captured the sinner Ra'ad and offer him to you.'

Soorat Nigar was delighted with Sarsar and awarded her with a heavy khalat robe and seated her in a place of honour. After a while, when Sarsar had left, Soorat Nigar said, 'Summon Princess Almas to our durbar so that she can execute her brother's murderer herself.' Almas Fairy-face had been strolling in the hills with several of her companions when she was summoned and came to the durbar adorned in rich robes and jewels. Soorat Nigar glowed with pride at seeing her beautiful daughter and made a gesture to ward off any evil eye. By this time, Ra'ad too had gained consciousness and Soorat Nigar greeted him with a volley of abuses.

Almas looked at Ra'ad and saw a young man, about twenty-two years of age, whose handsome, noble face shone like the moon. Almas Fairy-face lost her heart a thousand times at this sight and felt as if she could die for her beloved. At the same time, she was aware of the hopelessness of her situation and began weeping softly. Soorat Nigar, unaware of Almas's thoughts, tried to comfort her by saying, 'My daughter, your tears will not bring your brother back to life, you will just ruin your health with your grief.' Others in the durbar fussed over Almas as well. When their attention was focussed on her, Ra'ad looked up and saw a beautiful young damsel watching him with tears in her eyes. The young sahir sensed her longing and fell in love with her as deeply, but remained helpless and silent.

Just then, Soorat Nigar received a message from her husband that urged her to take the young prisoner to Hairat's camp. The message said, 'We can behead him in full view of his friends and punish anyone who tries to rescue him.' Accordingly, she ordered her officers to keep Ra'ad in chains within a circle of magic flames that night. After the guards took him away, Almas felt restless and asked her mother if she could retire for the night as she was exhausted. After her mother gave her permission to leave, she returned to her pavilion with her special attendant, the eunuch Mian Ishrat, who was in charge of her litter, riding alongside.

We will now return to Mahrukh's camp where Ra'ad's capture had caused a great uproar. Barq Mehshar was sick with worry over her son's disappearance and Amar promised her that they would find Ra'ad. Amar left the camp to look for Ra'ad and met Barq on the way. Barq decided to assist Amar in his search for Ra'ad and soon enough, came upon Soorat Nigar's camp. Barq, disguised as a sahir, began wandering through the camp, and saw Ra'ad being led out of the durbar in chains. Immediately, he began thinking of ways to rescue him.

A little later, Barq saw Princess Almas and her attendants. When he realized that she was Mussavir's daughter, he followed her to her pavilion. He observed that Mian Ishrat, who had escorted the princess back to her tent, was now enjoying a smoke in a secluded place. Barq managed to engage the eunuch in gossip about Hairat's camp and soon overcome him with drugged vapours. Barq dragged him behind some bushes and then quickly disguised himself as the eunuch.

Princess Almas Fairy-face was still thinking of Ra'ad and dismissed her attendants as she wanted to be on her own. Barq approached her tent stealthily and overheard her sighing, 'O Ra'ad, I could die for one more glimpse of you!' Barq realized that Almas was in love with Ra'ad and went forward to speak to her. On seeing the royal attendant, the princess tried to compose herself, but Barq whispered in her ear, 'Princess, I am aware of your secret; do not hide it from me. I am your devoted slave. If you so desire, I will try and pluck stars from the sky for you.' Thus reassured, the princess confessed that she was in love with Ra'ad. At this point, Barq decided to take her into confidence and told her, 'Princess, I am not your eunuch but an ayyar and have come to rescue Ra'ad. Tell his guards that you want to interrogate your brother's killer. Once they open the ring of flames around him for you, I will manage an escape.'

The princess laughed like a blossoming flower when she heard this and lost no time in sending for her palanquin. Barq, still disguised as Mian Ishrat, accompanied her. Folad, the captain of the guards, received them both and on the princess's request, dispelled the ring of flames around the prisoner. While the princess was with the prisoner, Barq offered Folad and the guards drugged wine and when they fell unconscious, he promptly beheaded all of them. This was followed by total darkness and the camp resounded with the wailing of their spirits. The princess was terrified and Ra'ad's magical shackles melted with Folad's death. Barq wanted to leave the camp with Ra'ad immediately, but Almas insisted that her tent would be safe for Ra'ad to rest after his ordeal.

The news of the prisoner's escape soon reached Soorat Nigar who flew around the camp looking for him. She thought of warning her daughter against the escaped prisoner and walked into her tent, only to see Almas Fairy-face and Ra'ad in each other's arms. In sheer rage, she cast a spell that made the earth under them tremble and fly upwards. Ra'ad and Almas found themselves flying in the air and Ra'ad tried to chant a spell to release them both, but realized that he was tongue-tied. Then, Soorat Nigar cast another spell that made the piece of earth on which the lovers stood divide in mid-air. The two pieces of earth took Ra'ad in one direction and the princess in another and the lovers wept on seeing that they were being drawn apart. Soon, they were out of each other's sight.

Barq, who was watching all this anxiously, did not know which one of them to follow. Eventually, he went straight to Barq Mehshar and related to her all that had happened. Barq Mehshar rushed like lightning to the enemy camp and fell upon the piece of earth carrying the princess first. She caught the princess and flew upwards, holding her by the waist. Soorat Nigar saw what was happening and cast a spell that made several puppets fly towards Barq Mehshar. Soon, the puppets had brought her down to the ground.

Soorat Nigar now wrote something on a piece of paper and gave it to a messenger puppet that promptly vanished. Moments later, the earth cleaved open and a sahir emerged from it. Soorat Nigar addressed him solemnly, 'O Zalim Black-face, I have summoned you to entrust my daughter and these two prisoners to your custody. Taking them back to my camp will bring us disgrace. Everyone will come to know that the daughter of Mussavir is in love with a traitor. Moreover, it is easier for ayyars to rescue them if they are in the camp.' Zalim immediately conjured a tower around the three prisoners.

Soorat Nigar confronts the rebels

Soorat Nigar flew back to her camp and ordered that they were to move. The next day, they reached Hairat's camp and after the usual courtesies, Soorat Nigar confided in Hairat, 'We are both naked in the same bath my sister! Your daughter Khubsoorat is in love with Mahrukh's son and my daughter Almas is infatuated with that traitor Ra'ad Jadoo! Strike the battle drums in my name as I am determined to destroy the rebels and avenge my son's death!' The drums of battle were struck on both sides and the night was alive with the sound of armour being prepared for battle the next morning.

Mahrukh and Bahar were the first to enter the battlefield the next morning. They conjured rainfall to settle the dust on the field and their soldiers fell into battle formations. Soorat Nigar and Hairat emerged with great ceremony, surrounded by their commanders. Soorat Nigar went forward on her magic dragon and challenged the rebels. Bahar Jadoo decided to face her first.

Soorat Nigar initiated the battle by smashing a coconut. Thousands of shadows emerged from it and rushed menacingly towards Bahar. In turn, Bahar smiled and a long string of pearls materialized before her. Bahar climbed up on the string, and conjured flames that fell on the spectres and burnt them to ashes. Soorat Nigar then sketched a portrait of Bahar and flung it on the string of pearls. The portrait came to life and expelled flames from its mouth that burnt the string of pearls. Bahar fell down, but recovered quickly and plucked a few strands of hair off her head, which she flung at the portrait. The strands of hair coiled around the picture like ropes and dragged it to Bahar, who shredded it with magic scissors.

Bahar then threw a bouquet that expelled a shower of gold and silver flowers at Soorat Nigar and her companions. In no time, they were all enchanted and swayed as they chanted lyrics in praise of Bahar's beauty. Just then, the earth opened and puppets emerged from it and gathered the enchanted flowers. They called out to Soorat Nigar, 'Malika, you are the wife of the grandson of Samri and you have been enchanted by a mere slip of a girl. Remember your status!'

Soorat Nigar was jolted back to awareness on hearing these words and fell upon Bahar with her sword. Hairat ordered her troops to attack at the same time and Mahrukh's army also joined in the fray. As the armies clashed with each other, there were fierce storms and bursts of flames and rain. The battleground looked as if it was blooming with flowers of blood. In the midst of battle, Soorat Nigar turned to Hairat in fury and declared, 'That chit of a girl Bahar has embarrassed me today. Tonight I will draw magic portraits of all enemy commanders and will kill them tomorrow!' 'As you wish,' replied Hairat. As they were talking, the earth before them split open as a slave-boy emerged from it and gave Hairat a message from her husband. Afrasiyab had summoned Hairat to meet him at the Dome of Light and Hairat left the battlefield to adorn herself for him. Before leaving, she ordered Sarsar to protect Soorat Nigar against tricksters.

That night, Amar and his comrades tried to kidnap and trick Soorat Nigar several times and even succeeded a couple of times. However, Sarsar was more than a match for them and saved Soorat Nigar from being executed. When Hairat returned the next morning, Soorat Nigar looked visibly pale and distressed and said, 'If it were not for Sarsar, my sister, you would have found me dead for sure.' As Hairat and Soorat Nigar talked to each other, Afrasiyab also arrived at the camp. After learning of Soorat Nigar's troubles with the ayyars, he said, 'Why do you bother to fight them? Rest easy and I will deal with the rebels now!' He sketched a magical sign in the air and within minutes, there was a shower of golden raindrops from the sky that came together to form a sahir. 'Baraan Jadoo, I appoint you as officer to confront the rebels. Arrest them for me!' said Afrasiyab to the young sahir, who kneeled low in obeisance. Then Baraan disappeared from sight in a shower of golden raindrops. A little later, Afrasiyab too returned to the Garden of Apples.

A magical shower or Baraan Jadoo

The youthful and confident Baraan Jadoo lost no time in assembling his army to confront Mahrukh's forces. Before settling into his quarters, he decided to call on the enemy and set off for Mahrukh's durbar. He walked into the durbar before his entry could be announced and calmly sat down on an empty chair. Then he addressed the rebel commanders in a contemptuous tone, 'Be warned you traitors, I have come to punish you for your treachery.' The durbar was too stunned by his audacity to respond, but Amar quickly flicked his whip and trapped Baraan in its coils. Baraan, in turn, transformed into a vaporous cloud and vanished amidst thunder and lightning. Amar turned to Mahrukh and asked, 'How does his magic work?'

'Khwaja, Baraan conjures a magical rainfall and the raindrops transform his enemies into trees,' explained Mahrukh. 'He was always a subordinate of Ra'ad and Barq Mehshar. Alas, had they been with us, we could have vanquished him with ease.' Amar decided that the two captured sardars needed to be released urgently and went to the edge of his camp. He summoned his ayyar colleagues using Zafeel, the whistle of ayyari. After directing them to find Barq Mehshar and Ra'ad, Amar and all the ayyars went off in different directions.

Baraan entered the battlefield early next morning. Too arrogant to lead the fight, he gestured to some of his officers to commence battle. Sardars like Surkh Mu Deadly-locks disposed of them with ease. Seeing this, Baraan angrily strode into the battleground and immediately muttered a spell that caused a large black cloud to drift in over the area where Mahrukh's forces were standing. As they looked up uneasily at the cloud, it released deadly raindrops and many of Mahrukh's soldiers slowly turned into trees with branches and leaves sprouting from them.

Mahrukh's sardars responded with counterspells, but they had no effect. Bahar Jadoo conjured a magic shield to protect herself from the raindrops and stepped forward to confront Baraan with a bouquet in her hand. Knowing how powerful she was, Baraan flew towards her and threw a pinch of the magical dust of Jamshed on her that made her unconscious.

The sardars panicked and fled to shield themselves from Baraan's cloud, which rained even harder and very soon, Mahrukh's army became a forest of leafy trees. Baraan returned to his camp jubilant, but was secretly worried about the ayyars. As a precaution, he conjured a huge tank of water in which he took refuge.

The ayyars of Islam saw what befell their army from a distance and decided to first deal with Baraan. Zargham Sherdil was the earliest to reach Baraan who came to know of his presence from within the tank and easily caught him. Just as he was about to execute the ayyar, a message arrived from Afrasiyab commending Baraan on his victory over the rebels. The message read, 'Transport these prisoners to the shores of the River of Flowing Blood, Amar is bound to attempt to rescue them there and we will arrest him easily. I will invite Shaitan Bakhtiarak to execute Amar, for I have been humiliated before him and Khudawand Laqa and would like to make up for it now.'

Baraan emerged from his tank and ordered his army to move. The soldiers of Mahrukh's army who had been magically transformed into trees were loaded on to carts for the journey. On reaching the shores of the River of Flowing Blood, Baraan assembled all the carts in a huge cordoned space guarded by his men and relaxed for the rest of the evening. That evening, he also managed to arrest Jansoz, who had tried to get past the guards of Baraan's tent.

Khumar captures Amar

Afrasiyab received a message from Baraan confirming that he was now camped with his army and the prisoners besides the River of Flowing Blood. He smiled with satisfaction and addressed Khumar, 'Princess, all the rebels except Amar and three ayyars have been captured. This is your chance to vindicate yourself. Find Amar who shaved your head and humiliated you before Khudawand. Take your sister Makhmoor with you.'

Both the sisters flew off to find Amar. Khumar went first to Baraan's camp and recognized Amar who was disguised as a sahir. She greeted him casually but he sensed that she knew that it was him and promptly disappeared. She looked everywhere for him and eventually reached Baraan's tent, completely exhausted.

Baraan received her with due honours as she was a close associate of the King of Sahirs and offered her refreshments. Khumar told him that Amar was in the vicinity and asked him to provide her with a sandalwood stool. 'I will use it to invoke a special spell to find Amar,' she said. Baraan sent for the stool while Khumar purified herself to invoke the spell.

Amar entered Baraan's tent behind the attendant carrying the sandalwood stool for Khumar's spell. First, Khumar bathed and dressed in a fresh sari, after which she poured wine and pig blood on the stool and started chanting her spell. Still invisible in Galeem, Amar sat right behind her as she invoked her magic. Khumar tried very hard but as the spell was designed to inform her where Amar was, she only learned that Amar was nearby. She gave up and exclaimed, 'Amar is impossible to locate!' Baraan responded, 'He is not an ordinary mortal that he will be drawn by your spell. Do not forget that he is one whose powers were extolled by the god Samri himself!'

As they talked, the attendant, whose clothes Amar had earlier stripped, walked into the tent stark naked. Everyone looked at him askance and Baraan harshly asked him to explain himself. 'Please tell me first,' the attendant asked in bewilderment, 'am I alive or dead?' Hearing this, his companions doubled up with laughter. Baraan consoled the confused attendant who told him that a stranger had tricked him into eating some fruit. 'That was Amar,' said Baraan, and looking towards Khumar, he added, 'How is it that your magic failed to locate him?' Khumar looked sheepish and Baraan gently reassured his attendant that he was not dead but merely the victim of trickery. Amar, who was still in the tent and invisible, now escaped into the forest beyond the camp.

Then Khumar conjured a pillar of smoke to find Amar. This time she was successful as Amar had emerged from his Galeem in the forest. Within moments, the pillar of smoke deposited Amar in front of Khumar who addressed him harshly, 'Amar, you have killed so many sahirs and you have shaved my head! How shall I punish you?' Amar responded, 'My master Hamza ordered me to kill and punish sahirs. If you want to employ me I shall only do your bidding!'

'You rascal,' railed Khumar, 'you are now trying to trick me with your glib talk! I will take you right now to Afrasiyab who has invited Shaitan Bakhtiarak to execute you!' Amar quaked inwardly at these words but cried defiantly, 'Do not talk nonsense or threaten me with talk of your lover Afrasiyab! The last time I shaved your head, but this time I think I will cut your nose off!' Enraged by his insults, Khumar rendered him unconscious, tied him up in a sheet and left Baraan's camp.

The end of Baraan

The ayyars Mehtar Qiran and Barq Firangi were still trying to locate their imprisoned sardars. Barq stumbled into the ayyar girls Sarsar Sword-fighter, Saba Raftar Fleet-foot and Tez Nigah Dagger-woman in the forest and they attacked him together. Barq fought back, but Sarsar rendered him unconscious with a narcotic bubble and tied him up in a sheet. Just then, a magic panja flashed down from the sky and transported the three ayyar girls along with Barq to Soorat Nigar's pavilion. They greeted her respectfully and Sarsar asked her, 'Why have you sent for us?' Soorat Nigar said, 'Sarsar, you have saved my life so valiantly in the last few days that in gratitude I appointed this magic panja to watch you and save you if you are under attack.'

Sarsar smiled and replied, 'Malika, your generosity knows no bounds! However, we are tricksters and have to be left free to plan our moves. How will we achieve anything if the panja keeps whisking us off? Order your panja to not follow me any more.'

Soorat Nigar was embarrassed and dismissed the magic claw. She then turned to Barq and abused him roundly before summoning Zalim, the sahir in charge of her prisoners. She told him, 'Take this man and imprison him with Ra'ad and Barq Mehshar.'

The sahir flew off with Barq in his clasp. Qiran, who had remained hidden in Soorat Nigar's camp, followed Zalim to the magic dome where the prisoners were imprisoned. He thought of a plan and disguised himself as an eccentric fakir. He smeared his body with mud and wore nothing except a tattered loincloth. Nibbling a lump of clay, he approached the dome and started shouting, 'On this dome is perched a dove but he swallows a deer! In the deer's tail hides a camel! A horse is swallowing an elephant!'

Zalim heard these extraordinary claims and rushed out of the dome crying, 'Who are you and how dare you make such a din!' The false fakir retorted, 'You are blind and cannot see! Eat this lump of clay to open your inner eye!' Zalim could not refuse the offerings of a holy man and nibbled at the clay cautiously. The clay was actually a drugged sweetmeat artfully prepared by Qiran and as soon as he tasted it, Zalim greedily swallowed the whole lump and fell unconscious. Qiran immediately beheaded him. With Zalim's death, the magic dome vanished and Qiran found Barq Mehshar, Ra'ad Jadoo, Almas Fairy-face and the ayyar Barq lying unconscious on the ground. He woke them up by sprinkling water on them and told them about how the army had suffered because of Baraan's magic.

Barq Mehshar stood up in rage and thundered, 'Afrasiyab sent him because we were out of the way. Baraan is no sahir! If he comes before us, his death is certain. Let us see what that haramzada can do to us. If I do not kill him, I swear I will change my name!' Baraan was arranging for the king's arrival in his camp when he heard Ra'ad's thunder from a distance and saw Barq Mehshar's lightning crackling through the clouds. Stunned by their arrival, he turned to flee but Ra'ad stamped his way into the earth and emerged near Baraan. He screamed so loudly that the sahir fell unconscious. Within moments, Barq Mehshar fell from the skies as a flash of lightning and sliced his body into two parts. With his death, the enchanted soldiers transformed back into their true forms and fell on Baraan's forces in vengeful fury. After several hours of fierce fighting, Baraan's army was decimated. The attendants of the River of Flowing Blood fled from their posts to inform the Shahanshah about this latest disaster while Mahrukh and Bahar led their army back to the camp in triumph.

Afrasiyab was unruffled by the news of Baraan's death. 'Return to your camp,' he told Hairat, 'because Khumar is on her way with Amar. We will now pray at the Emerald Well and destroy the rest of the rebels. Just wait for my orders.' The Islamic army had just relaxed after their exhausting ordeal with Baraan when they came to know about Khwaja Amar's capture. On hearing this, they all raised their hands in prayer for his early release.

∽

8   MAKHMOOR AND NUR AL DAHAR, SON OF BADI-UZ-ZAMAN

Let us get back to Khumar, the shaven sahira, who had captured Amar and was taking him to Afrasiyab's court. She crossed the River of Flowing Blood and passed through the Red Agate, Emerald and Lapis Lazuli mountain ranges. Beyond the mountain ranges was the beautiful Valley of Saffron, its slopes covered with saffron plants as far as the eye could see. The kingdom of Saffron was in the invisible Tilism of Batin and its ruler Zafaran Jadoo was Afrasiyab's niece.

The Valley of Saffron, with its verdant slopes and bubbling streams was Princess Zafaran's favourite retreat. On the highest hill was a pavilion of ethereal beauty with honey-coloured curtains. The pavilion was furnished with silken masnad seating and every comfort was provided for there. The princess, dressed in saffron-coloured robes, was reclining on a throne of white sapphire. She held a wand in one delicate hand and an orb of yellow agate in the other. Her attendants, who were all dressed in saffron, stood around her.

Everyone in this gathering was engrossed in the nautch being performed for the princess. Suddenly, one of her attendants saw Khumar Jadoo in the distance, holding a pushtara and informed Zafaran about this. The princess rose from her throne and called out gaily, 'So my friend, you are passing through my realm without even so much as a greeting, as if we are strangers!' Khumar went towards the hill with her hands folded and said, 'Princess, I beg of you to let me pass this time. I will come here once again.' Zafaran replied, 'Upon my honour, you must share a betel leaf with me! At least have a goblet of wine to refresh yourself.' Khumar said, 'Very well princess, if that is your wish.' After Khumar was seated with courtesy, Zafaran asked her, 'What is your hurry and what is in that bundle that you are carrying?'

Khumar responded, 'Princess, this is the infamous Amar ayyar. I have arrested him and the King of Sahirs awaits my arrival impatiently!' The youthful princess flushed with excitement and said, 'I have heard of him. Let me see what he looks like!' Khumar shuddered and warned her, 'Huzoor, he is a deceitful rascal. As soon as he is released, he will either run off or cause trouble. All the effort of arresting him will have been in vain! Shahanshah will be angry with you as well!' Zafaran was annoyed and mumbled, 'Very well then, do what is in your own best interest.' Khumar did not want to offend the Shahanshah's niece and so reluctantly released Amar from the sheet, but kept his limbs lifeless to prevent him doing from any mischief.

Amar woke up and saw that he was in splendid surroundings where several beautiful women were looking at him curiously. He quickly ingratiated himself with Zafaran using exaggerated greetings and words of praise for her beauty and long life. 'I believe he is a gifted singer huzoor!' whispered one of Zafaran's attendants into her ear. Zafaran addressed Amar, 'O Amar, we are anxious to hear you sing, pray entertain us for a while!' Amar said dramatically, 'My God, such rumours are a slur on my reputation! I have also been called the slayer of sahirs and the beard-shaver of kafirs, although I have never hurt even a lowly ant. Princess Khumar even accuses me of shaving her hair off! Now if you make me sing, who knows what might happen! Perhaps a few more heads will be shaven . . . perhaps Khumar may lose her nose this time!'

Khumar was embarrassed by Amar's reference to her hair, but Zafaran laughed and exclaimed, 'At least sing a little for me!' Amar said softly, 'Princess, I am not in my senses right now. Khumar is taking me to be executed. My limbs are lifeless. How do you expect me to sing in this condition?' Amar wept as he said this and looked so sad and helpless that the soft-hearted Zafaran's eyes filled with tears as well. Everyone in the durbar begged Khumar to release Amar from her spell. Even though she protested that Amar was deceitful and that he would attempt to escape, she eventually succumbed to the clamour for his release. Amar now sat up and showered Zafaran with blessings and prayers for a long life.

Zafaran declared, 'I swear by Samri and Jamshed, I will award you richly; I will even persuade the Shahanshah to forgive you and bestow rank and lands on you. Now sing for us!' Amar replied, 'Huzoor, I will try and please you. Just provide me with a *peshwaz* costume of rich gold embroidery and emerald jewellery. I need to adorn myself to sing and dance for you. Do not think I am a thief who might run away with your clothes. However if your humble servant substitutes the real costumes with false ones, surely you will not blame me!' Zafaran laughed and said, 'Khwaja, you are rare wit and a fit companion for royalty.'

Zafaran's attendants brought trays of heavily-embroidered costumes and jewellery for the trickster. Amar wore the garments in a corner and painted his face to look like a beautiful maiden. When he emerged in his new form, Zafaran marvelled at his transformation and thought, 'Samri has gifted him; first he was human and now he is a parizad!'

Amar danced and sang for Zafaran until the afternoon sun set and the shadows lengthened in the pavilion. Zafaran's handmaidens lit the durbar with glass lamps and candles. They suspended chandeliers exuding the light of heaven on the trees. Amar continued dancing and at the same time, began deftly dropping pellets of drugged incense into the lamps and candles. After some time, the fumes began affecting everyone's senses. As her head began swimming, Zafaran got up to wash her face in the stream; but as soon as she stepped forward, she fell unconscious. Khumar rose to assist her, but she too succumbed to the fumes. Within minutes, everyone in the durbar, except Amar, lay unconscious.

Amar remained conscious because he had stuffed his nostrils with artfully-crafted flowers of consiousness. He took out the blessed Net of Ilyas and within minutes, stripped the durbar bare of all the precious items and furniture. Then he decided to kill Khumar and Zafaran. At that moment, Khumar's sister Makhmoor Red-eye, whom Afrasiyab had sent to help Khumar, suddenly arrived on the scene and chanted a spell that made Amar's limbs lifeless again. She then conjured rose-coloured rain that woke up the unconscious women. Zafaran awoke to find her summer palace in ruins and looked askance at Khumar who cried, 'Now do you believe me, Princess? Were it not for the blessings of Samri, this scoundrel would surely have killed us. I was watching him carefully as he usually does his mischief while serving wine. I still cannot make out how he made us unconscious!'

The young princess shuddered and cried, 'For the love of Samri and Jamshed, take him away from here. I am also leaving because this dangerous scoundrel may have made this entire place unsafe!' Khumar left with Amar bound and tied up in a sheet. Makhmoor too took her leave of Zafaran and followed her sister. Just as she was leaving, however, it occurred to her that it was not wise to make an enemy of Amar. She thought to herself, 'I am privy to the secrets of Tilism and know full well that it will end soon. I also know that Amar will not be killed by any one of us. Perhaps the right thing to do now is to save his life so that he does not harm me in the future.'

After making up her mind to win Amar's goodwill, Makhmoor acted swiftly. She hid behind a hill and chanted a spell that made a small cloud appear above Khumar's head. It released a few drops on her and instantly made her unconscious. Makhmoor then went there and released Amar from the pushtara. She folded her hands and told him, 'Khwaja, please think of me as your handmaiden and please also do not kill Khumar or I will be in trouble. I cannot take you across the magic river as there is very little time. I suggest that you hide somewhere.'

Amar looked at her meaningfully and then ran towards the nearby hills. Makhmoor also left the scene after reviving Khumar with another magical shower. Khumar awoke to find her prisoner missing and was very vexed. She sprouted magical wings and flew across the River of Flowing Blood to Hairat's camp where she related her story to Hairat. She said, 'I am not going to the Shahanshah on my own. There is some mischief afoot; besides, he will be very angry with me for not bringing Amar to him as promised.'

As Khumar was talking to Hairat, the King of Magic arrived in his wife's camp in great splendour. Hairat welcomed him with her sardars and led him into her durbar. Khumar explained to him what had happened to her. 'It seems,' mused the King of Magic, 'that Amar has a powerful ally in Tilism Batin. He cannot cross the River of Flowing Blood unless I help him. Perhaps one who is privy to the secrets of Tilism can take him across. It is time to invite Shaitan Bakhtiarak from Mount Agate. I will capture Amar in Tilism Batin any time now.'

Afrasiyab whispered a spell and a lion and lioness came roaring out of the jungle and sat down before him. He gave the lion a message that read, 'O Khudawand, send the Shaitan of your durbar here so that he can enjoy the sights of Tilism and also execute his enemy Amar.' He then chanted a spell and a powerful white hawk flew into the durbar. A wide, low stool, encrusted with gems and covered with silk and brocade cushions, was tied to the hawk's back with a rope. Afrasiyab told the lion, 'The Shaitan will be mounted on you till you reach the border of Tilism-e-Hoshruba. Then the hawk will bring him to me in Tilism Batin. Tilism Zahir is crawling with ayyars and it will be safer to fly through it.' The lions bounded off in the direction of Mount Agate, while the hawk flew overhead.

Amar in Batin, the invisible Tilism

Now listen to what happened to the master of the art of ayyari and the king of deception. After Makhmoor rescued him, Amar remained hidden and spent the night in the branches of a large tree. The next morning, he tried to find a way out of Batin but found traps and snares everywhere. With his usual cunning, he also tricked and slaughtered several of Afrasiyab's officers who were on the lookout for him.

Frustrated with his failure to cross the River of Flowing Blood, Amar was wandering around when he saw five men dressed like sahirs. That is, they wore costly garments and turbans. The men also wore medals of rank around their necks and broad bangles on their wrists. Amar decided to rob them of their garments and precious jewellery and disguised himself as an old woman. Leaning on a staff and holding a plate of sweets in one hand, he followed the sahirs and called out in a quavering voice, 'My sons, come and help out an old woman.' The sahirs turned around and spoke kindly to the woman as she seemed frail and needy. The woman said, 'I have walked a long way from my home as I could not find anyone to read the Prayer of Samri and Jamshed on these sweets. Could you kindly oblige me?'

The sahirs chanted an incantation over the sweets with great reverence. At the old woman's insistence, each of them tasted the sweets. When they fell unconscious, Amar stripped them of their clothes, thick gold bangles and medals. He wrote a note to the King of Sahirs and slipped it into the hand of one officer. The note read: 'I am the beard-shaver of kafirs, the sahir-slayer, Amar bin Ummayyah. Listen to me Afrasiyab, haramzadeh! Take pity on yourself and the residents of Batin; let me cross the river or I will destroy your Tilism. You foolish man, no one actually invites an enemy to his home! You will be ruined. The rest is up to you.'

The officers awoke and realized that they were naked, and were only too relieved to be alive. They took the note to Afrasiyab whose countenance darkened as he read it. Sarsar Sword-fighter, who was present in the durbar at the time, suggested that she could find Amar provided someone whose magic was powerful accompanied her. Afrasiyab then directed Shagoofa Magic-maker, a powerful sahira, to accompany Sarsar and told her, 'Leave some sign or symbol in this durbar so that we will be warned if you are in trouble.' Shagoofa removed a pearl from the string of pearls that she was wearing and planted it on one side of the throne. Within minutes, a tree bearing fruits and blossoms sprouted from the earth. 'Huzoor,' announced Shagoofa, 'if I am dead, this tree will shrivel up. If it remains in bloom, you will know that I am alive and well.'

Shagoofa then left with Sarsar to find Amar. The two women reached the wilderness where Amar was hiding. Amar saw them and deliberately revealed himself to them. Sarsar shouted to Shagoofa that she had seen Amar and ran ahead with her sword drawn. By the time, however, Amar had ducked behind some bushes and slipped into a cave. Sarsar was looking through the bushes when Shagoofa cried, 'My sister, can you hear that hissing sound?' They peered behind the bushes and saw a python with rubies for eyes (cleverly contrived by Amar), lunging out of the cave, expelling flames from its mouth. The women ran away in fright, with Amar following them secretly.

A little later, Shagoofa felt the call of nature and went to relieve herself behind some bushes. Amar waited for her to finish and then ambushed her just as she was getting up. He rendered her unconscious with a narcotic bubble and divested her of all her outer garments. Then he painted his face to look like Shagoofa, wore her garments and joined Sarsar. After walking with Sarsar for some time, Amar disappeared into Galeem. Sarsar assumed that as Shagoofa was a powerful sahira, she had vanished magically. But Amar had actually disappeared because he had spotted a sahir in the distance.

Amar walked towards the sahir and suddenly appeared before him. This sahir lived in Batin and so recognized Shagoofa. 'What are you doing here?' he asked her. The false Shagoofa whispered, 'I am looking for Amar, but come closer, I want to say something to you!' When the sahir came closer, Amar made him unconscious and dragged him behind a bush where he painted the sahir's face to look like his face.

Meanwhile, Sarsar, who was wandering around looking for Shagoofa, saw her emerge from behind some bushes holding Amar. Sarsar excitedly tripped up to her and cried, 'This is why you disappeared! Because you had seen him! Huzoor, only you could have captured him for he is a slippery fellow. I do hope though that you will tell Shahanshah that I had him captured, for it is for us ayyar girls to capture these ayyars!'

The false Shagoofa said, 'Should we not wake him up and interrogate him first?' Sarsar looked horrified and shouted, 'Do not make that mistake! Once he is up, he will escape and we will never find him again. In fact, hand him over to me. I will be honoured because of you.' Amar smiled and handed over the sahir to Sarsar who laid him down on a sheet and then tied it around him tightly. The two women began walking happily towards the Garden of Apples with their prisoner. On the way, Sarsar suggested that they could go back to the durbar through a special magical route. The false Shagoofa readily agreed to this idea.

They reached a forest where the grass, the trees, the earth—virtually everything in sight—was made of pure gold. Indeed, the forest looked as if it was on fire because the vegetation there glowed in the sun's light. Amar thought of how rich he would be if he could only put the whole forest into Zambil. Since that was not a possiblity, he consoled himself that in any case, the forest was a magical illusion.

After walking through the golden forest, they reached a crystal wall. Sarsar stopped there and called out, 'For the love of the Shah of Tilism, give us way!' The wall parted before them and when they walked through, they saw a large camp of sahir soldiers before them. The commander of the camp stopped them and said, 'Why have you taken this route? It is used exclusively by the Shah of Tilism.' Sarsar explained to him that they had captured Amar and needed to reach the Shah as soon as possible. The commander asked them to wait and sent one of his soldiers to confirm with Afrasiyab whether Sarsar's story was true. Of course, the Shah declared, 'Let them through!'

Sarsar and the false Shagoofa now moved on and reached the rear entrance to the Garden of Apples. They passed through a splendid gem-inlaid archway that was guarded by hundreds of sahirs. Although Amar had seen the garden several times already, he was overawed each time by its beauty and freshness that was magically enhanced. It was as if a thousand springs bloomed in it every day.

Sarsar and the false Shagoofa walked through the garden and entered a magnificent durbar where Afrasiyab sat resplendent on his throne, surrounded by his nobles, who stood with folded hands. Sarsar laid the bundle down before the Shahanshah with an exaggerated account of how cleverly she had caught Amar. For this, she received a robe of honour and other gifts. When Shagoofa came forward, Afrasiyab rewarded her richly and exempted her from paying state tribute for a year.

Makhmoor in Mount Agate

Afrasiyab then turned to Makhmoor Red-eye who was present in the durbar and said, 'It has been some time since the lion and lioness went to fetch Shaitan. Will you follow them to Mount Agate and escort Shaitan on his journey to Tilism?'

Makhmoor had some misgivings about this mission but did not dare disobey the king. She returned to her palace and left for the journey with a large number of attendants. Meanwhile, the pair of lions had who reached Mount Agate caused immense fear in Laqa's durbar. Soon enough, a huge golden cloud gently rolled over Fort Agate and there was a shower of rubies. 'That must be Makhmoor Red-eye,' said some sahirs in the durbar. Within moments, Makhmoor appeared, accompanied by two thousand attendants. Dressed in royal robes and adorned with jewels from head to toe, she descended from her throne with infinite grace. Makhmoor prostrated in front of Khudawand Laqa and offered him nazar. Laqa invited her to sit on a chair of honour and asked her, 'My daughter, what brings you here?' Makhmoor then conveyed Afrasiyab's invitation to Shaitan Bakhtiarak to go to Tilism and execute the captured Amar.

The Shaitan laughed aloud on hearing this and said, 'Capturing Amar is difficult and almost impossible. I am not going to Tilism to lose my life. Even if Amar has been captured, he will manage to behead Shah and will disappear by the time I reach there!' Makhmoor smiled and said, 'Malik-ji, Shah cannot be killed unlessTilism is defeated. You can come without fear.' After much resistance, Bakhtiarak finally relented and agreed to go to Tilism. He mounted the white hawk that Afrasiyab had sent for his safe passage and the pair of lions accompanied him.

Makhmoor also bade farewell to Laqa and thought to herself, 'Since I have come all this way, I should at least see the lashkar of Hamza Sahibqiran.' After she left Fort Agate, she flew on her magic throne to a safe height above the Islamic camp and looked down to see the lashkar. Her eyes alighted with wonder on the Pavilion of Solomon with its pillars of pure gold. On either side of the pavilion, she saw clean, wide roads where water-carriers were sprinkling water from bowls of silver and gold to settle the dust. There were markets of gold and precious gems; and markets of European wares and goods from China. She saw vast tents where food was being prepared in hundreds of precious vessels. Some of the soldiers were practising archery and fencing, while others were absorbed in their prayer books. The scale and majesty of the Islamic camp astonished Makhmoor and she gazed entranced at the scene below her.

She was alerted to the arrival of an obviously important person at the Pavilion of Solomon by cries of 'Move out the way!' Water-carriers began clearing the path by spraying rose and *kevda* water, and a cluster of fine-looking young boys emerged next holding oudh and umber incense holders. Soldiers mounted on steeds and wearing gold embroidered uniforms followed them. Finally, attendants holding bouquets and miniature trees made of precious gems, walked behind them.

As Makhmoor watched this procession with fascination, Prince Nur al Dahar, grandson of Hamza, pride of the faithful, Sahibqiran bin Sahibqiran bin Sahibqiran, rode in on a magnificent horse. He was surrounded by sardars whom he had vanquished in battle, each one of them a prince in his own right. Makhmoor looked at the noble visage of the prince and was stunned by his beauty. This young warrior had a face that could put the shining sun to shame and his bravery and valour made the story of the great Persian wrestler Rustam seem trivial in comparison.

Makhmoor fell in love with him at first sight. She would have happily sacrificed her life for him a thousand times. She felt dizzy with the sudden rush of feelings and her attendants dabbed her face with rose water. By this time, the entourage had passed out of sight and this left Makhmoor feeling lovesick and restless. After some time, she left for Tilism holding the secret of her love deep in her heart. She thought, 'The only way that I can gain my beloved is by joining Amar. I should return to Tilism and help him across the River of Flowing Blood, and then join Mahrukh Magic-eye.' Thus, Makhmoor returned to Tilism deep in thought even as she shed tears of blood.

Bakhtiarak in Tilism

Meanwhile, the white hawk had carried Bakhtiarak across the borders of Tilism and from there on, the pair of lions escorted him to the invisible Tilism of Batin. Afrasiyab received him royally and took him first to Hairat's war camp in Zahir, the visible Tilism. The sounds of the magic kettledrums of Tilism resounded across the realm as Hairat, Soorat Nigar and their sardars received Shaitan Bakhtiarak. They showed the rebel camp in the distance to Bakhtiarak and then led him to the royal pavilion where he was entertained with wine and dance.

Afrasiyab called out, 'While Malik-ji is in the camp, a few sardars should prepare the Garden of Apples for the feast tonight. Adorn all its pavilions and palaces, replace the floor seating, arrange the glassware and furniture, stock the maikhana and supervise the royal kitchens!' The sahira Shagoofa (still Amar in disguise), stepped forward and begged to be given this assignment. Afrasiyab gave his assent and sent a message to the guardians of the River of Flowing Blood that Shagoofa was to be allowed safe passage.

Thus, the false Shagoofa crossed the river with her companions and reached the Garden of Apples. She sent for the officers in charge of the royal household as well as the stewards of the maikhana and the kitchens and told them what to prepare for the royal feast. Amar arranged the wine flasks himself and gave a powder to the steward to mix with the wine. He then went to the kitchens and mixed a drugged powder into the food being cooked. He told the chefs, 'This is special blend of spices prepared by me at great expense. Today Shahanshah will enjoy this food and because of me, all of you will be rewarded.' Amar went on to decorate the durbar beautifully and sprinkled a drug into all the unlit tapers and candles.

Afrasiyab escorted Bakhtiarak to the durbar at the Garden of Apples that evening with great ceremony. He was pleased with Shagoofa's management of the feast and bestowed a khalat on her. The guest of honour was seated on the head-throne; the garden was illuminated and fairy-faced dancers began entertaining the durbar. Makhmoor Red-eye also arrived in the durbar and joined the feast. Afrasiyab then sent for the rolled-up pushtara with the captured Amar in it (the reader will recall that Amar had disguised a sahir to look like him) and asked Bakhtiarak to kill Amar with his own hands.

The cautious Shaitan first examined the unconscious body of the false Amar. He prised open the right eyelid of the false Amar to check for the telltale mole that identified Amar. On finding it missing, the Shaitan broke into a little jig and shouted, 'O Afrasiyab, let me leave, there will be trouble here any moment. I knew that Amar could not have been captured!' As the King looked at him in astonishment, Makhmoor quickly reassured the Shaitan, 'Malik-ji have no doubt! This *is* the real Amar and Shahanshah has confirmed this.' The Shaitan, who was still dancing, responded, 'All praise be to Allah, I am a Muslim! I cannot kill an innocent man and why do you insist on killing someone who is probably a fellow sahir? This is certainly not Amar and really I have no hair left on my scalp because of all the shoe beatings that I have received from him!'

After saying this, Bakhtiarak removed his cap and showed everyone his scalp, which was in fact quite bald and shiny. The people in the durbar laughed and nudged each other while murmuring, 'This man really is the devil!' Afrasiyab gestured to Makhmoor to execute the prisoner even as Bakhtiarak warned, 'You laugh now but you will be weeping soon!' Sure enough, as soon as the prisoner was executed, his spirits howled in

rage, 'You have killed me, my name was Farhad Jadoo!' Sheets of flames
and stones cascaded down on the durbar. Bakhtiarak jumped up and
cried, 'Did I not warn you that no one could capture that paragon of
purity, that companion of kings, that benefactor of poor people like us—
the great and noble Amar!'

Afrasiyab felt very humiliated. He thought at first that Shagoofa was
false and examined her tree (readers will recall that the real Shagoofa
had conjured a tree in the Garden of Apples that would wither if she
died). As the tree still blossomed, he suspected her of having being tricked
into arresting the wrong Amar. It did not occur to him that Amar could
be posing as Shagoofa in that very gathering! Afrasiyab returned to the
masnad and said to Bakhtiarak, 'Malik-ji, you were right. Amar has not
been captured, but please enjoy the feast in your honour and rest assured
that he will be captured soon!' Bakhtiarak pleaded, 'I think I have had
enough—let me return to Khudawand!' Afrasiyab implored the Shaitan
to stay a while longer and asked for a round of wine to be served.
Cupbearers served the wine that Amar had drugged and as golden voiced
singers entertained the durbar, everyone relaxed with goblets of wine.

Afrasiyab soon began to feel light-headed because of the drugged
wine and sensed that something was amiss. He examined his hands to
check his fate (the reader will remember that his right hand revealed the
good that would befall him and the left hand, the evil that was imminent)
and realized that he had to leave the durbar quickly as he would be
humiliated if he stayed. Afrasiyab disappeared quietly and left a double
in his place. The whole court now lay in a deep sleep. Amar, who remained
conscious, decided to revive the Shaitan in order to torture him a little.
The Shaitan awoke to find death lurking on his head in the form of
Amar holding a sword to him. He bowed low at once and said, 'I remain
your humble servant!' Amar smiled and said, 'Malik-ji, I know that you
came here to participate in my death. No matter. Just start stripping
these sahirs of their clothes and jewels while I dispose of the furniture.'

In mortal fear of Amar, the Shaitan willingly did what he was asked to
do and was thrashed soundly the moment he faltered. Amar then ordered
Bakhtiarak to assist him in blackening the faces of the unconscious sahirs.
Amar stopped when he reached Makhmoor Red-eye for he remembered
that she had rescued him from Khumar earlier. He left her but shaved
everyone else's heads and blackened their faces. He tied strings around the
genitals of the sahirs and wrapped the ends of the strings around trees.
After he made sure that he had divested the unconscious sahirs of all their
jewels, he thrashed the Shaitan once again and told him to start beheading
the sahirs. Bakhtiarak immediately began to slaughter the sahirs and the

din created by their spirits was akin to doomsday. Amar wrote a note that read: 'This is the work of the noble Amar!' He left it on Afrasiyab's throne and then hid in a corner of the garden.

Now hear of something amusing. The real Shagoofa, who had been made unconscious by Amar and left in the wilderness, woke up and began looking for Sarsar. As she did not find her, she assumed that Sarsar might have captured Amar and returned to the durbar. Shagoofa arrived just when Amar had hidden himself and left Bakhtiarak to do the rest.

Shagoofa saw Bakhtiarak killing the unconscious sahirs and thought that he was Amar in disguise. She chanted a spell that made his limbs lifeless and lashed out at him with her whip. Bakhtiarak (having seen Amar disguised as Shagoofa) thought that this was Amar and pleaded, 'Huzoor, I did as you asked and killed so many sahirs; do not beat me any more!'

Shagoofa whipped him even harder and Bakhtiarak screamed in pain: 'Blast this Afrasiyab who invited me here to be beaten!' Just at that moment, the real Afrasiyab returned to the durbar. He saw Shagoofa whipping the Shaitan and thought that Amar, disguised as Shagoofa, had drugged everyone into falling unconscious and was now punishing Shaitan. In a moment of impulsive rage, he waved his fingers and a bolt of lightning fell from the skies on Shagoofa, killing her instantly. Darkness descended on the ruined durbar and her spirits howled and lamented her death.

Afrasiyab immediately looked towards the tree Shagoofa had planted and found it withered. He now glowered at the Shaitan, who he thought could be Amar. The Shaitan cried out, 'First this sahira beat me to pulp and now you look at me suspiciously! Did you invite me here to humiliate me? O Afrasiyab, do you see how the Righteous Teacher has tricked you? It is appropriate that you send me back to Khudawand right now.'

Afrasiyab realized that he had been deceived once again. He waved his hand and a magical shower of rain revived all his courtiers. It was a comic scene when they woke up for they were tied to each other, their faces were blackened, their heads were shorn of hair, and most of them were in a state of near-nakedness. Despite his rage, Afrasiyab burst into laughter and urged his courtiers to clean themselves.

Makhmoor Red-eye, who was also woken up by the shower, found that her clothes were intact and that her hair, clothes and ornaments were untouched. She realized that Amar had spared her for doing him a favour earlier. Meanwhile, Afrasiyab consulted the oracle Book of Samri and apologized to Bakhtiarak for suspecting that he was Amar in disguise. Hundreds of attendants restored order to the court and the courtiers returned after washing themselves and changing into clean robes.

Afrasiyab ordered some sahirs to look for Amar but just then, Shaitan Bakhtiarak fell at his feet and begged to be sent back to Mount Agate: 'I cannot bear to be beaten again. Look at my poor body, bruised and cut in several places! In the name of all that you hold dear, send me back to Khudawand.'

Afrasiyab tried to persuade the Shaitan to stay, but he was adamant about leaving Tilism. By this time, it was almost dawn and as the night sky left with its army of stars, the Shahanshah of the East appeared in golden robes. Afrasiyab now sent for Sarsar Sword-fighter. She had anticipated the Shahanshah's wrath and appeared before him trembling with fear. Afrasiyab rose with a whip in his hand and shouted, 'You slut, is this how you have captured Amar?' Sarsar wept and confessed that Shagoofa was the one who had arrested Amar. 'This time, I promise, I will find him huzoor, just give me another chance!' she said. The soft-hearted Afrasiyab relented and Sarsar left the durbar to find Amar again.

Afrasiyab then sent another note to the grandson of Samri, Mussavir the magic artist, reminding him of his promise to fight the rebels. Mussavir had actually set off from his realm to fight the rebels after they had killed his son Tareek. However, he had returned to his kingdom when he remembered that he had to go into seclusion for forty days to pray to his exalted ancestor, Samri. Afrasiyab pleaded humbly with Mussavir that he had been very troubled by Amar's presence in the visible Tilism of Batin. He wrote in his note, ' . . . If huzoor graces us with your presence, perhaps we could share the burden of administration of the Tilisms of Zahir and Batin.'

Mussavir was flattered by Afrasiyab's message and wrote back: 'O Shahanshah of the Skies! O Virtuous and Mighty Monarch! O King of the World and Ruler of Noble Sahirs! I have received your message of love and please rest assured that I am determined to destroy the rebels in Zahir.' Afrasiyab was delighted to receive this message and wrote to Hairat that the grandson of Samri was to be treated with every courtesy.

Amar and Khumar

Amar, who had been hiding outside Afrasiyab's durbar, saw Khumar Jadoo leaving and decided to follow her to find a way across the river. He knew that Khumar had an amorous disposition and disguised himself as a comely youth. Wearing costly garments with a cap of pearls on his head, he stood in her path forlornly, reciting sad verses. Khumar noticed him as she passed by and asked him kindly what troubled him at such a young age. The youth wept softly and replied, 'I am in love with Princess Bahar, but she has joined the rebels. What can I do except weep?'

Khumar gave an understanding smile and said, 'Why do you destroy yourself for love?' The youth said, 'If you sympathize with me, then you should do more. Accept me as your devoted slave.' He added slyly, 'I am rich and have no heir.' Khumar was amused and emboldened by his smiles; Amar held her hand and then embraced her.

Khumar protested half-heartedly and said, 'If someone should pass by, my reputation will be in shreds! You certainly have nerve to become so familiar with me!' Amar ignored her cries, lifted her and carried her to one side. He sat down with her and took out a small casket of betel leaves. He told her, 'I am addicted to these, will you not join me?' Khumar willingly ate a *gilori* and promptly fell unconscious.

Amar quickly stripped her of her expensive robes and jewellery. As she had lustrous pearls sewn into her hair, he shaved off her head again and was just about to kill her when there was a sudden gust of strong wind. Amar sensed trouble and bolted out of sight. Magic dust-whirls spun around the unconscious Khumar and transported her to Afrasiyab. The Shahanshah graciously covered the naked Khumar with his shawl before he woke her up.

Later, Khumar said, 'Amar has humiliated me several times. I will not rest till I find and kill him now!' Afrasiyab asked her to wait and addressed his durbar, 'Sarsar went to look for Amar. I would like one of you now to help Sarsar in her quest. Arrest the person she identifies as Amar.' Khumar was still smarting from her last encounter with Amar and volunteered immediately: 'Huzoor, your handmaiden will go at once and find that rogue!'

Now hear about Amar. He had infiltrated a wedding party disguised as a sahir and managed to render everyone unconscious by drugging the wine. He stripped everyone of their clothes and valuables and then began slaughtering the men. The sound of the wailing of their spirits reached Sarsar and Khumar. They were rushing towards the marquee when suddenly, Sarsar said, 'There is Amar! He is sitting on top of that man and is about to kill him!' Khumar transformed into a hawk, swooped down on Amar, and within moments, flew off holding him in her talons. Amar was furious and called out, 'Sarsar, you trollop, you had me captured? Now see how I punish you! As for this Khumar, this time I will cut her nose off!'

Sarsar rushed to the durbar and reached there before Khumar. 'Huzoor,' she panted after greeting the Shah, 'I have had Amar captured and Princess Khumar is bringing him to you!' Afsasiyab was delighted and bestowed a robe of honour on Sarsar. Moments later, Khumar arrived with Amar. She had rendered his limbs lifeless and threw him before Afrasiyab. The King of Sahirs looked down at Amar and said, 'Did you anticipate a day like this?' Amar tried his usual tactic in difficult situations, 'O Mighty King, is it my fault that Khudawand Laqa keeps sending me to Tilism to punish sahirs?' Afrasiyab replied, 'You have humiliated me before Khudawand's Shaitan! Now I will send your head as a gift to him!' Amar retorted, 'If Khudawand has ordained my death at your hands, it will be so. If not, then I will kill you. All will be as He has ordained.'

Afrasiyab said, 'We will see who kills whom!' He wanted Khumar to take Amar across the river to execute him, but Sarsar suggested that it would be best to kill Amar right away before one of his friends tried to rescue him. Afrasiyab saw the wisdom of her argument and sent for the executioner. Makhmoor Red-eye, who was still pining for Nur al Dahar, thought that she would never gain favour with her beloved if Amar was executed in Tilism. So she stepped forward and pleaded with folded hands, 'O Shahanshah, the respected Shaitan left here after being humiliated. Now that our enemy has been caught due to your grace, invite the Shaitan once again to execute him.'

Afrasiyab agreed readily with Makhmoor and dictated a nama to his scribe that read, 'O Khudawand Laqa, your humble slave is overcome with remorse that your Shaitan came to my durbar and was humiliated. Earlier, I could not serve him in any manner, but now, I have captured his enemy Amar and hope that he honours me and gains satisfaction by seeing Amar executed before him.' Afrasiyab asked Khumar to take the invitation but she was reluctant to carry the message as she had been shamed in front of Laqa the last time she visited Mount Agate. Afrasiyab sent the message through a noble sahira called Nafeer Jadoo instead. Nafeer adorned herself for the occasion and left for Mount Agate on her flying throne. On reaching her destination, Nafeer descended from her throne and started walking towards Laqa's durbar. The ayyars from Hamza's camp were always loitering around Laqa's durbar and Chalak bin Amar spotted her from a distance.

He quickly painted his face to look like the Shaitan Bakhtiarak and walked past her on purpose. Recognizing the Shaitan, Nafeer hailed him, 'Where do you go, O Shaitan of Khudawand? I have come to meet you!' The false Shaitan told her that he was on his way to meet some holy men to give them divine food that would increase their life spans. Nafeer begged him to let her taste the food as well. After making her plead for some time, he offered her a *sheermal*. Nafeer said a prayer before eating and became unconscious after a few bites of the bread. Chalak quickly searched her person and found Afrasiyab's nama to Laqa. He substituted the nama with a false one, then calmly shaved her hair, blackened her face and left her to wake up on her own.

Nafeer woke up and walked to the durbar in drugged confusion. She prostrated before Laqa and handed him Afrasiyab's nama. Laqa received her graciously and gave the nama to his *munshi*, who read the abusive message that Chalak had written and quitely handed it to Shaitan. Bakhtiarak read the message and laughed aloud, 'My dear princess, someone tampered with this letter and also shaved your head. Tell us, why did the Shahanshah send you?' Nafeer felt her head and began sobbing as she explained, 'Malik-ji, the King of Magic has invited you as Amar has been captured.' Bakhtiarak said, 'God forbid that the King of Tricksters should be captured! Even if that happens, he will kill a few sahirs and escape!'

Suddenly, someone shouted, 'I am Amar bin Ummayyah!' Chalak, disguised as his father, ran up to Laqa, hit him hard and whisked his crown off his head. Laqa shouted, 'Catch that impertinent mortal!' Nafeer ran towards Chalak but he burst a narcotic bubble in her face that made her unconscious. Laqa's courtiers threatened Chalak from a distance but no one dared go close to him for they knew that if he was harmed, his fellow ayyars would kill them in vengeance. Chalak went close to Bakhtiarak and lifted his eyelid to show him Amar's telltale mole. Seeing this, Bakhtiarak became convinced this was the real Amar. Chalak slapped him a few times for good measure and bolted out of the durbar.

Bakhtiarak rubbed his stinging cheeks before turning to Nafeer who had woken up by this time and said, 'Princess, did you see Amar here? Are you convinced now? Please tell the king about what happened here. I will certainly not go to Tilism now. It is bad enough that I am subjected to shoe beatings here; I have no desire to be thrashed even more in Tilism!'

Amar in Mount Agate

Trembling with shock, Nafeer returned to Afrasiyab's durbar. One look at her shaven head told him what had happened and he sent for the prisoner. 'Who are you? Tell us the truth now!' he shouted. Amar looked at Nafeer and realized that someone had helped him out in Mount Agate. He kneeled and wept bitterly. 'Huzoor,' he said, 'I am your lowly subject. I was on the banks of the river when two women arrested me, painted my face and told me that if I do not admit to being Amar, they would destroy my family.' Afrasiyab immediately released him and awarded him twelve thousand rupees. After the prisoner left, he sent for Sarsar and Khumar and threatened to whip them for this deceit. 'Huzoor, why did you not consult the Book of Samri first?' Sarsar replied.

There was an almighty roar of rage from Afrasiyab as he realized that he had been deceived yet again. Amar had already disappeared into his cloak. Afrasiyab angrily smashed a magic orange on the floor and rose from his throne. Suddenly, a million stars emerged in the twilight and as everyone watched, Afrasiyab transformed into a handsome dark youth, wearing a priceless diamond crown and strings of pearls and diamonds. A golden sash was tied around his waist and a magic sign was traced on his forehead with sandalwood paste.

Hundreds of cloves and black peppers were placed in incense burners; a thousand bells pealed and unseen heralds informed all the citizens of Tilism that the real Afrasiyab had emerged from behind the magic mirror. There was an uproar in Tilism and people rushed to catch a glimpse of the true form of their ruler. Thousands of sahirs fell at his feet with tributes of gold coins.

Amar also saw the treasure from a distance and his mouth watered at the prospect of plundering the gold. He said to himself, 'How long will you hide? Either lose your life or kill the Shah of Tilism!' He drew closer to the gold coins to cast his Net of Ilyas on the treasure when Afrasiyab trapped him in a pillar of smoke. Afrasiyab consulted the oracle Book of Samri that advised, 'Do not keep Amar here for he cannot be executed by you.'

Afrasiyab then summoned the sahirs Hizar and Inzar Jadoo and told them, 'Proceed with an army of sixty thousand men to Mount Agate and destroy Khudawand's enemies. Take Amar with you; Khudawand will know how to punish him.' Makhmoor Red-eye, who still pined for a glimpse of her beloved Nur al Dahar, realized that if she went with the army, she could perhaps see him again. She stepped forward and asked for Afrasiyab's permission to go and pay homage to Laqa.

At that moment, the body of the young and handsome man who had emerged as the real Afrasiyab caught fire and disappeared. Bells pealed and trumpets blew, and a loud voice called out over the din, 'Attention all sahirs! The Shahanshah is within the magic mirror. This was not him, but his double who was governing on his behalf!'

The durbar dispersed and Makhmoor returned to her palace to prepare to meet her beloved. She chose forty fairy-faced maidens to accompany her and then attended to her toilette. She selected the most exquisite robes and jewellery for herself, and looked as if she had immersed herself in a river of jewels. She stained her palms and soles with henna and rubbed *missi* to darken her mouth. Thus adorned, the dazzling Makhmoor summoned her flying peacock and reached Mount Agate before the sahirs who were travelling with the captured Amar.

Laqa was in his durbar with his sardars when there was a shower of flowers of gold. Moments later, Makhmoor Red-eye appeared before him in all splendour. She prostrated before offering nazar to Laqa, and declared, 'Khudawand, Afrasiyab has sent two sahirs with an army of sixty thousand soldiers to destroy Hamza. They will bring the real Amar, tied up in chains, with them.' Laqa tilted his crown with pride and cried, 'O my mortals, do you see my miracles?' Bakhtiarak slapped his own buttocks in sheer joy and cried, 'Princess, my eyes were thirsting for a sight of you! Let us go together and receive the Shah's sahirs.' Makhmoor just wanted an excuse to look for her beloved and insisted that the Shaitan was not to trouble himself, as she could receive the sahirs by herself.

After she left, Bakhtiarak asked Laqa, 'Khudawand, you and I are alone now; tell me, has it been ordained that Amar will be executed by you today?' Laqa replied joyfully, 'I had ordained ninety thousand years ago that when he is captured in Tilism and sent here, he will be executed!' Makhmoor went towards the lashkar of Islam but did not go too close to it. She looked eagerly for a glimpse of her beloved, but the mirror of her eyes did not reflect his image. Eventually, she sent a message to Hizar and Inzar that Khudawand was waiting for the prisoner. Later, the sahirs were received with honour by the ruler of Mount Agate, Sulaiman Ambreen Kohi, who made arrangements for the vast army to camp right across from Hamza's lashkar.

The two sahirs arrived at Laqa's durbar with the chained Amar and threw him in front of Laqa. Laqa said to Amar, 'You blasphemer and sinner—you will now die in great anguish!' Amar retorted, 'My only Khudawand! It is not my fault! You willed me once to anoint your beard with my urine before shaving it off. Surely you must have willed something similar this time!' Laqa was outraged by Amar's reply and the Shaitan whispered to him that it would be best to execute Amar at once. Amar then turned to the Shaitan and said, 'Malik-ji, it's best not to whisper in front of me! Do you know who I am?'

The Shaitan immediately kneeled before Amar and squeaked, 'O king of ayyars, I have tried to persuade this haramzada Laqa not to make false claims of divinity but this idiot will not heed me! No matter, he will surely go straight to hell!' Laqa roared, 'Haramzadeh Shaitan, what are you saying?' The Shaitan shouted back at Laqa, 'I speak the truth. Release the honourable king of ayyars now or your face will be blackened, your head shaved and you will receive a shoe beating!'

The enraged Laqa screamed, 'Call the executioner and tell him that this cursed Shaitan should be executed with Amar as well!' The Shaitan retorted, 'If you have awarded me the status of devil, I am bound to be blasphemous! Otherwise take this collar of my cursed office and make someone else Shaitan!' Laqa saw the logic of this argument and forgave Bakhtiarak. He then declared that Amar was to be executed within sight of the Islamic camp.

Laqa's men led Amar to the plain below the walls of Fort Agate and threw him on a bed of nails thinly covered by a rough sackcloth. Heavily-armed executioners swaggered around the platform with their swords drawn. Laqa's lashkar watched the newly-arrived sahir army who were a formidable sight. A legion of archers stood ready to kill anyone who dared come to Amar's rescue.

The news of Amar's imminent execution spread like wildfire throughout Mount Agate and the surrounding areas, and huge crowds gathered to witness the execution. Makhmoor stood to one side with her handmaidens and thought, 'Why did I come here at all? Now I will be party to this execution and will never gain my love!' Laqa emerged from the fort on an elephant and nodded at the executioners. They drew a line with charcoal around Amar's neck and said, 'O traveller of doom, you may eat if you wish and say your last words for any moment, the cup of your life will be filled with the wine of death!'

The ayyars of Islam ran back to the Pavilion of Solomon and informed the Shah of Islam, 'O King of the Worlds and the Skies, today some sahirs brought Amar in chains from Tilism. Laqa is about to destroy the flower of his life!' The Shah looked at his grandfather Emir Hamza, who rose from his seat and cried, 'Alas, my loyal friend!' The sardars and Hamza's sons rose as well. The lashkar mobilized for battle but the Emir did not wait for anyone. He left for Fort Agate alone, mounted on his great horse Ashqar from Koh Qaf, the land of fairies and *dev*s. His sons and grandsons, Qasim, Nur al Dahar, Iraj and Alamshah, rode close behind him along with sardars such as the faithful Landhoor. Shah Saad bin Qubad emerged on his throne flanked by several *tajdar*s. The Naqara of Alexander was struck and its mighty sound caused the sky to tremble.

Emir Hamza was the first to reach the execution site. He drew his sword out as he announced: 'I am Hamza the Arab, of the family of the Prophet; mounted on Ashqar!' Laqa's army trembled with fear as they heard his call, but Bakhtiarak started jumping in his seat and called out to Laqa, 'Allah ho Akbar! O infidel, convert to Islam now before Hamza brings misery to your life. As for me, I have been a Muslim from the very beginning!'

Laqa shouted at the executioners to behead Amar quickly but Makhmoor whispered an incantation that froze their bodies. The sahir army attacked the Emir with magic oranges and coconuts but he recited the Great Name and destroyed hundreds with his tegha. Qasim, Nur al Dahar and the other sardars soon joined in the fray. The forces of Islam fell upon Laqa's army like their nemesis and Laqa's army responded with vigour. The battleground resounded with clashing metal; the woodcutter of death cut the heads of braves that fell like autumn leaves; naked teghas produced blossoms of blood, while fresh wounds smiled like flowers.

Prince Nur al Dahar was one of the sardars fighting this bloody battle with Emir Hamza and Makhmoor kept whispering spells to prevent sahirs from harming her beloved prince. The ayyars of Islam decided to attack the sahir army as they knew that from their camp, only Hamza was impervious to magic. A hundred and eighty thousand ayyars burst smoking hookahs over the sahir army. The air became dark with smoke and the faces of several sahirs were seared by the heat of the smoke; many of them even fled the battlefield in panic. The Emir's faithful companion, Muqbil, the legendary archer, let forth a volley of arrows that killed many sahirs. He shot the sahir leader Inzar in the chest just as he was flying up towards the sky. Struck by the arrow, Inzar somersaulted back to the earth and died in great agony.

Inzar's death released Amar from his magical shackles. He jumped on Laqa's throne and snatched his crown after landing a great blow to his head. Bakhtiarak said cheerfully, 'Bismillah! May I offer these humble gifts to you as well!' He held out his fine *pashmina* shawl and gold turban cloth to Amar. Amar accepted these gifts, even as he fended off the attacks of Laqa's companions. He fought his way to his master Emir Hamza and kissed Ashqar's stirrup. The Emir dismounted and embraced Amar with warmth but the battle was not yet over; after a brief respite, the Emir continued to fight Laqa's men. Just as the Emir closed in on Laqa's throne, Bakhtiarak had the drums of peace struck, admitting defeat.

Emir Hamza returned to his camp in triumph and his sardars showered gold coins on him in jubilation. Amar protested loudly, 'Friends why do you waste your money? Give me all of this for I am needy!' Emir Hamza laughed and said, 'Khwaja, there will be more for you!' The greedy Amar, however, cast the Net of Ilyas on the heap of gold coins and deposited it in Zambil. Amar was led into the Pavilion of Solomon and seated on the exalted Hoopoe Chair. The Shah and the Emir awarded him with several trays of precious gems. Amar related all his adventures in Tilism in detail. Emir Hamza also heard of the exploits of the ayyars and sent for heavy robes of honour for them. Amar accepted the robes on their behalf and said, 'Ya Emir, I will not spoil my disciples yet but will tell them that the Emir has sent you khalats, wear them on Eid day!'

The Emir and everyone in his durbar roared with laughter at Amar's remarks. Then he took his leave and went into the women's pavilions. The women greeted him warmly but his many wives surrounded him and immediately asked for living expenses and gifts. 'Husband,' they teased him, 'you must surely have brought us some presents from Tilism!' Amar cried, 'I have been bankrupted by my expenses in Tilism and was hoping to now sell your jewellery to raise additional funds!' The women giggled in disbelief and continued to pester the ayyar for gifts. Eventually, Amar reached into the Zambil and with great aplomb presented his wives with synthetic gems, some old nails and turmeric roots. He told them, 'You people do not understand my plight. Now I am completely ruined!' Later, Amar went to his favourite wife Princess Saro Seemtan, who met him with great respect and affection. Amar finally relaxed in her calming presence.

In the enemy camp, Laqa returned to his durbar looking very gloomy and dejected. The surviving sahir officer Hizar went to Laqa and said quietly, 'Khudawand, the sahir army is no more. I will take my leave of you. If you have a message for Afrasiyab, I will convey it to him.' Laqa said, 'Tell him to send a powerful sahir to help me. This time, I will ordain the deaths of these blasphemous mortals.' Bakhtiarak heard this speech and said, 'Khudawand, you had also ordained that Amar would die today; instead Inzar lost his life. Why did you reverse their fates?' Laqa blustered, 'The pen of providence moves with my will. You should not meddle in divine matters.' Bakhtiarak fell silent and Hizar left the durbar.

Makhmoor also bade Laqa farewell and mounted her magic peacock. As the peacock flew upwards, Makhmoor looked down at the Islamic lashkar yearningly. The sardars had returned to their tents after Amar had left the durbar. Nur al Dahar was at that time standing outside his tent. Princess Makhmoor Red-eye, the beautiful bird who had flown into the highest realm of love, saw him and could restrain herself no longer. She told her companions to wait for her on the border of Tilism. After they left, this royal prisoner of love and devotion flew on her peacock down to the Islamic lashkar and called out, 'O unfaithful one, is this a rule of love that I should pine for you and you should remain unaware of me?'

The prince looked up and saw the star of the sky of lovers, a pearl of the river of devotion, a vision of loveliness that could illuminate any gathering. He lost his senses and fell in love with her at first sight. As he moved closer towards her, Makhmoor smiled and turned her face away. She said, 'Now do not declare your love for me just because you have seen me!' The prince who was hopelessly smitten with love cried, 'O beloved, why do you punish me that you first cast your shadow on me like a fairy and then you turn away from me!?'

Makhmoor was silent and floated out of the camp on her peacock. The prince followed her reciting verses of love, but the beautiful sahira did not respond to him. Makhmoor descended from her mount when she reached a mountain ravine and said, 'Why do you follow me sir? Well, here I am. Ask me what you will.' The prince's cheeks were wet with tears. Makhmoor wiped the tears gently and said, 'It is not good to be friends with me prince. My master Afrasiyab watches me closely and I must return to him.'

Nur al Dahar asked her quietly, 'Are you a sahira?' Makhmoor nodded. The prince fell silent. Makhmoor parted her ruby lips and laughed as she shed these pearls of speech: 'O faithless lover, I am not one of those sahiras who are over a hundred years of age and use magic to remain youthful. I am just fourteen years old.' The prince looked relieved and smiled, 'O comfort of my heart, I was merely thinking of how my grandfather Emir Hamza will never consent to my marriage with a sahira.'

Makhmoor laughed, 'How you do run on! How can you talk about marriage at this time! I admit I love you but nothing is possible until Tilism is destroyed.' Nur al Dahar embraced her but she was nervous and urged him to let her leave. 'I am yours,' she said, 'but I have to be cautious. In my heart I have converted to Islam; after Tilism is destroyed, Inshallah, I will abjure the practice of magic. For now, I have to assist Amar in Tilism and somehow escape from the Shahanshah.'

Now hear about Amar. After he bid farewell to his favourite wife, he thought of returning to Tilism. He went to the border and came across Makhmoor's attendants waiting for her. Disguised as a sahir, he asked them, 'Hizar has returned to Tilism and we are leaving as well. Why are you still here?' They said, 'We are Princess Makhmoor's handmaidens. We are waiting for her to join us before we return to Tilism.' Amar was happy when he heard this and thought, 'The Almighty has provided a way for me to return to Tilism.' He said, 'If one of you can come with me to my relative's house nearby, I can send wine and kebabs, for you must be weary of waiting here.'

So, one of the handmaidens went with him. After they had walked some distance, Amar burst a narcotic bubble in her face that made her unconscious. He wore her outer robes and painted his face to look like hers. He went back to the rest of Makhmoor's handmaidens with bottles of wine and claimed that the sahir had sent them. The wine was not drugged as Amar did not intend to render them unconscious. Thus, he waited with them for Makhmoor.

In the mountain ravine, Makhmoor sighed deeply and said to Nur al Dahar, 'For now, my love, farewell and may God be with you. I must leave before Afrasiyab is alarmed by my long absence.' As she rose to leave, Nur al Dahar's eyes filled with tears. Makhmoor wept as well and both lovers were distraught as they parted.

Amar and Makhmoor

Makhmoor found her handmaidens and they all flew back to Tilism on a magic peacock. Amar mounted the peacock-mount of the woman he had made unconscious (as long as she was alive, her magic was also alive). Makhmoor kept weeping softly all the way back to the invisible Tilism of Batin where she lived. As they flew over the Tilism of Zahir, Amar tried to land near his camp, but his peacock flew straight to the Garden of Apples. Makhmoor told her companions, 'You must be tired from the journey. Return home and I will follow you soon after meeting the Shahanshah.'

Makhmoor walked into the durbar with a heavy heart. She greeted the King of Magic and sat down next to her sister. Khumar made the traditional gesture of taking on her troubles and embraced her. She looked closely at Makhmoor and said, 'What ails you my sister? You look so pale and sad!' Makhmoor made up an excuse about being tired from the journey. At that time, Hizar entered the durbar. He greeted the Shahanshah and related all that had happened in Mount Agate.

The Shahanshah looked thoughtful and then said quietly, 'I know everything. O Makhmoor, come here.' Trembling with fear, Makhmoor went forward, but could not meet Afrasiyab's eyes. He stared hard at her emerald armbands carved with images and called out, 'Tell me what really happened!' The images came to life and recited all that had transpired between her and Nur al Dahar, and added, 'O Mighty King! Makhmoor wept to prove her love to Prince Nur al Dahar.' Afrasiyab laughed bitterly and said, 'You treacherous woman! What do you have to say for yourself now?' Makhmoor replied in a small voice, 'I wept for all our companions who were killed in battle.' She fell on her knees and pleaded, 'Forgive me huzoor!'

Afrasiyab said stonily, 'Not before you receive a hundred lashes as punishment.' He knocked in the air and two hideously black sahirs emerged from the earth with leather whips in their hands. At one signal from Afrasiyab, they started whipping Makhmoor mercilessly. Within a few minutes, the delicate and pampered Makhmoor lay with torn and bloody garments in a crumpled heap. Her sister Khumar bravely came forward, looked Afrasiyab in the eye and said, 'Shahanshah, have you no respect for our dignity and honour?' Afrasiyab replied that the images on the armband had confirmed Makhmoor's guilt. 'They are manipulated by magic,' wept Khumar, 'will you take my sister's life for their word?' Only when she threw herself on her sister to protect her did Afrasiyab signal to the sahirs to stop, after which they vanished back into the earth. Afrasiyab said, 'Khumar, I punished her to set an example. I do not care how many lovers she has, but to consort with my enemies in unforgivable.' Khumar replied, 'We are your handmaidens and would never disobey you!'

Khumar lifted the unconscious Makhmoor in her arms and carried her out of the durbar. Khumar then conjured a throne and carried Makhmoor to her palace where Amar was present along with the other women. As they fussed around their mistress and tended to her wounds, Makhmoor woke up and looked into her sister's worried eyes. 'What really happened there my sister?' whispered Khumar.

Makhmoor lost her temper and shouted, 'This pimp Afrasiyab will surely reach his doom! I am not his slave that he treats me in this manner! I am a princess of the realm with my own country and treasures. Now I will support Amar with my heart and soul!' Khumar looked around in alarm and hushed her, 'My sister, where will we go if we fall out of favour with Afrasiyab? We cannot live in the river and fight with the crocodile!' Makhmoor hissed, 'Please just fold up your advice and keep it with yourself! What can that joker do to me? For that matter, what has he been able to do to Bahar? I am a princess not a slave that I should remain silent after being whipped. My name is not Makhmoor if I do not have him beaten to a pulp by my prince! As long as I remain here, I am vulnerable. I have to leave.' Khumar said in a resigned tone, 'Well, it is your business after all. You are too angry right now and I will leave.'

She left Makhmoor to nurse her painful wounds and brood over her love for Nur al Dahar. 'Alas, I should have confided in Amar,' she muttered half-deliriously, 'I would have been spared this humiliation.' Amar, who had been hovering around as a concerned companion overheard this and whispered in her ear, 'Princess, I can make Amar available to you right now!' Makhmoor was startled and said, 'Have you lost your mind? You were with me in Laqa's durbar. Hamza rescued Amar and took him back to his camp. What are you saying? Are you making fun of me?' Amar whispered, 'Whatever you say is the truth. Nevertheless, if you are willing to part with gold, I can produce Amar right away.' Makhmoor said, 'If what you say is possible, I will reward you with great riches.'

'Princess,' Amar said in his own voice, 'I am Amar!' Makhmoor was stunned and the ayyar proved his identity by removing his disguise. In sheer joy, Makhmoor rewarded him with heaps of precious stones.

Now let us return to Afrasiyab. After he had punished Makhmoor, he regretted his actions. She had always been his favourite like Bahar and the thought of losing her to the rebels was unbearable. He brooded for a long time before sending her a message that read, 'Will you not grace my durbar again?' Makhmoor received this message and although she was still very angry with Afrasiyab, she was also highly intelligent. She knew that if she did not obey him now, he would consult the oracle Book of Samri and discover that Amar was with her.

She reached durbar a few minutes after receiving the message. Afrasiyab was overjoyed to see her and said, 'Princess, do not be angry with me; you are so very dear to me.' Makhmoor said softly, 'You are the ruler and I will remain loyal to you.' Afrasiyab awarded her with a robe of honour and made her the ruler of several kingdoms. Makhmoor wore the robe and returned to her seat in the durbar.

Amar strikes again

Afrasiyab then addressed Khumar, 'As you know, I had sent Qeher Nigar and Ghaddar Jadoo to fight the rebels. They have captured them and kept them by the banks of the River of Flowing Blood. I had thought of reasoning with the rebels so that they return to their senses, but now feel that they have destroyed my house. It is better to execute them.' Khumar said, 'I think that they should be executed right away, but huzoor knows best.' Afrasiyab called out, 'Jallad Jadoo, present yourself!' A sahir shot out of the earth and performed a mujra-greeting before the Shah. Afrasiyab said, 'Join Qeher and Ghaddar and execute all the prisoners. Have no mercy on anyone; Mahrukh and Bahar should also be killed.'

After Jallad had taken his leave of Afrasiyab, the Shahanshah decided that it had been a long day and dismissed his durbar. Makhmoor returned to her palace looking worried. Amar emerged from a corner and asked her what was wrong. Makhmoor whispered. 'Afrasiyab has ordered Ghaddar and Jallad to execute the sardars!' Amar said, 'Princess, just send me across the river and watch what happens. Ghaddar and Jallad will be killed and I will rescue Mahrukh.'

Makhmoor pondered for a while and then came to a decision. 'If I am with you, then I have to help you!' she declared. She reached into her magic pouch and took out a thorny twig. As she chanted a spell over it, the twig transformed into a human hand and clasped Amar around his waist. 'Good luck Khwaja,' cried Makhmoor, 'please do not forget this humble friend of yours in your prayers!' The magic hand flew off with Amar and deposited him across the River of Flowing Blood within minutes.

Amar first kissed the earth in gratitude to the granter of wishes. He moved on and saw that Ghaddar's lashkar was spread out beside the river. As he was watching this scene, Jallad Jadoo arrived with his army and was welcomed by Ghaddar. Amar saw that the executioners had erected scaffolds to execute the sardars the next morning.

Amar assumed the face and form of Khumar Jadoo and came to the camp holding a tray of fresh fruits. Qeher and Jallad knew Khumar and greeted her with courtesy. Khumar said solemnly, 'The King of Sahirs has sent this fruit for you and was insistent that you have it right away.' The unsuspecting sahirs ate the fruit and even served it to all their companions. After some time, their mouths felt dry and they asked Khumar, 'What kind of fruit is this that we are feeling intoxicated?' The false Khumar replied, 'It is from Afrasiyab's garden and you know that the fruit there is nurtured with wine.'

In a little while, the tongues of the sahirs had gone numb and they realized they had been drugged. They looked suspiciously at the false Khumar who glared back at them and called out, 'Fools, I am the doom of sahirs, Amar bin Ummayyah!' The sahirs looked aghast and rose to attack Amar but the drugged fruits had weakened them and they collapsed. Amar tried to behead them with his *khanjar* but realized that they had steeled their bodies magically against attacks. So, Amar took out gunmetal from Zambil, melted it over a fire, tore open their mouths and poured the metal down their throats. The sahirs died in great agony; their deaths caused a black storm and horrifying voices called out their names. Amar plundered the durbar of its precious items and ran for cover.

The imprisoned sardars were now released from their magical shackles and fell upon the enemy lashkar in a furious onslaught. Within moments, there were piles of dead bodies all around. Ra'ad plunged into the earth and emerged thundering amidst enemy ranks. Barq Mehshar shot up to the sky in a flash of lightning and fell upon enemy soldiers and scorched them alive. Mahrukh hurled iron balls that expelled deadly snakes, which then bit the cruel sahir soldiers; and Bahar conjured enchanted gardens that destroyed the tree of life of many sahirs.

After the lashkar was decimated, Amar addressed all his sardars, 'The Shah of Tilism will learn of this rout and will wreak vengeance. Each one of you should return separately to the camp. I will join you soon.' The sardars obeyed Amar—some of them flew back to the camp while others plunged into the earth to travel beneath it. The ayyars also ran off in different directions.

Now hear about what happened to Afrasiyab. He arose the next morning and appeared in the durbar behind a magic glass. 'Any moment now,' declared Afrasiyab to his courtiers, 'we will receive the decapitated heads of the rebel sardars.' As he was speaking, two birds, one red and one green, flew into the durbar. They trilled, 'Shahanshah, Amar crossed the River of Flowing Blood and killed your sahir officers. The prisoners escaped and destroyed their armies.' The birds vanished after making this announcement.

After a stunned silence, Afrasiyab wrung his hands in remorse and struck his knees several times as he cried, 'This ayyar has humiliated us time and again. What I cannot understand is how did he come into Batin and who helped him across the river. When we sent him to Khudawand, he was rescued by Hamza. He could have only managed escaping from Batin if someone very powerful and known to me supported him. No matter, I will find this person and punish him so hideously that the fishes of the river and the birds of the desert will weep for him.' Afrasiyab then vanished behind the magic glass. His courtiers looked at each in fear and wondered who among them would be punished next.

∽

9 MAKHMOOR'S SECRET IS REVEALED AND SHE JOINS MAHRUKH'S LASHKAR

Amar is trapped in Afrasiyab's Tilism

Afrasiyab was restless and agitated when he disappeared behind the magic mirror. He materialized on the far shores of the River of Flowing Blood and cast a spell that created a miniature Tilism in the strip of land between Mahrukh's camp and the river. It was as if the visible and invisible Tilisms were compressed into that space. He appointed notable sahirs as the guardians of this Tilism and vanished.

During this time, Mahrukh Magic-eye got a much-needed respite to gather her scattered forces. The camp was reorganized and the bazaars were re-opened. When Hairat saw the enemy camp being rebuilt she began to wonder how the rebels had escaped. Soon, Sarsar arrived at

Hairat's camp with her trickster companions and briefed the queen about the bloody battle that had occurred and about how the prisoners had managed to escape. She added, 'The Shahanshah came across the river and has left for the Garden of Pleasure.'

Now hear about Amar and the other ayyars. They were going to their camp through the desert. However, before they could reach it, they were trapped in the minature Tilism that Afrasiyab had conjured. Amar crossed the desert and suddenly found himself in a valley enclosed by huge mountains. He walked through a gully in the mountains and came upon a lush green meadow where there were two identical white marble palaces, almost fairy-like in their ethereal beauty, with walls inlaid with precious stones.

Amar stealthily investigated both palaces and found that they were richly furnished. He said to himself, 'Allah has placed these palaces here for my benefit! Who is there to stop me? So let me begin with Allah's will.' He entered the palaces and saw no owners, custodians or guards. He cast his blessed Net of Ilyas and soon emptied both palaces of all furnishings, precious objects and even curtains, and secured them in Zambil. On his way out, he heard an unknown voice booming, 'Where will you go now, you thief? You are trapped!'

Amar ran as fast as he could and took refuge in a hill where *molsri* trees cast a pleasant cool shade. There, a sahir sat cross-legged under a tree, clad in a silk loincloth with golden stripes; he wore armbands with tiny jewel-studded figurines and a string of pearls around his neck. Amar tried to dodge out of sight but a female puppet shot out of the earth and cried, 'Khursan Jadoo, this wretched thief is fleeing from you!'

Amar told himself, 'Let me get this sahir's wealth as well. I may be captured but it is all Allah's will!' Thus Amar approached the sahir and said, 'Brother, who are you?' Before Khursan could reply, the puppet piped up, 'This was the thief who plundered the magic palaces. Thieves usually look for money, but this rascal even took the curtains away!' Khursan got up to capture Amar, who protested loudly, 'Are you blind? That thief must be someone else. I am a trader!' Khursan said, 'But this puppet says you are a thief!' Amar replied, 'This wretched puppet lies!' 'Impossible!' Khursan declared, 'The magic puppet cannot lie!' He then read a spell that made Amar's feet stuck to the ground.

Following this, Amar said in a conciliatory tone, 'Brother, the magic puppet is right, but I am also truthful.' This interested the sahir and Amar continued with his yarn, 'Now hear me—I was in dire need of six lakh rupees to re-pay my debts and prayed to the great gods Samri and Jamshed to bless me with wealth. My prayers were answered and the gods provided these two houses full of treasures. Has this caused your father or this puppet any loss? Why have you captured me?'

Khursan laughed and said, 'Had the gods so willed, they could have given you mountains of gold! Why would they give you someone else's property to plunder?' Amar bowed his head and said, 'Do not be angry with me, I can lead you to the cave where I stored the goods.' Khursan readily agreed but the puppet cried out, 'You wily thief, you deceive us with this story of a cave. Why, I saw you swallow the goods before my eyes! Khursan, do not go with him lest he harms you!'

Amar laughed in derision and Khursan looked puzzled. 'What nonsense is this,' he asked the puppet, 'and how is it possible for a human being to consume such large items?' The puppet swore by Samri that she spoke the truth but Khursan ignored her and followed Amar. The ayyar pointed to a distant cave and the moment Khursan turned to walk in that direction, Amar quickly stabbed him in the back. The din that usually arose in wake of a sahir's death brought another sahir to the scene and he promptly captured Amar. Qiran, who had been watching all this from a distance, quickly ran to the sahir and Amar. The sahir asked him, 'Who are you?'

Qiran retorted, 'Worry about me later brother; look, a man behind you is about to attack!' The sahir turned around, and in a flash, Qiran drew out his mighty sword and smashed his skull. There was a huge dust storm and bodyless voices wailed, 'Alas! You have killed Khoonrez Jadoo!'

Amar embraced Qiran in gratitude but Qiran looked visibly distressed. 'My teacher,' he said, 'I have been wandering around this place, but cannot find a way out. May Allah protect us! I think we are trapped in some powerful enchantment!' He abruptly jumped back and ran away. Amar saw him disappear out of sight and thought, 'There is no one around; why did he run away like that?' Amar was still thinking about this when another sahir appeared before him and called out, 'Amar, will you kill the whole world? O cruel one, this place is full of sahirs; have some mercy! You must have heard the saying, "A single strike of the blacksmith's hammer has more impact than a hundred strikes by the goldsmith!" You will be caught eventually!' Amar thought, 'That is all I need! Do I really want his advice?' He remained quiet but quickly donned Galeem to become invisible.

Amar and the gullible Afrasiyab

After running for some distance, Amar reached the end of the forest. A great wall of mirrors divided it from a desert that lay beyond it. Amar jumped over the wall and was now truly trapped in the invisible Tilism of Afrasiyab's making. Amar ran around the desert like a whirlwind but could not find any way out. He recalled that the last sahir he met had warned him that he would be eventually captured. After some time, he felt as if his tongue was hanging out with thirst. He took out a pitcher of water from Zambil but felt even more thirsty after he had drunk from it. He wept bitterly, 'For how long will I take water out from Zambil? I will become penniless. Whenever Hamza was thirsty in the desert, I would sell him a pitcher of water for thousands of dinars. Alas, today I will have to take out not only water from Zambil, but also food!'

Amar tried to keep walking further on but his extreme thirst compelled him to take out another pitcher of iced water from Zambil. That did not assuage his thirst either. Then he ran in great agony towards a distant grove of trees and when he reached there, found the ground carpeted with soft green grass. Amar felt calmer in the shade of the trees. As he rested, a shimmering wall of silver and gold materialized before him. The wall had a finely moulded door of solid gold with two panels of glass through which Amar could see a garden that blossomed in a magical springtime. Its flowerbeds bloomed with narcissi and the fragrance of *sumbul* grass permeated the air. The streams in the garden bubbled merrily and *bulbul* birds perched on the trees heralded the advent of spring.

In the middle of the garden was a vast crystal platform with soaring pillars made of rubies. Sapphire peacocks perched on the steeples of the canopy with strings of pearls hanging from their beaks and the canopy was trimmed with tassels of pearls that moved in the breeze like a river. The platform's floor was covered with embroidered silk that sparkled with silver glitter. On a throne, sat Afrasiyab in all splendour.

Amar realized this was a trap and thought, 'I should turn away from here although it is a great loss not to plunder this rich garden!' He ran for several miles, but the desert around him seemed infinite. A golden-feathered peacock that was circling over him cried, 'I am very hungry!' Amar suddenly felt a rush of hunger and took out crusts of dried bread from Zambil. But when it was taken out in the hot, dry air of the desert, the bread crumbled like dry clay. Amar placed his hand in Zambil and called out, 'Grandfather, Ya Ab-ul-Bashar, I had looted some barfi from Jallad's lashkar. Kindly give it to me for it would still be fresh!' The barfi emerged from Zambil but turned to dust when he took a bite. Amar spat it out and quickly drank some water but then felt as if his throat was on fire.

Eventually, Amar fainted with thirst and want of nourishment. He woke up with a rush of cold air and opened his eyes to see that the earth had parted to reveal a woman who told him, 'Amar, go into yonder garden where Shahanshah holds court and beg for food and water in Shahanshah's name. Only then will you survive here!' Amar sighed deeply and looked reproachfully at the sky, 'Alas, I will now have to beg for charity from Afrasiyab!'

Amar returned to the grove and entered the garden through the gold door. There, some women approached him and asked him who he was. 'I am a weary traveller who was trapped in the desert. I am thirsty and hungry. I trust you will help me!' said Amar. The women giggled and rolled their eyes as they told each other, 'Look at this pathetic creature; as if he does not know anything although he has not even left trees behind when he plunders!' They turned to Amar and said, 'Unless you give us your real name, no one will help you here. Although we know who you really are (after all, your infamy is known to all and your name is engraved on the hearts of all sahirs), these are the orders of the Shah. Give your name and you will be given food and all other comforts.'

Amar realized that the Shahanshah wanted to humiliate him and thought, 'These women know me well. I will not debase myself by giving my name.' Just at that moment, a few more women came out to announce that the Shahanshah wanted to see Amar. The great ayyar thought in fear, 'Now what does this wretch intend to do to me? With God's will, either me or that joker Afrasiyab will win today!' When he finally stood in front of Afrasiyab, Amar greeted him respectfully. Afrasiyab played along and said in mock deference, 'Khwaja sahib, are you doing well?' Amar replied to this question with equal deference, 'I am thankful a thousand times to Almighty God who has brought me here.'

Afrasiyab then asked, 'Amar, will you truthfully answer one question?' Amar replied, 'I have never lied. Ask me and I will tell you what I know.' Afrasiyab said, 'If you answer me truthfully, I will release you. Otherwise you will perish in this desert.'

'Are you asking a question or threatening me?' Amar retorted. The King of Magic continued, 'What I have to ask you is this: who helped you across the River of Flowing Blood and how did you return to Tilism from Mount Agate?' Amar laughed out aloud and cried, 'O Shahanshah that is no secret! I am the favourite of my god and when I could not go across the river, I appealed to him to help me. He sent me a houri from heaven who took me across the river.'

'Who is your god?' Afrasiyab asked Amar. Amar laughed and replied, 'How many times have I told you my god is Zamurrad Shah Bakhtri or Laqa as you call him? I am his Angel of Death and he sent me to Tilism to punish sinners. To tell you the truth, I believe only in him and not the hundred and seventy-five gods you believe in. Khudawand Laqa and I share secrets that you cannot even imagine. The worship of Samri and Jamshed is abhorrent to Khudawand. He believes that if any god dies, his divinity dies with him. He appears to be well-disposed towards you but he is not happy with you right now. Therefore, he has sent me to kill those who worship gods other than him. O King of Magic, understand this! You know that you are so much more powerful than I am; it is only because Khudawand is annoyed with you that you lose to me!'

'You may be right,' Afrasiyab said slowly. 'Now tell me, how exactly did the houri take you across the river?' 'She hoisted me on her back,' replied Amar readily, 'and walked into the river. The water came up to my head and I was about to drown when I saw a boat with Khudawand Laqa in it. He rescued me and rowed me across the river himself. However, I fainted from the odour of the foul stench that came from him. When I became conscious, I was on the other bank.'

Afrasiyab was outraged but asked him calmly, 'Why do you say Khudawand smelt foul?' 'Because,' explained Amar with mock patience, 'Khudawand does not perform his daily ablutions. He never cleans his teeth, they are fungus-ridden and emit a horrible smell. The reason is that he has no time. He has to reward some, punish others, and make some rich, others poor. You tell me, how can he then attend to his personal hygiene?'

'You refer to Khudawand in a very blasphemous manner, but I suppose you could be right. I have such a hard time dealing with just this Tilism and Khudawand has the whole world to run! However, tell me this, why does there seem to be enmity between you and Khudawand Laqa? Shaitan Bakhtiarak is your sworn enemy. What does that mean?'

Amar improvised on his web of lies. 'I will tell you why. Khudawand Laqa created Shaitan Bakhtiarak in a moment of carelessness. But when Shaitan started to mislead humanity, Khudawand decided to create someone who could dominate both Shaitan and him. It took a hundred thousand years for him to create me. He has told me, "Amar, you are my father; there will be times when you will humiliate and thrash me and even shave off my beard!" For the time being, however, he has given me the titles "Angel of Death" and "Slayer of Sorcerers and Magicians".'

Afrasiyab was too stunned to speak and muttered after a while, 'How can us mortals divine the ways of providence? Amar, please tell me, since Khudawand helped you cross the river, what has he destined for us now?' Amar replied, 'He did not say anything specific, but yesterday, his Angel of Grace delivered a letter to me.' Afrasiyab asked Amar to reveal the letter's contents to him, but Amar declared solemnly,

'I have already spoken too many secrets. I am not allowed to reveal more and nor should I!'

Afrasiyab persisted in a conciliatory tone, 'Amar, please do not be angry. If you have already said this much, just tell me what does the letter say?' Amar said, 'Very well, I'll tell you! Khudawand says that Shah of Tilism has helped him; therefore, I should not harm him but join him instead. However, I think I will consider it first.' Afrasiyab declared, 'If you obey Khudawand and pledge loyalty to me with your heart and life (on the condition that you show me the letter first), I will forgive all your actions and elevate you to a high rank.' Amar replied quickly, 'The letter is with me. You can see it right away!'

Amar took out an envelope embossed with the seal of Laqa from Zambil. He handed it to Afrasiyab who kissed the seal and opened the letter with great reverence. It read, 'O Amar, you should be loyal and obedient to the Shahanshah of Tilism. Do not deceive him and surrender to him along with Mahrukh, Surkh Mu, Bahar, Ra'ad and Barq Mehshar, and all the ayyars. The King of Magic should also consider Amar to be a friend and must reward him handsomely.'

Afrasiyab immediately presented Amar with several bags of gold coins and precious jewels. He also offered a jewel-inlaid chair to him to sit on and asked him to round up the rebel sardars. 'How would I do that when I cannot escape from this enchanted desert?' asked Amar. Immediately, Afrasiyab knocked in the air and the wall of mirrors he had conjured vanished from the desert. As soon as this happened, the other ayyars who had been wandering around, quickly found their way back to their camp. Amar too bade the Shahanshah farewell and left for Mahrukh's camp after promising to deliver the rebels to Afrasiyab soon.

After Amar's departure, Afrasiyab sent a note to Hairat and asked her to make arrangements for a durbar at the Garden of Pleasure. Hairat left her camp and travelled to the garden to adorn it for the King of Sahirs. Afrasiyab reached the durbar in great splendour and twelve hundred drums were struck magically when he entered the garden. Hairat offered eleven hundred gold coins in homage to him and led him to the throne.

Once Afrasiyab was seated on his throne, female puppets began dancing for him. Sarsar Sword-fighter and her ayyar girls were also present in court. Afrasiyab smiled at them and triumphantly declared, 'Sarsar, your services will not be required any longer for Amar has joined me and I will be giving him a high rank in this kingdom.' On hearing this, Sarsar tried to stifle her laughter, but Afrasiyab sensed her derision and was furious. 'Do you think that I jest, you impertinent hussy!' he shouted.

Sarsar folded her hands and said, 'Huzoor, I respectfully beg to submit that I think Amar has tricked you once again.' Afrasiyab was furious when he heard this and Hairat admonished Sarsar for her impertinence. 'Leave her, my queen,' roared Afrasiyab, 'for very soon, she will have to eat her words!' Then he called out, 'O Gauhar-badan, come to me!' A female puppet covered with jewels appeared before him. Afrasiyab said, 'Go to Amar's camp; give him my greetings and tell him to grace this garden with the spring of his arrival. Tell him that I am waiting for him and his companions in the Garden of Pleasure.'

Gauhar-badan went straight to Mahrukh's *bargah* with the Shahanshah's message. The sahirs in the durbar were alarmed to see her and drew out their magical weapons. Gauhar-badan said, 'I am not here to fight you but to bring the king of ayyars a message from my master, the Great Shahanshah!' Amar's heart leapt with fear but the puppet approached him with a smile and said, 'Shahanshah sends you prayers and good wishes. He waits for you to fulfil your promise.' Amar saw Qiran poised behind the puppet with his bughda and quickly signalled to him not to strike her. He took the puppet aside and whispered a message for the Shah, 'Give Shahanshah my respectful greetings and tell him that with his blessings, I have convinced all my sardars and will present them to him tomorrow.'

Gauhar Badan flew back to the Garden of Pleasure and conveyed Amar's message to the Shahanshah. Afrasiyab smiled and said to the ayyar girl, 'Sarsar, have you heard my friend Amar's message?' Sarsar smirked and said, 'Quite right huzoor; to be sure, he will bring them all!' While saying this, she looked meaningfully at Saba Raftar who could not suppress her giggles any longer. Afrasiyab controlled his fury and said, 'You will be punished for your impertinence tomorrow when Amar arrives.' Sarsar retorted, 'Huzoor, you are my master and can say anything but I know he is deceiving you with these messages!' Afrasiyab declared, 'Well, this might convince you!' He sent for the puppet again and said, 'Go back to Mahrukh's durbar and convey our good wishes to Amar. Tell him today is as good a day as tomorrow is!'

Amar trembled with fear when Gauhar-badan appeared again. He sent back a message with the puppet: 'Huzoor, I will not come to the Garden of Pleasure but to the velvet pavilion under the Dome of Light on this side of the river.'

Afrasiyab looked at Sarsar when the puppet returned with Amar's message and said, 'Sarsar, they are all going to come. Now, how should I punish you?' Sarsar remained silent and Afrasiyab turned to his servants and instructed them to prepare and adorn the velvet pavilion. He sent another message to Amar, inviting him to a feast at the Dome. Amar called Mahrukh, Bahar, Surkh Mu, Barq Mehshar and the other sardars and said, 'I have given my word to the Shahanshah. All of you will have to beg his forgiveness.' On hearing this, the sardars walked away from Amar after declaring that they would rather die instead.

Amar whispered to Mahrukh, 'I was merely testing your loyalty. Hide now with the sardars in a separate pavilion because there will be trouble soon.' After Mahrukh went with all her sardars to a private tent, Amar signalled to his ayyar comrades to serve drugged wine to them. Mahrukh, Bahar, Surkh Mu, Shakeel, Ra'ad and Barq Mehshar with hundreds of other sardars fell unconscious after drinking the wine and Amar dropped them all in Zambil. The ayyars then rounded up several minor sahirs and sahiras from the camp, painted their faces as substitutes for the real sardars and instructed them that they were to beg for forgiveness from Afrasiyab. Amar warned them sternly, 'Remember, you are not to reveal your true identities or I will punish you!'

Among the ayyars, Qiran refused to participate in this plan because he felt that he would give himself away. The rest of the ayyars accompanied Amar and the false sardars to Afrasiyab's durbar at the Dome of Light.

Afrasiyab had already convened the durbar in the velvet pavilion when he heard the drums heralding Amar's arrival with the sardars. He sent his notable sahirs to receive the rebels. The false sardars entered the pavilion and immediately fell at Afrasiyab's feet. 'We have sinned greatly!' they cried, 'Punish us as you will but we will remain loyal to you forever!' Afrasiyab generously embraced all of them, patted them on the back and declared, 'You were not to blame; the gods had destined this for us!' He awarded each of the rebel sardars with robes of honour. Amar received the heaviest robe as well as a tray of jewels. He also sat next to Afrasiyab.

Sarsar, who was present in the durbar, realized that these were not the real sardars. 'Have you noticed,' she whispered to her friend Saba Raftar, 'Bahar's teeth never protruded like that; look at those fine black lines around her eyes; see how cleverly these faces have been painted!' Saba Raftar whispered back, 'Princess, you are so right! By Samri, I would never have guessed!'

Amar saw the two ayyar girls whispering and observed their lips carefully. He realized what they were saying and angrily called out, 'Sarsar, why are you observing us all so closely? Perhaps you think this is trickery. Do you seriously think I could deceive the King of Magic? Can a lamp be lit in the darkness?' Following this, Afrasiyab too admonished her,

'Sarsar, if you utter another word, I will punish you. Are you not ashamed that as an ayyar girl you have been wrong about everything so far?' Sarsar feared the Shah's wrath and remained silent.

After a while, Saba Raftar left the pavilion on an errand. Barq Firangi followed her and on seeing her hurrying off, realized that she would not be back for some time. Quickly disguising himself as Saba, he returned to the durbar where Sarsar was in a state of inner agitation. She thought, 'This fool Afrasiyab is determined to destroy himself today; he has gone mad and will not listen to anything. However, I have eaten his salt and do owe him my loyalty. Let me try and warn him once again.'

She tried to get closer to the Shah but Barq, disguised as Saba Raftar, held her hand and whispered, 'Come out with me, I have to consult you about something!' Sarsar went with him willingly. Barq led her to the edge of the forest around the Dome of Light and burst a narcotic bubble on her face that made her unconscious. He tied her to a tree deep in the forest and woke her by slapping her face. 'So my teacher's beloved,' he said, 'you were thinking of exposing our trickery? I should cut your nose off for this!'

Sarsar let loose of a torrent of abuses: 'You vile ayyar! I will bury your teacher in the deepest grave and make halwa out of you! May you die young and may you depart from this world unloved and unwanted! Your limbs should be broken before you die!' Barq laughed at her abuses and when he left her, called out over his shoulder, 'You can do nothing from here!'

Meanwhile, Amar had begun humming to himself in Afrasiyab's durbar. As his musical voice was a blessing of the prophets, Afrasiyab's soul was stirred by it. He said. 'O Amar, if you do not mind, could you sing for us?' Amar replied modestly, 'It would be better if a beautiful young damsel sang. I am old and spent; what is the point of making me sing?' Afrasiyab said, 'You must not make excuses. I have heard you sing several times; no one in this Tilism can sing like you!' Amar relented after some time and transformed into a beautiful damsel in a corner. The damsel had hair as long as the dark night; her cheeks shone like the moon; and her lowered eyes could hasten the final day.

Afrasiyab looked with wonder at this vision and sent for a costly dancing costume and gold jewellery. Amar adorned himself with these and began dancing for the Shahanshah. The damsel's dancing was so skilled that the Old Man of the Sky stopped to watch. After the whole durbar was mesmerized by his dancing, Amar took out his flute and started playing a soulful tune that moved everyone to tears. The King of Magic was in a trance-like state when Amar began singing a love ballad. Suddenly, in the middle of a song, Amar stopped abruptly and sighed deeply.

Afrasiyab asked him with concern, 'Why do you look so sad?' Amar wept and said, 'I was reminded of my master Hamza who would reward me richly for my performances and for whom I would arrange unbelievable displays of lights.' Afrasiyab signalled to one of his viziers and soon there was a heap of gold coins in front of Amar. 'Why do you deprive us of your skills?' asked Afrasiyab. Amar laughed and produced lamps and candles from Zambil to light the durbar. He lit the chandeliers and lamps; and placed perfume holders and bouquets of flowers around Afrasiyab's throne. The lamps and candles were actually cleverly crafted fireworks. As flowers of flames burst from them, everyone applauded Amar and claimed they had never seen lamps like this before. Amar resumed his singing as the drugged vapours of his candles and lamps began to overcome his audience.

Hairat, swaying with the music, turned to Afrasiyab and said, 'Golden snakes from the lamps are attacking me!' Afrasiyab replied drunkenly, 'They just want to kiss you!' Turning to Amar, Afrasiyab slurred, 'So what will happen after this?' Amar looked at him carefully and retorted, 'After the light, there will be darkness; the moment the lamps go out, your turbans will vanish!' No one paid the slightest attention to Amar's open warning as by this time, a combination of the wine and drugged vapours had dulled their senses. One of Afrasiyab's sahirs announced loudly, 'These servants are fools; they have placed the chairs upside down!'

Everyone rose and overturned their chairs. They fell down as they attempted to sit on their chairs again. Soon, the whole court, including Hairat and Afrasiyab, were unconscious. Amar and the other ayyars woke up the sahirs from their own camp. Amar instructed everyone to pile all the furniture, carpets and other precious items of gold and silver from the durbar in a heap. After Amar had deposited everything in Zambil, he drew out his sword to kill Afrasiyab. However, an unseen hand pushed him away every time he went near Afrasiyab. Amar was pushed away several times and thought to himself, 'Alas, what am I to do now?'

Suddenly, a voice thundered in the sky, 'I am Afrasiyab Jadoo!' Amar quickly vanished under his cloak and the other ayyars ran out of sight, while the false sardars from Amar's camp dived into the earth. A magic cloud appeared on the horizon and a bolt of lightning from the cloud wrapped itself around the unconscious sahirs of Afrasiyab's durbar. In a moment, it flashed out of sight with them.

Without much ado, Amar fled to safety of the mountains. He knew that Afrasiyab would be furious with him and that if he was captured, Mahrukh and the sardars (who were in Zambil) would also be captured with him. He took *chandini* sheets out from Zambil and spread them on the ground. Then he brought out the unconscious sardars from Zambil, laid them on the sheets and sprinkled cold water on them to revive them. Mahrukh and Bahar sat up and exclaimed, 'We were just in our pavilion! What are we doing here?' Khwaja then related how he had tricked the Shahanshah. Mahrukh, Bahar and the other sardars laughed and said, 'You did well, but Afrasiyab will be furious and vengeful now. There will be trouble!'

Amar smiled grimly and said, 'I am not afraid of any trouble, but tell me, how does one kill Afrasiyab and Hairat?' Bahar replied, 'Khwaja, Afrasiyab cannot be killed without the Lauh-e-Tilism. No one has seen the real Afrasiyab and Hairat's double cannot be killed so easily either.' Amar was thoughtful for a while and then suggested that they move back to the camp and wait for Afrasiyab to make the next move.

Afrasiyab's revenge

The magic lightning had transported Hairat and the other sahirs to the Garden of Apples. As we already know, there were two Afrasiyabs, one behind the magic mirror and one, who was now unconscious. The real Afrasiyab woke everyone and the double disappeared. The sahirs awoke to find that not only had they been stripped bare of their clothes, their faces had also been painted to look like monkeys and pigs! Some of them smiled at the farcical situation they were in, but Hairat and the other sahiras moaned in shame and tried to cover their naked bodies with their tresses as they rushed out of the durbar.

Later, when everyone congregated once again in the durbar, washed and dressed, Afrasiyab addressed his wife in a subdued voice, 'O Hairat, I have the power to capture this rascal Amar right now. What has Samri decreed that he has escaped so many times? This time, he humiliated me beyond measure. Sarsar was so right and I was punished for not heeding her warning.' The Shah consulted the Book of Samri and discovered that Sarsar was tied to a tree deep in the forest. She was immediately rescued and Afrasiyab awarded her with a robe of honour.

Afrasiyab then turned to Hairat and said, 'I want to consult my grandmother in Zulmat. She is bound to know who is destined to kill Amar.' After dismissing the durbar, Afrasiyab held Hairat's hand and they flew on their throne to the Veil of Darkness. They travelled for hours before they reached a mountain made entirely of gold. Four golden statuettes were guarding its base. The statuettes were covered in jewels and wore garments that were heavily embroidered with precious stones. As Afrasiyab neared the mountain, the statuettes laughed aloud. One said, 'Afrasiyab is approaching!' The second one said, 'Why should he not come?' The third statuette said, 'It is his need that brings him here!' The fourth one cried, 'Well, if he has come, why does he stop and not come any further?'

Afrasiyab heard the statuettes, but continued to hold Hairat's hand and climbed up the mountain. On the summit stood a building that was more splendid than the palace of the sky. Afrasiyab had reached the doorway when he heard a loud crack from the back of the palace that was followed by a dark storm. Within moments, the storm abated and a throne flew in from the sky carrying a toothless old hag, wrapped in a white silk Mehmoodi shawl, who seemed to be several hundred years of age.

Afrasiyab and Hairat greeted her deferentially. The old lady (whose name was Afat Four-hands and who was the paternal grandmother of the King of Magic), prayed for his long life and opened her arms wide. Afrasiyab leaned forward and put his head on her bosom. Afat held him with affection and kissed him. As she spoke, her mouth expelled flames and her face looked fearsome. 'You silly boy,' she said, 'it seems you could not manage Tilism, could you?' Afrasiyab replied meekly, 'What am I to do grandmother? Khudawand Laqa has decreed that Amar should overwhelm me!' Afat laughed aloud on hearing this and said, 'Listen boy, do not talk nonsense! How can Laqa decree anything? Amar and his friends constantly humiliate him. You fool! It was your favourite Makhmoor Red-eye who helped Amar across the magic river!'

Afrasiyab was shocked to learn of this ultimate betrayal and listened quietly when Afat Four-eyes related the contents of the secret conversations between Amar and Makhmoor to him. Afat went on to advise him, 'Listen, even if heaven and earth are overturned, and even if Tilism is destroyed and all the sahirs are dead, there are four things you must not do. First, do not overturn the sacred laws of Tilism; second, do not meddle with the Seven Cells of Doom; third, kill Asad only after eleven months and not before that as you risk violating the laws of magic; and fourth, no matter how dire your situation, do not send the twenty-one sahirs of Samri's times to fight the enemy. Go now and convene a fair at the Well of Emeralds. All the rebels will be drawn to it and you can easily capture them. However, beware of Amar! Ever since he has entered this realm, I have been looking out for his name in all the divine prophecies. There is no mention of his death; it seems he is indeed the slayer of sahirs. My son, you have to remain vigilant. Now go home and do as I have told you!'

Afrasiyab and Hairat bowed low to take their leave of Afat. The old sahira signalled and her throne rose into the skies. The four statuettes spoke again. The first one cried, 'If you have to go, go now!' The second one said, 'If you are leaving, then leave now!' The third one warned, 'What is wax will surely melt!' The fourth statuette declared, 'There will be a fire!' That is exactly what happened—as soon as they started climbing down the mountain, the stones on the mountain burst into flames and the mountain and palace caught fire. Afrasiyab and Hairat did not wait to watch this and hurried on. The King of Sahirs was furious and swore, 'I will kill this disloyal Makhmoor after torturing her!'

Afrasiyab returned to the Garden of Apples where a cool breeze stirred the leaves. It seemed as if they were clapping. Birds sang sweet melodies that made the trees sway with the music. Afrasiyab went straight to the main pavilion where two hundred fairy-faced handmaidens stood guard. Two hundred more handmaidens were inside the pavilion. No one, other than Afrasiyab and Hairat, had ever seen them or the inside of the pavilion. As Afrasiyab approached the pavilion, the handmaidens greeted him and lifted the curtains of the pavilion to reveal its secrets. The faces of the handmaidens who stood inside glowed so radiantly that the ones outside looked pale in comparison.

The king stood before a curtain in the middle of the pavilion. A handmaiden parted the curtain and revealed a stone statue of the King of Magic on a throne. Afrasiyab called out, 'My namesake, come to me!' The statue got up and stood before the king, who ordered it, 'You and I are one; go now and capture Makhmoor!' The statue fell on the floor, vaporized into smoke and spiralled out of sight. Afrasiyab now sat on the throne with Hairat besides him. He chanted an incantation that made all the plants in the garden bloom with flowers. Birds of many hues shot out of the flowers, rolled on the ground and transformed into beautiful fairies in multicoloured robes. Afrasiyab then relaxed with his wife as the fairies danced before him and the handmaidens served rose-hued wine.

Now hear about that captive of love, Makhmoor. After helping Amar across the River of Fire, she returned to her palace and couldn't help but pine for her beloved Prince Nur al Dahar. Suddenly, the ground before her cracked open and Afrasiyab's namesake sprang out of the earth. Makhmoor felt very alarmed but composed herself and greeted him. She said, 'The Shahanshah has honoured me by visiting my humble abode.' Afrasiyab's namesake did not reply and after holding her by the waist, flew out of the palace. Within moments, he threw Makhmoor in front of the King of Sahirs and Hairat. Both of them looked at

Makhmoor angrily and when she greeted them, Afrasiyab thundered, 'You disloyal, shameless wretch, how did I wrong you that you helped Amar across the river?' Makhmoor realized that her secret had been exposed and remained silent. Afrasiyab signalled and two hideous-looking sahirs who were holding leather whips emerged from the earth. Each of them lashed the beautiful Makhmoor in turn till her delicate skin was torn apart and her chemise was in tatters. When it seemed as if that the bird of her soul was about to fly out of the cage of her body, Hairat begged the Shah to spare her life. Afrasiyab signalled to the sahirs to stop and conjured four slave-girls who placed the unconscious Makhmoor on a flying throne and took her back home.

Makhmoor's companions and handmaidens wept to see her in this condition and placed her gently on her bed. Makhmoor was motionless as if she was dead and the women tending to her cursed and abused the King of Sahirs loudly. Suddenly, Makhmoor's body went into spasms and she hiccupped as if she was about to die. There was uproar in the palace and her attendants wailed, 'Alas, she who had never even been hit by flowers has been whipped so cruelly!' To cut a long story short, Makhmoor's wounds were stitched and healed with magic salves, and she was revived with powerful cordials. (As her servants tend her back to health, we will have to wait to know about what she does and where she goes after recovering.)

Meanwhile, Afrasiyab had returned to his durbar in the Garden of Apples. His courtiers rose to greet him as drums sounded magically and incense burners lit up spontaneously. Afrasiyab sat on his throne and ordered his vizier Baghban Qudrat to capture Amar immediately from the Islamic camp. He turned towards Hairat and asked her to return to her war camp as he would send another sahira or sahir to help her. Hairat left for the camp but instructed a couple of her servants to keep her informed. 'Let me know when Amar is captured,' she told them, 'for my heart is in flames for revenge, I would like to slap him a few times myself!'

Sarsar Sword-fighter and Saba Raftar Fleet-foot welcomed her back in her camp and cried, 'Huzoor, how does the Shahanshah intend to capture Amar now?' Hairat sat on her couch in the pavilion and mused, 'Sarsar, who is this man? Is he a genie or a ghost that even when he is captured he deceives everyone and vanishes? Baghban has gone to get him this time, so let us see . . . the Shahanshah will surely kill him if he is captured! I am disappointed that you have not achieved anything. You have never pleased the Shahanshah with your tricks.' Sarsar pleaded that they had actually captured Amar several times, but that he had managed to escape each time. She told the Malika, 'Huzoor, we have to go home for a few days and will try again when we return. By that time, Baghban Qudrat should have some results.'

The two girls took their leave of Hairat and left for their land. On the way, they came across Tez Nigah who asked them where they were headed. 'Home,' replied Sarsar wearily, 'you can come with us as well.' Tez Nigah readily joined them. 'Have you heard,' Saba Raftar said conversationally on the way, 'that Baghban Qudrat has gone to capture Amar this time?' Tez Nigah went pale on hearing this and Sarsar realized that it was Barq Firangi who was posing as her friend. Sarsar snapped, 'You think you can fool me, you silly boy? Tell your teacher to be wary of Baghban Qudrat. He is a mighty and powerful sahir!' Barq held out his hand to Sarsar and said, 'My teacher's beloved, why are you angry with me? It is out of love for you that I came to see you, but you are always so harsh on me!' Sarsar snapped back, 'To hell with your love! Look at how this wretch mocks me! I will set you and your teacher on fire!'

Amar's trickeries and arrest

Barq was anxious about Baghban and slipped away to his camp to warn Amar. Mahrukh advised Amar to hide but the ayyar remained unruffled when he heard the news. 'I almost killed Baghban the last time he came for me. This time he is asking for his death!' he said. Amar then went to his tent and took out a prisoner from Zambil. He painted the prisoner to look like himself and told him, 'I am releasing you on the condition that you proclaim yourself as Amar! Do not deny this however much you are bullied and threatened or you will have me to reckon with!' The prisoner, who was formerly a Rumi wrestler, agreed and Amar sent him to occupy his seat in the durbar. Hungry and thirsty from his sojourn in Zambil (where inmates were given only stale bread to eat!) the Rumi greedily guzzled the wine offered to him and asked Mahrukh for food. Since Mahrukh thought that he was Amar, she immediately ordered her servants to serve him hot food in a small courtyard behind the pavilion. The Rumi fell hungrily on the delicacies served to him and then stretched out in a semi-stupor on a couch in the courtyard.

Baghban Qudrat travelled below the earth and emerged in Mahrukh's camp precisely at the spot where the false Amar lay sleeping, snoring loudly. With a shout of triumph, Baghban caught the wrestler by the waist and flew off to Afrasiyab. Meanwhile, the real Amar had travelled some distance from his camp in Zahir and saw a house in the forest. A woman sat outside the house and two boys played besides her. Amar immediately disguised himself as an aged woman and called out, 'May the blessing of Samri be upon you! I am very hungry; do you have anything for me?' The housewife led her into the house and fed her. The old woman cried, 'Samri and Jamshed will bless you and your children for feeding a hungry beggar!'

The housewife asked the old woman if anyone looked after her. Amar replied, 'I am cursed and have outlived everyone. If you give me food, I will live here with you.' Amar then showed fifty gold coins to the housewife who asked her, 'What will you do with these?' The old woman replied, 'This is for my bad days. I go without food for three days at a time but do not touch these. I have other things as well but I will show them to you in a private place.'

Amar led the housewife into the store under the pretext of showing her the treasures, but rendered her unconscious there. He put her in Zambil and disguised as the housewife, emerged from the store. He summoned the servants and declared, 'This old woman was wily. She just vanished into the earth. Make sure no one comes in now!' He then turned to a handmaiden and cried, 'Hurry up, the master will be here soon!' The girl replied, 'I have prepared the curry already and only need to make roti.' Thus, Amar busied himself in domestic affairs.

Baghban Qudrat reached the enchanted Garden of Apples and deposited the prisoner in front of his master. The Rumi wrestler was overwhelmed by the grandeur of his surroundings and went around bowing obsequiously to the king and all his sahir knights. Afrasiyab smiled contemptuously and said, 'So Amar, here we are again! You will now be punished for your insolence.' The Rumi wrestler replied, 'Forget about what happened before. Just feed me and I will live here forever!'

Afrasiyab was enraged, 'You low-caste rascal, are you trying to deceive me again?' The wrestler too lost his temper and said, 'You and your father must be low-caste, you rude arrogant fool! Is this how you address a decent man?' Afrasiyab became purple with rage and shouted, 'Oye haramzadeh! How dare you speak to me this way?' The Rumi retorted furiously, 'You are a haramzada from a line of haramzadas! I can wring your neck right now!'

As they shouted at each other, the sahirs in Afrasiyab's court became uneasy and nudged one another. One sahir said, 'Brothers, we should leave; Amar seems angry this morning. There is bound to be trouble!' Another said, 'What kind of men are you? He can only abuse but do nothing else as he is powerless!' The first sahir replied, 'Yes, yes we have been through this before! Within no time he will be disguised as a woman and then we will get shoe-beatings and our faces will be blackened!' A couple of sahirs rose and muttered that they had to relieve themselves but that was the last anyone saw of them.

At Afrasiyab's signal, Baghban drew his sword and was about to execute the false Amar but his eyes fell on a magic amulet of Jamshed tied on his arm. A warning stating, 'This man is not Amar!' flashed on the amulet and the vizier stopped abruptly, dreading the Shahanshah's wrath. Afrasiyab looked at him questioningly and a sheepish Baghban held out the amulet for the Shahanshah to read.

Afrasiyab looked furious and said, 'Release this poor man. I will not rest till that wily ayyar is captured!' He chanted a spell and knocked in the air and a bareheaded sahira with uncombed hair emerged from the earth holding a hand mirror. She looked somewhat startled but greeted the Shah respectfully. Afrasiyab took the mirror from her and handed it to Baghban. The king said, 'O Baghban. Look into his mirror. Wherever Amar is hidden, he will be revealed to you.'

At that time, Amar, disguised as the housewife, was serving dinner to the husband, a sahir named Biyaban Jadoo. Baghban looked in the magic mirror and saw a man and his wife having dinner in their lush garden. Looking at Baghban's bewildered face, the Shahanshah smiled and said, 'My simple Baghban! Do you not observe that woman in the mirror? See how she is just pretending to eat with her husband but is hiding the morsels in her sleeves or under her robes. She is actually that deceiving rascal Amar! Now go to Biyaban Jadoo's house and arrest Amar!'

Within minutes, Baghban flew to the house and went straight to the garden. Biyaban left his dinner and rose to greet the vizier. He said, 'It is a rare honour to receive the Grand Vizier in my home.' The vizier ignored him and threw a grain of rice in his false wife's lap. The wife, that is Amar, wanted to disappear but found that his lower body was lifeless and started so began writhing on the floor in agony, pretending to be in pain. Biyaban begged the vizier to cure his wife of this affliction as he loved her very much. Baghban said, 'You fool, this is not your wife but Amar ayyar!'

Biyaban smote his forehead in anguish, but Amar held his hand and said, 'Sahib, why do you weep? I am your wife. This man is lying!' Baghban smiled and conjured a cloud that expelled drops of rain on Amar's face. The paints of ayyari were washed off and Amar's real face was revealed. Biyaban now threw himself on the floor and howled, 'O Amar, for the love of your faith, tell me what have you done with my wife?' Amar replied calmly, 'I was hungry and ate her. If Baghban had not come I would have eaten you as well.'

Amar now turned to Baghban and snarled, 'You better not take me to your master. Do you not remember how I humiliated you once before? It will be much worse for you this time for I am the angel of death for sahirs and sorcerers!' Unmindful of Amar's threats, Baghban caught Amar by the waist and flew to the durbar where he flung him at the Shahanshah's feet. Afrasiyab laughed at Amar's plight and said, 'You are a guest in this world for a few moments now!' Amar replied shamelessly, 'O King of Kings! You have every power and an ordinary mortal like me cannot harm you! You must release me just this time, and let your pen of mercy overlook my list of crimes. I will be grateful to you for the rest of my life!' Afrasiyab's viziers, the brothers Sarmaya and Abriq exclaimed in unison, 'Huzoor, he will only be silent after his head his cut off. Do not talk to him!'

Afrasiyab consulted the Book of Samri that advised him, 'Hand Amar over to Queen Hairat who should take him to her house in the city you have founded for her!' Leaning over to his wife, Afrasiyab said playfully, 'My queen, look at what the book says!' Hairat smiled meaningfully and after reading the text of the book, decided to move with Amar to her city. She was about to fly off with the prisoner when Afrasiyab stopped her and said, 'Why should you carry prisoners my love? Tell your women viziers Yakut and Zamurrad to take him. You can follow at leisure and finish him off later.'

Hairat looked happy and said, 'Huzoor, you honour me with your words and may you live till there is water in Ganga and Jamuna!' Yakut and Zamurrad cast a spell on Amar that made his body lifeless and then conjured a magic couch. They threw him between themselves on the couch and flew to the city of Napursan. Amar's eyes were open and his tongue worked, but his limbs were lifeless. He gazed upon the mountains and forests of Tilism and remembered God as they flew in the air.

Eventually, they reached a city which had outer walls made of mirrors with landscapes of deserts, gardens and forests etched on it. The gate was so lofty that its height could not be measured. Its turrets and towers soared into the sky and thousands of sahirs guarded the gate that was open. Yakut and Zamurrad entered the bustling city whose beauty could make the stars of the night sky seem dim in comparison. Amar vowed to himself that he would plunder the city at the first opportunity. Soon, they came to the garden of the wife of the ruler of Hoshruba. Words cannot describe this garden's loveliness. It had stone palaces encrusted with precious gems and its riches were mind-boggling.

Zamurrad and Yakut freed Amar from their spell and locked him in a small shack. They bolted the door and put three locks, the size of a camel's thigh on it. Then they cast a spell that created a wall of flames all around the shack as well as fiery dragons that guarded it from all sides. After these security arrangements we made, they adorned the garden like a new bride and waited for their mistress.

Amar in the city of Napursan

As soon as the women left him in his cell, Amar took out his sword and tried to dig his way out of the shack. He found that the ground was made of stone that was harder than iron. Amar was now truly frightened but composed himself and prayed to the saints to help him. As he was the favoured one of many prophets, he suddenly hit upon a strategy to escape. He pulled out a prisoner who had been sentenced to death from Zambil. After rendering him unconscious, he painted his tongue with a tincture that caused it to swell. Then he painted the man to look like himself and sat near the door, invisible in Galeem.

Hairat reached her durbar in all splendour and her courtiers rushed to pay homage to her. She turned to Yakut and Zamurrad and asked them where they had kept Amar. When they told her about their security arrangements, she turned pale and said, 'You should not have left him untied; he must have escaped by now!' Both women assured the queen that it was impossible for the trickster to escape. 'Huzoor,' they said, 'come with us and see how we have imprisoned him.' Hairat accompanied the two women to the shack where Zamurrad dispelled the magic dragons and the flames and opened the door. The real Amar, who was near the door but invisible in Galeem, quietly slipped out of the shack. Hairat saw the false Amar in dead sleep and asked Zamurrad to drag him out. 'Look at this wily rascal,' she screamed, 'he is pretending to be asleep!'

Zamurrad went into the hut and Hairat stood outside, chanting spells to prevent their prisoner from running out. The false Amar was dragged out of the shack and Hairat sent for her executioner, who beheaded the prisoner promptly. Rivulets of blood gushed out of the body as it went into its last spasms. Hairat ordered her minions to throw away the body and placed the severed and bleeding head with her own hands on a silver tray. She covered it with a silk cloth trimmed with gold tassels and handed it to Zamurrad and Yakut. She ordered, 'Deliver this to the Shah with my greetings and ask him where he would like to celebrate his enemy's death.'

The feast in the Garden of Pleasure

Zamurrad and Yakut deputed an attendant to carry the tray on his head. When the two women reached the Garden of Apples, the Shah of Tilism and his courtiers saw the tray with its ornate coverlet and speculated, 'Malika must have sent fruit from her garden!' Afrasiyab thought, 'Could it possibly be Amar's head? But it would be difficult to kill Amar!' Zamurrad smiled knowingly and submitted, 'This is a happy day. Malika has sent a rare gift!' Afrasiyab gingerly removed the coverlet with his own hands and saw Amar's freshly cut and bleeding head. He got up with excitement and prostrated in the direction of Mount Agate in gratitude to Khudawand Laqa. 'It is only through his grace that it has been my honour to execute Amar,' he declared triumphantly, 'for surely, he could not be killed by anyone else!'

The people in the durbar called out, 'Huzoor, this is due to your good fortune!' Afrasiyab laughed aloud as he tossed his crown into the air with sheer joy and cried, 'All of you should laugh with me!' There were shouts of laughter from all corners of the durbar and sahirs slapped their own bottoms to express their mirth. Afrasiyab embraced each one of his nobles who congratulated him. Afrasiyab declared, 'We will celebrate tonight! Tell Malika to make preparations in the Garden of Pleasure. It is beautiful and spacious enough to accommodate our guests comfortably.'

Yakut and Zamurrad left first to inform the queen and the King of Magic followed them in a glorious procession. Magic kettledrums were struck in unison and eight-thousand beautiful sahiras, dressed in rich garments and adorned like brides, accompanied the king. As they swarmed around him, it seemed as if stars were twinkling in the night sky. Parizads floated over the flying throne of the king and fanned him with gossamer-thin wings while tossing handfuls of gold and silver glitter in his path. A rain of pearls cascaded from magic clouds as the King of Magic left for the Garden of Pleasure with seventeen thousand powerful sahirs in his entourage.

The Garden of Pleasure

Queen Hairat reached the Garden of Pleasure before the king. She bathed and wore rich garments, and adorned herself with priceless jewels. Her mouth was darkened with missi and her eyes glittered with black kohl. She then turned to the garden and began preparing it for the celebration. She had fireworks placed at the entrance and the trees were decorated with jewels and gold glitter. She chanted an incantation that made each blade of grass in the garden sprout flowers the colour of rubies. Finally, the garden and its pavilions glowed with the light of a thousand bejewelled lamps and chandeliers.

Just when the garden was completely illuminated, Afrasiyab arrived in his magnificent procession. Hairat received him at the entrance to the garden, where Afrasiyab embraced her and smashed a magic coconut that made thousands of fragrant flowers fall from the sky. Afrasiyab and Hairat strolled through the garden hand in hand, accompanied by the highest-ranking courtiers. Hundreds of pretty and young female gardeners, laden with jewellery and with scarves tied around their waists, worked on the flowerbeds with gold and silver spades. Some of them were stringing garlands of fresh flowers. Beautiful dancers performed all around the garden while female water-carriers sprayed rose water on the flowerbeds.

The garden's marble pavilions were enclosed with velvet curtains and filled with glittering mirrors and crystal lamps. Each pavilion was furnished with jewel-inlaid chairs and thrones. A raised platform in the middle of the garden, encrusted with precious stones, was covered with a canopy of gold and sliver that rested on eight hundred emerald pillars. Peacocks crafted from rare gems were perched on the pillars. The canopy's silk ropes were secured with gold and silver nails and its golden tassels gleamed like the rays of the sun. The royal throne was made entirely of jewels and was flanked by emerald chairs. Several red and green crystal flagons with grape wine were arranged on the platform and the air was fragrant with the smoke of oudh and umber incense.

Afrasiyab settled on his throne with Hairat. Hundreds of fairies sat on swings and sang monsoon ballads; the bells on the trees rang in tune to their swinging; some of the fairies sprayed coloured water on each other. The garden resounded with the sound of music and beautiful girls, whose faces glowed like the moon, danced before the king. In the far end of the garden, golden and pink pomegranate blossoms of fire burst in the sky. All Praise to Allah, what a gathering of pleasure that was!

Precious gems were showered on everyone and the King of Sahirs declared, 'Whoever asks me for anything will be granted their wish this evening!' Hairat rose from the throne and stood before him with folded hands. The King embraced and kissed her fondly, and asked, 'By Jamshed, ask me what you will and I will grant you your wish my queen!'

'Huzoor,' said the queen, 'it is my hope that you will forgive Makhmoor Red-eye for my sake and invite her to this joyous feast.' Afrasiyab nodded and immediately sent some sahirs to bring Makhmoor with all honours to the garden. Now hear about the one stricken by love. Makhmoor had recovered from her wounds but still pined for Prince Nur al Dahar. She often shed tears for her beloved and every day, she would sacrifice the moth of her heart to the flame of thorns. In the depths of her despair, she heard of Amar's death being celebrated in Tilism and fainted with grief. After she was revived, she cried. 'O woe that I should live and Amar should die. I should have died with him!'

She wore simple white garments and thought of going to the Garden of Pleasure to find out how that helpless prisoner had been killed. She was just about to leave for the garden with some attendants when Afrasiyab's messenger arrived and said, 'Congratulations! You are indeed fortunate that Hairat appealed to the Shahanshah to forgive you! Come and join the celebrations now.' Since Makhmoor had been planning to go anyway, she left for the garden on a magic throne. She shed tears when she saw the garden and berated herself inwardly, 'O Allah! I am here to witness the celebration for a friend's death! Well, whatever Allah wills!'

Thus lost in thought, Makhmoor entered the garden and bowed in mujra-greeting before the queen. Hairat then led her to Afrasiyab who was really very fond of Makhmoor. He embraced her warmly and awarded her with a robe of honour, after which she stood behind him and fanned him with her handkerchief. The Shah declared, 'I think I should send Amar's head to the durbar of Khudawand Laqa. This will dishearten Hamza's forces and they might stop being such a nuisance to Khudawand!' The *durbari*s murmured their assent. Afrasiyab had the false Amar's head placed on a gold tray, covered it with a gleaming embroidered cloth and sent it to Laqa with other gifts.

Afrasiyab's messengers crossed the mountains and the River of Seven Hues and reached Laqa's durbar. Shaitan Bakhtiarak saw them carrying a tray and assumed that Afrasiyab had sent fruits from Tilism. He asked Laqa, 'O Khudawand, what fate have you decreed? What is on this tray?' Laqa replied promptly, 'We know, but we shall not reveal it to you!' The Shaitan thought inwardly, 'This joker never knows anything; what can he reveal?' By this time, the sahir messengers had prostrated before Laqa and placed the tray and other gifts before him.

Bakhtiarak's sharp eyes noticed that the messengers seemed to have come from a celebration as their clothes were smeared with colour and they looked excited and happy. 'What has Shahanshah sent through you?' Bakhtiarak asked them. They replied eagerly, 'Malik-ji, he has sent the head of your greatest enemy, Amar!' The Shaitan rose and did a little jig in sheer joy. He tossed his turban in the air and shouted, 'Khudawand, you have made my wish come true today!' Then he lifted Amar's head from the tray and held it aloft for the durbar to see.

'This is the man,' he called out, 'who made a *hareesa* of my father and wanted to make a halwa of me. This is the man who used to regularly beat me with his shoes so many times that no hair grows on my head, and I had to pay him what I would have paid the barber for a year! But what surprises me is that his God should have let him down; it seems unbelievable!'

Placing the head in his lap, the Shaitan checked under the left eyelid to locate Amar's telltale mole, the true proof of his identity. He could not locate the greenish mole despite looking very carefully and shook his head in remorse. 'What is it?' cried Laqa. The Shaitan snarled back, 'This is not Amar! The mole is missing; a thousand curses on Afrasiyab for this cruel hoax!' Laqa was also crestfallen but quickly recovered and said, 'Amar is our special servant. I never believed that he could be killed.'

'A thousand curses on you and your divinity!' shouted Shaitan. 'What kind of fate do you decree that causes me grief after so much joy?' Laqa comforted Bakhtiarak and declared that the next time, fate would be kinder to him. Afrasiyab's men looked puzzled with this turn of events. 'Where is the King of Sahirs?' Shaitan asked them. 'In the Garden of Pleasure,' they replied. Shaitan said, 'Then return now. You will find it all destroyed with the tree of the Shahanshah's life cut down. Tilism will be in mourning!' They continued to look disbelievingly at him, so Bakhtiarak sent for warm water to wash off the paints of trickery on the severed head. This revealed the face of the prisoner from Zambil and Bakhtiarak said, 'Are you convinced now? Now leave quickly for Hamza will hear of your arrival with this head and will attack us. Khudawand will be thrashed and your lives will not be spared either!'

Afrasiyab's messengers left in haste. Meanwhile, Hamza's spies reported the whole incident to their master. The sardars laughed as they heard of what the Shaitan had to say. 'Allah will look after Amar,' declared Emir Hamza, 'and he will triumph with Allah's will!'

Back in the Garden of Pleasure, Afrasiyab was in a good mood and fondled his wife who was pretending to be annoyed. 'Shahanshah,' she cooed, 'do not tease me in front of the durbar; look, my robes are in disarray and I am perspiring with shame!' The messengers arrived looking obviously distressed. Seeing them, Afrasiyab thought, 'Perhaps Amar really was Khudawand's special man or he would have sent robes of honour for me and rewarded the messengers.' He asked them, 'Is all well with you?' The messengers showed him the head, which was now washed of its disguise, and related what had happened. On hearing their story, Makhmoor rejoiced in her heart but kept very still.

Afrasiyab turned on his wife in rage. There was a torrent of explanations from Hairat, Yakut and Zamurrad. They swore that the prisoner was the same man that Vizier Baghban Qudrat had delivered to the Shahanshah. 'I will kill you both on the spot!' Afrasiyab said looking at Yakut and Zamurrad. 'What happened to Amar?' he shouted. The two women shook with fear as they told him that they had locked Amar in the garden shed. He asked, 'When you opened the door, were there two Amars or one?' The women replied, 'If one wretch has caused so much trouble, two of him would be the end of us all!'

The durbaris laughed at this reply and requested Afrasiyab to consult the Book of Samri. He struck his knee in frustration and said, 'I must have been mad not to consult the book before sending this head to Khudawand! When Baghban had captured Amar, I had consulted the book and that was the real Amar. Anyway, whatever is destined will happen.' Afrasiyab then plucked a petal out of the flowers lying before him and threw it towards the garden. Moments later, a magic peacock flew in with the Book of Samri. Afrasiyab read in the book, 'Your attendants were negligent and did not bind Amar with magic when he was in the shack. He is still in Hairat's city but will leave in a few days.'

The Shahanshah closed the book and wearily asked, 'How long before this night ends?' It was very late and almost daybreak by then. Afrasiyab told Hairat to return to Napursan and told her that he too would join her shortly after resting.

The sahir courtiers returned to their homes while Hairat and her officers left for their city. Afrasiyab retired for the night in his pavilion in the Garden of Pleasure until the Sultan of the Stars dismissed the gathering of planets and the Sahir of the East appeared with flaming chains to capture the cruel darkness of night.

Amar and Ghubar Jadoo

Now hear about Amar. He stayed in the garden at Napursan until Hairat and her companions had left for the celebrations in the Garden of Pleasure. He threw flowers of unconsciousness on the lamps and candles that made the few remaining handmaidens fall into a deep slumber. Amar then cast his blessed net on all the furniture and precious items in the garden; he even divested the unconscious handmaidens of their costly garments and jewellery!

Amar left the garden disguised as a sahir and roamed the city. He wandered into a part of the city that had craters and depressions in the earth and where the houses were in a state of disrepair. He took refuge in one of the craters to spend the rest of the night. After a while, Amar thought, 'There are many powerful sahirs in this city and I will be found here. There is also no joy in remaining invisible. I should only use Galeem when I have no other way to escape.' He thought for a while and then began digging a tunnel in the crater.

Having a fair idea of the layout of the city, Amar managed to tunnel his way towards the inhabited area and penetrated the storeroom of a *bania*, where sacks of grain and rice were stored. Amar covered the entrance to his tunnel with one of the sacks and started digging in another direction (he cleared the way by shovelling the loose mud into Zambil). This time, he emerged in the courtyard of a baker and found the baker and his family asleep. Amar quickly filled up this opening and dug further into the house. He emerged again in their storeroom where piles of *sheermal* and kulcha bread lay covered with a sheet. Amar cleverly covered the opening in such a way as to allow him easy access and returned to the tunnel. He dug his way to a wine merchant's cellar next, where bottles of the choicest wines, colourful and pleasing to the eye, were stored. Amar covered this opening too in a skillful manner.

Amar was about to dig in another direction when he heard voices and realized that it was daybreak. Amar quickly crawled back to the crater, stretched his limbs to relax his strained muscles and slept deeply. (He had placed the Net of Ilyas at the mouth of the crater to trap anyone who tried to enter it, but no one came.) He awoke some time later and took out some water from Zambil to perform the necessary ablutions for a belated morning prayer. Afterwards, Amar felt very hungry and crawled back through the tunnels to the bakery and wine cellar to pinch some sheermal and a bottle of wine.

All night, the city of Napursan was on the alert for thieves with shouts of, 'Find him! Catch him!' Gongs rang and alarm bells pealed as sahirs ran around in circles. Hairat returned from the Garden of Pleasure to find her palace plundered. She was furious and wanted to find Amar herself, but Ghubar Jadoo, an officer of the King of Sahirs, arrived and submitted that the Shah had sent him to capture Amar.

Ghubar went out of the garden and scooped a fistful of earth and sniffed it while chanting a spell. 'Amar is hiding below the ground,' he declared triumphantly to the Queen, 'and I will go and arrest him now!' He went into the city, sniffing the earth occasionally, to locate Amar's precise location. A throng of excited citizens followed him until he persuaded them to leave him alone by saying,

'Amar will be forewarned if you are with me, so let me do this alone.' The crowds fell back and Ghubar proceeded alone until he reached Amar's hiding place.

Amar was aware of his presence, but rather than giving away his refuge, decided to come out in the open. He covered himself with a sheet and lay in Ghubar's path like a corpse. He filled his mouth with some powder of unconsciousness and it seemed as if his limbs were limp and his eyes lifeless. Ghubar sniffed the ground and was informed by his magic that Amar was right there; he looked around, but only saw the inert figure under a sheet. He removed the sheet and was startled on seeing a dead body. As he leaned forward to examine the face, Amar quickly blew the drugged powder from his mouth on to Ghubar, who sneezed and fell unconscious. Amar slit his throat right away and this was followed by darkness as Ghubar's spirits howled with rage. The citizens of Napursan found Ghubar with his throat slit and took his body back to Hairat's palace. Meanwhile, Amar had already slipped back into his cave.

Amar and Shola Fire-eater

Afrasiyab was in the Garden of Pleasure in conversation with Mussavir when Ghubar's body was brought to him and he was informed about the tragic circumstances of his death. Afrasiyab writhed with anger like a snake with its tail cut off. After some time, he knocked in the air and called out, 'O Shola Fire-eater, present yourself!' No sooner had he said this than a firmament of flames extended over the garden. The flames parted and a sahir fell on the ground. His eyes shone like flames and his body was blue, and when he spoke, smoke emanated from his mouth. Afrasiyab acknowledged his greeting and told him to find Amar in Napursan. Shola Fire-eater flew upwards, disappeared into the fiery firmament and left for Hairat's city.

While this terror of the sky was on his way to capture Amar, the city of Napursan was in turmoil. Amar emerged from his tunnels frequently, disguised as a merchant or jeweller. He robbed several shops by asking to see their wares and then depositing the goods into Zambil right in front of the shopkeepers. When they howled in protest, Amar would quickly become invisible and emerge in another part of the city. Very soon, the harrassed merchants of the city closed down their shops and went in groups to Hairat to protest. She compensated them with money and advised them to secure their goods. She sent out a message to her people: 'There is a thief in the city and he can become invisible at will. Please remain alert and hide your wares.'

Hairat instructed the magistrate of Napursan to make a public announcement in the city that from then on, no one would be compensated for stolen goods and that it was up to the citizens themselves to secure their goods and houses. There was general pandemonium in the city after this announcement was made. Shops closed, merchants secured their wares in underground stores, women dug holes in the ground to hide their jewellery and savings, and the city looked deserted with only stray dogs barking in the streets. Hundreds of sahirs divided into bands of fifty men started looking for Amar, who had by this time returned to his hiding place.

Hairat sat in her garden perturbed by the unrest in her city when it was suddenly covered by a firmament of flames. Moments later, Shola Fire-eater came spiralling down to the ground and greeted Hairat. He sat on the masnad-seating, but declined the goblet of wine offered to him and said, 'O Malika, I shall only eat or drink after I have captured Amar!' Hairat said, 'Very well then. I am sure you will find that wretched thief. I have sent hundreds of my men but they could not locate him.'

Then Shola went and sat under a grove of trees. He placed some cloves and garlands on the ground and muttered a spell as he counted prayer beads. After some time, he raised his head and said, 'O Malika, Amar is not in the sky.' He continued counting the prayer beads and declared that Amar was not on earth either. The third time, his magic informed him that Amar was under the earth. Shola declared, 'I will make it impossible for him to remain there! As soon as he emerges, we will arrest him!'

Hairat was afraid that Shola too would be killed by Amar and said to him, 'I will come with you!' She followed Shola out of the garden, accompanied by Zamurrad, Yakut and a host of other sahirs. Shola looked back at them and said, 'If you accompany me, Amar might just be alerted and will vanish! Very well, I will cast a spell that will force him to leave his hiding place.'

Shola stood in the city square and flung a magical coconut towards the sky. Immediately, a sheet of flames fell on the city and was absorbed by the earth. Amar felt the searing heat in his underground cave and quickly crawled into the grain merchant's store. He made his way towards the sacks of grain piled in the store and hid in one of the sacks where the temperature was somewhat cooler.

Shola smiled at Hairat and said, 'Huzoor, surely Amar must be dead by now!' Hairat snapped, 'I think that Amar is most probably quite safe, but my people are suffocating in this heat! Terminate your spell at once!' Shola muttered a spell that made the hot flames dissipate. He then cleared the ground before him, coated it with pig's blood and moulded puppets out of lentil flour. He threw lentil grains on the puppets and chanted a mantra that made the puppets come to life. Shola said to the puppets, 'Dive into the earth and find Amar. Leave no cave or pit unsearched!'

A hundred magic puppets dived into the earth and spread out under the city. Amar was still in the bania's store, hidden in the sack of grain. As it happened, the bania had his strongbox in the storeroom. Amar heard the bania counting his money and then locking it in the box. The clinking of the gold coins when the bania counted them was too tempting for the greedy ayyar to bear. He waited for the bania to leave the store and crawled out of the sack to get the gold. Just as he about to return to his sack of grain, one of Shola's puppets suddenly shot out of the earth. Amar tried to trap the puppet in his net but it dived back into the earth. Amar then left the grain store and crawled into the bakery.

The puppet rushed back to Shola and disclosed Amar's hideout. Shola assured Hairat that he had located Amar and would capture him soon. He left with the puppet for the bania's house. When the bania saw Shola, he assumed that he was a rich client who had come to purchase at least two maunds of grain. He greeted Shola enthusiastically and said, 'Huzoor, rest assured that my prices will be lower than anyone else's in this city!' Shola ignored him and walked into the house with the puppet. The bania was startled by his behaviour and thought that Shola was the thief who was plundering the city. He wanted to shout for help, but the puppet silenced him by telling him that the thief was in his house already and that they were about to capture him.

The bania kept quiet and allowed Shola to open the store. The puppet pointed to the sack of grain where Amar had been hiding but the ayyar was long gone. Shola overturned all the sacks and probed the grain but could not find Amar. In sheer frustration, he breathed on the puppet that went up in flames. Meanwhile, the bania was horrified to see his grain sacks in a state of disarray as well as his strongbox missing, and protested loudly.

In another part of the city, one of Shola's puppets saw Amar in the baker's store and immediately reported this to his master. Shola ran with the puppet to the baker's house but Amar had already left for the wine cellar and was nowhere to be seen. In sheer fury, Shola breathed on this puppet as well. Another puppet came running to inform him that Amar was now in the wine seller's house. The wine seller looked suspiciously at Shola and said, 'The thief is a good excuse for you to plunder our houses. I just heard the bania complaining about you!' Shola was furious when he heard this, but controlled his anger. He sent for a few traders and told them, 'I am now going to enter this man's house; you will stand witness that I will not steal anything from him!' Naturally, Shola could not find Amar in the wine cellar for he had now returned to the grain store.

Eventually, after several failed attempts at capturing Amar, Shola knocked in the air. A peacock emerged from the sky and flew down. Shola asked him, 'Why can't we find Amar?' The peacock opened its beak and laughed when he provided the information, 'Amar has dug tunnels underneath three houses; as soon as you locate him in one, he crawls into the other. Right now, he is in the grain merchant's house.'

Shola now conjured three dragons to guard the entrance to each tunnel. Amar found his way blocked, but was never short of ideas! The wily trickster hid in the sack of grain and opened up Zambil so that anyone looking for him would only see the wondrous world that existed within the magical pouch.

When Shola returned to the bania's house, the bania cried, 'Sahib, you have just searched my place! Why are you here again?' Shola growled at the bania, 'Keep quiet! He has returned to your house!' The bania wailed, 'This thief seems to have singled out my place! The last time, he took my money; let us see what happens now!'

Shola inspected all the sacks of grain carefully and eventually came to the one where Amar was hiding. As he peered into the sack, he did not see Amar but the phenomenal sight within Zambil—forests and rivers, cities with magnificent buildings and soaring turrets, laughing parizads, active market places and throngs of people engrossed in their lives. Shola was vastly amused and thought, 'Amar is also a great sahir and has conjured Tilisms in this sack of grain. But I am a greater sahir and will find him in there!'

Shola jumped right into the mouth of the Zambil and Amar quickly closed the straps of the pouch to trap him. A little while later, he thought, 'As long as this wretch remains alive, his magic dragons will continue to block the tunnels and I will not be able to escape!' So, he reached into Zambil and took Shola out, and quickly smeared his face with an unguent that made him unconscious. Amar then slit his throat. There was an almighty roar of spirits after Shola's death, the skies went dark and his magic puppets and dragons caught fire immediately. The bania heard the din in his storeroom and fled from his house with his wife and son. 'Run for your lives!' he shouted, 'We are all in peril! I have been robbed and he wants to kill me now!' The hapless citizens of Napursan, who were already terrified, thought that Amar's allies had arrived to help them and abandoned their homes.

Amar took advantage of the situation and cast his net on the deserted shops and homes, and scooped up everything in sight. He attacked several people who were running by leaping on the shoulder of one man and decapitating the other. Very soon, dead bodies lay everywhere in the streets and women covered their faces with veils and wailed, 'Ya Samri and Jamshed! Save our husbands from this peril Amar!' Hairat came out of her palace in alarm with bare feet and without her veil. She saw the citizens of her city running around in sheer panic while houses were on fire and there was loud wailing in every house. Some of her officers informed her that after Shola Fire-eater's death, Amar had begun plundering the city. Hairat beat her head in frustration and wailed loudly, 'Shola was a great favourite of the king! What do I tell him now? Where is his body?'

Hairat cast a protective spell around herself before she went to the bania's house. The magistrate of Napursan made an announcement assuring citizens that there they could return to their houses without fear as there was no enemy in the city other than Amar and that he would be captured shortly. When Amar heard the heralds, he immediately became invisible in Galeem and returned to his hideout. Hairat, accompanied by Yakut, located Shola's corpse and took it back to Afrasiyab. She left her vizierzadi Zamurrad in charge of the city. Thus, that day of murder and mayhem ended in Napursan.

Late that evening, Amar emerged from his cave again and slipped into the palace gardens. He saw that the gardens were illuminated and that Zamurrad Jadoo was reclining on a masnad with the ministers and advisers of the state around her. Handmaidens stood by her with folded hands and there were guards everywhere, for fear of Amar. Amar hid in a grove of trees until he saw a maidservant walk past him. Amar ambushed her with his whip and before she could shout for help, rendered her unconscious. He wore her outer garments, painted his face to look like hers and then joined her companions who were lighting up the candles and tapers in the durbar.

Amar pretended to work with them and furtively sprinkled some powder into the burning candles and torches, that soon made everyone unconscious. Amar was afraid of the guards and quickly hid Zamurrad in a box in the palace storeroom. Then, after wearing her clothes and disguising himself as her, he returned to the durbar and sprinkled water on everyone to wake them up. 'I was trying out a spell,' the false Zamurrad informed the durbar by way of an explanation, 'and I will now use it to find Amar myself.' There was a murmur of praise from the durbaris for her magical powers.

'I want to meet the representatives of all the merchants and jewellers of the city,' the false Zamurrad declared later. When these men assembled in front of her, she said to them in a conspiratorial tone,

'Tonight, we are determined to capture Amar and since he can become invisible, it is unsafe everywhere. If you want to save your money, deposit all your wealth, jewels and wares in the state treasury, so that the state can compensate you for any loss. Otherwise, we cannot be responsible for your security.'

Some merchants decided to hold on to their goods, but most of them brought their treasures to the false Zamurrad. After the traders had left, she sent for wine and graciously had it served to everyone in the durbar. Naturally, Amar had drugged the wine. As soon as the durbaris were unconscious, Amar first cast his net on the treasures deposited in the durbar and then proceeded to slaughter the prominent sahirs.

The deaths of the sahirs caused dark storms and sheets of flames fell on the city. The army rushed to the palace gardens while the citizens of Napursan fled from their houses again in fear. People began shouting about how Amar was on the rampage again. Someone else said, 'He must have killed Hairat!' Another person cried, 'That slut Hairat has gone off to meet her lover! She should be killed for bringing Amar to our city!' A third person called out, 'I have heard Zamurrad has been killed!' The merchants and jewellers who had deposited their wealth with Zamurrad were most concerned and thought, 'If Zamurrad is dead, who will return our goods? That wretch Hairat will probably deny any responsibility!'

Hairat's army now surrounded the palace gardens and Amar could no longer slip in to kill Zamurrad. He thought it was now prudent to return to his hiding place under Galeem. He saw that the streets were deserted and that the houses were locked. He smiled grimly and said to himself, 'We are meant to cause unrest wherever we go!' He returned to his cave and after performing the early morning prayers, dozed off.

While this harbinger of trouble slept, Hairat reached her husband. She greeted him and tears streamed down her face. Afrasiyab looked at Shola's body and asked, 'O light of my eyes, Amar burned the tree of his life too? What happened?' Hairat tearfully related all that had happened and said, 'Huzoor, Amar will destroy this Tilism and we might never catch him!' Afrasiyab trembled inwardly but thought that any sign of cowardice on his part would dishearten his courtiers. He comforted his wife and said, 'My queen, this is a war and we must expect casualties. We will cremate Shola's corpse and I will think of something else or will go to Napursan myself.'

Amar and Zulmat Jadoo

After Shola's corpse was carried off for its last rites, Afrasiyab said to Hairat, 'It is not safe for you to return to Napursan. You stay with me and I will send someone else to govern the city and capture Amar.' He chanted an incantation and called out, 'O Zulmat Four-eyes! Come to me!' There was a loud crack of thunder and a sahir with a gigantic body and a face that looked as if he had come straight from hell descended from the sky.

As he bowed low in greeting, Afrasiyab said, 'I have appointed you governor of Hairat's kingdom, but the condition is that you have to find Amar who is in the city and has eluded capture so far.' Before Zulmat could respond, messengers from Napursan arrived to apprise the king of the looting of the treasury and the merchants, as well as Zamurrad's disappearance. Hairat wept for her missing companion and Afrasiyab immediately consulted the oracle Book of Samri. He read that Zamurrad was locked in a storeroom while Amar was asleep in a cave. 'I will send my puppet right now to arrest him,' the Shah declared.

Zulmat begged Afrasiyab to leave Amar's capture to him. 'If you send the puppet, what need is there for me to go there?' he asked. Later, Afrasiyab ordered Yakut to escort the new ruler of the city and to release Zamurrad as well. There was a wave of cheer and well-being in the city when the new ruler took over. Merchants opened their shops and a general feast was declared in Zulmat's honour. Flower and perfume merchants arranged their wares in trays to offer as tribute to Zulmat. Amar, ever on the lookout, also accompanied the merchants disguised as a servant.

Amar saw that people who took gifts of perfume and bouquets for Zulmat were rewarded with gold coins and was overcome by greed. Zulmat declared that he would convene his durbar in an open place from where he could look upon the whole city. Accordingly, a large pavilion was set up in the city centre with royal furnishing, gold-embroidered masnad seating and jewel-inlaid cots. Zulmat came to the pavilion with a huge procession of four thousand notable sahirs. Attendants laid out Roman *utlas*-silk as dining sheets and served Zulmat and his companions a magnificent feast of tasteful dishes.

When he saw the food trays being carried into the pavilion, Amar thought of a plan. He disguised himself as a chef and shaved his hair. He wore a square muslin cap, a loincloth down to his knees, a cloth tied around his waist and a cotton waistcoat. He then prepared a tray of pastries and exotic desserts. Each pastry had several layers and each layer tasted salty, sweet or tart. The desserts glistened with syrup and were moulded to look like birds or fruits. The whole array had been doctored with such a deadly poison that anyone who smelt or tasted it would literally melt to death.

Amar walked into the pavilion and after greeting Zulmat, placed the tray before him. Zulmat marvelled at the red and green sweets shaped like animals or fresh bunches of grapes, and at the layers of *khajla*-pastry that gleamed like emerald tablets. Pleased with the presentation, Zulmat had some sweets served separately on a gold tray for Afrasiyab and Hairat with a note that read, 'Huzoor, this is a unique offering from the city of Napursan.' Meanwhile, Hairat's vizierzadi Yakut rescued Zamurrad from the box where Amar had placed her and was telling her about the new governor of the city when Zulmat sent for them and asked them to take the tray of sweets to the Shahanshah.

Zulmat then began eating the sweets with his courtiers. Everyone praised the chef loudly and Amar bowed low in acknowledgement. One of the courtiers asked Amar, 'What is your name?' Amar replied, 'Your humble servants is called Ustad Charb Dast; I am also known by the name Khurd Burd!' The courtiers were amused and said, 'Both names reflect your talents. How beautifully you have crafted these sweets!' Somebody said, 'Mian Charb Dast, can you make a bird that can actually fly? Amar quipped, 'Huzoor I will make you a rooster that will fly back with you to your home!'

Thus, Zulmat and his companions consumed the array of sweetmeats happily. After dinner, Zulmat rinsed his hands and settled back to munch betel leaves and smoke a hookah. 'I can employ you at a salary of five hundred rupees per month,' he told Amar who was still in the durbar. Amar muttered, 'If you remain alive I will accept your offer.' Zulmat heard that statement despite the soporific effect of the wine and food he had consumed. 'What is that you said?' he slurred, the effects of the poison already working in his body. 'Huzoor,' Amar replied ingratiatingly, 'you are on the dangerous mission of capturing Amar. What I meant was that once you achieve success, you can employ me.' After saying this, Amar left the court and became invisible in Galeem.

As soon as Amar left, Zulmat felt ill and wanted to lie down. He tried to get up, but could not and asked his companions to give him a hand. 'Do you think I have overeaten?' he asked. 'Oh no, huzoor,' his companions protested a little too loudly, 'children eat much more than you did; you hardly touched anything!' As they carried him to bed, they sniggered and whispered to each other, 'This oaf had never seen delicacies like this before. He has stuffed himself through sheer greed and will now pay for it!'

Very soon though, the deadly poison affected them as well and within minutes, Zulmat and his companions and several other courtiers were very ill. Zulmat's stomach swelled to alarming proportions and he could no longer speak. His attendants tried to cure him with digestive salts and tinctures but all their efforts failed. Several hundred sahirs along with Zulmat died in agony. Rocks and flames rained from the sky when they died and their attendants fled from the palace. The citizens of Napursan were panic-stricken once again. Amar immediately cast the Net of Ilyas on all the furniture, precious goblets and even the floor seating. He stripped the sahirs of their outer clothes and jewels and left the ruined pavilion. The whole city had plunged into darkness following the sahirs' deaths and Amar killed anyone who crossed his path and plundered houses to his heart's content.

Amar and Danai Jadoo

Meanwhile, Yakut and Zamurrad reached Afrasiyab with Zulmat's offering of food and sweets. He was also stunned by the sheer beauty and variety of the sweets Amar had artfully prepared and asked Hairat, 'All these years you have been ruler of Napursan, you never offered such food to me!' Hairat said, 'My cook does not have such talent; this must be someone new!' Zamurrad interjected, 'This is a new cook called Ustad Charb Dast and he operates on his own.'

Afrasiyab was about to taste the sweets when Samri's grandson Mussavir held his hand back. 'Be careful,' he warned Afrasiyab, 'Amar is in the city, and it could be a trick.' Sarmaya, the vizier also agreed with Mussavir and said, 'In all my years I have never seen such food huzoor.' Afrasiyab looked amused and asked, 'Is Amar a cook as well as an ayyar?' Sarmaya replied respectfully, 'He is an ayyar huzoor! He is trained in every skill. Please consult the Book of Samri first.'

Afrasiyab trembled with rage and fear when he consulted the oracle Book of Samri. It read, 'This is all Amar's handiwork and he has killed Zulmat already. Had you tasted these sweets, you would have been instantly killed; be very cautious in the future!' Afrasiyab ordered that the sweets be buried and sent a message to a sahir called Danai Jadoo to immediately present himself in court. Danai sat on his flying throne of yellow agate that shone like the sun and within moments of receiving the message, appeared before Afrasiyab.

The King of Sahirs left for Napursan with Mussavir, Hairat, and Danai. The route that Afrasiyab took to the city was through a gully in a mountain that was pitch-dark. Afrasiyab chanted a spell and called out, 'O Mah Jadoo, let there be light!' No sooner had he uttered these words than two magic moons rose in the sky and illuminated the mountain. The city of Napursan was just beyond the mountain. Afrasiyab explained to his wife and friends that this was a secret passageway known only to him. Once in Napursan, Afrasiyab brought order to the frightened city, consoled the suffering populace and asked Danai Jadoo to take over as its ruler.

Afrasiyab then received a message from his maternal grandmother, Mahiyan Emerald-robe, who asked him to meet her immediately. Afrasiyab never ignored summons from his elders and after urging Hairat and Danai Jadoo to exercise extreme caution in Napursan, sped towards the Veil of Darkness where his elders resided.

After Afrasiyab's departure, Danai Jadoo began considering various strategies to trap Amar and eventually decided to take advantage of Amar's greatest weakness: his greed and love of wealth. So, the wise Danai went on a tour of the city of Napursan. Attendants in uniform held his throne while porters carried bags of jewels and gold coins. When he reached the city centre, Danai reached into the bags and drew out fistfuls of coins and jewels to throw at the poor and the needy. This led to a wave of excitement and cheer among the disheartened citizens of Napursan.

Amar, who had emerged from his hiding place in Galeem, saw a golden shower of gems and coins and thought to himself, 'This is nothing but a ruse to capture me.' He was soon overcome by his greed and took out the Net of Ilyas to scoop up the coins in mid-air. Mystified by the disappearance of the coins, Danai looked at his magic puppet that had been on the lookout for Amar. The puppet whispered, 'It is Amar my lord! Open two more bags quickly!' The sahir emptied the contents of the bags on the ground and just as Amar flung the magic net, the puppet jumped on the trickster's neck and held him in a vice-like grip. Amar was now truly caught and ran as fast as he could, but the puppet remained on his shoulders and dug its feet into Amar's ribs, riding him like a horse.

The puppet manipulated Amar straight into Hairat's durbar and was followed by an amused Danai Jadoo. The queen looked up and exclaimed, 'Why, Danai, you look so happy, almost as if you have arrested Amar!' Danai grinned and replied, 'It is as you say Malika!' Hairat saw the puppet riding on the back of a sahir and asked, 'Who are you?' Amar said, 'I am Khudawand Laqa's servant. He had lost a hawk and I was looking for it.' The puppet called out, 'Malika, do not be deceived by him; this is Amar!' The puppet conjured a cloud that released a few drops of water on Amar and the paints of ayyari on his face were washed away. Hairat called out triumphantly, 'So Amar, you are but a lowly ayyar after all and you will be punished for your crimes!' Always defiant, Amar replied, 'Hairat, I have killed many strumpets like you and now it is Afrasiyab and your turn.'

Hairat merely smiled and rendered Amar's limbs lifeless. She then sent a message to her husband about the latest turn of events. Afrasiyab was talking to his grandmother when Hairat's messenger reached him. He reacted angrily to her message, 'I told that trollop Hairat to kill Amar as soon as he is arrested! Why is she wasting time in sending me notes?' Trembling with fear, the puppet flew back to Napursan and when Hairat learnt of the Shahanshah's wrath, she immediately ordered that Amar be executed.

Makhmoor rescues Amar

The citizens of Napursan came out of their homes cheering when the drums rolled to proclaim the ayyar's execution. As Amar was walking towards certain death, he thought of Makhmoor Red-eye and said to himself, 'She is the only one powerful enough to save me in the Tilism of Batin, but where would she be now?'

The beautiful Makhmoor who had tactfully made her peace with the Shahanshah was still pining for her beloved, Prince Nur al Dahar. Her spies had been keeping her posted on Amar's trickeries in Napursan and they now brought her the news of his arrest and imminent execution.

Makhmoor went pale and looked up at the sky with her hand placed on her heart. 'If Amar dies,' she thought, 'I will never be reunited with my beloved!' Losing no time, she transported herself magically to the execution site and reached there just as the executioner was aiming to behead the great ayyar. Amar was still praying to the Almighty to save him when Makhmoor flung a metal disc that sliced off the executioner's hand. There was a sudden flash of lightning that made everyone close their eyes. The sky went dark and under the cover of darkness, Makhmoor swooped down in the form of a golden hand and whisked Amar out of sight.

Furious at this new turn of events, Hairat and Danai began following the golden hand that was the only visible part of Makhmoor. It too disappeared within minutes. After she had flown some distance, Makhmoor flung a puppet that looked exactly like Amar in Hairat's direction. When Hairat saw Amar catapulting towards the earth, she retrieved him and assumed that her spell had forced the rescuer to drop Amar. She handed Amar to the executioners and ordered that he be killed right away.

Makhmoor flew with Amar to her garden and ordered her astonished attendants and handmaidens, 'I am going to my Aunt Nastran's house in Tilism-e-Zahir. Bring all my valuables and belongings there.' Amar had become unconscious during the flight and Makhmoor now laid him down on a flying throne and woke him up. She flew to the River of Flowing

Blood and clutching Amar by the waist, jumped into the river at a point known only to Afrasiyab, Hairat and her. (Makhmoor was a powerful sahira and knew many secrets of Tilism that will be revealed later.)

When Amar's eyes opened, he saw that the river was flowing all around him, but the place where he stood was dry. Hundreds of sahirs in the form of crocodiles and beautiful fish darted through the waters. Deeper in the river, Amar saw a huge iron wall that was actually a doorway. The door had a lock the size of a camel's thigh and Makhmoor took out a golden key from her hair and opened the lock. She pushed the wall aside and took Amar to the other side, after which she slid the iron wall back into place. When Amar opened his eyes, he saw that they were already across the river.

Amar genuflected in gratitude to the Protector of Lost Travellers and looked at Makhmoor who acknowledged his unspoken compliment with a salaam. Suddenly, a revolting-looking sahir with a pig-like face appeared before them. Naqoos Jadoo lived in this wilderness and on seeing Makhmoor with Amar, realized that she had betrayed the Shah. He called out harshly, 'You treacherous wretch! You have betrayed Afrasiyab and escaped with this ayyar?! You will not escape from me!'

Amar immediately bolted out of sight and sprinted up the nearest hill. Makhmoor looked at Naqoos scornfully and said, 'Listen you useless wretch, why do you want to lose your life in vain? Do not try and stop us and be on your way!' Naqoos shouted, 'I will never let you go! I will capture you and take you to Shahanshah!' Makhmoor replied confidently, 'Well, if you insist on making your wife a widow, go ahead and do what you will!' Naqoos flung a magic coconut at her, but Makhmoor managed to deflect it and threw a magic ball in his direction. Naqoos flew upwards to avoid it and landed on the hill where Amar was hiding.

Naqoos did not see Amar as he was busy throwing an iron ball at Makhmoor. She caught it, but her hand shook with the impact. Naqoos was overawed by her strength and thought, 'This harlot is a favourite of the Shah of Tilism; she will not be killed with magic. I should attack her with my sword.' He drew out his sword and attacked her ferociously. Amar saw them fighting from the hill and thought to himself, 'Makhmoor is a woman and will be defeated by him!' He quickly placed a large stone in his catapult and shot it at Naqoos. The stone smashed his stubborn head right off his body. This was followed by thunderous sounds of, 'You have killed Naqoos Jadoo!'

Makhmoor was delighted with Naqoos' death and asked Amar, 'Brother, what is this sling that you carry with you?' Amar explained, 'This is a weapon of war and it is called a gophan.' Thus, chatting with each other, Amar and Makhmoor made their way to Malika Nastran's palace. Nastran was in her durbar when Makhmoor reached and greeted her. Nastran embraced and kissed her niece and asked, 'What brings you here my daughter?' Makhmoor silently showed her the wounds on her back and said, 'The Shah of Tilism had me whip-lashed.'

Nastran embraced her niece and wept in sympathy when she saw her wounds. She led Makhmoor into her garden, all the time muttering angrily, 'I would like to bury that wretch in a deep grave! I would like to sacrifice him seven times in the place where your nursemaid washes her hands! That wretched Afrasiyab threatens you with his power. I cannot get over the nerve of that wretch who inflicted such horrible wounds on my child!'

Nastran arranged for a bedchamber for Amar with a comfortable couch and appointed pretty handmaidens to attend to his comfort. She then turned to Makhmoor and said, 'My child, the Dome of Jamshed is near my palace. You and I should spend the night there and awaken our magic, for we have to confront the Shah of Tilism.' Makhmoor agreed readily to this plan and left with her aunt. After they left, Amar disguised himself as a sahir, just in case someone recognized and captured him.

Makhmoor travels to Mahrukh's camp

Now hear about Hairat. She fell into despair on discovering that the prisoner she had executed was actually a puppet moulded from lentil flour. The city of Napursan too was plunged into gloom following Amar's escape. Afrasiyab returned from his grandmother's place in Zulmat to find Hairat and the others looking downcast. After Hairat had related what had happened, he ordered a sahir to check whether Makhmoor was in her house. Makhmoor's handmaidens told the sahir that the princess had been away since the previous day. Afrasiyab turned to Hairat and said despondently, 'My queen, this was the doing of that traitor to the salt, Makhmoor! You had pleaded her cause and we are now paying the price. I will have to kill Makhmoor now for she knows too many secrets of Tilism.'

The next morning, Makhmoor's servants reached Nastran's palace with all her possessions. She advised her aunt to empty her palace and accompany her to Mahrukh's lashkar. Accordingly, Nastran ordered her servants to load her possessions on to mule carts and to then proceed towards Mahrukh's lashkar with Makhmoor's servants. Makhmoor, Amar and Nastran left separately on a flying throne.

On the way, Amar complained to Makhmoor, 'Malika, I have been in Tilism-e-Batin for so long but have not been able to find any of the treasures of the Shah of Tilism.' Makhmoor replied, 'Khwaja, if you desire treasures, I can offer you forty thousand gold coins from my treasury. When Shah is killed, I will take you myself to his treasury. He has emerald peacocks that are filled with precious rubies and pearls; there are puppets crafted from gems and their stomachs are filled with gold coins. There are gold saddles and bridles for eighty thousand horses. I even know where the horses are stabled. However, it will be impossible to conquer Tilism without the Keystone.'

Amar declared confidently, 'Princess, the Maker of a Thousand Tilisms and Universes will make it possible for us to find the Keystone.' Amar was delighted at the mention of forty thousand gold coins and his mouth watered at the prospect of the other treasures. Thus speaking pleasantly to each other, Amar, Makhmoor and Nastran travelled to Mahrukh's camp. As they approached it, Amar jumped off the throne and went into the durbar pavilion to announce Makhmoor's arrival.

Mahrukh declared, 'All the sardars should receive Makhmoor and the lashkar should also proceed to welcome her. Accordingly, the Naqara of Happiness was struck and the army moved to receive Makhmoor. Bahar, Nafarman, Surkh Mu, Afat and Hilal, and Ra'ad and Barq Mehshar too were dressed in rich robes when they went to receive Makhmoor who descended from her throne and embraced each of them as they greeted her formally. There were cries of '*marhaba*' and jubilation as the sardars led Makhmoor and Nastran through the camp and threw fistfuls of coins among the soldiers.

Mahrukh was waiting outside her pavilion when Makhmoor walked up to her and bowed low in mujra-greeting. Mahrukh embraced her and said, 'My daughter, are you well? Your arrival has strengthened the lashkar and gladdened my heart!' Mahrukh then bestowed a jewel-embroidered robe of honour on Makhmoor. Nastran was welcomed just as warmly. Mahrukh led Makhmoor into the durbar and offered her a ruby chair next to her own throne. Makhmoor then made an offering of five thousand rupees as tribute to Mahrukh, along with other gifts.

Following this, Mahrukh declared that the celebrations were to commence. Melodious, golden-voiced singers arrived with musical instruments and the gathering that evening was worthy of the great Persian kings, Faridun and Jamshed.

10 AFRASIYAB SENDS HOSHIAR KUTNI
TO CAPTURE MAKHMOOR

The keepers of the walled gardens of meaning and the flower gatherers of the meadows of words convey this through the scratching of their pens: Afrasiyab's bird messengers reported Makhmoor's grand welcome in Mahrukh's camp to him. The furious King of Sahirs wanted to capture Makhmoor himself, but was dissuaded by his companions like Mussavir, the grandson of Samri, who said to him, 'We have just seen the havoc Amar can cause here. In his own camp, he will be even more impertinent. It would be prudent to send someone else to arrest Makhmoor.'

A sudden thought occurred to the King of Sahirs. He turned to Hairat and said, 'Summon the five *Kutni*s from your realm.' The Kutnis soon arrived, dressed in robes of dishonesty. Their sinister and devious schemes were beyond the realm of human imagination and each one of them could give the devil himself lessons in treachery and deceit. In the durbar, they bowed before the Shahanshah who asked them, 'What can you do for us?'

The five women circumambulated Afrasiyab's throne with their hands folded to indicate that they would sacrifice themselves for him. Then they said, 'Huzoor, what can we tell you about our work? We have destroyed countless homes and have ruined and sold hundreds of people. We have deceived thousands of people to sell them as slaves. We have arranged many engagements, marriages and then divorces! We have caused dissent between the most loving parties; we have defamed the most virtuous girls and married women with vile rumours of lovers and adultery! We have revealed the secrets of rich merchants to thieves and robbers; and have reported on places where even air cannot enter. No foul deed or trickery is beyond our skills. We pose as friends and act like enemies! We can bring you gold leaf from the sun; we can tear the sky and patch it up! We can set fire to water and cause the heavens to tremble . . . '

'That is quite enough. Which one of you is the cleverest?' interrupted Afrasiyab, much amused. The women pointed to the eldest among them, Hoshiar Kutni. 'She is the great-aunt of the devil himself,' they said, 'and has taught us all that we know.' Afrasiyab instructed Hoshiar Kutni and told her that her sole assignment was to capture Makhmoor stealthily. He told her, 'I can send powerful sahirs to capture her but they can be killed by ayyars. It is necessary to fight trickery with deceit. If you can accomplish this you will be rewarded with the riches of the world.'

Afrasiyab bestowed a robe of honour on Hoshiar and dismissed the other Kutnis after giving them costly gifts. A sahir took Hoshiar Kutni across the River of Flowing Blood and informed the guards at the Bridge of Smoke that the Shahanshah wanted her to have easy passage across the river at all times. Hoshiar disguised herself as a beggar woman and entered Mahrukh's camp, calling out for alms. After a few days, she made her way to Mahrukh's pavilion. Mahrukh was absent-mindedly watching the landscape when the old woman came into sight, begging for alms. Mahrukh sent for her and asked her who she was. Hoshiar Kutni lied, 'Huzoor, I have lost everyone in my family; I did find a job but I am not used to taking orders from anyone and eventually, they threw me out. I was forced to start begging but now I am content. I beg the whole day and sleep wherever I can.'

The kind-hearted Mahrukh declared, 'You can spend the rest of your life here. You will get meals twice a day as well as clothes to wear and a tent to live in. A servant will attend to your needs and you will not need to work.' As it happened, none of the tricksters were in the camp at the time as they were guarding the camp from a distance. Besides, Amar spent most of his spare time with Makhmoor. Consequently, the devious Kutni managed to spend many days with Mahrukh, endearing herself to her by relating anecdotes and stories. One morning, she insisted on cooking for her mistress and prepared a fragrant, tasty pilaf. Mahrukh sent a message to Makhmoor, inviting her and Amar for lunch. The message read, 'I have hardly seen Khwaja Amar since you came to our camp. Come and share a meal with me.' Amar and Makhmoor promptly arrived and sat down for the meal. Mahrukh said, 'Khwaja, I have engaged a new servant who has many skills, even cooking. This pilaf has been prepared by her.'

Amar immediately became suspicious and thought that the new cook could be Sarsar in disguise. He took a spoonful of the pilaf, sniffed it and asked Mahrukh, 'Where has this new servant come from?' Mahrukh related how she had taken pity on the old beggar woman and had given her shelter. On hearing this, Amar asked Mahrukh to summon her. The Kutni arrived, head bowed down modestly. Amar looked closely at her and declared, 'She is not a ayyar, but is probably a Kutni. She seems too clever and her intentions are bad.'

'My good woman,' said Amar, 'look at me.' Hoshiar Kutni looked up at him straight in the eyes. Amar pretended to be satisfied. A moment later, he said, 'Let me look at your eyes again.' The woman looked up once more and Amar declared, 'Did you see that? She looked at me in a different manner each time! This woman is a Kutni and her mother was a Kutni too. If you want, I will get her to confess with my whip!' Just as he took out his whip from Zambil, Hoshiar fell at his feet and pleaded, 'king of ayyars, you are indeed without an equal! I am Hoshair Kutni! Afrasiyab paid me millions to capture Makhmoor. I make you a promise now that I will not betray Malika Mahrukh; I will spend the rest of my life at her feet for she has been very kind to me.' Amar retorted, 'I will never let you stay here because as they say, the bad one will never refrain from doing bad deeds!'

Mahrukh had become very attached to the old woman and when she realized that Amar would not let her stay in the camp, she pleaded, 'Khwaja, she has promised that she will not betray us; let her stay!' Amar replied, 'You are the leader of the camp so do as you wish but I do not think you should let her stay close to you!' Mahrukh said, 'She will remain in a corner and I will not have anything to do with her!' She gestured to the Kutni who slunk out of sight. Amar continued with his meal and the matter was closed.

Hoshiar remained inside her tent for a couple of days and made sure that no one paid any attention to her. One night, she slipped over to Hairat's camp and related what had happened. She added, 'If a powerful sahir can support me, I will capture Makhmoor in no time.' Hairat sent a nama to Afrasiyab conveying Hoshiar's message. Afrasiyab, in turn, asked Baghban Qudrat, his vizier, to go and help Hoshiar. Just as the vizier rose from his chair, his wife whispered to him, 'Why do you want to get killed for Makhmoor?' Baghban whispered back to her, 'He is my master, I have to obey him!' Afrasiyab saw them whispering amongst themselves and looked at Baghban questioningly. 'It is Gulcheen,' the vizier explained, 'she does not want me to go for this assignment.'

Afrasiyab said, 'I am pleased that you have been honest with me. Now go and capture Makhmoor.' Gulcheen followed her husband out of the durbar and nagged him on the way, 'It will not do to make an enemy of Amar. Why do you want me to become a widow?' Baghban replied irritably, 'Stop talking nonsense and stay in your garden! I have to do as the Shah says.' He flew to Hairat's camp where the Kutni was waiting for him. She made him change his face magically and took him to her tent in Mahrukh's camp. The next morning, she went over to Makhmoor's pavilion. As it happened, Amar was away at the time and Hoshair got the opportunity to open the door of deceit.

She greeted Makhmoor and said, 'I have crafted a rare bird that you should see.' 'What is so special about it?' asked Makhmoor. Hoshiar replied, 'It can conjure porcelain puppets that fight with each other and even sing.' Makhmoor was intrigued by this and accompanied the Kutni to her tent where Baghban was waiting for her. As soon as she entered the tent, he quickly threw a pinch of Jamshed's magic dust on her head that made her unconscious. The next moment, he put his arm around Makhmoor's waist and flew out of the camp while the Kutni fled from the tent. Her soldiers saw just a rope tied around Makhmoor as she flew in the air. They raised an alarm that alerted the tricksters and sahirs. By that time, however, Baghban had already flown across the River of Flowing Blood.

Hoshiar had reached the banks of the river when Amar spotted her from a distance. He called out, 'You slut, stop right there! Where do you think you are going?' Hoshiar ran to the Bridge of Parizadan where the guardians of the river moved forward to aid her. Amar realized that she would escape and so shot a huge stone from his gophan right at her head and smashed it to pieces. Sahir-guards ran after Amar but he became invisible in Galeem and turned to his camp. He related what had happened to Mahrukh and declared that he would try to save Makhmoor. Everyone tried to dissuade him by saying, 'Makhmoor will be helped by Allah, do not follow her. You will not be able to cross the magic river!' Amar remained adamant and left immediately. The other ayyars also followed him.

Hairat heard that Makhmoor had been arrested and travelled to the Garden of Apples feeling very happy. The King of Sahirs was in Zulmat at the time of her arrest. Baghban Qudrat had revived the unconscious Makhmoor after making sure that she would not be able to escape. Hairat reached the garden and subjected Makhmoor to a torrent of abuse: 'You disloyal trollop, how did the Shahanshah wrong you? He raised you from dust; he made you into a princess. You were respected by every royal of Tilism and yet you have made Amar your lover!?'

While Hairat was talking, a crimson cloud emerged on the horizon and the King of Sahirs arrived with his entourage. Afrasiyab sat on the throne and spoke to Makhmoor even more harshly than Hairat. Makhmoor thought, 'I will surely die now. Alas, I will not see my beloved Nur al Dahar and will leave this world deprived of his love!' Annoyed at her indifference to his insults, Afrasiyab taunted her, 'Is Amar your lover as well?' Makhmoor smiled contemptuously and declared, 'He is old enough to be my father. However, I am not bound to you and will have as many lovers as I please!' Afrasiyab shouted, 'You have so much confidence in Amar that you think he will be able to save you now?'

Makhmoor replied, 'I have confidence only in the Almighty. As for Amar, he can save me even if I was in the sky! You know that he is capable of shooting arrows through your nostrils!' Afrasiyab raved in fury, 'You harlot! You dare to threaten me! I will now burn you alive in front of him!' He turned to Hairat and said, 'Return to your camp and arrange a pyre in the plain in front of Mahrukh's army. Immolate her before her allies.' He then ordered a distinguished sahira, Rangeen Seher, to stand guard on the prisoner and assist Hairat in arranging the pyre.

According to her orders, Rangeen Seher went across the river with thousands of her sahir soldiers. She camped in front of Mahrukh's camp and ordered her men to collect wood for the pyre. As her men began to chop trees and pile them in one place, Amar, who had set off to rescue Makhmoor, passed by their camp. On seeing this operation in progress, he quickly disguised himself as a sahir and asked Rangeen's men why they were stacking the logs. When they told him about Makhmoor, he set about planning her rescue.

Meanwhile, the King of Sahirs consulted the oracle Book of Samri for he knew that Amar would try to rescue Makhmoor. The book informed him that Amar was standing next to the stack of logs disguised as a sahir. Afrasiyab told Hairat, 'Well! Her lover Amar is standing right next to the pyre. I will now burn the pair of them!' Afrasiyab sent a message to Rangeen Seher and ordered her to capture Amar at once. Amar saw her looking for him and vanished in Galeem.

Amar then summoned his wily pupil, Barq Firangi and said to him, 'My son, Makhmoor is to be burnt alive today. Assume my face and go in front of the soldiers who will capture you. I will see what I can do after that.' So Barq disguised himself as Amar and went towards the stack of logs. He saw that Sarsar Sword-fighter had also been sent by the King of Sahirs to assist Rangeen. Barq deliberately sauntered past Sarsar who lost no time in attacking him with her sword. Barq defended himself, but Rangeen's men soon overpowered him.

Rangeen immediately wrote to the King of Sahirs that she had captured Amar and that Sarsar had identified him too. Afrasiyab looked satisfied and said, 'My queen, prepare to leave and take Makhmoor with you. I will follow you so that I can watch them both burn!' Hairat left with several thousand sahirs and there was uproar in the invisible Tilism of Batin. All of Makhmoor's friends were grief stricken and decided to see her one last time. Her enemies thought, 'Let us see her in this plight and gladden our hearts.' Thus, both her enemies and friends travelled across the river. Hairat had Makhmoor shackled in iron chains and travelled on her magic peacock with thousands of sahirs guarding her and the prisoner. The King of Sahirs followed them in a grand procession.

Amar rescues Makhmoor

Now hear about Amar. After Barq's capture, he went to Rangeen Seher's tent and saw her seated on a masnad with her attendants hovering all around. Invisible in Galeem, he called out loudly, 'Rangeen Seher, I am Khudawand Laqa's angel and he has sent me to summon you. He is close by and wants to reward you for Amar's capture with immortality.' On hearing the disembodied voice, Rangeen was convinced that it was divine and followed its directions. She ordered her men against following her, 'This was a divine call meant only for me. Wait here!'

The voice led her to a lonely spot where Amar revealed himself to her as an awesome figure with many hands and fire emanating from his mouth and ears. Though this apparition intimidated Rangeen, she accepted the plateful of succulent fruit that the angel handed to her. He told her, 'Khudawand could not wait but left this fruit for you. Eat it and your life will be prolonged!'

The angel vanished after saying this and the gullible Rangeen tasted some fruit right there. She turned to walk back to the camp with the plate but fainted after just a few steps. Amar then emerged from his cloak and removed her outer garments. He painted his face to look like hers, wore her garments and returned to the place where the prisoners were to be burnt alive. He took out sticks of unconsciousness from Zambil that were crafted to look like dynamite and ordered Rangeen's men to lay them with the logs. The entourage of the King of Sahirs arrived at that time and Hairat brought forth the shackled and bound prisoner of love, Makhmoor.

Hairat conjured a gem-like bungalow for the Shahanshah to sit in and thousands of sahirs swept on to the plain to witness the execution. The false Rangeen went up to Hairat and said, 'Huzoor, remove your spells from Makhmoor so that I can place her on the pyre.' As Hairat released Makhmoor from her spells, the false Rangeen lifted her and placed her on the pyre along with Barq. Barq saw the sticks of dynamite in the pyre and thought to himself, 'May the name of my Teacher live forever. He has still not come to release me and I will be remembered for sacrificing my life for him!'

As she thought that she was with Amar, Makhmoor cried bitterly, 'Why did you put your own life in jeopardy for an unlucky woman like me Khwaja? It would have been better for you to have lived and related my misfortune to my beloved Nur al Dahar. Perhaps then he would have come to see my dust!' The false Amar, actually Barq standing in for his teacher, consoled Makhmoor, 'Princess, remember how the Almighty has helped us at every stage. Anything can happen at any moment. He will not let us down now!' Just then, Rangeen Seher approached them and shouted at Makhmoor, 'Stop weeping you foolish, treacherous woman and repent for your sins. There is still time for you!'

Alerted by the familiar voice Barq peered at the sahira and immediately recognized his teacher. Makhmoor shouted back at the false sahira, 'Do you think you can frighten me with death? I will never compromise with the King of Sahirs again!' The false Rangeen turned to Afrasiyab and Hairat who had come to witness the burning and waited for a signal. 'Move back from the pyre Rangeen,' Afrasiyab commanded and gestured to one of his officers to light the pyre. Just as the sahir went forward, another sahir blocked his way and smashed his head with a club. This was Mehtar Qiran in disguise. The skies darkened as they always did after the death of a sahir and under the cover of darkness, Qiran ran away, Barq leaped off the pyre, and Amar untied Makhmoor and placed her safely in Zambil.

Amar and Barq both fled the plain with sahir soldiers pursuing them. Amar turned and flung smoking hookahs on the pyre that caught fire and began to burn fiercely. The sticks of unconsciousness that Amar had placed on the pyre burst and released powerful narcotic fumes. Thousands of sahirs fell unconscious and Afrasiyab and Hairat succumbed to the fumes in their magic bungalow. Qiran ran to his camp and informed Mahrukh, who was battle-ready with her army, to attack immediately. She attacked the enemy ferociously and the sahirs who were conscious fled from the plain. Within moments, rivers of blood flowed on the battlefield. Suddenly, the earth quivered and parizads emerged from the ground with pitchers of water to revive the royal party.

Amar signalled to Mahrukh that parizads would revive Afrasiyab very soon and shouted across to her, 'The Shah is going to be mighty displeased when he regains his senses and it's best to be out of sight for a while.' Back in their camp, Mahrukh's son Shakeel declared, 'It is time we seek an ally as powerful as Afrasiyab.' Amar agreed, 'Yes, yes, but is there such a man?' Shakeel nodded and replied, 'His name is Kaukab the Enlightened and he is the ruler of Tilism-e-Nur Afshan. He has a daughter who is talented and beautiful, but the way to that Tilism is unknown, except to a privileged few. The River of Seven Hues separates it from Hoshruba, but no one I know has been able to sail on it, let alone cross it. There is another way to that Tilism, but it is through Mount Agate and is reputed to be treacherous.'

Amar declared, 'Treacherous or not, I will seek out a way to this Tilism.' Makhmoor was listening carefully to this conversation and now spoke up, 'Khwaja, I know the way to the River of Seven Hues and I will speak to Kaukab myself.' Amar wanted to leave immediately with her but the other sardars urged him to stay as everyone relied on his leadership. Makhmoor returned to her pavilion to prepare for the journey.

Meanwhile, the parizads had woken Hairat and Afrasiyab from their stupor. They awoke to see burning tents; several of their men lying burnt besides the pyre; thousands of bodies covered with gore and dust on the plain; and no Amar or Makhmoor. It was as if a flame of wrath burst within Afrasiyab who cried, 'It was a mistake to bring Makhmoor across the river, but they will surely die soon at my hands.' He vanished from where he was sitting and left to bring Ghurbal Jadoo, a powerful sahir who had a magic net that could trap any enemy. We will learn more about him later.

⌀

11 Princess Burran Takes Amar to Tilism-e-Nur Afshan

The one intoxicated by the wine of love, Makhmoor, made preparations for the journey to Tilism-e-Nur Afshan. She went to the durbar pavilion to bid farewell to all the sardars and set off for the River of Seven Hues on her magic peacock. Amar thought to himself, 'I should follow her. If nothing else, I might learn something about the secrets of Tilism. There is little to be gained by staying here.'

Meanwhile, Makhmoor had reached the edge of the camp on her peacock. Sarsar had been hiding in the ravine of a nearby hill thinking of ways to capture the ayyars when she saw her float by. She quickly disguised herself as Amar and called out, 'O Princess, wait for me! I have something to tell you!' Just as Makhmoor brought her peacock down to the ground, Sarsar approached her and burst a narcotic bubble on her face that made her fall unconscious.

Amar had been observing Makhmoor's peacock from a distance and saw Sarsar sprinting off carrying a bundle on her back. He called out angrily to her, 'Where do you think you are going? I have come now!' Sarsar laid Makhmoor on the ground and drew her sword on Amar. Even as he warded off her blows, Amar managed to lift and toss the bundle into Zambil. Sarsar was livid when she realized that she had lost her prisoner and fought with all her strength.

A sahir who lived on nearby mountain was intrigued by the sight of the fierce fighting between Amar and Sarsar. He chanted a magic incantation that created two claws that whisked Amar and Sarsar into the air and brought them before him. He asked them, 'Who are you and why do you fight?' Before Sarsar could speak, Amar said, 'This is my wife but she has become wayward!' Sarsar let forth a torrent of abuse and screamed, 'May I burn your wife's face and burn the face of anyone who calls me his wife! I can happily offer you as a sacrifice on Tuesdays and Sundays!' She cried out to the sahir, 'Do not be deceived by the words of this treacherous liar! I am the ayyar girl of the King of Magic and he is Amar!' The sahir looked confused and said, 'I am just an ordinary citizen and am not employed by the Shah. I will have to take you both to the durbar.' He then tied Amar and Sarsar to two pillars in his house.

Amar looked around in the sahir's house and noticed that though it was furnished simply, a number of musical instruments were lying about. Amar started humming to himself while still being tied to the pillar. The sahir, who heard his melodious humming, looked at him admiringly and said, 'You have some skill in the art of music.' Amar replied. 'If you free me, I can demonstrate my skills to you.' After a moment's hesitation, the sahir untied him, ignoring Sarsar, who was gesturing frantically.

'Please sir,' he urged Amar respectfully, 'will you not oblige me now?' Amar took out his flute and skilfully played both the sahir's sitar and his flute simultaneously. Amar's musical talents have already been mentioned earlier in this book. Within minutes, he had the sahir eating out of his hand and offering wine and sweetmeats to him. Amar doctored the wine as Sarsar watched him furiously. He poured out a goblet for the sahir, who paid no attention to Sarsar's warnings and drank the wine, and soon fell unconscious after a few sips.

Amar pranced up to Sarsar to steal a few kisses while she was tied up and helpless. Sarsar screamed at him, but inwardly marvelled at the way he operated. Very soon, Amar had stripped the sahir's house of all its valuables and returned to fondle Sarsar again. She cried, 'You worthless one, now that you got what you wanted, let me go!'

Eventually, Amar left Sarsar tied to the pillar and took Makhmoor out from Zambil. She was shocked to learn of how Sarsar had trapped her. 'This is why I wanted to accompany you,' explained Amar. Makhmoor had earler assumed that if she had a travel companion, she would probably have been distracted from the thoughts of her beloved. She conjured a flying throne on which both Amar and she could travel.

Ghurbal and his magic net

After vanishing from the battlefield, Afrasiyab materialized on a mountain in the invisible Tilism of Batin. The slopes of the mountain were covered with blossoms and on the summit stood a lavish bungalow made of sandalwood. Ghurbal Jadoo and his companions were relaxing on the masnad when Ghurbal's magical spirits informed him of the Shahanshah's arrival. Ghurbal quickly went out of the bungalow to receive him. Afrasiyab nodded in acknowledgement and said, 'Ghurbal, go with your magic net and capture all the traitors!' Ghurbal said, 'I will obey your orders with my heart and soul, but now that huzoor has come to my humble abode, will you not rest a while in my bungalow?'

Afrasiyab accepted Ghurbal's invitation graciously and sat down on the masnad. He had just begun to relax with a goblet of wine when bird messengers flew in to inform him of Amar's latest trickery at the musical sahir's house. Afrasiyab simply looked at Ghurbal meaningfully. The sahir did not say anything and left in a great rage with his lethal weapon, the magic net that could trap anyone, no matter how powerful.

Amar and Makhmoor had just flown a short distance when the skies darkened. When it became light again, they saw that they were caught in a vast golden metal net that spread for miles around them. Ghurbal immediately sent a bird messenger to Afrasiyab that said, 'Shahanshah your lowly servant has captured the sinners!' Afrasiyab was overjoyed when he heard this and arrived on the scene. He called out, 'Amar, this is the end to your mischief! Have you seen what has happened to you?' The sound of his voice was amplified magically and Amar and Makhmoor fainted in sheer fright. Afrasiyab now ordered Ghurbal to proceed to Hairat's camp with his net in order to capture the rest of the rebels.

The ayyars of the Islamic camp were the first ones to witness Ghurbal's arrival and reported Amar and Makhmoor's capture to Mahrukh Magic-eye. She visibly paled on hearing Ghurbal's name and wept for her two captured sardars. Soon she announced bravely, 'Alert our men and strike the battle drums for tomorrow.' The next morning, the sight of Ghurbal's vast golden net with the two prisoners dangling by their necks sent a wave of fear through the rebel army. Barq Mehshar and her son Ra'ad went forward and challenged one of Ghurbal's officers to fight. They had just disposed of him with their dual act when Ghurbal cast his net on them and they too became suspended by their necks from the net.

The rest of the Islamic sardars fought gallantly and killed several of Ghurbal's officers. Mahrukh Magic-eye in particular fought with great skill by diving underground whenever Ghurbal came near her to trap her; she would re-emerge behind him and kill another of his men. Afrasiyab, who was watching the battle from a nearby hill was amazed by Mahrukh's bravery. He came to Ghurbal's rescue and ordered his sahirs to close in on Mahrukh from all sides. Eventually, Nafarman, Bahar, Surkh Mu and almost all the other sardars and soldiers were caught in the net. The only ones to escape were Shakeel and the four ayyars. They watched Afrasiyab from a distance as he destroyed their camp and bazaars, but could only weep helplessly.

Afrasiyab ordered that one end of the net was to be tied to his pavilion and the other to the Dome of Light in Napursan. 'Be on the lookout for the four ayyars,' he warned Ghurbal, 'for they will come to rescue their companions during the night. Be sure to use the net against anyone you suspect. We will slaughter them all tomorrow morning!'

Ghurbal decided to keep watch with his men that night while Afrasiyab and Hairat went to rest. The next morning, a light-hearted Afrasiyab awoke early and after dressing carefully for the occasion, went to check on the prisoners who were still suspended from the net. Many of them had even died during the night. Afrasiyab sent for all his hangmen and executioners. Swords and knives were sharpened for the slaughter and the residents of Tilism came in droves to watch the greatest executions in the land.

Tilism-e-Nur Afshan

While these preparations are going on, let us observe the strategy of the True Protector that proves that the enemy can do little when a friend is favourable. In the neighbouring Tilism of Nur Afshan, the great Shah Kaukab had just convened his durbar. All the tajdars and sardars of Tilism were present there. Kaukab's daughter, Burran Sword-woman, was sitting next to him on a jewelled chair. The Grand Vizier Mirzan stood behind the Shah, fanning him slowly. Beautiful dancers performed before the Shah and golden-hued wine was being served. After some time, Kaukab declared, 'I feel like a turn in the gardens this morning.' He descended from his throne and walked with his courtiers behind him.

That vision of loveliness and the glory of the garden, to whom the sun and the moon were enslaved, Burran Sword-woman, also accompanied her father with her companions. After some time, Burran said, 'Honourable father, let us walk to the verdant plains in front of the Dome of Samri. My companions and I can have a flying contest there. That might entertain your royal self!' Kaukab smiled indulgently and said, 'It seems you have still not outgrown your childlike habits daughter! Very well, let us witness your games. I believe Princess Gauhar Afshan is a champion flier. I would like to see her take off.' Thus, the whole gathering left for the plains that were as beautiful as the legendary Gardens of Shaddad.

Burran's fair young companions tied their scarves around their waists and flew up to the sky. When these moon-like beauties with their gleaming clothes floated up, it was as if a thousand suns were shining in the sky. Most of the girls flew well, but Princess Gauhar Afshan soared up to such a height that people could not see her anymore even though they used magic binoculars. There were shouts of praise from the whole gathering for her flying skills. Then Kaukab said to Burran, 'My child, demonstrate your skills as well. Fly high enough to bring back a souvenir from Hoshruba!'

Thus instructed, Burran tied her scarf around her waist. She opened her tresses and took out the Akhtar Marvarid—the magic pearl from the Dome of Samri—that was tied in her hair. The pearl gave her extraordinary powers and when she held the large pearl in her palm, it emitted rays that were bright like the sun. At one signal from Burran, the rays formed a chain-like formation up to the heavens themselves. Then that pearl of magic, Burran, held on to the chain and flew upwards. The rays from the magic pearl transformed into pearls when they fell on the earth . . . what a glorious sight that was! The sky glowed as if a thousand lamps and torches were alight and pearls rained on the earth!

Burran flew up so high that she had could view the entire world. She looked down on Hoshruba and was startled by the curious spectacle unfolding below her. She saw the vast golden Net of Ghurbal, which spanned for several miles from the Dome of Light to the royal pavilion across the River of Flowing Blood. Thousands of prisoners were suspended by their necks from it. Some seemed to be suffocating, while others were moaning in pain; several more appeared to be dead. A large army stood in formation around a scaffolding for executions where executioners were strutting about with bare swords. Burran flew downwards to get a closer look when the sight of Amar startled her. She thought that this unusual-looking creature was a magical apparition caught in the net. What a strange appearance he had with a small round head on a thread-like neck, eyes like cumin seeds, cheeks like kulcha bread, small pearl-like teeth, rope-like limbs and the most curiously elongated body.

Burran thought, 'I should rescue this poor creature and take him as a souvenir for my father!' She signalled to the pearl and its rays came together to form a large shining disc like the sun. Burran jumped into the disc as it descended. It began hovering above the prisoner. Suddenly, the disc cracked open and Burran emerged from it to fall like a hawk on the net. The net tore and Burran managed to release Amar, who went catapulting down to the ground. Burran dived down to catch him and prepared to fly upwards again. However, when the golden net broke, it sagged and tilted. Ghurbal and Afrasiyab were alerted by the shouts of their soldiers who noticed that something was amiss. Ghurbal attended to the broken net and repaired it, while Afrasiyab swiftly pursued the golden disc now spinning rapidly out of sight.

Burran had travelled a short distance when the King of Sahirs caught up with her. He transformed into a large flying dragon and exhaled flames that wounded the delicate Burran. Her body erupted in boils and she wept with the pain but held on to the prisoner and bravely shot the magic Pearl of Samri at Afrasiyab. He jumped aside just in time to avoid the pearl that would have gone through his chest. Even so, its powerful radiance transformed him from a dragon to his real self.

Burran caught the pearl that flew back to her. The Shahanshah now went after Burran with a snare-rope. She tried to break free, but it caught her round the waist. The snare-rope cruelly cut into Burran's delicate body and she bled as Afrasiyab dragged her towards him. Burran was immensely powerful but was no match for the King of Sahirs and was pulled towards him helplessly.

Now hear about Kaukab. He was now worried about his daughter who had been away for an unusually long time. He thought of sending someone after her, but then felt that it would be quicker for him to find her himself. After flying high enough to view Hoshruba, he witnessed the shocking sight of his daughter caught in Afrasiyab's snare-rope. A livid Kaukab fell on Afrasiyab like a bolt of lightning. Afrasiyab hastily conjured a live dummy and vanished. Kaukab incinerated the rope that had trapped Burran and she managed to escape and fly homewards with Amar. Afrasiyab returned as a bolt of red lightning and Kaukab saved himself just in time by leaving a puppet in his place.

Kaukab reappeared bearing the mirror of Jamshed. Afrasiyab responded by holding out his powerful armband, a gift from Samri. As both the kings looked at these powerful magical objects, they fell unconscious and went spinning down to the ground. The earth split open and Afrasiyab's guardian puppets emerged to break his fall. Golden slave-boys mounted on magical birds flew in from the direction of Tilism-e-Nur Afshan and caught Kaukab before he hit the ground.

At that moment, a huge fish with emerald scales suddenly emerged on the scene. This was Mahiyan Emerald-robe, Afrasiyab's maternal grandmother, who was always vigilant on his behalf. The emerald fish opened her mouth wide and swallowed Afrasiyab. By that time, the golden slave-boys had revived Kaukab. The fish called out to him, 'Kaukab, why is there a fight between brothers? I agree he is at fault for attacking your daughter. I am taking him now and will talk to him. My son, you should also return to your realm.'

Kaukab returned to Tilism of Nur Afshan and flew down into his garden where his courtiers awaited him anxiously. They greeted him warmly and Kaukab sat down on his throne. Burran had already arrived with Amar and had laid him on the ground. She removed the broken links of the net that were still around his neck and applied magic salve to his wounds. Amar felt some relief but was very weak and lay half-conscious with his eyes closed. Burran first asked her father about the battle and then said, 'Respected father, I have brought this prisoner so that you can satisfy my curiosity about him. Is he a man, a bird or a genie? What is he? Why did Afrasiyab imprison him and why was he so furious about his escape?'

Kaukab looked closely at Amar and asked his courtiers, 'Can you recognize this man?' Several people ventured opinions, each one more preposterous then the other. One person said, 'This is a rare magical bird belonging to the King of Magic!' Another opined, 'He must be a demon from Zulmat!' Kaukab turned to his astrologer Fahim Faroos and said, 'Surely you can tell us who he is! You, who are wise and powerful!' Fahim said respectfully, 'The elders of our Tilism have cast a horoscope of this Tilism and have written down all that will happen here. With your permission, I can fetch that now. Perhaps they will have written about him as well?'

Kaukab declared, 'I know all about him; that is why I am called the Enlightened. Khudawand Samri wrote in his book about this infamous ayyar, Amar. Wherever he sets foot, Samri's faith is destroyed! Burran seems to have unleashed a demon in our realm! Anyway, bring the horoscope and we shall see what it will reveal.'

While Burran and the rest of the durbar looked disbelievingly at Amar lying in a crumpled heap, Fahim brought the ancient leaves of the horoscope and gave it to Kaukab. The horoscope revealed that in the last age of Tilism-e-Hoshruba, it would be invaded by Prince Asad bin Hamza Sahibqiran who would eventually conquer it. The horoscope went on to pronounce that the Shah of the Tilism-e-Nur Afshan would release Amar from captivity. He needed to become an ally of Amar for greater glory and to retain his empire. If not, he would be as disgraced and humiliated like Afrasiyab.

Kaukab read the horoscope quietly and gave it back to Fahim. He turned his attention to Amar who was now fully conscious. Even though Amar had seen many palaces and Tilisms, he was overawed by the magnificence and splendour of Kaukab's durbar. Kaukab addressed Amar with great respect and offered the jewel-inlaid chair next to his throne to him. Amar was hesitant, but at Kaukab's insistence, sat on the chair and explained the reason for his journey to Nur Afshan. He added, 'I am a poor man. Sahibqiran used to be very charitable towards me. I am at your service and await your generosity.'

Kaukab graciously sent for jewels for Amar and said, 'Khwaja, if it was not for my daughter, you would be dead by now. Your companions are still trapped in the magic net. Afrasiyab is with his grandmother right now. Once he returns, he will surely send everyone on the final path. Near the River of Flowing Blood, on the summit of a mountain, stands a house with steps made of gold leading to the basement. Ghurbal stays there. If someone can kill him, the magic net will disintegrate and the prisoners will be released.'

Amar remained silent but thought inwardly, 'It seems that my luck has turned. These people are also sahirs. If they become our allies, it will be good; if not, I should go and kill Ghurbal and release my friends. But before I leave, I should plunder this palace!' So, Amar started humming a tune. Kaukab looked at him with interest. Burran and the others were captivated by his voice and requested him to sing for them. Amar said, 'I am but a poor man in a dire situation; how can I sing?' Burran bestowed several gifts on him and Kaukab asked him to sing as well.

Amar then obliged them by singing a haunting ghazal that moved everyone to tears. Amar kept singing till it was afternoon and then stopped suddenly. Since everyone was enthralled by his voice, they called out to him to continue singing. Amar protested, 'My song is not for hearts of stone; there is neither wine nor meat here!' Kaukab signalled to a cupbearer who offered Amar a goblet of wine. Amar said, 'What good is one goblet? Let me serve wine to you today as I served the Shah of Islam!' Kaukab smiled and sent for flasks of wine for the trickster.

Amar poured the wine into decanters and stealthily added the powder of unconsciousness to it. He arranged the red and green decanters into a bouquet, poured wine into a goblet and served it to the Shah with a flourish. Kaukab graciously accepted the goblet from Amar's hand but he was as powerful a sahir as Afrasiyab and the wine caught fire just as he was about to sip it. Kaukab tossed the goblet aside and addressed Amar with the utmost contempt, 'You are a treacherous rascal. The fault is mine for trusting you, for to be kind to someone like you is worse than being unkind to someone good! Is this how you repay my favours?'

Amar tried to make amends by apologizing and said that he was merely testing the king's powers. Kaukab was angrier still when he heard this and thundered, 'No Khwaja, your word cannot be trusted. Return to Hoshruba for you deserve Afrasiyab's shoe-beatings!' He pressed his hand against Amar's chest and pushed him so hard that Amar felt like he was falling into a pit and closed his eyes in fright. When he opened his eyes, he saw that there was no garden, palace, durbar, vizier or king. Instead, he was standing near a mountain with the River of Flowing Blood running near by.

As Amar collected his senses, he marvelled at the power Allah had given to one individual. After a while, Amar realized that he was close to the hill where Ghurbal lived and thought, 'It seems that Kaukab is secretly my ally. Despite his anger, he had my army's interest in mind. If he had not sent me back, they would have been executed by Afrasiyab in the morning. Indeed he is a man of honour.'

Amar disguised himself as Afrasiyab and climbed up the mountain towards Ghurbal's house. He called out to him imperiously and Ghurbal emerged looking mystified for his magic had informed him that Amar was summoning him. Before he could do anything, Amar handed him a phial of perfume and said, 'I am concerned about you Ghurbal, for Amar will be a threat to you now. This is the perfume of invisibility to protect you from your enemies. Use it now and good luck to you!' After saying this, Amar suddenly vanished. Ghurbal was now convinced that this was Afrasiyab because he felt that only the real Afrasiyab could possess such powers. He returned to his house with Amar following him in his cloak of invisibility.

The first thing that Ghurbal did in his room was to rub the perfume on his face to see if it worked. Just as he looked at the mirror to test its powers, the narcotic worked and made him sneeze and fall unconscious. Amar emerged from Galeem and slaughtered Ghurbal instantly. The house went dark and his spirits howled, 'Surround him! Catch him! He has done a terrible deed and killed Ghurbal Jadoo!' Amar calmly plundered the valuables and went out of the bungalow.

While Amar was busy plundering, Ghurbal's death made his magic net unravel and all the prisoners were released. Hairat and her officers were unprepared and still waiting for Afrasiyab's return from Zulmat when the magic net disintegrated. Mahrukh, Bahar and all those who had been trapped in the net were released. Some of the prisoners were unconscious and began falling down to the earth, but the conscious ones conjured magic claws to save their friends. Mahrukh also chanted spells so that they revived quickly.

Hairat and the others rushed to attack the freed rebels. Mahrukh, Bahar and Makhmoor were so furious about their capture that they responded very aggressively. Even though the rebel soldiers were weak after their ordeal in the net, they rallied valiantly around Mahrukh. Bahar's bouquets weaved their hypnotic magic on thousands of Hairat's troops while Makhmoor hurled magic goblets of wine that besotted the rest. Ra'ad roared like thunder while Barq Mehshar fell like lightning and executed hundreds of troops. Only Hairat could confront each of them and counteract their magic. She chanted spells to conjure rains and rivers of fire. Only she could defend her own army and attack the enemy in the same breath. Soon, dead bodies were strewn all over and rivers of blood flowed in the battlefield.

This fierce confrontation continued until evening. Eventually, Hairat thought it wiser to strike the drums of peace and returned to her pavilion with a heavy heart. Mahrukh's camp was set up again and she took her place on the throne. Amar also arrived in the durbar and met his friends. Everyone was overcome with happiness and gratitude at this unexpected triumph and people embraced each other in joy.

The reader will recall that Afrasiyab's grandmother Mahiyan Emerald-robe had whisked him off when he had fallen unconscious during his skirmish with Kaukab. Mahiyan had appeared as a huge fish and had literally swallowed him. She took him to her palace and disgorged him there. Afrasiyab awoke and after greeting his grandmother, said, 'Why did you bring me here? Kaukab must have released my prisoners and destroyed my army!' Mahiyan looked angry and cried, 'You foolish boy, when Burran released Amar, you should have met that exalted one and asked her for the reason instead of fighting with her! It is not wise to be aggressive with people who share your faith. You should send Kaukab a message of peace or your enemies will gain a strong ally!'

Later, Afrasiyab returned to Hairat's camp and saw that it was in complete disarray. A tearful, distraught Hairat informed him about Ghurbal's death and the rebels' release. Afrasiyab rubbed his palms in dismay and wanted to set out to capture the rebels immediately. Hairat cautioned him, 'It seems that Kaukab has joined hands with them. All this is his doing. Do not go after them now. Instead, compose a message for Kaukab.'

Mussavir's encounters with the ayyars

Mussavir the magic artist and his wife Soorat Nigar reached Hairat's camp on Afrasiyab's request to avenge their son's death and destroy the rebels. In a private conversation with his wife, Mussavir revealed that he could trap Amar easily as he had drawn his magical portrait. Barq Firangi, who had been snooping around in Hairat's camp disguised as a maidservant overheard this and reported it to Amar, who was alarmed by the news and said, 'Somehow, my son, you must get hold of Mussavir's portrait of me!' Barq promised to do his best and left immediately. Amar too left the camp disguised as a sahir.

The Shah had instructed Sarsar and her companions to guard Mussavir against the tricksters. Mussavir appointed a large number of guards outside his tent and wore Amar's portrait around his neck so that he would be instantly alerted if Amar was around. Meanwhile, Barq had insinuated himself into the durbar disguised as one of Soorat Nigar's companions. He was even witness to a fight between Mussavir and Soorat Nigar when she caught her husband dallying with one of the maidservants. Barq followed Soorat Nigar to her tent where she vented her anger on her maidservants by picking on them unnecessarily. A little later, Barq offered her a drugged goblet of wine, which she sipped in a moment of carelessness, and after that, she instantly fell asleep.

Barq dragged Soorat Nigar, left her under the bed and disguised himself as her. Late at night, Mussavir entered his wife's tent and begged her forgiveness. The false Soorat Nigar pretended to be angry and turned away from him mumbling, 'Go back to your hussies and do not touch me!' Mussavir swore undying loyalty to her in the future and the false Soorat Nigar pretended to relent. She offered him a perfume phial as a peace offering. Mussavir immediately succumbed to the drug in the perfume and after sneezing once, fell into a drugged stupor.

Sarsar Sword-fighter and Saba Raftar Fleet-foot, who were patrolling the camp, heard him sneeze and immediately became suspicious. They looked into the tent and saw Mussavir unconscious and alone for Barq had slipped away when he heard their voices. They revived Mussavir who soon became distraught because of his wife's disappearance and ran to the Garden of Apples. Afrasiyab, however, was not very sympathetic and said with a smile, 'This is just the beginning my lord. You know I have also suffered grievously at the hands of these ayyars. You have to be patient and in any case, your wife cannot die unless Tilism is conquered.' Mussavir kept fretting and just to appease him, the Shah sent one of his magic claws to capture Barq who was with Amar at the time.

When the claw appeared above them, Amar quickly became invisible. The claw managed to catch Barq and immediately transported him to the Garden of Apples. Barq greeted the Shahanshah who smiled and said, 'Barq, just tell us where you have hidden this man's wife and I will release you.' Mussavir added, 'Yes, and I pledge to personally escort you across the river.' Barq lied with aplomb, 'Well, actually I have handed her over to Amar. If you really love her, you should send him a gift of money and robes of honour. Perhaps then I can persuade him to release her.'

An elated Mussavir immediately obliged him with the gifts and Barq wrote a note to Amar begging him to release Soorat Nigar in exchange for his life. Amar was in the durbar when a messenger arrived with the gifts and Barq's note for him. Realizing that Barq was actually tricking the enemy, Amar wrote back, 'O Exalted Son of Samri, I would never release a prisoner even for my son's life, but Barq means more than a son to me. Therefore, I am willing to exchange your wife for Barq. Bring him across the River of Flowing Blood and take your wife from me.'

Mussavir was delighted with Amar's message and immediately transported Barq across the River of Flowing Blood. Meanwhile, Amar took out a woman from Zambil and said to her, 'I have sold many slaves, but I took pity on you and will not sell you. You will be disguised as Princess Soorat Nigar and live a life of luxury. Just maintain your new identity and if they ask you to prove it through magic, tell them that your stay in Zambil erased all knowledge of spells and magic from your memory.'

The poor woman was relieved to escape the drudgery of her life in captivity and readily agreed to Amar's instructions. Then the ayyar took the woman to Mussavir who was waiting for him. Mussavir embraced his false wife warmly and presented Amar with more gold and presents. Amar was curious about his portrait so Mussavir held it out to him. Amar realized that the picture reflected him exactly and even showed the clothes that he was wearing at the time. On seeing this, Amar praised Mussavir lavishly: 'Never in all my years have I seen advanced magic of this kind!'

When Amar and Barq returned to the durbar laden with gifts, everyone complimented Barq for hoodwinking the sahir lords. 'Indeed,' Amar agreed solemnly, 'thanks to my disciple, I have managed to collect a few rupees. I am going to reward him with two muslin shirts.' Barq replied in jest, 'Sir, you have given me enough already! Please do not burden me with more gifts.' This caused a ripple of amusement among the sardars who were aware of Amar's miserly nature.

Meanwhile, Mussavir returned with his newly-found wife to the Shahanshah's durbar. Hairat and Afrasiyab greeted the false Soorat Nigar and looked closely at her. 'Your colour has changed!' exclaimed Hairat. 'Naturally,' replied the woman, 'who can remain healthy in prison?' The durbaris were eager to learn about Zambil so the woman described the wonders of the magical pouch—its seas and deserts, the harsh treatment meted out to prisoners there, and the meagre rations of a dried piece of bread with molasses that was served only once a day.

As she was speaking, Sarsar Sword-fighter and Saba Raftar Fleet-foot walked into durbar. They greeted the false Soorat Nigar but whispered amongst themselves because she did not seem genuine to them. 'Since you have spent so much money,' they finally asked Mussavir, 'did you not make sure that this is your wife? Ask her if she remembers magic.' Mussavir looked confused but the woman simply repeated Amar's instructions about forgetting magic in Zambil.

Sarsar remained unconvinced by her reply and declared, 'Sir, I am a trickster, not a she-donkey. This is not the real Soorat Nigar. Give me a whip and I will make her acknowledge it just now!' Perturbed by Sarsar's attitude, Mussavir requested the Shah to consult the Book of Samri. The oracle book revealed that Soorat Nigar was unconscious under her own bed and that the maidservant who Barq had tricked was lying unconscious elsewhere. Afrasiyab immediately vented his anger on Sarsar and screamed, 'You useless hussy, I had sent you to guard the camp! Is this how you serve me?' When Sarsar remained silent, the Shah sent Mussavir back to the camp to find his wife and then turned to Hairat and said, 'My dear, Mussavir may be the son of Samri but he is too gullible to deal with the ayyars. Let us try another tactic now. We will arrange a fair at the Emerald Well to trap the rebels. Prepare to leave for Zulmat and bring me the Ring of Jamshed.'

Hairat gets the magic Ring of Jamshed

Afrasiyab sat on his royal throne in the Garden of Apples while Hairat prepared for the journey to bring the Ring of Jamshed. When Hairat mounted her peacock throne, four jewel-inlaid peacocks perched on the four corners of the throne rose and formed a canopy over the queen, and hundreds of drums sounded magically. The King of Sahirs prepared a gilori with his own hands and lovingly offered it to the queen. Nobles in the durbar laid tributes of gold coins before her and the king held her arm and breathed some spells on her so that she looked younger and even more beautiful.

Thus, Hairat left for the Veil of Darkness in great splendour to get the Ring of Jamshed. She travelled through a beautiful wilderness where the air was as cool as the breeze of paradise, and savoured the beauties and wonders of Tilism. Finally, she reached the base of a magnificent mountain.

Meanwhile, Afrasiyab told his officers, 'Strike the magic naqaras of the realm and let all the heralds announce throughout my kingdom that a week from now there will be the feast and worship of Jamshed and Samri at the Emerald Well.' In no time, sixty-four thousand kettledrums suspended throughout the kingdom began to thunder and boom and the news spread like wildfire. Mahrukh paled as she heard the announcement and said to Amar, 'There is no escape for us now.' Amar asked her to keep faith and summoned his band of ayyars to discuss this latest development.

Elsewhere in Tilism, Hairat reached a large palace with a hundred soaring minarets of rubies that cast an eerie red glow over the area. As Hairat approached the main door, it opened silently. Inside, she found herself in total darkness. Minutes later, an arch that opened to the seven secret houses of Tilism began to reveal itself gradually. The first six were treasuries of gold, silver, rubies, emeralds, sapphires, and diamonds. The seventh house had seven secret chambers, each with its own fearful demon. (These demons will be used against Mahrukh's armies later on.)

Hairat avoided the demons and approached the house of gold. She stood before the magnificent golden structure with its intricate *kundan* inlay-work and called out, 'O Kundan, come to me!' Amidst the distant sound of bells and a shower of petals, a throne came flying towards the house. A beautiful girl, entirely made of gold, sat on the throne and asked Hairat, 'What is your purpose my queen?' Hairat replied, 'I need you to open the house of gold as the King of Magic has sent for Jamshed's ring. He offers these trays of precious gems in homage to Jamshed.'

Kundan looked at the offering and laughed. She said, 'This will not do my queen! Return to Shahanshah and get the real offering from him to get the ring. I will wait right here for your return.' Hairat was puzzled by this but returned to Afrasiyab and conveyed Kundan's message to him. Afrasiyab then tapped in the air. There was total darkness that dispelled within moments and revealed an ancient *pir* seated on a large throne. Everyone in the durbar rose to greet him. The old man asked the king abruptly, 'Why did you summon me here?'

'I need you to tell me what offering I need to make to obtain Jamshed's ring,' replied Afrasiyab. 'Do not even think about it!' the pir said dismissively. But Afrasiyab insisted and said, 'I have to! The religion of Samri and Jamshed is under threat. The kingdom is slipping out of my hands!'

The pir was silent for a while and then said, 'You will not be able to bear the pain.' When Afrasiyab persisted, the pir gestured lightly and a magic puppet holding a dagger and a silver bowl appeared before them. The pir said to Afrasiyab, 'You will have to cut seven pieces of your flesh and place them in the bowl—two from your hands, two from your feet, two from your ears, and one from your chest.' Afrasiyab performed the task unflinchingly and when he dropped each piece into the bowl, it transformed into a large ruby. The pir disappeared while calling out, 'String these rubies together into a bracelet for Jamshed and heal your wounds with the blood in the bowl!'

Hairat returned to the Veil of Darkness where Kundan was waiting for her. Kundan looked at the ruby circlet and prostrated in front of the door of the gold house. As soon as she inserted the key in the lock, the door opened with a loud crack. Hairat entered the house and saw that the chamber had several rooms with an inner sanctum hidden by curtains. Hairat prostrated in front of the sanctum and then stood on one leg with her hands folded in supplication. Soon, the chamber resounded with the sound of drums and bells, and the curtain lifted up to reveal a stone idol of Jamshed. The idol asked Hairat, 'O Princess of the Realm, what is your wish?'

Hairat said, 'The Ring of Jamshed.' The idol smiled and extended a stony finger towards her. Hairat tried to remove the ring off the finger but screamed in pain as the stone finger burnt her hand. 'Place the ruby bracelet around my wrist and then remove the ring!' the statue commanded. Hairat did as instructed and the ring came off with ease. There were thunderous sounds of drums and bells as the curtain closed on the image of Jamshed once again. Hairat prostrated in gratitude and then withdrew from the chamber.

Hairat left for the Garden of Apples with the precious ring. Magic birds flew over her to shade her from the sun and due to the power of the ring, the ghouls and spectres of Tilism were visible to her. Thus, the queen travelled in stages towards the Garden of Apples. Before approaching the garden, she stopped in another garden and placed the ring on a gold tray and covered it with a gleaming gold *zardozi* cloth. She also adorned herself in jewels and rich garments.

When the Shahanshah heard the sounds of drums and bells and a thousand voices singing in praise of Jamshed, he left with his courtiers and nobles to receive Hairat and led her into the garden. After reaching the garden, the Shahanshah suddenly vanished. After some time, the trees in the garden began sparkling with glitter, flowers began glowing and plants started singing praises of Jamshed. The throne in the baradari became magically enclosed in glass case and the fragrance of *bukhoor* incense filled the air.

The King of Magic materialized behind the glass in all his glory, wearing a dazzling crown on his head and a robe that had such bright rich colours that the robe of the sky seemed dull in comparison. Hairat was the first to pay homage to him and held out the ring. Afrasiyab smiled and prostrated in reverence to Jamshed before wearing the ring.

The stone on the ring was more dazzling than the sun and seemed to be inscribed with magic symbols.

Afrasiyab suddenly clapped his hands. Moments later, a peacock with the face of a parizad materialized before the Shah who said to it, 'I have sent for you magic peacock to test the ring.' The peacock replied, 'Whoever wears the ring commands not only me but the whole realm.' The Shahanshah ordered, 'Then go and bring the ayyar Amar who rebels against Khudawand Laqa!' The peacock flew straight to Mahrukh's durbar across the River of Flowing Blood and swooped into the pavilion. It called out, 'Khwaja Amar, Shahanshah summons you now.' Amar was about to flee but was enchanted by the peacock's voice and turned to say, 'The slave hears and obeys.' The peacock flew off with Amar and threw him at the Shah's feet.

Amar had never seen Afrasiyab in such splendour and shook like a leaf. The Shah graciously offered him a chair and said, 'I have sent for you Amar to warn you that even if you and your friends hide in the skies, you will not escape capture. Therefore, return to your camp now and persuade them to come with you. If you convert to the religion of Samri and Jamshed, perhaps you can save your life.' Amar replied with some fear, 'I can only speak for myself. I can convert to the worship of Samri right now! I will try and persuade the others, but it is their decision finally!' Afrasiyab said, 'I cannot trust your word; however, go now and speak to them or you will be severely punished!'

After the peacock left with Amar, Afrasiyab said, 'Amar will indeed try and persuade the rebels to capitulate today!' Hairat looked doubtfully at him and said, 'He is deceitful and I respectfully remind you that it is unwise to test someone who has been tried before. How many times has he slipped out of our grasp with his wily ways?' The Shah looked thoughtful and then cut out a paper puppet. He touched the puppet with the Ring of Jamshed and it transformed into a man. Afrasiyab ordered the puppet to spy on Amar.

When the magic peacock deposited Amar back in his durbar, the sardars were very relieved. As the peacock left, he warned Amar, 'Do not go against your word now, or you will be punished horribly.' Amar collapsed in his chair, pale-faced and sweating with fear. After some time, he gathered himself and related Afrasiyab's message. The sardars spoke in unison: 'Khwaja, we will do as you say!' Amar asked them, 'What is the way out of this?' The sardars sighed and said, 'Absolutely nothing Khwaja! Even if all the sorcerers in the world attack Afrasiyab, the ring will protect him.'

Amar looked at them and said, 'Look, I am never going to submit to that devil. I can promise you that this Tilism will be conquered by Asad, the grandson of Hamza. Once the sons of Hamza step into any land, they are always victorious. However, I am worried about all of you. If you declare your loyalty to the King of Sahirs, your kingdoms will be restored to you.' Mahrukh, Bahar and the others cried, 'Khwaja, Allah protect us! We are willing to lose our lives and leave this world, but we will never return to the King of Sahirs!' Once he heard this, Amar was convinced of their loyalty and urged them to hide. Mahrukh smiled and said, 'There is nowhere to hide; once Afrasiyab summons us we will have to go to the fair!' Amar replied, 'Stay here then and trust in God's mercy!'

Afrasiyab's paper puppet heard this conversation and reported it verbatim to his master. Afrasiyab looked furious and declared, 'These rebels are asking to be destroyed. I am now going to the Veil of Darkness to invite my elders to the fair. I will deal with the rebels when I return.'

Afrasiyab then tossed a citron into the air and the brass sky of the Garden of Apples split open. A pair of dragons emerged from the crack and descended, balancing a naqara between them. Afrasiyab then rubbed the ring on another citron and threw it towards the drum. A mighty sound resounded throughout the realm and cast a spell on every person that compelled them to travel to the Emerald Well.

The well was the size of an enormous water tank and was located in a vast area called the Garden of Jamshed near the Dome of Light. The well would be filled with offerings for the god by the end of the day. Afrasiyab had his pavilion set up under the Dome of Light and ordered his officers to adorn the Garden of Pleasure and the Garden of Jamshed for the royal guests coming to the fair.

Within hours, Afrasiyab's officers laid out roads paved with multicoloured mosaic stones and built stalls and shops for the wares that would come from all over the kingdom. Chandeliers and lamps were fixed on either side of the roads, and bejewelled trees were adorned with sprays of gold and silver. The frantic preparations went on until it was night.

The sky reddened over the fair and there was a shower of golden flowers. After some time, the sky split open and dragons and peacocks flew in with gold-embroidered velvet pavilions. Sahir workers erected the pavilions on the vast plains between the Dome of Light and the Garden of Jamshed. The pavilions soared up to the skies with pillars of emeralds and rubies and perched on these pillars were bejewelled peacocks that held strings of pearls in their beaks. The flooring was made of fine leather and jewel-inlaid thrones were placed under canopies of cascading pearls. Incense was lit and perfume holders were left open to make the air fragrant. All through these preparations, Hairat was engaged in the worship of Jamshed out in the wilderness, but more of that later.

When these arrangements were complete, a part of the sky radiated light and the fair grounds resounded with the sounds of conch shells and kettledrums. Royal processions from all over the vast realm began to converge on the Garden of Jamshed, dazzling the onlookers with gold showers and other magical phenomena.

One particular procession commanded people's attention more than the others for the fair maiden who sat on the throne was Lalaan Red-robe, the daughter of the Living God Dawood, who was the most exalted grandson of Samri. It was rumoured that Dawood had power over life and death; that if he drew a line with a knife on the portrait of any king, that king would be found dead, even if he were hundreds of miles away. Dawood was also quite elusive and the few people who glimpsed him merely saw a light shining on the throne. Since Lalaan Red-robe was an honoured guest, she was led into Afrasiyab's personal pavilion under the Dome of Light. The princess was indifferent to the splendour of her surroundings and complained, 'Has Afrasiyab become so arrogant now that he cannot come to receive me?'

Just when Lalaan said this, Afrasiyab entered the pavilion bearing gold trays heaped with jewels. He greeted the princess deferentially and apologized for not being able to welcome her earlier. After mollifying the irate princess, he ordered his officers to take special care of her. He then took his leave of her and went across to the wilderness adjoining the Garden of Jamshed, where Hairat had been standing on one leg, reciting magical incantations. She was so absorbed in worship that she was trembling.

Afrasiyab sent for his gold betel leaf container and lovingly prepared a gilori. He placed it in her mouth and as she chewed the leaf, she shook her head. Afrasiyab signalled to his men to draw back. Suddenly, Hairat began emitting red flames from her mouth. Within moments, the flames expanded to cover her entirely. Afrasiyab called out admiringly as she emerged from the sheet of flames, 'Praise be to you Malika; you seem to be blessed by Jamshed himself!' Hairat replied modestly, 'Your lowly handmaiden now takes your leave to worship in the Emerald Well!'

The mela in the Garden of Jamshed

Now hear about what happened in Mahrukh Magic-eye's camp. Amar recited holy verses and the Prayer of Abraham all night so that no one fell under Afrasiyab's spell and felt compelled to go to the fair. The next morning, after saying their prayers, Amar and his ayyar companions left to go to the fair. When they reached there, they saw cloth canopies erected at the edge of the fair where commoners sat watching dance performances. They too joined the crowd and saw musicians playing sitars, *sarangi*s and flutes. There were silver-plated platforms covered with carpets where courtesans in ornate robes were reclining on silk bolsters. They wore thick gold bands around their throats and silver glitter on their foreheads and in their hair, which they had left open. There was a tobacco stall where people were enjoying communal pipes and a marijuana stall where the leaves were ground into sweetened cold milk and consumed with relish. There were wine bars with saffron and ruby-coloured flasks of rare wines from all over the realm. Young bloods were involved in fencing and archery competitions under some canopies. As it happens in such a large gathering, pickpockets and thieves were quite active and many people lost their money pouches that night, despite the vigilance of Afrasiyab's guards and magistrates.

Amar and his companions walked past the food stalls. The shops gleamed like mirrors and the air was fragrant with the smell of tasty dishes. There was an array of pilafs and sweet saffron rice, sheermals, kebabs and *baqar-khwani*s, and parathas and kulchas. There were curries of all kinds and fish kebabs fried on iron griddles were the most popular item. Just ahead of the ayyars were young girls dressed in costly skirts with baskets of vegetables and fruits like pomegranates, guavas and custard apples. Hawkers walked around, loudly drawing attention to delicious snacks: *dahi-bara*s, *gol-gappa*s, spicy fruit salad and *halwa sohan*.

On the other side sat the cloth merchants with bales of precious cloth. Their agents beckoned people to examine the wares. Just ahead were jewel merchants with precious rubies, glowing corals, flawless diamonds and emeralds that they examined with care. Brahmins marched through the bazaar with sacred markings on their foreheads and bodies smeared with sandalwood paste as they rhythmically banged their iron bangles. The ayyars were tempted to buy some of the goods on display and Barq asked Amar if he would give the ayyars expenses for the fair. 'My son,' replied Amar seriously, 'this fair has been arranged for our destruction; it is not right for us to celebrate here.'

So, the ayyars walked ahead and saw tiered stalls covered in white cotton that displayed toys, knives, scissors, hand-mirrors, umbrellas and other fine English goods. Below these stalls sat artisans making silk flowers and laces. Nearby, other artisans sat stringing pearls and engraving gemstones, while still others sold rings and bracelets fashioned to please the customer. The stalls of *gota* and *lachka* sellers gleamed with rolls of gold and silver braids and throngs of people were examining the rolls—some wanted wide braids while others demanded delicate edgings for veils. Betel leaf sellers were sorting various varieties of betel leaves that they spread out in neat rows. Gleaming silver containers held betelnuts, cloves, cardamoms, and mounds of *katha* and *choona*. Perfumers assailed the senses of clients with their fragrant wares while florists displayed blooming spring flowers. The ayyars roamed through the fair until it was night and yet had not seen all of it. They saw that the fair grounds were illuminated with lamps and jewel-inlaid chandeliers suspended from trees for miles. As night fell, a dazzling display of fireworks lit up the earth and the sky. Merchants wearing long garments walked about with young boys and courtesans sat in all their finery, surrounded by groups of admirers; inevitable fights broke out over the favours of particular courtesans or young boys. Male and female acrobats entertained people with their acrobatic and dancing skills. Families were relaxing on rugs that were laid out under shady trees.

The next day, Hairat emerged from the Emerald Well and Afrasiyab went to the Garden of Apples. He was wearing the Tilismi crown that radiated the light of a hundred suns. The royal guests of Tilism soon emerged from their pavilions and formed a procession to accompany Afrasiyab to the magic well. Hairat's entourage also joined this procession. Amar followed the procession at a distance until it rached the Emerald Well, which was now overflowing with gold coins and jewels paid in homage to Jamshed. As the Shahanshah's entourage came closer to the well, there were thunderous calls of 'Ya Samri! Ya Jamshed!' from the crowds that stood around the well. Afrasiyab walked into the royal pavilion to the sound of conch shells and kettledrums. People rushed to offer *nazrana* to him and the royal guests sat in the durbar.

'It is now time to send for the rebels,' declared Afrasiyab. By this time, Amar and the ayyars had already returned to their camp. Amar was describing the wonders of the fair to Mahrukh when the magic peacock flew into the pavilion and said, 'Rebels, you are being summoned by the Shahanshah!' The ayyars ran out of the durbar and Amar became invisible in Galeem. He saw a sudden transformation in Mahrukh and Bahar at the sound of the bird. They both cried, 'This wretched Amar has misled us. If we find him we will cut him into a thousand pieces!'

Bahar arranged for a hundred and one trays of precious gems as nazrana for the King of Sahirs. She donned rich saffron robes and looked as if she had dived into a river of jewels. Similarly, Mahrukh adorned herself and was ready to leave with offerings of gems and gold coins. The other sardars tied their hands with scarves and cried, 'We regret! We regret!' They too mounted their thrones and magic birds to form a procession to leave for the fair. The ayyars met Amar and said, 'Ustad, our lashkar has turned against us and left. Any moment now, we will be summoned by magic and will be forced to go as well!'

Amar replied calmly, 'Just trust in God and come with me!' The ayyars whispered amongst themselves as they walked behind him, 'This is beyond reason. What does he have in mind? How can he plunder the fair as he has declared! Oh well, we shall see!' Amar and the ayyars went to the Emerald Well in disguise. They saw Bahar and the other sardars fall at the Shahanshah's feet, begging for forgiveness. Afrasiyab looked down at his rebellious sardars and quietly ordered, 'Send for the hangmen!'

His courtiers looked shocked and said, 'Huzoor, they are repentant. Why do you want to execute them now?' Afrasiyab smiled and said, 'They are only like this because of the power of the ring. He then held his hand out and addressed the ring, 'Release the rebels from your magic!' There was a sea change in the attitudes of the sardars as they came to their senses. They turned their faces away from the Shah in disgust when he said to them, 'So Mahrukh and Bahar, do you still pledge your loyalty to me?' The sardars answered in one voice, 'Don't be ridiculous, we can sacrifice our lives for Amar. Khwaja will be here soon and make you forget all this splendour and posturing as a holy man!'

Afrasiyab now turned to his durbar and asked them, 'Sahibs, have you heard them? Have I any other choice but to execute them?' All the nobles in the durbar said, 'You were right huzoor, they deserve the most hideous punishment.' Afrasiyab declared that they would be executed as soon as the tricksters were also apprehended. He ordered his men to shackle the rebel sardars in heavy iron chains and keep them in the Garden of Jamshed. He did not cast a spell on them as he wanted them to be in their senses and shed tears on their dire condition. He also had the rest of the rebel soldiers surrounded and disarmed. After these arrangements, the King of Magic sent a whole army of magic peacocks to find the ayyars.

At this time, Amar took out his blessed Tent of Danyal and extended it so that the ayyars would be sheltered under it with him. Due to its powers, no one could find them. The magic peacocks returned to Afrasiyab and admitted that they could not locate the ayyars. Afrasiyab then sent Tilismi ghouls and spectres to find the tricksters but they too were unsuccessful. Finally, Afrasiyab asked the ring where the ayyars were hidden. A voice called out, 'They are right here in the mela, but cannot be seen!' Afrasiyab then sent for his mount to look for the ayyars himself.

Meanwhile Amar had taken out Laqa's beard, which was thirty feet long, from Zambil. (The reader needs to know that Amar had divested Laqa of his beard on an earlier occasion and had kept it in Zambil to use later.) Each hair of that magnificent beard had pearls, rubies, and corals sewn into it. Amar disguised himself as Laqa by wearing a cardboard life-like mask of Laqa's face. Barq wore a robe of a hundred and twenty-one panels and transformed into Shaitan Bakhtiarak, that profane blasphemous kafir, with a stunted neck and low forehead. Qiran transformed himself into the Angel of Death with hideously deformed lips and ears, and flames emanating from his mouth. He held a fiery whip in one hand and stood to the right of the false Laqa. Zargham disguised himself to look like an Angel of Mercy with a glowing body and pure white wings. Every time he moved his wings, there was a whiff of oudh and umber incense in the air. Jansoz became a handsome young attendant and stood with flasks of wine and goblets on a silver tray.

When these preparations were complete, Amar placed his hand on the blessed tent and invoked a blessing on the soul of Hazrat Danyal. The tent miraculously extended itself into a magnificent pavilion with pillars of rubies and emeralds. The pavilion changed colours and was alternately red, green, yellow, black, orange or violet. Amar then blew on the white conch shell that made jinnis dance, and called out loudly, 'O my people, come to me, your Khudawand!' His voice boomed across the fair and everyone rushed to catch a glimpse of divinity. Those who recognized Laqa prostrated immediately in front of his pavilion.

Within moments, the whole fair was buzzing with the news of Khudawand Laqa's arrival. It was the miracle of a lifetime for many. Sari-clad witches, their anklets tinkling, ran bearing trays of jewels and offerings of sweets. Others brought lit oil lamps with flowers of camphor and cloves. Soon there was a heap of treasures in front of Amar. 'Prostrate once again my people,' he called out and scooped up the treasure and the offerings of sweets in the blessed Net of Ilyas. When his devotees raised their heads, they realized that their offerings had vanished. 'My divine hand took your offerings,' announced the false Laqa as they murmured in awe, 'Indeed, your divinity knows no bounds!'

Messengers informed Hairat that Khudawand Laqa was in the fair and she rushed out with the other princesses of the realm. They prostrated before the false Laqa and were astounded by the sight of his angels. The ayyar girls Sarsar Sword-fighter and Saba Raftar Fleet-foot were with the queen and Sarsar whispered, 'I hope this is not trickery.' Amar saw their lips moving and shouted in rage at Hairat, 'Your ayyar girls suspect us of being ayyars! Very well, use your magical weapons on me. We are leaving!' Hairat was furious with Sarsar and hissed, 'Have you seen how Khudawand divined your thoughts. Now leave as he is angry with you!'

Hairat apologized but the false Laqa pretended to remain incensed. 'I will only be happy,' he declared, 'if everyone attacks us.' Reluctantly, the royalty of Tilism aimed magical citrons and coconuts at the pavilion but could not damage it, and when many of them tried to step inside, they found themselves suspended by their feet at the entrance. The false Laqa said, 'Hairat, we will never come to your house for you had us insulted by your ayyar girls!' Hairat and the other princesses beseeched the false Laqa to forgive them and to grace the royal pavilion at the Well of Jamshed with his presence. After much pleading, Amar relented and reduced his pavilion to cover only his throne. When they reached Afrasiyab's pavilion, Khudawand asked for the Shah and was informed that he was out looking for Amar.

The false Laqa smiled and said, 'We will bring him to you! Who else has rebelled against you? I will make them all subservient to you?' Hairat led him to the prisoners where he called out, 'Fall at my feet now, you apostates!' The sardars let forth a torrent of abuse against Laqa and Jamshed. Amar jumped off his throne, walked up to them and condemned them to eternal damnation. However, he managed to secretly reveal his hidden mole to them and signalled, 'I am Amar and have come to rescue you so do my bidding now.'

As they recognized him, the sardars played along; they fell at his feet to beg forgiveness and chanted in unison, 'O Khudawand, you are the righteous one. Only you can persuade Afrasiyab to spare our lives!' Amar told Hairat to release them from their chains and to offer them seats. After the durbar assembled, the false Laqa asked Jansoz to offer his chosen congregation of worshippers with heavenly wine in order to bless them and prolong their lives. Hairat and the rest of the durbar eagerly sipped the wine and in no time fell down, deeply unconscious.

At Amar's signal, sardars like Mahrukh, Bahar, Makhmoor, Hilal and Afat flew up to the sky and attacked the mela with their magical weapons. There was chaos in the wake of this unexpected attack and within minutes, the whole fair was in disarray. Meanwhile, Amar divested the royal guests of their robes and jewels, and ordered his disciples to plunder the royal tents and to bring him the pillars of rubies and emeralds. He then went to the royal durbar and scooped up everything—the pillars, thrones, tables and chairs, even the carpets.

Finally, he reached the holy Emerald Well. The worshippers had fled leaving only the keepers of the well. Invisible in Galeem, Amar threw the Net of Ilyas on the well to take all the offerings and treasures. The keepers desperately tried to retaliate, but who could they attack? There was no one in sight. The second time that Amar cast his net over the well, he emptied the tank down to the wet earth at its base. Only a large pit remained where once there had been the opulent tank. (To remind the reader, the blessed Net of Ilyas was impervious to any form of magic. Even if it fell on Afrasiyab, it could pull him in. The reason Amar did not use the net except for plunder was Emir Hamza's strict injunction against using it to trap an enemy, unless there was no other recourse.)

Sarsar and her companions who had been disgraced and sent out of the garden returned to the durbar and woke Hairat, who wept at the ruined state of the fair. Meanwhile, Amar and his sardars had finished their work and retired to the Black Mountain, and Afrasiyab, who had left the garden to look for the tricksters, found hundreds of people rushing out of the garden, their faces blackened and their clothes in disarray. He hastened to the Garden of Jamshed and found it in shambles, its stalls looted and burnt.

Afrasiyab found Hairat weeping in the royal pavilion and the royal visitors in a state of shock. They said to him, 'This event does not augur well for the future of this Tilism. Give us leave now to return to our kingdoms.' Afrasiyab was embarrassed and humiliated and bid them a quiet farewell. He used his magic to clear the plundered fair and comforted his distraught citizens. He compensated the stall-owners for the loss of their plundered goods and ordered the restoration of the holy tank and the Garden of Jamshed to their former splendour.

The next morning, Amar left to meet Shah Kaukab with Makhmoor. As these two depart, the two armies are still at war. The humble one now ends this volume. It was written in haste and this lowly one does not claim to be a scribe. Therefore, the reader should overlook my mistakes and pray for my welfare.

II

12 AMAR DEPARTS TO MEET KAUKAB THE ENLIGHTENED

The sardars of the Islamic lashkar held a war council and decided that Makhmoor Red-eye and Amar needed to leave for Tilism-e-Nur Afshan immediately to enlist the powerful Emperor Kaukab's help in the war. Soon, Makhmoor and Amar bid their companions farewell and embarked on their perilous journey through Tilism-e-Hoshruba. Hairat came to know of their departure and was about to send a message to her husband when a magic bird sent by the King of Magic flew into her durbar and alighted on her knee. Hairat opened the scroll tied to the bird and read the message: 'Malika, do not go into battle until I am there with you.'

Hairat sent the bird back to Afrasiyab with the message that Amar and Makhmoor had left for Kaukab's Tilism. As soon as Afrasiyab read this message, he knocked in the air and a dark cloud formed on the horizon. The cloud descended on the durbar and parted to reveal a sahir who stepped out of it and greeted the king. Afrasiyab said to the sahir, 'Sabai Jadoo, Amar and Makhmoor are on their way to Kaukab, but are still within my realm. Arrest them immediately and bring them to me.' Sabai Jadoo bowed low and returned to his cloud that swiftly floated away.

Now hear about the travellers of magical realms, Amar and Makhmoor, the Praiseworthy! They were passing through a verdant meadow fragrant with spring blossoms when Sabai Jadoo materialized before them and called out, 'Makhmoor, come with me and I will ask Shahanshah to forgive your sins!' Makhmoor called back, 'Who is he to forgive me? As for you, do you think I will leave you alive, shameless one?' Sabai was furious when he heard this and hurled a magic citron at her. The lion-hearted Makhmoor quickly dodged it. Then Sabai drew his sword on her and she responded by drawing hers. Their swords flashed like lightning when they fought. Sabai soon realized that he was outclassed and took out a pinch of the dust of Jamshed from his magic pouch and blew it at Makhmoor, who immediately fell unconscious.

Amar ran and pretended to throw himself at Sabai's mercy. He pleaded, 'This woman is indeed dim-witted! Despite your many warnings, she did not listen and actually deserved this punishment. However, I am hopeful that you will get Shahanshah to forgive my crimes. I am now convinced that no one can oppose him and survive. He must be very powerful if he has illustrious sahirs like you with him.'

Sabai Jadoo was so flattered by Amar's words that he did not arrest him. Sabai Jadoo set off with Amar and the unconscious Makhmoor for Afrasiyab's durbar, but, on the way, Amar burst a narcotic bubble on the unsuspecting sahir's face. Sabai reeled and fell into a ditch filled with rainwater with the unconscious Makhmoor on his back. Both Makhmoor and the sahir revived when they hit the cold water; however, before Sabai could stand up, Makhmoor leaped out of the ditch. Sabai had just turned towards Amar to vent his fury when Makhmoor growled, 'Where do you think you are going?' She waved her fingers and before Sabai could react, magic lightning flashed down from the sky and slashed the sahir into two. It became completely dark and the sahir's magical spirits raised a din. After some time, the dead sahir's skull burst open and a bright green bird flew out in the direction of the Garden of Apples where it swooped down and wailed, 'Shahanshah! Amar and Makhmoor have killed the keeper of the magic house in the land of Princess Nur.' A flame spewed out of the magic bird's beak and incinerated it.

Afrasiyab had just relaxed on a masnad after a long meeting with the *nazim*s of the Tilism when the bird made this announcement. The king immediately chanted an incantation and knocked in the air. As if in response, a fierce gale blew in and moments later, a sahir riding a mighty dragon materialized before Afrasiyab and bowed humbly. Afrasiyab regarded him benignly and said, 'Balai Jadoo, Amar and Makhmoor have killed your brother Sabai. Arrest them and bring them to me. If you cannot capture them, at least bring their heads for me. Leave at once!'

After Balai took his leave of Afrasiyab, the king sent a letter to Hairat that read: 'My dear, do not lose heart. I will soon be deputing a powerful sahir to help you. Please let Murshidzadeh know that I have bestowed the magnificent velvet pavilion next to the Dome of Light upon him. He should dispose of these betrayers of our salt, and you, O Malika, should extend all courtesy and honour to Murshidzadeh.'

Mussavir's magic warrior

When Hairat read this letter, she happily handed it to Mussavir the magic artist who was very pleased and declared, 'I will only accept the pavilion after I am victorious!' He went into his tent and declared,

'Congratulations! I am the chosen one who will triumph in this war! See how Shah honours me!' Soorat Nigar, however, looked gloomy and said, 'The tricksters have humiliated us already. It seems impossible to win with them around. You should not interfere in Afrasiyab's war because we could lose our lives this time!'

Mussavir, however, remained resolute on fighting the ayyars. That evening, he went to an isolated hollow in the hills. There, he purified the earth before lighting a sacred fire, into which he tossed fiery red chillies and resin from the holy *googal* tree. Once the fire died down, he waited for the ashes to cool and scattered them in one direction. In a while, a sudden dust storm arose and a magic rider came towards Mussavir from the plains. Mussavir quickly laid out bottles of wine and the liver and tongue of a pig and offered it to the rider who eagerly consumed everything. Once he finished eating, he looked at Mussavir who commanded him, 'Go now and appear in the battle tomorrow to destroy my enemies!' Mussavir then went back to his camp.

Ravi, the narrator, tells us that Mussavir the magic artist knew how to use magical sketches as weapons and that, in this case, he had drawn this warrior on paper. He brought the drawing to life by suffusing it with a magical spirit. In order to secure his magic, he released several hawks in the desert as decoys. We will learn more about this mystery later in this story.

When Mussavir returned to his camp, he asked Hairat to announce that a battle would be fought the next morning in his name. Both the armies converged on the killing plains the next day and the rows of soldiers looked like the raging waves of mighty rivers. Heralds exhorted the soldiers to be courageous. Mussavir went forward and read a spell while looking towards the mountains. There was a sudden duststorm and the magic rider rode into the battlefield. Mussavir called out to the rebel forces, 'O betrayers of Afrasiyab's salt! Confront this warrior and go on the path of your doom!'

On the other side, the Queen of Spring Bahar Jadoo asked Mahrukh Magic-eye for permission to send her forces into battle. The magic warrior, however, was immune to attacks and spells, and by the afternoon, had killed ten of Bahar's officers. Bahar decided that she had to face him herself; but Mahrukh stopped her just in time. 'This appears to be a warrior puppet of Mussavir's magic. He cannot be killed!' said Mahrukh. Bahar replied, 'Well, let us then enchant this cuckold Mussavir into senselessness! He can be made to destroy the warrior!' She was about to raise her wand when Mussavir had the drums of peace struck. He called out, 'Rebels, you will all die tomorrow, so make your peace with Shahanshah if you want your lives spared!'

Mahrukh's soldiers responded with a volley of abuses and both armies returned to their camps. Later, the ayyars met Mahrukh Magic-eye and asked her, 'Do you know anything about this rider and where he comes from?' Mahrukh replied, 'I drew an astrological chart and concluded that he is a puppet moulded by Mussavir the magic artist. It is impossible to kill him unless Mussavir himself is killed.' Barq Firangi declared, 'I will find a way of destroying him.'

Meanwhile, Mussavir had not let the magic warrior vanish into the desert and said to it, 'It takes too long to summon you. We have to fight tomorrow morning, so why should you go anywhere?' He assigned the warrior a tent near his own. As the magic warrior was suffused with a fiendish spirit who had a voracious appetite, Mussavir also assigned attendants to bring food and wine for him. While these arrangements were being made, Barq managed to enter the enemy camp undetected and lured one of the warrior's attendants to a secluded area where he rendered him unconscious. He then entered the tent disguised as the attendant. The magic warrior was stretched out on the bed, munching pomegranate seeds. Barq stood at the head of the bed and began fanning him. With his free hand, he dusted some narcotic powder on the warrior who sneezed and slumped unconscious. Barq released more powder and everyone else in the tent collapsed as well. Barq drew his sword out to kill the magic warrior but was startled to find that his head had turned into solid stone. Barq thought to himself, 'Who should I kill now?' Eventually, he woke up the other attendants and said, 'Sahibs, all of you went to sleep and the warrior has turned into stone. Who are we meant to serve here?' The attendants were mystified by this and informed Mussavir Jadoo who came and read magical incantations over the warrior until he reverted to his original form. The warrior looked confused and asked, 'Did I go off to sleep?'

'It seems that some trickster tried to kill you!' said Mussavir. 'In that case,' the warrior said, 'I will vanish now and appear at the battle tomorrow.' Mussavir was satisfied with this arrangement and returned to his pavilion. Barq devised another strategy to defeat the warrior. He slipped out of the warrior's tent and went towards Hairat's pavilion disguised as a sahir. He signalled to one of her servants and said, 'Mussavir wants you.' The servant looked astonished and asked eagerly, 'Do you mean he actually knows me by name?' 'Of course he does,' declared Barq, 'and you will probably get an award from him.' The unsuspecting servant happily trotted along with Barq and was soon overcome by the trickster. Disguised now as the manservant, Barq handed Mussavir a forged note from Hairat that read, 'My Lord, I was just informed that your magic rider was harmed by a trickster. I am concerned for his life. Tell me how you have safeguarded him or I shall not be able to rest tonight!'

The gullible Mussavir wrote a note for Hairat that read, 'Malika, rest easy. In the mountains close to the camp, there is a clearing where a number of hawks are flying. They have all been conjured by me. One of these hawks is the strongest and the largest. Only if anyone kills this particular hawk and then sprays the magic warrior with the hawk's blood, can he die.'

Barq promptly returned to Mahrukh Magic-eye with this letter. Mahrukh was overjoyed when she read it and immediately left for the mountains. She found the clearing among the hills where a number of hawks were gliding in circles in the sky. She focused on the largest one and chanted mantras until it dropped down on the ground. Mahrukh cut its throat with a magic knife and drained its blood into a glass phial. Then she flew back to her tent and disclosed her secret to no one.

Meanwhile, the two attendants whom Barq had duped found themselves lying naked in different corners of Hairat's camp. By this time, they were quite used to the ways of the ayyars and were relieved that Samri had spared their lives. They returned quietly to their duties and did not tell anyone about their experience.

When the glorious sun reappeared with a resplendent golden turban in the durbar of the sky and the world became alight, young and old awoke from their slumber.

Mussavir first went to check on his magic warrior and was happy to see him alive. He then summoned his commanders to discuss battle strategies. After he warmed himself with a few rounds of wine, he ordered that the battle drums be struck. Mahrukh Magic-eye too responded with magic trumpets and drums as her army organized for battle. Hairat and Mussavir entered the battlefield with drums booming all around. The sky was overcast with dark magical clouds that began spewing sheets of flames and stones making the battlefield as hot as a fiery oven.

Mussavir chanted an incantation and moments later, the rider came in thundering from the desert. Mahrukh Magic-eye took off her crown and laid it on the throne after kissing it. The flags of her lashkar were unfurled in all their glory. Many sardars presented themselves before Mahrukh to the rhythm of battle drums and requested permission to begin the battle. She ordered them to stay in their places and mounted a peacock. She then went forward to confront the magic rider and invited him to attack first. Mahrukh flew her peacock closer to the warrior who drew his sword on her. Just as the warrior was about to attack Mahrukh, she threw the hawk blood at him. As soon as the drops of blood fell on him, the magic rider's body caught fire and he was reduced to a pile of ashes. The Islamic army broke out into shouts of praise for Mahrukh Magic-eye. A furious Mussavir wanted to attack Mahrukh immediately, but his wife begged him to desist and instead ordered her officers to attack. The battle between the two forces raged till the evening, by which time a despondent Hairat struck the drums of peace and returned to her pavilion. Mahrukh returned in triumph to her durbar with her sardars, where they unwinded with wine and nautch performances.

The kingdom of Nurania

Let us now see how Amar and Makhmoor fared on their perilous journey through the deserts and valleys of Tilism. After killing Sabai Jadoo, they came across a house that seemed to be empty. Amar was divesting it of its furnishings and valuables when he reached an inner chamber and saw a box suspended in the middle of the room. 'I am sure,' he told Makhmoor, 'that this must be full of treasures.'

'I am equally sure,' retorted Makhmoor, 'it is there to trap us!' Amar said in a dismissive tone, 'That is a nonsensical suggestion. You keep frightening me unnecessarily. Do you want me to be a pauper?' Amar found a stool and climbed up on it to reach the box. When he tried to open it, there was an ear-splitting scream. As Amar and Makhmoor blocked their ears with their hands, the box expelled two chains of fire that magically wrapped around them. Makhmoor looked at Amar meaningfully and said, 'I hope you are satisfied with the treasure you have found, and I hope your poverty has been alleviated.'

Amar thought to himself, 'If I show any weakness now, she will surely laugh at me even more. This is the time to talk like a man.' He said, 'Just trust in Allah! You know that we always come across thorns in a beautiful bed of flowers; where there is happiness, there is also extreme sadness; that is the way of the world. But tell me, why have these chains not burnt us?' Makhmoor explained how Amar was protected by the magic ring and bracelet presented to him by her aunt Nastran and she, by her magical powers.

While they were engaged in this discussion, a crystal slave-girl shot out of the box and flew away towards the fort of Nurania. Afrasiyab had appointed Nur Jadoo as the ruler of the kingdom of Nurania. When Amar and Makhmoor were trapped, Nur Jadoo was resting in a garden with seventeen hundred handmaidens in attendance. She was adorned with precious jewellery and her beauty dazzled the moon. Sabai Jadoo who had been killed by Amar had been the chief of guards of Nur's palace. The crystal slave-girl from the box landed before Nur and after greeting her courteously, said, 'Since the day Tilism-e-Hoshruba was founded, your slave-girl has never been touched by air. Today, the box was opened and I have come to you.'

Nur was stunned by this and thought, 'Who could have been courageous enough to release the magic slave-girl? I should go and see for myself.' She quickly reached the house where Makhmoor and Amar were trapped by the chains of fire. Nur had not yet learnt of Makhmoor's rebellion against Afrasiyab and exclaimed, 'My sister Makhmoor! What are you doing here? Have you applied henna to your feet that you have not visited me for so long? For months, I do not see you and now you cause all this trouble! I did not expect this of you!' Makhmoor realized that Nur was unaware of her defection and salvaged the situation by responding airily, 'You are not worth visiting! You see me tied up with this chain, and yet you stand around talking? It is true that even a dog has the courage of a lion in its own domain! When you come to my house, I will treat you in a similar manner!'

Thus chastised, Nur stepped forward and recited an incantation. The chains of fire released Amar and Makhmoor and flashed back into the box. The crystal slave-girl also disappeared into the box and its lid snapped shut on its own. Nur held Makhmoor's hand and said, 'Now spit out your anger and tell me what brings you here. Who is this lout for whom you court danger? Why are you alone with him? There seems to something going on here!'

Makhmoor smiled and whispered, 'Why don't you come to the point? He is yours if you like him so much!' Nur was not amused by Makhmoor's comment and said, 'By Samri, tell me the truth!' Makhmoor took her aside and whispered, 'My sister, this is the infamous ayyar Amar who has caused Shahanshah much grief. I have promised Shah that I will arrest him and pretend to be on his side for a while. I am now roaming the wilderness with him so that I can overwhelm him in a moment of weakness.' Nur whispered with some excitement, 'In that case, bring him to my home and I will arrest him for you.' 'Impossible!' Makhmoor cried, 'He will never agree to go to your place.' Nur ignored this and spoke aloud for Amar's ears, 'My sister, heaven knows when I will see you again. Do come to my house for a while!' Makhmoor responded formally, 'If Khwaja sahib agrees to go, I have no objection.' Nur turned to Amar and begged him to honour her house with his presence.

Amar thought, 'She is adorned with costly robes and jewels; moreover, she is the ruler and her house must be full of treasures. I will surely profit by going with her.' To Makhmoor's dismay, Amar willingly accepted Nur's invitation. Makhmoor tried to make more excuses, but she was helpless in the face of Amar's greed and had no choice but to go along with him. Nur transported her guests on her flying throne over forests and lakes till they reached the walled city of Nurania. Amar saw that the city had fine houses, shops brimming with goods and citizens who looked prosperous and content.

The royal palace was lavish and richly furnished. Nur led them to her garden that was heaven on earth—lush green and full of blossoms and trees studded with precious stones. The baradari in the middle of the garden had gem-inlaid pillars. Its floor was covered with soft silk carpets and it was provisioned with many comforts and luxuries. Nur led Makhmoor to the gold-embroidered masnad with great affection and courtesy.

Amar noticed that the carpets were held down with thick gold carpet weights and pretended to stumble and fall down on one. He wailed loudly that he had hurt himself and slipped the gold weight into Zambil. When Nur's attendants helped him get up, they noticed that the weight was missing and exclaimed, 'What happened to the carpet weight lying here?' Amar retorted, 'Do you invite me to your home to accuse me of theft? You can search me if you like!' He walked away grumbling and within moments, another carpet weight vanished. When the attendants raised a clamour Amar looked at Makhmoor and angrily said, 'Let us leave, these people consider us to be thieves!'

Nur placated Amar and said, 'Be seated, these maidservants are misbehaved and talk nonsense!' She admonished her attendants, 'Go away and stop making such a fuss. The weights will be here somewhere!' The attendants looked furious but remained quiet. Nur then offered a goblet of wine to Amar. He took it and said, 'Princess Nur, look at how that maidservant glares at me!' When Nur turned to look, Amar quickly added a powder to the goblet and said, 'Princess, I will drink this only if you sip it first. This place is full of my enemies and I am beset with doubts!' Nur smiled and sipped the wine without fear. Amar got up from the masnad and said, 'I will serve the wine myself.' He ordered the attendants, 'Bring me fresh flowers, I will infuse the wine with their fragrance.'

While Makhmoor engaged Nur in conversation, Amar mixed sleeping powder into the wine flasks. When the attendants returned, he graciously poured a goblet of wine for each one. Very soon, everyone except Makhmoor and he were unconscious. He tossed Nur into Zambil, disguised himself as her and revived the attendants. As they opened their eyes, he shouted, 'You strumpets, Amar doctored the wine in your presence and has run away. Jamshed has been generous or he would have killed us all!'

Makhmoor complained, 'Sister, all my hard work has been wasted! How will I face Shahanshah and where will I find that rogue now?' The false Nur replied, 'What is done is done! I am afraid that he may now plunder the fort! Sister, you wait here, I need to make some arrangements.' Amar went with an attendant to Nur's durbar and summoned her ministers and counsellors. After consulting them, the false Nur ordered, 'Make announcements in the city that Amar ayyar, whom I had captured, has escaped. All citizens should be alert. Merchants and jewellers can deposit their goods in the state treasury. When this crisis is over, their goods will be returned to them minus the interest. The state will make up any loss if it occurs in the treasury but we will not be responsible if goods are plundered on their premises.'

Panic spread through the city when this announcement was made. Wealthy merchants rushed with their goods to the treasury while ordinary citizens brought their valuables for safe keeping. The goods were placed according to their value in several houses specially cleared for this purpose. This continued for two days. Every evening, Amar would rest in the garden and convene a durbar in the morning. The third morning, the false Nur sent for the *darogha* of the treasury and said to him, 'I am feeling uneasy this morning. Give me the keys to the treasuries and show me the inventory.'

The darogha led her to the treasury and handed her the keys. The false Nur dismissed the darogha as well as the guards before taking out his blessed Net of Ilyas to sweep up all the goods. He returned to Makhmoor who stood waiting in the garden and declared, 'Prepare to leave now and think of spells that will cause pandemonium in this city. I will plunder it and meet you beyond the walls of the city.' Amar then summoned Nur's attendants and said, 'Stay and guard me in case Amar comes here.' Once they had surrounded him, Amar released artfully crafted moths of oblivion that settled on the lanterns and candles. The fumes rendered all the maidservants unconscious. Amar proceeded to pillage every valuable item in the garden. He even stripped the maidservants of their clothes and jewellery and dropped everything in Zambil.

Then he brought Nur out from Zambil. He pierced her tongue with a needle and tied her to a pillar in the garden before reviving her. As she looked at him in horror, he coldly declared, 'You must join me. I have plundered your treasury and will execute you!' Nur shed tears of despair and signalled her refusal to betray Afrasiyab. Amar beheaded her at once. There were terrible sounds when she died followed by a burst of fire and brimstone. Amar promptly beheaded her attendants as well. The radiant city of Nurania was plunged into darkness and filled with fearful noises. Many of Nur's servants and guards rushed towards the garden, only to become the victims of Makhmoor's magic arrows.

There was a stampede in the city as the ill-fated citizens began fleeing to save themselves from the unknown assailants. Makhmoor continued to attack with her magic arrows, while Amar took advantage of the prevailing darkness and left the garden. He tossed flame-bombs into houses as he ran through the city. The citizens of Nurania were already terrified of Amar's reputation; when they saw their city burning and arrows flying towards them, they thought that Amar had brought an army. The brave amongst them valiantly stood to fight but who could they confront? Makhmoor was attacking them invisibly from the sky and Amar was not to be seen anywhere. The royal guards and citizens were in such a state of panic that they attacked each other. The streets of Nurania flowed with blood and the city was alight with burning houses.

By the next morning, Amar had finished destroying and plundering the city, and escaped with the fleeing citizens. Makhmoor who was waiting for him on a hilltop was stunned by Amar's audacious and ruthless behaviour. She saw him trotting off at a distance and flew across to join him. They continued on their journey in a lighthearted mood. A little later, a hideous-looking sahir mounted on a dragon challenged them to a fight. Makhmoor pushed Amar behind her and responded to his challenge with phenomenal magical attacks. Balai Jadoo realized he could not defeat her and made her unconscious with a pinch of the magic dust of Jamshed.

Amar went forward and shouted, 'Oye haramzadeh, dispel my magic if you can!' Amar took out a citron and showed it to the sahir. Balai Jadoo assumed that Amar knew magic and started chanting another spell. In that time, Amar aimed the citron at the sahir's nose. The citron burst in the sahir's face and released narcotic bubbles. Amar was about to behead the unconscious sahir when something flashed in the sky. Sensing trouble, Amar picked up Makhmoor and ran for his life. A ray of light swooped down towards Balai Jadoo in the shape of a hand and whisked him off to the King of Magic.

After some time Makhmoor revived in Amar's arms. When he explained to her what had happened, she said, 'That was not lightning but Afrasiyab's guardian hand. Let us leave this place before we get into more trouble!' Amar said lightly, 'If the hand was there to guard the sahir, what is it to us? We will walk at our own pace and enjoy the sights!'

Nur Jadoo's attendants carried her corpse to the Garden of Apples. Afrasiyab, who was resplendent on his throne heard them wailing at the entrance and summoned them. They laid her corpse in front of him and wept as they related how she had been deceived and murdered. Afrasiyab was about to send an army to capture Amar when the magic hand dropped the unconscious Balai Jadoo before him. The King of Tilism was now very angry and revived the sahir by sprinkling magic water on him. He asked him coldly, 'Is this how you went to capture Amar?' Balai Jadoo paled with shame and declared, 'I will go back and capture him!' The King of Magic was sceptical and said, 'What will you gain by going? You will certainly die this time!' Balai said, 'Whatever happens, I will go!'

The magic sindoor

Amar and Makhmoor continued on their way and came across a mountain that looked exactly like a crouched lion from every angle. Amar asked Makhmoor, 'What is this dreadful place that seems even more frightening than Black Mountain?' Makhmoor explained, 'This is the legendary Mount Asad, abode of many fearsome lions.' Without warning, she threw a grain of lentil on Amar that rendered him unconscious. Then she dragged him to the nearest cave, conjured two magic slave-boys and ordered them to guard Amar against capture.

Makhmoor Red-eye climbed fearlessly up the mountain. She reached the walls of a fort where a lion sprang out of the earth and growled, 'Who are you to come here without fear?' Makhmoor said, 'Go and inform your master that Princess Makhmoor Red-eye is here to meet him.' The lion went and conveyed this message to Bubbar Jadoo, the custodian of the mountain. A surprised Bubbar exclaimed, 'Why did you stop the princess? Go in haste and lead her here with great respect!' The lion went back to Makhmoor, tucked his paws inwards with respect when he kneeled before her, and said, 'Come with me, he is calling you.'

Makhmoor was led to a house where she saw a sahir with the head of a lion sitting on a low stool. The lion who stood beside him was the keeper of the desert of flames. Bubbar rose and greeted her respectfully, and said, 'Princess, you have honoured us with your visit. Sit down and bless us with your company!' Makhmoor said, 'I have no time to lose. Has Amar been here? Shahanshah ordered me to pursue him but he eludes capture every time.' Bubbar replied confidently, 'No one has come here. If he had, he would have been captured immediately!' Makhmoor continued, 'He disappeared before my very eyes on this mountain. I am afraid to look for him in case one of your lions harms me.'

Bubbar declared that he was at her service and gallantly offered to accompany her in her search for Amar. He held her hand as they searched the mountainside for Amar. Meanwhile, Balai Jadoo managed to trace the fugitives to Mount Asad. He reached the cave where Makhmoor had hidden Amar and saw two magic slave-boys guarding the entrance. Without any delay, Balai breathed out fire and incinerated them. When he discovered Amar lying unconscious in the cave, he heaved a sigh of relief. He took Amar out of the cave and first thought of beheading him, but it occured to him that Afrasiyab would want him alive. Just at that moment, Makhmoor and Bubbar appeared on the scene.

Makhmoor whispered to Bubbar, 'Alas, Amar has been captured in your area, but not by you. This sahir will take all the credit for his capture in front of the Shah. I wish I had continued looking for him instead of seeking your help. Now I will also be humiliated before Shah!' Bubbar was naturally provoked by her words and roared at Balai, 'Wait, you mule-head! Where do you think you are going and how dare you come into my area without taking my leave?'

Balai turned around and saw Makhmoor with Bubbar. He cried out, 'Bubbar, do not be deceived by this woman! She has revolted against our master and has joined Amar.' Makhmoor again whispered, 'Bubbar, this is his devious strategy. He wants us to quarrel so that he can slip away. Tell him that he should hand Amar over to you and that you will take us both to Shahanshah. If he does as you ask, then he is surely speaking the truth and you can capture me immediately. However, if he does not hand him over, you must not let him get away!'

As instructed by Makhmoor, Bibran demanded that Amar be handed over to him. The arrogant Balai replied, 'Have you lost your mind? Why should I hand my prisoner over to you after having combed the desert for him? Do I seem dim-witted to you?' Makhmoor said to Bubbar, 'Did I not warn you about him?' The lion-man was already incensed by Balai's rejoinder and smashed a magic citron on the ground. Suddenly, the lion that was in Bubbar's house shot out of the earth and sprang at Balai. The sahir quickly hurled a magic egg at the lion that froze him in his tracks. Bubbar now sank into the earth and emerged just moments later, holding a small red casket. He handed the casket to Makhmoor as if to demonstrate that he was so powerful that he could get ask an outsider to kill his enemy. 'This is the magic sindoor of Tilism,' he said to Makhmoor, 'apply it to the lion's forehead and command him to kill Balai Jadoo!'

Makhmoor immediately opened the precious box and applied a *tika* of the gleaming red powder on the lion's forehead. She commanded, 'What are you looking at? Kill him now!' The lion leapt on Balai with an almighty roar and ripped his stomach open. This was followed by total darkness and magic spirits screeched and howled before carrying away Balai's body to the Shahanshah. After Balai's corpse was taken away, Makhmoor chanted a spell to revive Amar. Just as he was about to speak to her, Bubbar threw a grain on him that made him fall, writhing in pain, on the floor. Makhmoor said to Bubbar, 'Why did you do that? I have come a long way to find him! I will take him back to Shahanshah.' Bubbar growled menacingly, 'Treacherous woman, Balai was speaking the truth. You have indeed revolted against Shahanshah! This time you will not escape. I will kill you both!'

Now Makhmoor had manoeuvred this whole business in order to get hold of the magic sindoor that would help them find a way through the desert of flames. She calmly dabbed another tika on the lion's forehead and said, 'Get this man as well.' As the lion sprang at Bubbar, he desperately chanted mantras to ward off the beast, but nothing could stop him. The lion was compelled to obey anyone who applied the magic sindoor on him. He slapped Bubbar with his paw so that he died instantly. May Allah protect us! Bubbar's spirits raised such an almighty din that the mountain and desert shook with huge tremors. His house on the summit of Mount Asad burst into flames and whirls of dust transported his corpse to the Shahanshah.

The desert of flames

Now hear this: beyond Mount Asad lay the desert of flames and the lion who killed Bubbar Jadoo was its keeper. The creators of Tilism-e-Hoshruba had designed the desert to provide safe passage through the flames only to the owner of the magic sindoor of Tilism. The area beyond the desert of flames fell under the jurisdiction of Gesoo Long-locks. Gesoo's magic alerted her to the lion's arrival in her realm and she sent a guide to meet him. We will learn more about this later in the story.

Makhmoor was aware of the secret passage. She dabbed the lion's forehead for the third time with sindoor and ordered him to lead them through the desert of flames. The lion nodded and said, 'You will have to climb up on my back for the journey.' Once Makhmoor and Amar mounted him, the lion went around Mount Asad and entered a narrow gorge. For two days and nights, the lion bounded through the dark passage, filled with the sounds of snakes and pythons hissing at them as they passed through. On the third day, at sunrise, the travellers emerged from the defile into the terrible desert of flames. From the earth to the sky, they could see nothing but fire. The desert was a blazing pit of flames with caves that were as blistering hot as a blacksmith's forge. As the flames crackled and sparked it seemed as if trees of fire were rising from the ground. Nimrod's fire pit for Abraham would not have been as hot as this desert! The lion carried Amar and Makhmoor to one side of the desert. There, a beautiful woman with flaming cheeks and eyes glittering like lamps stood waiting for them near a large tank of red hot flames. Without a word, she handed Makhmoor a piece of paper that read, 'Lead the lion into the tank and do not be afraid.'

The lion, compelled to obey Makhmoor's commands, promptly dived into the burning tank. Amar closed his eyes and thought, 'Without doubt, the robe of our destiny will burn in these flames!' He began reciting passages from the Holy Book hoping that the tank of flames would became the Garden of Khaleel. After some time in the tank, they came up to a bank on a vast plain. In front of them was a wall that reached up to the sky and seemed to extend as far as the eye could see.

Here, the lion suddenly shook them off his back and smashed his head hard into the wall. As his skull split open, he wailed, 'Alas! How cursed I am that I led the enemy to this place!' As the beast died in great agony, the burning desert and tank, which were actually illusions, suddenly vanished. Makhmoor and Amar saw that they were in a wilderness and Mount Asad loomed in the distance.

Princess Gesoo Long-locks and the Dome of Samri

A doorway gradually opened in the wall where the lion had smashed his head. A beautiful, flower-like girl walked through the doorway and looked at the travellers with unbridled hostility. This was Qaash Jadoo, sent there by Princess Gesoo, who had also sent the woman with flaming cheeks and glittering eyes to receive them at the tank. After the first woman had left, Gesoo thought of confirming the identity of the visitors, in case the King of Magic had sent someone important. She consulted the magic paper of Samri and was outraged on learning of the havoc caused by Makhmoor. As a result, she sent Qaash Jadoo to capture Makhmoor and Amar.

Qaash called out to the two, 'Wait, you betrayers of salt! How dare you come to this forbidden area?' Amar reacted swiftly and cast the Net of Ilyas on Qaash and scooped her into Zambil. Amar then painted his face to look like Qaash and wore her robes and jewellery. He called out to Makhmoor, 'Use your magic to look like me.' After perfecting their disguises, the two travellers went through the doorway in the wall. They walked for a while and reached a huge fort with high ramparts. The moat around it was brimming with water and a wooden bridge led to a massive elephant gateway where forty sahirs stood on guard. They saw the false Qaash and called out to her, 'So did you manage to get Amar?' Qaash retorted, 'Are you blind? Can you not see that I have enchanted him so that he follows me of his own accord?' The guards laughed at this and let them through.

Amar and Makhmoor had just entered the fort through the gate when two sahirs materialized before them and said, 'Qaash, the princess summons you!' Amar retorted sharply, 'I am going to her! Do you want me to walk on your heads?' Qaash then followed the sahirs to a palace where the beautiful Gesoo reclined on a masnad. Amar went forward and greeted the princess, who asked her, 'So Qaash, what happened?' Amar replied, 'Huzoor, I have brought Amar to you!' The princess looked at Makhmoor posing as Amar and frowned, 'Where is that betrayer of salt, Makhmoor Red-eye?' Amar mumbled, 'I could not find her.' Gesoo immediately became suspicious and looked at the magic mirror lying beside her. She was shocked to see Amar in Qaash's clothes and Makhmoor as her real self reflected in the mirror. She rose in fury and cried, 'Wait you wily rascal, I recognize you!'

Gesoo hurled a magic citron at Amar that was deflected by Makhmoor, who burnt her hand in the process. Makhmoor quickly tied a magic scarf around Amar's neck that made him immune to Gesoo's magic. Gesoo shot an iron ball and a magic arrow at Amar, but both collapsed in mid-air. She realized that her magic was ineffective against Amar and shouted to her attendants, 'Get them!' Rows upon rows of handmaidens materialized and surrounded Amar and Makhmoor.

Amar realized that Gesoo and her forces were strong enough to overwhelm Makhmoor and decided to act quickly. He flung smoking hookahs that made the area around Gesoo and her handmaidens full of smoke. In the ensuing darkness, Amar trapped Gesoo in the Net of Ilyas and vanished out of sight. He went to a secluded part of the palace and stripped Gesoo of her jewels and outer robes before tossing her into Zambil. He then placed his hand on blessed Zambil, prayed for the miracle of transforming into Gesoo and wore her robes and jewels.

Amar returned to durbar in the form of Gesoo and saw that her attendants were bombarding Makhmoor with fiery spiders and a volley of magic citrons that burst into flames. It was clear that Makhmoor would be overcome very soon. The false Gesoo called out to the handmaidens, 'Leave her alone. I will handle this myself!' The handmaidens drew back as Amar approached a wary Makhmoor and pointed to the mole under his eyelid to reveal his identity. Makhmoor played along and wept, 'Forgive me princess, I had been led astray by Amar!'

The false Gesoo embraced her warmly and said, 'Amar is just a fair-weather friend. Look how he abandoned you while you were surrounded by enemies!' Makhmoor and the false Gesoo sat on a masnad and sent for flasks of wine to refresh themselves. Later, the false Gesoo had the treasury opened on the pretext of showing her treasures to Makhmoor. Amar cleaned out the treasury and returned to Gesoo's durbar. He sent out heralds to announce, as he had done in Nurania, that since Amar ayyar was in the city all goods and treasures were to be deposited in the royal treasury for safekeeping. No one could prevent the false Gesoo from making an inventory of the treasury and secretly plundering the valuables.

The next day, Amar instructed Gesoo's ministers to remain alert and left with Makhmoor on a flying throne. The nobles and citizens bid them a fond farewell as they were under the impression that their ruler had gone to capture the notorious ayyar Amar. The two travellers journeyed in stages until they reached the base of a towering mountain. They got off the throne and walked up the gentle slopes enjoying the lush greenery and mountain streams until they reached the summit. There they saw a vast dome made entirely of gold and rubies and it seemed as if the sun itself had descended on earth. The air resounded with the sound of bells and conch shells.

Amar looked at Makhmoor who explained to him that this was the sacred Dome of Samri and that its keeper was the cruel sahir, Hawai Jadoo. Amar said, 'Let us go in then and see what we can find there.' Makhmoor knew it was impossible to thwart Amar's greed and sighed, 'As you wish!'

Amar, who was still disguised as Princess Gesoo, walked towards the dome and the priests greeted her deferentially. Amar ordered them to unlock the door to the Dome, but as soon as he stepped inside, there was a fierce gale and a rush of hot air knocked him out cold. He was pushed out of the dome by unseen hands and a voice boomed, 'This is the first time that a Muslim has stepped in here. This dome has been desecrated!'

Sahir-guards rushed to arrest Amar, but Makhmoor swiftly whisked him up and flew to safety. Afrasiyab was immediately informed of Amar and Makhmoor's adventures in Gesoo's kingdom and of the desecration of the Dome of Samri. 'Let them go,' he said, 'I am not afraid of them reaching Kaukab. In fact, I will write to him now and who knows, he might just arrest them for me!'

13 Amar Reaches Kaukab's Tilism and Princess Burran Falls in Love with Prince Iraj

The River of Seven Hues

Amar and Makhmoor Red-eye continued on their journey after escaping from the Dome of Samri. They reached a verdant glade where Makhmoor's mother, a powerful sorceress by the name of Asrar Jadoo materialized before them. Asrar was a gifted astrologer and had calculated the time when her daughter would reach this place. As soon as she appeared, a startled Makhmoor immediately fell at her feet in respectful greeting. 'My daughter,' said Asrar weeping softly, 'You should not have rebelled against Shah. He was a good master to you and had honoured you with a kingdom and high rank. Look at your state now!' Makhmoor also wept and said, 'Mother, he whipped me until my body was torn to shreds. My wounds still hurt! Had your sister, my aunt Nastran, not helped me flee to Amar's lashkar, I would have died. The truth is that Amar saved my life.'

Asrar sighed deeply, 'I know all of that. I suppose we cannot fight our destiny.' She turned to Amar and said, 'I should have welcomed you in my home but this is not the right time. I will join you at some stage, I promise.' Asrar then led the fugitives through a ravine from where a river gushed out in the seven colours of the rainbow. Makhmoor explained, 'Khwaja, this is the River of Seven Hues that surrounds Tilism-e-Hoshruba.'

Asrar stood on the shore and recited incantations until a golden boat came into view, floating on the river. The boat slowly drew close to the bank and Asrar invited Amar and her daughter to climb on the boat with her. As the boat moved on its own towards the middle of the river, the rainbow-hued waters flowed around them in magical bands of colours that charmed the two travellers.

There were trees and dense vegetation on the banks of this river and the earth on the Hoshruba side was a bright green while it appeared to be blood red on the far side of the river. 'You would not have found the ravine without me. This river is the border between the realms of Afrasiyab and Kaukab,' Asrar explained. 'Afrasiyab owns three and a half colours, as does Kaukab. The sahirs who live in this river only obey the keeper and give way. I am the keeper for Hoshruba and that is why we can go across it.' Indeed, Amar saw a thin silver line running through the strip of colour in the centre to ensure that there were three and a half colours on each side.

Asrar called out, 'Princess Mahi Parizaad, hear my call.' A huge silver fish leapt out of the water and Asrar said to it, 'Come closer for what I have to say to you is secret.' The fish emerged near the boat and Asrar leaned down to whisper to it, 'Amar ayyar who fights my Shahanshah wants to meet your Shahanshah to enlist him as an ally. I can take him across or you can, but it's dangerous to stay here.' The fish was silent for a while and then said, 'You can take him across and then return.'

The fish turned its head towards Makhmoor and asked, 'Who is she?' Asrar replied, 'This is my daughter Makhmoor who is acting as his guide. It is because of her that I have brought him here, otherwise my Shahanshah wants him killed.' The fish dived back into the water while Asrar escorted the fugitives across to the far shore. When they reached the bank, Asrar said to Amar, 'Khwaja, this red earth belongs to Kaukab. When you meet him, convey my felicitations.' The moment Amar and Makhmoor got off the boat, Asrar turned it around to her side and vanished out of sight.

Amar happily declared, 'Praise be to Allah! My labours have been rewarded!' Makhmoor held his hand and they walked about leisurely viewing the landscape, until they came upon a magnificent apple orchard. Makhmoor whispered, 'This is Kaukab's Garden of Apples and beyond it is the Plain of Pomegranates where his army camps. The fruit here is magical; watch what happens now.' Moments later, a cool fresh breeze blew through the garden and all the trees started swaying. Ripe golden apples dropped from the trees and split open to release hundreds of birds that flew out of the garden. Amar and Makhmoor continued their journey while the birds flew straight to Kaukab's fortress to inform him of their arrival.

Kaukab looked towards his ministers who advised him to summon the court astrologers. The leading astrologer of the land, Kahin Jadoo, who had prepared Kaukab's natal horoscope, read out the charts, starting with the position of Saturn and Jupiter at the present time, then predicting Amar's arrival on this date and most important, the subsequent alliance of Kaukab and Amar. Kaukab was already aware of these predictions and had merely sent for the astrologer to convince his ministers who looked visibly uncomfortable as the astrologer read out his predictions. Kaukab then dictated a nama for his daughter Burran Sword-woman, asking her to welcome Amar in the Palace of Seven Hues.

One of his ministers, a sahir called Mah Jadoo, cleared his throat before addressing the Shah nervously, 'Huzoor, please heed my advice and do not offend the gods by welcoming this *maleech* into our realm.' Kaukab smiled benignly and replied, 'You are probably not aware of Amar's powers and talents.' Mah Jadoo said derisively, 'What powers are those? I can kill him this instant for you if you so command.'

'Very well then,' Kaukab relented, 'You have my permission to cut his head off. But he is not a sahir, so do not attack him without warning.' 'Makhmoor will try and defend him,' said Mah, 'and I am not afraid of her, but Amar might just disappear while I take her on.' 'We will separate both of them for you,' said Kaukab, 'you will have Amar all to yourself. Now go and get him in the Golden Garden.'

Amar and Mah in the Golden Garden

Amar and Makhmoor continued their journey and came upon grassy slopes verging on the shores of a clear blue lake. Thousands of gold and silver trees lined the lake, as if skilled artisans had created the image of heaven on earth. An octagonal crystal platform stood in the middle of this surreal landscape. Amar felt very happy to be in these beautiful surroundings and remarked that the crystal platform reminded him of the throne of Solomon. As soon as Amar and Makhmoor stepped on the platform, however, there was a sound like a thunderclap and it flew upwards.

Makhmoor forgot her magic and Amar could not jump off. When the platform had gained height, it cracked in the centre. Thus, Amar was on one part and Makhmoor was on the other. The two parts flew in different directions and though the travellers were dismayed at parting, they also felt helpless and resigned to their fates. Amar's half of the crystal platform took him to a place where the ground was pure beaten gold and golden trees produced blossoms and fruits of precious gems. It was as if the treasures of Qaroon had sprouted on this earth. As soon as Amar stepped off the crystal platform, it vanished.

Amar was bewildered but calmed himself and took out a crown of emeralds from Zambil. He wore the crown, a loincloth of brocade and strings of precious pearls around his neck, and squatted on the golden ground—the veritable image of a powerful sahir. Moments later, Mah Jadoo appeared in the golden forest. He saw Amar and assumed that he was the custodian of the magic gardens. Mah walked up to the false sahir and asked him politely, 'Brother, have you been here for some time?' Amar replied, 'This is where I live. Shah Kaukab has appointed me guardian of the Golden Garden.'

Mah asked eagerly, 'In that case, did you see Amar ayyar here?' Amar grimaced and said, 'He came here but he must be with the king now. Have you come to receive him?' Encouraged by his tone, Mah sighed deeply and said, 'No my brother, Shah Kaukab has turned away from the religion of his ancestors and is inclined to the worship of the Unseen God. I have promised Shah that I will kill Amar first. I will now return to durbar and kill that rascal there.'

Mah returned to the durbar and looked around for Amar, but could not see him anywhere. Kaukab asked him, 'Well, have you brought us Amar's head?' Mah protested, 'Huzoor, you sent me to the Golden Garden and sent for that rascal here?' Kaukab laughed and said, 'What? Are you declaring me to be a liar as well?' Mah looked ashamed and said, 'How can I be such a traitor huzoor? The custodian of the garden swore that you had sent for him!' Kaukab laughed even harder and said, 'Which custodian? You foolish man, that was Amar himself!'

Mah felt humiliated but declared bravely, 'I will return and find him now!' Still laughing, the king waved him off and said, 'Do so at the risk of certain death. I promise you Mah, I will not save you from him!' Mah descended on the Golden Garden in great wrath and called out to Amar from a distance, 'You wily thief, you have shamed me before my master. Prepare yourself for I will soon have your head!' Mah then disappeared to give Amar some time to prepare. In that time, Amar took out a prisoner from Zambil. He painted the man's face to look like his own and told him, 'Khudawand Laat sent me to rescue you from Amar. He will test you first, so if someone asks you who you are, declare yourself to be Amar, or you will be punished.'

The prisoner agreed to these conditions, so Amar left him and vanished in Galeem. Mah returned and addressed the prisoner, 'I have given you enough time and will now fulfil my vow to Shah.' The prisoner who understood nothing of this shouted, 'What nonsense are you saying? I am Amar!' Within moments, Mah killed the prisoner. Since he was not a sahir, there were no magical signs after his death. Delighted with his easy success, Mah cut his head off and thought, 'Well, that was simple! To think the king thought so much of this rascal's powers.' Just as he was preparing to fly away, Mah heard the sound of bells. He looked up and saw a beautiful fairy-like damsel floating down through the trees. It was as if the sun and moon had descended on earth, so glowing was her beauty.

Mah's heart filled with love for this incomparable creature. He cried, 'O vision of loveliness, I am returning to Shahanshah's durbar. We should keep each other company and travel together.' That fairy-faced beauty smiled knowingly and said, 'Go on with you? Have you lost your senses? I can see through your scheming mind. I am not a complete fool! Look at the nerve of this lout that he asks a lone, fragile girl like me to accompany him! If you are overcome by the devil of lust on the way, I will be ruined! You will eat me alive!'

Mah was amused by her innocent protests and boldly held her hand. He declared, 'I will not go without taking you with me!' The lovely damsel frowned prettily and cried, 'I will see how you will take me with you! No sahib, I will not go with you. Whoever hears about this will say, "Were you a little girl that you went off with a lout like him in this isolated place?" Even if I protest my innocence a thousand times, do you think they will believe me? They will surely say, "She is making excuses;

she is a strumpet and eager to go off with this young man!" No, I am not so foolish as to ruin my reputation by going with you! Go on your way and do not fret for me!'

Mah almost died with love when she spoke. He held her hand and said, 'I swear my hands will not touch you in a sinful way!' The flower-face retorted, 'Stop and touch your mother in a sinful way! Listen sahib, no one can cast an evil eye on me! I have been in the royal household for years and have been alone on many occasions. I have travelled with Princess Burran, long may she live! No one can claim to have even seen me laughing with anyone! Samri always protects me!' Mah Jadoo became even more captivated by her and pulled her towards him. The reader should know that the parizad was none other than Amar.

The damsel slapped her forehead and cried, 'I should never have come here. I swear by Jamshed that what I feared the most has happened! Very well, I will go with you but if you touch me at all, you will see what happens!' As they walked together, she took out a gilori and chewed it daintily. Even though Mah had not asked for it, she waved her thumb at him as if denying him the betel leaf. Mah thought she was softening and said, 'Will you not offer me a gilori, my love?'

The damsel pouted and said, 'Certainly not!' Mah shrugged her refusal off and cried, 'Keep it then, I will not offer you my perfume either!' He took out a glass phial and held it out to her. That fair damsel laughed and said, 'I don't need your perfume; my attendants tuck perfume phials in my bodice!' The false damsel then put a hand under her veil and covered Mah's eyes with the other hand, 'By Samri, do not look now as I have taken off my veil. May Samri blind anyone who tries to peek at me!' Thus with more of such provocative banter Amar took out a phial of drugged perfume. He gave it to Mah who sniffed it eagerly and instantly fell unconscious.

Mah woke up and saw that the damsel had disappeared and a thin, reedy-looking man stood in front of him with his sword drawn. 'What do you have to say for yourself now?' taunted Amar. He was about to behead Mah when a crystal slave-boy burst forth from the ground, held his hand and said in Kaukab's voice, 'That is enough, O king of ayyari! This is my special companion and has been punished enough for his stupidity.' Amar and Mah both fell unconscious when they heard the slave-boy's voice.

Later, Amar opened his eyes and found himself in a splendid house surrounded by gardens. Mah still lay unconscious, but the crystal slave-boy stood in front of Amar with folded hands and said, 'Shahanshah Kaukab sends you greetings and compliments you on your trickery. He says that this was a test and is now over. Please rest in this garden and you will be provided every comfort here.' The slave-boy picked Mah up and returned to Kaukab's durbar. Kaukab revived Mah there and said, 'Mah Jadoo, what happened? Have you brought us Amar's head?' Mah looked shamefaced and said, 'You are indeed right; it is impossible to vanquish Amar. The man is a chameleon of disguises. He is sometimes a man, sometimes a damsel! I am a believer now. Let me now carry the message to the princess.'

Princess Burran Sword-woman

Mah Jadoo left for Burran's durbar immediately. The princess was seated on her throne in great glory. Hundreds of her companions and ministers sat on chairs while her handmaidens, who looked as if they had dived into a river of jewels, stood behind her. A band of young slaves in golden clothes and sashes stood before her with folded hands. Everyone was the picture of awed silence as the princess watched a nautch performance.

Mah Jadoo reached the durbar and bowed low in mujra greeting. The princess bestowed a khalat robe on him and asked him about the reason for his visit. Mah Jadoo held out Kaukab's nama to her and her vizier Marzan took the scroll to her. The princess made a symbolic offering of gold coins to the king's nama and held it to her forehead and eyes. She read the contents and ordered, 'Marzan, Amar bin Ummayyah is in the Garden of Pomegranates. Escort him here respectfully. When the Fort of Seven Hues is adorned we will arrange a feast for him there.'

In the garden, Amar had conducted a survey and had settled in a large marble pavilion. He took out a magnificent crown from Zambil, dressed in rich robes and waited for Shah Kaukab to summon him. In a while, Vizier Marzan arrived at the gardens with a large contingent of sahirs. He entered the doorway of the marble pavilion with a few select companions who held gold trays filled with treasures. They gingerly entered it and saw Amar in all his splendour, conversing with empty chairs. The vizier was overawed and thought, 'Amar must be a great king and seems to have brought an invisible army with him.'

The vizier greeted Amar with great respect and said, 'O king of ayyars, Princess Burran sends you her greetings and has sent me in your service. She apologizes for not receiving you as she is engaged in state matters. The princess is, however, anxious to meet you. She requests that you honour us by staying in Moti Bagh this evening and she will receive you in the Fort of Seven Hues tomorrow.'

Amar signalled to the vizier to be seated and suddenly vanished out of sight. The vizier was astounded and thought, 'Is he a man or jinni?' Amar then disguised himself as a servant and appeared before him with a costly khalat robe. He said, 'The king of ayyars is changing his robes in his camp. He has sent this offering in your honour.' The servant then disappeared abruptly. Amar reappeared in his real form and told the vizier to close his eyes so that his servants could collect Burran's gifts. When Marzan closed his eyes, Amar scooped all of Burran's offerings in the blessed Net of Ilyas. The vizier opened his eyes to find the treasures gone and became even more convinced of Amar's power over an army of invisible jinni. Marzan escorted Amar out of the garden and seated him on the peacock throne as kettledrums were struck and the eye of the sky watched with wonder when they went past the Fort of Seven Hues towards Moti Bagh. A hundred lovely maidens emerged with bouquets to welcome Amar and led him into the gardens of Moti Bagh.

Tilism of Mirrors

Now hear about Afrasiyab. The King of Magic moulded a slave-boy from earth of the Garden of Apples and sent him to fetch Afat Swordfighter. Within moments, a crimson cloud floated into the durbar. A sahira sat on that cloud, laden with gold jewellery. She greeted the King of Magic, kissed the base of his throne and performed the ritual circling to take his troubles upon herself. The Shah affectionately patted her back and permitted her to sit down. Afat performed the mujra greeting before settling on her chair. Afrasiyab said to her, 'I have summoned you as Khudawand Laqa has asked for our help. Sofar Jadoo and Nazuk Soft-eye are there already. Go to their aid and be blessed with the vision of Khudawand!' The sahira was gifted a khalat robe by the Shah. Afat wore it and returned to her fort to mobilize her army of twelve thousand sahir soldiers. She soon left for Mount Agate on her magic throne in great splendour.

Afat had to go past the Tilism of Mirrors whose ruler was the powerful sahira Ayeenadar Jadoo. Half of the Tilism of Mirrors was in Hoshruba and the other half, in Nur Afshan. Accordingly, Queen Ayeenadar paid tribute to both Afrasiyab and Kaukab. Afat passed by the Tilism of Mirrors, and decided to call on Ayeena, who was a friend. After all, she was going to confront Muslims who were reputed to be the slayers of sahirs. Perhaps, she thought, Ayeena would give her a magical gift to help her in her battle. Thus, Afat ordered her commanders to lead the army to Mount Agate while she paid a visit to Ayeena.

Afat then flew into the Tilism of Mirrors. Its keepers knew her and allowed her to proceed on the magical path to the fort. Ayeena received her friend warmly and once they were in her palace, Afat said, 'I had not seen you for ages and as you know, whoever confronts the followers of the One God does not remain alive. If Samri saves me, I will meet you again; otherwise, let us be grateful that we meet now.' Ayeena declared, 'Do not worry. There is a feast in your honour tonight. Tomorrow, when you leave, I will send my magic warrior with you. He cannot be killed by anyone and will destroy the Muslims within moments!'

Afat was delighted with this assurance and went with Ayeena to her garden where a splendid feast of wine and meats had been laid out for them. They were entertained with soothing music as they ate. At that time Ayeena received a message that her friend Nazuk Soft-eye had come to visit her. Ayeena sent her nobles to receive her.

Now hear about Nazuk Soft-eye. Her lover Nasir Kohi had joined the Muslims and her daughter had already been killed in battle. Nazuk had gone to the Tilism of Mirrors to seek Ayeena's protection. Ayeena was fond of Nazuk whose kingdom bordered her own and she ensured that Nazuk was protected magically so that she would not die unless struck by a magic sword that was stored in Ayeena's treasury.

Nazuk met Afat and wept as she related her trying encounters with Laqa's enemies. Afat felt apprehensive about her own mission but Ayeena encouraged her friends to remain calm. At dawn, the ruler of day awoke to see his reflection in the mirror of the sun. Ayeena left the fortress with her friends and rode into the wilderness. She led them to a gully in a mountain where they came upon a stone *hujra* built into the rock. Its door was secured with a lock as large as a camel's thigh. Ayeena recited an incantation to open the lock, and a crystal figure the size of a hand emerged from the hujra on a miniature crystal horse. Within moments, the magic figure transformed into a life-sized warrior mounted on a magnificent silver stallion.

Ayeena ordered the rider, 'Go with Malika Afat and capture the worshippers of the One God.' After the magic warrior silently rode off, Ayeena addressed Afat, 'My sister, go now and in the battlefield, call out to Tilismi rider. He will appear and obey your orders. No one can vanquish or kill him. Only one who has the magic sword of my Tilism can destroy him!'

Afat looked satisfied and told Nazuk, 'There is no need for you to ask for anything now. The rider will serve both of us.' Ayeena also reassured Nazuk, 'Sister, why should you worry. You are magic-bound and you will not die except by the magic sword that I have kept safely!'

Nazuk thought, 'She is right; I should use the Tilismi rider to capture my lover and kill the Muslims.' Both friends left on a flying throne after a fond farewell to Ayeena. They crossed the borders of Tilism-e-Hoshruba, and the Tilism of Mirrors to reach Mount Agate. In Laqa's durbar, Afat prostrated before Khudawand. The army she had dispatched earlier was already encamped besides Nazuk Soft-eye's lashkar.

When the wizard of time allowed the darkness of night to invade the pavilion of daylight, Afat ordered that a battle be announced. Her sahirs sounded magically amplified trumpets; the brave ones struck battle drums with wooden mallets; and *sarod* masters played their instruments. Afat rose from her chair as heralds proclaimed battle and said to Nazuk, 'Sister, I give you into Samri's care and will try my luck in the battlefield.' Nazuk replied solemnly, 'Go with Jamshed!' Afat then folded her hands before Laqa and asked for his permission to fight. Laqa declared, 'Go and my divinity will protect you.' Shaitan Bakhtiarak added, 'Khudawand holds your death in his hand, you will not be killed! Go and face the enemy without fear!'

Afat happily went to the battlefield to demonstrate her magical powers. She caused trees to sprout out of the earth and conjured sheets of flames to frighten the enemy. She called out, 'You who deny the existence of Khudawand Laqa, your end is near. Confront me so that I can show you the final path!' One of the sardars of Islam cantered on to the battlefield to fight her. When Afat saw him rushing towards her, she called out, 'Tilismi rider, come forth!' A swirl of dust arose in the desert and the magic rider galloped on to the battlefield, roaring like a lion. The sardar of Islam tried to avoid the rider's lance, but succumbed to the powerful magical blow. Prince Nur al Dahar, son of Hamza, challenged him next, but was also defeated. Thus, the Tilismi rider defeated a hundred sardars before the shadows lengthened and he rode off into the desert.

Afat had the drums of peace struck. Emir Hamza and Shah Saad returned to their pavilion with heavy hearts and the tricksters set out to rescue their commanders. Afat and her friend Nazuk Soft-eye met with joy. Laqa showered jewels and coins on Afat and arranged the feast of Nauroze that evening. During the feast, Shaitan Bakhtiarak warned Afat that the tricksters of Islam would try to rescue their sardars. 'Show them the final path so that their numbers decrease!' said the Shaitan. Afat became thoughtful and said, 'Malik-ji, I want to capture Hamza before I destroy them.' Later that night, Afat sent a message to her friend Ayeenadar informing her of the number of Muslim sardars captured by the magic rider.

Prince Iraj in the Tilism of Mirrors

Earlier, Emir Hamza's grandson, Qasim, had fallen in love with Princess Nargis whose father's kingdom bordered the Tilism of Mirrors. Besotted with Qasim, the princess had given him a magic sword. Nargis was engaged to be married and her parents kept her under house arrest in Mount Nargis, in case her future in-laws got wind of her amorous adventures. Qasim had also been arrested and thrown into the dungeon. His replica moulded from lentil flour was sent to Hamza to convince him that his son had been killed. Hamza breathed the Great Name on the corpse and was much relieved to find that it was a magical illusion. Qasim's son Iraj left from Mount Agate to solve the mystery of his father's disappearance, but was whisked off by a magical claw to an unknown destination.

The mirrors of the real and the imagined reflect the travails of noble lovers in the Tilism of Mirrors thus: When the magic claw captured Prince Iraj, it flew over Princess Sanobar's garden high in the mountains. The sight of a claw carrying a youth whose noble visage was as radiant as the sun startled Sanobar. She made an invocation that made the claw freeze in mid-flight and descend with its passenger in the garden. As the claw vanished Iraj opened his eyes and saw a masked figure in male attire who was quite obviously a woman. He asked her politely, 'Who are you and why have you summoned me?' The maiden unmasked her face and replied, 'I have rescued you from a magic claw. I would like you to stay in all comfort with me!'

Iraj was entranced by her beauty while that envy of the moon was already smitten with him. She smiled and said, 'Come, fill the goblet with the wine of your lips and I will be honoured!' She held his hand and led him to a pavilion with forty pillars, a gleaming floor and a magnificent ivory throne. As they sat on the throne in all splendour, fairy-faced handmaidens served them goblets of wine. The prince declined the wine and said, 'Unless I know your faith and your background, it is not seemly to impose on you.' The princess smiled and said, 'Sheheryar, I am the niece of Hanzal, whose daughter Nargis eloped with a Muslim. She arrested him and sent him to the dungeons of Tilism of Mirrors.'

Iraj was relieved to hear that his father was alive and said, 'Princess, I am the son of the prisoner you mention. He is Qasim, grandson of Hamza. If you love me, give up the worship of Samri and Laqa and turn to the One True God. Otherwise, we can have nothing to do with each other.' Thus, Princess Sanobar along with her servants and handmaidens willingly pledged allegiance to the true faith. Sanobar declared that she would formally convert after the Tilism of Mirrors was vanquished.

It so happened that Hanzal, who was devastated by her daughter's betrayal, had sent one of her officers to summon her niece. The officer, Mareekh Jadoo, flew to garden in the mountains and was outraged to see Sanobar and the prince engrossed in a meeting of pleasure. Mareekh called out angrily, 'Wait, you living disgrace to your family! Why are you shameless girls causing so much trouble?' He recited an incantation that made Sanobar forget magic and Prince Iraj lose control over his limbs. Mareekh swooped down, caught both of them and headed straight back to his mistress in order to avoid Sanobar's father, who, he felt, would surely try to rescue his daughter in a moment of paternal weakness.

Halfway through his journey, Mareekh descended on a hill to catch his breath. Two ayyars, Shahpur and Sayyara from Hamza's camp, who were looking for the prince disguised as sahirs, saw him from a distance. They came closer and greeted him casually. Mareekh looked at them suspiciously and asked, 'Who are you?' The wily ayyars replied, 'We are the same as you! Tell us about yourself!' Mareekh sighed deeply and said, 'Brothers, these girls will be the ruin of the house of sahirs! They fall in love with Muslims and cause endless peril to us!' He then related the story of the two princesses and their paramours. The ayyars were delighted to learn that both Qasim and Iraj were alive, but exclaimed, 'Brother, these Muslims should be killed without warning wherever we find them. But who is that behind you who disagrees with us?'

As Mareekh turned in alarm, Shahpur caught him in the coils of his snare rope. Before he could respond, Sayyara burst a narcotic bubble under his nose that rendered him unconscious. The ayyars were quick to behead him and waited for the din of his magical spirits to cease before greeting the prince. Sanobar also recovered from the effects of the sahir's spell and greeted them warmly. The ayyars asked her if both of them could accompany her, disguised as Mareekh and her handmaiden. 'Meet your aunt and leave the rest to us,' they told her. Once they were disguised, they advised the prince to remain there while they went with Sanobar to her aunt Hanzal's palace.

Hanzal had been waiting for her niece and greeted her affectionately when she saw her. Some time later, Sanobar ordered her handmaiden to serve the fruit she had brought for her aunt. The handmaiden (in reality, the ayyar Sayyara) brought a salver full of the choicest fruit. Sanobar lovingly offered it to Hanzal who ate a few grapes to humour her niece. The fruit was then offered to everyone in the gathering and in no time, everyone was unconscious. The ayyars tied Hanzal to a pillar in the garden, pierced her tongue with a needle and revived her. Hanzal opened her eyes in alarm and looked at Sanobar for an explanation. The ayyars stepped forward and said, 'We are from the Islamic camp and your niece has joined us. If you want to save your life, you must release Prince Qasim and join us as well.'

Hanzal thought, 'Indeed, the faith of the Unseen God is powerful. I have already lost a daughter and now a niece to these people. It is better to join them and retain my kingdom and my honour.' Accordingly, she signalled her compliance with the ayyars' demands. They immediately untied her from the pillar and took the needle out of her tongue. Very relieved, Hanzal assured them that she was on their side and that she would formally convert after the Tilism was conquered. They informed her that Prince Iraj was waiting for them in the hills and was to be brought to the fort. Hanzal promptly revived some of her unconscious officials and sent them to escort Prince Iraj to her palace.

When Iraj arrived, she respectfully rose to greet him and offered him a place on the masnad. She then addressed her counsellors, 'I have allied with this noble prince. If you remain with me you will have to support the adherents of Islam.' All the sahirs of her durbar swore their allegiance to her and the prince. Hanzal then arranged a feast of pleasure in which wine and meat kebabs were served. After the meal, the prince requested Hanzal to release his father. Hanzal sent a respectful message to Ayeenadar at once that read, 'Malika of Tilism, I would be grateful if you could send my prisoner back to me so that I can dispatch him to the King of Magic in Tilism-e-Hoshruba. My husband is with Shah and I will rest easier if the prisoner is in his care. Tilism of Mirrors is too close to the Islamic lashkar for comfort.'

She sent this message through two loyal officers after swearing them to secrecy about her allegiance to the prince. The officers reached Ayeena's durbar and submitted the message to her. She handed the prisoner over to them and said, 'Tell your mistress that her friendship is more valuable to me than the fate of this prisoner. In fact, I am relieved that you are taking him away for I am afraid of a Muslim invasion if he stays here!'

The sahirs took Prince Qasim back to Hanzal's durbar on a flying throne. There, he was released him from his magical fetters and shackles. Iraj embraced his father and wept to see his matted hair and nails that had grown long in captivity. Eventually, Qasim went to bathe in the hammam and returned, dressed in fresh robes. He embraced his son and placed his hand on Sanobar's head affectionately. Hanzal went back to her palace and hugged her daughter Nargis. She gave her fine robes and jewels to wear and sent her to Prince Qasim in a golden palanquin.

Meanwhile, Qasim could not mention his beloved's name in durbar, although his heart longed to see her. Therefore, he was overjoyed when he was led into a chamber where Nargis sat waiting for him. A round of roseate wine was served and this gathering of pleasure came alive with laughter and joy.

Princess Bilour and Iraj

It so happened that young Prince Iraj expressed a desire to hunt in the forests around Hanzal's fort. Hanzal arranged the hunt for him and the next morning, Iraj rode out into the wilderness on a frisky Arabic hunter. He released swift flying hawks to pounce on the birds in the forest and hunted down several animals in the area. Eventually, the prince settled down on a hill under the shade of a tree and leisurely sipped wine as he enjoyed the splendid landscape around him.

The reader will remember that Sanobar had saved the prince from the clutches of a magic claw. Princess Bilour, daughter of Ayeena Jadoo of the Tilism of Mirrors had seen Iraj earlier when he had set out to look for his father and had lost her heart to him. She was the one who had sent the magic claw to abduct the prince. When the claw returned to her and assumed its human form, it said to her, 'I was bringing the prince to you when Princess Sanobar seized him from me!' Princess Bilour was livid when she heard this and summoned her companion Hoor Jadoo. She burst out angrily, 'The nerve of this Sanobar to waylay our prisoner! To think that these people who are vassals of my mother should defy us in this manner! I am going to reduce their forts to bricks and dust or change my name! Go and mobilize my army; I want you to come with me!'

Hoor clicked her fingers as a gesture of taking on the princess' troubles upon herself and said, 'Bibi, rest assured, Sanobar could not have known that huzoor had sent for that man or she would not have dared to be so impertinent. I will go now and bring the prince for you!' She sprouted wings and flew to the place where the prince was reclining on the hill. She thought it best to catch him unawares and waved her fingers to conjure a bright light that blinded his companions. She then fell upon him in the shape of a claw and flew off with him.

When the prince's companions regained their senses, they looked around frantically for him, but could find no trace of their master. They rushed back to Hanzal to inform her of his disappearance. Hanzal's niece Sanobar was alarmed and left at once in search of her beloved. Hanzal ordered her officers to investigate the prince's disappearance, and his ayyar, Shahpur, also left in pursuit of Iraj.

Now hear about the prince. Hoor left him on a hilltop and went to meet her mistress. Princess Bilour saw her smiling and knew that she had plucked the flower of her wishes. She suppressed her own excitement and casually asked her, 'Where were you and what did you do?' Hoor Jadoo smiled and replied, 'That will soon be revealed and it would not be appropriate to mention it here!' All doubts in Bilour's mind were now banished. She quickly made arrangements to receive a guest in the garden that served as her retreat.

The prince opened his eyes and saw that he was in a beautiful bungalow on a hilltop, set amidst a garden in full bloom. He was enjoying the view from the hill when a group of flower-like damsels, whose beauty was the envy of the sun and the moon, approached him. The prince also stepped forward and the lovely maidens asked him archly, 'Young man, how have you reached this place for even birds seek permission to land here! This is the garden of Princess Bilour!' Iraj replied, 'I am just a lost traveller!'

The maidens trilled with laughter and one of them exclaimed, 'Look at this rascal trying to deceive us with words! Women are infamous for their deceitful ways, but he surpasses them!' A second one said, 'As if he is so innocent that he lost his way!' A third one added, 'As if someone has brought him here!' The fourth one cried, 'Why would anyone one abduct you? Have you seen yourself in the mirror? You are not that attractive that someone should be in love with you!' The last maiden laughed, held the prince's hand, and said, 'Do not be so proud of your fair face. Now that you are here, come and meet our princess!'

Iraj was amused by their banter and retorted, 'I would not even have looked at you, but since your mistress wishes to meet me, I will go with you!' The damsels frowned and pouted at him; one of them protested, 'Do you think we are easy women that you talk to us in this manner? Why sahib, do you think you are so good-looking that we are besotted with you?' The second one piped up, 'My dear, the more attention you give this rascal, the more he thinks of himself!' Yet another exclaimed, 'Let us leave, if he wants to follow us, he will!' The fourth one met his eye, laughed, and said, 'You should come with us; you will not regret it!'

The prince smiled and went with them to the bungalow. He saw an exquisite maiden sitting inside, so graceful and fragile that a mere gust of wind would have harmed her. Flasks of roseate wine and gold-inlaid crystal goblets were arranged neatly in front of her. She looked up and smiled at the prince, beckoned him to sit besides her on the masnad, and offered him a goblet of wine. He declined it and raised the question of his faith. The princess laughed and said, 'I cannot refuse anything you ask for because you are my honoured guest.' Thus, this gathering of pleasure commenced with a round of wine and dancing.

While the prince was engaged in these pleasurable activities, the envious sky played him another hand; Ayeena Jadoo's messenger arrived at the garden and sought an audience with the princess. The princess was reclining in her lover's arms at that time, and instead of wine, he was drinking the beauty of her eyes; instead of food, he was nibbling her sweet lips. Her loyal handmaidens who were standing guard stopped Ayeena's messenger from going inside the bungalow. They entered the princess's chamber and gave her the scroll that read, 'O light of mine eyes, we are intending to travel to Mount Agate. Apart from being blessed with a vision of Khudawand Laqa, we will also witness the execution of Hamza's sardars captured by our magic rider. Therefore, you must return from your tour and reign in our place.'

The princess drafted a brief reply: 'Honoured mother, forgive me as I am not too well today. I will present myself tomorrow.' Her handmaidens handed this scroll to the messenger who delivered it to Ayeena Jadoo.

Now, though the princess had assured Iraj that she was sympathetic to his cause, in fact, she really had no understanding of his origins. She happily declared, 'Thank Samri that these enemies of Khudawand have been captured and will be executed!' Iraj was dumbfounded when he heard this and his eyes filled with tears at the plight of his companions. The princess was startled and tried to wipe his tears away with her scarf as she murmured, 'What did I say? How have I erred?'

Iraj responded quietly, 'You are happy to learn of the capture of those who are my kin and dearest companions! I am the son of Qasim bin Alamshah bin Hamza. Alas, I sit here in comfort while my lashkar is going through such hardships. I am leaving now and by my faith, I will slaughter the sahirs who have caused them harm or die by my own dagger! Return to your home and I will return to Emir's lashkar.'

As he rose from the masnad, the princess grasped the hem of his robe and cried, 'Kill me before you leave!' Iraj replied firmly, 'Princess, it is useless to stop me!' The princess saw the determined look on his face and pleaded tearfully, 'Forgive me and as penance for my crime, accept a weapon that will overwhelm any sahir and also destroy Tilismi rider!' Iraj stopped in his tracks and asked, 'What is it?' She explained, 'The rider of Tilism can only be vanquished by a sword that has been designed to destroy it. That sword lies is in my mother's treasury. Stay here and I will bring the sword to you tonight. Then you can return and send Afat and Tilismi rider straight to hell. However, remember that one who is the captive of your love will be waiting forlorn in the mountains.'

Iraj looked at her and said, 'I will not be able to find this place on my own!' The princess smiled and replied, 'Just go to the foothills of Mount Nargis and I will fetch you myself!' To her relief, Iraj resumed his place on the masnad and she renewed her pledge to convert to Islam.

That night, Princess Bilour left with a handmaiden for the fort of the Tilism of Mirrors, but avoided her mother's palace and went straight to the treasury. Since her mother trusted her absolutely, Bilour had the keys to the treasury. She unlocked the doors and opened a box that contained four magic swords. She took out the one meant for killing the Tilismi rider and went to the next chamber, where she found the magic horse. This horse could cover huge distances within moments and could take its rider wherever he wished. She took the sword and the horse with its harness and trappings back to her garden in the mountains. It was late at night when she returned to the prince and the two lovers slept in each other's arms. The night of union is always brief and soon it was dawn.

The prince rose and performed the dawn prayer before embarking on his journey. Bilour handed him the magic sword that he slipped in his belt. He then mounted the magic horse, bade the princess a fond farewell and soon rode out of sight. The princess returned to the bungalow with a heavy heart and went to her bed, where she lay down listlessly with her eyes covered.

Iraj in confrontation with Afat Jadoo

In Laqa's camp, Afat Jadoo decided not to wait for her friend Ayeenadar and struck the battle drums, hoping to capture the rest of the sardars of Hamza's camp. The next morning, when heralds announced the commencement of battle and flags of both armies fluttered colourfully in the field, the Tilismi rider cantered on to the battlefield and challenged the enemy. Prince Iraj greeted the Shah and after gaining permission from him, entered the battlefield in all glory. Bakhtiarak exclaimed, 'Ya Khudawand, your grandson seems to be in rare form today!' To remind the reader, two of Laqa's daughters had eloped and married Hamza's sons. Therefore, Iraj was also Laqa's grandson.

The magic rider, unaware of his doom, aimed his lance at the prince. Iraj stopped it with his own lance and after a fierce confrontation, sliced the rider in half with his magic sword. Afat was stunned by this outcome and there were loud calls of '*Takbeer*' in the Islamic lashkar. The sounds of victory drums and bells filled the air; Bakhtiarak stood on his elephant, recited the Muslim call to prayer like a parrot, and then abused Laqa loudly. Afat and Nazuk Soft-eye furiously ordered their armies to attack the adherents of the One God. Within moments, soldiers from the two armies converged on the battlefield like dark monsoon clouds. Emir Hamza moved forward and Iraj called out his signature battle call.

Afat and other sahirs cast ferocious spells and conjured huge mountains that fell on the Muslims. The magic sword protected Iraj while Emir Hamza recited the Great Name of Allah to make the mountains disintegrate and fall instead on Laqa's soldiers. When Iraj fought his way right up to Laqa's throne, Afat became nervous and had the drums of peace struck. The armies stopped fighting and Emir rode back to his camp, all the while showering Iraj with gold coins.

On the other side Afat, Laqa and their companions were crestfallen with the destruction of the Tilismi rider. Shaitan Bakhtirak could not resist teasing Afat, 'Malika, how neatly the noble prince slashed that rider into two pieces. I was so impressed with his swordsmanship!' Afat squirmed uncomfortably in her chair and asked, 'Who was that young man?'

'That was the grandson of Alamshah,' Shaitan informed her, 'and the great grandson of Emir Hamza. He was missing for a month, but seems to have returned in all glory!' Afat looked thoughtful and said, 'Malik-ji, I have no secrets from you. I had brought Tilismi rider from Tilism of Mirrors.' Shaitan grimaced and said, 'Then it is certain that some young woman from that land must have fallen in love with Iraj and presented him with a magic sword or instructed him to strike his sword on a hidden mark on the rider's body. Anyway, what have you decided now?' Afat declared, 'As long as I am alive, I will keep fighting but your conjectures about the Tilimsi rider's destruction seem plausible. I will wage one more battle against the Muslims before I go to the Tilism of Mirrors!'

The next morning, Afat conjured a magic rider of her own to confront Iraj, who destroyed it in no time. Afat suffered a resounding defeat in the ensuing battle and had to strike the drums of peace yet again. Emir Hamza gave away a lot of gold to avert the evil eye from his great grandson and held joyous celebrations that evening.

Afat left the battlefront and journeyed to Ayeena Jadoo's palace in the fort of the Tilism of Mirrors. Ayeena was informed of her arrival and received her warmly. Ayeena held Afat's hand when she came in and offered her a seat before saying, 'Sister, how are you doing? Has the Tilismi rider served you well? I had to delay my visit to you as my daughter is not well.' Afat responded drily, 'Malika, your rider caused an uproar in the enemy camp. He wounded whoever confronted him and captured many sardars. On the third day, however, Hamza's great grandson rode in from the wilderness and with one stroke of his sword, cut the magic rider in half!'

Ayeena looked shocked and cried, 'Sister, what are you saying?' Afat replied, 'I swear by Samri I am telling you the truth! Apart from your rider, I had conjured a warrior of my own but he was also destroyed. I came here because I thought you could perhaps explain how this happened. It is certainly beyond my understanding!'

Ayeena frowned and said, 'I made a grave error by invoking the Tilismi rider! We are only meant to use such magical weapons if Tilism is in grave danger. I may have broken a hidden taboo. I just hope this Tilism survives now!' She rose and told Afat she would be back in a minute. She went straight to the treasury, broke open the locks on the box that Bilour had opened, and found only three swords in it. She knew that only her daughter Bilour had the keys to the box and thought, 'I should ask her about the missing sword!' Ayeena locked the treasury and was about to summon Bilour when it struck her that if Bilour had been up to mischief, there was no point in exposing her to Afat who was bound to defame her.

Ayeena returned to her durbar quietly and sat down with her face averted from Afat, who was puzzled by her behaviour. After some time, she asked her, 'Why are you so quiet? You have not given me an explanation and now seem to have marbles in your mouth!' Ayeena snapped, 'Sister, spare me your complaints! If a friend extends a helping hand, do you need to cut it off? If you are that cowardly, why did you leave your house at all? You should have asked Afrasiyab to assign someone else to fight! First, you have my magic rider killed and now you want me to destroy my Tilism for you? I was a fool to help you and flout the magical laws of Tilism!'

Afat was stunned by this outburst and angrily said, 'Sister, you have the loyalty of a parrot! You are upset about a mere rider—people cut off their own heads in friendship! Why should I be patronized by the likes of you?' Ayeena replied, 'You were the one who came begging for help. If it were not for the rider, you would have been in your grave today! Anyway, let us see how you can confront the Muslims now!' Afat became livid when she heard this and cried, 'May Samri save me from friends like you! I am sorry that I caused your rider's death! I curse myself for accepting a favour from you!'

Afat left the Tilism of Mirrors in a rage and thought, 'Let me return and capture Iraj with the spell suggested by Afrasiyab!' She reached her camp but was too upset to present herself in durbar. For a whole day and night, she awakened her magical powers. She lit the sacred fire and fed *mohan bhog* to magical spirits. The next day, she sought Laqa's permission to fight. Shaitan Bakhtiarak said to her, 'Malika, you have struck the battle drums in your name and my heart trembles for your safety. Nothing is lost yet! Go back to Tilism-e-Hoshruba!' Afat declared, 'Malik-ji, it is either my head or his today! I am going to capture Iraj!'

Afat went to the battlefield and called out, 'Young Iraj, I have come here only to fight you. Come and confront me now!' When Iraj came forward, Afat smashed a magic coconut on the ground. The coconut burst and released thick black smoke that engulfed the young prince. The smoke made him feel so dizzy that he dropped his sword and fell off his horse. At Afat's signal, her men seized the sword and the magic horse. Afat saw the sardars of Islam moving forward to help the prince and fell upon him in the shape of a claw to whisk him out of the battlefield. The two armies clashed fiercely as Afat rushed to her camp with the prince. She sent word to Laqa that she had captured the enemy and so there was no need to continue fighting. Laqa had the drums of peace struck and the two armies returned to their camps. Emir Hamza and the Shah retired crestfallen to the royal pavilion, and their ayyars set off to rescue Iraj.

Afat had Iraj bound in the shackles of cruelty and sent him to Laqa's durbar. Laqa had just returned from the battleground and was engaged in pursuits of pleasure when Iraj was brought into the durbar. Afat walked behind the prince and announced, 'I have brought him here to be executed!' Shaitan Bakhtiarak said, 'You are a wise woman and do not need advice. Still, you must remain vigilant. It is not every day that the enemy is at your mercy!' Afat said, 'I want to execute him in front of his own camp!' Thus, the execution ground was prepared and sahir-guards dragged Iraj towards it. Laqa sat on a throne placed for him and asked Iraj, 'O mortal, prostrate before me!' Iraj retorted, 'I curse you and your followers a million times.' Laqa was outraged by this remark and shouted, 'Execute this impertinent mortal right now!'

Bilour rescues Iraj

Now hear about the beautiful, loyal and faithful Bilour. After Iraj had left, she spent the day adorning herself and her garden in anticipation of meeting her lover that evening. She sent Hoor and her handmaidens to wait for the prince at Mount Nargis, but when they returned without him, she was distraught. Hoor tried to comfort her and said, 'Bibi, restrain yourself. The Provider will show us the day when the prince will return!' Bilour became even more upset and wept, 'If you want me to live then find out what has happened to him!'

Hoor flew to the Islamic camp and was startled to see everyone standing on the battlefield, desperately praying with raised hands while a chain of flames seemed to be preventing them from approaching Laqa's camp. She changed her face magically and approached a water carrier at the edge of the lashkar, who stood weeping in despair. 'What has happened here?' she asked him. He barely gave her a glance as he responded, 'Afat has captured Iraj and is about to execute him!'

Hoor was stunned by his reply and flew back to inform Bilour. The princess took her aside and asked her eagerly, 'What was he doing? I am sure he was with another woman! Was he embarrassed at meeting you? Did he ask after me?' Tears rolled down Hoor's cheeks when she replied, 'Bibi, what are you saying? The prince is about to be executed! He is bound and shackled and sits under the shadow of a sword!' Bilour paled visibly and cried, 'Alas, I am so unfortunate that I let him go myself!'

The princess burned in the fire of love and her heart twisted with pain. She swiftly flew to a wilderness in the Tilism of Mirrors and reached the Four Hills. She went to a house that stood in the middle of the hills, opened its lock and proceeded to a hujra deep inside. Within the hujra was a box, a hundred yards long. The princess tried to lift the box but her companions who had followed her there lifted it for her. The princess locked the house while her companions placed the box on her flying throne. She moved swiftly like zephyr blowing over a garden. Her companions followed her and muttered, 'She is so drunk on love that she is heedless of her fate. What will happen when her mother hears of this?' Another said, 'Indeed, love brings its own perils! Look what happened to Qais and Laila!'

Soon the princess took off and left them far behind in her haste to leave the Tilism of Mirrors. She reached the execution ground after Laqa had given the second order for Iraj's execution and the executioner was only waiting for the third order to strike him. Iraj was reciting the verse of affirmation when the princess untied her hair and took a crystal ball out from it. She flung it on the chain of flames Afat had conjured to keep the Islamic lashkar at bay. Immediately, dark rain clouds floated in and burst over the chain. It was as if rivers were flowing from the sky to extinguish the flames.

Bakhtiarak exclaimed, 'O Afat, what peril is that?' Afat looked up and cried, 'I recognize you!' when she saw Princess Bilour. She tried to cast a spell, but the princess flashed down in the form of a sword and forced Afat to quickly sink into the earth. Bilour assumed her real form and flung magical citrons and limes in all directions, causing mayhem among Laqa's soldiers. In the melee, the executioners dropped their swords and fled. Meanwhile, Afat emerged from the earth and ordered her sahir army to attack Bilour. Magical onslaughts and an avalanche of stones and flames from the sky were directed at her.

At that time, Bilour opened the box she had brought with her. It contained forty thousand crystal statuettes that spilled out and instantly became life-sized warriors. They attacked the sahir soldiers with their lances and swords, and killed thousands. The soldiers responded with magical weapons but could not damage the invincible warriors. Now that the barrier of flames had been destroyed, the soldiers of Islam also joined the fray. Meanwhile, Bilour fought her way to the execution ground. Afat rushed forward and screamed, 'Shameless hussy, you dare to rescue my prisoner?!'

She tried to attack Bilour with her dagger but the princess conjured two slave-boys that held her back. Bilour then attacked Afat with her sword. Afat conjured a magic shield to protect herself, but the magic sword cut right through it. Afat ducked to save her head and the sword only sliced her arm. Afat quickly flew upwards and fled the battlefield. Nazuk Soft-eye saw all this from afar, but thought it would be useless to confront Bilour who had the magic forces of the Tilism of Mirrors supporting her. She too fled from the scene. The sahir armies were alarmed by their commander's desertion and there was a stampede on the battlefield as the soldiers attempted to escape. Bilour read an incantation and the crystal warriors shrunk to their miniature size and marched back into the box. She then released the prince from his magical shackles.

On seeing this, Laqa ordered his soldiers to stop Bilour from rescuing Iraj, but they were too busy defending themselves from Hamza's men to carry out his instructions. Bilour held Iraj by the waist and whisked him out of sight. She called out, 'O sardars of Islam, do not worry about the prince's safety. I am his friend and am taking him away!' Hoor and her other companions followed the princess with the box that contained the magic warriors. The drums of peace were struck and the sardars of Islam picked up their dead and returned to their camp. After burying the dead soldiers with full honours, they went to the durbar and related the events of the day to the Shah. Everyone was happy about the prince's rescue from certain death and enjoyed a feast in celebration.

Ayeenadar kidnaps Bilour

Meanwhile, Bilour did not return to the Tilism of Mirrors but descended into a lush valley in Mount Agate. Hoor and her other companions who joined her there suggested that they rest in the valley and discuss a plan of action as the princess had revived Iraj by then. Hoor asked her, 'Well, huzoor, where do we go now?' Bilour looked worried and said, 'What can I say? I cannot return to Tilism of Mirrors for Afat was injured and will give my secret away. My mother is bound to punish me!' Hoor murmured that she too was afraid to returning to Tilism. The prince looked at Bilour and her companions and said, 'Princess, what are you talking about? You cannot return to Tilism of Mirrors now! Come with me to my camp and Emir will be delighted to receive you. Besides that, you are battle weary and need rest.' Hoor added, 'Huzoor, the prince is right. Let us go with him to the Islamic lashkar before there is trouble!' The princess then opened the hundred-yard box. When all the Tilismi warriors emerged from the box, she ordered them to return to Tilism of Mirrors on their own.

Later, Bilour and Iraj proceeded to the Islamic camp on her flying throne, with her handmaidens following her. The entourage entered Hamza's camp in all glory and reached Iraj's pavilion. His mother, Princess Gaiti Afroze, Qasim's mother, Princess Khurshid, Alamshah's mother, Princess Rabia, and Emir Hamza's wives and daughters had gathered to receive them. As the princess descended from her throne, they welcomed her affectionately.

A herald called out that Emir Hamza was coming to meet his daughter-in-law. Princess Bilour suddenly felt very shy and pulled the veil low over her face. As the Emir entered the pavilion, she bowed and offered him nazrana. The Emir embraced her and gave her a present of a hundred and one sets of diamond jewellery. He said to her, 'My child, I am grateful to God that you have chosen the path of the Provider of the universe. Now recite the Kalma-e-Shahadat and reject the way of evil!'

The princess and her companions then recited the verse sincerely and foreswore the practise of magic. Emir took his leave of the new converts and soon after he left, the royal ladies also returned to their tents. Princess Bilour was seated on a jewel-studded throne in the pavilion with bouquets of flowers arranged all around her, and Emir Hamza had also sent trays of fruit, sweetmeats and food for her. When Prince Iraj heard that she was alone, he joined her for an evening of pleasure.

Meanwhile, the defeated and wounded Afat Jadoo who had fled from the battlefield reached the Tilism of Mirrors. When Ayeena saw her covered in blood with her left arm severed, she cried in alarm, 'Sister, what happened to you?' Afat panted as she said, 'This is all your daughter's doing! Come with me now and I will show you where she is.' Ayeena flew with Afat to Mount Agate and descended on a hill overlooking the Islamic lashkar. Afat transformed into a bird and hovered over Prince Iraj's tent while Ayeena sent a gust of cool magical breeze that made the sentinels and ayyars guarding the tent dazed and blank. The Turkish and African slave-girls appointed to attend to Bilour's also slipped into deep slumber. Ayeena then entered the tent and saw the lovers sleeping in each other's arms. Princess Bilour's chemise had climbed up her waist and it looked as if the sun and moon were lying together in one bed.

Ayeena was enraged by this sight and roughly pulled the princess out of her bed. Bilour opened her eyes and saw that she was in the clutches of the angel of death. She called out, 'Farewell my prince! Your handmaiden will be sacrificed in your honour today!' The prince awoke with a start and on seeing her captive, picked up the magic sword lying on the couch. Afat Jadoo, who was seething with resentment against the prince, could wait no longer and after transforming back into her real self, rushed into the tent crying, 'Where do you think you are going?' The prince struck a hard blow on her in his fury. Afat tried to shield herself magically, but could not recall any spells and Iraj's sword fell on her head and sliced her body in two. There was a tremendous din as her magical spirits wailed her death and sheets of flames and stones fell in the ensuing darkness. Ayeena Jadoo took advantage of this chaos and flew away with her captive daughter.

Iraj wept in despair when he realized that Bilour had been kidnapped and thought of going to Mount Nargis to enlist Hanzal and Sanobar's help to reach the Tilism of Mirrors. Sanobar, who had been searching for Iraj, saw him riding towards her garden in the mountains and rushed to his side. Together, they returned to her aunt Hanzal who welcomed the prince and enquired, 'Huzoor, where were you?' The prince related all that had happened and confessed his love for Bilour Jadoo. He declared, 'I will not rest until I destroy Tilism of Mirrors!' Hanzal looked thoughtful and replied, 'Huzoor, I am not privy to the secrets of that Tilism but am ready to give up my life for you!' Iraj said, 'Just show me the way and leave it to me. I do not need help as my Provider will be with me!'

Hanzal then decided to lead the prince and the ayyar Shahpur declared, 'Prince, I will also go with you!' Shahpur informed the prince's father Qasim of the prince's plans and Qasim ordered his ayyar Sayyara to accompany Iraj and Shahpur. Hanzal handed over the charge of her fort to her niece Sanobar and left with the prince and the ayyars on a magic throne. She flew over vast plains and deserts until they reached a mountain range. There, she said, 'Huzoor, the borders of Tilism of Mirrors lie in these mountains, but I cannot cross them.' Iraj told her to stay there with the tricksters and set off across the mountains himself.

In the Tilism of Mirrors, Ayeena Jadoo slapped her daughter Bilour hard across the cheeks. 'Shameless hussy, did you have to find a Muslim lover? May you live the life of a dog and may Samri destroy you! What have you done? You have cut off our nose before our very family!' After abusing her for some time, Ayeena dragged Bilour to a pavilion in a beautiful garden behind the palace. She made her sit on a golden throne and tied her legs to the throne with gold chains. She magically summoned a lion from the wilderness, tied him to the throne with a chain and ordered, 'Lion, if anyone approaches this woman without my permission, you can kill and eat him. Guard her well for she is a traitor!'

After assigning a few handmaidens to attend to the princess's needs, Ayeenadar wrote a letter to her sister Sholadar who lived in Tilism-e-Nur Afshan. The letter read, 'My sister Sholadar, there is trouble between us and the Muslims here. Your niece Bilour is in love with a Muslim by the name of Iraj. I have confined her to the palace for now, but I know that her lover is planning to conquer my Tilism. There will be a mammoth battle. You must come here at once to help me.'

Burran and Iraj

Princess Burran Sword-woman had been arranging a grand welcome for Amar in the Palace of Seven Hues in Tilism-e-Nur Afshan. The nazims of the Tilism had begun gathering outside the Fort of Seven Hues and there was a flurry of activity inside the fort too.

In another part of the Tilism, Sholadar received her sister's message and was very perturbed. She thought, 'I should inform Princess Burran for she is preparing to honour this Muslim trickster. Perhaps she can intervene and save my sister's Tilism from destruction.' She went to meet Burran Sword-woman and with folded hands made an appeal: 'I have just received this letter from my sister. The Muslims are threatening to destroy her Tilism. Huzoor, if you send them a message, they might hold back. Please also give me leave to go to my sister.' Burran smiled and declared, 'Foolish one, we are now allied with the Muslims even if they destroy our Tilism. Go now to the keeper of the keystone and make sure that Iraj, the Tilism Kusha of Mirrors gets it. Tell Ayeenadar that this is a direct order from us. She should not dare to disobey or she will be punished!'

Sholadar was shocked at Burran's words and pleaded, 'Huzoor, please do not get angry. I will convey your orders to my sister.' Sholadar returned to her home and left for the Tilism of Mirrors with a few attendants. After she left, Burran realized that as a gesture of goodwill towards Amar, she could hand over the magic keystone of the Tilism of Mirrors to the prince herself. However, she knew Sholadar would warn her sister and anticipated some resistance from Ayeena, who was close to Afrasiyab. She knew that Ayeena would not part willingly with the keystone.

She prepared to leave at once to capture the keystone. Just before leaving, she realized she did not know what Iraj looked like. So, she sent for the master of the archives to find a portrait of the noble Iraj. When the portrait was shown to her, the princess was as silent as an image. The prince's face was etched in her heart and she was overwhelmed by her feelings for him. After seeing Iraj's portrait, Burran prepared for her journey as if in a daze and left with just one attendant. She flew to the Plains of the Tilism of Mirrors and sent her attendant to summon Mukhtar Jadoo, the keeper of the magic keystone. Mukhtar had great respect for Princess Burran and quickly arranged to meet her. She took several trays heaped with jewels as offerings for the princess and left with a few attendants for the Plains. Once in the Plains, she saw the princess who was resplendent on her throne under the shade of a tree. It seemed as if an unexpected spring had come to the wilderness.

Mukhtar greeted her deferentially and said, 'Huzoor, your presence has converted this wilderness of thorns into a garden of blossoms; but why did you not grace your devoted handmaiden's poor dwelling?' Burran replied, 'I did not come to your house for Ayeenadar would then have been alerted to my presence and I wish to punish her. I have come to get the keystone from you.' Mukhtar was happy to hear these words because Ayeenadar was a haughty ruler and had treated her contemptuously. She eagerly said, 'Huzoor, the keystone is yours. I wear it around my neck all the time, in case Ayeena is tempted to steal it!' Mukhtar took off the keystone and offered it to Burran along with the trays of jewels that she had carried for the princess.

Burran Sword-woman accepted the keystone, placed her hand on the trays and graciously returned the tribute. After Mukhtar left, she took out the magic Pearl of Samri and sliced slivers off it with her knife. The slivers coalesced together to form a slave-boy. Burran asked the slave-boy, 'Where can I find Iraj, Tilism Kusha?' The slave-boy replied, 'Huzoor, may God keep you safe, the prince is crossing a mountain at the border of Tilism of Mirrors.'

At that moment, Iraj was actually walking through a gorge as dark as the night. He recited the many names of Allah as he bravely continued walking. Suddenly, the darkness dispersed and revealed a lush dell full of blossoms. The prince relaxed in the beauty of the dell and saw a wall made of rubies. The noble Iraj was irresistibly drawn to the wall and went closer to it. He saw that all the trees and vegetation adjoining the wall were bathed in its rosy light. He was gazing at the wall in wonder when there was a sharp sound and a doorway emerged in the wall before him. The prince walked through the arch into a luxurious house. There, he beheld a beautiful maiden with a face that shone like the sun. The maiden sat reclining on a jewel-studded throne.

The prince was overwhelmed by the sight of that vision of loveliness but composed himself. The maiden was none other than Princess Burran who had conjured the ruby wall to attract the prince's attention. As she looked at his handsome face, Burran was quite overcome and swooned with love. Her handmaidens sprinkled rosewater on her to revive her and she ordered one of them, 'Go and ask that man who he is and where has he come from.'

The attendant greeted Iraj respectfully and conveyed Burran's message to him. Iraj sighed and replied, 'Tell your mistress that once I was the prince among princes, but now I am a poor weary traveller who seeks a path in this wilderness. Alas, I am the grandson of Hamza, abandoned and forlorn with only the True God with me!' The handmaiden giggled and said, 'Mian, you have made such a long speech that I can barely remember it. However, I will convey whatever I can to my mistress!' She returned to the princes and said, 'My princess, he has related such a sad, convoluted story about himself that I could hardly understand him!'

The princess said, 'Summon him here then.' The handmaiden led Iraj to Burran who imperiously said to him, 'Sit down and state your purpose.' Iraj boldly sat down next to her. Burran felt as if her heart would burst with joy and asked Iraj shyly, 'What is your will?' The prince said, 'As God is my witness, I am stricken with love!' Burran playfully retorted, 'Then God protect me from your shadow. Stay away from me!' Iraj sighed, edged closer to her and whispered, 'Princess, even my shadow runs from me in this condition.' Burran said, 'Sahib, be still! It does not behove you to sound so defeated. I confess that I too am in love with you. There is no need for you to demonstrate your love for me. Your sighs tear at my heart.' Iraj whispered, 'At least you are being merciful.' Burran remained silent and the prince restrained his ardour.

Burran poured a goblet of wine and offered it to Iraj, who asked her, 'You who have robbed me of my senses, to which faith do you belong?' Burran laughed and said, 'Pray do not worry, I am an ally of Amar; he is in my house even now. Consider me one who is a believer and drink this wine without fear.' The prince's face glowed with relief. He accepted the goblet happily and the night of pleasure passed by too soon. The prince sat close to that moon of loveliness, Burran, and kissed her softly. At dawn, Burran's eyes filled with tears and her sighs sounded like the morning breeze. The prince too looked sad. Burran whispered, 'Young man, speak to no one about my secret. I am the daughter of Kaukab the Enlightened, ruler of Tilism-e-Nur Afshan. I came here to give you the keystone, but instead seem to have been caught in the coils of true love. Here is the keystone. Return to your camp as soon as you conquer the

Tilism of Mirrors. If my father and Amar remain friends, we might meet again, otherwise, heaven knows what will become of our love!'

The princess sobbed as she left Iraj behind and climbed on to her flying throne. She remained disconsolate throughout the journey back to her Tilism. Once there, she managed to compose herself to receive Amar.

Iraj and the keystone

With the keystone in his possession, Iraj moved on confidently. However, he had only travelled a short distance when the sun began to bear down on him and he felt stricken by pangs of love. He sat down listlessly and stayed that way until the afternoon passed by. Eventually, he forced himself to continue with his journey.

A curious thing happened when Iraj got the keystone. The ayyars Shahpur and Sayyara who were still waiting by the mountain that led into the Tilism of Mirrors abruptly turned to Hanzal and said, 'We are going to enter Tilism. The prince is Tilism Kusha so why should we be afraid?' Hanzal declared, 'I will also come with you!' Thus, she entered the ravine with the ayyars and after some time, they reached the place where the prince and princess had met. They saw wilted garlands, wine bottles and goblets that lay upturned on the grass as if they had lowered their heads to recall the gathering of pleasure. Hanzal took a pinch of the dust and sniffed it. She said happily, 'I can make out that the blessed feet of the prince have walked in this place!' She then conjured a travelling throne and sat on it with the ayyars to look for the prince. Presently, they heard a plaintive voice and saw the prince spouting verses of love. Hanzal and the tricksters quickly descended and greeted him.

When they asked him if he was well, Iraj sighed, 'I am in a state of enchantment, but I have obtained the keystone with the blessings of the Provider. Kaukab's daughter sent it for me as Amar is now their ally.' He related the information Burran had given to him but did not reveal that she had come in person to deliver the keystone and that he had fallen in love with her. Hanzal was happy to hear this and thought, 'These people have really got good fortune. Indeed, they will defeat the King of Magic as well!'

Ayeenadar on the warpath

Now hear this. Until Burran Sword-woman was in the Plains of the Tilism of Mirrors, the keepers of the Plains were under her spell. After her departure, they could not approach the prince because the power of the magic keystone protected him. Instead, they went to report the prince's entry in the Tilism to Malika Ayeenadar. They performed a mujra greeting and deferentially informed her, 'O mighty badshah, Tilism Kusha has entered Tilism of Mirrors. We went through a strange experience and lost our magical powers briefly. For a while, all we could see was an unending ruby wall and after it vanished, there was darkness. Today, our powers were restored partially, but we could not arrest Tilism Kusha as he has the magic keystone!'

Ayeena's heart sank when she heard this. Just as she was wondering what to do next, her sister Sholadar arrived from Tilism-e-Nur Afshan. Ayeena briefed her on what had occurred and then asked her, 'What is the news of Princess Burran Sword-woman?' Sholadar replied, 'You ask me about Burran? Well, she has joined the Muslims. Amar ayyar is in her realm and she has summoned the nazims of Tilism to receive him. Everyone is preparing for his visit. I showed her your letter and she ordered me to give the keystone of the Tilism of Mirrors to Iraj.'

Ayeena was even more distraught when she heard this and cried, 'It seems that the princess has already given the keystone to Iraj! The keepers of the Plains also confirm this. Sister, please go to Mukhtar and secure her loyalty! I will be busy mobilizing the resistance against Tilism Kusha.' Sholadar went to Mukhtar Jadoo's house and was received warmly there. Mukhtar knew all about Amar and Burran but heard her friend out attentively. When Sholadar had stopped speaking, Mukhtar said, 'Sister Sholadar, you and I have to ally with Tilism Kusha; the reason being that these Muslims are men of honour. Moreover, an enlightened ruler like Kaukab has become their ally! Do you think Tilism of Mirrors can survive now?'

Sholadar looked worried and said, 'Ayeena will kill me!' Mukhtar said to her, 'Now that the keystone is with Tilism Kusha, what can she do? Yes, if she appeals to Afrasiyab and if he comes to fight personally, maybe then she can put up some resistance! Sister, I am only concerned about your welfare. If you want to save your life and your property, then come with me. You know I have always been on Kaukab's side. If he allies with someone then I will also be with them!'

Sholadar was convinced by Mukhtar's argument and agreed with her. Mukhtar said to her, 'Let us now seek out Tilism Kusha for once the keystone begins to guide him, he will come here to seek me and we might be killed!' She told her servants to remain vigilant and left with Sholadar in the direction of the magic plains, carrying trays of jewels and gold coins. They travelled in the plains for a while before they saw the prince and his companions sitting under a tree. As they approached them, Hanzal saw the two sahiras and warned the prince to stay back. She went forward and flung a magic citron in their direction. Mukhtar waved her hand magically to make the citron fall on the ground. She cried, 'We are not your enemies but Princess Burran's friends!'

The prince signalled to Hanzal to stop attacking them and stepped forward. Mukhtar ran towards him and placed her head at his feet. He smiled and embraced her before greeting Sholadar who also pledged her allegiance to him. The keeper of the keystone, Mukhtar, now asked the prince, 'Huzoor why the delay in vanquishing Tilism? Although the sky cannot cloud the mirror of your good fortune, the enemy should not be given a reprieve!'

The prince then purified himself and looked into the keystone but no words appeared in it. When this happened, Iraj thought that perhaps he was not Tilism Kusha after all and decided to pray for guidance. He was about to perform his prayers when another thought nudged his mind, 'If I had not been Tilism Kusha, I would not have received these things so easily. I would not have obtained the keystone or the magic sword. A princess of the realm would not have fallen in love with me. These events should be regarded as heavenly signs!'

Mukhtar Jadoo saw him struggling with these thoughts and asked what troubled him. When the prince told her that the keystone was blank, she said, 'Huzoor, these Tilisms are complex creations. The secret of the keystone is in a fish that swims in a river flowing towards the west. If you dip the keystone in the river, the fish will leap out. It has to be sliced in half just as it emerges and its blood will purify the keystone, after which it will produce words. Your handmaiden knows this because I was the keeper of the keystone. You will have to leave at once for the river!'

Iraj was grateful for her advice and left for the river alone. The two ayyars followed him secretly and the sahir party left on flying thrones. Iraj enjoyed his journey across many mountains and lakes before he reached an immense river. He had barely reached it when the ayyars and the sahiras arrived as well. Mukhtar Jadoo said, 'Huzoor, Ayeena Jadoo will reach this place anytime now. The ayyars will roam around this area in disguise and will come to your aid if you are in trouble. Sholadar, Hanzal and I will be safe within a magic circle that Shah Kaukab taught me to conjure in case I lost the keystone. I will appear once you have vanquished Tilism of Mirrors.'

Meanwhile, Ayeenadar had consulted her book of prophecy, which showed her that the prince was journeying to the West River and that

Sholadar and Mukhtar had joined him. She rose from her seat in great fury and flew towards the river like a storm unleashed. The prince was about to dip the keystone in the river when the earth shook with the sound of booming kettledrums, and the army of Ayeenadar moved in the sky like a river of iron. Iraj looked up and saw that Ayeenadar had arrived on her throne, dressed in royal robes and wearing her crown, with an army of three lakh sahir soldiers armed with magical weapons.

Ayeena Jadoo approached the prince with folded hands and said, 'O Prince of the World, why do you need to destroy my Tilism? Do not summon the fish and regard me as your handmaiden. I have released Princess Bilour as well. Come to my fort so that we can solemnize your marriage to her.' The prince thought to himself that if the ruler had surrendered, there was no point in destroying her Tilism. He was about to go with Ayeena when his tricksters, who had moved closer to the prince when they saw the army, called out, 'O Noble Prince, if she had truly come to surrender, she would not have brought her army. It looks like she is deceiving you. If she had released Bilour, why did she not bring her along? Tell her that you will accompany her only after you have purified the keystone!'

The prince returned to his senses when he heard this and questioned Ayeena as the ayyars had suggested. Ayeena realized that her deception had not worked and ordered her troops to arrest the prince. As the army moved forward to capture him, Iraj quickly dipped the keystone in the river. Almost immediately, there was a commotion in the water and thousands of magic archers carrying bows and arrows emerged from the river. They began shooting rapidly at the advancing army and killed many sahir soldiers. While the archers held back Ayeena's soldiers, a large fish leapt out of the water and landed before Iraj, who promptly sliced it in half. He then washed the keystone in the stream of blood that flowed out of it. The keystone began glowing with the light of the full moon and words appeared on its surface. As soon as that happened, the magic archers sank back into the river. Iraj looked at the keystone for help and it advised him to recite the moon incantation. When the prince recited the incantation, the river's waves surged out and drowned hundreds of sahir soldiers.

The surviving soldiers flew upwards and began attacking the prince from the skies, but their magical weapons were ineffective against him because the power of the keystone protected him. Iraj recited the moon incantation again and this time, parizads in white jewel-embroidered robes rose from the water and flew up to the skies. They held out magic mirrors to the flying sahirs who froze when they saw their reflections and dropped unconscious into the river. Ayeenadar was now terrified and fled with her diminished army scurrying behind her.

The prince saw that the parizads had vanished into the river and looked at the keystone again. It advised him, 'Recite the incantation once again and invoke blessings on the Prophet Mohammad, Peace be upon Him. A boat, as bright as the new moon, will emerge from the river. Get on to the boat without fear and it will take you across the river. Consult the keystone once you are on the far shore. Remain alert for every blossom in this place is like a thorn for you, every garden nurtures a snake, and a friend can be the enemy!'

The prince recited the incantation and climbed confidently on to the crescent-shaped boat. It took him across the river in no time, where the prince consulted the keystone again. It read, 'O Victor of Tilisms, rest for a while and then walk towards that far mountain where you will see a gigantic python. Recite the magic words that I will teach you and witness the miracle of God.'

The prince waited on the shore till the hour of the moon had passed and the hour of Saturn began. He then began walking towards the mountain that soared into the sky and recited the magical words to the giant python he encountered there. An old man walked out of the mountain and cried, 'O Magic Python, this is indeed Tilism Kusha; we must ally with him!' He said to the prince, 'Sheheryar, I will be your obedient servant provided you give the keystone to me!' The prince looked at the keystone that warned him against trusting the old man and advised him to order the old man to kill the python first. The prince said, 'O Holy Man, if you want to join me, then you must first kill the python for he is the enemy of man. If you can do this, I will hand the keystone over to you!'

The old man clambered up the mountain and lifted a heavy stone that he flung at the python. The python's head was smashed to smithereens and darkness descended on the mountainside. When it became light again, the old man came down the mountain and again asked for the keystone. Meanwhile, the keystone had already told the prince what to say in response. Iraj said, 'I will give it willingly to you, but you will need to jump over the python's body and accompany me to the river. The reason is that one must jump over the enemy's body to dispel bad luck and purify oneself in the river to receive the blessed keystone.'

The old man leaped over the python and went to the river with the prince who asked him to dive in. When he emerged from the river, the old man felt a great itch all over his body and began rolling on the ground to alleviate his discomfort. Within moments, he transformed into a magnificent stallion. The prince, still following the keystone's directions, found a saddle and bridle hanging on a tree nearby with which he tried to harness the stallion. The animal resisted him fiercely and the prince succeeded in subduing it only after whacking him hard with his fists. At that time, an old woman dressed in black materialized before him. Her head was shaking with age and her cheeks sagged like cotton wool. She leaned heavily on a walking stick and cried, 'My son, is this how you punish one who did you a service?'

The prince consulted the keystone and said, 'At times you have to beat up a donkey to transform him into a horse! But do not despair, once I reach yonder garden, I will transform him back into a man!' Iraj mounted the stallion and lashed him a couple of times to get him moving towards the garden. The old woman hobbled behind him. After some time, the prince saw a garden enclosed within emerald walls with a beautifully carved emerald arch over a locked doorway. He consulted the keystone and harshly called out to the horse, 'Listen, old man, if you want to become human again then fly into this garden! If you try any tricks, I will kill you!' The horse sprouted wings and flew into the garden. The moment he landed there, there was a loud blast and the doorway began falling apart. The prince managed to leap out of harm's way, but the doorway crashed on the horse. Iraj removed the rubble and was distressed to see that the horse had died.

The keystone reassured him that the horse was still alive and was just pretending to be dead. The prince stroked him and murmured, 'If you really want to die I can kill you right now!' The horse reared up at once and this time, the prince fed him fruit from the garden and led him to a water channel. Later, he tied the horse to a tree and walked to the marble pavilion in the centre of the garden. The old woman who had reached the garden by this time began to shout, 'Come and see, there is a thief in the garden!' The prince saw a contingent of armed sahirs, led by a dark sahir, riding towards the garden. He quickly looked at the keystone, which urged him to kill the sahir before he entered the garden. Iraj ran out of the garden as instructed and fitted an arrow into his bow. When the sahir came closer to him, he called out, 'Wait, you black-faced stubborn one!'

On hearing this, the dark sahir lifted his trident to attack Iraj, but the prince's arrow pierced his heart and he fell from his horse. The rest of his army now attacked the prince ferociously. He fought back valiantly and continued fighting until evening, when he consulted the keystone. It read, 'You left the garden when Jupiter was in the ascendant and you were fighting during the time of Mars, the ruler of war and strife. Go back into the garden because you will soon become invisible to these soldiers. They will begin fighting with each other. Your adventures in this place commenced in the hour of the moon and will end in the hour of sun.' As instructed, the prince fought his way out of the army and slipped unseen into the garden.

Iraj spent the remainder of the night in the worship of the Creator. After performing his dawn prayer, he left the garden to find that most of the soldiers had slaughtered each other. The few who had survived fled when he attacked them. The old woman and the horse had also disappeared. The prince looked at the keystone for guidance again and it revealed, 'The span of Mars is followed by the span of the Sun. Rest during this time and when the period of Venus begins, sit under a tree and recite these magical words that will ensure your control over the spirits of Venus. They will bring you magical garments and weapons. You have to face the badshah of Tilism of Mirrors now and these items will grant you victory over her!'

This humble scribe will now leave the prince in the auspicious period of Venus and relate the story of the triumphant army of Hamza the auspicious and Laqa, the misleading one.

Nazuk Soft-eye declares battle

After Afat Jadoo's death, Nazuk Soft-eye had promised her army that she would wreak vengeance on the Islamic army for her friend's death, but did not appear to be in much of a hurry to do so. One day, in Laqa's durbar, Shaitan Bakhtiarak tried to provoke her into declaring battle and said, 'Malika, ever since you arrived, Sofar also stopped fighting and Afrasiyab has sent no one to help us either!' Nazuk retorted sharply, 'Malik-ji, if I am in your way then order whoever suits you to fight for you. I will leave for Tilism at once!' Laqa stepped in to soothe the irate sahira, 'O mortal woman, do not pay any heed to Shaitan. He is merely teasing you!'

Nazuk genuflected before Laqa and requested him to strike the battle drums in her name. The sounds reached the exalted Islamic camp and they, in turn, struck the Naqara of Alexander. The brave ones spent that night servicing and preparing their weapons. After the early morning prayers, Emir reached the royal pavilion. As the Shah entered, everyone bowed low in mujra greeting and escorted him to the battleground.

As soon as they reached there, lightning bolts flashed in dark clouds that spread over the arena. Large, black battle flags fluttered into sight and the sahir army settled into battle formations. Laqa was visible on his elephant mount, surrounded by thousands of wicked sahirs. Nazuk Soft-eye appeared and Prince Alamshah went forward to confront her. She called out in a hypnotic, magical voice, 'Prince, why do you confront me? Go and worship your true god and do not be misled by Hamza!' Prince Alamshah became dazed when he heard these words and went straight towards Laqa to worship him. Several other sardars tried to pull him back, but they too were mesmerized by Nazuk Soft-eye.

Realizing that Nazuk Soft-eye was playing tricks, Alamshah's father Emir Hamza went forward to confront the sahira himself, but there was a sudden flash of lightning in the sky and darkness descended on both armies, blinding everyone. When people regained their sight, the Emir was nowhere in sight. The Islamic warriors thought that Nazuk Soft-eye had abducted him, but realized that was not the case when she called out angrily, 'O Muslims, have you also employed sahirs to save you in dire conditions? Emir Hamza cannot hide from me forever!' The sardars replied, 'Listen, you evil witch! We do not believe in such devious tactics! It is devil worshippers like you that resort to deception and trickery!'

Nazuk Soft-eye was enraged at these words and tossed a magic citron at the sky. It split open and released thick smoke that engulfed the Islamic lashkar. She then conjured a cloud that exploded and rained iron balls and stones over her enemies. This led to pandemonium in the ranks of the Islamic army that did not cease until that evening, when Nazuk Soft-eye dispelled the war clouds and light returned to the battlefield. Before striking the drums of peace, she called out, 'O rebellious mortals, have you seen how the might of Khudawand Laqa transformed day into night? If you do not submit to him now you will see the black day!'

The Shah of the Islamic lashkar looked around and saw thousands of dead bodies and several thousands of his men lying wounded on the battlefield. Many horses and camels had also become casualties of the relentless bombing from the magic cloud. The Shah's eyes welled up with tears and he looked around for Ashqar Devzad, Emir Hamza's horse from Koh Qaf, the land of fairies, but could not see him. He assumed that the horse had escaped into the desert when his master was abducted. He turned his attention to the burial of the dead and supervised the arrangements himself.

In Laqa's durbar, Shaitan Bakhtiarak looked towards Nazuk Soft-eye and began weeping. Alarmed by his behaviour, she asked him, 'Malik-ji, is all well with you?' He replied, 'I weep for you! Alas, your beautiful face will be covered in dust and the flames of a funeral pyre will consume your body! Malika, the day these Muslims are defeated, the next day, the sky blesses them with divine rain and the earth creates new defences for them. You should not have spared Shah of Islam yesterday! Now, whoever has picked up Emir will bring him back honourably. One of his sons or grandsons will turn up and defeat us. We will have to flee and Khudawand will be humiliated!' Nazuk Soft-eye cackled derisively when Shaitan said this and replied, 'Malik-ji, who can kill me in this world? My end is not destined at the hands of a Muslim and I can execute Shah at any time! Very well, for your sake I will destroy them tomorrow. Just strike the battle drums in my name!'

The next morning, the remaining sardars arrived, ready for battle, at the royal pavilion. The Shah had not retired to his bedchamber the previous night. After the sardars performed a mujra greeting, he mounted his horse and left for the battlefield to the sound of kettledrums and bugles. Nazuk Soft-eye also appeared in the sky and descended on the arena. She prostrated before Laqa and sought his permission to begin battle. The Shah wanted to respond to her challenge, but the noble badshah from Hind, Landhoor bin Sadaan, moved forward on his elephant mount and sought permission from the Shah to confront the sahira. His elephant swayed like the meeting of two lovers and he swung his mace as he called out, 'O shameless one, attack with any weapon you please!'

Nazuk Soft-eye flung some grains of lentils in the air and the battlefield was plunged into darkness. Now, only Landhoor and she could see each other. He swung his mace to attack her, but she chanted an incantation that rendered him unconscious. She handed him over to her soldiers, dispelled the darkness and challenged the Shah again. Several sardars confronted the witch, but one by one, all of them were arrested. Shaitan Bakhtiarak was getting restless and impatient with the slow pace of the battle and sent a message to Nazuk claiming that Laqa wanted her to destroy the Muslims quickly.

Nazuk Soft-eye read the message and decided to speed up matters by conjuring the magical darkness again. This time, however, the Islamic lashkar managed to attack Laqa's forces and a river of iron flowed from both sides. The Shah was also on the battleground and killed hundreds of enemies before he succumbed to Nazuk's magic and fell unconscious. The noble sardars who were around him became unconscious as well and there was a stampede as the soldiers tried to flee from the magic cloud. The Islamic lashkar was grief-stricken, while the sahir army was celebrating. We will leave them here and turn to the experiences of the victorious Prince Iraj, who spent the night in the garden reciting magical words as instructed by the keystone.

Iraj and Hamza

Several fearsome apparitions of gigantic dragons and raging rivers materialized before Iraj, but he continued reciting the incantations fearlessly. When he had uttered the last magical word, two *saqqas* holding jewel-inlaid pitchers and crystal bowls arrived and asked the prince to purify himself. The prince consulted the keystone and then told them to bring him the magical armour and garments of Tilism. They vanished from sight and returned moments later with the magical items. As instructed by the keystone, the prince wore the garments and the armour, and then asked the saqqas to summon Rangeen Jadoo, the keeper of the enchanted garden.

The men vanished and reappeared with a sahir. The prince raised his sword to execute Rangeen Jadoo just as the keystone asked him to. However, Rangeen Jadoo cried, 'O Tilism Kusha, I knew this day would come when you would want to execute me. For this reason, I kidnapped your grandfather from the battlefield. If you release me, I can take you to him!' The keystone confirmed that the sahir's claims were true and urged the prince to go with him. Rangeen Jadoo led the prince to a hujra at the far end of the garden. The prince walked into the hujra and saw Emir Hamza sitting on a throne. The prince rushed forward and placed his head at the Emir's feet. The Emir embraced him and asked, 'My son, have you discovered the whereabouts of your father Qasim?' Iraj replied that his father was safe in Mount Nargis and went on to relate his recent adventures to the Emir.

Emir Hamza and Iraj then emerged from the hujra and the prince looked at the keystone for further instructions. It read, 'Tell the sahir to take you to the Tilismi army.' The prince requested Rangeen Jadoo to take them to the Tilismi army, and the Emir and prince were led through a doorway at the back of the garden to another hujra that stood in a hilly area. Rangeen opened the lock and took out the same trunk that Princess Bilour had carried to Mount Agate. When he opened the box, forty thousand crystal figurines mounted on miniature crystal horses spilled out of it and became life-sized warriors on magnificent steeds. The sahir also brought horses for the Emir and prince, both of who mounted them and left with the Tilismi army in great splendour.

The final battle for the Tilism of Mirrors

Meanwhile, Ayeena Jadoo was smarting from her defeat at Iraj's hands. She summoned her commanders and declared, 'I will have to fight Tilism Kusha once again. Those of you who are prepared to lose your lives, come with me, and those who want to remain safe, should leave me now!' Her commanders pledged loyalty until death and mobilized an army of three lakh men. Ayeena Jadoo emerged from her fort on her magic dragon and had just travelled a short distance when she came face to face with Iraj, who was leading the Tilismi army. Iraj ordered the magic warriors to attack Ayeena's army without any delay. Rangeen Jadoo protected Emir Hamza while Iraj was impervious to magical attacks due to the power of the keystone. Thus, the crystal warriors caused havoc in Ayeena's army. Ayeena, in turn, fought ferociously and incinerated hundreds of crystal warriors by conjuring sheets of flames. Her tridents pierced through their hearts and rivers of blood flowed. The prince glanced down at the keystone that revealed these words: 'Unless you kill Ayeenadar, you will not be victorious. Flash the keystone in her eyes to blind her with its rays and aim for her head to kill her. If she survives, she will be a nuisance!'

The prince continued fighting and kept moving close to Ayeena. When he was close enough, he jumped off his horse. Ayeena saw his horse without a rider and shouted in triumph, 'O brave ones, Tilim Kusha has fallen down from his mount. Behead him quickly and seize the keystone!' She happily jumped off her dragon and ran towards Iraj's horse when the prince suddenly appeared and blinded her with the keystone. Ayeena's eyes closed and her mind went blank. In a moment, the prince jumped and struck such a hard blow with his sword that it went right through her skull and sliced her body in two.

There were deafening sounds as if mountains were crumbling and huge craters appeared in the ground. The streams and rivers of Mirrors boiled and dried up while hurricanes and gales swept through the land. After a long time, a voice called out, 'Alas, you have killed me; my name was Ayeena Jadoo!' This caused pandemonium in the sahir army and eventually, they raised the flag of peace. Iraj stopped fighting as sahir commanders approached him and kissed his saddle to pledge their allegiance to him. Iraj bestowed honours on each one of them. He looked around and saw that the crystal wariors had vanished. It seemed that with the death of the ruler of their Tilism, they too had been destroyed.

As the prince moved forward with the commanders following him, some officials of the Tilism appeared and said, 'Felicitations on vanquishing Tilism of Mirrors. We are the keepers of the treasury. We will lead you to it.' The prince accepted their homage and walked on. At that time, Hanzal and Sholadar along with the ayyars Sayyara, Shahpur and Mukhtar Jadoo walked out of the protective circle. They congratulated him warmly and entered the Fort of Mirrors with him. It was deserted as the populace had fled; its magnificent buildings and shops were empty like the heart of the forlorn lover. The prince went to the royal palace and sat down on the throne of honour. He had heralds announce amnesty for the inhabitants of the city.

Throngs of citizens flocked to the royal palace with offerings for their new ruler. Soon, the temples of Samri and Jamshed were destroyed and replaced with mosques and prayer houses. After he had finished the business of the day, Iraj turned to Hanzal and said, 'There is no sign of Princess Bilour, we must look for her!' The officials of the palace then led the prince to a garden that was in full bloom. A marble pavilion stood in the garden and was covered with long golden curtains with tassels of pure silver thread. The prince walked in and saw that Princess Bilour was tied with gold chains to a throne and a lion stood guarding her. She was murmuring, 'O lion, eat me up for it would be easier to dream of him in the land of finality than grieve for him in this world!'

The prince wept when he heard these words and saw that Bilour's face was scratched, her eyes were sunken and her clothes were covered in dust. He immediately checked the keystone for advice. As instructed, Iraj threw the keystone at the lion and witnessed a miracle of God. When the lion was hit by the keystone, he somersaulted several times and collapsed as his head burst into pieces. The prince unchained Bilour from the throne and held her closely. Both of them wept and related the trials that each had undergone after they had parted. Since they were already married, Iraj spent that night with the princess and tasted the sweet sherbet of intimacy.

The next morning, Iraj surveyed the treasury and found two swords. He read the writing on their hilts and realized that one of the swords was intended to execute Nazuk Soft-eye and the other could kill sahirs anywhere in the world. Iraj took both swords and had all the goods in the treasury, including the horses and tents, loaded on carts. The Emir crowned Bilour the queen of the kingdom of Mirrors, Rangeen Jadoo was given a high office and Sholadar and Mukhtar were appointed as counsellors. Finally, the Emir and prince prepared to leave.

Iraj ordered some men to bring the Emir's horse Ashqar from Mount Agate. It was then that Rangeen Jadoo confessed that Ashqar had gone missing in the wilderness when he had abducted Emir Hamza. The sahir also informed the prince that the Islamic lashkar was in distress. Iraj was alarmed when he heard these details and decided to return to Mount Agate in haste. His father Qasim also left for Mount Agate with an army from Hanzal's kingdom.

The end of Nazuk Soft-eye

Now hear about the followers of Islam: the next morning, Nazuk Soft-eye subjected the Islamic lashkar to more punishment. The sahir army attacked them even as Nazuk's magic smoke blinded the soldiers. Though the ayyars made a valiant effort to defend the army from the pavilion of Solomon that was protected from magic, everyone called out to the Impervious One to help them in this hour of need. Suddenly, a cloud of dust was seen on the horizon and Nazuk Soft-eye stopped fighting abruptly. Bakhtiarak stood up in his *howda* to see the cloud clearly and called out, 'Welcome, welcome! This wretched witch has raised her head too high and does not listen! Send her straight to hell!'

Laqa barked, 'Oye Shaitan! What are you babbling about?' Shaitan replied, 'Run away now! Nazuk Soft-eye's fate has overturned and she is about to die!' The witch glared at him and cried, 'Malik-ji, what nonsense are you spouting?' He wailed, 'Until today, you were alive, but consider yourself a corpse now! If you survive, you need not call me the devil! Their worst hour has passed and their God always helps them!'

Prince Qasim emerged from the dust, flanked by hundreds of soldiers. When Nazuk Soft-eye saw this, she flew up and cried, 'O Qasim, I drove your grandfather out and arrested all the sardars! What harm can you cause me?' Incensed, Qasim aimed a stone at her chest, but it glanced off her body. She then pounced on him in the form of a claw. She left him in her camp and returned to the battlefield, where she proceeded to conjure thick black smoke on his army.

Yet another dust cloud came into view on the horizon and Shaitan called out, 'Malika, look at the message of doom! Your star is on the decline and you will be annihilated soon!' Nazuk Soft-eye said derisively, 'You are the devil and will continue to talk nonsense!' The dust parted as and Prince Iraj cantered towards the battlefield on his magic horse, followed by a vast army. Iraj and his army ploughed through Laqa's forces—their teghas shone in the darkness like stars in the firmament of deep blue and their swords were thirsty for blood. In the heat of the battle, Nazuk Soft-eye fell on Iraj in great fury and aimed a magic citron at him. It split open but could not harm him due to the double power of the keystone and the magic sword he had found in the treasury of Mirrors.

The prince finally drew out the sword that could kill Nazuk and attacked her. Until the last moment, she was was so certain that no ordinary sword could harm her that she bowed down, as if accepting her doom. The prince decapitated her at once and there was a trememdous din as her magic spirits swirled around in fury. The darkness she had conjured vanished after her death, but there was a rain of arrows from the sky and deafening sounds filled the air, almost as if Doomsday had descended on the battlefield.

Shaitan exclaimed, 'Well, well, this is what I would call a job neatly performed. Khudawand, you should now create another destiny for yourself

or you too will suffer the same fate. Your grandson is invincible today!'
Laqa looked distressed and ordered Sofar Jadoo, 'Arrest this impertinent
mortal!' Sofar leapt forward and attacked the prince with magic tridents
and coconuts, but, of course, could not harm him. Instead, Iraj pulled him
off his dragon mount and captured him. Meanwhile, Ashqar Devzad, the
horse from fairyland, galloped in from the desert when he heard Emir
Hamza's thunderous battle call. The magical shackles of the sardars Nazuk
Soft-eye had captured in battle melted after her death. She had also left
only sixty guards to watch over them, convinced of her victory. As the
sardars were all warriors, mightier than the legendary Rustam, they
overcame the guards easily and left for their camp. The army of Islam that
had so far been blinded by the magic smoke woke up and joined the battle.
Seeing the tide turn, Bakhtiarak snapped at his mahout, 'Listen you! Make
this elephant run! Do you want Khudawand to die?'

Thus, Laqa fled from the battle and did not stop until he reached the
safety of Fort Agate. The sardars of Islam, who were pursuing him, drew
back only when the bridge was pulled up from over the moat. After the
Islamic camp had been restored to its former glory, Emir Hamza had Sofar
Jadoo tied to a pillar in the pavilion of Hasham. This treacherous, devious
man signalled his obedience to become a Muslim and recited the verse of
affirmation like a parrot when he was released, but his heart remained
dark and deceitful. Unaware of Sofar's devious designs, Emir Hamza
bestowed a khalat robe upon him and also gave him a seat of honour.

The treachery of Sofar Jadoo

Sofar Jadoo's defeated and diminished army remained in Fort Agate for
several days while the soldiers who had deserted earlier straggled back
home. Sulaiman soothed the disheartened Laqa and wrote a letter to
Afrasiyab, briefing him on what had happened with Afat, Nazuk and
Sofar. He added, 'In case no one comes to his help, Khudawand's wrath
will fall upon you for he is much enraged with us mortals at this time!'
The letter was as usual placed on the mountain and a claw came for it
when the magic drum was struck.

Now hear about Sofar who had deceived everyone by pretending to
convert to Islam. Emir Hamza had given him a high rank, opulent living
quarters and planned to bestow a kingdom on him as soon as the festivities
were over. All this while, Sofar kept a close eye on the badshah of the
lashkar, who was tired as he had not slept for several nights. When he
finally retired to a secluded pavilion to rest, Sofar followed him and cast
a spell that put the Shah and his attendants in a deep sleep. He then flew

off with the Shah towards the desert. He did not want to return to his own camp just yet, as he knew that would be the first place where the ayyars would investigate the Shah's disappearance. So, he hid the Shah in a cave deep within a ravine and returned to his pavilion.

The next morning, Sofar read an incantation to revive the sleeping attendants. As soon as they found the Shah's bed empty, they raised a clamour. There was uproar in the lashkar and loud wailing was heard from the harem. The Emir was distressed beyond measure, the throne of Solomon was empty, and sardars and ayyars wept unashamedly. Emir Hamza composed himself and urged the ayyars to find the Shah as soon as possible. Chalak bin Amar declared, 'Grant me three days and if I do not find him, I will not show my face to you again!' He armed himself with the tools of trickery and set off. Chalak wandered around for a couple of days, but could not find any trace of the Shah and thought, 'I had promised to find him in three days! How can I show my face to Emir now?'

He sat on a rock and kept brooding until he was struck by a sudden thought: 'Sofar is new to our camp and his brow looks dark and suspicious. Perhaps his heart is still loyal to Samri and Jamshed. I should investigate him!' Therefore, Chalak dressed up as a holy man. He wore metal hoops in his ears and on his wrists, twisted his hair into dreadlocks, tied a loincloth around his waist and smeared ash all over his body. He went to Sofar's magnificent pavilion and told a guard to inform Sofar that a holy man from the garden of Samri and Jamshed had come to meet him.

Sofar flushed uneasily when the guard announced this and replied quickly, 'I am a Muslim now! What do I have to do with Samri and Jamshed? Tell him there will be no meeting!' The guard had already turned to go when Sofar changed his mind and said, 'Very well, bring him in. Let us hear what he has to say!' The guard had almost left the tent when Sofar called him back and whispered to him, 'Take the holy man to your tent; I will meet him there!'

After some time, Sofar went to the guard's tent and looked visibly happy to meet the holy man. He said, 'You have honoured me with your visit but I am a Muslim and you should have nothing to do with me!' The holy one smiled knowingly and said, 'I am the custodian of the garden of Jamshed and he often blesses me with his visions. Only yesterday Jamshed revealed to me, "Our special being has converted to Islam but he has not really converted in his heart. He has exalted our faith by abducting the Shah of Islam. Meet this rare mortal of faith and love." O Sofar, I salute you for you are truly steadfast to your faith and a favourite being of Jamshed!'

Sofar was stunned when he heard these words and remained silent. Chalak thought, 'This bastard has really taken the Shah!' He pretended to be offended and cried, 'I will complain to Khudawand Jamshed that you thought I was raving and did not respond to me!' Sofar said softly, 'How can I say anything to you as I know that you have spoken the truth! Khudawand Jamshed indeed knows the hearts of men. This place is crawling with enemies and I cannot openly acknowledge the truth. Anyway, I will do what I have to in this place and you will see how I destroy our enemies.' Chalak whispered conspiratorially, 'It is best you do not say anything. I think it is safer to keep the Shah in the garden of Jamshed. Tell me where you have hidden him and I will take him there.'

Sofar looked around and said in a low voice, 'Very well. The Shah is in a cave located in a ravine. I have blocked the entrance with a large rock.' He then explained in detail the exact location of the cave and added, 'The Shah must have died by now for I had rendered him unconscious with a pinch of magic ash.' Chalak wanted to kill Sofar right then, but restrained himself and said, 'I will go now but do something magical so that the stone moves and I can see the cave.' Sofar read an incantation and assured the holy man that he would find the cave easily.

Sofar returned to his pavilion and Chalak left to locate the cave. He lifted the unconscious Shah and brought him straight to the Emir in the pavilion of Hasham. Emir Hamza said, 'Take him to Solomon's pavilion and I will sprinkle the water of the Great Name to revive him!' Chalak cautioned the Emir that to do so would alert Sofar, and advised him, 'Hide the Shah from sight and call Sofar to this place!' Emir arranged for the Shah to be placed in a box with openings for air and sent a guard to Sofar with the message, 'Emir would like you to stroll with him in the moonlight!'

Sofar promptly presented himself at the pavilion of Hasham where the Emir greeted him cordially. At that time, Chalak walked in, still disguised as the holy man. Sofar looked shocked and tried to flee, but Chalak's snare-rope spun around his neck and Emir recited the Great Name so that Sofar was unable to remember any magic. Chalak pierced his tongue with a needle and tied him to a pillar before he brought the unconscious Shah out of the box and asked Sofar to revive him. Trembling with fear, Sofar revived the Shah with a pinch of the dust of Jamshed. While the Shah was being attended to, Sofar was told that if he was truly repentant, he would be forgiven. Sofar signalled that he would rather die in the name of Jamshed and as a result, he was executed summarily. Darkness fell on the lashkar for a long time after his death.

Later, when everyone had congregated in the durbar, Chalak heard a man wailing. Chalak went out to investigate and saw a sahir who looked badly wounded, howling with grief. Chalak asked, 'Why are you here and for whom do you weep?' The man sobbed, 'I am Nazuk Soft-eye's servant and mourn her death. I am here so that you should execute me as well!' Chalak said, 'You should accept the true faith and your wounds will also heal quickly.' Chalak went on to speak so eloquently in praise of the True Provider that the rust of falsehood melted off the mirror of the man's heart and he asked to meet the Emir.

Chalak took him to the Emir who embraced him affectionately and taught him the Takbeer. The sahir recited the verse and converted to Islam in all sincerity. Emir then sent for the blessed salve of Solomon and applied it on his wounds. The man became Chalak's disciple and, in gratitude, made him an offering of a magic ring. 'I took this off Nazuk Soft-eye's hand as it provides protection against all form of magic.' Chalak accepted the ring and wore it from that day on while the disciple settled into Sofar's former pavilion in comfort.

Now hear about Hoshruba. The survivors of Nazuk Soft-eye's army had returned to report their defeat to Afrasiyab. To add to his woes, a messenger bird brought Hairat's missive to Afrasiyab: 'Shahanshah, we hear that Amar is being given a warm welcome by Kaukab. You should think of executing Asad Lion-heart now for that would dash the hopes of the rebel lashkar. Otherwise, we will face an almighty war!' The King of Magic laughed and declared, 'I do not believe that Kaukab will go against me. However, I will send him a message of peace. He should send Amar back to me with his hands tied or else I will punish him as well!'

Afrasiyab then ordered his scribe to compose the nama. The scribe duly wrote it and presented it to the King of Magic. Afrasiyab stamped his seal on the nama and enclosed it in a gold-embroidered pouch. He summoned a high-ranking sahir and asked him to take the letter to Kaukab with some gifts. When the messenger was about to leave, Afrasiyab said, 'Do not take the route that Amar took for that will delay you. Take the route where molsri trees mark the borders of the two Tilisms and where two puppets sit on a tree. Tell them that you are carrying a message from the King of Magic. They will take you to Kaukab.' The messenger tied the pouch around his waist and left the durbar. We will hear about him later.

Afrasiyab now wrote a letter to Hairat: 'My lady, I have sent a nama to Kaukab. Once I get his response, I will execute Asad. Until then, say this to Mussavir, "Murshidzadeh, how long will you remain in prayer? You must punish these rebels and betrayers of salt!" Malika, I am certain that Murshidzadeh will destroy all the rebels in battle. I will also send other sahirs to assist you soon. Do not lose heart.'

Afrasiyab tied the letter around a magic bird's neck and watched it fly off. Hairat was happy to receive her husband's message and did as he instructed. Let us now witness the meeting between Amar and Burran Sword-woman.

సా

14 AMAR MEETS PRINCESS BURRAN AND KAUKAB REPLIES TO AFRASIYAB'S MESSAGE

The Palace of Seven Hues

Princess Burran returned from the Tilism of Mirrors after she gave the keystone to Iraj. She had the Palace of Seven Hues decorated and waited for Amar by the river. She ordered Vizier Marzan to bring Amar to the palace through the picturesque route along the river and the noble vizier left with a large procession of prominent citizens. Amar was on the roof of the garden pavilion when he saw them arriving. He returned to the baradari and dressed with care to meet Princess Burran. He wore his richest robes embroidered with emerald stars and a crown studded with rubies and pearls; around his neck was a collar of rubies that shone like a thousand moons.

Vizier Marzan entered the garden and approached Amar deferentially. He said, 'The princess is waiting to meet you by the river. Will you grace her garden with the flower of your arrival?' Amar smiled in assent and followed the vizier out of the garden where a bevy of beautiful maidens greeted him. Notables of Tilism-e-Nur Afshan met him warmly and made offerings of precious jewels that Amar generously declined. He was led to a river where jewel-studded boats bobbed on the water. Amar sat on a gilded state barge that moved majestically through the river. The water of the river was so translucent that fish darting through it seemed to be made of quicksilver.

When Amar reached the palace, Princess Burran descended from her throne and walked to the edge of the water. Amar said a prayer in praise of the Lord when he saw this maiden for she had such incomparable beauty that it seemed as if a houri from heaven had come down to the earth. As he stepped out of the barge, the princess bowed her head in greeting. Amar murmured 'My dear daughter!' and embraced her. After the formal salutations, the princess and Amar left for the City of Seven Hues. The gateway into the city had been adorned like the gateway of Rizwan. Hundreds of sahirs bowed to Burran as her entourage entered the gates of the city. What can one say in praise of this city? It seemed as if the Maker had built it with his own hands.

Now listen to this: one Burran was escorting Amar through the city, while the other, real Burran was seated in her palace, watching the procession in a magic mirror. The procession came into the royal palace and Amar saw an edifice that soared to the heavens. Here too Amar was welcomed and offered tributes of gilded trays heaped with gold coins. Amar accepted the offerings and promptly deposited them in Zambil. No one could understand where the coins disappeared near his waist. The reader is reminded that the blessed pouch Zambil was visible only to Amar.

As the procession approached the palace, the real Burran placed the jewel-studded crown of state on her head, held her magic sword and left with a hundred and one trays heaped with treasures as tributes for Amar. At that time, Vizier Marzan said to Amar, 'Princess Burran is approaching, perhaps you will wish to dismount.' Amar was astonished and thought, 'Burran is with me. What is he talking about?' He turned to see that the Burran sitting next to him had vanished and realized that she had been an illusion. As he stepped out of the *hawadar*, the real Burran came out of the palace, surrounded by hundreds of fair-faced maidens. She looked like the full moon and bowed low before Amar, forming the shape of a crescent.

Amar embraced Burran once again and said, 'My daughter, why did you trouble yourself? I was coming to you anyway!' Burran presented trays of gold coins to Amar and he accepted them with a smile. He soon took out a handful of coins from Zambil and showered them on the princess. Burran made a speech in praise of the great trickster, held his hand and led him into the palace. There princesses of the realm and women of high rank greeted him and offered homage. Amar was seated besides Burran, after which he requested her to seat the gathering.

As soon as everyone settled on their chairs, fair-faced saqis appeared in the durbar with jewel-inlaid flasks of wine. The princess filled the goblet with her delicate hands and while offering it to Amar, said, 'This is the wine of friendship. Honour me by accepting it.' Amar declined the wine diplomatically, but Burran whispered, 'You can drink the wine without fear. I am of the faith but cannot reveal it at this time.' Amar then joyously accepted the goblet and drank from it.

The eternal child

Presently, Kaukab's relatives joined this gathering of pleasure. Each one of them greeted Amar and then took their places in the durbar. Amar was struck by the sight of a young girl walking into the durbar amidst a throng of handmaidens. She was like a moon shining within its halo, a jewel sparkling in its setting. She looked like she was about five years old, but even at that young age, she stood out for her beauty and grace. She was dressed in a shimmering kurta of a diaphanous material with loose pyjamas. Her hair was neatly tied in tight plaits, her eyes were lined with kohl that had run down her cheeks and she wore a tiny pearl nose ring. She trotted up to Burran, calling out, 'Mother, mother!'

Burran picked her up, hugged her and said, 'My child, you have not greeted our guest!' The child hopped off Burran's lap, went up to Amar and greeted him prettily, then returned to Burran's lap. After some time, she approached Amar again. He kissed her and took out a handful of jewels from Zambil for her to play with. The child's nose was running and she was about to wipe it with her sleeve when Burran leaned forward and wiped it with a handkerchief. The girl looked up at Amar and lisped, 'Do you think I am greedy for these? My mother has plenty of jewels!'

On hearing these words, Burran looked at her sternly and the child sulked as she hopped back on to Burran's lap. Amar stroked her cheeks and said to Burran, 'Do not scold her. She's just a child!' Burran smiled and said, 'Khwaja, you do not know her. This is Princess Majlis Jadoo, the king's niece. She is a sorceress of exceptional powers and keeps herself permanently at this age through her magic. Her magic weapons are toys and dolls and she insists on calling me mother.'

Amar was amazed by this disclosure. Majlis put her arms around Burran and cried, 'Mother, tell me the truth. Who is our guest?' Burran told her that their guest was the slayer of kafirs and sorcerors, the incomparable Khwaja Amar. Majlis then climbed on to Amar's lap and lisped, 'Khwaja, are you at war with that wretched Afrasiyab?' When Amar nodded, Majlis asked him, 'Did you know my serving maid Junain has run away to Hoshruba?' Amar murmured, 'I believe Afrasiyab has given her a high rank.' Majlis looked angry and shouted, 'I will have that disloyal servant arrested right now!' Amar tried to placate her and said, 'Leave it my child. Let bygones be bygones.' Buraan intervened, 'Khwaja, she is a quite remarkable. The spells that we learned in ten years, she mastered in a few days. Just watch what she can do!'

As Amar watched, Majlis plucked a pearl from the string of pearls around her neck and lisped an incantation that made the pearl fly upwards. Moments later, a magic slave-boy holding a chain of fire materialized in front of her. He bowed before his young mistress and asked her, 'What is your will?' Majlis said, 'Listen, I am ordering you to arrest that wretch Junain and bring her back to me. Have you heard me, my good little slave? May Samri keep you alive! Do this at once and do not take too long!' The slave-boy laughed at her innocent patter and shot up to the sky to vanish in the direction of Hoshruba.

At sunset, the baradari was illuminated; crystal chandeliers lit up the garden and candles shaped like lotuses floated on the lake, casting a soft glow on the water. Burran entertained her guests with a tour of the gardens while her attendants spread brocade and silk dining sheets in the durbar pavilion for the feast. Khwaja Amar and Burran rinsed their hands and sat down for a fragrant meal served on gold platters.

Later, when the gathering was at ease, two sahirs materialized before Burran holding trays covered with rich gold cloth. They told her that these gifts had been sent by the great king, Kaukab, for Amar. Burran removed the covers and revealed beautiful jewels, the likes of which Amar had never seen in his life. There were strings of lustrous pearls, precious rings of rubies and emeralds, and crowns studded with the nine precious gems.

Burran read out from Kaukab's letter to Amar, 'Tell Khwaja sahib to accept these humble gifts from me. Afrasiyab's messenger has reached the molsri trees on the borders of our Tilism, send for him.' The princess then told her maidservants, 'Lay these gifts aside. We will be presenting our guest with other gifts.' Amar thought that Burran would also return the gold trays on which the gifts were placed and quickly said, 'Princess, these gifts are precious to me for they have been sent by my benefactor. I will not let you keep them!' He took out the blessed Net of Ilyas and deposited the jewels, along with the gold trays, into Zambil; then he mumbled, 'I am sorry I took the trays as well. I should return them.'

Burran exclaimed, 'Please do not heed what I said and do keep the trays!' Amar, who did not intend to return the trays anyway, declared, 'Princess, you and your father have such a generous disposition that I cannot find the words to praise you!' The princess arranged for a bed inlaid with precious gems for Amar to sleep on. Perfume holders placed around the pavilion made it fragrant and handmaidens massaged his limbs. The princess retired to her own chambers for the night.

The next morning, Amar awoke early to perform the dawn prayer and enjoyed the lavish breakfast the princess had sent for him. Later, she asked him to accompany her to the durbar, where she ordered her men to bring Afrasiyab's messenger to her. The messenger was awed by the splendour of the Palace of Seven Hues and greeted the princess with courteous formality. The princess signalled that he be seated and served wine. After consuming a goblet of wine, the messenger's heart gained courage and he declared, 'I am the messenger!' Burran asked him, 'Who has sent the message?' The messenger declared proudly, 'This message is from the ruler of Tilism-e-Hoshruba, the King of Magic, Afrasiyab Jadoo.

I have orders to convey it to Shah Kaukab and wait for his reply.' Burran ordered her officers to escort the messenger to Kaukab and returned to the palace with Amar.

Kaukab's message to Afrasiyab

The messenger arrived at Kaukab's durbar and waited to be announced. A herald called out, 'O King of Kings and Sultan of the World, Afrasiyab's messenger is here!' Kaukab looked up as the messenger raised his right hand to his forehead in a mujra greeting. The messenger went forward and presented the royal missive to Kaukab. The Shah handed it to his scribe, who read it out aloud. Kaukab declined the gifts and offerings Afrasiyab had sent for him, but asked the messenger to sit down. The Shah then asked his scribe to compose a reply from him. 'The text should be infused with humour. Commence with the praise of the Unseen God and the Seal of Prophets. Although I am not Muslim, this letter should be enough to convince Afrasiyab that I am allied with them. This should put a stop to any form of communication between us.' Accordingly, the scribe composed a reply that read:

'The pen writes in praise of the One True Lord who has floated rivers in the air. He who can elevate and He who can disgrace. He is the symbol of all life. After Him, we turn to the Star in the Firmament of Prophets who illuminated the world with his radiance. Now we address you, O Sultan of the World; You, before whom a mountain is as low as grass. You have crowned me with honours by sending your letter of friendship. You have complained about how you have been betrayed and humiliated. I must confess that it made me laugh as it did everybody in my durbar to think that you are so desperate. It is unwise to consider so many people inferior to you. It is absurd to declare that Amar is a swindler and a rogue. Amar is the King of Kings and the strength of believers. If you think that he needs help, you are wrong, for who can help one who is helped by God? I am saddened by the thought that your house is being destroyed. I advise you in all sincerity to shed your pride and arrogance or else you will certainly be defeated.'

Afrasiyab's messenger left Kaukab's durbar with a heavy heart. He was escorted to the Fort of Seven Hues where the message was shown to the princess and Amar, who was happy to hear the contents of the king's reply. The princess asked her officers to escort the messenger to the border of Tilism-e-Hoshruba, from where he travelled in stages to the Garden of Apples. When the messenger arrived, Afrasiyab was about to order a sahir to fight the rebels. He had not yet given the order when the messenger reached the durbar and greeted the Shahanshah. Kaukab's nama was handed to a scribe, who read it out aloud.

When the Shah of Tilsim heard the message, he bit his hand and trembled with rage. He then tried to put on a brave front for his companions by declaring in jest, 'Look at this! Kaukab is so afraid of Amar that he has lost his faith! Why should I be offended by the likes of him? I would have sent my armies against him, but he will be coming to fight himself and will be suitably punished.'

A slither of pythons

A magic claw brought a message from Hairat that made the Shah even angrier. After a while, he addressed his durbar, 'Who should I send against these traitors of salt? Whoever goes is deceived and killed by ayyars! Where can I find a sahir who does not live in this world? One who lives in the sky and does not succumb to their tricks!'

His courtiers suggested, 'Perhaps it should be someone who does not have human form!' The Shah looked at them thoughtfully and said, 'There might be a way. There is a sahir in Mount Sapphire who lives in the belly of a python. Azlam Python-dweller only emerges for battles. Let me send for him.' Soon, a monstrous python slithered into the durbar, followed by forty fearsome pythons. Sahirs emerged from the bellies of the snakes and greeted the Shah. Afrasiyab rewarded them with khalat robes and ordered their commander Azlam Python-dweller to fight the rebels. He cautioned them against the ayyars and said, 'Make sure that you remain within the pythons all the time!'

The sahirs listened to the king attentively and stepped back into the bellies of their pythons. The ground of the durbar shook as the gruesome pythons left for the battlefront. They reached Hairat's lashkar where she welcomed them cordially. They were shown into an open area with a few tents where they could assemble for their meals. Servants assigned to them were given magic badges and strict instructions to look out for ayyars. Azlam Python-dweller emerged from his python and attended Hairat's durbar, where his hideous face repulsed everyone. That evening, battle drums were struck in the ill-fated Python-dweller's name. In the rebel camp, Mahrukh declared, 'He is a powerful wizard, may God save us from his mischief. Let us strike our battle drums as well.' Sardars returned to their pavilions to prepare for battle. Azlam also took his leave of Hairat to join his comrades for dinner, and later returned to the belly of his python.

The next morning, Mahrukh and Bahar emerged in great pomp and splendour with an army of sahirs and braves, and headed for the arena.

On the other side, the proud and haughty Hairat come into sight with her army. Lightning flashed on the horizon, trees ignited, magic clouds burst into rain, the plains were cleared of dust and made ready for battle. The band of pythons slithered in, snapping at each other and emitting poisonous flames from their fearful jaws that made the air turn green. Azlam emerged from the python and approached Hairat for permission to commence battle. He returned to his python and slithered on to the battlefield.

Azlam expelled flames that filled the air with venomous smoke that blinded Mahrukh's army. There was chaos in the rebel lashkar as some people conjured magic turrets around themselves for protection, while others fled. Mahrukh Magic-eye had bravely moved forward when Azlam's python-dwellers emitted more flames. God protect us, no one could withstand those flames and delicate, fair-faced sahiras were scorched to cinders. The deadly smoke of the pythons penetrated the earth and turned the grass blue; the immortal Khizar himself would have looked for an antidote to their poison. The open jaws of pythons looked like vast caves on the battleground.

At Hairat's signal, her army attacked with magical tridents and spears. Half the rebel army had already been blinded and the other half could not resist the magical flames and fled. Only the brave Mahrukh Magic-eye and a few commanders were left on the battlefield. Yet, Mahrukh killed thousands with her spells, while Ra'ad thundered and his mother Barq flashed in the air. Mahrukh Magic-eye transformed into a mighty python and fell upon Azlam's pythons. She emitted flames that defeated the pythons and they slithered out of the battlefield. Azlam rallied forth to confront her and shouted, 'Where will you go now, you traitor to the salt?' Mahrukh retorted, 'Eunuch, you call yourself a man and then hide behind a python to fight me! You are nothing but a coward!'

Her taunts penetrated even Azlam's thick hide and he called out, 'Do you think I am afraid of you? Tomorrow, I will fight you alone!' Mahrukh yelled in reponse, 'If you return alone, you will get shoe beatings that you will remember for the rest of your life!' Azlam controlled his anger and asked Hairat to have the drums of peace struck. Hairat protested, 'Why do you want to draw back from certain victory? Only Mahrukh and a few sardars are left and will be easily captured.' Azlam related how Mahrukh had taunted him and Hairat again tried to convince him that Mahrukh was merely trying to save her life. Azlam, however, refused to listen to her because of his arrogance. Mahrukh said a prayer of gratitude to God for allowing her to retain her honour and returned to her camp with the remaining sardars. She wept when she saw the camp's deserted bazaars and empty tents. That evening, Mahrukh invoked magical powers to prepare for the next day's battle.

Barq Firangi and the Python-dwellers

The ayyars had witnessed their lashkar's disastrous rout from a distance. They returned to Mahrukh's pavilion and saw that she looked worried. They consoled her and promised that they would find a way to destroy the evil Azlam. The ayyars held a meeting and Barq announced that he would go first to the enemy camp. After he left, Qiran and Jansoz also disguised themselves to infiltrate enemy lines. Barq assumed the form of a gruesome sahir and strolled through Hairat's camp until he reached the place allocated for the pythons. Barq watched them carefully as they frolicked in the dust.

Suddenly, the stomach of one python opened and a sahir, dark and hideous as an ogre, emerged from it. Barq trembled with fear, but steeled his heart and remained where he was. The wizard approached him and asked, 'Who are you?' Barq snapped back, 'I am what you are! Don't you know me?' The sahir said, 'There are forty-one of us, including our commander. Where have you come from and where is your python?' Barq replied weakly, 'I have a python! Why do I need to explain anything to you?' The sahir became suspicious that Barq was be a trickster and shouted, 'Wait, you rascal, I recognize you!' By this time, however, the fleet-footed Barq was far away. The sahir ran after him and Barq quickly jumped into a trench to evade him. The sahir peered into the trench, but the very next moment, he was trapped in the coils of Barq's whip. He tried to chant a quick spell to escape, but Barq jerked the whip and throttled the sahir. The sahir's eyes bulged out and as he rolled into the ditch, Barq took out his dagger and sliced his head off.

There was an almighty roar followed by a burst of fire and brimstone. A voice called out, 'You have killed the Wine-drinker!' The dead sahir's python suddenly caught fire in the camp and there were dreadful sounds. Azlam and his companions emerged from their pythons shouting, 'What has happened?' They were so unnerved that none of them thought of taking a head count of the pythons. It never even occurred to them that one of them was dead as they felt they were invincible.

Barq disguised as Sarsar

Barq stayed on in the trench and disgiused himself as Sarsar. He painted her to look so beautiful that the ayyar girl herself would not have dreamt of having such beauty. Azlam and his sahirs were milling around, still bewildered by recent events, when they heard the sounds of anklet bells. They turned around and were stunned to see a beautiful woman walking towards them, staggering under the weight of a dead man. The woman laid the corpse at Azlam's feet and said, 'Look at him? Is he not your companion?' Azlam recovered his senses and said, 'Alas! Yes, this was the Wine-drinker!' The other wizards looked down mournfully at their murdered companion.

'What happened to him?' Azlam asked, to which the false Sarsar replied, 'An ayyar came into our lashkar and slaughtered him.' Azlam looked hard at her and said, 'Then why did you not arrest him?' She explained. 'Huzoor, I am Sarsar, the ayyar girl, not a sahira. I ran after the rascal, but could not catch him. Anyway, you should remain on your guard now, I have to leave!'

Azlam Python-dweller ran after her and caught her hand. He was smitten by her beauty and thought, 'She is just an ayyar girl. I am sure Shahanshah will not mind my dallying with her!' The false Sarsar frowned and said, 'Mian, return to your senses, I am not a prostitute! Sahib, I travel all over Tilism and my reputation is intact. I have never come across a rogue like you before!' Even as she admonished him, she languidly stretched her arms and made sure that the outline of her bosom were quite visible. Azlam was instantly overcome with desire and embraced her. She protested loudly, 'Look, I will scream now! By Samri, if you touch me, I will kill myself! Look at the audacity of this man that he dishonours me in broad daylight; I curse his unbridled lust!'

Azlam lifted her and began walking towards his tent even as she screamed, 'Listen, you will regret this! Do not think I am just anyone! An ayyar might come at any moment. Go and hide in your python you fool!' Azlam ignored her protests and put her down on his masnad. He instructed his servants to enter the tent only when summoned and his companions returned to their pythons. Once they were alone, Barq knew that the real Sarsar would be inquiring about the dead python-dweller and give him away. He decided to do something to prevent this and looked around apprehensively. Azlam asked him, 'O delicate one, why do you look around like this?'

The false Sarsar cried, 'You only want to have fun! Do you not realize that ayyars are always after me? They will follow me to this place!' Azlam declared arrogantly, 'I am here and they dare not enter!' The false Sarsar said, 'You will not know them. What if they will be disguised as me? They will accuse me of being ayyar and call themselves Sarsar! You will become my enemy and if they see me making love to you, they will tell everyone that I am a whore! By Samri, I will lose my life and my reputation!' The false Sarsar struck her forehead and made such a mournful face that Azlam held her hand and pleaded, 'My fair trickster, even if the enemy comes as the King of Magic, I will punish him severely!'

Barq was relieved that Azlam could be easily manipulated and now tantalized him with coquettish behaviour. When Azlam tried to become too intimate, he gave him a tight slap and the wizard fell back, sheepishly stroking his cheek. Barq then pulled him up and said, 'Control yourself, we have plenty of time!' One of Azlam's servants was watching Barq's antics and thought, 'Since when has Sarsar become so bold with Shahanshah's men? I should inform Hairat.' So, he ran to the durbar and related everything to his mistress. The real Sarsar was present there and started abusing the manservant, who protested, 'Why do you blame me? Go and see for yourself!'

Hairat said, 'He is right. It seems as if an ayyar is disguised as you. Don't blame this poor man and find out what is happening there first.' Sarsar said, 'Bibi, that ayyar is there disguised as me. Even if I manage to capture him, this Azlam is already enamoured by my face. If he overpowers me, the pearl of my honour might be tarnished!'

Hairat snapped back, 'My innocent, why did you train as a trickster if you are so frightened? You should have stayed at home and guarded your honour! Don't make excuses and find out what's happening in Azlam's tent!' Sarsar was reluctant to go there, but did not dare disobey her mistress. She walked cautiously up to Azlam's tent, where his guards looked at her and said, 'Bibi, wait here! Another one of your face is inside! There is something strange going on.' The guards called out, 'Huzoor, another Sarsar is at the door!' Barq heard this and suddenly put his arms around Azlam seductively. 'Do you want to be intimate with me now?' he whimpered. Azlam thought that she was finally attracted to him and cried, 'Dear heart, I love you a thousand times!' The false Sarsar pouted, 'First you must take care of the one who is outside posing as me. I told you my reputation would be ruined and what I feared most has happened. I will hide myself while you summon him inside and capture him!'

Azlam was annoyed by the interruption, but could hardly tell the guards that he was about to go to bed with his beloved. He ordered the guards to let Sarsar enter. She came in and greeted him, but kept scanning the tent for Barq. Azlam asked her to sit down, but Sarsar saw his bloodshot eyes and thought, 'What if he misbehaves with me?' She edged backwards and stammered, 'The one who poses as me is an ayyar!' Azlam saw her shrinking from him and thought, 'This must be an ayyar trying to run away.' Without a moment's delay, he chanted a spell that made her collapse.

Azlam tied her to a pillar and cried, 'Wily rascal, do you think I am a fool? Wait and see how I torture you to death!' The real Sarsar screamed, but he slapped her hard. Barq emerged from under the bed and called out, 'Hit him harder! These bastards deserve this treatment!' He hopped about, slapped Sarsar a couple of times himself, and whispered, 'My teacher's beloved, you have exposed so many of my trickeries, you should be punished for it! In fact, today I will cut your nose off!'

Sarsar tried to warn Azlam repeatedly, but Barq shouted to drown out her protests and slapped her again. Even when Azlam had drawn back, Barq egged him on to hit her again. Sarsar's voice was now hoarse and her body was covered with bruises for she had been raised as an indulged princess. The roses of her cheeks had turned into blue *sosan* flowers, her chemise was tattered and her hair, tangled. Eventually, Sarsar thought that she would die and signalled silently to Barq that she would not expose him if he released her. Barq took pity on her, and held Azlam's hand as he said to him, 'Leave him, he has been punished enough. Let us now drink wine and kill him later!'

Meanwhile, Hairat was concerned when Sarsar had been gone a long time. She discovered what was happening through her magic and moved quickly to save her. Just as she took a few steps, she sneezed. Being superstitious, she thought that her sneezing was a bad omen. So, she sent for a sahir, Samak Jadoo, and ordered him, 'Go in haste to Azlam and tell him that the one he has tied up is the real Sarsar!' Samak flew up and burst into Azlam's tent. Azlam reacted aggressively to Samak, assuming that he too was a trickster. Samak shouted, 'Have you lost your senses? You have tied up Sarsar and dally with an ayyar!' Barq cried, 'A curse on ayyars and their disguises! Azlam, he is another ayyar!'

The confused Azlam tried to attack Samak, but he was a powerful sahir. Samak read a spell that stunned both Azlam and Barq. He breathed on Barq and the paints of trickery peeled off and revealed his real face. Azlam felt contrite and fell at Samak's feet, begging for forgiveness. He tied Barq to a pillar and untied Sarsar, all the while pleading, 'Bibi, pardon me for this grave error!' Sarsar was unforgiving and abused him roundly before she left. Azlam turned to Samak and said, 'Will you take this ayyar to Malika Hairat? I will get back into my python!' Samak retorted, 'I am not going to be responsible for these ayyars! Send someone else.' Crestfallen, Azlam said, 'In that case, just ask her if she wants him executed and I will behead him.' Samak simply nodded and walked out of the tent.

The ayyar Qiran had been standing outside, posing as one of Hairat's attendants. He had seen Barq's capture and thought of a plan to rescue him. Just as Samak emerged from Azlam's tent, he approached him and said, 'Tell Hairat that Azlam has been killed!' Samak was stunned to hear this, but before he could react, Qiran sprinted off. Samak realized that he too was an ayyar. Fearful of his own life now, he sprouted wings and flew back to Hairat's durbar.

Meanwhile, Qiran walked into Azlam's tent, disguised as Samak. Azlam was pacing his tent with his dagger drawn, just waiting for Hairat's orders to execute Barq. He saw the false Samak and said, 'Brother, has Malika sent the orders for his execution?' Qiran whispered, 'Walls have ears in this place! Come closer to me.' Azlam went closer to Qiran, who said, 'Look! Who is that man peering into your tent?' When Azlam turned to look, Qiran smashed his skull with his mighty cleaver and split it open.

Instantly, darkness engulfed the camp and Azlam's spirits howled and raged. The other pythons were actually creations of Azlam's magic and suddenly burst into flames. The sahirs in their bellies leaped out of the pythons, scorched by the flames. Qiran untied Barq, set fire to the tent and both ayyars ran off, shouting out their names. A voice boomed out, 'You have killed Azlam Python-dweller!'

Samak and Sarsar were just relating recent events to Hairat when she heard fearsome sounds and cried, 'What has happened now?' Azlam's servants rushed into the durbar and gasped, 'Azlam has been killed!' Hairat could only strike her knee in dismay. Eventually, she regained control of her senses and had Azlam's corpse taken to the Shah with a letter explaining how he had been killed. The ayyars managed to return to their camp amidst much jubilation and Mahrukh rewarded them with khalat robes.

Hairat's officers arrived like messengers of doom with Azlam's corpse when the King of Sahirs, accompanied by his ministers and counsellors, was fishing on the shores of the River Zakhar in Batin. Hundreds of maidens, fair of face and covered with jewels were standing in attendance with wine flasks. This scene of festivity, cheerfulness and relaxation was destroyed when Afrasiyab saw Azlam's corpse, and looked as if he was drowning in a river of grief. That gathering of pleasure turned into a gathering of mourning. Afrasiyab rubbed his palms in sheer frustration and cried, 'Alas, these ayyars have caused too much damage!'

He wrote to Hairat, 'My lady, ask Murshidzadeh if he is intending to fight at all! Tell him that this war is now his responsibility.' Hairat read the message and passed it on to Mussavir the magic artist who sheepishly said, 'Shah has rightly admonished me. Indeed, I have taken too long to begin fighting. However, I have prepared a spell with which I can hang all these ayyars as if they are fruits on a tree!'

We will leave Mussavir to prepare for the battle and return to Kaukab's guests, Amar and Makhmoor Red-eye.

Amar in Burran's court

Amar stayed on in Princess Burran's palace and the princesses and nazims of the land remained in his attendance. During the daytime, Amar was taken for tours of the wondrous land of Nur Afshan. In the evening, he was served goblets of the intoxicating amber liquid and entertained with nautch performances. Majlis the infant enchantress would sit on his lap and charm him with her innocent chatter. One day, she said, 'My dear, dear uncle, my beloved Khwaja, I have heard such praises of your singing. You are known to play the flute like Kanhaiya. Will you not sing for us?' Amar looked embarrassed, but she continued, 'By Allah, what will happen if you sing; will you lose pearls from your mouth?'

At her insistence, Amar took out his reed flute and sang a ghazal by the poet Atish that entranced the whole gathering. Even the trees and birds of the garden became still when he sang. Burran and Majlis were overwhelmed by his melodious voice and remained in a trance even when he stopped singing. Majlis ran to him and cried, 'Khwaja, do not leave us in this fragile state. Please go on singing!' Amar realized this was an opportune moment to state his purpose and wept as he said, 'How can I continue? My dear son Asad Lion-heart is in Afrasiyab's prison. God only knows how Afrasiyab is making my companions suffer in my absence.'

Burran tried to placate him by saying, 'God willing, my father will send a huge army to defeat that monster!' Amar replied, 'Princess, that is what I had hoped for, but my heart is heavy. I miss Makhmoor who was always there to encourage me.' Burran smiled and said, 'I will send for Makhmoor right away!' She ordered her officers to escort Makhmoor Red-eye from another garden where she had been staying with Amar's replica. When Makhmoor arrived, Amar stood up to acknowledge her and then she greeted Burran formally. The princess and her companions accepted Makhmoor's greetings with all courtesy and gave her a seat of honour. Majlis suddenly piped up, 'Now that I have seen Princess Makhmoor, I am reminded of the slave-boy I sent to Hoshruba. I wonder how he has fared!'

The magic artist and the parizad

Now hear about the rebel camp. Mahrukh and Bahar were bracing themselves for another battle while Mussavir was busy practising his magic. The night Amar was entertaining Burran's durbar in Tilism-e-Nur Afshan with his reed flute, Hairat informed Mussavir that battle drums would be struck in his name. Mussavir rushed to Hairat and told her not to strike them yet. He explained, 'The King of Magic mocked me in his letter. I want to go to the enemy camp alone and try and bring them around. If they are still not willing, I can finish them off on my own.' Hairat said, 'In truth you are the grandson of Samri and can capture them easily, but I would advise you not to venture there on your own.' Mussavir said, 'Malika, this is something I have to do, You cannot stop me now!' He then announced to the durbar, 'If there are any ayyars in disguise here, I want you to warn your sardars that I am coming to confront them on my own!'

Mahrukh Magic-eye was informed of Mussavir's challenge by her spies in Hairat's court. She, in turn, sent a message to Bahar that read, 'The one you are preparing to enchant is coming to visit us alone.' As soon as she read Hairat's message, Bahar lit a sacred fire in her tent and began chanting an invocation. She moulded a female figure with lentil flour, dressed her in saffron-coloured robes and adorned her with jewellery made of flower petals. After making sacred offerings and reciting a magic incantation, she tossed the figure into the sacred fire. She joined Mahrukh in the durbar just as heralds announced that Mussavir was approaching their camp in battle dress.

Bahar quietly recited an incantation and knocked in the air. Mussavir was just about to enter the durbar pavilion when he heard the sound of bells. He looked up and saw a lovely maiden glowing with an incandescent, unearthly light, floating in the sky. Mussavir was stunned by her beauty and the mirror-faced woman floated down and held his hand. She whispered softly, 'Why, you unfaithful one, have you forgotten me?' Mussavir thought to himself, 'Who is this flower-like creature who appears to know me?' He whispered, 'O lovely vision, wait for me while I capture these traitors of salt! Then I will take you to my camp.'

The parizad laughed and said, 'Listen to the man! As if I will wait for him until he wins the battle! Are you in your senses? Do you think I am my own mistress? Just accept this gift and I will leave.' She extended a basket of flowers towards him. Mussavir stroked her petal-like cheeks and told her, 'Light of my life, do not be angry! Tell me who you are and who sent this gift for me?' The parizad sighed, 'Unfaithful one, if you do not recognize me, why I should give you my name? Look into the basket and you will know who sent the gift.' Mussavir was wondering which fair damsel could have sent him a formal gift through the parizad, and when he removed the basket's golden coverlet, he saw fresh jasmine garlands and bracelets infused with a delicate scent. 'Who could have sent these for me?' he asked the parizad. The flower-faced one murmured, 'Inhale their fragrance and you will know who has sent them.'

Mussavir reverently kissed the garlands and bracelets and inhaled the fragrance deeply before wearing them. Bahar's magic worked powerfully as soon as he inhaled the scent of the flowers. The parizad had not revealed Bahar's name to Mussavir, as he could have become hostile if she had taken the name of his enemy. The parizad laughed in triumph and cried, 'Do you know the name now? Look at the flowers closely. That garden of perfection has used narcissi stems to write a message for you on the petals!' Mussavir eagerly examined the garlands and found the petals etched delicately with a magical script that read: 'Princess Bahar has sent this gift of flowers to Mussavir. The fairy-faced handmaiden is also at his service.'

Mussavir was now completely enchanted and clapped his hands in delight. He lunged at the parizad and pulled her towards him. She was so delicate that upon his touch, her body disintegrated, her head rolled off and her limbs fell out like petals. Mussavir cried out in anguish, 'What is this? O my dear heart, I had no idea you were so fragile!' He tried to pull her head into his lap, but that too burst like a water bubble at his touch and melted into a pool of water. The nightingale of Mussavir's despair wailed, 'I only want that! I only want that!'

Mussavir began repeating this phrase in a frenzy of unrequited passion. Princess Bahar had the pavilion curtains drawn up and the sardars of the Islamic lashkar laughed at Mussavir's frantic and distraught state. A crowd gathered around him and men asked, 'Mian, what *do* you want?' He ignored them and desperately repeated, 'I only want that!' Eventually, urchins from the lashkar clapped their hands and ran after him, making ribald remarks. One shouted, 'Come to us, we will give it to you!' Another called out, 'Do you want us to call your wife?' Mussavir chased them away in rage, but continued his ceaseless refrain.

Mussavir the magic artist, though enchanted, was still a descendant of the great Samri. In his rage, he thought, 'I should capture Bahar so that she can lead me to my beloved!' However, the effect of the magic garlands was such that the person adored Bahar and in the next moment, he thought, 'If I confront Bahar and destroy the garlands and flowers in the battle, I will lose the only mementoes I have of my beloved. I should keep these in my lashkar and return to fight her!' He turned to his camp, still being followed by the band of urchins who were clapping and whistling behind him.

The urchins fell back when he entered his lashkar, where his own people began following him. Hairat heard the din and asked, 'What is that noise?' Her servants ran outside and returned to inform her, 'Murshidzadeh wants something!' The next moment, Mussavir burst

out loud, 'Ya Ali!' The forest trembled with the boom of his voice and a lion emerged roaring from the bushes. Qiran called out, 'Wait, you desert dog! Where are you going?' The lion roared and leapt at him, but Qiran dodged him and managed to land an almighty blow on the lion's forehead. The lion fell on the ground with the shock of the blow and Qiran unleashed a torrent of blows and slaps on the beast until it was tamed.

The ayyar then tied a leather saddle on to the lion's back and reined him with straps. He transformed himself into a monstrous sahir with massive limbs, a coal-black face and a huge red tongue that lolled out of his mouth, open like the gates of hell. He wrapped long black snakes around his body while deadly spiders crawled on his hairy black chest. Holding the longest snake as a whip, he mounted the lion that was now as meek as a kitten.

Thus disguised, Qiran rode into Qirtas's lashkar, striking terror amongst the sahirs who greeted him deferentially as he made his way to the royal pavilion. Qirtas had just collapsed on his bed after a bout of hard drinking when he was abruptly woken up by his servants screaming, 'The lion comes!' He was startled by the sight of the monstrous sahir on the lion and cried, 'Come in, come in!' Qiran dismounted and handed him a nama stamped with the seal of the King of Sahirs. Qirtas kissed the royal seal reverently and held the nama up to his eyes before opening it.

The nama read, 'We have consulted the oracle Book of Samri and discovered that you have captured Bahar and have travelled with her towards Tilism-e-Nur Afshan. We think it is not advisable for you to take her with you to enemy territory as Amar might rescue her there. Therefore, when the noble Nahir brings you this message, hand the prisoner over to him for he will guard her well. Be aware that this is an order and you will be duly rewarded.'

Qirtas immediately sent for Bahar and her handmaidens. The fair princess was bound with iron chains and was still unconscious. Qiran said, 'Release her from her chains and I will deal with her myself!' Qirtas readily agreed and Qiran brought out a garland of cloves from his pouch. Bahar awoke suddenly when Qirtas dispelled his magic and tried to escape, but was rendered unconscious once again when Qiran put the garland of cloves around her neck. Qiran mounted the lion with the unconscious Bahar in his arms and said, 'Release the handmaidens, they can run behind me!'

The handmaidens saw a strange sahir riding off with their mistress and thought it was not wise to attack him in a crowd of sahirs, lest they were captured again. Thus, they trotted off meekly behind Qiran. This convinced Qirtas that the king's man was a powerful sahir.

When they reached the safety of the forest, Qiran released the lion that scampered off into the forest. He then revived the princess and removed the garland of cloves from around her neck. Bahar opened her eyes to see a black-faced sahir hovering above her and was about to invoke her magic when Qiran put his hand over her mouth and said, 'Princess, it is I, Qiran. You have lived with us for so long and are yet not familiar with the ways of trickery!' Bahar was overjoyed to hear this and embraced her rescuer warmly. She said, 'O Qiran, the way you are disguised today even Khwaja Amar would not have recognized you!' Bahar's handmaidens, who had been following Qiran, came upon them as they talked and were happy to see their mistress rescued. Qiran summoned Barq by blowing Zafeel and he too had a warm reunion with Bahar.

Barq as Princess Gulzar

After resting a while, Bahar said, 'Qiran, wait here while I teach this pig Qirtas a lesson he will not forget. I will turn him and his men into raving lunatics!' Qiran said, 'Princess, listen carefully to me. You are here on your own and he is a powerful sahir with a large army. If he recaptures you, it will be difficult to rescue you again. Moreover, we have pursued him for some time. If we cannot kill him now, we will lose face before our fellow ayyars from Emir's lashkar. Leave him to us!'

Bahar agreed with Qiran as she had a great deal of respect for him. He asked her to hide somewhere while they killed Qirtas. Bahar asked, 'Very well, but should I leave my handmaidens with you?' Barq replied, 'Yes, that is a good idea. Leave them behind.' Bahar turned to her handmaidens and ordered, 'Stay with Mehtar sahib and do as he says.' Bahar then magically transformed into a bird of many hues and hid in a tree to observe the trickery.

The ayyars spoke to each other quietly and hatched a plan. Suddenly, Qiran got up and walked off into the forest, and Barq ordered the handmaidens, 'Change your faces magically as Qirtas might recognize you!' The handmaidens muttered incantations and altered their looks and clothes. Then Barq said, 'Now conjure a magnificent house provided with all comforts.' Since Bahar's handmaidens were trained in the art of illusion, they smiled at Barq and knocked in the air. Within moments, a beautiful garden materialized around him. In the middle of the garden was a magnificent palace, which looked like a befitting place for a tryst of royal lovers.

Barq said, 'Two of you go to Qirtas and convey the message that this area is called the Forest of Gulzar and belongs to Princess Gulzar Jadoo.

Tell him that he has camped without permission, and may cause damage to her agricultural land and gardens. He must remove his camp at once!' The handmaidens flew off to the camp and conveyed this message to Qirtas. The sahir was visibly annoyed but controlled his temper as he did not want to get into a fight before he reached Nur Afshan. Therefore, he pleaded softly, 'Tell the princess to be kind to travellers. We are only here this night and will depart for the Fort of Seven Hues tomorrow. We would have left tonight, but my men are weary after a long journey. Tell the princess that there will be no damage to her crops and we will be gone tomorrow.'

Barq heard this message and said, 'Return to him and say that if he is our guest, we must honour him with our hospitality, or else Princess Burran will chastise us. Invite him to our palace and tell him that we are alone in our garden and anxious to meet him. He can spend some time with us and leave whenever he likes.'

Qirtas had not yet gone back to his tent when the handmaidens returned with the second message. He looked worried and asked, 'Now what message have you brought?' The handmaidens repeated Barq's message to Qirtas, who thought, 'Perhaps this princess did not know who I am. Now that she is aware of my rank, she hastens to invite me.' He said to the handmaidens, 'You will have to excuse me this evening as I am travel weary. I will visit her in the morning.' The handmaidens turned away and giggled amongst each other, 'Sister, let us leave. This lout seems to think that he is exalted enough for princesses to summon him! As if she is going to wait for him until the morning! He is not grateful that instead of turning him out of her area, she has taken pity on him!'

Qirtas thought, 'I am being foolish. A beautiful young woman is inviting me to meet her alone; perhaps she has something else in mind! Moreover, she is a princess and might be a useful ally in the future!' He called out to the handmaidens, 'Do not be angry! I will come with you to meet the princess.' Qirtas went to his tent and wore expensive robes and jewels, and dabbed perfume on himself. Thus groomed, he went with the handmaidens.

Meanwhile, Barq used the paints of ayyari to transform himself into a beautiful maiden. He wore heavy robes and jewels and reclined on a masnad. Qiran dressed up as a sahir with costly robes, a huge turban and a shawl draped over his shoulders. He stood at the entrance and greeted Qirtas when he reached the garden.

Qiran bowed low and offered tribute to Qirtas in the form of gold coins. After some time, Barq emerged languidly, supported by Bahar's handmaidens. When Qirtas saw her, he felt as if he was witnessing a celestial vision that could fulfil all his latent dreams. He felt dizzy with desire and would have fallen had it not been for that enchanting one who came close to him, held his hand and whispered, 'You are welcome! By Allah, you have certainly made me wait! You must have known how eager I was to meet you!'

The false princess laughed after she said this and led him into the garden. Qirtas became even more excited when she sat close to him on the masnad and his heart began thumping loudly. He thought, 'This was an auspicious journey for me as this maiden seems to love me.' Meanwhile, the false princess looked at him with eyes brimming with the wine of love and poured him a goblet of the roseate liquid. Qirtas drank it eagerly and struggled to keep awake as the drug mixed into it began affecting his senses. Qiran stood behind them fanning the false princess. Barq looked at the giddy sahir and spoke in his normal voice, 'Why Mian Qirtas, how do you feel now?' Qirtas groaned, 'Princess, I am not too well. With your permission, I wish to lie down!'

Barq laughed and said, 'You silly joker! Don't you recognize me? I am Barq ayyar!' Qirtas was startled and tried to attack him, but Qiran, who stood behind him, kicked him hard on his buttocks. Qirtas fell down on the floor and became unconscious. Barq calmly decapitated his impure head with his dagger and ignored the howling of his spirits when he died. Hearing strange sounds, Qirtas's soldiers hastily mobilized and ran towards the forest.

Bahar had been watching the ayyars at work, disguised as a bird. When they killed Qirtas, she flew upwards and beckoned to her handmaidens to follow her. They quickly cleared the illusion of the magic palace and gardens they had created and flew after her while the ayyars fled into the forest. Whirling columns of dust whipped up the dead sahir's corpse and carried it off to Afrasiyab. Bahar, who was hovering over the sahir army as it rushed towards the forest, took out a tiny ruby casket from her topknot and chanted an incantation. The casket lid opened magically and released smoke that formed stormy dark clouds and spread over the army. A sudden and powerful flash of lightning blinded the soldiers.

When they opened their eyes, they beheld a wondrous scene of an enchanted grarden bathed in moonlight. Some women emerged from the garden and called out, 'O fortunate lovers! Come and hear the message of your beloved Princess Bahar!' The soldiers swept forward, reciting verses of love. The handmaidens put garlands of fresh jasmine flowers around their necks and told them that their beloved Bahar had sent this message for them: 'Are you not ashamed that you declare your love for me before each other. I am alone and the whole lashkar claims to be in love with me! It would better if you consider each other rivals and kill each other. I will acknowledge the lone survivor as my lover instead of suffering this humiliation!'

This magical message fired the passions of the sahir soldiers against each other. Each threatened the other, 'Listen, if you ever utter the name of my beloved, I swear by the name of that beautiful one that I will kill you!' The other would respond, 'I also forbid you not to lose your heart to my beloved or you will lose your life!' Rows and rows of love-stricken soldiers fell into battle formations and attacked each other with their magical weapons. By the time the fair maiden of dawn had overcome the dark dev of night, Qirtas's army of twelve thousand sahirs had destroyed itself. The mass killings of sahirs caused untold chaos unleashing harsh gales and storms while the shrieks of mourning spirits sounded like a foretaste of Doomsday.

At daybreak, the few surviving officers staggered back to Bahar, bleeding from their wounds. Bahar looked at them and knocked in the air so that the magic garden vaporized and the jasmine garlands withered. The officers came to their senses and realized that they had been enchanted. They wanted to attack Bahar, but saw her handmaidens threatening them with magical weapons and fled.

Qiran and Barq emerged from the forest and applauded Bahar's magic. She said, 'This was an ordinary spell. You had already killed Qirtas! Anyway, it is time we returned to our camp.' She conjured a flying throne for the ayyars and herself. Barq climbed on the throne and said, 'Now that we are here we should at least tour this area.' As they flew over rivers and forests, Qiran said, 'We should not wander into Tilism-e-Nur Afshan. It would be humiliating to be arrested by Kaukab's men and rescued by Khwaja Amar!' So, Bahar made the throne fly in a another direction and soon they approached a sandalwood forest.

Kaukab sends Amar's replica to meet his friends

The guardians of the plains where the ayyars had killed Qirtas related what had happened to Kaukab. The Shahanshah laughed and wrote a letter to his daughter Burran Sword-fighter that recounted how Barq and Qiran had tricked and killed Afrasiyab's messenger and rescued Bahar. The message said, 'They are now in the sandalwood forest. Should Khwaja sahib wish to meet them, he can, otherwise, we will host them before they leave. His magical replica should assuage their desire to meet him.'

Burran laughed as she read about the tricksters and showed the letter to Amar. He thought, 'Perhaps Kaukab is testing my patience. I should not leave Burran until I have got what I want out of them!' He turned to Burran and said, 'Princess, I am so content in your company that I really do not need to meet anyone. Tell Shah that he can feast them and send them off.' Kaukab smiled to himself when he read Burran's note. He conjured a figure that looked like Khwaja Amar and sent him to the sandalwood forest along with some high-ranking sahirs.

Bahar and the ayyars were resting in a garden in the sandalwood forest when they heard the sounds of drums. They rushed to the garden's entrance and saw a magnificent procession with elephants in the forefront and drummers and pipers seated on camels. High-ranking officials followed on thrones, while maidens dressed in costly robes and jewels sat on palanquins. Water carriers sprinkled the earth with rosewater and young boys holding incense burners marched behind them. Finally, Khwaja Amar appeared on a throne surrounded by liveried guards. He wore golden robes embroidered with jewels and a dazzling crown on his head.

Barq cried, 'This is Ustad's procession! I am going to call out to him!' Qiran looked sternly at him and said, 'That would be discourteous!' Barq looked chastened and restrained himself. After some time, a sahir came to the garden entrance and said, 'Come with me. Khwaja sahib remembers you.' Bahar said, 'We thought he would rest in this garden!' The sahir replied, 'No, this is my humble abode, it is not worthy of him!' The sahir took Bahar and the ayyars to a garden enclosed by walls made of pure gold. Sahirs and guards standing at the entrance greeted them courteously. When they walked into the garden, they felt their hearts lift as their old companion sat in splendour before them.

Khwaja Amar was sitting on a gem-studded throne with a golden canopy. Several sahirs of high rank sat on chairs in an arc around his throne, while throngs of handmaidens stood in attendance. Bahar, Qiran and Barq greeted Amar who embraced them warmly and offered them chairs of honour beside him. At his signal, handmaidens came forward holding gold trays heaped with robes of honour, strings of rare pearls and precious jewels for Bahar and the ayyars. They were served goblets of wine and the friends talked late into the night. Amar then led them to a pavilion where a feast of many fragrant dishes was laid out. When the night came of age later, it was time to rest. Bahar was led to a chamber that glowed in soft candlelight with fresh spring blossoms strewn on her bed.

Bahar rested on the bed and thought it was strange that there was no one to fan her or press her feet. Immediately, she felt a cool breeze and saw that one of the flickering candles spluttered into a strong flame, from which a voice called out, 'Princess, if you wish, this slave-girl can press your feet!' Bahar asked, 'Who are you?' The voice answered, 'This is your handmaiden Shola, friend of Princess Burran!' Bahar was astonished but said, 'Very well, you can come!'

The candle split open and released a flame that transformed into a fairy-like maiden as delicate as a flower. She stepped forward shyly with her head bent. As Bahar looked at her in wonder, the maiden kneeled on the floor and started massaging her feet. Bahar was drifting into sleep when she was startled by the sounds of laughter that seemed to emanate from a bouquet placed besides her bed. Bahar stared at the flowers that opened like a beloved's lips and a musical voice called out, 'If the princess permits me, I can relate a story to entertain you.' Bahar asked the bouquet, 'Who are you?' The voice tinkled back, 'I am your handmaiden Gulzar and Burran's friend!' Bahar smiled and said, 'Join us by all means!'

One of the flowers burst into petals and fell on the floor where it transformed into a lovely maiden clad in a robe of flowers. She kneeled on the floor besides Bahar's bed and related the story of the great Persian king Nausherwan and Emir Hamza. She described the immense love between Nausherwan's daughter Meher Nigar and Hamza and the birth of their son, Qubad. She went on to narrate how Qubad got married to Princess Mah Seema, who gave birth to Saad bin Qubad. The maiden talked about Saad's noble beauty, his skills as a leader and warrior, and his appointment as the Shah of the Islamic army with such eloquence that an arrow of love pierced Princess Bahar and she felt a rush of love for this prince, yet unknown to her. Bahar kept her eyes closed as the flower maiden Gulzar, softly narrated the legendary stories of Emir Hamza late into the night.

The dark visage of the night paled and the yellow sun hovered on the horizon like a restless lover. Khwaja Amar's replica emerged from his chamber and sat on his throne. The two ayyars and Bahar greeted him. Amar's attendants brought fresh robes and jewels for all of them, and after they had bathed and changed, they joined Amar in the garden again. There was a round of wine and the ayyars plucked up enough courage to ask Amar, 'Huzoor, when will you leave this place?' Amar said, 'When Allah wills it!' The ayyars looked at each other and then said to Amar, 'In that case, we will take your leave.'

Amar said, 'Although it is difficult for me to part with you, I am obliged to do so. Leave then and go with God!' For the third time, the ayyars and Bahar were presented with jewels and robes of honour and were again served a sumptuous meal. Amar then ordered some sahirs to lead his guests out of the north gate of the garden. As soon Bahar and the ayyars left the garden from the north gate, they found themselves in the wilderness with no sign of the sandalwood forest, the garden or the wall of gold.

Bahar smiled at the astonished ayyars and conjured a flying throne. As the ayyars sat on the throne with her, Qiran said, 'Princess, did you realize that this was not Khwaja Amar?' Bahar said, 'How could you tell?' Qiran shrugged and replied, 'Ustad would never have been this generous with robes of honour and other gifts!' A grinning Barq agreed, 'You are absolutely correct! This was indeed not Ustad but his magic replica probably created by Kaukab!'

Bahar and the two ayyars gazed upon the many wonders of Kaukab's Tilism as they flew towards the borders of the Tilism of Mirrors. By this time, Prince Iraj had conquered it and it had been divested of its magical buildings and illusions. Bahar could not recognize it and said, 'It seems I have lost my way!' The ayyars suggested that they descend anyway. They disguised themselves as sahirs and went off to make discreet inquiries. After a short while, they returned to Bahar and said, 'It seems this is the land of Mirrors and leads to Mount Nargis and Hoshruba. First we will have to travel to the fort of Gulfamia, from where we can either travel to Hoshruba or to Mount Agate and the lashkar of Islam.'

Bahar was outwardly calm, but trembled with excitement when she heard the words. She thought, 'Losing my way was not without meaning. My destiny calls for me to see my true love.' She said to the ayyars, 'I have long wished to meet Emir Hamza! If you think it's appropriate, we could go to Mount Agate.' The ayyars too had been longing to meet their friends and family in Hamza's lashkar and readily agreed to take her there. The cautious Qiran, however, decided that all three of them needed to travel separately as their crossing the border together could raise suspicions.

Gulfam captures Bahar

Stricken with the arrows of love, Bahar left for Mount Agate before the ayyars. Whenever she was tired of flying, she continued her journey on foot. When she reached the kingdom of Gulfamia, she stopped to rest on a flat rock and fell asleep, exhausted by continuous travel. The custodians of the kingdom came upon her as she slept and recognized Afrasiyab's beloved and Hairat's sister at first glance. They were too overawed to approach her directly and went off to report to their ruler Gulfam, 'The powerful Bahar Jadoo seems to be in some trouble for she is in our land alone and is sleeping on a rock like a vagrant!' Gulfam laughed and said, 'I heard that she has joined the rebels in Tilism, which makes her a fugitive. We should arrest her as she would be a suitable offering for Khudawand Laqa!'

Gulfam went with the custodians to arrest Bahar and saw that she was lost in sleep. Nature itself was hushed at the sight of her beauty and radiance. Flower buds had not opened, in case the sound woke her up; blossoms were not laughing for fear of disturbing her slumber; and the morning breeze tiptoed softly and fanned her like a handmaiden. Gulfam lost his heart a thousand times and felt as if he was a bulbul bird in eternal adoration of this beautiful rose. He chanted a spell to disable her and was about to pierce her tongue with a needle, when Bahar opened her eyes abruptly. She was startled to see the sahirs surrounding her, but could not remember any spells. She cried, 'Shameless coward! If you are a man fight me openly!' Gulfam smiled and said, 'You are a traitor and deserve punishment! Shah has ordered me to fight Hamza. I will offer you to the Khudawand Laqa and seek his permission to marry you as my wife is dead!'

Bahar thought, 'Well, at least he will be taking me close to my beloved Saad!' Nevertheless, she warned him that such an act would only lead to his destruction. Gulfam ignored her threats and rendered her unconscious. He returned to his fort, where he locked her up in a box. He then mobilized his army of twenty-four thousand sahirs and left with the box for Mount Agate on his magic dragon. Magical birds darkened the sky as they swarmed ahead of the army and sahirs exploded magical fireworks that created craters in the earth. As the army moved in stages, Gulfam made sure that Bahar was kept alive. Every few hours, he removed the needle from her tongue so that she could eat and drink. Finally, he reached Mount Agate after journeying for several days.

Laqa was expecting him and sent his sardars to welcome him. They assigned an open area for his troops and escorted him to Laqa's durbar. Gulfam prostrated in front of Laqa and was awarded with a robe of honour. He did not mention that he had Bahar with him, but declared that he would battle against Hamza the very next day.

The next morning, Emir Hamza waited at the mosque for Saad, the king of the lashkar, to emerge from his pavilion. As the Shah's procession moved forward towards him, Hamza kissed the base of the throne and led him into the heart of the lashkar.

The ill-starred Gulfam took permission from Laqa and went out into the battlefield. He produced a few insignificant illusions and called out, 'This will be the battleground of your doom!' The noble Folad frowned in irritation and sought permission to confront Gulfam first, after which he rode into the battlefield like an enraged lion. Gulfam smashed a magic coconut on the ground that burst open to release spirals of musky smoke. The smoke formed the shape of a horse that Gulfam mounted. He rode towards Folad, who invited him to attack first. Gulfam was wearing a belt of his own hair around his waist, which he untied and threw towards Folad like a snare rope. Folad struggled to cut the belt with his dagger but got entangled in its coils. Soom, he fell off his mount and Gulfam handed him over to his men.

Other sardars who confronted Gulfam succumbed to the same fate. Eventually, Hamza's right-hand man, the Indian king, Landhoor bin Sadaan, went forward on his elephant mount. Landhoor read the prayer of Abraham that made Gulfam's magic belt limp and powerless. Then, his elephant kneeled to allow him to take aim at the sahir. Gulfam quickly chanted a spell that made the earth around Landhoor billow with smoke. A pale hand flashed through the smoky darkness and whisked Landhoor off towards the sahir army.

Shaitan Bakhtiarak advised Gulfam to attack the sardars of Islam one by one so that Hamza did not get the opportunity to confront Gulfam. Shaitan said, 'If he comes on the battlefield, he will neutralize your magic and you will be helpless.' Gulfam did as advised and by the evening, he managed to capture over a hundred of Hamza's noble sardars with the magic rope. The drums of peace were struck and the two armies returned to their camps.

Bakhtiarak met Gulfam that evening and said, 'May you remain safe from the evil eye! Today you have accomplished a great deal. Where have you kept the prisoners?' Gulfam replied, 'For the moment, they have been imprisoned in a tent. As soon as I have captured more sardars, I will execute them!' Bakhtirak looked delighted and said, 'A wise man does not need advice. However I suggest that you remain wary of ayyars!'

The next morning, Qasim, the leader of the left flank of the Islamic durbar, rode up to the battleground on his magnificent Sulaimani steed. Again, Gulfam wielded his magic snare-rope of hair and captured him easily. The sardars of the left flank followed their leader and each of them succumbed to the deceitful Gulfam's magic rope. As the drums of peace were struck that evening, the brave warriors of Islam called out to Gulfam, 'You have had your way for two days. Tomorrow Hamza Sahibqiran himself will confront you.' Gulfam shouted, 'I also wish to fight no one but Hamza tomorrow!'

There was jubilation in Laqa's durbar that night. Laqa awarded Gulfam a precious robe of honour and declared, 'O Blessed One, after your final victory, I will confer prophethood on you and present you with a maiden from my heaven!' Gulfam was overwhelmed by this and prostrated before Laqa. Wine flowed in the durbar and Bakhtiarak asked Gulfam, 'Why are you delaying the executions of the sardars?' Gulfam said, 'Malik-ji, once I capture Hamza tomorrow, I will execute them all!' Bakhtiarak smiled cynically and said, 'You too have succumbed to the daydream of arresting Hamza? Tomorrow will be a terrible day for you for he is the master of the Great Name and you will die!' Gulfam looked thoughtful and then said, 'You are right. I have to do something about that!' Within moments, the sahir vanished from his chair.

Now hear about the lashkar of Islam. The badshah declared that he would not convene durbar that evening as the camp was disheartened by the capture of their sardars. He turned to his grandfather and added, 'Ya Emir, if the enemy strikes battle drums, we should respond likewise. Do not wait for my orders.' Chalak bin Amar supervised the guard duties that night while the sardars asked their respective ayyars to stay vigilant and retired to their tents. Night watchmen roamed the camp with occasional cries of 'Remain awake! Remain alert!'

Late that night, Chalak and other tricksters set off to infiltrate the enemy camp and get to Gulfam. Meanwhile, Gulfam, who had vanished from the durbar, reappeared at the edge of his camp. He saw Chalak and his friends furtively dart into his camp and thought, 'There is no point in arresting them. I will take a leaf from their book and go to their camp in disguise.' He transformed himself magically into Chalak and walked past the guards of the Islamic lashkar easily. Emir Hamza had gone to the mosque for his evening prayers and was on his way to the pavilion of his wife, Meher Gauhar.

Gulfam, disguised as Chalak, greeted him deferentially and said, 'Ya Emir, I went to the enemy camp and heard that Gulfam is determined to erase the Great Name from your memory. Will you recite it now so that his magic does not affect you?' As the Emir recited the Great Name Gulfam quietly muttered a spell. The Emir walked on, but felt a certain heaviness of spirit. He tried to recite the Great Name, and realized that he could not remember it. He quickly returned to his own pavilion and recited the prayer of Abraham to calm himself.

Meanwhile, when the Islamic ayyars could not find Gulfam anywhere, it occurred to them that he could be hiding magically from them. They consulted each other and finally decided to leave and tackle him on the battlefield the next morning. Later, Gulfam appeared in Bakhtiarak's pavilion and whispered to him that he had taken care of Hamza. Bakhtiarak congratulated him and urged him to remain hidden until the next morning.

Gulgoon kidnaps Hamza

Now witness the miracle of the Divine Strategist. Had Emir Hamza remained in the camp, he would have confronted Gulfam the next morning and succumbed to his magic. He was spared the humiliation in this manner. There were a number of forts in Kohistan. One of them was the fort of Gulgoonia and its master was Gulgoon Kohi, a Laqa worshipper with a passion for the art of ayyari. Gulgoon had spent many years learning the wiles of ayyari and had twelve thousand disciples living with him in the fort. He had long nursed an ambition to confront the infamous Amar and outwit him before Laqa.

Gulgoon said to his disciples, 'I really wish to meet Khudawand, but I should offer something unique to him.' The disciples suggested, 'Amar would have been ideal for that purpose, but since he is in Tilism, why don't we capture Hamza? That would really please Khudawand.' Gulgoon was very happy with this suggestion and began preparing for the journey to Mount Agate. Armed with the weapons of trickery, he set forth with his disciples. The night that Emir had forgotten the Great Name, Gulgoon had been wandering in the Islamic camp disguised as a handmaiden.

Hamza's childhood companion, the legendary archer Muqbil the Faithful, was guarding the Emir's pavilion that night. He looked at the false handmaiden suspiciously and asked her, 'Who are you?' The handmaiden gave him a name that startled Muqbil. His thoughts went back to the old days when Nausherwan's daughter, Meher Nigar, was married to Emir Hamza. He was reminded of his own wife Zehra Misri, daughter of the king of Egypt, who was handmaiden to Meher Nigar. Most of all, he was reminded of that terrible day when Meher Nigar and her handmaidens committed suicide by consuming poison. Muqbil sighed deeply as the memories overwhelmed him and began weeping silently.

Gulgoon was very puzzled by his behaviour, but before he could say anything, Emir Hamza emerged from his pavilion after performing his prayers. He saw his old friend in tears and asked him what was wrong. Before Muqbil could respond, Gulgoon murmured words of comfort and wiped the old archer's tears with a corner of his veil infused with a potion of unconsciousness. When Muqbil sneezed and slumped forward, the Emir looked at Gulgoon suspiciously, but the very next moment, Gulgoon managed to burst a narcotic bubble in his face and made him unconscious. Gulgoon unfolded the sheet of ayyari and tied the Emir in it with his snare-rope. He hoisted the bundle on his shoulders and darting behind tents for cover, finally reached the wilderness. He then made for the fort of Gulgoonia. Once he reached there, he untied the sheet and locked up the Emir in a box.

Meanwhile, Muqbil the Faithful woke up with a jerk. He rushed into the pavilion, but there was no sign of Emir Hamza there. Muqbil shouted out to the guards to check the camp. The ayyars of Islam too checked the camp thoroughly, but there was still no sign of the Emir. They found an unknown footprint just outside Emir's pavilion but it did not match the footprints of any of Laqa's ayyars.

The next morning, when Gulfam went to Laqa before commencing the battle, Laqa's spies reported that there was chaos in Hamza's camp because he was missing. Gulfam smiled at Shaitan and said, 'Malik-ji, it seems Hamza was too cowardly to face me and has run away.' Shaitan said scornfully to the sahir, 'Have you lost your mind? Even Hamza's slaves would not dream of hiding from danger! He is a noble warrior with the courage of a lion. Even if he was convinced of his death, he would not hide from you! I can swear to you, he is not deceitful!'

Laqa added, 'O mortal, you are not aware of our celestial strategies. It was our divine hand that actually whisked Hamza from his camp. We have captured him to spare you a fight.' On hearing this, Gulfam kissed Laqa's feet and said, 'Indeed, you are all-powerful!' Bakhtiarak cried out, 'For the sake of your divinity, please do not claim that you have captured Hamza my lord! You know what the son of my Teacher Chalak bin Amar will do to both of us if he finds out!' This terrified Laqa, who stuttered, 'I did not mean that I actually kidnapped Hamza. What I mean to say is that not a leaf moves without my divine will!' There were murmurs of admiration from Laqa's worshippers as they gazed up at him in awe and said, 'Indeed, there is no doubt about it, nothing happens against your will!'

Chalak bin Amar and his ayyar companions were present in durbar at that time in various disguises. Chalak heard this fatuous conversation and realized that both Laqa and Gulfam had no clue as to Hamza's whereabouts. Chalak then left the durbar and returned to his own camp. He entered the durbar and saw the Shah looking worried and the sardars in a state of grief. The badshah said quietly to Chalak, 'Alas, in Amar's absence, the camp is in such a state of disarray that someone could infiltrate and first erase the memory of the Great Name and later kidnap Emir!'

Chalak said, 'I am to blame for I should have remained in the camp last night. God willing, I shall now depart and find Emir or not show my face to you again.' He signalled to ayyar Abul Fateh to accompany him and left the durbar.

Meanwhile, in Laqa's durbar, Gulfam declared, 'There is no point in fighting an army without a commander. Who knows when Hamza will return? This may be a prolonged war.' Bakhtiarak suggested, 'You should use this time to destroy the rest of his camp. When Hamza returns, you can capture him as well.' Gulfam said, 'How will I get them to attack?' The scheming Shaitan replied, 'Prepare to execute the prisoners. Badshah will definitely try to rescue them. You can then cast a spell and capture the whole army.' Gulfam was pleased with this idea and ordered his commanders to prepare for the executions. Since he wanted to provoke Hamza's army, he asked the heralds to announce that the enemies of Laqa would be put through extreme torture before their public executions—a lesson for anyone who even dreamt of rebelling against Khudawand.

The ayyars of Islam reported the announcement to the Shah, who promptly ordered the army to prepare for battle. Kettledrums were struck and many braves donned their shrouds, ready to die in combat. The Shah himself wore his battle dress and mounted his black steed. Battle flags were unfurled and thousands of foot soldiers spread out in orderly formations.

Bahar's magic garden

Finally, in Laqa's durbar, Gulfam hesitated and then said, 'There is another prisoner in my custody. It was not appropriate to mention this before.' Laqa interrupted him, 'Our divinity knows already, but you should have spoken before!' Gulfam looked sheepish and said, 'I have captured Princess Bahar who is allied with Amar in Tilism-e-Hoshruba. She is a powerful woman, but I captured her while she was sleeping. I have kept her in a box. I think that she should be killed along with the prisoners if she still turns away from our faith.'

Laqa nodded sagely and asked him to bring Bahar to the durbar. Gulfam sent for the box and helped Bahar out of it. Bahar took deep breaths of the fresh air and looked around her. Being a woman of great intelligence and also someone who had learned a great deal in the company of Amar, she thought, 'If I am defiant now, it will be difficult for me. I should deceive them now and punish them later.' Accordingly, the lovely princess mournfully prostrated before Laqa and then stood silently with her hands folded. Laqa looked delighted and called out, 'O Gulfam, this princess is our favoured one! We have endowed her with beauty, grace and unique skills. Release her at once!' Shaitan Bakhtiarak quickly said, 'Khudawand, in the name of your divinity, leave this matter alone!'

Infuriated, Laqa shouted, 'Shaitan, you speak nonsense! If Gulfam goes against my wishes, I will bring my wrath upon him!' Gulfam looked terrified and quickly removed the needle from Bahar's tongue. Bahar looked gratefully at Laqa and said, 'Khudawand, your humble handmaiden longed to get a glimpse of you. Fortune gave me the opportunity to kiss your feet at last!' Laqa swelled up with pride and said, 'My favoured one, I accept your homage. This is our special mortal Gulfam whose wife has died. We want you to accept him as husband and together you can rule Hoshruba! We will remove the King of Sahirs!'

Bahar looked downwards, as if overcome with shyness, and Gulfam almost burst out of his clothes in sheer happiness. He released her at once from his binding spells and cried, 'As long as I live, Princess, I am your man!' Bahar felt her body getting lighter and realized that her magical powers had been restored. Gulfam even offered her a chair, but she smiled and said, 'You captured me while I was asleep, but be warned that I will fight you while you are fully awake!'

Bakhtiarak called out, 'That's the spirit! The blessings and peace of Allah upon the Prophet Muhammad! A thousand curses on this haramzada Laqa! I warned him but he did not listen to me! Princess, punish this fool and this kafir Gulfam!' Bahar simply walked away, leaving Laqa and Gulfam stunned. Gulfam soon rushed out after Bahar and ordered his commanders to attack her.

The sahirs hurled magic citrons, clove garlands and needles on Bahar, but the fair princess flew up and descended in the middle of the plain. She recited an incantation and cried, 'O magic spring, come and wither the tree of Gulfam's life!' There was a sudden gale and dark clouds spread over the plain. This was followed by a loud crack of thunder and lightning that blinded everyone. The very next moment, the plain seemed to be streaming with sunlight. A beautiful garden materialized with hundreds of neat little flowerbeds. In the middle of this garden, a clear crystal platform glowed like the light of heaven. Bahar was nowhere in sight, but a maiden of moon-like beauty who was adorned with flowers lay reclining on a silk masnad.

Gulfam lost his heart to the maiden and rushed towards the garden, reciting verses of love. The maiden saw him and called out, 'This is Princess Bahar's garden and strangers are forbidden here. Enter, and you will lose your life!' Gulfam did not heed her warning and stepped into the garden. That fairy-faced beauty rose from the masnad and glided towards him saying, 'Shameless one, I did warn you and now you will be punished!' She held out her arm and a branch snapped off one of the trees. As soon as it touched her outstretched hand, it transformed into a long sword. She smiled at Gulfam and brought the sword down on his head with force.

Gulfam tried to ward off the sword's blow, but could not remember any incantation in time. The sword split his skull open and went straight through him. His impure body fell apart into two pieces and his guardian spirits howled and raged. The sardars who were under his spell recovered their senses and charged at the guards with their broken chains. The executioners dropped their swords and ran for their lives, while the army of Islam attacked at the same time. Bahar, who was still hovering in the air, chanted powerful words that made the sardars of Islam immune to magic. The dust of hundreds of sahir lives was scattered by the ferocious swords of the courageous; the lamps of their existence were extinguished and their bodies piled up in the plain.

Bakhtiarak advised Laqa that it was best to barricade themselves in Fort Agate as the Muslims would attack them next. Laqa, who was already shaking with fear, gasped, 'I had destined this already!' The sahir army was defeated and the survivors fled for their lives. At the end of the day, the army of Islam returned to their camp with the released sardars, where the Shah reinstated them and bestowed robes of honour on them. He was informed that the beautiful enchantress Bahar Jadoo had killed Gulfam. He felt a warm glow when he heard Bahar's name and the seeds of love were planted in his heart. Outwardly, however, he remained impassive and graciously said, 'We should express our gratitude to the noble princess. Some of you go to her garden and escort her to our durbar.'

Chalak finds Emir

Now hear about the Emir. Chalak and Abul Fateh roamed everywhere, but found no trace of him. They decided to investigate in the areas beyond Mount Agate and were far from their camp when they passed by the fort of Gulgoonia. Ayyar Gulgoon was on his way to Laqa with twelve thousand men and had set up camp in the plains below the fort. Chalak saw that this appeared be a camp of ayyars with hundreds of them milling around in various disguises. Some of them were playing musical instruments, while others energetically ran up the trees and down into their tents. Several of them were guarding the vast pavilion in the middle of the camp. 'My instinct tells me,' Chalak whispered to his companion, 'that Emir might be in this camp.'

The ayyars of Islam disguised their real faces, but as they were already dressed like ayyars, they did not need to change their appearance much before they marched to the large pavilion. When the ayyars guarding the entrance stopped them, they protested, 'We are here to meet your leader. Why do you arrest us?' Gulgoon heard the row and sent his ayyars to escort the strangers inside. He looked sharply at the two ayyars and asked where they had come from. They replied, 'We live in Kohistan and always wanted to have a contest with you as you have made a great name in the profession of ayyari. We heard that you are on your way to the Khudawand Laqa and thought that we should have this contest there. We think that you are greater than the ayyars of Islam and if we defeat you, it means we have defeated all ayyars, for you are the best.'

Gulgoon was flattered and got up to embrace them. He told them, 'It is indeed gracious of you to say such kind things about me. Only those who are supremely talented and confident attribute others with the same qualities.' He offered them places of honour and asked, 'What are your names?' Chalak declared, 'We have many names but are popularly known as Makkar Slippery-tongue, and Ghaddar Lying-tongue.' Gulgoon laughed when he heard these names and served goblets brimming with wine to his guests.

They declined the wine politely and said, 'We cannot eat and drink with you if we intend to fight a battle of wits with you. Tell us, what special gift will you present to Khudawand Laqa?' Gulgoon looked at them suspiciously and thought that they could be spies from Hamza's camp. Abul Fateh rose abruptly and said to Chalak, 'Brother, we should leave now. Why should we suffer anyone's hostility? We can find our own way to Khudawand!'

Chalak also rose to leave, but Gulgoon caught his hand and said, 'Do not be offended my friends. I have been trained in the art of ayyari. A wise man is alert to even a hint of danger. For a moment, I thought that you might be from the enemy. Any ayyar who ignores his instincts does not deserve to be in this worthy profession!' They looked at him searchingly and said, 'Brother, you are so right. Now do you mind if we say something?' Gulgoon nodded his assent. Chalak said smoothly, 'It is clear to us that you have someone in captivity. If you had wanted to keep your secret, you would not have reacted this way!' Gulgoon was stunned and said, 'You are indeed very intelligent and skilled ayyars.' He presented them with two splendid scimitars and said, 'Accept these with my compliments!'

Chalak accepted the gift and said, 'We would have to return the compliment! Very well, if it is acceptable to you, we will leave now and bring you a gift from the lashkar of Islam. Perhaps even Hamza himself!' Gulgoon laughed and his disciples looked at the guests admiringly and murmured, 'Makkar, you really are an exceptional man!'

Chalak looked closely at Gulgoon and said, 'Surely you are testing me? It seems you have done something remarkable already!' Gulgoon said, 'Why do I get the feeling that you are here to discover my secrets? Very well, I have nothing to hide! Since you have already guessed that we have someone, I will be open with you. I have kidnapped Hamza.'

Chalak and Abul Fateh laughed derisively, 'Indeed, you must have Hamza!' Gulgoon frowned and said, 'Do you have any doubts?' Abul Fateh replied, 'Is Hamza a giant of a man with outsized limbs?' Gulgoon looked puzzled and said, 'He is smaller in stature than us Kohistanis!' The two ayyars laughed harder and exclaimed, 'Indeed that must be Hamza!' Gulgoon was rattled and snapped, 'What is so amusing?' Abul Fateh replied patiently, 'Brother, we have heard that the real Hamza lives in a cave. The ayyars of Islam disguise different men to look like him and sleep in his bed every night. It could be a grasscutter or a guard. Anyway, we have found out where Hamza remains hidden. We will bring him to you. You are welcome to present him to Khudawand. If not, then offer him the false Hamza you have captured!'

The ayyars jumped out of their chairs and left the pavilion. Gulgoon was very confused by this and postponed his departure to Mount Agate. He thought, 'It seems plausible. It is quite likely that I have caught the wrong man.'

The real and false Hamza

Chalak and Abul Fateh left the camp relieved that they had found their beloved Emir. Both had a mischievous streak and thought of ways in which they could humiliate Gulgoon before Laqa. They headed straight for a garden close to Fort Agate. The ruler Sulaiman Ambreen's wrestler nephew, Mansoor Kohi, spent his nights there, secretly dallying with a courtesan. The ayyars were of course aware of his secret. Abul Fateh volunteered to capture Mansoor in order to pass him off as Hamza. He disguised himself to look like a hideous apparition and peered over the garden wall. He saw that the garden was fragrant and bathed in moonlight, with a cool breeze wafting through it. The dais in the middle was covered with a rich golden carpet and Mansoor Kohi was reclining on cushions with the young and comely courtesan.

Abul Fateh jumped over the wall and landed with a bang in the garden. The courtesan pushed Mansoor Kohi away and screamed, 'Who is that?' Mansoor Kohi rolled up his sleeves and swaggered towards the wall, determined to punish the intruder. Abul Fateh suddenly materialized before Mansoor and frightened the wits out of him. Abul Fateh said to Mansoor, 'I am the angel of Laqa. He ordered me to bring these grapes to you because he said you lead a life of debauchery. This will make you forever young and virile.'

Mansoor genuflected before the angel and reverently received the fruit. He took it to the courtesan and shared the good news with her. The false angel said to them, 'Eat it quickly for it is divine fruit and will not remain long on this earth!' Mansoor and the courtesan eagerly consumed the grapes and were soon unconscious. Abul Fateh left the courtesan there and returned to Chalak with the unconscious Mansoor. They painted the wrestler's face to look like the Emir's face, changed his clothes, and tied him up in a sheet.

The next morning, they went to Gulgoon and threw the bundle before him. Gulgoon smiled and said, 'Who is this? Is it one of Hamza's sons?' They replied, 'We have brought the Father of the Lashkar, Hamza himself! It was not easy to find the vault where he was hidden but we managed it!'

They untied the sheet and Gulgoon was startled to see the unconscious man. His face seemed to be the same as the man he had kidnapped, but he was a veritable giant of a man with huge limbs and a neck as thick as a bull's. Gulgoon in his ignorance thought that this man could indeed be the legendary Hamza. He ordered one of his men to bring the box containing the Hamza that he had. Chalak followed the guard and told him, 'I will help you lift it!'

Chalak saw that the box had a lock that was as large as a camel's thigh. He burst a narcotic bubble in the guard's face and rendered him unconscious. Then he turned to the box. Chalak was Amar's son and such locks were child's play for him. He took out a set of keys and found one that fitted the lock. He opened the lid and saw Emir Hamza lying unconscious inside. Hamza was a strong man which is why he had survived three days without nourishment. Chalak revived his master with some incense of consciousness. When the Emir opened his eyes and looked questioningly at Chalak, the ayyar whispered, 'A trickster kidnapped you. I have duped him into believing that you are not the real Hamza. If he interrogates you, please tell him that you are not Hamza. I know that you are averse to lying, but this is the need of the hour. We are after all fighting kafirs!'

Emir remained silent. Chalak rendered him unconscious again and locked the box. Chalak revived the guard who looked at him furiously and said, 'Tell me, why you did this to me? I will have to report this to my master!' Chalak folded his hands and said, 'My life and honour are in your hands! When I saw this box, I thought it was full of treasure. When I opened the box, I saw a man in it and closed it again. That is the truth!' For added measure, Chalak pressed a handful of gold coins into the guard's hand and made him promise not to utter a word to Gulgoon.

They took the box to Gulgoon, who unlocked the box and revived Hamza. 'Tell me truthfully, who are you?' Gulgoon asked. The Emir said weakly, 'Who has brought me here? I have been deceived by a rogue of an ayyar!' Gulgoon said impatiently, 'Why do you talk in riddles? Tell us the truth!' Hamza replied, 'The truth is that I was Nausherwan's servant. I am now with his son Faramurz who came to Kohistan with Laqa. An ayyar promised me a lot of money to sleep in Hamza's bed but I have been punished for my greed!'

Gulgoon turned to Chalak and asked him to revive the real Hamza to hear his version. Chalak shuddered, 'It seems you do not value your life. You want me to revive the man who is capable of breaking the heaviest iron chains! If you doubt his identity, take your prisoner to Khudawand and we will take ours. We were doing you a favour by bringing the real Hamza to you, and you repay us by doubting our integrity?'

Gulgoon stood up and pleaded, 'I did not mean to offend you, merely to hear what Hamza had to say. You have indeed saved me from making a fool of myself before Khudawand! You are right! If Hamza is revived, it will be impossible to control him!'

The real Emir had been standing patiently during this exchange. Gulgoon pressed some gold coins in his hand and said, 'You can leave now, but do not talk about this matter in Khudawand's camp!' The Emir silently walked out of the pavilion. Gulgoon then placed Mansoor Kohi in the box and placed it in a heavily guarded tent. Chalak and Abul Fateh soon got up to leave. Gulgoon said to them, 'I thought you were travelling with us.' Chalak replied, 'We have four hundred disciples who are waiting to travel with us in a grand procession to Khudawand. We will reach there at the same time as you.'

By this time, Laqa's durbar was buzzing with the rumours of Mansoor Kohi's inexplicable disappearance. The believers turned to Laqa and cried, 'Omnipotent one, you will know where he is!' Laqa put on a mysterious expression and declared, 'Our divine hand has taken him to our heaven!' He was saved from further explanations by the news that the ruler of Gulgoonia had arrived with a large army. Laqa sent some people to receive him.

Gulgoon entered the durbar and prostrated in front of Khudawand. Laqa awarded him robes of honour before declaring that the durbar would be convened in the plains outside to provide the faithful with a glimpse of his divine self. Chalak and Abul Fateh heard that Gulgoon had reached Laqa's durbar and decided to amuse themselves at his expense. They painted their faces to look like Makkar and Ghaddar and asked four hundred ayyars to meet them in the forest beside Mount Agate. Once they had all gathered there, they formed a grand procession and proceeded to Laqa's durbar. They greeted Laqa and made an offering of gold to him, but made sure that they did not prostrate before him. It was obvious that Laqa was offended. To placate him, the ayyars came forward and said, 'O Divine One, we are not merely soldiers and ayyars, we also follow your injunctions faithfully. In your divine books, you have urged your followers to do the opposite of whatever the Muslims do. You declared that since Muslims always worship their God in a state of purity, your own followers should pray to you in an unclean state! As we have just bathed and are in a state of grace, we did not genuflect before you!'

Laqa cried, 'O faithful followers, do not reveal these secrets to all and sundry! You are indeed great scholars of the true faith!' Laqa's durbaris gathered around Makkar and Ghaddar and kissed their hands murmuring, 'You are the chosen ones and will guide us in the mysteries of faith.' Only Bakhtiarak realized that they were mocking Laqa and thought that they were probably from the Muslim camp. Before he could voice his suspicions, Gulgoon announced that he had brought Hamza as an offering for Laqa. He sent for the box and took Mansoor Kohi out of it. 'This is not Hamza!' exclaimed Bakhtiarak. 'Since when did he develop such large limbs?'

'What are you saying?' said Gulgoon. 'I have managed to capture the real Hamza from his hideout with great difficulty.' Bakhtiarak looked puzzled and asked, 'What do you mean, the real Hamza?' Gulgoon explained, 'His ayyars hide him every night and put someone in his place!' He then repeated Chalak's falsehoods word for word. When he was done, Bakhtiarak laughed and did a little jig in front of his chair. He sang, 'Someone has taught you well. Indeed, you have found the true Hamza!'

Gulgoon hissed furiously, 'Can you do anything apart from making a fool of yourself?' Shaitan retorted, 'I may be a fool, but someone has certainly made a fool out of you! Tell us, did you meet anyone on your way here?' Gulgoon related how he had kidnapped Hamza and the subsequent meeting with the two ayyars. He pointed at Chalak and Abul Fateh, 'These were the two ayyars I met!' Shaitan exclaimed, 'I knew it already! I had a feeling that the sons of our Teacher were here!' He looked at the two ayyars who stood up and glared at him defiantly. He recognized them at once and greeted them with mock deference while everyone else in the durbar seemed quite bewildered.

At that time, Mansoor Kohi woke up and cried out, 'O Divine One, how have I erred and why do you punish me? I am your faithful servant Mansoor Kohi!' Laqa looked reproachfully at Gulgoon who realized that he had been deceived. In his fury, he rushed at Chalak with his sword. Abul Fateh landed a mighty blow on his back just in time, while Chalak ducked and tried to leap out of the durbar. He landed on the slippery cornerstone at the entrance and tumbled down. Gulgoon's men moved swiftly and caught Chalak as he fell. Though he struggled and hacked at the coils of their snare-ropes, he was captured and bound. Abul Fateh, however, managed to escape and ran back to his camp

Meanwhile Laqa's men had washed the paints off Mansoor Kohi's face. Gulgoon felt humiliated and declared that he would execute Chalak right away. Shaitan was uncomfortable and thought that if he were present at the execution of Amar's son, the ayyars would skin him alive. He excused himself from durbar and returned to his tent.

Abul Fateh went straight to the ayyar Qasim of the Aad tribe, a veritable giant of a man. He asked him to transform into a dev and painted himself to look like Amar. This was easy enough as Abul Fateh was Amar's nephew and resembled him. Qasim moulded a hideous mask on his face, attached two horns on his head and a tail on his back. He fastened an iron chain around his waist and completed his transformation by fixing wings on his shoulders. He hoisted Abul Fateh on his mighty shoulders and bounded off to Laqa's camp. He leaped ten yards at a time and it seemed as if he was flying through the air.

They landed right in front of Shaitan Bakhtiarak's tent, who was stunned at the sight of Amar mounted on a fearsome dev. He presented the false Amar with whatever treasures he had in the tent and said, 'It is my good fortune that you visited me today. My eyes longed for a glimpse of you and at last my wish has been granted!' The false Amar took out his dagger and held it at Shaitan's throat. Shaitan collapsed on his bed and hurriedly recited verses from the Quran. Abul Fateh said to him, 'Haramzadeh, do you think you will live when my son is killed?' Shaitan declared bravely, 'No one can kill him in my lifetime!' The false Amar drew back and allowed Shaitan to run towards the durbar shouting, 'Do not kill him! I forbid you from killing him!' The false Amar mounted on the dev followed close behind Shaitan.

On the way to the durbar, Shaitan asked the false Amar, 'Has Tilism been conquered? How is it that you are here?' Abul Fateh replied, 'I spend a couple of months there and return occasionally to Mount Agate. It is easier now that we have devs under our control. If you doubt me, I can tell this dev to take you on a tour!' Shaitan touched his ears and said, 'I was at fault for asking you; forgive me!'

Shaitan entered the durbar and called out, 'Be warned that *he* is here! No one should execute Chalak!' Laqa snapped, 'What nonsense is this? Who has come?' Shaitan looked meaningfully at him and cried, 'Leave all that! I will explain everything if we live! Just let the boy go!' Gulgoon looked furious and shouted, 'I am not going to listen to this!' He drew his sword on Chalak, but Bakhtiarak threw himself dramatically on Chalak and shielded him with his body. He cried, 'My brother, I will give my own life for you!' As a result, Gulgoon was forced to release Chalak from his chains. As soon as he was free, Abul Fateh called out to him and both the ayyars ran out of durbar. Gulgoon ran after them, but the fleet-footed ayyars eluded him easily. He returned to durbar and told Bakhtiarak caustically, 'Malik-ji, I lost them both because of you!'

Shaitan said, 'We have been saved from terrible danger! I thought it was *him*, but it was not.' Gulgoon was now terribly irritated and shouted, 'Who are you talking about? Who is *he*?' Bakhtiarak shuddered and muttered, 'Let it go. If you mention it *he* might just appear!' Gulgoon gave up and sank back in his chair. 'Well,' he warned Bakhtiarak, 'it's clear to me that the ayyars of Islam are a menace. Never mind, I will capture them all! Do not interfere in my business next time!'

Bahar strikes again

The messengers who were sent by the Shah to invite Bahar could not find the fair princess or her magic garden. They reported this to the Shah, who was disappointed, but remained calm. Meanwhile, Bahar had dispelled her magic garden and was looking for someone to lead her to Hamza's lashkar. Suddenly, a sahir approached her and said, 'Princess, I will be honoured if you use my humble abode to refresh yourself. I will be at your service with all my heart!' Bahar was tired and smiled gratefully at him. 'Brother,' she said, 'if that is your wish I will gladly go with you.' The sahir happily led her to his garden nearby. He offered Bahar a goblet of his choicest wine and watched her as she sipped it without suspicion. He laid out refreshments for her and insisted on refilling her goblet after slipping a drug into the wine flask. Within moments, Bahar slumped on the cushions, dead to the world.

The sahir read spells to keep her unconscious and hoisted her on his back. He flew to Mount Agate where Laqa's durbar was still furiously arguing about the ayyars who had escaped. He threw her before Laqa and after prostrating, informed Laqa how he had deceived Bahar. Laqa cried,

'My Chosen One, you have indeed performed a wonderful deed!' The sahir folded his hands, and said, 'I am hopeful that Khudawand will award her to me.' Shaitan interjected, 'This is the same rebel princess who conjured the deadly garden. Have her killed right now and award this sahir with a houri from your heaven!' Laqa accordingly told the sahir, 'My son, this woman is destined to die but I will reward you beyond your expectations!'

Laqa sent for his executioner and his camp buzzed wth the news of Bahar Jadoo's capture. The ayyars who had returned to Laqa's lashkar in different disguises heard about Bahar's impending execution as well. The resourceful Chalak quickly transformed into an executioner and walked into the durbar calling out, 'Where is the criminal? Tell me quickly and I will free her of her life with one stroke!' Shaitan said, 'Strike this woman who lies here unconscious!' Chalak said, 'Revive her so that I can fulfil her dying wish!' Shaitan snapped back, 'There is no need to revive her! Kill her now!'

Chalak nodded and addressed the man who had captured Bahar, 'You are a sahir. Come and stand by me so that no ayyar interferes with my work!' The sahir obligingly came closer to Chalak who whispered, 'Khudawand seems to be signalling to you!' The sahir looked at Laqa, thus giving Chalak the oppurunity to strike him hard. The sahir's head rolled off and landed near Laqa. This was followed by a fierce gale and darkness as the sahir's spirits swirled through the durbar, howling out his name.

Chalak quickly revived Bahar and cried, 'Let us get away from here and I will explain everything!' Meanwhile, light returned to the durbar and Laqa's sardars and guards surrounded Chalak and Bahar with their drawn swords. Bahar thought that it was best to escape now and ask for explanations later. She cast a spell of darkness in the durbar, held Chalak by the waist and flew out. Laqa panicked during the darkness and hid under his throne while Shaitan hopped about, calling out to the Holy Prophet for help. Sardars fled from the pavilion and there was an uproar in the camp. The army began to mobilize for battle and shops closed for the day.

Bahar had created a temporary diversion to help her escape and the darkness did not last long. Bakhtiarak helped Laqa out of his hiding place, sardars returned to the durbar and the agitated camp calmed down. Laqa declared, 'O mortal men, I wanted to hand over the princess to her captor and Shaitan wanted her executed. He interfered in our divine will and the river of our rage boiled over! Did you witness what happened when I was disobeyed?' His sardars murmured in reverence, 'Indeed you are true! You are the Righteous Khudawand! No one can dare go against your will!'

Bakhtiarak thought in his heart, 'A curse on this liar!' For Laqa's sake, however, he cried out, 'Khudawand, indeed I have sinned! I should never have opposed your will and interfered in this matter!' Everyone trembled when they heard Shaitan and thought, 'If Khudawand can make Shaitan repent, we mortals have no standing!'

Meanwhile, Bahar had flown to safety with Chalak and landed in the wilderness. She asked him what had happened and he explained, 'A sahir had captured you. Laqa was going to execute you while you were unconscious, but I created a diversion by killing the sahir. Where were you? The Shah had sent sardars to invite you to our lashkar.'

Bahar looked grim as she related how the sahir had deceived her. She added, 'Return to your camp and inform the Shah that his humble handmaiden will follow soon to pay her respects to him. First, I want to teach this Laqa a lesson he will not forget in a hurry!' Bahar then flew off in the direction of Fort Agate.

Within moments, dark clouds floated down from the mountain and spread over Laqa's camp. Everyone swayed with pleasure as a fresh cool breeze blew over the plain. Princess Bahar had conjured these dark clouds to enchant Laqa's people. There was a sudden flash of lightning and the next moment, Laqa's army saw that the bride of the plain was wearing a diaphanous red veil and spring clouds glowed like the setting sun. Beautiful parizads emerged with flasks of wine and poured goblets for the entranced army. Soldiers threw away their weapons and lay down on the grass reciting verses of love. Laqa's sardars, Bakhtiarak, Sulaiman, Mansoor and Gulgoon started dancing frantically. Laqa called out, 'My chosen mortals, I feel like dancing naked today and want you to be naked as well!'

Laqa rushed out of durbar, stripped off his clothes and started jumping around. His sardars threw off their clothes as well and danced around him. They guzzled large quantities of wine and smeared each other with mud. Bakhtiarak drunkenly shouted, 'We need a clown among us!' Everyone fell on Laqa, who was jumping up and down, stark naked. 'What do you want, my chosen ones?' cried Laqa. They did not answer and instead painted half of his face black and the other half, red. Laqa looked a strange sight indeed. He was a giant of a man with a beard that was thirty yards long. The revellers covered his head with a torn robe and tied a drum around his waist. After they had finished with the foolish Laqa, they turned to Shaitan and made him kneel on all fours. They forced Laqa to sit on him and clapped as Shaitan moved like the donkey he was. Some fanned Laqa with brooms while others hit his head with slippers.

This bizarre procession then moved towards Hamza's camp. When the procession came into view, sardars placed their handkerchiefs over their mouths and laughed silently, while the Shah looked disgusted. Emir Hamza came out and made Laqa dismount Shaitan. He breathed the Great Name on him so that Laqa could come back to his senses. He did the same to the sardars and took all of them to a separate tent where they washed themselves and wore fresh garments. Then he led them to the durbar where they were welcomed by the sardars of Islam.

Emir Hamza asked Laqa, 'Who did this to you and your sardars Zamurrad Shah?' Laqa remained unrepentant and said, 'My divinity knows, but I will not reveal the name!' The Emir sighed and looked at Bakhtiarak, who rose and comically went around the Shah's throne reciting the verse of affimation and declaring that he had always been a Muslim at heart, all the time darting anxious looks at the ayyars standing in the durbar. After these antics, he said, 'A rebel princess Bahar Jadoo had been captured and brought to us. Chalak rescued her. It must have been her for she has done this before.'

Emir looked sternly at Chalak and sent him to the magic garden to convey this message to Bahar: 'This was not a good thing to do as you have cast a shadow on our reputation. The armies of Islam do not rely on magic to help them in war. Neutralize this spell and come to us in durbar.' Chalak went to the garden and called out to Bahar. When the beautiful princess emerged from the garden, he conveyed the message of the noble Emir to her. Bahar's heart was full of admiration for the Emir and she thought, 'All praise is to God and the chivalrous spirit of Sahibqiran. Anyone else would have been triumphant at his enemy's humiliation.' She bade Chalak convey her greetings to Emir and added, 'Apologize for me. I will come to durbar presently.'

That incomparable woman of magic then chanted a spell that created a crimson cloud between the dark ones, which burst to release crimson rainfall. Within moments, the garden and parizads vanished. The soldiers of Laqa's camp were also jerked into consciousness. When they opened their eyes, they felt remorseful and said to each other, 'Brother, what is this we have done? We stripped ourselves naked and made Khudawand dance! How could we commit this sacrilege? Perhaps this was part of Khudawand's divine will!'

Meanwhile, Emir Hamza signalled to the cupbearers to serve wine to their uninvited guests. After they had been sated, Emir dropped these pearls of wisdom from his mouth: 'Zamurrad Shah, why do you persist in these false claims of divinity and walk in the wilderness of hell? I promise that if you accept the true faith, I will endow you with all the kingdoms I have conquered. I will even carry your throne on my shoulders!' Laqa repeated the words Shaitan had advised him to say on such occasions,

'On the day you defeat and capture me, I will do as you say!' Emir sighed deeply and declared, 'Alas, you will never follow the righteous path!'

Laqa and his companions took their leave of the Shah of Islam and returned to their camp. The nobility of Emir's conduct towards them made a deep impression on Araz Kohi, one of Laqa's sardars. He was now convinced that Laqa haramzada was a liar and misled people with his claims to divinity. He returned to Fort Agate and sent for his commanders to tell them, 'I have decided to accept Islam for how can a true Living God succumb to magic? The conduct of the sardars of Islam towards us has convinced me that as soldiers and warriors, we must ally with them for they represent all that is noble and good!'

The commanders too pledged their support to Araz. He told them to sound the drum of travel and announce their departure for Hamza's camp in case they were accused of being deserters. Meanwhile, Laqa sat on his throne of pride and addressed his followers, 'O Chosen Ones, did you see how I influenced Hamza's heart into supporting us? Do you think an enemy ever behaves like he did? I can make him prostrate before me any time I want. I do not make him do so because he is my commander-in-chief. He punishes those who do not believe in me and worships me secretly at night! Look how I made you dance and then returned you to your senses. This is a small example of my powers!' His faithful believers swayed with the power of his words and sang his praises when his agents came in and informed him that Araz Kohi was leaving to join Hamza.

Laqa first impulse was to arrest Araz Kohi, but Bakhtiarak advised him against it as they had just emerged from one ordeal. If they attacked Azar, Bhatiarak reasoned, Hamza and his forces would fall upon them, the consequences of which would be terrible. When Araz Kohi reached Hamza's lashkar, the Shah got word of his arrival and sent his sardars to receive him. They led him to the durbar with great esteem and honour.

Bahar and the Shah

That evening, Bahar reached Hamza's camp on her flying throne and was overwhelmed by the sight of the Shah's pavilion that soared into the sky. Its moorings were as firm as the moorings of the earth. Beyond the pavilion was a great bazaar offering all manner of goods. Comely young sales boys clad in costly clothes and jewels courteously served their noble customers. A bevy of beautiful handmaidens in golden robes and jewellery approached the princess. They surrounded her throne and escorted her to the pavilion on a path illuminated with glass lamps. Bahar was entranced at the sight of a stream on which hundreds of multicoloured goblets floated on the waters and gleamed in the moonlight. The entrance to the Shah's pavilion was through a row of swaying poplars, but from the outside, only the stream and the trees were visible.

A throng of handmaidens greeted the princess as her procession approached the entrance. Bahar descended from her throne and went past the sentinels who opened the security chain for her. As she walked through the parted golden curtains, she saw that the pavilion was vast and lofty, and fragrant with bouquets of fresh flowers and incense holders. Twelve thousand crystal lamps inlaid with precious stones illuminated the pavilion and crystal chandeliers suspended from the roof of the pavilion were lined with jewels. Rare Persian carpets covered the floor and the chairs were studded with rubies and emeralds. The royal throne had a jewelled canopy and was flanked by forty pillars. On the throne sat a young man for whom the world and the sky itself could die a thousand deaths.

Bahar had fallen in love with Saad even before she had seen him. As she looked upon him now, she felt dizzy with the rush of feeling for him. The Shah of Islam was also overwhelmed by her beauty and gazed at her as if in a trance. Handmaidens revived them both with fragrant rose water. The Shah rose from his throne to welcome this paragon of beauty and held her hand. The princess murmured, 'I have travelled from a great distance and was overcome with weakness just now!' The Shah said, 'I was overcome with weakness just by looking at you!' The princess smiled archly and said, 'Now why would you fall ill on seeing me? Do not mislead me with such talk!'

The Shah said, 'The only ailment I have is that I am entangled in your winsome locks!' The princess asked, 'What will cure this ailment?' The Shah looked deep into her eyes and whispered, 'The sweet sherbet of your love!' The princess shyly looked away but the Shah kept holding her hand and led her up to the throne. His handmaidens drew the curtains aside and revealed a landscape gleaming under the monsoon moon. The Shah filled a crystal goblet with the nectar of grapes and held it lovingly to the princess's lips. Later, she refilled the same goblet and offered it to him. The wine removed their inhibitions, but their eyes were downcast to hide their desires. The Shah tried to pull her towards him, but she smiled and pretended to be annoyed. She whispered, 'Sahib, be still! By Allah, I do not approve of such familiarity. I dislike being pawed like this. Who could feel comfortable with such behaviour?'

The Shah began pleading and when she smiled, he boldly took her in his arms. She frowned and pulled away saying, 'You will have to curb your ardour lest we are mocked by friends and strangers. We will have to burn in the fire of separation and live in the hope of seeing each other again!' The Shah suddenly became very emotional. His eyes filled with tears and he said, 'O fair one, even though I am the Shah, I will always remain your slave!'

The princess wiped his tears with her sleeve and said, 'Sahib, I do not like men who weep!' As she laughed and went closer to him, the Shah could not restrain himself any longer and embraced her passionately. The princess struggled at first, but her heart was singing with joy and she returned his love. At last, they pulled themselves apart as they were conscious of the fact that they had to remain chaste and honourable.

The Shah led the beautiful Bahar to the back of the pavilion into a garden bathed in moonlight. The beauty of that garden cannot be described in words. There, the princess related to the Shah all that had happened in Tilism, how Afrasiyab had been besotted with her and how she had protected herself. She related her encounter with Amar, the manner in which he had converted her and their alliance with Kaukab. Finally, Saad and Bahar exchanged rings and promised each other that they would remain true to their love.

The night of separation was upon them and the courageous princess wept and said, 'My dearest love, Allah will be your Protector. Do not forget me and do not make me weep for you!' By this time, the Shah was also in tears and both the lovers wept with the grief of parting. In time, that garden behind the pavilion was lit by the rosy hue of dawn. Nature itself was heartbroken at Bahar's departure—waterfalls and streams wept for her while nightingales and peacocks cried forlornly as she left. There was a hushed silence as Bahar ascended her magic throne, constantly turning back to look at her beloved. The Shah gazed at her as men gaze at the moon of Eid until she disappeared into the sky and then returned to his pavilion with a heavy heart.

༄

16 Amar Sees the Wondrous Sights of Tilism-e-Nur Afshan, Princess Burran Arranges a Meeting between Mahrukh and Amar

Amar was now getting quite restless, having stayed in Burran Sword-woman's palace for so long. There was no news of the war with Afrasiyab and Kaukab had still not summoned Amar to meet him. One morning, Burran held his hand affectionately and said, 'Khwaja sahib, let me show you the wonders of our Tilism today.' Amar was reluctant to go on a tour at that point and said, 'How can I enjoy the sights of Tilism when my heart is torn with the thorn of anguish?' At Burran's insistence, however, Amar relented and left with her and a few selected sardars. As they emerged from the Palace of Seven Hues, Burran read an incantation that made a thick white mist envelope the travellers. Their eyes closed by themselves and the very next moment, they found themselves in a lush green plateau.

They walked towards the banks of a river, the waters of which were as pristine and clear as silver leaf. Burran invoked her magic and the travellers found themselves on the far bank. After walking a while, they came across a high wall of crystal that seemed to be stretching to infinity. Burran stood in front of the wall embellished with gold etchings in geometrical patterns and called out, 'Parizads of Tilism, come hither!' At the sound of her voice, there was a loud crack and a doorway made of rubies materialized in the wall. Through this door, the guardian fairies of Tilism emerged with a ruby throne and greeted Burran deferentially. Burran sat on the throne with Amar as several winged white horses with bejewelled saddles and silk reins flew through the doorway as mounts for Burran's sardars. The sounds of drums and trumpets filled the air as Burran's procession moved through the doorway.

On the other side of the magnificent ruby doorway stood a row of palaces made of silver bricks. These enchanting palaces were studded with precious pearls, emeralds, rubies, sapphires and diamonds. The procession stopped in front of the last palace that also had a lofty dome. They walked into the domed palace and saw that its interior glowed with the light of twenty-one spheres, virtual suns studded in the dome. As Amar went around admiring the priceless gems placed in the dome, he could not suppress his greedy instincts and asked Burran, 'Can anyone take these treasures or are they here just to be looked at?'

Burran smiled and said, 'You are welcome to partake of the treasures, but Kaukab has built this dome especially for the war with Afrasiyab. This dome has several magical properties—from here, you can view any place, no matter how distant, and reach any place within minutes.' When he heard this, Amar's endless greed took flight and he eagerly asked, 'Princess, show me Mahrukh's army from here!' Burran laughed and spoke some words that made a smiling parizad emerge from one of the suns. 'Arrange for Khwaja Amar to see Hoshruba from this dome!' Burran ordered.

The parizad went to a doorway and signalled towards one of the suns. It slid down and hovered in front of a shut doorway before going right into it. The door glowed with light and opened. Burran led Amar to the open door and said, 'Look down and you will see the camp.' Amar looked and saw that Mahrukh Magic-eye's army was trapped within a magical circle. The soldiers seemed to be in a state of complete chaos and were on their knees, worshipping the magic line, while the sardars were praying for deliverance. Hairat's latest ally, the ill-fated Nahoosat Jadoo, stood looking triumphant.

Amar was naturally agitated at the sight of his beleaguered army. Burran said calmly to him, 'Khwaja, stay strong and witness the miracle of God.' Even as she spoke, Mahrukh's army heard the boom of battle drums and trumpets. Princess Akhtar Jadoo arrived from the direction of Nur Afshan with a huge cavalry of sahirs and soldiers. Four sahirs of Nahoosat's army had conjured the magic line that trapped the soldiers of Mahrukh's army, and sixteen thousand magic slaves stood guarding it. Before Akhtar had left for battle, Burran had explained to her that once the four commanders were killed, the slaves would be destroyed automatically. So, the lovely Akhtar chanted an incantation that made five magic pearls materialize in the air. The pearls fell like arrows on the magic circle and the four sahir commanders. The sahir commanders were instantly killed and fell into the sea of infinity. As they died, the magic slaves also vanished.

Mahrukh's army immediately came to its senses and attacked Hairat's forces. Nahoosat fled for fear of his life, but Bilour Jadoo pursued him and called out sarcastically, 'Mian Nahoosat, how are you faring now?' Nahoosat flung a citron at him in anger, but Bilour deflected it easily. Princess Akhtar joined Bilour and waved her fingers that made a magic pearl shoot down from the sky and smash Nahoosat's skull. Hairat and Mussavir, who had been fending off Akhtar's army, fell upon Akhtar in fury. Meanwhile, Mahrukh and her sardars, Bahar, Barq Mehshar and Ra'ad, attacked Hairat's army with renewed fervour. The two armies met like the mighty waves of the rivers Qulzum and Zakhar and magic swords flashed in the battlefield. Nahoosat's army fled after the death of their commander, but Hairat's army continued fighting half-heartedly. Eventually, Hairat had the drums of peace struck.

Mahrukh, Bahar and the other sardars showered their saviour Akhtar with jewels and praised her magical skills. Akhtar met each of them warmly and assured them that Khwaja Amar would also be joining them in great glory very soon. Mahrukh said, 'We are hopeful that you will honour us by staying with us tonight.' Akhtar replied, 'You are my respected elder and it is my privilege to serve you. I would stay, but I have to report to Burran and Khwaja about your welfare. I need only your permission to leave.' Thus, Akhtar left the camp with Nahoosat's head as a war trophy.

Back in the palace in Nur Afshan, Burran looked at Amar and said, 'Are you satisfied now?' Amar looked disbelievingly at her and said, 'Princess, this was probably a magical illusion. My heart is full of doubt. Hoshruba is very far away from here. I think you may have conjured an image of victory to assuage my concerns!' Burran laughed and said, 'I will send for Akhtar right now and perhaps then you will believe me!' She signalled to the parizad of one of the virtual suns and ordered her to fetch Akhtar. The parizad vanished back into the magic sun that abruptly flashed out of the dome and appeared in front of Princess Akhtar, who was on her way back from Hoshruba.

Akhtar looked at the sun suspiciously and was about to attack it when a voice called out, 'Princess Akhtar, you have been summoned by Princess Burran. She is in the magic dome and watches you from there.' Akhtar ordered her army to go on without her. After they left, the guardian parizad of the sun held Akhtar by the waist and vanished into the sun. Within moments, the sun was shining back in its place in the dome. Akhtar, who had been unconscious during her journey with the parizad, was revived. Akhtar greeted Burran and Amar and presented Nahoosat's severed head to them.

Burran looked at Amar and said, 'Now are you convinced?' Amar laughed sheepishly and said, 'Princess, was that the real Mahrukh who was fighting in the battlefield?' Burran replied, 'It was indeed your own army and Malika Mahrukh herself. However, for your peace of mind, I will arrange a meeting between Mahrukh and you for you have not met her in a long time.' She summoned another parizad and said, 'Bring Malika Mahrukh back with you with due honour and courtesy. Take my ring with you for she is a powerful lady.'

Mahrukh visits Tilism-e-Nur Afshan

The parizad slipped the ring on her finger and vanished into her virtual sun. Mahrukh Magic-eye was in her durbar when the virtual sun and the parizad materialized before her. She greeted Mahrukh and said, 'Come with me, Princess Burran Sword-woman wants to meet you.' Of course, no one believed her and thought that this was yet another magical ploy by Afrasiyab to capture their regent. Mahrukh remained calm and said, 'I cannot leave my lashkar at this time.' The parizad persisted, 'I have my orders, I cannot return without you!'

This convinced everyone that the King of Magic had indeed sent her. Barq Firangi, who had slipped behind the parizad, tried to trap her in the coils of his snare-rope, but the parizad shivered and shook off the coils. She furiously addressed Mahrukh, 'You people are determined to be hostile. By my faith, if the princess had not urged me to be soft on you I would have reduced you all to ashes! I would urge you to come with me otherwise I will have to take you by force. The princess is waiting and I have been here too long!'

She went towards Mahrukh's throne and extended her hand to Mahrukh, who slapped her hard. The force of that blow would have severed an ordinary person's head, but the parizad remained unscathed. She fell upon Mahrukh like a bolt of lightning and flew off with her. Before anyone in the durbar could react, she was out of sight. In her haste, the parizad had not returned to her virtual sun. When she had flown some distance, she remembered this and stopped to summon it. At that time, Mahrukh suddenly became conscious and kicked the parizad with all her strength. Though Mahrukh was a powerful sorceress, the parizad managed to slap Mahrukh before she fell unconscious with the force of the blow.

Now, both Mahrukh and the parizad were unconscious and plumetted down to the earth. The magic ring that the parizad was wearing had several guardians and so invisible hands retrieved them and took them to Burran. The princess summoned the virtual sun wih a spell and then revived the two women with rosewater. The parizad woke up and cried, 'Princess, you sent me to fetch such an aggressive harridan!' Burran, however, scolded the parizad and embraced Mahrukh, to whom she said, 'She was very rude to you and I apologize for her behaviour. She could not have overpowered you if she was not wearing my ring.'

Mahrukh and Amar were overwhelmed on seeing each other and embraced and wept for some time. Burran murmured soothing words to them and then sent for Makhmoor, who met them with joy. After some time, Burran signalled to all the parizads, who vanished into their virtual suns. She then recited words that made everyone fall asleep. The next moment, the guests woke up in a vast plain with bubbling streams, trees laden with blossoms and birds singing in the branches. The sky was overcast with dark monsoon clouds and the evocative cries of peacocks filled the air.

Burran led her guests to a pavilion that opened out to four different vistas—an arid desert, lush mountains, a view of the Zakhar river and a garden in full bloom. As they sat down on the golden masnad seating, Mahrukh turned to Burran and said, 'Princess, you have kept Amar here with you for some time. If it had not been for the other ayyars in our camp, we would have been destroyed by now!' Burran replied, 'Indeed, your grievance is justified. However, this decision does not rest with me. Amar is Shahanshah's guest and can leave only when Shahanshah gives him leave.'

Afrasiyab kidnaps Mahrukh Magic-eye

As everyone relaxed with food and wine, the sight of a garden blooming with spring blossoms captivated Mahrukh. Even though she had seen Afrasiyab's phenomenal Garden of Apples, Mahrukh was fascinated by Burran's garden where each plant bloomed with flowers of many hues. While the others were busy talking, she slipped out quietly and walked through the charming and twisted paths in the garden. Unknown to her, Afrasiyab had been stealthily watching the garden from his Tilism. When he saw Mahrukh strolling alone in the garden, he swooped down and whisked her up into the clouds.

Poor Mahrukh did manage to call out, 'Princess Burran, help me!' However, a nautch performance had been arranged for Burran in the pavilion and no one heard her. Only the attendants of the garden saw a sahir shoot out of the garden holding a woman and raised a clamour. Burran ordered the dancers to stop and got up to check. Amar realized that Mahrukh was missing and wailed, 'Alas, the badshah of my lashkar has been captured!' Burran was about to go in pursuit of the sahir when Kaukab's voice resonated, 'Stay where you are daughter. Reassure Amar that I will bring Mahrukh back.'

Kaukab sent word to his vassal kings, 'The enemy will be flying over your lands. Do not intercept him at all. I will deal with this myself.' Thus, Afrasiyab was not stopped anywhere. Kaukab did this because he thought, 'There will be an uproar in my Tilism if it becomes known that Afrasiyab dared to kidnap my guest from right under my nose. If I attack him here, people will think that I am using all my powers against one man. I should pay him back in the same manner by retrieving Mahrukh from his domain.'

Afrasiyab flew at a great height as he did not want to stop anywhere on enemy territory and carried the rebel leader straight to Hairat's camp. His officers received him there and led him into the durbar. Afrasiyab made sure that Mahrukh was bound before he sat on the throne. He told the officers to summon Hairat and Mussavir from their pavilions to witness the execution and the royal party hastened to the durbar in great joy. Afrasiyab ordered his men ro revive Mahrukh, who closed her eyes as though she was having a bad dream when she saw the King of Magic before her. The Shah called out, 'O betrayer of salt, this is not a dream, but reality! Have you seen how my exalted self snatched you from that desert fox Kaukab's house? By my faith, if I want to, I can destroy his entire Tilism!'

Meanwhile Kaukab had reached Hoshruba and was hovering high above Hairat's camp. He chanted a spell that ensured Afrasiyab remained heedless of any external threat. It did not even enter his mind that the person whose domain he had violated was not a grasscutter but a king who might just retaliate. Up in the sky, Kaukab moulded Mahrukh's replica from lentil flour and gave it to one of his guardian spirits with instructions that it should replace Mahrukh when Kaukab rescued her. After the replica vanished, Kaukab conjured dark monsoon clouds that swiftly spread over Hairat's lashkar. Hairat said, 'Huzoor, look at those clouds. It seems someone is here to rescue the prisoner!' Afrasiyab lost no time and flew out of durbar. All eyes were on the King of Magic as he flew up towards the mysterious clouds.

Kaukab silently slipped out of the clouds and breathed a spell on Afrasiyab's durbar so that for an instant, everything went pitch black. The next moment, everything seemed to be back to normal. The prisoner was sitting in the same place with her head bowed. In that short moment of darkness, Kaukab did what he had to—he rescued Mahrukh and returned to his own Tilism. His guardian spirit had also placed the replica of Mahrukh in Afrasiyab's durbar. Meanwhile, Afrasiyab reached the magic clouds that disintegrated and vanished. The King of Magic remained in the air for a while and then returned to his durbar. He sat on his throne and boasted, 'Hairat, did you see that the moment I was there, the person who had come fled out of fear!' Everyone in the durbar called out, 'O Mighty Shahanshah, who would dare confront you?'

Meanwhile, the news of Mahrukh's capture had reached her camp. Bahar tore her garments and flung her crown away in grief while the sardars wept in despair. A decision was taken that everyone would fight until death, as the confrontation would be with the King of Magic. Battle drums were struck, sahirs hastened to arm themselves with magical tools while ordinary soldiers used conventional weapons. Bahar mounted her magic peacock and led the army that moved like a river in flood towards Afrasiyab's camp.

Bird spies informed the King of Magic that Bahar was coming to fight him. The Shah laughed and said, 'This is why I wanted to execute this betrayer of salt in Tilism Zahir. I want her friends to watch as the flower of her existence withers away! I want them to shed tears like the morning dew and be unable to do anything!'

Afrasiyab got up and flew to the River of Flowing Blood. He touched it with his wand and commanded, 'O Magic River, overflow your banks so that no one can reach Hairat's lashkar.' The river began churning and flowing towards the plain between the two battle camps. The ayyars, who had gone back to their camp to consult the sardars, could not return to Hairat's camp. They went to Bahar and told her that it was impossible to approach Hairat's lashkar. Bahar was plunged into a river of grief when she heard this. She threw herself off her mount and rolled in the dust like a fish out of water. Eventually, she stationed herself on the banks of the magic river from where she could see the execution site.

Meanwhile, Afrasiyab sent for his executioners. The durbar awnings were pulled up so that the royal party could view the execution. The plain was filled with thousands of soldiers and many sahirs flew in the sky to prevent any access from there. In addition, the Shah of Tilism had chanted a spell that reinforced the earth with rocks so that no one could dig a tunnel. Executioners holding huge swords prepared a mud platform in the middle of the plain. They brought the prisoner, seated her on the platform and called out, 'Sinner, if you are hungry, eat now! If you are thirsty, drink, for you will soon be satiated with the goblet of eternity.' The lentil flour substitute of Mahrukh remained silent. The executioners waited for the Shah to tell them how he wanted his prisoner to die—to break her neck, flay her alive or shoot arrows at her.

The Shah indicated that he wanted her shot with arrows. Mahrukh's replica was tied to a stake and at the king's signal, a volley of arrows were shot at her. Besides herself with grief, Bahar was about to dive in the river when Qiran ayyar ran up to her and said, 'Princess, you should not be so hasty! Just think, she was Kaukab's guest and kidnapped from his house. He is not going to remain silent. Moreover, Khwaja Amar is with him. He would have been the first to rescue her. Just wait and keep faith in the Almighty.' Bahar restrained herself and waited to see what would happen.

Meanwhile, a volley of arrows went through the body of the lentil flour figure posing as Mahrukh. Kaukab's guardian spirit made the sky darken and screamed out, 'I have been killed! My name was Mahrukh Magic-eye!' As soon as he heard these sounds, Afrasiyab ordered his men to strike a thousand naqaras of happiness and celebration. Later, Afrasiyab ordered the River of Flowing Blood to return to its original course and proceeded to Zulmat, the Veil of Darkness.

Kaukab and Mahrukh

Kaukab had flown back to his country with Mahrukh, who was unconscious. He landed in a vast plain and placed her gently on a rock before vanishing out of sight. Mahrukh opened her eyes and saw that she was in a magical plain that stretched endlessly so that the bird of thought could not envision its limits. Hundreds of streams rippled through the plain and it was green and lush. Mahrukh was completely bewildered but braced herself and started walking. Kaukab, disguised as a sahir, materialized before her. Mahrukh saw that the sahir was dressed in costly robes and had an intelligent and noble face. He greeted her and said, 'Shah Kaukab rescued you from Afrasiyab's durbar. He has assigned a cavalry of twelve thousand invincible soldiers to serve you. Take them and wreak vengeance on the enemy. The Shah sends you greetings and says that his daughter Burran and Amar will join you soon with a large army.'

Mahrukh asked the sahir where this cavalry was, so he led her through the plain until they reached a mighty dome. When he chanted an incantation, the dome opened and hand-sized iron men mounted on miniature iron stallions spilled out of the doorway and instantly transformed into formidable human warriors in battle armour. The sahir then signalled and a giant hawk spiralled out of the sky to land before him. The sahir addressed the hawk, 'You are to take Malika Mahrukh across these magic plains to Hoshruba.'

Mahrukh Magic-eye mounted the hawk that swooped upwards with her and the stallions of the magic warriors also flew and followed the hawk. The twelve thousand warriors spread in the skies like monsoon clouds where their armour flashed like lightning and their battle drums boomed like thunder. The earth trembled and the sky looked like it was virtually covered in steel. Thus, Mahrukh led this majestic army to Hoshruba. When she reached Hairat's camp, she recited magical words that rained sheets of flames on the tents. Hairat's soldiers, who had been celebrating Mahrukh's death, were taken by surprise. They made a valiant effort to defend themselves, but the invincible iron cavalry soon overwhelmed them.

Hairat rushed out of her durbar and saw burning tents, bodies piling up in the camp and her army in disarray. In between, she heard cries that Mahrukh's ghost was avenging her murder. The ayyars of Islam rushed back to Bahar and said, 'Congratulations! Mahrukh is alive and well! She is here with an army and in confrontation with the enemy!'

Bahar heard the news with joy and re-mobilized her army. She mounted her magic peacock and sounded the trumpets of war before attacking Hairat's lashkar. Hairat was helpless aganst the iron warriors who seemed to be impervious to physical attacks and magic. They killed thousands of Hairat's soldiers and everyone was now convinced that Mahrukh Magic-eye had indeed returned from the dead with an army of ghostly warriors. Hairat was stunned when she saw Mahrukh and immediately flew to the execution site, where she saw the lentil flour replica moulded by Kaukab. She realized that they had been deceived and returned to the battlefield to attack the magic warriors with every spell she could recall. Eventually, Hairat had the drums of peace struck and fled to the River of Flowing Blood. Striking it with her wand, she shouted, 'The wife of Shah of Tilism needs your help!' The river roared into action and moved towards Mahrukh's army.

Mahrukh who was well aware of the river's destructive powers, struck the drums of peace just in time and retreated to her camp in triumph. Bahar opened the doors of the treasury and showered gold coins on her soldiers as they returned to the camp. Mahrukh sat on the throne and each sardar came by to pay homage to her. She embraced them and awarded them with robes of honour. The celebrations commenced with cupbearers serving goblets of wine. Mahrukh informed her sardars, 'God willing, Khwaja and Burran will be here soon.'

Naqoos Lion-rider

Hairat was distraught at the sight of her shattered camp. Almost half her army was dead and the other half had fled. Tents and pavilions had been burnt to cinders. Hairat wept and crossed the River of Flowing Blood, where she conjured a magic claw and ordered it to take her to the Shahanshah wherever he was. The claw transported her to the Veil of Darkness where Afrasiyab was watching a dance performance to celebrate Mahrukh's death. A throng of parizads surrounded the throne. As the magic claw brought Hairat to the Shah, he looked at her dishevelled state and cried out, 'My dearest love, is all well?' Hairat howled and sobbed out her story, while Afrasiyab shook like a leaf when he heard the account of his latest humiliation.

The King of Sahirs calmed his wife before chanting some magical words. A swift gale darkened the sky and a sahir mounted on a lion emerged before the Shah. He looked disdainful and greeted the Shah arrogantly. The king motioned that he could sit and a parizad brought him a goblet of wine. The sahir smiled and said, 'How can I drink in the king's presence? Tell me, why you have summoned me?' The king said, 'Kaukab's Tilismi warriors have slaughtered my army. I want you to mobilize the forty thousand magic warriors you have been entrusted with and show Kaukab's warriors the final path!' The sahir declared, 'Why do I need the magic army? Your humble servant alone can punish them!'

The king smiled and said, 'Indeed, Naqoos Lion-rider, I expect nothing less of you! However, we need reinforcements as much of our army has been decimated. In addition to the magic army, you should take one lakh men and confront the enemy!' The sahir bowed in submission and took his leave. Afrasiyab turned to Hairat and said, 'Dear heart, return to your camp and watch how our enemies are destroyed!' Hairat was comforted with this reassurance and conjured a magic claw to transport her back to her camp.

Naqoos Lion-rider returned to his fort and mobilized an army of one lakh sahir soldiers. He travelled though the plains and reached a dome deep in the jungle. As Kaukab had done earlier in his domain, the dome in Hoshruba opened and forty thousand tiny figures burst out on miniature horses. They became life-sized in the open and their giant steeds sprouted wings. Naqoos flew his lion in the air, conjuring fire, smoke and water in his wake, and the Tilismi warriors followed him. He went across the River of Flowing Blood where Hairat's officers received him and led him to the durbar. Naqoos ordered that the battle drums be struck immediately. Mahrukh's bird spies informed her of his arrival and the rebel army retaliated by sounding their battle drums too. Mahrukh prayed in the great durbar of the Almighty for victory and left for the battlefield. Bahar emerged on her magic peacock and Kaukab's magic warriors rode to the battlefield in great splendour.

On the other side, Hairat emerged on her throne in all majesty. She was leading a large army of sahir soldiers who shed tears in memory of their slain comrades. Naqoos organized his mammoth army of magic warriors and sahir soldiers and once they were in battle formation, the kettledrums and heralds announced the impending battle. Naqoos sought Hairat's permission and rode to the middle of the battlefield. He called out to the rebels, 'You are well aware of my expertise in magic warfare! There is no need for me to demonstrate my skills, as I will be practising them on you! Come and confront me!'

From Mahrukh's side, a magic warrior galloped towards him. As he came closer, Naqoos drew his magic sword and struck him in the head. A flame leapt out of the wound and incinerated the warrior and his horse within moments. Naqoos looked at the rebels triumphantly and shouted, 'That should be enough for you! How long will I fight you one by one? I want to finish this war! Be warned that I will erase your image from the page of existence!'

Naqoos flew on his lion across to where the rebel soldiers stood in battle formation. On seeing him, the souls of dead kings called out for mercy, the sky brought out its golden shield and the formation of magic warriors stirred into action. Mahrukh moved her throne and prepared to attack. There was a clash of steel in the sky as forty thousand steel warriors attacked with Naqoos. Hairat's soldiers were about to follow them when Naqoos called out to Hairat, 'This is my battle; no one should interfere with me!'

That shameless one then fell on the rebel army. A volley of magic citrons, limes and other magical weapons were flung at him and rebel sahirs also assailed him with conventional weapons like arrows, swords and spears, but his impure body repelled all their attacks. Their guardian spirits informed them that they were helpless before this adversary. Naqoos began decimating Kaukab's magic warriors and with one stroke of his mighty sword, fifty warriors were destroyed at a time. The battlefield piled up with dead bodies and the hands of time moved to the land of annihilation. Naqoos slaughtered his way into the lashkar and caused destruction there as well. He set fire to Mahrukh's pavilion and killed all her guards. Eventually, he attacked Mahrukh. The noble malika jumped off her throne as Naqoos called out to his own magic warriors, 'You can finish these betrayers of salt now!'

Naqoos Lion-rider then returned to Hairat's lashkar to refresh himself, where his attendants served him wine and swine meat. Hairat went to him and said, 'O warrior of your time, all compliments to you!' Naqoos, who was too arrogant to acknowledge her greeting, merely flexed his biceps and pretended to examine them. Meanwhile, his magic warriors killed thousands of Kaukab's warriors and then turned on the rebel army. Mahrukh realized that her army was no match for the magical creatures and moved forward to confront them. Bahar thought that if Mahrukh died, the consequences would be terrible. So, she held her back and moved forward herself. Two of her own commanders, Larzan and Zilzila, begged Bahar to let them go instead.

The magic stream of Laat

Larzan and Zilzila moved fearlessly into the ranks of the magic warriors. They plunged into the earth and caused tremors that made the land and mountains shudder. Naqoos Lion-rider had returned to the battlefield and laughed as he swayed arrogantly on his mount. Bahar called out, 'O shameless one, this is not the moment to wage war but to celebrate the advent of spring!' A light flashed in the sahir's eyes that temporarily blinded him. Naqoos opened his eyes to a vision of narcissi and violet flowerbeds. Gentle breezes wafted through the garden, rows of red poppies swayed as if intoxicated and bulbul birds whispered on branches laden with blossoms.

Naqoos Lion-rider stopped fighting and walked into the magic garden. He swayed with enjoyment as cool breezes caressed his face. Suddenly, he saw the embodiment of spring itself, the lovely Bahar dressed in the colours of the rainbow. He looked at her yearningly as she smiled at him. A handmaiden approached him and said, 'O mighty warrior, are you not ashamed that your army is also claiming your beloved?' Naqoos looked back and saw that his army of one lakh sahirs was approaching the garden reciting verses of love and devotion. Hairat had previously retreated with her army and Mahrukh also drew her army back to make way for the enchanted soldiers. Naqoos was overcome by a jealous rage and had just turned to annihilate his soldiers when a mighty peacock swooped into the garden.

The peacock caught Naqoos in his claws and flew off. Bahar tried to trap it in a magic net, but the powerful bird shot up with the wretched sahir and was soon out of sight. Hairat saw that Naqoos' soldiers were still enchanted and quickly struck the drums of peace in case they caused more damage. Mahrukh was also grateful for the respite and attended to the wounded and dead in her army.

Meanwhile, the mighty peacock took Naqoos to a stream. It dived into the water with the sahir and then laid him down on the bank. The dive into the magical waters restored Naqoos' senses and he was no longer besotted with Bahar. Naqoos looked at the peacock inquiringly and the bird spoke, 'O Warrior of Tilism, it is surprising that a wise and cautious sahir like you should fall for the trap of that chit of a girl Bahar!' The peacock was in reality the King of Sahirs. He continued, 'Khudawand Laat rinsed his hands in this stream and its waters have special properties. Take some of its water back with you and sprinkle it on the magic garden. It will be destroyed and your soldiers will return to their senses!'

The bird gave him a jar of the magic water and flew off. Naqoos Lion-rider returned to the battlefield and sprinkled the magic drops on the garden, that promptly went up in smoke and vanished. At the same time, Bahar fell unconscious in her pavilion. The last time she had been to her palace in Aram Koh, she had prepared a concoction that could revive her when she became unconscious. Her handmaidens quickly sprinkled that magic water on her to restore her.

Later, Naqoos returned with his soldiers to Hairat's durbar. She tactfully did not refer to his humiliation at her sister's hands and treated him with respect. That evening, Naqoos declared that he would fight again the next day. The next morning, Mahrukh and Bahar set out with great determination for the battlefield. Hairat and the ill-intentioned Naqoos arrived at the same time and their armies spread out in battle formations. Naqoos Lion-rider sought Hairat's permission and moved forward shouting, 'Be warned as I am attacking your lines again!' He held his great magic sword aloft in one hand and flew on his lion once again towards Mahrukh's lashkar. Though her soldiers assailed him with iron balls and daggers that transformed into bolts of lightning and fell on his head, he remained impervious to all attacks. No spell or incantation worked on him. His spells discharged thousands of arrows that pierced through the chests of rebel soldiers and his sword expelled flames that annihilated the fabric of their existence.

Princess Bahar watched him wreak havoc on the army and moved her throne forward. She shouted, 'O shameless one, yesterday you were saved from me but where will you run today? Come here so that I can send you straight to hell!' Naqoos turned his lion around and called out as he flew towards her, 'O brazen one, I was looking for you as Shahanshah wants you captured alive!' Bahar flung a magic bouquet at him, which he incinerated with the magic waters of Laat's stream. He then sprinkled the same water on Bahar, but she very quickly dodged him and left a magic figure in her place. The figure looked exactly like Bahar and the water landed on her. As Naqoos watched in horror, the false Bahar was burnt to cinders on the spot.

Naqoos was stunned by this and thought that the Shahanshah would punish him cruelly for killing her. The real Princess Bahar now materialized behind him but she had transformed herself magically into Hairat. This was a clever move as Naqoos was deep in rebel lines and could not see Hairat. The false Hairat hit her bosom repeatedly and wailed, 'Alas, what have you done! You have killed my sister!' Naqoos looked devastated and cried, 'Mistress, I had no idea that this water incinerated sahirs, otherwise I would not have used it on her!' The false Hairat said, 'Give me the water jar, perhaps I can find a way of restoring her!' Naqoos obligingly handed her the jar. Bahar now assumed her real form and called out, 'You mule-head, I am Bahar Jadoo!'

She scooped the water in her hand and moved towards him. Naqoos fled for his life for the peacock had informed him that the water could annihilate the most powerful sahirs. Bahar continued to pursue him, followed by her army. Naqoos rushed back to Hairat and cried, 'O mistress, strike the drums of peace as your sister is after me!' Hairat could not help smiling at his plight for she had resented his arrogant attitude towards her. He hid behind her as she then ordered her commanders to attack the rebel forces. Mahrukh, who was leading her army, laughed at the terrorized sahir. Naqoos was terrified as Bahar still had the magic water and flew upwards and out of sight; but the two armies clashed fiercely. Eventually Hairat realized that the rebels were gaining and struck the drums of peace. Mahrukh showered gold coins on Bahar's head as they returned in triumph to their camp.

Barq and Naqoos

Meanwhile, Barq ayyar had used the oils and paints of ayyari to transform into a beautiful sahira. It seemed as if nature had moulded her from sandalwood and roses. She gleamed like the light of heaven and her tresses were as dark as the night. Snakes coiled around her head and she wore large gold hoops in her ears. She was draped in a sari embroidered with silver and gold sequins and was covered in jewels from head to toe; even her magic pouch was embroidered with gold thread. After this complete transformation, Barq went to some sahirs from Makhmoor's army and said, 'I am Barq. You have to give me a throne and accompany me to Hairat's lashkar with trumpets and drums!' The sahirs were stunned at the sight of the false princess and Barq had to convince them that it was really him before they did as he asked.

They arranged a magnificent flying throne for the false sahira. Barq headed for Hairat's lashkar and Makhmoor's companions flew alongside him on bird mounts. They reached Hairat's lashkar with great fanfare, where Hairat thought the Shah had sent a sahira and sent her nobles to receive her. Barq entered the durbar and saw Hairat on the throne while Naqoos Lion-rider was on the chair besides her guzzling wine. The false sahira greeted Hairat and made an offering of gold coins. Hairat directed her to the chair next to Naqoos. The warrior, in turn, looked at the beautiful sahira and lost his heart at first sight. The false sahira graced him with the dagger of her smile and said, 'I have heard much about your reputation as a warrior. Shahanshah speaks highly of you!'

Naqoos said, 'Shahanshah is kind to me. In truth, I have fought three fierce battles. I stopped because of the magic water, otherwise I would have finished the rebels by now!' He then related the story of his encounters with Bahar. Meanwhile, Barq's ayyar companion, Jansoz, had also infiltrated Hairat's camp. At that very moment, he was fanning Hairat disguised as an attendant. The cupbearers offered the false sahira a goblet of golden wine. She raised it to her lips, made a face and said, 'This wine is too strong for me!' She turned to her attendants and ordered, 'Bring me the wine that I drink!' Barq, of course, had already instructed the attendants what to do. They brought out flasks of drugged wines and presented it to the false sahira. Barq filled a goblet and offered it first to Hairat saying, 'Huzoor should drink it first.'

Hairat sipped the wine without hesitation. The next goblet was offered to Naqoos, who was overjoyed at being offered wine by his beloved. Barq then signalled to his attendants to offer goblets to everyone in durbar. Meanwhile, in the Garden of Apples, Afrasiyab consulted the oracle Book of Samri to find out how to counteract the waters of the magic stream. The oracle read, 'Worry about the water later and save your honour at this time. Barq disguised as a sahira is about to snuff out everyone's life in Hairat's durbar!'

Afrasiyab invoked magic that made a magic slave-boy shoot out of the earth before him. He gave the slave-boy a letter for Hairat that warned her about Barq. The slave-boy appeared almost instantly in Hairat's durbar and handed her the letter. Jansoz, who was standing behind her, read it too. He thought that Barq's trickery would be wasted and quickly scattered some powder of unconsciousness towards the Malika. She was just preparing to attack Barq when she felt dizzy. Jansoz offered her some flowers and whispered, 'Huzoor, everyone in durbar seems to be in a strange condition. Breathe in the fragrance of these flowers and return to your chamber. Once you are better you can tackle the situation here.'

Hairat did not suspect that her attendant was also an ayyar and gratefully took the flowers from him. She returned to her chamber inhaling their fragrance and fell heavily on her bed. In the durbar, Barq thought that it was not possible to render everyone unconscious and decided to lure Naqoos Lion-rider out of the pavilion. He got up and looked meaningfully at Naqoos, who jumped up and said, 'I am coming with you!' He held the false sahira by the waist and took her to his own pavilion. She protested, 'Why have you brought me here? My reputation will be in shreds! What will your servants say?' Naqoos dismissed his attendants and was now alone with Barq.

After Barq had left the durbar with Naqoos, Jansoz went to Hairat's chamber where she had passed out on the bed. He drew out his dagger and was about to kill her, but two magic slave-boys materialized and stood guard over the unconscious Malika Hairat. Jansoz realized it would be difficult to kill her and painted his face to look like Hairat. He could not get to her robes because of the slave-boys, so he wore his own robes.

In the Garden of Apples, the king consulted the oracle again. It warned him about the dangerous ayyars in Hairat's camp who could cause much damage. Afrasiyab got up to leave, but Vizier Abriq said, 'Huzoor, do not trouble yourself. I will go.' Afrasiyab briefed him on what had happened and told him to go and revive Hairat quickly. The vizier reached Hairat's bedchamber just as Jansoz emerged from it disguised as the queen. The vizier recognized Jansoz immediately, but to deceive the ayyar, greeted him as he would Malika Hairat and then firmly held his hand, as if to arrest him. Jansoz quickly said, 'Get inside quickly! Qiran is sitting on Hairat's bosom and is about to slaughter her!' Vizier Abriq was so startled to hear these words that he let go of Jansoz and rushed into the chamber.

Jansoz returned to the durbar and called out, 'Those sahirs who accompanied the princess should leave for we have been discovered.' Barq's attendants immediately flew out of durbar. Everyone else in the durbar was confused and thought, 'First came the unknown sahira, then the magic slave-boy appeared, Malika Hairat went to her bedchamber and when she emerged, Vizier Abriq tried to arrest her. She said something to him and he let her go. Now these sahirs have flown away! What on earth is happening?'

Meanwhile, Abriq had revived Hairat in the bedchamber. She looked at him and asked, 'Vizier Abriq, what brings you here?' Abriq explained how the ayyar had drugged her. Hairat returned to the durbar, where everyone seemed to be half-conscious. She revived them with cold water and asked about Naqoos. When she heard that he had left with the unknown sahira, Hairat looked at Vizier Abriq in alarm and said, 'The ayyar who had posed as a sahira will surely kill the warrior of Tilism now!' Hairat and Vizier Abriq immediately left for Naqoos's pavilion.

During this period, Barq had made some progress. He had got Naqoos alone and played on the sahir's desire for him by crying, 'Sahib, now that we are alone, what is in your heart? By Samri, I know your intentions, but I am not one who will give in so easily to a strange man. Listen, sahib, to tell you the truth I am attracted to you, but I have restrained my heart. Why should I take a bite of an ant-ridden kebab?'

Naqoos pleaded, 'Light of my heart, I will remain devoted to you and no one else!' The fair sahira laughed and said, 'You have a wife, do you not? This is just empty talk. I know that you are insincere!' Naqoos declared, 'Once we live together, I will not have anything to do with my wife!' Barq smacked his forehead dramatically and cried, 'Samri have mercy on you! You talk about leaving your wife for me! She must have been married to you with so much pomp and ceremony! You are an unfaithful man and I refuse to have anything to do with you!'

Naqoos was inflamed by these words and embraced her passionately. Barq kicked him hard and cried, 'My chemise is riding up, you lustful lout! What do you think you are doing?' Naqoos rubbed his head on her feet and begged her for mercy. Barq now had the sahir where he wanted him and said coyly, 'Just allow me to prepare a spell and I will fulfil all your desires!' Naqoos sulked, 'You are making excuses!' The fair damsel pouted prettily and cried, 'By Samri, can you not be quiet for a while? If I do not prepare the spell as Shahanshah had directed, I will forget the recipe. Send for a cauldron and some wax. I will prepare pellets from it and confront Bahar. It will not take long and later we can enjoy ourselves!'

Naqoos was delighted with her promises and promptly ordered his servants to provide a cauldron and wax. The fair sahira dismissed the servants once they had brought these items and told Naqoos to light a fire under the cauldron. Once the wax started boiling, Barq sprinkled some powder of unconsciousness on the fire and declared, 'The fumes of the dust of Jamshed will magically energize these pellets!' Naqoos was close to the fire and breathed in the noxious fumes. Within moments, he fell unconscious. The sahira, who was actually Barq, broke the sahir's front teeth with the hilt of his dagger and after tearing his mouth open, poured the boiling wax down his throat. From the throat to the stomach, a hot rod of wax hardened in the sahir's body and he died in agony. His guardian spirits raised an almighty din and a fierce gale swept through the camp, followed by sheets of flames from the sky.

Hairat and Abriq had just reached the pavilion when this commotion took place and a voice boomed, 'Alas you have killed me! My name was Naqoos Jadoo!' The ayyar ran out of the pavilion and shouted, 'I am Mehtar Barq Firangi!' Hairat wept when she saw this and the vizier flew back to Afrasiyab with the news that in the time that he had revived Malika Hairat, the ayyar had murdered Naqoos.

Afrasiyab's face went visibly red when he heard this and the flames of rage consumed him. He bit his hands anxiously and thought anxiously of who could go next to face the rebels. Meanwhile, the commanders of Naqoos'army retrieved his mutilated corpse and left for Zulmat.

III

17 SANNAT MAGIC-MAKER SPELLS DOOM FOR MAHRUKH'S LASHKAR, AT THE LAST MOMENT AMAR COMES FROM KAUKAB'S TILISM AND DEFEATS SANNAT

Now hear about Afrasiyab, the ill-intentioned one. He realized that Hairat would be downcast after so many defeats and decided to go and comfort her. As he rose to leave, several hundred comely, young damsels appeared in the durbar, holding aloft a magnificent throne studded with precious jewels. Many of them balanced gold and silver pitchers on their hips and held luminous bulbs. They smiled and swayed as they went towards the Shah, their bosoms gleaming like crystal orbs through transparent robes, and lowered their heads to greet him.

The Shah of Tilism then climbed the steps of the throne that his handmaidens had brought and sat in it in great splendour. Thunderous sounds of conch shells and gongs filled the garden as the throne rose in the air. A diaphanous crimson cloud extended over the throne and burst into a shower of pearls, after which the Shah set off on his journey to Hairat's camp.

Hairat was in her durbar with her commanders and sahirs. They were alerted to Afrasiyab's arrival when a crimson cloud materialized on the horizon and drumbeats began sounding in the distance. Hairat emerged from the durbar with her commanders to welcome the one with evil intentions. As Afrasiyab descended from his throne, Hairat bowed low in mujra greeting and rotated several trays of gold coins and jewels over his head, which were later distributed among the poor.

Afrasiyab affectionately tucked her arm into his and Hairat drew closer to him as they walked into the pavilion. The Shah sat on the throne with Hairat beside him, while the others settled on chairs. Goblets of wine were served in the durbar and a nautch performance began.

The badshah declared, 'I have invited my spiritual brother Taaq One-eye to this camp. He will arrive and destroy these rebels. They will wither like autumn leaves and he will blow them away like a swift gale.' Hairat was happy to hear such good news.

Mahrukh's agents were in Hairat's durbar too and realized that everyone in the camp was celebrating following Afrasiyab's declaration. There was much talk of how the Shahanshah's spiritual brother Taaq One-eye would destroy the betrayers of salt. The spies returned to their camp, where they greeted Mahrukh with deference and prayed for her long life before stating, 'The enemy camp is celebrating Taaq One-eye's arrival to fight us.' Mahrukh replied, 'Afrasiyab will find sahirs like Taaq One-eye to face us now! However, God is our protector!'

Barq Firangi happened to be in durbar at the time. He noticed that Mahrukh had gone pale on hearing the news and was silent while the other sardars were discussing their latest adversary. Barq rose and casually said, 'I am going over to see what Taaq One-eye is like!' As he approached Hairat's camp, he said to himself, 'The sahir you seek has not arrived yet. You should somehow reach Hairat's durbar and remain there disguised as one of her sardars. When the sahir comes, you can show him the final path!' Accordingly, he disguised himself as a sahir sardar and walked into Hairat's camp.

The maidens who had accompanied the Shahanshah were standing near the entrance of the durbar. One of them felt the call of nature and walked out of the camp, where she found an empty spot and squatted to relieve herself. Barq followed her and waited with his face averted. As she rose, he flung his snare-rope at her. The girl belonged to the area around the River of Light and was handmaiden to the King of Sahirs. How would she know of the deceptive ways of the tricksters?

She was caught in the coils of Barq's snare-rope and fell down heavily. The ayyar immediately set to work and rendered her unconscious. He stripped off her clothes and jewels, and buried her in the sand. Then he painted his face to look like hers and sauntered back to the durbar in her clothes, intending to mingle with the other women.

Now the handmaidens of the River of Light were protected by Afrasiyab's magic. When Barq left the maiden after burying her, a claw materialized and retrieved her from the sand. It transported her back to the River of Light and informed Afrasiyab that Barq Firangi was approaching the durbar disguised as the maiden. The Shahanshah therefore was aware of the ruse and laughed when he saw Barq, now a vision of loveliness, slipping into durbar.

Barq saw the king laughing and smiled back at him invitingly. The Shah signalled to the false handmaiden to come closer and mockingly asked, 'So what do you do my fair maiden?' Barq batted his eyelashes and shyly whispered, 'Huzoor, I attend on you when you are travelling and do whatever is asked of me.' Afrasiyab said to her softly, 'From now

on, you are excused of all other duties. Just press my feet every night.'
The maiden looked down shyly and remained silent.

Afrasiyab could not keep his eyes off the lovely maiden even though
he knew she was Barq ayyar in disguise. He thought to himself, 'These
wretched ayyars even surpass the artful ways of courtesans!' He whispered
a spell and a gleaming octagonal marble stool fitted with a red velvet
cushion circled down from the sky. Still smiling, Afrasiyab invited Barq
to sit on it. Barq was delighted and thought, 'This clown of a badshah
will send for me to sleep with him in the Garden of Apples tonight, and
I will show him the final path there!'

Barq swayed his hips provocatively as he walked and settled down
on the stool. Afrasiyab laughed and said, 'Dearest heart, do not go
anywhere! We are quite smitten with you!' Barq's ears pricked up at the
Shahanshah's words and the ayyar immediately realized that his bottom
was firmly fixed to the seat of the stool that was now slowly rising off
the ground.

Afrasiyab nimbly jumped on to the stool and cried, 'Mian Barq, are
you keeping well?' Barq replied, 'I humbly pay my respects!' When
Afrasiyab laughed heartily, Barq continued, 'Why do you laugh at me?
This time I came here not to trick you or fight with you, but to see you.
See, I have a bad habit that when I meet a person a couple of times, I
start missing him. I had not met you for some time and when I heard
that you were here, I came at once to see you! How did I know you
would treat me this way?'

Afrasiyab frowned and said, 'Oye, you almost killed my handmaiden
when you buried her! My magic claw saved her and took her to the
River of Light. Now you are trying to deceive me with this talk? I am
determined to execute you today!' Barq looked pained and replied, 'You
are right to accuse me! However, if I had not replaced her, how else
would I have had access to you Shahanshah? As for executing me, that is
entirely up to you. I know you are all-powerful, you are Shahanshah,
and no one can confront you. You can execute anyone, what will you
gain from killing me? If you release me now, you will be remembered for
your mercy!'

The gullible Afrasiyab felt pity for the ayyar and was about to release
him, when Hairat realized what was happening and cried, 'Shahanshah,
he is just misleading you! What is this nonsense about devotion to you?
He is a wily and deceitful liar. Your pir brother, Taaq One-eye, is expected
here any moment and this rascal will be a nuisance to him!' The chastened
Shahanshah replied, 'Malika, you are so right. I will treat him as an
enemy and he will die of hunger and thirst!'

The Shahanshah jumped off the marble stool and threw a lentil grain at it. The stool went circling up into the sky and stayed there, suspended in mid-air. Barq saw that he was now without a friend or well-wisher, and food or water, and he had very little chance of survival. It was as if he had been sentenced to purgatory.

Afrasiyab's teacher, Hissam

Let us first meet Afrasiyab's pir brother, the deceitful Taaq One-eye, who was afflicted with the disease of falsehood. He was the ruler of the kingdom of Lajwardia in the Veil of Darkness. The kingdom took its name from the range of lapis lazuli mountains that surrounded it. Taaq One-eye was in a state of ecstasy as his spiritual master Hissam had blessed him with a visit.

Taaq One-eye received him with reverence and seated him in a place of honour. He arranged for a gathering of pleasure and summoned comely cupbearers and fairy-like dancers to entertain Hissam. Meanwhile, goblets of roseate liquid were already being circulated in the durbar. The letter Afrasiyab had dispatched to Taaq One-eye reached him while he attending to his teacher. He read it carefully and dolefully said, 'The King of Magic wants me to destroy the rebels. What am I to do? I am helpless for I have to attend to my own problems. I cannot understand how to respond to this message!'

His teacher asked him gravely, 'My son, what is your opinion of me as a sahir?' Taaq One-eye was astonished by his question and said, 'Ustad, why do you ask this? There is no one like you, not just in Tilism, but in the whole world! It was after you trained him that Afrasiyab became the King of Magic. I am your humble slave, but even then, there is no one to match my powers. I say only this that even the great Samri must have been only as powerful as you are. You are the very spirit of Samri himself!'

Ustad-ji swelled up with pride when he heard his student's tribute. It is said that troubles come without warning. Heedless of what was to come, Hissam laughed with joy and said, 'In that case my son, send me instead of you!' Taaq One-eye was delighted with the idea. He summoned his commanders immediately and ordered them to move with the army at once. In preparation for battle, Hissam wore garlands of bejewelled crystal balls and sat on a flying throne with a trident and brazier of burning coals placed in front of him. He smeared his body with ashes and sindoor powder and tied his pouch of magical tools around his waist. An army of two lakh sahirs stood behind him. As Hissam set off with the army, the sound of conch shells and kettledrums made the spectators tremble with fear. Hideous-looking witches breathed out flames and ignited fires on mountains and in deserts, turning night into day.

Hissam, the ill-fated one, travelled in stages and crossed the River of Flowing Blood to reach Hairat's camp. The Malika's bird spies informed her of his arrival and as he was the Shahanshah's teacher, she met him with officers of state outside the camp to escort him to her durbar. Hissam decended from his throne and Hairat greeted him deferentially. In turn, he embraced her and blessed her with prayers for her safety. Hairat then led him to a gold-embroidered pavilion furnished with every comfort. His army camped besides Hairat's lashkar and the bazaars soon buzzed with activity.

Hissam sat in Hairat's durbar and consumed wine for a while. He asked her about the rebels and said, 'I can destroy them right now if you wish!' Hairat replied, 'No one can speak before you, however, you should strike battle drums for now and rest for the night. The enemy will also not complain that they were not warned. Tomorrow morning, you can show them the evening of annihilation!'

When the battle drums were struck, the rebels responded by striking their own magic war drums in mid-air. The ones who were willing to fight and die looked forward to the impending battle against Hissam while the dishonourable and the cowardly were alarmed. Mahrukh dismissed her durbar and the sardars returned to their tents to inspect their battle armour.

The next morning, Afrasiyab's teacher left for the battlefield with his army of two lakh sahirs behind him, while Hairat left her pavilion in great splendour with her formidable army. On the other side, Mahrukh and her army proceeded to the battlefield like a river in full flood. Hissam drew his magic sword from the scabbard, smashed one coconut on the ground and tossed another one up into the sky. A deep reverberation and a thunderous sound shook the earth and heavenly bodies. Suddenly, the earth beneath the lashkar of Islam gave way like a dark and fearsome grave—the pit of infinity itself! As the army sank into the pit, Mahrukh wept in dismay and the enemy sahirs laughed. The coconut Hissam had hurled at the sky formed pitch-black clouds and descended over Mahrukh's army. Sheets of darkness descended from this cloud and blocked out all light.

While Mahrukh's soldiers cried out in terror, Hissam called out, 'O wayward rebels! I could destroy you right now, but I have heard that the noble Shahanshah is inclined towards your surrender rather than destruction. I will give you a night and day to think about your plight. If you do not surrender to Shahanshah, the black cloud will annihilate you with flames and the earth in which you have sunk will close over you like a grave!'

Hissam then had the drums of peace struck and turned back to his lashkar. Hairat's soldiers wanted to plunder the rebel camp, but she stopped them and said, 'This is Ustad's battle. Do not interfere or you will be executed!' At her bidding, the soldiers restrained themselves and Hairat led Hissam to durbar, from where she sent message to Afrasiyab about his teacher's victory. Afrasiyab, who was in the Garden of Apples at that moment, remained in touch with Hairat's camp through his bird agents. He was overjoyed to hear about Hissam's victory and sent gifts and trays of jewels as homage to his teacher.

Barq and Hissam

Hissam was battle weary and left the durbar to retire to his pavilion. After dinner, he had the pavilion awnings pulled up and had a couch placed outside his tent in the moonlight. He idly lay down there, reflecting on his triumph, and looked up at the sky. Suddenly, his eyes alighted on a shining object that seemed to be suspended in the air, as if the residents of the heavens had hung a chandelier or a shooting star had descended from the sky.

Intrigued by this sight, the short-sighted Hissam used his magic binoculars to take a closer look at the star. What he saw was a marble object that gleamed in the moonlight. Hissam read a spell and Barq's stool started descending towards him. Barq Firangi had been weeping over his miserable state for he had been trapped on the stool without water and food for two days. He watched his army's rout from that height and was convinced that no one could rescue him now. He was deep in his misery when the marble stool suddenly started to descend to the ground in wide circles.

Barq peered down and saw that the stool was heading towards a sahir's tent. Barq's disguise as the handmaiden had been fading due to lack of nourishment and exposure to the elements, so he quickly touched up his disguise with the paints of ayyari before the stool reached the ground. When the stool landed, Ustad-ji was utterly stunned and gaped at the vision of the heavenly creature in precious clothes and jewels perched on the stool. He asked her, 'Fair maiden, who has punished you so cruelly? O parizad of the sky, whither are you flying? There is a royal medal on your forehead . . . perhaps you are Shah's handmaiden?'

Barq smiled coyly as he replied, 'You foolish sahir, have you lost your mind? Do you want to lose your life as well? I have been punished by Shahanshah himself!' Hissam cried, 'Light of my heart, why has he punished you?' Barq replied, 'If you do not send me back right now, there will be terrible consequences! Shahanshah has punished me because I stumbled and dropped a goblet of wine on him. For that, he suspended me in the sky to starve to death. If he finds me talking to a strange man, he will surely kill me right away!' Hissam said to the maiden, 'He must have been intoxicated at the time, otherwise yours was not such a serious crime. I will speak to him on your behalf.'

Hissam thought, 'I have accomplished such a mighty deed for Shahanshah today. Surely he will not grudge me this handmaiden!' He asked Barq, 'O lovely maiden, tell me truthfully, has Shahanshah ever touched you?' Barq lowered his head and replied shyly, 'No, I swear by Samri and Jamshed he has not even looked at me in that sense. Why should he? I am afraid of all men, my heart jumps in fear if I even see a man!' The false handmaiden then stretched her arms out provocatively so that her bosom and belly were clearly visible through her flimsy garments. Hissam looked as if he would die of desire. The damsel said, 'To tell you the truth, I loathe all men, but since I have seen you my heart feels something else. I have met many handsome young men, but there is something compelling about you!' Hissam was captivated by her innocence and chanted a spell that released her from the marble stool. He then wrote a note that read, 'O King of Sahirs, I have released the captive maiden from the sky and she is now in my service.' He placed the note on the marble stool and breathed a spell on it, after which it spiralled off to find the Shahanshah. Barq realized what was happening and thought, 'Once the stool reaches Afrasiyab, he will come running to his teacher's rescue. I should do something very soon!' So, he curled up next to the old sahir, who tried to caress his false beloved. The maiden sobbed softly and whispered, 'Wait, wait, my clothes are in disorder and your servants are watching. This is an open area. Do you think I am a common prostitute? Even they are not treated in this manner!'

Hissam brought down the awnings of his tent and dismissed his attendants. Meanwhile, the maiden had produced a marigold from within her bodice and asked coyly, 'Do you know what this is?' Hissam was charmed by her childlike query and embraced her as he murmured, 'It is a marigold, my love.' She pouted prettily and said, 'You don't know anything! This is a rose from the garden of Jamshed. Shahanshah plucked several of these when he went there and gave me one. Smell it if you do not believe me!'

Hissam looked puzzled and took the flower from her. He inhaled its deadly scent and suddenly fell unconscious. Barq immediately beheaded him with his dagger. It was if the heavens had fallen and Doomsday had arrived. Sheets of flames descended from the sky and terrible voices called out, 'O cruel one, you have killed the teacher of sahirs!' Taking advantage of this commotion, Barq managed to escape from the camp.

Afrasiyab was in the Plain of Poppies when the marble stool spiralled down from the sky. Afrasiyab read Hissam's letter and screamed, 'What has Ustad done? He has brought down his own doom from the sky!' Moments later, Hissam's guardian spirits swirled around him and related how Hissam had been hoodwinked and murdered. The King of Magic wrung his hands in dismay and lamented, 'There is no remedy for the damage we do to ourselves! Alas, I should have killed Barq when I had arrested him! Why did I have to imprison him? Well, I suppose it is as Samri wills!' On the other side, Mahrukh and her army were released from the pit of hell when Hissam was killed and returned to their camp, where there was great jubilation that night.

Taaq One-eye comes to fight

When the noble ayyar Barq killed the ill-fated Hissam, his wailing servants transported that rascal's body to Taaq One-eye, the dishonest one, in his kingdom of Lajwardia. Taaq One-eye was so outraged that he writhed on a bed of hot coals and the flames of wrath consumed him. He immediately mobilized his army of a lakh and twelve-thousand sahirs armed with magical and conventional weapons. They mounted magical birds while Taaq One-eye sat on his fiery dragon mount. Thus, this army set forth for Hairat's camp in a splendid procession.

When Hairat emerged from her camp to welcome him, he exclaimed, 'Dear sister-in-law, why did you trouble yourself for me?' As she was a princess of the realm, he kneeled down and made an offering of gold coins to her. Hairat ceremoniously accepted his offerings and led him into the durbar. She bestowed a khalat robe on him and beckoned him to the seat of honour. Meanwhile, his army set up camp besides Hairat's lashkar.

That evening, Hairat arranged a sumptuous feast for Taaq One-eye. He wolfed down the food and consumed several goblets of wine. When his brain was warmed by the wine, he cried, 'Sister-in-law, there is no need for delay. Let us strike the battle drums!' She replied dryly, 'Very well, since you are here specifically to fight.' He continued, 'I will not be long in destroying the rebels. My soldiers are marked with stars on their foreheads and their bodies are magically armour-plated. No one can kill them!' Hairat murmured, 'There is no doubt about that. After all they are your soldiers!'

Mahrukh Magic-eye's army also began preparing for the battle, but late at night, Bahar whispered to Mahrukh, 'What is the point of preparing the army? You and I have to exercise our magic alone.' Accordingly,

Mahrukh and Bahar slipped out of their camp on magic peacocks and flew to a mountain some distance from the camp. Mahrukh took out a coconut from her pouch of magic and smashed it against the base of the mountain. There was a sudden gush of water and rivulets began pouring out of the ravines. Within moments, the waters surged like the stormy Zakhar river and began flowing right in between Hairat and Mahrukh's war camps.

The two paragons of magic and enchantment, Mahrukh and Bahar, then flew back to their camp and stood on the banks of the river. When Bahar read a spell and breathed on the river, tiny flowerbeds and trees made of jewels materialized on their side of the bank. It was a wondrous magical springtime in that miniature garden; its trees were laden with fruit that gleamed like fairy wings, while its flowers sparkled like stars in the sky.

Bahar said, 'My sister, it is almost dawn. Should we play a round of *chausar*?' Mahrukh replied, 'Very well, send for it!' Bahar muttered a spell and a maiden with a rosebud mouth and the face of an unfolding flower emerged from the trees holding the game. She laid out the board before them and as they sat down to play, she began fanning them with a handkerchief. As they started playing the game, the river suddenly rippled with activity. Washermen materialized on the banks and their rhythmic splashes filled the air; river ducks and swans floated downstream and colourful fish dived in and out of the magic river.

Taaq One-eye, the ill-fated one, rose as the star of his destiny plunged into doom. He went to Hairat, who was just about to leave for the battlefield, and cried, 'Dear sister, in the name of my brother Shah of Tilism, you are not to go to the battlefield today! Please stay in durbar and be entertained while I cut their heads off in no time. By Samri, I will be hurt if you do not listen to me!'

Since Hairat could not refuse the king's spiritual brother's request, she returned to her pavilion. Her army stood at ease while Mahrukh's forces remained armed and ready for battle. Taaq One-eye, the defiant one, left with his soldiers whose foreheads gleamed with magic stars. In their sky blue uniforms, they looked so belligerent that it seemed as if the sky itself was determined to be merciless that day. Taaq One-eye's spies soon informed him that Mahrukh had conjured a river and was playing chausar some distance from her lashkar.

Taaq One-eye laughed heartily and exclaimed, 'Has she created the river to stop me? Does she think I will not be able to forge it?' He summoned his commanders and asked them, 'Should we fly over the river or swim through it?' They all shouted in unison, 'Huzoor, we should jump into the river and erase its existence! We will cut that harridan's head off. We are strong warriors and she is one woman! How can she confront us?'

This plan appealed to Taaq One-eye who was an arrogant man. He flew on his dragon to the river, but stopped abruptly when the magic waters came into view. He looked upon the river in wonder, slowly dismounted and walked into the water with his army behind him. As the water rose up to their waists, Taaq One-eye cried, 'My friends, this water is so refreshing and cold, we should drink it!' They replied, 'Huzoor, we feel the same way!' Taaq One-eye cupped his hands and drank several scoops of the water. Mahrukh's magic then began working on him. His rage against her subsided and he began feeling well disposed towards her.

Taaq One-eye's army also swallowed the waters as they swum across it and forgot their earlier intention of erasing the river. When they had reached the far bank, Taaq One-eye signalled to his army to stay back and approached the magic garden where Mahrukh and Bahar squatted on the grass, completely engrossed in the game of chausar.

Taaq One-eye confidently entered the garden and did not suspect that the air in the garden belonged to another world. Mahrukh declared calmly, 'Rise Bahar, the enemy is here!' Bahar retorted, 'All in good time! Let us play another round first!' She then looked straight into the enchanted sahir's eyes and called out, 'Taaq One-eye, can we start a new game?' Taaq One-eye folded his hands and said, 'O beautiful enchanter, I am your unpaid slave! How can I dare stop you?'

Bahar and Mahrukh turned back to their game. Mahrukh suddenly cried, 'This is my bid!' Bahar responded, 'Accepted!' Mahrukh smiled and asked, 'How can you accept it? You have lost all that you possess during the night. What can you offer now?' Bahar looked up and said, 'Why not? After all, my sister is Hairat and my brother-in-law is the King of Magic! How can you doubt my wealth? Continue with the game, you lose faith so quickly!' Mahrukh replied, 'You have no power over your sister! If you are that confident, are you willing to stake her life on this game? Arrest her first and if you lose, she will have to die!' Bahar calmly said, 'That will not be difficult!'

She looked up at Taaq One-eye and asked, 'Sahib, what am I to you?' Taaq One-eye cried, 'I am your slave! I will carry out any orders you give me!' Bahar continued, 'My sister Hairat has rebelled against me. Bring her to me dead or alive! I can then continue my game!' Taaq One-eye thought, 'If you want a union with this malika of beauty, do not hesitate and be as pliant as that chausar board before her! Fortune smiles on you today for she is one whom the King of Magic lusts after, but she rejects him!'

He looked at Bahar and humbly submitted, 'I will immediately bring that wretch Hairat to you! She is watching a nautch performance in her durbar!' Bahar said airily to him, 'Yes brother, bring her quickly or I will lose the game!' Taaq One-eye went back to his army and called out, 'Are you with me or with Shah of Tilism?' They replied in unison, 'We do not know Shah! You are our lord and master!' Taaq One-eye then told his soldiers, 'I am going across to capture Hairat. All of you should attack her army!' The besotted sahir then crossed the river and approached Hairat's camp. The guards let him through as they knew he was the Shah's ally.

Taaq One-eye's army rushed in behind him to attack Hairat's guards with magic citrons and limes. Tents and pavilions started burning and there was an uproar in the camp as the unsuspecting soldiers died in large numbers. The ones who did retaliate could hardly fight the armour-plated soldiers with stars on their foreheads. They seemed to be impervious to magic and no weapon hurt them.

When they reached Hairat's pavilion and slashed her tent's ropes, she rushed out in alarm. She mounted her magic peacock and bravely retaliated as the bodies of her soldiers piled up around her. Death played its destructive game and the heads of soldiers fell like pawns in a game of chess. When Hairat realized that she had lost this round, she fled to the River of Flowing Blood. Taaq One-eye saw her take flight and cried, 'Do not let that whore escape! I have been a while and my beloved might lose her game on my account!'

Thus instructed, his soldiers descended on Hairat like dark monsoon clouds. Hairat was now surrounded and about to be captured, but she was a powerful sorceress and fought back valiantly. She fended them off with her magical attacks and plunged into the earth, leaving a puppet double in her place.

Afrasiyab rescues Hairat

Afrasiyab had appointed a few magic slave-boys to brief him on Taaq One-eye's progress in the battle against the rebels. He was idly watching a nautch performance in the Garden of Apples, daydreaming of imminent victory, when the slave-boys rushed into the durbar and cried out, 'O Shahanshah, a terrible thing has happened! Taaq One-eye is killing them!' Shahanshah smiled and said, 'That is good. He was meant to kill them!' The messengers cried desperately, 'No, no, he is attacking Malika Hairat!'

The Shahanshah looked annoyed and said, 'Have you lost your senses? Do you mean that he is attacking Mahrukh?' The slave-boys replied, 'O Mighty King, we are telling you the truth! Mahrukh and Bahar conjured a river and a garden overnight and set up a game of chausar. After Taaq One-eye returned from the garden, he began wreaking havoc on our army!' Afrasiyab struck his knee and cried, 'This is terrible! I will have to destroy his army. A lakh and twelve thousand troops will die! Mahrukh and Bahar have invoked invincible magic. No one else can remove it.'

Afrasiyab blazed out of his throne in the form of a bolt of lightning and fell some distance away in a dark and fearsome forest in Tilism. He read out a spell that made one lakh stars fall from the skies, and at the same time, thousands of magic warriors emerged from the earth. The stars flashed down from the sky and locked themselves into place on the foreheads of the warriors. Afrasiyab then led this formidable army to a place deep in the forest where there were black marble domes. He entered one of the domes and saw a stone puppet seated on a chair, holding a coconut in one hand.

Afrasiyab called out, 'Hand me the coconut and the keys to the magic fortress for there is going to be a mighty war.' The statue smiled and asked, 'Have you lost your senses? Do not even think of using Tilismi lashkar! If it is destroyed now, then who will fight Tilism Kusha?' Afrasiyab coldly replied, 'Do not argue with me. Just do as I have told you.' The stone statue reluctantly reached out for a citron hidden in its hair and handed it to him along with the coconut it was holding.

Afrasiyab hastened with the two items to Hairat's camp where she was still desperately trying to save herself from Taaq One-eye's soldiers. Afrasiyab chanted a spell and breathed towards the sky. A lakh and twelve thousand stars shot down like arrows and pierced the foreheads of Taaq One-eye's soldiers. When the stars touched their foreheads, the soldiers exploded like fireworks and were incinerated within moments. At the same time, two magic claws picked up Taaq One-eye and whisked him away.

Afrasiyab ran towards Hairat and lifted her in his arms. She looked utterly spent—her veil had slipped off her head, her forehead was wet with sweat and her cheeks were smeared with kohl. She looked white as a sheet and was trembling with fear. Afrasiyab gently wiped her face and carried her to the pavilion. Mussavir, Soorat Nigar and other commanders who had fled when Taaq One-eye's star army attacked the camp now returned to the durbar. The King of Magic arranged the restoration of the burnt tents and pavilions of the camp, and had the plain cleared for the last rites of the four lakh soldiers who were lying dead in the battlefield.

Finally, Afrasiyab went to the magic river conjured by Mahrukh. He stood on the bank and tossed the coconut he had taken from the puppet into the waters while saying, 'Go back to where you came from!' The river retreated with a mighty roar and disappeared into the mountains. Mahrukh and Bahar had been watching the destruction of Hairat's forces from the far bank. However, when Afrasiyab removed the magic river, they returned to their pavilions to avoid facing him. They ordered their armies to remain alert, in case the King of Magic attacked them suddenly.

Afrasiyab joined his wife in the royal pavilion and spent some time comforting her as she was still in a state of great distress. He also sent for the ayyar girls Sarsar and Saba Raftar. Though the ayyar girls normally roamed the wilderness, they also had permanent tents in the camp. They had fled when Taaq One-eye attacked the camp and returned when they heard the Shah had salvaged the situation. When they arrived in court, he told them to convey this message to Mahrukh and Bahar: 'I am not going to strike battle drums but be warned that I will be fighting you. Prepare all the spells you can recall—let me also see how good you are as sahiras!'

After Sarsar left the pavilion, the Shahanshah muttered a spell and the magic claws that had retrieved Taaq One-eye from the battlefield transported him to the durbar. The Shah chanted an incantation over some water and then sprinkled it on the unconscious Taaq One-eye. When Taaq One-eye opened his eyes, he saw the King of Sahirs looking at him. He realized his folly and was overcome with shame. After some time, he said, 'O Mighty King, you are my teacher in place of Ustad. Forgive me!'

The Shah replied, 'You are not to blame! You were in a state of enchantment and not in your senses. This was one of my spells used against you; otherwise, no sahir can overpower you! You are my childhood friend and I do not like to see you hurt. Oh my brother, I am overcome with sadness when I remember how you and I, and Kaukab and Azhdar Zulmati used to get together in the *maktab khana*; how we laughed and joked together; how we abused each other in good humour. Do you remember those carefree days? Alas, we are all kings of large realms now but our hearts and minds have changed!' Afrasiyab then ordered, 'Let the nautch commence for my brother!' Thus, Afrasiyab graciously arranged a gathering of pleasure for his old friend.

Meanwhile, as Sarsar approached Mahrukh's camp, she met the ayyar Zargham, who mockingly asked her where she was going. Sarsar did not respond in her usual fiery manner and quietly said, 'This is not the time to tease me. Shahanshah has brought the magic forces of Tilism to fight you and sends a message for your Malika.' Zargham immediately led Sarsar to Mahrukh Magic-eye who was in counsel with her sardars. When Mahrukh heard the king's message, she was terrified, but tried to look outwardly calm. She said, 'Sarsar, tell Shahanshah we are all eager for the battle as well. Do not hold back in any way!'

When Sarsar left her durbar, Mahrukh trembled in fear. Bahar, who noticed this held her hand and said, 'Malika, why should we be afraid of dying? The point is to die with honour as some day all of us have to leave this world!' Mahrukh drew courage from Bahar's words and emerged with her sardars to lead her soldiers who were already on high alert to the battleground.

Afrasiyab calls upon the Tilismi host to fight the rebels

Sarsar returned to the durbar and repeated Mahrukh's message to the King of Magic. Afrasiyab's face grew dark with anger and he writhed in his chair like a spiral of smoke. He looked so furious that no one dared utter any word. He went out of the durbar and chanted an incantation. Within moments, it seemed as if his whole body was made of fire. He held a bolt of lightning as a whip in one hand and his sword flashed on his waist like a live flame.

The silhouettes of thousands of ghostly horses thundered in from the desert as the Shah moved forward with Hairat, while his commanders walked behind him deferentially. He stopped and took out the citron given to him by the Tilismi puppet. He smashed it on the ground and the earth shuddered and split open in a vast chasm. A grotesque sahir sitting on a monstrous elephant emerged from the cleft—the elephant of the sky was no match for it. The sahir wore gold-plated armour studded with gems while live red and black snakes were coiled around his head. He held a flag with the image of a boar on it.

A number of similar monster elephants laden with gold and silver kettledrums emerged next, followed by a formidable army of gigantic fire-breathing dragons. The sahirs sitting on the dragons exhaled flames from their nostrils and held long black cobras instead of whips in their hands. Behind them, an army of magical birds—peacocks, hawks and swans with beaks as sharp as daggers and swords—flew out of the chasm. Once these animal armies had settled on the plain, a cavalry of twelve thousand young soldiers mounted on horses emerged from the pit. They wore blood red uniforms with ruby-studded gold crowns and armour, and their scabbards were also made of rubies. Their horses trotted in orderly formations and settled into position behind the king.

Afrasiyab watched impassively as one phenomenal army after another emerged from the cavernous pit before him. Finally, a huge shadowy stallion with a jewel-encrusted saddle reared out of the pit. The Shah mounted this Tilismi stallion and the phantom horses that emerged from the pit formed a procession behind him. The air resounded with the sounds of a thousand unseen drums and gongs.

The forces of Mahrukh and Bahar who had followed their leaders to the battleground froze at the sight of the magical army. No one faltered or stepped backwards, but they felt like living corpses wearing shrouds for uniforms for they saw death confront them from across the battlefield. Bahar whispered in Mahrukh's ear, 'No one except Tilism Kusha can fight this host! Indeed, it seems to be the end for us. Let us pray in all sincerity to Allah to grant us mercy and save us today.'

They lifted their hands and prayed in all sincerity. Soon, their prayers were granted in the Highest Durbar. The Shah of Tilism was supervising his magical army when clouds of many hues, some red and some yellow with flames bursting within them, floated into sight. After a few moments, thousands of elephants, dragons and other wild animals materialized under the clouds. Lightning flashed through the clouds and there was a loud clap of thunder. An egg-shaped object shot out from the clouds and fell at Afrasiyab's feet. It burst open and released an emerald tablet that floated into the king's hand.

Afrasiyab looked down at the tablet and read the message inscribed on it: 'Your humble handmaiden will die a thousand times for you! Huzoor, why have you taken this terrible step? Are all your slaves and handmaidens dead that you confront these unfortunate rebels yourself? In the name of Samri, please stay back. Your humble handmaiden Sannat Magic-maker is about to arrive!' Afrasiyab flung the tablet away and called out in anger, 'Where was the handmaiden until today? It is too late for such talk. I will do my own work from now on! I am not dependent on any slave or handmaiden!'

As soon as he said this, an army of four-hundred thousand flame-throwing dragons flew in. Monstrous sahirs were riding these dragons. A throne that was mounted on four dragons then came into view. On it sat a middle-aged woman dressed in costly robes. She descended from the throne and went around the Shah with folded hands. She pleaded, 'Huzoor, behold my army!' Afrasiyab looked up and saw her lashkar of sixty lakh sahirs. A mighty river flowed on one side of the army and on the other side, the earth shook with powerful earthquakes. Afrasiyab looked unimpressed and said, 'What is the point of these illusions now?' On hearing this, Sannat beat her head repeatedly and wept, 'O Mighty King! Has it come to this that you should bring Tilismi host to face these worthless rebellious slaves? I will cut my throat before that happens! O Great Monarch, the sky itself is the canopy of your pavilion and the planets are your sentinels!'

As she continued in this vein, her words flowed like iced water upon the flaming rage that was consuming the King of Magic and the blazing river of his wrath subsided. He gestured lightly so that sixty-four thousand kettledrums resounded in the air; and the magic forces disappeared into the chasm from whence they had emerged. The king dismissed the magic host he had brought from the forests of Tilism and returned to Hairat's pavilion. On the other side, Mahrukh and Bahar kneeled down in grateful prayer right there and returned to their camp much relieved.

Sannat Magic-maker fights the rebels

Sannat's army camped on the vast plains along the banks of the River of Flowing Blood. A massive pavilion was erected for Sannat. Bazaars opened in the lashkar and were adorned with goods. The camp buzzed with activity as sahirs settled into their tents. Sannat went across to Hairat's camp and presented herself in the durbar. When she sat on the couch next to the royal throne, the nautch commenced, the *rubab* started playing and cupbearers served goblets of wine to the gathering.

In the laskhar of Islam, Mahrukh Magic-eye returned to her pavilion and sat on the royal throne. Ayyars who had left the camp when the Shah brought his magic forces now returned to the durbar. As Barq settled on the golden chair, Mahrukh exclaimed, 'O Barq, Allah extended his blessings on us today by saving us from Tilismi forces!'

In the enemy camp, Hairat and Sannat sat with each other companionably after dinner, sipping wine as they talked. In time, the light of dawn erased the night like an erroneous phrase. Sannat rose from her bed of inky blackness like the untrue word. The magic trumpet was sounded and echoed like a hundred trumpets throughout the massive army of sixty lakh sahirs. Barq, who was snooping around the enemy camp, heard the uproar and ran back to his camp to inform Mahrukh. Trumpets were sounded there as well and the lashkar mobilized in no time. Sahirs mounted magic birds, and Mahrukh emerged from her pavilion and left for the battlefield on her throne. Her army of several lakh sahirs marched behind her. Bahar, Nafarman, Zilzila and Larzan, all mounted on golden peacocks, looked alert and sharp.

As the two majestic armies faced each other, the universe itself was overwhelmed by the sight. The world cried, 'Today this wilderness will be further destroyed!' The sky whispered, 'If I could, I would myself flee!' The two armies settled in orderly files and heralds announced the battle. Sannat spiralled out like a whirlwind from her camp and called out, 'Mahrukh, send someone out to confront me!' Mahrukh was about to move forward herself when the brave Surkh Mu called out, 'O Malika, she is bound to kill all of us eventually! Allow me to confront her first!'

As Surkh Mu moved forward to confront her, Sannat laughed derisively and said, 'You can attack me first!' Surkh Mu had spent months perfecting a lethal magical weapon in the form of a citron, which she now took out of her waist band. Sannat was almost as powerful as the King of Sahirs, and her guardian spirits warned her just in time about the deadly citron that had been thrown at her. She flew off her lion mount just before it reached her, but the citron managed to hit the lion and incinerated it. This was followed by sudden darkness and Surkh Mu shouted triumphantly, 'I have killed her and finished this battle!'

Sannat descended from the sky cackling and asked, 'Whom have you killed you foolish woman? Let me teach you how to fight a war!' As she said this, she flung a huge iron ball at Surkh Mu. Her adversary, however, had also come into the battle fully prepared with several guardian spirits to protect her. They formed a bulwark against the iron ball thrown by Sannat and protected Surkh Mu, but were annihilated in the process. Surkh Mu jumped off her peacock, and dived into the earth. The iron ball then incinerated the peacock and several hundred elephants standing behind it. It went on to destroy thousands of soldiers standing behind the elephants before losing its momentum.

Surkh Mu then emerged from the earth and Sannat was furious on seeing her alive. She picked up a twig from the ground that she transformed into a deadly sword, forty feet in length. With this sword, Sannat attacked Surkh Mu, who read a counterspell that conjured forty shields to protect her. May God shield us, Sannat's sword could not be stopped now! It burnt Surkh Mu's guardian spirits, slashed through the shields and struck the young princess on her brow. As she fell unconscious on the ground, Sannat went forward to behead her, but a magic claw whisked Surkh Mu from the battlefield. Her sister Yakut, who had sent the claw to retrieve Surkh Mu, attacked Sannat with her sword, but the sahira conjured seven hundred iron chains to protect herself.

Yakut found it impossible to cut through all the chains and drew back helplessly. Sannat used the twig sword on her as well and wounded her. A magic claw whisked Yakut too before Sannat could make her next move. Mahrukh Magic-eye was enraged at the sight of her fallen commanders, She called out furiously, 'Wait you harridan, you have caused terrible injuries to my sardars, may God save them!' Sannat called out, 'I was waiting for you Mahrukh!' She stamped hard on the earth so that two iron chains coiled out of the ground, clamped around Mahrukh's ankles and rooted her on the spot. Sannat was about to slice her head off when Bahar called out, 'Sannat! Is that a sword you are holding or a wand made of flowers?' Bahar's words were magical and instantly transformed Sannat's sword into a harmless wand of flowers.

Sannat looked at Bahar, and smiled as she said, 'Bahar you were not a servant of Shah but his beloved woman. That is why your magic has affected me. Very well, I will release Mahrukh and bewitch you instead. Your wand of flowers is for me and my sword is for you! You will now use this sword instead of me!' Sannat's words were also magical and as the chains around Mahrukh's ankles snapped open, Bahar found herself holding the forty-foot sword. She jumped off her peacock and turned around to attack her own army.

The ayyars were also present in the army in various disguises. On seeing Bahar bewitched, Barq acted quickly and trapped Bahar in the coils of his snare-rope. As she tripped and fell, he burst a narcotic bubble in her face and made her unconscious. He ran off the battlefield with her and deposited her in Shakeel's tent, as it was closest to the battlefield. He made sure that she remained unconscious and returned to the battlefield. Sannat became even more furious and signalled to the cloud of many hues floating overhead. There was a loud crack of thunder and a blinding flash of lightning, as the next moment, the cloud began expelling large rocks on Mahrukh's army.

The sahira was so brutal that Mahrukh's army sustained serious injuries. Her stones smashed the mirrors of their hearts and everyone suffered. Sannat added to their suffering by slashing through their ranks with her magic twig sword. It flashed like lightning and annihilated line upon line of soldiers. The sardars conjured magic shields on their heads, but even this could not protect them. Mahrukh, Nafarman, Larzan and Zilzila were all badly wounded. Sannat signalled her army to attack at the same time and only the flash of swords and magic lightning could be seen on the battlefield.

Amar arrives from Nur Afshan

Let us now return to Tilism-e-Nur Afshan where, as the reader might recall, the great ayyar Amar bin Ummayyah continued to enjoy the hospitality of Shah Kaukab and his daughter Burran Sword-woman. He occasionally went on tours of the Tilism, but mostly spent his days drinking wine and watching nautch performances. His days were festive and his nights, celebrations. That day, he was engrossed in a gathering of pleasure when a gold puppet mounted on a lion flew into the durbar. Princess Burran acknowledged his greeting and the puppet handed her a nama from Shahanshah Kaukab. Burran read in the nama, 'My child, I have come to know that Sannat Magic-maker has come to fight Amar's army. That wretched woman is a powerful sahira. You must bring Amar to the Garden of Pleasure from where he can proceed to Zulmat of my Tilism and reach Hoshruba in a day. I can also meet him in the garden and give him leave to depart.'

Amar saw Burran's face change colour as she was reading the letter and asked her if all was well. She related the contents of the message to him. Makhmoor who was also present wanted to know if she was to leave as well. Burran told her, 'You will be given leave with Khwaja.' Makhmoor immediately rose to say her farewells and the princesses Imran, Akhtar and Majlis were in tears as they embraced her. Burran was in a hurry to leave and said, 'Khwaja will visit us often, but let us leave now as Shah has summoned us urgently!'

She put her arm around Amar's waist and flew off alone with him. Amar's eyes closed with the velocity of the wind. He opened them some time later and saw that they were in a wondrous garden of eternal spring. Burran led him to a pavilion where he saw Kaukab of the radiant conscience reclining on a throne. Amar bowed deeply and greeted Shah Kaukab, who emerged from the pavilion to meet him. They exchanged formal compliments before Kaukab led him by the hand into the pavilion and seated him next to the throne. He signalled to his daughter who disappeared into the pavilion. She emerged some time later with a bevy of lovely handmaidens holding gold and silver trays. These trays were laden with rare jewels and gifts of Tilism that even the eye of the sky had not seen before.

Kaukab presented these to Amar and said, 'Understand that this is not a formal farewell. You are being sent to confront Sannat. Once you have defeated her, you can stay for a night in your camp to meet your friends and then return to us. You can use the same route to reach this Tilism. Burran will watch over you and I will be coming to confront the King of Magic myself. You must leave now as the battle has begun.' Kaukab then turned to his daughter and said, 'Open the doorway into Zulmat and lead Khwaja to Hoshruba's boundaries. Mahi Parizad, Sailan and Baraan Jadoo are to take their armies and go with him.' The princess nodded and asked, 'What are your orders for Makhmoor?' Kaukab replied, 'That is entirely up to the noble princess. She can remain here or return to her lashkar.'

After Amar took his formal leave of Kaukab, the Shah suddenly vanished. Burran led Amar out of the garden to a place where they saw a huge golden gateway that soared into the sky. Burran stopped here and called out, 'O Sailan and Baraan Jadoo! Shah Kaukab commands you to accompany Khwaja Amar to Hoshruba.' There was a loud crack of thunder and a thin strip of light appeared above them. Amar and the princess walked in the glow of this light until they reached a mountain. Burran called out again, 'O Bahrain Jadoo! Appear now to accompany Khwaja's procession.'

A huge army of elephants emerged from the ravines of the mountain holding gifts for Amar. The princess draped Khwaja with the rich garments Kaukab had sent for him and placed a magnificent crown on his head. She tied magic amulets around his arms and protective rosaries around his neck. She told him, 'Use the noble Kaukab's gifts in the battle and do not linger there beyond one night. This horse will bring you back to our Tilism when you order him to do so.'

She recited an incantation and Makhmoor arrived on a flying throne. She was also overawed to see the preparations for Khwaja Amar's departure. Burran embraced them both and said, 'Go with God and return in victory.' Burran then disappeared and the procession moved forward. When they entered Zulmat, everything went pitch black, but the procession continued moving as if it was daylight. The oppressive darkness alarmed Amar who eventually cried, 'My friends, I cannot see anything! Where has this Burran brought me?' No sooner had he said these words than there was a loud crack of thunder in the air and a moon materialized above them, illuminating the world. Amar looked up and saw Burran's radiant face visible in the moon. She called out, 'Khwaja, do not be alarmed, I am with you.'

The moon stretched out into a thin line of light that illuminated the path all the way to Hoshruba. When they reached Tilism, the line contracted to form the moon again and Burran called out, 'Khwaja I was with you until now, but I will take your leave here. God be with you, for this is the land of Hoshruba. You will find your lashkar just ahead.' As the moon disappeared, Amar could hear the sound of a fierce battle. He travelled some distance and saw that his army had retreated to their last post. Its pavilions and tents had been destroyed, stones were raining from the skies, and the earth could not be seen for the number of dead bodies strewn on it. The ones who were still alive had received the message of their doom. Sannat's magic sword was flashing in the battlefield; its deadly flames were withering the tree of existence of Mahrukh's lashkar.

Mahrukh Magic-eye saw the magic clouds on the horizon and the army of elephants approaching the battlefield and thought that Afrasiyab had sent reinforcements. She cried, 'We come from Him and to Him we shall return! If this is another magical army, it is certainly the end for us!' Barq Firangi heard her and said, 'If that is true, we are indeed all dead! However, let me find out for sure first!'

By this time, Amar had reached the edge of the battlefield and called out, 'I am Amar bin Ummayyah!' Barq rushed forward and saw his teacher's homely face under the Tilismi crown. He bounced back to Mahrukh, laughing and tossing his cap in the air. 'Congratulations!' he shouted. 'Ustad has arrived from Tilism Nur Afshan and this is his army!'

Amar took out a magic pearl given to him by Kaukab and tossed it up towards Sannat's cloud. The cloud roared and moved over Sannat's army to pelt it with rocks instead. Sannat was alarmed and quickly read a spell so that the cloud evaporated and vanished. Amar brought out another gift, an incense, given by Kaukab. He aimed the stick of oudh incense at Sannat, who quickly dived into the earth and escaped having her head severed. Khwaja called out to Mahrukh, 'Get this harlot now!' Just as Sannat emerged from the earth, a hundred and eighty thousand troops of Kaukab's army charged towards her with their swords drawn shouting, 'We are Amar's slaves!' When they heard these calls, Mahrukh's soldiers and the ayyars ran forward shouting, 'We are Amar's slaves!' Hordes of sahiras from Kaukab's army also called out, 'We are Amar's handmaidens!'

Sannat then flung a huge iron ball at Amar, who calmly held out a golden goblet with the face of a beautiful woman engraved on it. The woman in the picture sighed so that the ball lost speed and fell mid-way. Sannat stamped on the ground in fury and a hideous sahir appeared, holding a burning torch. At Sannat's signal, he threw the torch at the rebel army and it produced a flaming river of fire that flowed with great speed over the battlefield. Its fiery waves blazed up as if they would burn the sun.

Amar saw that his army could be reduced to ashes within minutes and raised his hands. Two sahirs materialized above him holding an emerald bowl and a wand. They struck the bowl with the wand and smashed it. A fish with the face of a beautiful woman emerged from it. The fish released water bubbles from her mouth that burst forth and formed a great river. The fish then dived into the river and the two sahirs called out, 'I am Baraan Jadoo and Sailan Jadoo!' before they vanished from sight. It started raining furiously and from the river came the cry, 'I am Mahi Parizad!'

The two rivers of fire and water met and the waters of the magic river were boiling as they rushed towards Sannat's army. Sannat started retreating while her companions held shields over her head to prevent the magic raindrops from touching her. Her army, however, could find no reprieve from the boiling waters of the magic river and thousands of soldiers drowned.

Mahrukh and Amar's armies rallied together and attacked them with their swords. Rivers of water and blood flowed in the battlefield. Eventually, Mahrukh was persuaded that she could seek revenge on another day. There were shouts of victory from Mahrukh's army as Sannat turned and made a humiliating and inglorious retreat.

Sarsar and Amar

Now hear about Hairat's camp that was buzzing with the news of Amar's timely arrival. Earlier, the King of Sahirs had chastised Sarsar and Saba Raftar harshly after Barq had tricked and murdered his teacher Hissam, shouting 'Look at how active the ayyars of Islam are compared to you! You have achieved nothing!' The two girls knew the Shah would be even more furious now and thought that they should cause some mischief in Amar's camp to avoid the Shah's wrath.

Accordingly, they disguised themselves as beautiful young witches in rich garments and jewellery. They went towards Amar's camp and were overawed by the grandeur of the army he had brought from Nur Afshan. The entrance to the royal pavilion was crawling with sahirs from Kaukab's army and since they could not really identify anyone, they let the ayyar girls through easily enough. Sarsar entered the durbar and saw that there was much jubilation there. Sardars were crowding around Amar, congratulating him. Amar looked resplendent on an emerald throne and Sarsar was impressed with his elevated status. She thought, 'Surely this Tilism will be vanquished and these ayyars will achieve greatness.'

Amar was chatting with his friends when he noticed a beautiful sahira standing in a corner. Khwaja's skills as an ayyar were unmatched. He recognized Sarsar at first glance but looked away quickly and continued talking to Mahrukh Magic-eye. Sarsar mingled with the crowd in the durbar and furtively slipped behind Amar's throne. Amar was aware of her movements, but pretended to be absorbed in the conversation. He squatted on the throne in a relaxed manner so that he appeared oblivious to his surroundings.

When Sarsar finally stood behind Amar, he suddenly tumbled backwards and landed right on her. She tried to run away, but Amar caught her in the coils of his snare-rope. Qiran, who was sitting in the durbar, saw Amar's manoeuvre and suddenly sprinted towards the entrance. He tackled Saba Raftar who was standing there confident that no one would recognize her. Qiran lifted her and brought her back to the durbar. Meanwhile Amar smiled at his astonished friends and explained, 'This slave-girl had run away from me, but I have found her now.'

He lifted Sarsar in his arms and rubbed his cheek against hers. He murmured, 'You heard I was here and came to see me?' Sarsar wriggled in his arms and screamed, 'You wretch, I would only come here to set fire to you! O Amar, by your faith, do not talk to me in this manner. Shahanshah will turn me out! Dishonourable one, are you not ashamed of fondling me this way in public?' Amar grinned and replied, 'There is no shame in true love!' Sarsar shouted, 'I will sweep your love with a broom! Samri will scorch your mouth for dishonouring me!' Amar said to her, 'I will be here for one night, but will send you to Kaukab's Tilism. When I return tomorrow, I will have my way with you!' Sarsar continued heaping abuse on him: 'Am I your chattel that you will send me there? Do you think that Shahanshah (may God protect him always) will allow you to do that? Have you ever seen your face in a mirror?'

Amar calmly tied her up as she shouted and placed her next to the tied-up Saba Raftar. He summoned one of Kaukab's commanders and ordered him to take the ayyar girls to Tilism Nur Afshan. Sarsar was now quite alarmed and cried out, 'I will make life impossible for you there and Kaukab will banish you from his kingdom!' Amar laughed and said, 'You will not get that opportunity for you will remain by my side day and night!' As this farcical situation continued, there was a sudden rush of wind and everything went dark. A golden claw flashed into sight and whisked Sarsar and Saba Raftar out of the durbar before anyone could move. Amar's companions dispelled the darkness and saw a sahir flying off with the ayyar girls. Hundreds of Amar's sardars sprouted wings to pursue him, but Afrasiyab had specially chosen the flying champion Hanood Jadoo to rescue Sarsar and none of the pursuers could reach him in the sky.

❧

18 MEHTAR QIRAN CAPTURES VIZIER BAGHBAN QUDRAT

The dishonest King of Sahirs, Afrasiyab, sat arrogantly on his high throne with Vizier Baghban Qudrat, the divine gardener, standing respectfully before him. 'My good vizier,' spoke Afrasiyab, 'is it possible that you capture that rascal ayyar Barq for me and lead his friend, that black-faced Qiran, to the end he deserves? Will you cut his head off and impale it on the highest turret of my fort?' Baghban replied, 'Huzoor, I only need your good wishes! I will arrest them right away and bring them to you, mighty Shahanshah.' Afrasiyab graciously presented the vizier with robes of honour to mark his departure.

As Baghban left the durbar, his devoted wife Gulcheen looked wistfully at her husband. Afrasiyab smiled and asked her, 'Why princess, should we not send your husband on this mission?' Gulcheen replied respectfully, 'I am Shahanshah's handmaiden and my husband his humble slave. How can I dare stop him? In fact, I would like to accompany him.' Afrasiyab laughed, 'You will not be content without your husband! Very well, I give you leave to follow him.'

Gulcheen left the durbar and hastened back to her garden. She summoned a maidservant and ordered, 'Go quickly and find vizier sahib. He has just left the Garden of Apples for the wilderness and will not have gone far. Tell him that I want to see him urgently before he embarks on his mission!' The maidservant found the noble vizier and delivered the message to him, much to his irritation. 'The woman has to involve me in some petty domestic issue just when I am about to carry out Shahanshah's orders!' the vizier grumbled, but returned home nevertheless.

Gulcheen greeted her husband warmly when he returned. She held his hand, led him to a masnad and poured him a goblet of wine. When she handed him the wine, her lovely eyes filled with tears. She said, 'Listen sahib, I called you because I want you to realize that you will lose your life if you set out to arrest the ayyars. You must not at any cost confront them or have anything to do with them!' The vizier smiled and replied, 'Sahib, you know once a master gives orders, his servant has to obey even if he has to lose his life!' Gulcheen lost her temper at Baghban's reply and shouted, 'I will set fire to such a job and spit on loyalty that endangers my husband's life! No sahib, I will not let you go! Should I become a widow to keep Mian Afrasiyab safe? He can fold up his job and keep it with himself! We cannot pay such a high price just because you are the vizier! If my husband is safe, he can find ten other jobs! If not, we can both survive by begging for our livelihood or leave this land! Are we tethered to Hoshruba?'

Baghban frowned at his angry wife and said, 'Listen sahib, you have crossed all limits! As long as I got the salary, honours, land and awards, everything was fine. You were the wife of the vizier and enjoyed every luxury. Now that I have been assigned a dangerous mission, you are talking this way! Wife, remember that those who are true to the salt do not grudge sacrificing their family and wealth to obey their master. This will bring me honour in the eyes of both man and God!' Gulcheen was even more furious and screamed, 'Listen, you oaf! Stop talking nonsense and return to your senses! I am the mother of five children, not a little girl that I do not understand things. What has this Shahanshah against you that he wants you to face the ayyars? Does he not realize that they are the most wily and devious creatures in this world? They transform into women, men and spectres within moments. They cajole and bully and dissolve like colour into every kind of water! They kill sahirs as people crush headlice or bedbugs! Surely Shahanshah is your enemy for sending you against them!'

Baghban replied heatedly, 'That is quite enough! Shut your mouth right now! I swear by Samri that I will never be disloyal to Shahanshah even if it costs me my life!' Gulcheen stood up and frantically beat her chest as she shouted hysterically, 'People, stop this man! He is determined to make me a widow! People, my husband is being taken from me!' Baghban looked around in alarm and tried to calm his distraught wife. 'Try and control yourself my dear,' he said, pacifying her. 'If we have a hundred friends,' he continued, 'we also have a hundred enemies! Someone is bound to report this to Shahanshah and I will be disgraced for no reason. Why are you afraid? I promise I will be very careful and alert. I will not let anyone come near me nor eat anything. I will be suspicious of whoever approaches me, whether they are friends or strangers. The ayyars will not be able to trick me!'

The vizier went on this vein and when his wife was reassured, he left the garden. Gulcheen wept and wailed for some time and shed tears like a melting candle. Her companions consoled her and said, 'Bibi, do not bring bad luck upon yourself by weeping this way. Pray that your husband returns in victory!' Gulcheen, however, was not content with Baghban's reassurances and eventually decided to follow her husband and save him from the ayyars herself.

Vizier Baghban and the ayyars

Now hear about Barq and Qiran, the ones who brought sustenance to the garden of ayyari and heightened the colours of spring in the garden of deceit. They were together in a ravine in a mountain and decided that before infidel sahirs caught them together, they should part company. Barq transformed into the image of an impure sahir. He dangled a pouch of magic around his neck and used sindoor to adorn his naked chest with an outline drawing of Samri. He wore wooden sandals, held a garland of skulls in one hand, a trident in the other and left the ravine. Qiran stayed in the same place, but was also dressed up as a sahir.

Barq was wandering around when he saw a man in the distance who appeared to be searching for someone. Barq recognized Vizier Baghban Qudrat at first glance and approached him. Since Baghban had promised his wife that he would be wary of any stranger, he looked at the approaching sahir through the eye of magic and realized that this was Barq ayyar. Baghban called out to the false sahir, 'Brother, where are you wandering? Come and eat with me!' Barq said, 'May Samri bless you, I am not very hungry right now!'

Baghban asked the sahir, 'Where do you come from?' Barq had a ready reply, 'I belong to this area. In fact, my grandfather and great grandfather were born here.' The vizier laughed and said, 'You rascal ayyars, you never slip up do you?' Barq realized that the vizier had recognized him and hurled an egg of unconsciousness at the vizier's nose. The vizier reacted speedily and made the egg shoot upwards magically before it reached him. The vizier then drew a line on the ground and said, 'Fall at my feet right now!'

Barq rushed towards him and fell at his feet, completely mesmerized. The vizier clicked his fingers and a heavy iron chain burst out of the earth to bind Barq. The vizier held one end of the chain and dragged Barq behind him. Meanwhile, Qiran had emerged from the ravine and saw Baghban arresting Barq. He approached the vizier to trick him, but Baghan's guardian spirit called out, 'Baghban stay on your guard! That is Qiran!' Qiran dodged out of sight and Baghban whispered to his spirit, 'I am alert but what did you do? Your warned me and alerted the enemy!'

Qiran disguised himself this time as a holy man with his hair tied up in a high bun on his head. He wore broad steel bangles around his wrists, smeared sandalwood paste on his face and body, and strolled past the good vizier in this form. Baghban saw him and reached into his pouch of magical tools. Qiran knew he had been recognized and called out, 'Mian, instead of groping in your pouch look out for the one who is about to ambush you from behind!' Just as Baghban jerked his head to look behind him, Qiran leaped out of sight.

Qiran realized that Baghban was the powerful vizier of the King of Magic, and no disguise or ruse could deceive him. He devised another plan to defeat him. He stopped and explored the garden of trickery for inspiration. Eventually, the flower of wishes bloomed for him, the breeze of hope and success swept through the garden, the threads of thought tied the bouquet of deception together. Qiran laughed and drifted off like the fragrance of blossoms. As he walked, he cut as many blossoming branches as he could from trees and shrubs in that wilderness. Within no time, he had managed to get a substantial number of flowers of all hues. He selected a tree that was standing alone on a grassy plain for nature had shaped this tree to appear round with supple, glossy leaves.

Qiran weaved the blossoms he had collected through the branches of the tree and adorned it as if it were a new bride. He worked so skilfully that it seemed as if the tree had sprouted blossoms in every colour. Satisfied with the startlingly beautiful results, Qiran sprayed the blossoms with drugged perfume. He filled a silver ewer with water from a nearby stream, added rosewater and perfume to it, and placed it under the tree. He then suspended a tablet on a branch that read, 'Khudawand Jamshed planted this tree with his own hands. He is seen here sometimes, frolicking amongst the branches in the form of a bird. The blossoms of this tree have magical properties and confer health and longevity. The silver ewer contains the sacred water of Jamshed. If applied to the eyes, the user becomes invisible to the eye.'

A little while later, Vizier Baghban wandered into this place, still looking for Qiran. As he entered the meadow, his senses were assailed by the drugged perfume of Qiran's tree. He looked around and was startled to see the artfully crafted tree. His eyes fell upon the tablet and when he read it, he took his shoes off in reverence. He dropped Barq on the ground and went around the tree with his hands folded in prayer. While doing this, he inhaled the drugged perfume from the blossoms. Later, he kissed the stone tablet permeated with the same perfume. The drug affected the vizier so much that he sneezed once and fell down quite unconscious. Barq too succumbed to the powerful vapours.

Gulcheen and Qiran

Qiran had been watching the vizier from a hiding place and was waiting for just this moment. As he laughed triumphantly and ran forward holding his great bughda to smash the vizier's head, Baghban's wife Gulcheen arrived on the scene to find her husband lying helplessly on the ground with a heartless ayyar poised for the kill. Gulcheen was so alarmed by the sight that she forgot all magic. She ran forward pleading, 'In the name of your God, do not destroy my reign! Do not remove the shelter over my head! Do not kill my husband and turn me into a widow!'

Qiran held back his bughda and Gulcheen sobbed as she addressed her unconscious husband, 'Did I not warn you not to take on these ayyars? Look at you, how helpless you are! Where is your bravery and courage now?' As Gulcheen went close to the tree, the fragrance of the blossoms saturated with the drug caused her to sneeze and fall unconscious. No sooner had she fallen, tiny puppets of clay emerged from the earth and revived her by sprinkling water on her face. Gulcheen recovered immediately and chanted a spell so that Qiran's feet were rooted to the ground. He aimed his bughda at Baghban's head in anger and called out, 'Wait you ill-fated one! You may have caught me but I will kill your husband first.'

Gulcheen realized that before she could stop him with a spell, he would smash Baghban's skull. So, she released Qiran, folded her hands and asked him to forgive her. As she drew closer to the tree, she felt dizzy again and fell to the ground calling out, 'What trickery have you played here that a person keeps falling unconscious!' Her magic puppets revived her again and Gulcheen ran off to stand at a distance from the tree. Qiran thought that since the vizier's wife was so contrite, there was a chance that she and her husband could become allies. Meanwhile, Gulcheen had chanted an incantation that froze Qiran's limbs.

Gulcheen pleaded again, 'Listen ayyar, I give you my word that I will never betray you! If you are ever captured in Tilism, I will secretly come to your help. For the love of your Prophet and saints restore my husband to me and revive him from his stupor so that he can distinguish between friend and enemy!' Qiran said disdainfully, 'You should have stopped your husband from challenging us. Anyway, I take pity on you now and will let him go. Do not think that you captured Qiran with your magic. I am the favourite of the great pir, the miracle worker, Mushkil Kusha of this world! I can resist your magic anytime.'

Gulcheen said, 'Mian, may my life be sacrificed for him, your Mushkil Kusha is a powerful pir. I have heard of him as well. This spell on your limbs was just to save my husband. Here, I release you now!' After she released him, Qiran rubbed his numbed limbs and said, 'Release my brother who has been chained by your husband.' Gulcheen willingly obliged. When Barq was freed, Qiran lit the incense of consciousness and held it under his nose.

As the ayyar revived, Qiran stuffed his nostrils with wads of cottonwool to prevent him from falling unconscious again. Barq looked at Qiran's handiwork with the tree and complimented him. Qiran then handed Gulcheen the incense and said, 'Pinch your nose and use this to revive your husband. Tell that ignorant one that he is not to confront us again or I will kill him in his own house and cut your nose off!'

The tricksters left the meadow and hid themselves while Gulcheen revived Baghban with the incense stick. He opened his eyes and asked, 'What is happening here?' Gulcheen replied, 'I will tell you everything! Let us first move away from this cursed tree.' Once they were at a safe distance from the tree, she cried, 'Mian listen, it was as I feared! You were lying prostrate on the ground and had I not followed you would have been finished.' As she explained the trickery to him, Baghban looked stunned. He looked at the tree of deceit and thought, 'What an audacious trickery and how skilfully he caught me! I, Baghban Qudrat, the divine gardener, was deceived by an artfully created tree!'

Gulcheen kneeled at his feet and cried, 'Mian, for the love of Samri and Jamshed do not confront the tricksters. My nose will be cut off and I am afraid for your life! I have given them my pledge and you have to forswear this mission!' Driven by his loyalty to the King of Sahirs, the vizier said, 'You may be right but I cannot betray my master!' Gulcheen became hysterical when she heard this and screamed, 'If you do not listen to me I promise I will kill myself by swallowing poison or will cut my own throat. Listen sahib, if Shahanshah cannot do anything to Mahrukh and Bahar who have rebelled against him, what can he do to you?' Faced with this argument, Baghban faltered in his resolve and said, 'Princess, I am in a dilemma right now. I really do not know what I should do or not do! Give me a few days and I will give you a reply.'

Just then, a loud voice resonated in the air, 'Baghban come here at once!' Baghban trembled with fear and said, 'That sounds like the King of Sahirs!' The vizier sprouted wings and flew at once to the Garden of Apples. Afrasiyab controlled his rage and smiled as he softly asked, 'So Baghban, what reply will you give to your wife?' Baghban kneeled, kissed Afrasiyab's throne and said, 'Shahanshah, I am your lifelong slave. I will never betray you. I am not a tree that gives bitter fruit. I said that to put off my wife who is a woman of little intelligence. If my words have clouded the mirror of your noble heart I pray now that you will bestow the robe of forgiveness upon me!'

Afrasiyab replied, 'Baghban I used to consider you the strength of my right arm; I thought that you were true to the salt and my well wisher! I was deeply distressed to hear such words from you. Your reply should have been that even if you died a thousand deaths, you would still not ally with the tricksters! This time I forgive you, but if I hear anything like this from your wife or you again, I promise I will kill you in a dreadful manner. The fish in the rivers, the birds in the skies and the people of this world will pity you, but I will not be merciful!'

The vizier shook with fear and walked around Afrasiyab's throne holding his ears and begging forgiveness. Afrasiyab also realized that it was wiser not to make an enemy of Baghban. When Baghban completed his circumambulations, the king laughed and embraced his vizier, and said, 'Your punishment is that you go and capture the ayyars!' The vizier then left again to do the king's bidding.

✍

19 Afrasiyab Locates Jahangir Bin Hamza in the Valley of Dragons and Learns That Jahangir Is Unaware of His Lineage

Afrasiyab was desperately trying to find a Tilism Kusha who could destroy Kaukab's Tilism-e-Nur Afshan. His quest took him to Mount Sapphire, the highest mountain in Tilism Hoshruba. The ruler of the mountain and surrounding regions, Neelum Jadoo, was a powerful sahir and close to Afrasiyab. He regarded himself as Afrasiyab's equal and Afrasiyab reciprocated this sentiment by not demanding any tribute from Neelum.

Afrasiyab did not really want to visit Neelum in his palace and landed on Mount Sapphire itself. Neelum's spy birds, however, informed him of the Shahanshah's arrival and Neelum came out to welcome him with trays of jewels. After the formalities were over, Neelum suggested, 'I have built a small palace on this mountain that is used as a hunting lodge. Huzoor can grace it with his presence and rest for a while.' The king declared, 'When I come the next time, I will surely accept your invitation. This time, however, I have something else on my mind. Can you make some arrangements right here?'

Thus instructed, Neelum selected an alpine meadow on the mountain and sent for silken carpets and luxurious masnad seating. His attendants erected lofty canopies embroidered with gems and pearls and laid out ornate gold-inlaid chairs. Afrasiyab sat on a high chair as comely cupbearers served him goblets of wine that enchanted the senses. When Afrasiyab was rejuvenated with the wine, he recited an incantation. There was a sharp gust of wind and a parizad adorned with green robes and emerald jewellery flew in bearing a small golden casket. Afrasiyab took the casket from her and uttered some magic words to open it. Inside the casket lay a magic telescope that could show a view of the world. Afrasiyab had gone through so much trouble for he had read in an ancient book of prophecy that at about this time, a Tilism Kusha would appear to vanquish Tilism Nur Afshan. Afrasiyab wanted to find this Tilism Kusha and control Kaukab through him. His idea was that if Kaukab was busy fighting Tilism Kusha to save his Tilism, he would not be inclined to help Amar.

Afrasiyab began surveying the kingdoms of this sapphire range through the magic telescope when his attention was caught by a fortification in the Valley of Dragons. It appeared to be readying itself to face an attack and a row of archers guarded its battlements. The fort was facing a vast plain where two huge armies were standing facing each other, ready for battle. Lines of soldiers stood alert with drawn swords while two champions confronted each other in the battlefield.

Afrasiyab, who was watching the confrontation carefully, saw that a warrior emerged to confront the army poised to attack the fort. He was a barrel-chested, giant of a man with a dark, blood-thirsty face, enormous limbs and the strength of a mountain. He was riding a monstrous dragon and his pouch of magic hung around his neck. Confronting him from the other army was a young man of incomparable beauty and nobility. It is impossible to describe his feline grace and strength.

This noble young prince rode into the battlefield and foiled all the blows of the ogre-like warrior with his lance, dagger and sword. After some time, they jumped off their mounts and engaged in a fierce bout of wrestling. They wrestled for nearly two hours and finally, the young man hoisted his adversary aloft, threw him down on the ground and pinned his arms to the earth. He asked the warrior to concede defeat and when he refused, the young prince tore him from limb to limb with his bare hands. The warrior's army rushed towards the young victor shouting revenge, but he jumped on his horse and rode straight into their ranks, slashing away at the soldiers with his sword. His army fell upon them as well and the wrestler's army finally retreated and fled into the fort.

The gates of the fort were barricaded and the attacking army was subjected to a volley of arrows and cannon fire. The young prince of lion-like courage continued advancing while he deflected cannon balls with his mace. At that time, it seemed as if the whole plain was on fire; the battlefield was stained with the blood of slain soldiers and the air was thick with smoke as cannon balls smashed into the advancing lashkar. The young warrior dodged his way to the moat and swung his mace before flinging it across to lodge it in place on the fort's wall. He leaped off his mount, shimmied across the chain of his mace and managed to cross the moat.

The soldiers had stopped firing cannons from the fort and began pouring boiling oil down from the battlements. The brave prince smashed the gates open with one swing of his mace and by this time, his army had followed his example and crossed the moat. There was pandemonium in the fort as its guardian sahirs tried every protective spell at their command to no effect. The defiant ones of the fort were killed and many of them were captured. Eventually, the general populace of the fort waved flags of truce and surrendered to the young prince.

Jahangir Bin Sahibqiran

Afrasiyab was impressed with this young warrior and asked Neelum, 'Do you know anything about a fort in the Valley of Dragons and the young man who has subjugated it? I just witnessed his remarkable victory through the magic telescope.' Neelum took the telescope from the king, and after looking through it for some time, said, 'Huzoor, this is the fort of Zard Koh and the mighty wrestler who was torn apart was its ruler. The brave young man you just saw is the son of Malik Khurshid Taj Baksh, the ruler of Fort Khurshidia, and his name is Jahangir Bin Khurshid. He has a brother called Mehtar Chabak who is not a warrior like Jahangir, but is skilled in the art of trickery. Malik Khurshid himself is a powerful sahir. He has protected Jahangir against all magic with an invisible tablet that hangs around his neck. Jahangir has conquered several forts in this area, and in his fighting prowess, he surpasses Rustam and Saam! I have heard that there is some mystery about the origins of these brothers and they are not Khurshid's real sons. Both boys were averse to learning magic; one has excelled as a warrior and the other as an ayyar.'

As soon as he heard the story, Afrasiyab was satisfied and realized that his quest was over. He had observed Jahangir closely through the telescope and noticed the greenish mole and prominent vein of nobility on his radiant face, as well as his long hair that curled at his shoulders—all unmistakable signs of the tribe of Hashemites. He suspected that Jahangir was related to Emir Hamza and thought, 'I should extend my hand of friendship to Malik Khurshid and send this young man to conquer Kaukab's Tilism.'

Afrasiyab kept the magic telescope back in the casket and handed it to the parizad who flew off towards an unknown destination. He stayed with Neelum for some time drinking wine and sharing reminiscences before returning to the Garden of Apples. Ministers and counsellors of state welcomed him and paid homage. Afrasiyab presided over durbar on his throne and sent for the head scribe. He dictated a nama and stamped it with his seal. He ordered Aqeel Jadoo along with a contingent of a hundred sahirs to deliver the scroll to Malik Khurshid in Fort Khurshidia.

Kaukab's strategy

Now Shah Kaukab was also aware of the ancient prophecies and concerned about the threat to his Tilism. He shared his concerns with his teacher and the sage, Nur Afshan, who conducted a magic ritual that informed him about Jahangir. He wrote back to the Shah: 'Kaukab, be assured that the keystone of your Tilism is in a safe place. However, there is a new development—Afrasiyab has invited Jahangir bin Khurshid to Hoshruba. This prince is of the family of Hamza. If he accepts the invitation, the King of Magic will send him to conquer your Tilism. You should remain alert against this eventuality.'

When Kaukab read this letter, he conjured a magic claw and ordered it to summon Amar who was with Burran at the Palace of Seven Hues. The last time Amar had been to the Shah's durbar was when he had tried to trick Kaukab, who pushed him out unceremoniously. Amar found the durbar as splendid and grand as the last time and greeted the Shah with great deference. Kaukab dismissed the durbar and when they were alone, he consulted Amar on the problem at hand.

Amar said, 'You should also send an emissary to Khurshid and invite him here. It is likely that when two kings invite him, he may not go to either one. Second, send me to Fort Khurshidia. If I establish the fact that Jahangir is from the tribe of Hamza, I can inform him of his antecedents and bring him on the right path. Third, you should write to Mahrukh and tell her to send an emissary to Khurshid with appropriate gifts. Maybe he will consider an alliance with her.' Kaukab was pleased with Amar's counsel and acted accordingly. Mahrukh received Kaukab's message and selected her son Shakeel to lead a delegation to Khurshidia, as Shakeel was familiar with Tilism Hoshruba and its geography. The ayyar Barq Firangi accompanied Shakeel. We will see what happens to them later.

Now hear about Kaukab the Enlightened: He picked a sahir called Zufunoon Jadoo and several other high officials. His scribe adorned the bride of paper with the jewels of eloquent composition and the Shah stamped the nama with his seal. He also gave Zufunoon rare gifts and trays heaped with jewels and gold artefacts for Khurshid. Zufunoon's delegation also included Khwaja Amar, and soon the group left from the doorway to Zulmat that Amar had travelled through earlier.

Meanwhile, Afrasiyab's emissary travelled along the shores of the River of Seven Hues and bypassed Mount Agate to reach the kingdom of Khurshidia. Shakeel and Barq left the Tilism at the same time. Afrasiyab was informed of their departure but did not stop them, as he was interested in Khurshid's response to Mahrukh's invitation. The guardians of Tilism's frontiers were ordered to let the ambassadors travel to the land of Khurshidia.

The kingdom of Khurshidia

Thus, all three delegations arrived in Khurshidia at more or less the same time. They saw a land that was verdant and beautiful with trees blossoming in green pastures, and orchards abundant with fruit. Fresh water streams and rivers flowed throughout this gentle land and irrigated its fertile fields, and its people were warm and friendly. All three delegations set up camps just outside the walls of the city of Khurshidia. Amar had come with Kaukab's emissary Zufunoon, but slipped out of his delegation unnoticed and disguised himself as a sahir.

After occupying the fort in the Valley of Dragons, Jahangir had returned to his adopted father's durbar, where Malik Khurshid was celebrating his son's latest triumph. Cupbearers were serving goblets of roseate wine when Khurshid was informed of the arrival of the three envoys. He sent high-ranking nobles to escort them to his durbar. The nobles met the three envoys and said, 'Come with us—huzoor has summoned you.'

The envoys wore splendid robes of state for their meeting with Khurshid. They entered through the lofty gold-inlaid city gateway and saw that hundreds of mounted guards were guarding the entrance. The city had blooming flowerbeds, tall buildings, symmetrical and sturdy, with shiny gold cupolas that soared into the sky, and shop fronts that were arched and decorated with colourful arabesques. Its gold and textile bazaars were overflowing with the finest goods and buzzing with eager customers. They also observed that the city squares were piled with heaps of grain.

The envoys were duly impressed with this display of wealth. When they reached the durbar, they performed the mujra salutation at an appropriate distance from the throne and once they got the royal nod, they approached Malik Khurshid. They presented him with the gifts and the royal scrolls, and Khurshid had the curtains of the durbar drawn to view the gifts of elephants, horses and camels sent by the kings. When the ambassadors read out the namas, Khurshid listened to the contents intently and then smiled at Jahangir as if inviting him to speak. The noble prince declared, 'Although Kaukab's letter implies that we are not of the true faith, I am impressed by his conviction and sincerity. His nama is elegantly composed and he espouses a noble cause that warrants our alliance. Afrasiyab is the King of Sahirs and to join him would go against all my principles as a warrior.' Then Malik Khurshid said, 'In my opinion, we should support Afrasiyab for he is allied with Khudawand Laqa. We share the same beliefs and at this time, the godless ones have besieged him.' Jahangir replied, 'Well, let us consider all the options and compose appropriate responses. Meanwhile, commence the feast to welcome the noble ambassadors!' In response to his signal, comely cupbearers emerged with decanters of the choicest wines and melodious court singers began entertaining the guests.

After a while, a mace-bearer entered this gathering of pleasure and announced that an old musician was requesting an audience with the king. Prince Jahangir gave permission for him to be presented. The old man shuffled into durbar slowly so that everyone saw that he was of great age. His eyelashes were white and a snowy beard flowed down to his waist. He wore a kurta of the finest muslin, gulbadan pyjamas and a fawn-coloured turban. He had tucked his flute into his waist and carried a large drum.

The old man sketched a mujra greeting and said, 'May Samri keep huzoor safe. I have travelled a long distance in the expectation that I will leave this durbar a rich man!' Jahangir asked him, 'Where are you from?' The old man replied, 'I live in Umm al Jabbal and arrived in this land yesterday. I am a needy man, beset with monetary problems.' Jahangir said to him, 'Very well, demonstrate your skills.'

The old musician took out his flute and tried out a few notes before he began playing it in earnest. The whole durbar was in a trance as he played and it seemed as if the heavens and earth stood still to hear this music. When he stopped playing abruptly Jahangir cried, 'O skilled artist, for the love of your religion, do not leave us in this unfulfilled state!' The old man smiled and replied, 'O Great Prince, this old man is partial to wine. If you let me handle the maikhana today, you will enjoy the performance even more!'

Jahangir ordered the cupbearers to hand over the flasks and decanters of wine to the old man. The reader should know that this old singer was really Amar ayyar in disguise. Amar, in his time-honoured style, arranged the wine bottles deftly while adding a sleeping potion to them. Just as he was serving the goblet of wine to the prince, Jahangir's trickster brother, Mehtar Chabak, who had been away from the durbar suddenly made an appearance.

Chabak had read the annals of ayyari and had studied the trickeries of the legendary Amar, he was also aware of Amar's talents as a musician and singer. He realized at once that the old man was the ayyar in disguise who had probably come with one of the delegations. He took the goblet from the prince's hand and handed it back to Amar saying, 'Old man, drink this yourself before you serve anyone else.' Amar accepted the goblet without batting an eyelid and looked up to see a wiry young man, watchful and alert, armed with all the tools of ayyari. Amar also noted the young man's resemblance to his own sons. He tried to slip an antidote pellet into the goblet but the clever Chabak caught his hand just before he could slip the pellet in. Amar thought, 'Well he has exposed me but I will punish this wretched pup as well!' Amar suddenly twisted his hand and wrenched it out of Chabak's grasp. He then struck a blow to Chabak's head and sprinted out of the durbar.

Chabak was humiliated but cried out, 'No sahir here should attack this man! I will capture him myself.' Meanwhile, Amar had leaped over the palace walls. There was an uproar as palace guards and soldiers pursued him, but Chabak stopped them and said, 'That ayyar is alone and I should also confront him alone. If all of you attack him it would go against the principles of ayyari!' Thus, Chabak pursued Amar on his own. Amar saw him coming and took out a shield from Zambil as he ran (we will speak of this shield later). He tried to trace a way out of the city but found himself at a dead end. Chabak reached the street and called out, 'Wait you disgraceful one! Where will you escape to now?' Amar drew his sword and snarled, 'Come then, you are bound to die young!'

Chabak attacked him like a bolt of lightning. Amar dodged out the way a couple of times. When Chabak attacked him with his sword, Amar deflected it with the shield he had brought out of Zambil. The shield was actually mounted with paper and contained some dust of unconsciousness. As the sword struck the shield, it burst open and released the dust on Chabak's face, who sneezed several times and collapsed on the ground.

Amar quickly took his shirt off and wore it himself. He painted Chabak's face to look like himself and then placed his hands on the blessed Zambil to ask for the miracle of transforming into Chabak. He bound Chabak with a rope, hoisted him on his shoulder and returned to the durbar. Jahangir was delighted to see his brother unharmed and said, 'Let us tie him to a pillar and revive him!' The false Chabak said, 'He will be a nuisance if he is conscious. Once this gathering of pleasure is over, you can revive and execute him!' Jahangir had the unconscious prisoner tied to a pillar in the durbar. The false Chabak then whispered to Jahangir, 'It seems that ayyars have come to our land with these envoys. Dismiss all the attendants and cupbearers from durbar and let me serve the wine.'

Jahangir trusted his brother implicitly and followed his advice. After all the attendants had left the durbar, Amar took over the wine flasks.

He laid some aside and declared they were drugged, he fiddled with some more flasks and in the process drugged the entire stock. He poured a goblet and first served his brother and then everyone else in durbar. Very soon, the entire gathering was unconscious.

Amar first deposited Kaukab's messenger and Shakeel Jadoo in Zambil. He then revived Chabak and greeted him mockingly. Chabak woke up to find that he was tied to a pillar and that everyone else in the durbar was unconscious. He realized that Amar had outsmarted him and was intensely annoyed by this. To irritate him even more, Amar began plundering the durbar. He divested the unconscious men of their expensive robes and jewels and took the crown off Malik Khurshid's head. However, he left Jahangir as he was.

Meanwhile, Afrasiyab was getting restless and anxious about Jahangir's reaction to his message of alliance. He sent for the oracle Book of Samri and focussed on Khurshid's durbar. He saw the image of the unconscious gathering with an unknown trickster plundering and looting. Afrasiyab exclaimed, 'Alas I am dead! Amar is in the land of Khurshidia and about to kill everyone!' Afrasiyab first thought of sending someone there, but realized that Amar could kill everyone before anyone reached there. This was something he would have to do himself since he was the Shah of Tilism and could travel very fast. He thundered up into the sky and within moments, he flashed over Khurshid's palace. Amar was about to put Jahangir into Zambil when he heard the roar of thunder and saw a flash of lightning. Amar knew there would be trouble and quickly became invisible in his cape.

Afrasiyab flashed down into durbar and conjured a heavy shower to revive the gathering. They were shocked by their nakedness and rushed off to find other robes while Afrasiyab untied Chabak from the pillar. Malik Khurshid recognized Afrasiyab and greeted him deferentially. He said to Jahangir, 'My son, rise and greet Shahanshah and pay him homage. It is our good fortune that he visits us!' Jahangir greeted Afrasiyab who kissed him affectionately on the forehead and made him sit next to him. He said, 'O Noble Prince, did you see that wily rascal? If I had not reached in time, he would have killed everyone. He is the one who has caused this upheaval in my Tilism. It is incumbent upon you now to ally with me. Destroy Kaukab's Tilism for he is Amar's ally. Hamza is bound to come to help Kaukab. If you manage to defeat him as well, you will have the world at your feet and everyone will worship Laqa. This is my sincere advice. Of course the decision has to be yours!'

Jahangir was already fuming at Amar's audacity and cried, 'O Shahanshah, I will invade Kaukab's realm and cause rivers of blood to flow with my sword! I will punish that wretched ayyar so severely that he will remember it for the rest of his life!' Jahangir looked around for Kaukab's envoy and declared, 'He must have brought that ayyar with him. Although it is not appropriate to execute an envoy, he must be punished for this misdeed!' When he could not find either Zufunoon or Shakeel, he vented his anger on their delegations and ordered them to leave immediately. He added, 'Take your gifts as well and warn your masters that we are on our way!'

Khurshid arranged a royal feast in Afrasiyab's honour and cast protective spells so that Amar or Barq could not find their way into the royal palace and were blinded every time they tried. The feast commenced with a round of roseate wine and the nautch performances were followed by a splendid banquet of artfully prepared dishes. The feast lasted throughout the day and continued late into the night. The next day, Afrasiyab left Khurshidia after Jahangir assured him that he would join him as soon as he mobilized his army.

After Afrasiyab had departed, Jahangir sent messages to the vassals of all the forts he had vanquished, ordering them to accompany him in his war against Kaukab. From all corners of the realm, armies moved towards Khurshidia. Jahangir equipped his own army and within a few days, he had mobilized an army of twelve lakh cavalry and infantry troops with each soldier alert and prepared for combat. Once the preparations were over, Malik Khurshid sat on his travelling throne while the prince mounted a spirited, untamed horse of Arab lineage. From another direction, Chabak emerged on the box of ayyari with several thousand of his disciples. Many of them played the *iktara* while some of them leaped about in sheer exuberance. Thus, this magnificent lashkar travelled to Hoshruba in stages along with Afrasiyab's envoy.

Jahangir in Hoshruba

As Jahangir and his family approached the frontiers of Hoshruba, the nazims and rulers of that area came forward to make offerings of gold and escorted them into Tilism. Afrasiyab was happy to hear of Jahangir's arrival and promptly sent a message to Hairat that said, 'Malika, the honoured guests are coming closer. Send your highest ranking nobles to receive them and spare no effort in providing every comfort to them!' Hairat read the message and sent many of her nobles, including the Shahanshah's viziers, Sannat and Abriq, to welcome her guests.

The viziers met Malik Khurshid on the way and escorted him with due honour to the camp. Hairat had the drums of joy struck and emerged out of her camp to meet them. She affectionately patted Jahangir on his back and led the guests into a pavilion especially erected for them. It was furnished richly with an emerald throne for Malik Khurshid, a high chair studded with rubies for Jahangir and a jewel-inlaid chair for Chabak. High-ranking nobles sat on chairs around them. A little later, the King of Magic also joined his guests. In this exalted gathering, Prince Jahangir asked Afrasiyab about the war in Tilism. Hairat replied, 'O Noble Prince, a few ayyars have incited some of our sardars to rebel against us. The ayyars of Islam are a nuisance and manage to infiltrate every gathering like unforeseen trouble. Indeed, they must be present here as well!'

As soon as she said this, Chabak looked around sharply. Ayyars Zargham and Jansoz who were in durbar, signalled to each other, 'Chabak is looking for us. We should reveal ourselves even if puts us at risk!' They then looked defiantly into his eyes and signalled, 'We are here to take care of you!' Chabak's first thought was to expose them to the Shah of Tilism, but he reflected that if the ayyars were daring enough to declare their presence, he needed to respond in the same vein. He signalled to them, 'This dagger that I carry is for your necks!' The ayyars responded by touching their heads and then pointing to their feet to indicate, 'Khwaja Amar gave you a shoe-beating in your own house! We will treat you in the same manner here!' Chabak remained impassive and signalled, 'Beware, I will be coming to your camp!'

He then beckoned Zargham, disguised as an attendant, and asked for water. Zargham immediately offered him a goblet of water after adding the powder of unconsciousness to it. Chabak was prepared and had already kept an antidote in his mouth. He drank the water Zargham gave him and took out an egg of unconsciousness from his waist that he held up to Zargham. 'Tell me servant,' Chabak said, 'do you know which creature could have laid this egg. It seems to have a peculiar aroma?'

Now Zargham had seen him take the egg out and had quietly secured a plain egg in his sleeve. He took the egg from Chalak so cleverly that it slipped up his sleeve and the plain egg rolled down on his hand. He inhaled the egg deeply and exclaimed, 'Indeed, huzoor, its fragrance is that of musk. This is not really an egg but the umbilical cord of a musk deer! Here, huzoor would you like to smell it now?' He flexed his wrist slightly before holding his palm out so that the plain egg went back into his sleeve and Chabak's egg rolled out into his palm. Chabak took the egg in one hand and casually rubbed his nose with the other hand. He had dipped his forefinger earlier in the scent of consciousness and he confidently inhaled the drugged egg.

Once the ayyars had taken measure of each other, Chabak rose and addressed the Shah, 'O Exalted Badshah, I will return after I cut the heads of your enemies!' Zargham and Jansoz slipped out of the pavilion undetected and returned to their camp where they informed everyone of Jahangir's reception. 'Chabak has declared openly that he will be confronting us,' they warned, 'so all sardars should remain alert and watchful!'

Chabak in the rebel camp

Chabak left the pavilion, found his tent and sent for some of his disciples. He told them to procure certain items and slip into the forest secretly. After they had left, he sat in front of a mirror and painted his face. Chabak was youthful looking with a smooth, unlined face and could easily transform himself into a young damsel of unparalleled beauty. After he was satisfied with his appearance, he adorned himself with rich garments and costly jewels, covered himself in a black shawl and stole out into the wilderness.

Chabak's disciples disguised as musicians were waiting for him with a bullock cart. The back of the cart had sackcloth tied to it in the form of a pouch packed with violins and drums. Two ayyars dressed as musicians were sitting in the carriage. Chabak sat down with them and looked like a full moon shining through dark clouds. One disciple nudged the bullocks with a stick and clicked his tongue to get them moving while the musicians sitting with Chabak put their hands on their ears and belted out a loud folk song. Thus, this bizarre ensemble left for Mahrukh's camp.

The cart stopped as they drew near the Islamic camp and the fair damsel alighted from it. Her beauty attracted a great deal of attention and young men recited love verses as she swayed past them, some youths followed her and whistled in admiration. That lovely damsel sauntered on, flashing smiles at everyone and asked the way to the darogha's tent. When the darogha met her, he offered the loss of his senses as tribute to her dazzling beauty. He fussed around her and asked what he could do for her. The damsel rolled her eyes at him seductively and simpered, 'We are professional singers and dancers. We hope to earn a few coins today with your assistance!'

The darogha was captivated with the hidden promise in her eyes and asked her to wait for a while. He went with a determined air to the durbar pavilion, approached Mahrukh Magic-eye and said, 'I would like to present a courtesan who is so beautiful that huzoor will be compelled to believe the goddess Venus has descended from the skies!'

The ayyars became suspicious when they heard this and said, 'You do realize that no stranger can be admitted to durbar in these times!' The darogha replied, 'Huzoor, I have known her a long time but was hesitant to present her earlier. Today, she was really very eager to make herself known to you, so I have taken the liberty of asking you!' Since the ayyars trusted the darogha, they relented and said, 'Since you know her, there is no harm in it!'

The darogha returned to his tent and grinned smugly at the damsel. He said to her, 'Dearest heart, I have done what you asked for. Sarkar summons you now!' The damsel smiled gratefully at the darogha and hurried back to her cart. She summoned her musicians and the darogha himself escorted her to Mahrukh's durbar. As the august gathering in the durbar beheld her radiant beauty, they all lost their hearts to her. Though Zargham watched her carefully, he did not recognize her at all. The ravishing courtesan then danced and sang so beautifully that everyone was captivated. Zargham, particularly, was so smitten that he could have died a thousand deaths for her.

The sardars then generously bestowed costly jewels and gold coins on her. She thanked them prettily and said, 'If you allow me to serve you wine, I will come into form and make you lose your senses!' Everyone was so besotted with her charms that heedless of danger, they happily made her in-charge of the maikhana. She skilfully blended the wines, drugging the flasks in the process, and danced provocatively as she served each person in the durbar. After some time, the drug in the wine began to overwhelm her enthusiastic audience. They were too well bred to lose control by fighting or arguing, and eventually, all of them were unconscious.

The false courtesan or Chabak secured the curtains at the entrance and drew his dagger to kill the sardars. However, the Creator of the Universe is also the Supreme Protector. Mehtar Qiran, who usually kept to the forest and seldom came to the durbar, arrived in the camp at that very moment. He was walking past the pavilion when he noticed that it was unusually silent. He slashed his way in and saw a comely maiden holding a dagger over the unconscious sardars. He realized instantly that she was an ayyar.

Qiran roared like a lion, 'Stop you impertinent youth!' Chabak turned around startled and nearly died with fear at the sight of a huge black ayyar lunging at him with a mighty bughda. He tried to flee but Qiran moved quickly and was about to smash his head when a claw flashed into sight and whisked Chabak out of the durbar. Afrasiyab's magical spirits had informed him that Chabak was in danger and he saved Chabak in the very nick of time.

Qiran leapt out of the pavilion when he saw the magic claw, but returned to revive the unconscious sardars. He vented his rage on the two ayyars Zargham and Jansoz: 'You call yourselves ayyars and are tricked by a callow youth this way! You useless wretches, you should die for shame than court such dishonour!' As Qiran berated the shamefaced ayyars loudly, they listened respectfully with bowed heads for Qiran was the khalifa of ayyars. Eventually, Qiran returned to the desert.

The next morning, Afrasiyab complimented Chabak on his brilliant impersonation and said, 'I would like you to rest easy now. Let us first accomplish the purpose for which you are here. You will have plenty of time to tackle these ayyars later!' Chabak readily agreed with Afrasiyab as he was quite shaken by his encounter with Qiran. The King of Magic then cast protective spells around Hairat's camp so that no ayyar could infiltrate it. The ayyars of Islam did make some attempts, but blackness descended on any path they took and they had to retreat and stand guard around their own camp. At the feast in his honour that evening, Jahangir said, 'Shahanshah let us prepare to move as soon as possible!'

Queen Hairat's rival

Now hear about Khwaja Amar, the good-intentioned one, who left Fort Khurshidia with Barq Firangi, who had come with Mahrukh's envoy. They travelled to Tilism Hoshruba, killing random sahirs they encountered on their way. As they approached the border, they decided that they would need a sahir's help in entering the realm as keepers of the gateway would stand in their way.

Amar climbed a hill and surveyed the land around him through binoculars. He saw the Neel river and the forts along its shores. On the other side were the arid mountains of Kohistan and the River of Seven Hues. As he moved the binoculars to focus on the plains of Tilism, he saw a sahir encampment.

Both ayyars climbed down the hill and walked towards the camp. As they drew closer, they saw that the golden boundaries of the camp stretched for miles. Colourful flags marked its bazaars and bands of sahir-guards marched through the camp. Hundreds of sahirs milled about and there were rows of cavalry and infantry soldiers. The sounds of sitar and tablas resonated in the air, large cauldrons bubbled with oil and sahirs were chanting prayers around sacred fires. Several worshippers were taking sacred baths in the streams flowing beyond the camp while sahiras practised magical spells.

The main durbar tent pavilion in the middle of the camp contained an ivory throne surrounded by chairs shaped like peacocks. A young woman who seemed to be the queen of all beauties sat on the ivory throne in gold embroidered robes and jewellery. Amar was impressed by the aura of power emanating from her and the sheer size of her army. He casually engaged a sahir in conversation and asked him, 'We are natives of this area and you are travellers. Who is this princess and what brings her here?' The sahir replied, 'She is Princess Zulmat. The King of Magic has invited Zulmat to share the throne of Hoshruba with him. That is why she has left her place and is travelling to be with Shah.'

Amar took Barq aside and said, 'We should kill her now for she will be a nuisance to us later!' Accordingly, Amar assumed the disguise of a fakir, dressed in just a loincloth with a begging bowl and a staff. He went around the lashkar begging for coins and approached the durbar pavilion. He called out to Zulmat who looked at him closely as her guardian spirits warned her that he was Amar ayyar who had come to kill her. Zulmat then sent for her strongbox, from which she scooped out a handful of gold coins and called out, 'Fakir, come and take these!' Khwaja's sixth sense warned him that she knew that he was an ayyar. He went forward with his hand stretched out and said, 'May you have a long life!' She gave him the coins and held his wrist with her other hand. Amar had already greased his hand and twisted it out of her grasp. He somersaulted and kicked her hard on her chest. Zulmat fell backwards and when her attendants rushed forward to help her, Amar quickly became invisible in Galeem.

Zulmat was helped up and sat on her throne again. Her guardian spirits informed her that Amar was now disguised as a sahir and wandering around the bazaar in her camp. She ordered one of her officers to saddle a horse and said, 'Escort Amar to me with due respect.' The officer took the horse to Amar in the bazaar and said, 'Princess Zulmat summons you!' Amar wanted to run away, but the officer stood blocking his way. He reluctantly mounted the horse and went to the sahira.

Zulmat rose from her throne to greet him and offered him a chair next to her. She sent for a casket and, 'This casket is the repository of a thousand spells, therefore, I would advise you not to try any tricks on me or you will regret it!' Amar promised solemnly, 'Inshallah, it will be as you command.' The sahira thought that Khwaja had reformed and immediately sent for trays heaped with treasures to present to Amar. The wily ayyar suddenly exclaimed, 'Princess who is this standing behind you?' As Zulmat looked behind her, Amar put the casket of spells in Zambil and called out, 'We are leaving now!' When Zulmat turned around, Amar had already vanished into Galeem. Zulmat thought, 'He is not someone who can be convinced to change his ways. Why should he when he has challenged the King of Magic himself?' She then ordered two of her officers to find Amar and chop his head off.

Meanwhile, Amar found Barq and related what had happened. He added, 'This sahira cannot be tricked. She sees through every disguise. It is not safe to remain here!' The two ayyars left the camp quickly and took cover in the wilderness. They saw two men looking for someone and knew that they had come for Amar. After a quick consultation, Amar disguised himself as a holy man in a loincloth and Barq dressed as his disciple. They lit a fire and sat around it, sorting marijuana leaves. The holy man's beard flowed down to his waist while the disciple had a shaved head and no eyebrows. Zulmat's officers saw them and called out, 'Baba-ji, have you seen a man running out of the camp?' Amar replied, 'Not a soul my sons, but you look weary. Smoke a pipe before you leave.'

The two officers sat down in all reverence and Amar and Barq offered them hookahs filled with marijuana leaves and a drug of unconsciousness. After a few inhalations they fell unconscious and the ayyars promptly cut their heads off. Their guardian spirits howled in protest and informed Zulmat about the manner in which Amar and Barq had killed her officers. She was furious on hearing this and transformed into a bolt of lightning to look for the ayyars. Amar and Barq were poking the dead bodies to look for valuables when a bolt of lightning flashed in the sky and snapped around their waists like a chain.

The next moment, Amar and Barq found themselves in Zulmat's pavilion, shackled and gagged, with the sahira looking furiously at them from her throne. She abused them roundly and sent for a large iron cage. She pushed them both into the cage, pulled out an amulet from her hair and held it against the bars of the cage. She then summoned a sahir called Mateen Jadoo, gave him the amulet and instructed him, 'This amulet was prepared by Jamshed. The cage will not open unless the amulet touches it. Keep it safely on your person and keep constant watch on the prisoners. Remain alert and do not let anyone come near the cage!' Mateen took the cage to his tent and suspended it over his bed.

The quarrel between Afrasiyab and Hairat

Zulmat ordered that the drums of travel be struck and journeyed in stages to reach Hairat's camp. Afrasiyab's spy birds informed him of her arrival. Afrasiyab was still in Hairat's camp after arranging Jahangir's departure for Tilism Nur Afshan. He sent prominent sardars to receive Zulmat and told them, 'All of you should acknowledge and respect her as you would my wife!' Malika Hairat frowned as she heard these words and said, 'Why sahib, since when did you arrange another palace? Mian, since the day I was unfortunate enough to come to your house you have caused me nothing but heartbreak and unhappiness. Do you think you will make someone else happier? Do not forget that it was because of my kismet that I became malika of this realm, otherwise your fate was to serve Lacheen and Tajdar. It is because of me that you became king. If it is in my destiny, I will be in comfort wherever I am. This empire is as lowly as my shoe to me! Why should I tolerate a common whore like Zulmat?'

Afrasiyab was outraged by Hairat's speech and said, 'That is quite enough from you! I have suffered enough abuse from you over the years. By Samri, I have been patient long enough. Anyone else would have cut off your nose! What does a wife have to do with this? Men have a hundred concubines! Badshahs have several harems! Do their wives leave their palaces for this reason?' Hairat slapped her cheeks and shouted, 'May I grind anyone to dust who dares to mention my nose! May Samri destroy him! Sahib you are already so enamoured of that harlot that you talk of cutting off my nose! I will slaughter her in a place where my serving woman washes her hands!' She addressed the durbar and said, 'Look at this man! He has not seen her face yet and he threatens to cut off my nose. Once she is in bed with him, he will cut off the noses of everyone around him! I would rather wash corpses on Tuesdays and Sundays than stay married to him! No sahib, we cannot continue this way!'

Afrasiyab shouted back at her, 'Shut your mouth or I will whip your hide off! What do you think I am that you let your tongue run away with you this way? I swear I will send for my executioner and cut your head off right now!' Hairat jumped off her throne, beat her breasts and wailed loudly, 'I will set fire to this empire and dismiss this marriage to hell!' Afrasiyab raised his hand to hit her but her handmaidens and ladies in waiting rushed forward to ward off his blow. His counsellors murmured, 'Mian, she has been with you through all your trials. How can you even think of raising your hand on a woman?'

The women tried to mollify Hairat and said, 'Bibi, one should not argue with men. Everyone knows that no one can take your place. Women like her will come and go. Bibi, there is no point in taking offence. He is after all a man who will keep replacing his shoes. At least he happens to be badshah. Nowadays, even poor men seem to be bursting out of their loincloths and their poor wives suffer quietly. Let it go!' Some women fell at Shahanshah's feet and cried, 'Huzoor, please say no more to Malika, she has a sensitive heart!' Afrasiyab then sat down on his throne, still trembling with anger, while Hairat's attendants took her to a garden not far from the camp. They tried to console her as well as they could, but she remained distraught.

Meanwhile Afrasiyab's powerful ministers and nobles went to receive Zulmat on flying thrones. They met her on the way and bowed their heads as they offered nazar to her. In turn, she bestowed robes of honour on them. When they escorted her to the camp in a grand procession, Afrasiyab emerged from the durbar and lifted her from the hawadar in his arms. His army presented arms to her lashkar and they were assigned an open space to the north of the camp. Now there were three armies in the area.

Afrasiyab became almost dizzy at the sight of Zulmat's beauty and assigned Hairat's royal pavilions for her residence. While the King of Magic and Zulmat enjoyed intimacies that night, lip to lip and bosom to bosom, Hairat was overcome by fainting fits in the Garden of Pleasure. One of her handmaidens said, 'Bibi, a man's love is always fickle and not to be relied on. If he has discarded a parizad like you, how long do you think he will remain with this new hussy? It is just a game he will play for a few days!' Another woman piped up, 'You are so right! She will dominate the durbar for a few days and then see what happens! He will probably not even talk to her!' A third woman added, 'Sister, mark my words! This lowborn who has been enthroned now will not be able to even sell berries to anyone in a few days' time!' An elderly housekeeper told Hairat, 'Bibi, a mian-ji who lives near my house is known for his black magic. If Malika of the World orders me, I can bring an amulet from him!' The Malika's old teacher too gave her own opinion, 'To get rid of that hussy, Malika should call out her name and throw neem leaves and salt in an old well for seven Thursdays!'

Thus, the women continued babbling while Hairat shed tears. In her agitation, it suddenly occurred to her that she should secretly send for her sister Bahar and with her help, show Zulmat the path to hell. Having made up her mind, Hairat turned on her companions and cried, 'Your useless chatter makes my head ache, leave me alone now! I feel restless in a crowd. My heart is beset with fears!' Her woman attendants sheepishly filed out of the pavilion.

The secret rendezvous between Hairat and Bahar

After making certain that she was alone, Hairat sat near a candle, shedding tears as that candle shed wax, and wrote a note to Bahar. 'My dear little sister,' the note read, 'come to me so that I can see you one last time. Who knows whether I will live or die!' After this, Hairat took out a tiny golden statuette from her hair. The statuette rolled on the floor and transformed into a life-sized parizad. Hairat handed her the note and said, 'Give this to my sister Bahar, wherever she is.' Bahar had just returned from the durbar to her own pavilion when the parizad found her and greeted her politely. Bahar read the note and after the parizad informed her about the exact location of Hairat's garden, she said to the parizad, 'Tell my sister I will be there soon.' The parizad returned with this message to Hairat who reduced her to her former size and tucked her back in her hair. Meanwhile, Bahar adorned herself with fresh clothes and jewellery. She conjured a throne and sat on it with an ayyar and some of her handmaidens before calling out, 'This throne should take us to Hairat's place!'

The throne vanished and the next moment, they were in Hairat's garden. Hairat was anxiously waiting for her sister in her baradari. She rose and flung out her arms saying, 'Dearest, the sight of you cools my eyes, my heart was distraught without you!' As Bahar lowered her head, Hairat hugged her tightly, made a sign of blessing and wept softly. Bahar asked her, 'Baji, what has happened?' Hairat sighed deeply and said, 'My daughter, it was written in my fate that your brother-in-law would replace me with a courtesan. He has thrown me out like someone would flick a fly out of milk.' Hairat sobbed softly as she related the story of Zulmat's arrival and enthronement.

Bahar looked thoughtful and then said, 'Baji, I am much younger than you, and you should not think that I am taking advantage of your vulnerability. Take my advice and come with me to Amar's camp. I will ensure that you will be Malika there. My brother-in-law will realize that he has to pay a price for hurting you and indulging himself with other women!' Hairat was silent for a while and then replied, 'My daughter, although you are absolutely right, I am loyal to this man because I do not want to dishonour my parents.' Then recalling something with a start, she continued, 'Oh yes, I was told that this wretched Zulmat has captured Khwaja sahib and Barq Firangi on the way here!' As she said this, Zargham ayyar, who had accompanied Bahar disguised as a handmaiden, stepped forward to say, 'Huzoor, if you tell me where they are imprisoned, I will rescue them.' When Hairat asked, 'Who are you?', he replied, 'I am Zargham ayyar.' Hairat was startled by this and was all admiration for the perfection of his disguise.

She readily volunteered, 'There is a tent besides Zulmat's pavilion that belongs to a sahir called Mateen Jadoo. The ayyars are in a cage that hangs in his tent. Several hundred men guard that tent and Mateen stands guard inside. He cannot be killed by anyone for the magic amulet of Jamshed protects him. It is imperative for anyone mounting a rescue to get hold of that amulet because the cage will not open unless the amulet touches it. The amulet will also ensure that people leaving the tent will become invisible.'

Zargham rescues Amar and Barq

Zargham was determined to leave for the tent right away, but Hairat urged him to wait until he had reached his own camp. A little later, Bahar took leave of her sister and promised her that Zulmat would be disposed of very soon. Bahar left with her entourage, though Zargham stayed behind. He slipped out of the garden and followed Hairat's directions to find Mateen's tent in Zulmat's war camp. When Mateen's guards stopped him at the entrance to the tent, Zargham, who was still disguised as a beautiful handmaiden, archly said, 'Do you all want to lose your jobs that you stop me? Here, read this!' Zargham then produced a paper with the seal of the King of Magic stamped on it. It read, 'O Mateen, we are well pleased with your efficiency. You could not attend the celebrations of our marriage to your mistress; therefore, we have sent you something to remind you of it.'

The guards fell silent as they read the letter and Zargham sauntered past them into Mateen's tent. He saw that the tent was richly furnished and glowed in soft candlelight. The floor was covered with soft carpets and Mateen lay dozing on a gem-inlaid bed. The cage with the two ayyars was hanging just above him. Zargham lightly put his hand on the sahir's chest and Mateen woke up with a start. He rubbed his eyes and saw a vision of sun-like beauty standing above him, a vision that must have sent many to the sleeping chamber of the grave. In short, he saw a bold and seductive damsel bending over his bed.

Mateen got up smiling and held the flower-faced maiden's hand. She suddenly pulled away, hit her forehead dramatically and cried, 'O Samri, why is it that wherever I go men like to take advantage of me? They are so shameless that they only think of their own lust! Mian, did you have bad dreams? Do you want to lose your life? I would rather sacrifice a job like this that leads to my dishonour! I told Malika Zulmat not to send me alone to a strange lout! It is as I feared; you think I am an easy woman!' Mateen was even more charmed by what he thought were an innocent maiden's protestations. They were alone in the tent and overcome by lust, he cried, 'My dearest, do not be angry with me, my heart is not in my power right now!' That flower-face smiled at him and said, 'You can save such declarations and see the royal gifts first! I realize that you have loved me for some time. May you live long and remain safe!' The false maiden sat besides Mateen on the bed, took out a golden *khasdan* from her waist band and gave it to him. He opened it and found betel leaf giloris arranged on a bed of precious gems. The maiden gave him a letter that said, 'Mateen, this is a token of our appreciation for your services. Since we never send only one gift we have also sent you the betel leaves.' Mateen was very pleased to receive such benevolence from his mistress and turned to the maiden, 'O destroyer of my life, put this betel leaf in my mouth with your own hand!' The maiden dressed in wine-coloured garments teased him by showing him her thumb. She then picked up a giloris and cried, 'Mian, you are a very demanding. What other indulgences do you have in mind? You have virtually trapped me here! Well alright, open your mouth, I hope it chokes you!'

Mateen eagerly opened his mouth and chomped on the betel leaf. He tried to get intimate with the pretty maiden, but the drugged betel leaf overpowered him and he fell unconscious. Zargham first thought of killing him, but then reflected that such an act would alert the guards. He frisked the sahir to find the magic amulet and found it secured to his chest. He knew its powers and rubbed it against the cage.

The bars of the cage fell apart like twigs, freeing Barq and Khwaja. They left Mateen unconscious and walked right out of the tent. As they had the magic amulet, the guards did not stop them for it was as if they could not see them at all. They returned to their camp and met the sardars and Bahar told Amar about her meeting with Malika Hairat. Khwaja declared, 'You should rest assured, we will kill Zulmat very soon!' That night, Afrasiyab remained with Zulmat and imbibed the wine of intimacy. As they lay with each other later, Afrasiyab noticed that Zulmat looked worried. When he asked what troubled her, that exquisite creature opened her flower-like mouth and said, 'I fear the ayyars. I hope the amulet of Jamshed is secure and Amar does not escape!' She got up from the bed and sent for one of her officers. When he came, she ordered him to present Mateen before her. The officer reached Mateen's tent just as he woke up from his drugged stupor and was rubbing his eyes.

The officer conveyed Zulmat's orders and Mateen promptly rushed to her pavilion without looking up at the cage. When she asked him to produce the magic amulet, Mateen rummaged in his clothes and when he could not find it, thought that it had dropped on his bed. He told Zulmat, 'Huzoor I will just bring it to you!' He rushed back to his tent and naturally, did not find it. It was then that he looked up and saw the broken cage. He returned to Zulmat wailing and beating his head and related the incident of the beautiful maiden with the casket of betel leaves. Zulmat slapped her cheeks in alarm and cried, 'Shahanshah, a terrible thing has happened! That deceitful rascal Amar has escaped!'

The confrontation with Zulmat

Zulmat then chanted an incantation to summon a magic bird that flew into the pavilion and perched on her knee. Zulmat said, 'O lowly bird, tell me, which ayyar rescued Amar last night!' The bird trilled its melodious reply and told her about how Zargham deceived Mateen disguised as a handmaiden. Zulmat looked very angry and asked, 'Where is he now?' The bird told her that he was wandering in the wilderness at this moment. Zulmat made the bird fly off, sprouted wings herself and flew out to look for Zargham. At that time, Zargham was on his way back to Hairat's garden with Bahar following him at a distance. Zulmat spotted him in the forest and rendered him lifeless with a spell. She descended and had drawn out her dagger to kill him when Bahar arrived and called out, 'Wait you evil sahira! You are the one who has travelled in stages to become a rival of my sister!'

Bahar drew a magic bouquet from her pouch and flung it in Zargham's direction. The bouquet opened and a peacock materialized from its petals. The peacock fell on Zargham, extended its claw to hold him around his waist, soared into the sky and disappeared from sight. Zulmat was enraged at losing her prey and lashed out like a wounded lioness. She hurled a magic coconut at Bahar who deflected it and flung one back at Zulmat.

Mahrukh's well-wishers in that area informed her that Bahar was fighting Zulmat by herself. Mahrukh acted quickly. A blast of battle trumpets alerted Mahrukh's army and her troops rushed to prepare for combat. Mahrukh left a few sardars and sentinels to guard the camp and its livestock and left with a throng of her sardars. Zulmat saw them coming and moved forward ominously, tossing a coconut in one hand as she impatiently brushed a loose strand of hair off her forehead.

Mahrukh also moved forward and both sahiras engaged in a spectacular magical confrontation. Mahrukh conjured a sheet of flames on that spitfire, who, in turn, doused it with a heavy rain shower. Mahrukh then conjured a bolt of lightning on Zulmat, who deflected it and produced heavy stones that fell on Mahrukh's army. By this time, Zulmat's commanders had mobilized her army and were marching towards the arena. Mahrukh cast a spell so that the same stones fell on Zulmat's troops. Zulmat muttered some words so that Mahrukh's soldiers began decapitating themselves. Mahrukh managed to overturn this spell soon enough and cast a spell that caused the enemy lashkar to lose their minds. Zulmat retaliated with an incantation that made her hair emanate inky blackness that radiated on the rebel army. Mahrukh tried to dispel the darkness, but within moments, it had enveloped her army entirely. Zulmat then called out to her army, 'Attack these betrayers of salt! Do not spare them!' Her commanders rushed forward with teghas drawn crying, 'Get them! Get them!' Mahrukh's army, blinded as they were, bravely moved forward with teghas and daggers to defend themselves.

Kaukab's beloved mistress Princess Henna

Let us leave the rebel lashkar here and hear what happened elsewhere. In Tilism Nur Afshan, Kaukab the Wise, had kept himself informed of Khwaja Amar's adventures in the kingdom of Khurshidia. He heard of his capture by Zulmat and his rescue by Zargham. He had just learned of the confrontation between Zulmat and the rebels, and felt deeply disturbed by this turn of events. He flew to the home of his beloved mistress, Princess Henna, who greeted him affectionately and led him into her garden. His loyal beloved noticed that the Shahanshah's normally radiant countenance looked clouded and asked him what was wrong. Kaukab then shared his concerns with her.

Henna looked thoughtful and then said, 'Zulmat is a powerful sahira for she was trained by the terrible Tareek. However, with your permission, your handmaiden can confront her and kill her with your royal blessings.' Kaukab sat up and said, 'O eternal spring of the garden of colours, how will you destroy a thorn that is determined to ruin the garden?' The flower-faced Henna replied, 'I had gone on a visit to Hoshruba before the great mutiny when you and Afrasiyab were friends. On that visit, I also went to Tareek's abode in the Veil of Darkness. Tareek took me to the Dome of Samri, where she was given a number of gifts, and where I too received one coconut. It was revealed to me that apart from the Shahs of Tilisms, no sahir, however powerful, can survive the onslaught of this coconut. I have been saving it for a confrontation with a powerful sahir.'

When Shahanshah heard this, his face cleared and he agreed to the proposition of the love of his life. He said, 'If Shah of Tilism confronts you, your devoted lover will come to your aid. Leave now and I entrust you to the care of the True Creator!' The envy of the garden, the gentle Henna, then summoned her companions and handmaidens and ordered them to mobilize the army. Soon, the army arranged itself in orderly rows, and armed itself for battle. Kaukab saw that red, yellow and white clouds floated above the army, loaded with gold and silver kettledrums. Occasionally, magic slave-boys emerged from the clouds and struck the drums. This phenomenon was followed by dark monsoon clouds loaded with tents and pavilions. The clouds drizzled lightly to settle the dust raised by the vast lashkar.

Thus, in such pomp and splendour, Kaukab's beloved crossed all the stages of travel with greet speed to confront Zulmat. Mahrukh was on the retreat, completely overwhelmed by Zulmat's devastating magical onslaughts when the sound of kettledrums and trumpets filled the air. Princess Henna's army arrived and settled in battle formation. The princess signalled Mahrukh to draw back and came forward herself to fight Zulmat. It was a wondrous sight as the mistresses of the two monarchs hovered in the air, facing each other. It was as if two radiant moons were moving in the firmament of beauty, as if two lustrous royal pearls were gleaming with the patina of hostility. Zulmat swayed as she moved forward, loosened her glossy black tresses and shook them slightly. An inky blackness emanated from them and moved like fragrant zephyr over Henna's army. Her soldiers lost their senses and started reciting verses in praise of Zulmat's beauty.

Henna saw that the fragrant darkness had a lethal effect on her army. So she read an incantation and knocked against invisible glass in the air. A throne materialized before her from which sprouted henna plants. Henna plucked some leaves off the plants and rubbed them in her fair palms. There was a flurry of fresh cool breezes, and monsoon clouds rolled in from the horizon to drizzle softly. Zulmat's soldiers were utterly enchanted and tore their clothes as they recited verses in praise of the weather and Henna's radiant beauty.

Zulmat reacted by exploding a coconut that made darkness spread over the battlefield, and the enchanted scenery was hidden from sight. Her soldiers suddenly came to their senses. Princess Henna then laughed and expelled a bolt of lightening from her rosebud mouth. Zulmat's magic darkness turned into ominous monsoon clouds and burst on her forces. In turn, Zulmat conjured a false sun that made the dark clouds burst into flames over Henna's magical garden. She then attacked Henna with a magic sword. Henna foiled the attempt by conjuring a claw that stopped the sword in mid-air. Zulmat burnt the claw and tried again, but this time Henna conjured several shields to protect herself. At that time Henna called out, 'Be warned, you harridan!' She produced the magic coconut from Samri's dome and spun it towards Zulmat. The sahira read several spells to stop the coconut, but it smashed right through her forehead and her brains spilled out. Her body went spinning down to earth and she died in great agony.

There was uproar in the battlefield and fearful howls pronounced her death, 'A thousand pities that the spring of Zulmat's life was destroyed by the autumn of death! Alas, that beautiful flower withered just as it bloomed! Alas! Alas!' Eventually, her guardian spirits carried her body off to the King of Magic and the darkness dispelled. Zulmat's soldiers were heartbroken by her death and furiously attacked the rebels. Mahrukh, Bahar and Henna retaliated in equal measure. Slabs of ice and sheets of flames fell on Zulmat's soldiers, magic lightning destroyed the trees of their lives, the breeze of destruction swept through the battlefield, and young men were trampled in the dust. The soldiers stood their ground and fought valiantly, but could not succeed. Eventually, each one of them was killed.

After the air had cleared, Mahrukh and Bahar met Henna and asked her to convey their gratitude to Kaukab. They entreated her to rest for a while in the camp, but the wise Henna told them, 'The King of Magic is bound to vent his fury on us after he hears of his beloved's death. Kaukab will then have to confront him. There is no advantage in prolonging this battle. It is best for me to return to Nur Afshan right now as Shah Kaukab is waiting for me.' The sardars agreed with her reasoning and waited until she left before returning to their camp.

Afrasiyab and Hairat reconcile

Afrasiyab was heartbroken ever since he learnt of his beloved's fate and was too grieved to even think of revenge. He had pursued Zulmat for years and was blissfully happy for those few short hours in her company. He complained to his courtiers, 'We have been through such a traumatic event, but Malika Hairat has not even pretended to condole with us. Do kings not keep mistresses? Do their wives become so envious that they treat their providers like an enemy?' His viziers murmured, 'She is indeed not wise, but huzoor should forgive her!' They agreed with Shahanshah publicly, but secretly sent Hairat a message, 'Malika, it is imperative for you to dispatch a letter of condolence to the king and make your peace.'

Hairat was jubilant over Zulmat's death, but took heed of the sensible advice of the king's companions. She immediately wrote a conciliatory letter to her husband that read: 'Badshah, I am truly grieved to hear about the sad and untimely death of your beloved. By Samri, I did not resent her arrival, but it so happened that I got into an argument with you in the durbar. I deeply regret my inappropriate conduct and pray that you recover from this grievous event. I pray that your friends remain happy, your enemies are destroyed, your servants stay in good cheer and that your fortune is exalted!'

Hairat's vizierzadi Zamurrad went to Afrasiyab with the letter. She offered nazar and went around his throne with her hands folded. Finally, she offered the letter saying, 'Malika has filled vessels with her tears and keeps praying that Samri should console you for your heartbreaking loss. She urged me to tell you that she can sacrifice her life for you any time! Huzoor, please come to her and appease her.' Afrasiyab smiled sadly and said, 'She is the queen of my heart and of my kingdom. Who else will console me in my grief?' Afrasiyab then accompanied Zamurrad to Hairat's garden where handmaidens greeted him. Her companions made the gesture of sacrificing themselves to him and Hairat wept when she saw him. The Shah gently wiped her tears with his own hands. Thus, they reconciled and their hearts were one again. The evening of pleasure commenced and they imbibed goblets of wine. When finally they were alone, they tasted the wine of intimacy.

Later, the King of Magic brought Hairat back to the durbar seated on his own throne. He also placed the crown of state on her head. Nobles in the durbar came forward to pay homage to her and the pavilion resounded with shouts of jubilation as they congratulated Hairat. Heralds announced that Malika Hairat was the ruler of Tilism once again, and a wave of happiness flowed in the realm.

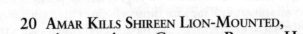

20   AMAR KILLS SHIREEN LION-MOUNTED, BAGHBAN ARRESTS AMAR, GULCHEEN RELEASES HIM, AFRASIYAB'S WRATH, BURRAN ATTEMPTS TO RESCUE AMAR

After Afrasiyab sent the noble Prince Jahangir and his army to Tilism Nur Afshan, he sought refuge with his wise minister Sannat Magic-maker. The King of Sahirs was still disconsolate after losing his mistress Zulmat, and wept as he spoke about his loss to Sannat. She made a gesture to take his troubles upon herself and said, 'May I die for you, there are a thousand beautiful women in Tilism. If you give the word, I will perform any service for you! Your enemies should suffer instead of you breaking your heart like this!' Sannat finally persuaded the badshah to rise from the bed of his grief. She ordered a nautch performance and signalled to the cupbearer to serve him goblets of richly-coloured wine. Thus, Sannat managed to distract Afrasiyab with this gathering of pleasure.

Now hear about Shireen Lion-mounted, the ruler of a fort with an army of twelve thousand sahirs. Shireen had been preparing his army for the battle with the rebels. Sahir soldiers mounted magic dragons and birds, and drums vibrated while cymbals clashed. Shireen tossed his pouch of magic on his shoulder and though he had no special magical powers, he did possess three powerful gifts—a *kashkol*, a brazier and a stone tablet. If the kashkol was filled with dust and scattered in the air, enemy forces would become careless and forgetful. The stove was capable of emanating smoke that could blind the enemy, and the magic tablet could reveal the name of anyone approaching its owner, no matter in which disguise.

Shireen had these powerful items taken out of his treasury and placed them in his pouch. He mounted his dragon amidst fierce magical gales and dust spirals. He and his twelve thousand sahir soldiers flew in the air as their guardian spirits raised a deafening clamour. Thus did this foolish owl of the desert of sorcery and the idiot of the wilderness of cruelty cross the River of Flowing Blood to approach the camp of the heartless Hairat. She was in the durbar pavilion when she heard of the arrival of this arrogant one. She sent her officers to receive him and Shireen came to the durbar to pay homage to Hairat.

At that time, a magic slave-boy sent by Sannat brought a letter for Hairat that read, 'Malika, Shahanshah is resting in a pavilion on the shores of the river near the mountain of wonders. He is still grieving for his dead mistress. You must go there and lighten his grief with the glow of your cheeks and render happiness to his royal self!' Hairat read the message and thought, 'Shahanshah's grief for his beloved is still fresh. I should not be envious for the heart has its reasons. It will take a while for him to forget her. I should be of some comfort to him in this hour of his sadness.'

She turned to Shireen and said, 'I am going to meet Shahanshah. You must carry out his orders here.' Shireen said, 'Huzoor, you should leave without a care. I will attack the rebel lashkar and with Samri's help, I will capture all betrayers of salt!' The queen felt reassured and retired to her pavilion. She bathed and made a special effort to adorn herself with rich robes and jewellery, and enhanced her beauty with cosmetics. She selected a few handmaidens to escort her and went to the King of Sahirs. She sat close to him and used her seductive wiles to comfort his grieving heart.

After Hairat had left her camp, Shireen went to his tent to rest. Later, he collected his magical tools, mounted his fire-breathing lion and left for the rebel camp on his own. Mahrukh Magic-eye and Bahar had returned to their camp after bidding farewell to Henna and the army was at ease after a hard battle. Shah Kaukab had sent a claw to bring Amar back and he was now with Burran in her palace. Mahrukh had convened her durbar and Qiran, who had made one of his rare appearances in the durbar, was sitting next to Barq on a chair. Zargham was away checking security arrangements in the camp while Jansoz had gone to spy in the enemy camp. When Shireen left for the rebel camp, Jansoz sprinted back to inform Mahrukh of this new development.

She was alarmed by this unconventional visit from the enemy. As soon as she learned that the sahir had entered her camp, she sent a few of her commanders to receive him. Shireen did not acknowledge their greetings or speak to them. He rode through the camp amazed at its size and splendour and shook his head as if thinking, 'These rebels have the effrontery to challenge Shahanshah with such a mighty force and trappings of power! There is nothing that is wanting in this camp.' Thus, burning in the flames of hostility and envy, this being of fire reached the royal pavilion. Again, Shireen was completely overawed by the magnificence and grandeur of Mahrukh's durbar. He was so intimidated by her exalted presence that he performed a mujra greeting deferentially. Mahrukh graciously acknowledged his greeting with a nod. She waved her hand to an empty chair and signalled a cupbearer to serve him a goblet of wine.

Shireen suddenly realized that he was there as an enemy and not a supplicant. He addressed the durbar aggressively, 'O rebellious, arrogant ones, I have been sent as the messenger of your destruction by Shahanshah. It is intolerable that you dare to challenge Shahanshah in his own Tilism. Now tie your hands with your handkerchiefs and come with me so that I can have you forgiven!' Mahrukh and the others remained silent, but Barq rose from his chair. While Shireen was still threatening the sardars, he lassoed him from behind so that he fell off his chair. Suddenly, a lion sprang from the earth and roared at Barq. The terrified ayyar dropped his snare-rope and ran out of the durbar. The lion, however, caught Shireen in his mouth and vanished into the earth. He disgorged Shireen deep inside the earth. There, Shireen cut the coils of Barq's snare-rope and decided to walk under the earth all the way to his camp. He emerged from the ground and ordered his army to gear up for battle. As the army prepared itself to the sound of battle drums and trumpets, Mahrukh's spies rushed back to convey the news that the enemy was approaching. Battle drums and bugles alerted her army as well and the brave ones prepared to fight.

Shireen mounted his lion and looked quite fearsome for he had smeared ash on his face, coiled live snakes around his head and worn a garland of skulls and the magic stone tablet around his neck. His magic brazier was smoking and he held the kashkol in his hands. His army stood in battle formation behind him. Shireen was seething with rage as he approached the battleground and called out, 'Whosoever kills first is the victor!' He tilted the stove and its ashes blew down and mingled in the dust. A fierce gale swept in from the forest and whipped up the dust in the battlefield. Within moments, the whole world seemed to have become invisible in the dust. The mirror of the sun was dark and the stream of sunlight clouded over it. It seemed the sky itself were raining dust. The dust enchanted Mahrukh's forces and they were unable to distinguish between friend and foe. Their hearts were overcome with humility and they forgot that they were in battle. They jumped off their horses and bird mounts, and folded their hands as they praised the King of Magic. At his orders, Shireen's army surrounded them.

Shireen had Mahrukh, Bahar and other prominent sardars shackled and told his army to continue surrounding the Islamic army. 'I will take the rebel sardars to Shahanshah. When you receive my orders, you can kill the rest of them.' Mahrukh's soldiers tried to follow him, but Shireen ordered them to remain there and in their enchanted state, they were obedient to his every command. Shireen left with his prisoners for the River of Flowing Blood.

Amar and Shireen

Amar was with Princess Burran Sword-woman in Tilism Nur Afshan. In the middle of the gathering of pleasure that the princess had arranged in his honour, he said, 'Princess, Afrasiyab has just lost his beloved. He is bound to take revenge on my army. Have you got any news about them?' The princess immediately sent two magic slave-boys to Hoshruba through the shortest route. They returned very soon and reported the army's capture by Shireen.

Both Khwaja and Burran were alarmed by this and Burran declared that she would rescue them. Amar held her back saying, 'It is not appropriate for you to confront an ordinary sahir like Shireen. If Afrasiyab comes to his aid, he might capture you and I will not be able to face your father! Give me leave and I will dispose of that evil sahir as soon as I reach there!' Burran was reluctant and told Amar, 'He has some potent weapons of magic. You will not be able to overpower him.'

'Let me assess the situation for myself,' Amar suggested, 'and if I am in trouble, you can always come to my rescue.' Burran agreed to this arrangement and ordered the same slave-boys who had brought them the news, to escort him to wherever Shireen was at the time. The magic slave-boys transported Amar to a place that Shireen was just about to pass through with his prisoners. Amar told the slave-boys to hide behind a hill and inform the princess if he was in trouble.

Amar selected a grove of trees and took out a few vessels from Zambil. He filled them with water and suspended them on the trees. He laid a straw mat on the ground and piled dry logs around it. He disguised himself as a holy man with his hair coiled in a topknot and a large metal hoop in one ear. He smeared his naked body with dirt, tied a loincloth around his waist and sat on the mat. He set fire to the logs around him and pretended to chant holy words while counting a long string of prayer beads.

Very soon, Shireen appeared and saw the holy man in the grove from a distance. Shireen was suspicious of everyone he came across and looked down at his magic tablet. It warned him that the yogi was actually Amar in disguise. Shireen laughed and said, 'It seems these ayyars are destined to die at my hands!' He looked at Barq and cried, 'Do you know who that is? It's your father!' Barq barked back, 'He is your grandfather!' Shireen snorted angrily, 'Oye, this is Amar ayyar!' Barq wanted to shout out a warning to Amar, but Shireen threw a lentil grain at him and rendered him speechless. Amar realized that the sahir had seen through his disguise and sprinkled large quantities of the dust of unconsciousness on to the pyre before folding his hands in prayer. Shireen thought, 'This deceiving rascal wants me to think he is conducting pooja!' He moved forward to capture Amar. Barq frantically waved his hands to warn Amar who deliberately ignored him.

Shireen laughed as he approached the false yogi and thought, 'Let me have some fun at this rascal's expense before I capture him!' He mockingly cried, '*Saeen*-ji, my salaam to you!' Amar replied, 'O man of the world! Go your own way. This is a path of deceit. Ayyars disguise themselves as fakirs to kill people!' Shireen was startled by these words and thought that perhaps the yogi was not Amar after all. He glanced at the magic tablet that again confirmed Amar's identity and called out, 'You wily scoundrel, how will you escape from me now?' Amar snapped back, 'You will not live to capture me haramzadeh!' Enraged by the reply, Shireen tried to attack Amar, but as he had already inhaled the narcotic fumes and the sudden movement caused him to fall unconscious.

Amar stepped out of the ring of fire and tried to stab the sahir with his dagger, but it glanced off Shireen's body. Amar then took out an iron poker from Zambil, heated it on the flames and plunged it through the sahir's rectum. Allah save us, his intestines, heart, and liver were scorched and that being of fire died in great agony. His guardian spirits raised an outcry, slabs of stones and ice fell from the skies, and a voice called out, 'You have killed Shireen Lion-mounted!' Mahrukh, Bahar and the other sardars returned to their senses and declared furiously, 'We will now go and destroy his army!' Amar quickly rummaged in the sahir's magic pouch and found the kashkol, magic brazier and tablet, and deposited them in Zambil.

The vizier and his wife

As mentioned earlier, the King of Magic had ordered Vizier Baghban to capture Amar whenever he returned from Kaukab's Tilism, and the vizier had been keeping an eye on Amar's movements through his spy birds and puppets. He could not capture Amar during Zulmat's brief reign as everyone had been warned not to interfere in Zulmat's affairs. Baghban was sitting with his wife in her garden when a bird spy flew in and informed him that Amar had killed Shireen on the opposite bank of the River of Flowing Blood. The vizier jumped up to leave and his wife cried, 'Listen sahib, do not capture Amar as you will lose your life!' Baghban ignored the words of his faithful wife and left quickly. Gulcheen promptly followed him.

Baghban reached the spot near the grove of trees where Amar had killed Shireen and quickly muttered a spell that made Amar unconscious. The vizier threw a citron on Shireen's lifeless body and the corpse came to life as a creature with the body of a man and the head of a lion. This creature put an arm around Amar and flew off in the air. Barq, who had darted out of sight when he saw the vizier, ran back to the camp to inform Mahrukh of Amar's arrest.

Baghban went to Vizier Sannat's place, where Hairat had earlier gone to comfort the King of Magic. Sannat was seated on a golden chair near Afrasiyab and Hairat who looked resplendent on their throne and comely maidens attended to their every need. Baghban greeted Afrasiyab formally and invoked magic that caused Shireen's corpse with Amar in its clasp to fly into the pavilion. The corpse cried out, 'Badshah, I have been slain by Amar!' and collapsed lifeless on the floor. Now Afrasiyab was too delighted with Amar's capture to grieve Shireen's murder. He ordered a few officers to dispose of Shireen's body with due honours and then turned to Amar, who was still unconscious because of Baghban's spell.

Baghban released him from his spell and Amar opened his eyes to see the King of Magic towering above him. He quickly closed his eyes and cried, 'A curse on Shaitan! I must be having a nightmare for I am facing a cruel tyrant!' The King laughed at his effrontery and called out, 'Khwaja salamat, how are you doing?' Amar replied, 'I am in Allah's protection, but tell me huzoor, what kind of trouble are you facing at this time?' Afrasiyab laughed heartily at Amar's response and replied, 'You are right! I am the one who is in chains and facing my direst enemy!' Amar mumbled, 'The brave do not fear chains!' The King of Magic, however, ignored this and continued, 'Perhaps you are relying on that man of the desert, Kaukab, to rescue you. He will never confront me openly! That girl, Burran might be foolish enough to try to rescue you but Amar, this time I will not spare you!'

Amar replied calmly, 'God is my Protector! Shah Kaukab does not need to come here. He can take care of you from a distance. If you try and harm me, with God's will, you will either break a leg or an arm.' The King of Magic was incensed by these impertinent words and leaned on his sword to rise from the throne, but tripped on his robe and fell flat on his face. Amar smiled and said, 'Did I not tell you that you will break your leg?' When the Shah fell, everyone rushed towards him. Sannat helped him up and restored the crown on his head saying, 'May I die for you! Do not pay attention to this rascal's jibes. He has already lost his life. Any one of your servants will cut off his head right now!' Afrasiyab muttered, 'I got up just to frighten him!'

Meanwhile, Gulcheen had followed her husband to the durbar and was appalled that her husband had captured Amar, 'Those ayyars will not leave him alive now!' she thought as she greeted the royals and slipped into the chair next to Baghban.

Gulcheen rescues Amar

The King of Sahirs was about to give orders for Amar's execution when Sannat suggested, 'Huzoor, you have endowed me with estates in this area. I have built a house here that is a furnace from within. Let us throw that rascal in that house. He will die instantly!' The Shah was pleased with this idea and said, 'Very well, send him there. I would like him to suffer a hideous death!' Sannat ordered her men to take Amar there and told Afrasiyab, 'Huzoor, a meal has been laid out for you. Will you honour me by tasting a morsel or so?' Afrasiyab got up to accept her invitation and removed his spell on Amar for he thought that he would be dead in a short while.

Two magic claws then materialized to take Amar to the house of fire and he glared at Baghban as he left. Gulcheen was now truly alarmed and thought, 'If Amar escapes now, he will surely kill my husband; if Amar dies, Barq and Qiran will certainly kill him for capturing Amar! I should release Amar to save my husband. Let someone else capture him again!' As everyone in the durbar followed Afrasiyab, she slipped out and found the house of fire before the claws had reached there with Amar. She saw that its walls, pillars and rooms were all blazing with flames and it was truly a tower of fire.

Now Gulcheen was the wife of a vizier and a powerful sahira in her own right. She conjured a snowball and chanted a spell over it before hurling it at the house. That fire-pit of Nimrod suddenly transformed into the Garden of Abraham and became as cool as a tranquil heart from inside, although its outward appearance remained the same. Moments later, Amar, dragged forth by the magic claws, was thrown inside, and the claws immediately vanished for fear of being scorched. Amar saw the fires of hell all around him, but was astonished that the flames seemed to be staying away from him.

Suddenly, Gulcheen materialized before him with her hands folded. She greeted him respectfully and said, 'Khwaja sahib, this humble handmaiden is here to serve you. I do keep urging this wretched lout of my husband to desist from interfering with the ayyars, but he does not listen to me. He is so taken up with his high office and claims that he cannot betray his master's salt. Please have mercy on this handmaiden and do not kill my husband for the love of your God!' Amar replied, 'How long will you protect him? Do you not recall the saying, "How long will the goat's mother celebrate her child's life? One day she will see the butcher's knife on its throat!" If he continues to harass us, he will surely die.' Gulcheen pleaded, 'Forgive him this time, if he harasses you again, you know best what to do!' Finally, Khwaja declared, 'Very well, this time I forgive him. Now help me escape this furnace!'

Gulcheen threw a lentil grain on him so that the chain around his legs fell apart. She then read an incantation to open the door and Amar rushed out of the flaming doorway. Sannat had earlier assigned guardian spirits to protect the house, and they raised an outcry when the door was opened. Amar quickly became invisible in Galeem as the spirits swept through the air like flames looking for him. When they could not find him anywhere they wailed, 'Alas! Alas! The criminal has escaped!'

Afrasiyab had just returned to his throne after a meal when he heard the din of the spirits and looked at Sannat inquiringly. Sannat said, 'Huzoor, Amar is in the house of fire. These must be his screams as he burns to death!' Even as she spoke, guardian spirits flew into the durbar in the form of birds and cried, 'A criminal has escaped from the house of fire!'

Sannat rushed to the house of fire only to find Amar missing and thought furiously, 'I should have let Shah execute that rascal! He has escaped from my prison and Shah will hold me responsible. How did he escape at all? Someone must have helped him!' In her rage, she stamped on the earth that split open. A tiny female figure shot up from the fissure and cried, 'Princess, why are you losing your temper? A spy from its own house destroyed Lanka! Princess Gulcheen came to the house earlier. She threw a snowball to cool it down, and opened the door for Amar to escape!'

Gulcheen was still hiding in the house, waiting for the right moment to escape. She overheard the slave-girl and realizing that Sannat would arrest her any moment, she immediately flew out of the house. The guardian spirits of the house rushed after her and Sannat sent some officers to pursue her as well. After escaping from the house of fire, Khwaja said to himself, 'Amar, you should humiliate Afrasiyab and kill Sannat if you can!' Accordingly, he disguised himself as a manservant, entered the durbar pavilion and stood unobtrusively in a corner. At that time, hundreds of magic slave-boys were present in the durbar. Afrasiyab was concerned about Amar's escape and was looking about desperately, when suddenly he met Amar's eyes across the tent. His magic informed him that this was Amar.

The ayyar also realized that he had been recognized and tried to bolt out of the durbar. The King of Magic read an incantation so that one of the slave-boys seized the end of his robe. Amar quickly slashed the garment and tried to leap out of the pavilion. The Shah shouted, 'Catch him! He should not escape!' At his command, hundreds of slave-boys fell on Amar and rendered him lifeless.

Baghban in disgrace

The Shah said, 'Tie him up and bring him to me!' The slave-boys tied Amar's limbs and dragged him before the Shah. Just then, Sannat returned from the house of fire and declared, 'Huzoor, your vizier's wife Gulcheen has turned traitor! She helped Amar escape from the house of fire!' Afrasiyab said, 'No harm done! He has been recaptured and I will soon arrest that treacherous woman!'

Now hear this tale! Barq had returned to his lashkar and informed everyone about Amar's arrest. Mehtar Qiran happened to be in durbar at that time. He got the ayyars in a huddle and said to them, 'We need to find out where the King of Magic is and then set off to rescue Khwaja!' Qiran snooped around in Hairat's camp and discovered that the Shah was in Sannat's estate along the river.

Armed with this information, Qiran disguised himself as a sahir and hired a prostitute from Hairat's camp. He walked towards the wilderness with her and rendered her unconscious before painting her face to look like Gulcheen. He wrapped her in a sheet and took her to Afrasiyab's durbar just when the badshah was about to find Gulcheen with his magic. Qiran greeted the King of Magic formally and when Afrasiyab asked him, 'Who is in the sheet?', Qiran replied, 'Badshah, it is Gulcheen. Please bind her and release Amar from your magic so that I can decapitate him with one strike! This rascal has tormented me and plundered my house several times!' Afrasiyab readily removed his spell and ordered his officers to untie the false Gulcheen.

All eyes were on Gulcheen at that time. The false sahir quickly hoisted Amar on his shoulder and slowly backed into a corner before he slashed the pavilion with his sword and slipped out. He defiantly called out, 'I am Qiran ayyar!' before leaping out of sight. Afrasiyab heard him and cried, 'Get him!' Sahirs rushed to find Qiran, but he was nowhere to be found and Amar had become invisible in Galeem.

Meanwhile, the false Gulcheen woke up and cried, 'Have mercy on me, Shahanshah! A sahir bribed me with gold and reduced me to this state!' The Shahanshah had her face washed and saw that she was a dark-skinned woman, certainly not the fair Gulcheen. He released her and ordered one of his officers to escort her to Hairat's camp. After she left, Sannat said, 'Huzoor is not to worry! I will bring that deceiver to you right away!' Sannat then threw herself on the floor and lighted up like a candle. The candle emitted a spiral of smoke that rose into the air and out of the durbar. In the meantime, Afrasiyab signalled to the guards who marched up to Baghban Qudrat the divine gardener and surrounded his chair. Baghban did not say a word, but bowed his head and wept silently.

The flower of the garden of loyalty, the brave and beautiful Gulcheen, who was now a fugitive, swept like zephyr into a verdant plain. She saw that the plain was blooming with spring blossoms. This flower of the garden of honour fell on the grass like a dewdrop and magically transformed into a brightly coloured blossom. She selected a tree that was laden with flowers of all hues, floated up, and attached herself to one of the branches. The sahirs who were pursuing Gulcheen looked for her in the meadow but turned back after a futile search.

Amar is arrested again

The other fugitive on the run was that flower of the garden of ayyari, Khwaja Amar. Qiran suggested, 'Ustad, let us hide in yonder ravine. I can cook rice and lentils. Eat a little!' Khwaja declared, 'I only hunger after the lives of sahirs! Until I kill a powerful sahir, I will not feel hungry or thirsty!' Qiran went off alone to the ravine and Khwaja walked on, thinking of just which trickery he could employ next. He had taken off Galeem as he did not like being invisible for very long.

He had walked just a little distance when a column of black smoke suddenly enveloped him. Within moments, the smoke coiled around his neck and shoulders in a vice-like grip. Black misfortune overtook him and he realized that this was the dark moment of his arrest. As Amar lamented his fate, the chain of smoke blew him right into Afrasiyab's durbar. The black smoke transformed into Sannat again who declared, 'Huzoor, I had sworn to myself that I will execute this wretch as soon as he is captured. I just need your permission!' Afrasiyab exclaimed, 'Kill him right away!' Sannat duly summoned the executioner—a dark-skinned, brutal looking man dressed in a rough homespun loincloth, who was holding a huge sword in one hand and a dagger in the other. Shahanshah ordered, 'Take this criminal outside and execute him immediately!' The executioner dragged Amar out of the durbar. The Shahanshah also went outside to watch the execution. The executioner constructed a mound of sand for the execution, spread the reed-mat of poverty and misfortune on the mound, and made Khwaja sit on it. The mound was soon surrounded by thousands of sahirs wanting to witness Amar's execution.

Burran Sword-woman attempts a rescue

The reader will recall that Burran Sword-woman had sent two magic slave-boys to escort Amar to Tilism Hoshruba. Those slave-boys had remained hidden to report on Amar's progress. When Vizier Baghban arrested Amar, they went back to Burran and informed her of his capture. The princess shared the information with her cousin Huma and said, 'How will we show our face to anyone? Khwaja has been arrested and we should not sit idle. Huma, keep this to yourself; I am going alone to rescue Khwaja!' No sooner had she spoken, Burran vanished like the fragrance of flowers. After she had gone, Majlis Jadoo came in. She saw that Huma seemed very quiet, as if worried about something. She put her arms around Huma and said, 'My good mother, tell me truthfully, why are you so quiet? What is bothering you? Swear by my life and tell me now!'

Huma frowned and said, 'You are always indulging in foolish talk! Now you are after me! Why should I be worried about anything?' Majlis looked closely at her mother and asked, 'Very well, just tell me where Princess Burran is? If you do not tell me, I promise I will lose my life!' Huma gave in and whispered, 'My daughter, do not disclose this to anyone! Amar has been captured and she has gone to rescue him!' Majlis did not react and distracted her mother by changing the subject.

After some time, she left her and went on the roof where she declared, 'I have had too much wine and would like to rest!' She dismissed her handmaidens and scolded the ones who dared to stay behind. She slapped one and cried, 'You evil one, you pushed me on the stairs!' She looked at another and said, 'Why do you keep staring at me?' She turned to the third and said, 'You keep whispering against me to the others!' Thus, she accused everyone of something and was finally left alone. Majlis locked the door leading to the stairs and chanted a magical verse to summon a hawk that swooped down on to the roof. She hopped on its back and left to help Burran.

First, hear about Burran Sword-woman. She left for Hoshruba magically transformed into a full moon flashing amidst dark clouds. She brightened the mountains and forests as she travelled above them and finally appeared in the place where Khwaja was sitting under the shadow of the executioner's sword. Looking up at the sky, the Shahanshah remarked to his companions, 'Look at that beautiful formation of clouds!' Hairat remarked, 'The season of rains is upon us!' Soon the dark monsoon clouds extended over them, there were gusts of cool breeze and everyone seemed mesmerized by the sight. Sannat was a canny woman and sensed that the clouds augured trouble. She ordered the executioner, 'Cut this sinner's head right now!'

When the executioner moved forward, Amar looked heavenwards in despair. At that time, lightning flashed in the clouds and tapered into a full moon. That moon split into two halves and one half fell on the executioner while the other half descended on Amar and radiated a light that blinded everyone. That crescent worked like a sword on the executioner and sliced his body into two pieces. The half-moon over Amar extended a claw that whisked Amar up into the air.

As the light dimmed, the King of Magic saw that all his officers were unconscious, the executioner was lying dead and the magic moon was carrying off Amar. Afrasiyab recognized Burran's handiwork and thought, 'She is the daughter of the ruler of Tilism and will not be captured unless I use a powerful Tilismi weapon against her.' Accordingly, he reached for his pouch of magical tools and took out a tiny dome—a gift from the

Dome of Samri—whispered an incantation on it and flung it in the direction of the half moon. The dome went spinning into the air expanding as it gained height. When it reached the moon, one-half slipped under the moon, the other half covered it from above like a lid and snapped into place. The moon, or rather Princess Burran, was now trapped in an enormous magic dome.

Burran was undaunted by the fact that she was in hostile terrain and pitched against the King of Magic. She flew up with all her strength and burst out from the roof of the dome in the form of lightning. She wounded her skull with the impact and Amar fell out of her grasp back into the dome. Burran continued flying until dazed with pain, she fell in the wilderness. She had been so intent on her escape that she had forgotten about Amar.

The anguish and distress of that moon of loveliness were heart wrenching. The force of the impact had split her skull and her hair was reddened with blood as if filled with sindoor. Her forehead too was wet with blood. She wanted to return and smash the magic dome, but then reconsidered, 'You have been injured and will not be able to destroy that powerful magic in this state. You should also find some Tilismi gift equally potent to overcome it.'

Burran bravely resumed her flight with a heavy heart and came across Majlis, who had followed her on the magic hawk. Majlis asked after her noble self and Burran related what had happened. Finally, she said, 'My child, let us return now. We will prepare ourselves fully and try again.' Majlis returned with her and once they reached the Palace of Seven Hues, they tried to devise a fresh strategy to rescue Amar.

Meanwhile, the Shah of Tilism learned from his magic that Burran had escaped, but Amar was still within the dome. Since the roof of the dome was broken, Afrasiyab feared that the wily ayyar would escape from it. The King of Magic flew up to the roof of the dome and made a sign over it so that the gap repaired itself. Khwaja was in the dome, lying unconscious. He would wake up occasionally in the pitch black darkness and sink back into oblivion. It was just as well that he was unconscious for if he had woken in that dreadful darkness, he would have surely died of sheer terror.

The King of Sahirs then descended and breathed on the unconscious sahir officers to revive them. He looked at Sannat and declared arrogantly, 'Kaukab's chit of a daughter has escaped from the dome. She had come to snatch Amar from me but how could she confront me? I took pity and let her escape. As for this wretched ayyar, he will be imprisoned in the air, and will die of hunger and thirst in two days. Let me see who can rescue him from the Dome of Dread. This is an opportune moment—Kaukab will be worried about the Tilism Kusha whom I have sent to his realm and Amar has been captured. We should find a powerful sahir to execute the betrayers of salt. I am going to Neelum Koh. I will send the witch who is the ruler of the gateway to Mount Agate to destroy Hamza's lashkar. Sannat said to the king, 'O Shahanshah, this is indeed an excellent strategy!' Afrasiyab turned to Hairat and said, 'Malika, you should return to your war camp.'

When the king was about to leave, Sannat folded her hands and entreated, 'Huzoor, I am hopeful that you will forgive Vizier Baghban. He has committed no crime and has remained true to the salt!' Afrasiyab was in a generous mood and decided to release Baghban. He ordered him to return to his house, and astonished and relieved at this turn of events, Baghban went in search of his errant wife, but we will return to them later.

✐

21 CHALAK BIN AMAR ENTERS TILISM

The narrators of lively prose step into the Tilism of Paper in this manner. Afrasiyab sent a sahir to confront the rebel forces and flew on to Neelum Koh. The ruler Neelum Jadoo received him deferentially and arranged for Afrasiyab's every comfort on the mountaintop. Afrasiyab sent for the magic telescope as he had done earlier and focussed it on Mount Agate. He saw the formidable lashkar of the noble Emir Hamza spread out for miles in great splendour. The exalted state of that lashkar has been described many times already.

Afrasiyab turned the telescope around and focussed on the impure Laqa's lowly lashkar. He saw that it looked depressed and disheartened—its tents were torn and burnt, and its soldiers seemed discontented and unhappy. The pavilions were pillarless and tottered like feeble men, the bazaars were empty and lifeless, and the royal stables appeared worse than a donkey's lair. The camp was poverty-stricken and its inmates were being eaten by worries. Their lives seemed to weigh heavily on them. Afrasiyab was heartbroken at seeing Laqa's lashkar in this piteous state and sighed deeply as he said, 'Do you know what is on Khudawand's mind right now?'

Neelum replied, 'The news from Mount Agate reveals that Khudawand is extremely distressed. Many of his close companions have been killed and there are rumours that he might just ascend to the highest heaven in despair!' Afrasiyab gave the magic telescope back to the keeper who left with it. He whispered to Neelum, 'I am worried as to who I should send next to Khudawand's aid. The ayyars kill everyone who is sent there!' Neelum submitted, 'Huzoor, I suggest that you send Sheeshadar Jadoo for this purpose!' The Shah looked uncertain and said, 'I have reserved her services for something else!' Neelum persisted, 'Huzoor, you still have the inmates of the cells of doom! If you use one Tilismi gift, it is no loss to you!' Afrasiyab reflected on his words for a while and then got up. He declared purposefully, 'Very well, I will send her right away!' Neelum said, 'This humble slave will accompany you for the darkness on the way might disturb your exalted self!'

Neelum knocked in the air and two flame-emitting dragons writhed out of the earth. They had wooden saddles tied on them and flew off in the air after Afrasiyab and Neelum mounted them. They landed in a wilderness where the earth seemed to be on fire. The two kings dismounted and walked through the wasteland that was smouldering like the heart of a rejected lover, scorched by a burning breeze that could make the dejected suitor even more feverish. The blistering heat of the sun withered any surviving trees in that hell. Some of the trees were ablaze and their branches were crackling like fireworks. There were bushes that were as dry and arid as poverty and there were signs of streams that once flowed here and which had now evaporated in the heat.

The Shah and Neelum walked to the edge of the wasteland where they came upon a dark and fearful cave that was the abode of a family of cobras. The snakes hissed and released sparks that flashed in the darkness. It was as dark as ink in the cave, but hideous spectres appeared occasionally to vanish again. The King of Magic told Neelum to provide some light and Neelum breathed a spell on the cave so that it became a well of light. A magic sphere emerged in the sky and filled the wasteland with light. The cobras and the spectres vanished in its glare.

Afrasiyab then threw himself into the cave and catapulted down its length with Neelum falling close behind him. They landed in a verdant meadow blooming in magical springtime. The Shah and Neelum strolled through the meadow and reached the gateway of a garden. As the Shah stepped inside, a soft, cool breeze playfully swept through the garden and rain clouds materialized over it as if a parizad had cast her shadow over them. Neelum walked ahead and informed the ruler of the garden that the Shahanshah had arrived. Afrasiyab saw that a sun of beauty emerged from the baradari—her shiny long tresses as black as the deeds of sinners and her face as fair as the deeds of the righteous. From head to toe, she was a seductress worthy of a king's attention. She greeted the Shah and said, 'This abode is not worthy of your exalted self, but now that you have honoured it with your presence, pray come and rest in the baradari.'

The Shah walked to the baradari with that captivating maiden and saw that it was adorned with rich carpeting, soft masnad seating and gleaming glassware. He reclined on a masnad while that fair moon of beauty offered him a goblet of roseate wine. After drinking a couple of goblets, the Shah said, 'Princess, I want to send you in the service of Khudawand Laqa.' The maiden murmured that she would be honoured to do so. The Shah continued, 'Go to Mount Agate with water from the blessed stream of Samri. There you will find the lashkar of the Muslims and their leader Hamza, who has frustrated Khudawand. Destroy him and his lashkar but remain alert against the ayyars!'

That flower-face laughed and said, 'Badshah, you are well aware that when I travel, I give up food, water and wine; I can survive without sustenance for years. When I am hungry, I just have to think of food and I am instantly assuaged. The thought of water quenches my thirst and the thought of wine intoxicates me! I am invisible at night and can remain invisible at my will. How can any ayyar bother me then? I will not be there for long. With your generosity and Samri's blessings, I have received a precious gift of the magic waters. The moment I sprinkle it on the enemy forces, they will turn to stone. Even if someone breaks the jar, the waters will spill out and cause greater damage.' Afrasiyab warned her, 'Hamza can counteract magic. You will have to conduct yourself carefully or you will lose your life!' She retorted, 'We will see! Hamza may dispel magic, but I have a gift of Tilism that only a Tilism Kusha can destroy!'

Afrasiyab stayed a long time in the baradari, explaining the dangers and pitfalls of the expedition to that proud one, even as he consumed wine and watched beautiful statuettes dancing before him. Finally, he rose and said, 'Princess, after your victory, come to visit me in Tilism. I do not want to go through the discomfort of travelling here again. Or, you can go to Neelum Koh and send a message to me.' She assured him that with Samri's will that is what she would do. Their task accomplished, Afrasiyab and Neelum returned to Neelum Koh taking the same path they had travelled on earlier.

Sheeshadar in Mount Agate

The next morning, Princess Sheeshadar (for that was the name of the beautiful maiden of the cave) adorned herself with rich garments and jewellery studded with precious gems and pearls. She carefully placed the jar containing the magic waters in her pouch of magic and emerged from the dark cave. She travelled to Mount Agate on a flying throne alone, without even one handmaiden to attend to her. As Mount Agate was close to her garden, she reached Laqa's lashkar very soon.

That shameless one was presiding over his durbar when the flash of lightning startled him and he called out, 'O Shaitan of my holy abode, go and see what destiny I have decreed now!' Shaitan Bakhtiarak hastened to the entrance of the durbar just as the sahira was entering and greeted her formally. Sheeshadar entered the durbar and genuflected before Laqa, who called out solemnly, 'Raise your head so that I can shower you with my blessings!' Sheeshadar got up and sat on a chair next to Laqa. She stayed there for a while and then retired to a heavy golden pavilion that had been provided with every comfort and luxury for her. The news of her arrival spread through the lashkar and she had several callers who wanted to meet her. That day, she kept to her pavilion to recover from her journey. The next day, when the wizard of day brought forth the mirror of doom from the East, the sahira rose and presented herself in the durbar.

Sheeshadar prostrated before Laqa and said, 'Huzoor, come with me and a few of your companions to the summit of Mount Agate and witness the destruction of the forces of Islam!' Laqa, accompanied by a few of his counsellors and Shaitan Bakhtiarak, rode to the summit with her. Hamza's lashkar stretched out for twenty-four miles and extended to the base of Mount Agate. Thus, Laqa and his party had a bird's eye view of the camp. It was a beautiful morning—the sky was overcast with monsoon clouds and there were occasional light drizzles. Peacocks were shrieking in the forest and melodious birds seemed to be trilling with joy. In the Islamic camp, the awnings of the Pavilion of Solomon had been raised and the sardars were tempted to go out on an excursion. They addressed the noble Emir, 'Huzoor, the weather is so beautiful that we are all inclined to venture outdoors. Moreover, we have heard that a sahira has arrived in Laqa's durbar. She is determined to cause us harm and has taken Laqa the Misguided to the summit of the mountain. If you accompany us to the edge of the lashkar, we can enjoy the weather as well as keep an eye on her movements!' The Emir graciously assented to this plan. He left a few sardars to attend to the badshah and emerged from the durbar to ride with the others to the base of the mountain. We will return to them later.

The beloved son of Khwaja Amar, the best of the Mehtars, Mehtar Chalak bin Amar had obtained the noble Emir's permission to leave for Tilism Hoshruba. Abul Fateh took over Chalak's duties in the camp.

However, every morning, Chalak would bid his companions farewell to leave for Tilism, but could not find the most appropriate way. Eventually, he remembered that sahirs from Tilism frequently visited Laqa's durbar, and thought that he could use one of them to lead him to Tilism. On the way to Laqa's durbar, he saw Laqa and his sardars riding up the mountain with a fair sahira. Chalak followed them stealthily and hid in a ravine when they reached the summit. He heard the Shaitan crying out, 'Princess, have you brought Khudawand here to enjoy the view?' In response, Sheeshadar explained the properties of the magic water of Samri to them. Chalak overheard her and thought, 'It was just as well that I did not leave for Tilism. This wretched sahira will cause a lot of trouble and I should dispose of her now!' Chalak checked if all his tools were in his pouch of ayyari, and arranged his bow and arrows, catapult and hookahs in preparation for his attack on the sahira.

Meanwhile, Ambreen Kohi, the ruler of Mount Agate, heard that Laqa had ventured out with a few companions. He exclaimed, 'I cannot understand what fate Khudawand had in mind when he left without the army to protect him! If he were a mere mortal, one could question him, but how can the divine one be so careless?' Ambreen Kohi then ordered his troops to spread out at the base of the mountain to protect Laqa.

From the other side, the noble Emir and his sardars were also riding in the same direction. Bakhtiarak said to Sheeshadar, 'This is not good. Hamza comes with his sardars and their forces are behind them. He will not spare anyone of us!' Sheeshadar laughed and said, 'Malik-ji you are as afraid of Hamza as a goat is of a butcher or bird of its keeper! Do not be alarmed, I will erase them like the erroneous word!' Sheeshadar took out a glass container filled with the magic water of Samri and looked down. She did not realize that the army stationed at the base was there to protect Laqa because he had come with her alone. She tossed the water at the army confidently, believing it to be Hamza's army. As the powerful spray fell on the army, there was a gust of cool breeze and the horrifying spectacle of men turning to stone. There was stampede in the lashkar and soldiers rushed around crying, 'Have mercy on us!'

Bakhtiarak looked down and recognized the commanders of his army. He was aghast and cried, 'Well done Sheeshadar! Did you bring Khudawand here to see his men being turned to stone?' Sheeshadar was equally shocked and shouted, 'Who asked you to bring your own army here and why did you not identify them before? Now tell me quickly, where is Hamza and his army?' When the Shaitan pointed them out to her, she angrily held the jar aloft to fling the water in that direction. Just at that moment, Chalak shot a large stone from his catapult that hit the glass container and smashed it into smithereens. The rest of Laqa's unfortunate army stationed below the mountain suffered hideously as their bodies erupted in flames. Men of fire sparked as if they were fireworks while the earth below them also burst into flames. They shouted, 'O Khudawand, we are burning!' Eventually, all of them went straight to hell.

Emir Hamza and his companions witnessed this turn of events with great interest. The sardars laughed as Shaitan Bakhtiarak wailed, 'A thousand blessings on the Prophet of Allah and cursed be this Laqa! How blessed are the Muslims that the doom intended for them targets our own house! The arrows for their deaths shoot us in the heart! It seems that they cannot be killed!' Sheeshadar vanished out of sheer humiliation and when she reappeared, she did not look anyone in the eye. In her frustration, she looked around and spotted Chalak who had emerged from his hiding place to watch the carnage. The sahira fell on him in anger and flew up in the air with him. Shaitan called out to her, 'Princess, wait a moment! This buffoon Laqa is still alive! Kill him before you leave!'

Sheeshadar ignored him and flew straight on to Tilism thinking, 'How can I fight now? My Tilismi gift is no more! If I fight with my own powers, I will be here for years. I have not even brought my army. I should hand this ayyar over to Afrasiyab and tell him that he was right about the ayyars. They are a confounded nuisance! He is well aware of their antics. Perhaps he may award another magical gift to me.' With these thoughts churning in her mind, Sheeshadar flew with Chalak and did not pause until she reached the foothills of Neelum Koh. She intended to go to the summit, but was exhausted and humiliated. Her body was wet with perspiration, her face was covered in dust and her garments were travel-worn and crumpled. Her petal-like lips were bruised for she had bitten them in sheer rage. Her arm ached as she had carried the ayyar and most of all, she felt the call of nature.

Sheeshadar dropped the unconscious Chalak on the ground and drew a magic circle around him so he could not escape. She took out a mirror from her pouch and wiped her dusty face, combed out her hair and adjusted her clothes. She then moved out of Chalak's sight and sat down to relieve herself. Chalak regained consciousness and wanted to run away, but felt an invisible wall around him. He realized that although the sahira had drawn a magic circle around him, he could move his limbs. He then coiled his snare-rope around himself in such a manner that if anyone touched the sheet tied around him, the snare-rope would entrap that person. He then lay down, pretending to be still unconscious. After some time, Sheeshadar returned and first removed the magic circle around Chalak. She was just about to touch the sheet when the artfully arranged coils of the snare-rope snapped around her neck and waist. As she stumbled, Chalak burst a narcotic bubble in her face that made her sneeze and fall unconscious.

Chalak carefully disguised himself as Sheeshadar and wore her outer garments. He soaked a bandage in the tincture of unconsciousness, tied it around her forehead and nose and threw her in a well. As he was climbing up the mountain, Neelum Jadoo, who was in the area recognized the false Sheeshadar and flew downwards towards her, calling out, 'Welcome princess! How are you here? Have you finished our enemies?' Chalak replied blithely, 'I defeated them some time back! I did not spare even one of them and showed them the final path of doom!' Neelum gave a shout of delight and said, 'Princess, you have performed a great deed! We must share the news of your victory with the King of Magic and celebrate with him. Let us fly for we will reach sooner!'

Chalak panicked and thought, 'How am I supposed to fly?' He acted quickly and collapsed on the ground groaning with pain. 'Princess, what has happened?' Neelum asked with concern. 'I suffer from an occasional epileptic fit,' cried the false Sheeshadar, 'and I think it's upon me now!' Even as she spoke, her eyes rolled up, her teeth clenched on her tongue and she pretended to be unconscious. Neelum immediately conjured a flying throne to transport the sahira up the mountain. Neelum's magnificent palace on the peak of the mountain was adorned with every luxury and could restore an invalid to good health. Neelum carried this flower-body and laid her down on a bed. He summoned his handmaidens to attend to her and they clustered around her, fanning her head and massaging her feet.

Chalak lay back and enjoyed the attention, thanking providence for allowing him to reach Tilism. Neelum returned to his fort and sent for his resident scribe. He dictated a news report that read, 'The King of Magic and the nobles of Tilism are informed that Princess Sheeshadar has destroyed the Muslims of Mount Agate. Only Hamza has survived because of the Great Name and has fled the scene. The rest of his lashkar was killed.' Neelum sent this report to the badshah and circulated it among all the notables of Tilism. Afrasiyab read the report and smiled broadly. He shared the good news with the durbar and was pleased with the jubilant cries of his courtiers. Afrasiyab immediately sent for forty trays of gems and gold from the treasury and sent it to Laqa with the following message, 'Khudawand, you are all-powerful. First, you created powerful rebels and no one could destroy them, then you endowed us with such strength that one of our servants Sheeshadar killed those disobedient beings within moments. We cannot find the words to praise you. We send you a thousand felicitations on this great victory that destroyed the enemy and provided a moment of triumph for your humble mortals.'

Sohail and Qahir Kohi in Mount Agate

A distinguished sahir by the name of Sohail Jadoo was given the honour of conveying Afrasiyab's message to Laqa. Sohail mounted trays of gifts on magic peacocks and left with forty other noble sahirs for Mount Agate. He had crossed the mountain pass when he heard the distant sounds of a battle. As he drew closer, he saw that Laqa was sitting on an elephant, watching his troops fighting a losing battle against Hamza's forces. As he prostrated before Khudawand, Laqa looked at Shaitan Bakhtiarak and asked, 'So, who are these mortals that I have created?' Shaitan looked closely at Sohail and said, 'They look like sahirs and have probably been sent by the King of Sahirs.' The Shaitan then asked Sohail, 'Who are you?' Sohail confirmed that the King of Magic had indeed sent him to meet Laqa. Shaitan laughed bitterly and said, 'The King of Magic has sent many like you. The last one was Sheeshadar who destroyed our own troops. Let us wait to see what you do to us!' Sohail looked mystified and asked, 'Malik-ji, I am glad you have reminded me. The Muslims have been destroyed. Who do you fight now?' Malik-ji responded solemnly, 'This battle is with the greatest of warriors, the mighty Emir Hamza, lord of the conjunction, whose lowly escaped slave is this Khudawand of yours!' Sohail was shocked by the Shaitan's blasphemy and slapped his own cheeks as he cried, 'Malik-ji, what are you saying?' Shaitan continued, 'I am right! He cannot find a place to hide! In fact, a slave is a thousand times better than him!'

Laqa now intervened and placated the outraged Sohail by saying, 'O my mortal, do not pay any attention to him! He is the Shaitan of my durbar and it is his job to try to set people against me! Tell me what brings you to this place.' Sohail explained, 'The King of Magic heard that you had overcome the rebellious mortals and has sent you a message of felicitation and trays of precious offerings. My companions are waiting with the offerings at Fort Agate. Order your troops back and I promise I will arrest the Muslims within moments!' The Shaitan interposed, 'Please spare us! Khudawand is not dependent on your offerings that he should withdraw from battle. His loyal mortals are fighting valiantly at the moment.' Sohail replied, 'You should listen to me and do not complicate a simple task. The final decision is of course yours!' Now Shaitan Bakhtiarak's real intention had been to provoke the sahir into helping them. When Sohail persisted, he said, 'Khudawand, ask for the drums of peace to be struck. These armies cannot otherwise be separated!' At Laqa's nod, Shaitan ordered their commanders to strike the drums of peace.

Among Laqa's troops were the ferocious warriors of Kohistan who reluctantly drew back at the sound of the drums. The two lashkars that were fighting hand to fist now separated. Qahir Kohi had just lost a brother in battle and was itching to avenge his death. In his frustration, he confided in his friend Ansar Kohi, 'What is wrong with this Khudawand? If he is so afraid of a battle, why does he fight at all? If we had continued I would have killed Hamza and the war would have been over!' Ansar suggested reverently that Khudawand must have had his reasons, which he would reveal in time. Qahir Kohi was not convinced and complained bitterly as they withdrew from the battleground.

Bakhtiarak addressed Sohail, 'Our lashkar has pulled back, now let us see what you can achieve!' Sohail immediately flew up in the air. Emir Hamza was returning to his pavilion, now that the battle was over. The deceiver Sohail cast a spell on him from above so that he suddenly felt drowsy. He managed to utter, 'Carry me back!' before he slipped off his horse and fell unconscious. As everyone rushed to his side, a deafening sound caused a wave of fear in the lashkar, horses reared up in the air and galloped off with their riders, and several men fell off their saddles. The Shah's counsellors and high-ranking nobles surrounded the throne of Solomon, anxious to escort the Shah back to the safety of Solomon's pavilion, but the earth went dark and a veil of black evil descended on the lashkar. There was an uproar among the soldiers as they called out to the True Provider to have mercy on them.

Another loud sound reverberated in the air. It was so fearful that the Bull of the Earth would have wanted to give up its existence and flee; the sky would have shrunk in fear. The hearts of thousands of soldiers burst and they died while many others fell unconscious. The forces of evil and magic obscured the light of Islam and the lashkar lost its lustre. Sohail kept the Islamic lashkar captive under the shroud of darkness and went to Laqa's durbar with the trays of precious offering from the King of Magic. Laqa's disgruntled warrior Qahir Kohi had been involved in his brother's funeral and came to durbar a little later with his friend Ansar Kohi. He saw a sahir occupying the place of honour next to Laqa and was even more enraged.

He controlled his anger and sat next to the Shaitan, to whom he said, 'Malik-ji, we were their match in battle today! Why did you strike the

drums of peace? Our brother was killed and we were seeking vengeance—
we would have taken Hamza's life or died ourselves!' The Shaitan replied,
'Khudawand had overturned fate and sent for this sahir from Tilism to
achieve instant victory! It was not destined that you should win today!'
Qahir muttered, 'So what has been achieved now? Has he destroyed the
enemy completely?' Bakhtiarak snapped, 'As to that you should ask Sohail
himself.' Sohail's attention was also caught by this exchange and he looked
enquiringly at the Shaitan.

'Qahir Kohi asks,' said the Shaitan maliciously, 'what have you
achieved today?' Sohail looked derisively at the two Kohistanis and
declared, 'What I achieved today is quite obvious! These warriors had
been fighting all afternoon to no avail but I disposed the enemy with one
spell!' Qahir, who was already seething with resentment was furious at
the aspersion that they had fought in vain. He addressed his friend Ansar
Kohi sarcastically, 'You useless, good for nothing Kohis, I spit on your
standing and curse your existence! The only true warriors seem to be
these sahirs!' Sohail Jadoo laughed and said, 'Indeed there can be no doubt
about that! If it were not for us, you would not have seen this day!'

Qahir became even angrier and shouted, 'You talk nonsense sahir!
Only cowards resort to using spells in battles. Indeed these Muslims are
very brave and triumph over us because they use no deceit in their battle
strategies!' Sohail could not really follow Qahir's words as he was
speaking in his native Kohistani dialect. He looked at Bakhtiarak and
asked, 'What is he saying?' Bakhtiarak, who loved to provoke a fight,
added fuel to fire by declaring with a laugh, 'He is abusing you!'

Sohail rose from his chair and shouted at Qahir, 'You worthless duffer,
what are you saying?' Qahir shouted back, 'You are the biggest duffer,
your father is a duffer and your Afrasiyab, Jamshed and Laqa are all
duffers! How dare you take me on, you low caste?' Sohail put his hand
on his pouch of magic and Qahir thought he would have to do something
so that Sohail would be unable to cast a spell. He pretended to collapse,
clutching his side and groaning loudly. Sohail walked closer to see what
had happened to the Kohi. Qahir quickly grasped him by the ankles and
began spinning the warrior in the air.

Sohail forgot all his magic as Qahir spun him faster and faster. Laqa's
durbaris shouted at Qahir to stop from a distance, but were too afraid to
go near him. Sohail's men heard the din in the durbar and rushed in, but
by that time Qahir had spun the sahir one last time and smashed his
head against a wooden pillar in the durbar. Darkness descended on the
durbar and a voice boomed, 'You have killed Sohail Jadoo!' Soon, sheets
of flames and stones rained down on the durbar.

Sohail's death instantly removed the shroud of darkness over the Islamic army. Emir returned to consciousness and everyone was released from the magic spell. Emir did not believe in fighting at night and returned to his pavilion in joy with his sardars The lashkar celebrated its release and rested in peace. However, there was uproar in Laqa's camp following Sohail's death. Sohail's contingent of forty soldiers could hardly question what had happened in Khudawand's durbar and returned with the corpse of their slain leader to the King of Sahirs.

Uqab Jadoo rescues Sheeshadar

When Afrasiyab convened his durbar in the morning, he sent for the forty sahirs who had accompanied Sohail. The sahirs related the events in Mount Agate leading to their commander's death. Afrasiyab turned to his ministers and exclaimed, 'I just do not understand! Sheeshadar was supposed to have destroyed the enemy, but according to these men, Hamza's lashkar was fighting Khudawand's army. Why did a Kohi who is a Laqa worshipper kill my man? Whatever the reason, I will also tear him from limb to limb!' Afrasiyab sent for his scribe and ordered him to compose a letter of complaint to Laqa. The scribe composed the following message, 'Khudawand, is this how you reward me for my devotion that an ordinary Kohi can kill my messenger? I am dispatching Uqab Jadoo and a large army in your service. Kindly deliver that nasty Kohi to this sahir so that he is punished for his crime. Any delay in this matter will tax the patience of your devotee!' Afrasiyab stamped the letter with his seal and handed it to Uqab saying, 'Mobilize fifty thousand men and proceed to Mount Agate. Execute Qahir Kohi and then finish off Hamza's forces. I am leaving for Mount Sapphire to resolve the mystery of Sheeshadar and her claims to have destroyed the enemy.'

Uqab returned to his estate and embarked on the journey to Mount Agate with fifty thousand sahir troops. The route that Uqab took led him through Mount Sapphire. It was mid-afternoon and the sun was at its zenith. His sahir soldiers could barely sit on their magic birds in that heat and happily descended on the verdant slopes of Mount Sapphire. The soldiers settled under trees and were engaged in various tasks. Some stretched out on makeshift beds, others assuaged their hunger, yet others set off to find wells and tanks to bathe. One or two of them found a well and tossed a metal pail attached to a rope to draw out water. The pail did not splash into the water and seemed to land on something soft like leather. The soldiers peered into the well and saw a dead body with the pail resting on its belly.

The soldiers reported this event to Uqab who came to the well with a few soldiers and had the body pulled out carefully. He was startled to see that it was Princess Sheeshadar in a strange condition. She appeared to be naked apart from a shabby sheet torn and mended in several places that was tied around her breasts and private parts. This was clearly the work of one of the ayyars of the Islamic lashkar. The ayyars always covered a woman they had to render unconscious in this manner and did not lay their eyes upon her naked body. If any of them did so and the Emir came to know of it, he was likely to kill that person!

Uqab saw that she had wads of cotton wool stuffed in her nose and a bandage soaked in the tincture of unconsciousness tied around her forehead. He opened the bandage, drew the wads out of her nostrils and sprinkled water on her face. After a long time, Sheeshadar regained consciousness. Uqab sent for women's garments and dressed her before bringing her back to his tent. There, he had food and wine served to her. When she had revived completely, she asked him, 'How did you come here and find me?' Uqab informed her that he had been sent to help Khudawand and found her quite accidentally in a well.

The sahira looked grim and said, 'This is undoubtedly the handiwork of the ayyar I had captured. O Uqab, you should continue your journey and I will not rest until I search and find that wily rascal and chew him up alive!' Uqab tried to warn her, 'Princess, you should offer thanks to Samri for preserving your life! Do not start pursuing ayyars and do not fight Muslims without Shahanshah's orders! There is something not right in Mount Agate. A Kohi has killed Sohail. Only Samri knows whether Shahanshah intends to help Khudawand after this incident. I only know this that if Khudawand does not hand over this Kohi, Shahanshah's relations with him will be strained!' The sahira thought for a while and replied, 'Very well, I will not fight but I have to find and execute that ayyar!' After this conversation, Sheeshadar conjured a flying throne to leave for her abode and Uqab continued on his journey to Mount Agate.

Afrasiyab and the false Sheeshadar

Afrasiyab, the Ill-fated One, left for Neelum Koh after dispatching Uqab on his mission to Mount Agate. The false Sheeshadar, that is Chalak, pretended to be ill for a day. The next morning, when Neelum came to ask after her, she frowned and pouted so prettily that Neelum was captivated and asked, 'Princess, how are you feeling now?' The false sahira sighed, 'With the blessings of Samri I am a little better, but I still feel very weak!' Neelum was happy to attend to her and was occupied thus when Afrasiyab's entourage reached the mountain. Magic birds trilled, 'Ya Afrasiyab! Ya Afrasiyab!' to herald his arrival and trees swayed as gusts of fresh, cool breezes swept through the mountain. Neelum and his officers rose immediately to receive him. Chalak also got up and saw that the Shahanshah was resplendent on a gem-inlaid throne. Hundreds of parizads and comely slaves accompanied him, and his handmaidens fanned him with branches of fragrant blossoming trees. Thus, the Shahanshah's throne descended in splendour on Neelum Koh. Afrasiyab dismounted and walked towards the palace. At that time, Neelum and the false Sheeshadar came forward to pay homage to him. The King of Magic gazed at Sheeshadar's breathtaking beauty and lost his heart. He held her hand as he entered Neelam's fragrant palace and made that flower-like beauty sit next to him on masnad. As parizads served roseate wine to the royal party, Shahanshah filled a goblet with his own hands and offered it to the unfaithful saqi sitting with him.

The false Sheeshadar rolled her eyes seductively and declined the wine saying, 'I have been ailing since yesterday and have only just recovered! If I consume even one goblet, I will be unconscious. Let me serve you instead!' The Shah smiled in assent and this mischievous one served him wine without adding any drug to it. As she poured him a goblet, Afrasiyab asked, 'How did you fare with the Muslim army?' The false Sheeshadar claimed breezily, 'Oh, I finished all of them!' Afrasiyab persisted, 'After you went there I sent Sohail, but he was killed there. His men claim that the battle was going on with Hamza's army. If you had destroyed all of them, then who was fighting from their camp?'

The false Sheeshadar explained, 'I am not sure about the size of Hamza's army, I killed whomever I saw there. If he sent for reinforcements after I left, I would not be aware of that!' Afrasiyab nodded understandingly, 'You are so right princess! His sons and grandsons leave lashkar on the pretext of a hunt. They venture far and wide to conquer kingdoms and then bring huge armies back with them!' Afrasiyab now spoke of other matters and the false Sheeshadar entertained him with her wiles. The Shahanshah did not go beyond talking with the sahira as Neelum and his nobles were also present there.

Uqab in Mount Agate

Now hear about Uqab who had travelled in stages and reached Laqa's camp in Mount Agate. Laqa sent his nobles to receive him and they allotted space to his army at some distance from the Kohis. Uqab Jadoo came to the durbar and genuflected in front of Laqa before calling out, 'I am the Messenger!' Laqa read the message and shook his head as he could hardly think of suitable response to it. Bakhtiarak took the letter from him and after reading it, said, 'Khudawand, who is this haramzada Qahir Kohi and what is he to us? Hand him over right now. The King of Sahirs is your ally and special devotee. Do not give him cause for offence!' Laqa looked doubtful and told the Shaitan, 'The Kohi was also our special devotee! However, we must oblige the King of Sahirs.'

Bakhtiarak then sent for Ansar Kohi and asked him to bring Qahir Kohi to the durbar. Ansar was no match for Qahir's strength and had to ply him with a great deal of wine in order to lure him into the durbar. When Qahir realized Laqa was handing him over to Afrasiyab's envoy, he begged him to spare his life. 'I apologize for my unfortunate behaviour Khudawand,' he cried, 'and hope to have your blessing for the future.' Laqa ignored his entreaties and tears and declared solemnly, 'Whosoever acts against our will must be punished!'

Laqa turned to Uqab and said, 'Here is the King of Sahir's offender! Punish him as you will!' Uqab, in turn, ordered his sahir soldiers to take Qahir outside and execute him immediately. They dragged poor Qahir Kohi out of the durbar and summoned the executioner. The Kohistanis raised a clamour when they realized that their commander was going to be executed. At that time, Qahir called out to his tribesmen, 'O Kohis, you are my kin therefore you are obliged to carry out my last request!' Some of them cried, 'We are listening and if we can, we shall fulfil your will!' Qahir said, 'After I am dead, take my corpse and hand it over to the Muslims for burial. The reason is that I accept Islam and curse this swindler Laqa, misleader of humanity. Now I will recite the Kalma. Bear witness to this event and confirm it to Emir Hamza.'

After this speech, Qahir Kohi read the true words of the Kalma-e-Shahadat and denounced idolatry. The ayyars of Islam who had come to watch the spectacle of Qahir Kohi's execution shed tears at the sincerity of Qahir's eloquent speech and returned to the pavilion of Solomon to convey the news to Emir Hamza. The Emir immediately got up from his seat and declared, 'If he has converted to Islam, we are honour-bound to help him!' He emerged with his hand on the sword of Solomon and mounted Ashqar. Within moments, the parizad horse had conveyed him to Laqa's camp. Everyone there looked intimidated by the Emir and let him pass without resistance. They nudged each other as he rode past their ranks and whispered, 'The fun will begin now!'

The Emir called out, 'Allah is Great!' just when Qahir was praying for the last time and Uqab was about to decapitate him. The thunderous call of the Emir announcing his presence reduced the enemy's lustre to water. Bakhtiarak ran towards Hamza and cried out, 'Your old slave greets you! I have been advising this useless sahir to desist from spilling the blood of a Muslim, but he is determined otherwise. Look how he stands with his sword drawn!'

Uqab was already quite stunned by Hamza's roar. When he heard Bakhtiarak, he realized that Hamza was there to rescue the prisoner. He balanced his sword on both hands and recited an incantation so that the sword flashed on Hamza's head like lightning. Emir recited the Great Name and the lightning was transformed back into the sword. Uqab then assumed the form of a monstrous fire-breathing dragon. He opened his fearsome jaws like the gates of hell on the Emir, who once again recited the powerful words and reduced the dragon back into Uqab.

An exasperated Uqab called out to his officers and ordered them to attack Hamza. His army surrounded Hamza and subjected him to a volley of magic citrons and coconuts. Meanwhile, Uqab had become helplessly trapped under the shadow of Emir's sword. He tried to fly into the air, but toppled down when Emir recited the Great Name. He then tried every spell at his command, but not one of them worked against the power of the holy words. Emir forcefully brought his sword down and sliced the sahir like a cucumber. By this time, Emir Hamza's sardars had also arrived on the scene to fight with their commander.

Once this happened, the Emir hastened to cut Qahir Kohi free of his shackles. The grateful Kohi went around Emir and held the reins of Ashqar on the way back to the Islamic camp. Laqa was in his durbar when he heard the din outside and tried to escape from the back of the pavilion. Bakhtiarak saw him and called out, 'Why are you running? This whole business is on the heads of these sahirs. No one will say anything to you! On second thoughts, perhaps we should all leave!' Thus, these kafirs were the first to leave. On the way back, Qahir asked Emir, 'With your permission, may I teach this Laqa the misleader a lesson?' Emir smiled and replied, 'He has already fled with fear. You can tackle him another day.'

Afrasiyab in Mount Sapphire

Now hear about Afrasiyab. He had earlier informed Uqab that he would be travelling to Mount Sapphire. Uqab's officers who had fled from Mount Agate now sought him out in that place. Afrasiyab was enjoying the company of the false Sheeshadar when he heard the sound of wailing and said, 'Find out who are these people!' Neelum's men presented Uqab's officers to the Shah. They performed mujra greeting before announcing, 'Uqab was killed by Hamza!'

The Shah asked, 'How did that happen?' They replied, 'Khudawand Laqa had arrested Qahir and handed him over to Uqab. When Qahir was about to be executed, he declared that he had converted to Islam. Hamza was informed by his ayyars and he came and killed Uqab with one mighty stroke of his sword. There was a fierce battle but we were defeated by the Muslims and have come to you!' Afrasiyab heard this and looked down at the ground, crestfallen. The false Sheeshadar declared, 'Badshah, let your shoe worry about this! Now your handmaiden will erase their existence like the erroneous word! I will put them to sleep in the lap of the nursemaid of the grave!' The Shah cheered up on hearing her reassurances and started drinking wine again. He signalled to Neelum that he needed some privacy. Neelum and Uqab's men withdrew from the room along with the handmaidens and other attendants.

The Shah looked at the apparition of loveliness beside him, at her reddened lips and kohl-filled eyes. He was quite drunk by now and lust overcame him. He stroked her thigh and cried, 'Dearest heart, come closer to me!' The ayyar gave a soft sob and gently removed his hand. Afrasiyab said, 'O destroyer of my honour, do not deprive me anymore. O beautiful statue, I am besotted with every gesture of yours. Come and warm my side and do not pretend to be so cold towards me!' Thus, the badshah and ayyar engaged with each other for different purposes. The badshah was eager for intimacy and the ayyar intended to render him unconscious.

The real Sheeshadar

Meanwhile, the real Sheeshadar had returned to her abode and had managed to re-awaken her magical powers. She then returned to Mount Agate to look for the errant ayyar in Emir's lashkar. She used her magic to search for him, but could not locate him anywhere. Eventually, she moulded a figure from lentil flour and breathed on it to make it come to life. The figure asked, 'Princess, what do you want to know?' Sheeshadar replied, 'Tell me the truth—where is Chalak ayyar?' The figure laughed and stated, 'He has assumed your form and is sitting in the lap of the King of Magic!' After saying this, the figure emitted a flame from its mouth and incinerated itself.

As soon as she heard this, Sheeshadar travelled to Mount Sapphire in great rage. Neelum's officers who were stationed on the slopes were surprised to see another Sheeshadar arrive when they had just left one with the Shah of Tilism. They were so confused that they did not stop her and she walked straight into Neelum's palace. She approached the durbar room quietly and saw that a person with her face was sitting close to the badshah who was nuzzling her cheeks. Convinced that this was Chalak bin Amar, Sheeshadar was livid at the sight and thought of striking a magic blow to Chalak's head to reduce him to ashes.

She tiptoed into the room, intending to stand behind them when the badshah suddenly looked up and saw her. Chalak also turned around and as he saw her, he threw himself on Afrasiyab and cried, 'This is the same ayyar who had thrown me in the well!' The King of Magic was now quite drunk and annoyed that he was interrupted in his session of pleasure with the false sahira. He looked at the real Sheeshadar with fury and blew his breath out in her direction so that she was hurled back against the wall and fell unconscious.

The badshah called out, 'Oye Neelum, come here at once!' Neelum rushed into the room and Afrasiyab barked, 'Revive this ayyar who is disguised as Sheeshadar and I will kill him myself!' Neelum approached the unconscious Sheeshadar while Chalak realized that he was now in danger, as she would reveal his secret once she was conscious. He got off the Shahanshah's lap and cried, 'Badshah, I am so terrified that I might relieve myself right here! I will just visit the privy.' The Shah called out to two maidservants to accompany the princess. The privy was located outside the main palace. Chalak told one maidservant to wait outside and took the other one with him. Once inside, he said, 'Put the water jug on the floor. Massage my navel and back so that I can relieve myself with ease!' As the woman bent down to place the water jug, Chalak smeared her nose with the unguent of unconsciousness so that she fell down on the spot. He quickly exchanged clothes with her and assumed her form.

Meanwhile, Neelum revived Sheeshadar who looked alarmed as she opened her eyes. The Shah shouted, 'Oye stubborn ass, who are you?' Sheeshadar was enraged at his tone and beat her breasts as she cried, 'A curse on you! You are not fit to rule a kingdom! You blind fool! That moment when you sat on the throne should have been destroyed!' Sheeshadar then hysterically slapped her cheeks, thus convincing Afrasiyab that she was the real sahira. He regretted his behaviour and apologized profusely until he had placated the furious Sheeshadar. He said, 'You should hide and emerge only when he returns from the privy.' Sheeshadar seethed, 'I will kill him in the privy!' She drew out her dagger and headed for the privy.

She reached it just as Chalak came out disguised as the maidservant. The sahira signalled to ask if the ayyar was inside. Chalak signalled back that indeed he was. The sahira pushed the door open and immediately decapitated the unconscious maidservant. As the woman did not have any particular magical powers and did not possess guardian spirits who would raise a clamour at her death, no one was alerted to her real identity. Sheeshadar took the severed head to Afrasiyab and cried, 'Here, I have brought it with me!' The Shah shuddered and said, 'Princess, do not touch this maleech! Throw him off the parapet! These people are enemies of Samri and Jamshed, it is forbidden to touch them!' Sheeshadar threw the head in the palace courtyard and said, 'Let it remain here so that we can see it and be happy!'

She went and sat with Afrasiyab who apologetically said, 'Princess, I am deeply ashamed that I did not recognize you and treated you badly!' The princess folded her hands and said, 'Huzoor, we are your lowest ranking handmaidens. At that time, I was very angry and you doubted me. Thus, I may have uttered some impolite words. Shahanshah, I will always remain obedient. If you desire my company, then come to my humble abode. Here you will suspect me of being an ayyar and I will suspect you! I have to confess I see ayyars everywhere now! My house is quite secure and you can stay there as long as you like!'

The Shah looked benignly at her and said, 'Princess, first I have to kill this ayyar's father Amar whom I have captured! After doing that I will definitely come to your house!' He embraced the sahira and kissed her on the brow. She then sprouted wings and flew off to her abode while the Shah left for the Garden of Apples.

Meanwhile, Chalak had fled from the palace and dived in a mountain stream. He remained under water for some time and when he emerged, he disguised himself as a sahir. He saw that Sheeshadar was flying off the mountain. Chalak dodged and darted behind bushes and trees and followed her as she flew overhead. After Sheeshadar had covered a great distance, she descended in the wilderness to rest. She sat under a tree for a while and then went to relieve herself.

Chalak was watching her from behind a tree and when he saw that she was not on her guard, he thought, 'This is the right moment, kill her now or she might kill you!' He took out his gophan and loaded it with a heavy stone. He took aim at her head and released the stone that went spinning towards her. There was a loud crack as her skull was severed from her body which shuddered and then went still. Her spirits raised an almighty din and darkness fell on the world. The desert of dread that the Shah had crossed to reach her garden was destroyed, as was her garden and palace.

The King of Magic was flying towards Tilism when he heard the uproar of her guardian spirits calling out, 'Alas, you have killed Sheeshadar

Jadoo!' The Shah turned around to find out what had happened while he glanced instinctively at his left hand. The signs on it warned him that the next few moments could be fatal for him and that he was not to travel anymore. Afrasiyab felt frustrated when he saw this, but could not do anything other than pay heed to the sign.

ᘐᘐ

22 Burran Rescues Amar from the Dome of Dread, Afrasiyab Condemns Her to the Dungeons of Zulmat

Tilismi herald

Shah Afrasiyab, the misguided one, travelled to the breathtaking Feroza Koh. The architect of the seas and skies had created this mountain entirely from turquoises and it was a reflection of His perfection. The earth for miles around the mountain was a deep turquoise blue, reflecting the colour of the mountains. When Afrasiyab reached the mountain and read an incantation, hundreds of melodious birds perched on blossom-laden trees trilled in response and flew to Fort Feroze Nigar that stood at the foothills of Feroza Koh. The ruler of this region, Feroze Shah Tajdar Jadoo, was presiding over his durbar in great splendour when birds flew in, sang his praises and announced the arrival of the Shah of Tilism.

When the badshah of the fort heard this, he and his counsellors and ministers rose and arranged trays of offerings. Feroze Shah presented himself to the King of Magic, and bowed his head respectfully. He led the Shah to a bungalow overlooking a lake and soon, roseate wine flowed and the nautch commenced. After he was refreshed, the King of Sahirs spoke solemnly, 'Feroze Shah, you are the royal herald of this Tilism. I will be executing Amar. You have to make an announcement throughout Tilism so that our friends can watch the spectacle of his execution!'

After Feroze Shah listened intently to the Shah he read an incantation. There was a fierce gale and a monstrous black ogre with an outsized head materialized before them. His mouth was open like the gates of hell, his teeth protruded like an elephant's tusks and his head was like the dome of a fort. A mammoth drum was tied around his waist and he held wooden rods almost as large as pillars in each hand. Feroze Shah ordered, 'O Herald of Tilism, strike your drum throughout Tilism and make it known that Amar will be executed on a given day. The residents of Tilism should come and witness this spectacle. Begin the strikes near the armies of Hairat and Mahrukh and make sure you are heard.'

The ogre smiled and declared, 'I have a Tilismi drum and I only exist for this one purpose. When I strike my drum, all the residents of Tilism can hear it! Its sound reaches fifty to sixty *kos*.' The Tilismi herald balanced his drum and flew from Koh Feroza to Hairat's camp. There, when he struck the drum with the enormous wooden mallets, the sahirs of both camps stood still and listened attentively.

The herald roared like thunder, 'Hear this! Shahanshah of the land of the gods, Samri, Jamshed and Laqa, has ordered that on the eighteenth of this month; on Tuesday, the day of Mars, Amar ayyar will be brought out from the Dome of Dread and executed! His enemies should enjoy the spectacle and his friends should prepare to fight!' After making this announcement, the Tilismi herald struck the drum twice and left to make the announcement in other parts of Tilism. A horde of spectators and young boys followed him as he left the camp.

Now hear about Amar: He was in the Dome of Dread when he heard the sound of the Tilismi drum and the date of his impending execution. He thought, 'I should plan an escape strategy soon.' Meanwhile, Feroze Shah followed the Shah's orders and composed letters to the nazims and kingdoms in the realm. He dispatched the letters through magic slaves and birds throughout Tilism. In the Garden of Apples, the Shah of Tilism sent for Baghban and said, 'We forgive your wife's misdemeanour. Find her and proceed to Malika Hairat's lashkar. Clear the plains from the shores of the River of Flowing Blood to the desert of Fanaa and the Dome of Light! The wilderness and the slopes should be even and balanced. If there are any trees in the plain, have them chopped and pull out random shrubs and thistles. The plain should be pure and as clean as a mirror and there should be no stones or pebbles either. The ground should be prepared for the nazims of Tilism who will camp there. Strike the drums to announce that Amar will be executed. Whoever thinks they can rescue him should remain alert!'

The vizier left the durbar and pondered about where he could find his fugitive wife. His instincts led him to the wilderness of blossoms that was abundant with colourful blooms. Baghban rested under a tree, which happened to be the one where that flower of the garden of goodness was hiding. As he sat under the tree, the flower that was Gulcheen fell into her husband's lap and said, 'I am a marigold in my lover's lap!' Baghban was about to pick up the stray flower when it assumed the form of Gulcheen. She garlanded her husband with her arms and watered the garden of her beauty with the dewdrops of her eyes; her husband wept as well. He told her that the Shahanshah had forgiven her transgression and had assigned them both the task of organizing Amar's execution. His wife replied, 'You are again saying things that burn my heart! I will not let you organize Amar's execution. May God save you from the machinations of ayyars! Why did you agree to do this task?' The vizier declared, 'Whatever happened has happened! Come let us serve Shahanshah. If he orders us to do something we dare not disobey him!' Gulcheen replied, 'Alas, what I should do! Where should I flee after setting this badshah's house on fire?' The vizier lost his colour and whispered, 'Wife, do not say anything against badshah! He has just forgiven us. Let us not invoke his wrath again. Come home with me, I do not have to leave right away!'

Baghban led his wife home gently, advising her on the way to curb her tongue. Gulcheen was grateful to be home again, where all comforts awaited her. Handmaidens heated water for their baths and after the vizier and his wife had bathed, they wore rich garments and summoned nautch girls. They watched the dancing for some time before they were left alone to imbibe the wine of pleasure.

Preparations for an execution

Later, the vizier wore the turban of his office and proceeded to carry out the Shahanshah's orders. His wife also left with him to serve Hairat. They travelled to the pavilion of the wife of the Shah and presented themselves in the durbar. Baghban informed Hairat, 'Shahanshah has sworn that he will execute Amar and sixty thousand nazims of Tilism will be arriving to watch the spectacle. Huzoor, we have to prepare for them!' Malika Hairat immediately sent for the camp *baildars* and ordered, 'Clear the forest between the Dome of Light, the River of Flowing Blood and the desert of Fanaa! Take some sahirs with you so that they can produce magic lightning to burn the trees and conjure gales to blow out the dust. Your team can fill caves or ditches, and level the ground. Water carriers are to spray the area and settle the dust. Hills and ravines should be sparkling like mirrors!'

The baildars thus set forth to carry out Malika Hairat's orders. The *jamadar* of baildars was wearing the red turban and badge of office to lead his team. A technical team of map-makers went along with their tools. Hundreds of sahirs holding administrative posts accompanied these teams. The Malika herself went to the edge of the camp where she had a tent erected. The vizier and his wife were also involved in this clean-up operation.

The baildars first cleared the forest—they cut down trees that were in the way and sheared the rest before adorning them with silver glitter and crystal globes and bulbs to illuminate the area. The doorways of mountains opened like the hearts of generous philanthropists and the baildars laid out gardens and planted flowering climbers there. They placed uncut rocks of gems in the gardens and grafted trees with bright spring blossoms. They dug canals to channelize waterfalls that flowed down from mountain streams and lined them with bricks and brightly painted parapets. The sahirs of Hairat's lashkar shaped water birds like swans, ducks and herons from wax models and transformed them into bejewelled creatures that walked about while gem-inlaid birds perched on branches trilled melodiously.

The baildars then turned to the rocks in the area and sorted them out so that a few of them were retained as milestones. They planted flowering vines to adorn them, transformed the smaller slopes in the area into miniature gardens with flowering shrubs, and opened pathways into mountain ravines. Finally, that wilderness looked as bright and alive as the shining disc of the sky, and a virtual city of tents and pavilions stretched out for miles in sight.

Nazims of Tilism

Malika Hairat returned to her pavilion and waited for the guests with her attendants and handmaidens. Suddenly, an unearthly light illuminated the earth, sounds of kettledrums and bugles filled the air and the plain began humming with activity as rows of magic birds and dragons descended on it. There was a vast congregation of sahirs as far as the eye could see.

If you looked at the fire-breathers, it seemed as if the plain was on fire; if you looked at the ones clad in yellow, the world seemed to be yellow with fear; where there was a throng of ones clad in green, it seemed as if the world had consumed poison. In another direction, witches clad in black robes exuded a darkness that dimmed the world. Fearsome lions roamed the fields, magic elephants loomed on the horizon and pythons surrounded this plain of fear; that now looked like the Plain of Doomsday.

Hairat was watching this spectacle when the rulers of kingdoms and frontiers of Tilism started arriving. The sound of trumpets heralded their arrival and the boom of hundreds and thousands of drums deafened the ear of the sky. Millions of coloured flags inscribed with the praises of Samri, Jamshed and the speaking calf that had mesmerized the people of Moses came into view on the plain. Sahirs mounted on magic dragons were carrying these flags aloft. After them materialized thousands of elephants with painted foreheads and intricate gold howdahs that were trimmed with strings of pearls. Behind them, appeared palanquins draped with gold-embroidered curtains. She-camels emerged next, adorned with bells that tinkled as they ambled and swayed.

There were crackling sounds as throngs of sentinels and royal attendants flew past in the air. Rows of saqqas sprinkled water to settle the dust in the plain. Thousands of sahirs and sahiras held braziers glowing with oudh and umber incense and the air was heavy with the fragrance of perfume holders. Finally, the royal parties appeared resplendent in their tiaras and crowns; gleaming with jewels and garments embroidered with gold threads. They sat on thrones and bungalows that rested on enormous magic dragons. Some flew in on golden-feathered peacocks and others rode on magnificent stallions. Miniature gold turrets fixed on each corner of their thrones held trays with a variety of condiments. These were aromatic piles of betelnuts, cloves, lentil flour, thorn apples, sindoor, googal and musk incense, saffron, cardamoms and whole black peppers. Each nazim had brought a lashkar of sixty or seventy thousand men along with them. Sahir soldiers, foreheads smeared with ashes, held tridents and carried magical offerings while little piglets squealed in their laps. Their faces were magically transformed into hideous masks.

There were so many lashkars that hardly had one nazim arrived than the next one's arrival was announced. It was an endless stream and for three days and three nights, the guests of the Shah continued to land with their huge armies on the site arranged for them. Every lashkar brought tents and furnishing loaded on magical dragons. They had also brought skilled workers of every craft with them. Hairat's servants were run off their feet as they settled each army into the area allocated for it.

Vizier Baghban and his wife made sure that the royal pavilions did not lack any comfort. Every badshah or princess that arrived first met Hairat to greet her. Hairat had barely rested for three nights as she had been supervising the arrangements. Eventually, all royal guests settled into their pavilions, bazaars opened in each lashkar and there was a carnival-like atmosphere for miles around. Many rich traders had accompanied their rulers and it was a gathering like no other in Tilism.

The rebel army reacts

While these lashkars were settling down, Mahrukh Magic-eye was also aware of the activity in the enemy camp. She had emerged from her pavilion with all her sardars and was observing the spectacle of the nazims from a high place. She returned to her durbar and ordered that magic trumpets were to alert her army. When her lashkar of seven lakh soldiers was ready, she ordered her commanders that two lakh men were to guard the camp and five lakh were to accompany her and the sardars. She wanted to mount an attack before the Shah of Tilism arrived on the scene and sat on her throne to lead the army. Suddenly, she heard thunderous sounds from the sky as four hundred magic hands materialized in the air. There was a shower of rose petals and magic birds called out, 'Spring is here! Spring is here!'

Everyone looked up and saw that the life of spring and the ruler of all lovers, Princess Bahar had arrived. She was seated on a peacock throne, laden with flower garlands and held a wand of flowers in one hand. Four thousand of her handmaidens were also with her. The flower-body Bahar was returning from her abode in Aram Koh where she had gone to awaken her magic. We have mentioned this place earlier in detail.

Mahrukh met her warmly and said, 'You have returned at the right moment for this is the last time that we see each other! We were all setting forth to die!' Mahrukh went on to explain the gathering of the nazims of Tilism and said, 'Our army is to this vast lashkar as a pinch of salt is to a sack of lentils! Compare millions of soldiers to an army of five lakhs! However, we are prepared to die and make a name in this world!' In response Bahar declared, 'I am with you all the way and will undergo whatever you suffer. I was in my home when I learned that the rulers of my neighbouring kingdoms were travelling to this area. Then I realized that all nazims were travelling to the same place and I returned here as soon as I could to find you. Malika, my advice is that you should not take any initiative yet. Have faith in God's mercy. Wait to see what emerges from the veil of invisibility!' Mahrukh saw the wisdom of her words and turned back. She ordered her commanders to keep half the lashkar on full alert in case the enemy attacked them unawares. The commanders executed her orders and she returned to her pavilion.

Nazims of Nur Afshan

Now hear about the situation of Princess Burran, the auspicious one. The young Majlis came to her and said, 'The Tilismi Herald has struck his drum to announce Amar's execution and it will not be long now!' The princess reflected, 'If Amar is killed, there will be terrible consequences. We should mount a rescue as soon as possible!' She happened to be strolling in the slopes just beyond her garden when she decided this. She scooped up mud and kneaded it to mould magic slave-boys, placed guardian spirits within them, and ordered them, 'Go and inform nazims of our Tilism that they should mobilize their armies and reach Hoshruba!' The magic slaves flew off to the four corners of Tilism Nur Afshan to inform the nazims and rulers of the frontiers. The nazims prepared to leave at once with millions of sahir soldiers. When they set forth with their vast armies, the face of the earth darkened and there was turmoil in the universe.

From the Fort of Seven Hues, Burran emerged, leading her own army. Millions of battle flags inscribed with verses in praise of Kaukab the Enlightened and the elders of Tilism Nur Afshan fluttered in the air. Thousands of gold and silver kettledrums boomed, powerful sahirs demonstrated their skills and magical illusions materialized for miles around. Magic rivers flowed—one of them the colour of rubies with bridges and boats of flames while animals made of fire floated down its length.

There was a shower of pearls from the sky as a thousands of magic moons peered through dark clouds and then vanished to reappear as suns. Sometimes, there was total darkness as millions of shooting starts darted across the skies. The desert seemed to be alight with sparks twinkling like fireflies. Cloud formations floated by with millions of porcelain and crystal statuettes perched upon them. Lightning flashed in the sky and the roar of thunder was deafening.

A garden of fire then materialized in one direction with hundreds of trees sparking within. Flowers of flames blossomed in the garden and birds of fire were enclosed in cages outlined with flames. Hundreds of giant bloodthirsty dragons struck terror in the hearts of viewers as they tossed their heads and expelled jets of flames. A parallel world floated above this spectacle with millions of towers and domes made with silver, gold and precious gems. Occasionally, there was a shower of tiny stars from these formations. Sahirs with heads of elephants, lions, and dragons leaned out from the buildings and called out, 'Jai Jai Samri!'

Princess Burran's white elephant sometimes appeared as a colossal mountain, sometimes, as a giant sun. The princesses of all vassal kingdoms surrounded her throne, mounted on peacocks and herons. Eighteen thousand handmaidens armed with pouches of magic struck their mallets on gongs and sounded conch shells. Shadowy maidens formed a canopy above the princess, and some of them danced and sang in front of her.

So radiant was this caravan that the sky had hidden the face of the sun in shame and Venus was faint with envy in the third heaven. Camp provisions like tents and pavilions, and hundreds of necessary items were loaded on giant birds and this procession lacked nothing. Thus, it proceeded in great pomp and splendour towards Hoshruba.

The morning of the execution

At dawn the next morning, the hand of the sun extended its glowing fingers. The rider of radiant victory travelled from the realm of darkness to illuminate the universe. Hairat's camp resounded with the sound of drums and heralds called out, 'This is the day of Amar's execution! Whoever wants to mount a challenge should remain alert!' These calls also reached Mahrukh and Bahar's ears. The army of victory reverberated with the sound of war drums and gongs. The brave ones hastened to arm themselves with swords that were in readiness to destroy the enemy. They prepared to sacrifice lives and adorned themselves in suits of armour that shone like mirrors of triumph on all sides. Their lances were like rising stars that could sicken the hearts of the enemy with the awareness of their inferiority. Their daggers were thirsty for the blood of the enemy.

In the land of valour, the hearts of braves swelled up with pride. Sahirs had awakened their magic all night and their guardian spirits were ready to consume the lives of enemies. Calls of 'Get them! Catch them!' resounded in the camp. The cavalry rode into the plain of death while the infantry dashed out cheerfully to give up their lives. Hordes of sahirs swooped through the sky. The forces of mischief and danger descended from the air like doom.

Mahrukh, Shakeel, Bahar, Nafarman and Makhmoor, Ra'ad and Barq Mehshar, and Afat and Hilal along with other leading commanders mounted thrones of magic. The sound of conch shells and kettledrums filled the air, magical birds fluttered colourfully in the sky and cool morning breezes uplifted the hearts of fearless warriors. The desert sparkled with dewdrops and refreshed the garden of the Islamic lashkar. Flowers listened intently for good news and young blossoms asked what was happening. Stars in the sky hid in fear and lances shone like morning stars. Thus, this lashkar moved in all glory to die in the battleground.

Hairat too had adorned herself. She wore glittering robes and the jewellery of a new bride. She knew that the princesses of Tilism outshone parizads in their beauty and allure and thought that the bazaar of her beauty would appear cold in comparison to theirs. Thus, she was determined to heighten her charms so that the Shahanshah would have eyes only for her. Her natural beauty was also such that the moon and stars paled before her. Hairat's beauty and grace have been described frequently in this book.

While she was adorning herself thus, the vast multitude of royal camps were also preparing to fight and millions of flags fluttered in the plain. The world trembled with fear and there was peril in the sky. The sound of trumpets and gongs reached the dome of heaven as Hairat emerged on a bejewelled throne mounted on the royal elephant. The battlefield could hardly be seen today for the wilderness and mountains were crowded with throngs of sahirs. Armies settled into battle formation within their camps for their intention today was not to fight, but to execute Amar and prevent his allies from rescuing him.

When these armies were fully prepared, magic clouds rolled in from the four corners of the earth to settle the dust. The forces of mischief and conflict rose and prepared to send off the forces of dead souls. The angel of death sat on the throne of state, the river of iron surged up, and battle flags were unfurled as far as the eye could see. Suddenly, the thunderous sound of eighty thousand trumpets and drums reverberated in the air. The River of Flowing Blood churned violently as heaven and earth trembled in anticipation of Afrasiyab, the dishonest one. As multitudes of sahirs stopped to watch, the signs of splendour and power emerged on the horizon. Thousands of magic slave-boys appeared with battle flags and eleven hundred beautiful young maidens emerged holding badges of office. Hundreds of parizad maidens floated in the air, rotating ruby grindstones and hundreds more frolicked behind them, spraying coloured water from golden hand-pumps.

Afrasiyab emerged next on a turquoise throne enclosed with a parapet of rubies. As the mammoth crowds watched, a gigantic white horse with a gold saddle flew down from the skies. Afrasiyab leaped on the horse and flew upwards. From that height, he shouted '*Manam* Afrasiyab!' Mahrukh's lashkar heard him and froze. Barq Mehshar lost her spark, Ra'ad stopped breathing and the ayyars fled far away from the camp. As the rebels watched him, petrified with fear, Afrasiyab took out a magic citron from his waist band and dropped it on the rebel army. The citron burst in mid-air, there was a light drizzle and a drop of water fell on each person in the lashkar.

The King of Magic rode the white horse to the edge of the rebel army and called out, 'Mahrukh, Bahar and the rest of you, retreat now with your army. Weep as much as you can and beat yourself as much as you can! Writhe in agony and throw dust on your heads, for I am now going to execute Amar. How can you not mourn him who is so close to you? It would be disloyal of you not to grieve for him. Now, throw away your weapons and bags of magic and mourn him to your hearts' content!' The Shahanshah's magical words had such an effect on the rebel army that they tore their shirts and ran to the desert weeping and wailing for Amar. Mehtar Qiran saw this from a distance and thought, 'Alas, I am dead! What calamity is this?'

Qiran disguised himself as a sahir and slipped into the enemy camp unobserved. The King of Magic had just dismounted from the magic horse and the nazims of Tilism were hastening to greet him and offer nazar. Driven by his anger, Qiran ran towards Afrasiyab and brought his mighty bughda down on his impure head. Instantly, magic shields materialized to protect the king and Qiran had to run away to save his own life.

The King of Magic, who had been conversing with the nazims, looked unperturbed at this interruption. He called out, 'O earth of Tilism, hold him!' At once Qiran was rooted to the earth and thought, 'Oh Allah, this is the end!' Afrasiyab looked sternly at the ayyar and said, 'Qiran I can erase you like the erroneous word from the page of existence! However, go now and watch your teacher's execution!' As he spoke, the earth released Qiran's feet. He ran into the forest and summoned his companions with Zafeel, the whistle of ayyari. Barq, Jansoz and Zargham came running up to him and Qiran declared solemnly, 'You have seen how the office of our lashkar was turned upside down! What do you suggest we do now?'

Barq, Jansoz and Zargham cried, 'When they execute Ustad, we will draw our daggers and fall on the enemy.' Qiran replied, 'Yes, that is what we will have to do in any case! Let us find a high place and turn to the durbar of the Ghareeb Nawaz and call out to the Almighty in all humility to have mercy on us!' Qiran then led his companions to a place from where they could see both their own army and the army of the King of Magic. They were saddened at the sight of jubilation in Afrasiyab's camp while their own army was torn apart with grief.

Amar's execution

While the rebel army was wailing and weeping, the King of Magic recited an incantation and breathed in the direction of the Dome of Dread so that it vanished in a puff of smoke. Amar could now be seen in a pitiful state. Everyone saw that his body was pale and weak, and marked with weals and blisters. Afrasiyab laughed and called out to Amar, 'Khwaja, if you know any magic you can try it on me!' Amar replied softly, 'I curse all sorcerors.' Afrasiyab cried, 'There will be no time for you to curse us when your head is severed from the body!'

Afrasiyab consulted the oracle Pages of Jamshed that warned him, 'Execute Amar at once and do not waste time in talking to him or he will be released. It was not right to remove him from the dome. He should have been kept captive.' Afrasiyab quickly read a spell so that dust blew up from the earth to form a bungalow around Amar. 'When I make this house disappear,' Afrasiyab instructed his sahir soldiers, 'all of you attack Amar with your swords and chop him into pieces!' Hundreds of sahirs drew their swords and tools of magic out and positioned themselves around the house of dust.

Suddenly, the air resounded with the sound of a thousand conch shells and kettledrums. The Shah looked up and saw millions of fire-breathing dragons coming towards the plains. Two sahir soldiers sat on each of them, holding flags inscribed with verses in praise of Shah Kaukab and Amar. Afrasiyab looked at Hairat and sneered, 'Malika, look! It looks as if Amar's supporters have arrived. Why, I think that gypsy Kaukab himself is here in person!' Hairat said anxiously, 'In that case, execute Amar immediately!' Afrasiyab smiled confidently, 'Let them reach here as well so that they can vent their frustration. Watch how I destroy them now!'

Afrasiyab tossed a magic citron up in the sky. It burst in the air and expelled dense smoke that formed a huge cloud and spread over Kaukab's army. There was a light drizzle and sahirs disintegrated like paper puppets and collapsed with their dragons mounts on the earth. Four lakh flags fell in the dust. Afrasiyab laughed triumphantly and the royal guests cried, 'All praise to you Shahanshah! Even Samri could not have known this spell!'

Their cries of jubilation were drowned by the sound of trumpets from another direction. A cavalry of four lakh soldiers appeared in golden uniforms, riding on magic steeds. The King of Sahirs saw them and chanted another incantation that made two magic riders materialize before him. They asked him, 'What are your orders?' He said, 'Let us see how this army of riders fight with each other!' As the two riders vanished the army of four lakh suddenly parted and settled on two sides, creating a battleground between them. They then attacked each other. Swords flashed, fountains of blood stained the air and the flowers of wounds blossomed in the garden of death. The sound of metal against metal filled the world.

A princess from Nur Afshan saw the soldiers fighting against each other. She flew her throne to Princess Burran and said, 'Malika of our time, eight lakh of our soldiers have been destroyed. They have not succeeded against Afrasiyab.' Princess Burran immediately took out the Pearl of Samri, placed it on her palm and pronounced, 'Afrasiyab's magic should be incinerated and our forces should return to their senses!' A streak of bright light radiated from the pearl and vanished. The two

Tilismi riders of Afrasiyab's magic who were fighting each other suddenly ignited and burnt to ashes. The moment that happened, Kaukab's army returned to their senses and stopped fighting. The King of Magic warned the royal guests, 'Beware! The enemy has arrived!' The armies of the nazims were already armed and prepared, and drew out their poisoned swords and tools.

On the other side, Princess Burran addressed the nazims of Nur Afshan and said, 'O lions of the land of magic and valour, this is the moment! Your prey is standing in front of you—spring on him!' Princess Burran vanished after saying this, but Kaukab's armies advanced forward to the beat of kettledrums. There was such an uproar that Doomsday seemed pale in comparison. The armies of Afrasiyab stirred on one side while from this side, the armies of Kaukab moved like a tidal wave. As the two armies clashed, it appeared as if there was a collision of two worlds. The reverberation reached the inhabitants of mountains and deserts for miles around. There was no sound other than that of clashing metal and soldiers shouting 'Get them! Kill them!' It was as if the lamp of the world was being extinguished.

The ship of existence was sinking on dry ground as waves of calamity raged, bringing death in their wake. In the first attack, deadly arrows pierced the chests of thousands of men. Their faces were streaked with blood as they attacked each other with daggers and swords. The place where hawks flew seemed now to be the domain of arrows. When the royal rulers of the two Tilisms attacked each other, it was as if two suns or two mighty rivers were rushing into each other. The heart of the universe shook with the sounds of swords clashing, the rush of arrows and the ferocious thrusts of lances and daggers. Conventional weapons were thus used effectively.

As for magical warfare, it seemed as if the fruit trees of the world produced only citrons and limes, the fruits of death. Each coconut shattered the chests of thousands, and guardian spirits did not spare any lives. Millions of magic suns had emerged in the sky and thousands of magic moons had risen. Magic stars were flashing in the sky while there was an endless display of bolts of lightning. Magical creatures were also engaged in bizarre warfare with each other. Lions fought against tigers, snakes against spiders, elephants against hippopotami while pythons were coiled in deadly combat.

Slabs of ice fell from the sky as dark clouds floated over the plains and caused the earth to tremble. Clouds of dust in the air gave the illusion that the earth itself had moved up into the sky. Stones flew up from mountains and pelted down on the armies and mountains pounded against each other. The rivers of the earth had run dry and coconuts rained down like musk balls from the bellies of the stags of death.

The King of Magic, who had flown up into the air to cast spells on the enemy, was calling out, 'O devotees of Samri and Jamshed, do not be alarmed and do not lose heart with the might of the enemy! Watch how I destroy them all!' Princess Burran, who had vanished after exhorting her armies to attack, now materialized besides him and called out, 'Afrasiyab, if the Pearl of Samri appears before you, what will you do?' As Afrasiyab turned towards her, she flashed the great pearl in his eyes so that he trembled and felt dizzy. The sahirs who were beside him recited incantations that made heavy monsoons clouds envelope him and break his fall.

Before he could revive, Princess Burran hurled a magic citron on his army that burst and killed thousands of men. The cacophony of their guardian spirits added to the din. Burran then entered the fray with her magic sword and the Pearl of Samri in her hand. She killed forty men with each strike of her sword. Her companion Princess Mah fought alongside her with her magic crescents. When she hurled a crescent, it reproduced hundreds more that fell upon enemy warriors and slashed them to pieces.

When Hairat saw this carnage, she moved forward and called out, 'Shahanshah, where are you?' Afrasiyab happened to be within the magic cloud. Who was there to respond to her? Hairat was convinced that the Shah had left. She threw a magic citron towards Burran that hit her hard on the chest and caused her to collapse. At that time, Vizier Baghban came forward and caused his deadly flowers to fall from the sky. Burran's companion Princess Qamar drew out a fistful of gems and threw it at him so that a volley of arrows wounded the vizier.

When Burran revived, she saw young Majlis watching her anxiously. Majlis then returned to the battle in her usual manner: she used toys and games as magical weapons. Burran asked the princesses with her, 'Who aimed the citron at me?' They informed her that it was Hairat and Burran aimed a magic arrow straight at Hairat. It hit Hairat's elephant and she was thrown off the howdah. A magic hand caught her in the air and took her to Burran. Angered by this, Hairat called out, 'Burran the magic claw will carry me off and the earth will swallow you!'

Burran suddenly found herself waist deep in the earth of Hoshruba. She called out, 'O Hairat, the claw will release you and earth will release me.' The magic claw set Hairat down gently while the earth expelled Burran. Both of them immediately flew upwards to resume fighting. At that time, Afrasiyab emerged from the monsoon cloud and thought, 'This battle is for Amar. I should execute him right now!'

Chalak enters the scene

Now hear something else. Chalak bin Amar, who had entered Tilism and deceived Afrasiyab in Neelum Koh, now emerged on the scene. Chalak had gained powerful sahir allies on his journey who brought him this far. Chalak and his sahir friends were on a flying throne and looked down amazed at the armies of Mahrukh and Bahar beating their chests and wailing loudly. They saw the ayyars huddled on a nearby hill and praying in desperation. Chalak approached them and they briefed him about the situation, but did not recognize Chalak.

Chalak braced himself and looked at his companions Sarshar, Sulaiman and Sultan. He asked them, 'Is there a way to remove this spell?' They shook their heads and replied, 'We cannot possibly dispel the magic of the King of Sahirs!' Then Sulaiman looked at Sultan and said, 'I seem to recall that on Nauroze the King of Sahirs had made you a gift of a copper amulet. He had enchanted a wedding procession and made them lose their senses. He then told you to immerse the amulet in water and sprinkle that water on the procession to return them to their senses. Do you remember?' Sultan exclaimed, 'You have done well to remind me! I still have that amulet on me!' Chalak jumped off the throne and filled a goatskin bag with water from a mountain stream. Sultan brought out the magic amulet and immersed it in the water. He flew up into the air and sprayed the army with drops of the magic waters. A sharp gale swept through the area and the army fell unconscious. When they woke up, they gathered their tools of magic and started attacking Afrasiyab's forces.

At that time, Qiran and the other ayyars met Chalak and said, 'Brother, we were so absorbed in praying for our army at that time that we did not recognize you. Join us now and fall upon the enemy to rescue Khwaja Amar with the power of God!' Chalak told his companions to accompany his ayyar friends and said, 'All of you go ahead and I will join you presently!' He leaped off the hill and went in one direction; meanwhile, Qiran and the ayyars disguised themselves as sahirs and accompanied Sarshar and the other sahirs to the battlefield.

Burran Sword-woman rescues Amar

As the armies of Mahrukh joined the fray, noise levels in the plains increased ten fold. Afrasiyab was about to execute Amar in the House of Smoke, but stopped dead when he saw the rebel army and wondered who had revived them. Burran saw that he was distracted and rose in the air. She transformed into a bolt of lightning and fell upon the House of Smoke.

As Afrasiyab turned towards her, Qiran struck him with his bughda. Magic shields instantly appeared over Afrasiyab's head to protect him. Afrasiyab tried to capture Qiran, but Barq caught him in the coils of his snare-rope, which burnt down instantly. The Shah ran after Barq, but Zargham attacked him with a dagger. A magic claw stopped the dagger, but Jansoz quickly burst a narcotic bubble in his face. The badshah reeled with the impact of the narcotic on the spot and would have fallen down, had it not been for magic puppets that materialized under him to break his fall.

In the meantime, Princess Burran fell on the House of Smoke as a bolt of lightning so that the smoke vapourized and vanished. Burran saw Amar, quickly held him by the waist and flew up in the air. The reflection of the magic Pearl of Samri fell on Amar and revived his strength. Sahir soldiers saw her shoot up with Amar and rushed after her shouting, 'Get her! Catch her! She is taking him!' The princess flashed the magic pearl at them and they fell down unconscious. The princess now flew with all her strength and vanished from the sky.

By this time, Afrasiyab had regained consciousness. He heard the cries of his sahirs as they followed Burran even though Mahrukh's sahir soldiers created hurdles in their way. Afrasiyab shot up in the air in great fury shouting, 'I will not leave this girl today!' The sahirs of Kaukab's army tried to prevent him from flying, but were no match for his powers and he vanished into the sky behind Burran.

The nazims of Tilism Hoshruba felt so humiliated at Amar's rescue in their presence that they were ready to sacrifice their lives. They began fighting ferociously. The flame of magic was so fierce that the sun itself was feverish with its heat. Black forces caused the world to become a house of darkness and for miles around, severed heads littered the plain while bodies writhed in the throes of death. Alongside the magic River of Flowing Blood, another River of Flowing Blood flowed—body and soul were parted from each other.

The combined armies of Burran and Mahrukh fell upon the enemy. Malika Hairat tried desperately to win this battle, but was defeated. Eventually, she tired of combat and had the drums of peace struck. The armies stopped fighting and separated from each other. Kaukab's royal vassals returned with the great Mahrukh Magic-eye. Their armies set up camps next to the rebel camp and there was a veritable sea of armies on either side.

Hairat already had a vast army of sahirs as has been described earlier. Now Mahrukh's side also had vast hordes of sahir soldiers. As far as the eye could see, there were armies and yet more armies. Soon, the ayyars left for the wilderness in search of Burran and Amar. Mahrukh met Sarshar, Sulaiman and Sultan who had released her lashkar from its enchanted frenzy. She awarded them with robes of honour, assigned pavilions and fixed salaries for them. Thus, everyone settled in great splendour and ease.

We will leave them here and relate what happened to the King of Magic who had followed Burran. She had travelled some distance and realized that she could not be victorious in a hostile Tilism Hoshruba, especially when she would have to confront the Shah who was surely in her pursuit. It would be prudent to think of an escape strategy. Accordingly, she descended into the wilderness. She placed the unconscious Amar in a cave and hid in a ravine thinking, 'If someone dies after consuming sugar, what is the point of killing him with poison!'

Moments later, Afrasiyab reached the same place, desperately looking for the two fugitives. He tried to find where Burran was hiding, but the powerful Pearl of Samri protected the princess. Afrasiyab's magic merely informed him that the princess had returned to her own kingdom. The King of Magic turned back in great despair. He was too mortified to return to Hairat's camp and went to the Garden of Apples. He stayed there for a while, but feared that his Tilismi guests would come to see him there and was too embarrassed to face them.

Eventually, he went off to Zulmat, the Veil of Darkness. He took refuge in a house and lay down there, brooding darkly over his humiliation: 'A mere girl caused you so much dishonour today. This must be a sign of your fall. Even now you can hand over Tilism to Baghban and release Asad and Badi.' A moment later, he consoled himself with the thought, 'O Afrasiyab, you can capture Burran even from her own house! No one can rescue Asad from the dome and no one knows where you have hidden the keystone. Why are you getting so disheartened?' Thus, Afrasiyab lay there battling with such conflicting thoughts.

After Afrasiyab had left the area, Burran remained hidden for some time, but since this was the fourth day of battle, she felt very tired. She had spent the day as well in running and hiding, and felt hungry and thirsty. She emerged from the ravine and went to the cave where she had hidden Amar. She did not bring him out, but revived him inside and related what had transpired. 'Our lives were saved because of the Pearl of Samri, otherwise we would not have escaped from Afrasiyab!' she told Amar. Amar offered bouquets of appreciative words as offerings of thanks to that precious flower. He serenaded her like the nightingale of the garden of gratitude and said, 'Princess, God has spared my life because of you and I cannot thank you enough!'

Burran then led him out of the cave towards the slopes where she saw a pleasant meadow and recited an incantation. A few beautiful maidens emerged from the earth and Burran said to them, 'Bring forth some refreshments and items of comfort.' The maidens vanished and reappeared just moments later to arrange soft masnad seating by the mountain stream. The princess and Amar sat on the masnad as the maidens laid out bouquets of flowers before them. Then other women spread a dining sheet and laid out a sumptuous meal. They had also brought an urn and washbasin with them. Khwaja and Burran rinsed their hands and had dinner. Later, the maidens brought flasks of roseate wine.

Burran sipped the wine and looked about her. The moon had emerged on the horizon and cast a silvery glow about them. The waters of the brook gurgled and wild flowers blossomed in that wilderness. As Burran relaxed and enjoyed the moonlit scene, Amar sang softly to entertain her. At that moment, Mehtar Qiran appeared in the distance. Amar stopped singing and called out, 'Come and embrace me my son!' Qiran rushed forward and fell at Amar's feet, but Amar clasped him in a warm embrace. Qiran said, 'You should come to the camp where everyone is eager to see you and sardars are waiting to greet you!' The princess and Amar got up and said, 'Very well, let us go!'

Afrasiyab captures Burran

Amar, Burran and Qiran were about to leave when they heard Afrasiyab's thunderous roar, 'Manam Afrasiyab!' The moment he heard this earth shattering call, Qiran neatly dived into the nearest cave. He arranged his snare-rope at the mouth of the cave to trap anyone who tried to enter it and then started digging a tunnel to escape from it.

Amar fled as well, but greedy as always, he tugged at the carpet. Burran shouted, 'Let the carpet go to hell Khwaja, and save your life!' Amar let go of the carpet but dragged the dining sheet as he ran. At that moment, the earth shook, lightning flashed and birds flew off the trees singing, 'Ya Afrasiyab, Ya Afrasiyab!' Amar had no other recourse but to become invisible in Galeem. Burran was left alone to face the Shahanshah. A ray of light flashed in the sky and beamed down. The princess saw that a ruby statuette that looked like Afrasiyab stood in that ray of light. The princess looked unimpressed and smashed a citron on the ground. Where the citron touched the earth, it split open and spouted a stream that foamed into a river with enormous waves like the waves of the Qulzum and Zakhar rivers. A gleaming jewel-inlaid boat in the shape of the crescent moon emerged in the river and swerved towards the bank. The good princess quickly jumped into that boat.

The ray of light with the ruby puppet now began flashing on the banks of the river. At that time, the magic-maker Burran produced another spectacle and mixed water with fire. Waves of the river rose to transform into sheets of flames and fell on the ruby statuette. That statuette then transformed into the real form of the King of Magic and shouted, 'Manam Afrasiyab Jadoo!' With these words, the waves of flames ceased to crash on the banks. Afrasiyab called out again, 'Listen girl, this spell of yours would have caused any other sahir to fall madly in love with you. However, what can you do against me? You are the same child that I used to dangle on my lap! Tell me, what have you done with the person for whom you are sacrificing your life? Where is that thief Amar?'

Burran replied calmly, 'Amar ayyar escaped three days ago from your Dome of Dread. You are under the illusion that he is with me! Did you think he was dependent on me to rescue him! He is after all the king of tricksters!'

'He may have escaped, but where will you go?' the Shahanshah sputtered. 'Girl, if you fall at my feet and tell me, "You are my father in the same way as Kaukab is my father!" I might spare your life!' Burran looked at him with contempt and said, 'We do not eat what you give us, nor are we dependent on you! Why should we plead with you?' Afrasiyab looked at her with astonishment and asked, 'Will you fight me then?' The princess replied, 'I will fight a thousand times! If I had not intended to fight, why would I have left my house?' Afrasiyab muttered something and stamped hard on the ground so that the waters of the river froze. Burran jumped off her boat and faced him as the boat also vanished in a puff of smoke. Afrasiyab took out a huge iron ball and balancing it in one hand, said, 'Listen girl, there is no point in taking your life. It is necessary though to teach you manners!'

Burran laughed and said, 'Will you will teach me a lesson with this ball of wax that sticks to your hand?' These words were magical and the iron ball stuck to Afrasiyab's palm like a ball of wax. He recited an incantation and breathed on Burran so that she felt dizzy. She quickly said something so that a puppet emerged from the earth with a phial of rosewater. The puppet sprinkled the rosewater on Burran to revive her and vanished abruptly. Burran then flashed the Pearl of Samri at the Shah. He also fell unconscious and his puppets revived him in a similar manner. Burran threw the magic pearl on the ground and the King of Magic suddenly sank in the earth up to his waist. He called out, 'Girl you have been taught well by my disloyal childhood friend! However, where will you escape to now?'

Afrasiyab chanted a powerful spell and two claws materialized in the air. One pulled the Shah out of the earth and the other clutched Burran by the neck. According to one narrator, the King of Magic captured Burran, but Amba Prashad, a great dastangoh of Lucknow stated that magic claws conjured by Afrasiyab captured Burran. The princess cried, 'Ouf! The magic claws should burn!' and the claws instantly burst into flames. Afrasiyab writhed out of the earth, held out his hand and cried, 'Give!' A snare-rope materialized in his hand. The princess called out, 'Mingle with the dust!' As she said these words, the earth trembled under Afrasiyab, he stumbled to the ground and the snare-rope snapped around his body and throat throttling him.

At that moment, by sheer coincidence, the ayyar girl Saba Raftar appeared at a distance and saw what was happening. She quickly painted her face to look like Amar and called out to Burran, 'Well done princess! After all, whose daughter are you?' She moved forward as she praised Burran and burst a narcotic bubble on her nose. The princess fainted at once. Meanwhile, a crystal puppet materialized with a flask of water. He sprinkled it on Afrasiyab a few times and the magic snare-rope uncoiled itself from the Shah's body.

The Shah rose and first took the Pearl of Samri from the unconscious princess. He ordered the ayyar girl to pierce Burran's tongue with a needle. After she did as he instructed, the Shah said, 'Return to Hairat's durbar! I am going to imprison this shaven-haired hussy into the dungeons of Zulmat. When I return, I will reward you for this trickery for you have indeed performed a remarkable deed!'

Saba Raftar then set off on her way while the Shah took Burran towards Zulmat. He headed straight for the dungeons. When he reached there, he read an incantation to inform the keepers of the dungeons, Afih Seher and Azhdar Zulmati, of his arrival. When they presented themselves before him, the Shah ordered them sternly, 'Make sure that you use the strongest magic on her. She should be unable to move. Revive her only after she is in shackles. Give her a piece of bread and a bowl of water every eight hours. Guard her day and night. Be watchful and alert for this menace on earth is the daughter of Shah Kaukab. Do not underestimate her powers. If she escapes, she will kill thousands and we will not get our hands on her again!'

The two sahirs declared, 'O Mighty Shahanshah, she is nothing! If we use our magic on her father, even his honour will be as dust and he will not be able to escape from us! You should rest assured. This is the dungeon of Zulmat. For miles around it, you can see nothing except darkness! Where can anyone run to from this place? No person can find a way out of here and if he does, he dies in the process. We are here to guard this place and do not move from here. We will watch this princess day and night!'

The badshah looked satisfied and said, 'Yes, this is what I want!' He left Burran with the sahirs and returned to Hairat's camp. The keepers shackled and revived that lovely princess whose family had always protected and indulged her. When would she have seen a dark and narrow place like this one? When would she have suffered such grief and woe? When she opened her eyes, she saw that a black-faced sky had shown her the dark day and trapped her in a black dungeon.

IV

23 BARQ AND THE MAGIC DUST OF JAMSHED, THE STORY OF BURRAN'S RESCUE FROM THE DUNGEONS OF ZULMAT

Mehtar Barq Firangi set out from his camp one morning for conducting some ayyari. He went into the wilderness and after a while, saw a mound in the distance. Barq climbed up on the mound and looked around him. His eyes alighted on a huge sahir encampment in the jungle whose pavilions and tents seemed to spread over several kos. Barq saw the splendour and might of the lashkar and thought, 'These kafirs have also acquired great riches and comforts. O Barq, you should reduce their lustre to dust!'

Barq then considered several options and eventually thought of a plan. He disguised himself as a poor shepherd, tied a shabby loin cloth around his waist, a homespun turban around his head, and draped an old blanket on his shoulders. He held a shepherd's crook in one hand and walked barefoot into the camp, pretending to pursue a stray goat. He approached a group of soldiers and asked them, 'Sahibs, whose laskhar is this?' Their jamadar replied, 'This is the lashkar of Maheeb Lion-mounted who has brought a lashkar of one lakh, twenty-five thousand sahirs with him. Tomorrow, he will fight that betrayer of salt, Mahrukh and other rebels. He will either cut their heads off or capture them alive!'

'Sir, you gladden my heart with this good news,' Barq said to the jamadar who seemed inclined to gossip. 'By Samri, I hope that the ayyars and their allies will die as well! Master, I have heard that the rebels also have a large army. How will this young commander defeat them then?' The jamadar smiled at what he thought was a simple question and said, 'The difference between him and the other sahirs is the difference between heaven and earth! He has two unique weapons that can make even the King of Sahirs forget his magic and fall unconscious. He has the dust of Jamshed that can render the largest army unconscious and he has the magic Mehmoodi chador that shields the wearer from all magic. Apart from these gifts, the young prince is so strong he can vanquish a mad elephant without resorting to magic.'

Barq was stunned by these revelations and thought, 'Barq, you have come to the right place! This should be dealt with quickly!' He said with pretend innocence, 'Jamadar sahib, what you say is all true. How valuable these things must be! Perhaps they cost about two hundred rupees?' The jamadar laughed loudly and picked up his hand to hit the false shepherd in a friendly manner. Barq ducked and said, 'Sahib, do not be angry with me. Perhaps it is worth three hundred? The jamadar cried, 'You fool! These things cost millions! I doubt if there is even a price for them!' Barq rubbed his head and said ruefully, 'Mian, you are right! I am just a poor man in debt for twelve rupees. I make a living by selling goats for the herd owner. If I am lucky, I can make a few coins and feed my wife and children. I have never even seen a thousand rupees!'

The jamadar was a kind man and was moved by the shepherd's condition. He said to him, 'I will help you sell your goat at a profit today.' He introduced Barq to the darogha in charge of the kitchens and pleaded, 'Darogha sahib, this man is very poor. I have promised that he will get a rupee for this goat. Look, how fat it is! If you cannot procure it, some of us can try and pool in the money ourselves and enjoy a meat curry today.'

The darogha gave Barq a rupee and called one of the cooks to take the goat. He asked Barq whether he was staying or leaving. Barq replied, 'Huzoor, the blessings of Samri on you. If you give me a square meal, I will bring you a goat every day. Jamadar sahib promised me that I would be given food here.' The darogha then said, 'If you wait for a while, I will give you plenty of food.' Barq replied, 'My master, I am right here; where will I go now?' Barq then sat on one side and draped the blanket around him to give the impression that he was hungry and deprived. After some time, one of the cooks called out to him, 'Oye labourer, could you put a few coals on my hookah?' Barq walked into the kitchen tent to get the live coals and on seeing it empty, quickly added the drug of unconsciousness to all the cooking vessels. As he emerged from the tent, the head-cook who was resting on a string cot outside called out, 'Will you lower the flame under the rice pilaf and just watch it for a while.' Barq returned to the tent and managed to sprinkle some more of the toxic powder into the cooking vessels.

Later, the darogha returned and asked the kitchen staff to bring small portions of the food to his tent so that he could taste it before serving it to the royals. The staff arranged a tray for him and naturally, gave it to Barq, the labourer, to carry it to the darogha's tent. The darogha sahib was relaxing on his bed, smoking a hookah, when Barq placed the tray of food before him. He looked appreciatively at Barq and said, 'You seem to be a useful man and have worked hard today. After I have served my masters, I will give you so much food that you will not be able to carry it! Just wait while I taste the food first.' He took a few mouthfuls of the drugged food and fell into a deep slumber.

Barq immediately took his robes and turban and pushed him under the bed. He transformed himself into the darogha and emerged from the tent. The kitchen staff had already laid out the dishes for the royal party. The false darogha arranged the food on the tray and added some more drugged powder to it. Eventually, he got labourers to lift the trays of food and took it to the royal pavilion. He spread a dining sheet in the courtyard next to the pavilion and went into the pavilion. There, he saw the commander of the lashkar Maheeb Lion-mounted, who was fifteen years old, seated on a throne. He wore large gold earrings and snakes around his neck, and expelled flames with every breath. His two ferocious looking uncles sat besides him. To one side was the female enclosure, lined with velvet and hidden by screens. A group of courtesans and handmaidens were seated inside with Maheeb's mother, Jamosh. Her face was so hideous that the mother of the night of doom would be fearful of her.

Barq was terrified at the sight of these people, but braced himself and announced, 'Huzoor, dinner has been served.' Jamosh looked at him and ordered, 'Send it inside to mother first!' Barq ladled out portions of food in gold and silver dishes, and sent them to the women's enclosure. A dining-sheet was spread in there as well and the women sat down to eat. Maheeb sat down with his uncles and other relatives to have dinner. Barq quietly dished out steaming hot pilaf rice in plates and signalled to the attendants, 'Friends, I am your well-wisher as well. Taste this while it is still hot as you will not get dinner for some time. At least your hunger will be assuaged somewhat with this!' The servants gratefully sat in a corner with their plates while Barq waited on the royal party himself. Everyone in the royal pavilion succumbed to the drug after just a few mouthfuls of the food.

When Barq saw that everyone was unconscious he secured the flaps of the tent. He frisked Maheeb and his uncles and found the casket containing the magic dust of Jamshed. He went into the women's enclosure and pulled the magic Mehmoodi chador off Jamosh for that harridan wore it constantly. Barq then began beheading everyone. He started with the mother Jamosh and then decapitated the young commander and his uncles. Barq's razor-sharp dagger licked sahir blood. Darkness descended. There were fearful sounds and huge slabs of ice followed by sheets of flames that fell from the skies, as guardian spirits lamented the deaths of their masters. As each sahir died, it grew even darker and the din of spirits became deafening. The sahirs who had rushed to the royal pavilion were helpless and attacked Barq in unison.

Barq was aware of their intentions and escaped from the pavilion for he had disposed of the commanders of the lashkar. At that time, it was still dark and the sahirs lighted magic torches to pursue him, all the while crying, 'Get him! Catch him! He should not get away!' Some sahirs mounted magic hawks and eagles to fly after him, while others stamped on the ground and shouted, 'O Land of Tilism, the murderer of Maheeb Lion-mounted should not get away! Hold his feet!' They called out to their guardian spirits and cast powerful spells on Barq, but he was now protected by the Mehmoodi chador. Their spells bounced back on them instead. In no time, the lashkar was in a state of disarray and everyone had fled from there in sheer terror.

In his haste, Barq mistakenly ran towards Hairat's camp some distance away. What everyone saw was a young man who looked as if he was a lawyer or a darogha with blood-spattered clothes and bloodshot eyes, holding a dagger dripping with blood, as blood ran down his elbows. He ran towards Hairat's pavilion, pursued by hundreds of sahirs, their heads smeared with dust and their shirts torn. Hairat's guards flung magic citrons and needles at him, but he remained impervious to magic and turned around to slaughter a few sahirs with his dagger.

Hairat and Mussavir emerged from the durbar pavilion to see what was happening. In his frenzy, Barq ran to Hairat and attacked her with his dagger but a hand materialized and foiled the attack. Barq then threw a pinch of the magic dust on the hand and it vanished. He attacked Hairat again, but this time, a lion sprang out of the earth and roared at Barq, expelling flames from it mouth. Barq threw another pinch of the dust on the lion and it too vanished. Barq thought, 'She is a princess of the realm and will not be killed. Let me get Mussavir instead.'

Suddenly, there was the almighty cry of 'Manam Afrasiyab!' All the trees swayed and hundred of puppets emerged from the earth shouting, 'O enemy of Samri, where will you escape to from the King of Sahirs?' Barq was just about to slaughter Mussavir when he saw Afrasiyab in full regalia, his eyes full of rage. As he descended on the ground, Barq turned around and shouted at Afrasiyab, 'You low-caste haramzadeh! I will not spare you today!' He attacked Afrasiyab with his dagger, but four golden claws materialized to hold it back. Barq simply waved the magic chador and the claws vanished. The King of Magic was very surprised by this and glared at Barq. There was a strong magical force in Afrasiyab's glare and anyone else would have dropped dead on the spot. Barq, however, looked Afrasiyab in the eye and said, 'What are you staring at?'

Afrasiyab was astounded at his impertinence and thought, 'What is happening today? He seems to have acquired magical powers suddenly!' He looked around and saw that Hairat and hundreds of his sardars were lying unconscious, and the rest of the lashkar had fled for fear of Barq. It seemed as if a cruel tyrant had plundered the camp. He was thinking of flying upwards again to attack Barq from a height when Barq rendered him unconscious with a pinch of the magic dust.

Barq then tried to cut his head off with his dagger, but two lions made of fire materialized to attack him. Barq dispelled them with the dust, but two more lions appeared and walked around Afrasiyab, protecting him. Barq thought, 'I cannot waste the magic dust on these lions. This is the Shah of Tilism and he will not be easy to kill.' He turned to attack the sahirs who had returned to fight him. Meanwhile, a golden slave-girl wearing saffron-coloured robes appeared holding a water flask. That vision of beauty sprouted from the earth like a marigold. She revived the Shahanshah, who immediately woke up Hairat and the unconscious sardars.

Afrasiyab then took out an iron ball from his topknot. He had created this ball with his magic and it could overwhelm the greatest sorcerer. He aimed it at Barq's chest, but since the ayyar was wearing the remarkable magic chador, the ball ricocheted back on to Afrasiyab. He hastily read a spell so that the ball sank into the earth.

Afrasiyab then scooped up some dust from the earth and moulded it into the shape of a bird that came to life with a spell. Afrasiyab asked the bird, 'Tell us why magic does not work on Barq.' The bird related the story of how Barq had slaughtered the young commander and his family and obtained the magical weapons. The Shah started trembling with rage and threw an iron ball at Barq with seven hundred deadly needles sticking out of it. When the ball did not affect the ayyar, Afrasiyab attacked him with his sword. Barq calmly flicked a pinch of the magic dust on him to render him unconscious again. He then turned around to throw some dust on the soldiers who had rallied to attack him and slaughtered them mercilessly. At that time, the ayyar girls emerged on the scene and attacked Barq with whips and daggers as they cried, 'You scoundrel, what has come over you that you kill so many men today! You wretched man, come to your senses, it is not right to be so cruel! We know that you have the upper hand today, but for your own sake, stop right now. Those who fight Shahanshah cannot survive.'

Barq replied as he continued fighting with the soldiers, 'Ustani, I have come here with the intention of dying. I am warning you not to come near me today! I swear upon my teacher that I am in a mighty rage. If I retaliate, you might lose your nose or ear today, and then you might blame me for showing you disrespect. As it is, my teacher has told me that Sarsar has become very licentious and carries on with young boys. He said that he would not be displeased if I cut your nose off! He is no longer interested in you and says that if you convert to Islam, he will employ you to tend to his cattle!' A humiliated Sarsar attacked him with fresh fervour. She heaped abuses on him: 'You are a dead man! A thousand curses on you and your teacher! With Samri's will, may he drop dead! May a bullet go through you right now! His wives should have their heads shaved off and tend to horses!' She shouted to her companions, 'It will be a disgrace if this trickster escapes from us today. He has killed hundreds of men right in front of our master. We will not be able to face anyone in Tilism and people will accuse us of being involved with ayyars. Our reputations will be in shreds!'

Thus, the ayyar girls fought Barq fiercely. Mussavir had returned to consciousness and ordered his commanders, 'If he is impervious to magic, use conventional weapons to capture him!' His army moved with their lances and swords drawn to attack the ayyar. Barq was now surrounded on all sides and fighting for his life. He began to retreat. When his attackers came too close, he threw the magic dust on them to render them unconscious. Afrasiyab followed his progress and conjured rainfall to revive the soldiers who attacked Barq again. At the same time, Barq was subjected to a ferocious volley of bricks, stones, lances, eggs of unconsciousness, magic coconuts and citrons.

Barq had scattered so much of the magic dust that the casket was now empty and he was left with only the Mehmoodi chador. As Afrasiyab went after him, growling with rage, Hairat said, 'O Shahanshah, please do not go forward. He has made you unconscious twice.' The Shah replied, 'Malika, he cannot take the credit for that. He managed to do so with a unique gift of this Tilism. Return to your pavilion and remove the dead bodies. I will capture this ayyar very soon!' Thus, Hairat, the immoral one, retired to her pavilion with Mussavir and the others.

Afrasiyab, along with the ayyar girls and his whole army, managed to corner a wounded and exhausted Barq. He wanted to escape, but there was no way out as soldiers had surrounded him on all sides. At one point, he took a deep breath and leaped to one side, thinking that he would escape by flashing his dagger through the line of soldiers. He, however, headed straight for a tree and hit his head on an extended branch. He felt dizzy with the impact and fell heavily on the ground. Sahir soldiers fell upon him and black fate showed him a black day. They smothered him with blankets and he thrashed around, but could not escape. The soldiers tied his limbs and hit him harshly as they dragged him before the Shahanshah. Afrasiyab snatched the pouch of ayyari from him and found the casket of magic dust, but it was empty. He was furious and cast a spell on Barq so that he lost the movement of his limbs. Barq cried, 'Shahanshah, be warned! If an ayyar is arrested, his pouch of ayyari stays with him until he is executed. Return my pouch to me or it will not be good!'

Afrasiyab scornfully threw the pouch of ayyari at Barq saying, 'This is useless to me.' He ordered Vizier Sarmaya to keep Barq in captivity and dismissed the rest of his army. They returned to their tents and were at ease while Sarmaya kept Barq captive in a secret place known only to him. Afrasiyab then returned to Hairat's pavilion. He moulded a figure from lentil flour and breathed on the figure. The figure soon assumed the physical form of Barq and started speaking. Afrasiyab had the replica bound in shackles and summoned Hairat. He told her, 'Malika, you can now execute this Barq, who has extinguished exalted luminaries of magic today, in front of those traitors of salt, Mahrukh and Bahar. Make sure that you execute him in such a way as to cause him great pain. Hang his head before his lashkar, and tie the body to your elephant and have it dragged throughout the camp.' Hairat cried, 'Shahanshah, I am so happy that you have captured this rascal. He cut my plait off today!'

Thus, Afrasiyab handed over the false Barq to Hairat and did not disclose to her that the real Barq was with him. There were still some hours until daybreak, but Afrasiyab decided to leave right then for the Garden of Apples with the real Barq and Sarmaya. Hairat tied the false Barq to a pillar in the durbar pavilion and appointed several hundred sahirs to guard him. She then retired to her pavilion to rest. When Afrasiyab reached the Garden of Apples, he tied Barq to a pillar and summoned several Tilismi puppets to guard him. He read an incantation and there was a sudden gale. A treacherous, dark-skinned sahir materialized with flames leaping out of his mouth. He bowed before the King of Magic who said, 'Shareer Jadoo, I assign you the task of handing this prisoner to the keepers of the dungeons of Zulmat.'

Then, the Shah took out the Pearl of Samri that he had taken from Burran and handed it over to the sahir saying, 'This will light your way through the darkness of Zulmat, but guard it with your life! Go to the keepers and say that Shahanshah sends his good wishes and prayers. Tell them that I am satisfied with the way they have guarded Burran. Tell them that they should keep this prisoner in the same dungeon where that girl is imprisoned!' Shareer heard these orders from the impure one and secured the pearl in his belt. He transformed himself into an eagle and as he was leaving, he said, 'Huzoor, release this sinner from your magic!' When Afrasiyab removed his spell on Barq, Shareer clutched him with his talons and flew up into the sky.

The lovelorn sahir

Barq had been rendered unconscious by Afrasiyab. He revived mid-air and realized that he was in the clutches of a monstrous bird. However, he soon succumbed to the low air pressure and became unconscious again. He became conscious when the eagle landed in the ravine of a mountain that was as dark as the night of Doomsday. Barq revived and saw that the eagle had now transformed into a hideous sahir. He saw him holding a pearl that lit up the ravine and the surrounding area with a beautiful unearthly light. Barq was terrified and felt as if his soul would leave his body, but took refuge in the thought of the Merciful and Benevolent One. The sahir walked through the ravine with Barq hoisted on his back. Despite being frightened, Barq began thinking of ways to deceive the sahir. His limbs were lifeless, but he realized that he could move his tongue. Barq thought to himself, 'Even this poor wretch, hideous as he is, must have feelings of love for someone.' To test the sahir's feelings, he sighed deeply and recited some moving couplets of unrequited love.

So beautifully did Barq recite the poem (he was after all Amar's most talented pupil) that a stone would have shed tears at that time. It had the desired effect on Shareer Jadoo and tears began to roll down his scarred, black cheeks. Barq sighed deeply again and said, 'O lovelorn sahir, as I am caught by the chains of love, you are bound by the chains of a beloved's tresses! I am aware of your condition and know how you suffer. But what can I say to comfort you when I suffer from the agonies of love as well?' Looking heavenwards, Barq cried, 'Almighty Helper of all lovers, unite all lovers and for their sake unite me with my beloved!' Shareer was astounded by Barq's insight. He thought, 'This ayyar talks about his beloved at a time when he is going to be thrown into the deepest dungeons of Tilism. He does not seem to be concerned that he might lose his life. He must also be spiritually gifted for he seems to know about my beloved.' Shareer asked Barq respectfully, 'Sir, if you know about my love, you must also know what will become of me.'

Barq smiled benignly and said, 'I know that there is a woman whom you have paid a great deal of money to arrange meetings with your beloved.' Barq had shrewdly guessed that this must be the case as it was traditional in those days to reach one's beloved through a woman mediator. The gullible Shareer laid Barq down on the ground and went around him with folded hands. 'Sir,' he said, 'that is exactly the case. I am convinced that you know all my secrets! Now please advise me as to how I can win my beloved.' Barq laughed and said, 'Wonderful! You have paid the go-between such huge sums while you have tied me in chains and expect me to provide free advice to win your beloved! My limbs are lifeless. I cannot even scratch my body! How do you expect me to even think straight?'

Shareer immediately recited an incantation and Barq's limbs were freed from Afrasiyab's spell. Barq stretched his limbs in relief and thought he would test the sahir's loyalties by casually saying, 'My friend, why are you putting yourself in danger because of me? When Afrasiyab hears about my release, he will be furious with you! Hand me over to the darogha of Tilismi dungeons and take the receipt back for the badshah. Understand this! We people cannot be imprisoned for long. I will escape and return to my lashkar. At that time, you can come to me and I can advise you on how to gain your beloved!'

Shareer thought, 'If he is not prepared to advise me when he is in my captivity, why would he be interested in my affairs once he is free!' He began pleading, 'Sir, you should have mercy on me! Do this favour for me and I will release you. I will make some excuse to the Shahanshah and tell him that the prisoner escaped from me. He is well aware of ayyars and their devious ways and will not blame me!' Barq asked him hopefully, 'And in that case, will you become our ally?' The sahir folded his hands and said, 'I will never come to fight you, but I cannot convert to Islam.' Barq realized that this sahir was too black-hearted to convert and that it was best to get on with his trickery.

He told Shareer, 'I have special *attar* on which holy words have been chanted. After you have helped me escape from Zulmat, you can rub the attar on your face and go home. If possible, show your face to your beloved. If you cannot show your face to her, then send the attar to your beloved through the woman who is acting as the go-between for you. The moment she inhales its fragrance, she will come to you and will herself want to be intimate with you. Enjoy yourself with her and do not let her leave your home. Send a message to her father that his daughter is with you. If she is willing to go home, he can come over to fetch her from your home. If she is not willing, you can ask her father to think of his reputation and marry her off to you.' Barq then took out a glass phial from his pouch and said, 'Rub it on your face now and I can instruct you on how it works!' The sahir eagerly rubbed the attar on his face and inhaled the fragrance. He sneezed a few times and fell unconscious. Barq took the magic pearl from him and went through the now familiar ritual of painting Shareer's face to look like himself. He painted his own face to resemble Shareer's and wore his robes. He then tied the unconscious sahir in a sheet, hoisted him on his back and walked away.

The dungeons of Zulmat

As he was leaving the ravine, Barq saw that the land of Zulmat was dark and dreadful. The road running through it had immense stunted and dried pipal and banyan trees on either side. Barq's heart sank at the sight of cobras coiled at the edge of the road, but he continued walking for several kos. After some time, he saw two hills with sapphire trees that were billowing smoke. This was truly the Veil of Darkness. Two ancient forts stood between the two hills. One was locked and the other had sahirs guarding the entrance.

Barq went to the sahir-guards and asked them, 'Where are Afih Seher and Azhdar Zulmati? Shahanshah has sent me here!' The guards went inside and emerged to pronounce, 'Come with us, Azhdar and Afih are calling you!' Barq followed them into the fort with Shareer hoisted on his back. He saw two sahirs reclining on couches with trays of wine flasks, kebabs and fruit laid out before them. They held colourful goblets in their hands and were laughing as they sipped the wine and picked at the fruit. Occasionally, they leered drunkenly in the direction of the courtyard that would resound with music and melodious singing voices.

The sahirs got up respectfully when they saw Shareer bin Ashrar, companion of Afrasiyab. They made a place for him to sit beside themselves and said, 'Sir, you have honoured us. If we had known, we would have brought you here in comfort. Anyway, now that you are here, you are welcome. Tell us why you are here and what do you carry in this bundle?' Barq said, 'For many days, I have been eager to meet you both in friendship and affection, but could not find a way of coming to Zulmat. By Samri, my heart was anxious to see you again. Anyway, I found a way when the Shahanshah captured Barq Firangi, disciple of Amar bin Ummayyah. You have to keep him in the same place where Burran is imprisoned!'

The sahirs got up as they heard Barq and said, 'We will do as you say! Come with us.' Barq lifted the bundle and went with them. They left that place and went towards the fort that Barq had seen earlier. As he came closer, he realized that what seemed to him like locks from a distance were actually large black cobras coiled around the bolts in such a manner that they looked like locks. The sahirs recited an incantation that made the snakes melt away and the doorway was opened. The two sahirs muttered another incantation so that the pythons that covered the floor crawled to one side. This made the room seem brighter, and they then called out to the false Shareer to enter.

Barq took the name of Allah and walked in. The air in the room was so oppressive that it sent shivers down his spine, but he braced himself and moved forward. A large idol with a huge stone blocking its mouth stood in the middle of the room. Afih chanted words that shifted the stone to reveal a well that was pitch-black. They lit torches and descended into the well followed by Barq, who saw that the room was like a cramped grave. On a torn reed mat sat that flower amongst flowers, the delicate Princess Burran. She was bound in magical shackles and her eyes were wide open as she tried to peer through the darkness. The sparkle of her eyes had vanished like deer in the forest and the colour in her face had flown like the bird of the garden.

Barq rescues Burran

Barq was almost in tears at the sight of the princess, but controlled himself and untied his prisoner. The two sahirs shouted at the princess, 'O ill-fated one, why do you weep at your plight? Now you can weep for those whom you think are close friends of yours. Look, who comes here! Whose black fate has brought him to this place?' Burran looked at the prisoner and recognized Barq Firangi! The two sahirs then asked the false Shareer to revive the prisoner. Barq pretended to read an incantation and sprinkled some water on the prisoner.

The real Shareer Jadoo woke up to find himself in a dungeon and looked around in alarm. That was when his eyes alighted on a mirror image of him. He understood in a flash what had happened and cried, 'O Afih and Azhdar! I am Shareer bin Ashrar, companion of Afrasiyab. Shahanshah sent me here with Barq but this rascal tricked me on the way. He has come here disguised as me. By Samri, do not be deceived by him!' Azhdar and Afih were shocked by this disclosure and looked at Barq in alarm. Barq, in turn, laughed and said, 'Did I not warn you that the moment he wakes up, he will cause mischief? Have you seen how he weaves a web of lies?' They said, 'Do you think we believe anything he tells us even if he says it a million times?' Shareer shouted angrily, 'You useless ones! Does it not occur to you that you can use your magic to know me?'

The two sahirs were now really confused. They looked at Shareer and then at Barq. They had not yet released Shareer from the bonds of magic, in case he escaped. Burran looked closely at the false Shareer and realized that this was really Barq in disguise. She signalled to him that he should not have revived the real Shareer and that he should try and escape as soon as possible. At that moment, Barq laughed and held out the Pearl of Samri in one hand and drew out his sword in the other as he declared, 'Wait you infidels! I am Mehtar Barq Firangi, the illustrious disciple of Amar, the beard-shaver and slayer of kafirs! Have you seen how the one and only God brought me to Zulmat so that I release Princess Burran from your prison? Now you can do no harm to the princess or me!'

When those venal sahirs heard him, they hurriedly cast spells freeing the real Shareer. Barq flashed into action and attacked them with his sword. They conjured a thousand snakes to fall on him, but due to the miracle of the magic pearl, the snakes melted before they reached him. Barq was close to the sahirs and hurled narcotic bubbles at Afih and Shareer, who was now free. They fell unconscious at once and went spinning down to the ground.

Burran called out, 'O Barq, give me the magic pearl. I can use it well to defeat these immoral ones and escape myself!' Barq replied, 'Princess, this Azhdar is still conscious. Let me dispose of him lest he harm you!' He then turned to Shareer, who was struggling to get up. Burran called out, 'Barq, of what worth is this dirty dog Azhdar? Afrasiyab himself cannot harm me now and even Afrasiyab's father cannot do anything to me!' Barq finally reached her and handed her the pearl. He wanted to kill the two unconscious sahirs, but Shareer chanted an incantation that made Barq's hand wither to a stump. Shareer then hurled a magic lime at Burran.

Burran, whose chains had melted off by now, blazed, 'You low-caste wretch! You think you have the power to stop me! Afrasiyab's servants are the same as my father's servants!' She exhaled on the lime coming towards her and it split into two parts. One half shot back at Shareer, blasted through his chest and sent him straight to hell, while the other half smashed against the wall of the dungeon and set it ablaze. Burran started producing rays of light from the pearl. One of the rays beamed on Afih and he burnt to death and Barq slaughtered Azhdar with his dagger. When the keepers of the dungeons died, that underground chamber flew up in the air. A few of the sahir-guards fled from the scene shouting, 'Friends, nothing like this has ever happened before in the dungeons!' Others tried to stop Burran from escaping, but she cut the pearl and made a sign so that its rays sliced the guards into two pieces. The Veil of Darkness resounded with the sounds of their wailing spirits and after some time, whirlwinds transported the corpses of the three dead sahirs to the King of Sahirs.

Burran transformed into a powerful hawk and flew off with Barq in her talons. She descended in the same ravine where Shareer had taken Barq and said, 'I will return to my land now. I will need a gift from the Dome of Samri to punish this wretched Afrasiyab for the way he has treated me! If I do not destroy the Bridge of Smoke one day, you can change my name! You should make your way back to lashkar now. Once the corpses of the keepers reach Afrasiyab, he will begin looking out for you. Convey my greetings to Khwaja sahib and the others. If you meet the nazims of my Tilism, give them this message—the princess is disappointed that you did not lift a finger to rescue her! Tell them that they should kill this wretched Afrasiyab or lose their lives. Otherwise, they should return to their lands. When I return, I will reward the brave amongst them and punish the cowardly!'

Barq smiled at the hawk princess and said, 'I have not eaten since Afrasiyab captured me. Can we rest a while before we leave?' Burran felt very contrite and changed from a hawk into her real self. She conjured floor seating in the ravine and said, 'O Barq, you have done what no one else could have. I am immensely grateful and will reward you so well that this whole world and the universe will be envious of your rank and status!' She was about to use her magic to send for refreshments when Barq stopped her and took out some sheermal bread and kebabs from his pouch of ayyari. After they had eaten their fill, he produced a flask of wine and they sipped it at leisure. They rested for some time and then left in different directions.

The execution of the false Barq

Now hear about what happened to the false Barq. The reader will recall that Afrasiyab had moulded an effigy of Barq and handed him over to Hairat. She sent for her companions Yakut and Zamurrud, and said to them, 'I have guarded this wretch throughout the night. It is morning now and you should execute this rascal. He humiliated me yesterday. It would have been easier if he had killed me instead! It is better to have one rupee of honour than lakhs of rupees of dishonour! Now go and order the army to prepare and execute this dishonest, ill-fated ayyar Barq before the lashkar of that venal one, Mahrukh!' The Malika's orders were carried out promptly. At the sound of the magic trumpet, thousands of sahirs and sahiras armed themselves and prepared the maidan for the execution. The uproar in the area even shook the foundations of nearby structures.

Now hear about Mahrukh's spies who were in this camp. They reached her durbar agitated and distressed. They bowed their heads humbly and after praying for her life, they said, 'Malika of our time, the best of Mehtars and the most excellent Barq Firangi will be executed by Hairat, the immoral one. A colossal army of sahirs has gathered in the plain for this purpose.' The spies withdrew after saying this, but tears flowed out of Mahrukh's eyes and her sardars wept unashamedly. Mahrukh sounded the magic trumpet and her valiant soldiers who had grown tired of inactivity began readying themselves for battle. They eagerly armed themselves and the platoons and regiments resounded with battle cries.

Hairat was informed of the advance of Mahrukh and her army, who seemed to be coming with every intention of laying down their lives for Barq. She said to her servants, 'Do not wait for the executioners! Quickly go and cut Barq's head off!' A headstrong sahir heard these orders and flew off at once to fall on the false Barq as a bolt of lightning. The executioner standing next to the prisoner leaped out of the way and the lightning flashed back in the sky after decapitating Barq. There were triumphant calls of 'Killed him!'

At Hairat's command the drums of jubilation were struck. Her attendants tied Barq's body to an elephant's hind leg and hoisted his head on a pole in the maidan. The arteries of his neck were still gushing with blood, and since his eyes were open, he seemed to look helplessly at his fate. His light brown hair was covered with blood as if the beautician of death had coloured this brave warrior's hair with henna.

Magic birds wept and informed Mahrukh, 'Malika, Barq Firangi's sojourn in this world is over. He is now a traveller in the Garden of Eden! Hairat's army is celebrating!' Bahar and Makhmoor tore their clothes and a loud lamenting rose in lashkar. The army that was so impressive and resplendent crumpled into a state of grief and despair. Their sorrow overwhelmed them and they struck the drums of mourning. It seemed as if they would break their own heads with the mallet of grief.

24 The Story of Laqa and Afrasiyab, Maimar Qudrat Joins Mahrukh, Amar in Mount Agate

Afrasiyab ordered Zaivar Jadoo, daughter of Malika Saffak, to fight on behalf of Laqa. Zaivar mobilized her lashkar of twelve thousand sahirs and sahiras and left for Mount Agate in a shining procession. She travelled in all arrogance towards Laqa. Laqa was seated on his throne in his usual state of depression when there was a sharp sound in the air, a gust of cold breeze and unseasonal snowfall. Laqa cried out, 'I have summoned my mortal from Tilism!' The air cleared as a throne descended in durbar. Everyone looked in wonder at the beautiful young maiden covered with jewels who sat on the throne. Her gleaming earrings could have shamed the light of the sun. Her bangles and bracelets could manacle the mightiest ones. She wore strings of pearls and her face was fresh and innocent.

She held the hem of her heavily embroidered loose trousers and descended gracefully from the throne to prostrate before Laqa who cried out, 'O mortal one, rise for my blessed curses are upon you!' The young sahira rose and smiled charmingly as she went around his throne and offered tribute of precious gems. Bakhtiarak asked her, 'Princess, what is your gracious name? Are you alone or is your army with you?' She replied, 'Your humble handmaiden is called Zaivar Jadoo. Indeed, I have brought my lashkar as Shahanshah has ordered me to help the divine one!' Even as she spoke, many more thrones and magic birds descended from the sky with her companions, handmaidens and maidservants. They were blessed with the vision of Khudawand and offered their tributes to him.

Bakhtiarak addressed Laqa, 'Ya Khudawand, you create mortals who captivate everyone!' Laqa declared, 'We create beautiful creatures like her to become our honoured wives, but then have a lapse of memory. Once she seals the fate of Muslims, we will make her our honoured companion!' Zaivar merely smiled at these compliments as if a blossom was about to bloom. She sat on a golden couch and a round of roseate wine was served. A war council was held and Zaivar heard an account of the defeats Khudawand had suffered at the hands of the Muslims from Bakhtiarak. She offered words of comfort to Laqa and said, 'Do not lose heart. With your blessing, I will defeat the defiant ones within moments!'

Bakhtiarak retorted, 'Sahib, do not be in such haste! Let us feast on your beauty. Who knows when we will meet again! You know the saying that a boat made of paper is bound to sink in the lake!' Zaivar smiled and replied, 'Malik-ji, do not flatter me so much! Khudawand has created many beautiful maidens like me. Look to your own business! Look sahibs, he has taken one look at my golden skin and lost his senses!' Bakhtiarak laughed and replied, 'Princess, my eyes will remain thirsty for a glimpse of you! O life of this world, do be careful of ayyars. Let me brief you about their deceptive ways before you go into battle. May Khudawand protect you or this beautiful face might be covered with dust.'

The sahira stayed on in the durbar for some more time before she retired to her pavilion. The next morning, when she entered the golden pavilion adorned with jewellery, the sun wore a halo of adoration as it beheld her. She spent the day in durbar and towards evening, she awakened her magic in her pavilion while Laqa ordered his commanders to strike the drum of Jamshed.

The spies of Islam presented themselves before the almighty Shah, bowed their heads, raised their voices in praise of his royal presence and said, 'An ill-fated sahira who is fair of face has come to the aid of the failed Laqa. She intends to confront the righteous men of the highest durbar tomorrow morning.' The Shah asked Emir, 'What is your advice?' Emir ordered Abul Fateh to strike the battle drums. Abul Fateh struck the battle drum with the wooden rod and all the brave ones became aware that the next day was one of swords and arrows. Sardars left the durbar to return to their tents and the Shah retired to the pavilion of the night. The brave ones knew that they were helpless against magic. Let us see what their fate is the next morning—who will be the one to win this confrontation?

Zaivar Jadoo's Tilismi rider

The time came when the victor of the mountains emerged from the East and spread his army of light on Kohistan. Princess Zaivar Jadoo awoke from the dream of death. She led her lashkar of sahirs to the battlefield and disturbed the world with her magic. Sahirs mounted on dragons flew into the fields and tested their magical spirits. They transformed pebbles into mountains and reduced mountains into pebbles. They ignited trees, made rivers boil and caused tremors in the earth. Laqa, the wayward one, sat on a large throne that was mounted on several elephants with Shaitan Bakhtiarak beside him. His army of Kohistanis and Bakhtris lined up behind him, laughing with joy. Thus, when these two sides confronted each other on the battlefield, it was the confrontation of light and dark, of day and night. On the one side were the followers of the Only God with no equals, and on the other, were the followers of the false god. The righteous and the unrighteous faced each other on the battleground.

Princess Zaivar emerged on the battlefield like the shining sun. Emir looked at her face and commented, 'It would be good if Allah had guided her into the fold of Islam. The wealth of her beauty would not have been squandered this way!' Princess Zaivar moved gracefully towards Laqa and once under the shadow of that lowly one's elephant, she sought his permission to fight. That foolish one said, 'Go, I entrust you into my godly care!' Zaivar flew her throne into the battlefield and called out, 'O rebellious mortals of Khudawand, come and confront me!'

In response to her challenge, drums and bugles sounded from the left flank of Hamza's army. Tohmatun Khan of Khawar galloped up to the King of Kings and asked for his permission. The badshah entrusted him into the care of the Pure God. The brave one then swiftly rode out to confront the ill-intentioned sahira. She looked at him and laughed before she turned and called out, 'Are you lying dead somewhere? Why are you not here yet?' A cloud of dust blew in from the desert. As it came closer, a magic rider emerged from within on a Taazi horse. He was armed and swung his lance as he approached Zaivar. When he reached her, he said, 'Princess, I was right here. Do not be angry. I will do as you say!' Zaivar told him, 'This man who stands before me has come to kill me. Dispose of him and if anyone comes after him, kill him as well! These people have made life difficult for Khudawand!'

The rider pulled at his mount's reins and turned around to face Tohmatun Khan. He dug his heels into the horse so that it shuddered and emitted guests of dust from its saddle. The horse kept shuddering till the magic dust filled the air and the world went dark. The lashkar of Islam was blinded by the dust and the Emir also closed his eyes. When everyone opened their eyes again, they were horrified to see that Tohmatun Khan lay decapitated, his body still shuddering in a pool of blood. The earth was depressed where he had dug his heels and it was obvious that he had not died easily. The lashkar of Islam tearfully retrieved that believer's body.

Feroze Khan Khawari confronted the magic rider next. God only knows how much dust was filled in that horse! Every time it shuddered, it would darken the world. Moments later, a decapitated body lay on the earth with its throat cut and eyes open in horror. The magic rider stayed on in the battlefield until evening as members of the clan of Khawar went one by one to confront him and die. After forty warriors of the city of Khawar were executed, the Emir himself decided to confront the rider, but Bakhtiarak was aware of his intentions and quickly had the drums of peace struck.

When Princess Zaivar left the battlefield, the rider also disappeared into the desert. Laqa was laughing in jubilation and showered gems and jewels over Zaivar's head as he turned back for his camp. Emir also turned back with a heavy heart. Zaivar went to Laqa's durbar and was sipping wine when Bakhtiarak said, 'All praise to you princess, that was pure magic! However, you have not prepared for the Great Name. I knew that if Emir appeared, your rider would have been reduced to a mass of lentil flour or if he is a sahir, he would have gone straight to hell!' Zaivar declared, 'Malik-ji, I do not fight the battle of deceit! The sawar is Tilismi and not made of lentil flour! He will not be affected even if Emir comes as he cannot be executed or wounded. You should not worry and have the battle drums struck again. The enemy has a vast lashkar and I would like the matter to be settled quickly!' Bakhtiarak said, 'Princess, do not mention Tilismi rider in the durbar for our enemies are deadly and will not rest until they kill him!' The sahira said, 'Do you think I am mad?'

The next morning, the battlefield resounded with shouts of praise for Samri and Jamshed. Magic lightning crackled over the plain and swept it clean. Heralds rallied the armies. Zaivar sought Laqa's permission to go on to the battlefield and Emir Hamza was about to move forward when Abul Fateh approached him with folded hands and submitted, 'Sheryar, some of us were in the kafir durbar last night when this sahira told Bakhtiarak that the mysterious rider is magic bound and cannot be harmed by you. I beseech you not to go forward lest the Great Name is compromised and the lashkar doomed. Your lowly slave will discover the rider's whereabouts today and take steps to destroy him. Let other sardars fight him this morning.'

Emir decided to stay back and his sardars went on to confront the sahira. Once again, the rider appeared from the desert and his horse shuddered to release the magic dust from its saddle. Several sardars lost their lives by the evening. The sahira did not challenge Emir Hamza by name and nor did Emir himself come forward to fight. At the end of that day, the two lashkars turned back. Laqa was visibly delighted and complimented Zaivar all the way back to his durbar. Emir returned to his camp and rested after a long and difficult day.

The Tilismi rider is destroyed

Abul Fateh had been hiding in the forest in disguise, waiting to follow the Tilismi rider to his hiding place. When the rider returned from the battlefield, he rode to a fresh water stream. He looked around him first and then dived with his horse into the stream and disappeared from sight. Abul Fateh was astounded by this event, but was determined to destroy the rider that evening. He thought hard for a while and then transformed himself into a beautiful woman with lustrous tresses that anyone would be captivated by.

The false maiden went to the banks of the stream. She lifted a few boulders and threw them into the water so that the waters of the stream spilled over the banks. Within moments, the rider emerged from the stream without his horse. He saw the beautiful maiden standing by the bank and cried out, 'O pearl of delight and beloved of lovers, did you throw stones into the stream?' The maiden replied, 'Go away! What is it to you? The person for whom we threw the stones will come himself!'

The Tilismi rider went closer to the maiden and was overwhelmed by her beauty, and the bold and fearless manner of her speech. He said, 'My dearest, this was not a good thing to do! I was sitting in that stream and you threw rocks in it!' That fount of beauty retorted, 'How would I know that even wretched rivers have men living in them? Very well, I will not throw rocks now! Mian, are you hurt? If you are, then you can go ahead and kill me!' She looked heavenwards and cried, 'O lord, punish that rascal who has reduced me to this state!'

The rider asked her, 'Beautiful maiden, tell me, who has caused you to come to this lonely forest and throw stones in this stream?' The maiden sighed, 'Mian, there is no point in hiding my secret from you! I am a resident of Fort Agate and am not lowborn! I am of *uttam* caste, but all that is in the past. There was a young servant boy in my house who was besotted with me and I was flattered by his attentions. He instructed me to leave the house on the pretext of performing pooja. I waited for two days and had to return alone. This evening, he told me to come to this stream and throw stones in it. I expected him to emerge, but instead you came out. Tell me, did you make a similar promise to someone?'

The rider laughed at her innocence and said, 'It is not incumbent upon all lovers to hide in tanks!' He embraced the beautiful maiden and said, 'Beloved, Khudawand saved your honour today or you would have been ruined by that low-caste scoundrel. He is a lowly servant and you seem to be the daughter of a sardar or merchant. He is no match for you! That rascal must have been too afraid of this forest to come here and you are a brave girl to venture here on your own. Understand that he will always deceive you. O fair maiden, only the son of a sardar will be the right match for you. Never give up your honour for a low-caste. I am a sardar of Tilism Hoshruba. Princess Zaivar is a special companion of the King of Magic and I am in her service. She has looked after me well and I have come to fight Hamza. I will cherish you and give you riches beyond your dreams.'

The maiden said, 'I cannot start loving you suddenly. You must court me and come to my house frequently. Perhaps then, one day, I will love you!' The rider fell at her feet and pleaded, 'O light of my life, stop thinking of that servant boy and come to my home!' The maiden protested, 'Everyone must be waiting for me at home. That boy must have gone home as well and if he does not find me there, he will be angry. I love him and if he is annoyed with me, I will die!' The rider said, 'No one will be angry with you! I will get Khudawand Laqa to bring your parents around. He will vouch for your honour.' The maiden cried, 'Whatever happens I will not go with you! You will dishonour me. Mian, have you lost your senses?! Just because you think I am alone, you are taking advantage of me. I am not stupid. My nurse has warned me that men lure women and treat them as wives. Listen, I am not prepared to be a wife to anyone!'

The Tilismi rider was smitten by her innocence. He lifted her up in his arms despite her protests and jumped into the stream. When her eyes opened, she was in a house that was furnished richly with carpets and curtains with a jewel-inlaid bed and masnad seating on the floor. The rider sat on masnad with the maiden close to him and said, 'O light of my life, have a goblet of wine with me and I will take you home soon. I have loved Princess Zaivar for some time, but she is my mistress and I cannot confess my heart's secret to her. Khudawand has sent you to me instead. You are better than her!' He lunged at her and that flower-body cried, 'A curse on your ardour! Let me go home now for I am dying of hunger!' The rider said, 'There is food here. Eat and I swear on your head, I will take you home!' He got up to get the food, but she said, 'Tell me where it is!' He pointed to a shelf where the food lay covered with a cloth. The damsel went to the shelf saying, 'Let me see what you have. If I don't like it, I will not eat!' She inspected the dishes and quietly sprinkled the powder of unconsciousness on the food. The maiden or Abul Fateh in disguise then took the dishes and gracefully placed them in front of the rider, who protested, 'O flower-face, you should eat and I should feed you!' She said, 'Listen, I think I have feelings for you now. If you do not eat from my hands, I will take my own life!'

The rider happily opened his mouth and after a few mouthfuls, felt warm and uncomfortable. 'You continue eating,' he urged the false damsel, 'I will just have a drink of water!' As he rose from the masnad he was overcome by the drug and fell to the floor. Abul Fateh tried to kill the rider with his dagger, but it glanced off his body. Eventually, he heated wax in a container and poured it down the Tilismi rider's throat, burning his heart and liver.

The stream and the house disappeared and Abul Fateh saw that he was near a vast cave in the earth. He went into the cave and saw that all the sardars who had been executed in the battlefield were alive in the cave. The Tilismi rider's horse was tied in one corner and on closer view, Abul Fateh realized that it was made of lentil flour. As a final measure, Abul Fateh frisked the rider's magic pouch and found a magic tablet in it. He took the tablet and returned to the camp with the sardars.

That evening, Zaivar did not have the drums of war struck as the rider had been active for two days and she wanted him to rest. She was confident that he would remain safe from the Emir because of the magic tablet in his possession. She was awakened by the sound of wailing spirits late at night. She chanted a spell to lead them to her pavilion in the form of birds. They cried, 'Princess, a sahira came to the underground house with the rider and killed him!' Zaivar was alarmed by the news and thought, 'It will be difficult for me now!' She wondered who had discovered the secret of the stream. While she was in this quandary, Abul Fateh had already reached the pavilion of Solomon with the released sardars. The Emir had retired to his pavilion, but was overjoyed on meeting his sardars. Robes of honour were bestowed on Abul Fateh and the lashkar celebrated that night.

The next morning, Laqa convened his durbar. Zaivar also came and prostrated in front of him before gloomily sitting down on her chair. Bakhtiarak looked at her and said, 'O flower of the garden of beauty, why has the dew dampened your good spirits today?' Zaivar mumbled, 'Malik-ji, someone killed my rider last night!' Bakhtiarak exclaimed, 'Greetings to you! Did I not tell you that no one can remain alive after harming them? Listen Zaivar, this must have been the handiwork of ayyars. It was either Abul Fateh or Sarhang Kohi!' Zaivar asked him, 'Who is Abul Fateh?' Bakhtiarak then described the ayyars to her and how they operated. Zaivar declared, 'I will arrest that wretch right away!' Bakhtiarak cautioned her not to tackle the ayyar on her own, but she had already vanished from her chair and reappeared in the Islamic lashkar. She saw its splendour and its rich bazaars and looked around for Abul Fateh. As he was in the pavilion of Solomon at the time, she could not find him.

Later, when Abul Fateh left the pavilion, he recognized Zaivar walking through the bazaars. He was astonished and was thinking of approaching her in disguise when she caught sight of him. She waved her hand to paralyze him, changed magically into a panja and hoisted him up in the air. This led to an uproar in the bazaar, but she was soon out of sight. The young sahira landed with Abul Fateh on a mountain. The ayyar opened his eyes and remained silent as he saw his death hovering over him. Zaivar said, 'You ill-fated wretch, may you be destroyed! You did a terrible deed in killing my rider!' Abul Fateh replied calmly, 'Yes I did kill him. What do you want to do about it?' Zaivar exclaimed, 'The sheer nerve of you! Did you not know that the Tilismi rider had a master? Did you not think what the master could do to you?' Abul Fateh said, 'I know this. No one can kill me! I have killed hundreds like you and will kill you as well! I promise you that if you have mercy on me and let me go, I will not harm any other rider that you make!'

Zaivar cried, 'You wily rascal, I am aware of your tricks! Do you think you can deceive me so easily? Sahibs, listen to the rogue! He tells me he will not destroy the next rider I bring! I should forgive him for killing this one! Why should I not kill you right away?' Abul Fateh retorted, 'Everyone forgives two sins. You should let me commit three before punishing me! I have just committed one yet. Why are you so angry?' Zaivar said, 'What admirable advice! You have committed one sin and now want to commit two more before I punish you! You people will never refrain from your deceitful ways!'

Zaivar clutched him at the waist and flew off again. She took Abul Fateh straight to Laqa's durbar and declared, 'Malik-ji, look I have captured him!' Bakhtiarak exclaimed, 'Well done my lioness!' Zaivar then said to Laqa, 'Khudawand, I want to execute him now! What do you say to that?' Laqa nodded, 'He is your prisoner. We give you permission to execute him!' Bakhtiarak added, 'You should kill him as soon as possible. If his supporters arrive from the lashkar of Islam, it will be difficult for you!' Her companions piped in, 'Princess, Malik-ji is right! Kill this rascal right now! He has destroyed our rider!' An attendant who was standing behind Bakhtiarak with a fly-whisk leaned forward and whispered, 'Malik-ji, the world is becoming your enemy! You are advising the execution of Amar's nephew Abul Fateh! This will go around and you might lose your own life in the process. How will you face Amar? This sahira is about to kill him but it would be better for you if you do not witness the execution!'

Bakhtiarak looked up at the attendant gratefully and said, 'You are right!' He made an excuse and left the durbar. The attendant followed him to his tent and saw that Bakhtiarak was curled up in his bed. The attendant removed the sheet from his face and said, 'Malik-ji, why are you so indifferent to us?' Bakhtiarak looked up and on recognizing Sarhang Misri, almost died with fear. He stuttered, 'My pir and guide, what do you want?' Sarhang simply swept his hand across Bakhtiarak's face and rendered him unconscious. He shaved Shaitan's beard and blackened his face before pushing him under the bed. He then transformed into Bakhtiarak and wore his robes. He hastened back to the durbar, held Zaivar's hand and whispered, 'Hear what I have to say before killing this ayyar!'

When Zaivar went into a huddle with him, Sarhang whispered again, 'Princess, do we want to kill the enemy or do we want to publicize his execution? If you will do this in the durbar, you will court danger. There are ayyars present here who will smash your skull before you kill him. Take him into a tent and kill him there!' Zaivar whispered back, 'Shaitan of Khudawand, you are wise! This is why Khudawand has bestowed this title on you. This is why you can say whatever you like to him and he does not take offence!' She dragged Abul Fateh out of the durbar and took him into an empty tent. Her companions wanted to follow her, but she stopped them and sent for Shaitan.

She wanted to kill Abul Fateh in his presence, but he advised, 'Remove your spell from him so that he dies slowly!' At that time, the false Shaitan or Sarhang Misri burst an egg of unconsciousness in her face. As she fell and hit the ground, it opened and swallowed her. Sarhang released Abul Fateh who ran out of the tent and disappeared. Zaivar had been absorbed by the earth and revived in its chill to shoot out of it like a bolt of lightning. She found the tent empty and went outside to ask the guards where the Shaitan of *dargah* was. They said, 'He came with you but we have not seen him since!' She looked around for Abul Fateh and eventually returned crestfallen to durbar.

She asked for the Shaitan there, but those people also told her that he was last seen leaving durbar with her. 'Where did you leave him that you search for him now?' they asked her. Zaivar then related the story of how Shaitan had burst an egg of unconsciousness in her face and how she had been saved by her guardian spirits. Everyone looked grave when they heard her and said, 'It seems that Khwaja Amar has returned from Tilism. He must have taken Shaitan as well!'

Zaivar looked alarmed and left the durbar to find Bakhtiarak. She entered his tent and her eyes alighted on Malik-ji who was lying naked and unconscious. Zaivar was abashed and lowered her eyes as she cried, 'People, come and see his state in here!' One guard said, 'Bibi, a sweeper died last night. His corpse must be lying at the back!' Zaivar looked at him angrily, 'You silly wretch, I am telling you to look in the tent and you are talking about dead sweepers!' Eventually, a few people came to the tent and on seeing Bakhtiarak in that disgraced state, they said, 'It seems that someone had a joke at Malik-ji's expense!' They sprinkled water on his face to revive him and the princess said sharply, 'Oye Shaitan, go and put some clothes on!'

Bakhtiarak covered himself by placing one hand on his private parts, the other on his buttocks, and left the tent. After he had washed his face and worn fresh robes, he went back to the durbar with Zaivar and related his misadventures to Laqa, who said, 'O Shaitan of dargah, this was your punishment for your insolence and mischief!' Bakhtiarak replied meekly, 'Khudawand, you are so right! Your slave has got his just desserts, but how is it that your beard was not shaved off today? In the time- honoured tradition, whenever I am afflicted with misfortune, your fortunes also decline and the divine beard is shaved off!' Laqa retorted, 'It is all because of the fate that I decree. You were disgraced and I was spared! Who can control the pen of providence, it moves where it wills!' While they sparred with each other, Zaivar consulted the oracle Papers of Jamshed and learned that Abul Fateh had been rescued by the ayyar Sarhang Misri. The oracle went on to warn her that she should not strut about openly as ayyars would kill her the next time. Zaivar looked ashen as she read this and was as still as a corpse.

Suddenly, a magic slave-boy materialized to greet her and said, 'I have been sent by your esteemed mother, Malika Saffak. This is her nama and I am to take your reply back to her. Princess, I have been with you for two days. I will now inform her that this time Samri saved you from the ayyars, but the next time, you may not be so lucky. I will tell her that her daughter is surrounded by ayyars! Princess, you really are negligent of your safety. Look, even now two ayyars are here waiting for you! How will your life be spared this way?' Zaivar looked to where the slave-boy was pointing and indeed recognized two ayyars. She raised her hands to arrest them magically when they escaped. They shouted, 'Listen, you wretch, we cannot be captured!' Zaivar looked abashed and the slave-boy left the durbar. The two ayyars Sarhang Misri and Abul Fateh returned to Laqa's durbar in fresh disguises, still in pursuit of Zaivar.

Markakul Snake-hair and the magic Egg of Jamshed

Let us leave Zaivar in Mount Agate and meet her mother Saffak Jadoo in Tilism Hoshruba. She had sent her magic slave-boy to guard her daughter and then went to seek an audience with Afrasiyab. She first met Hairat, hoping that she would help her in obtaining permission from the Shahanshah to join her daughter in Mount Agate. She was with Hairat when the magic slave-boy materialized before her and said, 'Malika, your daughter Zaivar will be killed by ayyars!' He then related Zaivar's recent encounters with the ayyars.

Saffak desperately turned to Hairat and said, 'Malika, give me leave to go to Mount Agate. I cannot stay here now. I had beseeched the Shahanshah not to send her as she is just a young girl, but he did not listen to me! Sahib, my daughter is my life. I have not slept or eaten since she left!' Hairat said, 'Bibi, it is up to you, but I have no authority to send you to that place!' One of Saffak's attendants, Markakul Snake-hair, whose tresses were coiled like two pythons, came forward and said, 'If you give your permission, this lowly handmaiden can go and guard Princess Zaivar. I do not need Shah's permission to leave.' Hairat advised Saffak to send the sahira and Saffak replied, 'Very well Markakul, you can go and take your maidservants with you. You can take your tents and items of comfort, but there is no need to take a lashkar as your honourable daughter has already taken one with her.' Markakul declared, 'I do not need to take a lashkar with me. I have something that will not give Hamza any time to fight!' Saffak said to her, 'As soon as I have Shahanshah's permission, I will join you!' Markakul replied, 'Huzoor, I will dispose of the enemy before you reach there!'

Hairat looked at her curiously and asked, 'What do you have that is potent enough to destroy the enemy? We would also like to see it!' Markakul obligingly took out an Egg of Jamshed's hawk that was carefully secured in her hair. She showed it to Hairat and said, 'Huzoor, this has been in our family for generations. If I throw it, it will overturn the earth! If I throw it on the mightiest army, it will be destroyed in moments!' Hairat looked overawed with Markakul's explanation and said, 'Indeed, this is a rare object. Now I am satisfied!' She turned to Saffak and added, 'It seems that Markakul comes from a distinguished magical family! Very well Markakul, you go ahead and when you return victorious, Shahanshah will bestow a high rank on you!'

Thus, Markakul Snake-hair returned to her tent. There, she conjured a throne and left for Mount Agate with her handmaidens, while a magic dragon followed, carrying tents and other equipment. Saffak had told her to spend the night in Mount Lajward and bypass the land of Mirrors to reach Mount Agate and Laqa.

The reader will recall that Chalak bin Amar was in the rebel camp. He had been spying on Hairat's durbar for some time now and when Markakul left, he decided that this was the opportunity he had been waiting for to demonstrate his skills. He left before her and made his way to Mount Lajward at the speed of lightning. Markakul travelled the whole day and reached the mountain in the evening. She pitched her tent in a clean spot beside a stream. Her maidservants arranged masnad seating and she relaxed with a goblet of wine and enjoyed the peaceful scenery.

Chalak observed her arrival from a distance. He decided to kill the wretched sahira and take the Egg of Jamshed from her before she could wreak havoc on Emir's lashkar. He transformed into a beautiful maiden laden with jewels and sauntered past the encampment with her anklet bells tinkling. The false maiden greeted Markakul as she walked past but pretended to be continuing on her way. Markakul called out, 'My dear, where do you come from and where are you going to? You really seem to be in such a hurry! I know that you are wearing costly robes and jewels. I will not snatch them away from you! By Samri, it is not good to be so unfriendly! Stay a moment with us and you can leave soon enough!'

That delicate maiden laid her basket on the ground and went around Markakul with folded hands as she called out blessings. Markakul, who was just a lowly handmaiden in Saffak's durbar, was flattered by this demonstration and felt like her star was in the ascendant. She held the beautiful damsel's hand and cried, 'Do not elevate me like this! Sit with me and tell me about yourself.' The maiden squatted on the ground and said, 'Princess . . .' Markakul interrupted her and said, 'I am no princess! I am handmaiden to Malika Saffak, may she live for a thousand years!' The maiden retorted, 'Well, for me you are a princess! Very well Bibi, now listen to my wretched tale. My husband lives in a village nearby, but he is so cruel and suspicious that I cannot describe him to you!' When Markakul heard this, she said to her, 'Have some wine and stay here tonight. If your husband comes here looking for you, I will have a word with him. I will convince him that he has a flower-body for a wife and even if he is intimate with you once a month, he should consider himself lucky. You are the goddess Lakshmi incarnate!'

That deceiver said to the sahira, 'If you fill a vessel with water, I will add a herb that grows in this very forest. The water will become as rosy as wine. It will taste far better than wine and will be more potent.' Markakul smiled and said, 'Sahib, I would like to see this phenomenon!' The maidservants cried, 'Huzoor why don't we use the juice of oranges for wine this evening?' Markakul nodded and the women quickly squeezed oranges and filled a vessel with the juice. They placed it before the false damsel or Chalak and said, 'Now transform this into wine!'

Chalak skilfully poured the juice into flasks and then poured it back into the vessel. In the process, he stealthily added a reddish powder of unconsciousness. He then poured the juice into decanters and declared, 'Here, the wine is ready!' The women looked at her and said, 'You said you will be adding a herb to it!' Chalak retorted, 'Do you think I will do that in front of you? Just taste it and tell me whether this is wine or not! I know several recipes like this one, you will see!' Markakul cried, 'O auspicious one, if your husband fights with you, I will spend thousands to obtain a divorce for you and keep you with me! Sahibs, she is indeed a remarkable woman. She is an endless source of amusement!'

Thus complimenting the false damsel, Markakul poured the wine into goblets and offered it to all the women present there. She had two goblets in quick succession as the women shouted praises, 'It has a wonderful fragrance and tastes good as well!' After some time, the drug began working on them. One woman closed her eyes and cried, 'Samri, save me!' Another said, 'Why have you closed your eyes? Did you see something?' The first one cried, 'You must be blind! Look, what a huge serpent flies through the air!'

Markakul was wearing an amulet in her hair that was fastened with a gold chain. The woman sitting close to Markakul peered at it and thinking that it was a centipede, tried to brush it off her mistress' hair. When it did not move, she thought in her drugged state that she should hit it with her shoe. Accordingly, she took off her slipper and hit Markakul's head with it crying, 'Huzoor, there is a centipede crawling in your hair!' Markakul too started plucking her hair frantically. The maidservant shouted, 'People, our mistress has a centipede in her hair!' Chalak laughed and egged her on, 'Really, has the centipede bitten her?' Markakul was by now hitting her head with her slippers and the women rushed to get the imaginary centipede out of her hair. The sudden movement made them dizzy and they all collapsed. Markakul too was dead to the world.

Chalak first extracted the Egg of Jamshed's hawk from her topknot and then sliced her head off with his dagger. When her guardian spirits raised a din, Chalak quickly decapitated the maidservants before they woke up. Their guardian spirits raised an almighty roar and Markakul's attendants, who were some distance away, rushed to see what had happened. As Chalak had already got the magic egg, he thought there was no point in fighting with the servants and bolted from the scene in a flash. The attendants were horrified at the carnage and looked for the killer, but could find no trace of him. Eventually, they travelled back with the corpses of the women to Hairat's lashkar.

The next morning, Hairat had convened her durbar. Saffak and other sahiras were present as well when they were startled by the sounds of wailing. Hairat sent someone to investigate and they returned to inform her that Markakul's attendants were in a distraught state. Hairat sent for them and was startled by the sight of the corpses they laid in front of her. They wept, 'She had camped in Mount Lajward and was killed last night!' Saffak sat in stunned silence and then said, 'Alas, it is as if my mother died all over again! They were all loyal to my family!' Sarsar and Saba Raftar were also present and said, 'Undoubtedly they have been killed by an ayyar!' Hairat consulted the oracle Papers of Jamshed and learned that Chalak bin Amar had killed them disguised as a woman.

She looked at Saffak and ruefully said, 'Bibi, we should not have asked Markakul her secrets in open durbar. These tricksters are always spying here. A son of Amar called Chalak bin Amar heard her and went after her. He is the one who has killed her!' Saffak cried, 'By my faith, until I avenge Markakul's death, I will not be content. These rebels will have to pay the price for such cruelty!' Hairat murmured, 'Well, everyone will do what they can. I only know that this is their victory and our defeat!' Saffak declared passionately, 'If I do not destroy Mahrukh's lashkar, I will lose my name! I will cut this wretched Chalak into pieces and feed him to kites and eagles.'

Saffak then moulded two figures out of wax. She placed two fiendish spirits in their bellies and when they came to life, she ordered them, 'Go and guard Princess Zaivar. Remain alert and if any ayyar renders her unconscious, take her away immediately and do not let her be killed. Keep me informed about her welfare.' The puppets flew off to Mount Agate.

Saffak Jadoo confronts the rebel army

The archivists of the annals of valour and courage record this war on the arena of paper this way. The gallant Malika Mahrukh came forth to confront the lashkar of the unworthy Saffak. Magic lightning cleared the bushes and thorns off the battleground, rain clouds burst to settle the dust and the armies settled into battle formations. Battle drums were struck and heralds were called out. Saffak, mounted on her magic dragon, confronted Mahrukh's lashkar. She ordered the commander of her forces, Harmurz Jadoo to start the battle.

Harmurz flew his dragon mount into the field. One of Mahrukh's sahirs confronted him, but Harmurz attacked him with his magic sword and sliced that poor man into two halves. Mahrukh stood on her throne and flung a magic citron towards Saffak. She retaliated with a lime so that Mahrukh's citron cooled down and fell. The lime flew straight at Mahrukh. However, she foiled it with a defensive spell and shot an arrow at Saffak, who knocked in the air, causing a panja to materialize with a knife and cut Mahrukh's arrow.

Saffak then moved forward and called out, 'O Mahrukh, watch what havoc I wreak on you now! It will be impossible for you to escape from me today. This is the response to your arrow. Who has the time to fight a long battle with you? If your death has come upon you, what can I do about it?' Saffak took out an iron tablet drilled with holes from her pouch of magic. She threw the tablet on the earth and hit it with a citron. The iron tablet vanished and was replaced by an iron wall between Saffak and Mahrukh's armies. The wall was dotted with round holes and stretched out for as far as the eye could see. Suddenly, a volley of arrows burst through the holes in the iron wall on Mahrukh's army. It was as if the archer of death was taking aim behind the screen. Was it a wall or the firearm of finality? Death came in the shape of arrows and pierced the honest hearts of Mahrukh's soldiers. Within moments there was pandemonium in the army and thousands of Mahrukh's soldiers were mowed down by the magic arrows.

Mahrukh's valiant army was hit hard and the battlelines disintegrated. The army had begun to retreat when a cloud of dust appeared in the distance. The best of Mehtars, the best of the sons of the beard-shaver and slayer of kafirs, Mehtar Chalak bin Amar, dressed and armed with the tools of ayyari, emerged from the dust to see Mahrukh's army being destroyed. Chalak took out Jamshed's magic hawk's egg that he had obtained after killing Markakul. It was then that he noticed the gold letters inscribed on the egg that read, 'If this egg is flung on the mightiest army whose commander is the mightiest sahir, that army will be destroyed and its commander, be he sahir or non-sahir, will be killed!'

Chalak moved towards the iron wall with the egg in his hand and called out, 'Wait you useless and ill-willed, impure and shameless sahira Saffak and you black-faced, mulish, treacherous sahirs! Why do you will your own deaths? Why do you turn this world upside down? I have come! I am the harbinger of your death!' As Chalak leapt close to the wall, Saffak flung a gleaming spear at him. Chalak raised the egg and twirled it around so that it emitted a light as bright as the morning star. The spear fell and the light flashed through the holes in the iron wall like bolts of lightning.

Saffak lost her nerve when she saw the light. She stamped hard on the ground and was absorbed by the earth. Her magic arrows stopped appearing through the holes of the wall and Chalak flung the egg on the wall. There was a thunderous, terrifying sound and it seemed certain that the firmament of the sky itself would burst open. The wall trembled and collapsed. Although it was made of iron, it disintegrated like the dust of the earth. As it collapsed, its particles fell on Saffak's soldiers like iron spears and pierced through their heads and bodies. The air was filled with cries of 'Ya Samri, save us! Ya Jamshed, save us!' As sahirs died, their guardian spirits too raised a din and there were black gales and a hail of stones from the sky.

The valiant lashkar of Mahrukh, the exalted one, moved forward with magical weapons and swords. The sahirs were completely destroyed and each one was shown the cave of doom. As the palace of their bodies disintegrated, the souls that lived within it ran out in alarm. Where could they go? Only the gates of hell were open to them and that was where they took refuge. Chalak decapitated hundreds with his dagger and there was a stampede in Saffak's lashkar, but it was difficult for them to save their lives. Saffak emerged from within the earth after a long time and wept tears of blood as she saw her army's destruction. She took out an iron ball and went for Chalak, crying in great rage, 'Is your name Chalak? You are destined to die young! I fought this battle because of you! How will you escape me now?' Chalak snarled back, 'You shameless wretch, I was looking for you. Come closer so that I can tear your legs apart!'

As the two confronted each other, the earth between them split open and a frail, old woman, ninety years of age, emerged from within. She was the grandmother of the earth itself, ancient and shameless, bent from the waist and holding a stick. Her name was Ghubara Jadoo and she was Saffak's nanny. She pulled Saffak's hair roughly and cried, 'You stupid, ill-fated one, why are you determined to lose your life? Your shoe should not mourn a maidservant like Markakul! Hundreds others like her can be sacrificed for you! When powerful sahirs could not defeat these people, how did you think you could vanquish them? These betrayers of salt have the upper hand now. No one will defeat them! I read the oracle Papers of Jamshed and rushed to save you. I hurt my foot in the process and may have broken my knee! It is true that a foster mother's love is great. Do you not understand that one who has the hawk's egg will also have the ring of Jamshed? Come away and do not face this cruel one!'

Thus, holding Saffak by her hair, the old woman disappeared with her into the earth. Meanwhile, Saffak's camp was in disarray. Most of her army was destroyed—some of them had managed to fly away while others hid within the earth. The ones who survived escaped to Hairat's camp. Mahrukh's soldiers set their tents and pavilions on fire. They plundered the treasury and returned in victory to their camp. Chalak was led to the camp in great jubilation and honoured by Mahrukh.

When Ghubara Jadoo disappeared within the earth with Saffak, she did not emerge from it until she was a good distance from the battlefield. Saffak wept as she saw the dire condition of her army. Ghubara comforted her and took her back to her fort. Saffak mobilized a new army while her daughter was still in Mount Agate, in confrontation with the Emir. We will hear of them presently.

The noble Maimar Qudrat

Shahanshah Kaukab invited Amar to spend a few days in Tilism Nur Afshan to recover from his harrowing ordeal in Afrasiyab's magic Dome of Dread. Kaukab arranged royal feasts for Amar over two days. The third day, after dinner, Amar, Burran and Kaukab sat together watching a nautch performance. After some time, Kaukab dismissed the durbar and spoke confidentially to Amar, 'I had sent a message to my friend Maimar Qudrat, the divine builder, some days ago, but there has been no response from him. If he is angry, we should make amends as it is necessary for him to come here.'

'Badshah,' Amar suggested, 'if you think it is appropriate, perhaps you can send me to him!' Kaukab thought for a while and then said, 'In the wilderness of flowers, there is a place known as the Garden of Jamshed. The Jamshed river flows through that place and that is where Maimar lives. My father Shahanshah Akhtar Jadoo and his father, Tameer Qudrat Jadoo were the best of friends. That is why Maimar and I have been close since childhood. I invited him here as a friend. He is not my vassal or beholden to me for any reason and is a favoured one of Samri and Jamshed. Just as my family has been blessed by Samri with an empire and riches, his ancestors have always been proud of their lineage. O Amar, I have immense faith in his love. I am sure that if I indicate my displeasure at his lack of response, he will come running to me!'

Amar said, 'Sir, in that case, you have to do what seems right to you!' Kaukab of the radiant conscience sent for his writing implements. He inscribed a message on paper with his own hand and stamped it with the royal seal. He moulded a slave-boy from candlewax, breathed life into him and handed him the nama. 'Take it to Maimar Qudrat wherever he is,' Kaukab ordered the puppet, 'and make sure that he is alone when you give it him. Do not let the enemy get wind of this.'

The magic slave-boy set off with the nama and reached the Plain of Jamshed. All buildings and houses in that plain were the fruits of Maimar's imagination. Gusts of magical breeze warned Maimar that Kaukab's messenger had arrived in the area. Maimar exclaimed, 'Kaukab honours us by remembering us this way. We were convinced that he had forgotten us and erased our old friendship from his heart!' Maimar ordered Durban Qudrat, 'Go and bring the messenger to us with all honours. Be warned that he is not to be interrogated or questioned!'

Durban Qudrat went in haste and brought Kaukab's messenger back with him. Maimar rose from his seat and declared, 'Sahibs, in truth, Kaukab the Enlightened is our overlord and ruler while we are his obedient servants!' Maimar opened the nama and read the contents of Kaukab's letter. In it Kaukab reproached him for forgetting their old friendship, briefed him on the situation with Afrasiyab and added that Burran and the army had already fought in Hoshruba. Kaukab concluded the letter by saying, 'O Maimar, we need to consult you on this matter urgently. In the name of our old friendship, trouble yourself by travelling to us as we think of you as one who gives us strength.'

After reading the contents of the royal letter Maimar remained silent for a while before declaring to his companions, 'Afrasiyab has always been arrogant and headstrong. Now he seems obsessed with needless provocation. Does he think that Kaukab is a minor overlord that he wants to destroy his kingdom?' Maimar's kinsmen Durban Qudrat, Benazir Qudrat and Sarshar Qudrat said, 'Huzoor, has Kaukab bin Akhtar sent this nama to you or is this from another badshah!' Maimar retorted irritably, 'Keep quiet! How dare you call him Kaukab bin Akhtar! He has written to me out of the generosity of his heart!' Durban Qudrat sheepishly submitted, 'Huzoor, you and the noble Shah are friends and it is appropriate for you to ally with him in this war!' Maimar pondered for a few moments and then pronounced, 'I have known Afrasiyab a long time as well. What I would like to do is to mediate between the two of them to make them friends and embrace each other again!'

Maimar awarded the messenger slave-boy with the robe of long life and said, 'Go now to your Shahanshah and tell him that I was indeed negligent in not presenting myself to him. I am on my way now.' The slave-boy flew back to Kaukab with the message, who smilingly asked, 'Tell me, did he reward you with anything?' The slave-boy beamed in reply, 'A long life huzoor!' Kaukab then said, 'Very well, go to the wilderness of wonders until I send for you again!' When the slave-boy left, Kaukab and turned to his daughter, 'My child, organize a gathering of comfort and pleasure for Maimar is on his way!'

Burran quickly took responsibility for the preparations. The palace was already quite magnificent and she enhanced its beauty with rare and valuable objects. First she removed the old furniture and replaced it with jewel-inlaid tables, chairs and thrones. She then adorned the palace like a new bride. In the Garden of Jamshed, Maimar prepared to meet his friend after the magic slave-boy left. His companions wanted to accompany him, but he declared, 'No brothers, I am going to be blessed with the vision of my badshah, there is no need for a large contingent. Kaukab knows me well and I do not need to impress anyone. When you all go to Jahandar Shah's durbar, tell him that I have gone to visit a friend.'

Suddenly, a magnificent house floated in. Maimar flew up and as he stepped into the house, it transformed into a bungalow with a garden that seemed to be blossoming in spring. Maimar was last seen sitting on the marble plinth in the garden before it veered up into the sky. Kaukab was eagerly waiting for Maimar when gusts of cool breezes swept through the palace. Kaukab looked at Amar and signalled so that with a loud crack, a wall of crystal materialized between them. Now the palace was divided into two parts with thousands of doors in each half. Kaukab had thoughtfully left Burran with Amar. Burran exclaimed, 'Did you see what a lovely sample of magic that was?' As she spoke, a saffron-coloured cloud with a flame-like glow emerged in the sky to the sound of unseen drumbeats.

Various apparitions appeared in the sky in quick succession. Amar saw a gem of a bungalow float in that was swiftly replaced by a solidly built mansion. It vanished and was followed by an opulent baradari with gold-embroidered canopies and drapes. Within moments, the sky was covered with a row of mansions and then forts with huge battlements and ramparts. It was a strange and wondrous experience to see these structures appear one after the other. When the apparitions came closer to the ground, Kaukab started pacing in his durbar as he knew that these were the signs of Maimar's arrival. Eventually, one of the houses descended slowly. Its bulwarks opened and the sounds of a thousand drums and trumpets filled the air. Kaukab walked out into the courtyard to receive his guest.

The first to emerge were forty Samri worshippers in loincloths, their bodies smeared with ash and molten gold lines drawn on their foreheads. Their eyes were bloodshot and they held braziers alight with coals in their hands. They were apparitions of Maimar's magic for he had left his place alone. A bevy of beautiful maidens who seemed to have dived in the river of beauty and jewels followed, holding badges of rank in their hands. Finally, Maimar emerged, clad in magnificent robes with a string of lustrous pearls around his neck. He saw Kaukab waiting for him in the courtyard and bowed his head in obeisance. Kaukab went forward to embrace him warmly and led him into a baradari.

Maimar did not want to sit on the same level as Kaukab as he was lower in rank and status, but the Shah insisted that he share his masnad and spoke affectionately to his friend. Maimar's servants sat down respectfully on the floor. Kaukab signalled to the cupbearer to serve roseate wine to Maimar.

When Maimar's heart was warmed with the wine, he said, 'O Great Badshah, it is my honour that you have remembered me! I know that you single me out for your royal favours. May Jamshed grant you a long life with all power and might as you appreciate a devoted old servant. Your royal message mentioned that you wish to consult me about the war with Afrasiyab. Tell me, are Shahanshah's servants and Afrasiyab completely at odds or is there a possibility of a truce with him?' Kaukab replied softly, 'O trusted and dear friend, you can try for peace, but I know that he will not agree to it and you will regret it. An augury of his misfortune is that he is fighting the Muslims. A person has invaded his Tilism and is allied with Mahrukh. Because of him, Mahrukh will be victorious even if there are thousand more Afrasiyabs!'

Maimar looked at the Shah in astonishment and asked, 'Who is this man and what is his name? Is he a greater sahir than Afrasiyab from a kingdom larger than Tilism Hoshruba? Which badshah can defeat Afrasiyab? By my faith, Afrasiyab is such a sahir that only Samri can fight him now. Every hair in his body commands a thousand spells!' Kaukab replied, 'Would you not have heard of this man? My brother, Samri himself predicted that he would be the slayer of sahirs. He is one who has urinated on Khudawand Laqa before shaving his beard off! He has destroyed many living gods and lives in Emir Hamza's camp. He has killed the mighty Damama Jadoo and destroyed the godhood of Nimrod. Now he has joined Mahrukh. How can Afrasiyab fight him now?'

Maimar started to tremble and said, 'You are talking about Amar. Badshah, do not even mention his name!' Kaukab smiled at his friend and said, 'Why not? Is his name so inauspicious that you tremble with fear?' Maimar replied, 'No it is not unlucky. He is the enemy of all sahirs! An enemy of Khudawand must be our enemy!' 'My friend,' Kaukab continued, 'he claims that he is not an enemy of Khudawand. In fact, he says that Khudawand favours him and has not destined his death! He is the one who has given him all these powers.' Maimar looked closely at the king and said, 'That may be so, but he is treacherous and deceiving. My heart shivers at his name! It seems that you have met him.'

Kaukab replied, 'I have not met him, but your niece Burran is very fond of him. He is with her right now. Although I have tried to dissuade that girl from this friendship, she will not listen to me.' Maimar looked at Kaukab in utter disbelief and cried, 'For the love of your faith, be open with me! Has this man persuaded you through trickery and deception to ally with him?' Kaukab sighed deeply and said, 'The truth is Maimar that this man went through great hardships to reach me from Hoshruba. He seeks my help, which is why I wrote to you. I have no secrets from you. You will suffer what I have had to endure! Brother, I pretend to be sympathetic and treat him with courtesy, lest he harms me with his ayyari. What advice will you give me? Should I kill him or turn him out of my realm? Should I ally with him or fight him? I will do whatever you recommend!'

Maimar laughed and said, 'Badshah, I am not as wise as you! When you have given him your pledge of support, you know very well that a badshah's word is everything. You cannot agree to help him and then back out of the agreement. If you do, he will publicly denounce you. If you say all this for my benefit and have already made up your mind, I will remain your friend and supporter, whatever your decision. Now, summon him before me. I am curious to see the might and splendour of one who insults Khudawand Laqa to his face and who brings down the kings of this world from throne to sarcophagus!'

Kaukab sent a magic slave-boy to summon Amar who had his ear pressed to the crystal wall all this while, knowing that Kaukab would find a way to bring him before Maimar. Accordingly, he took out a crown studded with pearls from Zambil and placed it on his head, wore a precious robe from the land of Koh Qaf, fastened his gem-inlaid belt and placed a pair of daggers with emerald hilts in it. He wore strings of precious gems and rings of rubies and emeralds in his fingers. Thus, he adorned himself like the king of seven realms and sat in splendour on a masnad with Burran.

The slave-boy arrived and trembled at the sight of this ghastly vision. After greeting Amar respectfully, the slave-boy squeaked, 'O rising sun of ayyari, Shah Kaukab the Enlightened has summoned you, huzoor. If you think it is appropriate, please go soon for he wants you to meet Maimar Qudrat who will not be here for long!' Burran rose and held Amar's hand to lead him into the baradari. She understood Kaukab's signal and called Maimar her esteemed uncle as she greeted him. Maimar responded warmly, 'My child, long may you live. My eyes were looking for you!' Kaukab looked at Amar meaningfully but could not tell him outright to greet his guest. Amar continued to stand in silence.

Maimar kissed Burran on her forehead and made her sit beside him. He then looked up to see the strangest creature he had ever come across. A man with a head like a coconut, cheeks like kulcha bread, tiny cumin like eyes, nose the size of an apricot, a belly that protruded like a drum, abnormally elongated limbs and torso, festooned and adorned with costly jewels and robes. Maimar's first reaction was that this was a divine creature moulded by Samri. He was unnerved as Amar stared hard at him with his beady eyes and stood up in fear saying, 'Ya Samri, save me from peril!' Then he recovered and said, 'Salaam to you as well Khwaja sahib!' You have honoured me by coming here.' Kaukab observed the effect Amar had on his friend and thought, 'Amar must have something in him to overawe such a powerful man.'

Kaukab addressed Amar, 'Khwaja sahib, this is Maimar Qudrat Jadoo whom I had mentioned to you earlier.' Amar said expansively, 'It is my good fortune that I meet you, O Maimar Qudrat Jadoo! After hearing praises of your noble self from Shahanshah Kaukab, I was eager to meet you!' Maimar replied carefully, 'I was also anxious to make your acquaintance. When Badshah wrote to me, I made haste to come here. Come and sit with us.' Amar sat down next to Kaukab without hesitation.

Maimar looked at him and said, 'There is one thing I wish to ask you. Now that Shah Afrasiyab and Kaukab are in dispute with each other, and your turban is caught in this as well, have you thought of a strategy to resolve this issue?' Amar retorted, 'I have tried to behead that monster twice, but he escaped from me. Where will he go? As you know well Maimar, it does not take long to behead someone. One of these days, my dagger will surely slice his throat! Sooner or later, I will kill him, never doubt that.'

Maimar looked stunned and said slowly, 'You are probably right!' Amar saw his expression and took out a paper tucked in his waist. He gave it to Maimar and asked him to read it. On it were inscribed details of the sahirs Amar had killed or humiliated and the episodes in which he had rendered Afrasiyab unconscious. Maimar almost lost his wits as he read the list. He braced himself to say, 'I am sure I will be able to broker peace between you and Afrasiyab.' Amar replied, 'There is no harm in that. We would be quite willing as well—if he agrees to marry Mahjabeen to Asad, becomes a vassal of Sahibqiran and offers half his kingdom and treasure as tribute. He would also have to propagate the True Faith in Tilism. Only then can we consider peace with him, otherwise he is doomed!'

Maimar asked eagerly, 'Whom did you say Mahjabeen should marry?' Amar replied, 'Asad Ghazi who is Tilism Kusha!' Maimar murmured, 'This is the very name that I have heard my elders mention. However, if the magic keystone of Tilism is not found, how can it be conquered? Khwaja sahib, what grieves me is that Kaukab's Tilism will be destroyed for no reason and you will be killed as well!' Amar pronounced, 'I am not destined to die, therefore who will kill me? I have killed thousands of sahirs. I have destroyed cities in Kashmir and Kashgar and killed the sahir Mishmish in his abode under the river.'

Maimar looked as though he was about to faint with these revelations when Kaukab interjected, 'Khwaja, why do you not let Maimar travel to Mahrukh's lashkar?' He whispered to Amar, 'Once he goes there, things will become so complicated for him that he will turn against Afrasiyab on his own!' Amar declared, 'Sir, since you are determined to prove your point and go to Afrasiyab, please do so. Speak to him and see what comes of it. Perhaps that arrogant, proud one will listen to you!'

Maimar conjured a fire-breathing dragon as a mount and after bidding Kaukab and his durbar farewell, he left for Hoshruba. At that time, Kaukab sent a magic slave to Mahrukh Magic-eye with this message: 'We have sent Maimar to you. He is a respected sahir and considers himself as our equal in rank and power. Receive him with full honours and do not let him be harmed in any way.' Kaukab's messenger reached Mahrukh before Maimar's arrival. The sahirs in Mahrukh's camp almost attacked the slave-boy, but he went straight to Mahrukh and delivered Kaukab's message. Mahrukh sat on a flying throne and went some distance to receive Maimar. She insisted that he sit with her on the throne and led him to her lashkar with the utmost respect and courtesy. At the time, ayyars of the lashkar, including Amar's son Chalak, were present in the durbar, as were Bahar and other high-ranking sahiras.

Maimar was lavish in his praise of Mahrukh and declared, 'A hundred compliments for bravely confronting Afrasiyab. However, we will clear the air between you both. We have convinced Kaukab and Khwaja sahib, but we had to consult you as well. Now we will call on Hairat.'

Sarsar kidnaps Maimar, Chalak bin Amar to the rescue

In time, Maimar asked to visit the privy. Attendants rushed to place a jug of water for ablutions in the privy behind the pavilion and led him there. Meanwhile, Mahrukh's entire army was buzzing with speculations about how Maimar Qudrat had joined them and would construct a magic fort for the rebel lashkar. Sarsar Swordfighter was prowling around in disguise in the Islamic camp at the time and when she heard the gossip, she thought, 'If he makes a fort it will be difficult for us; I should capture Maimar!'

She hovered at the entrance to the durbar and when Maimar rose to visit the privy, she followed him. The privy had no ceiling and when Maimar entered it, she managed to jump over the side walls. When Maimar turned around in alarm, Sarsar aimed an egg of unconsciousness straight at his nose and he collapsed instantly. Sarsar then tied him up in a sheet and slashed the tent's cloth to escape. As it happened, there was no one around the privy and she fled to her camp through the wilderness.

When Maimar had not emerged from his pavilion for some time, the attendants went into the privy to check on him and found that he was missing. There was an uproar in the durbar when they heard that someone had kidnapped Maimar. Chalak went to the privy to check and reported back to Mahrukh that he had identified Sarsar's footprints there. Mahrukh was even more distressed and said, 'Alas, what will Kaukab say about this? We should try and rescue him and if possible, we should stop Sarsar on the way itself!' Chalak declared, 'Malika do not worry, I will rescue Maimar and humiliate that wretch Sarsar or you can change my name!'

Meanwhile, Sarsar had managed to reach her own camp, but discovered that Hairat had gone to the Dome of Light. Sarsar crossed the Bridge of Smoke and was told that Hairat was not in the dome, but at a nautch performance arranged outside. Sarsar then went to Hairat and after greeting her, laid Maimar before her. Malika looked inquiringly at her as Sarsar explained, 'I have brought Maimar Qudrat.' Hairat was taken aback by this and exclaimed, 'He is the special companion of Jahandar Qudrat, master of the Desert of Jamshed! Where did you find him?'

Sarsar replied, 'He had come to ally with Mahrukh. Everyone in that lashkar was boasting about how he would build a strong fortress for them.' Hairat said to Sarsar, 'You have done well to nip this in the bud. Do you see the rooms of the Dome of Light? Place him on the bed in one of them, draw the curtains and appoint some guards to watch him.' Sarsar obeyed her mistress, confident that no one would be able to cross the Bridge of Smoke to rescue Maimar. Hairat then rewarded her with a khalat robe of twenty-one panels.

Chalak bin Amar had already set out to cross the Bridge of Smoke. As he set foot on the bridge, the River of Flowing Blood heaved and its waves rose like bloodshot eyes to glare at the intruder. Each time Chalak took a step, he felt as if was being pushed back a great distance, but soon some unseen power would put him back on course. Fire-breathing pythons and poisonous black cobras lunged at Chalak and the parizads of the bridge hurled iron balls at him while sheets of flames descended from the sky. Chalak remained safe as he was wearing the ring of Jamshed at the time and remembered God with every step he took on that perilous crossing.

Eventually, Chalak reached the other side and saw the Tilismi fort with its massive ramparts, lofty gates and the Dome of Light. Chalak strolled through the heavy iron gates admiring the many wondrous sights as he went towards the dome. He was overawed by the magnificence of Hairat's durbar and thought, 'It will be a miracle of Allah if we overcome sahirs like Afrasiyab and princesses like Hairat. What a country! What powers and treasures they have!' That was when he saw Sarsar hovering behind Hairat in her splendid robe of honour. Sarsar, who was alert to any newcomer in the durbar, recognized Chalak ayyar at first glance. As she met his eye, he realized that she had recognized him and quickly ducked out of sight when Sarsar leaned down to warn Hairat of Chalak's presence.

Hairat looked around in alarm, but did not see Chalak and was furious with Sarsar. She shouted, 'You silly wretch, are you drunk or drugged? How do you think Chalak crossed the River of Flowing Blood and how did he throw dust in the eyes of the guards at the gates of Napursan?' Sarsar thought, 'Malika is right. I must be delusional for it is impossible for ayyars to find a way here unless we bring them here. Only Barq has managed to get this far with the magic dust of Jamshed.'

By this time, Chalak had slipped out of the durbar and noticed a house with sahirs guarding it. He strolled over to them and said conversationally, 'How cool this place is! I had to leave the durbar because of the heat inside!' They responded guardedly, 'Brother, in truth, you work for Shahanshah as we do, and we live in the same Tilism, but we have to ask you to leave as we are guarding a special person. Do not take this amiss for we have to obey orders.' Chalak asked them, 'Who is this important prisoner?' When the guards told him the prisoner was Maimar Qudrat, he nodded his head knowingly and said, 'It is good that he was captured. He was making tall claims about making a fort to help the traitors of salt! Brothers, it will be a happy day when all the traitors of salt are captured this way!' Chalak continued, 'Brothers, I will leave! Why should I get you into trouble? It is so hot. Do you mind if I have a drink of water from your pitcher over there?' The guards smiled and said, 'Indeed yes, there is no restriction on drinking water here!' Chalak went to the pitcher and pretended to drink from it while he added the drug of unconsciousness to the water. He called out, 'Brothers, the water is indeed cold and has cooled my heart. Did you add ice to it? Well, Samri be with you! How ungracious you all are that you do not even offer me a smoke! If you have coals, I have tobacco and marijuana on me!'

Some of the guards were also marijuana addicts and they called out, 'Brother, come back. We will give you the coals!' They reassured the other guards, 'The prisoner is inside. What can he do to him when we are on guard?' The other guards were silent while the addicts beckoned Chalak to sit with them. He took out a pouch and opened it to show them the marijuana, boasting that it was the finest crop from Kashmir. Chalak arranged the marijuana leaves on their hookah and offered it to them. There was much banter as he insisted that the others guards should smoke it as well. After some time, they felt dryness in their throats and consumed vast amounts of drugged water from the pitcher. In no time, they all fell unconscious after sneezing.

Chalak entered the house and painted his face to look like Sarsar. He wrapped the unconscious Maimar in pushtara and left the house through another door. The guards at the back were surprised to see Sarsar and asked, 'How did you get into the house?' Chalak made up a story, 'The gods have given us the power to become invisible at times. How else could we overcome sahirs like Maimar? Look, I am taking him now to Malika Hairat!' Chalak then confidently marched away. He came across a number of sahirs guards on the way and was stopped at the gates by some of them who asked him, 'Sarsar, what are you carrying in that bundle?' Chalak replied, 'Malika Hairat has asked me to deposit something in her pavilion at the camp!' The guards persisted, 'But that looks like a man to us!'

Chalak decided to brazen it out and cried, 'Well, of course it is! Do you think we are labourers or thieves stealing treasures that you question us like this? I want to throw this bundle at you for your impertinence! If Malika asks me where it is, I will tell her to get it from her guards!' The guards felt intimidated and sheepishly said, 'Bibi Sarsar, you are right! It is your business to carry people in or out of this place. Please do not be offended and go ahead!'

Thus, the false Sarsar left muttering under her breath. As Chalak moved to the entrance he saw that it had vanished, as had the guards. He thought, 'This place is magic bound. I should consult the magic ring.' He looked at his hand and saw this message inscribed on the ring: 'Chalak, I have brought you this far but I cannot help you escape this magic dome. You will need the assistance of a powerful sahir to leave this place or be doomed to roam here till end of time!'

Chalak was alarmed by this message. At that time, there was also a sudden gale. An outcry in the city of Napursan revealed that the King of Magic had arrived. Hundreds of sahirs rushed out of the dome as a cool breeze swept through the city and a red cloud emerged on the horizon. The sound of bells, kettledrums and conch shells filled the air. Sahirs prostrated on the earth. Some of them fell headlong in their haste; others folded their hands in worship.

Chalak thought, 'I am truly caught now!' He looked around and saw stairs going up on the roof of the house from where he had rescued Maimar. Chalak sprinted up with his pushtara and found the roof deserted. He saw a turret through which he could see Hairat's lashkar and hid inside with Maimar.

Afrasiyab descended directly in Hairat's palace. Hairat bowed in mujra-greeting and offered a hundred and one trays of gold coins and jewels in homage to him. He held her hand affectionately and led her up to the masnad to sit beside him. Sarsar also came forward in her resplendent khalat robe and stood smugly before the Shahanshah, expecting him to award her as well. As the Shahanshah looked at her, she performed a mujra-greeting. He acknowledged it pleasantly and declared, 'Sarsar, you have performed a great deed in capturing Maimar. Go and bring him to me now.'

Sarsar went off with a few sahirs to the place where she had left Maimar. The guards stood up as they saw her and one exclaimed, 'Have you deposited your bundle safely?' The other guard cried, 'Brother, why do you have to ask. When she took it from here, she must have deposited it as well! You should not interfere with ayyars! How does it concern you?' Sarsar cried, 'What are you talking about? What did I take from here?' The guard said, 'You took the one you brought here earlier!' Sarsar lost her patience and shouted, 'Which harlot came here and whom did she take out of here? What are you saying, have you lost your mind?'

The guard said huffily, 'Why are you abusing us and yourself in the process? You are calling yourself a harlot! Even our shoe does not care whom you bring and take away!' Sarsar glared at the guards and growled, 'I will see you later!' She then went to the main entrance where she found the unconscious guards and rushed into the house, only to find Maimar missing. There, she recognized Chalak's footprints. Sarsar went outside to revive the guards and abused them roundly. They were still dazed with the drug and marijuana, and insisted that they had been awake all the while.

Sarsar returned crestfallen to the durbar and related the whole story to Shahanshah. Afrasiyab merely clasped his hands and opened them to release a slave-boy who hovered in the air before him. 'Call out that Chalak should bring Maimar to me!' Afrasiyab ordered. The slave-boy flew up to the Dome of Light and called out loudly, 'Chalak bin Amar, come out from wherever you are hiding with Maimar and present yourself now to the King of Magic!' As soon as he heard the call, Chalak felt the strongest urge to surrender. It was only because he was wearing the ring of Jamshed that he was able to resist the slave-boy's magical orders.

Even then, he was enchanted to the extent that he walked restlessly on the roof. Down below, the city of Napursan was in a state of panic. There were shouts like, 'Friends, close your doors and your shops! Once Barq had come here and plundered our shops! This time some Chalak is here. He is bound to live up to his name!'

Palace sentries spread out to stand guard on private houses, shutters were pulled down in shops and people were fleeing the city. Chalak thought, 'I am really in trouble now!' He remembered what the ring had said about a powerful sahir and thought, 'Maimar is a powerful sahir and he is with me. Perhaps he might help us escape!' He ran back to the turret and took Maimar out of pushtara to revive him. Maimar opened his eyes and saw that was in what appeared to be a turret with an ayyar from Mahrukh's lashkar bending over him. He murmured, 'What is going on?' Chalak explained how Sarsar had kidnapped him. 'I have done what I could Maimar,' Chalak added, 'but it is up to you to get us both out of here or we will both lose our lives. The doors of this dome become invisible if I try and leave this place. Afrasiyab's slave-boy keeps calling out to me magically and I feel a strong urge to surrender!'

Maimar laughed and said, 'Do not worry. I had come to make peace with Afrasiyab, but Kaukab was right. He is a stubborn and arrogant man. He will never listen to anything I say to him!' Maimar held Chalak by the waist and jumped down on the parapet. Hundreds of Afrasiyab's magic slave-boys were looking for the two fugitives and raised a clamour when they saw Maimar with Chalak. Maimar shot up into the sky and called out, 'Tell your master we are leaving!' The slave-boys repeated his words like parrots, 'They are leaving! They are leaving!' Afrasiyab heard the cries and rose up shouting, 'Maimar, you headstrong, black-fated one! Where do you think you are going? Do not think of escaping from me!' Maimar called back, 'You are talking nonsense! It seems that you are so blind with arrogance and false pride that you cannot see anything!' Maimar then flew up into the sky with Chalak and disappeared from sight. The slave-boy now sang a chorus of 'He has gone! He has gone!'

Afrasiyab was enraged at being called arrogant by Maimar and wanted to pursue him. Hairat held him by the waist so that he fell backwards and accidentally kicked her. She thought that the Shahanshah had kicked her deliberately and held her hips as she shouted, 'May this kingdom go to hell and may this union burn in fire! Sahib, you are so out of control that you do not think of people around you! You have actually kicked my womb so hard that by Samri, my back is aching! Do you realize how inauspicious it is to hit a woman's womb?' Afrasiyab immediately became contrite and embraced her saying, 'Dearest heart, it was not intentional. When you pulled me back, I fell and my leg hit you accidentally.' Thus, Afrasiyab cajoled his wife and Maimar managed to escape easily.

Maimar's arrest in the Desert of Jamshed

Maimar left the city of Napursan behind within minutes and reached the River of Flowing Blood. He was a powerful sahir with Tilismi gifts in his command and managed to cross the river, even though towering flame-like waves tried to obstruct him. The magic ring protected Chalak from the bloodthirsty waves. Mahrukh was relieved to see Maimar and was all concern for his recent ordeal. Maimar pointed to Chalak and said, 'If this brave young man had not rescued me, the King of Sahirs would have subjected me to much suffering!' Mahrukh arranged a gathering of pleasure that evening for her guest. Goblets of roseate wine were circulated in the jubilant durbar before the nautch commenced.

After the wine warmed his heart, Maimar declared, 'I have to leave now, but before I go I wish to leave my symbol on this battlefield!' Maimar emerged from the durbar and mounted his fiery python. He flew close to the river and selected a large field for his magic. He took out a white marble ball from his pouch, recited some magical names and smashed it on the ground. A thousand bolts of lightning emanated from the ball and it flashed into the earth with a blast, releasing so much dust that there was darkness all around. Maimar then knocked in the air to dispel the dust and everyone saw a towering minaret with eight tiers soaring up to the sky. Every tier had eight doors and every door had a turret with a man from Habsh blowing a trumpet that sounded like Doomsday.

Once this was done, Maimar took his leave from Mahrukh and the sardars. He flew back to Nur Afshan without looking back or pausing on his journey. Thus, he reached Kaukab in his fort. He met with Kaukab, Burran and Amar and related the story of his ordeal in Hoshruba. He added, 'This is how Chalak rescued me or I would have lost my honour and my life!' Amar asked Maimar guardedly, 'Maimar Qudrat Jadoo, now what do you want to do?' Maimar replied, 'Khwaja sahib, there is enmity between Afrasiyab and myself now. I will definitely fight him! He abused me to my face. At that time, since Chalak was with me and I was in his domain, I felt it was not proper to retaliate and left after some harsh words. Even if all of you make peace with him now, I will never meet him again. I will leave now for the Garden of Gulraiz. The ruler Jahandar Shah, is Jamshed's grandson and the custodian of the living image of Jamshed that talks and gives orders. I will relate all that has happened to Jahandar and submit my case to the living image as well. They will decide my fate. Well, brother Kaukab, may you remain in Samri's protection!'

Kaukab said to him, 'Brother, stay and have some wine and a meal with us and then leave!' Maimar replied, 'I have overstayed my visit as it is. I was due to go to Jahandar's durbar a day before I came here. Give me leave to go now!' Kaukab then said farewell to his friend who returned the way he had arrived, creating apparitions of houses and forts as he went back to his domain.

In Hoshruba, when Afrasiyab saw Hairat looking distressed, he said, 'Hairat, think of this! Amar has done no favour to the ruler of Gulraiz. I send him gifts worth millions every year because he is the grandson of Jamshed and the owner of the living image. When Jahandar Shah hears about this episode, I am convinced that he will be on our side and will not support Amar. It is vital to inform him now so that he arrests Maimar himself and hands him over to me or executes him there. He is Maimar's master and Maimar will never confront him.' Afrasiyab then arranged for gifts worth several lakhs of rupees, jewels and costly robes, four hundred flagons of rare wine from Hoshruba and beautiful maidens. He dictated a nama for Jahandar and selected a messenger to take the nama and the gifts.

Thus, the messenger left Hoshruba when Maimar reached his house in the Garden of Jamshed. Maimar had been travelling for three days and had been captured twice in Hoshruba. When he reached home, he decided to rest and visit Jahandar's durbar the next morning. Afrasiyab's messenger, therefore, reached Jahandar's durbar before Maimar.

Jahandar Shah in the Garden of Gulraiz

When Jahandar learned that Afrasiyab's messenger had arrived, he sent his nobles to receive him. They led him into the durbar with due honour. The messenger performed mujra-greeting before he formally presented the gifts Afrasiyab had sent and held out the nama. Jahandar rose from his throne to acknowledge his greeting and handed the nama to his special companions Qaim and Muqim Jadoo to read out in durbar. Muqim Jadoo read the nama and since he was jealous of Maimar's status in durbar, he read it with relish, emphasizing the negative inflections in the letter.

Jahandar face paled visibly when he heard the contents of Afrasiyab's letter. He addressed the durbar solemnly, 'My brothers, understand this! If Afrasiyab is no longer the ruler of Hoshruba, all of you sahirs will be ruined. The temples of Samri will be derelict with only donkeys to occupy them! What came over the wretched Maimar that he went to Hoshruba? He was heedless of his faith or my wrath!' Qaim Jadoo responded, 'O heir to Jamshed, Maimar is proud and thinks no one is equal to him. We should cut his head off and send it to Afrasiyab!'

Jahandar's durbaris murmured assent and trembling with rage, Jahandar sent his guards to summon Maimar. Maimar realized that something was wrong when he received the summons. He wore his official robes and presented himself promptly in the durbar. As he greeted him, Jahandar turned his face away in anger and said, 'You impertinent one! How dare you go to Hoshruba without my consent and cause mischief. Afrasiyab, the great monarch has complained about you bitterly in his letter!' Maimar responded quietly, 'O Exalted Monarch, Kaukab the Enlightened, Shahanshah of Nur Afshan is my close friend. He had confided in me about his problems with Afrasiyab. I thought I would broker peace between the two kings. I went to Hoshruba with only this intention but Afrasiyab had me kidnapped by his ayyar girl and was ready to execute me. Samri helped me at that time. I was also enraged and erected a minaret to threaten him. I returned here as soon as I could to inform you. I stayed home for a day and was preparing to come here when you sent for me. How am I at fault when Afrasiyab has become so proud and arrogant?'

Jahandar was even more incensed by Maimar's words and shouted, 'You ill-spoken wretch! How dare you express such disrespect for royalty. If he is proud and arrogant, then I am so as well! Your friendship with Kaukab has so turned your head that you think you are equal to kings. You have escaped from Afrasiyab but I will not spare you now!' Jahandar plucked out a pearl from his crown and threw it at Maimar while shouting, 'If this crown is a gift of Khudawand Jamshed, Maimar should be arrested!' Jahandar was the grandson of Jamshed and a powerful sahir. This particular weapon would overcome even Afrasiyab or Kaukab, so Maimar could hardly resist it. He fell down unconscious and Jahandar had him locked in a large iron cage. He ordered Muqim Jadoo, 'Keep him with you tonight. I will execute him tomorrow and will then send his head to Afrasiyab.'

As Muqim rose to obey Jahandar, Qaim Jadoo, who was excited about Maimar's downfall, said, 'Huzoor, I will take him to my house and watch over him!' Jahandar replied, 'Very well, you take him then!' Qaim had the cage placed on a throne and left for his house with several sahirs surrounding the throne, reciting magical mantras. Qaim had built his house like a royal palace and it was lavishly furnished and adorned. Maimar's companions and servants had heard the news of their master's misfortune and wept as they walked alongside the cage on its way to Qaim's house. Maimar called out to them as the cage was being taken inside, 'My friends forgive me if I have hurt you in any manner and if you can, inform Kaukab and Amar of my plight! I will remain in your debt till the end of time!'

Muqim scolded the servants and shouted, 'Why do you endanger your lives by talking to a criminal?' Maimar's companions returned to his house and consulted each other. They decided that they 'could not live in the river and fight with the crocodile'. In other words, it would be dangerous for them if they conveyed Maimar's message to Kaukab and Jahandar got to know about it. However, Maimar had one loyal servant, Shehnaz Jadoo, who thought, 'Even if my life goes in this process, I must return the favour of salt and help in my master's release!' He left the house secretly and made his way to Kaukab's Tilism. Meanwhile, Kaukab, who had been anticipating trouble for Maimar, had appointed magic slaves on the border between his kingdom and the Garden of Gulraiz and had ordered them to remain alert to any call of help. As Shehnaz Jadoo approached the border in the dead of the night he called out, 'O Kaukab! Let me come to you!'

In response, a magic claw grasped Shehnaz by the waist and whisked him off to Kaukab's fort. Shehnaz appeared before the Shah and wept as he related what had happened to Maimar. Finally, he told him, 'Tomorrow morning, he will be executed and his head will be sent to Afrasiyab!' Amar wept as well on hearing this and said, 'Alas! Our dear ones go through such trials on our behalf. If only I could reach the Garden of Gulraiz I would rescue him and play a trick on Jahandar that he will remember for the rest of his life! O Shah Kaukab, if you can help me reach there, then do so in the name of faith and religion!' Kaukab agreed readily and conjured a throne that transported Amar to the edge of his Tilism. There he clasped him by the waist and flew up into the sky. They eventually landed on the borders of Gulraiz. As soon as he put Amar down, Kaukab flew upwards and disappeared.

Amar rescues Maimar

Amar had closed his eyes in the rush of air as he flew with Kaukab. Now that he opened his eyes, he found himself in an eerie and petrifying desert that made his soul ready to leave his body. He braced himself and took a step forward. As soon as he did this, the earth of the desert started churning and produced thick black dust. After that, the wilderness turned a deep shade of red and Amar had to close his eyes again. He opened his eyes again to find that the wilderness was in flames. He prayed to the Almighty for deliverance and noticed that the flames were not real. The hills and slopes sprouted red flowers that gave the illusion of flames. As Amar looked around in astonishment, the flowers opened to release tiny figures that called out, 'O Visitor to the Garden of Gulraiz, where are you?'

Amar realized that he was in danger and could be captured any moment. He took out Galeem and draped it around himself to become invisible. The figures kept calling out to Amar, but their magic did not affect Amar. After some time, the figures rolled on the earth and transformed into colourful birds. The red flowers grew into trees and called out, 'Parizadan of Tilism, why do you want to show the king the sign that leaves no sign!' The birds then flew and perched on the flame coloured trees and sang so melodiously that Amar felt an urge to reveal himself, despite being in Galeem. He recited verses from the Quran to resist their call and continued with his journey. After some time, the birds vanished into the blossoms and the trees too disappeared. The wilderness appeared as before, desolate and dreadful. Amar was still invisible and continued walking as strange voices called out, 'This is a calamity! He is trespassing in our domain and has blinded us so that we cannot see him!'

Thus, Amar continued on his perilous journey. Whenever he emerged from Galeem, the blossoms reappeared and Amar had to quickly become invisible again. Towards dusk, Amar reached a plain surrounded by mountains with rivers running through it. There was a road cutting through the rivers and mountains. A gigantic chain of flames stretched out from one mountain to the other. Flames from the blazing chain were being absorbed by the earth and re-emerged as flaming warrior figurines. These figurines then flew around the chain like birds and were absorbed back into the chain. Amar watched this endless cycle and thought that the flaming chain had been summoned from hell itself. 'How do I get across this inferno?' he speculated as he watched the figurines emerge from the flames, circle the chain and then get reabsorbed into the chain once again.

Amar delved into the garden of ayyari, but could not find the flower of wishes. He dived into the river of deceit, but did not find the pearl of wishes there either. Eventually, Amar explored the wilderness of nature and achieved his purpose. It occurred to him that the blessed ankle-guards of Gabriel could help him jump across the chain! Accordingly, Amar tied the ankle-guards and took a flying leap over the chain of flames. Although it expelled high flames, they did not reach him because of the ankle-guards and he landed unscathed on the other side. No sooner he had landed, there was a mighty dust storm, the desert burst into flames and a dreadful sound shook the earth. Jahandar Shah felt the tremors in his distant palace and raised his hands in prayer to Jamshed in sheer terror.

Amar had taken refuge behind his Galeem during the mayhem and remained safe. Kaukab, who was hovering in the air, marvelled at Amar's courage and flew back to his own land for safety for he was in peril in the land of the living image of Jamshed. When the dust storm and noises abated, Jahandar Shah declared, 'It seems a stranger has trespassed in our land today. How far can he go? He will soon be caught.' Amar saw that all was peaceful now that he had crossed the chain. He disguised himself as a sahir with iron rings in his ears, plain steel bands around his arms and a pouch hanging around his neck. He walked some distance and reached the outskirts of a magnificent city.

Amar walked into the city and asked a man, 'Brother, where is Qaim Jadoo's house?' The man exclaimed, 'Mian, you can see his house just in front of you! It is as high and imposing as Badshah's palace!' Amar found Qaim's house easily and walked in confidently, greeting the guards familiarly. Before they could interrogate him, Amar called out loudly, 'Oye Qaim Jadoo where are you? Come out at once!' Qaim Jadoo wondered who could be calling him out so rudely and hastily emerged from his room to investigate. He was impressed with the sight of Amar in his imposing disguise and folded his hands in greeting. Amar took one look at him and burst into tears. He wept for so long that Qaim became alarmed and asked, 'Tell me brother, how are you here and why do you weep when you see me?' Amar cried, 'I weep for you for any moment you may be dead. I am very fond of you otherwise who would put his own life in peril to alert you?'

Qaim suddenly felt apprehensive at these words and thought that someone in the durbar had turned the king against him. He clutched Amar's arm and whispered, 'Brother, I am grateful to you for doing me this favour, but tell me, what has happened?' Amar whispered back that he could not divulge state secrets so publicly. Qaim then held his hand and led him into his house. Amar looked at the throng of sahirs and guards in the house and said, 'Get rid of these people!' Qaim quickly asked them to leave the house. Amar saw that the house was richly furnished and illuminated, and adorned with precious objects and glassware. A large iron cage was suspended from a hook in the ceiling. Within the cage, the master of sorcery and illusion, Maimar Qudrat, lay huddled in a corner, weeping over his miserable fate.

After the guards had left the room Amar turned to Qaim and slapped him hard on his face. 'You useless man,' he shouted, 'can you do nothing right?' This enraged Qaim, but before he could respond, he crumpled on the floor as Amar's palm was smeared with the unguent of unconsciousness. Amar bolted the door and first stowed away every precious item into Zambil. He then brought Maimar's cage down. Since Maimar had been rendered lifeless with his magic, Amar decapitated Qaim. He did not allow his head to remain on his body for long and sent him straight to hell.

Qaim's guardian spirits wailed while Amar deposited Maimar in Zambil. A mighty gale destroyed the structures Qaim had conjured with his magic and the sahirs in them were buried in the rubble. There was so much noise and confusion that it caused a stampede in the city. Amar ran along with the sahirs shouting, 'Run brothers, we are in peril!' As they approached the gateway, Amar shouted at the guards, 'Have you seen anyone running out of here?' They shook their heads and Amar sprinted out of the gate before they could question him. He kept running until he reached the top of a porcelain mountain in the area and watched the mayhem he had caused in the city.

While Amar was comfortably ensconced in his hideout, the death of the sahirs had caused much panic in the city. Householders had closed their front doors and shopkeepers had drawn their shutters. Jahandar Shah heard the din from his durbar and cried out in alarm, 'Find out what has happened? Has someone been robbed?' His men went off to investigate and returned with the disturbing news of Qaim's murder. Muqim Jadoo rushed to his brother's house and found that most of it had collapsed and the servants had run away. He brought back Qaim's dead body to Jahandar, who declared solemnly, 'It seems that the wrath of Jamshed fell upon Qaim for Maimar's capture. This must be the work of either Kaukab or Amar. No matter, when I report this to the living portrait of my grandfather, he will destroy Tilism Nur Afshan and Kaukab will also die!'

The next morning, Amar left his hiding place thinking, 'I should leave this place now! I will probably have to spend my own money for food. It's a pity that I had to leave the city. I could have worked at a jeweller's shop for a few days. Surely he would have offered me jewels for my labours?' He stopped at the shore of a lake deep in his thoughts when he noticed that the earth beneath him sprouted shoots of grass on its own and colourful flowers blossomed within the grass. Amar was taken aback and feared that he might be captured any moment as sahirs were frantically searching for him and Maimar. Amar said to himself, 'It is best to enlist Maimar's help now for he is a powerful sahir and knows this land well.' He took Maimar out from Zambil and revived him. When Maimar looked at him in astonishment, Amar explained, 'For love of you I came here to rescue you and killed Qaim. Now you have to find a way out for both of us.'

Maimar looked shocked and said, 'Tell me dear sir, how did you reach this place of sorcery and magic? No one can invade this land and no one can escape from here!' Amar smiled and replied, 'I reached here dear friend with the help of Almighty Allah. Only He has the power to enable a humble mortal like me to such a place. He is forever our Saviour and Protector and He will save us as well. Do not now worry about how I got here but think of a way to escape from here.' All of a sudden, there was an ear-splitting sound like an elephant's trumpet. Amar vanished into his cape at once. Maimar was even more perplexed and thought, 'Where has he gone now? Perhaps he is also a sahir. More likely, he is a sahir disguised as Amar to deceive me. How could Amar kill Qaim? It seems impossible!' As he struggled with his thoughts, a sahir who seemed the Samri of his time appeared before him. He was monstrously large and strong with ugly black features and bloodshot eyes. He hurled a lime at Maimar that shot towards him like a ball of fire.

Maimar merely knocked in the air to deflect the ball. This was, however, Jahandar's man and Maimar could not resist him for long. The sahir brought out a chain from his pouch and threw it towards Maimar, calling out, 'Chain of Jamshed, capture this sinner right now!' Maimar resisted with counterspells, but could do nothing against the powerful chain that bound his legs and arms. The sahir then put an arm around Maimar to fly off with him. Just as he was taking off, his eyes alighted on an old grasscutter, bent with age and pitifully frail. He wore a loose turban and a loincloth. His wrinkled skin hung in folds, and his veins and ribs were clearly visible. His head bobbed like a wad of cotton wool as he worked. His hands trembled and the scythe kept slipping as he attempted to cut the grass. The sahir watched him continue with this unrewarding labour and called out, 'Old man, you are foolish! There is no strength in your limbs and you have come out to cut grass at this age! Do you not have a son or relatives who can look after you? If you had provided for yourself in your youth you would not have suffered at this time!'

The old man croaked, 'May Jamshed keep you safe. I have sons, wives and relatives. I have earned vast sums in my youth, but I will not accept any favours or be beholden to anyone. Sahib, there is a limit to what one can give and I am not prepared to share my wealth with my useless progeny! I have a treasure that even Jahandar Shah could not have seen or even heard about!' The sahir was amused and asked, 'Let us see what kind of treasure you have amassed in your youth! Tell me, for I am not your relative and will hardly make a claim on it!' The old man retorted, 'What kind of talk is this? Does anyone ever give details of his wealth that I should tell you? Go on your way! I have wasted precious time in talking to you instead of getting on with my task!' Given the old man's prevarications, the sahir felt even keener to see the treasure. Eventually, the old man relented and said, 'This is for your ears only. I have a pair of sweet zircons. My sons want them, but I resist giving it to them. You may not have seen them, but have you ever heard of sweet zircons?'

The sahir stared blankly at the old man who said, 'Well, you can see them now!' He took out two gems from his loincloth and held them in his hand. The jungle glowed with their radiance. The turquoise of the sky and ruby of the sun seemed to fade before their brilliance. Their lustre dazzled the jeweller of the universe. The sahir looked at them and marvelled at their luminosity. His mouth watered and he cried, 'Old man, if you permit me, can I examine them closely?' 'Certainly,' said the old man readily, 'since they are called sweet zircons you should taste them as well for they live up to their name!' The sahir took the zircons from the old man and turned them around to examine them. He exclaimed, 'Exalted are the ways of Jamshed who has bestowed such a marvellous treasure upon this grasscutter!' He put the zircons in his mouth. When he took them out of his mouth, they shone with a greater lustre and his mouth felt sweetened with their taste.

The old man was actually Amar who had artfully prepared the gems and sweetened them with a deadly poison. After he tasted them, the sahir felt euphoric and cried, 'Respected elder, I will pay you a good price for these!' Amar retorted, 'How can you pay their price? Their price is your sweet life! These gems have taken the lives of many people. Now that you are eager for them, your life is forfeit!' The sahir threw the gems on the ground and lunged at the old man, but collapsed with his legs pointing up in the air. Amar vanished in Galeem, removed the paints of ayyari and appeared in his real form. 'I am the king of ayyars!' he shouted. Maimar watched horrified as Amar killed the sahir by forcing boiling wax down his throat. The sahir died in agony and Maimar was freed from his chains. Maimar immediately clasped Amar by the waist and flew from the area. He told Amar, 'Khwaja, you are a cruel and merciless enemy!' Maimar could not go too far for fear of arrest and hid with Amar in the recess of a cave.

Jahandar and Amar

Meanwhile, whirlwinds transported the body of the dead sahir to Jahandar. Two colourful birds emerged from the sahir's skull and called out, 'O Grandson of Jamshed, he had captured Maimar when Amar deceived him in the guise of a grasscutter!' Jahandar declared calmly, 'It seems that Amar has set foot in our realm. We will have to do something about it!' He left the durbar and went to his sleeping chamber in the palace. There he stood before a mirror that was the height of a man. This was a magical illusion that revealed the past and the future. This mirror of prophecy had portraits of Samri and Jamshed etched on all sides and they seemed to be alive and laughing. The prophecies were inscribed as symbols on the Scroll of Jamshed that unfolded in the mirror. Only Jahandar could decipher these magical symbols. The mirror gleamed brighter than the mirror of the sun and could have rebuked Alexander to his face.

Jahandar went in front of the mirror with his hands folded and focussed on his desire to learn precisely where Amar and Maimar were hiding. He then recited an incantation so that the symbols formed words that read, 'Jahandar, you were a fool to arrest Maimar and encourage Amar to set foot in this realm. Did you think that Amar is someone you can defeat? He is the one who has driven all the living gods from earth to take refuge in heaven. Laqa runs from pillar to post because of him.'

As Jahandar read the text of the prophecy, his blood went cold in his body and he trembled with fear. He braced himself and kept the message to himself. He returned to durbar where a companion asked him, 'Sheheryar, is all well with you? You look pale and apprehensive! Share your worries with your devoted slaves.' Jahandar said, 'Brothers, what can I tell you except that the wrath of Jamshed has come upon me as Amar has invaded my realm. I just cannot understand how he managed to come here, but rest assured, he was drawn by his own death. I am not the grandson of Jamshed if I cannot finish him!' Jahandar then returned to his rooms with his companions and threw a few lentil beans at the mirror of prophecy. The door of the mirror closed on its own and after reading an incantation, Jahandar called, 'Bring Amar and Maimar to me!'

At the time, Amar was chastizing Maimar in the cave, 'O brother, how long will you hide in this cave? I would do better on my own for I would have earned something in the city. Be a man and leave this cave now!' Maimar explained patiently, 'Khwaja, we are safe in here. I cannot call upon my magical powers for three days. It is a long story and one day I will explain it to you. Now pray that we are not overtaken by some hidden peril!' Just as he was saying this, there was a flash of lightning in the cave. Amar reached for Galeem, but he and Maimar were suspended from a flaming chain and flung through the air. Amar cried, 'A thousand pities Maimar. Did I not say we should have left the cave and earned a penny or two?' Maimar thought, 'This man has nerves of steel! He is concerned only with earning money as if he is ignorant of death. He does not seem to care that he is in danger!' As the chain rose higher in the sky, both Amar and Maimar fell unconscious.

There was an uproar in the city. Men and women looked at the sky as the adherents of Islam look out for the new moon on Eid al Fitr. They called out, 'There they go! How tightly that chain holds them!' Others nodded sagely and said, 'The respected ones are caught at last. They will get what they deserve!' The flaming chain transported them across the city and into the royal palace, where it deposited them before the Shah of Gulraiz. Amar opened his eyes and saw that he was in a magnificent garden. The ruler sat on a ruby throne in a marble baradari and hundreds of nobles stood at attention. Amar made a face at Jahandar and did not bother to greet him.

Jahandar said, 'Are you Amar? Are you the one who rescued Maimar and killed Qaim Jadoo?' Amar laughed in response and said, 'Do you have any doubts about that? I can perform all these deeds with my left hand! I am indeed Amar. You cannot detain me here or think of killing me however great a king you think you are! Neither can that bandit of yours Jamshed do anything to me.' On hearing Amar's profane words about Jamshed, the sahirs present in the garden slapped their own cheeks and shoved their fingers into their ears. Jahandar angrily shouted, 'O Ghazabnak Jadoo, present yourself!' The earth in front of the Shah split open and an executioner rose from it with bloodshot eyes and a naked sword. He called out, 'I am present!' Jahandar commanded, 'In the name of Jamshed, swing your sword so that Maimar is executed first!'

The executioner approached Maimar brandishing his sword and crouched to take aim. Amar moved swiftly (Jahandar had released them both from the chain) and after gathering Maimar in the blessed Net of Ilyas, he tossed him into Zambil. There was an uproar as Maimar vanished. Ghazabnak Jadoo asked Amar, 'What did you do with Maimar that he vanished?' Amar remained silent and was about to vanish as well in Galeem, but Jahandar quickly read a spell that paralyzed his limbs and he was unable to move. At that time, Amar looked up in the sky and his eyes filled with tears. Some people asked him, 'Why do you look heavenwards and not give us a reply?' Amar responded, 'I look at the sky because there was a sudden flash of a celestial light. That light took Maimar to safety, but left me here. I know that the light was Jamshed and I am sure he will return to rescue me.'

The living image of Jamshed

Jahandar was quite bewildered and looked at his companions. He said, 'This is strange. This man abuses Jamshed who still seems to come to his aid. I will now summon the living image of Jamshed and find out the truth.' Jahandar descended from his throne and genuflected first, then called out, 'O keepers of the image bring the box of Jamshed hither!' He repeated this refrain several times. Suddenly, there was a thunderous peal of bells and gongs. Within moments, the durbar filled with noble sahirs and parizads holding elaborate fans of Huma and peacock feathers. A virtual sun appeared in the sky, flashing rays of light and there was a shower of pearls and gems in the garden.

Amar called out, 'O Jamshed, Why do you leave me yearning for your blessings? Look how I have been vilified in this durbar!' A sudden burst of gems fell in a heap near Amar and a voice called out, 'No one should take these from our favoured one!' Jahandar looked completely stunned and said, 'Did I not tell you this man must have the backing of the god!' A glittering throne held by four parizads descended from the air. The throne was gleaming with an inlay of gems and held a diamond-studded casket. Strings of diamonds and pearls adorned the casket and garlands of fresh flowers were heaped upon it. Jahandar and his nobles genuflected as parizads laid the throne in the baradari.

After some time, Jahandar looked up and pleaded, 'Huzoor, emerge from the casket!' The lid of the box opened and a disc that shone like a sun emerged. Jahandar laid a hundred and one gold coins in front of the casket. As the disc ascended in the air, a hand-sized statuette arose next from the casket. The statuette laid its hand on the heap of gold coins, signifying that it had accepted Jahandar's tribute. A thousand gongs and bells sounded in the air and sahirs raised cries in praise of Jamshed. Jahandar folded his hands humbly and asked, 'O image of my ancestor, I just want to know where Amar hid Maimar. Was he really helped by your divine power?'

Amar, who was lying helpless on the ground, called out, 'O Image of Jamshed, my salaams to you as well.' The statuette frowned and replied, 'You are a fool that you have brought my chosen one to your land. Maimar is hidden in his Zambil. Listen, we have given him this magic pouch in which there are seven cities and seven rivers. Your whole kingdom can vanish into this pouch along with a few other kingdoms. You will never be able to execute him. You can certainly try, but this was destined by the gods.' Jahandar placed another heap of gold coins in tribute. Once again, the sounds of bells and gongs resounded in the air. The golden disc descended and the stone image went back into the casket. Parizads lifted the throne but Jahandar called out, 'O divine parizadan, wait a while!' He turned to Amar once again, 'Amar, hand over Maimar to me!' Amar replied, 'I do not have him. The statue was lying to you and you believed him?' Jahandar said, I will give you forty thousand rupees if you give Maimar to me!'

Amar readily agreed and he said, 'O Jahandar, I would never have given Maimar to you. Indeed greed for money forces me to do so. Very well, send for the money!' Jahandar had forty sacks of gold coins placed before Amar who said, 'Now release me from your spell so that I can bring Maimar out of the Zambil.' Jahandar had heard about the blessed pouch Zambil from the stone image and readily released him. He saw Amar take out the Net of Ilyas and waited for him to bring Maimar out next. As he watched, Amar threw the net over the sacks. When Jahandar saw the money disappearing, he rendered Amar's hands lifeless again. The sahirs shouted, 'He has taken the money!' Amar laughed, 'If my hands were free I would have taken you all!' Jahandar drew his sword and stood over Amar saying, 'I swear by Jamshed, I will kill you for this!' At that time, there were angry noises from the box and the parizads flew out of the durbar with the throne. Jahandar looked up in fear and withdrew his sword only to be taunted by Amar, 'Why do you stop now? Let us see where your sword lands, on yourself or me!' Jahandar was enraged again and struggled to keep his composure.

Meanwhile, the throne of the living image flew straight to the temple where it was housed. The keeper of the temple was the venerated Aftab Jadoo, adopted son and disciple of the great idol Jamshed. Jahandar Shah accorded Aftab the same respect as his own father. The living image reached the temple and called out to Aftab, 'Go quickly before this dim witted Jahandar kills Amar! We will all be in trouble for Kaukab, Hamza, Chalak and all ayyars along with the Islamic army will leave Hoshruba and attack our land. Prevent him from doing this deed. I tried to stop him by showing my displeasure, but you should go and slap him. Do not, however, reveal the secret that I shared with you about the final victory of the Muslims. Just send Amar to Mount Agate!'

Aftab heard this and vanished from sight. He reached when Jahandar was just about to execute Amar. There was a flash of light in the sky followed by loud boom. The next moment, a virtual sun flashed down into the durbar and blinded everyone. When they opened their eyes, they saw a sahir mounted on a lion. His face glowed like the sun, his body gleamed like burnished gold and flames emanated from his nostrils and mouth. The whole durbar knelt to greet him. Jahandar also bowed low in mujra-greeting. Aftab Jadoo dismounted from the lion, slapped Jahandar on both cheeks and shouted, 'You insolent disobedient wretch! Did you not realize that the living image tried to stop you from killing Amar? The image of Jamshed admonished you earlier and is still angry with you. What has Amar done to you that you want to punish him? If he has rescued Maimar, how does that harm you? If Maimar has converted, he will suffer for it himself. Tell Afrasiyab that you were going to execute Maimar, but Amar came and rescued him. Tell him that now you have nothing more to do with Maimar. Afrasiyab can punish him or forgive him; it is nothing to you. This will not offend Afrasiyab and you will not be party to the execution of Amar, who is Samri's chosen one. You do not know of his stature, but we have read about him in all the divine books.' Amar called out, 'Thank God someone appreciates me! It is true that only an exalted one can recognize my true worth!'

Aftab Jadoo roared with laughter and said, 'Khwaja, you are quite right!' He moulded a clay figurine and order, 'Transport Khwaja in all comfort to Mount Agate in the Garden of Solomon. His master, the gracious Emir Hamza and Khudawand Laqa are both there. We do not have to interfere in their business.' The figurine came to life as it heard these words from the wise and blessed Aftab and put its arm around Amar's waist. Jahandar then removed his spell on Amar and life returned to his limbs. Thus, the figurine flew with Amar to Mount Agate with Maimar Qudrat still in his Zambil.

Marvarid and Sadaf Jadoo in Mount Agate

Let us now turn to Laqa's lashkar in Mount Agate. Saffak's daughter Zaivar Jadoo presented herself everyday in Laqa's durbar. Since her magic rider had been destroyed by ayyars, she had wanted to find a new weapon. The Kohis of Mount Agate were determined to either kill Emir Hamza or die in the next battle. Laqa was also disheartened by his many defeats, but continued to occupy the throne of arrogance. He was sitting and worrying about his future one morning when there was a flash of lightning in the sky followed by total darkness, after which pearls rained down from the sky.

Laqa declared, 'I have destined that one of my devoted beings is coming to sacrifice himself!' A throne descended in the durbar with two hideously ugly sahirs with braziers of live coals in front of them. They wore strings of pearls and other gold ornaments. They prostrated before Laqa and offered nazar. Khudawand bestowed robes of honour on them and offered them golden chairs. Meanwhile, Bakhtiarak went out and assisted their army to settle its war camp. Goblets of roseate wine were soon served in the durbar. When those shameless sahirs were warmed with the wine, they said, 'We live close to Mount Agate and wanted to be blessed with your vision, but never had the good fortune to do so till today. The young mistress Princess Zaivar Jadoo's mother Malika Saffak sent us a message, 'O Marvarid and Sadaf Jadoo, go to Khudawand and protect my daughter from the Muslims!' We have cordial relations with this maiden's mother and could not refuse. Moreover, we were eager to seek your blessings!'

Laqa declared pompously, 'We had also destined that you present yourselves at this time and achieve greatness!' They then asked, 'Khudawand, why have you bestowed such strength and power to these rebellious mortals? Why do you encourage their hostility by having mercy on them so that they are so impertinent and humiliate your devoted mortals? Can you not destine their defeat this time?' Laqa replied, 'These are the mysteries of divine will!' The sahirs looked perturbed and said, 'We had come here to fight on behalf of your divinity and punish these rebels, but if you have not willed their destruction, than we are helpless. Even Afrasiyab will not be able to destroy them!' Laqa replied, 'If we were not merciful, how would they remain alive? I am their creator and if I was angry with them, they would have no place to go! Look, all of you commit so many sins everyday, but I still forgive you!'

The sahirs looked awed by this logic and said, 'What you say is absolutely true. There is no one but you who can be merciful!' Laqa declared, 'However, I am angry with them now and secretly want to destroy them, but I wish to punish them through a chosen mortal so that my reputation will not be damaged!' Sadaf and Marvarid spoke in unison: 'Although we do not have the ability, if Khudawand casts an eye of mercy and generosity on us, we will remove them within moments and the wrath of divinity will destroy them!' Laqa said expansively, 'We entrust all of them to you and you can do with them as you will. In fact, their death will be at your hands!' Marvarid sketched an elaborate mujra-greeting before Laqa and submitted, 'Now that Khudawand has bestowed his benevolence on us, have the battledrums struck in our names and observe our devotion. See how we fight a new kind of battle!'

Bakhtiarak then said, 'We are convinced that you will prevail, but remain on guard against ayyars for they could teach you sahirs a trick or two!' The sahirs left saying, 'Malik-ji, we are not sahirs who can be tricked by ayyars. We will eat them alive!' Thus, both sahirs left for their camp and after dinner, they bathed in pig blood, laid cloves and thorn apples fruits before the sacred fire and awakened their magical powers. At dawn, the exalted Emir was praying in the mosque of Kirpas when the sardars of Islam sent for their mounts to present themselves before the Shah. When the grooms went to the stables, they saw that all the horses had turned to clay. They stood still and forlorn like statues in their stalls. The grooms went wailing to the sardars and cried, 'Huzoor, come and see how the skies have reduced our efforts to dust!'

The Emir had not yet finished his prayers when the faithful Muqbil ran into the mosque and said, 'O Esteemed Emir, we have witnessed that which has never happened before. We have fought with sahirs and non-sahirs, but no one ever targeted the animals and horses of the lashkar. All your sardars will have to fight on foot today for the horses have turned to clay!' The Emir responded calmly, 'Whatever my Provider wills! This is the devilish work of the devils we confront. These treacherous sahirs have caused this phenomenon.' He wore the gifts of the prophets on his sacred person and emerged from his tent. Only his mount, Ashqar Devzad, the horse from Paristan, had not been turned to clay, but his gait was slow and he looked fatigued.

When Emir mounted his horse, there was a clamour in the lashkar and the sardars came to greet their commander. As they performed their mujra-greeting, tears rolled down the Emir's cheeks to see them on foot. So, he jumped off Ashqar to walk with them. Thus, this lashkar with the Shah and the noble Emir reached the battlefield on foot and spread out in orderly formations. From the other side, the entourage of Laqa, the damned, arrived in great pomp and splendour. His allies, the Kohis rode alongside and flashed their teghas. The sahirs Marvarid and Sadaf were mounted on fiery dragons with thousands of sahir soldiers behind. Princess Zaivar Jadoo was resplendent on a throne with her companions and handmaidens milling around. Laqa's throne was tethered on several elephants and stood in the heart of lashkar.

Marvarid saw the sardars on foot and performed a mujra-greeting before Laqa. He looked triumphantly at Bakhtiarak and said, 'Malik-ji have you seen how we have arranged matters? The sardars of Emir have come to the battleground on foot. Today they look truly chastised as before this they were more exalted than those of the highest rank!' Laqa stroked his beard proudly and declared, 'O Chosen Mortals, have you seen how my divine will works?' Bakhtiarak retorted, 'Ya Khudawand, who amongst us jokers denies your divinity? However, hear this from me—if you destroy Hamza's lashkar today, that is good. If not, remember this that these rebellious mortals will occupy Fort Agate and you will have to refrain from divine pronouncements in the future!' Laqa shouted at the Shaitan, 'What nonsense are you spewing?' Marvarid smiled indulgently and said, 'Shaitan of divinity is happy this morning and therefore will say anything!' He then sought Laqa's permission to fight. Laqa pronounced, 'Go then and I entrust you to my divinity!' Upon hearing this, that kafir who was as proud as a donkey flew his dragon on to the battlefield. By this time, the battlefield had been cleared, the armies had spread out in neat formations, and heralds had made their proclamations and withdrawn.

Qasim obtained the Shah's permission with folded hands. Marvarid saw the prince followed by forty thousand men and realized that the Muslims were intent on destroying him. That evil one leaned down to draw a line on the earth between himself and Qasim and called out, 'This prince and his companions should turn to clay as their mounts did during the night!' The next moment, Qasim and forty thousand men turned to clay and stood still. The battlefield became a studio and that sahir artist used magic to create a battle frieze. Emir Hamza's heart twisted when he saw this. He thought of sprinkling water blessed with the Great Name on the clay statues, but it was not possible to revive so many thousand men. Moreover, he knew the clay soldiers were magical illusions and were not real.

Marvarid called out again, 'O Muslims, whoever wants to taste death should come before me!' The sardars of the right row moved forward. The spiritual heir to Hamza Sahibqiran, Landhoor bin Sadaan sought the Shah's permission and swung his mace on the way to the arena. Fifty thousand Hindis moved behind him. Marvarid thought since this man was the powerful king of Hindustan and Hamza's heir, he was not to be vexed for too long. He dismounted, drew a line on the earth and called out, 'O line-maker, Landhoor and his followers should also turn to dust.' Within moments, Landhoor and his men were transformed into clay statues. Emir saw this and wept, but was resigned to his Master's will.

A stream of sardars from the Maghreb and Greece who followed Landhoor were also turned to clay. Finally, that kafir called out, 'O Hamza, have you seen the fate of your supporters?' Emir replied calmly, 'O kafir of evil tongue, do you think you can cower me with your magical illusions? Even with my last breath I will only curse your Khudawand and you!' Marvarid was enraged by these words and called out for more sardars to confront him. Thus, Rumi, Gujarati or Isfahani, all nationalities went to fight him and turned to dust. Bakhtiarak saw this sight and exclaimed with joy, 'Your divinity, you have now decreed the right destiny. Until now we were being punished, but it is now the enemy who is suffering!' Towards the evening Marvarid struck the drums of peace and declared, 'We should leave now. Tomorrow I will find a way of vanquishing Hamza as well and erase the names of these rebellious mortals from the pages of existence!' Bakhtiarak said, 'That is exactly what needs to be done! You are a wise man for unless you dispose of Hamza, the lashkar of Islam cannot be destroyed!' Thus engaged in talk, they returned to their camp. Laqa entered his durbar and sat on the throne of divinity. Marvarid and Sadaf went to the durbar as well and Laqa bestowed precious robes of honour upon them. Cupbearers served wine and the gathering of pleasure and happiness warmed durbar. Meanwhile, Emir Hamza sent the Shah back to the camp and had a tent erected for himself, close to where his men had turned into clay statues.

Sarhang Misri kills Sadaf Jadoo

Bakhtiarak was truly a spawn of Satan and always intent on causing mischief. He said, 'Marvarid, we have heard that Hamza has set up camp in the battlefield tonight. Have you seen how he loves his sardars? It is certain that he will tear us to bits and we should think of what we have to do about him. He is master of the Great Name and is blessed by Harzhaikal, the blessed amulet as well. He is impervious to magic. He is so powerful that he has killed several devs. If you do not plan today, you will see ill-fated day that no one has seen before!' Sadaf Jadoo replied, 'Malik-ji, you are correct. Even if the enemy is weak, it is foolish to be careless and Hamza is a powerful adversary! Very well, I will leave now and capture Hamza after divesting him of the Great Name!' Sadaf took out a jar from his pouch of magic and left for the Emir's camp.

The ayyars of the lashkar of Islam were always spying in Laqa's durbar. When Bakhtiarak and Sadaf had this conversation, Sarhang Misri was present in the durbar in disguise. He slipped out of the durbar and followed Sadaf. When Sadaf was in an isolated area, he called out to him. Sadaf turned around to check who had called him and saw Sarhang, who went to him and whispered, 'It is late at night and you are going into enemy terrain. Be very alert as I fear some ayyar might trick you and cause you harm!' Sadaf said, 'I am quite alert. You can tell them at the durbar that they should be at ease. No one will harm me!'

Then Sarhang said, 'You say you are alert when someone is standing behind you at this very moment!?' Sadaf turned around startled and in that instant, Sarhang caught him in the coils of his snare rope and burst a bubble of unconsciousness in his face. The ayyar then tied him in pushtara and sprinted off with him towards the wilderness. There, he untied the sahir and tried to cut his throat with his dagger, but it glanced off his neck. Sarhang panicked and flung the sahir on his back again, and ran to his own camp. In his camp he saw a breadmaker stoking his oven that was emitting flames. Sarhang flung the pushtara with the sahir into the hot oven and he was burnt alive. His magical spirits raised a din and when he heard their wailing, the baker fled from his shop. Sarhang then went to the Emir and related the whole story. He stated, 'He had intended to make you forget the Great Name, but I sent him straight to hell!' Although Emir Hamza was dejected and depressed with the state of his lashkar, he could not help laughing at Sarhang's account.

Meanwhile, Sadaf's guardian spirits reached Marvarid and wailed, 'Sadaf Jadoo went to Khudawand Laqa's heaven courtesy of ayyar Sarhang Misri!' Marvarid was stunned by this information. His heart tore with grief and his face lost all colour. He roared with rage and took out a magic egg from his hair. He flung it up towards the sky where it burst and began to emit thick smoke that formed a cloud. It spread over the Emir's lashkar, where it burst and its merciless drops rendered every person unconscious in the lashkar. Only the Emir remained conscious. Within moments, there was torrential rain and no one could escape.

Amar and Emir Hamza

To recount briefly, when the king of ayyars, the noble Amar, reached the wilderness of Gulraiz, he rescued Maimar by hiding him in Zambil. The ruler of Gulraiz, Jahandar Qudrat arrested him and intended to execute him. At that time the image of the god Jamshed sent Aftab Jadoo, who stopped Jahandar from carrying out the execution and ordered him to send Amar to Emir Hamza.

A magic panja transported Amar to Mount Agate. Amar found himself on the summit of Mount Agate and saw that Laqa's camp was resounding with the sounds of drums and gongs and the kafirs looked happy and triumphant. The first thought that occurred to Amar was that if the kafirs were celebrating, the lashkar of Islam must be in trouble.

Amar climbed down the mountain and entered the Emir's camp where he saw that thousands of men had turned into clay statues. Amar was startled and then saw that everyone in the lashkar—sardars, soldiers and shopkeepers—had fallen unconscious. Amar was now very alarmed and rushed into the Emir's tent. Inside, he saw the noble Emir standing all alone with his hands raised in prayer, and calling out, 'O Creator of the Universe, you know well that this humble mortal is a lowly functionary of Khana Kaaba. The honour and authority you have bestowed upon this humble servant is due to your mercy and generosity, otherwise I was not worthy of having even one sardar loyal to me. I appeal to you that since you have honoured me earlier, you must maintain my good name. However, you are the Master and I am grateful to you at all times. Do what is in my best interest as I will remain obedient to you.'

Amar heard this speech and could not hold himself back any longer for he was devoted to Hamza. He called out, 'O Master of Amar, this slave is here to serve you!' Emir was overwhelmed when he heard the sound of Amar's voice. He turned around to embrace his old friend and said, 'O faithful friend and supporter, I swear by the One who has created both you and me that I think of you day and night. I wanted to see you again and am grateful to the Provider as at least we could meet in these last day' of my life!' Amar wept as he heard Emir's dejected words and after some time, asked him what had happened. Emir told him about the confrontation with Marvarid.

Later, Amar said, 'Ya Emir, you seem to not have eaten for some time!' Emir Hamza laughed and replied, 'How can anyone in these conditions think of food and nourishment?' Amar retorted, 'Hamza, you eat even if you lose a son! For God's sake, eat something! All these people will be released, they have just been caught by a spell!' He took out kababs and kulcha bread from Zambil and persuaded Emir to eat it. Then he offered him a drugged goblet of wine. Once Emir fell unconscious, he placed him in Zambil.

Amar left for the mountains and rested in a ravine. He sniffed the back of his hand and three hundred and sixty different kinds of deceits were revealed to him. He decided to use one and used the paints and oils of ayyari to look like a holy man with a large moustache. He wore metal hoops in his ears and iron bracelets on his wrists. He tied a loin cloth tightly around himself and held a smouldering brazier in one hand. Thus, looking quite formidable, he headed for Laqa's lashkar.

Amar in Laqa's Durbar

When he was close to Laqa's durbar, he called out, 'O Marvarid, haramzadeh and illegitimate spawn of Satan! Where are you? I will give you such a shoe-beating that you will become part of the floor!' His abuses caught the attention of several people from the camp who gathered around him and asked, 'What sin has Marvarid committed against you that you abuse him this way!' The holy man said, 'That ill-fated wretch does not know that the night emerges from the belly of a lizard and buffaloes lay eggs!' Such nonsensical talk convinced everyone that he was demented. Some went into the durbar to warn Marvarid that an fakir was coming to the durbar, abusing him roundly. Marvarid said, 'Let him come! Perhaps he is a devoted servant of Khudawand!'

Soon, the false fakir entered the durbar, still abusing Marvarid. The sahir stood up respectfully and said, 'Sir, since you are here, come and sit down and refrain from this madness!' The fakir said, 'You are mad and your father is mad! I have come from Laqa and ask you this—who ordered you to destroy the lashkar of the Muslims?' Marvarid smiled and replied, 'Come and sit down and I will tell you. Leave this madness!' The fakir continued shouting, 'Why do you call me mad when you are mad yourself?' At this, Bakhtiarak intervened and said, 'Sahib, do not abuse him. He has achieved a remarkable feat!' The fakir said irritably, 'That is why I abuse him! Why has he not cut their heads off yet? He should finish them off right away!' Marvarid explained patiently, 'First I must seal the Great Name, then I will do as you say!'

Suddenly, Bakhtiarak Shaitan felt a violent throb in his nerve of ancestors under his left rib. He looked around him in alarm and cried out, 'Friends, the wind has changed direction. I am convinced *he* is here!' He stood up and hopped around as he cried, 'O Marvarid, release the Muslims now! The page is about to turn! Within moments, there will be no you and no Laqa!' Everyone in the durbar thought Bakhtiarak had lost his mind and whispered, 'What happened to Malik-ji? He seemed to be fine a moment ago!' Bakhtiarak asked the fakir, 'What is your name?' To which the fakir replied, 'I am called Amar Jadoo!' Bakhtiarak heard the name and almost lost his breath with fear. Amar said, 'Malik-ji, I have to speak to you privately.' Bakhtiarak walked with him to an isolated corner of the durbar, where Amar whispered, 'Malik-ji, how are you?' Bakhtiarak replied, 'I am sustained by your prayers!' Amar pulled his right eyelid down to show his tell-tale mole.

Bakhtiarak lost the rest of his senses and fell on his knees, 'Huzoor, I am your slave! Punish this Laqa for he does not listen to me and continues with his mischief. Also, your lowly slave has kept twenty thousand rupees, twelve thousand gold coins, many jewels and shawls for your eminence. You know that I converted to Islam six months ago!' Bakhtiarak then began reciting the Kalma. Amar said to him, 'Because of you, I will be able to repay some of my debts, but you are a two-faced hypocrite! Listen, you devil's spawn, if you reveal my secret, I will kill you!' Bakhtiarak stuttered, 'The words will not cross my tongue!' Amar then went and sat in the durbar. Bakhtiarak also returned to his seat and called out, 'Peace be on Muhammad and curses on Laqa!' To this, Ansar Kohi asked, 'Why do you abuse our Khudawand?' Shaitan responded, 'It is an ancient tradition. You will say the same thing some day!'

Bakhtiarak signalled to Laqa that Amar had come to the durbar, and gestured angrily, 'What kind of fate did you decree!' Laqa whispered back, 'I could not bear that all my mortals should be killed!' Bakhtiarak turned to Marvarid and warned him that Amar was in durbar. Marvarid looked disbelievingly at Laqa and consulted the oracle Pages of Jamshed that confirmed that the fakir was actually Amar. Marvarid quickly chanted a spell on a lentil grain and shouted, 'Wait you villain, you will not escape me!' Amar sat up in his chair, but the lentil grain had paralyzed his lower body. At that moment, he brought out Emir from Zambil, revived him and said, 'Ya Emir, deal with Marvarid!' Emir Hamza was armed as he had just returned from the battlefield when Amar had rendered him unconscious. He drew out the sword of Solomon and struck the sahir hard, cleaving him in half. There was an almighty roar of spirits and a voice called out, 'You have killed Marvarid Jadoo!' The durbar went dark and Laqa jumped off his throne to flee. The Emir called out, 'Allah is great!' Laqa's sardars too fled from the durbar as Emir pursued them with his sword flashing.

With Marvarid's death, the Islamic army was restored to its normal state. The horses that had been turned to clay also came back to life. The grooms quickly saddled them for the sardars. Those lions of courage and valour mounted them and moved in for an almighty battle. The Emir was fighting Laqa's army all alone when his army fell upon them ferociously. The keeper of the sky trembled with the resounding calls of the brave ones. Mountains and deserts shuddered and the world was darkened by swarms of soldiers. Swords clashed and bodies piled up in the battlefield with rivers of blood flowing everywhere.

The next morning, the Shah of the world sat resplendent on his throne. Amar also presented himself and sat in his chair. All sardars and commanders sat in their allocated seats. The Emir presented Amar with a heavily embroidered robe of honour and the sardars embraced him. Amar embraced Karb Ghazi who asked after his son Asad. Amar replied, 'It is a long story, but Asad is alive!' He then related all that had happened in Tilism with Afrasiyab and Kaukab. The gathering of pleasure was served goblets of wine and entertained by melodious singers and dancers. On the other side, Laqa, in his humiliation, had taken refuge in Fort Agate. His sardars gathered around him and that donkey was made to sit on the throne of divinity again. Sulaiman

Ambreen sent letters appealing to his allies for help and arranged a gathering of pleasure in Fort Agate as well.

༺༻

25 THE TALE OF AMAR AND BAKHTIARAK, AMAR IS CAPTURED BY MAWAJ JADOO AND RESCUED BY MAIMAR QUDRAT

Amar bin Ummayyah disposed of Marvarid Jadoo and spent a day in the gathering of pleasure convened at the pavilion of Solomon. Towards evening, the noble Amar went to the pavilion of Princess Saro Seemtan to meet her. She was Amar's most beloved wife. The princess had adorned herself in anticipation and had arranged a gathering of pleasure for Amar. As he entered the pavilion, the princess went ahead to welcome him; she led him to a masnad and filled a goblet with roseate wine for him. When his heart was warmed by the wine, she said, 'You have come from Tilism after such a long time; what have you brought for me?'

Amar's eyes filled with tears and he said, 'I have come to you especially so that if you have any jewellery, I can take it. O Princess, I am very much in debt for Prince Asad has been in prison in Tilism. I am responsible for a huge army of several million sahirs. I have to give them monthly salaries. There are princes of rank whose salaries run into lakhs of rupees and I have to bear all these expenses. We confront a king like Afrasiyab and it costs thousands of rupees to perform ayyaris. How can I alone bear such expenses? Naturally, I have to borrow the money. If you give me your jewellery, perhaps I can carry on for a little longer!' The princess laughed and said, 'What do I know about your poverty or riches? I am only concerned about my needs! If wives do not get food, clothes and money to spend, how can they live?' She then probed around his waist. Amar exclaimed, 'Alas, women are only concerned about their own needs. Very well sahib, I will give you something!' He took out some rusty nails, old coins, broken utensils and homespun caps embroidered with artificial gems and presented them to her while saying, 'Sahib, take this and be content! If I had known I would be so vexed here, I would never have come to you!'

The princess picked up his offerings and made a gesture of sacrificing them over her head before tossing them away. Then she said, 'I would not foist these even upon my enemies!' Amar hastily collected them and put them back in Zambil. There was a good deal of laughter at his antics and after teasing him for some time, the princess ordered more wine to be served and the night went by pleasantly. The next morning after breakfast, Amar bade his wife farewell and went to the Emir's pavilion. Hamza's wives asked after Badi-uz-Zaman and Asad Lion-heart. Later, Amar met his other wives who also teased him about gifts and expenses. Eventually, Amar emerged from the female quarters and met the Emir and sardars to whom he declared, 'Ya Emir, I am now going to Fort Agate to see how I can return to Tilism. God willing, I will meet you again.' Amar then went around the Islamic camp and met all his ayyar friends. He disguised himself as a barber, wore an *anghrakha* and pyjamas and draped a turban around his head to look like a royal servant. He tucked a box of medicines and unguents under his arm and left for Mount Agate. At the gates, the guards let him enter easily and he made his way through the bazaars to the royal palace where Laqa was holding his durbar.

Shaitan Bakhtiarak suddenly realized that since Amar was in the area, his house could be plundered. He left the royal palace area and mounted a mule to go to his house. Amar saw him leave and called out, 'Malik-ji, my salaams to you!' Bakhtiarak was in such a state of panic that he did not recognize him. 'Who are you?' he asked. Amar retorted, 'Do you not recognize me?' Malik-ji peered at him and Amar showed him his signature mole. Bakhtiarak almost died and croaked, 'Welcome, welcome, your slave will dismount and you can ride instead!' Amar said, 'No. You go ahead and I will be there soon!' As the mule trotted off with Bakhtiarak on it, Amar dashed ahead of it and managed to reach the house before the Shaitan did. He summoned Bakhtiarak's darogha and said, 'Quickly, bring out all goods and money! Malik-ji is on his way!' Bakhtiarak reached the house at that time and the darogha asked him, 'Should I do as this barber says?' Bakhtiarak replied, 'Bring twelve thousand rupees, the silver betelnut holder and all the perfume containers.' Thus instructed, the darogha left for the treasury with a servant. Amar told Bakhtiarak that he would return in a while and followed the darogha. He called out to the servant and told the darogha, 'Sir, please go ahead; I have to speak to this man!'

The darogha hurried on and Amar led the servant to an isolated corner where he burst a narcotic bubble in his face. When the servant fell unconscious, Amar took his clothes off and wore them. He transformed his face to look like the servant and hid him in a ditch. Then he ran and caught up with darogha, who asked, 'What did the barber say to you?' Amar replied, 'Malik-ji sent a message that certain items were to be set aside.' The darogha opened the treasury and told the servant to put the items their master had indicated in an empty trunk. The false servant or

Amar, however, heaped everything on the floor. The darogha said sharply, 'What are you doing? I asked you to place all this in the box!' The false servant snapped, 'I will keep it when I am ready. If you are afraid the goods will be stolen, then so be it!' The darogha pushed him in anger and the servant slapped him hard. Amar's hand was dusted with the powder of unconsciousness and the darogha immediately collapsed. Amar left the heap of items on the floor, but scooped the rest of the goods in the Net of Ilyas.

He returned to Bakhtiarak with the items he had ordered and told him that the darogha was still in the treasury. Bakhtiarak then sent another servant to summon the darogha. The servant went to the treasury and found it plundered with the darogha lying unconscious inside. He rushed back to Malik-ji and told him what had happened. Malik-ji clutched his heart and went to the treasury himself. Finding it empty, he wailed, 'May God destroy that rascal! He has ruined me!' The servant, that is Amar, said, 'Malik-ji why do you grieve this loss? You must have four times the amount you had in this treasury! You should secure the rest of your goods!' Malik-ji looked alarmed and said, 'You are my old, loyal servant and you are right!' He went to another storeroom with Amar following him. Amar's fingers were like keys and he opened the lock easily while complaining, 'Malik-ji, this lock is faulty!'

As they stepped inside, Amar observed that the store was crammed with valuable goods. He said, 'Malik-ji, I have taken a *haveli* on rent. You can use it to store these goods for safekeeping. If you want, I can move them there right away!' Bakhtiarak cried, 'How will you do that?' Amar replied, 'That is not a difficult task. I can even move you there. I am so trustworthy that you will not see whatever you entrust to me till Doomsday!' Bakhtiarak heard him and recognized Amar in disguise with a sinking heart. He called out, 'Please take it. It is all yours and I am your slave!' Amar ordered him to close his eyes and Bakhtiarak reluctantly obeyed him. In an instant, Amar swept up all the goods in the blessed Net of Ilyas. Bakhtiarak opened his eyes to find the room empty. Amar said, 'I am leaving now. The devil will look after you!'

Bakhtiarak ran to Laqa's durbar beating his head and related what had happened there. Amar was also in the durbar disguised as a servant. Laqa was sorry for Bakhtiarak and gifted him gold coins and jewels. He turned to Amar (who was disguised as Bakhtiarak's servant) and ordered him to take the gifts to Bakhtiarak's house with a few men to help him. Amar revealed the mole under his eyelid to Bakhtiarak and said, 'There is no need for any men!' Bakhtiarak cried, 'Take it all! It belongs to you anyway!' Laqa was startled and shouted, 'Oye Shaitan, what are you saying?' Bakhtiarak wept and said, 'I am saying that your fate and mine has been overturned!' While these two talked nonsense, Amar deposited the jewels and coins in Zambil and left the durbar. He was now thinking of a way to return to Tilism.

Amar's arrest in Mount Agate

Now we return to the lowly Afrasiyab, King of Sahirs. Afrasiyab was in his palace, thinking of strategies to defeat Princess Burran in battle when messenger birds dropped before him and transformed into men. They said, 'O Mighty Shah, we have heard that Amar rescued Maimar Qudrat in the wilderness of Gulraiz!' Afrasiyab was shocked to hear this and said, 'Sahibs, it does not seem possible that Amar gained entry into the wilderness of Gulraiz!' His courtiers agreed with him, but Vizier Baghban Qudrat suggested, 'Huzoor, consult the Book of Samri and all will be revealed!' Afrasiyab sent for the ancient book and discovered that Amar was in Mount Agate. He cried, 'Baghban, if I don't believe the book, it negates my faith. If I believe it, I cannot understand how Amar ended up in Mount Agate! The kingdom of Kaukab, Gulraiz and Mount Agate are worlds apart! In any case, let us test the book now!'

Afrasiyab ordered a high-ranking sahir Mawaj Jadoo to capture Amar in Mount Agate and hand him over to Malika Hairat. He gave Mawaj a magic picture that could reveal Amar's real face, whatever disguise he assumed. Mawaj left the Garden of Apples and mounted a magic dragon to head for Mount Agate. After Mawaj left, Afrasiyab went to Hairat's camp. The sound of gongs heralded his arrival and sahirs prostrated before him. Hairat came out to receive him and led him into the durbar pavilion. Cupbearers served him wine and after he was refreshed, he said, 'I have sent Mawaj to capture Amar. The moment he brings him, you have to swear by my head that you will execute him summarily!'

Meanwhile, Mawaj flew straight towards noble Emir Hamza's camp in Mount Agate and looked around for Amar. At that time, Amar was in the wilderness, thinking of ways to return to Tilism. Mawaj saw him sitting alone and looked at the magic picture to confirm Amar's identity. He swooped down in the form of a panja and whisked Amar up into the air. When he reached a great height, he cried, 'You low-caste scoundrel! I should drop you from here!' He shook Khwaja several times and the ayyar cried, 'You monster, am I a man or a lizard that you shake me like this? You will regret capturing me!' Mawaj retorted, 'Shahanshah has sworn that he will not leave you alive this time! Why should I regret anything?' Mawaj then rose up in the sky and Amar had to close his eyes to avoid the rush of air. He flew with the ayyar to Hairat's pavilion, where he landed and said, 'I have brought this sinner!' Hairat had Afrasiyab's orders to execute Amar summarily and ordered Mawaj, 'O Brave Warrior, you should be the one to cut his head off!' Mawaj was standing at Amar's head with his sword drawn when the ayyar awoke. He acted quickly and took out Maimar Qudrat from Zambil to say, 'O that Maimar, this sahir captured me and this is that strumpet Hairat's pavilion. If you don't act now we will both be killed!'

Mawaj was startled by this and lunged forward with his sword. Maimar extended his hand like a shield so that the sword glanced off it. Maimar then slapped Mawaj with his magical hand and his head split open. Mawaj went straight to hell and in the ensuing darkness and mayhem, Amar cut off several sahirs' legs and leaped in the air to cut their heads off. There was an uproar in the durbar and sahirs shouted, 'Surround him! Don't let him escape!' Amar vanished in Galeem and called out, 'Maimar, I am leaving! Follow me!' Maimar had been fighting along with Amar and once he heard Amar, he too flew into the sky.

Following this, Hairat's camp lay in disarray. The spirits of the dead sahirs howled and the skies raged with thunder and lightning. Some sahirs thought of following Maimar, but then thought again, 'This seems to happen all the time here. Why should we put our lives in danger?' Thus, Amar and Maimar easily escaped from Hairat's camp. Just as he was informed of the state of Hairat's camp, Afrasiyab received an urgent message from Laqa that read: 'Marvarid and Sadaf Jadoo have been killed. As for Zaivar whom you had sent earlier, she is so intimidated by the ayyars that she has isolated herself in the desert. Moreover, she is not capable of fighting with the Muslims. It is incumbent upon you to send a powerful sahir in our service as soon as this message reaches you; otherwise, you will have to suffer our extreme wrath!'

Afrasiyab immediately chanted an incantation before exhaling in one direction. Within moments, the skies darkened and there was a gale and rainfall before a sahir materialized on a magic dragon. The ogre-faced sahir performed a mujra-greeting before the Shah, who said to him, 'O Qeher Nigah Jadoo, proceed to our esteemed Khudawand and finish the worshippers of the One God!' Qeher responded, 'Your slave will fight as no sahir has fought before!' After receiving a robe of honour, Qeher returned to his place and mobilized his army of one lakh men. The drums of travel were struck and sahir-soldiers darkened the face of eternity as they moved. Magic bird formations covered the sky with their feathers while lances, spears and tridents flashed in the air. The mighty steeds of the brave ones neighed and snorted while braziers and lamps exuded the light of a thousand suns. Thus, Qeher's lashkar swelled and roared like a river as it moved towards Mount Agate.

Ghubara, Saffak and Zaivar Jadoo

We will leave Qeher and his army here. Now hear about Princess Zaivar Jadoo. Earlier, her mother Saffak had confronted Chalak bin Amar and her foster mother Ghubara Jadoo had dragged her off the battlefield just as she was about to be killed. In her palace, Ghubara tried to reason with her foster daughter, 'My child, you are my strength and the light of my eyes. Do not confront ayyars and the worshippers of the One God. Otherwise, I may have to lament the loss of your life (may my mouth be full of dust for thinking this)! It is not right even for your daughter Zaivar to stay in Mount Agate as the noble Emir has one lakh, eighty-four thousand ayyars in his lashkar. Each of them thinks he is better than Amar. Look at how much trouble Chalak has caused since he entered Tilism!'

Saffak said confidently, 'When Khudawand is in Mount Agate, why should we worry about her?' Ghubara looked frustrated and struck her forehead. 'Alas,' she cried, 'how do I make you understand? Do you really believe in that false god? He is only good for sitting on his throne like a peacock and making idiotic speeches! Only those who do not believe him prosper! I am afraid that Princess Zaivar is in grave danger!' Saffak realized that Ghubara was serious and sobbed, 'Mother, what should I do?' Ghubara said sagely, 'In my opinion, you should distance yourself from Afrasiyab. Despite the fact that you pleaded with him not to send your daughter to fight, he did not listen, nor did he permit you to join her. He wants you to come to grief! Now write secretly to your noble daughter and tell her to return to you at once. Tell her that she should not worry about Shah's displeasure as you will intercede on her behalf. Once she is here, we will explain matters to her and will present ourselves to Mahrukh for we will be safe only with her! I am convinced that Afrasiyab will eventually be destroyed!'

Saffak shuddered and said, 'I cannot become a Muslim! The Shah will kill me!' Ghubara patiently led Saffak to the treasury and took out a casket. She brought out a key from her topknot and made Saffak open the casket. Inside the casket lay a piece of paper with the writing of Jamshed Jadoo, an ancient sage who was Saffak's ancestor. It read, 'I am writing this so that whoever reads it in this age should benefit from it. This is meant for the age when Muslim ayyars will invade this

Tilism and their princes will be imprisoned here. The Shah's army will rebel against him and ally with the ayyars. In the confrontation, Shah will be killed and Tilism will be vanquished. Therefore, our descendants should ally with the rebels and not endanger themselves with misguided loyalty to Shah. Otherwise, they will lose their kingdoms and their lives!'

Saffak was stunned by this message and then embraced her foster mother lovingly. She cried, 'Mother, you have saved my life!' She composed a letter to her daughter as Ghubara had advised her to. She worshipped the sacred fire for a long time and then moulded a slave-boy from flour kneaded with her blood. She breathed on it to bring it to life and handed him the letter to convey to Zaivar. So strong was the slave-boy that it could confront Afrasiyab himself and resist any pressure from the guardians of the frontier to take the message from him.

In Mount Agate, Zaivar Jadoo had distanced herself from Laqa and had set up her camp in the wilderness. She spent her days and nights in fear and was afraid both of the Shah's wrath if she returned to Tilism and of the Muslim ayyars in Laqa's camp. She had told Laqa that she had to stay in isolation as she was awakening her magic. At the time, it was dawn and she had emerged from her bedchamber to sit on masnad seating. The awnings of her pavilion had been drawn up and she watched the colours of the landscape at dawn and the blossoming spring flowers, brooding over her predicament.

There was a sudden hush in the air and she saw a magic slave-boy flying in towards her. He greeted her and handed her the scroll from her mother, adding that her mother wanted her to read the message privately. Zaivar dismissed her attendants and the two slave-boys that were guarding her before reading it. Zaivar was endowed with intelligence as well as beauty. She realized that events had taken another turn. She wrote back: 'O Respected Mother, the King of Magic will know when I return to Tilism and he will send a sahir to arrest me. If you could make arrangements for me to return in safety, I can leave at once.' Zaivar made an offering of wine to the magic slave-boy before it left with her message. The slave-boy shot up to become a lamp in the sky and landed in the city of Saffakia to give the message to his mistress. Saffak took the letter to her nanny who read it and exclaimed, 'Saffak, although noble daughter is young, she thinks like an elder. We will have to be very cautious and arrange her escape.' Saffak looked thoughtful and said, 'No one else can do this except Mahrukh Magic-eye.' The old woman whispered, 'I will secretly go to Mahrukh and explain the situation to her. Let us see how she responds!'

The old woman rolled on the floor and transformed into a bird before flying to the rebel camp. Mahrukh was presiding over her durbar when the magic bird flew in and called out, 'If Khwaja Amar is present here, could he come to the wilderness for this humble handmaiden wishes to speak to him. Please do not be afraid of me. I am a friend not a foe!' Amar at once rose from his seat. Mahrukh advised him not to act hastily, but he left the pavilion and called out to the bird that he would wait in a certain place. The bird flew off and Khwaja went to the ravine of a mountain as he had promised. He was armed with the tools of ayyari and looked very alert when he saw the old woman approaching him. She greeted him courteously and said, 'O shah of ayyars, I am Malika Saffak's trusted nanny. She wishes to ally with you and remain under your protection.'

Amar replied happily, 'If it is so then what is stopping her? Our house and its humble offerings are yours if she so wishes!' Ghubara explained the danger of Haseena's position in Mount Agate and said, 'I beseech you to help Malika Saffak so that once her daughter enters Tilism and is arrested by Afrasiyab, you can rescue her and bring her to your camp!' Amar declared grandly, 'Once anyone allies with us, we protect them with our heart and lives. Send a message to the princess that she should leave Mount Agate. I will travel to the borders of Tilism and with God's will, I will not let her be harmed. When she leaves that place her mother should immediately come to our lashkar!' Ghubara folded her hands and cried, 'If you make a pledge, then I will bring Saffak right away. When God has made you merciful towards us, then what have we to fear?' Amar smiled and made a solemn pledge to reassure her. The old nanny returned to Saffakia beaming and announced to Saffak, 'Send for your daughter. Khwaja Amar will protect us!'

Amar returned to the durbar where Mahrukh asked him, 'Khwaja sahib, whom did you meet!' Amar took her aside and explained the matter to her. Mahrukh said, 'Khwaja, then you will have to keep your promise. Either go to the border or send someone there.' Amar nodded and sent for select sardars to whom he whispered, 'My friends, I have promised Zaivar's mother that I will protect her on the border. Which one of you will guide me on the way and help me with God's command?' Hilal Magic-maker and Makhmoor said at once, 'We, your handmaidens, are ready to sacrifice our lives and will accompany you!' Makhmoor thought at the same time that perhaps the mission would allow her the opportunity of seeing her beloved Prince Nur al Dahar again. Amar left with the two princesses and their attendants quietly, not wanting to draw attention to their mission. He made them change their appearances magically and then took out an amulet Kaukab had given him. When

Amar held the amulet to his mouth, a horse materialized before him and flew with all of them to Kaukab's Tilism. Kaukab was in his fort when Amar came in and greeted him, 'I have come on your magic steed with several companions. Will you send for them here as I have urgent business with you?' Kaukab sent flying thrones for Amar's companions. Once they had arrived, Amar requested Kaukab to help them get to Mount Agate. Kaukab conjured magic birds for them to mount and ordered them to take Amar to the borders of Hoshruba and his companions to Mount Agate. Meanwhile, the magic slave-boy that flew with Saffak's message to her daughter in Mount Agate was waylaid by a powerful sahir Tairan Jadoo, who was one of the nazims of the border. The sahir read the message Saffak had written to her daughter, but released the slave-boy to go on to Mount Agate. Tairan copied out Saffak's letter and sent it to Afrasiyab. When the King of Magic read the letter, he consulted the oracle Book of Samri and learned that Saffak had allied with Amar who had left to protect her daughter at the border.

Afrasiyab laughed and exclaimed, 'The one I thought was my friend turned out to be my enemy! Oh well, where will that wretch escape to from me? She will be punished severely for her disloyalty!' Afrasiyab then sent messages to the keepers of the borders, warning them that Zaivar Jadoo would be entering Tilism and should be apprehended. He also ordered a sahir called Azlal Jadoo to arrest Saffak before she left for Mahrukh's camp. The King of Magic forgot to warn the keepers of the River of Flowing Blood not to let Saffak cross the river and later paid a heavy price for this error.

After her meeting with Amar, Saffak's foster mother Ghubara advised her to join Mahrukh as soon as possible, before the King of Magic moved against her. Accordingly, Saffak emptied the treasury, mobilized her army and left for Mahrukh's camp in great splendour. The fort of Saffakia was close to the Dome of Light and she easily made her way across the River of Flowing Blood where no one stopped her. As she approached Mahrukh's camp, she was intercepted by Azlal Jadoo who could not match her in magic, but rendered her unconscious by blowing the dust of Jamshed on her. However, Mehtar Qiran, who was disguised as a holy man, killed Azlal and rescued Saffak. Afrasiyab then sent another sahir to capture Saffak. He transformed magically into a giant python and swallowed Saffak along with her companions. Yet again, Mehtar Qiran disguised as a desert lion tricked the sahir into disgorging his prey and then killed him.

Saffak prostrated in gratitude to the One True God and exclaimed to her foster mother, 'Dai Amah, the ayyars of Amar's lashkar are truly remarkable! These people are truly noble for they put their lives at stake for their guests and allies. We should now leave this place very quickly!' Saffak flew ahead with Ghubara to the edge of Mahrukh's lashkar and waited there for her army to join her. The ayyars informed Mahrukh, 'Mubarak! Malika Saffak has reached!' Mahrukh then sent prominent sardars to welcome Saffak. Nafarman, Surkh Mu and Mushkeen met Saffak and led her army to an area levelled out for them. They led Saffak into the durbar where she greeted Mahrukh and offered nazar. Malika embraced her and offered her the chair of honour. The gathering of pleasure commenced with a round of wine and there was much happiness in the camp that evening.

Zaivar is captured by Tairan

Now hear about Princess Zaivar. Her mother Saffak's messenger slave-boy reached her after being released by Tairan and informed her that he had been trapped in Tairan's magic net. Zaivar was apprehensive, but decided to entrust herself to the Almighty's protection and left for Tilism. She wanted to bypass Tairan's area, but all other routes into Tilism were inaccessible to her as Afrasiyab's warning had reached the nazims. There was another way through the Tilism of Thousand Towers, but that would have taken years. Zaivar had no other recourse but to cross the border that was under Tairan's control. She stopped short on the banks of a raging, boiling torrent that seemed like a harbinger of Doomsday. Zaivar declared she would fly across the magic river, but saw that there was a firmament of iron above her that exuded an inky blackness.

Zaivar announced, 'It seems that Afrasiyab has been informed about our intentions and is determined to arrest us. We will now cross the river by boat and fight back. The Master of Deserts and Rivers will protect us!' Zaivar and her army managed to cross half the river, but the iron firmament expelled the darkness on them. When daylight returned, Zaivar saw that she was in the pavilion of a sahir and her army had been arrested. The sahir addressed her harshly, 'O betrayer of salt, you turned against Shah who had bestowed all honours upon you! You have lost everything in the river of dishonour!' Zaivar remained silent, but that shameless sahir travelled with her and her captured army to the city. He led Zaivar and her officers into the royal palace where the black-faced, ill-intentioned Tairan was sitting resplendently on his throne.

Tairan lost his senses when he beheld the incomparable beauty of the young princess; but since she was a royal prisoner, he remained silent. After composing himself, he launched into a tirade against her, 'Why, you brazen girl, did you not think about Shah's punishment when you went against his orders?' Zaivar responded haughtily, 'Listen, you shameless monster, I am not against Shah! Even if it is true, than what kind of a joker is that Shah of yours?' Tairan was outraged with her impertinence, but his advisers urged him to inform Afrasiyab before punishing her. They said, 'Huzoor, Shah of Tilism has the power over life and death. If he wants her alive, you should send her to him and if he wants her head, then you can execute her.' Tairan ordered his guards to imprison her separately while her officers and army were confined to one area. The princess was incarcerated in the dungeon of grief in a dark and confined cell.

Amar rescues Zaivar Jadoo

Now hear about Amar bin Ummayyah who was conducted to the borders of Kaukab's Tilism by magic birds. The birds trilled, 'O king of ayyars, the road on your right leads to Tilism-e-Hoshruba. The one going straight goes to Mount Agate and to your left are the paths to the Tilisms of Pearls and Hundred Towers. Anyone headed to Hoshruba will have to cross the River of Seven Hues, beyond which is hostile territory.' Amar said, 'God is our Protector. You stay in this place and I will go ahead and look for Princess Zaivar.' Amar and his companions descended from their bird mounts and rested for a while before Makhmoor and Hilal magically transformed into birds and flew into the sky. Amar, in turn, disguised himself as a sahir. He slung a pouch of magic around his waist, wore strings and beads around his neck and arms, and smeared sandalwood paste on his body before striding ahead, chanting the holy name of Jamshed.

He saw a river whose waters boiled expelled flames as he approached it. Amar quickly tossed Kaukab's magic amulet into the river. The flames subsided and some fishes leapt out of the river and greeted him deferentially. One of them had a wooden seat tied to its back. As soon as Amar sat on the seat, the fish dived into the waters and swam across the river. Amar jumped on to the shore and walked ahead. He walked through a varied landscape with verdant greenery had sahir dwellings in the most unlikely places. In time, he came across a fort with massive walls and turrets. Amar walked up casually to the city gates and chatted to the guards who told him that access into the city was difficult as a prisoner of the King of Sahirs was being held there. When the guards mentioned Zaivar Jadoo's name Amar made a silent prayer of gratitude and left. In the wilderness, he transformed himself into a beautiful young *jogan* and sang as he approached the fort.

Passersby were mesmerized by the jogan's beauty and melodious voice and very soon, there was a throng of people around her. The jogan stopped singing abruptly and moved away as her disappointed audience scattered. Some of them returned to the city and spread the word about her incomparable beauty and beautiful voice. Meanwhile, Amar, disguised as the jogan, started singing again and people gathered around her again. Rich and poor from the city rushed to catch a glimpse of her and each one was smitten by her beauty. The vizier also heard about her and was intrigued when he was told, 'Huzoor, you have to see her. It is as if Samri made her with his own hands!'

The vizier went out of the city and found the jogan surrounded by a swarm of devotees. As the vizier gazed at the lovely jogan, she arched her eyebrows to beckon him forward. Her signal was like a sword with two blades that smote the vizier's heart into a hundred pieces. He went forward, as if in a trance and when the jogan asked him how he was doing, he sighed, 'I am about to lose my life for love of you!' The jogan frowned prettily and said, 'Mian, men like you deceive women by swearing devotion. Who am I that anyone would lose their life for me?' Her eyes filled up with tears and she abruptly broke into a poignant love song that overwhelmed the smitten vizier. The jogan finished her song and moved away, but the vizier held her hand and lowered his head as he beseeched her to hear him. As she paused to listen, he requested her to grace his abode with her presence. She agreed readily and the vizier sent for a carriage as gentle as the spring breeze to take her into the city and to his home.

Meanwhile, the ruler of the city, Tairan heard that the celebrated jogan had come to the vizier's home and sent word that she should be brought to his palace first. The vizier was crestfallen as he knew that once his master saw her, he would want her for himself. With a heavy heart, he took the jogan to the palace where Tairan received her in the garden. As she reclined on the masnad seating in the baradari and started singing, even Tairan was moved to tears.

By the time she stopped singing, the evening sky was covered with stars and a soft breeze wafted through the garden that was bathed in moonlight. Tairan was now alone with the jogan and so enraptured with her that he tried to kiss her sweet lips. She slapped him hard on his cheek and cried, 'Come to your senses! Do you think I am an easy woman?' Tairan was startled, but pleaded with her and bent to kiss her feet. The lovely jogan smote her forehead and cried, 'O noble sir, why do you harass a holy woman?' Tairan said, 'I would give all just to kiss your sweet lips!' The jogan archly signalled refusal with her thumb and shook her head. Tairan could no longer control his ardour and embraced her passionately.

She leapt out of his grasp like lightning and continued to tantalize him for some time before offering him a goblet of golden wine mixed with the drug of unconsciousness. The false jogan artfully pretended to sip the wine first and offered it to Tairan while declaring, 'If you do not drink the wine that I have tasted, you will see my dead body!' Tairan, who was intoxicated with love, eagerly drank from the goblet and asked for more wine. After a few goblets, he lunged at the jogan, but she laughed and ran away from him. He ran after her but was overcome by the drug, and collapsed with his legs in the air. The false jogan or Amar quickly took off his garments, wrapped him in a rug and hid him in the baradari. He wore his clothes and changed his face to look like Tairan, and then called out to the attendants to resume their duties.

The next morning, Amar wore the royal crown and opulent garments and proceeded to the durbar. When Tairan's ministers and counsellors presented themselves along with the commanders of the army, he declared, 'Last evening, my vizier betrayed my trust! It will be entirely fitting to execute his entire family! Before finding out anything about her, he brought the jogan to my palace. That jogan was actually Amar bin Ummayyah, the ayyar!' The vizier turned pale and trembled violently. Others were in the same state for they had also loudly praised the jogan.

The false Tairan said benignly, 'Do not be afraid. I have not come across a cleverer person than him. I have converted to his faith as I am convinced it is the true one. Whoever wants to stay with me is welcome and whoever wants to leave can do so as well.' Tairan's viziers and commanders declared that they would remain faithful to him. Amar then recited the holy verse and they converted sincerely. At his orders, Princess Zaivar was released from the dungeons and offered a golden chair of honour. Idol houses were demolished and foundations were laid out for mosques. Heralds announced that anyone going against Khwaja Amar would die in great agony. After making these arrangements Amar returned to the palace gardens with Zaivar. He tied the unconscious Tairan to a pillar in baradari and pierced his tongue with a needle before reviving him.

When Tairan opened his eyes, Amar said, 'O Tairan, see how the Creator of the earth and the skies gave me the power to overcome you. Now what do you say in recognition of the One True God?' Tairan was truly astounded at the sight of the ayyar and thought, 'Praise Allah, what a remarkable man he is! He can assume the form of a woman or any other person. He risks his life to rescue anyone allied with him.

Indeed, his faith is the true one!' He signalled his assent and Amar untied him and pulled the needle out of his tongue. Tairan kneeled in front of Amar, who embraced him warmly.

After his conversion, they returned to the durbar and Amar revealed his real face to everyone's amazement. Their thoughts were, 'This is truly a miracle of the Great Creator that this man can assume so many different forms!' Tairan then offered several caskets of jewels in homage to him. Makhmoor and Hilal joined them as well and embraced Amar. Tairan took his army of sixty thousand sahirs and accompanied Amar for he knew that since he had converted to Islam, Afrasiyab would not leave him alive. They travelled to the Land of Seven Hues and took the route that Kaukab had arranged for Amar to reach Hoshruba. Amar was the first to reach Mahrukh's camp and met Saffak there. She was overwhelmed with gratitude at the news of her daughter's safe arrival. Mahrukh sent her sardars to welcome Zaivar and Tairan ceremoniously. There was great jubilation as the new army settled in the camp. Mahrukh Magic-eye arranged a grand feast and everyone celebrated in the gathering of pleasure. The news of Zaivar and Tairan's arrival in the Islamic camp reached Hairat, who became distressed and sent a message to Afrasiyab. He got into such a state of rage as he read the message that he became even more determined to destroy his enemies.

༄

26 Jahangir Gets the Magic Sword and the Lamp of Jamshed, Confrontation with Kaukab's Commanders, Tricksters and Trickeries

The reader will recall that the noble Prince Jahangir took his leave of Afrasiyab, the misguided one, and left to vanquish Kaukab's Tilism with a lashkar of several lakh sahirs. His adopted father Khurshid Jadoo also accompanied him. After travelling for several days in stages, they arrived at a plain that was as dark as the destiny of the enemy. Jahangir settled his army in the plain and left on his own to find the black dome.

He had to grope his way in the Plain of Darkness until he felt the dome, which seemed to be the abode of the demons of hell. He raised the magic amulet given to him by Afrasiyab to cast light on the dome and saw that it was inscribed with the large letters of a strange script. Jahangir recited some magic words as that is what Afrasiyab had instructed him to do. No sooner had he recited them than a bird flew out from behind the dome. Afrasiyab was in the Garden of Apples when the magic bird flew in and perched on his hand. Afrasiyab instantly vanished from his throne and within moments, he had reached the Plain of Darkness. With his arrival, the plain was bathed in daylight. Khurshid Jadoo arrived to receive him and wanted to accompany him further on, but Afrasiyab said, 'This is a dangerous place and you should remain in this place until it is time for you to move.'

Afrasiyab went alone to the black dome and found Jahangir standing there looking angry. Nevertheless, he greeted the Shah politely. Afrasiyab called out, 'Well done, my noble lion!' He conjured a torch and raised it so that the script on the dome could be deciphered and read easily. As Jahangir recited the words, the dome opened to reveal a gigantic, black-faced sahir, expelling flames from his mouth. He greeted the Shah, who held his hand and embraced him warmly. The sahir said, 'O Leader of Sahirs and King of Magic, how can this lowly servant serve you for that would be my honour!' The Shah said, 'Brother, it would be right for you to hand over the Lamp of Jamshed and the invincible sword to noble Prince Jahangir for he is Tilism Kusha!' Afrasiyab signalled to Jahangir to behave obsequiously towards the sahir, but the most the brave warrior could do was to embrace him.

The sahir was overawed with Jahangir's personality and readily agreed to the Shah's request. He led Jahangir into the dome, presented him with the lamp and the sword and pledged his allegiance to him. The sahir took Jahangir deeper into the dome where they came across a throne made of a dark green stone fixed firmly on the floor with iron pegs. Jahangir lifted the heavy throne with Sahibqirani strength and saw what appeared to be the mouth of a tunnel.

At that time, Afrasiyab returned with the sahir to Jahangir's camp. Jahangir jumped into the tunnel and fell for some time before landing in a dark wilderness again. Jahangir held out the Lamp of Jamshed and the wilderness began glowing with a celestial light, just as the heart of a kafir is illuminated with the light of Islam. When he returned to his camp, the King of Sahirs met Jahangir with Khurshid Jadoo and victory gongs were struck in the camp. Afrasiyab left after giving detailed instructions to Jahangir for the rest of his mission. The camp settled in the plain that evening. Chabak assigned guard duties and bazaars opened while a gathering of pleasure began in the durbar pavilion.

Jahangir is duped by Sarhang ayyar

When Jahangir had broken the spell of the black dome with the Lamp of Jamshed, the dome had disintegrated. Some of its keepers went to the fort of Anjum Hissar and informed the ruler Anjum Shah, who was also Kaukab's brother-in-law. The incensed Anjum Shah sent an army of sahirs to confront Jahangir. They were defeated and returned in a pitiable condition to Anjum who then sent for his personal ayyar Sarhang and asked him to hoodwink and capture Jahangir

The next morning, light clouds and the shadow of the Creator's blessing spread over the land. So pleasant was the weather that Jahangir and his companions spent the morning hunting birds and animals in the jungle. Towards noon, they returned to their tents to eat and rest. In the evening, they continued to enjoy bracing weather. Sarhang went to this camp in disguise and discovered that the young prince had gone hunting. So, he left the camp and went into the wilderness. There, he erected a rudimentary shack such as holy men use and placed a sitar and a flute in it. He then transformed into a beautiful young woman with unkempt hair tied in a topknot; a stray lock of hair caressed her cheeks like a wisp of dark cloud on the face of the moon. She wore loose homespun garments and settled down to wait for the prince.

As the day came to an end, Jahangir and his companions rode into their camp. Sarhang saw them approaching and played the flute to attract their attention. Jahangir heard the melodious notes and turned his horse to ride towards the sound. The prey itself approached the hunter. The young prince saw a vision of loveliness in the shack and got off his mount. He easily persuaded the false maiden to accompany him to his camp and housed her in a pavilion provided with every comfort—there was masnad seating on the floor, flasks of wine laid out on a low table along with perfume and betelnut containers, and a bejewelled bed with silken bedding. Jahangir sent costly robes for the maiden, but she declined wearing them.

Finally, when the robes of the day were replaced by the dark garments of the night and the camp was illuminated, the prince went to the tent of the beauteous one. Jahangir met her alone and tried to embrace her, but she looked tearful; when he withdrew, she tantalized him with smiles before saying, 'I have nothing to offer you except a rare wine!' She offered him a goblet that he consumed eagerly and then fell unconscious. The false maiden, or rather ayyar Sarhang, tied him up in pushtara and boldly walked out of the camp. Very soon, he reached the fort of Anjum Hissar where the ruler Anjum divested Jahangir of the magic sword. He shackled him with heavy iron chains and ordered that he was to be kept in the Tower of Sunddal.

The next morning, when it was discovered that both Jahangir and the mystery woman were missing, there was an uproar in his camp. Chabak declared, 'I had warned him not to bring that woman to the camp. I will try and find him if I can!' Chabak left the camp and searched many villages and settlements before he reached the massive walls of Anjum Hissar. He tried to scale the walls, but a roar of thunder rose and a bolt of lightning fell on him. The lightning snapped around him like a chain and took him to Anjum Shah, who had him imprisoned with Jahangir.

Khurshid Jadoo was informed by his spies that both his sons were being held in Anjum Hissar. Khurshid mobilized his army and attacked the fort, but it emitted deadly rays of lightning that seared the attackers. Eventually, Khurshid withdrew with his army and encamped at some distance. Anjum Shah sent a message to Kaukab through a messenger who travelled past several fortifications before reaching the River of Pearls, where a panja transported him to Kaukab's durbar. The messenger performed a mujra-greeting before handing over Anjum's letter. The Shah read the message and thought deeply before replying, 'My brother, I have received your message and commend you for your valour; however, do not think of executing them or I will lose my honour in front of Amar. I will think of what we must do, but do not worry about this matter. Rest assured that I will award you richly!'

The messenger left with this reply after Kaukab had bestowed a robe of honour on him. Anjum Shah was greatly troubled by Kaukab's message, but kept quiet. After a few days, he consulted his viziers who advised him, 'We cannot presume to question Kaukab's wisdom, but it is against reason to keep these people imprisoned indefinitely. The King of Sahirs will wreak his vengeance on us any time now.'

Jahangir and Princess Mah

Eventually, it was decided that the prisoners were to be executed within the fort. As they prepared for the execution, there was an outcry that the Shah's daughter, Princess Mah had arrived. Everyone gazed breathlessly as that moon of beauty entered the durbar. That beautiful princess saw the young prince Jahangir shackled cruelly and as she beheld his noble beauty, her heart felt constricted with love. She went past the execution ground and went to her father looking unusually quiet. Anjum kissed her brow and made her sit close to him. The princess plucked up courage and said, 'Father, I realize that this prince is an ally of Afrasiyab, but my uncle Kaukab must have his reasons for advising you not to execute him. It is not wise to go against his wishes in this matter. You must be aware of this yourself.' Anjum Shah looked worried and said, 'So what should I do then?' His daughter said, 'You can do nothing else except hold him in captivity. My uncle will find a way out of this soon; why do you worry?' Anjum Shah heeded his daughter's advice and sent that prisoner of love back to the dungeons while the princess returned to her palace, her heart heavy with grief. Jahangir was as smitten with her and thought that the chains of her love would bind him more tightly to this place than the heavy iron chains that bound him.

While he wept over his plight, the princess returned to her garden and lay down on her bed, her face the picture of despair. Meanwhile, her vizierzadi Gulzar who had been equally captivated by Chabak was in a similar predicament. She wandered over to the princess's apartment and was startled to see her so distraught. The two girls looked at each other meaningfully before the vizierzadi asked, 'Princess, tell me, why you are so aggrieved? There are no secrets between us!' The princess wept so desperately that Gulzar also wept in sympathy and said, 'It seems that your heart has been captured by Prince Jahangir! I am in a similar plight— my heart has been pierced by the arrows of love for his ayyar Chabak!'

All barriers were down now and the two girls whispered their secrets to each other. Eventually, they decided to confide in the ayyar Sarhang. He responded to the summons promptly and offered nazar to the princess before sitting in the seat of honour. The vizierzadi explained the situation to him. Sarhang was very fond of the princess and left vowing, 'My life is forfeit for you! I will bring him right away!' In no time, Sarhang managed to bring the two young prisoners to the garden. The princess was suddenly very shy and exclaimed, 'This Sarhang is so misbehaved! Did I ask him to bring them here? I had merely taken pity on them and ordered him to release them from the dungeons!'

She ran into her pavilion and closed the curtains, but Jahangir boldly walked in and said, 'O moon of beauty, are you angry with me that you hide your face?' The princess smiled and said, 'Sahib, you are very forceful. Very well, you are welcome here!' Jahangir sat down on the masnad confidently while the princess sat before him. Her pretty young handmaidens sang melodiously to entertain them while water channels in the garden sparkled in the moonlight. This gathering of pleasure lasted throughout the night. The next morning, when Jahangir entered the baths, the princess slipped into the armoury to retrieve the invincible magic sword. No one could stop her from doing so. She delivered it to Jahangir and continued to entertain him.

Later that morning, the keepers of the dungeons discovered that their prisoners were missing and wailed as they informed the Shah, 'That pearl in the crown of royalty has been lost!' Anjum Shah immediately sent another message to Kaukab that someone had rescued the prisoners. Kaukab read the message and conjured a parchment and a quill. A hand materialized in the air and wrote that Princess Mah and her vivacious companion, the vizierzadi Gulzar were entertaining the prisoners in their garden. Kaukab then wrote to Anjum Shah how the culprit was his own daughter.

An outraged Anjum Shah attacked Jahangir in the garden but was killed by Jahangir with the magic sword from his own armoury. Jahangir and Chabak them took over the city in the name of Afrasiyab. However, in the heat of the battle with Anjum Shah, both Princess Mah and Gulzar were abducted and later rescued by Amar.

Kaukab enlists Amar to capture Jahangir

After the messenger left, Kaukab looked worried and sent Amar this message: 'O loyal friend, the situation has become critical in my realm. Jahangir was captured after destroying the black dome, but the daughter of the ruler Anjum Shah helped him escape the dungeons. Come to me at once!' Khwaja Amar was in Mahrukh's durbar at that time. He replied, 'I will be with you God willing after I make Jahangir and his lashkar submit to you!' Amar then left for Kaukab's realm with his disciple Barq Firangi. Just before he entered it, he disguised himself as a bent old man with a long white beard. Barq transformed into a comely youth with plump cheeks, his fingers stained with henna and covered with rings.

They reached the fort of Anjum Hissar and rented a shop that they furnished with long silk curtains and all comforts. Amar took out portraits of beautiful young girls from Zambil and decorated the shop with them. He sent Barq out to spread the word that a flesh merchant was displaying his goods in the city. Among these pictures was the portrait of vizierzadi Gulzar. One of the visitors to the shop was Jahangir's ayyar Chabak who fainted when he saw his beloved's likeness. When he revived, he requested Barq to take him to his master.

Chabak entered the chamber and saw an ancient-looking man reclining against cushions. Chabak greeted him deferentially and with some hesitation, he mentioned the said portrait. Amar pretended to be furious and cried, 'Young master, this is my daughter's portrait. It was not meant to be displayed!' Chabak left after much pleading and went straight to Jahangir. He told him, 'This old flesh merchant has my beloved's portrait and refuses to sell it to me!' Jahangir then sent his attendants to bring the old merchant to him. When Amar refused to meet Jahangir, the prince decided to go meet him himself. Amar deposited everything back in Zambil before meeting Jahangir. The young prince greeted him politely and asked him to sell the portrait to them. However, Amar frowned and glared at him and said, 'I have told your friend that she is my daughter!' Jahangir persisted, 'Pray, do not be angry! After all, you will have to marry her to someone. Do us a favour and consider my brother!'

After arguing fiercely for a while, Amar suddenly relented when Jahangir offered him money and a garden that was the heir to the Gardens of Paradise. He took Jahangir and Chabak into a secluded place and presented a sword to Jahangir with great ceremony. When Jahangir pulled the sword out of the scabbard, it released a vapour that rendered both Chabak and Jahangir unconscious. Amar took the invincible sword from Jahangir and put both the brothers in Zambil. He wrote a message to Kaukab: 'You can send for your prisoners and Tilismi gifts they had appropriated.'

Since this was Kaukab's territory there were several known sahirs who lived there and one of them took the message to Kaukab. The Shah was happy on receiving the news, but also seemed worried. The ruler of Bari Bara, Malika Afaq Jadoo, was in his durbar that day and asked Kaukab about what troubled him. Kaukab replied, 'Tilism Kusha has been captured. I need to send a responsible person to bring him here.' Afaq Jadoo volunteered to go and after obtaining Kaukab's permission to leave, left with her army like a river in full flood.

Afaq Jadoo and her sahir army met Amar in the desert where he handed over the prisoners and the invincible sword to them and left for his own camp, warning Afaq to be very alert while travelling with the young prisoners. Afaq bound them in heavy chains and travelled with the prisoners placed in the heart of the lashkar. In no time, they faced a fierce attack from the forces of Jahangir's adopted father, Khurshid Jadoo and were almost defeated, had it not been for a magic sun that emerged on the horizon and a voice that boomed, 'I am Kaukab the Enlightened!' The sun annihilated Khurshid's forces, but Kaukab saw that Afaq Jadoo was badly injured too. So, he sent Afaq with the magic sword to her kingdom, Bari Bara.

Kaukab's servants erected a tent for him in the desert. The Shah sat on his throne still in a state of rage, and sent for an iron cage for Jahangir and Chabak. He conjured a magic dome and had the cage hung inside. The dome was surrounded by a trench that expelled flames to ward off intruders. He then sent for Princess Mah and slapped her, 'You shameless bold-eyed hussy, is this the way you bring disgrace on your family?' Mah's vizierzadi Gulzar was severely chastised as well and both girls were handed over to a sahira to be confined in her garden.

Afrasiyab tries to rescue Jahangir

Afrasiyab was engaged in business of the state in the Garden of Apples when his men informed him that Khurshid Jadoo had arrived, looking obviously distraught. Afrasiyab felt apprehensive as besides him, only Hairat knew that Jahangir had captured the fort of Anjum Hissar. He sent his sardars to welcome Khurshid, who entered the durbar wailing. He related the story of Jahangir's capture by Amar and added, 'I tried to stop the army that was taking my sons away, but Kaukab intervened. I have heard that he has now imprisoned them in the desert.' Afrasiyab became very distressed when he heard this. He flew into a rage and sprouted wings to travel to the desert at once. Everyone tried to dissuade him, but he flew towards the dome where the princes were imprisoned. He saw that the place was like hell on earth and its towering flames threatened to burn the heart of the sky.

Afrasiyab conjured a dark monsoon cloud that burst on the trench and cooled the flames. In no time, the fire vanished and was replaced by verdant greenery. He then turned on Kaukab's army that guarded the dome by enchanting them into fighting each other. Kaukab was also informed of this turn of events and arrived on the scene shouting, 'O Afrasiyab, where will you escape to now?' As soon as he heard him, Afrasiyab plunged into the earth and made his way to the magic dome. Kaukab thought that he had fled from him and restored order amongst his frenzied troops. By that time, Afrasiyab had flown out of the dome with the cage and its prisoners.

Kaukab deputed his companion Sahab Jadoo to look out for Afrasiyab as he tended to his army. Sahab surrounded the King of Magic with fifty thousand sahirs. Their combined magical attacks stopped Afrasiyab, who broke into a sweat and put the cage down. Sahab chanted a spell that opened the cage. As the prisoners fell out, Sahab tried to capture them, but Chabak ayyar sprinted out of her sight while Afrasiyab dispelled her magic and put Jahangir back in the cage. He conjured an inky darkness that descended on her army and shot up in the sky with the cage.

Kaukab was busy with his army when he was informed that Afrasiyab had flown off with the cage. Kaukab's first impulse was to go in pursuit of Afrasiyab, but at that time a paper materialized in the air and floated towards him. Kaukab snatched the paper that contained a message from his pir brother Brahmin, 'O Kaukab, do not think of pursuing Afrasiyab! Let him go and come to me at once!'

Meanwhile, Afrasiyab took the cage to Hairat's durbar across the River of Flowing Blood. He released Jahangir from the cage and asked,

'How are you feeling Sahibqiran?' When Jahangir did not respond, Afrasiyab looked at Hairat who suggested that he could be enchanted. Jahangir suddenly rose and stated, 'I am leaving!' Afrasiyab was now alarmed. He tried to stop Jahangir, but as he held his hand, the young prince melted into water before his eyes. Khurshid Jadoo started wailing for his son again and a highly embarrassed Afrasiyab realized that he had been outwitted by someone in Kaukab's realm.

Jahangir had actually been captured by Kaukab's pir brother Brahmin, a powerful sahir, who greeted Kaukab with deference. He said, 'O Badshah, I have brought Jahangir from the battlefield and left his double for Afrasiyab. He must be so ashamed now!' Brahmin pointed to his left where Kaukab saw Jahangir tied up with magical chains. Kaukab sent for a cage for his prisoner and asked Brahmin what they should do with him. Brahmin suggested that it was best to send Jahangir to their ally Qaisar Jadoo in Kohistan. Kaukab then asked a sahir called Nihal Jadoo to take the cage to Qaisar's kingdom for safekeeping.

Jahangir in Kohistan

Afrasiyab's spy birds informed him where Jahangir was being taken. Afrasiyab sent a message to his own ally Muheel in Kohistan and ordered him to attack Nihal and capture Jahangir. Muheel waited for Nihal and ambushed him before he could reach Qaisar's fort. In the fierce battle that followed, Muheel managed to open Jahangir's cage, but the young prince fled from the battlefield and hid in the ravine of a mountain.

Meanwhile, Qaisar came to know that Kaukab's men were being killed and he came to their rescue. Kaukab's envoy Nihal was worried about the missing Jahangir, but Qaisar reassured him, 'He will not be able to escape from Kohistan and will die for lack of water and food in these hills!' Nihal returned to Nur Afshan and conveyed this message to Kaukab, who looked satisfied and declared, 'Indeed, it will be difficult for him to remain alive in that area!'

Now hear about Jahangir. He remained in the ravine for two days and nights in fear of the sahirs. The third day, he was ravenous and emerged from his hiding place. He wandered around for two days, eating wild berries and leaves. That wilderness had no settlements of men and the young prince suffered great hardships. His robes were torn and he had to resort to tearing them into strips to tie as makeshift loincloths and turbans. Looking like a fakir, Jahangir eventually wandered into the city of Qaisariya—the same city where Kaukab had sent him to be kept in captivity. Jahangir walked past the food stalls and almost fainted when he inhaled the fragrance of freshly prepared food and sweets. He walked past the stalls with great self restraint and observed that the city was neatly laid out with lofty buildings, gleaming shops and brick-lined drains. Molsri trees cast a pleasant shade in the heat of the day, the city buzzed with activity and its citizens looked happy and prosperous.

The noble prince wandered around the city until he came upon the settlement of a holy man by the name of Dervaish Sack-robe. He lived with some of his disciples who were milling around him, even as devotional singers created a spiritual atmosphere with their rhythmic chanting. Jahangir wolfed down the lentil curry and bread the disciples were distributing among the poor and fainted after he had eaten for his body had become unaccustomed to solid food. After he had recovered, Jahangir saw that Qaisar Jadoo, king of this realm had come to visit the holy man. Qaisar arrived with much fanfare, but humbly sat on the reed mat besides the holy man who looked closely at him and observed, 'Qaisar, I see that you are a troubled man. What has happened?' Qaisar replied, 'Huzoor, do I need to say anything for all is known to you!' The holy man said, 'O Qaisar you pine for the daughter of Afaq Jadoo, mistress of the wilderness of Bari Bara.'

Qaisar fell at his feet and cried, 'O divine master, this is indeed the truth. That place is inaccessible and no message can reach there. I have even written to Kaukab about this matter, but he did not honour me with a response. Now it is up to you!' The fakir declared, 'O Qaisar, your wish is about to be granted for the Sahibqiran of our times is here in the guise of a fakir. He wishes to go to the same place and you will gain access to it through him.' Dervaish Sack-robe was so complimentary about Jahangir that Qaisar was intrigued and asked to meet him. Dervaish Sack-robe then called out to Jahangir, who rose from his seat. Qaisar saw a noble young man of radiant disposition in tattered garments. Dervaish Sack-robe and Qaisar both stood up to greet him, overawed by his personality. Qaisar then ordered his men to present a robe of honour to him. After he had worn the new garments, Jahangir joined them on the mat and sat quietly as the Dervaish Sack-robe to talk of his virtues.

After a few rounds of wine, Qaisar related his love story to Jahangir with tears in his eyes. Jahangir was so moved that he also wept for his lost love, Princess Mah. Dervaish Sack-robe reassured him that his wishes would be fulfilled. For the next two days, Qaisar feasted the prince. He was reluctant to let him embark on the dangerous journey, but Jahangir left after he declared that he was ready to lay his life down to reach his destination.

The Tree of Samri

After a long perilous journey, Jahangir and his army reached the fort of Bibrania. The prince saw that the walls there were massive and lofty and its colossal doorway swayed like a rogue elephant. Its handsome citizens had pleasant dispositions and laughed easily. Its shops were brimming with fine goods and the shopkeepers were well dressed and prosperous, while the towers and turrets of the city's buildings soared to the skies. Jahangir enjoyed walking through the city and reached the royal palace where King Bibran was seated in all splendour on his throne. Jahangir greeted the king who received him graciously and offered him a seat of honour. Cupbearers served them goblets of wine while pretty dancers entertained the gathering.

After he had been served a feast in the palace, they returned to the durbar, where the king asked Jahangir, 'Who are you, O prince?' Jahangir declared confidently, 'I am the son of Khurshid Taj Buksh and have been sent by Afrasiyab to destroy Kaukab's Tilism. I am on my way to Mount Bari Bara!' Bibran was stunned by this revelation for he was a Kaukab loyalist. After some thought, he said, 'Prince, we worship a tree here because after every few months, a puppet emerges from it and calls out that he is Khudawand Samri. Before leaving my kingdom, you will have to discover its secret or genuflect before it!'

Jahangir was eager to see the tree and Bibran rode with him to a wilderness in his domain. The prince saw that there was an abundance of greenery there. Soon, they reached a tree that was laden with blossoms. As they stood before the tree, its massive trunk split open and a puppet with a parrot's beak emerged from within to call out, 'I am Samri!' Bibran and his companions on kneeled the ground and genuflected, but Jahangir merely watched the proceedings quietly. As he stood watching, the tree's branches grew heavy with fruit. Bibran picked some of the fruit and shared it with Jahangir, who marvelled at its unusual taste and sweetness. By this time, the puppet had vanished back into the tree. Bibran turned to leave, but Jahangir elected to spend the night alone in the wilderness. At midnight, Jahangir returned to the tree and saw a wondrous sight. The wilderness was illuminated with lamps and lanterns. A carpet had been laid out near the holy tree with lavish masnad seating. A beautiful woman dressed in gold-embroidered robes sat on the masnad and her face glowed like the light of the sun. She was absorbed in the performance of the dancers before her.

Soon, she noticed Jahangir who was standing quietly in a corner and was drawn to his good looks. 'Who are you?' she asked. Jahangir murmured that he was a chance traveller and after she introduced herself as Bazm Jadoo, he said, 'Tell me, do you know anything about this tree and the puppet that emerges from it?' The sahira laughed and said, 'Young man, I am the one who has conjured this tree and the puppet!' Jahangir said to her, 'Since you have honoured me as a guest, I want to inform you that I have promised Bibran that I will discover the secret of the tree. Will you permit me to reveal this to him?'

Bazm Jadoo was quite smitten by the young prince and assented graciously. She kept asking him about his identity and Jahangir revealed everything about himself to her. They sipped wine and talked late into the night. The next morning, she provided a mount for him and said, 'Go ahead and your humble handmaiden will follow you presently.' Jahangir returned to Bibran's fort and related all that had happened. Bazm Jadoo also arrived there and Bibran received her with due honour. He now pledged to be Jahangir's firm ally and the prince declared that he would now leave for the wilderness of Bari Bara, Bibran said, 'You will come across Khursan Jadoo on the way who is a staunch ally of Kaukab on the way. I will accompany you with my army.'

The magic dome

As Bibran had said, Jahangir encountered Khursan on the way. Following an intense battle, Jahangir defeated Khursan Jadoo with the help of Dervaish Sack-robe and his new allies, Bibran and Bazm Jadoo. The city of Khursania surrendered to Jahangir and its nobles paid him homage. After a few days, the dervaish told Jahangir that it was time for him to visit Mehmal, keeper of Kaukab's magic dome. The next morning, Jahangir mounted his horse and left with a letter from the dervaish that read, 'O Mehmal, receive Jahangir Sahibqiran on our behalf and give him a tour of the magic dome.'

Jahangir travelled alone for several days and he reached a grassy plain. He saw a frail old man sitting alone in the plain. Not only his beard, but his eye lashes too were white. He wore snowy white robes and sat brooding with his head resting on his knees. Jahangir greeted him before handing over the letter. The old man read the letter closely and then rose to embrace Jahangir. He led Jahangir to the magic dome and opened a doorway that had been secured with a lock as large as a camel's thigh. When he entered the dome, Jahangir saw that the inside walls had large mirrors that provided spectacular views. Each of the kingdoms in Afrasiyab and Kaukab's Tilism were clearly visible. He could see Hairat's battle camp beside the River of Flowing Blood on one side and Mahrukh's armies on the other. The armies of Emir Hamza and Laqa could also be seen, along with Burran's Fortress of Seven Hues. Jahangir's was fascinated by the dome's powers. He saw that it was adorned with portraits of kings past and present and included his portrait too. Kaukab and Afrasiyab's portraits were also visible.

When they emerged from the dome, Mehmal said, 'Prince, I have a magic wick that can summon anyone you wish if you light it. As long as the wick is alight, that person will stay with you.' Jahangir pleaded with the old man to give him the magic wick for one night so that he could meet his lost love, Princess Mah. Mehmal took pity on him and gave him the wick for the night. He led him to a private area within the dome where he could spend the night.

Meanwhile, Princess Mah had been confined to her garden on Kaukab's orders with her companion Gulzar. That evening, she was about to doze off when Jahangir lit the wick in the magic dome. In the garden, her bed was lifted by the invisible keeper of the wick and the princess who did not know what was happening, fainted out of sheer fright. Within the blink of an eye, the bed was transported to Jahangir. After some time, the princess revived to see Jahangir in front of her, and both lovers were overwhelmed to see each other. Jahangir embraced and kissed her, but the wick burnt out in no time and the keeper took the princess back to her garden. The grief of her heart now spilled over as she cried, 'O cruel sky, you could not bear to let me speak or laugh with my beloved for a while longer? Alas, this is a fresh blow to my heart!'

Dervaish battles

After the princess vanished, Jahangir too was inconsolable and tears streamed from his eyes like a spring downpour. He found Mehmal and complained bitterly to him about the wick. Mehmal reassured him that the Supreme One would surely reunite him with his beloved. Jahangir then sent for his army from the fort of Khursania and travelled towards the fortress of Afaqia. The ruler, Afaq Jadoo wrote to Kaukab, 'Badshah, Jahangir has reached as far as Sohrabia with Dervaish Sack-robe's help. You will have to do something about him!'

A magic puppet took this letter to Shah Kaukab in his durbar. When he read the message, he became anxious and worried. He then wrote a letter to another holy man in his area, Dervaish Khizran Desert-dweller, that read: 'O Chaste and Holy Sage, Dervaish Sack-robe wants to destroy my realm and deserves to be punished by you.' Khizran read the message and in no time sketched a name with his finger on the sack upon which he sat. The sack flew up with him in the air.

At that time, Jahangir had reached Afaqia with a huge army. Afaq Jadoo heard of his arrival and opened the doors of her fortress to emerge with her own army. Conch shells and drums were sounded, magical clouds appeared in the sky and a battle camp was established to confront Jahangir. The next morning, noble Prince Jahangir emerged in all glory to confront his adversary, Afaq. The sahira went on to the battlefield first and took out lentil flour from her magic pouch, moulded it in the shape of a lion, and chanted an incantation to bring it to life. The lion assumed colossal proportions and roared as he attacked the enemy.

Bazm Jadoo confronted him, but the lion swallowed her easily and bounded back into his camp to expel her. Bibran and other sardars were also captured in the same way by the lion. At that time, Dervaish Sack-robe emerged on the scene and advised Jahangir to have the drums of peace struck. The same night, the dervaish made Jahangir learn a powerful incantation and gave him a magic ring. The next morning, Jahangir himself emerged to confront the lion. As soon as it roared and leapt forward to swallow him, Jahangir flung the ring on him and incinerated the lion. Afaq then conjured fierce wild boars that fell from the sky and attacked Jahangir, who again used his magic ring to hold them off for a while.

Now observe how the fates favoured Jahangir. The reader will recall that Kaukab had entrusted the invincible sword to Afaq Jadoo when he had sent her back to Bari Bara. Afaq also had a magic tablet that had the power to resist magic. Afaq's daughter, Gauhar, who was in love with Bibran, an ally of Jahangir, stole these two items from the treasury and sent them to Jahangir. The prince tied the magic tablet around his neck and attacked the wild magical boars with the sword. Eventually, Afaq and her army were roundly defeated and fled from the battlefield.

At that time, there was a sudden hush in the air and a voice called out, 'I am Dervaish Khizran Desert-dweller!' The dervaish descended from the sky and challenged Dervaish Sack-robe, 'O disloyal pir! You have done a terrible deed by deserting Kaukab and leading Jahangir to this place! You will not be spared now!' Dervaish Sack-robe engaged in a magical battle with the old man, but could not withstand his powers. Khizran read an incantation that made Sack-robe tie his own hands and surrender to his foe. Khizran had him locked in a cage and returned with Malika Afaq to her durbar.

Sack-robe was also taken to durbar in his cage and was severely chastised by Khizran. Sack-robe was so humiliated that he sighed deeply and stopped breathing. Though Khizran regretted his death, he did not waste any time and turned to Afaq and said, 'Consult the Papers of Samri to know who sent the magic tablet and sword from your treasury to Jahangir!' Just as she sent for the oracle papers, there was uproar that Jahangir was leading an attack against the fort to avenge Dervaish Sackrobe's death. Khizran declared angrily, 'I will deal with him right away!' After he vanished, Afaq was about to mobilize her army to confront Jahangir again when a voice called out, 'Afaq, there is no need for your army! Just watch what happens!'

Jahangir and his army were marching up to the fort when the earth split open before them and a river gushed out from it. Jahangir's soldiers fell into the river and turned into fish. Only the place where Jahangir stood became an atoll with the magic river churning around it. The magic tablet that Jahangir wore around his neck protected him from the river, but when he tried to move, the earth shook violently. He saw a huge crocodile in the water that seemed to be moving towards him. Someone called out, 'I am Shah Pir! Fear not Jahangir. Throw the magic tablet and the sword at the crocodile!'

Jahangir obeyed blindly in his panic. The crocodile immediately swallowed the sword and the tablet, and the voice called out, 'I am Khizran Desert-dweller! You have lost the tablet and the sword!' Dervaish Khizran then signalled to the crocodile to swallow Jahangir as well. Later, Khizran retrieved Jahangir from the crocodile's belly and took him to Afaq's durbar. There, he consulted the oracle Papers of Samri and informed Afaq, 'Your daughter Gauhar stole the magic tablet and the sword from the treasury and sent them to Jahangir through Nahang ayyar who is here with Jahangir's brother Chabak. Chabak is disguised as a singer and will try to rescue Jahangir!'

Dervaish Khizran waved his hand and lightning flashed in durbar. Both Nahang and Chabak were tied in chains instantly. Dervaish Khizran declared that Jahangir was to be executed right away. This announcement created ripples in the durbar and preparations were made for the execution. Jahangir was now convinced that he would die and began weeping silently. At that time, an unknown voice called out, 'I am Shah Pir, Afrasiyab's teacher!' Several panjas flashed into the durbar and rescued Jahangir, Chabak and Nahang.

Dervaish Khizran was too stunned to react, but recovered enough to chant an incantation that forced Shah Pir to become visible. Shah Pir descended from the air, but retaliated with magic that made Afaq Jadoo and Dervaish Khizran burst into flames. Within moments, they were reduced to ashes. Thus, Jahangir was declared the ruler of Fort Afaqia as well.

The fort of Badakshan

Jahangir spent a few days at Afaqia and then prepared to move forward into Kaukab's realm. Shah Pir informed him that the magic keystone of Kaukab's Tilism had been moved by Kaukab from the Tilism of Thousand Towers to the fort of Badakshan. The noble Jahangir thus travelled towards the fort in all splendour. He reached the fort the next day and saw that it was made entirely of silver and gold. Its vast gates were closed, but a jewel-inlaid figurine stood on the bastion with jewelled birds perched on her head. At Jahangir's signal a prisoner was ordered to approach the fort. The figurine uttered the words, 'Alas, Alas!' and merely looked at the man, who burst into flames and was reduced to dust. Jahangir's ally Bazm Jadoo (who had revealed the secret of the holy tree to him) then moved forward, but was also incinerated. Several other sahirs were thus burnt to death before Jahangir's adopted father, Malik Khurshid too was burnt before Jahangir's eyes. Soldiers hurled magical weapons at the figurine, but nothing could not harm her.

Chabak then devised an ingenious strategy. He sewed mirrors on his garments and draped a sheet around himself. He then put a veil over his face and rode towards the fort. Just as the figurine looked at him, he removed the sheet. The sight of her face reflected in the mirrors ignited the figurine and it burst into flames. Chabak gave a shout of triumph and was much praised for his ingenious plan. The ruler of the fort, Badakshan Jadoo, struck battle drums that evening. Jahangir's army retaliated with the answering call of war trumpets and prepared for battle.

The next day, Badakshan led his army in a fierce attack. Magic citrons, limes and coconuts burst like bombs and the air became thick with smoke. There were flashes of magical lightning and swords flashed in the battlefield. The angel of death did good business that day. The planet Mars was malevolent and blood flowed like water. Jahangir was in the thick of the battle like a ferocious lion. He fought with the invincible sword that protected him against magic and thousands were shown the final path by him. Afrasiyab's guru Shah Pir used his powerful amulets to destroy any spells conjured by Badakshan. Eventually, Badakshan was defeated and fled to a nearby dome that was constructed in the middle of a flowing river. Once he was secure in the dome, Badakshan informed Kaukab that he had lost his fort.

Kaukab was alarmed and wrote to his pir brother Brahmin Iron-body to help Badakshan. Brahmin left immediately and set up his tent besides the river. He summoned Shah Pir with a message that read, 'O Shameless One, present yourself at once!' The message was magical and

Shah Pir could not do anything but go to him. Brahmin touched the hem of Shah Pir's robe with a piece of meat and he caught fire like a torch and was incinerated within moments. Brahmin scattered his ashes in the air and then read a spell to conjure a wall of flames around the dome where Badakshan was hiding, and assured him that he would be safe within. After putting these measures in place, Brahmin Iron-body left the area.

Jahangir was very upset to hear of Shah Pir's dreadful end and tried to attack the dome, but did not succeed. After several days of inaction, Mehtar Chabak thought of a plan. He constructed a large metal fish. Jahangir and his sardars sat inside it and Chabak floated it down the river. That day, Badakshan had emerged from the dome and was fishing on the banks of the river when he caught the artificial fish and pulled it out. Jahangir and his companions jumped out of the fish and fell upon him. Badakshan resisted valiantly, but was no match for the powers of Jahangir's invincible sword. Afrasiyab was saddened when he was told about his tutor Shah Pir's horrible end, but was satisfied with Jahangir's triumph over the dome in the river.

Amar and Chabak in battle

Shah Kaukab was in his palace when Badakshan's servants brought his body to him. Kaukab was now seriously perturbed and sent a panja to bring Amar to him. Amar promised Kaukab that he would resolve this business once and for all and sent for Barq Firangi and Bahar Jadoo to help him. Kaukab also provided him with a large army. Amar declared that he would meet Jahangir in his durbar and try and win him over. 'Otherwise, I will seize the keystone and the magic sword from him!' he stated. Bahar and Kaukab's commanders tried to dissuade him from going alone, but Amar left on his own.

Jahangir heard he was coming and sent his sardars to receive him. He received the great ayyar deferentially and offered him the seat of honour before asking, 'What brings you here?' Amar said, 'Jahangir, I am here to advise you to turn back. You have the unmistakable birthmark of the Hashemite clan on your forehead. You will regret the havoc you have wreaked in Kaukab's land for you are Hamza's son and Kaukab is our ally. You must investigate the origin of your birth!' Jahangir was unmoved by this disclosure and declared, 'I will not turn back until I kill Kaukab!' Amar returned to his camp and struck the drums to announce a battle between Chabak and him. Chabak retaliated with his own drums and the two armies stayed up that night preparing for battle.

During the night, Amar disguised himself as an ayyar from Chabak's army and strolled over to Chabak's tent. They chatted for a while and Amar asked him for wine. When Chabak went in the tent to pour him a goblet, Amar unsheathed Chabak's sword, filled the scabbard with a drug powder and replaced the sword. After some time, Amar left and Chabak retired for the night. The next morning, Chabak went to the battlefield alert and armed with his tools of ayyari. Amar went forward to confront him and Chabak drew out his sword. The movement released a cloud of drug powder from the scabbard that made Chabak sneeze and fall unconscious. As Jahangir watched from his side, Amar lifted Chabak and returned to his camp shouting triumphantly.

Jahangir returned to his pavilion, very depressed by the capture of his brother. At that time, Barq Firangi assumed Chabak's face and walked into the pavilion. Jahangir was overjoyed and asked him, 'How did you manage to escape from Amar?' The false Chabak smirked and said, 'It was my double he captured! Come with me, I want to share a secret with you!' Jahangir readily went with him. In the privacy of Chabak's tent, Barq made him unconscious with drugged wine and tied him in a sheet before taking him to Amar in the fort of Zarafshan.

Afrasiyab again came to Jahangir's rescue by transforming magically into Kaukab. He took Amar aside and said, 'Amar, hand over Jahangir, Chabak and the magic keystone to me. You have seen what havoc they have wreaked in my Tilism. I am afraid that someone might exploit your greedy nature and get them from you.' Amar was offended by these words and brought the young men out of Zambil along with the keystone. Afrasiyab, in Kaukab's form, thus managed to fool Amar and escaped with the two brothers and the magic keystone as well. Later, he gave Jahangir the keystone and said, 'O Sahibqiran, may I felicitate you in advance as you will now triumph over Kaukab's Tilism with this keystone. Rest for a few days and then advance further. You do not need me any more!' Meanwhile, the real Kaukab had come to the fort of Zarafshan. When Amar saw him, he turned his face away scornfully. Kaukab was mystified by Amar's behaviour and asked him what was wrong. Amar said, 'You have insulted me by calling me greedy and taking the prisoners and the keystone!' Kaukab paled visibly and cried, 'Khwaja, by your faith, I am not aware of this.' Amar realized that he had been deceived by Afrasiyab and swore that he would retrieve the keystone right away.

Meanwhile, Jahangir was back in his camp and sat triumphantly with the keystone. When Amar entered his durbar disguised as a sahir, he heard him declare, 'I have no worries now. If I have got the keystone, it will not be long before I get Kaukab!' Finally, that day also ended and the time came when the dark night revealed its face. Amar tried his best to get the keystone, but did not succeed. Eventually, he used the oils and paints of trickery to transform into Afrasiyab. He took out the throne of ancestors from Zambil and used dyed cottonwool to contrive the red cloud that remained suspended over Afrasiyab's head. Then, dressed as Afrasiyab, he went to Jahangir's durbar on the throne, tossing a lime in his hand. Jahangir rose to greet him and led him to the place of honour. The false Afrasiyab said, 'O Sahibqiran, give me the keystone as I want my grandmother Mahi Emerald-robe to examine it. Amar is an ayyar and he may have exchanged the keystone for something else!' Jahangir willingly gave him the keystone and was startled to hear Afrasiyab say, 'I am Amar!' The ayyar vanished in Galeem. The throne of ancestors flew him back to his camp and he secured the magic keystone in Zambil.

~

27 Kaukab Sends for Emir Hamza to Defeat Jahangir, the Conversion of Jahangir and Ayyars' Trickeries

Kaukab, the wise, pondered over Jahangir and came to the conclusion that only Hamza or one of his sons would be able to vanquish him. He asked his childhood companion Maimar Qudrat, who was visiting with his brother Tajdar, to proceed to Mount Agate and bring the Emir back with them. In Mount Agate, Emir Hamza and his army had suffered heavy losses at the hands of the powerful sahir Paikan Jadoo, who had been sent by Afrasiyab to help Laqa. Paikan had burnt fifty Muslim sardars to death with the help of his hooded magic warrior. The same night, Paikan had declared in Laqa's durbar that he would erase the Great Name from Hamza's memory.

Right after making this declaration, Paikan vanished and returned to his tent. He moulded a bird from lentil flour and brought it to life by conjuring a flame in its belly. Paikan then transformed himself into Isfahani, a trusted ayyar in Hamza's camp. He tucked the bird in his palm and went to the Pavilion of Solomon. At the entrance, he sent a message to Hamza that he wanted to consult him privately regarding the possible revival of the destroyed sardars. As Emir emerged from the pavilion, Paikan released the magic bird that circled over Hamza's head and returned to perch on Paikan's hand.

Emir looked enquiringly at the false ayyar who shouted, 'I am Paikan Jadoo! Ya Emir, I came here to capture the Great Name! Do you remember it now?' Paikan then vanished, leaving Hamza stunned and bewildered. Paikan materialized in his own camp and sealed the magic bird in a glass jar. He summoned a giant and handed the jar to him after urging him to secure it. That night, he struck battle drums for another battle with the Emir.

Maimar and Tajdar arrived the next day and met the Emir, who related the sorry tale of Paikan's treachery the previous evening. Tajdar declared, 'I will confront Paikan and restore the Great Name to you!' He went to the battlefield and lobbed an iron ball that disappeared in the air. Within moments, a parizad floated down from the sky. Paikan quickly retaliated by summoning a giant who materialized holding the glass jar with the magic bird in his hand. The parizad swooped down on the giant and managed to smash the jar before clinging to the giant in a fiery embrace. Both the giant and the parizad were burnt and the Great Name was restored to Sahibqiran.

Paikan quickly had the drums of peace struck and returned to his camp. Tajdar said to the Emir, 'Ya Emir, return to the pavilion and I will return presently with the sardars who you thought had been destroyed!' Tajdar had used his magical powers to find out where the sardars were being held. He then rescued the sardars and left puppet doubles of the prisoners and their guards. He then brought back the sardars in triumph to Emir Hamza. Meanwhile, Paikan had the puppet doubles executed, but soon realized that he had been hoodwinked and that the sardars were safe with Hamza.

Paikan rose in fury to attack the Muslim camp, but Tajdar conjured a fort and captured Paikan and his sardars. The rest of his army was destroyed and Laqa escaped to the Fort Agate. When Paikan and his sardars were presented to Emir Hamza, they consulted each other and decided that the faith of the Emir seemed to be the True One and decided to ally with him. The Emir was happy to hear this declaration and bestowed robes of honour upon them.

After settling this matter, Emir Hamza travelled to Tilism Nur Afshan and reached Kaukab's lashkar. The time came when the king of the day was hidden by the veil of night. Jahangir ordered that battle drums be struck. The Emir was alone, but Jahangir's camp was up all night as sahirs awakened their magic with sacred fires and bells. Heralds called out to awaken the brave and inspired them with battle verses. All night, the camp was in a state of anticipation until the time came when the mighty King of the East emerged with the lance of sunlight in his hand and mounted the steed of the sky.

In the morning, Kaukab sent his army out with Emir Hamza who reached the battlefield in great splendour. The two armies faced each other in orderly rows and the field was cleared. Jahangir rode into the field and called out, 'Ya Emir come forth!' Emir Hamza flew on his great horse Ashqar and faced Jahangir, who greeted him politely. After Emir acknowledged his greeting, Jahangir said, 'Ya Emir, let us settle the battle by wrestling with each other!' The Emir jumped off Ashqar and both adversaries removed their armour and tied simple loincloths for the wrestling bout. They made their moves and smashed their heads together with such force that a wall of iron could be reduced to dust between them. On the seventh day of wrestling, Jahangir's strength was flagging and Emir managed to push him back several paces before jerking him so hard that he fell on his knees. The Emir looked down at Jahangir and declared, 'I will be making my battle call! Protect yourself and do not complain that I screamed to vanquish you!' A defeated Jahangir murmured, 'This is a vast arena. Scream as loudly as you want!' Amar called out, 'May Allah protect us! Block your ears with cottonwool! Emir's battlecry can cause pregnant women to abort!'

The sardars moved their horses and blocked their ears as Emir roared out his battlecry and lifted Jahangir up in the air before smashing him down on the ground. He tied Jahangir's limbs together and returned to his camp in triumph. That evening, Sahibqiran sent for Jahangir's uncle from his camp and asked him, 'Tell us now. Whose son is Jahangir?' The man declared at first that Jahangir was Khurshid Taj Buksh's son, but after much argument, finally revealed the truth.

'Ya Emir, do you recall the time that you married the parizad princess Shams Pari and Amar married her companion Durdana Pari? They gave birth to these two boys. One day, when they were pregnant, they emerged in the real world and went into labour right then and gave birth. Malik Khurshid Buksh happened to be there and coveted the beautiful babies. He transformed magically into a desert lion and roared at the women, who fled for their lives leaving their children behind. He kidnapped the babies and brought them up as his own sons. Thus, Jahangir is your son and Chabak is Amar's son!'

Sahibqiran went and embraced Jahangir while Amar put his arms around Chabak. Amar returned the magic keystone and the invincible sword back to Kaukab while Sahibqiran returned with Jahangir to Mount Agate. Jahangir and Chabak converted to the True faith before Jahangir requested his father to reunite him with his beloved Princess Mah. Kaukab willingly released the princess and her companion Gulzar and they were married off to Jahangir and Chabak.

V

28 Amar Rescues Prince Asad Lion-heart

The reader will recall that Princess Burran Sword-woman had sworn to destroy the River of Flowing Blood and the Bridge of Smoke. With her father Kaukab's blessings she made the arduous journey to the Crystal Dome of Samri. The ghost of Samri gave her a boon, after which she destroyed the river and the bridge. The other significant event was that Baghban Qudrat was magically blinded and imprisoned by Afrasiyab. He was rescued by Amar and regained his sight after he finally joined the rebel camp with his wife Gulcheen. Afrasiyab then decided to execute Asad Ghazi who had been kept a prisoner in the Dome of Light all these years.

Amar, after consulting Kaukab, Maimar and Mahrukh, decided to take his next big step, which was to set off alone to rescue Prince Asad. Everyone was apprehensive about his undertaking such a major mission alone, but the brave Amar embraced his friends and reassured them that for this crucial mission, it was best for him to travel alone.

Thus, Amar left his friends, who feared greatly for his safety, for an unknown destination. On his way, Amar saw a rich and opulent wedding procession. Ever on the lookout for making money, Amar took out the paints of ayyari from Zambil and disguised himself as a professional singer. The young singer was fair of face and wore a heavily-embroidered cap and earrings, and held a miniature sitar in one hand. He joined the wedding procession and began attracting attention by loudly praising the bridegroom, his father the *thakur*, and the family in general. The rich thakur requested him to sing a ghazal and Amar obliged readily. He soon had the audience spellbound with his melodious renditions and collected a great deal of money.

While Amar was entertaining the wedding procession, a powerful sahira Samankal Jadoo, one of Afrasiyab's special officeholders, heard him as she rested in her garden close to the site of the bridal party. Samankal heard Amar singing and flew upwards to investigate. When she saw the singer, she hovered in the air, entranced by the beauty of his voice. She was also attracted to the young singer's beautiful face and decided that she wanted him for herself. Samankal swooped down on the wedding party and whisked Amar up into the air, leaving the audience gaping at her. Amar fainted with the rush of air and when he woke up, found himself in a beautiful garden. At Samankal's request, Amar obligingly sang evocative ghazals. Naturally, he begged to serve the fair sahira with wine, hoping to play one of his usual tricks. Taken up with his singing, Samankal unsuspectingly raised the drugged goblet to her lips when a voice warned her, 'Beware princess, this is Amar ayyar!' The wine then burst into flames and the goblet was shattered.

Samankal came to her senses and drew her sword out on Amar. She shouted, 'You dare to deceive me, you thief! I will kill you at once!' Amar began weeping helplessly and gasped between sobs, 'Princess, you must do justice to me. I did not ask to come here! I sing professionally to supplement my income. You know that Mahrukh does not pay me even a single coin. In fact, she takes away whatever I make on such occasions.' Amar saw that the sahira seemed uncertain and continued, 'Samankal, you are a wise and far-seeing woman. Do not stain your hands with my blood. You must have read the divine books predicting that Asad is Tilism Kusha. Look how a great Tilism like Hoshruba is now under siege. Mahrukh grows in strength while Tilism is weakened day by day.'

The sahira heard him say this quietly and that encouraged Amar to press on, 'Look at your religion with an open mind. Samri and Jamshed were sahirs like you, but they eventually died. Only the One True God runs the universe, and every plant and every flower bears witness to his greatness. Save yourself now before He takes you to task when you die and when your own tongue will bear witness against you. Let the light of Islam illuminate your heart. You know that I am innocent!' As Amar spoke, Samankal's face went pale, her body started to tremble and she could barely form the words as she spoke, 'Khwaja, your words have filled me with the light of the One True God. Even so, it would be difficult for me to leave Afrasiyab for he will not leave me alive!'

Amar responded reassuringly to her, 'That is your fear speaking. What is Afrasiyab's strength compared to the ultimate Saviour? It is He who has saved Mahrukh, Bahar and all the others countless times.' Samankal folded her hands and said, 'Then I am with you. As soon as I get the opportunity, I will join your lashkar.' While they were talking Afrasiyab happened to consult the oracle Book of Samri in his durbar and jumped up in a rage crying, 'That harridan Samankal has joined the rebels!' Afrasiyab summoned a sahir and handed him a glass vial of magic water. He ordered, 'Go and arrest both Amar and Samankal from her garden.

She is powerful, so do not fight with her, just sprinkle a few drops of this water on her.' The sahir flew off to the garden and reached there within moments. He gave a mighty shout as he descended, 'You treacherous hussy! You dare to bring the enemy to your house! Did you not fear Shahanshah?'

Gulgoon Soft-Eye

Samankal looked up startled when she heard this. Before she could use a magical weapon against the sahir, he sprinkled the magic water on her and Amar, and they both fell unconscious. The sahir shouted in triumph and lifting both of them on his shoulders, flew off towards Afrasiyab. On his way, he was flying over the garden of another powerful sahira called Gulgoon Soft-eye. Now Afrasiyab had ordered all his nobles to hone their magical skills for he was planning to execute Asad Ghazi and expected his enemies to attack soon. Accordingly, Gulgoon and her companions were in her garden, practising war spells. Some conjured thunderstorms and lightning, while others produced huge flames. The rest experimented with transformations, and kept turning into eagles or shooting stars.

Just as the sahir was flying overhead with the Shah's prisoners, Gulgoon lobbed an enormous iron ball into the sky. As fate would have it, the ball landed on the sahir's chest and killed him instantly. Gulgoon watched in horror as the dead sahir and Amar landed in her garden, while Samankal fell beyond the garden and fled to a distant hill to hide. As she ran to hide, Samankal thought of how Amar's words had been prophetic—the Hand of God did indeed save them from the clutches of the sahir.

Gulgoon's handmaidens soon revived Amar. When Gulgoon asked him for an explanation, Amar said with practised deceit, 'I am but a poor singer. My name is Ustad Khurd Burd. This sahir seemed to like me more than my voice and kept making suggestive remarks to me all evening. Eventually, when I asked him for my payment, he flew off with me, telling me I would have to spend the night with him!' As her companions and handmaidens sniggered at the implication of Amar's words, Gulgoon scolded them and requested Amar to entertain her that evening. Amar touched his ears melodramatically and said, 'I have sworn never to sing again unless I am paid in advance!' The handmaidens cried out mockingly, 'Our princess will be very generous provided you do not dally with men again!' Gulgoon then sent for a sack of gold coins for Amar. He looked greedily at the plump and rosy-cheeked handmaiden who had carried it and said, 'Princess, if this lady commands me, I will sing!' Gulgoon smiled and teased him playfully, 'So my handmaiden Nargis is more important to you than my request?'

'Princess, this lady reminds me of my wife who is cheerful and plump. The only thing is that she refuses to breastfeed me, which is why I am so frail and thin! My grandmother had advised me to drink my wife's milk to become strong!' As Amar continued talking nonsense, the princess and her companions giggled and urged Nargis to sit with Amar. The handmaiden smilingly obliged, but when Amar tried to fondle her bosom, she kicked him sharply in the ribs. Amar laughed and then burst into a love song. Very soon, he had the whole company swaying to his songs. He then proceeded to the next stage, when he served them with drugged wine.

Overcome by the combination of wine and drugs, Gulgoon and her companions behaved in a highly comical manner. Some of them started fighting with each other while others stared fixedly into space. Some others ran towards the fountain and fell into the waters. Gulgoon finally lost her temper and admonished her staff for misbehaving, but soon fell unconscious herself. Amar prepared to kill the whole lot of them, starting with Gulgoon's companions. Meanwhile, Afrasiyab, who was waiting for the sahir to deliver his prisoners, consulted the oracle Book of Samri and screamed in anger, 'My friends, this is terrible! Amar is about to kill Gulgoon and I must fly there to rescue her!' Afrasiyab's viziers volunteered to go instead, but the Shahanshah was already flying off and called out, 'Stay here, only I can reach her in time!'

By this time, Amar had killed all of Gulgoon's companions and was about to slay the princess when he heard Afrasiyab's thunderous voice booming, 'Beware, you son of a camel driver! Do not dare to touch Gulgoon Soft-eye or I promise I will cut you into a thousand pieces! I will not leave a Muslim alive on this earth!' Amar looked up startled and ran off through the courtyard into the garden. Though there were several fine buildings in the garden, Amar took refuge in a small hut that was a storeroom for old carpets. Afrasiyab wasted no time in looking for Amar and revived the unconscious princess. She murmured drowsily as she awoke, 'Ustad Khurd Burd, how well you sing! Please continue to sing as hearts burst with love on hearing your voice!' Afrasiyab slapped the inebriated princess and said, 'Open your eyes, you silly girl! You could have been killed by this Khurd Burd!' Despite his rage, Afrasiyab was amused to hear Amar's pseudonym. He laughed out aloud as he thought, 'Amar changes his names to fit his disguises!' Gulgoon, however, looked around at the carnage in her palace with horror. 'I was expecting my sahir to bring Amar and Samankal to me,' said Afrasiyab. 'How did Amar come to your garden?'

Gulgoon sobbed as she told Afrasiyab about how she had accidentally killed his sahir. 'I did see a woman as well but she disappeared. That singer dropped into my garden. He was so entertaining huzoor and had such a beautiful voice. I am not sure what happened next.' 'That was no singer, you fool!' scolded Afrasiyab. 'It was Amar ayyar and he seems to have escaped. However, search your garden thoroughly and remain very alert.' When Afrasiyab left, Gulgoon promised that she would remain vigilant and began collecting the bodies of her dead companions for their funerals.

Maraan Earth-bound and her grandmother, Asrar

Amar was still hiding in the small hut, but was getting anxious about escaping from there as he knew sahirs would be searching for him. He was groping in the darkness when he encountered something hard on the floor. It turned out to be a large padlock on a secret door. Amar easily picked the lock and slipped into a passage leading down from the door. The passage was very dark and Amar stumbled down the stairs until he felt another door ahead of him. Amar picked the lock on this one as well and opened it. He blinked with astonishment at the wondrous sight before him. Amar saw that he was in a green and verdant plain that led to a doorway in the distance. Amar cautiously wore his cape of invisibility and walked toward the doorway that was the entrance to a beautiful garden. As Amar walked about the garden, he marvelled at the myriad aspects of Tilism Hoshruba, which seemed to be as limitless under the earth as above it. It was daybreak in the garden and several handmaidens were bustling about, while some of them were still rubbing the sleep out of their eyes. One of them went close to where Amar (who was still invisible) was standing, and squatted on the ground. Amar averted his eyes and decided that he could easily disguise himself as her.

He was about to blow a narcotic bubble at her when it occurred to him that she was young and would be frightened easily. Amar thought, 'It would be better to keep her in my Zambil. I could sell her for a good price to a rich merchant.' Accordingly, Amar removed the invisibility cape partially from his person and appeared before her as a horrible disembodied apparition. The young damsel took one look at him and fainted. Amar disposed of her in Zambil and carefully assumed her form so that he looked just like her. He joined the throng of handmaidens rushing around to get ready. One of them called out to the false maiden, 'Gulroo, make haste. Princess Maraan will be awake any moment now.' Amar realized that the maiden he was replacing was a special attendant to the princess. He snapped, 'Stop bothering me, I am not fully awake yet! Just tell me where is my room!?' Peals of laughter greeted this query as the maidens started teasing the false Gulroo, 'Listen to the hussy! She is so wanton that forgets where her own room is!' Another maiden cried, 'Mistress Gulroo is too important! She is the mistress of the robes and has so many men friends she forgets where she sleeps!'

Amar joined in their game and pretended to be angry at the insults. He slapped one maiden, pinched another's bottom, spat on the third one and threw a shoe at the fourth. Finally, he made his way to Gulroo's room. He hurriedly stripped the room of all its valuables and left only fresh robes to change into for the day. After making sure that his disguise was perfect, Amar joined the other handmaidens on their way to the princess's chamber. When he looked upon Princess Maraan's fairy-like beauty, Amar sighed in admiration and reflected, 'It was predicted that someone of her name would support us. O Allah, guide me in converting her to our side.'

Amar then looked around the chamber and heard the querulous voice of an old woman from behind a curtain. 'Who is in there?' he whispered to one of the maidens with him. She pinched the false Gulroo hard and whispered back, 'You silly strumpet! You are still drunk with last night's wine! You know well that behind that curtain is the princess's grandmother, Malika Asrar.' At that moment, Maraan's grandmother called out to her granddaughter. The princess entered the inner chamber surrounded by a bevy of her handmaidens, including Amar disguised as Gulroo. When the curtain was lifted, Amar saw a frail wrinkled old sahira lying on a bed with a gold spittoon placed next to her. Despite her advanced years, the old sahira looked alert and watchful.

Maraan embraced her grandmother and the old woman said with smoke billowing from her mouth, 'My child, please heed the times. You seem to do nothing but play silly games. Do you not realize that this is a crucial moment for you? Tilism Kusha is about to be executed, may Samri and Jamshed protect us from all harm! Ever since I have woken up today, my heart is heavy with fears. My magic has informed me that Amar ayyar has entered your garden. Please remember that you are the custodian of the Dome of Light. We dare not displease Afrasiyab. Now go at once and look for Amar among your handmaidens.'

Maraan had to try hard not to smile as she listened to her grandmother with her head bowed. She left her chamber and went into the garden with her handmaidens, dissolving into barely suppressed giggles. Amar kissed her feet and said, 'My princess, what does your grandmother say?' Maraan smiled as she said, 'Gulroo, my grandmother seems to be still drunk from the wine she had last night. She was telling me to look for Amar ayyar amongst my handmaidens. I ask you, how is it possible for Amar to find his way here? Not unless my cousin Gulgoon helps him to find the secret chamber and that is impossible. Do not worry, just prepare for the evening's entertainment. I want to enjoy the full moon tonight!'

Just as Amar breathed a sigh of relief at her reaction, Malika Asrar called out again to Maraan, 'Have you found Amar yet?' Maraan replied breezily, 'Not yet, although I have scoured the length and breadth of this garden!' Asrar shouted angrily, 'Do you think I am senile? Send one of your handmaidens with the Red Book to me right away! I will tell you where Amar is.' Maraan laughed and brought out the book of divination. She was about to take it herself when Amar volunteered to take it, planning to dispose of the troublesome old sahira before he was discovered. When he took the book into the inner chamber, the old woman looked at him sharply before opening the book to read it. Amar quickly attacked her with his snare-rope. Its coils wrapped around her neck and decapitated her quite unexpectedly. Amar was astounded and inspected the snare-rope closely when the wall of the chamber cracked open and Asrar's voice called out, 'You son of a camel driver! Did you think I was Hairat or Afrasiyab, or did you mistake me for Mussavir or Soorat Nigar?'

Amar turned around startled and tried to attack Asrar again, but she stamped on the ground and a flame leapt up to melt off the paints of disguise from Amar's face. Amar saw that the beheaded body of Asrar on the bed was actually an effigy made of lentil flour. Asrar now called out, 'My child, come in now! You thought I was losing my mind. Come and see how I have discovered Amar!' Maraan rushed into the chamber with her handmaidens and looked in horror at the sight of Amar standing there, his body trembling with fear. As Maraan paled visibly, Asrar said, 'I had informed you a week ago that Amar would enter this garden. Now send for your cousin Gulgoon so that we can hand over this rascal to Shahanshah.'

Maraan's handmaidens brought a large iron cage to imprison Amar but before they could push him inside, he folded his hands and said, 'O Malika Asrar, I will be honest with you. I have never come across a sahira of your calibre in Hoshruba. I have sent many sahirs to hell and killed many others like dirty dogs, but have not come across anyone who could predict my arrival a week before I came. I am now convinced that your religion is the mightiest. I just want to serve as your humble slave now. You are the perfection of magic and I am unmatched in ayyari.

We will go well together. Let me lead your army to destroy Mahrukh and then Hamza in Mount Agate. Convert me to your faith and I promise that I will drink cow's urine but never mention the Muslims again!'

Asrar heard him out and cackled in response, 'Well spoken Khwaja sahib, wonderful! You can deceive Afrasiyab and Mussavir with such double talk, but not me, Asrar. Your end is near and Asad is about to be executed. If that happens now, Tilism is safe. I have read the Samri Nama that states clearly that no sahir will kill Amar, but I have proved it wrong. Your life is in my hands.' Amar changed his tactics and defiantly said, 'In that case, a curse on your Samri and Jamshed! How can you kill me if this is what they predicted? If they were wrong, what kind of religion is this? You are right; I will never join you, but will kill your kind at every opportunity! My God is great and comes to the succour of every man. He blesses all individuals. He is the One True God, the wisest, the most generous, the most vengeful and the most forgiving. He will enable me to triumph over all of you. If you are as wise as you claim you are, then embrace Islam, do not worship idols like Samri. They were sahirs and died like dogs. I have shaved the beard of the one you call your living god Laqa who flees from Hamza from land to land. He is a mortal like you and me. He eats, he sleeps and he relieves himself. He has been captured and released by Hamza a hundred times, but is so shameless that he is still defiant. Malika, this is your religion.'

Asrar was stirred by the power and truth in Amar's speech; she remained silent for a while and then said, 'Stop talking now. If you are saved from certain death today, we will see.' Gulgoon had also reached Maraan's garden by now and on seeing Amar locked in a cage, clutched Maraan's sleeve nervously. Maraan whispered, 'Gulgoon, Amar has spoken in such a strange manner to our grandmother that my heart was shaken. How did he come from your garden?' Gulgoon whispered the details of Amar's descent into her garden and added, 'I cannot describe to you how beautifully this rascal sings!'

Asrar turned and scolded her granddaughters for whispering nonsense to each other, and urged them to take Amar immediately to the Garden of Apples. Gulgoon got her attendant to take Amar's cage into her garden above the ground. She was just about to leave with her prisoner when Samankal, who had been hiding close by, attacked her. Samankal was more powerful and managed to wound Gulgoon. Maraan and Asrar arrived just then, captured both Amar and his rescuer, and travelled with them to Afrasiyab's court. As they stood before the Shahanshah, Asrar said, 'Huzoor, you know best. My advice to you is to kill Amar today. I can give it to you in writing that if he remains alive, Asad will escape. If you execute Amar, Tilism cannot be conquered.'

Afrasiyab replied, 'You are my well wisher and I will do as you advise. We will announce his execution today and he will be killed tomorrow morning.' Afrasiyab handed the cage to his companion Gulrang Jadoo and urged her to guard the prisoner herself that night. Gulrang did that, but Amar was free to move around in the cage and kept tantalizing his keeper with phenomenal gifts from Zambil. Eventually, the sahira succumbed to her curiosity and asked him to show her the blessed pouch. Amar unfastened the cords around Zambil as Gulrang stepped into the cage to have a closer look at the city she could see from the outside. Amar quickly trapped her inside Zambil. Four monstrously black guards wearing black uniforms surrounded her as soon as she fell into the pouch and as Gulrang screamed, the guards ruthlessly stripped her clothes off, tied a muddy sarong on her and placed a heavy basket of wet mud on her head. One of them roughly asked her to walk towards a building site with her load. Poor Gulrang tried to remember her magic, but could not recall a single spell. Every time she stopped walking, one of the guards landed an almighty blow on her buttocks.

Meanwhile, Amar had also pushed Samankal (who was with him in the same cage) into Zambil. She, of course, received vastly different treatment as Amar's ally. He then took out a woman from Zambil whom he painted to look like Samankal. He also brought out a prisoner from Zambil whom he disguised as himself. Finally, he used the paints and oils of ayyari to transform himself into Gulrang. Amar was now ready to join Afrasiyab's durbar.

When he reached the durbar, he saw that Afrasiyab was quite drunk and casting lustful looks at the beautiful Maraan. Amar managed to drug the wine being served in the durbar and very soon, everyone including the Shahanshah, Asrar and Maraan were unconscious. This time, Amar did not succumb to his greed. He resisted stealing valuables from the durbar and drew out his sword to kill Asrar Jadoo. He thought, 'This woman is dangerous. How well she convinced Afrasiyab to kill me before Asad!'

Just as Amar was about to behead her, the ground beneath him trembled. Amar stepped back and saw that it parted to reveal Nur Afshan, Kaukab's venerable old tutor and adviser. Nur Afshan's face was covered with a layer of dust and he was sweating with the rigours of his underground journey. As the ayyar gaped at him, Nur Afshan held Amar's sword hand and said, 'O king of ayyars, you have done remarkably well but the prophecies tell us that Asrar will be on your side. If you kill her now, we will never be able to rescue Asad. I learned through my magic that you were about to kill her and travelled through the earth to reach you. It is not possible for most men to do that. Thank Allah I am here! Asrar has been reflecting on your speech to her earlier. She just needs you to convince her now.'

Amar looked down in shame and said quietly, 'Nur Afshan, you have done me a great service today. By Allah, I overlooked all this in my rage.' Nur Afshan then carried the still unconscious Asrar and Maraan to a secret place and revived them. Asrar woke up and looked at Amar and then at Nur Afshan, whom she knew well. Nur Afshan answered the silent appeal in her eyes by saying, 'O Malika Asrar, you know that this Tilism will be conquered. I have lived long like you. I was a companion of Samri and Jamshed. They were powerful, unscrupulous devils. Amar has shown me the right path. Afrasiyab's arrogance will destroy him and Tilism will also be destroyed. You above all are privy to all its secrets and know this already. Join us now.' Tears were running down Malika Asrar's cheeks by then as she said, 'My brother, I swear by the True Creator that your words have affected me deeply. You have cleansed my heart of the dust of infidelity. My mind is at peace now. My life is at your disposal. O Shah Nur Afshan, the night of Asad's execution will weigh heavily upon me and my life will be in danger. But that will be a test of my faith.'

Then Asrar placed Maraan's hand in Amar's and said, 'O enlightened guide, this young person will be with you until the eve of Asad's execution and will guide you through the magic path. I will have to remain with Afrasiyab in the Garden of Apples or he will become suspicious.' Amar replied, 'If God is with us, we will overcome all obstacles. It is close to daybreak now and Afrasiyab will be awake soon. Make sure that my double and Samankal's double in the cage are executed tomorrow. Distract Afrasiyab by celebrating the executions.' Asrar Jadoo then stated, 'O king of tricksters, tomorrow everyone is meant to gather in the Dome of Light. Afterwards, I am to accompany Afrasiyab to the Garden of Apples. Tomorrow night, Princess Maraan will travel with you on your journey through the magic path. Remain alert and look after yourself.'

After exchanging farewells, Nur Afshan put his arm around Amar and flew to the safety of Tilism Nur Afshan, while Asrar and her granddaughter Maraan went back to join Afrasiyab in his durbar. Everyone was still unconscious there and Maraan and Asrar pretended to sleep as well. The next morning, an unsuspecting Afrasiyab woke up to find Asrar in attendance. He was discussing the details of Asad's intended execution with her when some of his officials informed him that thousands of people had collected to witness Amar's execution. 'The thing is huzoor,' they said, 'everyone is very doubtful as Amar has managed to escape several times already!'

Asrar Jadoo was in the forefront of the counsellors who advised Afrasiyab to execute Amar immediately. Accordingly, the two prisoners were led out of the iron cage and beheaded. Afrasiyab's courtiers jostled with each other as they rushed to pay homage to him on the joyous occasion. Asrar advised him to inform only Hairat of the great event to avoid Mahrukh's attacks. She said, 'Let us announce Amar and Asad's executions together!'

The night of the execution

Amar disguised himself as a beautiful sahira to accompany Maraan on the magic path. She took him to her underground garden that had a secret passage all the way to the Dome of Light. The entrance to the secret passage was hidden in the floor under a heavy throne in her baradari. There, Amar disguised himself as her grandmother Asrar while Maraan threw herself on the ground and transformed herself magically into a huge serpent. Amar climbed on the serpent and it slithered into the dark passage, illuminating it with flames from its mouth. After some distance, the passage opened into a large chamber with rich furnishings. A sahir who stood guard there called out, 'Who comes?'

Maraan transformed into her real self while Amar identified himself as Queen Asrar and added, 'You must remain very alert as Tilism Kusha is to be executed this night. Even Shahanshah will remain awake in his durbar tonight.' The sahir Hoshiar welcomed the false Asrar and Maraan and deferentially took them to his inner chamber. As soon as they settled down, Amar presented Hoshiar with a small flask of drugged wine. He pretended to take a sip and insisted Hoshiar share it with him too. Hoshiar looked uncomfortable and said, 'Malika, we have been strictly forbidden to drink wine tonight. The papers of Samri predict clearly that Amar will come here tonight. I would like to remain alert.' The false Asrar cackled and said, 'My son, Amar's shadow cannot find this secret passage. Don't you know he has been executed this morning?' Hoshiar replied, 'Malika, you must have also read those papers which tell us Amar will offer me wine tonight.' Maraan was trembling at this turn in the conversation and marvelled at Amar's daring as he continued, 'Drink this or I will be very grieved. The Samri papers must be right! I am Amar and I am offering you this wine!' The false Asrar then held Hoshiar's ears playfully and cried, 'You cannot withstand my powers. Samri and

Jamshed will not be able to save you from me. After all I have to get a good price from the Muslims for your head!'

Hoshiar, who did not wish to offend the powerful Asrar, said, 'I dare not refuse you. Of course I will drink your wine.' As Hoshiar took the goblet of wine to drink it, the wine went up in flames. Maraan was about to faint with fear as Hoshiar called out, 'What is this? Wait you rascal, I recognize you!' Amar quickly took out the Net of Ilyas, scooped Hoshiar in it and threw him into Zambil. Maraan fell on her knees, weak with relief, and cried, 'Khwaja sahib, you are a living marvel. But the next stage in this path is even more perilous.' Amar got busy plundering all the valuables in the room and threw them into Zambil. Maraan looked shocked at his behaviour, but continued regardless, 'Listen carefully. The next post of the magic path is guarded by a sahir whose name is Nakhal Jadoo. There is a tree just in front of Afrasiyab's baradari in the Garden of Apples that has been conjured by Nakhal. If he falls unconscious, the tree dries up. If someone kills him, the tree will go up in flames. If that happens, Afrasiyab will turn on my grandmother in revenge for he will realize she has betrayed him.'

Amar said in a soothing voice to Maraan, 'My dear child, the Almighty has brought us here and he will guide us in the future. Let us go.' Meanwhile, Asrar Jadoo was with Afrasiyab in the Garden of Apples and was glancing nervously every now and then at the tree Nakhal had planted. She also had to prevent Afrasiyab from looking at the oracle Book of Samri. At one point, Afrasiyab was about to open the magic book when Asrar kept her hand on it and distracted him by singing his praises. Afrasiyab who was always open to flattery turned away from the book and said, 'Malika Asrar, I was told that Nausherwan, a mighty king known for his generosity, was in fact an illiterate man!' Asrar replied, 'Huzoor, he was a just king but untutored in the affairs of state. There can be no comparison with you. You are the bravest; you are indeed the lion of Hoshruba! The slightest tremor of your tongue can pull the skies down! Nausherwan could not even dream of the powers you have!'

While Asrar distracted Afrasiyab with her flattering words, Amar continued travelling down the magic path with Maraan. They proceeded for some time and came across another post. The monstrous sahir guarding it saw the python that was Maraan and called out for identification. Maraan identified herself and her grandmother. The sahir who was Nakhal said, 'Princess, who can dare stop you? Every stone in this path knows your grandmother. She is our officer.' Amar heard his words carefully and observed that Nakhal was not too pleased to have guests at this time. His words were soft, but his attitude aggressive. As Maraan passed by him,

Nakhal leaned forward so that his shadow fell over the two travellers. The paints of disguise on Amar's face peeled off and Nakhal cried, 'Maraan, you traitor, you have that son of a camel driver with you!'

Amar leapt off Maraan's back as quick as lightning and became invisible under Galeem. Nakhal threw an iron ball that burst into flames while Maraan changed from a serpent into a bolt of lightning and fell on Nakhal to decapitate him. However, Nakhal was a powerful sahir and an expert in magic warfare. He moved deftly to save himself and cried, 'Maraan, you have caused great damage. Samri's predictions had clearly warned me that Amar was due on this path tonight! I was fully prepared so that whatever disguise he assumed, he would be exposed by my shadow!' As he talked, Nakhal kept an eye out for Amar, who had disappeared. The youthful Maraan attempted a few more magical attacks on Nakhal, but could only wound him slightly. He swayed and called out loudly, 'Ya Samri!' once before stamping hard on the ground. Maraan immediately fell down in a crumpled heap, looking lifeless. Nakhal was about to behead her with his sword when Amar appeared before him crying, 'You are a shameless one for attacking a woman! Come and confront a real man for a change!' As Nakhal looked up startled, Amar hit him hard on the head with the mighty Hammer of David. The unfortunate Nakhal's head exploded into a thousand pieces and darkness engulfed the magic path. His guardian spirits wailed out, 'Alas, you have killed me—my name was Nakhal. Alas I have died and gave up my life to no purpose!'

Maraan regained consciousness and started beating her head in frustration. 'Why did you have to kill him?' she shouted at Amar. 'Why do you think?' Amar retorted. 'He was about to kill you!' Maraan started weeping and said, 'This is the end! Nakhal's tree of life will burn in the Garden of Apples and Afrasiyab will surely kill my grandmother for treachery. Let us run to the Dome of Light, there is no time to lose!' Amar sprinted behind Maraan as she ran on the magic path towards a hidden entrance to the Dome of Light that had materialized after Nakhal's death. Even as he followed Maraan, Amar began painting himself to look like Afrasiyab.

Afrasiyab learns the truth

In the Garden of Apples it was almost daybreak and Asrar Jadoo had successfully distracted Afrasiyab from consulting the oracle Book of Samri for some time. Suddenly, a flame fell from the sky on Nakhal's life tree and it started burning. Afrasiyab screamed and beat his forehead shouting, 'You whore Asrar! You did not let me see the book all night. It is clear you have joined the Muslims! Alas, the guardian of the magic path is dead! Amar must have killed him as predicted. Who could have guided him there except your granddaughter?' Afrasiyab rushed to the Dome of Light while Asrar attacked him with weapons of magic so that several swords, knives and daggers fell on Afrasiyab. The Shahanshah shrugged these off and hissed, 'Ouf!' As he flew into the skies, the hem of his robe wound itself around Asrar Jadoo's neck. Now, as Afrasiyab flew furiously, Asrar dangled from his robe, hardly able to breathe like a fish out of water.

By this time, Amar and Maraan had reached the dungeons of the Dome of Light, and Amar's disguise as Afrasiyab was complete. All the guards on duty knelt deferentially to their master and were delighted when he presented them with a flask of wine. He urged them to drink it with him and declared, 'I am very pleased with you as you have guarded the prisoners well. I will award you each with a city!' Very soon the guards succumbed to the drugged wine and were unconscious.

Amar quickly found the key to the dungeons and shuddered as he caught sight of Asad and Mahjabeen, manacled and shackled in heavy iron chains. Asad's hair had grown to his waist, and his eyes were sunken and without lustre; Mahjabeen looked no better. Amar felt an overwhelming urge to weep, but controlled himself and released them. He handed both of them carefully to the attendants of Zambil. Just when he and Maraan were turning to leave, Afrasiyab reached the Dome of Light and hovered above it with the old woman still dangling like a lizard from the edge of his robe. Just before he entered the Dome, Afrasiyab was relieved to see his wife Hairat on a massive flying throne with magic bouquets laid before her. She seemed to be accompanied by Vizier Abriq Mountain-breaker holding his weapons of stones, Mussavir Jadoo the magic artist carrying his portraits and Vizier Sarmaya Ice-maker holding snowballs in his hands. For the reader's information, these personages were in reality the ayyars— Chalak was disguised as Hairat; Barq as Mussavir, Qiran as Abriq and Zargham as Sarmaya. They had stolen into Hairat's camp at night and after rendering the top commanders unconscious, had stolen the artefacts of magic that were the signature weapons of each of them.

When Afrasiyab saw the false Hairat, he called out, 'O lady of my palace, we have been betrayed! This traitor Asrar did not let me consult the oracle book all night and Amar must have reached the Dome of Light!' Chalak disguised as Hairat called back, 'You go ahead my Shahanshah, but first hand me this treacherous whore Asrar!' Afrasiyab gestured and his robe released Asrar. She dropped down on the ayyars' flying throne. Just then, Amar made a thundering announcement on the white horn, the magic amplifier of giants, 'O sahirs of Islam, Allah has been kind to us. I have Asad and Mahjabeen in my possession!' As they heard his call, Bahar and Baghban Qudrat, who had also come to rescue Asad and Mahjabeen, attacked the forces of Afrasiyab collected at the base of the Dome of Light. Afrasiyab was startled at the sound of Amar's announcement and turned around instinctively when the quartet of ayyars burst narcotic bubbles in his direction. Afrasiyab could not withstand this sudden onslaught and went hurtling down to the ground.

Before he fell, however, he managed to move his fingers and the ayyars' flying throne was smashed to smithereens. Undaunted, the ayyars used the stolen magic weapons of the sahirs even as they fell to certain death from that height. Powerful sahirs from their army like Baghban and Bahar conjured magic claws to save them from falling. Asrar, who was with them on the throne also catapulted down when Chalak called out, 'Someone save her, she seems to be one of us!' A claw saved her as well. The magic weapons they had flung earlier fell on Afrasiyab's army. Hairat's bouquets scattered into deadly petals of flames that set thousands alight. Mussavir's portraits came alive and fought like demons. Sarmaya's magic snowballs fell like mountains of ice crushing many more, and Abriq's stones fell like giant rocks on the harassed army. By this time, Maraan had flown with Amar towards his camp, even though she was shaking like a leaf with fright.

Meanwhile, the city of Napursan had hosted Afrasiyab's guests who had come to witness Asad's execution the next morning. Among them were the powerful kings Neelum and Tausan who had remained awake all night with their armies. As the magic weapons caused havoc in their ranks, they emerged from their pavilions completely bewildered. Afrasiyab's faithful parizads saved him as he fell from the sky. When he woke up, the real Hairat was bending over him in concern. Afrasiyab jumped up red-faced and said angrily, 'Why Hairat! Should I not cut your nose off? Your magic has destroyed thousands of our supporters!' Hairat stammered, 'Shahanshah, I have been unconscious all night. I had specially prepared the bouquets to tackle the enemy!'

Mussavir, along with Sarmaya and Abriq, also came forward. Afrasiyab looked at Mussavir angrily and said, 'Murshidzadeh, you really are a haramzada! Stop your magic portraits right now!' Mussavir also lost his temper and said, 'Control your tongue and stop talking such nonsense or else I will have your Tilism destroyed by my grandfathers!' The reader will remember that Mussavir was the grandson of the great god Samri from a slave woman. Afrasiyab laughed derisively and said,

'Your grandfathers were useless idols. What kind of destiny did they decree? Do you realize that Tilism Kusha is now free?' Eventually, the royals stopped bickering and began destroying the magic weapons that had been unleashed on their army. As the magic storms abated, Neelum and Tausan informed Afrasiyab that the ayyars' strategy had led to the destruction of twelve lakh soldiers that morning.

Afrasiyab's revenge

The royal pavilion of the rebel camp was in fine form that evening as sardars thronged around Amar, praising his daring rescue of Asad. Amar had still not taken Asad and Mahjabeen out from Zambil and was happily accepting the praise along with heaps of gold coins and jewels that the sardars were showering on him. Suddenly, the earth quivered ominously and split open. Afrasiyab emerged from the earth within the celebrating soldiers and stomped into the royal pavilion. On seeing the sardars jubilant with triumph, he thundered, 'You traitors and Amar, you worthless son of a camel driver! You have caused me great grief. Now see how you are rewarded for your treachery!'

Before the sardars could reach for their magic weapons, before the ayyars could reach for their snare-ropes, before Amar could wear Galeem to become invisible, Afrasiyab waved his fingers in the air and everyone froze into lifeless statues. Afrasiyab emerged from the royal pavilion and saw that the rebel army stood motionless and in a state of shock. Hairat and the rest of the Shahanshah's nobles and guests had also reached the rebel camp by then. As Neelum and Tausan cried out, 'Huzoor, wait for us!' Afrasiyab stamped his feet and sank into the earth.

Everyone was silent and watched in fascination as the earth around the royal pavilion quivered and emitted smoke. Neelum and Tausan looked at each other completely mystified. Before they could say something, there was a thunderous call from the earth, 'I am Shahanshah of Hoshruba!' To everyone's horror, the gigantic royal pavilion containing seventeen hundred rebel sardars rose shuddering from the earth. As it gained height, everyone saw the mighty Afrasiyab holding aloft the earth supporting the pavilion on his palms. The strain of holding the huge structure was obvious as the Shahanshah's hands were bleeding and his bones were creaking under the weight; the cords fastening his robe were torn and his shoes were tattered. Despite the pressure of the earth on his hands, Afrasiyab walked on, his feet faltering with each step, his mouth frothing with the effort of sustaining the heavy load.

Almost everyone from the city of Napursan had come to witness the incredible display of Afrasiyab's power and courage. There were deafening calls of 'Ya Samri! Ya Jamshed!' and the crowds roared in praise of the Shahanshah. After taking a few steps, Afrasiyab stopped and looked at his supporters, 'Is there any among you who can help me with this burden and carry it to the city of Napursan?' he called out. His supporters replied, 'Huzoor, none of us is capable. Only you are Shahanshah of Hoshruba and the King of Sahirs! You are the living image of Samri and Jamshed!' Afrasiyab retorted in anger, 'My friends, at least try and hold it in unison. You mocked me for being soft on the rebels. See how I have all sardars and the six ayyars unconscious in this pavilion! I intend to carry them to the Napursan and execute them there!' Afrasiyab's supporters remained silent and trembling, and none of them dared to help him.

Hairat saw her husband holding the pavilion aloft and realized that he was about to collapse. His fingers were bleeding and his veins bulged at his temples from the sheer pressure. She could bear the sight no longer and beating her head, cried out, 'O Shahanshah, this lowly maidservant will help you!' Afrasiyab called back, 'Lady of my palace, do not think of coming under this piece of earth!' Hairat started weeping loudly, 'O Shahanshah, how can I bear it? I am afraid that you will lose your sight with the strain or break your limbs! For the love of Samri and Jamshed, find a way out of this immediately.' Afrasiyab continued to hold the earth aloft but began feeling the strain acutely. He could feel his ribs snapping and his heart felt as if it would burst with the pressure any moment. He thought, 'She is right, I will not be able to carry this weight to Napursan. There are so many great sahirs of Tilism here. They are all traitors at heart and would mock me if I falter now.'

Afrasiyab then called out loudly, 'O slaves of Samri. Come at once, I have great need of you!' The crowds witnessed that as soon as the Shahanshah uttered these words, four heavily muscled Zangi slave-boys emerged from the earth before them. When Afrasiyab gestured to them, each one of them ran to take position under the four corners of the piece of earth the Shahanshah was holding up. Afrasiyab called again, 'Now I will let go!' The slave-boys called back, 'By the will of Samri, please step outside huzoor. It is a matter of shame that you should carry such a heavy burden when you have slaves to do it for you.' Afrasiyab was thus released from his burden and emerged from beneath the earth, swaying as he walked. Hairat rushed to embrace him and his nobles bent to kiss his hands. They fell at his feet and sobbed, 'You are the greatest sahir! Only you are worthy of Hoshruba!'

Ahwal's sacrifice

In Tilism Nur Afshan, Kaukab learned of the misfortune of the Islamic lashkar and wept at their plight. He dressed for battle and mounted his swiftest horse to go their rescue when a magic messenger bird landed on his shoulder holding a note in its beak. The message came from his best friend and Burran's teacher, Brahmin Iron-body. It contained a desperate request, 'O Shahanshah, for the love of Allah, however great your need, do not step out of the palace of Jamshed. Your stars are inauspicious at this time and you will face certain humiliation and defeat if you venture out!' Kaukab felt frustrated as he longed to help his friends and broke out in a sweat as he struggled with his thoughts.

One of his ministers, the wise Khurshid, kissed his hand and gently asked him what troubled him. Kaukab burst out, 'The Muslim sardars have been overcome by Afrasiyab, but Brahmin has specifically urged me not to venture out at this moment. This is terrible! Amar has helped me so many times and I cannot help him now. If Afrasiyab kills him today, my reputation as a man of honour is finished.' Khurshid murmured soothingly that Kaukab could not defy fate and that Brahmin must have a reason for his message. Kaukab then sent a message to Princess Burran repeating Brahmin's message, and urged her to stay in her palace.

There was an uproar in Burran's palace as the message was read out. Burran wept and said to her companions, 'I cannot disobey my father, but how can we fail to help our friends?' A little while later, Burran had a visitor, who was none other than the noble Ahwal Jadoo. Ahwal was Kaukab's foster brother and the venerable Nur Afshan's student along with Kaukab and Brahmin. Burran clung to him and wept, 'My uncle, Afrasiyab will execute all the Muslim sardars in Napursan, but Ustad Brahmin forbade us from leaving the palace. How shameful it will be if we cannot save one who has saved us so many times!' Ahwal patted her head and said, 'My child, do not grieve like this. Afrasiyab will not dare to execute any of the sardars in my lifetime. I will rescue them with the Almighty's help.'

Ahwal then conjured a round shining metal dish that circled down from the sky towards him. He sat on the disc and gestured lightly, after which the dish started spinning slowly and then vanished from sight. Burran and her companions watched him leave and prayed for his safety. Ahwal travelled invisibly until he reached Hoshruba. There, he hovered in the air above Afrasiyab and his companions as they walked back to Napursan. Afrasiyab was laughing and leading a band of two hundred nobles. He twirled his moustache with pride as he boasted, 'Why Neelum and Tausan, had Samri and Jamshed been alive today, surely they would have kneeled to me! Who but I could lift a weight like that? I am the living god of Hoshruba, no one can match me in magic and bravery!' Afrasiyab's overawed nobles responded with exaggerated compliments.

Ahwal saw that Afrasiyab was occupied with his friends and flew on until he saw the royal pavilion on the shoulders of the slave-boys of Samri. Ahwal hid the flying metal dish in a cave and stealthily flew into the rebel pavilion. He was shocked at seeing the whole durbar sitting lifeless, but controlled his emotions as he thought of a way to rescue them. He did this by creating replicas of every sardar and ayyar present in the durbar with lentil flour. There was no time for Ahwal to remove Afrasiyab's spell on the real sardars and ayyars as the city of Napursan was very close now. He muttered a spell and conjured hundreds of iron claws that whisked the sardars out of the pavilion and deposited them in a secret hideout in the nearby hills. Elated with his achievement, Ahwal managed to slip out himself just as the gates of Napursan became visible.

As the Zangi slave-boys placed the rebel pavilion before the entrance to Napursan, Hairat and her companions rushed in to gloat over their enemies. Hairat saw her sister sitting lifeless with her head slumped down and shouted, 'Why dear Bahar, where are your supporters now? Where is that son of a camel driver and why is he not performing his tricks? Where is Mahrukh, malika of rebels? She has had to pay a heavy price for leading this lashkar!' There was naturally no response to her taunts and this seemed to enrage her even more. Afrasiyab heard her cursing the sardars and whispered to his viziers Sarmaya and Abriq, 'Do not let her harm Bahar and Makhmoor. I am still fond of both of them and would like to forgive them.' As Sarmaya moved forward to distract Hairat, she shook him off crying, 'Do not stop me Vizier or I will kill myself right now. I know Shahanshah still secretly loves Bahar and Makhmoor but I am the Malika of this realm. I can punish whomever I want!'

Hairat rushed towards Bahar, her face shining with joy and anger at the same time and pulled her hair roughly. Bahar's head rolled off along with the hair. Hairat looked shocked, 'What kind of magic is this? My sister has decayed!' She held Bahar's hand and that also came off. Hairat screamed in terror. Her companions rushed towards the other sardars and found that their limbs also dropped off at the slightest touch. Afrasiyab walked into the pavilion, still flushed with pride at capturing the rebel lashkar, followed by his nobles who whispered among themselves that surely the rebellion was over now. They were stunned by the spectacle of disintegrating bodies and Tausan and Neelum cried, 'Huzoor, someone has substituted the bodies with effigies of lentil flour. Who could it be, a man or a genie? He must have been a powerful sahir to have done this under your very nose.'

Afrasiyab realized that they were mocking him and rushed to consult the oracle Book of Samri. He started trembling with rage as he read the book. He then rolled up his sleeves and reached for his sword. Seeing him in this state, Hairat clung to him and cried, 'Tell us what has happened?' Afrasiyab replied, 'You are responsible for this! Had I been carrying the pavilion, no one would have dared to mount a rescue! While I was talking to all of you, Ahwal managed to do this. Still he has not taken them far. I can still get them!' Afrasiyab was about to leave, but his wife and nobles urged him not to be rash. 'One of us can confront Ahwal. Why should you bother to fight him?' Afrasiyab agreed, but was still furious and walked around restlessly as one of his sahirs flew off to tackle Ahwal.

Ahwal was about to reach the secret hiding place to accomplish the next stage of his mission, which was to remove Afrasiyab's spell from the sardars. Just as he reached the hiding place, a hideous black sahir challenged him from the sky. The sahir flung an iron ball at him while descending, but Ahwal deflected it and drew his magic sword on the sahir, thus decapitating him in an instant. Darkness fell on the area and the sahir's guardian spirits howled with rage at his death. Afrasiyab was still pacing restlessly when Hairat cried, 'Shahanshah look up and see that black bird. Surely it is a bad·omen!' The bird descended on Afrasiyab's shoulder and after shrieking and flapping its wings, dropped dead on the ground. Afrasiyab consulted the oracle Book of Samri and without saying a word to his companions, sprouted wings and flew off towards the desert.

Ahwal was just recovering from the sahir's attack when Afrasiyab thundered above him and shouted, 'Did you think you would rescue my prisoners and I would remain silent? Do you not know me? If you value your life, give me back my prisoners right now!' Ahwal snapped, 'You pompous fool, stop your nonsense! Do you think I am afraid of death?' Afrasiyab swooped down to gather some pebbles from the earth and flung them at Ahwal. The pebbles descended as huge rocks from the sky, but Ahwal deflected them with the silver dish he had earlier used for flying. One of the deflected rocks hit Afrasiyab on the chest and he fell from the impact. Ahwal laughed aloud and drew his sword to attack Afrasiyab, but the Shah had drawn out his own magic sword by then. Ahwal tried a few spells, but Afrasiyab attacked him fiercely. The brave Ahwal lost his life and as he died, there was a sandstorm as if the very earth mourned his death.

Afrasiyab straightened his crown and went to the secret hiding place to find the lost sardars, but it was pitch dark there. Afrasiyab hurriedly conjured a flaming torch and looked all over for his prisoners, but did not find any trace of them. Eventually, he rubbed his palm on his thigh and magic writing materialized on his palm and revealed to him that Burran Sword-woman, Kaukab's daughter, had secreted everyone out of the place and returned to her garden. Afrasiyab's fury was now terrible to behold. He swore to himself that this time he would not spare Kaukab's daughter and went after her.

Burran's garden

Burran was busy trying to remove Afrasiyab's spell on the sardars, but found it difficult to dispel the Shahanshah's powerful magic. Eventually, she took out the magic Pearl of Samri. She cut her forehead to draw blood and dipped the pearl in it. The pearl then looked like a precious ruby. Finally, she dipped the pearl in clean water and bathed Amar's face with it. Amar immediately woke up and recited the holy verse of affirmation. He saw Burran leaning over him and looked at her enquiringly. She told him all that had happened since Afrasiyab entered the royal pavilion and ended with the noble Ahwal's supreme sacrifice.

Burran had barely managed to restore the six ayyars when she heard Afrasiyab's thunderous voice calling out from a distance, 'Are you that determined to die, you chit of a girl, that you kidnapped my prisoners? Your uncle's body is not yet cold in that desert! Go and prepare him for his funeral!' Afrasiyab descended rapidly from the sky as his mouth frothed with anger. Burran bravely stood in front of the prisoners to confront him. Afrasiyab's magic at that moment was a remarkable sight and Burran was no match for the King of Sahirs. As soon as he stamped hard on the ground, she collapsed along with all her companions and their pouches of magic burst into flames. Afrasiyab went forward with a huge sword to kill them when a loud voice called from the sky, 'Stop you shameless man! I have reached!'

Afrasiyab looked up and saw Kaukab diving down with his sword held aloft. The two kings then confronted each other. Each practised a few lightning spells on each other, but eventually Afrasiyab threw his head back and called out, 'Is there anyone present?' Even though Afrasiyab was in an alien Tilism, his powers reached everywhere. No sooner had he called out than a beautiful maiden appeared, holding a golden tray with a dazzling magic crown. The maiden placed the crown on Afrasiyab's head and disappeared. Afrasiyab turned to Kaukab with fresh confidence. He lunged at Kaukab with his sword outstretched, but Kaukab chanted a spell just in time so that a sheet of flame came between them; Afrasiyab extinguished it with another spell. This continued for some time and finally, Afrasiyab seemed to have the upper hand for his dazzling Tilismi crown could blind Kaukab, who found it impossible to overcome his adversary. They fought in this manner for some time. Kaukab was clearly troubled when a voice called out, 'All praise to you Shahanshah, may the shadow of Samri, Jamshed always be on you, and may your enemies be defeated!' Afrasiyab was surprised to hear the familiar voice of his wife. He looked up and saw that Hairat was standing on the tree, having obviously just descended from her flight. He cried, 'Malika, do not come any closer. I have wounded Kaukab and he is about to fall!' Hairat jumped down from the tree and cried, 'Two hearts that beat as one have the power to destroy mountains!' Afrasiyab turned to fight Kaukab again and was startled to find himself trapped within the steely coils of a snare-rope. An all too familiar voice called out, 'I am the king of ayyars, the master swordsman, the mighty Amar!' The reader may have guessed that Amar had disguised himself as Hairat. Amar quickly burst a narcotic bubble under his nose that made the Shahanshah spiral down to the ground.

Amar shouted, 'Shah Kaukab, get him now!' Kaukab lunged forward, but the earth split before him and Mahiyan Emerald-robe, Afrasiyab's maternal grandmother, burst out of the cleft. As she emerged, she flung a few grains of lentils from her hand towards Kaukab and they fell upon him like deadly daggers. While he was tackling them, Mahiyan clasped the unconscious Afrasiyab by the waist and disappeared into the earth with him. Amar had as usual hidden himself at the first sign of trouble. As he emerged from his cape of invisibility, Kaukab rushed to embrace him and cried, 'O shay of ayyars, your help was most timely. Afrasiyab had almost finished me because I was blinded by the Tilismi crown.'

Amar pointed to his sardars who were still lying lifeless and implored Kaukab to revive them. 'Before I do that,' Kaukab said, 'tell me, do you really have Asad and Mahjabeen with you?' Amar smiled and said, 'My dear brother, they are now free from prison.' Kaukab's face lit up with delight and turning to his attendants, he ordered them to bring forth a phial of magic water. Kaukab bathed each sardar's face with the healing water himself to revive them. Mahrukh, Bahar, Nafarman, Shakeel, Ra'ad and Barq, along with Baghban Qudrat, Surkh Mu and scores of other sardars awoke from their near-death state and embraced each other in joy.

Burran's garden that had witnessed so much sadness recently blossomed with happiness. Its trees swayed with joy, its flowers bloomed in all colours and birds trilled merrily. Amar looked at his supporters with gladness in his heart and announced, 'We shall now return to our camp.' Kaukab bid them Godspeed, adding that he would soon follow to feast his eyes on Tilism Kusha.

✒

29 ASAD IN DAWOODIA WITH THE LOVELY PRINCESS LALAAN RED-ROBE

Afrasiyab's main concern now was that the magic keystone of Tilism should not fall into Asad's hands. Asad had recuperated after his harrowing sojourn in Afrasiyab's prison. With the help of powerful dignitaries like Mahrukh, Makhmoor and Bahar who were privy to the secrets of Tilism, Asad had travelled to the Garden of Seemab. This garden belonged to one of Afrasiyab's most trusted lieutenants, Seemab Jadoo, who had guarded the magic keystone. Afrasiyab reached there just in time to retrieve the magic keystone and returned with it to Crystal Mountain.

Hairat, Mussavir and his wife Soorat Nigar, along with the viziers Sarmaya and Abriq and forty other nobles also reached the mountains to meet the Shahanshah. Hairat saw that Afrasiyab was in a shattered state—his brow was covered with beads of sweat, his face covered with dust and his robe was tattered. Hairat clung to her husband and sobbed, 'Tell me, what happened at the Garden of Seemab?'

Afrasiyab held his wife closely as he replied, 'My dear, Mahrukh, Makhmoor and Bahar travelled with Asad to the garden through the magic wilderness. It must have been a difficult journey for them. I will not go into details about the battle there, except to tell you that my friend Seemab fought bravely. He had overcome the rebels, but Kaukab reached there with Burran and killed him. Tilism Kusha had almost reached the magic bouquets where Seemab had hidden the keystone when I reached. I managed to escape with the keystone but in my haste, could not kill Asad.' As Hairat wept silently, Afrasiyab turned to his nobles and said, 'Now I ask all of you, who should be entrusted with the keystone? Where will I find another Seemab who will die for me? Alas! I will never find another friend like him even if I sift the dust of this earth!'

The nobles looked at each other and remained silent, but Soorat Nigar said, 'Shahanshah, if you follow my advice, even Samri and Jamshed will not be able to find the keystone! Think of my brother-in-law, Khudawand Dawood, who is so powerful that he composes the oracle Book of Samri for you. If he wants, he can send the keystone to the heavens where his angels will guard it. The Muslims will never be able to find it on this earth!' Afrasiyab looked thoughtfully at the sahira and then said, 'You may be right, but will Dawood agree?' Soorat Nigar replied, 'Why do you not request an audience from him first? If he agrees, we can all travel there with the keystone. Perhaps he can also bless us with longer lives, as we are in constant danger from the Muslims!'

Afrasiyab smiled and said, 'O divine one, what a splendid suggestion. However, we must be extremely cautious. I do not want Amar infiltrating that realm. I think I will entrust Sarsar with this mission.' Everyone in the durbar agreed with this strategy. Accordingly, Afrasiyab wrote a message to Dawood that read, 'I am hopeful that you will accept the magic keystone and keep it safely with you. What can I tell you about the troubles that surround me at this time? Your mortal Kaukab has become my enemy along with several other nobles who are rebelling against me. Help me now and relieve me of all trials.' He then summoned Sarsar and gave her the message along with the strictest orders to be on the lookout for ayyars who might have infiltrated the city of Dawoodia. After Sarsar left, Afrasiyab sent for her friend Saba Raftar and gave her similar instructions.

Asad and Lalaan

The brave young warrior was separated from his companions after the fierce fighting with Afrasiyab in the Garden of Seemab. He stumbled out of the garden and walked blindly in one direction, distraught and miserable at having lost the magic keystone. Asad's mind was in turmoil as he reflected, 'How unfortunate I am to have almost got the keystone and then lost it. Alas, I should have fought Afrasiyab to the death. I would rather die than live with this shame! How will I face Khwaja Amar now?'

Asad thus walked on, brooding on his failure until he found himself in a verdant green meadow. The wounded Asad collapsed under a tree, exhausted by the long walk. A little later, a royal barge shaped like a peacock floated by in the river. It had a rich red canopy embroidered with gold thread. Under the canopy, reclining on the masnad with a bevy of damsels surrounding her, sat a princess of incomparable beauty. As the barge neared the shore, the princess saw Asad lying under the tree. She jumped off the boat and waded to the shore to investigate.

Asad groaned and turned on his side and the princess saw his face. She sighed at the sight of his youthful beauty and shuddered at his wounds. She kneeled down besides him and addressed her childhood companion and vizierzadi Nagin Jadoo, 'It seems that this young man comes from a noble background. Obviously, some thieves attacked him for his goods and left him in this wounded condition. How disgraceful that someone should be treated so badly in our realm.' Nagin and her handmaidens nodded in agreement and the princess ordered, 'Place him on our barge so that we can tend to him in our garden.' Within moments, Asad's unconscious form was gently placed on a masnad in the barge that turned around swiftly to head home.

The princess's garden was on the shores of the same river and surrounded by high walls. The princess herself helped her handmaidens carry Asad into the garden and was covered with blood from his wounds. Her handmaidens kept protesting that they could tend to the wounded youth, but by this time, the princess was far too deeply in love to listen to them. She lost her temper with them for she noticed that on the pretext of tending to him, they were caressing his cheeks and stroking his hair. She shouted at them, 'You silly strumpets, is this your father that you fondle him this way! Get away from him. He is my guest and I will tend to him myself!'

The handmaidens drew back sheepishly while the princess removed Asad's garments, cleaned and stitched his wounds and applied a magic healing salve on them. After dressing him gently in fresh robes, she sat besides him, sometimes rubbing his hands or his feet. Her eyes filled with tears as he remained unconscious and she asked helplessly, 'Why Saman and Yasaman, my dear Ghuncha-dahan, did you ever see such deep wounds? Do you think they will ever heal?' Her companions murmured soothingly, 'Of course they will huzoor! These are just surface wounds, they heal quickly!'

The princess, however, remained anxious and thought, 'Who is he and what is he doing here?' The day was just ending when Asad suddenly opened his eyes. He looked at the handmaidens bustling around with their chores and then turned around to see the princess with her head bowed in deep thought. Asad was spellbound with her beauty and sighed deeply. The princess looked up and found her patient gazing at her lovingly. Overcome with shyness, she covered her face with her veil and left Asad to sit on the masnad. 'Go to our guest Nagin,' she said half smiling, 'he is awake and bound to ask about me. Tell him that I am the daughter of Khudawand Dawood. He must come and kneel to me or I will be much offended!'

By this time, Asad was sitting on the bed although he was still weak from his wounds. Nagin approached him and bowed respectfully saying, 'Sir, do you feel better now? Tell me who you are and where you come from?' Asad retorted, 'I shall not tell you anything about me! It is obvious that the lady of the house does not welcome me or else she would not have left when I regained consciousness. It is useless then for me to stay here!' Asad supported himself with his sword hilt and got off the bed.

Nagin ran to the princess and whispered Asad's reply in her ear. The princess became quite agitated and urged Nagin to prevent her guest from leaving. She whispered urgently, 'Tell him that it was I who brought him back from the jungle and tended to his wounds! Why would I do that if I did not want him to stay?' Nagin went running back to Asad with this message and instructed him to prostrate before the princess. Since Asad was in any case just pretending to be offended, he walked up to the masnad and boldly sat down besides the princess. She did not know how to react to him and blushed as her companions started whelping, 'Kneel down, this is the daughter of Khudawand Dawood!'

Asad looked scornful and the princess scolded her companion, 'Stop this nonsense. Will I be a greater person if he kneels to me?' Turning to Nagin, the princess told her to question their guest. Nagin addressed Asad with folded hands, 'O brave warrior, will you not tell us who you are and who wounded you?' Asad sighed and addressed the princess, 'What can I tell you about myself? Every stone in Hoshruba knows my name and Afrasiyab knows me well. I am Asad the grandson of Sahibqiran. Afrasiyab had imprisoned me in the Dome of Light for a very long time. Along with my friends, Bahar, Baghban, Burran and Khwaja Amar, I tried to fight for the magic keystone in the Garden of Seemab, but lost it. Afrasiyab retrieved it at the last moment and I wandered off in my grief and pain. Allah is great that you found me. I thank you for tending to me.'

While Asad was still talking, the princess wept silently and whispered to Nagin, 'What calamity! The entire Tilism is the enemy of this brave lion. What am I to do now?' Nagin whispered back, 'There is no time to lose princess. Let us find him a swift horse and let him be gone from here. If your father gets to know our secret we will all be punished hideously!' The princess then rose from her masnad and took Nagin to one side of the garden. She put her arms around Nagin and a river of tears ran down her cheeks. 'My dearest companion and confidante,' she sobbed, 'if this young man leaves, I will surely die! Can you not help me and hide him in this garden?'

Nagin looked aghast at the suggestion and said, 'Princess, if he remains here we will all face certain death!' As she heard this, the princess collapsed right there, her face went pale and her limbs seemed lifeless. Nagin was heartbroken at seeing her childhood companion so grief stricken. She revived her with rosewater and promised that she would do her best for the princess. Princess Lalaan Red-robe (for that was her name) rejoined Asad on the masnad, but looked visibly distressed and tearful. Asad gently wiped her tears and said, 'What is the matter beloved? Will you not tell me?' Lalaan looked down, but Nagin replied quickly, 'It's nothing, just a personal matter between us.' Nagin then filled a goblet and handed it to Lalaan to offer to Asad. He declined the wine saying, 'My dear, I cannot have anything here unless you recite the holy verse of affirmation and convert to Islam.' Lalaan looked angry at this suggestion and Nagin said, 'Sir, how can you question the princess's faith when we have informed you that she is the only daughter of the greatest Khudawand Dawood?'

Asad turned to the Lalaan and said, 'Princess, how can the True God have families? Your father is a sahir, although he must be a very powerful sahir for having led so many people astray with his claim to divinity. The True God is all powerful and there can be no one like him.' Asad continued speaking in this vein and so moving were his words that the princess and her companions saw the true light and their hearts were purged of sin. Except for Nagin, all of them converted to Islam. She explained that as she was the only sahira in the garden, it was necessary for her to retain her identity. 'My powers may be needed before long,' she explained to Asad.

Asad then relaxed and shared a goblet of wine with Lalaan while her companions danced and entertained them. Sensing that she was still tense Asad said, 'Princess, do not worry. Tomorrow morning I will go to Dawood's durbar and expose him as a fraud.' Lalaan started weeping again and said, 'How can you even think of going to his durbar without any magical weapon with you? You may not be aware, but everyone in Tilism Hoshruba is afraid of his magical powers. The most powerful sahirs in the realm prostrate before him. Please do not even think of going to the durbar on your own. Nagin will bring us news of the magic keystone.'

❧

30 AMAR IN THE CITY OF DAWOODIA

We will leave Asad in the garden of the lovely Lalaan Red-robe and return to the exploits of that infamous ayyar Khwaja Amar. He had disguised himself as a sahir as usual and was on the lookout for some easy prey while searching for Prince Asad. He saw the walls of a settlement

in the distance and decided to investigate it further. He changed his form
to that of an impoverished Aghori fakir. He carried a bottle of cheap
wine and a skull that he used as a cup. He approached shopkeepers who
tossed a coin or two to him.

After earning a good sum of money this way, Amar made some discreet
inquiries about the settlement. He learned that this place was merely the
outpost of the great city of Dawoodia, home to the mightiest Khudawand
Dawood. Most powerful sahirs including Afrasiyab Jadoo visited
Dawoodia to pay homage to Dawood. Moreover, Dawood was the one
who composed the oracle Book of Samri for Afrasiyab that provided
him with instant knowledge about whatever was happening around him.
Armed with this information, Amar left for the city of Dawoodia that
was some twelve miles away. Ravi, the legendary narrator informs us
that Dawood was so powerful that in some ways he was even mightier
than Samri and Jamshed. He ruled over the kingdom of Dawoodia like
an absolute god and the sahirs of the world offered him rich tributes.

The city of Dawoodia had a colossal Dome of Samri over a large
tank of fresh water. Walls of crystal, quartz and silver extended from the
tank to the dome. Etched on these walls were hundreds of living statuettes
made of silver and gold. Dawood went to the dome regularly to meet
the statuettes, who kept him informed about the state of the Tilism.
Everyone in Dawoodia knew that the Khudawand visited the dome daily.
His devotees thronged the dome to catch a sight of him and to beseech
him for favours and wishes. People made numerous requests to him—
from barren women asking for a child to a man enquiring about a
daughter's marriage. Dawood would grant boons with a smile. If the
magistrate of the city took a band of rebels to him, Dawood merely
laughed and expelled a bolt of lightning that would shoot out from his
mouth and fall on the rebels, instantly reducing them to ashes. Dawood's
form of instant justice was famous in Tilism and there were constant
shouts of praise from the public, 'O Khudawand, praise to you and your
sense of justice. You are the essence of Samri and Jamshed. You are the
one who created and destroyed them!'

On this day Dawood was wearing the crown of divinity and obviously
relished the praise being lavished on him. There was a sudden hush in
the air and everyone fell silent on seeing the giant flying throne of
Afrasiyab approaching the city. As people shouted Afrasiyab's name, the
tiny statuettes of prophecy smiled knowingly amongst each other. When
Afrasiyab drew closer to the dome, one of them laughed and cried, 'O
handmaidens of Samri, beware!' As the flying throne drew even closer,
the statuettes rose in the air and cast their shadow over the visitor.

Dawood looked up and saw a curious sight. Instead of Afrasiyab, a strange-looking creature sat on the throne—a round head shaped like a coconut, full-blown cheeks like kulcha bread, a reedy neck, beady eyes and a potbelly. Dawood saw that the stranger's limbs were abnormally long and felt a twinge of fear when the magic statuettes called out, 'O Khudawand, Amar comes!' Another added, 'He dares to deceive Khudawand so openly!' Looking at the shocked faces of Dawood and his companions, Amar realized that he had been exposed and jumped off the throne just as it landed in front of them.

Amar fought his way out of the durbar as Dawood's guards attacked him. The ayyar displayed his extraordinary talents at this time by jumping several feet out of reach and then using his snare-rope, sword and tools of ayyari like narcotic bubbles and smoking pipes, all at the same time. Whenever he was cornered, he quickly disappeared into Galeem and then emerged to fight again. Dawood and his durbaris watched in horror as Amar killed and wounded several people in his bid to escape. The magic statuettes laughed in derision as they cried out, 'Khudawand, what kind of mortal have you created that he dares to kill your own men? Turn him into stone at once!' Dawood snapped back unconvincingly, 'What do you know of my intentions? He is killing these sinners at my behest. Do you not realize that I have appointed this misbehaved creature as the slayer of sahirs and have created his master Hamza to punish Laqa who dares to claim that he is my equal in divinity? Shut your mouths now and do not spout nonsense!'

By this time, Amar had escaped from the durbar and had vanished. The citizens of Dawoodia went weeping to Dawood to report the death of a brother or son and pleaded with him to restore their lives. Irritated with his inability to help, Dawood shouted at his guards to turn them all out and to tell them that the dead could not come back to life. 'If you people do not leave now you will all be turned into stone right away!' he shouted angrily. The citizens left the durbar weeping while others pronounced that the coming of Amar was a bad sign for all sahirs. Dawood then descended from his dome to inspect the throne Amar had flown on into the durbar. He became silent when he read a plaque on it that declared that this was a flying throne from the land of Jinni. He had the throne placed carefully and returned to his palace, still in a state of shock.

Meanwhile, Amar was hiding in a forest far way from the walls of the city when he spotted a sahir followed by forty labourers carrying sacks of gold coins. Amar quickly disguised himself as a Brahmin with a homespun loincloth and the characteristic shaven skull with only a thin plait of hair winding down on the back of his head. He found a well that lay in the path of the procession, filled an earthenware vessel with cold water and added a drug to it. As the sahir passed by, he offered the water to him. The unsuspecting sahir and his labourers slaked their thirst gratefully and were soon unconscious. Amar first deposited the sacks of coins in his Zambil. He then shaved off the sahir's beard and moustache leaving only one hair in place. He tied a message for Dawood on the single whisker that stated, 'Dawood Jadoo, I am the master of trickery and swordplay. Be alert for I have entered your kingdom. Keep my throne carefully. If you lose any gem from it, you will have to pay dearly!'

When the sahir regained consciousness, he went straight to the durbar to complain. Dawood was in his palace when he saw the near naked sahir shorn of all his hair. The sahir sobbed as he related what had happened and handed Amar's note to Dawood. He said, 'This was tied to the only hair that was left of my moustache.' Dawood was inwardly shaken as the message was read out to him, but calmly told the sahir that he would be compensated for his loss from the state treasury. After the sahir had happily left the durbar, Dawood ordered a massive hunt for 'that son of a camel driver'. His courtiers whispered amongst each other, mystified by Khudawand's cool response to Amar's provocative letter.

Aflaq Jadoo reveals Lalaan's secret

One of Dawood Jadoo's closest companions, a sahir called Aflaq Jadoo, was flying for the sake of exercise early in the morning when he flew over Princess Lalaan's garden. He heard the sound of singing from the garden and stopped above the garden out of curiosity. He was shocked to see the princess and the noble Prince Asad being entertained with early morning chants by Lalaan's companions. By this time, Asad was famous throughout the Tilism as Tilism Kusha and everyone was familiar with his face. Aflaq recognized him immediately and flew up hastily out of sight, his mind churning with thoughts of future glory once he reported his daughter's treachery to Dawood. 'Because of me Tilism will be rid of this troublesome thorn in its side forever and the rebels are bound to succumb to Afrasiyab!' Aflaq thought as he approached the durbar.

Dawood had recovered somewhat that morning and was receiving homage in his usual arrogant manner. His rather dim-witted vizier, Khurshid Jadoo, who had been given the title of prophet, was busy reassuring Dawood that Amar would be hunted down like a dog when Aflaq Jadoo landed in court looking visibly shaken. Dawood Jadoo saw his state as he genuflected and asked, 'My dear friend, what brings you here so early?'

Aflaq Jadoo replied, 'Khudawand, I have observed a sight so shocking that I cannot find the words to describe it to you!' Dawood looked at him inquiringly and Aflaq continued, 'Huzoor, today I saw an aspect of your beloved daughter that broke my heart.' Dawood said angrily, 'Why do you talk in riddles? Speak openly to me!' Aflaq begged Dawood to not punish him if he spoke the truth. After Dawood had promised not to harm him, Aflaq said, 'Huzoor, I was flying over Princess Lalaan's garden this morning when I saw her sitting besides Tilism Kusha Asad Ghazi. Her handmaidens were entertaining them with wine and music. I was shocked beyond measure and have come to inform you about this.'

Dawood Jadoo reacted terribly to this news and screamed out in anger. As his courtiers trembled with fear, he shouted at Aflaq to immediately behead Tilism Kusha and bring the princess to the durbar. 'I will whip that shameless girl until her skin comes off and burn her in my hell! But remember this Aflaq, if you are wrong I will turn you into stone and your tribe will vanish forever!' Lalaan's vizierzadi Nagin was also in the durbar at the time and reached the princess's garden before Aflaq. She came into the princess's presence looking pale and troubled. Lalaan immediately realized something was wrong and followed Nagin into a private chamber. Nagin crumpled on the floor and wept bitterly as she said, 'Princess, I had warned you to go inside this morning. What I feared most has happened. That wretched Aflaq Jadoo saw you with the prince this morning and now Dawood is sending him with an army to execute Asad.'

Lalaan went pale with fear and her body trembled as she said, 'I have no fear for my own life, but dear Nagin, save the prince somehow. He is far from his friends and allies. Who will come to save him? He is brave and will fight but will be helpless against magic.' Nagin wiped away her tears and said comfortingly, 'Huzoor, remain calm. We still have time. I will hide the prince with my magic. Continue to sit in the garden with your handmaidens. When Aflaq and Khudawand interrogate you, just deny the whole story and say you do not even recognize Tilism Kusha!' After counselling the princess, Nagin took Asad into the same room. He looked puzzled, but the princess merely looked down at the ground as Nagin recited powerful incantations that transformed Asad into a tiny green pea. Nagin then placed the pea in one of Princess Lalaan's anklet bells and sealed the opening carefully. She looked up at the princess with a smile and said, 'Huzoor, even Samri Jamshed will not be able to find him in there. Your beloved is with you and this humble handmaiden will make a timely appearance to save you. Just do as I have told you now.'

Nagin left the garden and the princess went back to her masnad after removing all signs of Asad's presence in the garden. Very soon, Aflaq burst into the garden with his soldiers. He did not bother greeting the princess and asked her to produce Tilism Kusha. He shouted, 'Do not bother to deny it princess. I have seen him with my own eyes sitting with you in this garden!' Princess Lalaan looked straight at him and said, 'Are you mad? What would Tilism Kusha be doing in a garden that no man can set foot in? My handmaidens entertain me every morning and disguise themselves as men sometimes, but if you still persist with this nonsensical claim, search the garden. Do not be harsh with my handmaidens for they are very dear to me.'

Aflaq signalled his soldiers to search the garden and grew increasingly frustrated as they hunted every room in vain. Aflaq himself searched every box and every flower bed, but could not find that flower of bravery anywhere. Eventually, he asked Princess Lalaan roughly to present herself in the durbar where her father was waiting for her. She climbed into the carriage he had brought for her and wept all the way to the durbar while her handmaidens followed her weeping and wailing. On the way, Aflaq tried to threaten and even cajole the princess into admitting that Asad was with her, but she remained silent while her handmaidens cursed him for casting aspersions on the princess's reputation.

Dawood Jadoo was pacing in the durbar with a leather whip in one hand. When Aflaq told him Asad was nowhere in the garden, he summoned the princess who came forward with her eyes lowered and her heart in her mouth. As she greeted her father, he turned away in anger and shouted, 'You harlot, who have brought dishonour on the family, tell me where have you hidden Tilism Kusha? Did you not fear my godly wrath when you sheltered that thorn in your garden? Tell me the truth now!' The princess collected herself and said softly, 'Honoured father, I do not know of any Tilism Kusha, nor do I know what he looks like.'

'You dare to lie to me?' shouted Dawood frothing at the mouth. 'You dare to imply that my companion is lying to me! Tell me at once or I will flay you alive with this whip.' Lalaan bravely denied knowing Tilism Kusha once again. Dawood now cracked his whip. There was pandemonium in the durbar as the princess crumpled on the floor, her robe in tatters and blood pouring out of her wounds. Before she fainted, she whimpered, 'Father I did not deserve this. Kill me right now with your sword.' Dawood's horrified companions and ministers clung to him to prevent him from using the whip again and pleaded, 'Huzoor, you have brought her up with so much love—she will die like this. Had she been lying, surely she would have admitted to it by now.' Aflaq Jadoo was also shaken as everyone turned to him, blaming him for making such an ignominious charge against the princess. 'Had she been guilty,' they asked, 'would she not have admitted to it by now?'

While his companions held Dawood back, the princess shuddered with the pain of her wounds and the anklet bell that held the pea opened with the movement. She watched in horror as the pea rolled away from her feet towards the wall. As she watched helplessly, a mouse emerged from a hole in the wall, lifted the pea in its mouth and vanished out of sight. Lalaan was truly shattered now with the pain of this greater misfortune. 'Alas I have suffered and gained nothing!' she thought. 'Alas, that this flower of Sahibqiran should lose his life in this ignoble manner!' She smote her forehead with grief and then fainted once again.

At that time, the durbar was startled by the loud voice of a woman cursing. 'Let this kingdom of divinity be destroyed! Let the heavens fall on the city of Dawoodia! Let the earth swallow this city and let no Khudawand remain in it!' Dawood looked around and saw Nagin approaching him beating her head in grief. She looked him straight in the eye and shouted, 'This cruelty from you O Khudawand on the flower of your own garden! May your hands be cut off for striking this innocent girl! What has she ever done to you?' Dawood was also very disturbed at that time and held Nagin's hand and said, 'My daughter, I cannot find the words to tell you what she has done, but just listen to me!' As Dawood repeated Aflaq's grave allegation, Nagin turned around to look at Aflaq and then bowed to him. 'Mian Aflaq,' she said scornfully, 'you have not been around to visit me for several days now. Will you not bring me any more sweets? I need new clothes; will you not bring me bales of costly material anymore? Will you not marry the princess anymore?'

She now turned to Dawood and said, 'Alas, you should have asked me before this unfortunate incident. This wretched Aflaq has been trying to bribe me for months with money, sweets and fruits. He promised to reward me richly if I could arrange an assignation with the princess for him. I admit to accepting the edibles, but I never touched the money and never mentioned any of this to the princess. Eventually, he threatened me and said, "You have deceived me and I will now punish your princess." Alas, I never took his threats seriously.' Dawood felt a rush of anger, and when Nagin swore by his ancestors that she was telling the truth, he turned around and shouted at Aflaq, 'You traitor, you dare to cast eyes on my daughter!' Aflaq tried to deny the charge and swore he had never been to Nagin's house, but Dawood was too enraged to listen to his companion. He picked up a pinch of dust and threw it on Aflaq who screamed with pain as flames engulfed his body. Within moments, Aflaq burnt to ashes and went straight to hell. A voice called out, 'Alas, you have killed me! I was Aflaq Jadoo. Alas, I gave my life in vain!'

Dawood then asked Nagin to take Lalaan back to her garden and heal her wounds, and to ensure that no stranger entered the garden.

Nagin obeyed with alacrity. Dawood then ordered Khurshid Jadoo to look for Amar and returned to his private chambers. There, he lay down on his bed, his heart wracked with guilt at the pain he had inflicted on his daughter. Meanwhile, Nagin had returned with the unconscious princess to the garden. She dressed her wounds with a magic salve and then revived her. Lalaan woke up and clung to Nagin weeping, 'I am ruined Nagin. My prince has gone forever!' Nagin looked unperturbed and said, 'Princess, now what has happened?' When the princess described what had happened to the pea, Nagin laughed and said, 'Princess, you are still alive! Why should we care about what happens to every little pea?'

The princess looked disbelievingly at her friend and cried, 'Nagin may your tongue be bitten by a snake! Is this the time for jokes?' Nagin replied casually, 'What is there to worry about? The pea is too big for a mouse to swallow. I will become a rat and kill that little mouse!' Lalaan started weeping with despair at this reply and picked up a dagger to stab herself when Nagin held her hand and said, 'Do not worry. When the pea was dislodged from your anklet bell, I transformed into a mouse and retrieved it. Then I transformed back to take care of that wretched Aflaq. What did you think of my little drama? Even Khudawand was deceived. Go into that room now, the prince is resting there. It is not good to break good tidings suddenly as you could have died of shock.' The princess laughed and embraced Nagin warmly, and praised her ingenuity and courage.

Amar and Dawood Jadoo

Let us now return to Khwaja Amar, who after robbing a sahir trader of his gold, was on the lookout for more victims. As usual, he had disguised himself; this time as an elderly sahir. From his vantage point in the shadow of a mountain, he spotted a travelling *halvai* who was holding a large tray of piping hot puris and barfi, obviously delivering an order somewhere. Amar waylaid him and asked, 'Will you sell this food to me?' The halvai replied politely, 'Sir this is Thakur sahib's order, it's not for sale.' Amar said, 'Go ahead then my good man. In my city, such large puris cost one rupee each and barfi is fifty rupees a seer. This place seems more expensive, so the puris must be for two rupees each and the barfi a hundred rupees a seer!' The halvai who had walked ahead turned back on hearing this and said obsequiously, 'Huzoor, this food is yours. But hurry as I have to rush back to make some more of these for the Thakur.'

Amar's eyes fell on the thick silver bracelets on the halvai's wrists and he offered him six gold coins for them. The trusting halvai took these off for Amar as well, who paid him for the bracelets and the puris. The halvai thanked him and rushed off. Amar returned to his hideout and slowly consumed the puris and barfi, thanking Allah for His Munificence in this wilderness. The halvai went home, eager to share the news of his morning sale with his wife. He whispered to her, 'I came across a very generous man who rewarded me richly with gold coins.' The wife happily untied the cloth into which he had tied the coins and was startled to see only a large golden *laddoo*. The halvai screamed and clutched his head, while his wife tasted the laddoo that was delicious. Both husband and wife went to report this event to Khurshid Jadoo, Dawood's vizier, who had set up a camp in the vicinity in order to look for Amar.

When the halvai told Khurshid that an old sahir had robbed him, he realized that it must have been Amar. He was already frustrated with his soldiers for not being able to locate Amar and announced that he himself would arrest the ayyar. As he emerged from his pavilion, he was struck by the sight of a distant whirlwind that on closer inspection turned out to be Afrasiyab's emissary, Saba Raftar. She was armed with the tools and weapons of ayyari and handed Khurshid a note from Afrasiyab that urged him to use her services in locating the wily ayyar. Khurshid was happy and went with Saba Raftar to the place where Amar had robbed the halvai. Saba Raftar walked ahead of him alertly, looking around for signs of Amar. Suddenly, she turned back and whispered to Khurshid, 'I have found him. He has hidden himself in that bush.' Khurshid tiptoed behind her and was startled to find himself trapped in the coils of a snare-rope. The next moment, he was unconscious.

The reader should know that Saba Raftar was in reality Amar disguised as her. He took out a prisoner from Zambil and painted his face to look like Amar, then calmly decapitated him. He wrapped the severed head in a scarf and went back to the camp disguised as Khurshid, laughing and crying at the same time. His soldiers rushed to receive him, as he babbled, 'No sooner did I go myself, I caught Amar. That Saba Raftar was no help! She vanished out of sight when I fought with Amar. People tell us that Amar is not a sahir. I am telling you now Amar was a very powerful sahir. Even now, his spirits are tormenting me. Friends, if I behave strangely, do not be offended. I have forgotten magic and want to cut my own throat right now!'

Khurshid's companions conjured a flying throne and flew with the false Khurshid to Dawood's durbar, greatly concerned by their master's behaviour as he muttered insanely on the way, 'Yes, take me to Dawood! He is the head of all demons! Only he can save me from these demons that surround me!' Thus, the false Khurshid landed in the durbar and placed Amar's decapitated head at Dawood's feet while screaming, 'Khudawand, save me from these demons. Your durbar is full of them. They will kill you as well. Hide Amar's head somewhere!' Dawood was overjoyed at seeing the decapitated head and thought, 'This will break the Muslims. Mahrukh and Bahar will never stand up to Afrasiyab now.' He looked at his distraught prime minister and led him into a private chamber where he offered him a goblet of wine and reassured him that the demons would plague him no more.

Amar had been waiting for this moment. He quietly doctored the wine and held it out to Dawood. He said, 'Huzoor, if you sip it first, I will benefit from it.' Dawood Jadoo unsuspectingly sipped the wine and as the drug went to his head, he cried out, 'Khurshid I can see the demons as well! Look there is Damama with her skirts raised and there is Mishmish leading an army of demons!' Within moments, Dawood succumbed to the drug and fell unconscious. Amar carefully placed him in Zambil and asked his darogha to look after him. He then painted himself to look Khudawand Dawood and emerged in the durbar wearing the crown of divinity. He explained Khurshid's absence by telling his courtiers that he had sent the prime minister to a safe place. He then conversed with Dawood's ministers and cleverly elicited information about events that had transpired in the durbar since he had last escaped from there.

Lalaan's friend Nagin visited the durbar regularly and was alarmed at the news of Amar's death. She ran back to Lalaan and gave her the news, adding, 'Do not tell Tilism Kusha, he will lose heart. I would urge you now to visit your father. He was discussing the incident with Aflaq this very morning with his ministers and seemed most concerned about you.' Meanwhile, Amar had come to know of the incident with Lalaan Red-robe and the fate of the unfortunate Aflaq at the hands of Dawood. He realized that Asad must have been with Lalaan but some wise person with her must have manipulated events to save her. 'I will get to the bottom of this matter soon, but meanwhile let me earn a little from my short-lived divinity—I will never get such an opportunity again!' he thought. Accordingly, Amar as Khudawand Dawood announced, 'I am concerned for my people who remember me in their prayers night and day. I would like to reward them. Tell all my people to bring their treasures and money to me. After some time, angels from my heaven will give them three times more than the sum they deposit with me.'

There was great excitement in the city of Dawoodia following this announcement. Profiteers and moneylenders tempted by the prospects of tripling their capital brought their money to the durbar and women borrowed jewellery to present to Dawood. Every house and every street in

Dawoodia buzzed with the news that the Khudawand was in a generous mood and that no one in Dawoodia would be poor any more. As Amar watched in satisfaction, cartloads of gold coins, precious gems and jewellery arrived at the durbar. Amar asked for it to be stowed in the treasury and occasionally visited the treasury alone to deposit the treasures in Zambil.

The next morning Nagin accompanied Lalaan when she went to meet her father. When informed of her presence, the false Dawood drew himself up and frowned. He looked angrily at the prostrated figures before him and killed a couple after saying, 'This is no time for worship!' As his courtiers looked in horror, the Khudawand ordered one of his guards, 'Cut this man's nose off so someone else can have ears!' When Lalaan entered the durbar, a few ministers whispered to her, 'Khudawand is in a mighty rage. Be careful!' Lalaan trembled with fear on seeing the bodies of Dawood's victims in the durbar and stepped back whispering to Nagin, 'This is not the time to face my father!' Nagin whispered back, 'Do not lose heart princess. We have come this far. Let us leave our fate to the Almighty.'

Encouraged by Nagin, Lalaan went forward. As Amar looked at her, he noticed that though she was pale with fear, her eyes were bright and there seemed to be a glow about her as if she had just met her beloved. Amar opened his arms to receive her with affection calling her 'light of mine eyes'. He kissed her forehead gently and offered her the jewelled chair besides his throne. Then he looked straight at Nagin who quickly bent down to kiss his throne and said, 'How are you today vizierzadi?' Nagin heard a strange note in his tone and was about to faint with fear, but composed herself to reply, 'I always pray to you my lord.' Amar looked at her smilingly and said, 'Come and sit with us. I know the secrets of all hearts. You are my daughter's well-wisher and I am pleased with you. I will reward you, but remember this: nothing is hidden from me and I know everything.'

Nagin lost all colour and her usually sharp wits eluded her as she thought, 'He does seem to know everything, he only has to say Asad's name now.' She and Lalaan exchanged meaningful glances, and Amar observed that Lalaan was shaking like a leaf with fear. He decided to stop teasing them for he realized that the princess could just die of fright. He was also now quite sure that Asad was with her and that he would find him soon. He stroked Lalaan's back gently and addressed the durbar, 'My friends, this is my daughter, the light of my existence, the most beautiful in this land. It is clear to me that she will rule Hoshruba.' The courtiers listened intently and murmured agreement as there was little else they could do at that time, terrified as they were by Khudawand's swift changes of mood. The false Dawood continued in this vein for some time and constantly referred to Nagin's wisdom and clever nature. He ended by once again emphasizing how he knew all that had happened and then turned to the trembling Lalaan. He said to her, 'Go now light of my heart to your garden and be at ease there.' Lalaan was relieved to hear this command and left the durbar holding Nagin's hand. They returned to the garden where Asad was waiting for them; Lalaan joined him silently. Nagin was also terrified inwardly, but kept a smiling face in case the prince suspected anything.

In the evening, Amar, still successfully impersonating Dawood, asked for the royal carriage. 'Take me to my daughter's garden!' he ordered. Dawood's carriage, surrounded by his companions and devotees, was seen from a distance by Princess Lalaan's loyal *mahaldar*, who had locked the garden from the inside and guarded the entrance. She rushed in to the princess and said breathlessly, 'Huzoor, for pity's sake, stop this singing and dancing. Khudawand, your father comes to visit you.' Lalaan became as still as a statue, but Asad held her hand and said, 'Do not fear anything. Let that shameless kafir enter! I will make sure that he forgets all claims to divinity by the time I am finished with him. By Allah, I will tear him from limb to limb! His death brings him here.'

The princess looked at him with a mute plea in her eyes, but Nagin fell at his feet and pleaded, 'Huzoor, do not get us all killed! Please hide yourself. We did not tell you this morning, but Khudawand said some frightening things in the durbar. It is clear that he knows you are here. He is the Lord of the Seven Worlds. How long could we have deceived him?' Eventually, Asad was persuaded against his better judgement to hide in a baradari. Nagin and Lalaan quickly tried to remove all signs of his presence from the scene, but did not have the time to remove the wine goblets. Lalaan Red-robe was dressed like a bride, laden with jewellery and fragrant with perfumed oils. She hastily tried to pluck afshan glitter from her hair and bit her lips to remove their redness. Even in this dishevelled state, she looked beautiful and radiant.

Her handmaidens were in a state of shock and whispered to each other, 'Today we must all surely die with the princess. What will happen now? She is a rare one for sheltering her lover without fear of her father. Even being whipped did not deter her from true love. Now Dawood will surely wreak vengeance upon us all and turn this garden into a living hell.' The garden door opened and Lalaan wrapped in a simple white shawl, greeted her father with her head bowed. Nagin stood besides her. Amar left his band of followers outside and walked in with Lalaan. He realized at once that Lalaan must have been entertaining a guest for there were clear signs that someone was sitting with her. Amar walked up to the masnad with Lalaan and Nagin on either side of him. He deliberately looked around him and said, 'Well Nagin, why is this gathering so solemn? Bring forth that braveheart. Do not hide him from us. You made me kill my own companion Aflaq, but I forgive you for that.'

Nagin remained silent and Amar turned to Lalaan and said, 'Light of my eyes, tell me now. Where is the master of your house?' Lalaan replied in a shaky voice, 'Honoured father, I am the mistress of this house. There is no other master here.' Amar continued patiently, 'Call your honoured guest for whom you arranged this evening. I would also like to meet him and perhaps give him a high post in my army.' Lalaan swallowed her fear and said, 'Huzoor I do not understand you. I have no guest here nor have I invited anyone.' Amar pretended to lose his temper. He brought out a huge iron ball that he balanced on one hand and shouted, 'Do you all think I am a fool? I will now cast a spell that will immediately turn your friend into a donkey and he will come running here. He will remain that for the rest of his life and I will give him in the service of a washerman who will work him hard!' Amar then tossed the ball and caught it again, calling out, 'Well Nagin will you not counter my spell?' As she looked away, he roared, 'Lalaan, the next time I toss this ball he will become a donkey!'

Asad had been listening to all this from his hideout in baradari and decided that it was better to attack Dawood before he could use magic. 'At least I will die fighting instead of living out the rest of my days as an ignoble donkey,' Asad thought and rushed out with his sword in hand. He shouted, 'Dawood Jadoo, do you only frighten women or can you fight a man? You infidel, you dare to claim divinity! Are you not afraid of your Maker?' Amar was overjoyed to find Asad again but stood up in alarm as he saw the prince rushing towards him with his sword unsheathed. Nagin and Lalaan were rooted to the ground, but Asad wanted to attack the sahir before he could cast his spell.

As the prince attacked the false Dawood, he leaped to one side, as no one knew better than Amar that one powerful blow from Asad would slice him in half. He challenged Asad from a safe distance, 'Throw your sword or I will make you into an animal! You dare attack my divinity!' This encouraged Asad even more as he attacked the false Dawood fiercely crying, 'You fool! Do you imagine brave men just throw down their swords?' Princess Lalaan and Nagin watched in disbelief as they saw Khudawand dodge Asad every time he attacked him. At one point, Asad had Amar cornered under the shadow of his sword and was about to decapitate him when Amar quickly revealed the mole on his left eyelid, whispering furiously, 'What is the matter with you? Do you not know me? Why are you pretending to be a big swordsman! I will just pull your ears off!'

As soon as Asad recognized Amar, he threw away his sword and clung to Amar, weeping loudly with relief. Lalaan looked at Nagin in dismay and said, 'This is terrible. Father has bewitched him! Look how he weeps!' Lalaan was about to collapse with fear when Asad called out, 'Princess come and greet my respected elder, Khwaja Amar bin Ummayyah!' Lalaan and Nagin looked stunned and Asad said, 'Huzoor bless them with a vision of your real face.' The false Dawood turned away for a moment and then turned again to reveal his real face. The princess and her attendants greeted him with all respect and presented him with trays heaped with gems as homage. Asad asked Amar, 'Huzoor, tell us what have you done with Dawood Jadoo.' Amar smiled and said, 'He is in my pocket!' He then went on to explain how he had taken Dawood's place. Lalaan and Nagin were even more astonished at these revelations and stared at Amar.

After some time, Amar advised Asad to stay in the garden with Lalaan while he continued to impersonate Dawood Jadoo. He said, 'God willing, we will obtain the keystone soon. However, Lalaan and Nagin should continue to visit the durbar occasionally.' Thus, Amar said his farewells to his friends in the garden, and after assuming Dawood's face again, returned to his divine duties as Khudawand of the city of Dawoodia.

∽๑∾

31 SARSAR AND SABA RAFTAR, BARQ AND ZARGHAM

The reader will recall that after the battle at the Garden of Seemab, Soorat Nigar had convinced Afrasiyab to give the magic keystone to her brother-in-law, Dawood, for safekeeping. Afrasiyab sent a message regarding the keystone to Dawood through his trusted messenger, Sarsar. He had sent the same message through Saba Raftar as well in case one of them could not reach the city of Dawoodia.

We now return to Khwaja Amar, who was successfully impersonating Khudawand Dawood. When Sarsar finally reached Dawoodia and sought an audience with Dawood, Amar began feeling very apprehensive. He knew that Sarsar was well versed in the art of ayyari and would be able to see through his disguise immediately. Accordingly, he murmured to his vizier, 'I have decided not to appear before everyone and therefore will wear a veil from now on. Only the select may have a glimpse of my divine visage.' The vizier faithfully provided a black veil with which Amar covered his face completely.

He then sent for Sarsar who prostrated before him and kissed his throne before presenting Afrasiyab's letter to him. Along with the royal letter, there was a handwritten message from Soorat Nigar, written in an informal familiar manner, urging her brother-in-law to do this favour for the Shahanshah, as it would provide with her an excuse to visit him, and who knows what might happen after that. Amar heard the contents of the letter and laughed, 'My sister-in-law loves me a great deal. Let her come and I will treat her to a shoe beating! She will not be allowed to leave for a week this time.' Sarsar listened to the voice intently and grew very suspicious, but her worst fears were confirmed within moments. When Amar had been pretending to be amused by Soorat Nigar's letter, at one stage, the veil flew off his face as he laughed heartily. The clever Sarsar recognized him immediately, but averted her gaze. Amar was lulled into thinking that she had not seen through his disguise. He adjusted his veil and said imperiously, 'Tell Afrasiyab that I create keystones like his every day—what would I want with another one?'

Sarsar was in a hurry to leave and took her formal leave of Khudawand. She left Dawood's durbar like the breeze she had been named after. As she raced back to her master, her mind was in a turmoil. She thought, 'Who would have thought this wretched ayyar could overcome Dawood and impersonate him. Let me hasten and reach Afrasiyab so he punishes him grievously. I am sure Asad must be here as well.' Meanwhile, Amar was presiding in his durbar, delighted that the keystone was on its way. After some time, Afrasiyab's second emissary, Saba Raftar, sought an audience with Khudawand. She was even sharper than Sarsar and recognized Amar as well. After taking her leave of the false Dawood, she left the durbar in the same state of mind as Sarsar. She thought, 'Saba Raftar, you have seen everything now! Khudawand Dawood has disappeared and Amar impersonates him! He really is the devil for who could have thought he would be in Dawoodia of all places! I had better report this to Shahanshah at once. He will know how to punish him.'

We now shift the scene to the ayyar Barq who was as usual wandering outside his camp. He had just risen after rinsing his hands in a natural spring, when he noticed a whirl of dust spinning away in the distance. On closer inspection, this turned out to be Sarsar who seemed to be in a great hurry to reach somewhere. 'I should waylay her and impersonate her. Let us see what happens after that,' the wily ayyar thought. Accordingly, he laid a trap for Sarsar by placing his snare-rope on the path and hiding it under ferns and leaves. As Sarsar's whirlwind approached the trap, she hesitated for a moment, some instinct warning her of danger. At that time, Barq roared like a lion and Sarsar became rooted to the spot. The next moment, Barq had her trapped within the coils of the snare-rope and rendered her unconscious with a narcotic bubble. He picked up her unconscious body and tied her to a tree. When Sarsar woke up, she found Barq greeting her with mock respect. She felt very frustrated and looked away, but Barq said mincingly, 'My dear ustani, my dearest mother, where are you going? Do you ever think of your poor sons like me whom you abandon on birth? A father is meant to be indifferent to his children, but a mother is not meant be unkind and hardhearted as you are!'

Sarsar retorted sharply, 'Do you really want to die? Afrasiyab had sent me on an errand and I will return to him now!' Barq looked at her searchingly and said, 'Ustani, your explanation does not seem to be truthful. You are covered in dust and sweat, it's obvious you went very far on some mission. I think I should search you.' Sarsar tried to stop him, but he rummaged through her pouch until he found the message from the false Dawood regarding the keystone. Barq laughed with delight at this discovery and said, 'Ustani, this is indeed very important news. It seems that Shahanshah is in Crystal Mountain and there is some Dawood who will be given the keystone for safekeeping.'

Sarsar lost all colour and remained silent while Barq deliberately took out his paints and colours of ayyari in front of her. As he transformed his face to look like hers, he urged her to advise him, 'Ustani, do guide me. Am I doing well or is there a flaw? Just tell me if I am missing something and instruct me accordingly. Do you think Afrasiyab will recognize me? I forgot you have a mole on your chin, yes, this should do the trick!' Sarsar was now thoroughly enraged and snapped, 'As if I care how you look! A thousand curses on your ustad and ustani.'

After Barq had perfected his disguise, he untied Sarsar from the tree trunk and holding her firmly, climbed up the tree to tie her to the upper branches, out of sight. He artfully cut and arranged the branches to make a rough seat for her, and then tied her firmly to the seat with his leather snare-rope. He said, 'Ustani, do you see how concerned I am for your comfort? Now stay in this nest and trill like a bird!' Sarsar replied, 'You swine, I will starve up here.' Barq murmured that no dutiful son would starve his mother. He took out some pieces of sheermal bread and poured water into a bowl that he placed in the branches besides her. 'You idiot,' Sarsar tried another ploy, 'how do you expect me to eat with my hands tied?' Barq looked patiently at her, smiled and said, 'You really are silly. Just lap it up like a dog!'

Sarsar did not know what to say to this and looked around in alarm as Barq hopped off the tree. She cried, 'You shameless wretch, I will be torn apart by wild animals here!' Barq smote his forehead and said, 'In truth, you indeed are the right woman for my teacher! I completely forgot that aspect.' Barq then produced a leather collar from his pouch of ayyari, stitched some anklet bells on it and tied it around Sarsar's neck saying, 'Ustani, whenever some bird or animal approaches you, shake your head and the sound of bells will frighten it away.' Finally, after securing Sarsar in the tree, Barq left for Crystal Mountain disguised as her.

The other trickster, Zargham Sherdil, was also wandering around the forest when he waylaid Saba Raftar who was returning from Afrasiyab's mission. He also found the message from Khudawand Dawood (in fact Amar) and tied Saba Raftar in a tree, before leaving for the Crystal Mountain disguised as her. Meanwhile, Afrasiyab anxiously waited in Crystal Mountain surrounded by his wife and a handful of loyalists like Soorat Nigar, Mussavir the magic artist, Sarmaya Ice-maker, Abriq Mountain-breaker and Sannat Magic-maker. Since he had the precious magic keystone with him, he had stayed away from all other business of state, determined to first place the keystone in safe custody. As he waited anxiously for his messengers, Soorat Nigar tried to reassure him that Khudawand Dawood would respond positively to his request. 'My brother-in-law loves me and would never refuse me even if I have to force him to accept the keystone!' she boasted as Afrasiyab bit his nails in anxiety.

From his vantage point in the mountain, Afrasiyab spotted Sarsar approaching from a distance, almost hidden by a haze of dust. She arrived soon afterwards and reassured him that Khudawand Dawood would not deny him his request. Soorat Nigar urged him not to lose any time before travelling to Dawoodia. Saba Raftar reached some time later. Barq disguised as Sarsar, was apprehensive that she would see through his disguise and tried to avoid her eyes. He soon realized that Saba Raftar was in fact Zargham. Both ran to embrace each other and exchanged secret signals as they met. Eventually, Soorat Nigar and the others persuaded Afrasiyab to travel to Dawoodia with the keystone. His wife and other loyalists accompanied him, as did the false Sarsar and Saba Raftar.

Afrasiyab meets the false Khudawand Dawood

Amar, who was impersonating Dawood Jadoo, was presiding over his durbar one morning with his advisers and viziers in attendance. Princess

Lalaan Red-robe and Nagin had just entered the durbar with the princess's companions when a messenger came running to announce that Afrasiyab Jadoo had come to Dawoodia. Amar sat up straight and adjusted his robe, and then sent Nagin to receive the royal party. The second messenger announced the names of those who were accompanying Afrasiyab. At the mention of the ayyar girls, Sarsar and Saba Raftar, Amar lost his colour. His body trembled with fear and he prayed earnestly that they would not recognize him as this was his only chance to get his hands on the precious keystone.

He prayed desperately, 'They will be the only ones to see through my disguise. Oh God, make them as blind outside as they are from the inside.' Meanwhile Zargham and Barq who were with the Shahanshah as Saba Raftar and Sarsar were equally worried. The Shahanshah had kept the magic keystone close to his person throughout the journey. 'Once he hands it over to Dawood Jadoo,' they signalled desperately to each other, 'it will be lost to us forever!' They followed Afrasiyab into the durbar and went through the motions of prostrating themselves before Dawood and kissing his throne. As they were going around his throne performing the ritual of worship, Amar accidently looked straight into the eyes of the false Sarsar and was delighted to recognize the warm brown eyes of his favourite disciple Barq.

Amar could not resist calling out, 'Sarsar how are you? Look me in the eyes my child, I am impressed with the stories I have heard about your achievements.' Barq looked up startled and saw the familiar twinkle of his teacher's eyes. He nudged Zargham and whispered, 'Look up at Khudawand!' Zargham also recognized Amar at once and the three ayyars were beside themselves with joy. Amar composed himself and seated Afrasiyab in the place of honour next to him. Soorat Nigar and her husband Mussavir sat on the other side. Barq and Zargham began praising the Khudawand lavishly and begged him to accept the magic keystone from Afrasiyab. 'Keep it in safe custody, huzoor, and also destroy the Muslims who condemn you and the pantheon of gods who are your brethren.' They then whispered to Afrasiyab to hand over the keystone immediately, but he remained uneasy and seemed reluctant to part with the keystone.

Amar pretended to ignore the ayyar girls and turned his attention to Soorat Nigar. She was behaving in a forward and shameless way with him while her husband Mussavir looked on in good humour and said, 'My dear brother, she pines for you especially at night when she kicks me out of bed.' Soorat Nigar snapped at Mussavir to keep his mouth shut and declared that she loved her brother-in-law and did not deny it. Then she turned to Dawood and said ingratiatingly, 'Will you not accept the keystone for my sake? Only you can send it to heaven where your angels will keep it safely.' Amar retorted, 'Shut up you old witch! What would I care about the keystone, I make and break hundreds like this one.' Soorat Nigar smiled archly back at the false Dawood and urged Afrasiyab to hand over the magic keystone.

As the foolish chatter swirled around him, Afrasiyab sat still, his heart pounding with an unknown fear. All his loyalists urged him in unison to give the keystone to Khudawand, but he seemed reluctant to part with it. Eventually, Soorat Nigar forcibly pulled it out of the folds of his robe while he lowered his head to hide his expression. Amar then went through the pretence of not accepting the keystone. As Soorat Nigar tried to force the keystone on him and he resisted, Princess Lalaan Red-robe stepped forward with folded hands and said, 'Honoured father, Shahanshah is special to you and you must help him secure the keystone.' Lalaan then took the keystone from Soorat Nigar and wore it around her slender neck. She said, 'Honoured aunt, I will make sure that Khudawand sends this keystone to his angels.'

Afrasiyab looked at the magic keystone with longing, but could not say a word. The false Dawood looked at Afrasiyab sternly and said, 'Afrasiyab, since my daughter is insistent, I will do this for you!' Afrasiyab managed to mutter a few words of gratitude, but Khudawand continued, 'Listen Afrasiyab, you have been the cause of your own undoing. However, my divinity will protect you from the Muslims. Give me the Book of Samri. It is the need of this moment that I correct it for you.' Afrasiyab who had been listening with his eyes lowered now looked up in alarm. 'Khudawand,' he said, 'I consult the book frequently. How will I do without it for a whole month?' The false Dawood smiled benignly and said, 'What takes a month can be accomplished in an hour. That is all the time I need to go to my heaven and compose a new book for you.'

Afrasiyab's face turned ashen, but Soorat Nigar took the book from Afrasiyab and handed it to Dawood. He stood up and announced, 'I will return in an hour.' He then walked into his private chambers reflecting, 'Amar, this wretched book has ruined many a ayyari. Let me erase it forever!' Amar then erased every word in the magic book with water. He took out a similarly bound book from Zambil, lamenting, 'Alas! I will have to exchange a book for a book. What a waste!' Amar next opened the book in the middle and wrote, 'In the name of Allah, the Compassionate, the Merciful.' After praising Allah and the Prophet, he went on to inscribe the following words, 'I am the king of ayyars, Khwaja Amar bin Ummayyah. Afrasiyab, I have tricked you into giving me the magic keystone and the Book of Samri. I have destroyed the prophecies and erased your ancestors' hard work.'

Meanwhile, Afrasiyab was waiting in the durbar biting his nails when he was startled by loud voices that appeared to be coming from Khudawand Dawood's private apartments. As everyone in the durbar listened intently, it seemed obvious to them that the divine one was talking loudly to someone, shouting one moment, laughing the next. Eventually, the door opened and the false Dawood staggered in, holding the oracle Book of Samri. He was sweating and covered with a film of dust. It was obvious that he had returned from a long journey. Everyone rose to greet him and Afrasiyab asked anxiously, 'Huzoor is the book ready?' The divine one frowned at Afrasiyab and said, 'O sinful mortal, I have suffered much on your behalf today. The book is ready but the words are still in a raw state; they have not settled into the book yet. Be very careful and do not open it for three days. During that time, you must pray to Samri day and night and you are not to have any wine or red meat either.'

Afrasiyab tucked the heavy book of prophecies tightly under one arm, in case it opened accidentally, while Soorat Nigar declared, 'We will remain with Shahanshah during this vigil and observe the same restrictions.' Amar then held Princess Lalaan's hand and said, 'I have no more time to talk. I must keep the keystone safely.' Afrasiyab ventured hesitatingly, 'Khudawand, please ensure that the keystone does not remain on this earth.' Amar frowned again at him and said, 'I will do what I consider best. You fool, I will destroy the keystone altogether so that your Tilism is safe for a thousand years! You will be invincible until then. I also have a plan for the Muslims, but all will be revealed at the proper time.'

Amar got up to leave with Lalaan and Afrasiyab came forward to kiss his feet. As the royal party was saying their farewells, the false Sarsar and Saba Raftar requested the King of Magic to allow them to stay a while in Dawoodia 'in case some ayyars drift in here and cause trouble'. Dawood also urged Afrasiyab to leave them behind, as he said they could be helpful against the Muslims. Afrasiyab agreed and then departed for Crystal Mountain with the rest of his party.

The conversion of Dawood

After Afrasiyab's departure, Amar went with Lalaan to her garden, almost light-headed with happiness. Asad was waiting anxiously for him when Amar appeared and led him into the baradari. He presented the keystone to him there and said, 'Bismillah, here is the magic keystone of Tilism. It is a miracle that a brilliant man like Afrasiyab should be so deceived that he should present the keystone to me with his own hands!' Asad happily wore the keystone around his neck and asked, 'Grandfather, what is this I hear about the Book of Samri?' Amar replied with a smile, 'I have destroyed that book of prophecy forever. Now we must rejoin our lashkar immediately. Afrasiyab is bound to attack us when he discovers what has happened.'

Princess Lalaan had followed Amar and Asad into the baradari and asked, 'Khwaja sahib what do you intend to do with my father?' Asad looked at the princess and said softly, 'The truth is Grandfather, I would not like Dawood Jadoo to be executed. I hope he sees the light and converts to Islam.' 'By Allah,' Amar exclaimed, 'I am also very partial to the name Dawood. It is a name of honour and greatness.' Amar then prepared to bring Dawood out of Zambil. Princess Lalaan fled into her room in sheer fright, but Amar made Asad sit on a high chair. The princess's companions and handmaidens took up posts in the garden, but were quaking inside at the prospect of facing the Khudawand.

Amar removed the paints of ayyari from his face and brought out the unconscious Dawood from Zambil. He tied him to a pillar in the garden and pierced his tongue with a large needle to prevent him from casting spells before finally reviving him. Dawood Jadoo sneezed loudly when Amar woke him up and called out with his eyes still closed, 'Come to me my people. Khudawand is awake!' Amar called out, 'Dawood Jadoo, open your eyes and look around you. See the destroyer of sahirs, the Tilism Kusha, before you. Treat him with respect. You have done yourself great harm by claiming to be God. You have misled thousands of the True God's people. You are an intelligent man. Have you thought of the time when you will face your Maker? Will you still claim to be God then? Do you think your magic will save you from the fires of hell?' Amar then eloquently described the afterlife and the retribution all men must face. As he talked, Dawood Jadoo turned pale and started shivering as if consumed by fever. Beads of sweat covered his face and eventually he cried, 'Khwaja Amar, release me now. Throw me at Tilism Kusha's feet and show me a way to repent my sins. I have done great wrong and must be punished.'

Dawood became increasingly emotional as he spoke and struck his head against the pillar in remorse. Amar was alarmed by this reaction and Lalaan wept as she saw her father's state. Amar quickly drew the needle from Dawood's tongue and released him from the pillar. Dawood rushed and kissed Asad's feet first. He then begged Amar, 'O man of faith, recite the holy Kalma-e-Shahadat for me so I can come into the fold of the Almighty.' Amar held him affectionately and said, 'Listen to me. Do not make the affirmation yet. Just be of the faith in your heart. Join Tilism Kusha in his jihad against Afrasiyab. You will be rewarded in this life and the afterlife.' Dawood looked at Amar with tears in his eyes and said, 'O favourite of the prophets, I am weighed down with sins. I dared to claim to be equal to the Almighty. I cannot bear the burden of my sins anymore.'

Asad stepped in and said, 'Grandfather, your words have made the deepest impression on his heart. He will not turn away from the faith now.' Thus, Asad and Amar instructed Dawood to purify himself through the Islamic ritual of holy ablution. Dawood recited the holy verse after them and came into the fold of Islam. After becoming a Muslim, Dawood made everyone in the city of Dawoodia follow his example. He sent for his attendants and directed them to construct a building in the form of a mosque for him. After the mosque was built, Dawood sat in it with prayer books and surrounded himself with people who read the Holy Quran to him. Thus, Dawood became a man of God. He wore simple clothes and consumed only dry bread and water.

After Dawood settled in the mosque, Amar declared that Princess Lalaan Red-robe would rule the city. He raised a large force of soldiers from the land of Dawoodia and left with Asad. He wrote a detailed letter to Mahrukh describing the events in Dawoodia and sent it to her, ahead of his arrival. He instructed Nagin to take special care of the princess's safety and left with Asad for the Islamic camp with the new army.

⁓

32 AFRASIYAB PANICS IN CRYSTAL MOUNTAIN, SOORAT NIGAR AND DAWOOD

Afrasiyab left the city of Dawoodia with the precious Book of Samri tucked tightly under his arm and was trembling with the effort of keeping the heavy book tightly sealed. His arm ached with the strain and his heart was filled with strange fears. He regretted leaving Sarsar and Saba Raftar behind and thought, 'Now why did Khudawand insist on keeping them? Had they been with me, they would have thought of ways of keeping the book intact.' Torn by such thoughts, Afrasiyab arrived in his abode in Crystal Mountain in great anguish. Hundreds of attendants welcomed him back and led him to the throne with great ceremony. His wife Hairat and his viziers Sarmaya and Abriq fluttered around him, but Afrasiyab snapped at them, 'Do you think I will be at ease on this throne when I have to recite the names of Samri and Jamshed for three days and nights?'

Soorat Nigar arrived as well looking very smug after her audience with Khudawand Dawood. 'Did you see,' she said happily to Hairat, 'how well disposed Khudawand was towards me?' She then lowered her voice and said, 'Actually he has been in love with me for a long time. Had it not been for you people, I would have stayed back with him. My husband Mussavir does not mind. After all, Khudawand is our creator. I cannot refuse him anything, even my body!' Hairat looked disgusted and hissed, 'He might be Khudawand, but that does not mean that he should be after our honour!'

On the third day of chanting, Afrasiyab was near breaking point with the strain. In the afternoon, he decided that he could wait no longer to read the book. 'Let the day go by,' Soorat Nigar advised, 'wait till tonight to open it.' Afrasiyab lost his temper with her and shouted, 'I am torn apart right now and you want me to wait till tonight! I cannot wait anymore. If a page or two is unformed, I will deal with that later. I have ruled Hoshruba for ages and have never heard of letters disappearing from a book. Now Khudawand has revealed something new to us. I am opening the book right now! Let us hope we do not regret this.'

Afrasiyab took out the book he had tucked tightly under his arm and took it out from its silk cover. Everyone crowded around Afrasiyab, looking closely at the book. Soorat Nigar was the most excited one amongst them and boasted about how the book was prepared so quickly because of her. She declared, 'Shahanshah would have had to wait for months for the book to be written!' Turning to Afrasiyab, she urged him to open the book quickly, 'Observe how each word will be a work of art!' Afrasiyab rudely told her to keep quiet, opened the book cautiously and found the first page completely blank. Soorat Nigar immediately said, 'We have acted contrary to Khudawand's orders and opened the book too soon. See, the words have disappeared!' Afrasiyab snapped, 'Will you hold your tongue? I fear something else here.' He turned a few more pages that were also blank. Eventually, the twentieth page seemed to have something written on it. Soorat Nigar piped up again, 'There you are, the words have emerged. You opened the book too soon so the words were unformed. By tomorrow, they will emerge as well.' Afrasiyab said angrily, 'You silly woman, can you see what is written here? I feel dizzy at the sight of it. Will someone call the Arabic and Persian scribes and get this writing translated.' Vizier Abriq said, 'Huzoor, I can read Persian and Arabic. Let me try reading this.' Afrasiyab chewed his nails and said, 'Then hurry up and read it. There seem to be only two pages with writing on them. How will this tell us what will happen in Hoshruba till the end of time?'

Abriq started to read the writing in the book and blanched visibly. After some hesitation, he said in a low voice, 'Huzoor, I have read the first line and it is the Islamic invocation to their unseen God which is 'In the name of Allah, the Compassionate, the Merciful.' I cannot read beyond this or you will be angry.' Afrasiyab told Abriq to read on, so the vizier said, 'Huzoor, I have read both pages. Do you want a literal translation or should I just summarize the text?' Afrasiyab said impatiently, 'Vizier sahib, are you playing with me? Just tell me what is written here!' Abriq said with resignation, 'Huzoor, these two pages have been written by Amar ayyar. He has tricked you into giving him the magic keystone by posing as Khudawand Dawood. He has destroyed the oracle Book of Samri and the work of all Khudawands that went into writing it.'

When he heard this, Afrasiyab clutched his head in despair and shouted, 'This is terrible! How did he reach Khudawand and what has he done with him? Soorat Nigar, you have ruined us! I also just realized that Sarsar and Saba Raftar who had accompanied me must have been false. Find them now and get me the Papers of Samri from my grandmother Mahiyan.' Abriq said, 'Huzoor, I will go at once.' There was pandemonium on Crystal Mountain as Afrasiyab's companions rushed to do his bidding. Soorat Nigar looked horrified at the turn of events and Afrasiyab turned on her in his fury. He shouted, 'You are responsible for this disaster. You were the one who rushed me into handing over the magic keystone and I will get it back from you now!'

Vizier Abriq returned from Zulmat, the Veil of Darkness, and presented Afrasiyab with the oracle Papers of Jamshed. Afrasiyab learned through the papers that poor Sarsar and Raftar had been tied up in trees. He ordered Abriq to rescue them, who flew off at once and found them both unconscious and tied to trees. He brought them back to the durbar and revived them. Sarsar and Saba Raftar opened their eyes to look at a strange sight—Afrasiyab sitting before them trembling with rage, Hairat looking distraught with her hair open and beating her head. Soorat Nigar looked even worse and the rest of the durbar looked visibly disturbed. Afrasiyab looked at the ayyar girls and said, 'Tell us what happened to you.' Both the girls related their experiences: 'We recognized that son of a camel driver Amar immediately, but he was surrounded by advisers and ministers and we felt it was best to report this back to you. As fate would have it, those rascals Barq and Zargham waylaid both of us on the way home. Huzoor, can you tell us what happened after that?'

Afrasiyab replied, 'They both impersonated you and went with us to Dawoodia, but I did not really heed their advice. This wretched Soorat Nigar was the one who made me give the magic keystone to Amar. You should have seen the way she behaved with him when she thought he was Khudawand Dawood. Amar also took so many liberties with her while this dishonourable husband of hers kept laughing. I have not come across a shameless couple like this before! Because of them I have lost the keystone and the oracle Book of Samri.'

Sarsar and Saba Raftar were stunned by these revelations and turned on Soorat Nigar who was clutching her head in remorse. They taunted her, 'Why Soorat Nigar, did you enjoy yourself then? Amar has always behaved like this. You should be glad you did not stay back or he would have disgraced you that night.' The humiliated queen started weeping now and wailed, 'Alas, I have lived to see this day when I am accused of such terrible things. I must redeem myself before Shahanshah by getting the keystone back. If Dawood Jadoo has converted, that is my misfortune for he is much more powerful than I am. But I promise I will succeed or not return alive!' Soorat Nigar then asked Afrasiyab's permission to leave durbar and left for the land of Dawoodia.

The holy man of Dawoodia

After his conversion to Islam, Dawood was had been living a life of prayer and repentance. He had turned away from all earthly pleasures and had forsworn magic. Soorat Nigar reached the city of Dawoodia disguised as a bird and perched on the branch of a tree wondering what to do next. She had learned that Asad had left with a large army and that Dawood had remained in the city. She also knew that even Afrasiyab himself could not fight Dawood's magical powers. After thinking for some time, she decided to investigate the matter further. As she flew over the city, she was intrigued to see an unfamiliar structure that looked like a mosque. As she circled over the mosque, she saw a frail old man deep in prayer. Soorat Nigar thought to herself, 'This man must be a true mystic. See how his face is radiant with the light of Islam.'

She looked at him closely and recognized the man as none other than Dawood Jadoo. She trembled with rage, but realized immediately that Dawood must have forsworn magic. There seemed to be no guards or sahirs around him and taking heart, Soorat Nigar transformed into her real self. She called out angrily, 'You traitor, it has come to this that you now worship the unseen God whereas we all worshipped you earlier? Your daughter was instrumental in giving Asad the magic keystone.

Repent now or I swear by all the gods that I will burn you in hell. Because of you, my reputation is in shreds. Afrasiyab has taunted me in a manner even my handmaiden would not tolerate!'

Dawood looked up at the sahira and replied softly, 'Soorat Nigar, it is useless to speak to me thus. I have given up the world. If you want a fight, go and confront Asad and Amar in the Islamic camp. I have seen the light thanks to Asad and have imbibed from the stream of truth. Do not bother me.' Soorat Nigar was even more incensed by these words and abused Dawood loudly. Dawoods's attendants sitting outside the mosque heard her shouting and ran to their master. They wept as they begged him, 'Badshah of the worlds, punish this wretched woman. We will provide you with the tools of magic. She cannot face you and you can destroy her with one lentil grain. O Shahanshah, it was for this day that Khwaja Amar urged you not to give up magic. This wretched woman who could not even meet your eyes before is daring to confront you! We cannot bear it any longer.' Dawood looked at his attendants sadly and said, 'My faithful companions, how can I sin again after having sinned for so long? How will I face my Maker after doing that?'

Soorat Nigar watched with grim determination as Dawood's attendants pleaded with him in vain to punish her while Dawood calmly proceeded to continue with his prayers. Encouraged by his attitude, Soorat Nigar drew out her sword to attack him. His attendants tried to stop her with magic spells, but she casually foiled them, killing hundreds of guards with her magic. After disposing of them, Soorat Nigar turned to Dawood. He had calmly continued with his prayers but looked up when she stood over him with her sword drawn. At that point he said, 'Soorat Nigar, I am warning you for your own good. Do not stain your hands with my blood or you will burn in the fires of hell forever.' Soorat Nigar bared her teeth with rage and struck Dawood who did not resist and lowered his head to receive the blow. His head rolled on to the floor as if still in worship of the Almighty.

Soorat Nigar deceives Lalaan

The citizens of Dawoodia ran in droves towards Princess Lalaan's garden to inform her. After performing this dastardly deed, even Soorat Nigar trembled inwardly for she was afraid of Amar and Asad's wrath. Eventually, she decided to penetrate Princess Lalaan's court in disguise for that would lead her to Tilism Kusha and the magic keystone.

We will now leave this deceitful sahira to her devices and follow Lalaan Red-robe to her hunting lodge outside the city. The faithful Nagin had persuaded the Princess to go there in order to distract herself as she was pining for Asad after his departure. The princess returned from the hunt that afternoon, her heart and mind refreshed by the forest. Towards the evening, however, even the nautch and music did not distract the princess as her heart grew heavy with a strange foreboding. She confided her fears to Nagin and said, 'I feel that there has been a calamity in our city. Can we get news of Dawoodia from here?' Nagin tried to reassure the princess that there was nothing wrong, but she remained unconvinced and troubled. Nagin was just about to leave for the city when they heard the sounds of wailing outside the lodge. Princess Lalaan and Nagin emerged from the garden hastily and met with women who wept loudly as they called out the names of their dead sons or husbands killed in the fight against the evil sahira.

Lalaan did not realize the scale of the calamity that had befallen her city until some of her father's surviving attendants followed the women, their faces caked with dust and blood. They wept as they related the treacherous death of their master at the hands of Soorat Nigar and the way she had brutally killed anyone who tried to save Dawood. Princess Lalaan threw herself on the ground and wept bitterly calling out to her dead father. Her attendants also started wailing loudly, but Nagin took the princess inside and assured her that Dawood's foul murder would be avenged. After a while, Lalaan told Nagin that they should escort her father's body to the Islamic lashkar where Amar and Asad could bury him according to the Islamic rites. 'They had converted him and they should say the final prayers for him,' she cried emotionally.

Nagin suggested that the princess stay on in the hunting lodge while she would go to the city to see if it was safe for the princess to return there. Nagin returned to the city to find it utterly deserted and several of her own relatives dead. As she mourned them loudly, Soorat Nigar who was hiding nearby recognized Nagin at first glance and cast a spell on her that made her go into a trancelike state. After that, it was simple for the sahira to execute Nagin and bury her right there. Soorat Nigar then magically transformed herself into Nagin. She smeared herself with dust, left her hair loose and went to find the princess who was now waiting for her just outside the city limits. She wailed as she met the princess, lamenting the destruction of the city by Soorat Nigar. The false Nagin's state of grief appeared so genuine that it was the princess who comforted her this time. She told her, 'If you are in this state, who is going to console me? I have lost my father and I am worried about my beloved Asad who is on the war front. You must be brave now for my sake.' Soorat Nigar howled even louder, 'Princess, I am ready to die for you, but my heart is heavy with the memory of your father who loved me and pampered me as much as you.'

In this clever manner, the false Nagin escorted Princess Lalaan into the city of Dawoodia. Lalaan Red-robe took over the administration of the city, had the dead buried and placed her father's body in a black coffin. The next morning, Princess Lalaan, dressed entirely in black robes, prepared to leave for the Islamic camp with her father's body. Several hundred attendants also clad in black mourning clothes accompanied her. The false Nagin saw to all the arrangements personally. Later, this mournful procession left the city.

After returning to his camp, Asad was reunited with Mahjabeen. Both wept as they saw each other after a long absence, but Mahrukh urged her granddaughter to thank the Almighty for bringing Asad back safely. They had barely walked into the royal pavilion when Asad heard the sound of wailing women. He went out to see a group of black clad women approaching him and recognized one of them as Princess Lalaan's special attendant Nargis. She ran ahead and threw herself at his feet sobbing, 'Huzoor, Princess Lalaan has been orphaned and has brought the body of her father to you for the funeral rites!'

Asad immediately left with the women towards the distant camp of the princess. In his haste, he did not inform anyone and only a few attendants followed him. On the way, Asad asked, 'What happened? Did Afrasiyab himself attack Dawoodia that this black day was inflicted on us?' Nargis then described the way Dawood had died, unflinching in his faith: 'It was Soorat Nigar who spilt his blood in the mosque itself.' Tears rolled down Asad's cheeks as he heard the terrible details of Dawood's death. His heart was torn as he approached Princess Lalaan's camp and saw the black funeral tents from a distance. Lalaan came out to meet him, followed by the wily Soorat Nigar disguised as Nagin.

Lalaan threw herself into Asad's arms and wailed that she had been orphaned. Asad led her into the pavilion and held her close. After wiping her tears, he said, 'Princess, I feel as if I have lost my father. Rest assured that this murder will not go unpunished. Khwaja Amar will not spare Soorat Nigar, just wait and see. Our priority now is to bury your father as you must have travelled with him for days.' Soorat Nigar trembled to hear these words, but acted as Nagin might have done by throwing herself at Asad's feet and crying, 'My prince, you are right. Please conduct the funeral of this noble king now. I know that we will weep for him for the rest of our lives!'

Asad had Dawood buried in the Islamic manner and conducted everything himself, from the burial to the funeral prayers. Despite herself,

Soorat Nigar could not help but be moved by the funeral. She steeled herself as she recalled that her purpose was to get the magic keystone from Asad. After the funeral was over, she whispered to Princess Lalaan not to let Asad return to his lashkar. Princess Lalaan waited for Asad to return and said, 'Sheheryar, you have honoured my father in his death and his spirit must be at rest now. Do not grieve any more and join me in my pavilion.' The false Nagin led them both into the pavilion and asked Asad to persuade the princess to eat with him as she had abstained from food and water since her father's death. Asad dined with the princess and later said, 'You must come with me to the Islamic lashkar where Mahjabeen, Mahrukh and Bahar will welcome you with open arms. I have to travel tomorrow to the Neel river with Baghban Qudrat for that is what the magic keystone advises.'

Lalaan looked confused by this, but the false Nagin suggested that since it was late, the princess could travel to the camp with Asad in the morning. Asad also felt that the princess needed to rest that night and assured her he would travel only when she permitted it.

Khwaja Amar is suspicious

Princess Mahjabeen had resented Asad's departure from the camp soon after he had returned to her. Her attendants further inflamed her jealousy by telling her that Asad would not return that night. Just at that moment, Amar entered her pavilion. He saw Mahjabeen in tears and surrounded by concerned companions. She rose on seeing him, put her arms around him and began weeping loudly. Amar wiped her tears and asked in concern, 'My child, what is the matter? I swear that you are dearer to me than my own son Chalak. If someone has hurt you I will gouge his eyes out!' Mahjabeen was too upset to answer, but her vizierzadi Dilaram said, 'Khwaja sahib, I will tell you. Your grandson's beloved Lalaan Red-robe travelled with the body of her dead father to find him. Prince Asad rushed to her camp and now we have been informed that he will spend the night there. Please tell me, was it appropriate for him to be so careless with Princess Mahjabeen's emotions and so readily spend time with her rival?'

Amar was shocked at hearing this news of Dawood's death, but composed himself to console Mahjabeen, 'My child, it is advisable for you not to say anything against Princess Lalaan. It was because of her that Asad got the magic keystone. For the love of him, she endured a whip lashing, but did not betray him. It is a great calamity that her father has died. Just remember that even if Asad has a hundred mistresses, all of them will bow to you. Therefore, do not grieve, but pray for Asad's safety.' Turning to Dilaram, Amar said, 'You should comfort the princess. She must not waste her time with petty jealousies. Asad is the grandson of Hamza Sahibqiran and will always remain steadfast and true to her.'

Mahjabeen looked more composed and happier after Amar's talk. Amar left her to hastily speak with Mehtar Barq Firangi, to whom he said, 'Have you heard, Asad has gone alone to Lalaan? I am worried about the magic keystone as there could be an agent of Afrasiyab's in Lalaan's camp. Go now to the camp and I will soon follow.' Amar also whispered secret instructions to Barq and sent him off.

Soorat Nigar suffers ignominy

Let us return to Princess Lalaan's camp where the evil Soorat Nigar in the guise of Nagin had plied Asad and Lalaan with copious quantities of wine. Later that night, she whispered to Asad that she would leave him alone to console the princess, as she still looked very depressed about her father. After taking leave of her masters, the false Nagin made sure that none of the princess's companions stayed back and ordered them to leave the lovers alone. Asad led Lalaan to her bed and gently tucked her in. He saw the tears in her eyes and said, 'Princess do not grieve anymore. I will not be able to travel if you are in this state.'

Lalaan held his hand and implored, 'Take me with you. Everyone in your camp will be loyal to Mahjabeen and will resent my presence.' Asad reassured her that he would introduce her to Mahjabeen himself and all the sardars would welcome her warmly. Even as Asad was speaking to her, she fell asleep, overcome by a combination of wine and fatigue. Asad was also feeling drowsy and lay down beside her. Soorat Nigar was watching them from behind the curtain and stepped forward. She looked at the magic keystone hanging around Asad's neck and trembled with fear at the thought of Asad's strength if he awoke now. She approached the bed and cut the cord of the magic keystone with scissors. She then wrapped the keystone in a scarf and placed it in her bag of magic tools. Feeling more confident, she decided to take Asad with her to Afrasiyab. Accordingly, she put an arm around his waist and prepared to fly out of the pavilion with him.

As it happened, Barq had been sleeping under Asad and the princess's bed for that was what Amar had asked him to do. He woke up with a start to see Asad in Soorat Nigar's grasp, and thought, 'We feared a professional ayyar, but this is Malika Soorat Nigar, wife of Mussavir.' Thinking quickly, Barq quietly took out his snare-rope and lassoed the sahira as she began flying. As she faltered mid-air, Asad fell from her grasp. She breathed a magic word and the coils around her went up in smoke, while Barq's limbs suddenly became lifeless.

Soorat Nigar rose from the ground and shouted, 'You pale-faced bastard, I will take you to Afrasiyab as well!' She was about to burst out of the pavilion with both of them when Amar, who was hidden outside, called out to her. He realized that she would get away and took out the blessed Net of Ilyas. As he tossed it over the sahira, it trapped her and her prisoners. Amar quickly aimed a narcotic bubble at her face and she soon fell unconscious. He took her out of the net, tied her with a rope and pierced her tongue with a needle. Amar released Asad and Barq from the net and dragged Soorat Nigar out of the pavilion. Princess Lalaan was now awake and began weeping loudly. Amar called out, 'Why do you weep now? All is well. I have caught the murderous woman who spilt the blood of my innocent friend. She will pay for it now!'

By this time, it was dawn and the news of Soorat Nigar's capture spread like wildfire in the Islamic camp. Mahrukh, Bahar, Maimar Qudrat, Baghban and other sardars rushed to Lalaan's camp. They tumbled into the camp to see Soorat Nigar tied to a post and Amar standing in front of her with a whip. His mouth frothed with anger as he shouted, 'You harlot, you killed that innocent holy man! Did you not have any fear? Where is Afrasiyab now and where is that pimp husband of yours, Mussavir?' Lalaan cried out, 'Ask her what she did with my vizierzadi Nagin?' Amar called back, 'What is the point? It is obvious she killed Nagin and impersonated her. But she will be punished for all the crimes she committed in Dawoodia!'

Mahrukh, Bahar and the other sardars had not seen Amar in such a rage before and were afraid to approach him. Amar called out to his ayyar companions, Barq and Zargham and handed them two whips. 'Strike this whore with all your strength. If either of you falters, I promise I will whip you to shreds!' Barq and Zargham tremblingly began to whip Soorat Nigar. She screamed as her flesh tore and her blood spurted in all directions. The moment Barq or Zargham faltered, Amar struck them with his own whip. Soorat Nigar screamed, 'Amar forgive me! I will be your slave forever!'

The enraged Amar shouted back, 'You scheming witch, do you think I believe you? You did not have mercy on that God-fearing man. Had he not renounced magic, you would not have dared to confront him. He was truly repentant and did not remain a sorcerer and apostate. He has gone straight to heaven, but I will send you straight to hell! I will kill you a thousand times before you finally die.' When Baghban Qudrat realized that Soorat Nigar was about to die, he held Amar back and appealed, 'That is enough, king of ayyars. She is after all the wife of a noble sahir, you have punished her enough.' Amar was weeping by now and calling out to the dead Dawood, 'My dear friend, alas, I was not with you when you died. What a shameful death you had!' When Baghban touched him, he turned on him and in a frenzy and whipped him as well as he cried, 'You traitor, you dare to speak for this evil wretch!' Baghban yelped in pain and drew back. Asad then whispered to the sardars, 'I have never seen him in this state before. It is best not to go near him right now.' Thus the whip lashing continued. The sardars tried to counsel Amar from a safe distance, but he was blind to reason at the time.

Afrasiyab and Mussavir in Crystal Mountain

Meanwhile, Mussavir the magic artist had been worried about his wife's abrupt departure from the durbar. Occasionally, he would say, 'My wife has gone on such an important mission—pray to Samri that she does not get into trouble.' Afrasiyab ignored him until a bird swooped down from the sky and perched on his shoulder. Afrasiyab smiled at the bird and gently extracted a message from its beak. He saw that the seal on the letter was Soorat Nigar's and cried out, 'Murshidzadeh, listen to this, your wife has written it!'

Afrasiyab read out from the letter, in which Soorat Nigar informed him of her progress in Dawoodia with details of Dawood's murder and her disguise as Nagin: 'I am going with Lalaan to find Asad and the magic keystone. I will not write again unless I am in trouble. Otherwise, I will return to you with the magic keystone.' Mussavir smiled arrogantly and said, 'Shahanshah, have you seen how my wife has vanquished a powerful sahir like Dawood who claimed to be our living god? She has a brave heart to infiltrate the enemy camp. She will not spare any of the rebels. In truth, Tilism will be ours now. We will decide who will be king here!' Afrasiyab was offended by Mussavir's words, but said, 'I do not know how Soorat Nigar managed to kill Dawood. Even I was afraid of him. It is indeed remarkable.' He later whispered to Hairat, 'If I win this war because of these two, they will become insufferable. I will turn them right out of Tilism. What nonsense this man is talking?' Hairat whispered back, 'You have to be diplomatic now. Wait till we get the keystone.'

Afrasiyab then presented Mussavir with the oracle Papers of Jamshed and said, 'I have to meet with my ministers now, but this will provide you information about your wife.' Afrasiyab was deep in conversation with his ministers while Mussavir smiled as he read the oracle; then he laughed loudly. Moments later, Afrasiyab turned and saw his face crumple with grief. Mussavir beat his head and cried, 'My wife, my poor wife!' When Afrasiyab asked him what had happened, Mussavir merely flung the papers at him and cried, 'Read these papers.' He then flashed upwards like a flame and disappeared within seconds.

Afrasiyab looked at Hairat bewildered and said, 'Murshidzadeh really is very strange. He kept calling out for his wife, but did not tell us anything!' Hairat smirked and said, 'Soorat Nigar always did have an eye for young men. She must be with someone right now and he will just make a fool of himself. I am sure her lover will give him a shoe beating and pluck his beard as well!' Hairat laughed loudly at her own joke, but Afrasiyab sent a spy bird to bring him news of Soorat Nigar.

Amar was still punishing Soorat Nigar when Mussavir flashed in the sky above the camp and shouted, 'Wait you Muslims! How dare you mistreat the daughter-in-law of the great Samri?' Mussavir threw a handful of lentils at the rebel sardars as he descended from the sky. Amar had already disappeared in Galeem as soon as he heard him. Mussavir's magic turned daylight into darkness and no one could see anything. Mahrukh and the other sardars tried to dispel his magic. Mussavir did not wait to untie his wife from the pillar and in his haste, pulled the pillar right out of the ground. As Mussavir flew upwards, Amar leapt up high and ensnared both him and his wife in the blessed Net of Ilyas. He then tied Mussavir and his wife to separate pillars; Mussavir struggled to get free and Amar called out, 'Did you think you could snatch my prisoner from me? You will know me today!' Mussavir looked at his wife's condition and shouted, 'Amar, you will pay for how you have mistreated my wife!' Amar laughed derisively and said, 'If you are alive after this day, you can do what you please.'

Amar then signalled to Zargham to whip Mussavir as well. Zargham cracked his whip hard on Mussavir. After a few minutes, Mussavir screamed with pain, 'O son of a camel driver! Have mercy on us or my wife will die!' He then turned on his wife and shouted, 'You harlot, you have brought this on us by murdering Dawood Jadoo! Who will save us now? Tilism Hoshruba can burn to ashes! We are Brahmin by caste, we can survive by begging for food and shelter. I swear I will never even dream of ruling a kingdom again!' To this Amar growled, 'You fool, you will also have to pay for your wife's crimes. She has murdered an innocent man and I want you both to suffer for it!' Amar had by this time taken the magic keystone from Soorat Nigar and had given it to Asad, who had worn it around his neck again. Asad could not bear Amar's brutality anymore and called out, 'Grandfather, please forgive them now. Your faith does not permit such cruelty!' Amar turned on Asad in his rage and lashed out, 'You dare to talk to me about religion! These kafirs have murdered an innocent holy man and should be burnt alive for their crime!'

Asad stepped back afraid that Amar would strike him as well and joined the other sardars who were silent spectators to Amar's cruelty. No one had the courage to speak to him. In Crystal Mountain, the atmosphere was a light-hearted one in Afrasiyab's durbar as everyone speculated about Mussavir's abrupt departure. Hairat suddenly said, 'Should we not consult the oracle Papers of Jamshed? After all, he seemed very distressed when he left.' It was then that Afrasiyab casually picked up the oracle paper and lost all colour as he read it. He beat his head and cried, 'O shame and dishonour!' Hairat looked questioningly at him and he explained what was happening to Soorat Nigar and Mussavir at the time. He then declared, 'I will have to rescue them myself. No one should follow me.' Afrasiyab shot up into the sky and disappeared.

By this time Mussavir and Soorat Nigar had been whipped so long that they were both unconscious. Amar told Zargham to revive them. 'They are just pretending right now,' he said, 'and I will not rest till only their bones are left!' At that time, Afrasiyab flashed into the skies above them and thundered, 'Wait you Muslims! How dare you mistreat the grandson of Samri?' At the sound of his voice, Zargham and Barq leapt out of sight and Amar vanished in Galeem. The sardars were terrified to see Afrasiyab and reached for their magic weapons. Afrasiyab merely looked at the sardars and a sheet of flames descended on them. As they tried to save themselves, Asad, who was impervious to magic due to the keystone, challenged Afrasiyab to a fight.

Afrasiyab trembled inwardly when he saw Asad with the keystone, but averted his eyes and swooped down on the pillar where the husband and wife were tied. He hauled it out of the earth as there was no time to release the prisoners. Afrasiyab was after all the Shahanshah of Hoshruba and endowed with tremendous physical strength. He rose swiftly in the air and held the pillar in one hand while throwing pebbles with his other hand that descended like huge boulders on the Islamic lashkar. As he flew towards the wilderness, the sardars tried to follow him, but could not match his magical skills. Several sardars were stunned as if they were footprints on the earth. Sheets of flames and boulders fell on the lashkar and Afrasiyab's spells destroyed hundreds of rebel soldiers as he doggedly made his way out of danger.

Suddenly, a cloud appeared from the direction of Nur Afshan and burst open to reveal the noble form of Kaukab the Enlightened. He shouted at Afrasiyab from a distance, 'Wait Afrasiyab, I have arrived!' Afrasiyab saw Kaukab and immediately descended on the ground. He stamped hard on the earth and created a fissure. Afrasiyab jumped into the fissure with Kaukab following close behind, roaring like a lion. Afrasiyab merely pointed forward for the fissure to open like a corridor before him. Afrasiyab ran through the corridor, still holding the pillar with Mussavir and Soorat Nigar tied to it. He protected them even as he fought off Kaukab's spells.

Kaukab was holding something in his hand that he kept trying to aim at Afrasiyab, but the King of Magic was weaving his way through the earth like a powerful python. What Kaukab held in his hand was a large magic ruby that he had conjured after months of hard work. Kaukab knew that the ruby would not kill Afrasiyab, but hoped that it would disable him for life. Afrasiyab had also seen Kaukab's fist clenched around the ruby and feared for his life. Afrasiyab was vulnerable at this time because he was protecting Mussavir and Soorat Nigar. Otherwise, the Shahanshah of Hoshruba outranked Kaukab in status and magical powers. He would never have run from him at any other time. Kaukab was waiting for the right moment to strike when he saw Afrasiyab turn to his extreme right. For a moment, Kaukab lost his quarry, but turned the corner to see Afrasiyab standing still with the pillar in his hand. Kaukab aimed the ruby at his foe with all his strength. The ruby struck Afrasiyab straight through the forehead so that his skull burst open and flames consumed his body.

Kaukab then read a spell so that the earth above him burst open. He shouted triumphantly once he was on the ground, 'I have killed him! I have destroyed the arrogant ruler of Hoshruba!' Everyone rushed to see the sight of Afrasiyab burning and burst into applause for Kaukab's magical powers. Kaukab acknowledged all the praise with smiles and described how he had conjured the powerful ruby with the help of his mentors Nur Afshan and Brahmin Iron-body. Suddenly, a dense cloud of smoke rose from Afrasiyab's burning body. As everyone watched in horror, a light flashed in the cloud and a voice boomed out, 'Kaukab, you are still immature. Practise your magic a few more days before you confront the sahirs of Hoshruba! I am Mahiyan Emerald-robe and you have wasted your precious ruby. You fool, this was not Afrasiyab but his image placed here to deceive you!'

The cloud of smoke then rose into the sky and vanished in a flash of lightning. Kaukab looked stunned and when Amar asked him what had happened, he said half dazed, 'Khwaja sahib, alas I was deceived cruelly. I wish Afrasiyab had escaped and I had not wasted the ruby. He was saved by that whore grandmother of his who is always on the lookout for his safety!' Asad Ghazi then put his arm around Kaukab and said, 'Let it go huzoor. God willing, Afrasiyab's death will be at my hands.' Kaukab then walked back to the Islamic camp with all the sardars. Asad sat in the place of honour with Kaukab besides him while the rest of sardars sat in their appointed places. After everyone was refreshed with goblets of wine, Amar suggested that it was time for sardars like Mahrukh and Bahar to bring Lalaan Red-robe from her camp. He said, 'We have witnessed in one night the miracle of the magic keystone being almost lost and then found again. Princess Lalaan needs to be safe with us. She has suffered much by losing her father who died for his love of Islam.'

As the sardars rose to do Amar's bidding, he added, 'Before you leave, you should speak to Mahjabeen. Explain to her that her rival is of high rank. Her father was a great king and sahir, and also the living god of Hoshruba. God had endowed him with wisdom. That is why he died in a state of grace in the house of Allah. Very few are blessed with such an end.'

Lalaan Red-robe and Mahjabeen Diamond-robe

Lalaan, who was still in her camp, missed her friend Nagin and would not be comforted by her other companions who assured her that Asad was safe with the magic keystone. When she heard that Asad had gone with the other sardars back to the Islamic camp, she moaned, 'Why would Asad return to me now?' Lalaan grew more and more distressed even though her companions assured her that Asad and Amar would never let anyone point a finger at her. Just then, Asad's ayyar, Zargham Sherdil, sought an audience with her. He kneeled before the princess and informed her that the sardars were on their way to escort her back to the Islamic camp. The sardars soon arrived in a procession accompanied by trumpets and gongs. As the sound reached her, Lalaan's face flushed. She changed into her richest garments and looked like she had virtually dived into a river of jewels.

The sound of trumpets drew closer and finally the curtains of the pavilion were parted to let the sardars in. Nafarman, Hilal, Surkh Mu and other sardars had accompanied Mahrukh and Bahar. Mahrukh bowed before the princess, prayed for her health and long life, and said, 'Huzoor, do not stay in the desert now. Princess Mahjabeen awaits you eagerly in the camp.' Princess Lalaan embraced the sardars happily as all her doubts dissolved with the prospect of reuniting with Asad. She was led out of the pavilion and into the bejewelled palanquin that had been brought for her. Pretty girls in smart uniforms lifted the palanquin while

Mahrukh and the other sardars surrounded it. Thus, Princess Lalaan was escorted with great ceremony to the camp.

Meanwhile, Amar had been thinking of a strategy to unite the two princesses. He brought Asad out of the royal pavilion and said urgently to him, 'There is bound to be trouble now. Mahjabeen has been supreme in this camp. She has powerful allies like her grandmother Mahrukh and her aunt Bahar. Poor Lalaan will lose her life for nothing. As it is Mahrukh has promised Mahjabeen that she will cast spells on Lalaan and burn her. Bahar has prepared magic garlands for Lalaan, once she wears them, she will die of kidney pain.' Asad was stunned to hear this and pleaded, 'Grandfather, do something to prevent these shameful deeds!' 'What can I do?' asked the wily ayyar. 'Mahjabeen is livid and complained to me about you. Even the sardars are hostile to me. Perhaps if you give me the keys to the treasury I can bribe the sardars involved in this conspiracy.'

Asad immediately offered two lakh gold coins from his own funds to Amar, who smiled and said, 'These are powerful princesses. Do you think Mahrukh and Bahar will be tempted by such a small sum?' Asad quickly pledged another five lakh. Amar made him sign a promissory note and said, 'I may have to borrow some more, but I will try and retrieve the situation.' Amar then went running to Mahjabeen's pavilion where the princess was sulking as she had heard about the sardars' departure to welcome Princess Lalaan. 'It is true,' she was telling her companions, 'that in adversity even your near ones turn against you. If Lalaan comes to my pavilion, she will regret it. Are you ready?' Hundreds of Mahjabeen's attendants who were lined up in battle formations with swords in their hands shouted their assent.

When Khwaja Amar entered her pavilion, Mahjabeen rose out of respect to greet him. Amar was trembling and his eyes were filled with unshed tears. Mahjabeen forgot her defiance and asked him, 'What has happened? Has Afrasiyab attacked us?' Amar replied, 'Forget Afrasiyab, it is Princess Lalaan who is coming here in a mighty rage. In the first flush of love, Asad had claimed that he had no woman in Hoshruba. Now someone has told her about you and she is very angry. Mahrukh and Bahar are like meek handmaidens with her.' Mahjabeen lost all her colour when she heard this, but Amar continued, 'She declares she will kill you first, and then punish the whole lashkar. She says she will take Asad with her to Dawoodia and help him in conquering Tilism. It seems her father told her all the secrets of Tilism. By the way, someone has also informed her that you have used harsh words against her.'

Mahjabeen lost all her bravado and started crying. She pleaded with Amar, 'You know I am not familiar with magic. I am surprised that my aunt Bahar has turned against me. Does she have no regard for me?' Amar said cynically, 'Bahar has to save her own skin. It is an old story; people are with whoever wields power. Lalaan is after all the daughter of a Khudawand. All the sardars are escorting her carriage and it seems like the procession of a mighty king. As for your Tilism Kusha, he is sitting alone in the pavilion.' As Mahjabeen looked at him in despair the scheming ayyar took pity on her and said, 'There may be a way. Prepare your attendants to give her a grand welcome. When that bloodthirsty wench arrives, embrace her warmly and say this, "My dear sister, I was waiting anxiously for you. Alas, your father, so pious and holy was murdered so cruelly. We mourn his death and we are grateful that you should have risked your life to get the magic keystone for Tilism Kusha." When you say this to her, your eyes should be brimming with tears. She will be more sympathetic if your attitude is humble.'

Mahjabeen readily promised to do as he advised. Amar added in an undertone, 'Give me some money as well so I can bribe her attendants to put in a good word for you.' Mahjabeen at once removed the costly ornaments she was wearing and handed them to Amar, who pocketed these and whispered, 'My child, do not mention this to Asad. Bribery is a great crime and both the giver and receiver can get into trouble.' After making sure that she would receive Lalaan graciously, Amar left her pavilion many times richer.

Princess Lalaan arrived at the camp, apprehensive about Mahjabeen's attitude, but found the princess waiting to welcome her with hundreds of attendants behind her. As Lalaan descended from the palanquin, Mahjabeen extended her arms and said, 'Sister, you are very welcome.' Lalaan also responded in kind and both embraced warmly while Mahrukh and Bahar watched in delight. Mahjabeen led Lalaan into her pavilion and seated her beside herself on masnad. Both princesses, equally matched in beauty and grace, looked very beautiful together. Mahjabeen also honoured Lalaan's attendants with robes of honour.

Meanwhile, Asad was waiting anxiously in his pavilion when Amar entered. 'Grandfather, has all gone well between them?' he asked. Amar replied, 'My son, I have done my best and spent a great deal of my own money in bribes, but have succeeded in uniting the two princesses. They are together now and being entertained with music and dancing.' Asad rose and said, 'Grandfather, I would like to join them.' Amar looked doubtful and said, 'That may cause a fight between them.' Asad insisted that he could wait no longer; so Amar said, 'If you give me one lakh rupees, I can arrange it for you.' Asad happily pledged him the money. Amar returned to Mahjabeen's pavilion where everyone got up to greet him. Mahjabeen requested softly, 'Huzoor, all of us are waiting for you to play the flute.' Amar smiled and said, 'This is a wedding gathering without the bridegroom. Mahrukh and Bahar, will you not bring Asad here as well?'

Several sardars then went to the royal pavilion to escort Asad into the pavilion. He sat between the two princesses like the sun between two moons. Asad saw the harmony between Mahjabeen and Lalaan, and looked gratefully at Amar and said, 'Grandfather, this is a day of celebration and calls upon you to play the flute.' Amar looked at Asad sitting so majestically in durbar and remembered his master, the noble Sahibqiran. He murmured a blessing for Asad and played his flute with such passion that the whole durbar was mesmerized. For two whole days, the lashkar of Islam celebrated the arrival of Lalaan. The two princesses exchanged veils as a symbol of their sisterhood and Lalaan's pavilion was erected next to Mahjabeen's.

کہ

33 THE TRICKERY OF SARSAR, ASAD LOSES THE MAGIC KEYSTONE

Afrasiyab reached Crystal Mountain with his clothes in shreds and caked with mud. He had wounds all over his body inflicted by Kaukab's magic, but was still holding on to the pillar with Mussavir and Soorat Nigar tied to it. Their condition was pitiable after their whip lashing by Amar. Hairat took one look at him and beat her head before clasping him round the waist. 'What have you been through Shahanshah,' she screamed, 'and who did this to the family of Samri?'

Afrasiyab laid the pillar down and almost collapsed on the throne before gasping out the details of his rescue to Hairat. After catching his breath, he continued, 'The fact is that we have been truly humiliated today. That son of a camel driver was in a great rage. In truth, Soorat Nigar committed a terrible crime by murdering the innocent Dawood in a mosque of all places. Hairat, if Dawood had just moved his lips he could have destroyed heaven and earth. He gave up his life but did not resort to magic. I have heard that among Muslims once you take a vow of repentance, you become innocent of all your previous sins. To break this vow is a great crime and Dawood remained true to his Unseen God. As a sahir he could have destroyed us. Thank Laqa that he is no more. Amar was in such a mad rage that if I had not reached, he would have surely killed these two. Alas, the news that Samri's grandson was whipped will spread like wildfire in Tilism. It is a matter of disgrace!'

Hairat sent for healers who came and tended to the wounded royals. Some time later, Mahiyan Emerald-robe also reached Crystal Mountain. 'Have you seen Grandmother,' Afrasiyab asked her, 'what that wretched Amar did to Murshidzadeh?' Mahiyan frowned at her grandson and said, 'Afrasiyab, your arrogance has led to this day. Had I not reached you, Kaukab would have finished you today.' As they talked, Sarsar Sword-fighter arrived in the durbar, covered with the dust of the long journey. Afrasiyab looked at her enquiringly and she smote her forehead to indicate frustration. She reported, 'Shahanshah, after you escaped with the prisoners, there were great celebrations in the Islamic lashkar as Amar brought about a happy meeting between the two princesses Lalaan and Mahjabeen. After the celebrations were over, Asad and his allies consulted each other. Asad will now proceed to Neel river with Baghban Qudrat and Amar. Barq will also accompany them for Amar claims that he is his most promising disciple. Mehtars Qiran and Chalak will stay back in the lashkar and Kaukab has promised to send help to Asad through Burran.'

Afrasiyab blanched as he heard these words and looked at his grandmother, who, in turn, looked disturbed and said, 'Afrasiyab, if the Muslims manage to reach the Neel river, this Tilism cannot be saved.' As she spoke, there was panic in the durbar and some people wept openly. 'We have to think of a way to stop them,' added Mahiyan. Afrasiyab got up in anger and shouted, 'Grandmother, return to Zulmat. I will cause rivers of blood to flow before they can reach Neel river.' Hairat wept and clung to her husband. She cried, 'I will not let you go to confront the Muslims. The sardars may not stand up to you, but Asad has the keystone. He will be impervious to magic. You cannot be humiliated by him. He can even follow you to the Garden of Apples.' Mahiyan also advised Afrasiyab not to fight Asad while he had the magic keystone. Afrasiyab snapped, 'So what am I meant to do now? Sit here and let them destroy my Tilism?'

Sarsar came forward now; she declared that she would try to steal the keystone from Asad. She said, 'Huzoor, wait for one more day. Once you have the keystone in your possession, you will be able to defeat them easily.' As Sarsar prepared to leave, her companion in arms, Saba Raftar also reached the durbar. She volunteered to accompany Sarsar on this sensitive mission, but Sarsar refused firmly and said, 'You are my childhood friend, but I must do this alone. Even if I die in this mission, I will be happy for I will have served my Shahanshah!' Even Afrasiyab tried to dissuade Sarsar from going alone, but she remained firm and left for the Islamic lashkar alone.

Sarsar reached her destination that evening and wandered around the camp disguised as an old beggar woman. She drifted over to Mahjabeen Diamond-robe's pavilion and kept a keen eye on the entrance. There was a flurry of activity as Mahjabeen's attendants emerged to question the guards on duty and then vanished inside. After a while, one of them returned and called out, 'One of you find out what is delaying Tilism Kusha, it is almost time for the evening meal.' Sarsar noticed that the maiden who was young and pretty lingered at the entrance and spoke archly with the guards.

Sarsar approached her slowly and in a quavering voice begged her for food. The maiden immediately gave her a coin, but Sarsar said, 'Huzoor, I am hungry, could you not spare a plate of rice for a starving old woman? The maiden ran into the pavilion and rushed back with a steaming plate of pilaf rice, but Sarsar had moved back into the shadows. As the maiden looked around for her, Sarsar called out, 'Huzoor, I am under this tree with my granddaughter.' The maiden walked over to the tree and Sarsar rendered her unconscious with a narcotic bubble right away. She stripped the maiden of her clothes and jewellery and painted herself to look like her. She walked back to the pavilion thinking, 'I should have found out what her name was.' As if in answer to her prayers, one of the guards called out as he saw her, 'Rose-bud, where were you and why do you not talk to me?' Sarsar retorted, 'Watch how you speak to me! Do you think I will speak to anyone here?'

Sarsar entered the pavilion where Mahjabeen Diamond-robe asked her anxiously, 'Have you any news of Tilism Kusha?' Sarsar replied glibly, 'Huzoor, I have just been told that he was on his way there, but Princess Lalaan insisted that he dine with her first.' Mahjabeen remained silent, but Sarsar noticed Amar entering the pavilion and casting a sharp eye on all the attendants. She quickly hid herself in the privy tent to avoid meeting him. Mahjabeen rose to greet Amar who embraced her warmly. Mahjabeen bowed her head and said softly, 'Grandfather, I am concerned about Tilism Kusha. He has a long journey tomorrow and must eat and rest here tonight. I am worried that Afrasiyab might try to snatch the keystone from him tonight.' Amar replied reassuringly, 'My child, I am also concerned and have been roaming in lashkar since the morning looking out for ayyar girls. You must also remain alert against strangers.'

As soon as Amar left the pavilion, Sarsar emerged from the privy and thought that if she did not act now, all would be lost. She lured Mahjabeen into the inner chamber and after seating her down, whispered, 'Huzoor, I have just heard that Tilism Kusha might be taking Princess Lalaan with him on the journey. He says that her father is dead and she cannot be left in lashkar where she might have enemies.' Mahjabeen's face turned red as she said, 'If he takes her with him, he will not see me alive again.' Sarsar saw that the princess was trembling with anger and said soothingly, 'Huzoor, it may be just a rumour. The prince loves you and will be here soon. Please have this gilori and do not fret.' Mahjabeen was still preoccupied with her thoughts and put the betel leaf in her mouth. Very soon, the drug in it started working and Mahjabeen stood up in alarm. 'What have you given me? It is causing my insides to burn!' Sarsar urged the princess to walk and after taking a few steps, Mahjabeen collapsed in a drugged stupor.

Sarsar then set to work very quickly. She hid Mahjabeen under the bed, covered her with a sheet and thought, 'If that son of a camel driver walks in now, he will know me and all will be lost. No matter, if I steal the keystone, he will remember me for the rest of his life!' She assumed Mahjabeen's face, changed into her robes and emerged smiling into the pavilion, although her heart trembled with fear. As she was struggling to keep calm, her attendants rushed in to inform her that Asad was on his way. The false Mahjabeen immediately ordered that dinner be laid out and everyone got busy. Meanwhile, she pretended to sit with eyes downcast and tearful. As Asad walked into the pavilion, Sarsar became even more afraid, but remained silent. Throughout dinner, the false Mahjabeen kept silent and then walked into her bedchamber. Asad followed her and sat beside her on the bed. He tried to put his arms around her, but the false Mahjabeen said, 'Have some wine and then rest. You have a long and dangerous journey ahead of you tomorrow.'

Asad then poured a goblet of wine and offered it to the princess. The false princess simpered and took a sip, then handed it back to him saying, 'Now it is your turn.' She had cleverly slipped a drug into the goblet during this exchange. Asad had the wine and at once realized that something was wrong. He looked at the princess and tried to speak, but fell back on to the bed, completely unconscious. Sarsar wanted to shout with joy, but controlled herself and carefully cut the cord of the keystone from around Asad's neck while guards roamed outside the pavilion, occasionally calling out to each other to remain alert.

Sarsar looked outside and saw that dawn was approaching. She took out a pair of daggers and started to tunnel her way out of the pavilion. Her fingers bled from the effort, but she persisted until she had dug a tunnel to the edge of the camp. She looked out to see if someone was around and finding the place deserted, fled from the camp still covered in dust. Meanwhile, Asad was stretched out on the bed still unconscious when the cockerel crowed to announce a new day. Amar had been roaming the camp all night and had just managed to catch a few winks of sleep in his tent when a disturbing dream awoke him. He came out of the tent and saw the morning star. Zargham was pacing at a distance and Amar called out, 'My son, where did you spend the night?' Zargham said he was on guard outside Mahjabeen's pavilion, but Amar remained uneasy. He summoned the ayyars and went to Mahjabeen's pavilion.

Baghban Qudrat was already there with several other sardars, waiting for Asad to come out. As Amar came nearer, Baghban said, 'Huzoor, you must wake up the prince. I am told he is still asleep.' Amar became even more worried and said, 'Let us see what happens today. Even I am anxious to see Asad.' Baghban looked at him closely and asked, 'What is wrong?' Amar had already entered the pavilion by then and called back, 'I had a bad dream.'

Dilaram and the rest of the attendants were standing in the pavilion, ready to welcome the royal couple. Amar asked her, 'Why is Asad not awake, Dilaram? Usually your mistress is the first to wake up.' Dilaram replied, 'Last evening, the princess was depressed and they went to bed very late.' Amar approached the bedchamber and called out. When there was no reply, he walked in and cried out when he saw Asad collapsed on the bed in an unnatural position. Amar's scream alerted the sardars outside and Mahrukh and Bahar rushed inside. Amar first revived Asad and asked about the magic keystone. Asad was still dazed from the drug but shouted in alarm when he found the keystone missing from around his neck. Amar examined the floor and declared that he recognized Sarsar's footprints. Someone spotted Mahjabeen under the bed and brought her out. Dilaram reminded her of the dinner with Asad, but she looked blankly at her.

Amar said, 'I will tell you all. When I came to visit the princess, she was real. Sarsar must have hidden herself when she saw me. She did this after I left, but where could she have disappeared from?' Qiran noticed the tunnel in the corner and pointed it out. He said, 'She could not take Tilism Kusha through this so she just escaped with the keystone.' There was great despair in the camp as the news spread rapidly. The sardars decided that they would die fighting with Afrasiyab, as it would be impossible to find the keystone again. Amar tried to reason with them, but they resisted all his calls to remain calm. 'It is no use now Khwaja sahib,' they said in unison, 'you did your best and got us the magic keystone after the battle in the Garden of Seemab, but we have lost it due to our own misfortune. You should put Asad in Zambil and travel back to your master in Mount Agate. We will fight it out and die here. It is hopeless to follow the magic keystone now. Afrasiyab will make sure it is in a place where even our thoughts will not reach.'

Amar embraced the agitated sardars and calmed them down. He said to them, 'You are brave and loyal, but just wait till I try getting the keystone back from Crystal Mountain. If I do not succeed, you can have your way.' Chalak and the other ayyars also reassured the sardars, 'Ustad is right. Sarsar cannot have gone far; one of us will stop her on the way. Otherwise, we will pursue Afrasiyab until we find the keystone from him. What all of you must do is to support Tilism Kusha for he needs to conserve his strength and not fall into despair about losing the magic keystone.' Mahrukh also consoled the sardars and convened durbar in the royal pavilion. Amar and his companions left for Mount Crystal in various disguises. Before leaving the lashkar, Amar had a secret conference with Barq and Asad.

Amar in Crystal Mountain

Afrasiyab was waiting anxiously in Crystal Mountain for news of Sarsar when he caught sight of a figure moving in the distance. He thought it could be Sarsar, but decided to wait until the person was identifiable. Meanwhile, though Amar and the other ayyars had caught up with Sarsar, she was travelling very fast ahead of them. She was well aware that she would be followed and at one point when she turned around, she saw a whirl of dust far behind her. She immediately called out, 'Shahanshah, I have brought the magic keystone, but I am completely exhausted and my feet are swollen. The ayyars are pursuing me!' Afrasiyab heard her call and ran to her rescue. He picked her up and said, 'Sarsar, you are indeed remarkable!' Afrasiyab flew back to the mountain with Sarsar and deposited her amidst the throng of courtiers.

Amar saw Afrasiyab flying off with Sarsar. He thought very quickly and disguised himself as a beautiful young sahira. He stealthily went up the mountain and joined the throng around Sarsar. One of Hairat's attendants asked the false sahira who she was and Amar laughed in reply, 'Have you lost your mind that you ask me this? Do you not recognize me? I am Shama Afroze, the illuminator. Without me, every gathering would be plunged into darkness.' Amar quickly moved on and mingled with the people congratulating Sarsar on her remarkable feat. At one point, Afrasiyab called out, 'Friends, do not make such a noise. We must remain alert against the ayyars of Islam.'

Sarsar then pushed her admirers aside, approached the Shahanshah and held out the magic keystone. She said, 'Huzoor, you are right. They were all on my trail and I even spotted Amar from a distance. That rascal may already be there, so here is the magic keystone.' Amar watched in great agitation as Afrasiyab placed the keystone besides him on the throne. There was no chance of getting the keystone with so many powerful sahirs around. By this time, the other ayyars had also reached Crystal Mountain and were mingling with Afrasiyab's courtiers. All eyes were on the magic keystone.

Afrasiyab brought out a tiny golden statuette from his topknot and breathed life into it. He wrote something on a piece of paper and handed it to the statuette who smiled and flashed out of sight. The durbaris were just speculating amongst each other as to what would happen next when a whirlwind appeared in the distance. Afrasiyab looked intently at the whirlwind that eventually turned out to be a magnificent bull that galloped up the mountain in a flash and went straight to Afrasiyab. As the Shahanshah stroked the animal's back and spoke to him in an unknown language, it nodded its head. The ayyars disguised as durbaris were so agitated that they would have jumped on Afrasiyab to get the magic keystone, but could only watch helplessly. The bull opened its mouth wide to receive the magic keystone and then bounded out of the durbar and down the mountain again. Within moments, it had disappeared into the desert. The ayyars signalled to each other, 'What are we to do now, how did this donkey summon a bull?'

As mentioned earlier, Amar had secret consultations with Barq and Asad before he left the lashkar. What he had actually done was to render both of them unconscious and put them in Zambil. He now set about luring Hairat away from the durbar on some pretext. After rendering her unconscious, he deposited her in Zambil as well and assumed her form.

After the neelgai had left, Afrasiyab looked relaxed and happy after several days of anxiety. When the false Hairat rejoined him on the masnad, he reached out for her, but was startled when she rapped his hand and cried, 'Don't you dare touch me or I will take poison or jump in the well! If you do not trust me then we are no longer married. They say that a wife hides her husband's worst traits even if he is a gambler or a drunkard. Since you consider me an enemy, I should not stay in your house; I should also betray your darkest secrets. I should tell people that you are sweet on a young boy, that he was a shepherd's son and you adopted him for your own pleasure. You visit him and then sleep with your back towards me! You can sign a slip divorcing me right now and I will go straight back to my parents' house.'

Afrasiyab was so stunned with this volley of abuse from his otherwise devoted wife that he immediately put his arms around her and embraced her tightly. Amar, who was impersonating Hairat, shook him off sharply, thinking to himself, 'God help you Amar, your profession leads you into such humiliating situations!' Afrasiyab tried to cajole his wife, 'Tell me what secret have I kept from you?' The false Hairat turned her face away and said, 'You have kept the secret of the magic keystone from me! You think I am your enemy. The moment I know the secret, I will betray you to Tilism Kusha! Is that what you think?' Afrasiyab started pleading, 'Malika, why are you so agitated? I kept silent about the magic keystone deliberately. Bahar, Makhmoor and Baghban were my confidantes earlier. Look how they betrayed me by leading Tilism Kusha to the Garden of Seemab!'

The false Hairat smote her forehead dramatically and said, 'You cruel, heartless man! You dare to compare me with those worthless chits Bahar and Makhmoor who first made eyes at you and then betrayed you! I am your wife and I will follow you to hell if necessary. Tell me or I will swallow this emerald from my ring right now!' Afrasiyab first looked around and then whispered, 'Then listen. If someone wants the magic keystone, he would have to first render me unconscious; then take out a tiny casket hidden in my topknot that contains a key. He would have to lift the heavy throne you and I sit and open the door to the secret passageway underneath with the key. This passage goes down several hundred steps and opens into a vast desert without any water. It takes several days to cross this desert and reach the Tilism of Sunddal. This person would have to conquer this Tilism, which is impossible for the ruler, Sunddal Jadoo, is an extremely powerful sahira. Let us imagine that by some chance that Tilism is conquered; even then, the enemy would have to conquer the Darband of Meher and Mah. I have sent the keystone to the sisters Meher and Mah Jadoo, also very powerful sahiras. Only if they are killed will our enemy get the magic keystone.'

Amar disguised as Hairat listened intently, but pretended to look bored. She slapped Afrasiyab playfully on the cheek and yawned, 'Well that is all fine then. I am exhausted and want to sleep, so do not bother me at night!' The false Hairat then stretched and muttered, 'Shaitan urged me to fight with my dear husband tonight. What exactly did you say to me Shahanshah? I could hardly hear you I was so sleepy. You told me that the magic keystone was hidden under the throne, did you not?'

Afrasiyab was so relieved that he said quickly, 'That is exactly what I said. You can rest easy now, but have some wine first.' As they moved to the bedchamber, Nairang, the palace mahaldar brought them goblets of wine. Amar carefully drugged Afrasiyab's goblet and offered it to him. He said, 'I am not too keen but will have some with you.' After the unsuspecting Afrasiyab had consumed the wine, he collapsed on the bed in a drugged stupor. Amar carefully removed the key for the underground passage from his topknot and then began thinking of a plan. He reached the conclusion that it was best to bring Hairat out from Zambil and leave her with Afrasiyab to allay his suspicions as long as possible. He also decided to bring Barq out from Zambil so that he could inform the sardars about Amar's destination.

Accordingly, Amar brought out Hairat from Zambil and drugged her as well so that both she and Afrasiyab would remain unconscious for hours. He then brought out Barq, who rubbed his eyes as he saw Amar in a splendid palace bedchamber with Afrasiyab and Hairat lying unconscious before him. 'Ustad, where are we?' he asked. Amar then related all that had happened to Barq and said, 'Everything depends on you now. Disguise yourself as an attendant and stay with Afrasiyab.' Barq wanted to accompany Amar, but he forbade him from doing so and said, 'It would be better for you to stay here and allay Afrasiyab's suspicions for as long as possible. Just make sure that you convey my message to our friends that I have left for the Tilism of Sunddal with Asad. Tell Baghban, Burran and Makhmoor that Asad will be alone and will need their protection.' Barq and Amar then went back to durbar that was deserted at this late hour; they removed the heavy throne together and found the entrance to the tunnel. Amar opened it with the key and handed it back to Barq. As Amar was descending into the pitch-dark tunnel, Barq clutched his hand and cried, 'Ustad, we do not know what horrors might lie beneath us. Afrasiyab is the master of magic and intrigue; he could have deceived you earlier.'

Amar smiled calmly and declared, 'I have to go through with this now.' Barq almost wept with anxiety as Amar descended the steps of the tunnel and disappeared into the darkness. Barq covered the tunnel with the carpet and dragged the throne back into place. He tucked the key back in Afrasiyab's hair. He now had to find a role for himself and went to examine the sleeping attendants in the back rooms. Selecting one attendant, he first made her unconscious and then dragged her to a deserted room where he exchanged clothes with her and painted his face to look like hers. After these exertions, he lay down quietly on her bed.

Barq in Crystal Mountain

As Barq lay next to the other attendants, he thought of Amar finding a way through the treacherous tunnel and said to himself, 'One needs a heart of stone to remain in the profession of ayyari.' He was full of admiration for Amar for undertaking the journey entirely on his own and for preparing to face the difficulties he would encounter on the way to the Tilism of Sunddal. The sun came out and Afrasiyab awoke, rubbing his eyes. He looked at Hairat sleeping beside him and felt guilty for having fallen asleep when she had so lovingly offered wine to him the previous evening. He shook her gently to awaken her, but she was dead to the world. Meanwhile, Barq saw that the Shahanshah had arisen and went forward to greet him. Afrasiyab recognized her as one of Nairang's special handmaidens, Saman Azar. He greeted her pleasantly and as Nairang Jadoo came forward, he said, 'Princess Nairang, Malika Hairat is angry with me this morning. Will you awaken her?'

Nairang woke the queen by kissing her feet. When Hairat woke up, she felt very confused. Her last memory was being in Amar's Zambil and she shuddered as she remembered her experiences there. Afrasiyab tried to speak to his wife, but she turned her back on him. He assumed she was still angry with him and kept quiet, but Nairang went forward with a bowl of scented water and asked her if she wanted to wash her face or needed something to eat. Hairat snapped, 'Why would I want to wash my face? I seem to have washed my hands off life itself!' As everyone stared at her in astonishment, Barq thought that the truth would be revealed before he could find a way of reaching his camp. He whispered to Afrasiyab, 'Huzoor, let us take Malika back to her lashkar. Perhaps she will feel better there.' Afrasiyab was pleased with the suggestion and held his wife's hand as he said, 'Come, let us return to your camp. Your sardars will be relieved to see you again. Perhaps Mahrukh and Bahar may have declared war again and you know how badly you will be needed then.'

Hairat looked at him blankly and did not say a word. Afrasiyab conjured a flying throne and led Hairat to it. Barq was afraid that he would be left behind in Crystal Mountain. He signalled desperately to the Shahanshah for permission to accompany Hairat. Afrasiyab smiled and sportingly invited Saman Azar to join them on the throne. As they flew over Tilism and the River of Flowing Blood, the false Saman Azar kept chattering while Hairat maintained a stony silence. Afrasiyab's viziers Sarmaya Ice-maker, Abriq Mountain-breaker and Sannat Magic-maker received the royal couple when they arrived and led them into the durbar pavilion. The false Saman Azar followed the royal party, smiling at everyone. Vizier Abriq stared at her and said meaningfully, 'How are you today Mistress Saman Azar?' Barq retorted archly, 'Sir, why should you care? Please do not stare at me like this. I am very fragile. If someone stares hard at me, I immediately go down with fever. Oh Samri, blind whoever looks at me harshly!' Abriq was stunned by this outburst, but his brother Sarmaya said wryly, 'Mistress Saman Azar, your tongue has sharpened since we last met!'

Meanwhile, Afrasiyab's female vizier Sannat Magic-maker noticed that Hairat was quiet and had tears in her eyes. She led Hairat to the throne and invited her to sit down there. Hairat looked at her and then at her concerned attendants, but silently ascended the throne. As Afrasiyab sat down beside his wife, Sannat said, 'Huzoor, Malika Hairat looks very distressed today.' Afrasiyab looked at his wife and sighed deeply. He said to her, 'Sannat, the matter is such that I am cursed if I say something and cursed if I don't.' Sannat looked concerned and asked, 'Huzoor, will you not confide in us your slaves?' Afrasiyab said eventually, 'The truth is Sannat, Malika has been angry with me since last evening. First, she screamed at me for hiding a secret from her so I revealed the secret to her. Later, I was exhausted with sleep and wine and went to sleep early. Perhaps she is annoyed about that now.'

At that moment, Hairat screamed and said, 'Will someone tell me if I am dead or alive? Is this my pavilion? Are these my servants?' Afrasiyab looked at Sannat meaningfully and said, 'Now this is another story altogether!' Sannat then said, 'Huzoor, be silent. I have never seen Malika in this state. She is a person of great wisdom and dignity. She can single-handedly run this empire. What could have happened to reduce her to this state?' Sannat went close to Hairat and asked, 'Huzoor, I am your devoted attendant and all other attendants and handmaidens are here to serve you. Tell me what troubles you.'

Hairat replied, 'Sannat, all I remember is that I was talking to Sarsar before I lost consciousness. I woke up to find myself in my worst nightmare. I was in Amar's Zambil. Oh Sannat, I tremble with fear even as I tell you. I heard Amar call out that I was the wife of the ruler of Hoshruba and should be treated properly, but soon the most hideous black creatures surrounded me. All of them were shouting that I was the wife of their master's enemy and that I should be stripped of my clothes and beaten. Some of them came with live coals and threatened to blind me; others wanted to sear my tongue for abusing their master with it. Just as I was about to faint with fright, the crowds of those frightful creatures suddenly parted and a beautiful parizad approached me. She was obviously a princess with a crown on her head, adorned in the costliest robes. She admonished the horrid creatures soundly and said, "She may be our master's enemy but she is a princess of a powerful realm. She in our custody now, but will be released soon. If you harass her now, she will be an even greater enemy to him. She cannot be faulted for fighting when her kingdom is threatened." The horrible creatures then slinked away and this angel came and comforted me. She assured me that their master was not a cruel man and would not hurt me. She offered me a glass of water and some betel leaf. If it had not been for her, I might have died in there. Later, I lay in a corner and went to sleep. I woke up in my own bed in the palace and have been hearing nonsense since then about secrets and wine and how angry I was last evening!'

Afrasiyab lost his colour and asked, 'So who was it who threw a fit last evening? Who threatened to chew her emerald ring? Who said "Divorce me, I do not wish to stay with you anymore?"' Hairat shrugged and said, 'How do I know? Once you had told us you were going to keep the secret of the magic keystone to yourself, why should I have bothered you again?' The Shahanshah clutched his head in despair and cried, 'Who was it then?' At this point, Sarsar spoke up, 'Huzoor, it must have been Amar. He must have disguised himself as Malika and extracted the secret of the keystone from you. He then brought out the real Malika to divert you for a while. He must be surely in pursuit of the keystone now.' Afrasiyab looked angrily at her and said, 'Stop talking nonsense! Malika threatened to kill herself unless I revealed the secret, so I told her everything. Wait a minute, the key to the tunnel is still on me. It could not have been Amar!' Hairat said, 'Well it was certainly not me who was with you last evening!' Afrasiyab looked at her with confusion while everyone in durbar began speculating about what might have happened. Hairat's attendants wailed about Hairat's sufferings in Zambil and as the noise level rose in the durbar, Afrasiyab called out, 'Friends, be quiet! I cannot hear myself think!'

Meanwhile, Barq disguised as the maid Saman Azar was clinging to a fat sahir's arm and whispered, 'Brother, please stay by me. I am so frightened with this talk that is going on in the durbar.' The fat sahir stood by the false Saman protectively and she called out, 'Huzoor, I know the truth! If you silence everyone in the durbar, I will tell you.' The Shahanshah silenced everyone and turned to listen attentively to Saman Azar. She said, 'Huzoor, listen, your lowly handmaiden was awake last night and saw that son of a camel driver disguised as Malika Hairat extract the secret of the magic keystone from you. After that, he made you drink drugged wine so that you were unconscious. Then he brought

Malika out from Zambil and laid her down beside you. He also brought out his disciple Barq Firangi from Zambil and told him that he would be going with Asad to find the magic keystone. He told Barq to disguise himself as an attendant and accompany the royal party across the river. Huzoor, I watched as Amar and Barq removed the heavy throne and then removed the stone that blocked the entrance to the tunnel. After that, Amar descended into the tunnel and Barq restored the stone and the throne back into place. Then he quietly lay among the attendants disguised as one of them. This is exactly what happened.'

Afrasiyab shouted, 'You foolish hussy, why did you not wake me up at that moment or make a noise?' Barq simpered, 'Huzoor, the reason was because my grandmother had always taught me never to be a tattletale. That is why I watched everything in silence and did not wake you up.' Afrasiyab was almost purple with rage now and screamed, 'You wretched woman, if you had woken me up, I could have captured Amar instantly.' Barq retorted, 'If you had, you would have killed that miserable wretch and I would have been blamed for the murder. My grandmother would have turned me out of the house for being an informer!' Afrasiyab got up in his rage and shouted, 'Beat up this disloyal strumpet! It seems as if she has joined Amar!' Barq called back, 'You idiot, why should I have my teacher arrested? Can you not tell who I am? I am Barq Firangi!'

After this announcement, Barq immediately killed the fat sahir next to him and the whole durbar went dark. Barq killed a few more sahirs and escaped from the durbar while it was still dark. Gradually, light returned to the stunned durbar. Afrasiyab looked ashen and cried, 'My friends, this is terrible. I never thought that the secret to the keystone could be revealed in this ignominious way. That son of a camel driver is my nemesis.' As Hairat began weeping in despair, Afrasiyab said, 'Do not worry at all. I will warn Queen Sunddal that Amar is on his way. She will arrest him soon. It is not easy to conquer the Tilism of Sunddal.' Afrasiyab dispatched a hasty letter to the ruler of Sunddal and then turned to his wife to comfort her.

Amar in the Land of Sunddal

After saying farewell to Barq, Amar descended into the magic tunnel quaking with fear. As Barq closed the tunnel, a stifling darkness engulfed Amar and he felt as if he was in his grave. He took a deep breath and lit a torch. He stumbled along the tunnel for some time until it opened into a vast, burning desert. Amar was disguised as a sahir as his real face was famous throughout the realm. He made his way under a scorching sun and looked for shade or water, but there was none available. Eventually, Amar reached a hill and rested under the shade of a rock. After some time, he saw a sahir in the distance. As he drew closer, Amar could see that he looked distraught and exhausted by the journey. Amar called out, 'Brother, where do you travel in the noon sun? Come and rest here with me or you will fall ill.' The sahir looked up in relief and approached Amar gratefully. 'Brother the sun is at its zenith. This is no time for you to travel!' Amar said. The sahir sighed and replied, 'I know, but my job depends on this mission.' Amar asked, 'Who is this cruel employer who sends you out in this heat? Has he no fear of Samri and Jamshed?'

The sahir looked around him furtively and then whispered to Amar that he was Afrasiyab's messenger on his way to the ruler of Tilism-e-Sunddal with a message from the Shah. As Amar looked interested, the sahir went on to relate the story of how Amar had deceived Shahanshah into revealing the secret hiding place of the magic keystone. Amar pretended that he was not even aware of the existence of the ayyar. After the sahir had completely relaxed with him and revealed the route to Sunddal, Amar took out a flask of cold water. The sahir gratefully had the water and fell into a dead faint. Amar dragged the messenger sahir behind the rock and went through the practised ritual of changing his form. He then set out for Tilism-e-Sunddal, happy with his success in the perilous mission.

Prince Sundlaan and Asad Ghazi

Amar had to travel a long distance on the route indicated by the messenger before he sighted a gigantic fort made entirely of sandalwood that was sprawling across the horizon. As he went closer, Amar saw that each of the turrets of this fort was manned by a parizad holding a shield made of pearls. The movement of the shields blinded anyone who looked up at the fort. A huge moat with clear running water ran around the fort. The gates appeared to be closed and there were no guards in sight. Amar went to the fort gates and called out loudly, 'I am the messenger of Afrasiyab for Sunddal Jadoo, ruler of Tilism.' There was absolute silence so Amar called out his message several times. There was still no response to his cries except from the parizads in the turrets, who kept smiling at him enigmatically.

Suddenly, a cloud of dust appeared in the desert. As Amar watched with interest, a cavalry of twelve hundred young men seemed to be approaching him, led by a young man of noble face and form. The young soldiers dismounted and within minutes, established a camp right there. The leader then led Amar by the hand into his pavilion and seated him respectfully. After refreshments were served, the young man said, 'O king of ayyari, I have wanted to meet you since long. My name is Prince Sundlaan Sunddal-Posh. I have always liked the Muslims and urge you now to leave before you are harmed in this Tilism.' Amar pretended to be startled and asked, 'What are you talking about? I am the messenger of the King of Sahirs.'

Prince Sundlaan laughed and said, 'Please do not try and trick me. Let me explain. I was averse to learning magic, but I have acquired skills as a warrior and wrestler. The ruler of this area, Princess Gauhar has been in love with me for some time. I often requested her to let me try my skills by confronting Hamza or one of his sons in a wrestling match, but she does not let me go. This morning, she suddenly said, "Amar is approaching disguised as a messenger. I will dispose of him right now." I persuaded her not to kill you until I had a chance of meeting you first.'

Amar admitted, 'You are correct. I am disguised as Shahanshah's messenger.' So, Sundlaan requested politely, 'Will you not show your real self to us Khwaja?' Amar reluctantly went into a corner and removed the paints of ayyari from his face. Sundlaan's comrades sniggered when they saw Amar's real face, but Sundlaan rebuked them and behaved even more courteously with his guest. He pushed forward a young cupbearer towards Amar and said, 'You can convert this child to Islam and then drink the wine that he serves you.' Amar did that and after their hearts were warmed with the wine, Sundlaan said, 'Khwaja, my dream is to travel to Mount Agate and engage one of Hamza's sons in a bout of wrestling. Either I will defeat them or become one of them forever.'

Amar smiled at the young man's enthusiasm and said, 'Are you really serious about this?' Sundlaan replied, 'Take me to Asad's lashkar right now and I will prove it to you.' 'In that case,' declared Amar dramatically, 'Asad himself will confront you tomorrow morning, so be prepared.' Sundlaan looked stunned as he heard this and looked at his companions, who whispered, 'This ayyar is just trying to escape. Arrest him now and hand him over to Princess Gauhar.' Sundlaan, however, felt that Amar was sincere and continued entertaining him.

Towards the evening Amar got up and said, 'Farewell my son, I will return at dawn tomorrow with Asad Ghazi for your wrestling match.' After Amar had departed, Sundlaan insisted on striking drums to announce the battle the next morning. His sardars were convinced that Amar had deceived their master to save his life, but could not refuse his orders. They struck battle drums and announced that there would be a wrestling match between Asad and Sundlaan the next morning. Meanwhile, Amar spent the night in a mountain ravine. He woke up at dawn and after saying his morning prayers, brought Asad Ghazi out from Zambil. The reader will remember that before leaving for Crystal Mountain to retrieve the magic keystone, Amar had put Asad in Zambil. Asad looked surprised when he was taken out and Amar quickly briefed him on the events in Crystal Mountain. 'I have found my way through the tunnel to this place and have arranged for you to confront a wrestler. Will you do it?' he asked Asad. Asad declared, 'Whatever you say, Grandfather. I can face Rustam or Sohrab and even jump into a river of fire for you!' Amar smiled wryly and said, 'There is no need for such tall talk. Shall we leave as he must have struck the battle drums.'

Asad said he was willing, but needed a mount. Amar replied there were no horses in this country. To this Asad said that though he was willing to go on foot, his opponent was bound to be mounted. 'It does not matter,' he declared airily, 'I will make sure that I dislodge him from his mount before fighting him.' Amar realized that Asad had outwitted him and said, 'I will try and find a mount for you. The last thing I want is for you to make a laughing stock of me and your ancestors by losing this contest!' Amar then left Asad and soon reappeared with a splendid steed that he stole from a witless merchant. He told Asad that the horse cost him five thousand gold coins. Asad immediately pledged that sum to him. Amar provided a saddle and reins from Zambil and they promptly left for Sundlaan's camp.

Sundlaan and his commanders were waiting for Amar and Asad to arrive when a cloud of dust rose from the desert. As they looked closely at the cloud, they saw the comic, skinny figure of Amar leading the reins of a great horse. The rider of the horse was a fine-looking young man with a muscular body. The contrast between the two men was so obvious that everyone in Sundlaan's lashkar looked with fascination at them. Sundlaan admired Asad's calm acceptance of an unexpected encounter without any supporters. He jumped off his mount and eagerly went forward to greet him. Asad smiled as he dismounted and embraced Sundlaan just as he was going to kneel at his feet. Sundlaan was so entranced and overwhelmed by Asad's personality that his condition became like that of a lover. His eyes never left Asad's face as he led him towards his camp. Asad looked amused and said, 'My friend, I am looking forward to a confrontation with you.' Sundlaan replied with a touch of arrogance, 'Sheheryar, you can try to attack me with whatever weapons you are carrying with you and my prowess will also be revealed to you.'

Asad laughed and said gently, 'Sundlaan, my faith will only permit me to react to your attack.' Sundlaan marvelled at these words and mounted his horse for the contest. Asad also mounted his steed and waited. Sundlaan aimed his spear straight at Asad's chest, but he caught it neatly and handed it back to him. At one stage, Asad came very close to Sundlaan and wrenched the spear out of his grasp. Sundlaan's face went red and he cried, 'Sheheryar, you have won the first round but my sword is invincible. I can cleave a mountain with my strength.' Asad continued to smile and very soon, Sundlaan lost his sword as well. Now disarmed, Sundlaan jumped down from his horse and prepared to wrestle with Asad. As the lashkar watched with interest, the two young men wrestled vigorously. Both were equally matched and it seemed like a contest between two lions. Very soon, both of them were sweating with the extraordinary effort and yet the contest continued.

Towards the evening, Sundlaan stopped and said, 'Sheheryar you have fought me well. Eat and rest now and we will continue tomorrow morning.' Asad looked up and panted, 'No brother, order some light and we will carry on fighting tonight.' Sundlaan looked at his commanders who immediately provided torches to light the field. Asad looked at Amar helplessly. In a rush of affection for Asad, the resourceful Amar produced beautiful Sulaimani chandeliers from Zambil. Everyone looked stunned and wondered how he had managed to conjure such precious objects. The contest continued with Sundlaan now looking exhausted. Asad, however, seemed as fresh as he was when he started. As the first rays of the sun lit the earth the next day, Sundlaan tried to dislodge Asad by pushing with all his might; but a mountain would have been easier to move than young Asad. Sundlaan gave up when his fingers were about to snap with the strain. It was now Asad's turn. He placed both hands on Sundlaan's shoulders and pushed him back even as the powerful wrestler resisted with all his might. Asad then hoisted the beaten warrior on his shoulders and spun him around several times. Just as he was about to throw Sundlaan on the ground, he gasped an admission of defeat and begged Asad to spare his life.

Asad stopped at once and gently put Sundlaan down, who immediately fell at his feet. He requested Asad to convert him to Islam and then turned to his companions and declared, 'I have sworn to serve Tilism Kusha. You are all free to follow your own conscience.' Sundlaan's lashkar of twelve hundred young men elected to embrace the faith as well and Sundlaan and his soldiers kneeled before Asad while Amar watched the proceedings with satisfaction. Suddenly, there was a cry from the skies, 'Wait Sundlaan.

Have you forgotten what you were sent for?' Amar ran for cover, but a lightening bolt from the sky fell on Asad, Sundlaan and the whole lashkar and blinded everyone. A little later, everyone was shackled and manacled, and Gauhar Jadoo was seen admonishing her paramour Sundlaan, 'You have betrayed me and your faith in Samri and Jamshed. Have you no fear of Afrasiyab? Even now, you should forswear your allegiance to Tilism Kusha. I will cut his head off and send it to Sunddal Jadoo.'

Sundlaan replied, 'I have embraced the faith of Islam and will not betray my master. If you love me, you will join me now.' Gauhar Jadoo started weeping and cried, 'Sundlaan, I love you dearly. Why are you intent on ruining me?' Sundlaan replied, 'Gauhar, I love you as well, but I am devoted to Tilism Kusha.' Gauhar Jadoo angrily confined the whole lashkar to a dungeon in the fort and wrote to Sunddal Jadoo, 'Amar entered this realm with Asad. He has escaped, but I have arrested Asad along with my paramour Sundlaan who has been bewitched by Asad and has sworn allegiance to him. Tell me what your will is now.'

Sunddal Jadoo immediately sent a message back to Gauhar instructing her to kill Tilism Kusha and find Amar as soon as possible. Gauhar Jadoo prepared an execution ground for Asad and warned Sundlaan that Asad's execution was imminent. After she left, Sundlaan wept and begged Asad to save himself. Asad replied calmly, 'Brother, do not be concerned. If I am not destined to die now, no one can kill me. If my death is ordained, then I will welcome it.' Sundlaan derived a sense of comfort from Asad's unflinching faith in his destiny. When all the preparations for the execution were complete, Gauhar Jadoo sent for Asad and the executioner drew a circle around Asad's neck with charcoal and raised his sword. As he brought it down, something happened in a flash and everyone saw the executioner's head splitting into two halves instead, while Asad remained alive and calm. Gauhar's soldiers told her that it seemed as if the executioner had brought the sword on his own head. She sent for another executioner, but he too suffered the same fate. No one realized that Khwaja Amar was standing amongst the crowd watching the execution disguised as a fakir, and was using his catapult to hurl stones at the executioners.

When the second executioner was killed, one of the guardian parizads perched in the turrets of the Sunddal fort smiled and a pearl from her armour split to release a puppet. The puppet flew downwards and settled around Amar's neck. To everyone's surprise, the paints on Amar's face evaporated as he squirmed to try and dislodge the puppet. Sahirs dragged him in front of Gauhar Jadoo, where Asad greeted him. Amar called out, 'My son, it seems the fates are against me.' Sundlaan cried out in despair, 'Badshah of ayyars, we are surely finished now.' Amar remained calm and said, 'Do not worry my son. The Almighty will help us in mysterious ways.' Gauhar Jadoo then decided to send Asad and Amar to Sunddal Jadoo. As some of her sahir-guards dragged them both away, Sundlaan cried out, 'Do not separate me from my master!' Gauhar Jadoo ignored him because she thought that separating Sundlaan from Asad would bring him back to his senses.

Just as Asad and Amar were about to be whisked off, whirlwinds of yellow sand swept in from the desert and there was a call from the skies, 'I am Bahar Jadoo, do not dare to touch our master!' The sahir-guards were immediately enchanted by her voice and started to tear their clothes off. Just then, one of the parizads merely looked at the cloud formation that hid Bahar and it disintegrated into hot smoke. Bahar emerged from the smoke badly singed and was about to catapult down to the earth when Baghban Qudrat appeared suddenly to break her fall. Baghban also became the target of the parizad's magic and could not fight any longer. Other Muslim sardars like Barq Mehshar, her sister Barq Lameh and Ra'ad Jadoo, who had followed Baghban, succumbed to the powerful magic of the parizads.

Hope was rekindled when the child sahira Majlis Jadoo announced her arrival, but she too could not withstand the deadly pearl weapons shot from the turret and fell unconscious. At that moment, Amar looked heavenwards and prayed desperately for help. There was a distant light in the sky and a huge black cloud blew overhead. The cloud parted to reveal a full moon, which meant that Princess Burran had arrived. The parizad then flew down from the turret to confront her and for while, only flashing lights in the sky were visible as the two clashed. The two opponents emerged from their shields of light in their real forms and drew swords on each other. Finally, Burran was exasperated with the prolonged fencing and took out her ultimate weapon, the powerful Pearl of Samri. She threw the pearl straight at her opponent and it went right through the parizad, destroying him instantly.

The skies went dark and there was a ferocious storm as slabs of ice fell from the skies. A voice called out, 'You have killed me, Mareekh Jadoo, a symbol of the Tilism of Sunddal. Alas, I have given my life in vain!' The sardars of Islam who had been rendered unconscious revived after Mareekh's death and attacked Gauhar Jadoo and her sahir soldiers, while Burran freed Asad and Amar from their chains. The moment he was released, Asad ran to free Sundlaan and his commanders from their chains. Gauhar Jadoo was fighting back with her sahirs when Bahar declared, 'Watch how I punish her.' Sundlaan was still in love with Gauhar and started weeping softly when he heard this. Asad looked at his grief-stricken face and rushed to plead with Bahar to spare Gauhar's life.

After a short bout of fierce fighting, they captured Gauhar and her sahir soldiers. Sundlaan persuaded his beloved to join him and she willingly came forward to pay homage to Asad. After resting that night, everyone decided to go their own separate ways. The sardars assured Asad that they would come to his rescue when necessary, while Gauhar advised Amar to be cautious. She said, 'I will hide with Sundlaan and come to your help when you find the keystone, but from what I know, Sunddal Jadoo cannot be killed by anyone!' Amar smiled and told her that the Almighty would come to their assistance. Then he took Asad's hand and continued on his journey.

Malik Akhzar helps Asad

As Amar and Asad travelled on, the land became verdant with shady trees and green hills. Towards nightfall, Amar found a hidden place in the hills and bade Asad to rest and pray for guidance. Asad Ghazi prayed almost through the night and as he nodded off early in the morning, a voice told him in his dream that to find the magic keystone, he would have to rescue the former ruler of Tilism-e-Sunddal. Asad woke up after the dream completely refreshed and glowing with happiness.

Amar who had been keeping guard returned and was happy to hear of Asad's dream. Asad expressed his concern that he had no clue as to where the former ruler of Tilism-e-Sunddal was. Amar kissed Asad on the forehead with affection and said, 'This was a direction from God. Rest assured we will find him.' Meanwhile, Afrasiyab had written a note to the keeper of the dungeons in Sunddal quoting the Samri Nama that clearly referred to the rescue of Akhzar Jadoo as the first sign of the destruction of Tilism-e-Sunddal. Afrasiyab went on to say that it was imperative to kill Akhzar Jadoo immediately. Afrasiyab's messenger was flying through the Tilism to deliver this message when a voice called out to him, 'Brother do not go any further or you will die a dog's death.'

The messenger froze in mid-flight and descended to the ground, fearing for his life. He came across a sahir sitting on a hill (actually Khwaja Amar in disguise). He barked at the messenger, 'Who are you and where do you think you are going?' The messenger was startled by this rudeness and said, 'Sir, you must learn to speak politely.' Amar retorted, 'Who needs to be polite with donkeys like you?' The messenger looked very cross now, so Amar changed his tune and said pleasantly, 'Well, what is it to me? You go ahead but when she sees your corpse, your wife is bound to be upset.' The messenger looked alarmed and begged Amar to explain. Amar, in turn, said, 'I will help you only after you tell me where you are going.' The messenger spilled out the details of Afrasiyab's message and told Amar that he was on his way to the Iron Palace. Amar cunningly extracted information about the exact location of the palace and later airily told the messenger to go on his way, warning him of the many dangers he could encounter on his journey. Amar then went to find Asad, who was still hidden in the hill. Amar whispered something in his ear and Asad nodded and said, 'Whatever you say sir.' Soon afterwards, both of them left the hill.

Sunddal Jadoo had imprisoned the former ruler of Sunddal, Malik Akhzar Jadoo, in the Iron Palace for a very long time. He was now blind, his hair and nails had grown long, and he was in a pitiable state. When the keepers of the dungeons received the orders for his execution, some of them felt compassion for Akhzar, who was an amiable prisoner and had caused them no trouble. Malik Akhzar received the news of his intended execution calmly. The leader of the keepers was a harsh and cruel man who confided in his colleagues that he was relieved with the order as they could all go home after they executed the prisoner. When Malik Akhzar was brought forth for his execution, the keeper taunted him by saying that Afrasiyab would reward them richly for Akhzar's head. Malik Akhzar calmly replied, 'No one can kill me today for this is the day of my rescue.' The keeper laughed and said, 'What nonsense old man! For the last month you have been telling us of your dreams and your rescue! What your dreams really mean is that we will execute you today! You should have joined Afrasiyab instead of remaining loyal to Lacheen.'

Just as the sahirs were preparing to execute Malik Akhzar, there was a sudden uproar as Afrasiyab appeared in the dungeon courtyard with his wife Hairat. The keeper along with his compatriots greeted the Shahanshah and asked him the reason for this unexpected arrival. Afrasiyab replied solemnly, 'The Samri Nama warned me that whoever tried to kill Akhzar would be blinded. Therefore, I decided to help you with your task. I need a pitcher of wine so that I can recite a special mantra on it. After you drink from this blessed wine, your task will be easier.' The keeper provided a pitcher of wine for Afrasiyab within minutes. The Shahanshah recited some words from an unknown language as Hairat smiled and held the pitcher. All the guards drank the blessed wine and very soon, all of them were unconscious. Hairat then cut the chains of the prisoner and declared in a man's voice, 'Malik Akhzar, be aware that Tilism Kusha is here and I am Amar bin Ummayyah!'

Malik Akhzar groped his way to Asad who was disguised as Afrasiyab and wept, 'Huzoor, I knew you would come today! You will have to do one more thing for me. My eyesight can only be restored if the liver of the prison keeper is roasted and its smoke enters my eyes.' Amar sprang into action and slaughtered the keeper as Asad lit a fire. He cut open his belly to extract the liver and threw it on the fire. The first whiff of smoke from the keeper's liver restored Akhzar eyesight and he looked gratefully at his rescuers.

Amar's natural greed now surfaced and he began searching the Iron Palace for treasures. He found each of the rooms brimming with valuables and used the Net of Ilyas to scoop up everything in sight. As he ran from room to room, he called out to Akhzar, 'There seem to be no treasures in this palace at all. It is all quite bare.' Akhzar looked puzzled and said, 'But this place was full of treasures.' Amar was obviously not about to expose his greed to Akhzar and Asad. As he ran into the next room, he called back, 'All I found was a jar of rusty old coins which I have thrown away.' Asad who knew Amar well called out sarcastically, 'No doubt the twelve thousand sahirs who guarded this palace must have existed on thin air.' Amar emerged from the room slowly and said, 'Son, that seems to imply that there was treasure here which has been stolen.' Asad looked away abashed and mumbled, 'Who said anything about a treasure?'

Later, Malik Akhzar released the other inmates of the Iron Palace who were actually his former servants, and persuaded them to join Asad. That night, he provided a splendid feast for his guests. The next morning, Akhzar travelled with Asad and Amar towards the fort of Sunddal to get the magic keystone of Tilism-e-Sunddal. As they took cover behind a hill, they could see the huge walls of the fort stretching for miles. They could also see a massive turret that rose inside the fort. There was a huge iron cage on the turret that contained a turtle dove that was hooting softly.

Malik Akhzar explained to Asad and Amar, 'The founders of this Tilism have placed the magic keystone within this dove's belly. If any stranger approaches the fort, the dove hoots three times. If the stranger turns back, she remains quiet, but if he comes forward, she flies out of the cage and throws her shadow on the stranger and then hoots three times. With the third hoot, she expels a flame from her beak that annihilates the stranger. Hundreds of innocent men have perished this way. If you both can wait here I will go and work on a spell to capture the dove and get the magic keystone.'

Looking at Asad, Akhzar warned, 'I am giving you these details in case you are tempted to go forth yourself. If that is what you intend, then nothing can save you.' After the former king left, Asad turned to Amar and said, 'Grandfather, how could you swallow the nonsense this old man was spouting? I can fell this dove with one arrow and get the keystone.' Amar looked alarmed and warned Asad not to try anything foolish, but the young warrior ignored him and stepped forward. The dove hooted softly while watching him carefully. As Asad continued moving, the dove burst forth from its cage and circled over Asad so that her shadow fell on the young warrior. As soon as that happened, Asad felt his limbs turning to water and a strange lassitude overcame him. With trembling hands, he shot several arrows at the dove. The bird destroyed the arrows by expelling flames from its beak. It was about to expel a flame on Asad when it was attacked by a gigantic hawk that circled in for the kill. The dove fought back fiercely, but eventually the hawk tore her to pieces. Asad and Amar saw the hawk swoop down to catch a shining object before the skies went dark and the massive walls of the fort shook as spirits lamented the death of the guardian dove.

After some time, Malik Akhzar or the hawk flew down from the sky in his real form and rushed to Asad, who was still shaken up. Amar looked gratefully at the old sahir and said, 'Malik Akhzar had you not made a timely appearance, Asad would have surely perished today.' Akhzar led them to their hiding place behind the hill and after handing the magic keystone to Asad, urged him to read the magic words on the keystone. Asad first purified himself and then looked at the keystone. It merely informed him that he would have to find a way to kill the ruler Sunddal Jadoo. When Asad said that the magic keystone had not suggested how he could kill Sunddal, Akhzar said, 'There is a mystery here that will be revealed to you later, but meanwhile, we must be prepared to face the ruler of this Tilism who must surely be on her way now.'

By this time, Akhzar's attendants and army had reached the site and established a war camp outside the fort. Akhzar led Asad into the main pavilion and seated him in the place of honour. 'Sheheryar,' he said, 'after leaving you I contacted a number of people who had remained loyal to me and rallied a huge army.' Asad looked satisfied and declared, 'Tomorrow after the morning prayers I will set forth to conquer the Tilism.' The next morning, Asad had just finished praying when Malik Akhzar rushed in to inform him that Sunddal Jadoo and her massive army were quite close. Asad calmly prepared for the battle and wore the magic keystone around his neck. He also wore a powerful magic ring destined to destroy Sunddal Jadoo. Through a series of fortuitous events, the ring had been provided to him by Princess Ajaib who had been entrusted with this precious relic. Only Amar was privy to this secret.

Sunddal's army arrived in great splendour with gongs and drums resounding and thousands of flag-bearers leading the march. Asad mounted his horse and led the attack from the Islamic side with Malik Akhzar and Amar following close behind him. Queen Sunddal was leading the attack from the other side. She trembled when she saw Malik Akhzar as she was his former officer and had betrayed him to get the throne of Tilism. Malik Akhzar called out, 'You traitor, I have my eyesight back because of this brave young lion fighting with me. Fall at his feet and I can still forgive you. Why do you want to die?' Sunddal turned away from him and thought, 'My death is not in their hands.' She avoided coming into direct confrontation with Asad who had the magic keystone, but killed hundreds with her magic. A cloud of dust that floated in revealed Sundlaan and Gauhar Jadoo with their armies. As both joined the battle, Sunddal looked at them and snarled, 'Look at this treacherous woman Gauhar who has joined Tilism Kusha with her paramour. I will destroy them first!'

Sunddal then paralyzed Sundlaan and his troops with one spell and was about to kill him when Gauhar swooped down and tried to fly off with him. Sunddal was a powerful sahira and injured Gauhar as well. Now the lovers were at Sunddal's mercy. Gauhar called out to Asad to save them and though Sunddal's army had surrounded Asad, he made an extraordinary effort to reach his friends. Sunddal sneered at Asad and said, 'Who can kill me?'

Asad took off the magic ring from his finger and Sunddal's composure crumpled for the first time. She tried to flee, but Asad's aim was swift and accurate. The ring landed on Sunddal's forehead and a huge blast ripped through Sunddal's body. She died in great agony and as the sky went dark, there were thunderous storms and stones and slabs of ice fell from the skies. Sunddal's guardian spirits howled, 'You have killed me, my name was Sunddal Jadoo. Alas, I died in vain!' Sunddal's army lost heart and admitted defeat. Gauhar Jadoo was now the most senior commander in the Tilism and led the defeated commanders to Asad in order to convert to Islam. Asad, Malik Akhzar and Amar spent the night in the fort that was now theirs; they thought about the next stage of the quest for the Tilism Kusha's magic keystone, which was to proceed to the Darband of Mah and Meher Jadoo.

Asad in the Land of Meher and Mah

Asad and Amar stayed in the fort of Sunddal for a week with Akhzar and his comrades to rally and train the large army. They left for Darband in an optimistic mood, certain that this time they would find the magic keystone. After travelling for several days, they reached their destination and found that the rulers Meher and Mah had established a battle camp and were waiting for them. The two rulers Meher and Mah were exceptionally beautiful and skilled sahiras. They stopped to stare at Asad's arrival in his war camp. They were stunned by his beauty and nobility and impressed with the might of his army. Meher and Mah returned to their pavilion still awestruck with Asad, but after consulting their sardars, decided to announce the battle for the next morning.

The leading wrestler of the sahir army, a powerful giant of a man called Shahour Elephant-face, went up to the two princesses and requested that he be allowed to confront Asad first. He said, 'I have long heard of the prowess of the sons of Hamza and I would like to make you proud by defeating Asad. The only request I make is that no one should use magic when I fight him.' Meher and Mah accepted his request and Shahour directed his mount to the middle of the battlefield, where he challenged anyone to wrestle with him. When Asad went forward, Shahour gaped at him, stunned by his beauty and youth. He thought that this youth had come instead of Asad to fight him and was even more startled to learn that this was the real Tilism Kusha.

When the bout began, Shahour was convinced that he could overwhelm Asad with sheer brute strength, but Asad fought back fiercely. At one stage, he was wounded by Shahour, but he managed to also wound the huge wrestler and killed his mount in the process. Shahour was now without a mount. His men saw that he was vulnerable and rushed forward to help him. From Asad's side, Sundlaan came forward with his men to Asad's assistance. There was fierce fighting for several hours during which Shahour and Asad wounded each other again.

Asad and Princess Shamim Flower-robe

Suddenly, Asad felt giddy because of the head wounds he had suffered and slumped forward. His horse cantered out of the battlefield until he reached a stream in a lush shady meadow. The horse gently shook himself so that his unconscious rider slid out of the saddle and on to the edge of a freshwater stream. As the horse drank thirstily from the stream, the wound on Asad's head bled into the waters and a trickle of red blood flowed through the stream into the water channel of a nearby garden. The owner of the garden, Princess Shamim Flower-robe, was sitting with her feet in the main fountain and was enjoying the feel of the cold churning water on her skin. She then noticed a long thin red ribbon flowing in the water. She leaned forward to examine it and realized that it was blood.

She turned to her attendants and said quickly, 'There is a stream beyond our garden that feeds the water channels. Perhaps someone is wounded there. Go and check at once.'

The attendants went to the stream and went running back to report to the princess that someone lay dead at the edge of the stream. Shamim decided to investigate this herself, angry that someone should have dared to commit a crime in her area. She gasped when she saw Asad lying on the edge of the stream. He looked as if the morning star had fallen from the sky. The princess went closer and she looked at Asad's shining young face, dreading that he might be dead. Shamim asked one of her attendants to check if the stranger was alive, but the young girl stuttered, 'Huzoor, I cannot touch a corpse! What if it seizes me?' Shamim was irritated and cried, 'You stupid girl, if it was a corpse, his horse would not have been licking his feet.' Her attendants were still terrified and Shamim checked Asad's breath herself. She cried happily, 'He is still alive!' She sent for a cot to carry the wounded Asad back to her garden, where her handmaidens attended to Asad's wounds. However, Shamim thought they were stitching his wounds too roughly. She snatched the needle from one of the women and poked her hard with it. The woman screamed with pain as the princess smiled and said, 'Now you know what it's like to feel pain?' Shamim herself stitched Asad's wounds and later as she gazed at his radiant, noble face she wondered who he was.

Asad opened his eyes and looked around in surprise at his surroundings. His eyes alighted on the beautiful maiden sitting on a chair besides his bed. Asad moaned slightly and the maiden started and then came closer to him. She put his head on her lap, stroked his face gently and inadvertently two large tears rolled down her cheeks and dropped on Asad's face. Asad opened his eyes again and on seeing his eyes upon her, the maiden made a move to leave. Asad reached out for her hand and said, 'Do not leave your patient, O angel of mercy.' Shamim replied shyly, 'I am not a physician, I merely dressed your wounds. I found you lying unconscious by the stream. Obviously someone wounded you in battle. Tell me who you are.' Asad lay back again and said, 'Beautiful lady, every stone in Hoshruba knows me! I am Asad bin Karb Ghazi.'

Shamim smote her forehead in horror and said, 'This is terrible! Meher and Mah have sent orders to all of us to capture you on sight. Anyone sheltering you will be severely punished.' Asad rose from the bed and declared, 'In that case, my beloved, I should leave you at once for I would not want anyone to be punished on my account.' Shamim held him back and said, 'I did not mean you to leave, but merely informed you what the situation is.' Asad turned away while saying, 'It is quite obvious that you would not like to shelter an enemy of Afrasiyab. It is better if I leave you now. Whenever the war is over I will return to meet you.' To this, Shamim said firmly, 'I will not let you leave in this wounded condition. You will be safe with me.'

Asad sank back on the bed, as he felt suddenly weak with the loss of blood. Shamim sent for wine at once and served him a goblet, but he said, 'I will not accept any food or drink from you unless you convert.' Shamim looked hurt, but Asad went on to speak eloquently in praise of the One True God. Shamim listened to him and realized the folly of equating so many deities with the Supreme God. She willingly converted to Islam and by this time, Shamim and Asad were also deeply in love with each other.

Despite the comfort of his surroundings and the company of his beloved, Asad was soon anxious to leave. Shamim was unwilling to let him go in his weak condition. It also happened that one of Meher and Mah's spies informed them that Shamim had given refuge to the enemy. The two sides had actually declared a truce at the time to retrieve their wounded and dead from the battlefield. The news that Princess Shamim Flower-robe had sheltered Asad spread in both the sahir and the Islamic camps like wildfire. Meher and Mah decided to lead the expedition to capture Asad themselves. Asad's allies like Malik Akhzar, Sundlaan and Gauhar Jadoo also prepared to rescue their friend, but Amar was the first to reach Princess Shamim's garden. When he saw two thousand sahirs on guard outside, Amar immediately disguised himself as an official herald of Afrasiyab. He wore a waistcoat and a starched white turban and held a silver wand of office engraved with the official seal of Hoshruba. He mingled with the soldiers and said, 'Brothers, Afrasiyab has declared that whoever will capture Tilism Kusha will be rewarded richly.'

The soldiers looked meaningfully at each other and mumbled, 'Tilism Kusha is right here in this garden. Princess Shamim Flower-robe is protecting him. We have tried to reason with her, but she will not listen to us.' Amar's eyes widened and he said, 'That is interesting! Tell me, are you all in her employ?' The guards shifted in a guilty manner and said, 'Well, we are really loyal to Afrasiyab, but Shamim is our mistress and we are honour-bound to obey her commands.' Amar beamed at them, 'I will commend you in my report, but first I must see Tilism Kusha with my own eyes in case these are just rumours.' The guards willingly let Amar into the garden and he walked in confidently. He was struck with the beauty of the garden and as he saw Asad reclining on the masnad with a beautiful maiden, Amar experienced a pang of pure envy. He thought, 'These sons of Hamza are really fortunate; wherever they go some lovely damsel is ready to help them!'

He decided to have some fun at Asad's expense and marched right into the gathering of pleasure. Asad looked up and said, 'Who is this man who walks in so casually to invade our privacy?' Before the princess could respond, Amar called out rudely, 'Princess Shamim, you have Shahanshah's enemy with you. Do you not recognize me? You will all be arrested any moment.' Shamim trembled with fear as she heard these words, but Amar turned to Asad and shouted, 'You there, beg for mercy and I may have you pardoned. After all I am the chief herald!' Asad was not used to such talk and rose in anger. He shouted, 'Stop talking nonsense old man. Go and inform Afrasiyab if you will!' Amar taunted him back, 'Remember, this is the same Afrasiyab who imprisoned you in the Dome of Light. This time he will definitely execute you. However, if you give me a small bribe, I will not tell him anything.'

While Asad spluttered at the sheer impudence of the man, Amar shouted at Shamim again, 'Why do you not speak? Give me your garments at once!' Shamim made a move to disrobe, but by this time Asad had had enough, 'Stop that at once Shamim! Afrasiyab can do nothing to us, this man is talking nonsense!' Asad drew his sword to attack Amar, who sprang back and said, 'You dare to attack me, I will make you forget any claims to be Tilism Kusha!' As Asad attacked him, Amar quickly pulled his eyelid down to reveal the telltale mole. Asad looked at him amazed and then embraced him warmly. Amar patted him on the back affectionately and said, 'You idiot, you are indulging yourself here while Meher and Mah are coming with a whole army to attack you!'

Asad then introduced Khwaja Amar to Shamim. Amar greeted her and said, 'Either escape now with Asad or hide him for you are both in danger.' Shamim bowed low in respect to Amar and responded, 'O king of ayyars, Meher and Mah Jadoo are very powerful sorceresses who can turn day into night. I am but a humble vassal of theirs. I suggest you take the prince with you. I will fight them one way or the other even if I lose my life.'

The battle with Meher and Mah

Asad was reluctant to leave the garden without confronting his enemies openly and told Amar he would not escape like a coward and disgrace his ancestors. As they discussed their next move, they heard the sound of trumpets and realized that Meher and Mah Jadoo had arrived already. Both of them rode golden peacocks and led a huge army of sahirs mounted on fire-breathing dragons. Amar vanished behind Galeem, but the impetuous Asad rushed out with his sword in hand to confront the enemy. Shamim Flower-robe followed him with her armed companions and tried her best to protect him from the spells of the sahir army. A sudden gust of cool breeze swept across the battlefield and it was obvious that Bahar Jadoo had arrived. She appeared with bouquets in hand and tossed one on the lashkar of Meher and Mah. The sahirs instantly fell under her spell and tore their clothes as they chanted her name in frenzy. Thousands of soldiers slit their own throats and the army was in complete disarray.

Meher and Mah read a counterspell that caused a sudden shower of heavy rain and the soldiers came back to their senses. They were fighting Bahar when Malik Akhzar appeared to help her. Meanwhile, other Muslim sardars also appeared and attacked the enemy. Ra'ad Jadoo sank underground and emerged within the ranks to shriek characteristically so that hundreds fainted or split their skulls. His mother Barq Mehshar fell as bolts of lightning and killed the ones still alive. Her sister, Barq Lameh assisted her by falling as another deadly bolt of lightning. The faithful Baghban Qudrat emerged beside Asad and protected his master by tossing magical flowers that split open to expel flames, killing hundreds of enemy soldiers.

To give Meher and Mah their due, the two sisters fought back valiantly. The fighting continued for several hours when a ruby-coloured cloud began glowing on the horizon. As everyone looked up in surprise, the cloud parted and Princess Burran emerged from it on a golden peacock. She attacked the enemy in great wrath and finished thousands with her spells. She intended to target Mah Jadoo, but Mah's loyal soldiers constantly got in her way. Eventually, Meher herself came forward shouting, 'Daughter of Kaukab! Your people have never dared to attack Hoshruba before. Now a few rebels have encouraged you to fight us!'

Burran merely smiled at the provocative words and aimed her powerful weapon, the magic Pearl of Samri, straight at Mah's chest. Mah tried every spell she knew to deflect the pearl, but it tore through her like a bullet and she died instantly. The skies darkened and a loud voice called out, 'You have killed Mah Jadoo!' Meher Jadoo, who was fighting at a distance, lost her footing when she heard the spirits. Her heart broke as she saw her sister's corpse and she rushed towards Burran, beating her head. She cried, 'You have done great harm and robbed me of my right arm! The full moon of Darband has been eclipsed!'

Burran called back, 'If you love your sister so much, perhaps you should be sent where she is!' The furious Mah responded with several deadly spells aimed at Burran who deflected them all with the mighty Pearl of Samri. Eventually, she hurled the magic pearl at Meher's forehead so that it smashed her skull and she fell on the ground. With her death, the battlefield was engulfed in smoke, huge trees swayed and leaves lamented the deaths of the two sisters. After a long time, light returned to the desert and guardian spirits announced Meher's murder. With the deaths of their commanders, the lashkar of Meher and Mah lost heart and tried to flee, but Asad's soldiers captured thousands of them. Camp advisers and ministers presented themselves to Asad with their hands tied with scarves to symbolize their defeat. Asad sheathed his sword and the fighting ceased at that time. The nobles of the capital city emerged to pay homage to Asad, while all the Muslim sardars thronged around Burran to praise her for vanquishing Meher and Mah. Everyone led Asad in a grand procession to Darband, showering him with jewels and gold coins, while trumpets of victory blared all around. Amar was the happiest person on that day for he felt they were now very close to the magic keystone of Hoshruba.

The magic keystone

After the victory celebrations were over, Asad prayed that night for some revelation about the magic keystone of Hoshruba. He prayed long into the night and when he dozed off, he dreamed that the skies opened before him and from there, an elderly man appeared on a shining throne. As he came closer, Asad rose to greet him and touched his feet in respect. The man asked, 'O noble soldier of Islam, why are you so distressed?' Asad replied, 'I am looking for the keystone of Hoshruba for the lives of so many people depend on it. If I do not find it, Afrasiyab will leave no one alive. I am hopeful that you will help me in this quest.' The stranger said slowly, 'O follower of the One True God, arm yourself and go eastwards early in the morning. In the fold of a mountain, you will find a venerable old saint. His name is Pir Zamin-gir. He will guide you on your quest for the keystone. Follow his directions and you will reach your destination.' Asad wanted to ask the stranger more questions, but at that moment, his eyes opened and he saw the morning star. Asad immediately purified himself and performed the Morning Prayer. He then returned to the pavilion and prepared for the journey ahead.

His sardars offered to go with him, but Asad insisted that the stranger had instructed him to go on his own. A mace-bearer announced, 'Huzoor, your ayyar Zargham Sherdil has come.' Asad's face lighted up with happiness and he said, 'Bring my loyal friend to me immediately.' Moments later, Zargham ran in and fell at Asad's feet weeping as he had been separated from his master for a long time. Asad gently raised him to his feet and embraced him saying, 'My brother, this is a time of joy. After many setbacks, the Almighty made us victorious and Tilism-e-

Sunddal was conquered. We have killed Meher and Mah Jadoo and I have had a revelation about the magic keystone. But tell me, how did you come here?'

Zargham informed the prince that he and Mehtar Qiran had set out together, but were separated on the way. 'Huzoor,' he said, 'I found my way to you after much difficulty. Now that I am here, may I accompany you on your journey?' Asad repeated that he intended to go alone, but Zargham merely said, 'Huzoor, you should go alone and I will proceed on my own.' Asad then turned to the sardars and asked them to pray for his victory. He also told them to keep the lashkar prepared as they would go to war as soon as he had the keystone. After bidding farewell to his sardars, Asad left to find the old man in the desert. Zargham Sherdil followed him secretly, making sure that the prince did not see him.

After Asad left, Malik Akhzar declared, 'It is not safe for the prince to travel alone. The deserts of Hoshruba are crawling with sahirs. The prince is brave, but he will be helpless against their spells. I intend to follow the prince. I will remain out of his sight by disguising myself as a hawk. That way, I can fly overhead and keep an eye on him.' The other sardars approved of this idea and Akhzar transformed himself into a hawk to fly after the prince.

Meanwhile, Asad had followed the directions of the stranger in his dreams and found the mountain of the saint. He jumped off his horse and walked into the ravine. As he turned a corner, he saw the ancient man with a long white beard sitting on a prayer mat, his forehead bruised with the characteristic prayer mark. As soon as he saw the prince, the old saint rose from the prayer mat. Asad was going to kneel at his feet, but the saint embraced him instead and kissed his forehead. He said, 'O lion of Sahibqirani, you are exalted! Your elders have spread the True Word in the darkness of disbelief. Come and sit with me and refresh yourself.' After Asad had rested and eaten, the old man said, 'Asad, about a mile from here, you will come across a *chinar* tree on the banks of a freshwater stream. Hide behind the tree until daybreak. When the sun rises, a bull will emerge from the desert to drink from the stream. When he comes closer, kill it with your arrow. Cut him open and you will find a casket with its key. The magic keystone of Hoshruba is in that casket.'

Asad said his prayers and took leave of the saint. He found the chinar tree and the stream and spent the rest of the night hidden behind the tree. Towards daybreak, he awoke to the sound of the bull's hooves thundering towards the stream. Asad took aim and killed the bull instantly. The bull was actually a sahir in disguise and his spirits lamented their master's death. With great joy, Asad cut the bull open and found the casket. Zargham Sherdil, who had been following his master, saw Asad bring out a shining object from the bull's stomach and ran forward calling out, 'Ya Sheheryar, have you found the keystone?' Asad happily replied, 'Zargham, I am about to take it out from the casket. The saint has guided me accurately so far.'

Just as Asad was about to open the casket, a voice called out from the desert, 'Wait my son, do not open the casket yet. I forgot to give you the magic name that will open the casket.' Asad turned around to see Pir Zamin-gir running towards him and unsuspectingly handed him the casket. The old saint wrapped the casket in a scarf and then sprouted wings to fly off. Asad suddenly realized that this was not the saint at all but a sahir, black of face and heart. The sahir rose from the ground saying, 'My master Afrasiyab had given me a pearl and had warned me that if the pearl splits open, I should know that the magic bull is dead. The old saint was the only other person privy to this secret, but I have killed him as well!'

Asad wept with rage at losing the magic keystone yet again. The sahir had flown some distance when he turned back and said, 'Tilism Kusha, perhaps I should take you with me as well. Afrasiyab will kill you and all will end well!' Zargham was now very afraid for his master and urged him to save himself, but Asad was in despair and said, 'Zargham, I will be happy if this sahir kills me now. How will I face Khwaja Amar now? I had the magic keystone in my hand and lost it so foolishly.' The black sahir was now hovering above them and was about to cast a spell on both Asad and Zargham when Malik Akhzar as a powerful hawk flew in from the desert. He realized that Asad was at the sahir's mercy and called loudly, 'Wait O shameless one! I am here now. Do not attack my master!'

The black sahir quickly transformed himself into a peacock and attacked the hawk fiercely. There was a violent confrontation in the sky between the two sahir birds. Zargham warned Akhzar that the black sahir had the magic keystone in his possession. The sahir managed to wound Malik Akhzar when Asad brought out his bow and arrow and took aim at the peacock. The sahir heard the swish of the arrow and dodged it quickly so that the arrow pierced Malik Akhzar straight in the chest. The sahir laughed loudly and disappeared into the sky while the loyal Malik Akhzar fell on the ground in his true form. Asad was horror struck at what had happened and wanted to take his own life in despair. At that time, Akhzar called out, 'Sheheryar, it was willed that I die in your service. I am blessed that you will perform my last rites.' Thus, Malik Akhzar breathed his last, leaving Asad greatly grieved and regretful.

The Garden of Zaivar

With heavy hearts, Asad and Zargham performed the last rites of Malik Akhzar. After they had finished, Zargham offered his master cold water from his flask and was just about to refill the flask from the stream when Afrasiyab's magic slave-boy fell from the sky. In moments, he clutched both Asad and Zargham by the waist and flew with them straight back to the King of Magic. At that time, Afrasiyab was holding court in the magic garden of a noblewoman, Zaivar Jadoo who with her husband Lahoot Jadoo was close to the Shahanshah. When the puppet flashed overhead with the two prisoners, Afrasiyab smiled and tilted his crown in joy while crying out, 'I am Tilism Hoshruba! Zaivar have you seen my power? I have already captured Princess Burran, Bahar and other sardars of Islam while Tilism Kusha was looking for the keystone. The magic keystone is secure with my loyal servant Makkar Jadoo! Now, Tilism Kusha is also in my power!'

Zaivar made the appropriate flattering response. Afrasiyab urged her to summon her husband so that he could hold the executions that evening. Asad and Zargham were dragged in front of the Shahanshah in iron shackles. Afrasiyab was bursting with pride at that moment and thundered, 'Bring the executioners right away! There will be rivers of blood here tonight!' However, he quietly whispered on the side to Zaivar, 'Persuade Bahar to leave the rebels. If something happens to her, I will regret it forever!' Very soon, he was shouting again, 'I will forgive no one! Everyone said that they will conquer Tilism! Even Samri and Jamshed had prophesied that Asad would be the conqueror! Where are Samri and Jamshed now? Let them come and see how I have proved them wrong! The astrologers' own stars are malevolent.'

Mehtar Qiran and Lahoot Jadoo

We return now to Mehtar Qiran who was separated from Zargham Sherdil when they were on their way to Tilism-e-Sunddal. Qiran was hopelessly lost in the desert and thought, 'Where could Zargham be now. He must have surely reached Sunddal now and will boast about his exploits in durbar while I will be ashamed and embarrassed.' As Qiran trudged along the wilderness, tired and weary, he saw a great shady tree in the distance. His heart gladdened at the sight of the tree whose leaves rippled in the breeze while birds sang perched in its branches. He stumbled in the sand in his haste to reach the tree and found that its shade was cool and a breeze calmed his senses. He leaned against the tree breathless with his exertions when the birds fluttered their wings and shouted in human voices, 'Be alert! There is a traitor under our tree. Catch him, he must not escape!'

Qiran was startled at the voices and fled just as the birds rolled down the trees transformed into sahirs. The sahirs ran after Qiran calling him by name, but the powerful ayyar used his mighty bughda as leverage and jumped several yards ahead at a time. Know this that the guardian tree had been conjured by Lahoot Jadoo, husband of Zaivar whom we had met earlier with Afrasiyab. The tree had been specially created to identify any ayyar who would take shelter under it. Qiran desperately ran for his life away from the sahir-guards. He spotted a deserted well in the distance and made a split-second decision to throw himself in it. The sahirs reached it moments later and decided to flush him out by throwing huge rocks and boulders into the well.

Qiran panicked and used his bughda to tunnel his way out of the well. He took the name of his master Mushkil Kusha, and smashed his bughda on the brick-lined wall so that it broke open. Qiran continued hammering a tunnel underground, thinking he was bound to reach somewhere safe. Covered in dust, his clothes in tatters and his fingers bleeding, Qiran dug his way through the earth.

We now meet Zaivar's husband Lahoot Jadoo who seemed perturbed after reading an urgent message from his wife. Turning to his companions, Lahoot exclaimed, 'This is terrible news! Shahanshah intends to execute all the rebels including Tilism Kusha in my wife's garden of pleasure. Samri Nama states quite clearly that wherever Tilism Kusha will be executed, the land will be cursed forever! What are we to do now?' Lahoot's companions confirmed his fears by adding that they had also heard that the land where Tilism Kusha's blood spilled would never be fertile again.

Lahoot retired for the evening to his chambers and tried to think of a way out of this new dilemma. He sat with his head bowed, deep in thought, when the earth before him cleaved open and a young man covered in dust and holding a huge bughda leapt out of it. Lahoot was so stunned at the apparition that his magical powers seemed to desert him at that moment. On his part, Qiran quickly determined that he had walked right into a sahir's domain. Before Lahoot could recover, Qiran caught him in his snare-rope and rendered him unconscious, after which he sighed in relief. After tying Lahoot to a pillar in the room, Qiran first pierced his tongue with a large needle. He brushed the dust off his clothes and cleaned himself. Then he revived Lahoot and sat down on a chair as Lahoot opened his eyes.

Lahoot regained consciousness to find a young man of powerful face and body sitting in front of him with a huge sword in one hand. As he looked at Qiran, the ayyar spoke, 'Do not look so perturbed. I am Mehtar Qiran, bughda-wielder and disciple of Khwaja Amar. The saints have blessed me. I was lost in the wilderness when sahirs pursued me, but the Ruler of the Universe helped me. I threw myself into a well and tunnelled my way into this palace. Now I have overcome a powerful sahir like you.'

Lahoot Jadoo looked terrified and Qiran continued, 'O noble sahir, curse the names of Samri and Jamshed. There is only One True Creator. He has created the universe, given light to the sun and the moon and made heaven and hell. Understand this, to equate him with false deities is a sure path to hell. This world is but a temporary place. Once you die, you will know the truth, but it will be too late to repent then. Look how Asad Ghazi and five ayyars entered this Tilism and with God's help we now have a lashkar of twenty lakh soldiers. Seventeen hundred sardars who held key positions in Hoshruba chose the righteous path. Kaukab the Enlightened, ruler of the Tilism-e-Nur Afshan, known for his wisdom and sagacity, converted to the true faith. All these people will never turn back for they know that even if they die they will enter the gardens of paradise.'

Lahoot was listening to Qiran's eloquence in rapt silence and felt the rust of disbelief melt from the mirror of his heart. He signalled to Qiran that he wanted to convert to Islam. Qiran rushed to release him heedless of the thought that the sahir might just be pretending. However, Lahoot was very sincere and fell at Qiran's feet, crying, 'O blessed of all saints, you have lifted the curtain of blackness from my conscience and shown me right from wrong. My life and all I own are yours!'

Qiran embraced him warmly and Lahoot anxiously told him about Afrasiyab's plan to execute Asad and the rebels in his wife's garden. Qiran went pale and begged Lahoot to help him in reaching the garden. Lahoot and Qiran discussed the situation at length; Lahoot felt that Qiran would be captured the moment he reached the garden. For one thing, the garden was magic bound and no intruder could escape from there. The other threat in the garden was Sarsar Sword-fighter who was bound to recognize Qiran even if he was in disguise. Eventually, Qiran reached the conclusion that he would have to present himself to Afrasiyab as himself. Qiran said to Lahoot, 'What you have to do is to tell Afrasiyab that I asked you to take me to the Shah's durbar as I want to work for him now. Tell him that it is up to him to decide if I am sincere or not. Leave the rest to me.'

Lahoot looked at Qiran with tears in his eyes and said, 'Qiran, you are blessed by the saints; how can I do this and be blamed for your death? These people are so suspicious of you that they will never believe you. They will execute both you and Zargham. Your friends will believe that I converted merely to lead you to certain death!' Qiran, however, insisted on this plan and managed to persuade Lahoot to do as he suggested. Lahoot reluctantly conjured a flying throne to transport both of them to Zaivar's garden. Qiran went as himself, fully armed with his sword and shield, and holding his signature weapon, the bughda. As they flew over the desert, Qiran tried to reassure Lahoot who was still very uncomfortable with the idea of presenting his new friend to Afrasiyab.

Zaivar's pleasure garden

Meanwhile, Afrasiyab, the Samri-worshipper, was drunk on wine and kept asking Zaivar where her husband was. There was a sudden flash in the sky that caught Sarsar's eye and moments later, she announced wryly, 'Well, well! Look, who is here with Lahoot Jadoo—none other than Mehtar Qiran and in his real form! Huzoor, do not be deceived by this Habshi today. Kill him instantly before he spreads his net of ayyari! Where could he have come across Lahoot Jadoo? The wonder of it all is that he has come undisguised!' Zaivar asked Sarsar in alarm, 'Who is this young man?' Sarsar responded sarcastically, 'This is the infamous Mehtar Qiran, better known as the bughda-wielder and the angel of death for all sahirs. He is the spiritual heir to the great Amar. You should really ask your husband what he is doing here.'

As the flying throne circled and descended into the durbar, Sarsar kept coaxing Zaivar and Afrasiyab to execute Qiran, but Afrasiyab said expansively, 'Let him approach me first. Obviously he will be put to death, but I am eager to hear which ayyari he has up his sleeve now.' As everyone in Afrasiyab's durbar whispered and speculated, the flying throne descended on the ground and Lahoot Jadoo kneeled before Afrasiyab in greeting. Qiran followed suit by sketching a salaam greeting. Afrasiyab could not contain himself anymore and burst out sarcastically, 'Mehtar Qiran, how are you here? Lahoot, where did you come upon the great bughda-wielder?'

Lahoot folded his hands and responded, 'Huzoor, your lowly slave was in his palace preparing to come to you when this man came to me in his real form and begged me to bring him to you as he has something important to tell you. Now it is up to you to determine if he is playing a trick on us or is genuine.' Lahoot managed to say this much, but was trembling inwardly with fear. Fortunately, all eyes were on Qiran and Lahoot sat down quietly.

Mehtar Qiran went forward and spoke ingratiatingly, 'O Exalted Shahanshah and Great Sahir! You know that I have always been your enemy and sought to kill you. I am a soldier and speak to you plainly. The thing is that Mahjabeen Diamond-robe does not appreciate me. Mahrukh Magic-eye is arrogant because she leads the lashkar. I am not going to complain about what has happened to me, but the truth is that I have grown to loathe the ways of Amar. I am a soldier and I have certain skills. I desire nothing more than employment in your durbar. You can test my skills by pitching me against Amar or Chalak. The only request I will make is that you do not try to convert me to your religion. Respect me as a soldier and I will fight devs for you.'

As everyone listened with bated breath, Qiran continued, 'If you want to test my loyalty, I will kill Tilism Kusha right now before you. You know that until now I have been your enemy. I have killed other mighty kings like you. If you had not been magic bound, I would have killed you as well. People like me have built Hamza's reputation. Understand this that after this day, no one will even remember Hamza the Arab! As for Mahrukh, she will knock around from pillar to post!'

Qiran's eloquence and overt sincerity affected Afrasiyab deeply and he said, 'If you are really sincere, I will elevate you to a position that even exalted kings might envy. To tell you the truth, my heart is still doubtful. You have come to me on the day that I captured Tilism Kusha. How do I believe you are not deceiving me?' Qiran replied, 'Huzoor, I have spoken plainly to you. Test me if you want and I will prove my sincerity to you.' Afrasiyab laughed and looked at Sarsar, who was looking very doubtfully at Qiran. She signalled to Afrasiyab, 'He deceives you with words of ayyari, do not treat this lightly.' Qiran understood the drift of her signal and said, 'Huzoor, do what your heart tells you. Do not listen to this wretch. You are a mighty and wise king. You do realize that had I wanted to I could have come here in disguise and she would have been clueless about my identity . . .' Afrasiyab was now convinced that Qiran was completely sincere, but hesitated to express his thoughts. Qiran continued to swear loyalty to the Shahanshah and kept requesting that he should be taken to Tilism Kusha in order to execute him and prove his sincerity.

Suddenly, a voice sounded from beyond the wall of the garden: 'O Exalted Shahanshah of Hoshruba! May the light of your empire extend forever! I have long yearned to work for you and today my stars are bright for I have seen your shining face!' Afrasiyab turned around and saw that the speaker was obviously an ayyar. However, he was dressed like a peasant with a shabby waistcoat, a hand-woven loincloth and a turban tied loosely around his head. He carried a rope on his shoulder and his leather sandals had been soaked in oil. He jumped down from the wall of the garden covered in dust and approached the Badshah of Sahirs with many more blessings and prayers. Everyone, Sarsar in particular, noticed that he had very large eyes.

'Who are you?' asked Afrasiyab. The stranger replied, 'I am your slave Sarhang Kohi. I live in the mountains and make my living by ayyari. I have killed hundreds of innocent travellers and filled wells with their corpses. I am weary of my ways now and have always wanted to work for you. I have heard that one Amar ayyar has many disciples. Tell me where he is and let me confront him.' Afrasiyab noticed that though the man spoke like a peasant, his manner was sly and deceitful. Mehtar Qiran seemed amused with the peasant's talk while Sarsar observed him closely, wondering who he was. Turning to Qiran, she said, 'O wielder of the bughda, do respond to this wily man. He claims to be an ayyar, but holds an ordinary rope instead of a snare-rope. He looks like a lowly cloth weaver, what would he know of the ways of ayyari?'

Mehtar Qiran laughed derisively and said, 'He is mad! One word from Shahanshah and I will tear his ears out right now. If he dares to confront me, I will deprive him of his nose with one blow and he will run out weeping.' Afrasiyab addressed the newcomer, 'This is a disciple of Amar. Fight him if you can.' Sarhang Kohi looked at Qiran contemptuously and said, 'Sahib, I use the likes of him to till my lands. As for this woman who just spoke, she looks like a whore to me!' Sarsar became livid when he said this and shouted, 'You low-born peasant, how dare you speak like this! Your own wife must be a whore!' Mehtar Qiran added, 'Huzoor, let me deal with this clown. If I defeat him, you can employ me.'

Sarhang Kohi drew his sword out and waved it in front of Qiran as an invitation to face him if he could. Qiran looked scornfully at the peasant and said, 'I am not impressed with your acrobatics!' Sarhang attacked him viciously with his sword, but Qiran deflected the blow with his bughda. There was a violent confrontation between the two and both seemed equally matched in the art of warfare. There were cries of admiration from everyone as the fight continued.

Sarsar exclaimed, 'Huzoor, in truth this wretched peasant is very skilled in swordplay. Only a man like Mehtar Qiran can avoid his blows.' Afrasiyab replied, 'If not, he would never have come to me with such a claim.' Sarsar continued as if she had not heard, 'Huzoor, Mehtar Qiran seems to be in trouble. Both are fighting with such concentration, but I think it is Sarhang Kohi who has the upper hand.'

The fight between Sarhang Kohi and Qiran continued for an hour and the gathering was completely absorbed. Eventually, Qiran held his mighty bughda aloft and cried, 'Peasant, never say I did not warn you!' He then brought the bughda down on Sarhang in one mighty blow. Afrasiyab observed that Qiran was now in a bad temper and almost hit the peasant, but Sarhang was too quick for him and kept dodging out of the way. At one stage, Qiran's bughda hit the earth so hard that the whole durbar vibrated with the shock. Sarhang Kohi backed out of the durbar as he dodged Qiran's blows. By this time, Afrasiyab and Lahoot, and Zaivar and Sarsar were all standing to get a better view, as was the rest of the durbar. Finally, the peasant just turned and fled for his life.

Qiran called out, 'You coward, where are you running? Are you not ashamed to show your back to me?' Afrasiyab also called out, 'Mehtar Qiran, all praise to you! Do not let him get away!' Sarsar was swaying with delight and said, 'Shahanshah, what a brave warrior Qiran is!' Look, how he has overpowered that wretched peasant. Where are his boastful claims now?' Lahoot Jadoo was the happiest man in the durbar and added, 'Huzoor, do you see how brave Qiran is? He is like a lion and can vanquish even the mighty Rustam and Sohrab!' By this time Sarhang Kohi had reached the far end of the huge garden and had jumped behind a curtain. Qiran looked back at the Shahanshah who urged him to follow the peasant behind the curtain. Everyone crowded behind Qiran as he tore the curtain aside. This part of the palace seemed to be a storage area for old furniture.

Qiran picked his way through the furniture and heard a clatter in the distance. 'It seems, huzoor,' Qiran called back, 'this man knows magic and has hidden himself cleverly.' Suddenly, a wild cat emerged from behind some old string cots, growling menacingly. Afrasiyab said, 'Quick Qiran, he has transformed himself into a wild cat!' Qiran called out, 'Listen peasant! Where will you run now? I will not leave you in any form!' The wild cat snarled at Qiran and ran towards a tree. Just as it was climbing it, Qiran killed him with one blow of his bughda. The wild cat fell on to the earth, but it was obviously not a sahir, as its body did not change shape, nor did any spirits call out. There was a hushed silence and Afrasiyab exclaimed, 'Qiran, what is this? This seemed to be a real cat! Had it been Sarhang Kohi, he would have turned back into a man. You should know, you who have killed so many sahirs! It certainly was the largest cat I have seen yet.'

As these speculations were going on there was a whiff of heavenly perfume from the far corner of Zaivar's garden. It seemed as if a thousand perfume phials had released their contents or whole beds of fragrant flowers had blossomed. As everyone breathed in the sweet air, Afrasiyab turned to address Zaivar, 'How is it that we smell musk and umber in your garden?' Zaivar said, 'Huzoor, I have never experienced such a fragrance in this garden. Perhaps this was the former abode of some saint. Let us take the names of Samri and Jamshed who have wrought a miracle of such aromatic perfumes here. What lies behind it I wonder!'

The Jinni King

Moments later, an unearthly light emanated from the corner of the garden. It was as if the sun itself was coming out. As everyone stared at the apparition, the earth shook with the sound of a thunderous voice that called out, 'O Afrasiyab, you unfortunate one! You arrogant fool, you have brought calamity on yourself! I am the King of Jinni!' Afrasiyab then saw a resplendent royal figure wearing a ruby crown and a magnificent robe encrusted with precious jewels. His face shone like the sun, he had a long black beard and the largest hazel eyes, which were brimming with tears of rage. He wore strands of enormous pearls around his neck that seemed to emit a heavenly fragrance. He also wore a huge emerald in the form of a locket that seemed to have words of an unfamiliar language etched on it. He was armed with a sword, a dagger and a shield of fresh flowers.

The Jinni King frowned and clasped Afrasiyab's hand roughly as he cried out, 'Ya Qahar, Ya Jabbar! Afrasiyab, why did you kill my servant? How did he harm or injure you that you punished him thus? You know that we jinni live in the world of men often disguised as cats or snakes. Forty-lakh jinni are ready to fight you to avenge their brother. Tell me truthfully, who is the murderer here? I warn you—my people are swarming in this area. You sahirs are so proud of your magic. That is why I have worn this emerald keystone as it protects me from spells. I invite you to cast your spells on me and I promise that there will be rivers of blood in this place.'

Afrasiyab shook with fright as the Jinni King shouted at him and even Qiran felt a tremor of fear. He threw his bloodstained bughda aside and hid behind Afrasiyab, pleading with him to protect him. The Shahanshah composed himself and invited the King of Jinni to sit on his throne. Afrasiyab said, 'Huzoor, I assure you of my loyalty. Your wish is my command.' The Jinni King was somewhat placated by

Afrasiyab's manner, but still frowned sternly. He urged Afrasiyab to attack him with spells but the Shahanshah merely folded his hands and said, 'Huzoor, how can I commit such an unpardonable sin? I am so blessed that you are before me.'

The Jinni King looked at Sarsar angrily and asked, 'Who is this woman who sits here wearing a sword? She appears to be wily and disloyal!' Sarsar looked terrified and the King of Jinni addressed her directly, 'Woman, tell me, what did my cat do? Had it stolen food or broken a vessel? Why do you not speak, you lowly wretch?' Sarsar was so terrified that she wet her pyjamas and hung her head in shame. 'O mighty king, I know nothing,' she whispered softly, 'the cat was not killed in front of me.' 'You lie!' shouted the Jinni King. 'You were right here. In fact, I suspect you were the one who encouraged the killer. I can smell him in this gathering. I know what is going on ten thousand miles away! Allah has given us Jinni all powers. It is a pity that Afrasiyab does not attack us with magic or I could have come up with some tricks of my own.'

The Jinni King now turned his attention to Qiran, 'So who are you then? You are obviously not one of these sahirs. I can wager that you are a Muslim.' Qiran turned a shade paler, folded his hands and said, 'Huzoor, you are correct. I am ignorant of magic but came here by chance. I did not see your cat being killed.' The Jinni King smiled and said, 'It is obvious from your words that you were involved in our brother's murder.' Qiran was terrified and looked at Afrasiyab imploringly to help him. Afrasiyab intervened, 'O Mighty Badshah, this man is a traveller. I will find your killer soon. Do not mention magic, no one here will dare to attack you. I am honoured to have you here this evening; give me the opportunity to entertain you for I feel proud to be in your company.' The Jinni King laughed and said, 'Afrasiyab I am moved by your modesty and good manners but rest assured, I will have to find my brother's killer.' Afrasiyab started to plead, 'Huzoor, be fair to us. Whoever killed him did so out of ignorance.'

While Afrasiyab was trying to placate his irate visitor, Zaivar whispered to her companions, 'Are there really the remains of a grave in the far corner of this garden?' They responded, 'Sometimes a ghost can be seen walking here in white garments. It seems that this is an abode for Jinni. We swear to you that we have not teased them.' One of the handmaidens whispered, 'My dears, one night I relieved myself here, and I was laid up with fever for two days. I placed garlands of flowers in the same spot and felt better. Now I will make it a point to pray here every Thursday!'

As the women whispered amongst themselves, the King of Magic managed to placate the Jinni King by begging him not to mention the killer anymore. The Jinni King still glared at Qiran who was sweating with fear. 'Huzoor,' he spoke at last, 'my master, the discerning and brave Hamza Sahibqiran stayed behind the curtain of Qaf for eighteen years.' The Jinni King smiled scornfully in response and took out a phial of perfume from his robe and said, 'Oye Habshi, you seem to be swollen with pride when you take the name of Hamza. Smell this attar and tell me if Hamza ever brought back a gift like this!' The Jinni King soaked a wad of cotton wool in the perfume and held it out to Qiran who accepted it with great deference. The moment the perfume phial had been uncorked, its sweet smell swept over the durbar and everyone inhaled the soul-refreshing fragrance. Afrasiyab looked longingly at the Jinni King who smiled, 'You can smell this as well. Although you have many wonders in your treasury, a whiff of this attar will eliminate the smell of pride and arrogance from your mind. Your soul will be refreshed and your eyesight will be stronger.'

Afrasiyab raised his hand in respectful greeting and extended it to the Jinni King who let a drop of the attar fall on it. The Jinni King was about to replace the phial in his pocket when Zaivar said, 'Why huzoor, will you deprive your humble handmaidens of this rare gift? I promise that I will personally attend to the grave of your relative who is buried in this garden and walks about in white garments. I will cover it with flowers and sweep it with my eyelashes!' The Jinni King responded graciously, 'Now that bounty is being distributed you will not be deprived!' He then added meaningfully, 'You will be very happy as your husband is a well intentioned man.' Lahoot trembled as he realized that the Jinni King was aware of his conversion to Islam. He thought, 'If he blurts anything in front of Afrasiyab, he will wreak hell on me!' Lahoot folded his hands and whispered, 'Huzoor, you know everything so why reveal it? Please give some attar to these women. My wife who lives in this garden will attend to the grave. I will have a mausoleum erected here, but please do not speak of good intentions!'

The magic garden explodes

Very soon, everyone in the durbar had breathed in the heavenly scent deeply. Qiran was the first one to fall unconscious, followed by Afrasiyab and the others. The whole gathering was lying on the floor when the Jinni King rose and called out loudly: 'I am Amar, Sahibqiran's ayyar! The world trembles with my treachery! I am the beard-shaver of kafirs, the most deceitful of men. I am faster than the wind!' Khwaja Amar revived Qiran quickly, who opened his eyes to see the Jinni King bending over him. He immediately folded his hands and cried, 'O Jinni King I did not kill your brother!' Amar responded rudely, 'Listen Kalia! I am the hand of treachery and deceit, the slayer of sahirs and the favourite of prophets! This is one sample of my ayyari. How is it that you who know me so well turn yellow with fear?'

Qiran looked astounded and threw himself on Amar's feet crying, 'Huzoor, this is not ayyari but a miracle, praise be to Allah! Tell me for God's sake, how you managed to change your eyes for that is how an ayyar can be identified?' Amar replied, 'Mehtar Qiran, the beauty of this ayyari was that I used glass eyes to hide my own.' Amar now took off his glass eyes in front of Qiran, who was awestruck by this trick and walked around Amar saying, 'Ustad, may Allah keep you safe, you have elevated the name of ayyari! Please revive Lahoot before Afrasiyab wakes up because I have converted him.'

Amar revived Lahoot and Qiran told him, 'Lahoot, kneel before the king of ayyars! He came first as Sarhang Kohi and then as the Jinni King. By Allah, even I did not recognize him!' Lahoot also went around Amar with his hands folded in respect. Amar said, 'Lahoot, free all the prisoners as Sarsar is still unconscious.' Lahoot replied, 'This garden belongs to my wife and it is magic bound. Without her spells, we cannot free Bahar and the others. I will revive her now and you should convert her to the right path by praising the Almighty.' Lahoot's advice was timely, as indeed Afrasiyab would have left no one alive once he woke up, and the fact was that without Zaivar's help, any attempt at escaping from the garden would be futile. Zaivar woke up to find her husband standing before her, Afrasiyab unconscious, and Qiran and Amar standing with drawn swords. She looked inquiringly at Lahoot who said, 'Zaivar, witness the power of the Almighty that Amar performed such a daring feat and brought Afrasiyab to his knees. We were all made unconscious by the attar. Now it is up to you to accept the true faith.'

Khwaja Amar then made an eloquent speech in which he elaborated on the incomparable characteristics of the One True God. Zaivar was filled with awe as she heard him and finally said, 'Khwaja, I am with you as is my husband. I am you with all my heart but we must make haste now.' Then Zaivar released Bahar, Burran and the others. She removed the needles from their tongues and cut the chains off Asad. An alarmed Burran said, 'Zaivar, I cannot remember any spells here!' Zaivar explained that the magic garden deprived sahirs of their powers. She conjured a magic throne for the leading sardars, while Mehtar Qiran and Lahoot sat beside Zaivar. They looked around for Amar and found that he was kneeling besides Sarsar, looking greedily at her. He felt a rush of lust for his unconscious sweetheart and stole a few kisses. Sarsar suddenly woke up when Amar was embracing and kissing her, and screamed furiously, 'You wretch, how dare you!'

As she struggled to rise, Amar folded his hands and pleaded, 'I am your slave. Just put your arms around me willingly for one kiss. I cannot bear to be without you now. Take pity on your lover, how long will you deny me?' Sarsar was even more enraged by this and attacked him with her sword muttering, 'The cheek of this wretch to even change his eyes while deceiving us.' Amar dodged her blows and said comically, 'My heart is in shreds because of your eyes! They fall upon me like two swords. Where do I escape from them?'

It was then that Zaivar called out impatiently, 'Khwaja, what are you doing? Afrasiyab will wake up any moment and then none of us will leave this garden alive.' Amar returned to his senses and jumped on to the magic throne crying, 'Don't leave me here!' Sarsar followed him shouting, 'Where are you going you scoundrel? Zaivar! Are you insane that you rescue the enemies of Shahanshah?' By this time, Zaivar's throne had risen in the air. Sarsar rushed back and revived Afrasiyab crying, 'Wake up huzoor, the prisoners are free and Zaivar flies off with them.' Afrasiyab opened his eyes and called out, 'O Jinni King, you maker of wonders and miracles! What wonderful attar that was!' Sarsar screamed, 'Huzoor, Zaivar and the others are escaping on her throne!' Afrasiyab looked up in horror and shouted, 'You traitors! Where do you take my prisoners?' Zaivar looked at Amar with resignation, 'It is hopeless now. I was planning to leave this garden magic bound so that it could be a refuge for us in the future. If I do not destroy the garden now, we will all die. My ancestors had built this garden painstakingly and filled it with magical wonders, but I will have to erase their legacy now!' Zaivar wept bitterly as spoke.

Afrasiyab was going to cast a spell to prevent them from leaving, but at that moment, Zaivar brought out a large iron ball from her pouch of magic and chanted a spell on it. She cut her forehead with a dagger so that her blood splattered on the ball and flung the ball on the garden while calling out, 'Ya Samri!' As the ball exploded, the garden and its palace shuddered, and its blossoms and flowers suddenly ignited. Ancient trees swayed and birds fell upon Afrasiyab making shrill sounds. The magic garden caught fire and its grounds burst open into fissures and pits. The blazing branches fell on Afrasiyab and had he not been the ruler of Hoshruba, Afrasiyab would surely have perished that day and his very bones would have turned to ashes. Afrasiyab seized Sarsar and shouted 'Ya Samri!' He shot up in the air like a leaping flame himself and flew to the Garden of Apples, covered with soot and ashes.

Meanwhile, after sacrificing her garden in her enthusiasm for her new faith, Zaivar brought her throne down upon a mountaintop. She removed the spells cast on Burran and Bahar, and all the sardars left for Mahrukh's lashkar in all glory and triumph.

Afrasiyab flew out of the magic garden holding Sarsar and furiously casting spells to avoid falling back into the blazing garden. He reached the Garden of Apples in a distraught condition, his garments torn, his crown lost and tears of rage in his eyes. Sarsar had become unconscious due to the rush of air during the speedy flight. Afrasiyab's attendants were horrified to see the Shahanshah in this condition and rushed to dust the soot off him. The King of Magic almost collapsed on the masnad and fainted with exhaustion. His attendants sprinkled rose and kevda water to revive him, while others massaged his feet. Afrasiyab regained consciousness after a long time and remained silent as everyone asked what had happened. Sarsar came forward and explained, 'Sahibs, what happened today was really terrible! That son of a camel driver made allies of Lahoot and his wife Zaivar. He rescued all the prisoners and got away from us. His ayyari today was truly a miracle. So overwhelming was he as the Jinni King that I literally wet myself. Look, my pyjamas are still damp! Leave me aside, even Shahanshah had lost his colour!' Afrasiyab asked quietly, 'Sarsar, how did he manage to change his eyes?' Sarsar replied, 'Huzoor, I really cannot imagine how he did so. His insect like eyes were even bigger than a gazelle's today! I am aware of all the tools of ayyari, but even I have not heard of any oil that can transform eyes!'

Afrasiyab suddenly remembered something and called out, 'Does anyone know where the magic keystone is? It could not have been on Asad or the puppet would not have been able to capture him.' Sarsar told Afrasiyab not to worry and said that she would look for the keystone. Just as the cupbearer served the Shahanshah a goblet of wine, there was a sudden flash in the sky and moments later, a puppet slave descended with Hairat in its arms. Hairat was unconscious and the coils of a snare-rope were still wrapped around her. Her robes were torn and her thin chemise was tattered so that her breasts were exposed. Afrasiyab looked shocked and rushed to hold Hairat in his arms. He looked at the puppet and asked it, 'Where did you find the Malika in this state?' The puppet responded, 'Huzoor, I found bibi unconscious in the battlefield. Your slave arrived just as Bahar was going to attack with a bouquet and dashed off with Malika in the nick of time.' Afrasiyab beat his head anguish as he heard this account.

The puppet disappeared, but moments later, a distraught and tearful Mussavir ran into the garden holding his wife's hand. Hairat's vizierzadis followed him wounded and weeping loudly. They ran towards Hairat and loosened the coils of the snare-rope that had almost cut to her bone. They revived Hairat with great difficulty. She took one look at the Shahanshah and let her hair loose as she wailed, 'I am beset with problems but what happened to you?' The bareheaded and distressed Shahanshah said, 'I will tell you later but tell me what befell you.' Hairat then described how she was fighting the rebel army when Amar arrived in the midst of the battle with Bahar and Tilism Kusha. She tearfully described how Amar had made her unconscious after trapping her in the coils of his snare-rope.

Afrasiyab heard her with mounting anguish and said, 'Friends, we now have to think if Asad reached his lashkar with the magic keystone. Perhaps Amar did not trust him to keep the keystone seeing how many times he lost it. Perhaps Amar has placed it in Zambil for safe keeping.' Hairat started wailing loudly, 'Alas! Tilism-e-Hoshruba will not survive now! Tilism Kusha will fight my husband and will be impervious to magic. O Shahanshah, ever since this wretched Laqa has come into our lives we have been doomed! We face a new disaster every day and the land of Hoshruba weeps for us!'

Afrasiyab secures the magic keystone

The durbar seemed to be in a state of shock as the queen wailed and even Afrasiyab was silent. Suddenly, there was a flash in the sky and Makkar Jadoo flew in, bathed in blood. Afrasiyab saw him with relief and called out, 'O true friend, tell me about the keystone. You must know that the magic bull was killed. How did you react?' Makkar Jadoo gasped, 'Shahanshah, your lowly slave has brought you the keystone. It was difficult, but I fought valiantly for it.' The colour returned to Afrasiyab's face as Makkar presented the keystone to him. He embraced Makkar warmly and declared that he would bestow a heavy khalat robe on him. Saqis appeared with carafes of wine and there were cries of jubilation and mubarak in the durbar

In the midst of celebrations, Afrasiyab addressed his sardars, 'Friends, advise me now. Whom should I entrust with the keystone? I cannot keep it on myself for I have a thousand responsibilities, I am here in the morning, somewhere else in the evening, how will I keep it safe?' The sardars made several suggestions, but none of them met Afrasiyab's requirements. He sat with his head bowed and was silent for a long time till the flower of hope blossomed on the branch of his wishes. Afrasiyab looked up with his face glowing with happiness and declared, 'Friends, I will do as I think best.' He ordered Vizier Sarmaya to write a letter. As Sarmaya prepared to write, Afrasiyab dictated, 'To the loyal and great sahir Zamharir, I need your counsel. Please come to the Garden of Apples as soon as you can.'

A little after the message was sent, a black-faced giant of a sahir appeared in the durbar. Afrasiyab met him warmly and led him to the seat of honour. Zamharir inquired anxiously about the magic keystone and Afrasiyab laughed, 'Who can reach the magic keystone? It is safe with me. Even if the Muslims fight for a hundred years and comb the dust of Hoshruba, they will never find it. As for the rebels, I can deal with them in a day. No, the reason I sent for you was that I wanted your company. Spend this evening with us and enjoy the nautch. I will send you off tomorrow morning for I am well aware that your abode is in Neel river. That dangerous river is your refuge.'

Thus Zamharir was served wine by saqis, and musical and nautch performances were held in his honour. It was obvious to the sardars that Afrasiyab had a plan in mind, but no one could think of what it was. Later that evening, Afrasiyab signalled to Sarsar to serve their guest drugged wine. Sarsar was astounded by this order but served the wine anyway. Afrasiyab himself took the goblet and offered it to his friend saying, 'Brother, drink this offering of love from me!' The unsuspecting Zamharir drank the wine and immediately felt uncomfortable. 'I feel as if my bones are on fire!' he exclaimed. Afrasiyab suggested that he walk in the garden to dispel the effect of wine. Zamharir rose from his chair, but stumbled and fell unconscious. Afrasiyab then calmly lifted his friend and went into a chamber in the garden. Hairat, Sarmaya and Abriq looked at each other in surprise. Sarsar whispered something to Hairat who thought for a while and then said, 'Let us not speculate any further. This is Shahanshah's business and we must not interfere. I am sure that he means no harm to Zamharir who is his friend.'

Ravi, the legendary narrator, tells us that Afrasiyab remained in that chamber the whole night and no one knew what he did. Early next morning, Afrasiyab and Zamharir emerged from the room laughing together. Afrasiyab presented his friend with a magnificent robe of honour and trays of jewels. As they said farewell, Afrasiyab said, 'Brother, return to your abode under the river. Do not leave it until I send for you. I will explain everything in a letter.' Zamharir travelled to the Darband of Dukhania, where he met his friends. They met him with affection and asked him why Afrasiyab had sent for him. Zamharir replied, 'There seemed to be no special reason. I spent the night in his durbar and he saw me off with several gifts. However, since I woke up this morning, I have been experiencing strange sensations; I feel as if I have extraordinary strength and my body feels heavy. When I walk, the earth seems to tremble under me.' His friend Dukhan Black-face was perturbed by this and said, 'It is strange that I cannot remember any spells when I sit beside you.' Zamharir's other friend, Firoza Turquoise-robe added, 'I am in a strange state as well for I too seem to have forgotten magic.'

Zamharir rose in alarm and said, 'Brothers, what could have Afrasiyab done to me? I feel surges of power and want to attack someone with my sword.' Dukhan Black-face suggested, 'Go at once to your brother Neelum. He will be able to advise you well.' Zamharir immediately conjured a magic throne and left for Mount Neelum. At that time, Neelum Jadoo had convened a durbar in the Palace of Samri and was surrounded by his advisers, Vizier Mawaj and his son Lutmah of a hundred years. Neelum's durbar was as magnificent as Afrasiyab's and he was a monarch of great distinction and power.

As soon as he got word of his brother's arrival, Neelum sent his ministers and counsellors to receive him. Zamharir came into sight and Neelum looked at him closely. Zamharir was covered with the beautiful robe and jewels bestowed on him by Afrasiyab. His hand rested on the hilt of his sword and he swayed like a mad elephant as he walked. As he came closer, Neelum noticed that his eyes were bloodshot and he frowned darkly. Neelum embraced him warmly and asked, 'What is the matter with you brother? It seems as if you are ready for battle, you look that angry.' Zamharir explained his state after he had left Shahanshah and added that his friends forgot magic in his presence. Neelum looked thoughtful and said, 'Now that I think about, even I cannot remember magic.' Neelum moved away from his brother and realized that his powers were back. He shouted in alarm, 'Brother what has happened to you? One forgets magic in your proximity!'

There was an uproar in Neelum's durbar as powerful sahirs tested Neelum's claim by standing close to Zamharir. Each of them forgot their magic spells and jumped away to have their powers restored. It was a game to the sahirs, but Zamharir looked at his brother and pleaded, 'What do you think Afrasiyab has done to me?' Neelum replied, 'It seems to be clear that Afrasiyab has somehow placed the magic keystone in your body. This is not an act of friendship for the Muslims will now look for you. How will you escape from that son of a camel driver? He traced Seemab and invaded the Dome of Light! It will be difficult to escape from him.' Zamharir was stunned, but Neelum continued, 'Brother you have to go straight to the Neel river and hide in your palace within. Be warned that you are not to leave it at any cost. Forget obligations like weddings and funerals. Samri Nama states clearly that there will be great bloodshed by the river once Tilism Kusha reaches there. A River of Flowing Blood will flow along the Neel river and the Tilism of Hoshruba will fall still. I do not want to alarm you, but I have read the oracles and am aware that our family in particular is doomed. Lacheen will be rescued and we will be his first target. Where will we hide from him? For the time being, just go and hide in the river.'

When Neelum had finished speaking, the simple Zamharir said, 'Brother, this is terrible! I will not be able to meet my brothers and sisters and will be denied all family occasions.' Neelum replied, 'What family occasions? Just be grateful that you will remain alive. It is best for you to take refuge in the river. This haramzada Afrasiyab should not have treated you this way. We cannot do anything now. Surely Tilism is in decline now. The prediction is that Asad Ghazi will vanquish Tilism. The founders of the Tilism have even described his very personality and lineage, there is no room for doubt anymore. These are terrible times, may Samri and Jamshed protect us. We must hope for deliverance and conduct special worship rituals. Pundits should cast our horoscopes and tell us about auspicious hours. Do not worry, I will visit you soon and you have everything you need in your palace under the river.'

Zamharir was listening intently to all this and almost turned yellow with fear. As he left for Neel river, Neelum cautioned him not to stop anywhere on the way. Zamharir promised that he would leave straight for his palace. After saying farewell, Zamharir left for his abode in great fear for his life. We will come across him again when the river will be under siege.

VI

34 THE BATTLE WITH SANNAT MAGIC-MAKER, KHWAJA AMAR'S AYYARI, THE DEATH OF SANNAT

There was fear and apprehension in Mahrukh's lashkar for their formidable opponent Sannat Magic-maker had awakened her magic to fight them. She had captured prominent sardars like Bahar, Baghban and Makhmoor. Surkh Mu Deadly-locks was Sannat's latest victim. Asad was ostensibly out of the camp on a hunting expedition, and managed to stay out of her way. Sannat returned to her camp with the captured sardars and had a magic circle drawn around it to prevent any invasion by the ayyars. Her lashkar then celebrated her victory with trumpets and kettledrums.

Mahrukh and her sardars returned to the durbar pavilion saddened by the day's events. Mahjabeen Diamond-robe took her place on the throne, but was distressed by Asad's absence from the lashkar (for his protection, he had been sent to a secret hideout). Khwaja Amar and his fellow ayyars were also present in the durbar, but were as silent as the rest. After a long time, Mahrukh addressed the durbar, 'O sardars of the lashkar of Islam, you have witnessed the power of Sannat's magic today. She has given us a week's reprieve. We must have a plan quickly for a week is not a long time.' Mahjabeen went up to Amar and affectionately put her arms around him. She said to him, 'Grandfather, suggest something. We cannot fight Sannat now.'

Amar patted her back and addressed the durbar caustically, 'Sahibs, you have people like Chalak and Barq in your lashkar. They claim they will enter the magic line and bring back Sannat's head! You do not need my advice when you have such stalwarts around.' Barq went forward and said, 'Ustad, how can we dare to claim anything in your presence? Huzoor, how do we go past the magic circle, please advise us.' Amar laughed and told him, 'Whenever I will it, Sannat herself will call me in the magic circle; she will dispel her own magic.' Barq tried to find out just what Amar had in mind, but Amar parried and said he would reveal all in good time. Barq was quiet, but exchanged glances with his companions and the four younger ayyars rose to leave the durbar. Amar immediately protested, 'Malika Mahrukh, these four good-for-nothing rascals are leaving. They will not achieve anything, but will ruin any plans I may have. I would like them to be arrested and kept in isolation.' The four ayyars immediately sat down and declared, 'No need to arrest us, we will not leave the durbar.'

Mahrukh turned to the other sardars, but Mahjabeen Diamond-robe was perturbed to see the ayyars arguing amongst themselves. 'Grandfather,' she addressed Amar, 'it is not right that you fight thus. What will happen to us if you fall out with each other? I cannot even turn to Asad for comfort for if Sannat discovers he is here, it will be the end for us.' Khwaja Amar embraced the distraught Mahjabeen and murmured comfortingly, 'Light of mine eyes, do not despair. God willing, we will formulate a plan very soon and the unworthy Sannat will be punished for her deeds.' While Amar was engaged with Mahjabeen, the four ayyars quietly slipped out of the durbar. When Amar turned around, he found them missing and exclaimed, 'These boys have gone. This is the end to any plan I would have made!'

Now let us add a few words about Sannat Magic-maker. She had transformed the sardars she had captured into birds and laughed as they fluttered desperately in their cages. She called out to them gleefully, 'Yes you wild birds do not forget to sing for us! Did you think that you would gain anything by rebelling against the King of Magic? You have finally been punished for your misdeeds!'

Suddenly there were distant cries of '*Ram naam satya hai*'. Sannat looked up to see a funeral procession at the edge of the magic circle. An impoverished Brahmin was seen walking alongside an *arthi*, holding an earthenware pot containing some leaves and ghee. The Brahmin was weeping as he walked along the corpse of his brother. As the small procession reached the magic circle, Sannat's soldiers ran forward and warned them, 'Turn back or you will all perish! Malika Sannat has drawn a magic circle here, you cannot walk through it.' The Brahmin said, 'Listen, a few yards yonder there is an old pipal tree. Our family members have been cremated there for generations. We are Brahmins and will not turn back now. Tell Malika Sannat that she should not offend Gisyan Brahmin *devta*.'

Sannat's soldiers asked the Brahmin to wait until they had obtained Sannat's permission. They rushed to their mistress and informed her of the situation, and added, 'Huzoor, it is a Brahmin's corpse. They have told us that they have to cremate it under that tree and nowhere else. They say that if we stop them, a hundred Brahmins will collect here, break their sacred threads and then starve themselves to death. A hundred of them will die for one corpse!' Sannat looked worried and asked, 'What should we do?' Sannat's handmaidens chimed in, 'Huzoor, if these Brahmins break their sacred thread, the sin will be upon us. How will we ever make up for it? Brahmins are a stubborn people, they will do as they say. They will sit besides the magic circle for their pooja and beat their drums and make life very difficult for us.'

Sannat lost her temper and shouted, 'You harlots, you are talking about sin! I am more concerned about the ayyars of Islam. They can pretend to be dead or alive. I am aware of their tricks.' Her handmaidens replied, 'Huzoor, you are right, but how can a corpse trick us? Huzoor should stand there while the corpse is cremated.' Sannat agreed doubtfully, 'Very well, tell them we will have to inspect the corpse before the cremation.' Her relieved handmaidens reassured her, 'Huzoor, they should have no reason to object to this condition.' 'Even so,' said Sannat, 'I still do not trust them. I will inspect the corpse myself.'

Sannat went out and stood under a tree while her handmaidens dispelled the magic circle. The handmaidens went to the edge of the lashkar and approached the funeral party. They said, 'Brahmin devta, now stop complaining and come with us.' As they removed the magic circle, two of the Brahmins lifted the arthi and the third followed weeping and wailing. They brought the cot and placed it under the pipal tree, then came to kneel to Sannat and requested that she provide wood for a pure funeral. Sannat asked them not to make such a din and said that she would provide the wood, but asked to inspect the corpse first. The Brahmins protested at this sacrilege, but Sannat insisted. As she approached the corpse, the three Brahmins made a great din by blowing their conch shells. Sannat bent down and opened the fastenings of the coffin. Her soldiers and handmaidens stood at a distance and trembled with fear as they whispered, 'How could Malika Sannat commit this sacrilege? To think she has actually opened the coffin. If she survives this year, it will be a miracle!'

Sannat was about to uncover the face when one of the Brahmins distracted her by asking her to open the feet first. As she turned around, the corpse moved so that its face was exposed. The handmaidens watched in horror as the dead body seemed to come to life. The three Brahmins took out their snare-ropes in a flash and attacked Sannat, while the corpse called out, 'You evil woman, your end is near!' Sannat was already alert and although the snare-ropes caught her around the neck, she shot up into the air like a bolt of lightning and incinerated the ropes.

The four ayyars fell upon Sannat's handmaidens and killed several of them. The skies darkened with the deaths of the sahiras and the ayyars tried to make a run for it. Sannat descended from the sky in her real form stunned by the attack, and saw her soldiers chasing the four ayyars as they ran for their lives. 'Let them run,' she called out, 'they will not be able to cross the magic circle.' Indeed, the ayyars stumbled and fell as they tried to cross the magic circle. Sannat's soldiers tied them and dragged them to where Sannat was standing. She screamed, 'You foolish ones, did you think I would not restore the magic circle after letting you in? Where is that sarbanzada? Have you not brought him with you? And where is that Kalia who goes around with a bughda?' After abusing them roundly, Sannat transformed the four ayyars into birds and incarcerated them with the other sardars of Islam.

Khwaja Amar's revolt

Several people witnessed the capture of the ayyars from the Islamic lashkar. They rushed to report this latest mishap to their sardars and wept as they addressed Mahjabeen Diamond-robe, 'Malika of the world, there is bad news. Chalak and Barq were captured along with Jansoz and Zargham. It was remarkable that they tricked Sannat into letting them into the magic circle. That wretch is too clever though. Eventually, she captured them and turned them into birds.' There was an outpouring of grief in the durbar at this news. The first to speak was Amar who declared, 'Sahibs, I will not interfere any more nor I will make any attempt to rescue them. These haramis have eliminated the chance to perform another ayyari! I do not wish to remain in Tilism Hoshruba, I will return to my master Hamza Sahibqiran. I am weary of planning ayyaris anyway!'

Amar then rose and embraced Mahjabeen. He said, 'Farewell Bibi, I will leave you now as there is nothing I can do here.' Mahjabeen held the hem of Amar's robe as he turned to leave and said, 'Respected sir, do not talk thus. After Allah, we rely only on you.' Amar muttered, 'They planned this unfortunate ayyari without consulting me. Had I planned it, I would have arranged a grand funeral with several mourners; we would have gone in blowing trumpets and drums. Sannat would have been convinced that there really had been a death. The moment she saw only three people, she must have realized that they were ayyars. They were caught for this oversight.' Mahjabeen persisted, 'Forgive us sir and please sit down. Nothing will be done without consulting you first.' Amar looked at her and reluctantly settled into his chair again.

At that time, there was a distant sound of trumpets and drums. The sardars realized that it came from the direction of Hairat's lashkar. Moments later, Mahrukh's spy birds flew into the durbar to announce that a sahira Zulmat Jadoo had declared war on behalf of Sannat against the Islamic army and there were great celebrations in Hairat's army for this reason. Amar declared, 'Bismillah! Let us also respond with drums and trumpets of war.'

The next morning, the sardars of Islam faced Sannat's forces with mixed emotions. They saw that Hairat and her forces had settled to watch the battle from a higher ground while Sannat herself came out to face them. After demonstrating a few examples of her dazzling magic, Sannat called out, 'Mahrukh, send someone to confront me soon, for your lives will be shortened now!' Princess Maraan Earth-bound (who had been instrumental in the rescue of Asad from the Dome of Light) asked Mahrukh's permission to fight. Mahrukh said, 'Light of mine eyes, may the Almighty protect you, Bismillah!'

As she swayed out into the battlefield, Sannat looked at the tender young face of Maraan and cried out, 'Maraan, for the love of Samri, have pity on your youth! I will get Shahanshah to forgive you. Do you think you can win against me?' Maraan responded, 'Listen, shameless one, my beginning and my end are all the same now!' There was a brief and fierce contest of magical spells between the two, but eventually, Maraan was injured on the head and fell down. Sannat immediately transformed her into a golden parrot. Maraan's grandmother Asrar then attacked Sannat and the two armies engaged in a prolonged and bloody battle. Sannat lost several powerful commanders and was wounded herself. As the battle ended at sunset, she announced that she would give the rebel army another week for them to reflect and beg for forgiveness from Hairat.

Meanwhile, Mehtar Qiran began pleading with Amar to suggest a plan to destroy Sannat. Amar replied with sarcasm, 'Kalia, you want a plan from me as well? Who is a greater ayyar than you? Your bughda is famous in Tilism Hoshruba. Go and strike Sannat with it. I promise you after her death all the sardars will be released. The rest of her army will not withstand Mahrukh and her forces. There, now I have suggested a plan of action. Go and act upon it.' Qiran looked crestfallen and said quietly, 'Ustad, if it was not for the magic circle I would have killed even her grandfather with my bughda. Please think of another plan.' Amar said seriously, 'Whatever strategy I had thought of for entering the magic circle was ruined by these wretched boys. All I said was that Sannat would invite us into the circle herself. Barq must have conceived that foolish plan after he heard me. Harami got all of them trapped! I am even more helpless than you are at this time.'

That evening, Mahjabeen Diamond-robe, Maimar Qudrat and the other sardars approached Amar with folded hands and offered to pay all his debts if he would just devise a strategy. Amar taunted them by saying they were in no position to relieve him of his debts. Mahjabeen sent for fifty sacks of gold coins at once while the other sardars offered whatever they could afford. Amar watched them impassively without saying a word. Eventually, he rose and deposited every offering into Zambil. Then, he said, 'Sahibs, there is no other way. I will now fetch my master Hamza who will recite the Great Name and destroy the magic circle. I will return very soon. It takes three months to reach Mount Agate and will take another three months to return. Within six months, everything will be resolved.'

Mahrukh Magic-eye lost all her colour as she heard him and the other sardars looked at him stunned. Everyone protested, 'Khwaja what are you saying? Do you think Sannat will leave us alive for six months?' Amar calmly declared, 'There is no other way. When Sannat comes to confront you, tell her honestly that your leader has gone to Mount Agate and you cannot fight till he returns. Six months will pass by in a flash. In fact, I intend to take a few sardars to accompany me as the way to Mount Agate is full of hazards. Maimar Qudrat, Lahoot, his wife Zaivar, and Malika Asrar will go with me, as will Mehtar Qiran. Do not worry, Sahibqiran will come and resolve everything.'

Everyone in the durbar protested loudly while Mahjabeen broke down and began weeping. Amar embraced her and wiped her tears. He said to her, 'Light of my eyes, these are matters of ayyari and you should not interfere. God will be merciful, this Tilism will be conquered and you will rule over eighteen hundred countries. Your marriage to Asad will be solemnized in great splendour and I will hold your children in my lap. We will return soon. Just trust in God and pray to him.' When the traveller of the day journeyed from the East and rested at last in the inn of the West, Amar told Qiran and the sardars that he had selected a lashkar of four lakh men. He asked them to leave in groups of ten or twenty and wait for him in the desert of Humania.

Amar himself prepared to leave late that night. Every person in the lashkar was convinced that he was leaving to save his own life now that he had managed to collect a good part of the treasury from the sardars. Some even suggested that they should ambush him and steal Zambil. Others feared this talk and said, 'Be quiet lest he hears you and raises hell.' Still others whispered, 'Look how he loads the treasure on carts! Now where will poor Malika Mahrukh find the money to pay us?' The weak-hearted ones suggested that it was best to desert as well and beg Afrasiyab for forgiveness. They said, 'He is a great king, surely he will forgive us. We should never have joined this sarbanzada!' Amar heard all the whispers and innuendos, but did not respond and bade farewell to the sardars. He urged them not to worry as he would return in six months. Mahjabeen whispered loudly, 'Grandfather, do not keep repeating this, it disheartens everybody.' Amar replied airily, 'You know that I do not lie. Why should I hide the truth?'

Mahjabeen clung to Amar and wept bitterly and Mahrukh looked as if she would faint any moment. Lalaan and the rest of the sardars also wept and there was an air of mourning in the camp as if someone had died. Amar left with a few words of reassurance and disappeared into the night. Meanwhile, Sannat was relaxing with a few of her companions and was drunk on wine and pride. The awnings of her pavilion had been raised and her soldiers could be seen sitting on fine carpets with beautiful glass lamps around them. Sannat's companions were inebriated and sang her praises, 'O symbol of Samri and Jamshed, surely Shahanshah will hand over the rule of Hoshruba to you. Malika Hairat does not matter any more.'

The wedding procession

Sannat's heart swelled with pride as she heard these words. Suddenly, a mysterious light emerged on the horizon. Everyone watched as the light increased and sounds of music and merriment were heard. Very soon, it seemed the whole jungle was on fire. Thousands of riders in robes of red and gold led what was obviously a wedding procession. They were followed by pretty young girls singing wedding songs and seated on thrones adorned with fine gold inlay-work. A bridegroom sat on an elephant that was being steered by a young mahout who wore expensive livery. A young warrior wearing a gold-embroidered uniform, armed with a shining sword and a pair of rare daggers stood behind the bridegroom. Behind them was a huge army in smart uniforms. Bands of soldiers on horseback held flags embroidered with gold lettering in praise of the hundred and seventy-five gods. The bridegroom was being showered with precious stones and the gold coins were received eagerly by leaping *shohdas* who would greedily call out for more. Cartloads of food and sweets followed.

As Sannat and her companions watched the dazzling procession in wonder, the bridegroom's elephant approached the magic circle. Sannat's guards rushed forward and warned them not to step over the line lest they fall unconscious. No sooner had they issued this warning, thousands of men stepped forward holding magic weapons and cried, 'Who has drawn this magic circle? Is this not the land of Hoshruba? If it is not and we have wandered elsewhere, we will cause the earth to overturn and destroy the creator of this circle.'

Sannat's guards were intimidated by the threats of the young soldiers and even more fearful of the hundreds of Brahmin priests who walked behind them chanting mantras. They called out to the commanders, 'Huzoors, respectfully, this is the land of Hoshruba and Malika Sannat has made this magic circle.' The commanders turned around and addressed the young man fanning the bridegroom, 'Sarfarosh Jadoo, this circle has been conjured by Malika Sannat. If you order us, we will destroy the circle right away!' Sarfarosh Jadoo called Sannat's guards closer and said, 'Tell Malika Sannat that this is the wedding procession of her nephew, the son of King Tajdar, ruler of the west countries. Could she remove the circle for a while so that we conduct pooja under that pipal tree? The bridegroom would also like to offer tribute to her.'

The guards ran back to Sannat to inform her. Sannat looked at her companions and admitted, 'Sahibs, this is indeed true. They had sent me an invitation, but I forgot everything because of this war. My absence must have been felt in the family.' Turning to the guards, Sannat said, 'Apologize on my behalf and tell them that my absence from the wedding was not of my will. I am one of them, but Shahanshah's prisoners are being held within this magic circle. Tell them that if it is not much trouble, can they proceed with the procession a few miles further as these are Shahanshah's orders?' Sannat's guards returned to Sarfarosh Jadoo with this message. On hearing the message, that honourable man went red with anger. He took out a huge iron ball splattered with blood and balanced it in one hand. He gave it a twirl and shouted, 'Ya Samri! Ya Jamshed! Servants of Sannat beware! I am Sarfarsoh Jadoo, son of Jan Nisar Jadoo, commander-in-chief of the army of Tajdar Jadoo. Beware for this iron ball of death has been especially crafted by Samri and Jamshed. It is not great magic—only eleven lakh men will die most painfully!'

Sarfarsoh Jadoo balanced the iron ball on his hand as Sannat's guards cried in fear, 'Mian Sarfarsoh Jadoo, have mercy on us poor soldiers. Give us time to try and persuade Sannat once again before you do anything.' That young man smiled and said, 'My heart is against it, but yes do try again. Tell Sannat she should not be this arrogant. Our vengeance will be swift and hard!' Sannat's guards returned to her beating their heads and wailing loudly. They threw themselves down before her and wept, 'For the love of Samri and Jamshed, save our lives! Sarfarosh Jadoo is angry. We have never seen the likes of iron ball he has. He claims that thousands will die from it. He has five lakh soldiers with him ready to fight or die. Huzoor, this Sarfarosh seems to be an eloquent and powerful sahir. Even our grandfathers could not have heard the magic words he used when he brought out the iron ball. When we spoke to him about changing the route of the procession, he was very angry. He says that by tomorrow morning, the procession has to reach the bride's house. Huzoor, shohdas alone are looting millions of gold coins. This wedding is worth six crore. We have heard that the bride's father is a rich merchant. The procession will remain in his house for seven days!'

Sannat's sardars added their voices to the guards and begged her not to cause a fight between people of Samri's faith. Sannat looked at her sardars in stunned silence and then said, 'So what are we to do?' Everyone suggested that she should remove the magic circle for a little while to let the procession pass by. They assured her, 'They will not take long as they are in a hurry to reach the bride's house.' Finally, Sannat relented and asked Zulmat to remove the magic circle. She ordered, 'I will be watching from the pavilion. I will apologize to Shah Tajdar later and will accept the tribute from this place. Restore the magic circle the moment the procession passes through it.' Zulmat and some of the other sardars went to do as she ordered.

Meanwhile, the bridegroom's elephant swayed close to the magic circle. Powerful sahirs stood nearby with their magic weapons aloft and called out, 'Mian Sarfarosh Jadoo, should we remove the magic circle? Should we overturn the earth and rain flames? Should we destroy your enemies?' Sarfarosh Jadoo replied, 'We will not turn away from death nor shall we sour family relationships. Wait till we get a reply.' As Zulmat and the others reached the edge of the lashkar, the sight of the militant sahirs terrified them. They heard pundits crying, 'The time for pooja is running out. This marriage will not be solemnized if we wait too long.' Zulmat removed the magic circle and called out, 'In Samri's name, the procession should move forward!' Mian Sarfarosh Jadoo urged the pundits to proceed with the pooja. Hundreds of pundits moved forward and Sarfarosh gave an order for the rest to follow. As soon as the order was given, the *atishbaz* with their sleeves rolled up briskly moved their carts forward, and then fanned out to lay fireworks throughout the area.

Sannat's soldiers tried to prevent the atishbaz, but they ignored the protests and continued with their work. Meanwhile, the bridegroom's elephant stopped close to Sannat's pavilion and musicians played their instruments. The singers were so loud their voices seemed to reach the sky. From her pavilion, Sannat watched fascinated as Mian Sarfarosh untied a white silk sheet and took out emerald tablets from it. The bridegroom, who was hidden behind a veil of flowers whispered something to Sarfarosh, who laughed and said loudly, 'My son, I know that these emerald tablets were selected by your esteemed father as tribute for Shahanshah of Hoshruba. However, you know that Malika Sannat Magic-maker is the most distinguished of Afrasiyab's sardars and a pillar of strength for him. She has no peer in the arts of magic and sorcery. I am well aware of her status for I have known her since her childhood when her toys were made of precious gems. She is the most generous, the kindest and the wisest. She has to be offered a hundred gold dinars and a hundred and one emerald tablets. Present these to her with great respect.'

Sannat heard these words of praise, as indeed she was meant to, and her heart swelled with pride. She threw caution to the winds and said to her companions, 'Sarfarosh Jadoo appreciates us and why not? He knows us since our childhood. He is a man of great distinction and taste. See how eloquently he speaks.' Her companions murmured, 'Huzoor, all Hoshruba is talking about how you have defeated the Muslims and saved Tilism from destruction!' Sannat emerged from her palace and called out, 'Mian Sarfarosh, descend from the elephant and rest awhile with us; you can always join the procession in the morning.'

Sarfarosh smiled and said, 'It is too late to stop now, but I promise to stay with you when I return. Please accept this nazar from us.' The elusive bridegroom now descended from the howdah and went forward with the emerald tablets held in his hands. It was obvious that the bridegroom was bathed in perfume and as he bowed before Sannat, everyone inhaled the heavenly fragrance emanating from him. Sannat extended her hand to accept the tribute while Sarfarsoh Jadoo called out, 'Yes friends! Light the fireworks to celebrate this occasion right now!' The night was illuminated by fireworks of all hues and there were explosions all over the plain. Meanwhile, as Sannat bent her head low to accept the tribute, the bridegroom, that is the incomparable ayyar Amar bin Ummayyah, shook his head slightly so that the veil of flowers covering his face moved. The flowers had been soaked in the attar of unconsciousness and as she breathed in, Sannat started and then stumbled as it affected her senses. Sarfarosh Jadoo, who was actually Mehtar Qiran in disguise, jumped down from the howdah. He held Sannat by her hair and held his bughda in the other hand.

Meanwhile, Amar quickly threw the veil of flowers off his face and plucked Sannat's precious crown off her head crying, 'O treacherous sahirs, have you now seen the ayyari of Khwaja Amar?' Qiran's bughda smashed Sannat's skull into a thousand pieces. At the same time, Sannat's soldiers fell unconscious from the drugged fumes of the fireworks. Amar's soldiers had already stuffed wads of cotton wool soaked in an antidote into their nostrils.

As Sannat died, a huge cloud of flames covered the skies, the earth trembled, there was a fierce sandstorm and stones fell from the air. Her spirits wailed in grief and after a long time, came the familiar call, 'You have killed me, my name was Sannat Magic-maker! Alas, I died and gave my life; and did not achieve my purpose!' The sardars of Islam whom Sannat had transformed into birds were restored to their real forms. Mehtar Barq Firangi ran for his life but Chalak bin Amar, who was as greedy as his father, went to plunder Sannat's tents. Baghban, Bahar, Makhmoor and the other sardars emerged from her prison to see that the earth was in flames while terrible voices were proclaiming Sannat's death.

∽

35 AFRASIYAB DECIDES TO OPEN THE HUJRAS OF PERIL, THE OPENING OF THE FIRST HUJRA AND THE DEATH OF MASHAL JADOO

Afrasiyab rose in anger as if awakened by a bad dream and declared, 'I am going to kill them all! Alas, my dearest companion and the most distinguished of all my sardars died in such an ignominious way!' Mahiyan Emerald-robe, Afrasiyab's maternal grandmother, was with him at the time and was trying to comfort him as best she could. A magic panja suddenly flew in holding Malika Hairat. The moment she landed, Hairat started wailing, 'Shahanshah, I will surely die or commit suicide. The Muslims have caused the ultimate humiliation. Have you seen how a farsighted and clever woman like Sannat fell into Amar's trap?'

Afrasiyab tried to placate his wife and said, 'Hairat, just have patience. Within a week you will not find a single Muslim alive even to be cured!' Hairat snorted, 'You say that every time!' Afrasiyab declared, 'I will go right away and bring back their severed heads.' Mahiyan intervened, 'It would be more advisable for you to send Hairat to face the rebels, but she must not declare battle. I intend to write to the supreme counsellors of Tilism. I will also appeal to my relatives in Zulmat. They will strike terror in the enemy ranks.' Afrasiyab looked unconvinced and said, 'You can write to whomever you like. Only I will decide who goes to fight the rebels.'

Mahiyan then left for Zulmat after pacifying her grandson, but the Shahanshah was pale with grief and worry. His heart twisted with pain as he pondered his latest defeat. When he was alone with his wife, he whispered, 'Hairat, I want to try and persuade Mashal Jadoo to confront the Muslims. They will all go up in smoke in one breath. You return to the battle camp. I will inform you of what happens next.' Afrasiyab then travelled with his entourage to the Fort of Light-rays to meet his trusted ally Zaal Jadoo, secret keeper of the Hujras of Peril. After a private conference with Zaal, Afrasiyab left with him on a flying throne. He landed in a distant fort in the wilderness. As Zaal entered the fort, he noticed that beautiful adolescent youths seemed to be its only occupants. He observed, 'Shahanshah, what kind of a realm is this? Afrasiyab explained, 'The ruler of this fort is Khurshid Taj Buksh. He is the uncrowned Shahanshah of Hoshruba. Many proud warriors kneel to him. If he marks their foreheads with his toe, they can hope to achieve a kingdom.'

Meanwhile, the youthful Khurshid Taj Buksh came out to greet the Shahanshah. Afrasiyab and Zaal were dazzled by the sight of the young boy covered in jewels, his fingertips stained with henna and accompanied by a throng of young companions. As he kneeled in greeting, the Shahanshah held his hands and gazed at him adoringly. Khurshid asked the Shahanshah gently what brought him there. Zaal could not take his eyes off the beautiful boy and Afrasiyab looked completely entranced. He composed himself in time and invited Khurshid to accompany them on their journey. Khurshid turned in excitement to his companions and asked them to prepare for the journey.

Zaal said, 'Khurshid you will have every comfort there. Come along with us.' Khurshid then excused himself and left for his chambers to bathe and change into even more splendid robes. He returned and said, 'Shahanshah, let us go wherever you please. I shall sing for you and serve you wine.' Thus, Afrasiyab returned with both Khurshid and Zaal to the Fort of Light-rays where a feast had been laid out for them. There, Zaal whispered to Afrasiyab, 'Shahanshah, while you are entertained here, I will leave to look for Mashal's place and also obtain Samri's sindoor for the worship.'

After Zaal left, Afrasiyab spent an evening of pleasure in the company of his young friend. Khurshid delighted him with his ardour and love, sometimes strumming the sitar and singing, sometimes putting his arms around Afrasiyab. At daybreak, Zaal Jadoo arrived to inform the Shahanshah that all preparations were complete and that they should leave at once. As they flew on magic thrones, this time accompanied by a lashkar of twelve thousand, Khurshid asked eagerly where they were going. Afrasiyab lied that they were just going for some fresh desert air. As the throne entered the Desert of Thorns, not a leaf stirred, the air was hot and oppressive and there was no sign of life. Khurshid's fresh young cheeks wilted in the heat and even Afrasiyab experienced a frisson of fear. After travelling a few miles into the desert, Afrasiyab saw a chinar tree in the distance without any foliage and it seemed as if the branches were on fire. As they approached the tree, Zaal signalled to Afrasiyab that they should land nearby, as this was where Mashal Jadoo lived. Afrasiyab took the throne down to the ground and the army of twelve thousand cleared the area to pitch their tents. The wilderness around them was covered with sand and had a strange haunted feel to it. Zaal walked under the tree and said, 'Shahanshah, recite the name of Samri and dig a hole with your own dagger. Only you can do this.'

Afrasiyab started digging and after going down the length of two hands in the earth, his dagger struck a solid surface. He cleared the sand and found an ancient door with a rusted lock in the bolt. Zaal then took out a small packet of sindoor and marked the young Khurshid's forehead with the red powder. The moment he had done this, it was as if a bad spirit overpowered Khurshid. He opened his hair and shook his head from side to side. He pleaded with the Shahanshah to behead him instantly, 'I entreat you to place your dagger on my throat. Let me meet Samri and Jamshed, I have had enough of this world.' Afrasiyab looked aghast and asked Zaal, 'What is going on?' Zaal replied calmly, 'Just do as he says. These are the secrets of Samri; we mortals cannot guess the reasons. Slaughter him as you would a wild bull.'

Afrasiyab reluctantly took Khurshid in his arms. He laid him out gently on the ground then reached for his dagger. Khurshid himself stretched his throat up to receive the dagger. Afrasiyab's hand was trembling, but he managed to cut open his young friend's throat. As his blood poured out, Zaal Jadoo quickly collected it in a crystal bowl. Khurshid's body was still twitching, but eventually, he lay still. Afrasiyab stood there shivering as Zaal handed him the bowl of blood and knocked on the door in the ground. A frail voice called out from inside, 'Who goes there?' Zaal called back, 'O companion of Samri and king of the art of magic, the King of Hoshruba, Afrasiyab Jadoo seeks an audience with you.'

The quavering voice called again, 'What does he bring us, why is he here?' Zaal replied, 'He has brought you the blood of his beloved for your drinking pleasure.' The ancient door opened noiselessly on its own. Afrasiyab hesitatingly entered the room and was confronted by a repugnant old sahir, whose flesh had eroded so much over the years that it seemed as if only his wrinkled, sagging skin held his bones together. Afrasiyab was revolted by the sight of his face. Suddenly, the old man yawned. Zaal nudged Afrasiyab who was holding the crystal bowl, to take it to Mashal's lips. As Afrasiyab raised the bowl, Mashal laughed loudly and bent over to slurp the blood from it. After drinking it to the last drop, he burped and swayed in ecstasy. He said, 'Zaal, you mentioned that Shahanshah of Hoshruba is here. Where is he?'

Zaal pointed to Afrasiyab. Mashal suddenly shouted, 'Impertinent one! Where is Shahanshah Lacheen?' Afrasiyab trembled with fear, but Zaal bravely said, 'Huzoor, Lacheen died and is with Samri now. Afrasiyab became the king then. It was he who slaughtered his beloved just outside your door and served you this life-saving beverage.' Mashal then beamed at Afrasiyab and declared, 'Indeed, he is my true friend. O Shahanshah of Hoshruba, sit down and tell me what has happened. How is it that you are here?' Afrasiyab replied, 'Huzoor, you must already know. The Muslims have invaded my kingdom, and seventeen hundred of my most trusted sardars have rebelled against me and joined them. I have managed to hide the magic keystone so that even the bird of their imagination cannot reach it, but recently, they struck a grievous blow and killed my vizier Sannat Magic-maker.'

Mashal laughed softly and said, 'Tell me, who is the biggest villain amongst them? Someone whom even Samri and Jamshed would fear.' Afrasiyab started to tremble, 'I cannot tell you his name for he might just find us here!' Mashal said, 'I understand completely. I have read the Samri Nama, I am aware of his identity. You have nothing to fear now. I will go with you and make you victorious throughout the world. You have served me nourishment that has renewed my soul. However, my body is decayed even if my spirit is young. Find me a young body so that I can leave this ancient one.' Zaal came forward with folded hands and suggested, 'Huzoor, the body of young boy whose blood you drank is lying just outside. You can use it if you want. The Muslims will think you are a cupbearer.' Mashal approved of this idea and so Zaal brought the body of Khurshid into the hujra.

Mashal inspected the body and was particularly happy with Khurshid's beautiful face. After Zaal had skilfully stitched the severed neck back on to the body and covered the wound with a dressing. Mashal addressed the King of Magic, 'Afrasiyab, I am now changing my form. I leave this body after two hundred years. You must remember two things, first, you must provide me with a sharp wine and second, a comely young boy to serve it. I have been thirsty for a long time and you must assuage all my needs.' Mashal suddenly jumped off the cot, put his mouth on the corpse's mouth, hiccuped three times and transferred his soul into the corpse. His desiccated old body fell in a heap as the young Khurshid Taj Buksh got up from the floor and declared, 'I am Mashal Jadoo!'

A stunned Afrasiyab thought, 'Truly, he can turn destiny around. Who can kill him?' Mashal had his old body cremated. He took Afrasiyab by the hand and went into the desert as Khurshid Taj Buksh. Afrasiyab's soldiers breathed with relief as they saw him emerge with the young wine boy as the heat of the desert was stifling. Afrasiyab led Mashal to his throne and the royal party left with the soldiers celebrating their departure from the Desert of Thorns.

On his way home, Afrasiyab wrote a message to Hairat that said, 'Lady of my palace, congratulations! I have made the supreme sacrifice and was blessed with the light of Mashal. Who will have the courage to confront him? Hairat, make preparations and tell Sarmaya and Abriq to procure the best wines.' This missive was conveyed to Hairat through a messenger who rode a she-camel to reach the durbar and declared, 'Shahanshah has unlocked the hujra of Mashal Jadoo. That peerless sorcerer and companion of Samri, Jamshed, Laat and Manaat will arrive any moment.'

Musssavir the magic artist cried, 'Whose blood was he given to drink? Whose life was cut short? Who did Shahanshah kill with his own hands?' The camel rider replied, 'Shahanshah comes with his wine boy Khurshid Taj Buksh. Rumour has it that Mashal comes as him. I do not understand this mystery. Perhaps Shahanshah's letter will explain it.' Hairat read the letter addressed to her and said, 'Let it be announced that King Mashal Jadoo is coming. Tell the Muslims that they should find snake holes to hide in.' This news was duly conveyed to the Islamic durbar by their spy birds. Baghban Qudrat cried out, 'Surely we are dead now! Indeed this is a terrible event. Find out whose blood did Afrasiyab offer? Hairat is still alive!' The messengers replied, 'We have heard that Afrasiyab slaughtered that shepherd who became his cupbearer, Khurshid Taj Buksh. Mashal comes in his form.'

Amar saw all his sahir sardars looking very disheartened and tried to comfort them. He said, 'My friends, take heart. Do not let your courage desert you now. Just be patient, I will kill this haramzada very soon.' Baghban Qudrat smiled weakly and said, 'Khwaja who will you kill? He returns in a different body each time.' Amar declared, 'Even then I will kill him. The Almighty has not created any life form in this world that is immortal. Do not let me hear these words of despair in durbar again.' While this discussion went on in the Islamic durbar, Zaal Jadoo led a procession into Hairat's camp. Afrasiyab followed, looking as arrogant as ever as he rode a magnificent horse. Mahrukh and Bahar came out eagerly to watch the procession and saw that a young man of incomparable beauty, dressed in gleaming robes and a crown, was being carried on a throne encrusted with diamonds. They looked at him closely and recognized the son of a shepherd whom Afrasiyab had adopted. Their hearts trembled with fear and they retreated in despair.

Hairat Jadoo greeted Mashal with the utmost reverence. The young man smiled at her while the five ayyar girls present in the durbar whispered to each other, 'This is surely the end for the Muslims. Who can trick this creature?' Once Mashal had been given the place of honour in the durbar, Afrasiyab told Hairat that he wanted to leave for Zulmat to convey the good news of Mashal's arrival to his grandmother Mahiyan Emerald-robe. He asked Hairat to entertain Mashal, but warned her against declaring battle before he returned from Zulmat.

Mashal Jadoo and Mahrukh Magic-eye

After the Shahanshah departed from the camp, Mashal turned his attention to Hairat and said, 'Who shunned the worship of Samri and joined Tilism Kusha? In particular, who leads them?' Hairat informed him that it was Mahrukh Magic-eye who led the sardars and the army. Mashal then declared, 'In that case, write to Mahrukh on our behalf and invite her to meet with us. Tell her that Afrasiyab will forgive her if we ask him to.' Hairat immediately dictated a message that was delivered to Mahrukh by an attendant. After reading it, Mahrukh told Amar that Mashal had invited her to meet him. 'Then go and meet him by all means!' said Amar. Mahrukh was reluctant and explained, 'I do not want him to extract my soul from my body!' Amar realized that Mahrukh was very agitated and asked to speak to her privately. A little later, Mahrukh emerged alone from the inner chamber and told everyone, 'Khwaja Amar has left to consult Shah Kaukab. I have decided to meet Mashal. After all, what harm can come from speaking to him?'

Everyone in the durbar was too much in awe of Mahrukh Magic-eye as the ruler of the camp to disagree with her and murmured, 'Bismillah, God be with you.' Mahrukh left for Hairat's camp with only a few handmaidens in attendance. Mashal was also informed that Mahrukh was on the way and he sent a few nobles to welcome her. Mahrukh Magic-eye entered Hairat's pavilion with great dignity and greeted everyone in the Islamic manner of greeting. She was given a place of honour to Hairat's right and was served wine by a young boy. Mahrukh declined the goblet of wine and said, 'O Shahanshah Mashal, you are supreme amongst sahirs and also perceptive, therefore you know that we cannot drink your wine. Accept our apology and tell us why have you summoned us.'

Everyone in Hairat's durbar was eager to hear the conversation between Mahrukh and Mashal and listened intently. Mashal declared arrogantly, 'I have come to destroy the enemies of Afrasiyab and to establish peace. As you well know, I am a miracle of nature. I cannot be killed. It would be folly to confront me. You are a wise and farsighted woman; join Afrasiyab now. The six ayyars and Tilism Kusha will be dealt with in our own time.'

Mashal continued to sing his own praises for sometime, but Mahrukh merely smiled in response. When he had finished, she said, 'Mashal Jadoo, you have said some very foolish things that no logical person can accept. Many sahirs like you came to confront us and died at our hands. Their pride came to dust as they were sent straight to hell. It seems as if you have also reached the end of your long life.' Mashal laughed and said, 'Malika of the world, you have spoken logically, but I have been blessed by Samri after years of worship. My soul is old but I have descended into this young body.' Mahrukh retorted, 'This is nonsense; what is so difficult about changing your face? Amar and his ayyars do it every day!' Mashal replied patiently, 'I have not changed my face; it is my soul that has descended into this body. If someone kills me, my soul will move into another body and I will fight again. That is why it is impossible for me to die.' Mahrukh said scornfully, 'Now this is difficult to believe. For how can I believe something that not only I have never seen but have not even heard of?'

Many people in the durbar nodded in agreement for many of them were also sceptical about Mashal's powers. Mashal smiled tolerantly and said, 'Malika, you are right! No one else has been blessed this way. It is after two hundred years of penance that I was given this boon.' Mahrukh declared, 'The only way we can believe you is if you actually die and then come back to life in front of us.' Mashal said, 'You will not deny me then?' Mahrukh replied, 'Bismillah, we are ready. We will kill you and you should come back to life. That is when we will have faith in you. But if you die at someone else's hands we will regard it as a magical trick.'

Hairat's durbar listened to this exchange intently and felt great admiration for Mahrukh's courage. Mashal nodded and whispered something in Hairat's ear. She excused herself and left the durbar. Mahrukh again addressed Mashal, 'If we kill you and you return to life, all our sardars will come and kneel to you.' Mashal said happily, 'In that case, sharpen your sword. We will just wait for Malika Hairat to return.' Hairat had gone into a private chamber, where she sent for a bird, twisted its neck and then wrapped it in her scarf. She then sent for Vizier Abriq and ordered him to strangle a young personable looking man and hide the corpse under her throne in durbar, 'When Mahrukh kills Mashal, I will immediately attach the bird's beak to Mashal's mouth and his soul will descend into the bird. What you have to do then is to bring out the corpse so that his soul descends into it. The corpse will come to life and declare, "I am Mashal!" Mahrukh will be convinced and the war will be over.' Abriq nodded and immediately carried out her orders. Hairat slipped back into the durbar with the dead bird hidden in the folds of her scarf while Abriq quietly pushed a corpse under her throne unnoticed by anyone.

Hairat nodded at Mashal who turned to Mahrukh and said, 'You can test my powers now!' Mahrukh rose from her chair and drew out her sword with a flourish. Mashal finished his goblet of wine and jumped down from his throne to face her. Mahrukh, who was actually Amar in disguise, leaned back and was intending to slice Mashal in half so that there was no question of him remaining alive to transfer his soul, when a voice thundered from the sky, 'You camel driver's son, what do you think you are up to? I am Afrasiyab Jadoo! Shahanshah Mashal, you have been deceived!' As they heard his voice, Barq and Chalak who had been disguised as Mahrukh's handmaidens leapt out of the pavilion. When Afrasiyab flashed down from the sky, Amar also ran out of the durbar with Afrasiyab, Hairat and Mashal running after him. Mashal's huge army with his commanders Ifrar and Iqrar Jadoo was spread out near the durbar.

Amar leaped fifty feet away from the durbar into an open area, held his sword on his shoulder and called out, 'O Mashal, you witless man! It seems that you only know how to return from the dead. I would have killed you now, but you have been saved. You shameless man, I am not a sahir and yet you pursue me? You have a huge army of sahirs here. Tell them not to use magic on me and then see how I confront them all. Afrasiyab are you not ashamed to target me with magical weapons? If there is a man here who can capture me now, I will immediately convert to your faith!'

Afrasiyab was overcome by shame and Mashal started to sweat as they saw Amar in his real form holding his sword and challenging anyone to capture him without using magic. Afrasiyab called out harshly, 'No one is to use magic. Only attack Amar with your swords and arrows and spears.' The lashkar of ape-like kafirs fell on Amar and he responded with a roar like a lion. Amar moved on the battlefield like a bolt of lightning. He decapitated sahirs so swiftly that no one was able to capture him. Afrasiyab and Mashal marvelled at Amar's courage as he destroyed their army. As the sahir soldiers seemed to be avoiding going anywhere near Amar, Mashal signalled to his commanders to attack him.

Iqrar Jadoo, who considered himself a great warrior, approached Amar crying, 'Be warned sarbanzade! I am Iqrar Jadoo, commander of the great Shahanshah Mashal!' Amar turned and saw a monstrous black sahir parrying and thrusting. He snarled at him, 'Stop these acrobatics and come closer to me. Can you not see that I am fighting your men right now? Very soon, I will send you straight to hell as well!' Iqrar ran forward with his sword drawn and attacked Amar who dodged out of the way. Iqrar fell with the force of his thrust and as he blow, Amar brought his sword down on him in an almighty blow so that it cleaved him in half. Amar happily recited a prayer and shouted, 'I have killed him!'

Ifrar Jadoo saw his brother being killed and clutched his heart in grief. In his rage, he lobbed an iron ball at Amar. As the ball shattered, Amar swayed and collapsed on the earth crying out, 'O Afrasiyab and O Mashal, shame on you! Your combined forces could not defeat me and this haramzada has finally attacked me with magic!' Ifrar ran towards Amar who writhed on the ground as his limbs were lifeless and he could not flee. Ifrar attacked Amar in this helpless condition. Everyone saw Amar's body being sliced in half as a cloud of dust descended on the battlefield. Afrasiyab called out, 'This is terrible! Amar's companions will not leave Ifrar alive now! However, it is just as well that he is out of the way. Now there is nothing to fear! This camel driver's son was arrogant and died in such a disgraceful manner today. This will weaken Mahrukh and Bahar. How will they fight us now? All Muslims will flee from Hoshruba henceforth!'

The dust dispelled and a voice called out, 'I have been killed, my name was Ifrar Jadoo!' Everyone looked in horror as they saw Ifrar's body writhing on the ground and no sign of Amar. Lightning flashed in the sky and a voice boomed, 'I am Shahanshah Kaukab! Afrasiyab are you not ashamed that your whole army could not kill a single man and eventually you had to resort to magic. No one can dare harm Khwaja Amar in our lifetime. See this is how I take him away!' Afrasiyab was horrified and made a move to attack Kaukab when Hairat clung to his waist and cried, 'Shahanshah, let him go.' Mashal Jadoo was in a towering rage at the death of his commanders. He declared, 'Afrasiyab, I will not leave the Muslims alive now. My sardars who were loyal to me for so long were killed today!'

Hear a word or two about Khwaja Amar now. He opened his eyes to find himself in the Palace of Jamshedi. Shahanshah Kaukab, Brahmin Iron-body, Princess Burran and Princess Hina were all present there. Kaukab embraced Amar warmly and said, 'Khwaja why did you go alone to confront Mashal?' Amar replied with resignation, 'Kaukab, I would have killed that haramzada today but Afrasiyab saved him!' Kaukab said thoughtfully, 'I am aware of that Khwaja and I was on the lookout for you. Ever since this monster arrived here, I have not been able to think of anything else. My venerable teacher, Ustad Nur Afshan Jadoo had written to me earlier and said he wanted to meet you. Now that you are here, he should be informed.'

After some time, Nur Afshan arrived in the palace on a flying throne along with his two beautiful daughters Princesses Aftab and Hilal. Nur Afshan embraced Amar and both his daughters greeted Amar respectfully while he responded with prayers for their long life. After he had settled down, Nur Afshan said, 'Shahanshah of ayyars, I have something important to discuss with you. Please listen carefully to me. Mashal is not like the other sahirs.' As Amar listened intently, Nur Afshan continued, 'Khwaja, when your sardars will face Mashal, he will first mesmerize them with his fiery magic and then capture their souls in birds. What he will do next is to have the lifeless bodies cremated. You must instruct your ayyars that they should prevent this from happening and somehow keep the corpses in safe custody. Guard them from all harm. Perhaps then the Almighty may bestow his mercy on us.'

Amar declared, 'Even if we are finished in the attempt, rest assured that we will keep the bodies safe and intact.' Later, Nur Afshan took Amar aside and they talked for a long time. Late that night, Nur Afshan, Brahmin and the others bid farewell to Amar and left for their abodes. Amar also bid Kaukab farewell and returned to Mahrukh's camp.

Mashal and Barq ayyar

Afrasiyab had arranged a separate pavilion for Mashal where he was provided with fair young boys and all the wine his heart desired. While Mashal indulged himself after two hundred years of abstinence, Barq Firangi left his lashkar, thinking of ways to infiltrate Hairat's camp. While he was walking through the forest, he saw Vizier Abriq with two young boys who were cruelly bound with ropes. As he dragged them through the forest, they howled in protest while Abriq tried to reason with them, 'You will be in attendance on Shahanshah Mashal. You will be given plenty of money and expensive clothes to wear. You are humble peasants now, but you will be gifted large tracts of land.'

The young peasants wept, 'This is how you lured our two brothers and they never returned to the village. Who knows what happened to them?' As Barq watched with interest, a group of angry peasants ran towards the vizier crying, 'This man is a kidnapper! Let us take him to the thakur!' Abriq was terrified that they would attack him with their hefty bamboo rods; he left his prisoners there and ran for his life. The peasants untied the boys and left for their village. Abriq also emerged from his hiding place and returned to his camp thinking, 'This is not good; the peasants know me now. I have no boys for Mashal now and Afrasiyab will be furious with me.' After witnessing this episode, Barq thought that this would be a good way to snuff out Mashal's life. He brought out the paints of ayyari and transformed himself into a youth of fifteen. He wore a gold-embroidered cap, a bright orange outfit embroidered with gold thread and matching shoes. He applied kohl in his eyes, tinged his mouth with missi and dabbed attar on himself.

He then deliberately walked past Vizier Abriq, looking like the very picture of a carefree youth, smiling and humming to himself. The vizier was delighted to see the comely young youth. He stopped Barq and said, 'Mian, come with me and I will introduce you to a powerful patron who will shower you with money!' Barq retorted saucily, 'So who is that wretch? Take me to him and I will ensure that he will never love another. I promise you he will be in my snares forever!' Abriq led the artless youth back to the camp chatting all the time, but thinking to himself, 'Ever since Shahanshah Mashal arrived here, we have not presented him with a beautiful youth like this one!' They reached Mashal's camp and Abriq went in first to inform Mashal, 'Huzoor, I have brought you a beautiful beloved.' Barq followed Abriq into the durbar and when Mashal laid eyes on the youth, his heart gladdened with joy. As Barq came closer, he reached out for his hand and tried to embrace him. Barq rewarded him with a tight slap and cried, 'You wretch! How dare you try to be so familiar with me?'

Mashal sheepishly rubbed his cheek, but seemed entirely captivated with the young boy. Soon, Barq pretended to warm to him. He entertained Mashal by singing lilting ballads. Mashal was in raptures and smilingly asked Barq to serve him wine. He pleaded, 'Perhaps if I drink from your hands I will be satisfied, otherwise no wine seems to quench my thirst!' Barq made Mashal drink several goblets of wine into which he had slipped drugs of unconsciousness. To his alarm, Mashal seemed to be impervious to them. He only laughed at Barq and complained, 'Your wine seems to be a little bitter.' Barq was about to faint with grief and disappointment when suddenly the curtains of the pavilions lifted and Afrasiyab entered. He was horrified to see Barq sitting close to Mashal and called out, 'Beware, this is Barq ayyar!' By that time, Barq had already leapt out of sight as he had seen the King of Sahirs.

The battle with Mashal

That evening Mashal ordered that battle drums were to be struck for the next morning. In the Islamic camp, Amar had a tent erected away from lashkar. He sent for the ayyars Barq, Chalak, Jansoz, Zargham and Qiran and held a secret meeting. Amar declared, 'O good ayyars, tomorrow's battle will be like the Day of Judgement for us. Nur Afshan has given strict instructions that the enemy will try and cremate the dead bodies from our camp. We have to ensure that this must not happen at any cost.' All five of the ayyars promised that they would keep the bodies intact even if their lives were lost in the process. Amar embraced each one and said, 'Brothers, in truth we will be in a difficult situation. It will not be easy to snatch the bodies while Afrasiyab stands there, but I will be with you and together we will do what we have to.'

The next morning, Mashal rode to the battlefield and inspected the arrangements Afrasiyab had made for him. Everyone saw that several corpses were laid out on string cots. About five hundred yards from the battlefield, there was a huge pyre of leaping flames. Several black-faced sahirs were pacing close to the pyre, determined to cremate the dead bodies of the rebel army. All six of the ayyars also mingled amongst them disguised as sahirs and tossed iron balls to express their enthusiasm.

As Mashal walked into the battlefield, Princess Nafarman came forth from the Islamic lashkar to confront him. Mashal looked at her scornfully and called out, 'Nafarman, try all the spells in your power!' Nafarman retorted, 'We are not in the habit of attacking first. If the Almighty saves me from your spells, I will respond then.' Mashal brought out an iron ball from his bag of magic and hurled it at her. Nafarman chanted an incantation and successfully cut the ball in half. They fought in this manner for a while until Mashal suddenly lost patience and leapt forward like a flame. He shouted, 'O Nafarman, look at me! I am Shahanshah Mashal, companion to Samri and Jamshed!'

Nafarman looked him straight in the eye; Mashal kept staring at her and held out his hands. It was as if he was a magnet and Nafarman was drawn to him involuntarily. As Mashal drew his hands back, she stood perfectly still. He repeated his actions and she began swaying on her feet. The third time Mashal moved his hands, Nafarman fell down lifeless on the ground. Mashal took the dead bird Afrasiyab was holding out and attached the bird's beak to Nafarman's mouth. Moments later, the bird came to life and spoke in Nafarman's voice. People in both camps were astounded at this unusual form of magic. The bird was put into a cage that Afrasiyab handed to Uqab Jadoo, who was to be in charge of the birds. Afrasiyab then called out, 'Throw Nafarman's corpse into the fire.' A huge black sahir came forward and hoisted Nafarman's body on his shoulder. He went towards the fire, but walked past it towards the hills. One of Afrasiyab's sahir guards stopped him to ask where he was going. The black sahir replied, 'I am burying Nafarman's body.' The sahir guard protested, 'But why bury her when the orders were to burn the bodies?' The black sahir replied, 'Should I obey your orders or listen to Shahanshah? Look, even now he is saying something.' As the sahir guard turned around to see Afrasiyab, the black sahir quickly drove a dagger through his heart and shouted, 'Shameless one, I am Zargham Sherdil! Would I burn the body of my own sardar?' As the sahir guard died, everything went black and Zargham stole into the hills in the darkness.

Afrasiyab wanted to pursue Zargham, but Mashal stopped him by saying, 'Shahanshah, let him go. We have her soul with us, what will you do with her lifeless body? The Muslims will weep to see her corpse and within a few days it will decay.' Afrasiyab saw the logic of this advice and turned back. Meanwhile, Zargham brought Nafarman's body back to his camp where the princesses came running out, beating their heads in grief. Nafarman's companions wailed in lament and some of them stated that they wanted to kill themselves. Khwaja Amar arrived and comforted everyone by murmuring, 'Do not be so foolish, she is merely the victim of black magic!'

Back in the battlefield, Mashal challenged his enemies, 'This was just an introduction to my powers. Send someone else now!' Nafarman's best friend, Surkh Mu, who could barely contain her rage, went forward to confront him. This time Mashal did not bother to read any spell, but merely repeated his mesmerizing gestures. Surkh Mu fell lifeless on the ground. Mashal transferred her soul into a dead bird and handed her body to Maheel Jadoo, who was well known to him. Maheel went towards the pyre when a large black sahir leapt out of a group of sahirs and smashed his head with a huge bughda. Afrasiyab turned to see Maheel writhing in his death throes on the ground, while Qiran was running off with Surkh Mu's body into the hills. There were wails of grief from the Islamic camp as Qiran arrived with Surkh Mu's limp body.

Baghban and Bahar succumb to Mashal's magic

Mashal called out again, 'Betrayers of salt, send someone powerful to face me. This has been too easy.' The noble Baghban could not resist this challenge. He jumped off his mount and after receiving the nod from Mahrukh, went forward to meet Mashal in all splendour and dignity. He deflected some of the iron balls Mashal lobbed at him, but did not look at his adversary. Mashal kept urging him to meet his eyes, but

Baghban kept his face averted while approaching him. When Baghban was within fighting distance, Mashal attacked him with his sword. Baghban deflected it with his magic shield. Mashal kept inciting Baghban to look at him, but Baghban drew his sword and after declaring his intentions, brought it down on Mashal's head.

Mashal tried to shield himself, but Baghban's sword cut through the shield and decapitated him in one swift blow. Baghban triumphantly shouted, 'I have killed him!' His friends jumped with joy and shouted praise for him. Baghban turned around smiling to acknowledge their cheers. Meanwhile, Afrasiyab transferred Mashal's soul into a dead bird and then again into the corpse of a young man. The corpse rose shouting, 'I am Shahanshah Mashal!'

Baghban was still waving to his friends the cheers and his wife was kneeling on the ground in gratitude to the Almighty, when he heard Mashal's call. He turned around startled to see a dark young man claiming to be Mashal. Baghban's eyes met the young man's in a fatal moment. Mashal extended his arms and Baghban was rooted to the ground. As Mashal's arms moved again, Baghban's colour faded and his eyes froze; with Mashal's third gesture, Baghban fell lifeless on the ground and his guardian spirits wailed for him. His wife Gulcheen raised her head from the ground and saw her husband's dead body on the ground. She rose like a fury and attacked Mashal with her dagger. She stabbed Mashal in his belly so that he fell writhing to the ground.

Gulcheen then wept over her husband's body, 'Sahib, I have avenged your death! I was a married woman this morning and am a widow now! How will I survive you?' Meanwhile Afrasiyab did the needful with a dead bird and in his haste, dragged the body of an old man forward to Mashal. The old man rose claiming he was Mashal. Gulcheen saw him approaching her and cried, 'Who are you, old fool? I have just killed Mashal!' Sure enough, her eyes met the old man's and Mashal mesmerized her with his unique magic. Gulcheen fell beside her husband and a wail of despair rose from the Islamic lashkar.

Mashal ordered Afrasiyab to make sure the bodies of the husband and wife were cremated. He then ordered, 'My soul was traumatized by them. There will be no more fighting today. I need wine and food to relax.' Afrasiyab signalled to twelve of his trusted guards to immolate Baghban and Gulcheen. As they dragged the bodies towards the pyre, they were waylaid by the ayyars who attacked them with snare-ropes, bughdas and every weapon of ayyari. After killing the guards, Chalak, Qiran and Zargham escaped with the bodies of their sardars in the darkness that ensued after the sahirs' deaths.

That evening, Mashal indulged himself with wine and kept requesting Afrasiyab to provide him with adolescent boys. He complained, 'I am lonely on my own.' Afrasiyab looked towards his viziers Sarmaya and Abriq, who reluctantly left to find boys from neighbouring villages. By this time, both the viziers were regarded in the area as suspicious characters. Wherever they were seen, peasants chased them with large sticks. With the greatest difficulty, they managed to find two boys, but Mashal did not like the look of them. Eventually, Afrasiyab asked him with folded hands if they could sound the battle drums for the next day. 'Indeed you should,' declared Mashal drunkenly, 'I only want you to be happy. Tomorrow I will finish the rest of them— just provide me with a list of the prominent sardars so that I can challenge them by name. Now that I have seen the world after so long, I have decided that I will not return to the hujra but stay with you!' Afrasiyab thought, 'This is not good for me. Where will I find beautiful children for him every day?'

The next morning, Mashal was ready for a fight. He reached the battlefield and called out, 'O worshippers of One God, whichever one of you wants to taste death should come out to confront me!' Bahar came out of the ranks of the lashkar to face him and there were cries of 'The garden of Islam will be withered. Bahar Jadoo goes to die!' Afrasiyab clutched his heart and said to Hairat, 'This is terrible! Your sister comes to confront Mashal. She may not survive.' Hairat Jadoo wept softly and said, 'Shahanshah, alas I did try to warn Bahar, but she did not listen to me and now she will surely die. How will I explain this to my father Hayat Jadoo? He will hold me responsible for her death.'

Meanwhile, in the battlefield, Bahar was careful not to meet Mashal's eyes. She took out a bouquet of fresh flowers from her bag of magic and after chanting an incantation, called out, 'Mashal, beware!' Afrasiyab exclaimed, 'She has thrown her bouquet, Mashal will be in trouble now!' As Bahar's bouquet burst into hundreds of fragrant blossoms, Mashal swayed on his feet. He picked up the blossoms and inhaled deeply while calling out, 'Princess Bahar, I long to see your lovely face. Show yourself to me.' Bahar kept her face averted and continued chanting her spell. Soon Mashal was in a frenzy. He tore his clothes and started to bang his head against a tree trunk. Afrasiyab realized that he was completely bewitched and could injure himself. The King of Magic quickly expelled his breath loudly so that Bahar's blossoms ignited into flames and the sweet-sounding birds she had created burnt to cinders. Mashal suddenly came to his senses and ran towards Bahar, abusing her angrily. Bahar was deeply offended and called out scornfully, 'Afrasiyab, is this shameless one the master of your Hujra of Peril that he needed your help to destroy my spell?'

Her face burning with rage, Bahar also jumped forward to confront Mashal and forgot to avert her face. As her eyes met his, Mashal extended his arms forward in his characteristic spell. Bahar stood rooted to the ground, her cheeks withered and her eyes filled with tears. With his next gesture, Bahar swayed and fell on the ground. Mashal quickly transferred her soul into a bird. As Afrasiyab's soldiers rushed to her corpse, the brave Makhmoor Red-eye threw a magic ruby into their ranks and it exploded like a bomb. Hundreds of Bahar's handmaidens also rushed into the battlefield and several of them were killed. In the ensuing confusion, Amar retrieved Bahar's body. Afrasiyab saw his beloved being carried off lifeless and called out in grief, 'Let the body of Bahar go. Alas that such beauty should leave this world. My heart is torn into pieces!' Hairat said, 'Recite such mournful verses later and watch how Makhmoor has fallen like a bolt of lightning on Mashal. This Mashal is a fool! He cannot withstand her spells!'

Indeed, Makhmoor fought Mashal and his army so bravely that the earth seemed to shake with her attacks. She was making her way to Mashal and intended to slice him in one blow so that she should expose the bastard's pretensions once and for all. Afrasiyab's soldiers were also retreating with the onslaught of her spells. The force of her attacks also shook Mashal. He tried repeatedly to meet her eyes, but she was too engrossed in destroying his men. At one point, Mashal injured Makhmoor on the shoulder, but she quickly bound the wound with a scarf and then fell on Mashal with her sword. She flashed a blinding magic light before his eyes that made him blink. Makhmoor then fell on him like a fury unleashed and sliced him in half.

There was an outcry when Mashal died and Makhmoor swayed on her feet and shouted, 'O lovely Bahar, I have avenged your death! I have blown out the lamp of Mashal's life!' In that time, Afrasiyab went through the procedure of transferring Mashal's soul into a dead bird and then into a young man's body. The body rose and called out 'I am Mashal Jadoo!' Makhmoor was still weeping bitterly for Bahar when a young man approached her. As she did not know him, she met his eyes and Mashal repeated his magical manoeuvre. When Makhmoor collapsed, Barq Lameh fell on Mashal like a bolt of lightning, but unfortunately, she too succumbed to his mesmerizing magic. The souls of Makhmoor Red-eye and Barq Lameh were transferred into birds, but the ayyars fought fiercely for their bodies.

The princesses of Nur Afshan confront Mashal

Mashal was still in the battlefield and drank copious amounts of wine served by his saqi boy. He shouted 'Ya Samri!' each time he guzzled the wine. As Mashal drunkenly called out for his next victim, Mahrukh Magic-eye herself prepared to meet him. At that moment, a light flashed in the skies. Everyone looked up and saw the sun of beauty and valour, Princess Burran Sword-woman mounted on a golden peacock. Mahrukh called out, 'O light of mine eyes and daughter of Kaukab! For God's sake do not go to the battlefield, but come to me!' Princess Burran called back, 'Huzoor, your lowly handmaiden begs your permission to fight. I know what has happened and cannot wait any longer!' Burran then descended on the battlefield as Afrasiyab's soldiers announced her presence. Afrasiyab looked at her with grim satisfaction and said to Hairat, 'Tilism of Nur Afshan is now doomed for Burran comes to fight. I will throw her body into the pyre myself!' Afrasiyab then was suddenly reminded of his own status and instructed a witch standing next to him, 'You pick up her body. Why should my exalted self be soiled by touching it?'

Meanwhile, Burran jumped off her peacock and confronted Mashal. She called out, 'Shameless one, enough of your tricks! Prepare for your end!' Mahrukh had already warned her not to meet his eyes and she kept her face averted. Mashal flung an iron ball at her which she sliced into two and aimed the magic Pearl of Samri straight at his chest. The pearl went straight through Mashal's deceitful heart. Burran flew up shouting, 'I have killed him!' While she was up in the air and straightening her garments in case she was exposed in any way, Afrasiyab went through the procedure of transferring Mashal's soul into the bird and then into a dead sahir's body.

Burran was just preparing to meet her friends in the Islamic lashkar when she heard a voice claiming to be Mashal. She then fell on him again with heightened rage. Ravi, the legendary narrator tells us that Burran killed Mashal three times with the magic pearl. The fourth time, however, she accidentally met his eyes. Within a flash, Mashal had mesmerized her and then transferred her soul into a golden bird. Afrasiyab reached Burran's body and flung a few magic pebbles towards the Islamic lashkar as he shouted, 'Be warned! No one should try and claim this body!' The witch Afrasiyab had spoken to earlier lifted Burran's body and carried it to the pyre with Afrasiyab striding beside her with his tegha. Afrasiyab kept shouting, 'No one should dare cross our path or he will be killed, may he be a friend or a foe!'

The five ayyars Chalak, Barq, Jansoz, Zargham and Qiran watched helplessly from a distance. Qiran said, 'Chalak, where is Ustad? Alas, the body of Burran might be cremated!' Chalak replied, 'My respected father has not been seen for some time. In truth, he will blame us for not saving her body. Even if we try we will just be killed for Afrasiyab is adamant on cremating her.' As the ayyars watched restlessly from a distance, Afrasiyab reached the pyre in a state of excitement. He saw his sahir commander, Atishbar Jadoo standing in the middle of the burning pyre and calling out, 'Shahanshah give me Burran's body!' Afrasiyab signalled to the witch, who literally threw Burran's body into the pyre as it was too hot to go near it. Atishbar Jadoo caught the body expertly, looked Afrasiyab straight in the eye and called out, 'Why Afrasiyab Khana Kharab, do you recognize your father? I am the seal of ayyars, the sun of ayyari and the acme of swordplay. I had captured your commander Atishbar and disguised myself as him. Look, I have his body with me! I rubbed the magic varnish on my body and it protects me from these flames. I have wrapped Burran's body in a sheet soaked in the same varnish and not a hair of hers will be burnt!'

As Afrasiyab watched in stunned silence, Amar tossed the body of Atishbaz into the flames. As soon as Atishbaz died, a sheet of flames fell from the skies. Hidden by the flames, Amar jumped into the tunnel he had dug previously and escaped with Burran's body. That tunnel took him half a mile behind the Islamic camp. Afrasiyab made a move to follow him, but several of his companions clung to his waist and stopped him, pleading, 'Shahanshah, he may have set a trap for you, please restrain yourself. What will you do with Burran's body anyway?' Meanwhile, in the Islamic camp, all the sardars had surrounded Burran's body. Amar was also stricken with grief and wept for a long time.

Suddenly, a light flashed in the sky. Princess Majlis Jadoo, who had followed Burran from Tilism Nur Afshan, arrived on the scene. She looked down from the sky to see Burran's dead body surrounded by the wailing sardars. She looked again and saw an unknown sahir challenging Mahrukh, 'Send someone else t-o face me now for I have extinguished the lamp of Nur Afshan.' Majlis realized at once that this man had killed her dear mother. She fell on Mashal like a fury unleashed from that height. Afrasiyab ran towards Mashal shouting a warning, 'Beware of this girl, she is a menace! She looks young, but is imbued with the spirit of Samri!'

As Majlis fell on Mashal, she struck him with her sword and cleaved him in half. Majlis flashed back into the sky when Afrasiyab went through the usual process with Mashal. As he came to life in another body and declared himself, Majlis looked down in surprise and bore down on the battlefield again. It is said that Majlis killed Mashal five times before she met his eyes and crumpled to the ground. Afrasiyab shouted, 'Someone get her body.' As one of his attendants rushed to the battlefield, another one cried, 'Brother I will come with you.' Afrasiyab assumed that both of them were his servants. The first attendant bent down to lift the body of the young princess while the second one stabbed him from behind and shouted, 'I am Mehtar Barq Firangi!' In the ensuing darkness of the sahir attendant's death, Barq ran off with the body. When he arrived in the lashkar bearing the body of Majlis, there was general panic in the ranks of soldiers and everyone was convinced that Mashal would spare no one. By this time, Mashal had declared an end to the day's battle. Meanwhile, there was great outpouring of grief in the Islamic camp as Majlis and Burran's bodies were laid out side by side.

The next morning, Amar went with Mahrukh into the durbar. As she ascended her throne, he urged her not to go on to the battlefield. He said, 'If you fall, it will be difficult to hold the lashkar together. Today, Inshallah, I will either kill this scoundrel or die myself!' Mahrukh looked at him with despair and said, 'What can be done before Afrasiyab?' Amar declared firmly, 'Nevertheless, it will be done.' He then signalled to Chalak and Barq who left the durbar with Amar following them. After they departed, Malika Mahrukh and the other noble sardars went out on the battlefield. On the other side, Afrasiyab's lashkar spread out in all its might before them. Mashal emerged and thundered out a challenge to his enemies. There was great fear in Mahrukh's lashkar and no sardar seemed to be willing to face Mashal. Mahrukh decided to confront him herself when there was a flash of lightning and Princess Aftab, daughter of Nur Afshan Jadoo emerged in the sky. She was adorned like a new bride, but appeared to be weeping. She saw Mashal shouting on the battlefield and realized this was Burran's murderer.

Mashal looked up startled as she announced herself and she fell upon him straight as an arrow. Before he could respond, she had cleaved him in half with her sword. She was just preparing to fly up into the sky when a sahir startled her by claiming to be Mashal. As she met his eyes Mashal repeated his mesmerizing magic and Aftab went pale in the face, eventually falling lifeless to the ground. When Mashal trapped her soul in a dead bird and handed it to Uqab Jadoo, even Aftab's enemies were saddened by the loss of that beautiful young princess.

Qiran smashed the skull of the sahir who was going to lift Aftab's corpse with his bughda. Afrasiyab watched with his mouth agape as Qiran leapt out of sight with Aftab's body. There was an outbreak of grief in the Islamic lashkar when Qiran appeared with her body. Mashal Jadoo was triumphant with his latest success when Aftab's sister Hilal appeared weeping and wailing in the sky. As she fell upon Mashal in sheer rage, she hurled a golden crescent at him. Mashal tried to deflect it but it fell on his throat and decapitated him immediately. Hilal flashed back into the sky shouting, 'I have avenged my sister!'

Amar captures Mashal's soul

Afrasiyab immediately went forward, twisting and turning a dead bird in his hands when a sahir tapped him on the back and exclaimed, 'Huzoor, there seems to be a great cloud floating in from the direction of Tilism-e-Nur Afshan. Perhaps Kaukab is arriving.' Afrasiyab turned and looked up at the sky. Meanwhile, Mashal Jadoo was writhing on the ground, anxiously waiting for Afrasiyab to transfer his soul before it left his body. A thin, elderly sahir jumped forward with a blue-throat bird and attached its beak to Mashal's mouth so that Mashal's soul entered the bird. Afrasiyab turned again and saw that an elderly sahir was sealing the beak of the blue-throat with a steel wire. The bird was trilling faintly and Afrasiyab could hear Mashal's feeble voice calling out that he had been trapped by Amar.

Amar shouted, 'I am the king of ayyars, the slayer of kafirs, Amar the honourable! O Afrasiyab Khana Kharab! Look I have trapped Mashal in this blue-throat and will extinguish him forever!' As Amar ran with the blue-throat, Mashal's voice became fainter and then stopped when Amar wrapped the bird in the Net of Ilyas and placed it in Zambil. Amar vanished in Galeem, but Afrasiyab was in a mighty rage and fell upon Mahrukh's army. Within moments, hundreds had perished with his magic. Still not satisfied, Afrasiyab ran towards the tent where the bodies had been kept, shouting, 'I will now burn these bodies, I have the souls already!' Mahrukh Magic-eye rushed to defend the tent while all the other sardars attacked Afrasiyab with their magic weapons. Afrasiyab remained impervious to their assaults and dismissed them with a few spells. He reached the tent and found Mahrukh and the sardars standing before it although many of them had been wounded by his spells. He called out, 'Mahrukh, hand Amar and the blue-throat to me and I promise I will spare your lives!'

Mahrukh replied firmly, 'Afrasiyab, we are prepared for death, but we have no control over Amar. Do what you will. We are ready to face you.' Afrasiyab faced the onslaught of spells from the sardars and responded by throwing a handful of pebbles at them. There was a shower of heavy stones from the sky and the sardars were badly injured. Eventually, everyone fled and watched him from a safe distance. There was total silence as Afrasiyab looked into the tent. The attendants who were watching over the bodies ran out at the sight of him. Afrasiyab was about to conjure a fire that would destroy the tent altogether when the whole tent was suddenly hidden from his view by a pall of black smoke. It was obvious that someone had conjured the smoke deliberately. Afrasiyab chanted a spell and aimed an iron ball towards the billowing smoke. A golden paw materialized in the smoke and tapped it so that it turned back and landed at Afrasiyab's feet. A voice called out from the smoke, 'Afrasiyab, do not give your life away for the bodies. The next time you throw the ball, it will land on your head. O *mardood*, when will your mind be rid of its arrogance? Go and look after your own house, see what has happened there!'

Afrasiyab became even angrier after hearing this. He glared at the smoke and shouted, 'Is anyone here?' No sooner had he uttered the words than there was a flash of lightning in the sky. A parizad holding a golden vessel containing iron balls flew down and handed it to Afrasiyab. As the parizad flew off, Afrasiyab lobbed another ball at the smoke. The golden paw reappeared and deflected it back so that it landed where Afrasiyab was standing. Afrasiyab jumped quickly to save himself. Afrasiyab was now in a great rage. He took another ball from the vessel and chanted a spell on it. He cut his forehead with his dagger and sprinkled his blood on the ball. Holding it aloft, he cried, 'If I throw this at the sky, it will fall down! If I smash it on the ground, it can destroy the earth!' He leaned back to throw the ball when a voice thundered from the smoke, 'O Afrasiyab Khana Kharab! You foolish arrogant man, do not throw this ball or it will fall back on your chest. We know that you are strong, but your bones will break and you will complain to your grandmothers for a long time!'

Afrasiyab looked up to see Nur Afshan Jadoo standing in the smoke and trembling with rage. Afrasiyab said, 'Nur Afshan move away. I will not leave without the bodies. I will burn each one of them.' Nur Afshan replied quietly, 'Afrasiyab, I have given you lessons along with Kaukab and taught you the ways of magic. For that reason, I will let you go or I would not have revealed my presence. Do not be arrogant about your powers or you will regret this forever!' Afrasiyab lost his temper and burst out, 'Nur Afshan I am the king of Tilism Hoshruba. There is no equal to me in magic or sorcery. It was a long time ago I came to you for lessons. If Samri and Jamshed were here, they would also acknowledge me as a superior. I am the creator of magic and the King of Sahirs. This iron ball will find its mark.'

Afrasiyab prepared to throw the ball again while Nur Afshan stood calmly before him. Suddenly, the earth parted and Mahiyan Emerald-robe shot up and clung to Afrasiyab. She cried, 'Afrasiyab, what are you doing? Nur Afshan is very angry at this time. He is the most senior elder of the Tilisms of Nur Afshan and Hoshruba. The consequences of attacking him now will be terrible. This tent only has the bodies. Go and burn those birds with the souls in them. What will we do with these lifeless bodies of dust?' Afrasiyab still resisted, so Mahiyan just swooped him up in her arms and dived back into the earth with him. Nur Afshan remained standing before the tent. The sardars witnessed all this from a distance and returned to the tent. The earth parted again and this time, Kaukab and Brahmin stepped out of it. Kaukab asked for Amar as soon as he emerged from the earth. Amar appeared right away as he was hiding in Galeem nearby and said, 'Nur Afshan, I was watching everything and admired your courage. *Mashallah*, how bravely you stopped Afrasiyab.' Nur Afshan bowed his head modestly and replied, 'O king of ayyari, ever since Mashal came, the one concern I have had is that the birds holding the souls of our birds should be safe from harm. He will surely try and immolate them now.'

Indeed, Afrasiyab went straight to the place where the birds had been kept and found that the keeper Uqab Jadoo along with twelve thousand soldiers had been killed and the cages were missing as well. No one seemed to know how this had happened. Afrasiyab returned to his durbar trembling with rage. He wanted to strike the battle drums and fight, but Mahiyan had given strict instructions to Hairat before she left for Zulmat that on no account should Afrasiyab be allowed to fight that day. Hairat Jadoo then tried to distract Afrasiyab as best as she could.

On the other side, Nur Afshan sent for all the scattered sardars and ayyars. After everyone arrived, Nur Afshan asked Brahmin, 'Son, what did you do?' Brahmin replied, 'Ustad, I killed Uqab Jadoo.' Kaukab added, 'I brought all the cages with me, none of the birds have been harmed.' Everyone then moved to the pavilion specially erected for the purpose; Sarsar and Saba Raftar were also present there in different disguises. Then Nur Afshan declared, 'king of ayyars, bring out the blue-throat now. Indeed, you have done well, but beware that if there is an opening, that wretch is like air, he can escape easily.' Amar replied, 'I have closed all its orifices with a steel wire and have also wrapped it in the Net of Ilyas.' Nur Afshan said, 'So what should we do now?' Amar said, 'Just tell me one thing, is there a chance that the sardars can be brought back to life?' Nur Afshan replied, 'Inshallah! For this day I had said that the bodies should be preserved.' Amar looked satisfied and said, 'Then I will find a way of killing Mashal.' Amar sent for the largest cooking vessel in lashkar. The vessel was filled with two or three maunds of oil and a fire was lit under it. When the oil started to boil Amar took the blue-throat out from the Net of Ilyas.

Sarsar and Saba Raftar who were present there watched carefully and there was complete silence in the durbar. Only the birds holding the souls of Bahar, Burran, Baghban and other sardars fluttered restlessly in their cages. Amar threw the blue-throat into the bubbling hot oil. There was a deafening explosion as the blue-throat burnt to death. Everyone in the durbar was stunned. Several people fainted and even an experienced sahir like Nur Afshan trembled in his seat. Dreadful voices called out, 'You have killed me! My name was Mashal Jadoo!' Mashal lived up to his name and burned to death. For a whole hour after Mashal died, there was no movement in the durbar. When everyone had recovered from the shock, Nur Afshan sent for the birds with the souls and after a great deal of effort, managed to transfer the souls back into the bodies of the sardars. It has been written that Nur Afshan, Kaukab and Brahmin spent three days in the process of restoring the sardars back to life.

For a week after they had come back to life, the sardars remained anxious and nervous. They could not recall spells as their souls had been weakened. The three great sahirs spent another week in the lashkar; they tended to the sardars and honed their magical skills. As Nur Afshan took his leave of Amar, he said, 'It will be the end if Tareek Shakal-kash decides to confront us. She is a peerless sahira; no one can match her magical skills.' Amar smiled and replied, 'O Nur Afshan, there is no problem that cannot be solved. A believer should never give up hope.'

Thus, Kaukab, Brahmin and Nur Afshan left for their abodes while the lashkar of Islam celebrated yet another victory.

◦◦◦

36 Amar Meets Malika Tareek Shakal-Kash, Tareek Comes to Confront the Lashkar of Islam; Eventually, Qiran Kills Her

Afrasiyab was reassuring Hairat, 'Malika, to tell you the truth, I wanted the light of Mashal's life to be extinguished to pave the way for Dai Amah, Malika Tareek Shakal-kash. I will now inform her that Amar captured Mashal and it is time she emerged from the Dome of Darkness. She will be quite glad to leave it. You know that I have not neglected her all these years. Every evening, ten men are presented to her. She plays with them all night and tears them to pieces in the morning before consuming them. This is just her breakfast! In addition, I have arranged for her to have as much wine as she desires. She consumes hundreds of goblets every day. Not everyone can reach her abode. I will send Ta'oos Jadoo to her with my request. I am sure that she will be happy to oblige me.'

Afrasiyab then sent for his companion Ta'oos, wrote a letter to Tareek and instructed Ta'oos to relate to Tareek whatever had happened to Mashal and added, 'Tell her also that this is a difficult hour for her son.' While Afrasiyab was talking to Ta'oos, Amar was standing close by invisible in Galeem. He followed Ta'oos out of the durbar and as the messenger was preparing to sprout wings to fly off, Amar rendered him unconscious with a narcotic bubble, dragged him behind a bush and pulled his clothes off. Disguised as Ta'oos, Amar set out for the Dome of Darkness.

After a long and arduous journey through Zulmat, Amar reached the Dome of Darkness. He saw that there were hundreds of sahirs holding drums and flutes standing at the entrance to the Dome. They were startled on seeing him and asked, 'O sahir, how did you manage to reach here? No spell can work here. How is it that you have not been burnt to ashes?' Amar declared, 'I am Ta'oos Jadoo, trusted companion of Shahanshah. I long wished to meet Dai Amah and Shahanshah obliged me by telling me the way to reach here. Tell Malika Tareek that her son's messenger is at her door and anxious to lay eyes on her peerless beauty.' One Brahmin approached the dome and called out, 'O Companion of Samri and Jamshed, the light of your eyes has sent his messenger Ta'oos Jadoo.' A loud voice that shook the whole dome boomed, 'Send the messenger in.'

Amar lifted the curtain and stepped into the dome. He saw an ogress with a head as big as a dome, her tongue lolling out of her mouth dripping saliva, swaying on the floor as she leaned on both hands. Ten young men sat on one side trembling in fear. Earthenware wine pitchers were arranged besides the ogress. She lifted one pitcher and drank from it until it was empty, then grabbed one of the young men and started munching on his leg, biting through the bone. After she had eaten him, she turned her attention to Amar. As he looked at her fearsome face, Amar was about to faint with fear. He was mute with terror and sweat dripped down his face. Tareek burped and her mouth emitted smoke that covered Amar's face. The paints of ayyari immediately peeled off Amar's face. He knew he was exposed and died a thousand deaths. Tareek smiled, 'How are you doing Khwaja sahib? What has happened to your disguise?' Even though Tareek had spoken gently, the dome resounded with her voice.

Amar fell at her feet and pleaded, 'Dai Amah, I long wanted to meet you. See how I bravely travelled through fire to reach you.'

Tareek probed his limbs and cried, 'Why, your body is nothing but bones!' She held him by his neck and was about to suck his blood when Amar desperately recited a verse in praise of her beauty. Amar sang the verse out so that Tareek swayed and said, 'You have a beautiful voice!' She dropped him on the floor and said, 'Come and serve me wine and sing a love poem for me. Your voice appeals to my ears.' Amar said, 'Dai Amah, how am I supposed to serve you wine from these pitchers? I will not even be able to lift one of them!' Tareek gave him a porcelain bowl to dispense the wine. Amar sat down respectfully before her and thought, 'Amar, she will not leave you alive, do what you have to right now. You are just a mouthful for her. Look how she chews up these young men and sucks their bones.'

Amar filled the porcelain bowl with wine and added a sleeping draught to it. Tareek finished the bowl in one gulp, but seemed to be impervious to the potion. She asked for more and this time Amar increased the dose. Tareek bellowed with laughter and said, 'Amar, you have pleased me today. For years I have been drinking this wine but it gave me no pleasure. I am so happy today. Mix what you will in it, and do not hide it from me.' Tareek was in a state of great excitement; she ran around the dome like a mad elephant, sometimes with Amar on her shoulders. Every time she burped, she exhaled black smoke. She even sang to Amar who was terrified by the deafening sound of her voice. Finally, she sat down again and asked Amar, 'Tell me what you have mixed in my wine? Bring it out. Amar reluctantly took out the sleeping potion and said, 'My master Hamza Sahibqiran is very partial to this potion. I believe it has strengthening powers. It improves the eyesight and refreshes the soul. It is because of this that Hamza can fight the mightiest wrestlers.'

Amar then added the rest of the potion to Tareek's bowl of wine. She drank it with satisfaction and threw a strand of pearls at the ayyar. Amar bowed low to thank her, but his limbs were quivering with fear as he wondered what would happen next. 'Amar, you will mix these potions in my wine every day,' declared Tareek, 'for from today I appoint you my special companion.' Amar gingerly took out Afrasiyab's message for Tareek. She smiled as she saw the letter and said, 'Khwaja, Ta'oos Jadoo whom you had rendered unconscious must be with Afrasiyab now. I had arranged it from here through my magical spirits.' Amar folded his hands and said ingratiatingly, 'Dai Amah, had I not disguised myself, how would I have been blessed with your vision?' Tareek shook her massive head and said, 'You wretch, you had come here to kill me. Draw your sword on me and let us see what happens. You fool, I have seen the eyes of Samri! Do not think I am like Mashal who used to stand all night with a lamp in his hands. You thought you could kill me, but what do you think of me now?' Amar fell at her feet and pleaded, 'Tareek, in truth I have never come across anyone with powers like yours. You really are the personification of Samri!'

Tareek laughed and replied, 'Khwaja, you are no less of an ayyar yourself. I will leave this hujra now, as I must save my child's empire. You will take my message back to him.' Amar protested that Afrasiyab would arrest him, but Tareek reassured him that she would instruct him not to arrest Amar, but reward him instead. She asked him, 'Tell me only this. Will you play a trick on me again?' Amar said he would leave Tilism and never turn his face towards the Dome of Darkness again. He added, 'I beseech you to give me leave and send another messenger to Afrasiyab.' To this, Tareek said, 'Why are you so afraid? I am doing you a favour. It is a long journey and you could wander around for ages in the mountains. With my help, you will reach there soon and you will be rewarded as well.'

Amar decided not to resist her further in case she lost her temper and gobbled him up alive. In her letter to Afrasiyab, Tareek wrote, 'Light of mine eyes, your message reached us through Amar. Indeed this ayyar has entertained and pleased us very well. When you receive this message, reward him well. Do not punish him for his past sins, but give him money. We will shortly emerge from our hujra.' Tareek then sealed the letter with her special seal and gave it to Amar. She moulded a peacock from lentil flour, breathed life into it and asked Amar to mount it. Amar mounted the peacock still trembling with fear. Tareek said to him, 'Magic bird, take Amar to Afrasiyab's durbar. He is my special companion and should experience no discomfort on the journey.' The peacock flew off with Amar, who slowly recovered his wits as he travelled back to Hoshruba. He took out a crown from Zambil and wore it while he was still on the peacock. He thought to himself, 'No point in worrying, the Almighty will look after me.'

Mahrukh, Bahar and the other sardars were sitting outside their durbar pavilion when Amar flew overhead on the magic bird. Soldiers shouted, 'The king of ayyars is flying on a peacock!' Mahrukh looked up and was startled at the sight of Amar wearing rich garments with a crown on his head. Bahar and Baghban rose to stop him, but Amar shouted down, 'I am the companion of Malika Tareek. Beware O Muslims, do not try and stop me or I will kill each one of you!' Amar also called out to the ayyars,

'You deceitful rogues, leave Tilism now or you will be torn apart and eaten by Malika of the world when she arrives here!'

Sarsar Sword-fighter and Saba Raftar Fleet-foot who were loitering at the edge of the lashkar also heard Amar and rushed to inform Afrasiyab. Sarsar laughed as she said, 'Huzoor, come outside and see Amar. He is on a flying peacock and abusing his own people. He claims he is the special companion of Tareek Shakal-kash.' Afrasiyab snorted, 'He must have heard of her somewhere. How can he claim to know Dai Amah? No one can reach the Dome of Darkness.' The bird took Amar into the durbar and then flew off again. Khwaja greeted Afrasiyab and then handed him Tareek's letter. Afrasiyab read Tareek's message and looked in awe at Amar. He asked, 'Khwaja, you went to the Dome of Darkness?' Amar retorted, 'Not only that, I am now in your service. Give me my salary as the letter instructs.' Afrasiyab said slowly, 'Indeed this is what the letter reads.' He offered Amar a chair and was still stunned when Hairat asked Amar, 'Tell me truthfully Amar, how did you manage to reach it?' Amar related his adventures on the journey while everyone listened to him in awe. Eventually, he rose and took his leave, adding, 'I will try and convince Mahrukh and the others to capitulate. Perhaps, they may agree.'

Afrasiyab presented him with a robe and five sacks of gold coins, as he could not go against Tareek's orders. Amar left the durbar happily and returned to his lashkar. Mahrukh had been pacing her durbar, and worrying about this new turn of events when Barq ran into the durbar and announced Amar's arrival. All the sardars clustered around Amar and Bahar clung to him as she asked, 'Khwaja, what was all this about?' Amar explained the situation to the sardars. Meanwhile, Afrasiyab happily prepared for his foster mother's arrival. He erected a gold-embroidered pavilion for her and instructed Sarmaya, Abriq and other noble sardars to arrange for huge vats of wine for Tareek. Just as the preparations were complete, messengers informed Afrasiyab, 'Huzoor, your respected Dai Amah has left the Dome of Darkness in splendour and is travelling with a lashkar of a lakh and fifty thousand sahir soldiers.' Afrasiyab set off on horseback to receive Tareek while Hairat left on a large flying throne with her companions around her.

Her spy birds also informed Mahrukh Magic-eye that Tareek was to arrive that day and that Hairat and Afrasiyab had left to receive her. The sardars looked at each other in alarm and Amar said, 'I had better hide. If she sees me she is bound to call me to her.' As he vanished in Galeem, the sardars turned to Mahrukh and said, 'Let that man-eater arrive. You should convene your durbar as usual.' At Mahrukh's signal, the durbar was convened outdoors. Asad left the lashkar after the sardars decided that he should be hidden away from the lashkar with his personal ayyar Zargham and a few other guards. The other ayyars also left the lashkar in various disguises. By this time, Hairat's litter had reached the edge of her lashkar. There was a feeling of anticipation as everyone waited to see Tareek. Soon, distant sounds of trumpets and drums could be heard. The earth trembled and a sahir army came into sight holding hundreds of flags. Amar watched from behind a tree when Afrasiyab rode towards Hairat and said, 'Malika, get ready! Dai Amah's throne approaches.' He then cantered off again at great speed.

A little later, everyone saw a huge black ogress seated on a throne, her tongue hanging out as she leaned forward on both hands. As everyone watched, she picked up a large vat of wine, guzzled it down, and then started munching on the raw leg of a bull. Fresh blood trickled down her chin and down her vast black bosom. She threw her head back, burped loudly and emitted thick gusts of black smoke. In the pavilion, Tareek made Afrasiyab sit next to her. After consuming several goblets of wine, she bellowed, 'Afrasiyab you have called me for nothing! Who am I supposed to fight—these miserable slaves? None of them can match me in magic. They are animals. I can tear them apart and eat them!'

Afrasiyab replied, 'Dai Amah, listen carefully. It is not just these rebels. They have the support of the King of Tilism Nur Afshan, Kaukab the Enlightened as well as his teachers Brahmin Iron-body and Nur Afshan Jadoo, who have become my enemies. Whenever the rebels are being defeated, Kaukab and Brahmin help them out.' Tareek laughed ominously and said, 'Son, who are Kaukab and Brahmin that they dare challenge the sahirs of Hoshruba? Look, I will use my magic amulet. Kaukab and Brahmin will soon be here with their hands folded!' Amar was also present in the durbar invisible in Galeem. He was alarmed by Tareek's claim and prayed to the Almighty to save his friends.

Meanwhile, Afrasiyab offered Tareek roasted sheep meat, but she laughed and said, 'My son, this will not satisfy me. I would prefer the flesh of two men as I am hungry after so much wine.' Afrasiyab looked down at the ground uncomfortably. The curtains of the pavilion had been pulled up and Tareek spotted two travellers in the distance. She rose from her throne and fell on the travellers like a bolt of lightning. She returned holding them both by the neck and tore them apart as she made a meal of them. She did not even leave their bones. Some people in the durbar fainted with fear while Amar thought he would die right there.

Tareek seemed satisfied after her meal and burped loudly. She brought out the magic amulet of Samri and said, 'Afrasiyab, look, this is what

magic is all about.' The ogress screamed, 'Ya Samri! Ya Jamshed!' and
the pavilion shook with the sound of her voice. Tareek held the amulet
in her palm and muttered words of magic. At the time, Kaukab of the
radiant conscience was presiding over his durbar in Jamshedi palace. As
Tareek held the amulet in her hand, Kaukab lost his colour and seemed
agitated. He started to tremble and looked visibly disturbed. His vizier
Khurshid folded his hands and asked, 'Shahanshah, is all well with you?'
Kaukab struck his thigh and said, 'O great vizier, I have made a grave
mistake by making an enemy of a mighty king like Afrasiyab for the
likes of Amar ayyar! You people should have advised me against it.' As
the vizier looked alarmed, Kaukab wept and said, 'O wise vizier, tell me
how can I get out of this situation in order to save my kingdom and my
children?' Khurshid replied, 'Huzoor, Afrasiyab is no one before you.
Look how many times you have confronted him and won.' Kaukab rose
abruptly and said, 'You people want me to lose my kingdom! I will consult
with my old and loyal friend Brahmin. I will do as he tells me.' Kaukab
then conjured a flying throne and left alone for Brahmin's palace in an
agitated state, leaving behind a completely mystified durbar.

Tareek's amulet had a similar effect on Brahmin Iron-body. His
companions asked, 'Huzoor, we find you agitated! Whatever is the
matter?' Brahmin cried, 'Friends, I am suddenly aware of my fate!
Shahanshah Kaukab did a terrible thing by quarrelling with a great
Shahanshah like Afrasiyab! He did not think of his misfortune!' His
companions retorted, 'Huzoor, who is Afrasiyab? We will knock his teeth
out and he will run from us in battle!' At that moment, a light flashed in
the sky and Brahmin looked up to see Kaukab's throne descend. Brahmin
rushed to greet him and kissed the base of the throne saying, 'Shahanshah,
I was about to visit you. I have learned that Afrasiyab has mobilized for
another battle.' Kaukab said, 'Brother, he does not need a lashkar. Tareek
Shakal-kash has arrived. She will first destroy Tilism Nur Afshan. Who
can stop her?' Brahmin replied, 'Shahanshah, we should both go to
Afrasiyab and fall at his feet. He is a generous monarch and is bound to
forgive our faults.' Kaukab then said, 'I am even more anxious than you
are. Let us go at once.' Both men left for Hoshruba as dressed as humble
supplicants. Kaukab took his crown off and wore an old cap. Brahmin
dressed in crumpled clothes. On the journey, both spoke to each other
pessimistically and feared the worst for themselves.

The flight took them over Nur Afshan's palace and they saw him
pacing on the roof, looking visibly disturbed. Kaukab said, 'My friend,
let us take Ustad with us as well.' 'You are right,' said Brahmin, 'he is the
one who is responsible for this mess.' Nur Afshan was waiting for them

as they landed and greeted them affectionately. Before he could say anything else, Kaukab said, 'Ustad, have you heard that Tareek is out of her hujra? Where will we hide from her? We have made an enemy of the powerful Afrasiyab! Both of us are going to Afrasiyab to beg for mercy. It is up to him now to forgive or punish us. Did you not anticipate this? You were our elder and should have advised us better.' Nur Afshan embraced both his pupils and said, 'Indeed, I have been at fault and I will do whatever you want me to. Tareek is my friend and has great affection for me. She will have us forgiven and we can fight Mahrukh and Amar from Afrasiyab's side. He will be very pleased.'

Kaukab and Brahmin looked relieved and urged him to accompany them at once. Nur Afshan, however, led them to the masnad seating and offered them wine to refresh themselves. Both Kaukab and Brahmin were reluctant, but Nur Afshan insisted that they have a goblet each. As soon as they had drunk the wine, they felt very sleepy and told him they would like to rest. Nur Afshan then led both his disciples to a sleeping chamber where they fell on the beds and fell into a deep sleep. Nur Afshan locked the chamber and then went to another part of the palace where the magic replicas of Kaukab and Brahmin emerged before him and left on a flying throne. Nur Afshan called out to them, 'You go ahead. I will be there soon.'

Meanwhile, in Afrasiyab's durbar, Khwaja Amar was still present hidden in Galeem when Tareek held the amulet in her hand and claimed that Kaukab and Brahmin would arrive soon. Amar thought, 'Will that really happen?' Suddenly, there were shouts from outside and some men ran into the durbar and informed Afrasiyab breathlessly, 'Kaukab and Brahmin have arrived on a flying throne but they look quite distraught.' Amar ran outside to look and was alarmed to see that Kaukab and Brahmin had really arrived. He wanted to waylay them, but they had already entered the pavilion. Both walked up to Tareek and greeted her. Kaukab said, 'Tareek, you have sent for us by the power of the amulet of Jamshed. Speak to us without the amulet. We will tell you what has happened between Afrasiyab and us. If we are at fault, you can punish us. If you really want us to speak to you, you should burn the amulet. We will not talk otherwise'

Tareek lost her temper and tossed the amulet into the nearest brazier. It burst into flames and emitted thick smoke. Tareek watched it burn and then turned to Kaukab, 'So now reveal to me the whole story of the rebellion and your role in it. I will make sure that Afrasiyab and you reconcile.' Kaukab laughed and said, 'Tareek, did you think you could actually send for Kaukab and Brahmin into your durbar? Did you really believe that your amulet could work on Kaukab, almighty monarch, and the valiant Brahmin? We are merely the slaves of Nur Afshan the magic-wielder. He sent us lowly slaves to blacken your face!'

Tareek watched in horror as Kaukab and Brahmin transformed into little Zangi slave-boys before her very eyes. She got up in a mighty rage, but the two slaves laughed and stamped hard on the ground so that it cleaved open. Before anyone could stop them, they disappeared into the earth. Tareek roared in anger, 'How dare Nur Afshan play this trick on me? He made me destroy the powerful amulet. Watch what destruction I cause now!'

Tareek's house of smoke

Tareek stamped out of the pavilion in a mighty rage. Afrasiyab was still in a state of shock, but Amar followed her out of the pavilion, frightened out of his wits. Mahrukh and Bahar were also informed by their spies that Tareek was in great anger. Both of them rushed out without shoes and veils in their eagerness to see her. As everyone watched fascinated, Tareek made her way to the open plain beyond the lashkar and squatted on the ground. She opened her foul mouth wide and emitted thick black smoke in vast quantities. The smoke billowed and assumed the shape of a huge house. Tareek conjured two slave-boys to guard the entrance and called to Afrasiyab, 'Send me my wine here. I have left the Dome of Darkness after two hundred years and feel like living in the open desert. I will fight tomorrow. Nur Afshan, Kaukab and Brahmin, Mahrukh and Bahar will all be destroyed. My magic will be revealed!'

That evening, there were excited speculations in Afrasiyab's camp. People said amongst themselves, 'Tomorrow morning, Mahrukh's lashkar will be destroyed. We will get rich when we plunder their camp. These people have amassed huge wealth. They get large tributes from the cities they have conquered!'

Both lashkars prepared for the battle the next morning in their own manner; Muslim soldiers kneeled on their prayer mats, while sahirs worshipped before their idols. Believers called on the Almighty for help, while sahirs called out the names of Samri and Jamshed. Afrasiyab woke up abruptly. He worshipped his gods and emerged in the battlefield to the sound of conch shells and kettledrums. Hairat also emerged on a wooden throne. Tareek came out from her house of smoke and laughed in derision when she saw the Islamic lashkar. She called out to Afrasiyab, 'They are a mouthful for me. I will finish them off in a day!' Tareek signalled to her slave-boy, 'Go and challenge them. I have a bad taste in my mouth. After wine, I would like some living flesh!' The slave-boy walked into the battlefield and called out, 'Traitors of salt and rebels, whoever amongst you wants a taste of death should come out now!'

Princess Nafarman confronts Tareek

Mahrukh's sardars responded to the challenge with fervour. The first one to come forward as usual was the brave Princess Nafarman. Baghban Qudrat protested violently to this, as did the other sardars, for they felt that it was better for everyone to attack together rather than go out one by one. Nafarman said firmly, 'Stop weeping now. You can weep for me after I have gone!' Everyone then blessed Nafarman as she walked forward. As Nafarman left the lashkar, her face seemed ashen, but her heart was content. Her attendants and companions were in a state of frenzy as she faced certain death. Some had opened their hair in grief while others wept openly.

When Nafarman faced the slave-boy, he threw a grain of lentil at her that she deflected neatly. Meanwhile, Tareek kept urging him to bring her human flesh. 'I am very hungry!' she shouted. The slave-boy screamed 'Ya Samri, Ya Jamshed!' once so that the very earth shook with the sound. Everyone saw Nafarman tremble like the morning flame of a candle and then fall in a dead faint on the ground. The slave-boy got hold of her leg and dragged her inert body mercilessly back to his mistress. Tareek emerged happily from the house of smoke, her body swaying, her face horribly distorted. She lifted Nafarman by the feet and ripped her apart before munching her flesh.

Afrasiyab trembled with fear while Hairat fainted right there. Tareek continued to consume Nafarman and even chewed her bones. Meanwhile, four of Nafarman's companions also came forward. The slave-boy and Tareek dealt with them in a similar manner. In the evening, Tareek drew back into the house of smoke and called her slave-boy back from the battlefield. As she disappeared, she called out, 'O Muslims, this was a small example of my magic!' Tareek continued to fight in this way for the next seven days. Several sardars met their ends and went to the Eternal Garden of Peace. Those shining stars hid behind the dark firmament forever. Mahrukh Magic-eye sent for Amar on the seventh evening and said, 'O king of ayyari, do something so that whoever falls in the fighting is kept in captivity. When we are all captured, then we can be punished or reprieved.'

Nur Afshan's plan

Amar was also very agitated at the turn of events and left immediately to meet Nur Afshan. Nur Afshan came out of his palace to welcome Amar and greeted Amar with great politeness and courtesy. After he had seated Amar in a place of honour in the palace, Nur Afshan began weeping and said, 'O king of ayyari, I am well aware of Tareek's menace but cannot think of what to do about it.' Amar said, 'Nur Afshan, you have known her for long. The Almighty has blessed you with the light of Islam while she is a devil. If you think it is appropriate, write a nama to her. Tell her that it is not proper to tear our sardars and devour them the moment she captures them. Tell her to behave like nobility. If they do not agree to her demands, she can then do what she wants with them.' Nur Afshan agreed to write the letter at once and said, 'I can either send it or give it to you.' Amar thought it best to take the letter himself and said, 'I will deliver it to her personally.'

Nur Afshan then carefully composed a letter to Tareek and handed it to Amar who went straight to Afrasiyab. As he greeted the King of Magic, Afrasiyab smiled benignly and asked, 'How are you Khwaja?' Amar replied, 'With the grace of the Almighty I am well. You are the victor now and we are the vanquished. It is not appropriate that your foster mother eats up whichever sardar she captures. I have brought a message from Nur Afshan. Please accompany me to her abode and present me to her. I will speak to her myself.' Afrasiyab agreed and Sarsar Sword-fighter, who was also present, remained silent. Hairat exclaimed, 'He might try and trick them!' Sarsar reassured her that he could not. She said, 'None of his tricks will work on Dai Amah. Wherever drugs do not work, the ayyar is helpless. Our lashkar also believes that we should capture the sardars, but not kill them in this manner. Only Asad Ghazi and the six ayyars should be put to death.'

Afrasiyab brought Amar to Tareek's smoky palace and asked her slave-boys to announce him to Tareek. A little later, she emerged from the smoke. Baghban Qudrat and Mahrukh Magic-eye watched from a distance as Amar greeted her and Afrasiyab sat down on the ground respectfully. As soon as Tareek laid eyes on Amar, she bellowed with laughter, 'My companion of old, have you concocted a potion for my wine?' Amar replied, 'I am trying but it is difficult to obtain all the herbs required for it.' Tareek grabbed his neck and cried, 'Why you wretch, you are lying to me! I will eat you right now.' As Tareek opened her mouth to swallow him, Amar yelped, 'I have got a little potion on me.' She let go of him at once and said, 'Then serve me some wine and sing me a love song. I know the reason you are here you wretch!'

Afrasiyab whispered to Amar, 'You had better serve her a few bowls of wine. She can eat you any time.' Amar reluctantly took out the powder of unconsciousness and mixed it in a bowl of wine, complaining to Afrasiyab that he was incurring a loss. Afrasiyab promised to make it up to him. Amar served the brimming bowl to Tareek, who lapped it up and burped loudly. 'Amar do you like my face,' she cried. 'You wretch, you seem to eat me up with your eyes! I like the way you sing, I feel great affection for you.'

Amar folded his hands and said, 'It has been a long time since I have forsworn love. Had I been younger, I would have dedicated my life to a beauty like you.' Amar handed her another goblet of wine. Tareek was delighted. She snatched a string of pearls off Afrasiyab neck and placed it around Amar's neck, then said, 'Amar, now sing me a nice love song. Praise my beauty. Samri and Jamshed used to really like me.' Amar forced himself to sing a poem in which he compared Tareek's tresses to snakes. After Amar had finished singing and plying Tareek with wine, she said, 'What brings you to me my companion?'

Khwaja Amar presented her with Nur Afshan's message. She read it, shook her head and said, 'This will not be acceptable to me!' When Amar persisted, she said, 'Khwaja, you will have to promise me my rations of live men. I will imprison whoever I capture, but you will have to provide me with ten men every day. This I do only for you and not for Nur Afshan. He was Samri's companion, but has turned his back on the ancient religion.' Amar was silent and after thinking for some time said, 'Very well, I promise. I will provide you with ten men every day.' Tareek then said, 'You had better keep your promise. If you do not, I will charge into your lashkar and eat a hundred men instead of ten. Make sure that I get my breakfast; otherwise, I will create hell for you. I have taken this long just to terrify Afrasiyab's former allies into submission again or I would have eaten them long since.' Amar promised that he would not go against his word and left the palace of smoke with Afrasiyab.

In Mahrukh's durbar, the sardars were silent and worried. As soon as Amar entered the durbar, Mahrukh asked, 'So what decision was taken Khwaja?' Amar sighed deeply, 'What can I tell you? She declared that she would leave no one alive. Eventually, I had to promise her ten men every day. In turn, she will imprison the sardars defeated in battle.' Mahrukh looked shocked and cried, 'How will you provide her with ten men every day?' Amar replied quietly, 'We will have to do it somehow and the day we cannot, we six ayyars will offer ourselves to her. Even today, I had to waste so much of my precious drug and it did not have the slightest effect on her. On the contrary, she wants to get the formula from me to enliven her wine! She picked me up as if I was a lizard! Only my Allah saved me from her or she would have eaten me alive! How does one fight an ogress like her?'

Amar then beckoned Qiran and Barq, whispered some instructions to them and then said, 'Tell the others as well.' Both ayyars said, 'Huzoor, do not worry, we will arrange this.' Qiran merely added, 'Ustad, this was a terrible promise you made to her.' Amar replied, 'My son, what else could I do?' That night, Amar and the ayyars wandered around trying to arrange a meal for Tareek. The night ended and the executioner of the day emerged on the horizon holding the sword of light in his hands. Both lashkars came to the battlefield. Tareek's head emerged from the smoke and signalled to her warrior slaves pacing outside. One of them approached the battlefield and called out, 'Malika Mahrukh, are you not going to send someone to die today?'

No sooner had he said this when Makhmoor Red-eye arrived on her magic peacock. As the slave-boys prepared to attack her, Afrasiyab's expression froze in fear and he called out, 'Makhmoor, run from him, he comes to attack you!' Makhmoor ignored him and faced her attacker. The slave-boy aimed an iron ball at her, but Makhmoor conjured lightning that shattered the ball. As Tareek watched through the smoke, Makhmoor fell on the slave-boys in a flash and sliced him in two parts with her sword. A fountain of blood spurted from the slave-boy's body and a voice called out, 'You have killed me, my name was Slave of Malika Tareek!' Tareek trembled with rage and signalled to the other slave-boy who attacked Makhmoor ferociously. Soon, Makhmoor's sword dropped from her hand and she fell unconscious. The slave picked her up and went towards Tareek. Amar rushed forward towards Tareek as well and said, 'Dai Amah, please keep your promise. Arrest Makhmoor and I will provide you with ten young men!' Tareek agreed to Amar's request and tossed Makhmoor into a corner of the house of smoke.

Qiran then came forward dragging ten men tied to an iron chain. Tareek happily took the chain from him and immediately set on the poor men. After Makhmoor had been captured, her attendants confronted the magic slave-boy, who captured them as well. Tareek tossed them into the smoke with their mistress. That evening, the defeated sardars of Islam returned to their camp throwing dust on their heads in grief and frustration.

Amar's duplicity

From that day on, Amar provided Tareek with ten men every day. Over the next few days, Tareek captured forty more sardars from the rebel camp. On the seventh day, several men from Afrasiyab's army came wailing to him. A startled Afrasiyab asked them if all was well. They wept and pleaded, 'Huzoor, there are strange things happening in Hoshruba!' Each in turn informed them of how their brother, son, and others went missing suddenly. 'We have searched everywhere for them. It seems that the earth has swallowed them or a lightning from the sky has annihilated them.'

Afrasiyab first thought that Tareek was eating them, but did not voice his suspicion. He comforted his men and promised to find their missing kin. After they left the durbar, Afrasiyab walked over to the house of smoke and found Tareek's slave-boys guarding the entrance. He was admitted in, where he said, 'Dai Amah, several men from my lashkar are missing. I hope you are not in the habit of pouncing on them at night.' Tareek replied, 'Afrasiyab, I swear on your head, I go hungry, but have never gone into your lashkar. That is the reason why I live away from camp. However, if I see a passing traveller, I cannot resist the temptation of pouncing on him. Besides that, Amar arranges my breakfast. He brings me the most succulent young men. You used to provide me with sickly, bony old men, but ever since Amar provides the men, I am quite satisfied.'

Afrasiyab persisted, 'But Dai Amah, what has happened to my missing men?' Tareek retorted, 'How should I know? You are badshah of your lashkar! Find out yourself! I am in seclusion here; it is no concern of mine.' Sarsar Sword-fighter, who was with Afrasiyab and listening to this exchange, suddenly laughed and exclaimed, 'Why not?' Afrasiyab looked enquiringly at her. Sarsar said, 'Shahanshah, I have just thought of something. Samri and Jamshed guard my tongue, perhaps I have the answer.' She then whispered in his ear, 'Huzoor, I was very surprised when Amar promised to deliver ten men every day. The adherents of Islam do not believe in class distinctions and respect their subordinates. Perhaps that is why they have such loyal followers. Maybe their ayyars kidnap ten men from your lashkar everyday and after disguising their faces, deliver them to Malika Tareek.'

Afrasiyab looked at Tareek guzzling down barrels of wine and burping. She had already torn and eaten four of the men provided for her breakfast. The rest were moaning in fright, clearly unable to speak. Sarsar said, 'Huzoor, all the signs are there. Look at their swollen throats. Perhaps the ayyars have gagged them with balls. Please tell Dai Amah not to touch them and we will find out who they are.' Afrasiyab approached one of the prisoners, peered into his mouth and extracted the ball stuffed into his throat. The man cried out, 'Huzoor, I am your coachman's brother!' The coachman rushed into the house of smoke and embraced his brother howling in relief. 'My brother,' he cried, 'you were so fair, what has happened to your colour.' Sarsar suggested that the prisoner's face be washed.

As real faces and identities emerged from underneath the paints of ayyari, the prisoners turned out to be related to someone or the other in Afrasiyab's lashkar. There was an outcry among Afrasiyab's men and they started to shout in protest, 'What kind of a ruler is this who has his own men killed. What kind of Dai Amah is this (may her mouth be filled with dust) who has eaten members of our families!' There was general resentment in the lashkar and the soldiers shouted loudly about deserting their posts: 'A curse on such a job, we would rather beg for our living. Amar has been so clever. He promised her that he would deliver ten of his own men. Instead, he delivered our sahirs. This wretched man-eater ate them without any qualms!'

On hearing wailing from the lashkar, Tareek shouted, 'Afrasiyab, what is happening? You have denied me my breakfast! I promise I will eat everyone alive here!' Afrasiyab came forward and said, 'Then eat me first! You are so inebriated all the time you have no idea of what you are doing. Amar promised you ten men and then delivered my men to you! This is how you have favoured me? You have destroyed my lashkar!'

Tareek's revenge

Tareek shook with rage when she heard this. She screamed, 'Do you mean to tell me that camel driver's son has dared to pull a trick on me and made me eat your servants?' Burping out smoke, Tareek rose from her place and stomped out of her house. Amar and the ayyars were confiding in Mahrukh, 'The secret will be out soon, Afrasiyab's lashkar is restless. We cannot find more men for her now; she has eaten hundreds of them already.' As they talked, there was an outcry in the lashkar. Mahrukh and the others emerged from the durbar pavilion to investigate and saw Tareek attacking their lashkar in a fury. She was reaching out for men, tearing them from limb to limb and chewing their bodies on the spot. Pavilions and tents were collapsing with a swipe of her hand and as people struggled to escape, she tore them apart.

The sardars of Islam rallied forth to save their lashkar from destruction. Barq Lameh flashed up as lightning in the sky and fell on Tareek. The ogress merely waved her hand and squashed her like a fly. The sardars tried the most powerful war spells on her, but could not hurt even a single hair of her body. Ra'ad shrieked and his mother Barq

Mehshar fell as a bolt of lightning; Mahrukh flung huge iron balls on Tareek, but she did not even wince. She continued on her path of bloody destruction, destroying pavilions and tearing battlelines. Afrasiyab wanted to follow her into the battlefield, but she shouted, 'Afrasiyab, don't you dare come here! I am not going to spare anyone today. Just watch the spectacle from a distance!'

Tareek then planted herself firmly in the midst of the Islamic lashkar. The sardars saw that Tareek's method of magic was unique. She neither chanted any incantations nor threw magic pebbles; she merely smashed enemy ranks and was impervious to all magical spells. Four hundred sardars attacked her in unison, but just managed to inflict surface wounds on her. Her skirt and blue shirt were covered with blood and she charged around the field like a mad fury. Within moments, there were rivers of blood all around. She tore young men apart and consumed them while tossing the older ones aside after sucking blood from their necks. Occasionally, she burped loudly and expelled smoke from her mouth.

Tareek spotted Mahrukh Magic-eye in the lashkar and called out, 'O Mahrukh, hand over Amar to me. He has tricked me and shamed me before my people. I will leave no one alive and will turn back only when I find that camel driver's son!' Mahrukh retorted, 'Malika Tareek, we have no authority over Amar. He saw you coming and fled in fear. He must have gone to his master Hamza. Please find him yourself and kill him but spare us your anger.' Tareek became even more enraged and shouted, 'You silly girl, do you think you can deceive me with such words? I honoured that wretch Amar by making him my companion and he dared to trick me?' Tareek once again fell on the lashkar and in sheer rage breathed fire on Mahrukh's pavilion, burning it to cinders. She then expelled flames from her mouth so that the trees caught fire like torches.

Finally, Mahrukh and her sardars and soldiers fled from Tareek in terror, hoping to hide in the mountains. Even as they ran, Tareek pursued them, terrorizing them even more. Afrasiyab stood besides his wife Hairat laughing at the plight of his enemies and cried, 'No one can face Dai Amah. Look at that rebel Baghban Qudrat flee now. Why did he go into the thicket in the first place? Did you see Dai Amah's magic today? She fights in the magical ways of Samri and Jamshed! I could have destroyed them as well but I thought it was better to subjugate them. Amar has destroyed them all today by trying to deceive her!'

Hairat was rubbing her palms in glee at the sight of her enemies fleeing when Sarsar came running and cried, 'Shahanshah, there is good news! The war will not be over even if Mahrukh and Bahar are killed. Tilism Kusha and his army will continue to fight. I have found out that after Tareek's arrival the Muslims arranged to hide Asad in a secret place two miles away. At this time, Asad does not know the dire state of his lashkar or he would have been the first one to draw his sword on Tareek. Just tell Dai Amah to attack his pavilion and eat him alive. Her appetite will be assuaged and your heart will also be at peace!'

Afrasiyab joyfully wrote a note to Tareek about this. She was still pursuing the Islamic army whose desperate cries could be heard for miles. They would run for a while and then turn to attack her, knowing very well that she was immune to their attacks. When Afrasiyab's message fluttered before Tareek, she snatched it from the air and read it with joy. Everyone was startled by the sound of her resounding laughter. Suddenly, Tareek turned away from the fleeing rebel lashkar and turned in the direction of Asad's tent. Mahrukh and Bahar stopped running and cried, 'Where do you think you are going?'

Mahrukh's son Shakeel had been deployed with a few other powerful sahirs to guard Asad. He almost lost his senses at the sight of the charging Tareek, but bravely stood in her path to stop her. Tareek was like an avalanche that no one could stop; Mahrukh's arrows merely glanced off her body. As Asad's soldiers attacked her with swords, she swatted them aside like flies and charged into the tent. She saw Asad seated on the masnad in great glory, his noble face shining like the sun. Tareek laughed loudly expelling gusts of smoke from her mouth that blinded everyone around Asad. Asad looked straight at her and reached for his sword, but Tareek screamed, 'You cruel wretch! You have been nothing but trouble for my son. You were probably not aware of me when you dared to claim yourself Tilism Kusha!'

Her screaming was so loud that Asad stumbled as he rose. She lifted him up, tore his legs apart and ferociously chewed his bones. Amar and the other ayyars had emerged from their hiding places in the hills. Amar wailed loudly, 'My friends, the time of death has come! I will not hold myself back now. Alas, she has eaten my brave boy. How will I face my honoured master now?' As the ayyars approached him, Amar looked at them and cried, 'Where is that young wretch Zargham? Where was he when his master was killed? I will strangle him with my own hands!' At that time, they saw Zargham running towards them from the desert. Amar saw him and shouted, 'Shameless one! Where were you when your master was eaten alive? Are you not sorry at all? Alas, my poor Asad did not even get a coffin or a proper burial! I am going to kill you here or take you to Tareek so you too can be torn apart! Perhaps then I will be content. I cannot bear to see you alive. There is blood in my eyes!'

Zargham protested lamely, 'Huzoor, how am I at fault? I had gone hunting when she attacked him. Did I tell her to do that? He was destined to die this way!' Amar was even more enraged, but Zargham put his arms around Amar and said, 'Sir just hear me first before you kill me!' He whispered something in Amar's ear and the great ayyar seemed to calm down. He called out, 'Friends, indeed Zargham is right. This was God's will.'

Baghban and the other sardars also declared in a similar vein, 'Our master has been killed—it was God's will. We will continue to fight and avenge his death which is like a black stain on our hearts.' Mahrukh whispered something to Mahjabeen and she too withdrew with her companions. Amar wrote an account of whatever had happened and sent it to Kaukab. The reader should be aware that the rest of the Islamic lashkar was highly agitated about Asad's horrible death.

Meanwhile, Afrasiyab began celebrating Asad's death. He now thought that the rebel sardars would beg his for mercy very soon. In his exultation, he sent a message to Tareek that read, 'Dai Amah, I will provide your special meals every day. I have stocked the maikhana with the choicest wines for you. Give the Muslims a week's respite; they will come pleading to join us again.' Accordingly Tareek sent a message to the Islamic camp, 'You can weep and wail for Asad for a week. We shall see then.' That week, Afrasiyab's army geared up for the final battle. Hordes of men rushed to be recruited in the army. Everyone talked about how Afrasiyab was after all a powerful Shahanshah who could destroy his enemies. Tareek paced restlessly in the palace of smoke. If she spotted any man passing by, she pounced on him like lightning, tore him apart and consumed him right there. Several of Afrasiyab's employees suffered this fate.

Vizier Sarmaya pleaded with Tareek, 'Dai Amah, this is your son's faithful servant, spare his life!' Tareek merely laughed and said, 'Sarmaya, this young man looked good to us. It is too late now, his death is certain.' She tore her victim apart in front of Sarmaya and gobbled him up. There was a wave of fear in Afrasiyab's lashkar as well for the men knew that Tareek did not distinguish between foe and friend when overcome by her fiendish appetite.

The final battle with Tareek

Thus came the last fateful night of the week. The moon trembled with fear as it passed into the Palace of the West with all the planets. From the House of the East, the sun-king emerged in the blue sky in all his glory. The people of Mahrukh's camp spent the night in agony and faced the terrible morning. The brave ones rose from their beds in trepidation and presented themselves in Mahrukh's durbar. Each met the other in great sadness and said, 'Let us embrace as we face this black peril today. It is certain death as Afrasiyab has vowed to destroy us all!' Malika Mahrukh Magic-eye emerged on her throne carried by her handmaidens. Mahrukh looked visibly sad. Bahar was the first among the sardars to bow down to her in mujra greeting. Mahrukh embraced her and then turned to the sardars to enquire after Khwaja Amar. They informed her that although they had seen him the evening before in a state of great despair, none of the ayyars were present at the time. Mahrukh declared, 'We know that Khwaja sahib must have a plan in his mind. He has sent Chalak somewhere and Barq and Qiran are missing. After all, they are not sahirs. They cannot fight with that shameless Tareek, but they will be thinking of us.'

Mahrukh's throne was surrounded by her sardars as it moved forward. They had not yet reached the battlefield when there were signs of Afrasiyab's arrival. As Afrasiyab rose from his throne, the air resounded with the thunderous sounds of a thousand bells and drums. He emerged into the battlefield accompanied by the beautiful Hairat who was seated on a throne carried by young, comely girls. Afrasiyab rode along her throne and to elevate her status, kept his hand on the base of her throne. Thus, this procession proceeded to the battlefield like a spring breeze. The sahir army called out, 'Indeed our Shahanshah can claim divinity. He is more powerful than Samri and Jamshed!' Afrasiyab's heart swelled with pride as he heard these cries. Meanwhile, Mahrukh and her army waited on the battlefield and watched Afrasiyab's arrival.

Tareek emerged from the house of smoke that was still guarded by her iron slave-boys. That morning, Tareek made an effort to adorn herself. She wore a richly embroidered wedding skirt and jewellery that appeared to be made of dark metal. Despite her nose ring, she looked as fearsome as the goddess Kali. Afrasiyab also trembled as he beheld her black face, while his sardars were quaking with fear. Tareek signalled to one of the slave-boys who strode out arrogantly and challenged the enemy in an abusive, insulting manner. Bahar, whose heart was heavy with grief, drew her magic peacock forward and asked for Mahrukh's permission to respond to the challenge. From a distance, Afrasiyab saw Bahar emerge and felt his heart constrict. He beat his chest and cried, 'Friends, look after her, lest she is torn apart by Dai Amah. Pray that her mouth fills with dust before she eats a beloved like Bahar!'

As Bahar drew closer, the magic slave-boy aimed an iron ball at her. Bahar smiled in response and the ball turned to head back towards the slave-boy. It would have burst in his chest, but the slave-boy quickly jumped out of the way. It fell instead on Afrasiyab's army and several men were injured. Tareek shouted, 'You shameless slave, capture her quickly so that I can whet my appetite now!' The slave-boy turned to attack Bahar again. Bahar swayed as she threw a bouquet in the air. There was an explosion of yellow dust and a shower of petals. Flower buds smiled and leaves clapped in joy, trees swayed on their trunks and yellow dust hid everything else from sight. Bahar intended the slave-boy to be completely enchanted so that he would attack Tareek at her behest.

Meanwhile Tareek was busy taking swigs of wine from a huge tub. After consuming it, she burped loudly emitting smoke, and called out, 'Is there any meat here?' The second magic slave-boy replied with his folded hands, 'O Leader of Samri Worshippers and Pride of Sahirs, ten men were provided for breakfast but you have consumed them. There is no meat left now.' Tareek roared in anger and looked towards the forest where two unfortunate travellers were on their way somewhere. Tareek swooped on them and after returning to her place, she tore them apart and munched on their flesh.

Bahar used this time to completely enchant the magic slave-boy who was now besotted with Bahar. He tried to get closer to her, but Bahar cried, 'Shameless one, do not approach me. If you claim true love, go and bring me the head of your maternal aunt Tareek! Fight my enemy for me!' She then placed a scimitar in the slave's hands and urged him to slay Tareek. The enchanted slave-boy turned to attack his mistress as Bahar returned to her own lashkar amidst a volley of praise from both sides. Afrasiyab was watching his foster-mother consume the two men and whispered to Hairat, 'This is terrible! Dai Amah does not spare even travellers now. My reputation in Tilism will be in shreds. If I had known this, I would never have opened the hujras of perils at all. After all, I am no less than anyone!'

While Tareek was busy consuming the travellers, the enchanted slave-boy returned and shouted, 'You cruel ogress, you dare to hurt Malika Bahar! I will punish you for this!' Tareek stood up in alarm and as the slave-boy attacked her with Bahar's sword, she held his hand and slapped him so hard that his head flew off his body. Tareek was now truly angry and shouted, 'Bahar, you dare to display such cheap magic tricks before me. I am one who defied even Samri and Jamshed! I have chewed up Asad Ghazi's bones. Today you will all meet your end!' Tareek went charging towards her enemies like a mad she-elephant.

The sardars of Islam saw the dreaded Tareek charge towards them and started running away. Some complained loudly that Bahar had really caused their deaths this morning; others suggested that if they fell at Afrasiyab's feet, he would forgive them. Most people, however, remained true to Mahrukh and put their faith in the Supreme Creator who had come to their rescue so many times before. Everyone girded up to face death as Tareek charged towards them and the earth trembled under her footsteps.

Brahmin and Tareek

Suddenly, the arrow of the prayer of innocent victims reached its target. There was a cloud of dust in the desert. As everyone looked, the dust clouds parted to reveal several lakh riders holding aloft flags inscribed with verses in praise of the Almighty. The flag-bearers were followed by Kaukab's brave commander Bilour Four-hands, who was leading a posse of several hundred armed riders. In the midst of this army, Kaukab's son Jamshed bin Kaukab sat on a ruby throne, while the noble Brahmin Iron-body rode besides him. Brahmin rode forward and saw that there was mayhem in Mahrukh's army. Mahrukh herself was bareheaded and praying desperately while Tareek was planted in the middle of the battlefield shouting, 'Bahar you have done a terrible deed with your magic. You have made me kill my own servant. Now you are hiding in the magic garden, but I will hunt you down there. It will be difficult to escape from me!'

Brahmin had seen enough. He jumped off his horse and approached Mahrukh Magic-eye. He kissed the base of her throne and said, 'O Monarch of the Worlds, permit me to respond to this wretch or die in your service!' Mahrukh embraced him as Tareek called out suddenly, 'O Mahrukh, send Bahar to me or I am coming. This wretched Brahmin child has come a long way. Why is he hiding and not coming before me?' Brahmin gently disengaged himself from Mahrukh. He walked to the battlefield like a brave lion with his sword balanced on his shoulder. Tareek started swaying as she saw Brahmin. She gestured to her slave-boy who came forward to confront Brahmin, who called out, 'O Tareek, you are now so arrogant that you send your slave to confront me?' Tareek fell silent at this. The slave-boy attacked Brahmin with his sword, but Brahmin held his wrist and wrenched the sword out of his grasp. The slave-boy tried to grapple with him, but Brahmin slapped him hard so that he fell on the ground. Brahmin then cut the slave-boy's head off and threw it towards Tareek.

Teachers of the word have written in this tale of glory and honour that whenever Tareek looked towards her house of smoke, a magic slave-boy would emerge forth crying, 'I am at your service.' Brahmin disposed of all of them with either his sword, with magic fire or with his bare hands. Tareek's eyes became blood red. She screamed in rage so that the earth trembled, the air became dense with yellow dust and buildings fell down. Hairat cried, 'Shahanshah, this is bad. Dai Amah is really angry!' Afrasiyab was also trembling and said, 'Malika, may Samri and Jamshed protect us. Brahmin's death is certain now.' Meanwhile Tareek and Brahmin were engaged in a fierce battle. Brahmin neutralized each of Tareek's ferocious spells. He wanted to get closer to her, but that firebrand screamed warnings and emitted flames from her hideous mouth. The trees in the forest burnt like torches. Tareek expelled smoke so that it formed a canopy in the sky and a sheet of flames descended from it on Brahmin. The incomparable Brahmin Iron-body conjured magic rain that cooled the flames and flew up like lightning to destroy the canopy of smoke.

He kept challenging Tareek to face him instead of hiding and casting spells. Enraged by his taunts, Tareek pulled the veil off her head and threw it at him. Everyone saw the veil descend on Brahmin like a sheet of blood and people cried, 'Brahmin is finished now!' Suddenly, Brahmin was seen flashing out of the sheet of blood like the glorious sun itself. As he emerged, he shot an iron ball at Tareek that hit her hard on the forehead. Tareek was spun off her feet with the impact, but steadied herself and bellowed so loudly that the ball shot towards the lashkar of Jamshed bin Kaukab and injured several hundred young men.

Brahmin continued to fight and Tareek realized that he was more than a match for her. She hurled a magic crescent at him and injured his shoulder. Brahmin then angrily attacked her with his sword and when she tried to resist him, he clamped her wrist with one hand and slapped her violently. Tareek's head would have blown off but she had breathed a counterspell so that Brahmin developed an enormous boil on his hand and his bones started to melt. He continued fighting, but was badly injured by then. Eventually, everyone saw Brahmin collapse on the ground.

Tareek triumphantly dragged Brahmin back to the house of smoke. Her cheek was swollen with the force of Brahmin's blow and she was injured and hungry. In sheer rage, she tore Brahmin's body apart and snapped her head down to bite his head; but, her tooth broke with the impact. She looked closely at the body and realized that it was made of clay while the head was made of stone. Everyone heard Tareek's howls of pain. Hairat returned to her pavilion and hid in fear. Afrasiyab rushed to be with her and saw that rivulets of blood were pouring out of Tareek's mouth and she was hollering in pain. He asked, 'Are you alright Dai Amah?

What has happened?' Before Tareek could reply, there was a flash of lightning in the sky and a voice called out, 'I am Shahanshah Nur Afshan! Tareek, you dared to eat the flesh of my son! Did you enjoy eating stone instead of meat? That was a clay replica I placed before you. Look, I am taking Brahmin away. Inshallah, I will deal with you later!'

Tareek wanted to fall upon Nur Afshan, but Afrasiyab held her hand and said, 'Dai Amah, let it go. Do not follow that old man!' Tareek shouted, 'I will tear that old man apart as well!' Afrasiyab held on to her hand and Tareek said to her foster son in disgust, 'Listen you wretch, I have been fighting and my belly is full of dust. My breakfast was digested long since. This Nur Afshan has given me a shock and I will kill every inmate of Tilism Nur Afshan in revenge. I am weak now, my mouth is bloody and my cheek is swollen. I protected myself with magic when Brahmin slapped me, otherwise I would have lost my head. Serve me wine and flesh quickly or I will eat you instead. My stomach is on fire!'

Afrasiyab was terrified and served her a vat of wine. In his haste; he got hold of two young men from his own army. They screamed for help, but their officers looked on helplessly as Afrasiyab threw them in front of Tareek. As the ogress tore their flesh apart, there was an outcry in the lashkar and Afrasiyab's soldiers started to desert in sheer terror. As they ran, there were cries of, 'Friends, save yourselves from this man-eater! The Shahanshah himself is helpless before her!'

The Turkish soldier

Mehtar Qiran and Barq Firangi were watching this spectacle from a distance. Qiran made himself up to look like a Turkish soldier with several war wounds and stitches. Barq and he decided that they would go and attack Tareek in her house to kill her, even if it meant risking their lives. They had just gone a few steps when they heard a voice saying, 'Brothers, do not go any further, wait for me!' Qiran and Barq thought Afrasiyab had recognized them when Nur Afshan appeared suddenly before them. He held Qiran's hand and said, 'O noble Mehtar, you cannot hope to vanquish Tareek. You are both very brave, but you will lose your lives.'

Qiran embraced Nur Afshan and wept helplessly. The old sahir consoled him and suggested that the three of them hold counsel privately. He led the two ayyars into the ravine of a mountain and said, 'O Qiran and O Barq, I have been more worried than you about this matter. I have brought the magic sword of Nur Afshan with me. This is the sword that is destined to kill Afrasiyab. The one who wields this sword will be impervious to any spells. I thought of fighting Tareek with this myself, but only you are worthy of holding it. I am sure your mighty blow will cleave that black-faced ogress in half. I will also be nearby to help you. Perhaps this plan may work.'

Qiran's face shone with joy and he said, 'O Nur Afshan, if magic does not affect me, I swear I can slay that man-eater. Otherwise, you can change my name.' Nur Afshan warned, 'Great Mehtar, do not think you can kill Tareek so easily. She is a highly intelligent creature. She is aware of the power of this sword! She will not allow you to come close to her. The whole army of Afrasiyab will surround you and Afrasiyab himself will fight you at the same time.' Qiran smiled and said, 'My God is my protector! Now just give me the sword and watch what happens!'

Meanwhile, Afrasiyab and Hairat were serving wine to Tareek after providing her with live men for her lunch. As she tore through her meal, Tareek said, 'Afrasiyab, for your sake, I left my ancient abode. I will now destroy all your rebels and make sure that you are the only power in this realm.' Afrasiyab was relishing her promises while Hairat softly urged her to spare the life of her sister Bahar. She pleaded, 'If she is killed, it will be a great slur on my name. I would like to just send her to my respected father, the noble Hayat.'

While they were talking, a guard informed Tareek that Afrasiyab's niece Armaan Jadoo had come with a Turkish slave and wanted to meet her. Tareek looked alarmed and said, 'Who is this Turkish slave with Armaan? I have a bad feeling about him.' Afrasiyab replied, 'He must be an old retainer. You know how protective her family is. They never let her go out alone.' The smoke parted to reveal a face whose beauty outshone the sun and the moon. The beautiful Armaan Jadoo walked in richly dressed and glittering with jewellery. A muscular young man armed with a bughda and a sword followed her into the house. As Tareek saw him, she began trembling. Afrasiyab looked at the young soldier curiously and asked Armaan, 'Who is this with you? I have not seen him before.' Tareek then jumped up and stamped hard on the ground. She screamed, 'Catch him, he is Mehtar Qiran! Barq Firangi has come disguised as Armaan!'

Qiran called out, 'Tareek, I am not afraid of being recognized. I am Mehtar Qiran, the killer of sahirs.' He lunged at Tareek with the magic sword of Nur Afshan. She screamed out to Afrasiyab to save himself. Magic shields suddenly materialized to protect her, but Qiran's sword cut through them. Tareek twisted out of the way, but he wounded her forehead. Qiran then turned on Afrasiyab and injured him as well. Hairat cried out, 'Shahanshah, what is this? Qiran seems to have been instructed in magical warfare by a very competent sahir!' A stunned Afrasiyab flung some magical pebbles at Qiran, but the sword protected him and they did not affect him. Tareek, Afrasiyab and Hairat fled from the house of smoke with Qiran fiercely chasing them. Mahrukh's agents informed her that Qiran was fighting Tareek, and she quickly rallied her forces to come to his help. Qiran was now in the battlefield surrounded by Afrasiyab's forces with Barq fighting valiantly besides him.

Qiran spotted Afrasiyab and Tareek talking with each other at a distance and fought his way towards them. Afrasiyab saw him approaching and shouted, 'Run Dai Amah, that lion of courage has come! It will be difficult to escape from him!' Afrasiyab bolted in one direction, while Tareek flew up into the sky like lightning. Mehtar Qiran looked up at her in despair. He continued to fight the forces surrounding him, but kept thinking of how to reach Tareek. Had he been a sahir, he would have sprouted wings, but all he could was pray desperately for help.

Suddenly, there was flash of lightning and a turquoise cloud emitting flames appeared from the direction of Tilism Nur Afshan. The cloud parted to reveal the noble forms of Nur Afshan and Kaukab the Enlightened. Kaukab rushed off to fight Tareek in the air even though Nur Afshan warned him not to go near her. Tareek saw Kaukab and shouted, 'Why Kaukab, it seems as if your star is also on the decline!' There was fierce fighting between Kaukab and Tareek in which Kaukab sustained many wounds. Tareek's spells caused a thousand knives to rain down on him and he found it difficult to defend himself. Nur Afshan stepped forward and managed to reduce the effect of Tareek's spells while shouting at Kaukab, 'Go down to the battlefield and save Mahrukh's forces from Afrasiyab. I will fight this cruel whore!'

Once Kaukab had flown down to the ground, Nur Afshan turned towards Tareek. She sneered, 'Old man, you have turned against the worshippers of Samri. Did you have no fear for your own life?' She leaned over and belched smoke all over Nur Afshan. He dispelled the smoke with a wave of his hands and then flung the powerful Net of Jamshed on her. Tareek was expecting him to cast a spell, but was startled as the magic net trapped her. Tareek was well versed in the ways of magic—she v.rithed like a fish out of water and tore the net, but fell down heavily on the earth. Qiran now leapt towards her, flashing the Nur Afshani sword. Tareek saw him approach and heaved herself into the sky again. Nur Afshan flung a second net on her that she managed to shatter as well. Nur Afshan also conjured boulders and stones and hurled them at her. The stones hit her hard and she somersaulted back to earth.

Mahrukh's sardars surrounded her. Bahar flung a bouquet at her and Makhmoor tossed magic flowers that had sharp edges and cut her like knives. Qiran ran towards her again, but Tareek defused the spells in an instant and rose up in the air as she called out, 'O Afrasiyab Khana Kharab! Look in my direction! I am surrounded by enemies. This old man's magic is bothering me!' Afrasiyab heard her and tried to go to help her, but Kaukab attacked him fiercely at that time.

Khwaja Amar had been standing under a distant tree bemoaning the fate of his army when he saw Afrasiyab and Kaukab fighting. He looked up to see Nur Afshan engaged with Tareek and was so heartened by this spectacle that he joined in the fray with his sword drawn. From a distance, a ruby-coloured cloud floated into the battleground. Everyone looked up to see the radiant Princess Burran Sword-woman dressed in rich clothes and jewellery and flanked by four hundred other princesses of Kaukab's realm. She fell upon Afrasiyab's army and called out, 'I am the daughter of the noble Kaukab!' The child-like Majlis, whose weapons of warfare were magical toys and dolls, followed Burran. Scores of her girl companions squealed their way into battle as well. Kaukab's son Jamshed and his commander-in-chief Bilaur Four-hands attacked from one side. Burran headed straight for Hairat and engaged her in battle. Majlis killed hundreds of men with her magical toys, while Bahar flung her bouquets far and wide. Makhmoor fought with deadly rubies that exploded like bombs, Surkh Mu Deadly-locks loosened her scented tresses that made darkness fall on the battlefield. Shakeel fought by his gracious mother Mahrukh's side. Asrar Jadoo's spells were mysterious and fatal, while her granddaughter Maraan conjured hundred of pythons and serpents that slithered on the battlefield and swallowed enemy soldiers.

Afrasiyab was trying to help Hairat and fight the other sardars at the same time with Kaukab on his tail. Afrasiyab had already sustained several wounds, but valiantly stood his ground and fought on a number of fronts. Hairat was trying to get away from Burran's attacks and somehow reach Afrasiyab's side, but Burran did not give her a chance. Her companions like Majlis, Shagoofa and Akhtar were also flashing around her to support her. Khwaja Amar took advantage of the battle in his characteristic manner. Whichever of Afrasiyab's sahirs tried to run, he reprimanded them for desertion and deprived them of all their money, valuables and clothes. As a parting gift, he cut their noses off, and when they howled in protest, he explained, 'You are lucky to be alive. Shahanshah had given orders that deserters should have their heads cut off. I have merely cut off your nose! If you are not satisfied I can present you to him!' The deserters decided that they were lucky to be alive and then ran off in tears. Amar also went around the battlefield prodding corpses to see if they had any valuables left on their bodies.

Other ayyars like Jansoz, Barq, Zargham and Chalak bin Amar were also fighting in the battlefield and burnt hundreds with their smoking hookahs. Meanwhile, Tareek was still fighting Nur Afshan and had destroyed several magic nets. She had wounded Nur Afshan with her spells, his clothes were tattered and his fingers bled, but he continued to ambush her with magic nets. Every time Tareek fell to the earth, Qiran would be waiting eagerly for her with his magic sword. The battle continued in this manner for three days. Nur Afshan was half dead with exhaustion, but had managed to weaken Tareek as well. Tareek had destroyed seven of his magic nets. In utter rage, Nur Afshan reached out for the eighth deadly net. Tareek hit him on the head with her sword. Nur Afshan then took out his dagger, but Tareek chanted a spell that made the dagger fly out of his hand. Tareek's death was now imminent for the dagger landed instead on her thigh. She moaned with pain and bent forwards and Nur Afshan used his magic net to trap her again.

Tareek just about managed to extricate herself from the net and fell heavily to the earth. At that time, a voice called out, 'Tareek how will you escape now? I am the bughda-wielder, the favourite of saints, the most loyal servant of the great and victorious Sahibqiran!' A startled Tareek tried to deflect his blow with her hands, but the magic sword slashed both her wrists and a river of blood poured forth. Tareek bellowed like an injured buffalo and a thousand flames burst from her mouth. Qiran flashed his magic sword and dispelled the flames, then took aim again. Tareek then screamed for help. In response, a slave-boy emerged from the earth and stood like a shield before her. Qiran's sword flashed like lightning. It sliced the slave-boy and landed on Tareek's head. Within the blink of an eyelid, the sword sliced her in half from head to toe, eventually resting on the earth.

As soon as the peril of the second hujra died, the desert darkened and everyone choked on their breath. A thousand birds flew off the trees and beat their heads with their wings while crying, 'Alas Malika Tareek!' As each one lamented, it fell on the earth in a heap of ashes. Nur Afshan hastily conjured some torches to light up the battlefield when frightful voices called out, 'You have killed me! I was Tareek Shakal-kash!' In his rage, Afrasiyab cast spells so that several desert lions appeared and attacked Nur Afshan. Nur Afshan started fighting with the lions, stunning several and tearing others apart. Meanwhile, Afrasiyab's grandmother Afat Four-hands was arrogantly presiding over her court in the Mountain of Ancestors surrounded by hundreds of ancestral magic slave-girls. Afat noticed that all of them looked depressed and asked, 'Why princesses, is anything wrong? You have been lookings sad for some time. I am worried now. Tell me if you are ailing. I will have you treated. I am at your service. Tell me how my child Afrasiyab is doing. You have not made any predictions for three days and I am completely in the dark about the future!'

One of the magic maidens snarled back, 'Leave us grandmother and look after your own affairs! Find out about Afrasiyab yourself!' Afat said gently, 'Princesses, you are the source of prophecy, you are meant to inform me. I do not understand you!' Other magic maidens called out, 'Foolish old woman, you are after our lives! When will you understand?' Another maiden called out, 'There is no point in speaking to this foolish woman. She will soon find out when bad news reaches her!' Afat started beseeching the magic maidens, 'I have served you for so long. Why are you treating me so harshly? I am heartbroken!' The magic maidens averted their faces and one of them cried, 'Stop bleating. The time has come when we meet Samri again. Alas, we will burn in the fires of hell!'

When Qiran's sword killed Tareek in the battlefield, the head of one of the magic maidens burst open and she wept, 'Afat, we leave your house now.' Drops of blood shot out from her skull and fell like flames around her. Other maidens burst into flames as well and the palace walls and furnishings started to burn. Afat desperately tried to save the remaining maidens by throwing them in the Palace of Darkness, but several hundred magic maidens were burnt to ashes. The ones whom Afat had saved kept beating the door of the palace, imploring her to release them. Eventually, Afat flew out of the palace and pounced on two young men. She brought them back to the palace, slaughtered them ruthlessly and filled a deep vessel with their blood. She pushed the tub into the dark palace where the maidens were wailing. As soon as they saw the blood, the maidens smiled in joy and called out, 'Now grandmother, why did you not think of this before?'

Afat locked the door on them and flew out of the palace again. She had only travelled a short distance when she heard spirits bewailing the death of Tareek. Afat reached the battlefield like lightning and saw that Nur Afshan and Kaukab's forces had destroyed Hairat's lashkar; Tareek's body lay covered with dust and blood while Qiran was preparing to attack Afrasiyab. The King of Magic was in tears over Tareek's death, his crown was missing and his clothes were torn. He had just turned to attack Qiran when Afat called out, 'You foolish, foolish man, do not confront him for he has the sword of Nur Afshan in his hand. This sword might cause your death. Do not go into the mouth of the dragon!' Afrasiyab looked up at her and moaned, 'Grandmother! I am destroyed! Dai Amah has left me!' Afat did not reply but swooped down and picked up Afrasiyab, Hairat and the other sardars in her magic net. Within moments, she flashed out of sight while calling back, 'Nur Afshan and Kaukab, your end is also near for I will punish you myself for your crimes.'

Nur Afshan wanted to follow her, but Amar held him back by saying, 'It is enough that with God's help we have killed such a powerful sahira!' Afrasiyab's forces fled once they saw their commanders disappear with Afat. Mahrukh's army plundered the enemy tents and treasures and the sardars of Islam attended to the injured and buried the dead. The masters of these tales tell us that for two whole days, no one could get any rest as corpses covered the earth. Eventually, the whole army moved several miles away from that terrible site.

Princess Mahjabeen Diamond-robe presided over her durbar after many days. Amar sent for Zargham Sherdil and declared, 'Zargham, in truth you have performed a noble deed. How did you hide Asad and save him from that man-eater? Everyone wants to know.' Zargham then explained, 'When I saw that Tareek consumed anyone in sight, I rendered the noble Asad unconscious and hid him in a cave. I persuaded a young man to take his place and warned Princess Mahjabeen to keep away from Asad for a few days. Thank God that my plan worked.' Mahrukh Magic-eye then bestowed a robe of honour on Zargham and praised him lavishly. Amar embraced him and declared, 'You are my strength and my true heir. You will inherit Zambil and other gifts. Now give me this robe so I can keep it safe for you!' Mahrukh awarded the other ayyars gifts and robes as well. Nur Afshan took the magic sword from Qiran and sent it back to his realm.

After several days, the sardars gathered in the durbar to celebrate Asad's life and their victory. Cupbearers served roseate wine to all present. At that time, Nur Afshan whispered to Mahrukh, 'Today the Almighty has delivered us and we are content. Can you not request Khwaja Amar to sing for us?' Mahrukh trembled and said, 'I dare not, but if Princess Burran asks him, he will not refuse her.' Nur Afshan kissed Burran on her forehead and repeated his request. Burran trembled as well and said, 'Huzoor, I am no one to make such a request, but Majlis Jadoo is his favourite. When she throws a tantrum he cannot refuse her.' Burran then whispered to Majlis, 'My child you have fought so bravely today. Khwaja sahib will surely sing for you if you ask him.'

Majlis Jadoo hopped over to Amar and jumped up on his lap. Burran admonished her for being so ill mannered, but Amar smiled indulgently and embraced the child. Majlis put her arms around Amar and said, 'Grandfather, look how I fought Hairat. I am wounded everywhere.' She lifted her shirt and showed him her back. Amar saw that she was indeed badly wounded with stitches and bandages in many places. His eyes filled with tears as he said, 'My child, God will protect you from harm. You are a brave girl and fight so valiantly.' Majlis then said, 'Grandfather, don't talk, just play your flute for me!' Amar said, 'My child, do not insist on this right now. Look we have gathered here after many days. The great Nur Afshan is with us. We need to confer with him and Kaukab about the next move against Afrasiyab for they will not stay with us for too long.' Majlis immediately threw herself on the floor, flung her goblet on the ground and started to howl and kick her heels. Everyone in the durbar laughed and Nur Afshan whispered to Burran, 'In truth, no one can match her wiles!'

Amar got up in alarm as he thought that the stitches on her back would tear open. He tried to lift her and assured her that he would do as she said, but Majlis struggled in his arms and cried even louder, 'It is no good now. You have hurt me and I will die weeping!' It took some time for Amar to console Majlis and wipe away her tears. Burran said, 'Khwaja sahib, do you see how you have spoilt this child with such indulgence!' Asad said, 'In truth, Khwaja sahib really loves this child. Look how he humours and cajoles her!' Eventually, Amar lifted Majlis off the floor and said, 'Alright my child, no more tears. Hear the flute now!'

Majlis called out loudly, 'Our esteemed Khwaja is playing the flute. Whoever speaks now will be turned out of the durbar!' Burran said sharply, 'Keep quiet! There are powerful sardars present here. You will offend them with your nonsense!' Mahrukh intervened, 'She is an innocent child. No one will take offence at what she says.' Majlis piped up, 'Huzoor, you should also remain quiet!' Mahrukh smiled and said, 'Child, once the music starts we will all be quiet.'

Majlis then turned to Amar and declared, 'Grandfather, everyone is quiet. Start playing now!' Amar had no recourse but to take out his flute. Thus, this session concluded happily with Mahrukh and the sardars waiting to see what happened next.

೨

37 THE MASTER OF THE THIRD HUJRA OF PERIL, AHQAQ JADOO COMES TO CONFRONT MAHRUKH, THE TRICKERIES OF AYYARS, AMAR'S PLAN SUCCEEDS

Afrasiyab went this time to the Desert of Terror to seek out the third hujra of peril which was the abode of Ahqaq Jadoo. He saw a contingent of twelve thousand soldiers and tents scattered at the base of a mountain. As he approached them, some of them stepped forward and called out, 'Who dares to approach the dwelling of the companion of Samri and the King of Sorcery, Ahqaq Jadoo?' Afrasiyab replied gently, 'O Companions of the Great King, please inform him that Shahanshah of Hoshruba, Afrasiyab, is here to kneel at his feet after a long, arduous journey.' The soldiers looked startled and immediately disappeared into the mountain. Ahqaq Jadoo sat up when he heard of Afrasiyab's arrival and told his companions, 'In truth, Samri and Jamshed had predicted that in the end, the ruler of Hoshruba will come to the Desert of Terror. I am anxious to meet him too!'

The soldiers emerged to lead Afrasiyab into the mountain. He saw a repulsive, black-faced sahir whose face resembled a pig, sitting on a stone throne and drinking wine. To one side was a throne studded with rubies with a golden naqara drum and a gold mallet placed on it. As Afrasiyab kneeled to greet him, Ahqaq said, 'O Noble and Great King, come closer. We had recently observed to our companions that there is rebellion in the realm and the ruler of Hoshruba will come to us. The end of the war will be at the powerful hands of our exalted self. You have come at a time when we longed for some meat with our wine!' Afrasiyab was prepared for this request. He sliced a slice of flesh off his thigh, roasted it over the fire and presented it to Ahqaq. The old sahir was pleased with the offering and exclaimed, 'Friends, today I have enjoyed a kebab with my *sharab*!' Meanwhile, Afrasiyab had turned white with the pain of the bleeding wound on his thigh. Ahqaq smeared some of his spittle on the wound and it healed immediately.

Ahqaq then turned to Afrasiyab and said with a smile, 'So what happened to Lacheen and how did you become king of Hoshruba?' Afrasiyab came out with his standard response of how Lacheen had died, but had nominated him as his successor in his lifetime. He followed with a brief account of how Asad the grandson of Hamza had arrived in Tilism and how several powerful sahirs had rebelled against him and joined Asad. He added, 'The king of Nur Afshan, Kaukab, has turned away from the ancient religion and joined Tilism Kusha. I have lost many kingdoms in Tilism. Mashal and Tareek fought and lost their lives. Now I have come to you.' Ahqaq laughed derisively and said, 'Of what worth was this shameless Mashal? He had the job of lighting torches and lamps in Samri's durbar. Who was Tareek? She swept the durbar and Samri used her to manage some forests and gave her other menial tasks. My exalted self was Samri and Jamshed's confidante and I am their true spiritual heir. I wielded the great magic Naqara of Samri's army. Even if the most powerful sahir army confronts me, when I strike this naqara, they will forget all magic. With my second strike, they will sway on their feet and with the third strike, they will lose consciousness. My army of twelve thousand soldiers then ruthlessly slaughters everyone. Afrasiyab you have provided me with heavenly nourishment. I will certainly accompany you now!'

At dawn the next day, Ahqaq sat on the ruby-studded throne with the magic naqara in front of him. His soldiers carried out the throne; Afrasiyab rode alongside and his army moved forward in stages. At every stage, Afrasiyab's vassals came forth to pay tribute. When they reached the kingdom of Fironia, Afrasiyab had a pavilion erected on the highest spot. Ahqaq sat on a throne with Afrasiyab besides him on a golden chair. Wine started to flow and a beautiful singer entertained the royal party.

The maulvi and the jinni

Suddenly, they heard a melodious voice coming from a distance. Everyone looked in that direction and saw a comely youth of tender years, wearing costly but torn and dusty garments. His beautiful face was troubled and smeared with dust. It was obvious that the boy was demented for he would sometimes run or laugh, then start weeping. Sometimes he would recite verses of unrequited love. Ahqaq and Afrasiyab were startled by this sight. Ahqaq said, 'O King, it seems as if he is of noble birth but has lost his senses because of some trauma. Look, he is about to fall in a well! Stop him!' The boy was actually near the well, but turned around to catch a bird and fell down.

A few sahirs tried to cajole him into coming with them, but he resisted fiercely and threw stones at them and cried, 'Do not come closer, there are swords here! Look the whole forest is on fire! Lions and elephants are fighting. The elephants have won!' The men wept to see him in this state and kept their distance from him, fearing that he would throw himself in the well. Afrasiyab ran forward and said, 'My son, do not be alarmed. Do not throw stones at us!' The boy saw Afrasiyab in his royal garments and a heavy crown and looked stunned. Suddenly, he cried out, 'Father, why did you leave me alone!' Afrasiyab played along and said, 'Yes my son, I had lost my way. Come home with me, your mother weeps for you.' The boy laughed and recited some verses. It was evident that he was educated. Afrasiyab said to his companions, 'Friends, he must be the son of some noble. Perhaps he has lost his senses because of an evil spirit!' As Afrasiyab cautiously approached him, the boy held his arms out. Afrasiyab lifted him and brought him back to the pavilion. He saw Ahqaq and cried, 'Grandfather, even you did not look for me!' Ahqaq held his arms out to the boy who hopped on to his lap and started to pluck at his beard. Ahqaq looked angry, but Afrasiyab pacified him by saying, 'Huzoor, he is not in his senses. Once the evil spirit is exorcized I will adopt him and make a sahir out of him.'

The boy was now shaking his head and glaring at everyone. A number of sahirs had gathered outside the pavilion to see this spectacle when they saw a maulvi heading towards them. The men asked him where he was going and he answered, 'I cured a landowner's daughter who was possessed by a jinni. The landowner promised me half a village, but he has fobbed me off with a couple of acres of land. No matter, I have trapped that jinni in a bottle. I am going to release him and order him to destroy the landowner and his family!' When Afrasiyab heard of this, he summoned the maulvi, who was reluctant to come over. Eventually, the sahirs lured him with promises of great wealth from the ruler of Hoshruba. As he came closer, Afrasiyab saw that he was dressed traditionally, with a loose kurta and turban, and his pyjamas hitched well above his ankles. As he entered the pavilion, he saw the boy and shouted, 'Wait you rascal, how did you come here! Look, your father is also here!'

The young boy, who had been swaying like an angry young lion cub, took fright and hid under Ahqaq's throne crying, 'Friends, do not let this maulvi come close to me! I fear his eyes!' Afrasiyab asked the maulvi to exorcize the bad spirit that had possessed the boy, and promised, 'You can ask for any price you want.' The maulvi explained patiently, 'Shahanshah sahib, this is not a matter of magic or sorcery. This is a particularly stubborn spirit. I have driven him away several times, but it may be more difficult today.' Afrasiyab led him into the pavilion and said to him, 'In truth, he is terrified of you. Look he is hiding under the throne shaking like a leaf!' By this time a swarm of onlookers had surrounded the maulvi, who shouted, 'Draw the curtains, only important people should remain here. The rest of you leave in case the spirit possesses you next!'

A number of people fled in fear, leaving only forty noble sardars, Afrasiyab and Ahqaq. The boy was still cowering under the throne. 'How will you bring him out?' Afrasiyab asked the maulvi. The maulvi declared, 'I will need a maund and a quarter of gold, incense, googal, peppercorns, two garlands of fresh flowers and some precious jewels. I do not need the gold. It is all yours. Later, you can give me my honest wages. I spit on wealth and it is like pig's blood to me!'

Within moments, the sahirs placed a heap of gold coins and the other ingredients before the maulvi. He noticed that the crowds outside were trying to peer inside and shouted at them, 'Whoever looks inside will be struck blind!' Afrasiyab and Ahqaq watched silently as the maulvi wrote something on four pieces of paper that he rolled into wicks and placed in the four corners of the pavilion. He placed four unlit lamps in the middle and declared, 'Please do not move from your seats, there will be a fight with the jinni.' Afrasiyab looked nervous and asked, 'Should I leave the durbar?' The maulvi laughed and said, 'Shahanshah, he will not hurt you. His fight is with me!' He suddenly shouted, 'Come out you coward! How long will you hide under the throne!' The boy grinned nervously and folded his hands. The maulvi threw a few grains of mustard seeds at him. The boy came out abruptly and approached the maulvi with bloodshot eyes, swaying on his feet. The maulvi ordered him to sit down and knocked in the air. 'What is your name?' he asked the boy.

The boy snapped back, 'I will never tell you my name you shameless mullah! I will eat you up as well!' The maulvi lit the googal and blew the smoke on the boy. This had an instant effect as the boy, who started rolling on the floor and then suddenly leapt on the old man. The maulvi threw him on the floor, slapped him hard on his face and said, 'Shameless spirit, tell me your name! I am not going to spare you today! I have travelled a long way for you and will lock you in a glass box!' The boy was trembling and foaming at the mouth now. A deep voice emanated from him, 'Maulvi sahib, my name is Qumqam. I live in the veil of Qaf. I like this boy and will take him with me. If you bother me, I will possess you as well!' The maulvi rose in anger and shouted, 'Qumqam, watch what I do to you!' He ran and lit the four wicks and the lamps, throwing some substance on the lamps so it emitted thick smoke that engulfed the durbar. Afrasiyab, Ahqaq and forty nobles rose from their seats in sheer panic as they inhaled the smoke. They shouted, 'Maulvi sahib, the jinni has possessed us as well! Many others have joined him, jinni and parizads and devs!'

Then Ahqaq began shouting, 'Save me maulvi, the devs are going to eat me up! Look, there is a river of fire here!' Afrasiyab shouted back, 'No, it's water!' To this Ahqaq cried, 'I am up to my knees in water!' Afrasiyab said, 'Do not be alarmed, I am a swimmer! Just hold me and pinch your nostrils.' Ahqaq replied, 'My son, let us leave quickly!' Afrasiyab continued, 'I will risk my life for you and jump into this fearful river!' He dived on to the floor with Ahqaq and the other sardars and fell unconscious. The boy straightened up and shouted, 'I am the Mehtar of Mehtars, the best of the best, Khwaja Amar!' The maulvi shouted, 'I am the lightning, Barq Firangi! Ustad, how did I do as the maulvi?' Amar hit him hard on his head and said, 'You will not be an ayyar for a thousand years you shameless fool! You asked for a maund of gold when I had specifically asked for five maunds, you idiot!' Even as he scolded Barq, Amar took out his magic Net of Ilyas and scooped up the gold coins and jewels. Barq cried out, 'Ustad, hurry up! Afrasiyab will not be killed, but we can dispose of Ahqaq. Mahrukh has already warned us about him and his magic naqara.'

Amar was now removing other precious items and called back, 'Do not attempt anything. I will put him in Zambil along with the magic naqara.' Barq did not listen and tried to kill Ahqaq with his dagger. It flew out of his hands and a magic slave pushed his way out of the earth, crying, 'Who are you that you attack the Companion of Samri?' As he emerged, the slave waved his fingers so that Barq fell on the ground, his limbs lifeless. Amar in his usual greed was stripping the sahirs of their clothes and valuables when he heard Barq's warning shout. He tried to become invisible in Galeem, but the magic slave stamped hard on the floor and Amar also fell down fluttering like a wounded dove.

The slave then revived Ahqaq by sprinkling water on him. 'Companion of Samri, you have slept enough. Awaken now for Amar and Barq were about to kill you! How can the naqara keeper of Samri's army be so careless?' Ahqaq woke up and saw neither the maulvi, nor the young boy. Writhing on the floor before him was a fair young man and a thin, ugly ayyar. Ahqaq revived Afrasiyab and said, 'Shahanshah, did you bring me out of seclusion just to have me humiliated by ayyars?' Afrasiyab trembled with shame and the magic slave also scolded him, 'Shahanshah, if I had not protected my master, he would surely have been dead by now! He certainly cannot go with you now! Amar has tricked you hundreds of times and yet you cannot recog nize him!' Afrasiyab shouted in reply, 'How dare you comment on us y ou shameless slave! These are rebels whom I can dispose of whenever I want!' The slave looked Afrasiyab straight in the eyes and said, 'That is utterly wrong. You cannot do anything against them. That is why you have been begging my master to help you!'

Afrasiyab rose in a fiery rage and screamed, 'Shut your loose tongue or I will burn you in the fires of rage and anger!' The slave retorted, 'Very good! You cannot vanquish your enemies and now turn on me? Well, I am not your slave but an ordinary servant of Shahanshah Ahqaq!' Afrasiyab slapped the slave hard on the face and he was burnt to ashes. A bird flew out of the ashes crying, 'Alas, alas! This is a sign that Hoshruba will not survive!' Ahqaq looked angrily at Afrasiyab and asked, 'What have you done? You have destroyed my loyal servant. Who will save me from my enemies now?' Afrasiyab retorted, 'Do not say a word! You have thousands of protectors who will die for you!'

The magic slave's death released its spell on the two ayyars and they were just about to escape when Afrasiyab signalled and they fell down helpless again. The attendants and soldiers who had left the durbar refused to come forth when they were summoned and said that they would be blinded if they returned. 'You fools,' one of the sardars called out, 'those two were ayyars. Shahanshah wants you immediately!' The attendants entered sheepishly and saw Ahqaq looking gloomy while Afrasiyab was still trembling with rage. The two ayyars sat before him with their heads bent low. The soldiers whispered to each other, 'Friends, these ayyars are two steps ahead of sahirs! Who could recognize them? They must be very fearless to deceive a great sahir like our master.'

Qiran and Ahwal

Suddenly, a dark and sinister cloud appeared on the horizon. As everyone watched, it came closer and parted to reveal a black-skinned sahir with his forty companions. He kneeled before Afrasiyab and explained, 'Shahanshah, I was visiting your honourable grandmother, Malika Mahiyan. She asked me about the important prisoner I have been keeping for you and then said, "My powers inform me that he may be released very soon." I assured her that this was not possible when she suddenly said, "Something else has happened. Amar and Barq have been captured. You should go there and take them to your own place; they will surely die there! That king of fools, Afrasiyab was hypnotized again by Amar's voice. He will never learn!"' Afrasiyab was embarrassed by this, but handed his prisoners over to the sahir named Shahab Jadoo, who left immediately. He arrived at his fort and made preparations to kill his two prisoners.

Now hear a word in this colourful story about Mehtar Qiran, who was looking for Amar and Barq. He ingratiated himself with Shahab's men and found out that the important prisoner in the fort was none other than Ahwal Jadoo, Kaukab's foster brother. The reader will recall that everyone believed Afrasiyab had killed Ahwal for humiliating him. That night, Qiran served drugged wine to prison guards and broke into the dungeons. He found Ahwal in a pitiable state, with sunken eyes and withered cheeks, weighed down with chains, his tongue pierced with a large needle. Qiran cried out, 'O noble Ahwal! Do not despair for God has been kind. I am Mehtar Qiran, Khwaja Amar's servant and Kaukab's ally.' Ahwal wept helplessly and signalled to Qiran to take out the needle from his tongue. Qiran gently took out the needle, freed him of his shackles and gave him a drink of water. 'How did you reach me?' Ahwal asked. Qiran replied, 'It is because of the hand of God himself. For years, everyone has been convinced that you were dead. But this is no time to explain, the guards will be conscious any moment.'

Ahwal and Qiran left in haste. Outside the dungeons, Ahwal told Qiran to return to his lashkar, as he wanted to tackle Shahab. He sprouted wings and swooped down on Shahab just when Amar was about to be executed. Shahab looked up in alarm at the spectre of Ahwal calling out, 'I am Ahwal! Look Shahab, my God has released me! Prepare now for your end!' After a fierce fight, Ahwal killed Shahab and his men. He released Amar and Barq who briefed him on the state of the war after his capture. When he mentioned Ahqaq, the naqara-striker, Ahwal went pale in the face and said, 'O king of ayyars, we must hurry, there is no time to lose!'

The Naqara of Samri

Meanwhile, Afrasiyab and Ahqaq had reached Hairat's lashkar in great pomp and ceremony. That evening, Ahqaq was drunk on wine and his own arrogance. He asked Afrasiyab to declare the battle for the next day. He said, 'I will dispose of these rebels and then we can proceed to Mount Agate to deal with Hamza!' The next morning, Afrasiyab asked Vizier Sarmaya to convey a message to his favourites Bahar and Makhmoor. Sarmaya called out to them, 'Bahar and Makhmoor, Shahanshah will be merciful and forgive your sins. Come and join us for he will restore you to your former glory. It will be difficult to save your lives today!' Bahar and Makhmoor were livid and shouted sarcastically, 'Tell Shahanshah, we are as concerned about his safety as he is about ours. It is clear that Asad is Tilism Kusha and will be his killer. We can intercede on his behalf and Tilism Kusha might spare his life!'

Ahqaq went forward on the battlefield accompanied by his blood-thirsty army of sahirs who were brandishing their daggers and calling out to each other, 'What a glorious day, for our daggers have been thirsty for blood all these years! Today we can quench their thirst by destroying this army!' Ahqaq called out arrogantly, 'Rebels, do not think I am Tareek that I will make my way through you tearing you up and consuming you. I just need to strike this naqara thrice to annihilate the most powerful army!' Mahrukh Magic-eye jumped off her magic peacock and went forward, angrily shouting, 'Ahqaq, do you think we can be threatened so easily? We have forsworn the cursed ways of Samri and Jamshed! With the help of the holy Khizar, we have reached the stream of truth and honour. Life and death are all the same to us now!'

Ahqaq was enraged by her defiance and in his fury, struck the magic naqara very hard with the gold mallet. It was as if Doomsday had descended on the battlefield. Sardars like Mahrukh, Bahar, Baghban, Surkh Mu, Hilal, Ra'ad, and Barq Mehshar and Barq Lameh, who had been standing proudly, heard the naqara and trembled and swayed on their feet. Their eyes filled with tears and they looked helplessly to the skies for help. As Ahqaq prepared for the second strike, everyone raised hands in prayer, calling out, 'O Supreme Creator, help us at this time. We have forgotten our magical powers and are about to collapse.' Suddenly, a bolt of lightning flashed in the sky as the noble Kaukab descended before Ahqaq and called out, 'Do not strike that naqara again Ahqaq! You are the famous Companion of Samri. Are you afraid of magical combat?' Ahqaq seemed transfixed by Kaukab's lion-like glare and stopped in his tracks

Afrasiyab ran forward shouting, 'Companion of Samri, do not make the mistake of fighting him. This is Kaukab, ruler of Nur Afshan!' Ahqaq once again reached out for the naqara when there was another flash in the sky and Nur Afshan came into sight. He did not descend for fear of hearing the sound of the magic naqara and had stuffed his fingers in his ears. He warned Kaukab to be careful just as Ahqaq struck the naqara again. This had a devastating effect on Mahrukh's army as they went deaf and dumb while Kaukab began swaying on his feet, completely powerless.

Ahqaq relished the spectacle of the helpless Kaukab and taunted him, 'You claim to be the ruler of Nur Afshan. Draw your sword and attack me! Show us the gems of your courage!' Kaukab glared back at him helplessly, but Afrasiyab kept shouting, 'Do not waste time in such empty talk! Strike the naqara again or you will regret it! The Invisible God of these people is very powerful! The Unseen Power will help them! Even as you laugh, your fate weeps for you!' Ahqaq was now in his element and called back casually, 'Why do you panic so easily? I will destroy them all. Even if Samri and Jamshed confront me, this naqara will stun them! I can pull in the skies at this time!' Ahqaq continued in this vein while the lashkar of Islam prayed for help. There was another flash in the sky and the cloud of mercy appeared revealing Amar, Barq and Ahwal.

Hairat was alarmed by this sight and gripped Afrasiyab tightly. She cried, 'O Shahanshah, what is this? You had killed Ahwal after he had rescued Mahrukh and the sardars! How has he come back to life?' Afrasiyab was also stunned and said, 'Malika, he is a very powerful sahir and learnt sorcery with Kaukab and me. He is also privy to the secrets of Hoshruba. I had not really killed him, but my trusted friend Shahab had kept him in his prison. I had recently handed over Amar and Barq to him as well. They must have tricked and killed him to release Ahwal. This is not a good sign. If only this fool Ahqaq was not being so arrogant!'

Meanwhile, Nur Afshan addressed Ahwal, 'Light of mine eyes, you have come just in time. We are in a terrible calamity now; I am powerless as is your brother Kaukab. With the third strike, the lashkar will become unconscious and these butchers will slaughter them. It will be the end of Tilism Nur Afshan as well. O lion-hearted warrior, this world is but an illusion, there is only one permanent abode in the kingdom of heaven. It is all up to you now. If you die now, you will be immortal in the afterlife.' Ahwal jumped off the throne and said, 'My master, I hear and understand. I know that life is less than a bubble and mine will be the greatest honour!'

Ahwal then flew to where the great drum lay and called out, 'Ahqaq, you shameless fool. Your end is at my hands. Look at the ways of the Almighty that I was imprisoned for so many years and released at this crucial moment. I leave this world now and sacrifice myself for my friends!' Afrasiyab was now cursing Ahqaq loudly, 'Ahqaq, you arrogant, dishonourable fool! As soon as he cuts his own throat, it will be Doomsday. The naqara will burst and you will not have a moment to breathe. Strike now!' Ahqaq rushed to strike again, but it was too late. Ahwal had drawn a dagger and sliced his own throat with it. As the noble Ahwal's blood spilt on the magic drum, it was as if somebody had thrown gunpowder on fire. There was a loud explosion and the drum burst into flames. Ahqaq screamed loudly for he did not think that Ahwal could actually perform such a deed. A green flame shot out of the drum and fell on Ahqaq to execute him on the spot. His army of twelve thousand soldiers also perished instantly while thousands of men in Afrasiyab's army fell unconscious.

The earth and the skies went dark after Ahqaq's death and loud, horrifying voices could be heard everywhere. Birds threw themselves against the mountains and wailed, 'Alas, the companion of Samri is no more!' After a long time a voice boomed out, 'You have killed me! I was Ahqaq Jadoo, the ruler of the third hujra! Alas, I died and did not achieve my purpose!' Nur Afshan, Kaukab and Mahrukh's army had regained their powers and fell on Afrasiyab's army vigorously. Afrasiyab was in a state of shock and stumbled as he tried to flee. Hairat, Sarmaya and Abriq also ran for their lives.

The reader will remember the twelve hundred golden magic maidens of Samri who were in the care of Afrasiyab's grandmother, Afat Four-hands. Several hundred of them were annihilated when Mashal and Tareek were killed. Afat was in her palace in the Mountain of

Ancestors when she saw the maidens change colour. This time, Afat merely uttered, 'Ya Samri and Jamshed! Keep the third hujra safe!' She was just about to secure them within the palace when a bright flame engulfed one of them who shrieked and held the next one. Several magic maidens immediately went up in flames. Afat managed to save three hundred of them and flew in great despair to the battlefield. She reached it and saw the terrible sight of trees burning and the earth spewing out flames. Ahqaq's corpse lay stiffening in the field and a sea of enemy sahirs surrounded Afrasiyab. Afat swooped down and shouted a warning, 'Nur Afshan and Kaukab beware! I am Afat Four-hands and I am here!'

As she dived down, Afat chanted a destructive spell that made the earth heave; thousands of rebels lost their heads and several were swallowed alive as the earth split open. There were fierce bolts of lightning and thunder, and a sandstorm blinded everyone. Afat reached Afrasiyab and picked him up. She called out to Hairat, 'Can you not see your husband is surrounded by enemies? I am taking him to the Garden of Apples—follow us at once!' Hairat fought her way out of the battlefield, followed by her sardars like Mussavir the magic artist, Sarmaya Ice-maker and Abriq Mountain-breaker. The rest of Afrasiyab's army also turned and fled. No sooner had they deserted, Amar went straight to the treasury and tricked Mahrukh's guards into leaving their posts. He calmly scooped all the treasure within the Net of Ilyas and deposited it in Zambil. The net did not leave a single coin and left a huge crater in the ground where the treasure had lain.

Mahrukh was livid when the theft of Afrasiyab's treasury was reported and accused her treasurer, who innocently declared, 'Huzoor, where do you think I could hide such a treasure? It was your man who did it!' Barq immediately knew that only Amar could have stolen the treasure. He was about to share his suspicions with Mahrukh when Khwaja Amar walked towards them with his head bent and sulking. Mahrukh said, 'O king of ayyars, Afrasiyab's treasury was empty today.' Amar responded, 'I had also heard that his army had not been paid their wages.' Everyone knew that Amar had stolen the treasure, but no one dared to accuse him. That day, they celebrated their miraculous victory against the master of the third hujra.

38 THE MASTER OF THE FOURTH HUJRA, SHEHNA NAWAZ, AMAR DISGUISED AS THE GREAT JAMSHED, THE DEATH OF SHEHNA NAWAZ

Afrasiyab bid farewell to his grandmother in the Garden of Apples and addressed Hairat, 'Malika, I am leaving now on a perilous journey.' Hairat pleaded with her husband to take her with him on this journey, but he said, 'My dear, there are stages on this journey that only I can cross and even that with great difficulty. No, it is better for you to remain here and confront Mahrukh in my absence.' Afrasiyab then embarked alone on the journey on his shining throne. As soon as Zaal Jadoo heard he was approaching, the old sahir beat his head and cried, 'My friends, I greet you on the latest death! It seems that Ahqaq sahib was sent straight to hell.' Zaal then went outside his fort with his sardars to welcome the King of Magic. After Afrasiyab became slightly drunk with wine, he declared, 'My friend and well wisher, this Ahqaq was killed because of his supreme arrogance. Now I would like you to take me to the fourth hujra of peril.

Zaal said, 'To hear is to obey. However, I would like to warn you that Shehna Nawaz has spent several lifetimes in prayer and devotion. He is a special being of the gods and is very arrogant. He will most probably refuse you.' Afrasiyab cried, 'Then I will bring him by the scruff of his neck! He will not dare to refuse me in person! Do not interfere in this. You are my guide, not my adviser!' Afrasiyab soon rode forth on the journey to the fourth hujra. They had just gone some distance when the Desert of Hasti erupted into flames and there were gusts of blistering breeze. The earth became so hot that flames leapt out of it. Several of Afrasiyab's men collapsed and died of the heat. A canopy covered Afrasiyab, but he began sweating profusely as it radiated heat. They marched across the merciless desert for the whole day and in the evening, Afrasiyab reluctantly ordered his men to rest for the night. Even then the hot breeze was relentless and the hills nearby emitted smoke. The next morning, they reached a forest. Zaal stopped the party at one place and called out loudly, 'Commander Palang Blood-thirsty, the King of Sahirs is here!'

A cloud of dust materialized and a huge blood-thirsty sahir emerged from the forest riding a ferocious wild boar. His face was as dark as the blackest night. He kissed Afrasiyab's feet and asked, 'Shahanshah, your face is flushed with the heat! Why did you make this perilous journey?' Afrasiyab affectionately embraced the sahir and said, 'I was so eager to meet you that I have destroyed three hujras! I have now come to fetch Shehna Nawaz.' Palang looked troubled and said, 'Huzoor, that old man has renounced the world and meets no one. Even I see him only once a year. He will not meet you, but perhaps I can convey your message to him.' Afrasiyab persisted, 'I insist on meeting him. As you know, I am the supreme sahir in the realm. I will not turn back unless I meet him now!'

Palang then led Afrasiyab to a cave located in a hill some distance away. Afrasiyab could hear a quavering voice chanting hymns as he drew closer to the cave. He walked into the cave behind Palang and looked in awe at the hideous old sahir who was bent from the waist with skin that sagged in folds on his naked body. Afrasiyab stood before him for a long time, but the arrogant old man kept chanting and did not bother to look up. Eventually, commander Palang called out, 'Master of Magic, the noble Shahanshah of Hoshruba stands before you.' The old man looked up and stared at Afrasiyab in some surprise. He asked, 'Commander, who is this man? Do you not recognize the ruler of Hoshruba? This is not the noble Lacheen, our friend and companion. It was because of him that I could become a hermit.'

Afrasiyab stepped forward and gushed, 'Huzoor, do you not recognize me? I was second-in-command to the great Lacheen. After he joined Samri and Jamshed in heaven, I became ruler. For the last twenty years I have been in your service and have been anxious to have the honour of kissing your feet.' Shehna Nawaz threw back his head and laughed derisively. He said, 'Afrasiyab, Samri and Jamshed come to me in my dreams, but I cannot talk about what they reveal to me. You have really elevated the spirit of Samri! Let me see, you have destroyed the three hujras, you have a formidable Tilism Kusha and a major rebellion in the realm. The Tilism of Nur Afshan is against you as well. Now what do you expect of me?'

Afrasiyab at once cut flesh from his thigh, grilled it on fire and presented it to the old man. Shehna was pleased with the offering and said, 'Lion of Hoshruba, I enjoyed this offering and am content. Your wish is granted and your enemies will be destroyed. You will be happy and they will be sad. O King of Sahirs and Protector of Samri Worshippers, I am dedicated to the memory of Samri, but I will send my trusted commander Palang, the blood-thirsty one, who is privy to my secrets. When he will blow my magic *shehna*, he will blow apart the enemy. Listen, these are bad times. If I stay here, I can come to your help later, but if I am harmed, your Tilism will be destroyed!' After the old man had convinced Afrasiyab of the wisdom of his words, he added, 'Afrasiyab, this magic flute of Jamshed will work for whoever has possession of it. Save Palang and the shehna from the trickery of ayyars, otherwise I may have to sacrifice my life.'

Afrasiyab promised he would never let Palang and the magic flute out of his sight. Then the old man described the wonders of the magic flute to Palang and Afrasiyab. He gave it to Palang and urged him to remain alert. He warned, 'Do not be complacent because Shahanshah protects you. He has already destroyed three hujras, but I am honour bound to help him after consuming his offering.' Palang promised to remain vigilant and left with Afrasiyab. The next morning, Shahanshah and his party crossed the dreadful Desert of Hasti again. Their progress was slow and agonizing, but Palang guided them. In the evening, they stopped travelling, but Afrasiyab could not sleep much that night.

The trials of Ahwal

Suddenly, the silence of the night was broken by the screams of a man undergoing extreme physical torture. Afrasiyab left his tent in alarm and went out to see that the desert was pitch black and the agonized voice seemed to be coming from a distant mountain. The screaming and whimpering went on for the rest of the night and tore at Afrasiyab's heart. As he stared into the night, he could make out flames burning on a distant mountain. It seemed as if some sinner was being punished for his misdeeds as a dreadful voice could be heard saying, 'You wretched sinner, you abandoned the worship of the true gods and accepted the Unseen God! You destroyed the companion of Samri without any hesitation! You will now undergo this torture for a hundred years!'

The next morning, Palang and Zaal Jadoo presented themselves to Afrasiyab. They found him trembling and sweating, his face pale as a sheet. Palang said, 'Shahanshah, is all well with you? I do not think we should travel today; yesterday's journey was hard on you.' Afrasiyab look dazed as he responded, 'O Palang Blood-thirsty, I feel as if I am about to die! There were dreadful sounds of someone being tortured for his sins in yonder mountain.' Palang looked thoughtful and said, 'Shahanshah, I have heard from my elders that Samri and Jamshed can be seen in this desert in strange forms. I also heard these dreadful sounds. The only explanation is that one of your former servants who joined the Muslims must be being punished after death.' Afrasiyab said, 'The sound of whimpering can still be heard. Let us have a look.' Afrasiyab led the way and they walked a fair distance to the highest mountain. Afrasiyab peered up and could make out a portrait in stone etched in the mountain with its mouth open and tears rolling down the stone cheeks; the eyes appeared be to be moving as well. Afrasiyab cried, 'Friends, this sinner has been trapped in stone but his face seems strangely familiar.'

As everyone looked closely, they noticed that the stone head had a body that was emitting smoke. It was obvious that a sinner was being burnt for his sins. Its moans and cried of pain moved everyone and they cried, 'Ya Samri and Jamshed, Ya Laat and Manaat, forgive us our sins.' Afrasiyab was about to turn back when the image cried out, 'O noble Shahanshah, stop in the name of Samri and Jamshed! Do you not recognize your old servant?' Afrasiyab turned back abruptly as he realized that this was the image of his old companion Ahwal. He called out, 'I recognize you now my old friend. After all, we were together since we were children. Alas, how you have suffered for your love of the Muslims.'

The image of Ahwal seemed to be emitting smoke from its mouth, 'Do not mention the wretched Muslims! Where is the Unseen God? There is only the mighty wrath of the old gods. Please save me for the love of Samri and Jamshed. Perhaps if you forgive me and pray for me, I will be free of this torture. You are an exalted person here. Whoever died for you is in wondrous gardens specially allocated for you!' These words had a profound effect on Afrasiyab's companions. Some of them fainted with fear and the others fell at Afrasiyab's feet sobbing, 'Shahanshah, you are the lord of this world and the next. You are the chosen one of the gods!' Zaal Jadoo and Palang said, 'Shahanshah, he has sinned grievously, but he is your old companion and has consumed your salt. You must overlook his disloyalty for great men forgive their inferiors. Please pray for his deliverance.'

Afrasiyab prayed for a long time while the sun beat mercilessly down on the stone image so that it emitted flames and screamed in agony. Chips of stone flaked off the image and Ahwal's screams became unbearable. Afrasiyab kept repeating, 'Gods, I have forgiven him; be merciful to him! Suddenly the stone image burst in the middle and Ahwal emerged from within. He appeared to be wearing the same clothes that he had worn before he slit his own throat, but they were tattered. His body was black and covered in boils. Afrasiyab's companions screamed, 'Huzoor look, he seems to be changing, he is smiling now. Look friends his face is clearing up, the boils have gone!' As they watched in wonder, Ahwal was restored to his former self and stood in front of them, the picture of a noble young man in splendid robes. Afrasiyab called out, 'Friend Ahwal, how are you now?' Ahwal called back joyously, 'May the blessings of Samri and Jamshed be with you forever! Your prayers were answered and this sinner was released. Just now, an angel released me from the stone prison and told me that I was forgiven because of you. I might be given a small garden to live in for a hundred years in isolation, but I will not be tortured any more. I cannot return to the world now, but I do want to do you a favour. Listen well! There is a place some distance from here called the perfumed forest. There is a special tree there. The trunk is hollow and Jamshed resides within it. Go to that tree and pray to him to help you in defeating the enemy. I know that he will answer your prayer.'

Jamshed in the Perfumed Forest

Afrasiyab and his companions bid farewell to Ahwal and immediately left to find the perfumed forest. After some time, they saw it from a distance, green and lush. As they approached it, they could smell its heavenly perfume. Afrasiyab saw that the largest tree had branches that shone like emeralds. Its trunk was so large that even if ten men joined hands, they would not be able to encircle it. There was a fine vertical line on the trunk and they could hear music from within. Afrasiyab cried, 'Friends, this is the abode of the Jamshed! He cannot hide from me! Stand back as I pray to him.' Afrasiyab's companions crowded behind him as he put his hand on the massive trunk and called out loudly, 'Ya Jamshed, fate has brought me here and I have found you! Do not hide from me. Mahrukh and her army have brought ruin to Tilism Hoshruba and your worshippers are being killed and harmed. Your companions, Mashal, Tareek and Ahqaq have been cruelly slaughtered. I will die here and not leave until you bestow upon me a view of your radiant self. Show yourself to me; do not deprive your humble ones!'

Afrasiyab sobbed as he spoke and raised his hands in prayer. There was a sharp noise and the seam in the tree split open like an open doorway. Afrasiyab saw that a ruby throne studded with other precious gems was placed in the hollow and a figure shrouded in red sat upon the throne. The air in the hollow exuded an unearthly fragrance. Afrasiyab kneeled down and clung to the base of the ruby throne. The shrouded figure spoke, 'Afrasiyab move away lest my shadow falls on you and you are burnt to ashes! Look up now!'

Afrasiyab and his companions raised their bowed heads and saw the figure remove the veil from one side to reveal the face of a handsome young man with light eyes and moustache. As they watched in wonder, the figure removed the veil from the other side to reveal the face of the most beautiful woman anyone had ever seen. They trembled with awe and cried out, 'O Jamshed, all glory to you that you have bestowed upon us the supreme honour of revealing yourself to us.' The voice called back, 'Move away, we will emerge now. Afrasiyab you are not aware that we have to fight the other gods daily on your behalf. Laat and Manaat want to remove you and bestow triumph on the Muslims. They want to eradicate all sahirs but we tell them that Afrasiyab is a king of supreme grace. He remembers us daily in his prayers and we would like to reward him. We did not intend to accompany you, but we now take pity on your mournful plight. Now close your eyes as we emerge from our place!'

Afrasiyab and his followers stepped back and closed their eyes. There was a sudden rush of air. They opened their eyes to see a mighty pavilion of gold pillars with gleaming curtains. The scent of musk and umber assailed their senses as they gazed upon the veiled figure, now resplendent on a throne within the pavilion. Afrasiyab, Zaal and Palang walked in and sat on chairs provided for them. They suddenly realized that they could not recall a single magical word. Jamshed called out, 'You fools, did you think that you could remember magic in the presence of the greatest magician? Go out of the pavilion and your powers will be restored.'

Afrasiyab and the others walked out and found that they could recall all their spells. More convinced than ever of the god's powers, they returned to the pavilion in a state of complete subjugation. They trembled as the voice boomed out, 'Palang Blood-thirsty, go into the forest and call out to the angel of death. Say that Khudawand Jamshed remembers him.' Jamshed then turned to Zaal Jadoo and ordered, 'Old man, go to the forest also and call out with great affection, to the angel of grace.' Palang promptly left the pavilion walked some distance. As he called out, he saw that a wall of flames came towards him from one direction. Palang was then terrified by the sight of a huge black man with a hideous face, with flames coming out of his mouth as he called out, 'I am the angel of death of Khudawand Jamshed!'

Palang was a brave warrior, but he fell on his knees in sheer terror, his teeth knocking against each other. The angel of death held him by the neck and said, 'Why are you so frightened? I can kill your father and grandfather, but this is not the time of your death!' Palang could not move an inch so the angel dragged him to the pavilion. Meanwhile, Zaal had called out to the angel of grace who appeared as a beautiful young man with long hair, singing hymns to Jamshed. There were ruby wings on his shoulders and his body was radiant with divine light. Zaal felt his spirits uplift as he accompanied this creature of light and grace back to the pavilion.

Afrasiyab came out of the pavilion in his eagerness to see the two angels. He was about to faint with horror at the sight of the angel of death and stuttered a greeting in his nervousness, but his heart swelled with joy as he saw the angel of grace. The two angels walked in, the angel of death looking as if he had never smiled and the angel of grace smiling in joy. Both went and stood behind Khudawand Jamshed. Palang sat down and readers should remember that Shehna Nawaz's magic flute was tied to his waist. Jamshed asked, 'What is this toy you are carrying with you? Are you still a child?' Palang folded his hands and said, 'Huzoor, you had bestowed this gift on your ancient companion Shehna Nawaz, the master of the fourth hujra. Shahanshah had gone to him for help. He is a hermit devoted to you and did not want to cease praying to you, therefore, he has entrusted the magic flute to me and I guard it with my life.'

Khudawand Jamshed declared, 'You fool, your god is with you now! I am responsible for my creatures! What need have you of this toy? Give it me and you can rest easy.' Afrasiyab echoed, 'The great god is right.' Palang offered the magic flute to Jamshed. He handed it to the angel of grace, who tucked it in his waist. Jamshed told Afrasiyab to leave the pavilion, as he would be travelling in it. The sahirs left the pavilion and saw that it diminished and transformed into a canopy shielding the great idol on his throne. As Afrasiyab and the army moved, the throne rose into the air and moved above them. As the news of Jamshed's presence spread throughout the realm, thousands of people walked alongside the army, striking kettledrums and ringing bells, and praising Jamshed. Afrasiyab sent a message to Hairat to prepare a welcome for the august presence. He wrote, 'I will explain in detail, but rest assured that Mahrukh and Bahar will now be destroyed!'

Hairat laughed as she read the message and declared, 'My friends, Shahanshah brings the god Jamshed with him. There is some perfumed forest where this vision appeared to my husband. He now accompanies him.' There was excitement in the durbars as sahir sardars said to each other, 'Did you ever hear of the perfumed forest? It seems like a place of miracles!' Sarsar Sword-fighter suddenly spoke up, 'Huzoor, may Khudawand Laqa protect us, but could this be another trick that camel driver's son plays on us?' Everyone turned on Sarsar and rebuked her for doubting the Shahanshah's word. Eventually, she left the durbar sheepishly, but whispered to Saba Raftar Fleet-foot, 'I have my doubts about this. It is likely that Shahanshah has been tricked again.'

The arrival of Jamshed

All night, Hairat Jadoo and her sardars were busy in preparations. The next morning, they rode out into the desert to welcome the divine presence. Mahjabeen and Mahrukh, along with the other sardars of Islam, came out of their pavilions to witness the arrival of Jamshed. They saw that a huge cloud of dust arose in the desert and there were resounding cries of 'Ya Jamshed'. Thousands of peasants playing tambourines and drums led the procession. The throne of Jamshed was flying high in the air, with the two angels on either side. The figure of Jamshed was shrouded in red, but glowed with light. Afrasiyab and the other sardars were walking underneath the throne and the sound of conch shells, bells and kettledrums was deafening. As Hairat prostrated before Khudawand, Sarsar also followed suit, but peered up in curiosity. Jamshed called out in anger, 'Hairat, this wily, deceitful woman with you doubts our integrity! She needs a shoe beating! Remove her from our sight!'

The crowds turned on Sarsar in fury and began thrashing her soundly. She implored loudly, 'O Khudawand Jamshed, spare me your wrath!' The angel of death then thundered out, 'She thinks we are Amar. We will leave now!' Afrasiyab implored the angel to have mercy. Sarsar's companions dragged her to Jamshed with her clothes torn and face swollen with the beating she had received. Sarsar kissed the earth thinking furiously, 'Sarsar, your instincts must be wrong. If this is trickery, it is miraculous!' Jamshed laughed and said, 'You disbeliever, you still suspect us of trickery. Clear your heart of all doubt or I will throw you into the fires of hell!' Sarsar lost her senses and thought, 'He must be true for he knows what is in my heart.' She held her earlobes to demonstrate her repentance and implored him for mercy. The procession then moved forward with more and more people joining it. At one stage, the deity's throne stopped in mid-air and then descended. The canopy shielding him expanded in size to transform into a magnificent pavilion. Hundreds of sahirs jostled with each other to get closer to the throne.

Back in the camp, Hairat led an exhausted Afrasiyab into her pavilion and said, 'I have made preparations to serve food and wine. Should I serve it now to Khudawand?' Afrasiyab sank on the masnad and said, 'Hairat, Khudawand has not troubled me in any way. He has not consumed any wine or food that we offered him on the way and nor did his angels. They are used to divine food and look down on our earthly offerings. We squandered so much money on Mashal, Tareek and Ahqaq and damaged our reputation in the bargain. Khudawand has brought me nothing but peace and joy untold.' Hairat left her husband to rest and returned to Jamshed's pavilion. She saw that his face was still hidden by the veil. His angels stood on either side of him while sardars like Zaal Jadoo and Palang Blood-thirsty sat before him in complete silence. As Hairat prostrated and went around the throne in homage, Jamshed laughed and said, 'Your kingdom will last till eternity, no more tears for you. Strike the battle drums this evening and I will fight for you. Do you realize that I have to manage the universe at the same time with the help of my angels?' Mahrukh

Magic-eye's response to the declaration of the battle was calm. 'We submit to our God's will! Strike our battle drums as well to inform everyone that the fight tomorrow is with Jamshed.'

The battle with Jamshed

The god of the sky appeared in shining glory the next morning and was soon followed by the sounds of the kettledrums and bells of Afrasiyab's army. Jamshed's throne floated into the battlefield with the jewelled canopy shielding him. His angels were flanking him and Palang stood below the throne while Afrasiyab's army was spread out behind the divine throne. Dignitaries from the realm started arriving to catch a glimpse of the supreme deity and were lavish in their praise of Afrasiyab: 'Shahanshah, you are truly exalted! Hundreds of holy men died, but did not have this honour while the god came with you of his own will.' Soldiers on both sides faced each other in a disciplined manner. Afrasiyab rode up to Jamshed's throne and he folded his hands to request, 'Will the shehna be given to Palang Blood-thirsty so that he can commence the battle?' Khudawand Jamshed scolded him, 'You have nothing to do in these matters!' He turned to the angel of death and said, 'You are the symbol of my ire and wrath. Go to the battlefield and capture Bahar, Baghban and Makhmoor. If they are willing to concede, it will be good for them, otherwise, I will burn them in the fires of hell.'

The black angel of death then jumped off the throne with a mighty roar. He jumped on to the battlefield and the earth trembled as he shouted, 'O rebellious Muslims, you are so fearless that you dare to confront Khudawand Jamshed? Come, worship him, and obey your former master Afrasiyab who is the beloved of Jamshed. Why do you court your own deaths?' The sardars called back in unison, 'A thousand curses on your god Jamshed. We are brave warriors and not afraid of losing our lives.' The angel of death called again, 'Let your beloved Bahar who captivates everyone work her magic on me!' There was a stir in the lashkar as Bahar rode forward on her golden peacock holding a bouquet in her hand. She called out, 'Are you a sahir or not? Show me your hand!' That young man laughed in derision, 'You foolish person, I have control over life and death. I hold sway over the north and the south, over the east and west. I have no need of magic or weapons. One sign from me is enough to pull the heavens and earth. A movement of my eye can cause such an upheaval that sahirs and non-sahirs will become lifeless!'

Bahar trembled in fear, but bravely called back, 'Stop talking nonsense and watch what I do to you!' The angel of death then brought out some flowers and threw them at Bahar saying, 'These should be enough for you!' Before Bahar could react, the flowers hit her in the face and she fell down in a dead faint. The angel of death pierced her tongue with a needle and dragged her away. He threw her before the throne of Jamshed, returned to the battlefield and shouted, 'Send Baghban to me now!' Baghban jumped off his mount and rushed to the battlefield, waving his sword. The angel of death cried, 'You dare to confront the controller of souls?' He parried Baghban's attack and held his shield aloft. Baghban was overcome by the fragrance emanating from the shield and fell down heavily. The angel tied him up as well and tossed him before Jamshed. The ferocious young angel was about to return to the battlefield, but Afrasiyab begged Jamshed that this was enough to teach the enemy a lesson. Jamshed called out in anger, 'Do not interfere in the ways of god! However, since you are the Supreme Commander of Samri Worshippers, we cannot refuse you! We will spare the enemy today.' Jamshed's throne then flew to where it had stood earlier and the canopy extended into a large pavilion. Baghban and Bahar were conscious now, but completely helpless and signalled to each other, 'How did we succumb so easily? What kind of magic was this?'

Afrasiyab and Hairat tried to enter the pavilion in order to save Bahar, but the angel of mercy stopped them outside and said, 'The angels of hell are with Khudawand. It is not appropriate for you to enter now!' A few minutes later, they were allowed to go in and saw no signs of Bahar and Baghban. Afrasiyab trembled while Hairat openly wept and said, 'What have you done to Bahar? She is my sister!' Jamshed laughed and replied, 'Hairat, a sinner cannot escape from hell, but I have taken mercy on your tears. I will collect her ashes and she will be reborn after the enemy is punished. Then I shall breathe in a new soul within her!'

Chalak bin Amar was watching this from one corner of the pavilion and was convinced that he was in the presence of a mighty sorcerer. He returned to Mahrukh and wept, 'Huzoor, he has hidden Bahar and Baghban somewhere. He claims he will recreate them from their ashes. I do not believe his nonsense, but he is a powerful magician. We will not be able to overpower him in any manner!' There was an outcry as the sardars wept in despair over the fates of Baghban and Bahar. Their tears spilled into the river of collective grief that flowed throughout the lashkar.

Meanwhile, back in Jamshed's pavilion, Afrasiyab, Hairat and the other sardars were flowing in the ocean of devotion. Jamshed declared, 'Tell us what you want. The garden of Hoshruba sprouts hidden thorns that will plague you for years and years. The angels of hell are here. There is no point in destroying the enemy one by one. We can destroy them all! Who is your greatest enemy?' Hairat spoke up, 'Huzoor, that camel driver's son is the one who is feared most. Let him burn in hell!' Jamshed looked at the angel of death and ordered, 'Capture Amar at once. The lady of the palace must be appeased. She is a woman of immense wisdom and intelligence!' The black angel went bounding out of the pavilion and within moments dragged in the unconscious Amar tied up with ropes. Jamshed rose and shouted, 'My creatures, close your eyes for the angels of hell are here.' Everyone shut their eyes tightly and could hear Khudawand ordering someone, 'Take this sinner and throw him in the same palace of hell where Baghban and Bahar burn. In addition, you can whip him with the fiery chain of flames. Let him recall his misdeeds! Let him burn seventy times before you collect his ashes for rebirth.'

After a pause, they opened their eyes to find Amar missing and Jamshed back on his throne. He then sent for Sarsar, who came forward shivering with fear. He shouted, 'Why you treacherous woman, Amar has not been in the lashkar for a week. His son Chalak has been passing himself as his father in this period. Were you not aware of this or are you secretly on their side? That ayyar had been hiding from me from me in distant forests but the angel of death caught him today.' Sarsar stuttered, 'Huzoor, I was unaware of this. Indeed, my friend Saba Raftar informed me about the deception of Chalak only this evening. You alone could be aware of such trickeries for you are all-knowing and supreme.' Sarsar was now completely convinced of Jamshed's divinity and had become the most ardent of his worshippers. As she kissed his throne, Jamshed laughed and cried, 'This wretched woman's heart is unclouded with doubt today.'

He then turned to Afrasiyab and said, 'In truth, Hamza has found one of our powerful names and is therefore impervious to magic. I cannot take this gift back from him for it would go against all norms of divine grace to bestow a blessing and then take it away. When Hamza enters Tilism, he will thirst in vengeance for his grandson and Amar. He is so blessed by us that he is bound to destroy you. Listen carefully, you foolish man, we have to secure the magic keystone. Tell us where you have hidden it. In fact, give it to us. We will keep it safe in our heaven for you! Where have you kept Lacheen and Badi-uz-Zaman? Their presence in Tilism is dangerous for you!' Jamshed sounded angry while saying this and Afrasiyab's friends were quick to echo his sentiments. They urged Afrasiyab to heed his words and Sarsar in particular said, 'Huzoor, the mercy of Khudawand enfolds you now. Tell him your secrets for I have understood what he means!'

Afrasiyab stood up and postrated before Jamshed and then said, 'I have placed the magic keystone in my friend Zamharir Jadoo's belly. He is hidden in the Neel river and never leaves it. As for Badi and Lacheen, they are in the magic dungeons of Tilism in the care of my friend Tausan, a mighty king.' Jamshed held Afrasiyab by his ears and shook him hard, 'My worshippers, did you ever come across a man as foolish as this one? I have decided now. We will leave these rebels to mourn Baghban and Bahar and travel to Neel river. We will take the magic tablet from him and secure it in our heaven. After that, we will proceed to Tausan's fort and kill Badi and Lacheen. On our return, we will either kill these rebels or make them your slaves. Let us tell you something about Hamza! He curses us in the day and at night he begs and pleads us to forgive him.'

The trickery revealed

Meanwhile, in the Veil of Darkness, Afrasiyab's maternal grandmother Mahiyan consulted the prophecy parchments of Jamshed and slapped her own cheeks in alarm. She cried, 'This is the end. Afrasiyab has been tricked by Amar!'

Just as Afrasiyab was preparing to leave with Jamshed for the journey, there was a shout from the sky, 'Beware you camel driver's son, I am Mahiyan! Afrasiyab you fool, Amar has tricked you! You shameless man, he has made you prostrate to him as well. He has been with you for a week and you could not recognize him? Do you never consult the oracles? Where is the magic flute? Have you handed that to Amar? Alas, you have killed Shehna Nawaz as well!' Amar saw Mahiyan descend like a bolt of lightning and shouted, 'Mahiyan, I have the magic flute. Had you been a little late I would have had the magic keystone and rescued Badi and Lacheen as well!'

Afrasiyab and his companions were horrified. Palang Blood-thirsty tried to leave the Tent of Danyal, but the angel of death who was actually Qiran leapt on him and pinned him to the ground. Amar removed the veil from his face as the Tent of Danyal diminished in size and flew him out of danger. Mahiyan wanted to attack the tent, but Afrasiyab held her back and said, 'Grandmother, do not go. That camel driver's son may have a trap in the tent!' Afrasiyab's soldier sahirs tried to attack the pavilion, but were strung upside down as soon as they entered it. Finally, Amar brought Bahar and Baghban out from Zambil, where they had been in all comfort. When they came out and saw Amar, they said, 'Khwaja sahib, Allah be praised, you are a marvel!'

Afrasiyab began chanting spells that made a sheet of flames fall on the tent. It remained unharmed, but the flames annihilated many of Afrasiyab's men. Sarmaya Ice-maker and Abriq Mountain-breaker conjured huge blocks of ice and large boulders to fall on the pavilion, but only damaged their own troops. Mahiyan and Afrasiyab kept their distance, but moved heaven and earth to overcome Amar despite failing each time. Meanwhile, Mahrukh Magic-eye's spies informed her that Amar's trickery had been exposed. She and the other sardars prepared to defend their friend and as Amar's throne drew nearer, they attacked Afrasiyab's forces with great strength. Eventually, Mahiyan persuaded Afrasiyab to accompany her to the Garden of Apples. As they left, she called out to Hairat, 'There is no use in fighting any more. We have lost the magic flute and thousands of our people are losing their lives in vain. Withdraw your forces now!'

The magic flute

That evening, Palang, who stayed back of his own accord, converted to Islam and asked Mahrukh to strike the battle drums in his name. Afrasiyab was in the Garden of Apples when his agents informed him, 'Huzoor, the battle drums have been struck for Palang. He claims that no one shall withstand the power of the flute, not even you.' Afrasiyab was stunned into silence and after some time, said, 'Friends, his claims are not false. If Samri himself confronts him, he will fall unconscious at the sound of the flute. What am I before Samri? Anyway, I shall have to do something.' Afrasiyab rose and stamped hard on the earth so that it parted. He made his way to Mahrukh's camp through the tunnel that he cut through the earth with his sword.

Meanwhile, Palang was resting in his pavilion. Amar was sure that Afrasiyab would try to retrieve the magic flute and was hidden nearby. Afrasiyab tunnelled his way and emerged into Palang's pavilion. He chanted a spell that made Palang drowsy and then attacked him. Even in that state, Palang tried to fight the king, but was eventually killed. There was darkness all around and his spirits announced his murder. Sahir soldiers rushed into the pavilion and Afrasiyab was forced to fight all of them. The magic flute had been lying next to Palang, but every time Afrasiyab killed a sahir, there was total darkness and he could not see a thing.

Amar woke up with the din and found Palang dead, and Afrasiyab fighting the soldiers. Amar took out the Net of Ilyas and scooped up the magic flute. He then challenged Afrasiyab after announcing himself. Afrasiyab took one look at Amar and the magic flute and ran outside with his fingers stuffed in his ears. Amar ran after him calling, 'Stop Shahanshah, at least enjoy the melodious tones of this flute!' By this time, the rest of the sardars were up and attacked Afrasiyab as he ran towards Hairat's camp. Amar handed the magic flute to Afat Jadoo, who began playing it relentlessly. It was a pitiable sight to see the great Afrasiyab in flight accompanied now by his wife Hairat and other prominent sardars. Even as he ran, Afrasiyab was more than a match for his enemies and felled many of them. Eventually, he ran out of sight of the Islamic lashkar.

After running for a whole day and a night, Afrasiyab reached a verdant plain. One of his vassals, Princess Zamurrud, was enjoying a day out with her companions on the slopes of a hill nearby when she saw the bizarre sight of Shahanshah running for his life. His wife Hairat was running too with her hair open and Afrasiyab's army were running behind them. Zamurrud ran forward and met Afrasiyab. She cried, 'Shahanshah, rest here for a while and eat a few morsels!' Afrasiyab almost fell on the food laid out by the sahira and asked Hairat to join him. Zamurrud left them to eat and went on to confront Mahrukh's sardars. She managed to wound Surkh Mu and Hilal Magic-wielder. Afat had also reached the battlefield with the magic flute when he saw his wounded wife and played the flute so loudly that Zamurrud and her attendants fell unconscious. Afat then held her by the legs and ripped her body apart. With her death, the verdant plain burst into flames.

Afrasiyab and his followers were forced to flee again as Afat went towards them, playing the magic flute steadily. As he ran, Afrasiyab cursed Samri and Jamshed and even swore at Laqa. In sheer rage, he turned to attack Afat, but Hairat screamed and held him back, 'For love of Samri, do not go near him Shahanshah, do you want to make me a widow? Look how loudly he plays the flute!' Afrasiyab fled out of his reach, but Afat managed to kill many of his supporters. It was an extraordinary scene with hundreds of bodies strewn in the plain and Afrasiyab's companions beating their heads. It seemed that any moment Afrasiyab would succumb to the sound of the flute as well. Suddenly, a light flashed in the sky. A wizened old sahir appeared on the horizon cursing Afrasiyab, 'O Afrasiyab Khana Kharab, it was for this day that I did not come with you earlier! I would have died like Palang and who would have saved you now?'

Shehna Nawaz flew down towards Afat and shouted, 'Afat you traitor to the old religion! Have you no shame that you destroy so many Samri worshippers? You abandon the gods and worship the Unseen One! Now you are after the life of the ruler of Hoshruba?' Afat was startled by this sudden onslaught and before he could recover, Shehna Nawaz hovered above him and slit open his own throat with a dagger. He scooped up his blood and threw it over the magic flute before falling on the earth. There was an almighty explosion and the flute burst into flames. A flame shot up from it and fell on Afat like a sword and that brave warrior went straight to heaven. Several people fainted with the sound of the loud explosions that occurred with the death of Shehna Nawaz.

In her palace, Afrasiyab's grandmother Afat saw the golden maidens change colour and realized what had happened. She managed to save many of them, but three hundred magic maidens lost their lives anyway. Afat reached the battlefield to hear sounds of 'You have killed me! I was master of the fourth hujra!' She saw Afrasiyab disconsolate and weeping while Mahrukh's army was preparing to avenge their sardar Afat's death. She fell from the skies shouting, 'Be warned that I am here! Do not move, or you will all be instantly killed.' Afat rescued Hairat and Afrasiyab and flew off with them, even as she called out to Sarmaya and Abriq, 'Return to your posts. Your king will return with a fresh army!'

<hr />

39 THE STRANGE TALE OF THE FIFTH HUJRA OF PERIL, PRINCESS YAKUT, LAL SUKHANDAN AND MALIK AKHZAR, AMAR'S TRICKERY ON AFRASIYAB, THE DEATH OF PRINCESS YAKUT

After Shehna Nawaz's death, Amar returned to his camp and sat in his chair in the durbar triumphantly. Princess Bahar said, 'Khwaja, we are not at peace yet. It is now the turn of the fifth hujra. Its master is Malik Akhzar, companion of Samri, who was married to Kaukab's sister-in-law. His daughters Yakut and Lal are renowned for their beauty and magical powers. Afrasiyab intended to marry Yakut, but had to marry Hairat instead. This was because Malik Akhzar wanted him to propose to Yakut in person, but Afrasiyab was too proud to do so. He will certainly make the journey now and persuade them to come with him. If they agree, the heavens and earth will tremble. They have two magical springs that accompany them wherever they travel. The waters of these springs are deadly and can annihilate millions. Malik Akhzar also has the crystal Globe of Samri that reveals everything. No one can dare trick these people. If you approach him in disguise, the magic globe will immediately reveal your true identity.' Amar smiled and replied, 'Bahar, are you trying to frighten me so that I lose heart even before I confront them? Remember the miracles of the Almighty. Did we think we could destroy the four hujras? He will guide us now and protect us.'

At that time, a message came from Kaukab that he was with Nur Afshan in the Palace of Jamshed and wished to consult Amar. Kaukab and Nur Afshan were meeting with some of their advisers and ministers when Amar reached the palace. They all rose to greet him respectfully. After Amar sat on the seat of honour, Kaukab said, 'King of trickery and deceit, let me be brief. My wife Naheed and Malik Akhzar's wife Akhtar were sisters and therefore Akhzar is my brother-in-law. Akhtar had two daughters Yakut and Lal Sukhandan, and my wife had Jamshed and Burran. The sisters had decided that Yakut and Jamshed would be married. After his wife died, Malik Akhzar broke relations with us and the engagement never took place formally. We heard that Malik Akhzar was considering Afrasiyab's proposal, but in his arrogance, wanted Afrasiyab to beg for her hand. Afrasiyab, on the other hand, thought since he was the ruler of the realm, it was Malik Akhzar's duty to offer his daughter as tribute to him. The girls also developed independent reputations as the chosen ones of Samri and no one proposed to them. Afrasiyab will most definitely go and propose to marry Yakut now that he wants Akhzar's help. Ever since I have forsworn the ancient religion, Samri worshippers are my enemies. Malik Akhzar will accept the proposal, especially as it means confronting me. They also have the dreaded man-eating ogre Afreet Tilismi, who will do their bidding and swallow everybody. Apart from him, they know many other magical spells of Samri and Jamshed. Now what I suggest is this. Before Afrasiyab reaches there, I will send a messenger proposing Jamshed's hand in marriage for Yakut. If they accept the proposal, Afrasiyab will have no recourse but to capitulate.'

Amar heard him silently and said, 'I agree with you. Send your messenger as soon as possible.' Kaukab then rose and led Amar to a secret room in the Palace of Jamshed. There, Amar saw a number of large boxes that looked like sarcophagi. Kaukab opened one of the boxes in which a young man lay sleeping. Kaukab called out, 'Asrar Tajdar, you have slept a long time. It is time to wake up!' The young man opened his eyes and sat up. he said, 'I am at your service.' Kaukab saw that Amar was looking puzzled and explained, 'Khwaja, this young man Asrar Tajdar has a honeyed tongue and will convey the proposal in a unique manner. Besides, he is the only one who can travel to that magic-bound land.'

Asrar Tajdar then wore a crown and royal robes. A party of forty counsellors and attendants were to accompany him and he conjured a large flying throne for the journey. Amar also took his leave of Kaukab, who bade him farewell. Amar walked a few steps and then disappeared.

A little later, Asrar Tajdar conjured a cloud that floated above the flying throne to provide shade and left for the fort of Yakutia.

Now hear about Afrasiyab. His grandmother Afat had rescued him with his wife Hairat and took them to the Garden of Apples. Hairat beat her head in grief and said, 'Our house will be destroyed now!' Afrasiyab looked at her calmly and said, 'Why do you weep? Accept my second marriage and all our troubles will be gone.' Hairat looked horrified, but Afat embraced her and said, 'Hairat, we were waiting for this day. You should consider yourself fortunate for your rival is one who was the beloved of Samri and Jamshed. She is the acme of magic. Who can confront her?'

The kingdom of rubies

Soon, Afrasiyab left for the fort of Yakutia and awakened his magical powers on the way. A white cloud showered him with pearls and five thousand companions and soldiers accompanied him on horses. After many hours, he saw the ruby fort from a distance. The walls of rubies glistened in the sun like rubies and hundreds of golden slave-girls stood on the walls as guards. As Afrasiyab neared the fort, one of the girls stepped in front of the contingent and cried, 'Who are you that you dare to ride into this forbidden place? Turn back at once!' Afrasiyab's men were as arrogant as he was and one of them attacked her with a spear. The magic slave-girl jumped up, slapped him hard, and smashed his head. The slave-girl then turned to the other riders and punished them in a similar manner.

Soon, there was an uproar among the soldiers. Afrasiyab looked up and asked, 'What is going on?' One of the soldiers rushed to him and said, 'Huzoor, there is a magic slave-girl who has killed several of our men. She refuses to let us proceed further.' Afrasiyab was furious as the golden slave-girl came up to him and laughed derisively before saying, 'Who are you that you dare to wear a crown here? Wear a cap at once and state the purpose of your visit!' Afrasiyab was even more startled when she jumped up and tried to wrest the crown from his head. Enraged, he slapped her hard and her skull split open. She screamed at her companions, 'This monster has shed my blood!' At her call, forty other slave-girls jumped down from the palace walls and fell on Afrasiyab's soldiers killing hundreds of them. One of them reached Afrasiyab and plucked the crown off his head. Afrasiyab furiously chanted spells, but the slave-girls seemed to be impervious to magic. Eventually, he called out loudly, 'Has Hoshruba been conquered? Has Tilism Kusha found the magic keystone? O Kundan, come here at once!' The earth trembled and a beautiful girl in golden clothes materialized in the sky. 'Whatever is the matter huzoor?' she asked with folded hands. Afrasiyab replied, 'Kundan, bring me the Tilismi crown at once! These shameless slave-girls have destroyed hundreds of my men!'

Kundan promptly vanished and reappeared just moments later with a gleaming Tilismi crown that she placed on Afrasiyab's head. Afrasiyab then attacked the slave-girls furiously and tore many of them apart. His Tilismi crown radiated rays that incinerated them and he destroyed twenty-five slave-girls. The rest scampered back to their stations on the fort walls and began screaming abuses at Afrasiyab from a distance. Afrasiyab was still wearing the magic crown when he approached the fort, but stopped when everything went dark around him. The light came back within moments and Afrasiyab saw that a wall of iron with hundreds of holes in it materialized before the ruby fort. The slave-girls looked at him through the holes and screamed, 'You heartless man, will you also attack this wall now? You have been merciless with the slaves of Samri!'

Afrasiyab furiously flung an iron ball at the wall, but it bounced back and killed several of his men. The slave-girls screamed, 'Why you arrogant fool, is this all the magic you know? Come across the wall and we will tear your flesh apart and teach you a lesson!' Afrasiyab was preparing to fling another ball when a light flashed and a voice called out, 'Wait Shahanshah! Your men should not have been so aggressive when they were guests in this place. If you had waited a while we would have come to receive you.' Afrasiyab looked up and saw an old man seated on a golden peacock calling out to him. Mussavir the magic artist was with the Shah and asked, 'Do you recognize this old man?' Afrasiyab replied, 'God knows who this fool is and what nonsense he is spouting!' Viziers Sarmaya and Abriq folded their hands and said respectfully, 'Huzoor, this venerable elder is the father of Yakut and Lal Sukhandan; companion to Samri and Jamshed, Malik Akhzar Pearl-robe. He is coming out of the fort to receive you.'

Malik Akhzar approached Afrasiyab and embraced him warmly. He murmured apologetically, 'Shahanshah, the slave-girls of Samri have caused you much trouble.' Afrasiyab was still smarting and said, 'I would have destroyed them all very soon!' Presently, the sound of drums filled the air and everyone turned around to see the massive gateway of the fort being opened to reveal a maiden whose beauty surpassed the sun and the stars. As Afrasiyab gaped at her, Malik Akhzar said, 'My younger daughter Princess Lal Sukhandan comes out to welcome you. The one for whom you have come lives in Yakut Nigar. We will send word to her and she will either summon us or come here herself.'

Lal came forward and held Afrasiyab by the hand. The King of Magic was entranced by her grace and beauty. It was as if the sculptor of nature had cast her face and body in a heavenly mould. She led Afrasiyab into the fort and then sent a message to Yakut. A light flashed in the sky and hundreds of song birds flew in followed by two magical springs. They unrolled like ribbons and rested on the ground. The birds trilled, 'The beloved of Samri arrives!' Malik Akhzar stood up to receive his daughter, as did Lal Sukhandan. The attendants in the durbar stood in rows to welcome her. Lal said to Afrasiyab, 'Brother, you should also rise as the elder sister arrives. She is the most exalted, the personification of Samri himself.' The waters of the springs then began to churn and the birds flew around in excitement. Everyone in the durbar, including Afrasiyab, lowered their heads in respect. After some time, Afrasiyab looked up and saw a maiden of unearthly beauty and grace. Afrasiyab was overwhelmed as he gazed at her flower-like face and her lips that were as red as rubies. His limbs trembled and his lips went dry, his heart felt as if it was constricted. He was about to faint with the rush of emotion when Malik Akhzar held his hand. Lal Sukhandan said, 'Brother, remain steady!'

Afrasiyab could not help staring at Yakut, who blushed as she took her place on the throne. Malik Akhzar said, 'Shahanshah, talk to us. What brings you here?' Afrasiyab sighed and said, 'Father, what can I say? I seem to have lost my senses!' Lal then parted her delectable red lips to say, 'Brother, say what is on your mind. Your heart's desire will be fulfilled for you are of an illustrious rank.' Afrasiyab had already written down the proposal of marriage on a letter and handed this to Akhzar. He said, 'This is my heart's desire.' Akhzar read the proposal and rose to embrace Afrasiyab warmly. 'Shahanshah,' said Akhzar, 'do not be despondent. You are close to victory for within a day my daughters and I will destroy every rebel. What is Asad and who is Amar before us? At the mention of Amar's name, Afrasiyab slapped his own cheeks and cried, 'For the love of Samri, do not take that monster's name! Shaitan Bakhtiarak of divine Laqa's durbar has explained this to me. If anyone takes Amar's name, wherever Amar is, he comes to know of it. If it is taken a second time, he sits with his face in the direction of that gathering. The third time you call his name, he reaches that place. After that, he is like the curse of Samri on that gathering and every one is disgraced with blackened faces and shoe beatings! Believe me this is the truth about him!'

Malik Akhzar laughed and said, 'Shahanshah, have you lost your senses? Look at the difficulty with which you have reached here and you are the monarch of this realm! How can that camel driver's son come here? I will take his name a thousand times. Let us see if he can reach here!' Lal added, 'How can he dare to come here!' The attendants cried in unison, 'If that wretched Amar comes here, we will cut up his flesh into tiny pieces and eat him!' Afrasiyab pleaded, 'Friends, be quiet and do not utter his name! That monster will indeed appear here. Khudawand Laqa is his loyal friend and obeys him in all things. Shaitan trembles with fear at his name and even Samri and Jamshed are in awe of him!' Malik Akhzar said scornfully, 'We have taken his name a hundred times now. Why has that camel driver's son not come here as yet?' Afrasiyab replied, 'Shaitan Bakhtiarak assured me that he is drawn like a magnet to any gathering where his name is mentioned.' Malik Akhzar retorted, 'It must be in gatherings that you hold. We will twist his neck if he comes here! Do you see the drawings of magical birds on these walls? They will reveal the identity of any intruder who comes here. There is open rebellion in your land, but this is a secure place.'

Afrasiyab called out, 'Khwaja Amar, you are the living model of Samri, save me from shame! Come and display your talents to Malik Akhzar!' Everyone laughed and Malik Akhzar said, 'Stop talking nonsense and hear some good news. We accept you as our son-in-law.' Yakut also nodded her agreement. Lal signalled and a handmaiden wearing red robes came forward holding a perfumed citron. Afrasiyab's reddened with joy as she rubbed the perfume on his chest. He then looked deep into Yakut's eyes and tilted his cap in triumph. There were cries of greetings from everyone in the durbar and pretty young girls sprayed everyone with perfumed coloured water. Malik Akhzar bestowed rich robes of honour on all of Yakut's attendants and Afrasiyab promised that his gifts would be sent from Hoshruba. Yakut and Lal were still smiling when an attendant announced that Kaukab's messenger, Asrar Tajdar was waiting to be admitted into the durbar.

Yakut said, 'Our uncle Kaukab has remembered us after a long time.' Afrasiyab intervened, 'Princess, your uncle is our enemy. It was with his help that Mashal, Tareek, Ahqaq and Shehna Nawaz were killed. Whenever we try to destroy the rebels, he comes to help them. Do not meet his messenger!' Yakut smiled and said, 'Shahanshah, we cannot abandon our kith and kin for you. Burran and Jamshed are blood relatives. I am sure that once we confront the rebels, they will turn their backs on them as well. If they have sent a messenger, we must receive him.' Yakut gave instructions that the messenger was to be welcomed formally and added, 'Asrar Tajdar is privy to the secrets of this realm, he must be give due honour.'

Asrar Tajdar was welcomed by several nobles and went to the palace with four attendants. He left his attendants outside and went into the durbar to present the message. He greeted everyone respectfully, but frowned when he saw Afrasiyab. The King of Magic was enraged by this and looked at Yakut meaningfully. She smiled and whispered, 'Shahanshah, you do not lose your rank if a messenger does not greet you!' Before he sat down, Asrar presented Kaukab's letter with both hands to Malik Akhzar, who took the letter and raised it to his eyes. Yakut and Lal tearfully said, 'Father, our uncle has remembered us after many years. If our dear mother had been alive, this message would have meant something. We will write back and complain to him.' Lal took the letter and read it out aloud as Yakut and Malik Akhzar listened carefully.

After Malik Akhzar heard Kaukab's loving proposal; he struck his knee and said, 'Your mother had agreed to this proposal, but died before she could formalize it. Now we have accepted Shahanshah. What reply do we give?' Yakut said in anger, 'Respected father, was our uncle asleep all these years? Tell him in clear terms that we have said yes to Shahanshah. Had his proposal reached us sooner, we could have considered it. Tell him that since he is now a Muslim, he will not need Samri worshippers anyway. He should seek an alliance with people of the same religion as his. I do not approve of his praise of the Unseen God in this letter.' Afrasiyab's heart swelled with joy at her words and he stroked his moustache arrogantly. Mussavir whispered to him, 'Shahanshah, this beloved of the gods is obviously inclined towards you. What an appropriate reply she has suggested! The old man looks quite stunned!'

Amar in the land of rubies

Malik Akhzar wrote out the response Yakut suggested and handed it to Asrar. Yakut and Lal signalled to the cupbearers to serve Kaukab's messenger with wine. A young damsel in bright clothes led the cupbearers. She held a flask of wine and sang melodiously as she approached the royal party. Her voice was so clear and musical that Malik Akhzar looked at Lal in surprise and said, 'You have trained your attendants well. Who is this young parizad? She has entranced us with her voice.' Afrasiyab also heaped praise on the singer whose name was Madhosh. She came forward still singing and filled Afrasiyab and Mussavir's goblets. She then turned to Malik Akhzar and said, 'Huzoor, I am your humble slave and longed for the honour of serving you wine.' The old man eagerly took the goblet she offered him, while Yakut watched the proceedings silently. The eyes of the birds drawn on the walls were also gazing down steadily. As Akhzar raised the goblet to his lips, one of the birds with wings of gold shrieked loudly. Yakut stood up and cried, 'Father, do not touch the wine! Madhosh, you rascal, I have recognized you! You cannot escape now!'

Madhosh, who was actually Amar in disguise, became invisible at once, but Yakut had already uttered the magic incantation 'gir'. Even though he was invisible, Amar's feet were fixed on the earth and he could not move. Akhzar saw that Mussavir and Afrasiyab were already unconscious and were snoring loudly. Yakut said, 'Father, the earth must have caught that rascal's feet. This earth is of the palace of Lal Sukhandan! This earth is an enemy of all Muslims!' As she waved her hands, birds flew in and trilled over Mussavir and Afrasiyab to revive them. Afrasiyab awoke and greeted his father-in-law in mock humiliation, 'Respected father, I greet you. Amar, my friend, you have honoured my word!' Lal said, 'Brother, stop praising Amar! He is invisible! Tell us where we can find him!' Afrasiyab exclaimed, 'My loyal friend must have worn his Galeem! Where are you Khwaja? Talk to me!'

A voice called out, 'Respected one, your slave is here, but my feet are almost breaking. My master came here to get married, how could his court singer not accompany him?' One of the attendants screamed and ran towards Princess Lal. 'He is standing next to me, but I cannot see him!' Malik Akhzar was too embarrassed to speak, but Afrasiyab declared, 'Malik Akhzar, Princess Yakut, even if you search for the rest of your lives, you will not find Amar! He will only appear if you promise him safe conduct.' Amar's voice called out again, 'Shahanshah, I am only afraid of you. This old man who is close to death is nothing before me. If I am not guaranteed safe passage, I promise you, I will destroy his magic crystal ball and fill this place with dead bodies!'

At this point, Yakut said caustically, 'Shahanshah, you seem to have great faith in Amar!' Afrasiyab retorted, 'Princess, he proved me right. I had warned you about him. I knew that he would come! I let Murshidzadeh drink the drugged wine and had it myself to prove my word. You would not have known, but for the warning from the magic bird!' Yakut said softly, 'Khwaja, we are keen to set eyes upon your noble visage. Indeed you are skilled in the ways of trickery.' The voice replied, 'You are too kind! I am an ordinary man, but remain my Shahanshah's slave. I always go where he goes. If you remove your spell, I will show my face to you.' Lal, who had been silent all this time, said, 'Friends, find out about Madhosh, what has happened to her?' Her attendants rushed to search for Madhosh and reported that she was not to be found anywhere. Afrasiyab smiled and said, 'My faithful friend must have deposited her in Zambil. Khwaja what did you do with Madhosh?'

Amar's voice replied, 'I was hungry and ate her.' Madhosh's mother was in the durbar and began wailing when he said this. Yakut said, 'Stop weeping! I will destroy heaven and earth to recover Madhosh. We have been deceived, but no one can keep our attendant! Khwaja Amar, what has happened has happened. You are indeed a great ayyar. I will remove my spell now. Show yourself to us!' Yakut merely smiled to remove her spell. Everyone was surprised to see Amar descending from the sky as if the earth had never caught him. Afrasiyab stood to greet him and said, 'Welcome shah of ayyars! We are all anxious to meet you.' Amar replied, 'I am at your service!' Amar looked his real self now, with Galeem on his shoulders, the snare-ropes of ayyari coiled around his arms, and his heavy sword suspended from his waist.

He greeted everyone respectfully and kissed Yakut's feet. He said to her, 'Huzoor, you must not waste your anger on lowly slaves like me. I would like now to sing for you.' As Amar hummed to himself, Afrasiyab declared, 'Indeed princesses, Amar is skilled in the art of music and his voice is famous throughout the world!' Yakut ignored Afrasiyab and said, 'Khwaja, you can get your own way by flattering Shahanshah, but we are different. It is because of his weakness that there is rebellion in Hoshruba. No one can pull a trick on us. Do you see the crystal ball that my father holds in his hand? The gods themselves created it! It is better than the Book of Samri and reveals the heart of all conspiracy. Anyway, let that be. Sing for us.'

Amar then sat with the musicians and sang so melodiously that there was a hushed silence in the durbar even after he finished. Lal impulsively took off the costly string of pearls around her neck and gave it to Amar. He looked at the King of Magic with a smile and asked him, 'Shahanshah, should I accept this gift from your sister-in-law? After all that you have given me, I can easily return it.' When Afrasiyab did not respond Amar put the string in his pocket and said, 'My master's in-laws have given me a gift. I will have to accept it!'

Suddenly, the missing handmaiden Madhosh's mother rushed forward and fell at Amar's feet. She cried, 'Khwaja, whatever jewellery I have made in my life I give to you. Give my daughter back.' Amar's reply was so evasive that Madhosh's mother appealed to her mistress Lal, who said, 'Khwaja, we are willing to pay your price for her!' Amar replied, 'I am in debt for one lakh rupees. My creditor has not told me what the interest is yet.' Afrasiyab nodded and smiled, as if to encourage Amar. Lal quickly said, 'I am willing to give you twenty-five thousand over a lakh.' Amar bargained, 'I am afraid that once you have Madhosh, you might not give me the money or worse, you will capture me. What we can do is this. We can go out of this fort. I will bring Madhosh out and you bring the money. We will make a fair exchange.'

Princess Lal agreed to these terms and sent her attendants to get the sacks of gold coins from the treasury. She went out of the fort with Afrasiyab and saw that Amar had spread an old carpet under a tree. As they watched, he brought Madhosh out and laid her out on the carpet. Madhosh's mother wanted to rush to her daughter, but Afrasiyab stopped her. He said, 'Do not be hasty, you might upset everything. Khwaja Amar has a method to what he does. Only I understand his ways.' Amar called out, 'Do not come near me. Just keep the money under that tree. When I go near it, you can come and get Madhosh!' Yakut had been watching the proceedings from the fort walls and was chewing her lips in anger. Amar walked towards the sacks of coins, flung the Net of Ilyas over it and scooped up the sacks of gold. At the same moment, Madhosh's mother screamed because when she embraced her daughter, her body came apart in her hands. Amar had vanished in Galeem by then. Afrasiyab roared with laughter, 'It seems as if my faithful old friend has been up to his old tricks again!'

Yakut Sukhandan called out, 'Sister, what has happened? Lal called back mournfully, 'Sister, he has taken the money and left a lentil flour figure for us!' Yakut reddened with anger and she furiously stared at the magic springs. Her gaze was magical and a bubble burst out of one spring and expelled a flame that shot up to the sky. Meanwhile, Amar had been running for his life. He stopped to rest under a tree and took off his cape. Suddenly, the earth under the tree heaved and parted. A mountain lion sprang out of the cleft and roared at Amar. The ayyar did not have the time to wear Galeem and ran towards the desert. By then, hundreds of lions were running after him. He turned around and ran towards the fort and saw that only one lion pursued him this time.

Yakut and Lal Sukhandan, Afrasiyab and Malik Akhzar were standing on the walls of the fort when they saw Amar running for his life towards them. He called out, 'Save me master from this lion!' Amar tried to wear his Galeem as he ran, but was too terrified to wrap it around himself. He ran up to Afrasiyab and clung to him in desperation. Yakut said, 'Khwaja, you tried to deceive us. You had better give us Madhosh or it will be even worse for you!' Khwaja Amar spluttered, 'I am in your power now so I will give Madhosh to you. But be warned that I will play a trick on you when you confront us in the battlefield and you will lose your magic ball.' Malik Akhzar shouted, 'You would not dare!' Amar replied, 'This is your moment, so of course you are right. You will understand when you go to confront Mahrukh.' He turned and addressed Afrasiyab, 'Huzoor, I played this trick to establish your word against theirs. Please guarantee that I will not be harmed and I will return Madhosh.' Afrasiyab gave his word that the princess would not harm the ayyar. After much persuasion by Afrasiyab, Amar brought Madhosh out from Zambil. She was clad in a soiled sari and looked distraught. Her mother embraced her and asked, 'Are you well my child?'

Madhosh began babbling: 'I would like a ride in the boat that sails down the river. The fair princesses beckon me, but their black-faced handmaidens frighten me. Amar has a vast kingdom with forts and gardens. I will also go to the gardens to see the spring blossoms. You must come with me. I gave my clothes and my jewellery, but they would not leave me alone!' Yakut remarked dryly, 'This Madhosh must be drunk on wine or perhaps she lives up to her name!' Afrasiyab signalled to Amar to leave. Asrar Tajdar went up to Amar and said, 'Khwaja, how did you reach here?' Amar replied, 'I came with you actually. I drugged one of your attendants and took his place. God save the lashkar of Islam.' Amar then returned to Tilism Nur Afshan with Asrar Tajdar.

Later, in the durbar, Yakut scolded her father roundly, 'My dear elder, you have a unique gift that tells you whatever is happening around you; why do you not look at it? At least that sarbanzada would not have humiliated us this way! Our worthy Shahanshah is completely under Amar's spell, but you must remain vigilant. He has openly claimed that he will take the magic ball away from you!' Malik Akhzar said with false bravado, 'He will not dare to!' Yakut became even angrier and shouted, 'I do not believe in such empty talk. You must remain alert with an enemy like Amar!' She turned to her sister and asked her to prepare for the journey to Tilism.

Yakut meets Hairat

The next morning, Lal's army of a lakh and fifty thousand fair handmaidens, armed with magical weapons, assembled in front of the fort. Yakut and Afrasiyab sat on a flying throne made out of rubies, while Lal and her father sat on separate thrones. Malik Akhzar's army of four lakh men were assembled behind them. A pink cloud floated in to shield them from the sun. The magical springs also moved along with the army. Thus, the procession of Princess Yakut moved towards Hoshruba in all pomp and splendour.

As the procession approached the two war camps, the sardars of Islam came out to see the famous family of the fifth hujra. The two magic springs rolled in first, their clear waters sparkling in the sun. As the royal party followed them, Bahar's eyes met her sister Hairat's across the battlefield and she mockingly signalled to her, 'Your rival comes, you should be prepared for shoe beatings!' Hairat signalled back, 'I will accept even death if it means that she will twist your neck!'

Afrasiyab cantered up on his horse and cried excitedly, 'Malika, come and welcome the princesses Yakut and Lal. My proposal was accepted.

Look how beautiful they both are. I will marry one and make the other my concubine!' Hairat said derisively, 'Are you not ashamed? I believe Amar deceived you even there!' Afrasiyab shrugged casually and said, 'He may have humiliated them, but I do not care. At least he proved my point. I must tell you all about it.' Hairat snorted, 'I will welcome them because they are my guests; otherwise my shoes would welcome them!' Afrasiyab then escorted her personally, shouting out 'Make way for Malika Hairat!' As the crowds parted before them, Hairat first greeted Malik Akhzar. Yakut rose to greet Hairat and made her sit on the throne beside her. Afrasiyab's heart burst with pride as he looked up at the two beauties. They were like two shining celestial bodies, two precious pearls in one setting.

Princess Lal had gone forward to inspect her camp as it settled down. She was close to the rebel camp and saw Princess Mahjabeen on a throne surrounded by all her sardars. Lal sighed as she saw the incomparable beauty of Mahjabeen, and asked, 'Who is she?' Sarsar, who was with her, said, 'Do you not recognize Shahanshah's niece, Mahjabeen Diamond-robe?' Lal looked startled and she placed her index finger on her chin before asking, 'Why is Shahanshah's niece with the rebels?' Sarsar then pointed out Asad and said, 'Do you see that lion sitting on the throne beside her? He is Tilism Kusha Asad Ghazi. Mahjabeen eloped with him! She is badshah of lashkar and the sardars pay homage to her.'

Lal looked closely at Asad and saw a young man of incomparable beauty and dignity, with hazel eyes and a noble forehead. Zargham whispered to Asad, 'Huzoor, sit up, Lal Sukhandan is looking at you.' Asad twirled his moustache and looked around. He met her eyes and was immediately entranced by her beauty. Lal turned away with her hand on her heart and Sarsar noticed her reaction to Asad. She said, 'Is Mahjabeen not fortunate? She is the beloved of the bravest of Hamza's grandsons. He can fight large armies and destroy their ranks. The young man besides him is his devoted friend Sundlaan Sandli Posh, the strongest wrestler in this realm. Asad defeated him in a wrestling bout and he has been devoted to Asad ever since. If it was not for the fact that Asad is unfamiliar with magic, he would certainly have defeated Afrasiyab.'

Lal said quietly, 'He may be all that, but what good is it to us? Mahjabeen is welcome to him!' Sarsar, adding fuel to fire, said, 'He has a formidable reputation as a lover. Besides Mahjabeen, he has another beloved, Lalaan Red-robe, the daughter of Khudawand Dawood. Both maidens are devoted to Tilism Kusha. They are both beautiful and accomplished and he spends alternate evenings with each of them.' Lal fell silent, but her heart was torn by her love for Asad, and she wondered how it would end for her. She busied herself in selecting a place for her army and eventually selected the base of the mountain of Nilofar.

Hairat returned to her pavilion with a heavy heart after having left Afrasiyab in attendance on Yakut Sukhandan. She was lying on her bed depressed and gloomy, when Sarsar came in laughing. 'What amuses you so much today?' Hairat asked. Sarsar grinned and replied, 'Huzoor, something new is brewing and someone will go astray. I have also added fuel to her fire!' Hairat got up abruptly and said, 'Tell me what has happened!' Sarsar whispered, 'Huzoor, remember that this was the day I warned you about! Lal Sukhandan is in love with Asad Ghazi!' Hairat sighed, 'No, Sarsar, that is impossible! She is also going to be my rival for Afrasiyab's affections.' Sarsar said confidently, 'Just wait and see!' Hairat said, 'May Samri and Jamshed bring this about. At least they will not taunt my sister any more!'

Malik Akhzar in Zambil

The next morning, the waters of the two magic springs churned in anticipation of the battle that day. Princess Lal inspected the rank and file of their army while Yakut and her father entered the battleground. A turquoise-coloured cloud arose from the direction of Nur Afshan. Below the cloud, Kaukab the Enlightened sat on a flying throne, resplendent in jewels and a ruby crown. Malik Akhzar looked away, but Kaukab addressed him loudly, 'Brother, praise be to Allah, you are so hard-hearted that you face your kinsman in battle? Had my sister-in-law and your late wife been alive today, would she have allowed this? It is certain that Burran and Jamshed will die in this battle for everyone knows of Yakut's powers. Whatever happens, I do not wish to remain alive to see the dead bodies of these four children.'

Malik Akhzar started to explain, 'Brother, we asked Burran to meet us, but she is too proud and completely under Amar's spell ...' Kaukab shouted, 'You fool, Burran is the same child who used to play in your lap. What does she know about anything? No, I have made up my mind! I will die today and these four children will carry my bier. I do not want to be alive to see any one of them dead. I am not an executioner like you. Everyone knows that Kaukab is a soft-hearted man!'

By this time, Akhzar was close to Kaukab's throne. Kaukab drew his dagger and declared, 'Look, I am placing this on my throat and will take my own life. My life's story has ended. I will leave you to witness the carnage of this battle.' Malik Akhzar became nervous and cried, 'Brother,

I will turn my armies around and accept Jamshed as my son!' At this, Kaukab smiled and said, 'I have just come here to sacrifice my life!' He then placed the dagger on his throat. Malik Akhzar leaned forward to snatch it from his hand, but Kaukab brushed him aside. Hairat and Afrasiyab were watching Kaukab carefully while there were cries all around them, 'Indeed, Kaukab is a man of sensitivity and honour!' Yakut and Lal were distraught and Yakut called out, 'Father, wrest the dagger from our uncle's hand. Samri preserve him, he loves us dearly! He has held us in his arms since we were babies. We will not go against his will now. May worms eat the marriage that extinguishes the brightest star of Nur Afshan!'

Meanwhile, Kaukab had already sliced his throat and his lifeless body fell on the throne. Malik Akhzar screamed in anguish and fell on the body, weeping loudly. Suddenly, the blood that was spurting out of Kaukab's throat shot up like a spray on to Akhzar's face and he fell unconscious. At that time, a smaller head appeared from within the cavity of Kaukab's throat and shouted, 'I am Amar!' As everyone watched in horror, Amar and Akhzar vanished within the turquoise cloud that went spinning out of sight. The cloud transported Amar within moments to the Palace of Jamshed where the real Kaukab was waiting for him. He jumped up and embraced Amar warmly. 'Khwaja,' said Kaukab, 'I watched everything. You have done a remarkable thing!' Kaukab then took the magic crystal ball out of Amar's pocket and said, 'This will be very useful to us in the future! You should take Malik Akhzar back, otherwise dreadful things might happen to you!' Amar smiled and said, 'Dreadful things happen all the time! Let this old man have a taste of life in Zambil for some time!' He dropped Malik Akhzar in Zambil and called out to the keepers, 'His name is Malik Akhzar. Do not subject him to hard labour. He is educated, so let him help you with the accounts!' Amar then returned to his lashkar.

Yakut was in a rage after Amar abducted her father right before her eyes. She had the battle drums struck in her name. Mahjabeen turned to Amar and said, 'Grandfather, let the battle drums be struck on our side with the will of the Almighty.' Baghban Qudrat lifted the golden mace with silver inlay and struck the largest drum himself. The rest of the seventeen hundred drums were also struck and the lashkar buzzed with speculations. People said to each other, 'Friends, Allah protect us. Khwaja kidnapped Yakut's father and she will fight against us. Did you know that she is a without a peer in her magical powers?'

The sardars flanked Mahjabeen as they left for the battlefield like the spring breeze. They saw that Afrasiyab and Yakut were waiting for them, and the magical springs were churning behind them. Yakut observed from a distance that Bahar was ready for battle with an array of her deadly bouquets. Lal was about to go forward when Yakut stopped her and said, 'It is not fitting for you to confront these people. I have a plan already.' She called out, 'Mistress Saman, go ahead and challenge Bahar.' Saman stepped forward from the ranks of the army and called out, 'Princess, I am waiting for you.'

Bahar then flung bouquets in four directions. A cool breeze swept through the battlefield, and trees swayed and birds sang melodiously. A garden appeared in the middle of the battlefield with tender young shoots and pleasing streams. As Bahar looked at the garden, the flower buds smiled and blossomed while birds burst into song. Saman was completely enchanted and walked towards Bahar with her hands clasped, pleading to be accepted. Bahar brought out magic flower bracelets to tie around her wrists. These would have turned Saman against Yakut, but Yakut quickly flung a pearl in her magic spring. The waters expelled a flame that fell on Bahar's garden and burnt it to ashes. The same flame rendered Bahar unconscious. Saman was herself again and at Yakut's signal, lifted Bahar's lifeless body and carried her back to her mistress.

Princess Burran stepped forward and called out, 'Well done Yakut for saving your woman and not having the courage to step forward yourself. Were you afraid of Bahar? What you did was entirely unethical.' Amar whispered to Burran that he was willing to exchange Malik Akhzar for Bahar. Burran called out to her cousin, 'Yakut, will you return our fair Bahar for your father?' Yakut agreed readily. She revived Bahar and sent her back to her camp saying, 'Just make sure our father comes back.' After Bahar's return, Amar brought out Malik Akhzar from Zambil. Burran arranged for someone to escort him back to Afrasiyab's camp. As Malik Akhzar approached his camp, his daughters went forward to greet him. The old man was silent and the girls thought that he was angry with them. They led Akhzar into the royal pavilion, but he remained silent and sullen. Eventually, Yakut put her arms around him and asked, 'Respected elder, why are you angry with us? We are not to blame for your capture. You should have consulted the crystal ball before Amar deceived you so shamefully. Talk to us!' Lal also put her arms around her father, but the old man still remained silent. Akhzar's companions and sardars pleaded with him in unison, 'Shahanshah Akhzar, talk to us. Embrace your daughters. Look how distraught they are and weep so bitterly. They have not eaten since Amar kidnapped you! Tell us what happened to you and where were you imprisoned?'

Malik Akhzar finally snapped, 'Who is Shahanshah and whose daughters are these? My daughter's name is Mankoria. I am sick of this

charade! My name is Bhola and I am a simple wine seller!' Yakut drew
back in horror and kicked the old man. He moaned in pain and the
paints of ayyari melted off his face to reveal a crude peasant dressed in a
loincloth and a dirty waistcoat. He cried helplessly, 'Mankoria, my
daughter, where are you? These wretched *goris* will not leave me alone.
Tell the thakur to come and rescue me!'

Yakut was enraged and slapped the old man so hard that his head
snapped off his neck. She shouted, 'These people will pay for deceiving
me!' She marched out to the magic springs and let out a blood-curdling
scream. When a scarlet bird shot out of the waters, Yakut caught him
and slaughtered him right away. She collected the bird's blood in a cup
and threw it in the direction of the rebel camp. The earth trembled and
cracked open. Everything went dark and the open earth released a vapour
that blinded Mahrukh's army. Burran quickly reached the place where
Yakut was standing and furiously muttering spells. She held her hand
and said, 'Yakut, it is not seemly to cast spells without coming out in the
battlefield. No one is averse to confronting you. You started by sending
your handmaiden to battle with Bahar and offended everyone.'

Yakut replied, 'That camel driver's son has betrayed my trust!
Everyone will choke to death unless my father is returned to us!' Burran
said, 'Come with me to our camp and your father will be restored to you
immediately. It is folly to take offence at the trickery of ayyars. This is
the way they work!' Burran eventually persuaded the reluctant Yakut to
go with her to the Islamic camp. When she got there, Burran seated her
in a place of honour. She turned to Amar and said, 'Khwaja, you will
have to give up Akhzar if you want to save our people. I have given my
word to Yakut!'

Amar was reluctant to part with his prisoner, but Burran insisted and
he brought out the real Malik Akhzar from Zambil. The old man was
naked except for a dirty loincloth. When he saw his daughter, he ran and
clung to her. Yakut turned to Amar and said, 'Khwaja give me the crystal
ball and his clothes.' Amar stood up leaning on his sword and said,
'Princess Yakut, you should be grateful I have given your father back for
I never give up my prisoners. I will not give you the magic ball or the
clothes now.' Malik Akhzar, still clinging to Yakut, began to babble, 'Let
those things go! I have been lugging heavy baskets of mud in there. It is
so cold near the river that hundreds of prisoners die there! They give us
only a thin shirt and a blanket to cover ourselves. My child, do not argue
with him and take me home. I am so hungry. All I had in there is hard
maize bread and it has given me a stomach ache. I will have to take a few
purgatives to feel better!'

Yakut wept as she heard her father speak. Akhzar hid behind her and trembled as he looked at Amar. He continued babbling, 'Ya Samri, Ya Jamshed! Amar's prison is worse than any Firangi's. He has villains and blackguards in there who scream for mercy, but cannot escape. He has several factories but most of us work on the land!' Yakut was embarrassed and asked her father to keep quiet as Burran and the other sardars suppressed their smiles. Eventually, Yakut removed her spell on the Islamic army and brought her father back to her camp. Malik Akhzar was still in a pitiable state and ran around the pavilion crying, 'Bring me my basket. It is two in the afternoon and I must report for duty. If any labourer is absent, he is lashed.' He then exposed his buttocks to the durbar and said, 'I had to grind flour, but I did not do it properly. Look, darogha subjected me to a dozen lashes!' His companions cried, 'Huzoor keep quiet. No one can force you to do labour. You are a great king!'

Malik Akhzar remained distraught and said to Yakut, 'My child, let us return to Yakutia, do not confront these people!' Yakut snapped, 'Respected father, return to your senses! No one can dare to cast an eye on you now. I will drown each one of them! I will spare no one! I will eat Amar alive. Wait to see how I avenge you!' Yakut had to wait another twenty hours to confront her enemies. Meanwhile, Lal Sukhandan went to the edge of the lashkar on the pretext of inspecting her troops. She stood under the shade of a tree and looked longingly at her beloved Asad, who was flanked by his friend Sundlaan Sandli Posh and his army of wrestlers.

Aqwal Leather-robe and Asad Ghazi

Suddenly a cloud of dust caught everyone's attention. A band of equestrians appeared holding battle flags with verses inscribed in praise of Laat and Manaat. A young man with the limbs of a giant riding a rhinoceros, followed them. He approached Afrasiyab who was standing outside the royal pavilion and kissed the ground before him. Afrasiyab smiled, 'What brings you here Aqwal Leather-robe?' The young man said, 'I have heard that some grandson of Hamza has come to conquer Tilism. I am eager to see him. As you know, you have blessed your slave! The lions of the forests and crocodiles in the rivers hide in fear of me. I fight several men at the same time. I will tear this Tilism Kusha limb to limb! Tell me, where is he? Is he endowed with bigger limbs than mine?'

Vizier Sarmaya pointed Asad out to the wrestler. Aqwal laughed and said, 'Huzoor, he is as delicate as a beloved. I will keep him by my side as a cupbearer! Allow me to challenge him to a fight. Please forbid anyone to use magic on him.' Afrasiyab nodded and the young man jumped off his mount and said, 'Huzoor, your slave departs now.' Lal Sukhandan, who was standing close by muttered softly, 'Go to hell!' Aqwal roared into the battlefield and shouted, 'O followers of the Unseen God, I have come to wrestle with Tilism Kusha. Do not try any magical spells on me or you will be punished by the King of Magic!' Asad rode out to the battlefield. As he drew close to the wrestler, Lal Sukhandan watched him closely, and was entranced by his grace and beauty. Her lips went dry and her face grew pale with fear. The two warriors attacked each other, first with swords and spears, and eventually engaged in hand-to-hand combat. Aqwal was powerful but Asad was a better wrestler. Aqwal tried to overpower him several times, but Asad managed to slip out of his grasp repeatedly. The giant wrestler was beginning to tire and eventually Asad held him in an iron grasp so that he could not escape.

Lal Sukhandan had been praying for Asad's success and thought, 'This shameless one has become a part of the earth. Tilism Kusha should poke him in the eye! Look at how he glares at that lion!' Asad dragged the giant wrestler around the field and punched him repeatedly. Aqwal's clothes were torn and his face was smeared with dust and blood. In this pathetic condition, Aqwal met Afrasiyab's eye and signalled desperately that he should rescue him. Afrasiyab turned his face away in disgust. He looked at Aqwal's companions and muttered, 'What kind of man is this? He wants me to cast a spell to rescue him. Does he think I will go against my promise?'

After some time, Aqwal pleaded with Asad, 'Young man, you have fought me like a lion. Let us pause for the night and resume the fight tomorrow morning.' Asad replied, 'This could go on forever. It has to be decided right away.' To this Aqwal cried, 'Look we are both hungry and thirsty and it grows dark.' Asad simply said, 'It is not a problem for great kings to turn night into day. You can send for your food right here and we will continue the fight after you have eaten.' Asad then looked at Mahrukh and called out, 'Huzoor, we will pause this combat until there is light in the field.' Mahrukh and Bahar cast spells that made golden slave-boys holding flaming torches emerge from the earth; Bahar flung garlands in all four directions so that the trees glowed like lamps; and even Afrasiyab awakened his magic to illuminate the desert.

Once this was done, Aqwal motioned to his companions, who brought forth pitchers of fresh milk and trays heaped with dried fruits. Aqwal consumed two or three pitchers of milk and munched on the dried fruits to restore his strength. All this time, Asad was pacing up and down. Aqwal said to him, 'Young man if your lashkar has not sent you nourishment, you are welcome to share this meal.' Asad declined politely and said, 'I should be worried that you have a full belly and you should be concerned that I am a hungry man!' Aqwal was embarrassed by Asad's comment and returned to the arena. He was refreshed and therefore more confident. He fell upon Asad with a renewed energy and the wrestling bout continued throughout the night. Towards dawn, Aqwal was beginning to tire again. Aqwal tried one last time to push Asad and managed to move him back by several feet. Lal's heart was in her mouth and she desperately prayed, 'O Unseen God, if you exist, then let Asad triumph over this mad elephant!' Just then, Asad stood his ground and pushed at Aqwal's shoulders so hard that he fell on his knees.

Lal immediately thought, 'The Unseen God must be true for my prayer was answered so promptly. Indeed, He is the Supreme Power and I believe in him wholeheartedly!' Meanwhile, Asad had completely overpowered his opponent and hoisted him high above the ground. Aqwal's companions rushed to their master's help shouting, 'Get him now!' Afrasiyab shouted, 'Where do you think you are going you uncouth ones!' But they called back, 'Do not interfere, he will kill our master!' Asad was about to throw Aqwal on the ground when there was a volley of arrows and spears from his followers. Aqwal slipped from Asad's hands as he tried to defend himself. Aqwal tried to fight him again with a sword, but Asad killed him in one blow. Aqwal's followers fell on their master's body and then ran towards Asad whose followers chased them away. Mahrukh and Mahjabeen rushed to Asad's side and escorted him back to the pavilion amidst cries of jubilation and triumph.

Asad Ghazi and Lal Sukhandan

That evening, Shakeel went to Asad and informed him that according to the camp roster, it was Asad's turn to keep watch over the camp. After dinner, Asad left with his ayyar Zargham and a few hundred troops. He rode all over the camp and the bazaars, placing his men in strategic places. Late that night, Asad said to Zargham, 'We will have to remain awake for the rest of the night. Let us find a place from where we can see the entire lashkar.' Zargham led his master to a distant knoll with a good view of the camp. Zargham laid out a rough cloth for Asad to sit on and then brought out a flask of wine from his satchel.

In Afrasiyab and Yakut's lashkar, every tent was smoking with preparations for the battle the next morning. After dismissing her durbar for the night, Yakut strolled back to her pavilion with her sister saying, 'Do you see how confident these rebels are? You must remain vigilant tonight; by tomorrow afternoon they will all be destroyed.' Later, when

Lal was with a band of companions, she longed to be alone. She got rid of her companions by appointing them on guard duty at various points. She then walked to the edge of her camp, thinking, 'How do I express my longing and love to that paragon of beauty and power!'

At that time, Lal heard the sound of melodious singing. She followed the voice until she came across Asad sitting on the grassy knoll, where Zargham was entertaining him with a ghazal. The lovesick princess gazed at her beloved with longing and love in her heart. Asad looked up suddenly and saw the same beautiful maiden who had enchanted him with her breathtaking beauty. Overwhelmed by the rush of emotion, Asad Ghazi fell into a stupor. Lal could not restrain herself any more. She went forward and cradled his head in her lap as Zargham massaged his master's feet to revive him. Asad inhaled the fragrance of her perfumed locks and his eyes opened as he felt her tears falling on his face. He looked up at her and slowly held her hand. He signalled to Zargham to pour wine in a goblet and offered it to the princess. She said, 'Sheheryar, this is not the time for wine. I have longed to meet you for some time and will no doubt pay for this folly. Tell me this, what has my cousin Burran done to ensure your safety?'

Asad replied gently, 'My safety is in the hands of my Sustainer, not Burran!' Lal was silent. Finally, she raised the goblet in her hand and said, 'If you do not mind, can I offer this to you?' However, Asad put his hand over the goblet and refused to drink from it. Lal's eyes filled with tears and she whispered, 'I realize that you are the beloved of the Shahanshah's niece. I have no expectations from you.' Asad wiped her tears and said, 'O ruler of my heart, renounce Samri and Jamshed and believe in the One True God. I promise you, I will drink wine proffered even by your lowliest handmaidens. Just think, Samri and Jamshed were sahirs like you. How can you believe they were gods and not be aware of the Supreme Being?' Asad spoke so eloquently in praise of the only True God that Lal's soul was stirred to its depths. The rust of doubt was removed from the mirror of her heart and she said, 'I believe wholeheartedly!' Asad smilingly took the goblet from her hand and drank from it, then filled it up for her to drink from it.

The two lovers now relaxed with each other. Zargham was happy to see them together and thought, 'With the Grace of God, they are well suited to each other, as two suns in the same orbit. Lal said, 'Sahib, what drew me here was the song. Brother Zargham, are you shy of singing before me? Do you want me to leave so that you can be private with your master?' Zargham replied, 'If he is my master, I am your slave!' He picked up his jewelled sitar and sang a poignant ghazal of unrequited love.

Lal sobbed silently as she heard him. She got up suddenly and said, 'I must say farewell. If I remain alive, I will meet you again. My sister Yakut has awakened the magic of the two springs and I am fearful for you.' She untied the amulet from her arm and said, 'This is a lowly gift that I offer for your protection.' She tied it around Asad's arm and said, 'Brother Zargham, you must make sure that this is always tied to your master for it will make him impervious to magical attacks.' Asad said, 'Princess, I rely only on the Great Provider. His name is always on my lips and He is always with me!' Lal said, 'Do not refuse this for tomorrow Yakut will make heaven and earth tremble!'

Before she left Asad said, 'Why do you have to leave now? You are of our faith and we will protect you.' Lal said, 'That is not possible just now. Yakut will not leave me alive if I do. At least this way I can be of some service to you.' Lal left in tears and kept turning around to look at Asad until she reached her camp. It was dawn by then and Asad rode back to his camp with Zargham. His men were anxiously looking for him there. Soon, the sardars presented themselves at Mahrukh's durbar. Burran and her companions had also come from Nur Afshan. A little later, Princess Yakut's lashkar emerged on the battlefield. The magic springs unfolded on the field. Their waters bubbled and colourful fish leapt out from the depths like flames.

The confrontation of Yakut and Burran

Burran drew forward and called out, 'Yakut, be warned that I attack!' She took out the magic Pearl of Samri from her topknot and it seemed as if the full moon was holding the morning star in its hands. Burran opened her flower-like mouth and sighed deeply to expel smoke that formed a dense cloud. Burran was absorbed into the cloud like a bolt of lightning and floated up to the skies. Her companion Majlis was waiting for her in the clouds. Burran called out, 'Majlis, Yakut is here with her magical springs!' As everyone watched, Majlis emerged from the clouds and opened her plaits. A round gold tank filled with water emerged out of the skies. Majlis transformed into a ruby fish and dived into the tank. As soon as she was underwater, thousands of fishes leapt out of Yakut's springs and fell upon Afrasiyab and Yakut's armies in the form of deadly daggers. Thousands of soldiers perished while Burran and Majlis shouted in triumph in the sky.

Yakut went red in the face and plucked a pearl out from her earring. She called out, 'Burran, do not boast yet. I will turn this spell around now.' She flung the pearl towards the wilderness and called out, 'Slaves of Samri, come at once!' She then plucked a second pearl and threw it towards Burran. A giant bubble appeared in the sky and circled towards Burran and Majlis. Baghban and Bahar flew upwards to protect their friends. Burran emerged from her cloud of smoke and managed to smash the bubble, but as it burst, its water fell on Burran, Majlis, Baghban and Bahar as leaping flames. Within moments, the flames burnt them and they tumbled down to earth.

Meanwhile, several golden slave-boys holding golden fishing nets emerged from the wilderness. Yakut ordered them to destroy the deadly fish and the slave-boys trapped the killer fishes in their nets. After all of them had been trapped, the slave-boys hovered above the lashkar of Islam and massacred the fishes. The veritable rainfall of blood incinerated those it fell on. There was chaos in the Islamic camp as the drops of blood fell on everyone. Yakut noticed that every time Asad was in danger, he would put his right arm forward. The drops would then fall on the earth and be absorbed. Even the golden slave-boys stayed away from Asad.

The Islamic lashkar was at its lowest ebb when help came from Tilism Nur Afshan in the form of Princess Haijoon Green-robe, who was holding the magic ball of Akhzar. Princess Haijoon chanted a spell and tossed the ball into the air. Suddenly, intense heat seared the golden slave-boys and as their bodies burnt, they ran screaming towards Yakut, abusing her loudly. They now sprayed their own army with the blood of the magic fishes. Seeing all this, Afrasiyab furiously knocked in the air and conjured four iron slave-boys. They fell on the golden slave-boys and tied them together. The deadly fishes fell on the earth and were absorbed instantly. Yakut eventually had the drums of peace struck and called out, 'Haijoon, you have used one of our spells to save your lives. You must also be aware that I can have you all eaten by Afreet. Convey a message to my uncle Kaukab that his niece will give her enemies a week's respite. On the eighth day, Afreet Tilismi will swallow everyone. As for Burran and Majlis, they must be as good as dead already. You should think of burying them now!'

After these harsh words, Yakut turned to her sister and held her hand as they walked back to the pavilion. 'Tell me, my dear,' Yakut asked her confidentially, 'why did the magic droplets not burn Asad? He seemed to have some magic gift with him that repelled the drops.' Lal went pale and stammered, 'Huzoor, our uncle Kaukab must have devised a way of protecting him.' Yakut looked thoughtful and said, 'This seemed like a gift from our own house. My dear, what I meant was that these Muslims are quite defiant; Afrasiyab is an ass. That fool dispelled my magic and destroyed my slaves. No matter, I only cast minor spells today. Afreet

Tilismi will consume them all in one mouthful. Tell me, what is in your heart. I can spare whomever you like.'

Princess Lal wept and said, 'My sister, you doubt me for no reason at all. Why should I want to save any of the rebels? I know that Tilism-e-Hoshruba is ours and Afrasiyab will ignore Hairat in your favour. As far as I am concerned, you can send for Afreet today and destroy these people.' Yakut was quiet, but her brow was troubled as she joined Afrasiyab in the durbar. Lal went straight to her tent, her heart heavy with secrets.

Lal Sukhandan's secret is revealed

Asad too had been thinking about his beloved since she had left him. His days were restless and he spent his nights counting stars. Finally, one evening, he approached his confidante Zargham and asked him to arrange a meeting with Lal. Zargham looked troubled and said, 'Huzoor it will be difficult to get in touch with her. Yakut has put her in charge of the lashkar and I have seen that she is very busy. However, for your sake, I will try my best.' Zargham went into the forest disguised as a sahir and Lal spotted him as she was flying overhead. She flew down and asked, 'Who are you that you are out on a dark night like this?' Zargham smiled and said, 'I was looking for you actually.' Lal looked puzzled and so Zargham wiped the paints of ayyari from his face. Lal recognized him and blushed, 'Brother, what are you doing out at this time?' Zargham replied, 'Princess, you have left my master torn with love for you. He is longing for a glimpse of you and I was wondering how I could send word to you. It was fortuitous that you appeared yourself. Come with me or my master might start looking for you on his own.'

Asad was pacing outside his tent when he saw Zargham leading Lal, who was wearing a veil. Asad eagerly held her hand and took her inside his tent. Zargham discreetly stayed outside. Princess Lal was silent and depressed and when Asad tried to embrace her, she burst into tears and said, 'Sheheryar, I cannot stay long. Pray do not love me so much. One glimpse of you is enough for me.' Meanwhile, Zargham saw Sundlaan and went over to talk with him. They were talking about the two lovers when Sarsar Sword-fighter who had been prowling around the Islamic camp in disguise peeked into Asad's tent. She went cold when she saw him consoling the love-struck princess and thought, 'This woman is shameless. She has betrayed her sister for her lover. She must be punished!'

Sarsar hid in the privy tent and after some time, when Asad went to the tent, she rendered him unconscious with a narcotic bubble. She tied him up in a sheet and left under the cover of the night. Meanwhile, Jansoz walked by and noticed that Zargham was not on duty outside his master's tent. He went inside and saw the princess sitting with her head bowed. Jansoz identified herself and asked after Asad. He was immediately suspicious when the princess told him that Asad had been gone for some time. He rushed to the privy and saw Sarsar's footprints on the floor. He went back to Lal and said, 'A terrible thing has happened! Sarsar has kidnapped our master!'

Lal was horrified and wept loudly, 'I must have brought your master bad luck that this has come to pass!' Jansoz told her as he rushed outside, 'This is no time for such talk. I must follow Sarsar!' He bumped into Zargham and Qiran outside and told them what had happened. All three ayyars left separately to waylay Sarsar and her precious cargo. Lal waited inside Asad's tent for a while and then thought, 'My secret will be revealed soon. It is better for me to try and save my beloved.' Meanwhile, Sarsar had reached the outer reaches of Afrasiyab's camp, but kept looking nervously over her shoulder. She was relieved to see Vizier Abriq keeping watch over the camp. 'Who goes there?' the vizier called out loudly. Sarsar called back, 'It is Sarsar Sword-fighter. I have brought Tilism Kusha. Help me for the ayyars must be following me!'

The vizier suddenly appeared before her. He held her hand and said, 'Put your burden down and inform Shahanshah. I will carry Asad.' Abriq held her hand so hard that Sarsar looked up. She saw that her wrist was in the paw of the lion. She realized that her saviour was none other than the bughda-wielder Mehtar Qiran. She recognized his eyes through the disguise and shuddered as he said, 'Mistress Sarsar, your end is near!' The terrified Sarsar dropped Asad, wrenched her wrist out of his grasp and ran away shouting, 'Awaken everybody! I had brought Asad, but Qiran waylaid me.' Meanwhile, Qiran quickly released Asad from the sheet; Zargham heard Sarsar's cry and rushed over to revive his master. Soldiers from Afrasiyab's camp came forward to attack them, but Qiran, Jansoz and Zargham flashed their swords and killed several of them. Asad then mounted the horse of one of the slain soldiers and joined the fray.

Afrasiyab heard the uproar in his camp and rushed out of his tent shouting, 'I am Afrasiyab!' He mounted a horse and cantered towards Asad, brandishing his sword. He attacked Asad ferociously, but his horse kept shying away from Asad and none of his spells worked on him either. At one stage, Asad leaned forward with his sword and shouted, 'O Afrasiyab Khana Kharab, if you are a man, try and foil this attack without your shield.' Before Afrasiyab could conjure a shield, Asad's sword fell on his brow and wounded him. Afrasiyab withdrew in shock.

As his sahirs attacked Asad, Afrasiyab waved his fingers furiously and conjured a magic flame. A voice called out, 'Shahanshah, what do you wish to know?' Afrasiyab said, 'O Flame of Samri, why is Asad impervious to magic? He wounded and humiliated me just now.' The flame burnt brightly and spoke, 'O Shahanshah, the princess of the fifth hujra, Lal Sukhandan is favourable towards Asad. She has tied the powerful amulet of Samri on his arm and he is protected from magic.'

Afrasiyab screamed with rage when he heard the explanation. Hairat had also come to her husband's side and heard the oracle. She bowed sarcastically and said, 'My greetings to you Shahanshah! I humbly state that the lady had been sequestered in her hujra all these years and probably longed for a man. She came here and the beautiful Asad captivated her. She has really disgraced her family! To think that she is the sister of the woman you will marry! Sarsar had warned me much earlier, but I did not believe her. All these years I have been faithful to you. I travel all over the realm and meet the handsomest young men, but have you known me to be anything but virtuous? Yes Asad really is a prize for your niece Mahjabeen, Lalaan and now, Lal Sukhandan!'

Afrasiyab was even more incensed by Hairat's words and roared, 'She will be punished for this, but before doing that, I must get the amulet from Asad.' Afrasiyab dismounted and ran towards his foe. Asad was a man of principles, and when he saw Afrasiyab dismount, he also jumped off his own steed. He shouted, 'Afrasiyab Khana Kharab! Stop shouting from that distance and face me like a man!' Afrasiyab knocked in the air and called out, 'I need a Zangi right now!' The earth parted and a powerful young Zangi slave sprang out crying, 'I am at your service.' Afrasiyab said, 'O faithful slave of Samri, confront Asad and take the amulet away from him for it belongs to the treasury of Samri!' The Zangi slave immediately went forward shouting, 'O Tilism Kusha, I am the slave of Samri and Jamshed! Why should Shahanshah confront you when he has devotees like me to do his work?' He attacked Asad with his sword, but Asad punched him so hard that he fell down. As he fell, he wrenched the amulet off Asad's arm. Asad was going to pin him to the earth to get the amulet back, but one of Afrasiyab's sahirs snatched the amulet from the Zangi slave's hand and wounded Asad with a spell. The sahir was about to cut Asad's head off when the Zangi slave urged him to first hand over the amulet to Afrasiyab.

This din had also awakened Yakut. She rubbed her eyes and asked her handmaidens what had happened. Lal Sukhandan had also reached the camp in pursuit of Asad and looked down in horror at the scene below her; Asad lay wounded and unconscious while a sahir holding the amulet was poised to kill him. Lal shouted, 'I am Lal Sukhandan!' As she dived, she threw an iron ball that killed the sahir and the slave instantly. She snatched the amulet and threw her earring at Afrasiyab that hit him like a bolt of lightning. As he tried to protect himself, she put her arm around Asad's waist and flew upwards swiftly and called out, 'Companions of Asad, come away from here!'

This was too much for Hairat. She went up to Yakut who had also emerged from her tent and snapped, 'My greetings to you. If the favourites of Samri behave in this manner, there are no more pure believers. Did you witness your sister's loyalty to Asad? Did you see how she executed the followers of Shahanshah to save him? Tell me, respected Yakut, how will we confront Asad now that he has your amulet to protect him?' Yakut replied angrily, 'Lady of the palace, spare me your taunts. I will punish that shameless wretch and whip her to shreds. I will not allow her to join the enemy! I will not stand by and wait for her to confront me on the battlefield. You and Shahanshah seem to have the patience of saints that you can tolerate the sight of Mahjabeen challenging you. I will not stand for it!' Hairat shrugged her shoulders and said, 'Well you can try. We have been fighting this war for twelve years. No one who has left us has ever returned!' Yakut hissed, 'Just watch and see what I do!'

The princesses Mahjabeen and Lalaan were weeping for Asad when the sight of a rose-coloured cloud spinning towards them startled them. Princess Lal suddenly appeared from the cloud, covered in blood and looking furious. She held Asad in her arm and took him into the royal pavilion. She did not speak and revived the unconscious Asad before tying the amulet on his arm. There were cries of jubilation in the lashkar Mahjabeen and Lalaan lovingly seated Lal beside Asad on the throne. Loud cries of praise for Lal filled the durbar. She modestly bowed her head and said, 'You are all too kind. As long as I am alive, I will not let Afrasiyab capture Asad. I have cast the dice now. I have left my house for love of Tilism Kusha and have defied my sister. Pray that I can keep my word.'

The sardars then appealed to Lal to cure the four sardars who were the victims of Yakut's deadly spell. Bahar, Baghban, Burran and Majlis Jadoo were in a poor condition for their bodies had been blistered with the water of the magic bubble conjured by Yakut. Lal wept when she saw their suffering. She said, 'I will try my best to cure them, although Yakut's magic is difficult to remove.' The six ayyars including Amar had come to the durbar and were watching carefully when Lal took out her dagger and stabbed herself on her forehead. She chanted an incantation and then sprayed the prostrate sardars with her blood. Within moments, their blisters burst and they were as active and healthy as they had been before. They had barely recovered when the earth trembled and Princess Yakut shot out in the form of lightning. She looked at Lal and said, 'Well done my sister! Was it for this day that I schooled you in magic? You are so benevolent towards my enemy that you have removed my spell and brought disgrace to the religion of Samri and Jamshed?'

Lal rose and stamped so hard on the floor that Yakut stumbled, but she recovered quickly and shouted, 'You harlot, you have disgraced our family!' Yakut then furiously expelled smoke from her mouth that blinded everyone in the durbar. In the confusion, Yakut lifted Lal and flew out of the durbar. Yakut's movements were so swift that the sardars did not have the time to react. Bahar aimed a bouquet at her, but Yakut smiled and the bouquet burst into flames. Barq Lameh was preparing to turn into a bolt of lightning, but Yakut smiled again and expelled a ray of light that wounded Barq Lameh. Baghban was so stunned that he could not recall any magical spells. As Yakut disappeared in a flash Asad rose from his seat and cried, 'This is terrible! Yakut will not leave Lal alive. I must save her even if I lose my life!' All the sardars also rose to accompany him, but Amar came forward and said, 'My friends do not follow her. You are not a match for her. Just wait here till I return.' Amar then left the durbar and signalled to the wily Barq to follow him. Chalak followed them secretly.

Yakut reached the desert with Lal in her clasp and saw that Sarsar Sword-fighter was standing under the shade of a tree calling out to her, 'Princess Yakut, Shahanshah is furious with us for letting you go to the enemy camp on your own. I would have brought your sister back to you.' Yakut snapped back, 'No one dared confront me there and I have brought her back!' Yakut landed on the ground and Sarsar came forward with her hands folded. She said, 'Huzoor, you have indeed done a remarkable thing. Quickly pierce her tongue with a needle lest she revives and casts spells. Oh look, Shahanshah is here as well. He was worried about you!' As Yakut turned to look, Sarsar burst a narcotic bubble in her face and Yakut stumbled to the ground unconscious. The false Sarsar, actually Barq Firangi in disguise, wanted to cut her head off when a golden slave-boy emerged from the earth and held his hand in a vice-like grip. The slave-boy growled, 'Why you rascal, you want to kill my mistress?' Barq tried to flee, but could not. Still holding on to Barq's wrist, the slave-boy revived Yakut. The slave-boy then waved a hand on Barq's face so that the paints of ayyari peeled off. Yakut awoke to hear the slave-boy say, 'Huzoor, this man was trying to kill you. He was disguised as a woman!'

Yakut drew out her dagger to behead Barq, but he pleaded, 'Princess, I am your slave. I swear I was not trying to kill you, but just wanted to save your sister. You would have killed her in your rage and regretted it later.' Yakut pressed the dagger down on his throat and Barq desperately shouted, 'Ask Shahanshah, he is always kind to us ayyars. My ustad Amar will kill you mercilessly if you take my life!' Just as Yakut was about to execute Barq, a voice called out, 'Beware princess, Shahanshah will be furious with you. These ayyars are very special to Khudawand Laqa!' Yakut turned and saw Saba Raftar Fleet-foot running towards her with a piece of paper in her hand crying, 'Do not kill him, just read this note before you do anything!' Yakut immediately suspected that this too was an ayyar and waved her hand once. The paints of ayyari peeled off the false Saba Raftar and Chalak bin Amar stared back at her. Yakut was about to kill both ayyars when she heard the rustle of leaves on a tree. She looked up and saw Hairat Jadoo in the tree. It was clear that Hairat had just landed from the skies. Hairat's finger was in her mouth as she looked down at Yakut and cried, 'What are you doing?' Yakut said, 'O lady of the palace, these two rascals would have killed me, had I not been so vigilant!' Hairat jumped down from the tree, held Yakut's hand and affectionately said, 'You are one in a million!' The next moment, the false Hairat rendered Yakut unconscious with a narcotic bubble. As Yakut stumbled and fell, Hairat, or Amar in disguise, drew his dagger to kill her, but at that moment Lal's eyes opened.

She held Amar's hand and said, 'Khwaja, she will not die this way and we will be instantly captured. We will take her with us!' Lal and Amar were about to carry Yakut off when Afrasiyab appeared on the scene and challenged Lal. Amar and the other two ayyars scampered off, but Lal bravely stayed there and threw an iron ball at Afrasiyab. While Afrasiyab dodged the ball, Lal stamped hard on the ground and disappeared into the earth as it opened for her. Afrasiyab then conjured magical rain to revive Yakut. She returned to the camp, but did not speak to anyone and looked visibly upset. She went straight to her pavilion and emerged a little later wearing rich garments and jewels. Afrasiyab was entranced with her fiery beauty as she declared, 'Let the battle drums be struck in my name. I will get Afreet Tilismi to come now. Do not wait for me tomorrow. I will appear in my own time!' After Yakut left, Afrasiyab went to Hairat's pavilion and said, 'Malika, you are to be congratulated. Yakut has left to get the man-eater Afreet. She was in a terrible rage. Let the battle drums be struck for the fight tomorrow!'

The man-eater Afreet Tilismi

The next morning, the two armies stood facing each other in the battlefield. Suddenly, a rose-coloured cloud appeared in the sky. Everyone saw Yakut flying in on a magic peacock, wearing a crown of rubies with robes encrusted with rubies and ruby jewellery. She flew straight to the nearest mountain and crashed into it. The mountain cracked open with the impact and an ogre as large as the mountain itself swaggered out. His head was the size of a dome, his limbs were as wide as the trunks of chinar trees, and his chest as wide as the desert. He screamed as he emerged and asked Yakut with folded hands, 'O beloved of Samri, is all well with you?'

Yakut said, 'O Afreet, these blood-thirsty rebels have spilt my blood. Eat all of them!' As soon as Afreet heard her, he turned around. He extended his foul hand and reached out for the rebel army. A bevy of handmaidens were the nearest to him. His dirty paw lifted two hundred of these beautiful girls and he began chewing them with relish. Within moments, all of them had perished in three mouthfuls. He then moved forward to the rest of the Islamic lashkar. Lal Sukhandan screamed, 'Friends, run for your lives! Save yourselves from this brutal man-eater! Look how he has chewed up the handmaidens without even spilling their blood. This is what I had feared! This is devastating!'

The sardars and the rest of the army fled, but how long could they run? The ogre's hand could reach out to two kos and his every step covered five kos. Whenever that shameless one reached out, he would swallow two hundred people at one time. Everyone knew that he was indeed their nemesis and his stomach was the pit of hell. He had already swallowed ten thousand people. Baghban chanted a spell that made Asad's horse canter away with his master on his back. Asad tried to control his horse by pressing his thighs and whipping it, but it did not stop. Princess Gauhar also protected her beloved, Sundlaan, who was not a sahir. Burran, Majlis, Bahar and Baghban attacked Afreet together, but he remained impervious to their magic. They tried to stop him with rivers of flames, but he walked through them unscathed. They conjured rivers whose monstrous waves engulfed him, but he drank his way out of them. Burran hit him with the powerful Pearl of Samri, but the only effect it had was that it stained the ogre's chest on impact. Eventually, the sardars wept and ran for their lives. Even after running huge distances, they found Afreet right behind them.

The masters of eloquent speech describe this strange tale thus. Lal Sukhandan transformed into a bolt of lightning and fell on Afreet's head. She tried to stab his shoulders with her dagger and run her sword through his stomach, but to no avail. She could not even dent his thick hide with her attacks. Princess Lal then conjured a river of fire, but Afreet walked through it. She changed a small stream into a mighty river, but Afreet called out; 'O beautiful beloved, I was thirsty and will quench my thirst now!' He stood by the river and scooped its water in his hands to drink it. Within moments, he had even eaten the sticky mud under the river. Gigantic crocodiles from the river attacked him ferociously, but he tore them apart and swallowed them. When all her magic failed, Lal ran weeping towards Mahrukh who was all praise for her magical powers. Lal sobbed, 'Huzoor, it was of no use. These crocodiles would have swallowed millions of people, but he destroyed them in a flash. All we can now do is save Asad and Mahjabeen and run for our lives.' A whole day and a night passed by and Afreet continued pursuing the Islamic army.

The reader should be aware that Afrasiyab, Yakut and Akhzar would catch up with Afreet every time his progress was suspended by the magic of some of the fleeing sardars. Yakut would then call out, 'Afreet, why have you stopped? Do not let them out of your sight!' Thus ordered, Afreet would resume his blood-thirsty activity. Afrasiyab, of course, was travelling with all comforts. His kitchen staff and saqi boys provided his party with food and wine at every stage. At one stage, they laid out a huge repast for the royal party. Hairat was about to start eating when she saw Sarsar weeping bitterly. Hairat asked her, 'What is the matter?' Sarsar replied, 'Huzoor, it has been three days and three nights since the Muslims have been running. Today, they were near a fortress whose owner was a former tributary of Mahrukh's. When he saw that they were hungry and thirsty, he laid out a meal for them. Your sister Bahar was very thirsty and had just taken a bite of the food before drinking water when she heard Afreet's loud roar. Bahar got up to run, but was so thirsty that she literally fell on a stream to drink from its waters. Afreet was close behind, so her handmaidens lifted her physically and ran with her. My heart broke when I saw her in this state. It is unbearable to see anyone suffer this way. These people are so staunch that they will not even think of surrendering.'

On hearing this story, Hairat began to weep and called out, 'Bahar, we had brought you up with so much love and comfort. Alas, my Bahar is now being torn apart by thorns in the forests!' Sarsar said, 'We must try and save Bahar at any price!' Hairat said, 'Sarsar, here are my orders. If Afrasiyab does not agree, I will leave his house! Go now and bring Bahar back to me. Tell her that I have forgiven her and that Shahanshah still loves her. Tell that unfortunate girl that I am anxious for her safety, perhaps she might listen to you.' Sarsar left as briskly as the morning breeze.

The third morning dawned with the lashkar of Islam collecting in the wilderness. They were all very tired and Mahrukh declared, 'Friends, we cannot run any further. Our feet are swollen and it is impossible to take another step. We will give up our lives in this place as we have enjoyed the pleasures of this world.' Just then, Princess Lalaan Red-robe arrived bareheaded and barefoot with her companions, who were beating their heads in anguish. Lalaan's delicate feet were pricked by thorns and the blisters on her heels were bursting with grief at their mistress's plight. The sardars wept to see Princess Lalaan in this state. Mahrukh forgot about Mahjabeen and rushed to embrace Lalaan. The princess cried, 'O Malika Mahrukh, leave me to my misfortune, just tell me where my beloved is. Afreet can swallow us all, but how can the lashkar remain if Asad is harmed?'

Mahrukh led Lalaan to a carriage and addressed her companions, 'Do not tarry with us but run with your mistress as far as you can. It is clear that the Great Provider has destined that we will all be food for Afreet, but you must save her at any cost.' Lalaan seemed reluctant to go any further. Mahjabeen went forward to embrace her and they both wept bitterly for Asad. At that time, Asad rode into the wilderness on his horse, followed by the faithful Baghban Qudrat. Behind them were Sundlaan and Gauhar Posh with their army of sixty-thousand soldiers. Both the princesses looked at Asad's face longingly. His horse had stopped and as he saw the two princesses with their blistered feet and scratched faces, Asad thought his heart would break. He said, 'Baghban, you have made me so helpless that I have had to see these princesses in this state. My life is as dust. I am not going to move from here now. If you make me flee with your magic, I will cut my own throat!'

Bahar had also reached the wilderness at that time, panting with exhaustion. As she stood in one place, Sarsar, disguised as one of her handmaidens, held her hand and said, 'Could I have a private word with you?' Bahar walked to one side with her and asked, 'Mistress Yasaman, what is there left to say now? Death looms over us all and we will all meet our Maker!' The false Yasaman folded her hands and fell at Bahar's feet. She cried, 'Huzoor, I am Sarsar. Your sister Hairat has sent me with this message: "I forgive you; take pity on your youth and come to me. How long will you run? This Afreet will go all the way to Mount Agate and spare no enemy of ours."' Bahar got angry and said, 'Mistress Sarsar, do you want to lead me astray from the righteous path? You are showing me the path to hell. Tell my sister she is welcome to keep her kingdom. Tell her that I will rest peacefully in my grave while she rules your world.'

Sarsar began weeping and said, 'Huzoor, I cannot bear to hear any more. I pray with all my heart that the Almighty helps you now and destroys this terrible ogre.' Bahar joined the other sardars and saw that they were clinging to Asad's feet and pleading with him to move on. Lal Sukhandan had transformed herself into a hawk and she rolled on the earth to return to her true form. She too pleaded with Asad, 'Sheheryar, for the love of God run from this place. Afreet is behind us. He is busy swallowing the army that had lagged behind. Afrasiyab is following in great jubilation. The kind of iron balls I aimed at Afreet would have destroyed mountains, but they left no mark on him. I had to escape as a hawk!'

Asad still refused to budge and no sardar was willing to flee without him. They saw Afreet's massive head appear on the horizon and Amar removed his cap to pray. He said, 'Friends, pray to your Saviour who can dispel all evil. This Afreet is nothing before him.' All the noble sardars kneeled to pray to the Almighty to save them and the arrows of their prayers reached their mark. As Afreet came closer, Kaukab and Nur Afshan Jadoo emerged in the sky. They called out to Amar, 'Khwaja you must be wise for this foul-mouthed Afreet will spare no one! We have also come to offer our lives for if we remain alive, we will be disgraced before the world. Everyone will say that we were so shameless as to have Tilism Kusha eaten alive. Please run as far as you can. We will not be able to destroy this monster, but we will try our best to stop him for a while!'

Afreet was just about to pick up another two hundred men when Kaukab landed a mighty blow on his wrist with his sword. Afreet was unmoved. Nur Afshan then hurled a massive iron ball at him, and Afreet fell back a few steps with the impact. Kaukab addressed Yakut, 'Shameless woman, are you such a coward that you brought this monster to do your work?' Nur Afshan shouted, 'Afrasiyab, are you afraid of my magical powers that you cower down there. The difference between you and I is that you run to your grandmothers for help while I rely on the True Provider!' Afrasiyab was enraged by these taunts and wanted to attack the old man, but Hairat held him back. Yakut also advised him not to be so hasty and said, 'Afreet can swallow a thousand Nur Afshans. Do you think these iron balls will affect him? Watch how I will incite him now!'

Yakut took out a pearl from her mouth and threw it on Afreet's back. She called out, 'O shameless one, are these two your relatives that you spare them? Eat them up at once!' Afreet went for Nur Afshan, who quickly brought out an iron ball. He smeared it with drops of blood from his own tongue and flung it on the earth. Suddenly, a gigantic python with a mouth like the door to hell attacked Afreet. Nur Afshan called out, 'Khwaja, this was only to grant you respite. For the love of God please run now!' The python struck Afreet hard with its tail so that the monster stopped in his tracks and trembled. The python was about to swallow Afreet when

Yakut screamed, 'You wretch, you are frightened by a magical rope! This is also a meal for you.' Afreet recovered and tore the python's jaws apart. He swallowed the python in two mouthfuls and went for his enemies again. Kaukab and Nur Afshan then tried to stop him with all the powers at their command. They drained their bodies as they cut themselves to throw blood on Afreet. The other sardars also joined Kaukab and Nur Afshan to create magical storms and rivers to stop Afreet.

Meanwhile, Baghban lifted Asad off the ground and ran like the wind with his master. He shouted, 'Huzoor, you have to come with me!' However, Asad struggled in his arms and threw himself on the earth. As he fell, he prostrated and held up his hands in prayer. By this time, the other sardars had caught up with Baghban. When Nur Afshan saw Asad with his head down in prayer with Amar was weeping nearby, he called out, 'Khwaja, I have lost all my blood to stop this monster. I would have destroyed a fortress of iron with my blood, but this shameless monster is untouched!' Nur Afshan added that he wanted to conjure a cloud to hide all the sardars, but Amar called out, 'Nur Afshan, let us leave Asad to his Maker. His prayers are pure and sincere, perhaps they will be granted.'

Afreet Tilismi and Mehboob Kakul Kusha

A cloud of dust then rose in the desert and one of the princesses from Tilism Nur Afshan, Mehboob Moon-face appeared with Makhmoor Red-eye. Mehboob saw everyone in a distraught state and cried, 'What is happening?' Her friend Princess Haijoon stepped forward and wept as she said, 'Princess, at last you are here. Look at this ruined lashkar. See how this garden dries up before autumn. Afreet has eaten hundreds of the faithful!' Princess Mehboob was silent as she heard this. Nur Afshan looked at her, held his heart and called out, 'Mehboob come to me. You are here just in time!' Mehboob said, 'O Great Master, your lowly handmaiden knows that we will not be in this world forever. I understand that this world is not permanent and those who thirst for it will be disgraced. I am at your service.'

As she stepped forward, her friends from Nur Afshan, Burran, Haijoon and Majlis, began beating their heads in grief and their black tresses became wet with their tears. Mehboob drew her dagger and placed it on her throat. She muttered magical words, drew the dagger and fluttered like the morning star as she fell. Haijoon Green-robe drained the blood from her throat in a bowl and then slit her stomach open to cut out Mehboob's heart and liver. Holding the bowl in her hands, she approached Afreet and called out, 'O shameless man-eater, look what I have for you. Your makers had destined that you should have this gift from Mehboob's body.' Afreet took one look at the contents of the bowl and danced with joy. He took the bowl, drank Mehboob's blood, and chewed her heart and liver.

After consuming this fare, he burped loudly and said with folded hands to Princess Haijoon, 'Princess, I have been seeking this meal since I was created. You have satisfied me with the heavenly offering and I am satiated. What can I do for you?' Haijoon said, 'Swallow the enemies of the one whose heart you have eaten. Fill your stomach with them and do not hesitate.' Afreet replied, 'Very well!' and turned around. Malik Akhzar was leading Afrasiyab's party with Yakut and Afrasiyab following close behind. He addressed his daughter and said, 'Yakut, we have a long journey ahead of us. We will not stop at Mount Agate, but continue on to the Khana Kaaba in Mecca itself!' Yakut said, 'I am sure Afreet must have eaten Tilism Kusha by now. I will only be satisfied once he consumes Kaukab and Nur Afshan!'

They were still talking when they saw Afreet Tilismi approach them smiling and looking satisfied. Akhzar shouted, 'O shameless ogre, why are you back?' The ogre, however, remained silent. Akhzar ran forward with his ebony stick and hit him hard. He cried, 'Go and make a meal of the Muslims!' The ogre screamed after being struck. He picked up the old man from the neck as if holding a lizard. Yakut shouted at him, 'Shameless one, what are you doing? Do not be disrespectful! This is Malik Akhzar my father and the companion of Samri, the keeper of the treasury of magic!' In response, Afreet put the old man in his mouth and chewed him up. He looked at the horrified Yakut and called out, 'You will be next. My mistress has fed me the heavenly meal Samri had promised me. He had written that I should obey the one who feeds me the heart and liver of Mehboob!' As Afreet extended his mighty arm, Yakut screamed and transformed into a hawk to fly out of his range. How could she escape the angel of death who covered five kos in one stride? He reached out into the sky and held the hawk's tail. Yakut fluttered wildly in his grasp, but he swallowed her without hesitation.

As the reader will recall, the remaining golden maidens of Samri were in the palace of Afat Four-hands, Afrasiyab's grandmother, in Zulmat. Afat was talking with the golden maidens when the skies went dark and resounded with the sounds of grief. Thousands of birds fluttered overhead, beating their wings and crying, 'Alas, Yakut Sukhandan, should we remember your youth or your peerless beauty? Today Samri and Jamshed have been left alone!' The golden maidens heard the birds and cried, 'Grandmother, today we leave you to the devil's care. Write down our last words for your information for we go to the gods. This year, Afrasiyab will die. Lacheen, former Shahanshah of Hoshruba will be released. Now this land will be a land of justice and the religion of the Unseen God will prosper here. Afrasiyab will be destroyed!'

Five hundred golden maidens flew to the skies to attack the birds who were lamenting Yakut. When the shadow of the birds fell on them, they were incinerated. The birds flew away calling out, 'Afat, today we were also released from the cages of Yakut. Samri and Jamshed had trapped us and we were in captivity for many ages. We will now enjoy our freedom in the jungles. Go and save Afrasiyab Khana Kharab who is running for his life. Afreet Tilismi has turned on him!' Afat beat her head in frustration and cried, 'Ya Samri, Ya Jamshed, punish this Afrasiyab for destroying the five hujras. I have lost everything! Who will predict the future for me now?' Her husband Nairang, whose camp was at the foot of the mountain where Afat's palace was, rushed up to the palace as he heard the din of the birds and the maidens. He saw his wife wailing and said, 'Why do you weep now? This foolish Afrasiyab has destroyed his own realm. Everyone was overawed with Hoshruba because of the mystery of the hujras of peril. Now they will know that Mahrukh and the others have destroyed the five hujras. Afreet would only turn against us if the Muslims provided him the required nourishment. Go to Magnet Mountain and call out for Muheet Jadoo. Tell him that the king of Hoshruba is in trouble and by the decree of Samri and Jamshed, he must save him!'

As Afat rose to do his bidding, Nairang added, 'Tilism-e-Hoshruba is a land of great mystery and wonder. Samri and Jamshed created it after years of loving labour. Now go to the mountain and save Afrasiyab!' After Afreet had swallowed Yakut, Princess Haijoon ordered him to attack Afrasiyab and his lashkar. Afreet picked up two hundred soldiers at a time and started swallowing them. Afrasiyab saved himself by sending for the forty iron slave-boys of Samri. They attacked Afreet with their swords, but eventually looked helplessly at Afrasiyab as the swords broke on his skin. Afrasiyab cut open his thigh and fed the slave-boys his blood. They fell on Afreet with renewed vigour, but eventually cried, 'We are helpless before him. All we can do now is to die for you!' They fell before Afreet who chewed them up as well. Although they were made of solid iron, he ate them as if they were made of flesh!

Afrasiyab was now truly alarmed. He cast spells that made the heaven and earth tremble, but could not stop the fearsome ogre. The distance that Afrasiyab and his lashkar had travelled over three days was now covered in a day and they reached their former base. Afreet followed them there and destroyed all the pavilions. The lashkar of Islam took possession of the treasury. Afrasiyab was now running for his life.

Suddenly, a light flashed in the sky and Afat Four-hands called out, 'Afrasiyab, you did not listen to me and opened the hujras of peril. Now you are in grave trouble. Do not worry, help is at hand.' Afat then flew to Magnet Mountain, crashed against it as a bolt of lightning and shouted, 'Muheet Jadoo, the life of the ruler of Hoshruba is in danger. Afreet Tilismi has turned on him.' The mountain trembled and burst open. After some time, an ancient sahir emerged from it. His veins were so prominent that they looked like black snakes on his body. He cried, 'Grandmother, did you not warn Afrasiyab of the dangers of opening the hujras? He was laughing and his fate was weeping!'

Muheet then conjured a throne and sat on it with his tegha and a book tucked under his arms. He reached Afreet just when he had chased Afrasiyab to Fort Rehania. Muheet's throne hovered above the man-eating monster and he cut his own throat so that his body fell upon Afreet. The ogre screamed and expelled a flame from his mouth that engulfed his whole body. He burnt like a torch and it seemed as if an entire mountain was on fire. The desert and the forest also burnt fiercely and several sahirs lost their lives. Afrasiyab was so distraught that he tried to save himself from the flames by blowing on them. He ran and picked up Hairat who was about to become unconscious. Afat descended from the skies with a huge magic net and scooped up Afrasiyab, Hairat and twelve thousand other nobles. She flung the net on her shoulders and took all of them to the Garden of Apples.

Afrasiyab's attendants rushed to revive their masters. After the durbar had been convened, Afrasiyab's maternal grandmother, Mahiyan also reached the camp, weeping and wailing. Afrasiyab was still in shock over the death of Yakut because he genuinely loved her. His eyes welled up with tears whenever he recalled her youth and beauty. Eventually, Afat consoled him and said, 'Why do you grieve so? She was no one special. She was a tributary like so many others in this realm. She was a ruler and was murdered. That is all!'

~✺⌁

40 The Murder of Mawaj Jadoo, Amar's Arrest, Asad's Capture, Lacheen, Badi and Tasveer

Malika Hairat Jadoo was in her durbar when Sarsar Sword-fighter entered in an agitated state and spoke with folded hands, 'Huzoor, do you have any news of Mawaj Jadoo?' Hairat said, 'He is meant to be here by now.' Then Sarsar said, 'I was spying in the enemy camp and heard that Amar, Zargham and Barq killed Mawaj and destroyed his lashkar of forty lakh troops. Toofan Jadoo has captured Amar. Can we verify this?' Hairat beat her head and cried, 'Sahibs, this is terrible! A sahir like Mawaj died without fighting. These ayyars will be the death of us!'

A little later, a cloud with seven hues appeared on the horizon and Hairat got up to welcome her husband. Afrasiyab came and sat down beside her and saw that she looked troubled. She met his eyes and began sobbing, 'The kingdom of Hoshruba is doomed!' Afrasiyab snapped, 'Now what has happened, who is dead, who has been robbed?' At that moment, sahir messengers informed Afrasiyab that ayyars had destroyed Mawaj and his lashkar and that Toofan had captured Amar. Afrasiyab turned to his wife and said, 'Do not weep Hairat! How can the death of Mawaj destroy Hoshruba? Be grateful to Samri and Jamshed that Amar is in Mount Sapphire. The ruler Neelum Jadoo will either execute him or send him to his brother Tausan. You know that Tausan's prisoners cannot escape his terrifying dungeons. The mighty Lacheen, Badi-uz-Zaman and Tasveer have been rotting in that place for so many years. Celebrate this moment for this is the end of Amar!'

On Mount Sapphire, the ruler Neelum Jadoo was in his durbar when a light flashed in the sky and Toofan Jadoo shot down from a height looking distressed. He was holding a strange-looking creature in his hands. Neelum asked, 'O wise minister, is all well with you?' Toofan sobbed helplessly and said, 'O Shahanshah, the walls of Mount Sapphire have been diminished today. Your prime minister was killed in such a heinous manner that I cannot bear to relate it to you. This Amar, who was disguised as a singer, destroyed the whole lashkar. Huzoor, your lowly slave had to avenge his master; I captured this rascal from the heart of his camp. Huzoor, this ayyar is the strength of lashkar of Islam!'

Neelum looked hard at Amar, then turned to Toofan and said, 'Toofan why are you storming at this miserable creature? How can he kill anyone? If I scold him, his breath will leave his body!' Toofan cried, 'Do not look at him scornfully! Afrasiyab claims that he is the executioner of many noble sahirs!' Neelum still looked doubtful and asked, 'O Toofan, how can I believe that this puny, sickly creature can be so powerful?' Amar interjected, 'I must have been mistaken for Amar ayyar! I am just a poor man who sings for a living. I am a Samri worshipper. Please employ me for I have many skills besides singing. I can design lamps and am also a chef. In the winters, I can make halwa sohan. Just give me three rupees and I will sing for you!' Toofan saw that Neelum was warming up to Amar and intervened,

'Huzoor, what are you thinking of? He deceived Mawaj in the exact same way. He will destroy the kingdom of Sapphire before you know it.'

Neelum was worried by this and suggested that Amar could be kept in an iron cage and taken to Tausan. Amar's beady eyes bulged out and he looked threateningly at the king. He screamed, 'Neelum, if you do not release me, your death will surely be upon you.' A stunned Neelum sent for an iron cage and after Amar was tied up, he locked the door with his own hands. As Toofan flew in the skies with the cage, the heat became very intense and Amar's skin erupted in boils. Toofan flew all through the day and reached a large fort. As he descended with his prisoner, curious sahirs surrounded and asked him, 'Brother, where do you take this ape-like creature?' They were startled when Toofan informed them that this was the monster referred to in the Book of Samri as the slayer of sahirs.

Toofan spent the night in this fort, but did not sleep a wink for fear of Amar escaping. It took Toofan seven days to reach Tausan's fort. The fort extended for miles around and its walls were massive and solid. Thousands of sahirs and sahiras were camped outside the fort walls. Toofan entered this fort of impressive palaces and bazaars and went straight to the ruler's durbar with Amar in the cage. Amar saw that the ruler seemed to be a powerful sahir with a court of seven hundred sahirs who sat on iron chairs. Amar was overawed by the durbar and he began trembling with fear. Toofan greeted the ruler Tausan Jadoo and presented him with the message that Neelum had sent. Toofan then prepared to leave. Amar became agitated when he realized that the one who had imprisoned him was actually getting away. He cried, 'Toofan it is a matter of shame for me that you leave here alive. Remember that I have mastered the art of astrology. I must have come here for a reason! As for Mian Tausan, he is a horse of a rare breed. I will surely mount him and ride him on thorny paths! He will not be able to rear his head and will gallop in whichever direction I want him to!'

Amar had been deliberately insulting to Tausan who shook with anger and said, 'Listen you camel driver's son, I am not Afrasiyab! Once I imprison you, only your death will release you. You will forget the horrors of Zulmat in my dungeons. You will not be able to tell night from day. The bird of your soul will flutter restlessly in your body of dust. You will forget hunger and thirst!' Amar trembled inwardly, but blustered, 'Tausan, I crush animals like you between my thighs.' Tausan responded calmly, 'Very well, you will now pay for your impertinence.' Tausan rose and picked up the cage. He sprouted a pair of wings and flew up into the sky until he disappeared out of sight. Amar fainted with the rush of air and his eyes opened in a place that was darker than the Veil of Zulmat. Amar could feel dust falling on him occasionally, but could not make out where the dust was coming from. The dark disoriented him and he felt like banging his head against the cage. He began to think that death would be more welcome than to be in this state.

A little later Amar's eyes became accustomed to the darkness and he could make out three other cages suspended besides his. Amar strained his eyes and saw that the largest one held an old man, who seemed worn out and frail and was sitting with his head lowered. In the second cage sat a younger man of immense nobility with an ashen face and circles under his eyes. The third cage had a young woman of incomparable beauty, her hair tangled in knots. She was shackled in heavy iron chains like the others. That moon-faced beauty said, 'Sahib, open your eyes and speak to me. My heart is heavy with grief today; it seems that some other unfortunate has come to these dungeons.' The young man raised his head with an effort and sighed so desperately that the earth trembled with grief. He replied, 'What can I say to you? The heavens have abandoned us.' He turned to Amar's cage and said, 'Who are you and why have you been brought to this dungeon? Perhaps you will not be here for too long, your friends and relatives will speak for you.'

Amar felt as if his heart would burst with grief and he said, 'Young man I cannot bear to hear you speak in such despondent tones. Tell me who you are so that my heart is at rest.' The young man said, 'Badi-uz-Zaman is my name and this lady who has suffered so much pain is Princess Tasveer.' Amar sighed so deeply that smoke came out of his mouth and he felt that his bones were on fire with so much sadness. He cried, 'My son Badi, you have been in this dungeon all these years? Alas Tasveer, you have come to this state! My son, tell me about the person in the third cage? I would like to hear his tale of woe.'

Lacheen, the former monarch of Hoshruba wept loudly and said, 'O king of ayyars, do not ask this unfortunate man who he was! O moon of the sky of ayyari, when I lost Hoshruba, I fought for seventeen years from my own fortress in Qalam Koh. I had no magic gift at my disposal for the traitor Neelum had handed the treasury of Tilism to Afrasiyab. Even in that condition, whenever I would emerge and challenge my enemies, they would run from me. I would then plunder their treasuries and grain to provide for my people in the fort. There was nowhere I could go. They had the forces of the Tilism and besieged my fort repeatedly. This shameless Tausan eventually captured my wife Bilqees and me. I do not know where he has kept that paragon of purity and virtue.'

Lacheen wept bitterly as he remembered his wife and said, 'Had we been together, we could have at least consoled each other. Khwaja, do you know why Afrasiyab rebelled against me? The reason was that I used to reflect on religious matters. I am a sahir and I understood that Samri and Jamshed were human beings who had declared themselves divine due to their magical powers. One day in the durbar, I inadvertently said, "Friends, does it not seem to you that our religion is very weak? I have been thinking and feel that we should follow another path!" My mistake was to speak my thoughts aloud in the durbar. This Afrasiyab became my enemy and convinced all the other sardars that the ancient religion was in danger. They joined him and I lost everything. They took my kingdom and my treasury; they threw me in this dreadful place and separated me from my wife. It was only then that I prayed to the One True God. I thank my Maker that He revealed himself to me in a dream and said that when Amar will be captured and brought here, I will be released.' Amar said, 'Lacheen, He will provide the way and we will be released. God willing we will be content!'

Meanwhile, in Tausan's durbar, his sardars whispered to each other about his abrupt departure with Amar, 'What could have happened to have made the king trouble himself? After all, he could have assigned the task to any one of us, his humble servants.' Suddenly a light flashed in the sky and they saw Tausan descending in a highly distraught state, covered with sweat, and holding a lion-like young man in his arm. The sardars rushed forward and asked, 'Sheheryar, who is this young man? On his face are signs of great nobility, he seems to be a great king!' Tausan replied, 'Friends, this is the young man who has caused Afrasiyab so much trouble. It is my good fortune that I was destined to arrest him. His name is Asad Lion-heart, the conqueror of Hoshruba, the grandson of Sahibqiran. All the great books tell us clearly that Asad will kill Afrasiyab. Today, I have caught him and saved Afrasiyab. No more will the angel of death lurk on his head. All of Hoshruba will be grateful to me!' Tausan's companions murmured in unison, 'You have always been the saviour of Hoshruba. It was you who captured Lacheen and kept him in such secret captivity that no one even knows that he is alive.'

Tausan paid no attention to their flattery and declared, 'Put him in chains immediately and send for the executioner so that he is executed as soon as possible. No sahir in Hoshruba will be safe if this young man escapes. All of Afrasiyab's powerful allies and loyalists will be killed. Friends, just remember this. Even if I decide to delay Tilism Kusha's execution, do not heed my words and go ahead with the deed!' Within minutes, the sahirs bound Asad in heavy chains. As Tausan removed his spell on him, he opened his eyes, looked around at the grand durbar around him and slowly got up, in spite of the chains. He greeted everyone in the Islamic manner and upset all the sahirs, who touched their ears and muttered, 'We will have to sacrifice something today. He takes the name of the Unseen God before us!' Seeing this, Tausan said, 'This man is like the setting sun, the lamp of early morning. Why do you take offence at something a dead man says?' The executioner presented himself in the durbar and Tausan ordered him to execute the young Asad right away.

The news of the Tilism Kusha's impending execution had spread like wildfire throughout the city. Eventually, the news reached Tausan's only daughter, Naheed, a powerful sahira. One of her handmaidens rushed to her and wept, 'Huzoor, your respected father is being very cruel today. He has brought a noble youth whose beauty has illuminated the durbar and is determined to execute him!' Naheed was curious and travelled from her place to her father's durbar with some companions. She found the entrance swarming with curious citizens. When she asked, 'What is happening here?', a dozen voices replied, 'Tilism Kusha is being executed!' Naheed quickly sent a handmaiden to ask her father not to kill Asad until she was present. Tausan agreed and said, 'Indeed, since her uncle Mawaj was killed, she has been inconsolable!' Naheed reached the durbar moments later as her companions moved people aside for her. She looked at the beautiful young Asad and her eyes filled with tears.

Asad also looked up and on seeing a houri-like maiden, sighed deeply. The arrows of love pierced both their hearts. Naheed walked up to Tausan's throne trembling like the morning candle and fell in her father's lap unconscious. Tausan was alarmed at her condition and her companions rushed to her. They sprayed that envy of the garden with rose water. She regained consciousness after a long time and said, 'Respected father, I was overwhelmed with memories of my noble uncle. He died the death of a dog because of this man and so many other noble sahirs have also been killed. I am grieved that this man should die such an easy death. I would like him to be stabbed all over and for us to sprinkle salt and chillies on his wounds, so that he should beg for death and not be released from his pain.'

Everyone in the durbar murmured, 'The princess is right; this man should be tortured before being put to death!' Naheed said, 'Father, let me take him to my garden. My African and Turkish handmaidens will torture him. At dawn, I will kill him with my own hands and send his head to you. I will throw his corpse in the forest where wolves and tigers can tear it apart. You can send the head to Afrasiyab who will show it to Mahrukh and Bahar to make them suffer!' Tausan laughed indulgently and said, 'My child this kingdom and its treasures are yours. You can take the prisoner but remember he has many friends. I do not want him to escape!' Naheed assured him, 'I will remain awake all night and his escape will be impossible!' She signalled to her handmaidens to take the prisoner to her garden without removing his chains.

As soon as Naheed reached her gardens, she took Asad into her chamber. She bribed the handmaidens to remain silent and cut off his chains. Asad bathed and changed into royal garments and sat on the masnad in all splendour. He was already smitten with Naheed and gazed at her completely entranced. Her cupbearer filled a goblet with wine and offered it to the princess. She said, 'Huzoor, our souls are in ecstasy in the presence of such an exalted guest; God has graced us with this blessing, He has brought the moth to the flame, the bulbul to the flower!' The princess smiled and accepted the goblet, and then offered it to Asad who said, 'You have a different faith to mine. If you love me, you have to renounce the religion of Samri and Jamshed and know the One True God!' As Asad explained the concept eloquently, Naheed's soul was set free. The mirror of her heart was cleansed and the rust of her doubt dissolved. She smiled at Asad and said, 'I believe in what you believe, but if I recite the Kalma, my tongue will lose the powers of magic. I give you my word that I accept Islam and hope that my powers can be of service to you when needed.'

Thus, the princess and all her attendants happily vowed to serve the true cause. Rose-tinted wine was served by young cupbearers and golden-voiced singers began entertaining the two lovers. After his heart was warmed by the wine, Asad declared, 'Princess, you have done me a favour by saving my life at a time when my life was like the last flicker of the candle. My mentor and supporter, the honourable Khwaja Amar was captured by Toofan. For me to drink wine in your company is against all norms of courage and honour. At dawn, I intend to attack Tausan even if my end is near.' Tears rolled down Naheed's cheek and she said, 'If you go to Tausan's durbar, you will surely lose your life for he is as powerful as Afrasiyab. No one knows the way to the magical dungeons, except Tausan. I will go to my mother and somehow discover the way to the dungeons; I will release Lacheen, Badi and Tasveer even if I lose my life in the process. Please give me your word that you will not leave this garden.'

The princess looked so distressed that Asad promised he would do her bidding. Naheed then left on a peacock with golden feathers, but instructed her companions, 'Find some peasant and disguise him as Tilism Kusha. Cut his head off and take it to Tausan. Do not forget to tell him that we tortured the man before killing him and threw his headless body in the jungle.' Naheed's mother Badban Jadoo was in her palace surrounded by companions when she was informed that Naheed had arrived to meet her. Badban smiled and said, 'Well, I am glad that this chit of a girl has stopped her frolics with her friends to remember me.'

Naheed went forward and bowed deeply. Badban welcomed her with a warm embrace. Naheed put her arms around her mother and said, 'Dear mother, have you heard that I tortured the Tilism Kusha for eight hours? Towards the end, he begged to be killed. It is your house that has saved Tilism and all sahirs from extinction!' Badban clicked her fingers in a sacrificial gesture and said, 'My child you have done well! Hoshruba now belongs to you.' Naheed continued, 'Mother, what worries me is that if someone wants to rescue Lacheen, Badi and Tasveer from the dungeons of the Tilism, how he would go about it?' Badban got into a rage and slapped her daughter in the face. She screamed, 'You shameless hussy, do you want to take your father's life?' Badban had never slapped Naheed before and she was very shocked. She threw herself on the floor, pulled her hair and kicked her heels in a hysterical tantrum.

Tausan had dismissed his durbar for the day and walked into the palace at that time. He came across the disturbing scene of his daughter on the floor and Badban standing over her with a whip while her companions tried to hold her back. Tausan rushed to his daughter and took her in his arms. 'What is happening here?' he asked his wife. She replied angrily, 'She is behaving very strangely today. She actually asked me how the prisoners of the dungeons could be rescued!' Naheed put her arms around her father's neck and pouted, 'Father, am I the enemy that this secret should be kept for me? I merely asked in the course of the conversation and my mother slapped me. I want to kill myself because of the shame.' Tausan whispered to her, 'My dear, your mother is just suspicious by nature. Come to me at night and I will divulge everything to you.'

Naheed returned to her garden and stayed with her lover the whole day. In the evening, she dressed like a new bride and went to her father's palace. She put her arms around his neck and wept, 'Father, am I your enemy? My mother has treated me like one. If I can kill Tilism Kusha, I can kill myself as easily or I will die weeping. If you want me to live you will have to confide in me.' Tausan comforted his daughter and said, 'Listen carefully my dear. If someone wants to rescue Shahanshah Lacheen and the others, he will first have to render me unconscious. I have hidden the key to the dungeons in my topknot. This throne would have to be removed. Forty people are required to move it as it is so heavy. Underneath is a black stone that blocks the entrance to a stairway going deep into the earth. It will lead to a door that opens into a vast desert. Once you cross the desert, the black structure of the dungeons becomes visible. The same key will open the dungeons as well. Twelve hundred princes who were loyal to Lacheen are also imprisoned in the outhouses.'

Tausan sighed deeply and said, 'Light of my eyes, I have revealed my darkest secret to you, but feel very uneasy now!' Naheed calmed her father by offering him wine. After he had consumed several goblets of wine, she quietly muttered a spell so that Tausan fell unconscious. Naheed then tied a cloth soaked in the potion of unconsciousness around his head to prevent him from waking up. She sprouted wings and flew back to her garden. Asad was waiting for her when she appeared in the night sky like the morning star. She looked distraught and said, 'Sheheryar, come with me I have discovered the route to the dungeons!'

Asad and Naheed returned with Asad to Tausan's palace in the dead of the night. She removed the key from her father's hair and they made their way to the Tilismi dungeons. By the time they found the dungeons, the sun was about to rise. They found a number of shabby houses where several prisoners with matted hair were staring out of the barred windows. They called out, 'Tilism Kusha, God has brought you to our rescue. We had a revelation about you in our dreams last night. We do not have the strength to bear our ordeal any longer!' Asad called back 'Friends, let me rescue your master first and I will return to you. With God's grace, there will be no more prisoners in this place now!'

Asad opened the dungeons and made his way to the place where the four cages were hanging. Amar saw him first and cried, 'O light of my eyes, your uncle Badi-uz-Zaman and aunt Tasveer are in these two cages. This one here is Lacheen Jadoo, former ruler of Hoshruba.' Asad brought down Amar's cage first and left it with Naheed to open. Lacheen watched Asad with unspoken longing in his eyes. Asad climbed up to get Badi-uz-Zaman's cage, but Badi said, 'Light of my eyes we must do the right thing. This great king has been incarcerated in this cage for the last twenty-two years, you should release him first. This venerable old man is already one of the faithful.'

Asad then brought down Lacheen's cage. Meanwhile, Naheed had cut Amar's chains and he was running around the dungeons looking for treasure. When Asad pulled the needle out from Lacheen's tongue, he moaned with pain and fell back unconscious. Badi and Tasveer's chains were also cut and revealed deep wounds underneath. As Tasveer moaned with pain, Badi-uz-Zaman hobbled painfully up to her and stroked her hair. Lacheen opened his eyes and said, 'Naheed, the keeper Bozeena and his men were guarding the dungeons. Where are they?' Naheed replied, 'Tilism Kusha thinks he must have gone off hunting in the night otherwise he would not have let us enter.'

Lacheen then explained, 'It has been twenty-two years since I practised magic. I have lost all my magic gifts. I will leave you for a week and awaken my powers. But first I must rescue my friends.' Lacheen stepped out of the dungeons and found his former allies and friends shouting, 'Shahanshah, God has shown us this blessed day when Tilism Kusha came here. We have spent twenty-two years in this prison, but thank the Lord that we remained steadfast and loyal to you.' Lacheen was bent with age and grief, but when he saw his friends, he stood up straight and colour returned to his cheeks. He ran around happily opening the doors to their cells and embracing them with joy. Amar had found rooms filled with treasure and had already dropped it all in Zambil. He then returned to the others with a long face to complain, 'There is no treasure in this place!' Naheed exclaimed, 'But this place is full of jewels!' Amar smiled and said to her, 'Light of my eyes, you can verify it yourself. There is nothing but dust in all the rooms!'

The next morning, when Tausan and Badban woke up, they realized their daughter's treachery. Tausan was in a rare rage and left with his wife and an army that swelled like the sea in pursuit of Asad Ghazi. The noble Asad had an army of twelve-thousand released prisoners from the dungeons. He had barely travelled five kos when he encountered Tausan's great army. At Tausan's signal, the sahir army heaved into motion. Badi-uz-Zaman saw the forces of evil intending to cover the moon of honour and announced himself as he led the battle. Naheed was alarmed by the size of her father's army. She fell upon it with her own force of twelve thousand companions. Her magic flashed in the battlefield in the form of iron balls, lightning bolts and flame-rains. She was not a match for Tausan, whose magic was so powerful that no one could withstand it. He killed hundreds with just one stroke of his sword. He was also attacking his daughter and wanted to rip her apart, but Badban Jadoo held him back. She marvelled at Tilism Kusha's courage in fighting the sahirs and murmured, 'Naheed is indeed a judge of rare gems. What a rare diamond she has found! Look how beautiful he is and just as courageous. No one can withstand his attacks!'

Badban's companions echoed, 'Huzoor how right you are! Indeed he is beautiful and has the courage of a lion!' Badban became distraught and cried, 'How can I attack them? Indeed, I want to shield them both. Look how fearless she is. She meets her father's eye so boldly and is not afraid for her life. I am afraid Tausan might disable her with his magic, I have reared her with so much love and I can see her being destroyed before my very eyes!' Tausan saw that his daughter had killed hundreds of his men. Naheed had just killed a sahir and in the ensuing darkness, was flinging lentil beans on her father's forces when Tausan emerged before her. He expelled a flame from his mouth that blinded her. He then flew up into the sky, holding her tightly by the waist. Badban looked up and saw that he was slapping her daughter repeatedly as she pleaded for her life. Badban flashed up like a lightning bolt and shouted, 'You shameless man, let go of my daughter, she is innocent! I have not seen a bigger eunuch than you. I am convinced now that Tilism Kusha is in the right!'

Tausan began abusing his wife loudly, but she aimed a magic ball at his wrist. Tausan was a powerful sahir and the blow did not break his wrist, but a large boil broke out on his hand. Naheed slipped from his hand and into her mother's arms. Badban descended to the earth and revived Naheed by spraying her with cold water. Naheed woke up and clung to her mother sobbing, 'My dearest mother, if you have saved me now, then give me your support. Consider that the pantheons of gods we believe in are false. Samri and Jamshed were mortals like us. They mislead millions of us by conjuring wonderful spectacles of magic. Where are they now? What kind of gods were they that they died? The adherents of Islam believe that their God has always been there and will remain forever. His Majesty will never diminish!'

Badban's heart was stirred by her daughter's words and she embraced her saying, 'Light of my eyes, I am with you with all my heart and soul!' Both the mother and daughter then attacked Tausan's forces ferociously. Badban's companions and handmaidens also joined in the attack. Tausan's magic wounded both his wife and daughter, but he was unable to mount an attack on Asad. His companions said, 'Huzoor, your wife and daughter are of no consequence, but we have to organize an attack on this brave lion fighting us. He has killed so many powerful sahirs. What is the source of his strength?'

Tausan stopped fighting and pondered. He then muttered a spell and a bird made of flames appeared before him. It called out, 'Why does the master summon me now?' Tausan said, 'O Bird of Samri, why is Tilism Kusha untouched by magic?' The bird declared, 'Princess Lal Sukhandan has tied the powerful amulet of Samri around his arm. Your magical spirits will not go near him!' Tausan barked in laughter and said, 'Sahibs, have you heard the bird? The religion of Samri is on its way out if the daughter of Malik Akhzar companion of Samri has joined Tilism Kusha! How disgraceful that our saviour now protects our enemy! I will snatch the amulet from him!' Tausan then attacked Asad with renewed fury.

Badban and Naheed prevented him from getting close to Asad, but Tausan's magic overwhelmed them. At that time, a fragrant breeze swept through the battlefield. Everyone looked up to see the joyous vision of the beautiful Bahar on a peacock with golden plumage. The incomparable Makhmoor was following her. As Bahar tossed a bouquet of flowers at the enemy, trees swayed in the cool breezes and two thousand of Tausan's men were enchanted. They rubbed dust on their faces and tore their garments as they pleaded with Bahar. She calmly ordered them to cut off Tausan's head. As they turned to attack their master, he reluctantly turned from his wife and daughter to confront and destroy them.

A little while later, a white cloud emerged in the sky. Tausan looked up in alarm and saw that the cloud parted to reveal the mighty Shahanshah Lacheen seated on a throne of rubies. He wore rich garments and a gleaming crown. An army of twelve thousand sahirs marched on the ground beneath him. He looked down at Tausan and shouted, 'I am the ruler of the kingdom of magic! You disloyal traitor, I have arrived. You dare use my former slaves to fight me!' Lacheen then opened a little casket and a bird with plumage of seven hues flew out of it. Lacheen called out, 'O magic bird, go and knock the enemy senseless, punish the traitors and my enemies!' The bird nodded and flew over the enemy. As its shadow moved over them, many of them dropped dead. Tausan tried to run, but knew that Lacheen was unforgiving. He thought, 'Asad is a noble warrior. If I convert, he will protect me!' Tausan then tied his hands with a scarf and fell at Asad's feet. He cried, 'Ya Sheheryar, save me!' He then wept so copiously that Asad's shoes were soaked with his tears. Tausan then folded his hands and said, 'I am indeed the greatest sinner. I betrayed Lacheen and treated him very badly. I handed him to Afrasiyab and forgot that there is a Higher Power!' Asad was convinced that Tausan was truly repentant. He embraced him warmly and said, 'O Tausan, do not despair, the mercy of the Provider is limitless. Every mortal sinner is forgiven by him.'

VII

41 THE BATTLE OF KAUKAB AND MAHIYAN, THE NEW TRICKERIES OF KHWAJA AMAR IN ZULMAT

The travellers of the paths of magic relate this story of valour and glory. Ever since Afrasiyab's grandmother Mahiyan Emerald-robe had killed Kaukab's grandmother Mushtri during a battle, Kaukab had sworn that he would not eat with his right hand unless he killed Mahiyan. Amar tried to dissuade him from embarking on this perilous mission but Kaukab was determined. As a result, Amar decided to follow Kaukab secretly. He disguised himself as a fakir and travelled far into the wilderness where he waited for Kaukab to pass by. Amar stopped by a river that had several temples along its banks where thousands of sahir devotees were praying. Cries of Samri and Jamshed filled the air.

Suddenly, a second sun appeared in the sky and bore down over the river. Its heat was so intense that several sahirs lost their lives. They wanted to run, but could not escape. The waters of the river boiled in the scorching heat and houses on its banks began to collapse. The fishes in the river leapt up, but the magic sun's rays cut their heads off and the river went red with their blood. As Amar watched all this from a distance, the sun of Tilism Nur Afshan, the moon of the skies, the sahib of glory and honour and courage, Shahanshah Kaukab the Enlightened emerged from the magic sun. Amar then saw a sahir, whose body had the scales of a crocodile and whose face was snarling in arrogance, charging out of the river to attack Kaukab. The sahir called out, 'Kaukab, you have killed my friends! I am Nahang River-dweller, the protector of this river as appointed by Mahiyan Emerald-robe. Return now for I will never let you pass!' Kaukab snapped, 'Shameless one, why are you determined to die? I will not turn back until I kill Mahiyan! This is just a river of water; even a river of flames would not have stopped me!' After a fierce fight with Nahang, Kaukab killed him. Amar saw that with Nahang's death, sheets of flames fell from the skies and the river went dry, turning the land into a desert. After some time, darkness fell and a voice called out, 'You have killed me, I was Nahang River-dweller!'

Within moments, a magnificent gateway appeared where the river previously flowed. Kaukab had sustained some wounds in the fight with Nahang and was in pain. He rode to the doorway with Amar following him invisible in Galeem. Kaukab smashed the gate with one mighty blow of his bughda. However, Mahiyan's officer Qumqam Jadoo was waiting beyond the gateway with an army of three lakh sahirs. Kaukab rode forward on his horse, completely alone with his blood-stained tegha in his hand. He called out, 'Shameless ones, get out of my way! I am Kaukab!' The sahirs attacked him, but Kaukab fearlessly fell upon this mighty river of sahirs. He used all his powers and annihilated thousands with his iron balls, lentil grains, mighty tegha, or with just a smile that conjured bolts of lightning. So nobly did Kaukab fight that Amar shouted impulsively, 'O Shahanshah, you are magnificent! Well done!' Kaukab was startled when he heard this and thought the voice was familiar; but it did not cross his mind that Amar could reach this place.

Eventually, Kaukab killed Qumqam with one ferocious blow of his tegha. Qumqam's forces tried escaping, but Kaukab continued attacking them. He destroyed the whole army and sustained several wounds in the process. Kaukab then rested in a nearby defile and tended to his wounds. Amar stood close to him, invisible in his mantle, but did not appear before him. Kaukab then conjured a bungalow in which he sat and watched the desert. Presently, he was startled at the sight of a magic moon that illuminated the desert. As he watched in fascination, seven stars came into view in the sky and crashed down on the earth. At that time, several songbirds flew out of the trees, rolled on the earth and transformed into young girls. They immediately set to work and erected a pavilion in the desert. The falling stars were actually young women whom the serving girls greeted with deference.

Kaukab looked closely and saw that the leader was a beautiful princess flanked by an ayyar girl who looked sly and deceitful. The other women were mere companions. He could hear their musical voices in the silence of the night. The ayyar girl, Saba Doe-eyed, was warning Princess Akhtar, 'Princess we must remain alert about the enemy!' Akhtar's response was, 'Saba, the enemy is indeed formidable!' Before they disappeared into the pavilion, Saba murmured, 'Lay a trap and he will walk into it himself.' Kaukab realized that they had actually come there to capture him; and that perhaps, the ayyar girl intended to trick him into defeat. Kaukab thought, 'I have been in the company of the great Amar himself. Who will try to trick me? The best thing to do is not to eat anything they offer to me.' Kaukab thought of mounting an attack on the pavilion, but then thought the better of it.

In the pavilion, the young maidens arranged a gathering of pleasure with wine and sweetmeats. The ayyar girl Saba had a beautiful voice and broke out into song. Kaukab began swaying with pleasure as he heard her sing. He picked up his tegha and swaggered over to the pavilion. The curtains parted magically and the princess emerged from within. She said, 'Greetings Shahanshah! What brings you here?' Kaukab replied, 'I have come to confront you as you seem to have blocked my way. Please go ahead and try your magic on me.' He then looked at the ayyar girl and said, 'Try all your tricks—drug the wine, lay out a trap for me with your snare-rope!' Saba folded her hands and said, 'Huzoor what are you saying? Our princess always comes to this spot in the desert to enjoy the moonlight.' Akhtar added, 'Huzoor how can we dare to stop you? In any case, if you are on your way to Zulmat, you must know this is not the route.' Kaukab restrained himself and said, 'Akhtar, do not deceive me with your pretty words. Everyone knows me for my intelligence. Now go ahead and attack me!' The princess looked down coyly and whispered, 'How can a handmaiden attack the king? In fact I have always longed to meet you.' She smiled and revealed her pearly teeth, while her eyes relayed an unmistakable signal to Kaukab, who felt the stirring of desire for this enchanting young woman.

Akhtar begged him to join her on the masnad and Saba added, 'Huzoor, come in. You have been in the company of Khwaja Amar. How can I trick you in any manner? You know all the ways of ayyari. Here, there can be no deceit in water or flower. I cannot lay a trap for you, I cannot drug your wine, and you are incomparable in magic and courage, who can dare to meet your eyes?' Kaukab thought, 'She is right; if there is treachery afoot, I can always confront it.' Akhtar then beckoned him into the pavilion and Kaukab found it adorned like a new bride. Just as he sat down on the masnad, Saba held a string of pearls in her hand and cracked them open. They released a narcotic vapour and when Kaukab inhaled it, he fell unconscious. Saba called out triumphantly, 'I am Saba Doe-eyed! Amar's guardian angels could not have been aware of such a trick! Only fools drug the wine, those who keep my company know better!' Akhtar pierced the unconscious Kaukab's tongue with a needle and sent for an iron cage. She locked the noble Kaukab in the cage and sent a message to Mahiyan that read: 'Malika Mahiyan, Saba Doe-eyed rendered Kaukab unconscious and we have him in a cage. Please come and kill him with your own hands.'

Amar rescues Kaukab

When Akhtar's message reached her, Mahiyan was in her durbar in Zulmat telling her companions, 'If this week goes by without an incident, then even Samri and Jamshed cannot kill me! This week my stars are malevolent, the heavens are after my life!' Mahiyan then read the note and was overjoyed. She said, 'My friends, the star of Akhtar overwhelmed the exalted star of Kaukab's magic. Saba Doe-eyed did the needful.' She wrote back to Akhtar, 'You have done well to capture Kaukab. Amar accompanied him on this journey. Tell Saba to find and arrest him as well. I will also send some people to find him.'

On receiving Mahiyan's message, Saba was about to leave the pavilion to find Amar, when she heard voices outside. The serving maidens came in and announced that Princess Hawai Jadoo, Mahiyan's niece, had brought Amar's head. Saba was perplexed, but Akhtar was ecstatic. Moments later, Hawai Jadoo entered the pavilion holding Amar's head tied in a handkerchief. She was panting as she laid the head before Akhtar and said, 'This is the head of that camel driver's son. He led the Muslims. I don't know why it is believed that ayyars cannot practise magic. He subjected me to such vicious spells that my body erupted in boils!'

Hawai inspected her limbs and found that her body had broken into boils, her face was pale and she was trembling. Akhtar took off her string of pearls and put it around Hawai's neck in appreciation and said, 'We must find Amar's body!' Saba said, 'I will go back with Hawai Jadoo and I will drag back that maleech.' Hawai Jadoo led Saba deep in to the jungle and cried, 'O look, there is his body!' As Saba turned to look, Hawai burst a narcotic bubble in her face. The reader must have guessed that Hawai was really Amar in disguise. Amar threw Saba in Zambil and called out to the keepers, 'Look after her. She is a rare ayyar girl, a veritable flower of the garden of ayyari. I will marry her to one of my sons; their children will be deceitful rascals!' Amar kept muttering in this vein as he returned to Akhtar disguised as Saba. He came across a peasant on the way back and killed him. He cut his head off, tossed it away and dragged the body to the pavilion. He started shouting, 'Come and help me somebody. This Hawai Jadoo has disappeared. Amar's spirits must have been after her. I managed to get hold of his body before they could harm me!'

Akhtar's serving maidens rushed out and saw that Saba was sweating heavily as she dragged the false Amar's body. They surrounded the babbling Saba, and Akhtar also emerged and gasped, 'It is because of Samri and Jamshed's blessings that you are safe!' The false Saba was very excited and asked, 'Huzoor where have you kept Kaukab?' Akhtar said, 'He is in a tent behind ours. Kufail Jadoo is guarding him.' The false Saba gasped and said, 'Huzoor that was not wise. Kufail is a drunkard! I need to go back there and check on him!' The false Saba then went to Kufails's tent and found him nodding off with sleep. She hit him hard and shouted, 'You donkey! Is this how you guard anyone? Have you heard that Amar has been captured and Malika Mahiyan is due here any moment?'

When Kufail looked sheepish, the false Saba immediately softened and said, 'No harm done. I know how fond you are of your wine. Look I have brought you a flask!' Kufail was grateful for this gift and immediately consumed the drugged wine. He was unconscious in a little while and fell down heavily. The false Saba or Amar then looked at Kaukab who lay in a cage with snakes coiled around his body. He said 'Shahanshah, how could you be so careless knowing that you were with strangers? Tell me how can I help you now?' Kaukab recognized Amar's voice and signalled to Amar to open his satchel. He pointed to a golden statuette in the satchel. Amar understood that he would have to anoint the statuette with a drop of Kaukab's blood. As soon as Kaukab's blood dropped on the statuette, it came to life and kneeled before Kaukab, who pointed towards himself. The magic statuette pulled out the needle from his tongue and tore the snakes off his body.

Kaukab came out of the cage and embraced his friend. Amar now disguised the unfortunate Kufail to look like Kaukab and threw him in the cage. Kaukab locked the cage with his spells and said, 'Khwaja, I am going to remain invisible. You should disguise yourself as Kufail. Let Mahiyan arrive. I promise you, I will either kill her today or lose my life. Khwaja, you are truly blessed that you have been safe even in these magical realms riddled with traps set by Mahiyan. I was as good as dead until you rescued me!' Amar replied generously, 'There is no need to mention that. You and I both did what we did. The important thing is that we vanquish the enemy.'

The next morning, Mahiyan's face was alight with joy when she heard that Amar was dead. She happily sat on a flying throne and set off to meet Akhtar, who had brought Kaukab's cage outside. Preparations were on for his execution when she heard the sound of trumpets and kettledrums. Mahiyan's throne flew in with several black-faced magic slave-girls and an army of twelve-thousand sahirs. As Mahiyan inspected Kaukab's cage, Akhtar went forward and simpered, 'Queen of the World, your lowly slave spent a difficult night. I was afraid that Kaukab might escape or a friend will release him. His biggest supporter Amar was also killed or he would have tried to deceive us!' Mahiyan smiled and awarded Akhtar a priceless necklace of rubies. The false Kufail said, 'Malika, surely I deserve to be awarded for guarding Kaukab all night. It was not an easy task. A golden statuette tried to release him, but I overpowered her after a tremendous fight.' Mahiyan replied, 'Indeed, you have done very well. Kaukab's magic protects him; he will not be executed easily. I will conjure a special iron ball to destroy him or perhaps burn him to death!'

As soon as Mahiyan uttered these words, one of the slave-girls laughed, while others smiled and moaned in succession. One said, 'This is incredible! Look how Amar disguised as Kufail makes a fool out of Mahiyan. The real Kufail lies in that cage. Malika has blinkers over her eyes. She accuses others of arrogance but does not look at herself!' Another slave-girl shouted at Mahiyan, 'Do you not understand? Do not kill your own servant Kufail. Attack the camel driver's son instead who is swaggering before you. Your time has come. The angel of death is on his way!' Mahiyan screamed at her niece, 'Have you heard what the slave-girls of Samri are saying? Catch Amar at once you fool! You have my faithful Kufail in that cage!'

Amar immediately leapt up and flung several hookahs on the people around him. The air filled with smoke and as the hookahs burst in the air, their flames burnt many of the sahirs. Mahiyan began screaming, 'Get him! Get him!' Suddenly, the earth before her parted and Kaukab emerged, declaring himself. Princess Akhtar was closest to him and the first to receive the punishment of his sword. She went straight to hell. Kaukab then turned on the rest of the army in his lion-like manner. The earth trembled with his magic and he was bathed in a river of blood. Mahiyan realized that Kaukab would destroy her army soon, so she jumped off her throne and fled to her palace. Kaukab turned to Amar and said, 'Khwaja, I am going after her. Do not follow me for that place is crawling with sahirs!' Amar replied, 'How can the shadow leave the body? You go ahead, God be with you!'

The death of Mahiyan Emerald-robe

As soon as Mahiyan reached her garden in Zulmat she asked her contingent of four hundred officers to quickly marshal the army to face Kaukab. Within no time, an army of seventeen lakh sahirs was defending Mahiyan's palace and shouting, 'Kaukab will not dare to enter this place! If he does he will be humiliated!' Mahiyan kept pacing restlessly in her garden when there was an uproar amongst the troops, indicating that Kaukab had arrived. Kaukab fought like a lion, heedless of his own life, although a shower of spears was directed at him. Finally, he destroyed the army and rushed into the garden. Mahiyan went forward and attacked him with her sword. Kaukab fenced with her and with his free hand, released a bird of many hues. As the bird flew around Mahiyan's head, she stood still and the colour drained from her face. Kaukab then brought down his sword on her. Even in that paralyzed state, several shields flew over Mahiyan's head to save her while magic birds swooped down to shield her from Kaukab's sword. The birds lost their heads and the shields were smashed to smithereens. Kaukab's sword sliced through Mahiyan's head, face and torso, and eventually kissed the earth. Kaukab shouted triumphantly, 'I have killed her!'

A voice called out 'Brother, well done!' Kaukab turned around and saw that Amar stood besides him, his face shining with happiness. The inmates of the garden panicked as darkness fell and several hundred birds flapped their wings as they cried, 'Alas, our queen!' The garden walls collapsed in the fierce storm and after some time, magic spirits wailed, 'You have killed me! My name was Mahiyan Emerald-robe! Alas, I died in vain and did not achieve my purpose!' A bird of seven hues then burst out of Mahiyan's skull and flew away wailing to the Garden of Apples. Mahiyan's army begged Kaukab for clemency and swore allegiance to Islam. At that time Kaukab finally stopped fighting.

◆

42 THE STRANGE TALE OF HAIRAT'S FATHER HAYAT JADOO, THE AMAZING TRICKERIES OF AMAR, THE DEATH OF HAYAT

Afrasiyab was overwhelmed with grief after the death of his grandmother Mahiyan. Hairat also looked the picture of sorrow. Afrasiyab's paternal grandmother, Afat Four-hands, travelled from the Palace of the Ancestors when she heard the news. Afrasiyab provided her with the details of Mahiyan's death and said, 'Today, the pillar of Hoshruba has fallen!' Afat tried to give him courage and said, 'Afrasiyab, I am still here. I will not let Tilism Kusha harm you!' Suddenly, royal messengers entered the durbar and informed Hairat, 'Your respected father, Hayat Jadoo, companion of Samri is arriving with an army of four lakh soldiers. He will be here tomorrow morning'

Hairat rose to welcome her father, but Afrasiyab frowned and said, 'Hairat, there is no need for your father to confront the enemy. We do not want to be burdened with gratitude to anyone at this time!' Hairat was deeply offended by these words, but left silently with her companions. She ordered her camp to prepare for her father's arrival and declared that the bazaars of her lashkar were to extend to the boundaries of her father's camp. The next morning, she went to her father's pavilion. Hayat Jadoo emerged from his pavilion to greet his daughter and embraced her warmly. Hairat informed him about all that had happened and said, 'My sister has become our enemy, but father, do not interfere in this matter. Afrasiyab is arrogant. Why should you be bothered for him? Remain our guest for a few nights and return to Fort Hayatia.' Hairat then led her father with due solemnity towards her camp.

The news of Hayat's arrival had reached Mahrukh's lashkar as well. Amar declared, 'At the time of Hayat's arrival we will all go fishing in the river close to Hairat's camp. All sardars should be dressed in their best robes and must accompany us.' The next morning, a large gold-embroidered canopy was erected along the banks of the river; Khwaja Amar sat in its shade on a throne, wearing a crown. All the sardars stood around him with their hands folded. Khwaja threw a line in the river and looked as if he was absorbed in fishing.

It so happened that Hayat Jadoo was passing by with his flower-like daughter, Hairat. He was shocked at the sight of a man with rope-like limbs, seated in all arrogance on a ruby throne while his fishing line dangled in the river. Hayat exclaimed, 'Hairat, who is this man who wears a crown in my presence? He does not rise to greet me. Does he not know who I am?' Hairat replied, 'Huzoor, this is the man who has destroyed Hoshruba. He calls himself the slayer of sahirs and beard-shaver of disbelievers! Indeed, he is all that he claims he is.' Hayat Jadoo said, 'My daughter, at least give me his name. There is no one equal to me except Afrasiyab. Even he has always deferred to me. He never wears a crown in my presence and always appears before me in a golden cap.' Hairat sighed and said, 'Huzoor, this is Amar ayyar. He is trying to offend you deliberately!' Hayat looked at Hairat and asserted, 'My daughter, he has insulted me by wearing a crown before me. He must be punished!' Hairat tried to tell him not to pick a fight with Amar, but Hayat ignored her.

(Hayat had two commanders in his army—Palang and Nahang. Nahang had accompanied his master and his hand was resting on the base of Hayat's throne. Palang was supervising the movements of the troops.) Enraged with Amar's behaviour, Hayat ordered Nahang to bring the ayyar to him. Now, Nahang was a hot-tempered young man and was outraged by the insult to his master. He shot up like a bolt of lightning and fell on the fishing party with such force that their eyes closed.

When they opened their eyes again, they realized that Amar was missing. The sardars were about to look for him when ayyars Barq and Qiran declared that they would go and investigate the matter as there could be great bloodshed.

Meanwhile, Nahang threw Amar before Hayat. Amar had become unconscious due to the rush of air. Hayat said, 'Call your brother Palang. He will execute him right away!' There was an uproar as Palang Jadoo came forward through the sahir army. He shouted, 'Huzoor, give him to me. I will tear him to pieces and swallow him!' Palang flung the unconscious Amar on his shoulder and handed Hayat a paper. He said, 'Huzoor, this is a list of the men we recruited today. You will have to determine their salaries.' As Palang swaggered out of sight, Hayat exclaimed, 'Hairat, are you happy now? Palang is a cannibal. He will eat up this wily rascal. The rebels will be running back to you and the war will be over!'

Hairat was stunned and thought, 'How could this happen? He cannot kill Amar! Perhaps his end was near. He was foolish to wear a crown in front of my father. He deserved to die!' Hayat was still talking to his daughter when they reached the durbar pavilion. Barq was present there, disguised as a sahir. Hairat said, 'Huzoor, do read the paper that Palang gave to you.' Hayat's jaw dropped as he read the paper that said, 'I am the bughda-wielder and favourite of the saints, Mehtar Qiran! O Hayat, you are courting your own death! You captured my master and I whisked him away from under your very nose. Your commander Palang is unconscious and hidden in a well. Rescue him or he will surely die!' Hairat tried to comfort her father and said, 'Dear father, these ayyars are a menace. They have tricked Shahanshah several times and Murshidzadeh has disappeared for fear of them.' Hayat composed himself and said, 'Do you think Amar has frightened me? Just watch what happens tomorrow! If all sardars and Amar do not kiss my feet and apologize, do not call me the companion of Samri anymore!' He then asked his men to rescue Palang from the well.

Afrasiyab also came to greet him and said, 'Do not trouble yourself! I have a plan for the Muslims.' Hayat said, 'I will finish them and conquer Tilism-e-Nur Afshan! Who is Kaukab? He is just a boy who grew up in front of me!' Afrasiyab tried to dissuade his father-in-law from planning anything against the ayyars, but Hayat spoke so arrogantly that Afrasiyab was offended and eventually he shrugged and said, 'Well, it is entirely up to you! Hairat, it is of no use to speak to your father. Hayat means life, but he will be remembered for his death which is surely upon him!' Hairat cried, 'How can you say such nasty things about my father?' Afrasiyab responded coolly, 'I have tried to reason with him, but now I will sit back and watch the spectacle unfold!' Hayat declared, 'You will see right away! My magic will work wonders. I will whip that camel driver's son so that he will beg for mercy!' Hayat knocked in the air and called out, 'Nairang magician, present yourself quickly!'

The boy magician

A young boy, about twelve years old, suddenly emerged from one corner. He was dressed for battle and bowed before Hayat. The old man said, 'Nairang, go to the Muslim durbar and tell them that Shahanshah wants to invite them for talks as it is better to resolve all disputes peacefully. If they resist, then do what you have to do!' Nairang nodded and left immediately. In Mahrukh's camp, he leapt into the durbar and shouted, 'I am Nairang magician who has been sent by Shahanshah Hayat Jadoo!' The young boy then marched straight up to Amar and said, 'Khwaja, rise for my master wants you!' Amar looked at Mahrukh and Baghban, who shook their heads. Then he declared coolly, 'I refuse to go with you!' As he spoke, Amar was planning to disappear, but Nairang waved his hand in the air. A bolt of lightning flashed in the durbar and everyone's eyes closed for a moment. Amar found himself fixed to his chair and blinked at Nairang, who said to him, 'I wanted to take you respectfully, but now I will drag you away!'

The sardars of Islam were distraught for they realized that they could not recall any magic. Mahrukh signalled to Amar, who said ingratiatingly, 'O Prince Nairang, we did not know how powerful Hayat is. Give us this day and we will accompany you tomorrow.' Nairang laughed derisively and said, 'Khwaja, do you think you address a child? You are an ayyar and if you disappear during the night, where am I supposed to find you? However, if all these sardars stand as your guarantors I may spare you tonight. If you deceive me then they will all be killed tomorrow!' The sardars who doted on Amar promised that Amar would be there the next morning. Nairang made them sign a declaration to this effect and sealed it. He said to Mahrukh, 'Tomorrow morning I will take Amar from you!' Nairang then waved his hand again and everyone recalled their magic. Nairang disappeared, but there was an uproar in the durbar. Mahrukh and Bahar fell at Amar's feet and said, 'For God's sake, leave for Mount Agate right away. He might be very nasty with you tomorrow. Look at the havoc he caused with one minor spell!'

Meanwhile, Nairang returned to Hayat and handed him the declaration the sardars had signed. He said, 'Huzoor, I have the measure of Mahrukh, Bahar and the others. They could not move a finger against an ordinary spell your lowly slave cast upon them.' Hayat stroked his whiskers and beard triumphantly and gloated, 'My daughter, have you seen the reality of these rebels that you have been fighting all these years? I have tested them in a day!' Afrasiyab was offended by Hayat's tone, but remained quiet. Nairang disappeared just as he had arrived. Afrasiyab remained sullen and cross with Hayat the next morning. Meanwhile, Hayat sent for Nairang and asked him to proceed to the enemy camp. He told Nairang, 'Tell all the guarantors to come with Amar. Assure them that they will not be pressurized in any way. We just want to speak with them.'

Nairang marched up to the rebel camp, held Amar's hands and said, 'Huzoor, come with me now. Shahanshah remembers you.' Amar had no other choice but to go with Nairang silently. Mahrukh, Bahar, Baghban, Ra'ad and Barq, along with forty other sardars, followed their leader, weeping in frustration. Ayyars Barq, Jansoz and Zargham also came forward, but could only watch their teacher helplessly as he walked behind Nairang. As Khwaja Amar followed Nairang into Afrasiyab's camp, the sahirs laughed at him and said, 'Hairat's respected father has certainly overpowered him, he cannot even run!' When Amar reached the royal pavilion, he stopped and said, 'O Prince Nairang, may I say something?' He looked so pathetic that Nairang felt pity for him and said, 'Khwaja, do not worry. I will intervene on your behalf with my master. You will have to do two things. One, fall at his feet, and two, agree to worship Samri.' Amar pleaded, 'O prince, he might just kill me on sight. If he accepts my servitude, I will make all the sardars fall at his feet. Asad has gone hunting, but I will bring his head and offer it. Look brother, I am only concerned about my own life. Mian Asad cannot bring me back from the grave. If I die, my children will be orphaned. I have so many wives who will be forced to beg for a living. I will not rest easy in my grave!'

When Nairang assured Amar that he would not let him die, Amar said, 'My brother Nairang, do not take me before your master in this manner. You know the ways of kings, they can do anything. I will wait here for you. Tell your master that Amar is here. He will worship Samri and Jamshed and hopes for your favours. After he cools down then come and get me.' Nairang was afraid that Amar would run away, but Amar assured him that he would not. He said, 'I give you my word as a man. I have found a patron like you who is the ruler of seven realms. Why should I not remain with you?' Meanwhile, Afrasiyab was whispering to Sarsar Sword-fighter, 'I cannot believe that Amar has capitulated. I would dearly like him to humiliate this old man. He is bragging a little too much for me!' Sarsar whispered back, 'I am also quite surprised.'

As soon as Nairang left Amar and went into the pavilion, Amar took out the blessed Tent of Danyal from Zambil. As Afrasiyab's sahirs watched him, Amar kept his hand on the folded tent and asked for a miracle. Within moments, it extended into a large pavilion. Amar led his sardars and ayyars into the pavilion, where he laid out a couch and appointed a few handmaidens, both of which he had brought out from Zambil. Then he wore a crown and a rich robe, and stretched out on the couch. The handmaidens began pressing his feet. Hayat's sahirs who were standing around asked, 'O Amar, what is this?' Amar responded by roundly abusing them. The sahirs rushed to attack him, but whoever entered the tent found himself dangling upside down. Amar took out a few strong men holding large sticks from Zambil. They cried, 'Master, what is your will?' Amar replied, 'These men are disturbing my sleep. Beat them up!' The men charged on the suspended sahirs with sticks and beat them to a pulp. The sahirs who were still outside were now too afraid to attack Amar, but cast thunderous spells. They conjured sheets of flames, but the tent remained intact and the flames burnt their own people.

One of the strong men from Zambil asked Amar, 'Master, there is no more candlewax in our stores. With your permission, can we make some more?' When Amar nodded, the villain stoked coals in a stove and placed an enamel bowl on it. He pierced the fattest sahir's head with a large needle so that his brain began dripping into the bowl. The sahir screamed with pain and Amar said, 'He disturbs me, cut his tongue off!' The villain obliged him instantly. Two companions of Hayat, Saam and Haam Jadoo, died at the hands of Amar's villains. The royal party heard the din of guardian spirits wailing the death of the two sahirs and were alarmed. Hayat turned to Nairang in fury and screamed, 'Haam and Saam were my companions! Who killed them?' Afrasiyab laughed and said, 'Perhaps Amar has lost his temper!' Hayat shouted, 'I will subject him to a shoe beating!' Nairang Jadoo begged him not to take Amar's life, but Afrasiyab knew what was happening and laughed derisively. He advised Nairang, 'First worry about your own life!'

Everyone stepped outside and saw the blessed tent with Amar stretched out on a couch and sardars seated on jewelled chairs. Qiran was pacing restlessly with his bughda and the other ayyars were also busy attending to Amar. A young girl was kneading Amar's feet when the ayyar kicked her hard so that she fell on the floor. She wept and cried, 'Master, how have I caused offence?' Amar shouted, 'Shameless hussy, how dare you knead my feet with henna on your hands. The colour of henna irritates my feet.' The girl sobbed and rubbed her palms on the floor until the skin came off, and then returned to her duties. Nairang was shocked to see this spectacle and shouted, 'You camel driver's son, what is this insolence? How dare you lie here with your feet stretched before my Shahanshah?' Amar retorted, 'Stay away or you will be beaten so hard that you will not forget the pain for many days. I intend to make candlewax out of you. The recipe is not effective unless we use an adolescent brain!'

Afrasiyab provoked Nairang even more by saying, 'Go and drag him out.' Nairang shot forth like a flame, but as soon as he reached the pavilion, he was suspended upside down and became helpless. Amar's villain stood over him with his stick. Amar said, 'Snatch the precious locket from his neck first. I was the one who gave him these pearls!' The villain first hit Nairang on the buttocks and then pulled the string off his neck. Amar counted the pearls and said, 'One pearl is missing. Cut off his nose instead.' One villain cut off Nairang's nose while the other hit him so hard that his skull split open. Amar rose and started whipping the villain, who cried, 'What fault have I committed?' Amar shouted, 'You fool! His clothes are bloodstained and you have caused me a loss. The price will be cut from your salary every month!' Afrasiyab could not help laughing at this, but Hayat Jadoo rolled up his sleeves and went forward. Hairat clung to him and implored, 'Father, where are you going?' Hayat said, 'Child, let me go. He has killed my dearest companion. I must punish him!' Hairat held him back and insisted, 'Father, your magic will not work on that tent and dreadful things will happen to you!' Seeing this, Afrasiyab said, 'Let him go Hairat. Perhaps you will be witness to the miracle of his magic. After all, elders like him teach all of us.'

Hairat beat her own head and screamed, 'Do you want that my father should be made into candlewax or that wretch should subject him to an ordeal in Zambil? You know you have tried to use magic on that tent and failed miserably each time!' Hayat was more enraged because Amar kept taunting him to come forth and attack. Whenever Hayat went forward, Hairat stopped him. Hayat tried every magical spell known to him. He conjured sheets of flames and huge slabs of ice that destroyed hundreds of Afrasiyab's men, but the tent remained intact. When Afrasiyab complained that he was destroying his soldiers, Hayat had to dispel his magic. Eventually, he called out, 'king of ayyars, what is it that you want?'

Amar replied, 'What kind of king are you? Is this how you invite a noble decent man to talk with you? If you want us to talk with you, then arrange a special pavilion for that purpose. My ayyars will supervise its erection. You can receive us there and we will answer all your questions with dignity and peace. What do you mean by sending a *shodah* to bring us over with force? We are men of honour. Shahanshah is well aware of this!' Afrasiyab called out, 'Indeed, Amar is right. Father committed a breach of etiquette!' Hayat was burning in his heart by now and thought, 'When he is talking with me I will cause a dispute and then cut this bastard's throat!'

Talks with Hayat

Hayat then did Amar's bidding and arranged an imposing durbar tent. The four ayyars supervised its erection and made sure that the tent had escape routes in case the talks failed. Hayat had the tent furnished with carpets and chairs for the talks. After all this, he called out to Amar, 'Khwaja, please come forth!' Amar then reduced the blessed tent into its original size (it was only as large as an umbrella) and put it back in Zambil. He led his sardars in a grand manner, dressed in a crown and a splendid robe, with his snare-ropes of ayyari coiled around his arms and Galeem flung over his shoulder. Hayat was waiting for him in the durbar tent. Afrasiyab thought to himself, 'Why is Amar coming here now? He will surely regret it!' When Amar walked into the durbar tent, there were cries of 'Bismillah! Bismillah! The king of ayyars has arrived!'

Hayat went forward to welcome him, shook his hand and asked him to sit down. Khwaja walked up to the throne while other sardars sat on chairs. The ayyars took their positions around the tent. Hayat watched Amar carefully. Suddenly, messengers informed Afrasiyab that Kaukab the Enlightened had arrived outside. Afrasiyab said while leaving to receive him, 'Amar's patrons have come!' Hayat hissed, 'He is a mere boy to me; I do not think anything of him!' Afrasiyab replied, 'Nevertheless, he is coming to our house. He must be welcomed properly.' Afrasiyab led Kaukab into the durbar tent and seated him in the place of honour. At this time, Hayat turned to Amar and said, 'Khwaja, you have created havoc in Hoshruba. It is better for you to compromise with Afrasiyab.' Amar frowned and replied, 'If Afrasiyab agrees to pay tribute, we will leave!' Hayat threatened, 'Khwaja, I will cause an upheaval. None of your sardars will be able to confront me!' To this Amar asked, 'Hayat, why do you think you are invincible?' Hayat replied, 'I am a powerful sahir, companion of Samri and well versed in the art of astrology. I can overwhelm anyone!'

Amar said, 'What would you know of the art of astrology? I know the stars. Ask me about anything or anyone and my powers will be revealed to you right now!' Hayat retorted, 'I can tell you what is happening at the distance of ten thousand kos while I sit here!' Amar's face flushed with anger and he said, 'O Hayat, if you are a sahir, I am a spiritualist. I control jinni and parizad. While you are all talk, I will make them appear before your very eyes.' Hayat declared arrogantly, 'What is the point of this talk? Ask me anything and I will provide answers based on my calculations.' Amar paused and then said, 'Very well, tell me what Laqa and Sahibqiran are doing at the moment.' Hayat did some calculations on his fingers and said, 'The stars reveal that Khudawand is in his durbar and Sahibqiran in his durbar. There is no fight between them.' Amar then pretended to do his own calculations and said, 'You are a liar! It is clear that there is a fierce confrontation between Laqa and Sahibqiran. Laqa has suffered a resounding defeat and is fleeing towards Hoshruba. Sahibqiran is following him and Laqa has lost many thousand men!'

Hayat said, 'Impossible! There is no mention of war in my calculations!' Amar's beady eyes almost popped out of their sockets with rage. He shouted, 'Hayat, do you dare to refute my words? Should I now prove this to you?' Hayat replied calmly, 'You do not frighten me with this insolent tone. You are talking nonsense!' Amar then took out a paper and a red pen. He drew a sign on the paper and shouted, 'Ya Jabbar! Ya Qahar!' The earth shook and Hayat looked alarmed. Amar rose from the throne and shouted again, 'King of Jinni, show this arrogant fool the spectacle of Laqa in flight or the twelve years I have spent in your service will go to waste!'

Laqa and Hamza in Hoshruba

Suddenly, everyone heard the thundering sound of hooves. The curtains of the durbar tent burst open and everyone saw the terrible Zamurrad Shah Bakhtri mounted on a large beast charge into the durbar. He wore a ruby crown on his head and brandished a heavy tegha of iron in his hand, but looked as if he had dived in a river of blood. Laqa stopped in the middle of the tent and shouted, 'Whose durbar is this?' The flaps of the tent lifted again and everyone was dazzled by the sight of the sun of the deserts of Arabia, the thunder of Solomon, Hamza Sahibqiran, riding in on his mighty horse, Ashqar Devzad. He held the tegha of Solomon in his hand and his face was covered with layers of blood and dust.

He announced himself and called out, 'Laqa, you cannot escape me. I have been following you for seven days. Who will save you from me?' Everyone in the durbar stood up in sheer awe, their limbs trembling in fear. Sahibqiran drew close to Laqa and attacked him with his sword. Laqa was a giant of a man, but could not fight Hamza. His iron shield was shattered into pieces and his mount collapsed. Laqa fell on the floor. Sahibqiran also jumped off his horse and both flung their weapons aside to wrestle with each other. As they charged around the durbar, carpets were torn to shreds and several chairs were overturned. Sahibqiran held Laqa's neck in the grip of the righteous and pushed him hard so that his knees buckled and he fell. Emir then called out his name and lifted him off the floor, first up to his knees, then to the level of his chest, and finally held him above his head. He spun Laqa in that position so that his crown, gloves and socks flew off him.

As he paused, holding Laqa aloft, Amar greeted his master. 'What are you doing here?' asked Emir. Amar said, 'Master, this old man has summoned me here. He is trying to force me to capitulate!' Sahibqiran addressed Hayat, still holding Laqa in one hand and his sword in the other, 'Who are you that you dare to send for my ayyar!' His tone was so majestic that Hayat trembled with fear and said, 'Huzoor, I had called Amar here for talks. I cannot put any pressure on him. It is up to him to agree or not!' Sahibqiran turned to leave and said, 'I am taking Laqa away. Will you not stop me? What kind of Samri worshipper are you?' Hayat replied, 'Huzoor, I do not belong to this place. I only intervened so that I could resolve any dispute by peaceful means.'

Sahibqiran then turned to Amar and said, 'Khwaja, these people deny your charges. Let us return to your lashkar now. They can stop us if they dare!' Amar called out, 'Hayat mian, I am leaving!' Hayat replied, 'By all means, go with your master. I will not stop you.' Sahibqiran then mounted his horse Ashqar and left the pavilion holding Laqa in his hand of righteousness. Amar followed with his hand on Ashqar's saddle and the other sardars surrounded Emir. The curtains of the durbar tent closed behind them. After their departure, Afrasiyab heaved a sigh of relief. Sarsar, who had fainted at the sight of Sahibqiran, was revived.

A little later, Afrasiyab said, 'Friends, a terrible thing has happened! Hamza captured the living god from right under our noses. Sarsar go to the rebel camp and find out what is happening to Khudawand.' Sarsar left right away. Kaukab went into Mahrukh's durbar and saw that Amar was sitting in his chair and Mehtar Qiran was changing his blood-soaked clothes. There was no sign of Hamza. Kaukab was alarmed by this and asked, 'Khwaja, where is Sahibqiran?' Amar laughed, 'Kaukab, Sahibqiran never came here. This too was ayyari! My heir and right arm, the mighty Qiran came as Sahibqiran. We found a giant of a youth to impersonate Laqa. This ayyari could not be pulled off by an ordinary person. Qiran is the favourite of the saints for a reason!'

Sarsar, disguised as a handmaiden, also heard this conversation. She rushed back to Afrasiyab with this news and said, 'Huzoor, look how cleverly he saved himself and humiliated us at the same time!' Hayat was livid, but Afrasiyab laughed and said airily, 'I knew all along but thought that respected father, companion of Samri might see through the charade. He had claimed that the ayyars had no standing. Only I could have tolerated a menace like Amar for so many years!' Hayat lost his temper and shouted, 'Did you want me to be disgraced?' Afrasiyab meekly protested, 'Oh no father!' However, behind Hayat's back, he grimaced at Hairat and signalled, 'Amar has really put rings around this old man!'

The battle with Hayat

Hayat ordered that the battle drums were to be struck in his name and declared, 'What can they do in the battlefield? I will blow them away in one curse. As for mistress Bahar, watch what I do to her tomorrow!' When the morning star twinkled in the night sky, the armies prepared to face each other. Afrasiyab was still annoyed with Hayat and left in the morning after telling Hairat, 'Try and send your father home as soon as possible.' Hayat reached the battlefield seething with rage. Hairat also joined her father. The confrontation with the rebels was not as simple as Hayat had anticipated. Mahrukh, Bahar and Maimar Qudrat caused havoc in Hayat's army. Bahar's magical bouquets drove his men to such a frenzy that they slit their own throats. Jahandar Shah had recently allied with the rebels. Together with his loyal commander Maimar Qudrat, he conjured towers and turrets that bombarded Hayat's army.

The battle raged for three days. Hayat managed to injure several top sardars like Surkh Mu, Hilal Magic-wielder, Shakeel and the noble Maimar, but realized that he would not be able to defeat the rebels. At one point, he had wounded Baghban and was about to kill him when Amar diverted his attention disguised as his companion Yakut. Hayat was pleased as the false Yakut praised his magic and said, 'Yakut, these sardars were the most exalted in Hoshruba! It will be impossible to kill them!' The false Yakut said, 'The cloud of seven hues appears. I think Shah is coming!' Hayat turned around to look at the cloud when a narcotic bubble knocked him unconscious. Amar was about to capture him when Hayat's guardian slave heaved out of the earth and attacked Amar, who quickly leapt out of its reach. The magic slave revived Hayat, who was badly shaken when he realized how close he had been to his death.

Hayat then flew to the midst of the battlefield where sahirs surrounded Mahjabeen's throne. He managed to disperse her guards with a few well-aimed magic iron balls and made off with the princess. Bahar and other sardars pursued him, but he subjected them to such ferocious spells that the earth and sky shook with his cruelty. He handed Mahjabeen to his sahirs and returned to the fray. There was a sudden light in the sky. Everyone was astonished to see the former ruler of Hoshruba, the noble Lacheen seated on a powerful flying hawk. Some of the allies he had released were with him. He called out, 'I am Lacheen, the mighty and famous enchanter!' Hayat and he engaged in a short fierce fight in which Hayat was injured. He fled from Lacheen, who let him go as he was not yet aware that Hayat had kidnapped Mahjabeen.

Hayat took advantage of the reprieve and left with the captive Mahjabeen on a flying throne. He called out to his officers to follow him to the golden desert. 'I will be conjuring the fortress of seven hues where I will be invincible. All enemy sardars will try and rescue Mahjabeen but my magic will trap them.' After her father left, Hairat struck the drums of peace and returned to the camp with her army. It was only when Mahrukh returned to her camp that she was informed about how Hayat had kidnapped Mahjabeen. Bahar and Lacheen immediately sent spies to find out where Hayat may have taken her. Asad had been sent to a safe place after Hayat's arrival. He returned from there and was naturally very upset when he heard the news. He sent Barq ayyar to follow Hayat.

Meanwhile, Hayat had conjured the invincible fortress of seven hues in the golden desert. He sent a challenging message to Mahrukh Magic-eye that read, 'Mahrukh if you are confident of your powers, then try and rescue Mahjabeen from my fortress. Tell Amar to try his tricks here!' Asad rose in fury and said, 'I will go myself!' Bahar fell at his feet and begged him not to go. She cried, 'Your humble handmaiden will teach this Hayat a lesson and rescue Mahjabeen.' The sardars eventually left Asad with Lacheen and Amar, and travelled to the golden desert to mount an attack on Hayat's fortress. They fought valiantly, but eventually, Hayat captured all of them. Hayat sent a message to Hairat asking her to come and execute all the captured sardars herself. 'Make sure that you travel with your ayyar girls,' Hayat added.

Hairat left with her ayyar girls and a small group of companions. At every stage, everyone had to wash their faces in case an ayyar was hidden amongst them. The news of the sardars' capture also reached Lacheen and Asad. Lacheen said, 'Hayat is powerful and his fortress is cunningly conjured. My calculations tell me that he will not be killed, but nevertheless, I should go myself.' Asad was keen on accompanying him, but Amar decided to leave for the golden desert and advised Asad to stay with the lashkar.

The holy man of the mountain

Amar and Qiran left together, but decided to travel separately to the golden desert. Qiran saw Hayat's army of sahirs spread for miles around the magic fort and decided to keep a watch on the fort after disguising himself as a fakir. He settled into a ravine from where he could see the fort and found some twigs to light a fire. Qiran sat behind the fire with a heavy heart and sang to assuage his grief. His voice was so melodious that the birds and deer of the forest gathered around him to listen. Some birds formed a canopy of wings over him to shade him from the sun. As this Solomon of his times sang, a light appeared on the hill. Qiran saw a fearsome sahir coming towards him. He was obviously moved by the verses of the song and tears rolled down his cheeks, but his eyes watched Qiran suspiciously. Qiran quickly threw a tablet of oudh incense into the fire and continued singing with greater fervour. The sahir swayed with appreciation and came closer. Soon, the drugged fumes assailed his senses and he fell unconscious.

Qiran quickly tied him up with a rope; pierced his tongue with a needle and then stood before him as his real self. When the sahir opened his eyes, Qiran called out, 'I am Mehtar Qiran, favoured one of saints and the best of ayyars! Tell me who you are and what are you doing in this lonely place? I can smash your skull with my bughda, but that is not my way. I will give you one chance to follow the righteous path.' Qiran then continued in a softer voice and made such an impact on the sahir with his eloquence and his sincere manner that he signalled, 'Remove the needle from my tongue and I will convert to Islam.' Qiran removed it without any fear and the sahir fell at his feet crying, 'O Qiran, I accept your faith with all my heart! I know why you are here. My name is Asrar Jadoo and I am Hayat's darogha. The dagger tied to my waist is the only one that can take Hayat's life. O best of Mehtars, it is impossible to get into the fort without Hayat's help. No one can get in there, not even me. However, this dagger is yours for better or for worse!'

Qiran felt that the sahir sounded sincere and that he had converted to the faith in all honesty. He accepted the dagger and both parted on good terms. Qiran then began thinking of ways to invade Hayat's magic fort. Meanwhile, Hairat was travelling to Hayat's fort with her ayyar-girls and some companions. They had stopped to rest in a lush meadow with blossoming trees that nestled at the base of a mountain. At twilight, they saw a man of pleasant disposition and a kindly face emerge from within the mountain with an emerald lantern that he placed on a rock. The lantern radiated an unearthly light that illuminated the whole area.

As he retreated into the shadows, Hairat said to Sarsar and Saba Raftar, 'It seems that he must a special worshipper of Samri in this mountain. There is not another lantern like this one in our entire kingdom!' Sarsar and Saba Raftar nodded in agreement. Moments later, an attendant holding a bejewelled staff emerged in the same place. He was dressed in expensive livery studded with precious gems. He stood for a while and then walked back into the mountain. An army commander wearing heavy armour emerged next. As he walked away, a nobleman walked out wearing a ruby crown, with several ruby ornaments and rows of precious pearls around his neck. As the women watched transfixed, the morning star twinkled on the horizon. A holy man of tender years then appeared on the hill. His face was smeared with a paste of pearls and shone like the rising sun. After he disappeared, the first man came to remove the lantern for it was daybreak now.

Hairat said, 'This fakir seems fit to be a king. I have never seen a more beautiful face. The people whom we saw must have been his attendants. Let us visit him and ask him to pray for us.' Sarsar and Saba Raftar were as keen as she was. Hairat approached the mountain confident that no one could equal her in magic. As they drew closer to the ravine from where the figures had emerged, their senses were assailed by a heavenly fragrance. Hairat murmured Ya Samri and turned the corner to find that a magnificent carpet was laid out on the ground. They found the fakir reclining on a hammock that seemed to be swaying on its own.

Sarsar and Saba Raftar looked at his fair feet that glowed like crystals and sighed deeply. The fakir looked at the women with a frown, jumped off the hammock and shouted, 'Who are you that you dare to walk into the abode of Samri and Jamshed? This is a secret place for their devoted servants!' Hairat tried to reason with him, but he drove them out and went back to his hammock. The women returned to their camp and Hairat said, 'Let us spend another night in this place. Indeed, this is a holy place. Sarsar have you ever seen a more radiant face?' Sarsar replied, 'Malika, you know how much I have travelled in your realm. I have met all your noble men. Hamza's children are renowned for their beauty. Asad Ghazi's face is like the lamp on the mountain of Toor, but comparing him to this fakir is like showing the sun a grain of dust! Indeed, his beauty and piety are incomparable. Even to receive a beating at the hands of such a holy one is a blessing!'

Hairat and the women went three times to the fakir's abode and were entranced by his beauty and radiance. Each time, he would drive them away but on the fourth day, Hairat went to him alone very early in the morning. She did not even wince when he hit her with his staff and fell at his feet begging for mercy. Suddenly, the fakir burst a narcotic bubble in her face and she fell unconscious. The young fakir, actually Amar in disguise, quickly painted Hairat to look like the fakir and placed her in the hammock. Then he sat disguised as Hairat on the carpet. Later, Sarsar and Saba Raftar found the false Hairat blowing flies off the young fakir and were overjoyed. They suggested that since the fakir was fast asleep they should travel to the fort with him. Hairat seemed pleased with the suggestion and sent for her companions to place the hammock gently on a throne. They were near the golden desert and reached Hayat's fort in no time. Hayat came out to receive his daughter and was startled to see the young man whose limbs seemed to be cast in pure light sleeping in the hammock.

Hairat, Sarsar and Saba Raftar then explained the miracles of the young fakir to the overwhelmed old sahir. Hayat took them all into the fort. Amar disguised as Hairat observed that apart from a few attendants Hayat had kept, the rest of his army was outside the fort. The place was magic bound and he saw his sardars sitting, as if in a trance. The young fakir's hammock was carefully suspended on one side. Sarsar and Saba Raftar pressed his feet as an act of devotion. The false Hairat ran across to the sardars with a drawn sword and called out, 'Father, I will kill these rebels right now!' Amar placed his sword on Bahar's throat and whispered, 'I am Amar! I have managed to reach here. What is the plan now?' Baghban, who was tied up besides her, whispered back, 'Something will have to be done now or no one will be able to kill him after tonight. Hayat is a sahir of remarkable powers and this fort is invincible.'

The unsuspecting Hayat then held his daughter's hand and said, 'My child, you are the wife of the ruler of Tilism. Why should you bother with these rebels? My executioner will appear tomorrow and dispose of them.' The false Hairat withdrew and said, 'Father, I had made a vow for your safety. I will now pray and prepare the sacrificial food with my own hands.' The false Hairat then performed pooja and prepared the *mohan bhog* herself. She offered the halwa to her father and said, 'O favourite of the court of Samri and Jamshed, taste this offering to the gods!' Hayat was overwhelmed by love for his daughter and eagerly consumed the entire plateful of halwa, while Saba Raftar and Sarsar also partook of the holy offering. Soon, Hayat fell down unconscious, as did the two ayyar girls. Amar then ran forward with a dagger to kill

Hayat. Baghban called out a warning, 'Khwaja do not try and kill him! He will not die but we will be further afflicted and Afrasiyab will also be warned!' Amar ignored Baghban and struck Hayat on the shoulder with his dagger. Hayat received a superficial wound, but instead of blood, the wound emitted smoke. The smoke rendered Amar and all the sardars blind. They cried out, 'Khwaja, what have you done? Why did you not listen to us? Our bodies are burning with this smoke and our bones smoulder like candles!' Even in that helpless state, Amar ran around trying to rob Hayat's fort of its valuables, although he could not see.

Meanwhile, Mehtar Qiran had decided to tunnel his way into the fortress. By sheer good luck, he emerged at the time the sardars were bemoaning their fate and Hayat lay unconscious on his throne. Qiran dragged him off the throne and the fort resounded with his ear-splitting call, 'I am Mehtar Qiran!' Qiran then decapitated Hayat with the magic sword. As soon as he died, the fort started collapsing around them. The sardars regained their sight and flew out of the fort with the two ayyars.

∽

43 THE MAGIC IN ZULMAT—THE VEIL OF DARKNESS, THE TRICKERY OF AMAR AND THE SARDARS OF ISLAM

The reader should know that previously, Sarsar Sword-fighter had abducted Asad Tilism Kusha and Afrasiyab sent him to Zulmat. It was decided that Amar should travel to Zulmat to rescue Asad and the sardars also arrived in time.

The shah of ayyars and sword play, deposited Barq and Qiran in Zambil and left for Zulmat. He reached a fort and discovered that its ruler was Mainosh Jadoo. Khwaja Amar then assumed Sarsar Sword-fighter's form and went into the fort. There, he requested for an audience with the king. Mainosh immediately sent for the false Sarsar, who presented him with a royal message that ordered him to move with his army to the Neel river. On reading this, Mainosh looked confused and said, 'Sarsar, I have already received such a message!' The false Sarsar then signalled that she had a secret message meant only for his ears. So, Mainosh took her into his private chambers where Amar rendered him unconscious and dropped him in Zambil. He then assumed the guise of Mainosh and disguised Qiran as one of Mainosh's advisers. He returned to the durbar and cleverly told his ministers that he had to travel to Zulmat right away. His ministers recommended that it was best to travel to his brother Sarshar's fort. They added, 'His prime minister is privy to the secrets of Zulmat. He will take you there as he had done before.'

Amar, disguised as Mainosh, travelled with his army of twelve thousand. When they reached Mainosh's brother Sarshar's fort, he received them and escorted the false Mainosh into the fort. There, Amar managed to render Sarshar unconscious and dropped him in Zambil. He then took Barq out, disguised him as Sarshar, and sent for the prime minister. When the prime minister and secret-keeper Razdar arrived, he informed him, 'It is necessary for us to leave for the Veil of Zulmat. Our Shahanshah wants us to execute Asad there!' Razdar readily agreed to be the guide on the journey. Amar in the form of Mainosh, Barq in the likeness of Sarshar, and Qiran, newly disguised as a minister, along with Mainosh's army, set out with Razdar. On the third day of their journey, they reached a ravine that had an unusual cloud cover of iris flowers and the forest around it was so beautiful that it could put gardens to shame. Razdar said, 'If huzoor can rest here a while, I will go find Princess Gauhar Pearl-robe. She will take you further.'

Razdar stepped forward and began chanting a name. There was a thunderous sound as a door materialized in the ravine. As it opened, a beautiful princess, who looked like she had dived into the sea of pearls, emerged from within. Twelve hundred handmaidens, who held crystal pumps of coloured water and were dressed in golden costumes, accompanied her. The princess announced herself as Gauhar Pearl-robe and called out to her handmaidens, 'This is the time of colour and music!' No sooner had she spoken than the handmaidens sprayed the lashkar with sparkling coloured water. A few drops fell on Amar, Barq and Qiran, and their paints of ayyari rapidly evaporated. Qiran immediately killed a sahir who was standing close by, and Amar killed another. In the darkness that followed, they fled after declaring their identities.

'Where is your king?' Gauhar asked the lashkar, but no one seemed to know. She then had a pavilion erected in the same place and sat in it, rather dejected. After some time, Sarsar Sword-fighter's arrival was announced. When Sarsar met Gauhar Pearl-robe, she said, 'Princess, Shahanshah is all praise for you for revealing the ayyars' trickery!' Gauhar proudly declared, 'Sarsar, no ayyar can dare enter Zulmat as long as I am alive!' At that moment, Saba Raftar suddenly entered the pavilion and said, 'Princess, Shahanshah has told me where the three ayyars are hiding. Come with us and we will capture them for you!' Gauhar Pearl-robe willingly accompanied the ayyar girls into the wilderness. Suddenly, Sarsar whispered, 'Princess, look Amar is hiding in the leaves!'

Gauhar immediately threw a lentil grain and the iris cloud emitted a bolt of lightning that caused the paints of ayyari to peel off the faces of the false Sarsar and Saba Raftar. Amar and Barq tried running away, but Gauhar captured them and handed them to her maidservant Sosan. She ordered Sosan, 'Keep them in your custody; I will execute them in the morning!' Sosan took them back to her tent and had them bound in heavy chains.

Amar and Barq in the dungeons

Later that night, a violent quarrel broke out between the two prisoners, Amar and Barq. As they kicked and pummelled each other, Barq cried, 'Ustad, give me my share!' Amar shouted, 'What share? This handmaiden is mine. If I catch another, you can have her! You have only sold five hundred women this year and now you fight me for a handmaiden?' Then Barq shouted, 'Today I will not listen to you! I am the one who traps the women and you want to possess them all?' At this point, Sosan walked in and was alarmed to see them in this state. Barq's head was bleeding as Amar was showering blows on him, but he was screaming, 'I will not spare you today even though you are my Ustad!'

Sosan was very perplexed and asked them, 'Why are you two fighting?' Amar replied, 'Princess, this is between the two of us—do not interfere! Listen, we are ayyars; we earn our living in different ways. We kidnap princesses and the daughters of noblemen from all areas. We sell them and distribute the money between ourselves. I am this idiot's teacher. I liked a handmaiden that I had kidnapped and wanted her for myself. He should respect her, but instead, he wants to sell her and take the money himself!' Sosan said, 'Why Barq, are you not ashamed of wanting to sell your teacher's intended bride? Indeed, you people are cruel to kidnap the daughters of decent people. You are slave traders!' Amar said casually that this was part of their profession and turned away. Sosan demanded to see the handmaiden, but Amar pretended to be reluctant to bring her out in front of Barq. Sosan then told Barq to turn around. Barq said, 'It seems that you and my master are collaborators in this. I will not turn away. I will tell Gauhar Pearl-robe that you are plotting against her with the prisoner!'

Sosan ignored him and said, 'Khwaja, he can do nothing anyway, just bring her out!' Amar asked for his handcuffs to be removed and then took out a young, fair and innocent-looking handmaiden from Zambil. She was wearing a large nose ring and silver jewellery and her beauty was the envy of flowers. Sosan was moved by her innocence and asked, 'Where is your home?' The young girl replied, 'I was born in Kohistan, but am Amar's captive now. He feeds and clothes me well!' While Sosan's attention was on the girl, Amar burst a narcotic bubble in Sosan's face that made her fall unconscious. Amar then freed Barq and disguised two prisoners from Zambil to look like Barq and himself. Amar soon dressed up as Sosan, while Barq disguised himself as her companion Gul Andam.

The next morning, Gauhar Pearl-robe had the two prisoners executed and sent their heads to Atishbar Jadoo, her immediate superior. Since the real Amar and Barq were still in the camp, that evening they tried to trick Gauhar Pearl-robe with their musical and dancing skills. When they presented her with drugged wine, a bolt of lightning shot out from the protective iris cloud and uncovered their disguises. A furious Gauhar captured them and ordered their execution. The next morning, they were led to the executioner's block in front of Gauhar and her companions. The executioner had raised his sword to strike them when, suddenly, his own head burst open. The same thing happened to the next executioner. The third executioner was Mehtar Qiran, who stepped forward and freed his companions. As all three ayyars tried to run away from the durbar, Gauhar looked at the iris cloud that began exuding an unearthly light. The ayyars were rooted to the ground and this time, Gauhar Pearl-robe stepped forward to execute the ayyars herself.

Amar, Barq and Qiran were praying desperately for divine help when the fragrance of Bahar wafted in. She reached moments later on her golden peacock and showered magical petals on the ayyars to release them. Bahar then killed several of Gauhar's attendants, but Gauhar managed to draw a bolt of lightning from the cloud that injured Bahar's head. Gauhar moved toward the injured Bahar to kill her, but sardars like Baghban and Surkh Mu arrived on the scene and fought fiercely with Gauhar and her army. However, the iris cloud injured them as well. That was when Kaukab the Enlightened arrived. He immediately flung four huge iron balls on the cloud that shattered it.

A hideous black sahir had actually been casting spells from behind the cloud. In sheer rage, Kaukab attacked him and tore him to pieces. Frightful voices called out, 'You have killed Sosan Jadoo!' Kaukab then turned to Gauhar Pearl-robe and her army. Although she was a formidable sahira, Kaukab was the king of a Tilism and injured her badly. She fled from him and took shelter in the wilderness where she was tricked and captured by Amar, who dropped her in Zambil. Then he disguised himself as Gauhar Pearl-robe and called out to her companions, 'Let us hide in the ravine!'

As soon as the false Gauhar and her companions jumped into the ravine, it closed over their heads. Amar was alarmed by this, but Gauhar's companions assured him that the ravine would only be destroyed if Gauhar was killed. So, Amar disguised as Gauhar Pearl-robe travelled with her companions to the abode of Atishbar Jadoo, who received the false Gauhar warmly. He told her, 'You have performed a remarkable feat by the sending the heads of Amar and Barq to me. Let us now go to Khoonkhar Zulmati.' Meanwhile, Kaukab and the other sardars had decided to camp at the edge of the ravine as Baghban, Bahar and several other sardars were badly wounded. A little later, Barq and Qiran informed Kaukab that Amar was missing.

The battle for Asad

The next morning, Kaukab changed his own face as well as the faces of his sardars magically and along with the ayyars, reached Atishbar's durbar. Meanwhile, Amar had tricked Atishbar and was now disguised as him. He recognized his companions in Atishbar's durbar and left with them for Khoonkhar Zulmati's fort. When they reached the fort, they saw that Afrasiyab and Hairat had also arrived there in all splendour. The gate of the fort was opened and Asad Ghazi was brought forth as a prisoner, weighed down with heavy chains. He was surrounded by a force of ten thousand black-clothed guards.

Kaukab and his party were anxious about rescuing Asad when the sound of kettledrums and trumpets sounded from the fort and Princess Khoonkhar Zulmati emerged from within. She was being carried on a throne that had four stone pythons coiled at its base and she was wearing arm bands made of tiny golden statuettes. Since Khoonkhar was a mature sahira with advanced magical powers, Afrasiyab greeted her deferentially and she made the traditional gesture of taking his troubles on to herself. Khoonkhar said, 'Shahanshah, I have heard that some strangers and ayyars have crossed the border of Zulmat. Let me now verify this news.' Khoonkhar then took out wads of cotton wool from her magical pouch and dropped a few drops of water on them. The wads floated upwards and expanded into clouds that burst into rain just above Kaukab and his party. Their real forms were soon exposed as the paints of ayyari evaporated from the ayyars' faces, while the magical disguises of the others just melted away. Everyone was startled to see Kaukab, Burran, Akhtar, Baghban and a host of other sardars with Amar, Barq and Qiran, all looking intently at the prisoner Asad.

As soon as they realized that they had been exposed, Amar called out a warning to Kaukab, who responded by bursting an iron ball. Bahar threw a bouquet; Akhtar, a string of pearls; Burran, the Pearl of Samri; and Baghban, magical flowers. The ayyars burst fireworks that filled the place with smoke and enemy sahirs called out to their gods in panic. Khoonkhar, Afrasiyab and Hairat recovered from the shock of finding the enemy in their midst and signalled to their armies to attack immediately. The fourteen Muslim sardars began fighting a lashkar of several hundred thousand sahirs. Kaukab shot up and fell on the enemy like lightning repeatedly and annihilated thousands.

Khoonkhar too was also flashing all over the battlefield. It was mid-afternoon by then and a hot blistering breeze was blowing. It seemed as if sheets of flames were falling on Zulmat. Khoonkhar chanted a spell that made the earth tremble and conjured sharp swords to fall on the sardars. Baghban, Bahar, Burran and Akhtar were badly wounded as a result. Kaukab kept on fighting on all fronts with great courage. He protected his wounded sardars even while foiling Afrasiyab and Khoonkhar's attacks. At one point, Afrasiyab's spells plunged the whole area into darkness. Kaukab conjured magic torches and dispelled the darkness, but was confronted with a greater calamity when he finally managed to fight his way to the place where Asad had been kept. There, he found the guards dead and Asad missing. Amar had also reached there at the time, though disguised as a sahir.

Kaukab slapped his own cheeks and said, 'Friends, all my efforts were in vain. Asad Ghazi has been kidnapped!' Amar and Kaukab looked for Asad among the bodies of the dead guards, but there was no sign of him. The sardars were distressed at this unfortunate event and beat their heads in grief. However, Amar remained calm and called out, 'Friends, God will look after our brave Asad. Just look after your own safety!'

Asad and Ta'oos

Now hear this: Khoonkhar Zulmati had a beautiful daughter named Princess Ta'oos Fairy-face who was also well versed in magic. She was sitting in her palace intoxicated by her own beauty when she heard that Tilism Kusha had been imprisoned in Zulmat. As soon as she set eyes on the radiant sun-like beauty of the honourable Asad, she was stricken with love. She had been wondering how to rescue her beloved and was present when Kaukab and the sardars were recognized. Ta'oos took advantage of the distraction caused by the fighting and rescued Asad. She took him to her garden and revived him there.

When Asad saw that fairy-faced beauty, he too fell in love with her. Ta'oos Fairy-face, however, rendered Asad unconscious and placed him on a throne. Her trusted companion Crimson-eye sat besides Asad to protect him. Just as the princess was setting off, her aunt Nastran Zulmati arrived and said, 'There is trouble in Zulmat tonight, where are you going so late at night!' Ta'oos retorted sharply, 'I am not answerable to you! I will go to Mount Zulmat and kill any Muslim that I spot from there!' Meanwhile, one of Nastran's handmaidens had flown upwards and saw Asad from that height. She shouted, 'Princess Nastran, she has Tilism Kusha with her!' The handmaiden then tried to grab Asad, but Crimson-eye killed her with her dagger. A fierce battle broke out between Ta'oos and Nastran's forces, and when Asad was conscious he too joined the fight. They continued fighting until daybreak; Ta'oos Fairy-face had killed hundreds of sahirs by then, but Nastran did not let her get away with the Tilism Kusha.

By this time, Khoonkhar had also been informed of her daughter's treachery. She was furious when she heard this and left for the garden, swearing that she would kill Ta'oos Fairy-face. Just as she had reached there, lightning flashed in the sky and the gracious Lacheen descended from the sky. He called out, 'Khoonkhar, you treacherous, black-faced woman, where do you think you are going?' Khoonkhar had been Lacheen's treasurer and flushed with guilt when she saw her old master. She lunged at him with her sword drawn, but Lacheen leaned back and flashed his sword so swiftly that it sliced Khoonkhar in two pieces. This was like the end of times in Zulmat. A fearsome voice pronounced her end, 'You have killed me! My name was Khoonkhar Zulmati! Samri's soul has been wounded today!' A bird flew out of her skull and called out, 'This month will be the last for Tilism Hoshruba!'

Afrasiyab, who had just arrived with Hairat, was alarmed to hear this prophecy and flung a magic grain of lentil on the flying bird that incinerated it immediately. Lacheen then turned to face Afrasiyab, but the King of Magic avoided him as he clasped Hairat by the waist and flew to the Garden of Apples. One by one, the sahirs of Zulmat emerged from their houses and fell at Asad and Ta'oos Fairy-face's feet, begging for clemency. The ayyars Amar, Barq and Qiran also appeared. Asad was carried along in a great procession with trumpets and drums to the black fort of Zulmat and everyone in the land swore allegiance to him. Kaukab and the other sardars finally rested after their long ordeal and tended to their wounds.

44 SARSAR STEALS THE MAGIC KEYSTONE, CHALAK DISGUISED AS NEELUM JADOO GETS THE MAGIC KEYSTONE AND GIVES IT TO ASAD, THE TRICKERY OF AMAR, THE BATTLE BETWEEN LAQA AND SAHIBQIRAN, THE DEATH OF AFRASIYAB

The reader will recall that after a mysterious ritual, Afrasiyab had placed the magic keystone in the body of his friend Zamharir. Asad managed to kill Zamharir and obtain the keystone. In the same campaign, he destroyed Elephant-body and Seven-heads the masters of the sixth and seventh hujras of peril. Pir Abrar, who had been declared Qutb of Hoshruba by the saints, guided Asad in the penance and prayers he had to perform to elicit information from the magic keystone. Asad also rescued Malika Bilqees, wife of Lacheen, former ruler of Hoshruba from the Fort of Seven-heads. Meanwhile, Afrasiyab suffered more losses. His grandmother Afat Four-hands and her husband Nairang were killed by Lacheen in battle while Amar had tricked and killed the grandson of Samri, Mussavir and his wife Soorat Nigar in their hideout. By this time, Afrasiyab had lost most of his territory and his replicas had been destroyed.

Afrasiyab had the battle drums struck in his name and waited for his enemies in the field. Kaukab was about to confront him when that paragon of courage and honour, Asad Ghazi, appeared in the battlefield, riding his horse at the speed of wind. When Afrasiyab saw Asad in all his splendour, he simply had the drums of peace struck and returned to his pavilion. His ministers and advisers were all present in the pavilion. A little later, sounds of triumph and jubilation arose in Afrasiyab's camp. Amar said, 'Will someone find out what is happening there.' Barq and the others ran over to find out what had happened and reported, 'An army of four lakh sahirs has arrived. Their leader is a powerful warrior by the name of Shaddad with the strength of an elephant. He has persuaded Afrasiyab to strike the drums in his name and makes empty threats that he will not return unless he kills Tilism Kusha!' Asad said calmly, 'My friends, why are you worried? Victory and defeat are all up to the Great Provider. Let us also strike the drums with God's will!'

The battlefield resounded with the boom of seventeen kettledrums and everyone was dazzled by the sight of the noble Asad on the battlefield. Flanking him was his army of sahirs, while Bahar, Mahrukh and Surkh Mu surrounded Mahjabeen's throne. Just besides them stood Malika Bilqees and her husband Shahanshah Lacheen, Malika Badban, and the princesses Naheed and Gulgoon, with several other sardars. Thousands of gold-embroidered flags of war were also fluttering in the breeze.

Afrasiyab emerged on the other side with the fair-faced Hairat on his side and four hundred tajdars, who stood surrounding them. Shaddad the wrestler appeared, swaying like a rogue elephant, with an iron chain tied to his waist. His lashkar of four lakh foot soldiers stood behind him and looked like black monsoon clouds. It was clear that Shaddad was supremely confident of his own strength. Afrasiyab also seemed very proud of Shaddad's courage and said to Hairat, 'There is no other wrestler in Tilism to match Shaddad. Perhaps Hamza could have confronted him, but this Tilism Kusha certainly cannot!' When the armies stood in formation, Shaddad approached Afrasiyab, who descended from his throne, embraced Shaddad warmly and said, 'You are the match of the great wrestler Rustam himself. If Tilism Kusha dies at your hands, I will declare you ruler of half my realm.' Afrasiyab spoke at length and the shameless one kept nodding in agreement. He charged into the battlefield on his monstrous rhinocerous waving his lance, as his lashkar applauded him.

Shaddad looked hard at the lashkar of Tilism Kusha where row upon row of lion-like young warriors stood at attention, eager to confront him. He called out, 'I will fight no one except Tilism Kusha!' Asad Ghazi responded by riding out on the field. His horse was swift and its tail was held aloft as he cantered like swift wind down the field. When Shaddad saw Asad thundering towards him, his heart trembled with fear. As Asad's mount drew closer, everyone saw that Shaddad's dragon lurched backwards several paces. Shaddad looked Asad in the eye and said, 'Young man, did you think there was no man in Hoshruba to face you? Try all your tactics to your heart's content. My tactics are the wrath of Laat and Manaat! If I throw this spear, it will pierce the heart of a mountain. My sword will cut down chinar trees. If I want I can lift that mountain!' Asad merely laughed as Shaddad continued bragging and quietly interjected, 'Stop talking nonsense and make the first move. If my Provider saves me from your attack, then I will also respond. It is not our tradition to be the first to attack in battle!'

Shaddad roared like a thunderous cloud and attacked Asad with his lance. Asad stopped him with his own lance. The two armies watched closely as Asad fought with great elegance. Soon, the lance slipped out of Shaddad's hand to the delight of Asad's supporters, who applauded wildly. Shaddad was sweating with shame by this time. He then drew his mighty sword and it seemed as if a fearful python had emerged out of its cave. He brought it down hard on Asad, who protected himself with his shield. Shaddad was powerfully built and his sword cut through the shield and hurt Asad on his head. The moment he was wounded, Asad frowned and roared like a lion as he attacked Shaddad with added fervour. Strong as he was, Shaddad's heart trembled and he could see his own death in the polished metal of Asad's sword. He realized that the sword would fall on him like lightning and scorch the tree of his life into black dust. He quickly jumped off his rhinocerous, but the sword went right through his beast. There was a gasp of appreciation from both the armies.

Asad did not want to attack Shaddad while he was still sitting on his horse, so he jumped off. Shaddad was now truly frightened and convinced that he would die at the hands of this brave lion. He said, 'O Tilism Kusha, stop your companions. I am alone and they are coming to attack me!' Asad turned around and called out, 'No one should come near me!' The shameless Shaddad had been waiting for just such an opportunity and attacked Asad while he was distracted. Asad had already sustained a wound and this time, his head was badly injured and he swayed and fell on the ground. The sardars rushed and rescued Asad before Shaddad could kill him.

The Dome of Light

For the next few days, Afrasiyab remained in confrontation with the rebels. His spells were so powerful that no one could withstand him. It should be kept in mind that Afrasiyab would manipulate Asad's lashkar into following him towards the base of the Dome of Light from which a volley of arrows, swords and daggers was being continuously rained down on the army. Whenever Asad came close to Afrasiyab, he would have the drums of peace struck as he knew that the followers of Islam would abide by a declaration of peace.

One evening, when the durbar had been convened after the day's fighting, Lacheen said to Asad, 'Sheheryar, in the last few days, so many distinguished sardars have gone to the Eternal Garden with their hopes unfulfilled. The fact is that Afrasiyab has been ruling Hoshruba for the last thirty years. I am not privy to the secrets of this magic dome. We cannot stop the volley of arrows and daggers from it. It has caused the greatest damage to our lashkar. Even today, scores of dead bodies are strewn all over the battlefield—forty thousand of Afrasiyab's and sixty thousand of our men.' The ayyars were also present in the durbar and Lacheen pleaded with Amar, 'O great ayyar and companion of the noble Sahibqiran, it is because of you that Tilism-e-Hoshruba has been vanquished. Now only Afrasiyab remains to be killed. You have observed the havoc caused by this dome that Afrasiyab has conjured. It is beyond my powers to save us from this calamity.'

Amar heard Lacheen quietly and said, 'The noble Asad is the conqueror of Tilism Hoshruba and you are the acme of magic. I am a poor man who does not count. All my wealth was squandered when we besieged Tausan's fort. I am plagued by moneylenders and I am penniless. There are countless messages from Fort Agate that Hamza has suspended all salaries and my family is in dire need. Where can I go and what can I discover? I am suffering while all of you are like lords on your thrones. I am also convinced that Afrasiyab will kill you and your wife. As for me, I will travel to my master in Mount Agate and say to him, 'You unjust man, while I was serving your children, you suspended my salary for the last three months!'

Lacheen, who did not know Amar that well, had no answer to this. Asad then wrote out a pledge for two lakh rupees and declared, 'Whichever ayyar solves the mystery of the dome will be entitled to this money.' Amar turned his face away, but Barq and Chalak rose from their chairs. Amar instantly subjected them both to a couple of whip lashings and shouted, 'You useless louts, you will achieve nothing. You are just greedy for the money.' Barq remained quiet, but Chalak said politely, 'Your humble servants will indeed solve this mystery.' Amar said, 'Give me the money now and I will go myself.' At this point, Asad folded his hands and said to Amar, 'As huzoor is aware, this money belongs to the brave soldiers and victors in this army. It will be placed in a special tent and when you get us rid of this calamity, you can collect it.'

Amar was very annoyed by this condition, but Asad remained calm and determined. Eventually, Amar rose from his seat in the durbar, muttering curses against Chalak and Barq. He said, 'It is because of these foolish boys that things have gone wrong for me. I should have had the money before I left.' He looked at Mahrukh and Bahar and said, 'Is this the reward I get for fifteen years of labour? I am now considered so unreliable that people think if they give me the money, I will run away with it. They think that because they are as untrustworthy, other people are like them!' Asad Ghazi remained impervious to Amar's taunts and turned his face away. However, Mahrukh and Bahar offered fifteen thousand rupees towards the expenses of Amar's journey. Amar then turned his attention to Mahjabeen and said, 'Bibi, you are a princess, but alas you are doomed to misfortune. You will be married to a mace-bearer's son. His grandfather Aadi is a mace-bearer in Hamza's lashkar and is known as a dacoit. I elevated his rank by arranging a marriage for him with Hamza's daughter. He was acknowledged as the son-in-law. Now his son thinks he is somebody, he has forgotten his origins. I am going to tell everyone about his true origins.' Asad retorted,

'You can tell everyone anything you like, but you will get the money only when the work is done!' Mahjabeen, however, was quite disturbed by Amar's diatribe and sent for one lakh rupees. Asad tried to warn her, 'You should promise the money, but do not give it yet and he will do the work properly.' Mahjabeen insisted on giving the money anyway. After taking the money, Amar bid a dour farewell to Lacheen and the others and left. Chalak bin Amar also left with him, but they soon followed separate paths to the magic dome.

Neelum Jadoo

First, the adventures of the Mehtar of Mehtars, Chalak bin Amar, were written this way: Chalak wandered around for three days. On the third day, he climbed on top of a hill and saw a group of desolate young soldiers milling around a rather worn and tattered tent. Chalak disguised himself as a holy man and wandered into the lashkar to discover more. 'Shah sahib,' he was told, 'this is how the mighty fall. When Neelum Jadoo was defeated, he was without any resources and came to this place. There was a day when Afrasiyab used to consider it an honour to visit Neelum in Samri Palace. This time, when Neelum informed him of what he had undergone, Afrasiyab did not send anyone to receive him, but sent a message back that he was in the same situation. Neelum is still a powerful sahir. If he joins Afrasiyab in battle, his magic will cause heaven and earth to move!'

Thus informed, Chalak left and disguised himself as Sarsar Sword-fighter. He returned to the lashkar and there was an outcry as everyone recognized the famous Sarsar Sword-fighter. Neelum himself emerged from the tent to meet her. The false Sarsar said, 'Huzoor, these are times when Shahanshah himself emerges in the battlefield and returns after killing a few sardars. If he has you by his side, the war will be won in a week.' Neelum declared, 'Sarsar, even in this condition, my spells will make Kaukab and Lacheen flee from the battlefield.' The false Sarsar then whispered to Neelum that she had to meet him privately as she had a secret message from Afrasiyab. Neelum was aware that he was an object of pity amongst his companions at that time. He eagerly took the false Sarsar into his tent where she asked him to send for a brazier of live coals. She explained, 'Shahanshah has given me a spell for you. He believes that you will corner the enemy with this spell while he will also attack them from one side. Asad Ghazi will be helpless on his own.'

After the brazier was delivered and they were alone again, the false Sarsar gave him incense powder and said, 'Burn this and a parizad will emerge from the flames. She will instruct you in the spell.' Neelum sprinkled a handful of the powder in the coals and was soon unconscious because of the fumes. Chalak quickly pierced Neelum's tongue with a needle and locked him in a box. He emerged from the tent disguised as Neelum and told his men to prepare to travel. They asked, 'Huzoor, what happened to Sarsar?' He replied, 'Friends, you are very simple. Who can see the wind? Shahanshah has sent for us in all honour. The war with Tilism Kusha will now be fought by us. We will be a curse to the enemy!' Neelum's men were waiting for just such an opportunity. They eagerly wore their shabby uniforms and brought an ancient *hawadar* for Neelum to travel in. Chalak loaded the box in which the real Neelum lay unconscious on a cart and left with his men to join Afrasiyab.

Sarsar captures Asad

Meanwhile, the real Sarsar Sword-fighter had promised Afrasiyab that she would get the magic keystone from Asad. She had been wandering through the rebel camp for several days and saw that a mighty river flowed through the area. Lacheen's army was on one side, while Kaukab's lashkar was camped on the other bank. Jahandar Shah's vast army was spread out in another direction. Sarsar came across the pavilion of Princess Tasveer, who was Badi-uz-Zaman's beloved. Sarsar found out that Tasveer had been unwell and that Tilism Kusha was due to visit her. Quaking with fear, Sarsar managed to render a handmaiden called Nargis unconscious and went into the pavilion disguised as her. She lured the unsuspecting princess to a private chamber and rendered her unconscious by giving her a drugged gilori of betel leaf. Sarsar then hid Tasveer in a box and painted herself to look like the princess. She sat on the masnad, but remained very nervous, in case she was identified by the ayyars.

Moments later, Asad entered the pavilion to meet his aunt. The false Tasveer rose and greeted him affectionately and asked, 'Well my son, how goes it with the war?' Asad replied, 'For many days now Afrasiyab has not struck the battle drums. When grandfather Amar returns, we will be able to plan a new strategy.' As they talked, Sarsar poured Asad a goblet of wine and offered it to him. Asad bowed and drank the wine and immediately fell unconscious. Sarsar divested him of the magic keystone and tied him up in a sheet. She dug a tunnel out of the camp and left the pavilion with Asad. She emerged from the tunnel covered in dust and darted behind tents to get away. Meanwhile, Afrasiyab was waiting for Sarsar to arrive and had also received news of Neelum's arrival. He told his advisers, 'My ally and strength Neelum is in a bad way. He has been my officer and colleague for long. Receive him with all honours.'

Several tajdars and ministers went quite some distance to receive Neelum. They were shocked to see him and his shabby companions in their impoverished state, but greeted him courteously while their hearts filled with pity at his humbled condition. Chalak, disguised as Neelum, greeted them cheerfully and laughed when he saw the enemy camp. He said, 'I am not impressed with the rebel camp. I can incinerate them all with one spell! No magic rain will be able to put out the fire. I may be without any resources, but I still have my magical skills. I will restore the empire of Hoshruba. Afrasiyab will be great again!'

Afrasiyab went out of his pavilion to meet his old friend and embraced him fondly. The false Neelum wept loudly and Afrasiyab asked him, 'My brother, why do you weep? All that I have left, my kingdoms and my life are yours!' Chalak cried, 'My lord, I will kill Bilqees and Lacheen in their beds tonight! I will behead Kaukab!' Afrasiyab happily led him into the pavilion. At that time, there was an uproar in lashkar that Sarsar Sword-fighter had captured Tilism Kusha. Afrasiyab turned to Hairat with a glowing face and cried, 'Neelum's arrival has won us the war!' Just then, Sarsar walked into the pavilion and laid Asad at Afrasiyab's feet. She offered him the keystone as nazrana. Afrasiyab flushed with happiness and performed some magic that made black snakes wind themselves around Asad's body. Barq, who had been spying in Afrasiyab's durbar, saw this and bolted back in alarm to his camp. He ran screaming into the durbar, 'While you sit here free of cares, Asad has been captured by Sarsar!'

Meanwhile, Afrasiyab was gloating over Asad's capture, while Hairat said to the false Neelum, 'My uncle, you have brought us good fortune!' Chalak was horrified to see Asad in that condition, but pretended to be jubilant. Sarsar came forward and said, 'Shahanshah, do not repeat your previous errors! Why are you delaying Asad's execution?' Afrasiyab placed the keystone on the throne and got up to execute Asad himself. The false Neelum also rose and holding Afrasiyab tightly around the waist, said, 'Shahanshah, you have always gone against the laws of magic and it has resulted in great calamity for you. Samri and Jamshed have made you ruler of eighteen countries and bestowed great honours upon you. Why should you need to execute anyone? Give me this task. The companions of Samri and Jamshed, the great malikas Mahiyan and Afat, always said that the ruler of Hoshruba should not kill anyone with his own hands, it will weaken his blood. For you to kill Tilism Kusha goes against the injunctions of the great gods.'

Then the false Neelum flashed his sword in the air and approached Asad. He said, 'Young man, were you not afraid of causing a rebellion in Hoshruba? Were you not afraid of this day? Have you seen the might of Shahanshah now? Where are those astrologers who predicted that the noble Asad will kill Afrasiyab? Who is the killer now?' Neelum then drew a line around Asad's throat with charcoal and called out, 'Shahanshah, give the first order, I am now going to execute Tilism Kusha.' On seeing this, Afrasiyab said to Hairat, 'This is true loyalty! How concerned brother Neelum is for me—he wants to kill Tilism Kusha himself. He has brought us good fortune today!' Chalak raised his sword and then dropped it when he saw the keystone on the throne. 'What is that?' he asked, pointing at the keystone. Afrasiyab replied, 'Dear brother, Sarsar did something remarkable today by bringing in Tilism Kusha and the keystone! If you go close to it, you will not be able to practise magic.' Chalak quickly said, 'Huzoor, may I read what is written on it? I do not understand what you are saying. We are sahirs who have no equals in magic craft. How can this keystone affect us?'

Afrasiyab protested, but Chalak picked up the keystone, handed it to Asad within a flash and shouted, 'Rise my prince! I am the Mehtar of Mehtars, Chalak bin Amar!' Before Afrasiyab could react, Asad had killed the sahir standing closest to him and snatched his sword, while Chalak ignited fireworks in the durbar. As the sahirs ran after Chalak, the earth opened as the former rulers of Hoshruba, Lacheen and his wife Bilqees emerged with magical weapons in their hands and the earth trembled with their attacks.

The battle with Afrasiyab

Asad's companions soon arrived with his suit of armour and weaponry. Asad was now seated on his horse with the sword of Nur Afshan in his hand. Afrasiyab saw that Asad was in full form and rushed out of the pavilion. His army hastily took up arms, but could not withstand the onslaught of the Islamic lashkar. Very soon, the battlefield was strewn with dead bodies.

The sahirs of Tilism Khurshid had surrounded Prince Nur-al-Dahar and Princess Makhmoor was by his side. Nur-al-Dahar's face shone like the sun, he held strings of rubies in his hand and wore the blessed amulet that protected him against spells. Afrasiyab was stunned by this sudden turn of events as his soldiers were mercilessly killed. His viziers, Sarmaya Ice-maker and Abriq Mountain-breaker, who were the commanders of his army tried their best to fight the Islamic army. Sarmaya Ice-maker conjured mountains of snow and killed thousands in avalanches. Finally, Maimar Qudrat aimed a few iron balls at Sarmaya's illusory mountains that made them vanish. Sarmaya's magic cloud was then floating overhead. He threw a few drops of blood on the cloud and it emitted a bolt of lightning that injured Maimar Qudrat. Sarmaya was about to kill him when Jahandar Shah came in the way and destroyed the magic cloud. Sarmaya attacked him with his tegha, but Jahandar foiled all his moves and severed his head with a mighty blow of his sword. There were fierce storms with Sarmaya's death and black clouds covered the sky. Voices called out, 'You have killed me; my name was Sarmaya Ice-maker!'

Abriq Mountain-breaker saw his brother's dead body from a distance and ran towards Jahandar with his sword drawn. Kaukab the Enlightened had also reached the battlefield and saw that Sarmaya and Abriq's army had surrounded Jahandar, who was fighting valiantly and protecting the wounded Maimar at the same time. Kaukab attacked Abriq who conjured boulders and stones which did not affect the great king. Instead, the boulders fell on Abriq's own army. Abriq then attacked Kaukab who held Abriq by the wrist and slapped him so hard that his head flew off his body.

Afrasiyab got into a mighty rage as he saw his viziers being killed. He went towards Kaukab and waved his fingers so that a bolt of lightning wounded Kaukab's shoulder. He also killed several hundreds of Kaukab's soldiers. The noble Asad realized that Afrasiyab had caused havoc in the ranks of Kaukab's army. In truth, Afrasiyab was casting such powerful spells that Kaukab's army could not stand up to him. His magical weapons were unique. He would sometimes throw a string of pearls or his diadem or even pieces torn from his robe and conjure flames and clouds that emitted drops of blood causing hundreds to ignite and die in agony. Asad then called out to Afrasiyab and went towards him, but the King of Magic saw him and fled from there. The masters of eloquent conversation have written that this battle lasted for three days. Afrasiyab succeeded in killing thousands of rebel soldiers, making sure that he was never close to Asad. Bilqees, Lacheen and the other sardars were convinced that no one would survive Afrasiyab's magic. His grandmother Afat's sister, Zulmat Four-hands, was now supporting him. She had cast a spell that caused darkness to descend on the battlefield and flashed like lightning, killing hundreds herself.

Malika Bilqees fought her way to Zulmat and called out harshly, 'You disloyal, black-faced, ill-fated woman! You dare to fight before me! You have spilled the blood of so many of God's people!' Zulmat turned around, faced Bilqees and shouted, 'O Bilqees, Afrasiyab destroyed his own Tilism by sheer stupidity! Who can be as foolish as he was that he deprived you of your crown and your wealth, but kept you husband and wife alive and now pays the price for it? Today, I will do what he could not do and kill you!' Malika Bilqees advanced towards Zulmat in great rage, held her by her hair and slapped her hard. As Zulmat stumbled and fell, Bilqees wrenched her head off her body and tossed it at Afrasiyab.

The King of Magic was heartbroken by this sight and conjured a bolt of lightning that wounded Bilqees on her head. Afrasiyab was now fighting in full form. He leapt and fought soldiers all over the battlefield. Every time he flew upwards, he flung daggers that decapitated hundreds of rebels. Asad was not able to reach him at that height and was forced to fight the rest of Afrasiyab's army. On the third day of battle, when the sun was at its nadir, a light appeared in the direction of the desert of Nuristan. For the reader's information, the wilderness of Nuristan is the place where the holy saint Abrar lived and prayed on the summit of a mountain. Abrar had earlier helped Asad in the campaign for the magic keystone and had informed him that he had been appointed Qutb of Hoshruba by the saints. As the light came closer, everyone saw Abrar with the saint Hakim Roshan Rai seated on jewel-inlaid thrones that flew towards the battlefield. They were holding amulets of the sun that they flashed before Afrasiyab's army. Hundreds lost their heads instantly. Each time Afrasiyab tried to rise upwards, they recited incantations that prevented him from flying. Afrasiyab tried to use his magic on them, but they were unaffected by his spells. He called out desperately, 'Friends, I was not aware of your intentions or I would never have let you stay in my realm. I was told that you are Samri worshippers!'

Meanwhile, Asad made his way to Afrasiyab, but the King of Magic fought his way to the dome and took shelter under its shade. As the armies of Mahrukh and Bahar followed him there, a volley of arrows, daggers and stones assailed them. Lacheen tried very hard to stop this assault, but the arrows pierced soldiers, the daggers decapitated people and the stones wounded hundreds. No one was safe near the dome except Asad, who was protected by the keystone. As Asad rode up to the magic dome, Afrasiyab turned to run inside but Asad called out, 'Where do you run? Do you have any shame?' Asad was in a great temper and as he had been fighting for three days, blood dripped from his elbows. His clothes were torn and his body armour was smeared with blood. On hearing Asad call out to him, Afrasiyab turned around and waved his fingers that made a thousand flames fell upon Asad. However, they vanished with the power of the keystone.

Asad lifted the tegha and brought it down hard on Afrasiyab's head. Afrasiyab gave a startled cry and conjured several iron shields to protect him, but the tegha cut the clouds of shields like lightning and wounded that arrogant, headstrong king's head. He moaned with pain and fell on the earth.

Asad jumped off his horse, but Afrasiyab recovered swiftly and ran towards the magic dome. Asad cried with desperation, 'Is there someone who can prevent Afrasiyab from running into the dome!' Jahandar Shah, brave and fearless soldier, heard his master and flew in to stop Afrasiyab, who intended to fly to the top of the dome. Hairat was already on the topmost tier of the dome that had seven tiers with several thousand soldiers. As Afrasiyab flew upwards, Jahandar Shah seized his leg. Afrasiyab then threw the metal bracelet he was wearing on his hand on Jahandar's head and smashed it. Jahandar's body catapulted to the foot of the dome and his death was followed by stormy darkness.

By then, Afrasiyab was in the dome and was casting fearful spells on his enemies. Asad wanted to follow Afrasiyab into the dome, but Bilqees and Lacheen held him back. After some time, a voice boomed, 'You have killed me; my name was Jahandar Shah, King of Gulraiz!' Jahandar's loyal companion Maimar Qudrat beat his head in grief and his army was plunged into mourning.

Afrasiyab's tactics

Bilqees and Lacheen persuaded Asad to return to their camp. They told him, 'Huzoor, this battle has dragged on for three days and so many thousands of our men have gone to the Eternal Garden.' Afrasiyab had also struck the drums of peace and sat on the top of the dome watching Asad's army. Asad returned to the camp and supervized the burial of his dead soldiers. His wounds were dressed and bandages covered his body. Lacheen, Bilqees, Mahrukh and Bahar were in their own pavilions, but remained alert.

Princess Hilal Magic-wielder, whose husband Afat had died earlier, had also returned to her tent. Her handmaidens were dressing her wounds. Meanwhile, Afrasiyab was watching like a hawk from the dome to see which of the sardars was most vulnerable. He saw Hilal resting and shot out of the dome in the form of a bolt of lightning. He flashed into Hilal's tent and slapped her hard so that her head flew off her body. Her handmaidens retaliated, but he killed all of them. Asad was still in his durbar when he was startled by a voice calling out, 'You have killed me; my name was Hilal Magic-wielder!'

Barq Firangi went running into the durbar and cried, 'Huzoor, get ready! Afrasiyab has come down from the dome and has killed Hilal Magic-wielder and thousands of her supporters!' Asad was grieved on hearing this news; he rushed out of the durbar with his sword drawn and challenged Afrasiyab. As soon as the King of Magic saw Asad, he flew right back to the dome. Asad went to Hilal's tent and was overwhelmed with grief on seeing the bodies of the princess and all her attendants. He sent for Lacheen and said, 'O wise Lacheen, what can we do about the wickedness of Afrasiyab? No one can reach him on the dome. He is sitting in the sky stalking us and attacks whoever is not alert!' Lacheen replied, 'Huzoor, we are all waiting for Khwaja Amar to give us the solution. It has been a week since he left us. What we have to do is to remain alert for twenty-four hours of the day. Afrasiyab has also forsworn food and sleep and watches us all the time.'

Asad had not yet recovered from Hilal's death when Afrasiyab swooped down from the dome to kill a few more sardars. Every time Asad Ghazi ran towards him, Afrasiyab flew out of his reach and called out, 'O Tilism Kusha, will you lead the war on your own? I will not leave anyone alive!' Each time, Asad turned back in great despair. Meanwhile, Afrasiyab found Neelum Jadoo in the box that Chalak had brought him in. He took him to the top of the dome and after reviving him, explained the situation to him. Neelum beat his head and said, 'Shahanshah, strike the battle drums in my name. I will fight them!' Afrasiyab said, 'Neelum, we are helpless before Tilism Kusha. No magical weapon can affect him.' Neelum retorted, 'In that case I will capture Lacheen. I will be as wily as the ayyars. I have nothing to lose. My crown and my kingdom, my status and honour are all dust! I am just burning for a fight now!' Afrasiyab advised him against such a risky task but Neelum was adamant. He left the dome, dived into the earth and cut a tunnel through to Lacheen and Bilqees' tent. He peeped out of the tunnel and found the husband and wife in battle armour, conferring softly with each other. Neelum's plan was to attack them once they were asleep. He thought, 'They will surely not remain awake all night!' At that moment, Bilqees said to Lacheen, 'Chalak told me he had brought Neelum here in a box. Afrasiyab must have found him by now. Let us consult the oracle Papers of Jamshed to see what Neelum is up to now.'

Lacheen consulted the papers and laughed to himself. Bilqees looked at him puzzled, and he whispered in her ear, 'Neelum is right here waiting for us to sleep. I will cast a spell that will make the earth quiver and force him to emerge. Do not let him escape!' Bilqees nodded and quietly drew her dagger out. Lacheen muttered a spell that made the earth beneath the tent very hot. Neelum's feet started to burn and he jumped out of the tunnel. He sprouted wings and tore the tent as he shot out of it in a hurry. Malika Bilqees followed him swiftly and called out, 'You worthless wretch, where are you going? You thought you could trick us? We remember the day when you betrayed us. You will pay the price for that disloyalty now!' Afrasiyab was watching all this from the top of the dome and saw Neelum shooting out of the tent with Bilqees flying up behind him. He saw Neelum casting a spell that made flames burst on Bilqees, who merely smiled to transform the flames into water. Neelum then conjured a bolt of lightning that wounded Bilqees in the head. She became furious and attacked Neelum ferociously. Lacheen also emerged from the tent and saw his wife battling Neelum, who was screaming to his magical spirits, 'Save me now! I have served you all my life!' As he was screaming, a magic Zangi slave and several killer birds attacked Bilqees. She incinerated the birds, while Lacheen killed the slave with a well-aimed iron ball.

Afrasiyab, who was watching the proceedings from the dome, called out, 'Old man, you should be in your grave! Wait, I am coming!' As Afrasiyab swooped downwards, Asad heard his call and quickly mounted his horse. Afrasiyab was in a rare rage and killed anyone who crossed his path. By this time, Lacheen had flown close to Neelum, who hurled a magic ball at him in defence. Lacheen stopped the ball, slapped Neelum very hard and severed his head. A voice called out, 'You have killed Neelum Jadoo!'

After Neelum's death, the sardars of Islam attacked Afrasiyab and he heard the Tilism Kusha's voice challenging him. Hairat realized that Afrasiyab was surrounded on all sides. She flashed down from the dome like a thunderbolt and flew away with her husband clasped in her arms.

Later, Afrasiyab confessed to Hairat, 'I am not going to appear before Lacheen now. Every time he calls me a traitor, I recall that I was his subordinate. I had the whole kingdom for so long, I never realized that it would end this way. It is just as well that Neelum has been killed. He was the one who incited me into rebelling against Lacheen.' In the rebel camp, Lacheen presented Neelum's severed head as an offering to Asad. Lacheen said to the Tilism Kusha, 'Sheheryar, this wily one had come to trick us, but with God's blessing he has gone straight to hell!'

The enchanted sardars

That night, Afrasiyab did not leave the magic dome. The next morning, when Princess Surkh Mu Deadly-locks woke up, she declared, 'My heart is restless this morning; I think I will go for a stroll in the forest.' As she left her tent, her handmaidens saw that she seemed tearful and upset. They wanted to accompany her, but she insisted on going alone and disappeared into the forest. Some time later, two other sardars, Khurshid and Yakut went looking for her and did not return either.

The next morning, Bahar Jadoo awoke in an agitated state and began laughing and crying at the same time. She left for the wilderness after declaring that she had to prepare a spell. The noble Asad was now worried and alarmed by this unusual situation. The morning after Bahar's departure, Baghban Qudrat emerged in battle armour from his tent. When Barq went forward and greeted him, Baghban laughed and then wept bitterly. Barq asked, 'Why great vizier, is all well with you?' Baghban only told him he was going for a morning stroll and set off. A suspicious Barq followed the vizier secretly and observed that his behaviour was totally out of character. After walking for some time, Baghban stood under the shade of a large tree, suddenly sprouted wings and flew up into the sky. After he disappeared from sight, Barq went to Shahanshah Lacheen's durbar looking disheartened and depressed. He found the rest of the sardars in the durbar as well and informed them about Baghban. Lacheen observed, 'Without a doubt someone casts an enchantment on them at night. The next morning they feel compelled to meet that person!'

While this discussion was going on, Mehtar Chalak bin Amar entered the durbar. After learning what had happened, Chalak suggested that he and Barq investigate the matter. He said, 'It must be a powerful sahir who can enchant Bahar and Baghban. I have been looking for Khwaja Amar, but he seems to have travelled away very far.' Asad laughed and said, 'His money is waiting for him here, so he is bound to bring us some useful information. Had we given it to him, he would not have tried so hard.' Soon, Chalak and Barq left the durbar, but decided to travel separately. Barq disguised himself as a sahir and waited in the wilderness. He saw Shakeel, the son of Mahrukh walking from the lashkar with tears in his eyes and thought, 'May God protect us; he too seems to be enchanted!' Barq quietly followed the prince, who walked for several miles until he approached the gates of a garden. A few young handmaidens were standing at the gate and called out to Shakeel as he walked towards them, 'O brave son of Malika Mahrukh, come forth. Princesses Barq Khatif, Barq Khundan and Barq Giryan are summoning you!' Shakeel cried 'I am at their service!' and ran into the garden.

Barq then took out his paints of ayyari and transformed himself into Sarsar Sword-fighter. He approached the handmaidens who recognized Sarsar and said, 'What brings you here?' Barq replied, 'Shahanshah is full of praises for you. He wanted me to supervise the execution of the captured sardars. He wants their severed heads!' The handmaidens said, 'In that case, wait here and we will inform Princess Barq Khatif.' After they left, Barq started chatting with the guards on duty and discovered that the three sisters had come from Zulmat to destroy the Islamic lashkar.

The three princesses were seated in a pavilion in the garden when Shakeel was brought to them. Barq Khatif said, 'O prince, pierce your tongue!' Shakeel willingly pierced his own tongue while Barq Tears tied him up with heavy chains. Handmaidens then led him into a house in the garden. As soon as he entered the house, Shakeel suddenly came to his senses and saw that Bahar, Baghban, Surkh Mu, Yakut and Khurshid were also in chains. Meanwhile, Barq Khatif said to her sisters, 'My sisters, activate your magic. Each of you should awaken the spell of laughter and of tears. Leave it to me to enchant the sardars at night. The day we capture Lacheen and Bilqees, we will invite Shahanshah to execute the rebels himself. He will then realize how the faithful serve him!'

At that time, their handmaidens informed them that Sarsar Sword-fighter was waiting to meet them. Barq Khatif smiled when she heard Sarsar's name and said, 'It seems that an ayyar has come to visit us!' She then opened her mouth and expelled a magic bird. She caught him in her palm and said, 'Magic Bird of Samri, bring Sarsar to us in her real form!' Barq Firangi was waiting at the garden door when the bird flew over him and cried, 'Sarsar beware! Reveal what is in your heart, there are no secrets here!' The bird burst into flames and its ashes fell on Barq's face and peeled away the paints of ayyari. The handmaidens and guards were startled to see Barq Firangi in his real form and were about to attach him, but Barq swiftly stabbed the nearest handmaiden and ran for his life. There were cries of 'Do not let this angrez escape!' but Barq had hid himself in a cave. Barq Khatif soon transformed herself into a bolt of lightning and went off in his pursuit. She looked around frantically, but could find no trace of him.

As it happened, Chalak bin Amar had also reached this place and had seen Barq escaping from the garden. He saw Barq Khatif searching for him and thought of a plan. Barq Khatif was thinking of returning to the garden when she heard the sound of wailing and someone calling out, 'Alas, this wretched thief has stolen my paandaan!' Barq Khatif turned around and saw an old woman in silk clothes and a mehmoodi shawl. Her fair face was wrinkled and she stooped as she beat her breast and wailed loudly. Had Barq Khatif been more alert, she would have observed that the curve of the old woman's back was the curve of a deadly bow and that her wrinkles were the wrinkles of perfidy and duplicity.

Barq Khatif kindly asked the old woman what had happened. The old woman cried, 'My mistress, just now a thief who was fair of face and dressed like an angrez with coat and trousers kicked me. I fell on my face and my silver paandan fell on the ground. He made off with it.' Barq Khatif asked her to show her the place where he had attacked her. The old woman led Barq Khatif into the forest. She stopped abruptly in one place and whispered, 'Look I can see him through those trees. He is burying the paandan.' As Barq Khatif stepped forward to peer through the foliage, the old woman swiftly caught her in the coils of a snare-rope.

Barq Khatif hissed loudly and the coils of the whip turned to ashes. Chalak tumbled on the ground and when Barq Khatif stroked his face, he screamed as the paints of ayyari burnt and peeled off. Barq Khatif slapped him hard and said, 'You wretch, tell me where Barq hides himself?' Chalak started weeping and said, 'Huzoor he is hiding nearby. Release me and I will lead you to him. He was the one who asked me to become an old woman and kill you, but I have not seen a more powerful woman than you!' Barq Khatif looked closely at him and asked, 'Who are you?' Chalak replied, 'Malika of the world, I will tell you everything about myself. If you can look after me, I will tell you how to capture every ayyar. I am Chalak bin Amar. I can lead you to the great Amar himself, but first I will take you to Barq. He is a sly and devious creature, so do not listen to what he says about me.'

Barq Khatif declared happily, 'Chalak, if you work for me I will raise you to such heights that Sarsar and Saba Raftar will envy you!' Chalak gushed, 'Huzoor, you can test me right away. Just remove your spell and see my handiwork!' Barq Khatif readily released him from her spell. Chalak then told her where Barq Firangi was hidden and suggested that she cast a spell right away to capture Barq. He told her, 'Once you have killed this light-haired rascal, Amar will be devastated for he is the best of his ayyars and very devious.' Barq Khatif muttered a spell that made Barq Firangi feel as if his body was burning. As he rushed out of the cave screaming in pain Chalak immediately captured him, tied him with a rope and said, 'Mian Barq sahib, no one will be safe now. I am now employed by Malika. I will make sure Amar is in chains as well!' Barq howled in protest, but Barq Khatif dragged him behind her while Chalak walked with her, all the while talking ingratiatingly, 'Malika of the world, once you have destroyed the Muslims, you can hold Hairat and Afrasiyab by the neck. They should give you the kingdom.'

Barq Khatif was duly flattered by such talk and assured Chalak that she would give him an exalted rank. She returned to the garden looking very proud and told her sister, 'Samri has been kind to us. Chalak helped me capture Barq or how would I have found him?' At that time, they heard the sound of a melodious voice singing and Barq Khatif asked her handmaidens to investigate the source of the voice. One of them went to the garden door and found an old man sitting there, singing and playing the *tanpura*. His beautiful voice had drawn animals out from the forest, who sat around him, entranced by his singing.

The handmaiden remained there, captivated by his golden voice. Barq Khatif sent another handmaiden, who also did not return. After several handmaidens had disappeared like this, Barq Khatif rose muttering, 'Where have all these wretches gone?' She saw them standing in a trance as the old man sang and was moved herself by his song. She nudged one of the women to tell the old man that the princess was summoning him. The old man stopped singing and snapped, 'Am I your mistress' slave? She must have sent for a young man to please her. What will I do with her?' Barq Khatif sent another handmaiden who told the old man, 'Our mistress is eager to hear you sing!' The old man replied rudely, 'Your mistress must have sent for her lover. What would I do there?' This time, the handmaidens surrounded the old man. One held him by the arms, another fell at his feet, and still another picked up the tanpura. The lecherous old man saw them milling around him and began fondling their bosoms. The handmaidens were surprised and outraged, and let go of him abruptly. The old man fell on the ground and shrieked, 'They have killed me!'

Barq Khatif then brought out her whip and lashed out at the handmaidens. She shouted, 'You harlots, you have traumatized the old man!' She then approached the old man and pleaded, 'Mian, come with me. I am anxious to hear you sing.' She led the old man into the garden and seated him in baradari. The old man struck the tanpura again and started singing. Barq Khatif swayed with the music and was so delighted with the singer that from time to time she took off a piece of jewellery and offered it to him. After some time, the old singer paused and yawned, as if he was fatigued. Barq Khatif asked him, 'What is your good name?' The old singer said he was called Ustad Khurd Burd and said, 'I am also saqi. I will serve you the wine off my head while I play the tanpura with my hands and dance with my feet!' Barq Khatif laughed and asked, 'Will you not spill the wine then?' The old man said archly, 'Try me now. Just send for the wine.' Barq Khatif asked the handmaidens to bring flasks of wine.

The handmaidens soon brought the flasks and placed them before the old man. He showed great dexterity in handling the bottles. He twirled them around a few times and filled several goblets. He served the handmaidens and then placed a goblet on his head. Singing and dancing at the same time, he went forward and kneeled in front of Barq Khatif, bowing his head and offering her the wine. Barq Khatif drank the wine without a thought and soon enough, felt her limbs getting heavy. The handmaidens were also in a similar state. A voice called out, 'I am the great ayyar Khwaja Amar!' Chalak who was standing besides Barq Khatif, immediately stabbed her with his dagger. The garden was plunged into darkness and spirits called out, 'You have killed Barq Khatif!' Her alarmed sisters Barq Khundan and Barq Giryan rushed into the baradari, but Chalak had already released Baghban, Bahar and other prisoners. They all took out their magical weapons and caused havoc in the garden. Eventually, the sardars and ayyars killed all three of the sisters and returned to their camps with their severed heads.

The secret of the dome

The king of ayyars, the great sword wielder and slayer of sahirs was worried. He had promised Lacheen and the others that he would investigate the mystery of the magical weapons in Afrasiyab's dome. In his absence, the lashkar of Islam had suffered the tragic loss of Shahanshah Nur Afshan. His death had renewed Afrasiyab's confidence. The Islamic lashkar had already forsworn food and rest due to his lightning attacks. The noble Asad remained prepared for battle at all times. Every time Afrasiyab attacked his camp, Asad would confront him with the keystone and Afrasiyab would flee from him. He succeeded in denying Tilism Kusha any rest. He cast spells and then disappeared. He conjured flame rains and deadly snowstorms, and in the process, ignited rebel tents and killed vulnerable sardars.

His teacher's death had devastated Kaukab, while his companions and army openly grieved for their lost mentor. Afrasiyab's attacks kept gaining vigour and caused great damage and loss to the Islamic lashkar. Asad desperately sent for the ayyars and told them, 'For God's sake, go and look for Khwaja Amar. Maybe he is in trouble.' Thus instructed, Chalak, Zargham, Barq, Jansoz and Qiran left to find Amar bin Ummayyah. Meanwhile, Khwaja Amar had been wandering in the wilderness for a week with little success. Disguised as a singer, he finally sat down under the shade of a tree and began singing. Birds of the forest perched on the branches of that tree to listen to him. His voice then reached Princess Gulzar, who was flying overhead. She was well versed in music and said to her handmaidens, 'This is the voice of a master singer. How well he sings this ghazal!' She looked down from her flying throne and saw that a frail old singer was playing his flute while the entranced birds and beasts of the forest seemed to be listening to him.

Gulzar signalled to one of the handmaidens, who swooped down, clasped Amar by his waist and flew back to Gulzar, who then took him to her garden. Gulzar sat down on the masnad as her handmaidens revived Amar, who had fallen unconscious. Amar opened his eyes to find himself in what seemed like the garden of paradise with a damsel of incomparable beauty seated on the masnad in front of him. Her handmaidens stood around her and were smiling at him. Amar realized that they had heard him sing and brought him to the garden, unaware of his true identity. He rose and cried, 'May Samri and Jamshed illuminate the lamp of your beauty forever! Who has brought me here?' Gulzar replied, 'O master of the flute, do not be alarmed. I have some knowledge of music and many accomplished artistes have performed in this garden. I liked your voice and brought you here. I will reward you with whatever your heart desires if you sing for me.' Amar replied, 'Princess, all the tajdars of the land are fighting along with the Shahanshah. Are you not with him?' Gulzar smiled and said, 'There is no one more loyal than us. It is because of us that the war is still on. Otherwise, Afrasiyab Jadoo would have been killed. My husband and master is a mighty king and the bright light of magic. He is Aftab Sky-dweller, the ruler of this realm. Our ancestors had prepared the magical weapons that attack Shahanshah's enemies from the magic dome. They designed these weapons so that wherever they are placed, they will destroy the enemy. My husband and I will soon be leaving for Hoshruba with our army of seven lakh soldiers. We have prepared some excellent spells to confront the enemy. I will fight Bilqees and my husband has sworn to kill Lacheen.'

Amar heard her silently. By this time, the day had passed. In the evening, Princess Gulzar had the garden illuminated and flecks of silver glitter adorned the trees, while cages of singing birds were suspended on the branches. Amar was awarded a robe of honour and Gulzar's handmaidens began strumming musical instruments. When Gulzar invited Amar to sing, he said, 'Princess, I have been thinking. Your husband has handed over such precious weapons to Shahanshah. If Afrasiyab does not appreciate his gesture, is there a way to dispel their magic?' Gulzar trembled and said, 'Do not mention such a possibility! Our ancestors designed these magical weapons with the guidance of Samri himself. Afrasiyab came in person to beg my husband to lend him these gifts. My husband was reluctant, but Afrasiyab gave my husband a written agreement that no one can dispel the magic of these weapons.' Amar was about to ask another question, but the princess glared at him and said sternly, 'O flute player, do not talk about such matters. My husband's life is at stake here. Just sing for us.'

Amar felt a twinge of alarm and kept silent, but his heart was in turmoil as he thought of what he needed to do to discover the secret of the magical weapons. He played the flute while the handmaidens matched his tune with their instruments. In the silence of the night Amar's voice filled that beautiful garden. He enthralled his audience for some time before stopping abruptly. As the princess looked at him enquiringly, Amar said, 'Princess, this gathering is without salt. We need to liven it up with wine.' Gulzar was amused and said, 'So you have an interest in such things!' She then handed him the keys to her wine store and asked him to fetch the wine. Khwaja Amar first doctored the wine bottles and then served the princess by balancing a goblet on his head and dancing at the same time. He lowered his head before her and said, 'A true lover of music should be served thus!' Gulzar was delighted and awarded him with a string of pearls. As she sipped the wine without fear, Amar served goblets to all her handmaidens. The night was almost over when, overwhelmed by the effect of the wine, Gulzar rested her head on the masnad and fell into a stupor. Her handmaidens also fell about unconscious.

Amar thought of killing the princess and plundering the garden. Not sure of what to do next, he explored the garden of ayyari and saw the flowers of deceit and fresh trickeries. He picked one of the flowers and its fragrance and colour advised him not to kill the princess as he would gain nothing by the deed. He deposited the unconscious Gulzar in Zambil and called out to the keeper, 'She is not to do hard labour or it will affect her price. My noble master's lashkar will be in Hoshruba soon. His sardars have an eye for beautiful women and will be happy to bid for her!' He then brought out the paints of ayyari and transformed into the very image of Gulzar. By this time, he was tired as he had been wandering in the wilderness for several nights without sleep. He wrapped himself in a shawl and slept soundly through the night on Gulzar's bed.

Gulzar's handmaidens stirred with the morning breeze. Nargis was the first to rise, Sosan woke up making a noise as usual, Ghuncha-dahan was quiet as always, and Shamshad stretched her limbs as she woke up. They conferred with each other and decided that the princess had overslept and that they should awaken her. These moon-faced handmaidens woke her up gently by rubbing her feet. Amar awoke rubbing his eyes. The handmaidens then saw that the princess was in a foul temper. She shouted, 'You wretches what have you done with my flute player?' The maidens cried, 'Huzoor, we were so overwhelmed with the wine we dropped off to sleep. You had given that old man so many sacks of gold it probably went to his head!' The false Gulzar pretended to be livid with rage and ordered, 'Search for him! If I do not find my flute player I will kill myself and murder you all!' She started weeping and the handmaidens fluttered around her anxiously. The false princess shouted, 'Nargis, I will pluck your eyes out! Sumbal, I will pull your hair! Shamshad, you will lose your head! Do not try to console me. I will not rest till you find him!' The handmaidens ran around the garden looking for the old singer, while the false princess sat sulking on her bed.

The magic mirror of Aftab Sky-dweller

Soon, the sound of kettledrums was heard and a magic cloud, crackling with a thousand lights, descended into the garden. The handmaidens ran to the princess and cried, 'Huzoor, your loving and devoted husband has come with his large army. It is so formidable that he is bound to destroy the Muslims in a day!' The false princess snapped, 'Harlots, are you trying to frighten me with his name? Let him come if he wants to! I am ready to give up my life—let him be entertained by you instead!' When Aftab stepped off his cloud, he was surprised to see that the princess had not come out to receive him. So, he walked into the garden and found her in an agitated state. Aftab loved his wife dearly and was concerned to see her so upset. He kissed her and pleaded, 'Princess, what have I done to annoy you? At one word from you, I am ready to pluck the stars from the sky or to lie beneath your feet!'

Even as Aftab was pleading, the false Gulzar noticed that he was holding on to a small casket. In response to his entreaties, she pouted prettily and said, 'What is this casket that you are carrying under your arms?' Aftab smiled and said, 'My princess, there are no secrets between us. Is this what is annoying you? This casket holds the life of Hoshruba!' The false princess said caustically, 'Well, do not tell me about it or I will join Tilism Kusha!' The unsuspecting Aftab took out a small key tucked in his topknot and opened the casket. In it was a mirror that seemed to emit an unearthly light.

As Gulzar stared at the mirror, Aftab said, 'You see princess, it is only a mirror!' The false princess pulled his hair and said, 'You wretch, tell me about the mirror, what is it used for?' She hid the mirror in her shawl and said, 'If you do not, I will smash it with stones!' Aftab explained, 'O ruler of my heart, the truth is that this mirror can destroy the magical weapons I have given to Afrasiyab. If someone flashes this mirror on them, they will be incinerated. This mirror can also destroy the magic dome. This is the reason why I keep this secret to myself; Afrasiyab's life depends on it.'

Amar then returned the mirror to Aftab and said, 'You shameless one, keep the mirror in the casket or next to your bosom. I do not want the mirror. I was not after the mirror. At least I have proof that you do not consider me your enemy! Now I will accompany you. I have prepared several spells that will put Hairat to shame and Afrasiyab will be happy with us!' The false princess put her arms around Aftab and said, 'I must have been foolish to fight with my husband. Did you think that I would let you go to fight alone?' Aftab's face flushed with happiness and he said, 'O dearest one, this mirror has been specially prepared by Samri and Jamshed. Apart from its destructive qualities, it also protects whosoever holds it from magic!' Amar replied, 'Now do not go on about the mirror. Keep it back in the casket and guard it with your life. This is the time to think of the battle ahead of us. The lashkar of Tilism Kusha must be in turmoil now with the death of the great Nur Afshan. We must first tackle Bilqees and Lacheen. That pair must be killed first!'

The very same day, the false Princess Gulzar and her husband Aftab Sky-dweller set off for the Dome of Light with two thousand handmaidens and their formidable army of sixty lakh sahirs. Amar told the handmaidens, 'Use your magic to fly my throne; I have sworn not to cast any spells till I reach Afrasiyab.' Thus, this procession travelled to the dome in all splendour.

Afrasiyab kidnaps Asad

Now hear about Asad Ghazi. He suddenly felt very anxious and began to pace about restlessly. He told his sardars that he was feeling uneasy and went to Mahjabeen's tent. She looked and him and asked, 'Sheheryar, is all well with you? You look off colour today.' Asad replied, 'Princess, I feel very uneasy today. I do not know why.' After some time with his beloved, Asad returned to his own pavilion. He covered himself with his *doshala* and lay down on his bed; the keystone was around his neck and the Nur Afshani tegha by his side. He fell into an uneasy sleep. Outside his pavilion, the guards also nodded off. Afrasiyab, sitting on his dome, saw that Asad's lashkar was quiet. He flew down and stealthily approached Asad's pavilion. He cast a spell so that there was a cool magical breeze and the guards and servants fell into a deep sleep. Afrasiyab entered the pavilion and found that the candles were still burning. He also saw that the magic keystone shone like the morning star on Asad's chest, while his magic Nur Afshani tegha lay besides him.

Afrasiyab first lifted the tegha, then quietly cut the cord of the keystone and took it off Asad. He then put his arms around Asad's waist and made off with him after leaving a note on the bed that read: 'Be aware that I am taking your sardar with me. I will execute him in a manner that the birds in the air and fishes in the river might have mercy for him, but I will not. Consult each other and join me, in which case I will forgive your sins. Otherwise, I will kill you mercilessly. I have been lenient with you all these years although I could have killed all of you at any time but I am determined to fight now!' Afrasiyab reached the magic dome with Asad who was unconscious. In a fit of anger, Afrasiyab pulled off his head with such force that it was severed from the body. He threw the head away and went to boast to his wife, 'Hairat, have you seen my power? I used to say to you that these are my servants and I can kill them any time! Asad's headless body is below this dome. If these rebels kiss my feet, I might forgive them.'

While Afrasiyab was talking to Hairat, Zargham Sherdil was making rounds of the Islamic camp, checking on the safety of the sardars. If any guard had fallen asleep, Zargham woke him up. He was startled to see the guards outside Asad's pavilion fast asleep, with the curtains of the pavilion lying open. He rushed in and saw the bed empty. Zargham first thought that one of the ayyar girls had kidnapped Asad, but when he found the note, he began beating his head in grief. He tore open his shirt, and went to Asad's uncle Badi-uz-Zaman. It was dawn by then and Badi-uz-Zaman was already awake for the morning prayers. He read the note and slapped his own cheeks.

By this time, the clamour had awoken the sardars who were awake and they rushed to Badi-uz-Zaman's tent just in time to prevent him from slitting his own throat. Asad's cousin Nur al Dahar was also distraught when he heard this news. Badi-uz-Zaman wept, 'How will I show my face to Sahibqiran? When my sister Zubaida Lion-heart asks me what I have done with her lion cub, what answer will I give?'

On hearing the clamour in Badi-uz-Zaman's tent, Mahjabeen Diamond-robe sent her vizierzadi Dilaram to investigate what had happened. She ran back beating her breast and wailing, 'Huzoor I have heard terrible news and my heart is in my mouth! The sardars are saying that our master has been kidnapped by Afrasiyab and killed. His body is lying under the magic dome!' Lalaan Red-robe and Lal Sukhandan had also emerged from their tents and heard Dilaram. The three princesses Mahjabeen, Lalaan and Lal, all fainted with grief while their handmaidens screamed and beat their breasts. The sardars wore their battle dress as if they were donning shrouds and were determined to fight and lose their lives. Suddenly, a cloud of dust blew in from the desert and Khwaja Amar emerged from it, looking very disturbed. Badi-uz-Zaman embraced Amar and cried, 'Something dreadful has happened! Afrasiyab has killed Asad Ghazi and we all go to our deaths!' Amar simply said, 'Very good!' and walked past the confused sardars.

The princesses too saw Amar and rushed to embrace him. They cried, 'O respected elder we are ruined! Afrasiyab has snatched our beloved. He has killed Asad Ghazi!' Amar turned to Mahjabeen and said, 'My daughter Mahjabeen, it is just as well! Go and reconcile with your father and be happy with him. He will marry you to some great king. Asad was merely Hamza's grandson. He acquired many pretensions in Tilism. I will go now and tell my master that I tried to stop his grandson, but he was stubborn and eventually lost his life! After all he was confronting such a powerful king, his end was inevitable!' Amar then turned around and addressed the lashkar, 'Friends, you are ready to die for Asad. Do you not want to find some way of bringing him back to life?' Shahanshah Lacheen said, 'Khwaja what way is that? Has anyone come back to life after dying?' Khwaja Amar smiled and said, 'If you spend some money, he can come back to life!' Lacheen asked how much was required. Amar said, 'This I do not know. Everyone will have to give as much as he can. My job is to bring him back to life; your job is to provide the money. The angel of death must still be on the way. I will go and offer him all that you give me. I will plead with him and say, "Leave Asad for a while. He is the grandson of a penniless keeper of Khana Kaaba. You will gain nothing by his death!"'

Lacheen immediately said, 'Khwaja, I will contribute one lakh rupees.' Badi-uz-Zaman promised the same amount. In this way, Amar got all the sardars to pledge large sums of money. He spread out a sheet for the money and everyone contributed according to their ranks. Mahjabeen and the other princesses gave away several caskets of jewels. Amar addressed the soldiers and said, 'You people should contribute a month's salary for your master's life.' After the soldiers too had paid up, he declared, 'This will pay the expenses for my journey. I am going to Khana Kaaba.' Amar was about to deposit the money into Zambil, but Badi-uz-Zaman held his hand and said, 'This money is not for you to go to Khana Kaaba. You promised you would restore Asad to us.' Amar retorted, 'Has your father given me this money? This is money that sardars have given me for my expenses!' Badi-uz-Zaman remained adamant that he should restore Asad to them, as did the other sardars. Amar said 'Leave me and I will speak to the angel of death. I will not go to Khana Kaaba.' Badi-uz-Zaman said, 'That is up to you.' Amar suddenly laughed and said, 'I will bring Asad to you!' He then took out Asad from Zambil and said, 'Here is Asad! I had to plead very hard with the angel of death for his life; I told him that he has young wives and I cannot bear to see them weep!'

The reader should know that when Amar was disguised as Gulzar Jadoo, beloved of Aftab sky-dweller, and resting at night, he dreamt of the elders of his faith telling him, 'Amar you are resting in comfort here, but your lashkar is in grave danger. Afrasiyab is determined to kill Tilism Kusha. You must go and save Asad.' Amar woke up instantly and decided on a plan. He disguised a handmaiden as Gulzar and laid her down on the bed. He then went back to his lashkar with such speed that he jumped over wells and ditches and was faster than the wind. He reached Asad's tent when the guards in front of Asad's tent were beginning to nod off. He put Asad in Zambil and painted a prisoner from Zambil to look like Asad. He then laid him on Asad's bed and replaced the keystone and Nur Afshani tegha with replicas. Amar quickly left with Asad and returned to Gulzar's place. A little later, Afrasiyab captured the false Asad and killed him. Meanwhile, in the Islamic lashkar, everyone cried out in happiness, while the camp resounded with the sound of gongs and trumpets celebrating Asad's return. Afrasiyab saw Asad from the dome and cried, 'Malika, this is a disaster! This was not the real Asad!'

Amar destroys the magic dome

Afrasiyab continued to keep watch on Asad's lashkar, while Asad remained alert in case Afrasiyab entered his camp. The next day, when the battle started, Afrasiyab intended to fight his way and escape from Asad. As the battle raged, a cluster of red and green clouds appeared on the horizon. Afrasiyab's spies came in to inform him that Aftab Sky-dweller was approaching with his army of sixty lakh to confront the enemies. Afrasiyab tossed his cap in the air and told his sardars to receive Aftab. He stood with his sword drawn and waited eagerly for Aftab. Everyone saw Aftab Sky-dweller and his wife Gulzar fly on two thrones. By this time, the lashkars of Asad and Afrasiyab had drawn closer to the dome while fighting.

A volley of magic arrows from the dome had already killed hundreds of Lacheen's soldiers.

Hairat had been fighting alongside her husband. She provided him with magical weapons and conjured spectacles of magic herself. She was nervous and shared her apprehensions with her companions, 'This battle is not going well. Let us see what happens today.' There was a sudden hush in the skies and Hairat looked up to see Gulzar Jadoo on a flying throne with her handmaidens. She seemed to be heading towards the magic dome. Hairat called out to her not to go too close to the dome lest there was fresh trouble. Gulzar called back, 'My sister, we will not turn unless the war is won! The reason we could not appear before was because we were preparing for this final day and awakening Samri and Jamshed's magic!'

As Hairat watched anxiously, Gulzar rose higher in the air. The reader will remember that Gulzar was actually Khwaja Amar in disguise. The false Gulzar had returned a fake mirror to Aftab during her mock fight with him and now had the actual magic mirror that could cause the dome's destruction with her. From a distance, Afrasiyab also felt uneasy when he saw Gulzar flying towards the dome. Under the shadow of the dome, the battle continued relentlessly. Afrasiyab's soldiers were fighting ferociously with Lacheen's men and the battlefield was strewn with corpses. The noble Asad was also fighting fiercely, even as the dome targeted the Islamic soldiers relentlessly with its magic arsenal of daggers and arrows. Gulzar's throne swayed as it approached the dome and she took out the magic mirror from the folds of her scarf. Aftab was also watching his wife and said happily to Afrasiyab, 'O Shahanshah, Gulzar has great love for you. She will conjure flames to descend on Lacheen's lashkar from that height.' Afrasiyab just managed to utter, 'Aftab, have you got the magic mirror with you safely?' Aftab said confidently, 'Huzoor, it is locked in this box and remains locked all the time. No one is allowed to even touch it and the secret is safe with me!' Afrasiyab relaxed and said, 'I know that both you and your wife are devoted to me! You will not let Tilism be destroyed.'

For the reader's information, the magic dome had seven tiers and housed eight lakh sahirs who targeted enemies from within. The dome resounded with the sounds of gongs and conch shells and had many treasures. The false Gulzar or Khwaja Amar quickly flashed the magic mirror at the dome. The mirror released a bolt of lightning that destroyed the magic weapons suspended on the dome. The knives, daggers and magical arrows went up in flames. The dome swayed on its axis and then went crashing down, killing all the sahirs inside. Afrasiyab screamed, 'Friends, kill that camel driver's son right now! O Aftab, how did that monster get to the mirror when you said you guarded it with your life?' Aftab merely stood there with an ashen face and beat his head in frustration. Meanwhile, Amar had announced himself and disappeared in Galeem. Afrasiyab's army lost heart with the destruction of the dome, though the fighting continued. Afrasiyab fought with great valour against both Lacheen and Bilqees. Aftab Sky-dweller fought alongside the King of Magic. Kaukab and Burran were also conjuring powerful war spells.

The final battle

At that time, a huge cloud of dust moved in from the desert. Afrasiyab's ally Anjum Atishbar arrived in the battlefield, leading an army of four lakh soldiers. He looked distraught as he neared Afrasiyab, who asked him, 'Where have you been fighting?' Anjum replied, 'Huzoor, I am being pursued by the grandsons of Hamza. I tried to stop them several times, but these lion-hearted braves can go through rivers of fire with ease!' Then, Anjum and his men also joined the King of Magic to fight the Islamic army. Their magical weapons were citrons and limes that exploded and caused great destruction. The earth trembled with this fresh onslaught of sorcery.

Anjum was just about settling into the rhythm of the battle when a wall of dust rolled in from a distance. As every one was watching, a gigantic man with long hair streaming behind him emerged from the dust, riding a rhinocerous. Thousands of sardars surrounded him and a host of sahirs and non-sahirs followed him. The size of this army was so immense that it seemed as if the Bull of the Earth would not be able to bear the burden of its weight. The giant-like man called out, 'O my people, beware I am Khudawand Zamurrad Shah Bakhtri. The river of my rage has burst and I will fight with my righteous hand!' From the other side, a sahir leading a huge army appeared and shouted, 'I am Kalang Fire-eater!' Kalang was another ally of Afrasiyab who was also fleeing from Hamza's forces. Kalang Fire-eater aimed magic citrons and limes at Asad's men that burst and killed several thousand people.

Afrasiyab's men, who had been demoralized by the destruction of the dome, got fresh impetus to fight with the arrival of Khudawand Laqa and Kalang Fire-eater. Sardars of Islam like Mahrukh, Bahar, Baghban Qudrat and others had not slept properly for a month due to the war, and were now fighting for their lives. Kalang Fire-eater and Anjum Atishbar fought fiercely to demonstrate their loyalty to Afrasiyab. They believed that Khudawand Laqa had destined their victory. Despite their ferocious onslaughts, Kaukab killed several enemy commanders, while Burran's magic Pearl of Samri destroyed the ranks of Hoshruba's soldiers. Kaukab's son Jamshed used the magic Rings of Jamshed as his weapons.

In the heat of the battle, two dust clouds arose from the desert and approached the battlefield like an avalanche. The left cloud of dust cleared to reveal thousands of soldiers carrying war flags, followed by Prince Iraj, great grandson of Hamza. He was on Ashqar and was leading an army of seven lakh men. Afrasiyab then turned to see the second cloud of dust that cleared to reveal a vast army. Afrasiyab's sardars said, 'Huzoor, that is Hamza!' The masters of written speech tell us that the area from Tausan's fort to the Neel river and the place where the magic dome once stood swarmed with Afrasiyab's sahirs. Swords flashed like lightning and rivers of blood flowed. Zamurrad Shah Bakhtri was also engaged in the battle, seated on his mighty rhinocerous. Shaitan Bakhtiarak had always wanted to see Afrasiyab fight. He had often said that such a powerful sahir would probably make the earth tremble with his magic. In truth, Afrasiyab was fighting with great courage that day.

Emir Hamza kept reciting the Great Name while the noble Asad flashed the magic keystone. Afrasiyab's magic seemed invincible that day. He avoided Tilism Kusha, but vented his strength on Mahrukh and Bahar. He also tried to get to Mahjabeen Diamond-robe, but it was not easy to kill her. A host of sahir and non-sahir sardars surrounded her throne, for she was ostensibly the ruler of the lashkar. Her uncle Shakeel, in particular, guarded her carefully. He felt proud that because of Mahjabeen's marriage to Asad Ghazi he would be related to Hamza. The powerful darogha of the Garden of Apples, Gul Afshan Jadoo, was also fighting and was hidden high up in the sky in a magic cloud. Lacheen and the other sardars were helpless before her. As soon as they rose into the air, she conjured blistering winds that stopped them mid-flight. She called out to Afrasiyab, 'Huzoor, why did you not send for me before. These people are worthless; I would have destroyed them in moments!' Afrasiyab snapped, 'Am I lower than you now? I need no one! Tilism Kusha will be alone and none of his allies will be left alive!'

Gul Afshan then saw the Tilism Kusha flying on a magic peacock towards the magic cloud. He flashed the keystone at the cloud that disintegrated and exposed Gul Afshan. She was alarmed by his proximity to her and thought, 'How could Tilism Kusha fly up on a peacock? These people are not familiar with magic!' She conjured a sheet of flames that fell on Asad, but when he flashed the keystone, the flames fell on Gul Afshan instead. She jumped aside, but her peacock was burnt to ashes. Asad Ghazi looked down at the tablet that read, 'O Tilism Kusha, look carefully at Gul Afshan. You will see a white mole on her forehead. Aim your arrow at this mole. Be very careful because if you miss, the arrow will go through your own skull! Gul Afshan is the keeper of the Garden of Apples and must not escape!'

Asad then fit his arrow into the bow and stretched it while taking careful aim at Gul Afshan's forehead. The arrow left his bow like a bird and pierced her head right through the white mole. Instead of blood, flames erupted from her shattered skull and her body caught fire. A voice called out, 'You have killed me, I was Gul Afshan Jadoo, keeper of the Garden of Apples!' There was a tremendous uproar of grief in Hairat's lashkar when she died. A fire instantly raged through the Garden of Apples and reduced all its palaces and walls to ashes. Thousands of sahirs within the garden perished in no time.

When this happened, Afrasiyab vented his rage on Kaukab and tried to cut his head off. Kaukab was a true soldier and never turned away from a fight. He stood where he was and faced the onslaught of Afrasiyab's men. Suddenly, there was a call like the roar of a lion. That was Asad who called out so loudly that the lashkar of kafirs fell on its knees, the hearts of the reckless and the rash bled with fear, while horses bolted out of the battlefield, throwing off their riders. How can I describe to you the swordplay of that time? Prince Nur al Dahar rode in, flashing the Sulaimani sword from one side, while Badi-uz-Zaman exhibited the gigantic tegha of Tilism Tahmaroos. Bahar and Baghban threw thousands of bouquets and there was a rain of petals with a magic breeze. Occasionally, Bahar conjured flower-like creatures who challenged Afrasiyab, 'Why do you run hither and thither like a shameless man? Stand and fight! We have come to see you fight!' For a few seconds, Afrasiyab would be enchanted by their magical tones, but since he was a powerful sahir, he would recover and keep fighting. He was assailed by the magic of Bahar, Baghban, Lacheen and Bilqees in the air, while Barq Lameh and her son Ra'ad attacked him on the ground. Afrasiyab was now in trouble. He could not fly up in the air for fear of Kaukab and Lacheen. At one point, he opened his mouth wide to expel smoke that blinded thousands of people. Asad just flashed the keystone to disperse the smoke and cool the sheets of flames Afrasiyab had conjured.

Asad was the descendant of Abraham (blessed by the Provider) who was thrown into the furnace that transformed into a garden. These people were of fiery temperament and thought nothing of magical flames. Asad flashed the tegha of Nur Afshan and attacked Afrasiyab, who thrust his own sword forward to meet it. Asad pulled his tegha back and brought it upon Afrasiyab's head with force. Afrasiyab could not escape either to the sky or below the earth. He managed to conjure a magic shield just in time to protect him. The Nur Afshani tegha shone like the new moon and cut right through the shield and the crown of pride that Afrasiyab wore on his head; it then cut through Afrasiyab's arrogant head down to his heart. His pride and conceit led to this day. Afrasiyab groaned and fell on the earth. How can I describe to you what happened then? Black dust arose from the earth, millions of birds flew to the skies, peacocks beat their heads with their wings, houses crumbled into dust, and rivers boiled and went dry. The effects of Afrasiyab's death were felt hundreds of miles away. After a long, long time, the inevitable voice called out, 'You have killed me! My name was Afrasiyab Jadoo! Alas, I gave up my life and died, but could not fulfil my destiny!'

Hairat was alarmed by this sound, while mighty kings who were fighting with Afrasiyab ran and fell at Lacheen's feet, begging for clemency. Hairat raged through the ranks of the army to get to her husband's corpse. She cut a tragic figure with her eyes brimming with tears and her hair streaming in the wind. In her anger she got back to fighting and threw magic grains that caused thousands to burn. As Hairat fought in her grief and rage, everyone thought Afrasiyab had come back to life. Her spells were so destructive that the eyes and the pen shed black tears; words flutter on paper like half dead birds. Hairat's angry spells wounded Baghban, Ra'ad and Barq Lameh and killed several prominent sardars. Finally, Malika Bilqees arrived in great majesty, holding a magic net. She stood behind Hairat and first released some magic birds that stunned Hairat and she was as silent as a portrait. Then, Bilqees threw the magic net over Hairat and captured her. Sixty thousand of Hairat's handmaidens were also captured along with her.

Aftab Sky-dweller saw Afrasiyab's corpse rolling in blood and dust; he saw Hairat captured and realized that the river of Sahibqiran's sword was in full flood. He continued to exhort his friends to fight by shouting, 'Friends, avenge your master's death! Do not run at this crucial moment!' On hearing this, Princess Burran took out the Pearl of Samri from her topknot and aimed it at Aftab. It went straight through his body and killed him. There were frightful sounds as he died and a voice called out, 'You have killed me! I was Aftab Sky-dweller!'

Though the war was won with Afrasiyab's death, some of his followers still kept fighting. Mahrukh Magic-eye disposed of many of them. The reckless died, but the rest pleaded for clemency. Some fell at Lacheen's feet; others begged Mahrukh Magic-eye and Bahar Jadoo, who requested Sahibqiran to give them mercy. The reader should know that when the war ended, Sahibqiran arrived in all splendour and met the noble Asad after several years. He wept when he met his son Badi-uz-Zaman. His grandson Nur al Dahar fell at his feet.

Despite the victory over the kafirs, Laqa continued to fight. Sahibqiran fought his way closer to Laqa to capture him, but several hundred brave young men surrounded Laqa's throne. Laqa was distraught and kept calling out to Bakhtiarak, 'O my Shaitan, what destiny have I ordained?' Bakhtiarak shouted back, 'Our destiny has taken a somersault! You are so unfortunate that just when you reached a man like Afrasiyab, he lost his life! Our only shelter now is the wilderness. There is no place to hide here. Your brother Namrood claims divinity in the city of Shikakia. He is reputed to be powerful with a large army. Let us go to him. O Khudawand, I regret bitterly that I did not see Afrasiyab at the height of his powers! He was the mightiest sahir and had no match in this world. I just saw one example of his powers when he captured Hamza's Great Name with just a movement of his tongue. Alas by the time we reached here, he went straight to hell!'

Laqa said to Bakhtiarak, 'That Namrood *mardood* is a lowly creature. I have a plan to eliminate him as well. I will never go to him. I will ordain that Hamza is destroyed!' Bakhtiarak was now truly worried because he knew that their capture was certain. Hamza's followers surrounded them and were determined to capture Laqa. Although Hamza's sardars were dropping with fatigue after fighting for a week without rest, they thought of only this, 'Asad has conquered Tilism. We should capture this hypocrite today.' Seven hundred tajdars flashed their swords and closed in on Laqa. He wanted to pray, but as he claimed to be god himself, whom could he pray to? In his heart, he was a believer and prayed, 'O Merciful One, I know what I really am and you are all powerful and strong. Save me from these people today!'

Within moments, a dark cloud materialized in the sky and expelled golden lights. Several hundred panjas fell from it and lifted Laqa, Bakhtiarak, Faramurz and the treacherous sons of Nausherwan in a flash. A fearful voice called out, 'Beware O Muslims, Khudawand Khurshid Iron-body has sent for his lowly creatures. Laqa is foolish and arrogant, but we will have mercy on him and will grant him a kingdom. Do not try and follow him there or you will be punished cruelly.' The dark cloud moved swiftly out of sight. Laqa's followers realized that a sahir had saved Laqa and that they were to meet him in the realm of Khurshid Nigar. They left for the wilderness and travelled through plains, mountains and deserts to reach their master. Back in the Islamic camp, the night went by in celebrations. At dawn, Sahibqiran and Asad met each other. Everyone embraced each other in joy.

❦

45 THE STORY OF HAPPINESS, THE WEDDINGS OF SARDARS AND PRINCESSES, AMAR AYYAR WEDS SARSAR

The legendary narrators tell us that the noble Sahibqiran travelled in stages to the Garden of Apples; Shahanshah Lacheen had adorned the palaces of the garden in a beautiful manner. At the time of Afrasiyab's death, the Garden of Apples had been destroyed, but Lacheen had restored it to its former splendour. When Sahibqiran arrived in great glory, Lacheen and Bilqees, along with eighteen hundred kings and nobles, received him. Malika Bilqees had arranged formal bridal chambers for the princesses Mahjabeen, Bahar, Makhmoor, Lalaan and Naheed.

The badshah of the lashkar of Islam, Saad bin Qubad, Nur al Dahar and Asad Ghazi followed Sahibqiran into the garden. Ruby-studded wedding stools were laid out for the three bridegrooms on which they sat down in all splendour. The badshah who was getting married to the flower-like Bahar, was adorned in saffron-coloured robes. Nur al Dahar and Asad wore similar robes. The garden was adorned with saffron-coloured flowers and decorations, and cries of jubilation filled the air. The morning breeze was heavy with the fragrance of love; flowers were filled with the wine of dew and there was happiness all around. There was an outcry to summon the qazis to conduct the marriage ceremonies.

The sons of the great Buzurjmeher were excited at the prospect of conducting these noble marriages for they knew that the rewards and gifts alone would enrich them for generations. As they prepared to conduct the weddings, a pleasant-faced attendant wearing saffron clothes rushed in and said, 'Hakim sahib, come quickly for you have to conduct the nikah of Shah, Nur al Dahar and Asad!' When the Hakim sahib arose to leave, the attendant stopped him and said, 'Why are you looking so pale on this joyous occasion? Sahibqiran will be offended. Have this gilori from my hands and you will feel better.' Soon after the Hakim began chewing the betelnut leaf, he felt like relieving himself and excused himself.

The attendant laughed and said, 'Wonderful, you are like the dog that relieves himself just as he is needed for the hunt! Please make haste as we are getting delayed!' Hakim sahib went into the privy and the attendant knew that he would be there for several days. He then locked the door from the outside. For the reader's benefit, the attendant was Khwaja Amar who had doctored the betel leaf with *jamal gota*, a potent laxative. He sighed with contentment and then took out his paints of ayyari to disguise himself as Hakim Umeed. He walked confidently to the palace holding the largest and longest prayer beads. As Khwaja reached the durbar, attendants came running up to him and urged him to make haste. He first conducted the Shah's marriage and fought to get the award that ran into hundreds of thousands of rupees. When he conducted Nur al Dahar's nikah, he went straight to his father Badi-uz-Zaman, who awarded him generously. After Mahjabeen was wedded to Asad, the princesses Lalaan and Naheed were also married to him. Khwaja collected his dues of trays heaped with gems and took off.

Lacheen and Bilqees hosted all these events personally so as to not offend anyone. Makhmoor's mother, Malika Asrar, gave her daughter several kingdoms as dowry. Lacheen and Bilqees provided Bahar and Mahjabeen with their dowers. The rulers of Tilism Nur Afshan also participated eagerly in these marriages. Asad's mother and Sahibqiran's daughter, Zubaida Lion-heart, sat with Mahjabeen in the palanquin and the procession returned to Mount Agate in all magnificence.

Shohdas accompanied the wedding processions and shouted, 'This Arab must be divested of his money before the procession returns!' Sahibqiran had showered them with several sacks of gold coins, but the shohdas were greedy for more. As he saw Sahibqiran carelessly toss coins at them, Khwaja Amar too was overtaken by greed. He painted himself to look like a shohda in a homespun loincloth. He joined the shohdas and called out, 'Throw us a handful then!' Sahibqiran threw another batch of coins and Amar jumped up higher than the shohdas and scooped up the coins in his hands, not letting even one drop to the ground. The shohdas watched in dismay as Amar snatched their rightful share. An old Rumi shohda whispered to the others, 'Friends, this miserable specimen of skin and bones is not one of us! Let us catch him for look at the way he jumps! Surely he must be a thief who scales walls at night and now has come to cheat us!'

The third time that Amar jumped up in the air to get the coins, a shohda grasped his ankle and pulled him down. Khwaja stuffed the gold coins in his mouth, but the shohda stuck his fingers into Khwaja's mouth, tore his mouth open and took the coins. Khwaja left the gathering disconsolate, his eyes filled with tears and his mouth bleeding as he approached Sahibqiran's mount. Sahibqiran looked down on his friend and said, 'Is all well with you?' Amar said evasively, 'Sahibqiran I fell down and hurt myself.' Sahibqiran laughed spontaneously and said, 'Khwaja, such behaviour is not worthy of you. I saw you mingling with shohdas and snatching their rightful share. What do you lack for that you resort to this?' Amar sighed, 'O Hamza, you have no idea of what I have to go through. My creditors harass me endlessly and I thought I might make something at these weddings to pay off their interest. I have spent a great deal on these marriages!'

The noble Emir gave his old friend several sacks of gold coins and Khwaja prayed at once for his long life, 'My dear master, may Allah keep you safe. At least this month's interest will be paid!' Thus, in such good humour and laughter, the noble sardars led their badshah and the other bridegrooms, the noble Asad and Badi-uz-Zaman. Several other sardars also married that day and wore saffron-coloured wedding robes. It was a happy day, even happier than the day of Eid. The beautiful brides with faces that shone like the moon entered the bridal chambers in the palace. When princesses Mahjabeen, Bahar and Makhmoor entered the palace as brides, Sahibqiran sent Khwaja Amar to them with this message, 'You have now recited the sacred words and have come into the enlightened circle of Islam. According to the rules of our religion, you will now have to be in purdah and you will be in seclusion.' Lacheen and Bilqees stepped forward and he said, 'The day the wedding festivities began, the same evening, I, your humble slave and all the sahirs of Hoshruba recited the sacred text and forswore magic.'

The marriage of Burran and Iraj

Shahanshah Kaukab left after Asad's marriage. Prince Iraj was getting married to his daughter Burran and he had to arrange the wedding. The sardars Alamshah, the noble Qasim and all the sardars of the Islamic lashkar who sat on the left row organized the wedding procession for Iraj. Kaukab sent a magnificent dower and showered so many gold coins on the way that the populace became rich. Alamshah, Qasim and Sahibqiran himself organized the bridal procession exquisitely. Young Iraj emerged from the place in saffron-coloured clothes.

Kaukab the Enlightened had adorned the Jamshedi palace like a bride of the first night. As Hamza Sahibqiran entered the fort of Jamshed, its streets thronged with people who jostled with each other to catch a glimpse of him. On the roofs of the palaces, the princesses of Nur Afshan watched the procession from behind curtains of real emeralds while poorer damsels erected string cots on their rooftops and draped their scarves and veils on the cots to peek at the procession. Every eye was on the procession; Sahibqiran flung sacks of gold that fell in the houses of the poor. There were cries of joy and gratitude and people said, 'May God preserve the bride and groom! Sahibqiran should come once again to celebrate his grandson's birth!'

Khwaja Amar let out howls of protest, 'Ya Sahibqiran do not waste your money on these shohdas. They will either gamble it away or spend it on cheap alcohol! God will punish you for such extravagance! Give it all to me and I will send it to Khana Kaaba in Mecca to earn you grace!' Sahibqiran ignored Amar and arrived at the palace of Jamshedi in this magnificent manner. The nobles and tajdars of Nur Afshan received the procession and showered the bridegroom with real pearls as they led him into the palace. Sahibqiran looked at the palace of Jamshedi and its adornments and praised it lavishly. Malika Naheed, Burran's mother, received the women in the procession. Singers greeted the bridegroom's family with traditional curses and songs and the two families exchanged gifts of land and money.

Suddenly, there was an uproar outside the palace that the qazi sahib had arrived to conduct the nikah. In reality, Amar, who had administered the deadly laxative jamal gota to the real qazi, was impersonating him. Burran was in the bridal chamber surrounded by her companions; her vizierzadi Shagoofa held the princess, while Malika Nahid stood near her daughter. The qazi approached the chamber and called out, 'You are being wedded to Prince Iraj, the son of the noble Qasim. Do you accept him?' There was no reply, as Princess Burran felt too shy to say yes loudly. As it happened, Shah Kaukab had also invited Sarsar Sword-fighter and Saba Raftar Fleet-foot to this wedding and they were present in the bridal chamber. The plan was that after Iraj and Burran's wedding, the five ayyar girls would be married to the five ayyars. After the fall of Hoshruba, the five girls had converted to Islam. Sarsar heard the qazi's voice and whispered to Burran's companion Shagoofa, 'This is the voice of the camel driver's son!' Shagoofa looked shocked and whispered back, 'Be silent! Qazi sahib is a man of God and he is one who conducts all marriages. Do not joke about such matters!'

Not convinced, Sarsar peered out of the bridal chamber and met the qazi's eyes. Khwaja Amar realized that she had recognized him and called out angrily, 'Who is this bold woman who stares at us so impertinently. She has seen us and that is a sin!' Sarsar quietly sent for Kaukab and whispered in his ear, 'This qazi is actually Amar in disguise!' Kaukab then went up to Amar, held his hand firmly and said, 'Khwaja Sahib, what do you think you are doing?' Amar said defiantly, 'This was my promise!' Sarsar's revelation caused a furore in the palace. People rushed to the qazi's house and called out to him, but there was no response. After a long time, a maidservant came out and informed them that qazi sahib was suffering from severe diarrhoea. Kaukab conveyed this information to Sahibqiran, who smiled and said,

'Everywhere, the qazi sahibs are fed laxatives! I will conduct Burran's *nikah* myself!'

Thus, in the midst of laughter and high spirits, Burran was wedded to Iraj while her companion Shagoofa was married to the ayyar Shahpur. Apart from the usual dower, Kaukab gave his daughter several hundred kingdoms. As Sahibqiran led Burran out of the palace, her mother Naheed clung to her and wept dearly. The princesses of the realm bid a tearful farewell to their friend. Porters carried out the palanquin and the sky gleamed with stars. Wedding singers sang about the occasion so poignantly that all those present who had daughters were overwhelmed by tears.

The young Iraj lifted Burran in his eager arms and seated her in the golden palanquin; in other words, he brought the full moon into the turret of the palanquin. Kaukab himself kept his hand on the palanquin and led his daughter's carriage out of the palace. As they reached the massive doors of the fort of Jamshed, Sahibqiran jumped off his mount and said, 'My Brother, it is time for you to return to your place with God's will.' Kaukab then kneeled down before Sahibqiran and wept, 'Huzoor, I offer my daughter as a handmaiden to do your menial chores! As God is my witness, I wish to inform you that last evening, your humble slave, my wife Nahid, my daughter Burran and all sahirs of Nur Afshan have recited the prayer of penance. We have thrown away all magical items from our palaces and obliterated the manifestations of magic like palaces and buildings from our realm. Your humble servant has recited the Kalma and converted to Islam. Your handmaiden Burran is the light and eyes of Tilism of Nur Afshan. Her mother will not be able to bear her absence!'

Sahibqiran said, 'O Kaukab, our Provider has fulfilled all the stages of my jihad. Please participate in Khwaja Amar's wedding. As for the young Iraj, I intend to leave him and your daughter with you for some time as I could not bear your grief at her parting from you.' Thus, Emir bid farewell to Kaukab and returned to the Garden of Apples. After several years of separation, Iraj and Burran reunited that night and had much to say to each other. Iraj attained the gem of desire from that rare pearl.

The ayyars' weddings

After these marriages had been conducted, Sahibqiran commanded the sardars of the Tohmatan, 'All of you must organize the wedding arrangements of Princess Sarsar and her companions. These five ayyars have spent many nights yearning for their love. We are thankful that the morning of their unions has dawned.' The badshah of Islam provided saffron-coloured robes to the ayyars and opened the doors of the treasury. The venue for their wedding celebration was the pavilion of Hasham. The badshah sat on the Throne of Solomon and all the sardars and ayyars were present in the pavilion. Khwaja Amar, Mehtar Qiran, Mehtar Barq, Jansoz and Zargham walked into the pavilion dressed in wedding apparel. Sahibqiran said, 'Khwaja, you conducted all the marriage ceremonies by pretending to be qazi. You gave laxatives to the real qazis. Today we will conduct your marriage. You must give us an award!'

Amar retorted, 'It does not behove the master to argue with his slave. I am an unfortunate, poor man. You must have heard of the saying, "Sugar from a bridegroom's house is equal to the water from the bride's well!" How that saying fits this occasion!' Amar then took out a broken cup from Zambil in which he put a single crumbly *batasha* and offered it to the Emir, saying, 'Bismillah, do not tarry in conducting the marriage!' Badshah smiled and said, 'Sheheryar, we will never get anything from Khwaja! However, to sweeten our mouth today, he can play his flute and sing for us! All sardars are present today and you will not have such a distinguished gathering on any other occasion.' Khwaja looked offended and said, 'Am I a professional singer? Does a bridegroom sing at his own wedding?' Barq Firangi flashed forward and said, 'Ustad, all the sardars are in a mood today for your performance on the flute!' Amar brushed off Barq, but signalled to Emir, 'You are my master and I cannot ever refuse you, but I will be humiliated before my bride.' Sarsar and her companions were dressed as brides and were waiting in an adjoining pavilion. Shameema, who was now Barq's bride, emerged laughing and said, 'Ustad do sing. Our mistress Sarsar is really in love with your voice!'

Thus, Sahibqiran solemnized all the marriages one by one. The brides were invited to sit in the main pavilion and the gathering of happiness was now complete. The news of Amar's performance had spread throughout the lashkar and eager listeners surrounded the pavilion. Khwaja sat proudly as the bridegroom and took out his flute from Zambil. He played it with fresh vigour and sang a poignant ghazal to accompany it. As Amar sang the ghazal, there were cries of praise from everyone, young and old. Lovers and their beloveds were moved to tears. Sahibqiran's eyes filled with tears and he took off strings of pearls, emeralds and rubies as offerings for Amar. There was a rain of rupees in the pavilion. Sarsar and Saba Raftar sat on their chairs, paragons of beauty and trickery, their eyes overflowing with rivers of tears.

Suddenly, the curtains of the pavilion lifted and a light flashed that blinded everyone for a while. When people returned to their senses, they saw a beautiful jogan walk into the pavilion. Every man looked at her, stunned by her beauty. The jogan walked into the middle of the pavilion and raised her hands in prayer, 'May the Almighty Provider preserve this gathering till Doomsday! This humble handmaiden also heard of Khwaja's wedding and has come to join in the celebrations.' Amar was also staring at the jogan. He sighed as he gazed upon the garden of her perfect beauty. Emir pointed her to a chair. That Venus of the sky of beauty then sat on a chair and looked at Amar. She exclaimed, 'king of ayyars, you have stopped singing as soon as we joined your gathering! We have come here because we are eager to hear you perform. Indeed, you have perfected the art of music! Grant us a few verses as well!'

Amar just gazed at the beautiful damsel, too stunned to respond. The Emir said, 'Khwaja, we must not disappoint our guest!' Amar slowly raised the flute and played a haunting melody accompanied by verses of love. The beautiful jogan swayed with pleasure as Amar performed. Amar looked only at her as he sang and seemed completely infatuated. Whenever that cruel one smiled, it was as if a bolt of lightning destroyed all senses. Amar sang for two hours with such skill and rapture that the whole lashkar became silent in appreciation. When he finally stopped, the jogan rose and stretched her limbs gracefully. She looked at Khwaja straight in the eye and said, 'Why Khwaja, you killed Afrasiyab with trickery and deceit? Do you now celebrate Afrasiyab's death with weddings? I am Princess Marjan Jadoo, handmaiden of Afrasiyab! You camel driver's son, you are the root cause of all the trouble!'

The jogan moved like lightning, put an arm around Amar's waist and flew out of the durbar. Kaukab and Lacheen saw her take off, but were too startled to respond. Kaukab thought he would sprout wings to follow her, but recalled his prayer of repentance and bowed his head. Before Sahibqiran could react, the jogan had become like a lamp in the sky. Kaukab slapped his own cheeks as he addressed Hamza, 'Sheheryar, this is disastrous!' Sarsar came forward weeping, 'Sheheryar, did I learn the art of deception so that my own husband should be in captivity? All his wives will now declare that I brought him bad luck. Your handmaiden will go now and bring you that woman's head! In truth, she is a powerful sahira. In his days of power, Afrasiyab bestowed an island kingdom in River Qulzum on her. I will know what to do there!'

Sahibqiran strictly forbade Sarsar from making any move and said, 'Sarsar, you are now obliged to remain in purdah and it is not appropriate for you to venture out. An ayyar is used to captivity. God forbid, if you are captured, Amar will be grief stricken. God is still kind to me and I remember the Great Name. I will kill the woman myself. I know that she is really after me and the Great Name. Her death is at my hands!' Amar's ayyar companions also did not approve of Sarsar's going anywhere and she reluctantly withdrew. Late at night, Sarsar awakened her four companions and whispered some instructions to them. Each of the girls armed themselves with the weapons of ayyari. In that black night, they left their house and went to the palace stealthily. Sarsar Sword-fighter rendered Sahibqiran unconscious, Shameema Tunnel-woman attended to Badi-uz-Zaman, Saba Raftar Fleet-foot took Asad, Sanobar Whip-lasher tied up Alamshah and Tez Nigah Dagger-woman captured Qasim.

The five ayyar girls left that night with the five sardars tied up in pushtaras and headed for Marjan's place. Marjan was alert that night and was guarding her lashkar. Late that night, she spotted a pillar of dust moving in the desert. Marjan turned to her commander Sohail and said, 'Go forth and see who approaches!' Sohail went forward and saw that Sarsar and her four companions were moving through the desert like the morning breeze. Sarsar saw Marjan from a distance and quickened her pace. She called out, 'Princess Marjan, be aware that we had been trapped by the Muslims. Now that we saw a ray of hope, we have also revealed our treacherous selves! We have brought with us the five sardars who are considered the pillars of the lashkar!'

Marjan heard this cry and ran towards the girls. She called out, 'Sarsar whom have you brought?' Sarsar said, 'Sahibqiran and the young Asad who is the murderer of our Shahanshah, Alamshah, Badi and Qasim, I have brought them all. O Marjan, kill them on this dark and treacherous night and let us leave immediately for the Veil of Zulmat. We must not linger here for tomorrow morning the murderous hosts of our enemies will fall on us. The Shahanshah was killed for his negligence in such matters. Alas Marjan, even ten seers of sandalwood was not available for Shahanshah's funeral pyre! There was no one left to see to his last remains. Send for your chain-keepers so that they can bind these prisoners. They are like burning flames. If they awaken, these silken cords will not hold them down. Marjan, if you delay their execution, you will regret it and die a dog's death!'

Marjan, Sohail and Marjan's handmaidens were brimming with excitement and brought Sarsar and the other ayyar girls into the main durbar tent. The handmaidens echoed Sarsar's warning and cried, 'Sarsar is right, kill them right away!' Marjan asked them to bring Amar. The handmaidens brought him in chained and gagged. He looked up and saw Sahibqiran, Asad, Alamshah, Badi and Qasim in Marjan's durbar. Sarsar called out harshly, 'Sarbanzadeh, did you think you would marry me? Now have you seen the fruits of your marriage? It will be the destruction of your house! I have avenged my Shahanshah!' She jumped forward to kill Amar herself, but Marjan held her back and said, 'Sarsar wait! I will just send for the executioners!' Sarsar squirmed in her grasp and cried, 'Let me go, I want to kill him with my bare hands! My heart is in flames! I have seen the helpless corpse of my Shahanshah!'

Just as Marjan's men tied Sahibqiran and his companions in heavy chains, the morning star emerged in the sky. Sahibqiran awoke to find himself tied up and Marjan standing before him, summoning the executioners. Sarsar went forward with her sword drawn and cried, 'You foolish one, what need is there of an executioner? We were trained to fight for this day!' She brought her sword down on Sahibqiran's wrist in a hard blow so that his chain was broken. She then called out, 'Sheheryar, break your chains! I am Sarsar Sword-fighter!' Sahibqiran understood Sarsar's tactics immediately and with a supreme effort broke free of his chains. Saba Raftar Fleet-foot released Amar while Shameema Tunnel-woman untied Asad; and Sanobar Whip-lasher and Tez Nigah Dagger-woman broke the chains of Alamshah, Badi-uz-Zaman and Qasim. These lions also roared and broke open their own chains as well. Sahibqiran picked up one of the chains and twirled it as he approached Marjan. Anyone who ventured too close to him was wounded by the chain. Amar and the ayyar girls then released narcotic vapours and smoking hookahs in the durbar.

Sahibqiran was now very close to Marjan, who flung an iron ball at him. The Emir simply recited the Great Name and her magic was dispelled. Marjan tried a few other spells, but they were all useless against the Great Name. By this time, Marjan looked worried and wanted to sprout wings to flee. She cried out, 'This Sarsar deceived me horribly. Alas, I could not see through her treachery!' As she flew upwards, the Emir held her by the legs and spun her around a few times before smashing her on the ground. Marjan's skull burst into a thousand pieces. The Emir then turned his attention on to the other sahiras whose face were already burnt by the smoking hookahs. Asad and the others then fought the remaining sahirs fiercely.

Back in the Islamic camp, there was an uproar at the news of the missing sardars. When the ayyar girls' tent was searched, it was also found to be empty. Everyone was convinced that they had kidnapped the sardars. The badshah and his sardars decided to follow their trail and reached Marjan's place just when the winds were howling and voices were calling out, 'You have killed me, my name was Marjan Jadoo!' Soon, all of them plundered Marjan's tents and Sahibqiran congratulated Sarsar.

There was an outcry that Marjan was killed because of Sarsar's trickery. Khwaja Amar went to all the captured sardars and cried, 'Sahibs, you have been freed by my wife! You should kiss her feet and thank her for saving your lives. What a marvellous strategy she devised!' Emir then led the five ayyar girls to a carriage and seated them in it tenderly before they returned to the base camp in all glory. Since the celebrations for Amar's wedding had been disrupted due to the appearance of the jogan, the badshah declared, 'The celebrations will continue. Praise be to the Lord who has saved our lives!'

The sardars enthusiastically organized the celebrations and the entire camp was illuminated. The badshah opened the doors of the treasury and generous sums were given to the poor and needy to celebrate the light of Sahbqiran's safety and life. That night, the lashkar remained awake in the celebration of happiness.

GLOSSARY

aatishbaz: one who makes and sets off fireworks

Aasman Pari: Sky Fairy; Hamza's wife in Qaf, the land of fairies

Ab-ul-Bashar: father of Bashar or man; keeper of Amar ayyar's Zambil

Afrasiyab: illusionist of water; character derived from the *Shahnama* ('The Story of Kings') by Firdausi. In that book, Afrasiyab is the King of Turan

afshan: silver glitter used by women of the Indian subcontinent to adorn the parting of their hair

Aghori: sect of Hindu fakirs who are devotees of the god Shiva

Akhtar Marvarid: star amongst pearls

Allah ho Akbar: Allah is the greatest, the first words of the *azan*, the Muslim call for prayer

anghrakha: traditional long sleeved, full skirted tunic for men, tied across the chest with an inner flap

arthi: Hindu funeral bier

Ashqar Devzad: a beautiful winged colt that bears Emir Hamza home from Qaf and stays with him until death

attar: perfume

ayyar: trickster

ayyari: the art of trickery, a profession with its own costumes, codes and sign language

Baba-ji: respectful way of addressing an elderly man

baildar: one who works with a spade; mason; gardener

Baji: a respectful way of addressing elder sisters in Urdu

bania: a Hindu caste of traders

baqar-khwani: a savoury puff pastry

baradari: pavilion with twelve arches

barfi: sweetmeat prepared from milk

bargah: the place for a gathering or audience

Barq: lightning bolt

Barq Firangi: Amar's talented disciple who is an Englishman; 'Firangi' is derived from Frank and is the term for foreigner in Urdu

batasha: thin sweet wafer the size of a coin distributed on happy occasions or at shrines

Batin: that which is hidden; the Invisible Tilism in Tilism-e-Hoshruba

Bibi: respectful way of addressing a woman, wife or sister

Bismillah: In the name of Allah

Brahmin: highest of the Hindu castes

bughda: cleaver; hatchet

bukhoor: Arabian incense made of wood chips soaked in scented oils and burned in incense burners. These emit thick perfumed smoke. Used to perfume homes and clothing

bulbul: nightingale

Bull of the Earth: derived from Persian and Indian mythology in which the earth rests on the back of a bull who is perched on a fish. According to another tradition, the earth rests on the bull's horns. When the earth becomes heavy with the sins of humanity, the bull shifts the earth from one horn to the other, thus causing earthquakes

Burzurjmeher: Nausherwan's legendary vizier, astrologer and seer

Buzurg Umeed: the late Buzurjmeher's son; astrologer and qazi in Hamza's camp

chinar: plane tree

chandini **sheets:** long white sheets used as floor seating

Charb Dast: slippery hand; thief; comic name used by Amar in his trickeries

chausar: Indian game of dice; backgammon

choona: slaked lime also known as hydrated or pickling lime

daftars: offices; ledgers; volumes

dahi-bara: savoury snack made from lentil flour and spiced yoghurt

Dai Amah: foster-mother

Darband: Persian word meaning Closed Gates; a narrow and difficult pass through mountains; the name of a fortress on the Caspian Sea

dargah: holy place, the abode or shrine of a saint

darogha: steward, keeper

dastan: epic, story

dev: a species of gigantic, powerful and occasionally cannibalistic giants or demons that inhabit the mountains of Qaf.

devjama: garment made of animal skin usually worn by warriors

devta: gods

doshala: Pashmina shawl with a double weave

durbari: courtiers

Eid al Fitr: Muslim festival marking the end of Ramadan, the month of fasting

Fajar: the dawn prayer in Islam

Faridun and Jamshed: legendary kings from the *Shahnama*

Galeem: Amar's cape of invisibility, a divine gift from the prophets

Garden of Khaleel: reference to the prophet Abraham whose sobriquet is Khaleelallah. He was placed in a burning pit by Nimrod for believing in the divinity of the One God. Due to a miracle, the pit transformed into a garden and he was saved

Ghareeb Nawaz: literally, one who is generous to the poor; a sobriquet of the Muslim saint Khwaja Muinuddin Chishti Ajmeri

ghazal: love lyric in Persian or Urdu

ghulam: male slave

gilori: betel leaf smeared with condiments and folded into a triangle

gir: from the Persian *giraftan*, sieze, hold or capture

Gisyan Brahmin devta: respectful deity of the Brahmins

gol-gappa: savoury pastry puffs served with spiced tamarind water

gophan: a kind of catapult used as a weapon of war by ayyars

gori(s)**:** fair; Urdu slang for a white woman

gota: gold or silver ribbon used as braiding on women's garments

Gulbadan: flower-body; expensive silk gauze material woven in central India

Habshi: from the land of Habsh; Ethiopian or Abyssinian

halwa: dessert made of milk and semolina

halwa sohan: hard brittle candy made of wheat germ and milk

harami: illegitimate; bastard; villain,

haramzada(*eh*)**:** of illegitimate lineage; villain

hareesa: Kashmiri dish made of pulverized meat, lentils and rice

haveli: private mansion

hawadar: an open palanquin carried by porters

Hazrat Ali: cousin and son-in-law of the Holy Prophet Mohammad and the fourth Caliph of Islam, especially revered by Shia Muslims

Hindustan: literally, the land of the Indus; derived from the Persian word *hindu*, derived in turn from *Sindhu*, Sanskrit for the River Indus

Holi: annual Hindu spring festival celebrated with colours

houri: beautiful female companion awarded to the faithful in heaven according to Islamic belief

Hoopoe Chair: Amar ayyar's chair in Hamza's camp. In Egypt, the hoopoe is known as the son of Solomon. The bird used to have a crown of real gold and was often killed for gold. It appealed to the Prophet Solomon who then prayed that its gold crown become a crown of feathers

hujra: hidden room

huma: a mythical high flying bird from the *Shahnama*; traditionally believed to confer kingship if it flies over someone; an equivalent of the phoenix

huzoor: sire; exalted one; presence

iktara: single stringed instrument

Ilyas: a prophet referred to in the Quran; associated with shipwrecks; a vizier or minister of Solomon

Indra: Hindu god

Inshallah: Arabic for 'God willing'

Ism-e-Azam: the greatest name among all the names of Allah, known only to the chosen few

Izrael: one who comes at night; the prophet Jacob who was born at night; the angel of death according to Islamic belief

jadoo: magic

jamadar: a rank in the army; head of labourers, cleaners

Jamshed: an ancient Persian king who had legendary magical powers

-ji: respectful diminutive attached to names in Urdu

jogan: Hindu holy woman

kafir: infidel, pagan

kahari: female porter

Kalma-e-Shahadat: the Verse of Affirmation for Muslims: 'There is only One God and Mohammad is His Prophet'

Kanhaiya: affectionate nickname for the Hindu god Krishna

kashkol: wooden begging bowl traditionally used by fakirs and holy men. Usually, the kashkol is presented to a disciple by his spiritual teacher as a symbol of his admission into the group

kevda: perfume distilled from the flowers of a tree of the same name; used in pilaffs and halwas

khajla-pastry: puffed pastry filled with dried fruit and boiled down milk

khalat: robe of honour

Khalifa: caliph; successor or representative

Khana Kaaba: the house of Kaaba in Mecca; originally built by Abraham and situated in the holiest mosque in Islam; the direction of prayer

Khana Kharab: one who comes from a dubious house or family

khanjar: dagger

khasdan: container for betel leaves and giloris

katha: the nut of the areca palm

Khizar: the Green One, associated with water and the environment; enigmatic immortal figure in Islam who guided prophets

Khudawand: master; divine one; lord

Khurd Burd: one who can make things vanish; comic name used by Amar in his trickeries

Khwaja: a man of distinction; rich man; owner; merchant; doctor; lord; master; teacher, etc. It could be related to the Persian root *'khw'* meaning desire. Anyone who can grant a desire is khwaja. That is why Sufi Chishti saints were called Khwaja. A Persian word, it became Hoja in Turkish

Koh Lajward: mountain of lapis lazuli

nargis: narcissi

Koh Qaf: the Caucasus mountains; in Persian tradition, the abode of fairies and devs

Kohi: a native of Kohistan

Kohistan: literally, the land of mountains. Kohistan is also a district in northern Pakistan spread on both sides of the Indus river, consisting almost entirely of rugged mountains. The Karakoram Highway, built over the ancient silk route to China runs through Kohistan. Could also refer to the Pamir mountains that spread from Tajikistan to Pakistan

kos: measure of distance used from the Vedic to the Mughal times

kulcha: small round bread baked in a clay oven

kutni: professional con woman

Laat: female deity worshipped in pre-Islamic Arabia; changes gender in the Tilism dastans

lachka: soft and shiny gold or silver braid

laddoo: soft ball-shaped sweet made from gram flour

Lanka: reference to a proverb about an incident in the *Ramayana* that talks of betrayal by one's own people

Laqa: vision; visage; face; to see

Maghreb: North African countries such as Tunisia and Morroco

mahaldar: keeper of the palace

maikhana: tavern or bar; in this case, the palace wine cellar

maktab khana: house of learning; school

maleech: one who belongs to no caste; derogatory term for non Hindus

malik: Arabic for king; tribal leader or chieftain

malika: queen

Manaat: female deity worshipped in pre-Islamic Arabia; changes gender in the Tilism dastans

manam: 'I am'

mardood: abusive term meaning 'the evil one'

marhaba: 'All Praise'

mashkeeza: goatskin bag used to carry water

masnad: soft floor seating of cotton mattresses covered with sheets, pillows and bolsters

maulvi: honorific Islamic religious title

maund: a unit of weight of about 40 kilograms

Mehmoodi: fine muslin

Mian: family name and title of nobility in the subcontinent

missi: herbal preparation that Indian women used to darken their lips

Mirror of Alexander: a mirror made by Aristotle and placed on the summit of a tower erected by Alexander at Alexandria

mohan bhog: sacred food for the gods; usually a halwa prepared with semolina

molsri: Mimusops elengi or the *bakul* tree known for its fragrant blossoms

mubarak: felicitations

mujra: a highly stylized form of greeting in court; also a dance performed for royalty on special occasions like weddings

munshi: secretary or scribe

Murshidzadeh: son or descendent of spiritual guide; in this case, Mussavir is the grandson of Samri and therefore revered

Mushkil Kusha: one who removes troubles or obstacles; sobriquet of Imam Ali bin Abu Talib, cousin and son-in-law of the Holy Prophet Mohammad

Naad-e-Ali: prayer to Imam Ali bin Abu Talib

Nabi Danyal: the Prophet Daniel; a prophet mentioned in the Quran and the Old Testament

Nafarman: Persian for violets; in Urdu, these flowers are called *banafsha*. The better known meaning of this word is 'disobedient'

nama: royal letter

nan: a variety of leavened bread baked in a clay oven

Napursan: disregard; 'City of Disregard' in Tilism-e-Hoshruba

naqara: kettledrum

Naqara of Alexander: Kettledrum of Alexander; reference to the *Hamzanama* where Emir Hamza is rescued in a sea storm by the miraculous appearance of an obelisk with a kettledrum placed on it. Hamza strikes the drum for the storm to abate. It is later gifted to him

Naulakha: necklace worth rupees nine lakhs

Nauroze: spring equinox; the ancient Persian new year and a Zoroastrian festival; also celebrated by the Kurds and others in Central Asia, Iran and Afghanistan

nazar, nazrana: a gift offered in homage to the monarch or deity, usually gold coins or food

nazim: administrator

neelgai: a large antelope, the male is also called blue bull

neemcha: sword from north-western Africa, especially Morocco

nikah: Muslim wedding ceremony

oudh: a kind of black aromatic wood; the best kind of oudh wood sinks in water

panja: hand; claw; in this case, a magical disembodied hand

pari: fairy, supernatural race that traditionally dwells in the mountains of Qaf. Pari, like jinni, are creatures of fire and invisible to the human eye. They have several powers including the power of flight. They can be the size of humans and are uncommonly beautiful. They can travel the world at will

Paristan: the mountains of Qaf, the land of parizads

parizadan: plural of parizad; pari-born; the name used for males of the Pari race; sometimes female paris are also referred to as parizad

peshwaz: literally, open from the front; a traditional outfit in which the robe is open from the waist down, worn over trousers

pir **brother:** spiritual brothers; disciples of the same teacher

pir: holy man; sage; teacher

pushtara: bundle; burden

Qahar and Jabbar: two of the ninety-nine names of Allah

Qais and Laila: legendary lovers whose love story ended in tragedy

Qaroon: cousin of the Prophet Moses; Qaroon was an alchemist and produced gold and silver. He had accumulated so much wealth that forty mules carried only the keys to his treasuries. When Moses asked him to donate one out of every thousand dinars to the poor, Qaroon became his enemy and wanted to harm him. Moses then cursed him and Qaroon sank into the earth bearing the weight of his vast treasury. He will continue to sink till Doomsday

Qulzum: the Red Sea

Qutb: an exalted rank in Sufi belief

Ram Naam Satya Hai: invocation to the Hindu god Ram chanted in funeral processions

Rangeen Hissar: colourful boundary or parameter

Rangeen Seher: colourful magic

Ravi: legendary narrator; one who passes on *rawayat* or traditions

Rizwan: the angel who is the gate keeper of *jannat* or paradise in Islamic belief

Rumi: man from Byzantine or Asia Minor

Rustam: wrestler with super human strength from the *Shahnama*

Saba: zephyr; morning breeze

Saeen-ji: respectful manner of addressing a holy man

Sahibqiran: lord of the seven realms; one at whose birth Jupiter and Venus are in conjunction; Hamza's title referring to his birth at an auspicious astrological moment; the founder of the Mughal empire Taimur used this title and the Holy Prophet Mohammad is also referred to as Sahibqiran in some texts.

sahir: enchanter; sorcerer; sahira for females

salaam: the diminutive for the Muslim words of greeting, *assalam-alaikum* or 'Peace be upon you'

Samri: maker of the Golden Calf that the followers of Moses worshipped in his absence; in the Persian tradition, Samri is a powerful magician

Samri Nama: a record of the prophecies of Samri

saqi: cupbearers who serve wine

saqqa: water carrier

sardar: leader of the tribe; commander

sarkar: the government; highest official

Sati: title given to a Hindu woman prepared to immolate herself on her husband's funeral pyre; in this case, however, Hilal Magic-wielder is not a Hindu, but a worshipper of Samri and Jamshed

Seal of Prophets: reference to the Holy Prophet Mohammad

seer: a measure of weight approximately more than a pound

seher: magic, enchantment

Shaddad: legendary Middle Eastern king who built a city that he claimed was heaven on earth. He was struck dead when he set foot in it

Shahanshah: emperor

Shaitan: Satan

sharab: wine

sheermal: rich unleavened bread, sometimes served with curry for breakfast

Sheheryar: keeper of the city; king of kings; just and wise king; elder of the city

shehna: Indian oboe

Sherdil: lion-heart

shodah: villain; layabout; vulgar; crass

sindoor: vermilion worn by married Hindu women in the parting of their hair

Slippery cornerstone: traditionally, a flawless rock was placed at the durbar of Persian kings to allow their minions and servants to kiss the stone before they were admitted into the presence of the monarch.

Sohrab: son of Rustam bin Zaal, powerful and legendary hero of the *Shahnama*. Father and son fought each other to death, ignorant of their relationship

Star in the firmament of prophets: reference to the Holy Prophet Mohammad

sumbul: hyacinth

sunddal: sandalwood

Taazi: Arabian horse

Tajdar: one who wears the crown; crowned heads; kings; monarchs

tanpura: Indian string instrument

tegha: Indo-Persian curved executioner's sword

thakur: from Sanskrit meaning idol or deity; title of respect for Rajput nobles

tika, tilak: mark made on the forehead with vermilion or sandalwood paste; also an ornament worn on the forehead

Tilism Kusha: destroyer of a Tilism; Asad Ghazi is the Tilism Kusha of Hoshruba

Toor: Mount Sinai which was called the Toor of Sinai; here, the lamp of Toor means divine light

umber: ambergris; incense that melts like wax when heated

ustad: teacher

ustani: female teacher; wife of the teacher

utlas-silk: expensive handmade silk from China

vizierzadi: feminine of vizier; daughter of the vizier

Zahir: that which is visible; the Visible Tilism in Tilism-e-Hoshruba

Zakhar: swelling with water; stormy waves

Zambil: a leather bag carried by fakirs or beggars; here, Amar ayyar's enchanted pouch that contains a whole world

Zamurrad: emerald

Zangi: native of Zanzibar

Zulmat: cruelty, darkness; the Veil of Darkness in Tilism-e-Hoshruba

Selected names and their meanings

Azhrang: the name of a demon

Aflaq: celestial bodies

Akhzar: green; dusky brown

Aftab: sun

Ahwal: squint-eyed man

Akhtar: star; omen, augury

Ambreen: fragrance

Asrar: secret; mystery

Ayeenadar: the mirror-holder

Azar: fire

Azhdar Zulmati: serpent of cruelty

Badi-uz-Zaman: inventor of the times

Baghban Qudrat: divine gardener or the gardener of nature

Bahar: the spring (season)

Bakhtiarak: lucky, fortunate

Balai: perils

Baraan: rain

Barq Giryan: lightning bolt that drops like tears

Barq Khatif: lightning bolt that is like thunder

Barq Khundan: lightning bolt that drops like laughter

Barq Lameh: lightning bolt that is shining and gleaming

Barq Mehshar: lightning bolt that is like Doomsday

Bazm: gathering

Benazir Qudrat: one who has no parallel in nature

Bibran: lion-like

Bilour: crystal

Bilqees: variant of Bilqis, the Queen of Sheba

Bubbar: lion

Burran: sharp, cutting

Damama: drum; lively atmosphere

Danai: wise

Darya Dil: heart like a river; generous

Dukhan: smoke

Folad Shikan: iron breaker

Gaiti Afroze: world-illuminating

Gauhar Afshan: pearl glitter

Gauhar-badan: pearl body

Gesoo: hair

Ghaddar: traitor

Ghazabnak: in a mighty rage

Ghazzal: deer, fawn

Ghuncha-dahan: flower mouth

Ghurbal: net, sieve

Gul Andam: flower body

Gulcheen: one who plucks flowers

Gulfam: flower-complexion

Gulgoon: rose coloured

Gulrang: rose-coloured complexion

Gulroo: flower-face

Gulzar: garden

Haijoon: tumult
Hairat: fresh and healthy; also surprise, wonder
Hanood: Indian
Hanzal: wild gourd, colocynth
Hilal: crescent
Hoor: houri
Hoshiar: alert, watchful
Intizam: arrangement; organization
Inzar: warning
Iraj: the sun; character from the *Shahnama*
Jahan Afroze: to adorn the world
Jahandar Shah: king of the world
Jallad: executioner
Jamosh: a buffalo
Jansoz: heart-consuming
Jan Nisar: one who is devoted and ready to lay down his life
Kahin: perspicacious; seer
Kalang: pickaxe
Kaukab: planet; pearl
Khoonkhar: bloodthirsty
Khoonrez: one who spills blood
Khumar: languor; mild state of inebriation
Khursan: like a bear
Kohan: mountains
Lacheen: a region in Central Asia
Lahoot: divine
Larzan: tremor
Madhosh: intoxicated
Mah: moon
Maheeb: formidable, terrible
Mainosh: wine drinker
Makhmoor: intoxicated
Makkar: cheat, swindler
Maraan: serpents
Markakul: hair curled up like serpents
Mushkeen: musky; dark
Mishmish: apricot
Mussavir: artist, painter

Nafeer: trumpet; flutist
Nahang: crocodile
Naqoos: gong
Nur: divine light
Nur Afshan: light dispersing
Nur al Dahar: light of the time
Qaash: splinter; slice
Qaisar: king
Qamar: moon
Qeher: rage
Qeher Nigah: eye of rage
Qeher Nigar: face of rage
Qiran: the conjunction of two planets
Qirtas: pages
Qumqam: genie from the *Arabian Nights*
Ra'ad: thunder
Rahdar: guide; angel who governs the zodiacal sign Cancer
Saad: felicity; fortune
Sadaf: pearl
Saffak: cruel; ruthless
Sahab: mover of clouds
Sailan: flowing rapidly
Samak: the fish on which the earth rests
Saman Azar: jasmine-fire
Samankal: of the same kind, similar
Samar: fruit
Sannat: product; skill; profession; work
Sanobar: pine tree
Sarfarosh: rebel; willing to lose one's head
Sarhang: commander; boatswain
Sarmast: leader of the intoxicated
Sarmaya: wintry, wealth
Saro Seemtan: willowy gleaming body
Sarsar: gale; stormy breeze
Sarshar: sated; replete; happy
Sayyara: planet
Seemab: boundary of water
Shagoofa: blossom
Shahab: shooting star; luminous
Shahbaz: king of hawks

Shakeel: handsome
Shama Afroze: lamp that illuminates
Shameema: scent; flavour
Shamim: fragrant
Shams: sun
sharab: wine
Sharara: spark
Sheeshadar: the glass-holder
Shehna Nawaz: flutist
Shireen: sweet
Shola: flame
Shola Rukhsar: flame-cheek
Sholadar: one who has flames
Sofar: ram's horn
Sohail: the star Canopus
Ta'oos: peacock
Tameer Qudrat: divine builder

Tareek Shakal-kash: darkness that creates images
Tarrar: fast; wily
Tausan: young unbroken horse
Tez Nigah: sharp eye
Uqab: hawk
Yakoot, Yakut: ruby
Yasaman: jasmine
Zafaran: saffron
Zaivar: jewellery
Zaal: old, white haired; warrior from the *Shahnama*
Zalim: cruel
Zamharir: moon; extreme cold
Zamurrad: emerald
Zilzila: earthquake
Zufunoon: one who has many skills